TWENTY THOUSAND LEAGUES UNDER THE SEA

TWENTY THOUSAND LEAGUES UNDER THE SEA

JULES VERNE

This edition published in 2021 by Arcturus Publishing Limited
26/27 Bickels Yard, 151–153 Bermondsey Street,
London SE1 3HA

Copyright © Arcturus Holdings Limited

All rights reserved. No part of this publication may be reproduced, stored in a retrieval system, or transmitted, in any form or by any means, electronic, mechanical, photocopying, recording or otherwise, without prior written permission in accordance with the provisions of the Copyright Act 1956 (as amended). Any person or persons who do any unauthorised act in relation to this publication may be liable to criminal prosecution and civil claims for damages.

Cover design: Peter Ridley
Cover illustration: Peter Gray

AD006511UK

Printed in the UK

MIX
Paper from responsible sources
FSC® C018072

Contents

Introduction 7
Translator's Introduction 9

FIRST PART

CHAPTER 1: *A Runaway Reef* 15
CHAPTER 2: *The Pros and Cons* 22
CHAPTER 3: *As Master Wishes* 28
CHAPTER 4: *Ned Land* 34
CHAPTER 5: *At Random!* 41
CHAPTER 6: *At Full Steam* 47
CHAPTER 7: *A Whale of Unknown Species* 56
CHAPTER 8: *'Mobilis in Mobili'* 64
CHAPTER 9: *The Tantrums of Ned Land* 72
CHAPTER 10: *The Man of the Waters* 79
CHAPTER 11: *The* Nautilus 88
CHAPTER 12: *Everything through Electricity* 96
CHAPTER 13: *Some Figures* 103
CHAPTER 14: *The Black Current* 110
CHAPTER 15: *An Invitation in Writing* 121
CHAPTER 16: *Strolling the Plains* 129
CHAPTER 17: *An Underwater Forest* 135
CHAPTER 18: *Four Thousand Leagues Under the Pacific* ...142
CHAPTER 19: *Vanikoro* 150
CHAPTER 20: *The Torres Strait* 160
CHAPTER 21: *Some Days Ashore* 168
CHAPTER 22: *The Lightning Bolts of Captain Nemo* 179

CHAPTER 23: *'Aegri Somnia'* 190
CHAPTER 24: *The Coral Realm* 199

SECOND PART

CHAPTER 1: *The Indian Ocean* 209
CHAPTER 2: *A New Proposition from Captain Nemo* 219
CHAPTER 3: *A Pearl Worth Ten Million* 228
CHAPTER 4: *The Red Sea* 239
CHAPTER 5: *Arabian Tunnel* 251
CHAPTER 6: *The Greek Islands* 260
CHAPTER 7: *The Mediterranean in Forty-Eight Hours* 271
CHAPTER 8: *The Bay of Vigo* 281
CHAPTER 9: *A Lost Continent* 291
CHAPTER 10: *The Underwater Coalfields* 301
CHAPTER 11: *The Sargasso Sea* 311
CHAPTER 12: *Sperm Whales and Baleen Whales* 320
CHAPTER 13: *The Ice Bank* 331
CHAPTER 14: *The South Pole* 342
CHAPTER 15: *Accident or Incident?* 354
CHAPTER 16: *Shortage of Air* 362
CHAPTER 17: *From Cape Horn to the Amazon* 372
CHAPTER 18: *The Devilfish* 382
CHAPTER 19: *The Gulf Stream* 392
CHAPTER 20: *In Latitude 47° 24' and Longitude 17° 28'* 403
CHAPTER 21: *A Mass Execution* 411
CHAPTER 22: *The Last Words of Captain Nemo* 420
CHAPTER 23: *Conclusion* 427

Introduction

Deservedly known as the 'Father of Science Fiction,' Jules Verne wrote of adventures to the unexplored regions of the world and wonderful inventions. On many occasions, his technological marvels, such as the submarine and space travel, predicted scientific advances that were years, or even decades, in the future.

Born on 8 February 1828 in the port city of Nantes, France, Verne always saw vessels come and go, wondering what adventures they were going on. As a young boy, he dreamed of one day having his own adventures on the sea, and at when 12 years old he smuggled himself onto a ship bound for India, only to be discovered and beaten for his disobedience. His relationship with his father, Pierre Verne, was a troubled one. Pierre, hoping to see his son follow in his footsteps, sent him to Paris to study law.

However, the appeal of writing proved too strong. He spent much of his time writing plays rather than studying law, and despite graduating in 1849, he showed little inclination to pursue a legal career. Encouraged by the writer, Alexandre Dumas, Verne decided to remain in Paris and write plays instead. His first production in 1850, *Blindman's Bluff*, was a lukewarm start to his ten year playwright career. Finding the love of his life, the divorced Honorine de Viane Morel, in 1856, Verne saw the need for financial stability and found work as a stockbroker to maintain his marriage. But the writing never stopped, and Verne would soon ignite his adventures off-stage with one of literature's greatest partnerships.

Verne and his publisher Pierre-Jules Hertzel were an exceptional duo. Recognising the untapped potential in Verne's seemingly crazy, futuristic ideas, Hertzel's masterful editing and knowledgeable suggestions kept his stories grounded and accessible enough for audiences to digest when Verne's original manuscripts would have been too far-fetched.

Equal respect and talent culminated in Verne's 1863 adventure novel, *Five Weeks in a Balloon*. With no experience in a balloon, let alone using one to cross the Atlantic, Verne researched Edgar Allan Poe's 'The Unparalleled Adventure of One Hans Pfaall' and travel magazines to familiarise himself with the experience. Verne continued to venture into the unknown, spawning titles like *Journey to the Centre of the Earth* (1864), *From the Earth to the Moon* (1865) and *Around the World in Eighty Days* (1872). One of his most visionary novels, *Paris in the Twentieth Century*, featuring skyscrapers, bullet trains, calculators, and gas-fuelled cars, was not published until 1994 due to Hertzel's belief that the subject matter was too subversive.

While Verne was fascinated with the progress of technology, he was also sceptical about its overpowering effect on mankind. This was most apparent in his nautical masterpiece, *Twenty Thousand Leagues Under the Sea* (1869). In this tale, rumours of a sea monster destroying ships leads the main characters, Professor Pierre Aronnax, Conseil, and Ned Land aboard the *Abraham Lincoln* to stop the creature. They survive the encounter only to find out the monster was a highly advanced electric submarine, *The Nautilus*, captained by the mysterious Captain Nemo. Having cut all ties with humankind, Captain Nemo imprisons our characters from the surface, but not from adventure. Discovering the lost city of Atlantis, fighting giant squids, and charting the unimaginable distance of the sea are just a day in the life aboard *The Nautilus*. But Captain Nemo's well-hidden intentions and dreary outlook on human existence entrances Professor Arronax, wondering whether this powerful craft will be used as mankind's greatest creation or their biggest downfall.

Jules Verne died 24 March 1905 from diabetes. A prolific writer throughout his life, the success of Verne's tales and worldwide appeal made him the second most translated writer of all time. He may have not been a scientist, but his work's innovations have influenced many writers and scientists, paving the way for one of literature's most exciting and thought-provoking genres – science fiction.

Translator's Introduction

'THE DEEPEST PARTS of the ocean are totally unknown to us,' admits Professor Aronnax early in this novel. 'What goes on in those distant depths? What creatures inhabit, or could inhabit, those regions twelve or fifteen miles beneath the surface of the water? It's almost beyond conjecture.'

Jules Verne (1828–1905) published the French equivalents of these words in 1869, and little has changed since. 126 years later, a *Time* cover story on deep–sea exploration made much the same admission: 'We know more about Mars than we know about the oceans.' This reality begins to explain the dark power and otherworldly fascination of *Twenty Thousand Leagues Under the Sea*.

Born in the French river town of Nantes, Verne had a lifelong passion for the sea. First as a Paris stockbroker, later as a celebrated author and yachtsman, he went on frequent voyages – to Britain, America, the Mediterranean. But the specific stimulus for this novel was an 1865 fan letter from a fellow writer, Madame George Sand. She praised Verne's two early novels *Five Weeks in a Balloon* (1863) and *Journey to the Centre of the Earth* (1864), then added: 'Soon I hope you'll take us into the ocean depths, your characters travelling in diving equipment perfected by your science and your imagination.' Thus inspired, Verne created one of literature's great rebels, a freedom fighter who plunged beneath the waves to wage a unique form of guerilla warfare.

Initially, Verne's narrative was influenced by the 1863 uprising of Poland against Tsarist Russia. The Poles were quashed with a violence that appalled not only Verne but all Europe. As originally conceived, Verne's Captain Nemo was a Polish nobleman whose entire family had been slaughtered by Russian troops. Nemo builds a fabulous futuristic submarine, the *Nautilus*, then conducts an underwater campaign of vengeance against his imperialist oppressor.

But in the 1860s France had to treat the Tsar as an ally, and Verne's publisher, Pierre Hetzel, pronounced the book unprintable. Verne reworked its political content, devising new nationalities for Nemo and his great enemy – information revealed only in a later novel, *The Mysterious Island* (1875); in the present work Nemo's background remains a dark secret. In all, the novel had a difficult gestation. Verne and Hetzel were in constant conflict and the book went through multiple drafts, struggles reflected in its several working titles over the period 1865–69: early on, it was variously called *Voyage Under the Waters*, *Twenty-five Thousand Leagues Under the Waters*, *Twenty Thousand Leagues Under the Waters* and *A Thousand Leagues Under the Oceans*.

Verne is often dubbed, in Isaac Asimov's phrase, 'the world's first science–fiction writer.' And it's true, many of his 60-odd books do anticipate future events and technologies: *From the Earth to the Moon* (1865) and *Hector Servadac* (1877) deal in space travel, while *Journey to the Centre of the Earth* features travel to the earth's core. But with Verne the operative word is 'travel,' and some of his best-known titles don't really qualify as sci-fi: *Around the World in Eighty Days* (1872) and *Michael Strogoff* (1876) are closer to 'travelogues' – adventure yarns in far-away places.

These observations partly apply here. The subtitle of the present book is *An Underwater Tour of the World*, so in good travelogue style, the *Nautilus*' exploits supply an episodic story line. Shark attacks, giant squid, cannibals, hurricanes, whale hunts, and other rip-roaring adventures erupt almost at random. Yet this loose structure gives the novel an air of documentary realism. What's more, Verne adds backbone to the action by developing three recurring motifs: the deepening mystery of Nemo's past life and future intentions, the mounting tension between Nemo and hot-tempered harpooner Ned Land, and Ned's ongoing schemes to escape from the *Nautilus*. These unifying threads tighten the narrative and accelerate its momentum.

Other subtleties occur inside each episode, the textures sparkling with wit, information, and insight. Verne regards the sea from many angles: in the domain of marine biology, he gives us thumbnail sketches of fish, seashells, coral, sometimes in great catalogues that swirl past like musical cascades; in the realm of geology, he studies volcanoes literally inside and out; in the world of commerce, he celebrates the high-energy entrepreneurs who lay the Atlantic Cable or dig the Suez

Canal. And Verne's marine engineering proves especially authoritative. His specifications for an open-sea submarine and a self-contained diving suit were decades before their time, yet modern technology bears them out triumphantly.

True, today's scientists know a few things he didn't: the South Pole isn't at the water's edge but far inland; sharks don't flip over before attacking; giant squid sport ten tentacles not eight; sperm whales don't prey on their whalebone cousins. This notwithstanding, Verne furnishes the most evocative portrayal of the ocean depths before the arrival of Jacques Cousteau and Technicolor film.

Lastly the book has stature as a novel of character. Even the supporting cast is shrewdly drawn: Professor Aronnax, the career scientist caught in an ethical conflict; Conseil, the compulsive classifier who supplies humorous tag lines for Verne's fast facts; the harpooner Ned Land, a creature of constant appetites, man as heroic animal.

But much of the novel's brooding power comes from Captain Nemo. Inventor, musician, Renaissance genius, he's a trail-blazing creation, the prototype not only for countless renegade scientists in popular fiction, but even for such varied figures as Sherlock Holmes or Wolf Larsen. However, Verne gives his hero's brilliance and benevolence a dark underside – the man's obsessive hate for his old enemy. This compulsion leads Nemo into ugly contradictions: he's a fighter for freedom, yet all who board his ship are imprisoned there for good; he works to save lives, both human and animal, yet he himself creates a holocaust; he detests imperialism, yet he lays personal claim to the South Pole. And in this last action he falls into the classic sin of Pride. He's swiftly punished. The *Nautilus* nearly perishes in the Antarctic and Nemo sinks into a growing depression.

Like Shakespeare's King Lear he courts death and madness in a great storm, then commits mass murder, collapses in catatonic paralysis, and suicidally runs his ship into the ocean's most dangerous whirlpool. Hate swallows him whole.

For many, then, this book has been a source of fascination, surely one of the most influential novels ever written, an inspiration for such scientists and discoverers as engineer Simon Lake, oceanographer William Beebe, polar traveller Sir Ernest Shackleton. Likewise Dr Robert D. Ballard, finder of the sunken *Titanic*, confesses that this was his favourite book as a teenager, and Cousteau himself, most renowned of marine explorers, called it his shipboard bible.

The present translation is a faithful yet communicative rendering of the original French texts published in Paris by J. Hetzel et Cie. – the hardcover first edition issued in the autumn of 1871, collated with the softcover editions of the First and Second Parts issued separately in the autumn of 1869 and the summer of 1870. Although prior English versions have often been heavily abridged, this new translation is complete to the smallest substantive detail.

Because, as that *Time* cover story suggests, we still haven't caught up with Verne. Even in our era of satellite dishes and video games, the seas keep their secrets. We've seen progress in sonar, torpedoes, and other belligerent machinery, but sailors and scientists – to say nothing of tourists – have yet to voyage in a submarine with the luxury and efficiency of the *Nautilus*.

F. P. WALTER
University of Houston

FIRST PART

CHAPTER 1

A Runaway Reef

THE YEAR 1866 was marked by a bizarre development, an unexplained and downright inexplicable phenomenon that surely no one has forgotten. Without getting into those rumours that upset civilians in the seaports and deranged the public mind even far inland, it must be said that professional seamen were especially alarmed. Traders, shipowners, captains of vessels, skippers and master mariners from Europe and America, naval officers from every country, and at their heels the various national governments on these two continents, were all extremely disturbed by the business.

In essence, over a period of time several ships had encountered 'an enormous thing' at sea, a long spindle-shaped object, sometimes giving off a phosphorescent glow, infinitely bigger and faster than any whale.

The relevant data on this apparition, as recorded in various logbooks, agreed pretty closely as to the structure of the object or creature in question, its unprecedented speed of movement, its startling locomotive power, and the unique vitality with which it seemed to be gifted. If it was a cetacean, it exceeded in bulk any whale previously classified by science. No naturalist, neither Cuvier nor Lacépède, neither Professor Dumeril nor Professor de Quatrefages, would have accepted the existence of such a monster sight unseen – specifically, unseen by their own scientific eyes.

Striking an average of observations taken at different times – rejecting those timid estimates that gave the object a length of 200 feet, and ignoring those exaggerated views that saw it as a mile wide and three long – you could still assert that this phenomenal creature greatly exceeded the dimensions of anything then known to ichthyologists, if it existed at all.

Now then, it did exist, this was an undeniable fact; and since the human mind dotes on objects of wonder, you can understand the worldwide excitement caused by this unearthly apparition. As for relegating it to the realm of fiction, that charge had to be dropped.

In essence, on July 20, 1866, the steamer *Governor Higginson*, from the Calcutta & Burnach Steam Navigation Co., encountered this moving mass five miles off the eastern shores of Australia.

Captain Baker at first thought he was in the presence of an unknown reef; he was even about to fix its exact position when two waterspouts shot out of this inexplicable object and sprang hissing into the air some 150 feet. So, unless this reef was subject to the intermittent eruptions of a geyser, the *Governor Higginson* had fair and honest dealings with some aquatic mammal, until then unknown, that could spurt from its blowholes waterspouts mixed with air and steam.

Similar events were likewise observed in Pacific seas, on July 23 of the same year, by the *Christopher Columbus* from the West India & Pacific Steam Navigation Co. Consequently, this extraordinary cetacean could transfer itself from one locality to another with startling swiftness, since within an interval of just three days, the *Governor Higginson* and the *Christopher Columbus* had observed it at two positions on the charts separated by a distance of more than 700 nautical leagues.

Fifteen days later and 2,000 leagues farther, the *Helvetia* from the Compagnie Nationale and the *Shannon* from the Royal Mail line, running on opposite tacks in that part of the Atlantic lying between the United States and Europe, respectively signaled each other that the monster had been sighted in latitude 42° 15' north and longitude 60° 35' west of the meridian of Greenwich. From their simultaneous observations, they were able to estimate the mammal's minimum length at more than 350 English feet;[1] this was because both the *Shannon* and the *Helvetia* were of smaller dimensions, although each measured 100 metres stem to stern. Now then, the biggest whales, those rorqual whales that frequent the waterways of the Aleutian Islands, have never exceeded a length of 56 metres – if they reach even that.

One after another, reports arrived that would profoundly affect public opinion: new observations taken by the transatlantic liner

---

1 Author's Note: About 106 metres. An English foot is only 30.4 centimetres.

Pereire, the Inman line's *Etna* running afoul of the monster, an official report drawn up by officers on the French frigate *Normandy*, dead-earnest reckonings obtained by the general staff of Commodore Fitz-James aboard the *Lord Clyde*. In lighthearted countries, people joked about this phenomenon, but such serious, practical countries as England, America, and Germany were deeply concerned.

In every big city the monster was the latest rage; they sang about it in the coffee houses, they ridiculed it in the newspapers, they dramatised it in the theatres. The tabloids found it a fine opportunity for hatching all sorts of hoaxes. In those newspapers short of copy, you saw the reappearance of every gigantic imaginary creature, from 'Moby Dick,' that dreadful white whale from the High Arctic regions, to the stupendous kraken whose tentacles could entwine a 500-ton craft and drag it into the ocean depths. They even reprinted reports from ancient times: the views of Aristotle and Pliny accepting the existence of such monsters, then the Norwegian stories of Bishop Pontoppidan, the narratives of Paul Egede, and finally the reports of Captain Harrington – whose good faith is above suspicion – in which he claims he saw, while aboard the *Castilian* in 1857, one of those enormous serpents that, until then, had frequented only the seas of France's old extremist newspaper, *The Constitutionalist*.

An interminable debate then broke out between believers and sceptics in the scholarly societies and scientific journals. The 'monster question' inflamed all minds. During this memorable campaign, journalists making a profession of science battled with those making a profession of wit, spilling waves of ink and some of them even two or three drops of blood, since they went from sea serpents to the most offensive personal remarks.

For six months the war seesawed. With inexhaustible zest, the popular press took potshots at feature articles from the Geographic Institute of Brazil, the Royal Academy of Science in Berlin, the British Association, the Smithsonian Institution in Washington, DC, at discussions in The Indian Archipelago, in *Cosmos* published by Father Moigno, in Petermann's *Mittheilungen*, and at scientific chronicles in the great French and foreign newspapers. When the monster's detractors cited a saying by the botanist Linnaeus that 'nature doesn't make leaps,' witty writers in the popular periodicals parodied it, maintaining in essence that 'nature doesn't make lunatics,' and ordering their contemporaries never to give the lie to nature by believing in krakens, sea serpents, 'Moby Dicks,' and other all-out efforts from drunken seamen. Finally, in a much-feared satirical journal, an article by its most popular columnist finished off the monster for good, spurning it in the style of Hippolytus repulsing the amorous advances of his stepmother Phædra, and giving the creature its quietus amid a universal burst of laughter. Wit had defeated science.

During the first months of the year 1867, the question seemed to be buried, and it didn't seem due for resurrection, when new facts were brought to the public's attention. But now it was no longer an issue of a scientific problem to be solved, but a quite real and serious danger to be avoided. The question took an entirely new turn. The monster again became an islet, rock, or reef, but a runaway reef, unfixed and elusive.

On March 5, 1867, the *Moravian* from the Montreal Ocean Co., lying during the night in latitude 27° 30' and longitude 72° 15', ran its starboard quarter afoul of a rock marked on no charts of these waterways. Under the combined efforts of wind and 400-horsepower steam, it was travelling at a speed of 13 knots. Without the high quality of its hull, the *Moravian* would surely have split open from this collision and gone down together with those 237 passengers it was bringing back from Canada.

This accident happened around five o'clock in the morning, just as day was beginning to break. The officers on watch rushed to the craft's stern. They examined the ocean with the most scrupulous care. They saw nothing except a strong eddy breaking three cable lengths out, as if those sheets of water had been violently churned. The site's exact bearings were taken, and the *Moravian* continued on course apparently undamaged. Had it run afoul of an underwater rock or the wreckage of some enormous derelict ship? They were unable to say. But when they examined its undersides in the service yard, they discovered that part of its keel had been smashed.

This occurrence, extremely serious in itself, might perhaps have been forgotten like so many others, if three weeks later it hadn't been reenacted under identical conditions. Only, thanks to the nationality of the ship victimised by this new ramming, and thanks to the reputation of the company to which this ship belonged, the event caused an immense uproar.

No one is unaware of the name of that famous English shipowner, Cunard. In 1840 this shrewd industrialist founded a postal service between Liverpool and Halifax, featuring three wooden ships with 400-horsepower paddle wheels and a burden of 1,162 metric tons. Eight years later, the company's assets were increased by four 650-horsepower ships at 1,820 metric tons, and in two more years, by two other vessels of still greater power and tonnage. In 1853 the Cunard Co., whose mail-carrying charter had just been renewed, successively added to its assets the *Arabia*, the *Persia*, the *China*, the *Scotia*, the *Java* and the *Russia*, all ships of top speed and, after the *Great Eastern*, the biggest ever to plough the seas. So in 1867 this company owned 12 ships, eight with paddle wheels and four with propellers.

If I give these highly condensed details, it is so everyone can fully understand the importance of this maritime transportation company, known the world over for its shrewd management. No transoceanic navigational undertaking has been conducted with more ability, no business dealings have been crowned with greater success. In 26 years Cunard ships have made 2,000 Atlantic crossings without so much as a voyage cancelled, a delay recorded, a man, a craft, or even a letter lost. Accordingly, despite strong competition from France, passengers still choose the Cunard line in preference to all others, as can be seen in a recent survey of official documents. Given this, no one will be astonished at the uproar provoked by this accident involving one of its finest steamers.

On April 13, 1867, with a smooth sea and a moderate breeze, the *Scotia* lay in longitude 15° 12' and latitude 45° 37'. It was travelling at a speed of 13.43 knots under the thrust of its 1,000-horsepower engines. Its paddle wheels were churning the sea with perfect steadiness. It was then drawing 6.7 metres of water and displacing 6,624 cubic metres.

At 4:17 in the afternoon, during a high tea for passengers gathered in the main lounge, a collision occurred, scarcely noticeable on the whole, affecting the *Scotia*'s hull in that quarter a little astern of its port paddle wheel.

The *Scotia* hadn't run afoul of something, it had been fouled, and by a cutting or perforating instrument rather than a blunt one. This encounter seemed so minor that nobody on board would have been disturbed by it, had it not been for the shouts of crewmen in the hold, who climbed on deck yelling:

'We're sinking! We're sinking!'

At first the passengers were quite frightened, but Captain Anderson hastened to reassure them. In fact, there could be no immediate danger. Divided into seven compartments by watertight bulkheads, the *Scotia* could brave any leak with impunity.

Captain Anderson immediately made his way into the hold. He discovered that the fifth compartment had been invaded by the sea, and the speed of this invasion proved that the leak was considerable. Fortunately this compartment didn't contain the boilers, because their furnaces would have been abruptly extinguished.

Captain Anderson called an immediate halt, and one of his sailors dived down to assess the damage. Within moments they had located a hole two metres in width on the steamer's underside. Such a leak could not be patched, and with its paddle wheels half swamped, the *Scotia* had no choice but to continue its voyage. By then it lay 300 miles from Cape Clear, and after three days of delay that filled Liverpool with acute anxiety, it entered the company docks.

The engineers then proceeded to inspect the *Scotia*, which had been put in dry dock. They couldn't believe their eyes. Two and a half metres below its waterline, there gaped a symmetrical gash in the shape of an isosceles triangle. This breach in the sheet iron was so perfectly formed, no punch could have done a cleaner job of it. Consequently, it must have been produced by a perforating tool of uncommon toughness – plus, after being launched with prodigious power and then piercing four centimetres of sheet iron, this tool had needed to withdraw itself by a backward motion truly inexplicable.

This was the last straw, and it resulted in arousing public passions all over again. Indeed, from this moment on, any maritime casualty without an established cause was charged to the monster's account. This outrageous animal had to shoulder responsibility for all derelict vessels, whose numbers are unfortunately considerable, since out of those 3,000 ships whose losses are recorded annually at the marine insurance bureau, the figure for steam or sailing ships supposedly lost with all hands, in the absence of any news, amounts to at least 200!

Now then, justly or unjustly, it was the 'monster' who stood accused of their disappearance; and since, thanks to it, travel between the various continents had become more and more dangerous, the public spoke up and demanded straight out that, at all cost, the seas be purged of this fearsome cetacean.

CHAPTER 2
The Pros and Cons

DURING THE PERIOD in which these developments were occurring, I had returned from a scientific undertaking organised to explore the Nebraska badlands in the United States. In my capacity as Assistant Professor at the Paris Museum of Natural History, I had been attached to this expedition by the French government. After spending six months in Nebraska, I arrived in New York laden with valuable collections near the end of March. My departure for France was set for early May. In the meantime, then, I was busy classifying my mineralogical, botanical, and zoological treasures when that incident took place with the *Scotia*.

I was perfectly abreast of this question, which was the big news of the day, and how could I not have been? I had read and reread every American and European newspaper without being any farther along. This mystery puzzled me. Finding it impossible to form any views, I drifted from one extreme to the other. Something was out there, that much was certain, and any doubting Thomas was invited to place his finger on the *Scotia*'s wound.

When I arrived in New York, the question was at the boiling point. The hypothesis of a drifting islet or an elusive reef, put forward by people not quite in their right minds, was completely eliminated. And indeed, unless this reef had an engine in its belly, how could it move about with such prodigious speed?

Also discredited was the idea of a floating hull or some other enormous wreckage, and again because of this speed of movement.

So only two possible solutions to the question were left, creating two very distinct groups of supporters: on one side, those favouring a monster of colossal strength; on the other, those favouring an 'underwater boat' of tremendous motor power.

Now then, although the latter hypothesis was completely admissible, it couldn't stand up to inquiries conducted in both the New World and the Old. That a private individual had such a mechanism at his disposal was less than probable. Where and when had he built it, and how could he have built it in secret?

Only some government could own such an engine of destruction, and in these disaster-filled times, when men tax their ingenuity to build increasingly powerful aggressive weapons, it was possible that, unknown to the rest of the world, some nation could have been testing such a fearsome machine. The Chassepot rifle led to the torpedo, and the torpedo has led to this underwater battering ram, which in turn will lead to the world putting its foot down. At least I hope it will.

But this hypothesis of a war machine collapsed in the face of formal denials from the various governments. Since the public interest was at stake and transoceanic travel was suffering, the sincerity of these governments could not be doubted. Besides, how could the assembly of this underwater boat have escaped public notice? Keeping a secret under such circumstances would be difficult enough for an individual, and certainly impossible for a nation whose every move is under constant surveillance by rival powers.

So, after inquiries conducted in England, France, Russia, Prussia, Spain, Italy, America, and even Turkey, the hypothesis of an underwater *Monitor* was ultimately rejected.

And so the monster surfaced again, despite the endless witticisms heaped on it by the popular press, and the human imagination soon got caught up in the most ridiculous ichthyological fantasies.

After I arrived in New York, several people did me the honour of consulting me on the phenomenon in question. In France I had published a two–volume work, in quarto, entitled *The Mysteries of the Great Ocean Depths*. Well received in scholarly circles, this book had established me as a specialist in this pretty obscure field of natural history. My views were in demand. As long as I could deny the reality of the business, I confined myself to a flat 'no comment.' But soon, pinned to the wall, I had to explain myself straight out. And in this vein, 'the honourable Pierre Aronnax, Professor at the Paris Museum,' was summoned by *The New York Herald* to formulate his views no matter what.

I complied. Since I could no longer hold my tongue, I let it wag. I discussed the question in its every aspect, both political and scientific, and this is an excerpt from the well-padded article I published in the issue of April 30.

'Therefore,' I wrote, 'after examining these different hypotheses one by one, we are forced, every other supposition having been refuted, to accept the existence of an extremely powerful marine animal.

'The deepest parts of the ocean are totally unknown to us. No soundings have been able to reach them. What goes on in those distant depths? What creatures inhabit, or could inhabit, those regions 12 or 15 miles beneath the surface of the water? What is the constitution of these animals? It's almost beyond conjecture.

'However, the solution to this problem submitted to me can take the form of a choice between two alternatives.

'Either we know every variety of creature populating our planet, or we do not.

'If we do not know every one of them, if nature still keeps ichthyological secrets from us, nothing is more admissible than to accept the existence of fish or cetaceans of new species or even new genera, animals with a basically "cast-iron" constitution that inhabit strata beyond the reach of our soundings, and which some development or other, an urge or a whim if you prefer, can bring to the upper level of the ocean for long intervals.

'If, on the other hand, we do know every living species, we must look for the animal in question among those marine creatures already catalogued, and in this event I would be inclined to accept the existence of a giant narwhal.

'The common narwhal, or sea unicorn, often reaches a length of 60 feet. Increase its dimensions fivefold or even tenfold, then give this cetacean a strength in proportion to its size while enlarging its offensive weapons, and you have the animal we're looking for. It would have the proportions determined by the officers of the *Shannon*, the instrument needed to perforate the *Scotia*, and the power to pierce a steamer's hull.

'In essence, the narwhal is armed with a sort of ivory sword, or lance, as certain naturalists have expressed it. It's a king-sized tooth as hard as steel. Some of these teeth have been found buried in the bodies of baleen whales, which the narwhal attacks with invariable success. Others have been wrenched, not without difficulty, from the undersides of vessels that narwhals have pierced clean through, as a gimlet pierces a wine barrel. The museum at the Faculty of Medicine in Paris owns one of these tusks with a length of 2.25 metres and a width at its base of 48 centimetres!

'All right then! Imagine this weapon to be ten times stronger and the animal ten times more powerful, launch it at a speed of 20 miles per hour, multiply its mass times its velocity, and you get just the collision we need to cause the specified catastrophe.

'So, until information becomes more abundant, I plump for a sea unicorn of colossal dimensions, no longer armed with a mere lance but with an actual spur, like ironclad frigates or those warships called "rams," whose mass and motor power it would possess simultaneously.

'This inexplicable phenomenon is thus explained away – unless it's something else entirely, which, despite everything that has been sighted, studied, explored and experienced, is still possible!'

These last words were cowardly of me; but as far as I could, I wanted to protect my professorial dignity and not lay myself open to laughter from the Americans, who when they do laugh, laugh raucously. I had left myself a loophole. Yet deep down, I had accepted the existence of 'the monster.'

My article was hotly debated, causing a fine old uproar. It rallied a number of supporters. Moreover, the solution it proposed allowed for free play of the imagination. The human mind enjoys impressive visions of unearthly creatures. Now then, the sea is precisely their best medium, the only setting suitable for the breeding and growing of such giants – next to which such land animals as elephants or rhinoceroses are mere dwarves. The liquid masses support the largest known species of mammals and perhaps conceal molluscs of incomparable size or crustaceans too frightful to contemplate, such as 100-metre lobsters or crabs weighing 200 metric tons! Why not? Formerly, in prehistoric days, land animals (quadrupeds, apes, reptiles, birds) were built on a gigantic scale. Our Creator cast them using a colossal mould that time has gradually made smaller. With its untold depths, couldn't the sea keep alive such huge specimens of life from another age, this sea that never changes while the land masses undergo almost continuous alteration? Couldn't the heart of the ocean hide the last-remaining varieties of these titanic species, for whom years are centuries and centuries millennia?

But I mustn't let these fantasies run away with me! Enough of these fairy tales that time has changed for me into harsh realities. I repeat: opinion had crystallised as to the nature of this phenomenon, and the public accepted without argument the existence of a prodigious creature that had nothing in common with the fabled sea serpent.

Yet if some saw it purely as a scientific problem to be solved, more practical people, especially in America and England, were determined to purge the ocean of this daunting monster, to insure the safety of transoceanic travel. The industrial and commercial newspapers dealt with the question chiefly from this viewpoint. The *Shipping & Mercantile Gazette*, the *Lloyd's List*, France's *Packetboat and Maritime & Colonial Review*, all the rags devoted to insurance companies – who threatened to raise their premium rates – were unanimous on this point.

Public opinion being pronounced, the States of the Union were the first in the field. In New York preparations were under way for an expedition designed to chase this narwhal. A high-speed frigate, the *Abraham Lincoln*, was fitted out for putting to sea as soon as possible. The naval arsenals were unlocked for Commander Farragut, who pressed energetically forward with the arming of his frigate.

But, as it always happens, just when a decision had been made to chase the monster, the monster put in no further appearances. For two months nobody heard a word about it. Not a single ship encountered it. Apparently the unicorn had gotten wise to these plots being woven around it. People were constantly babbling about the creature, even via the Atlantic Cable! Accordingly, the wags claimed that this slippery rascal had waylaid some passing telegram and was making the most of it.

So the frigate was equipped for a far-off voyage and armed with fearsome fishing gear, but nobody knew where to steer it. And impatience grew until, on June 2, word came that the *Tampico*, a steamer on the San Francisco line sailing from California to Shanghai, had sighted the animal again, three weeks before in the northerly seas of the Pacific.

This news caused intense excitement. Not even a 24-hour breather was granted to Commander Farragut. His provisions were loaded on board. His coal bunkers were overflowing. Not a crewman was missing from his post. To cast off, he needed only to fire and stoke his furnaces! Half a day's delay would have been unforgivable! But Commander Farragut wanted nothing more than to go forth.

I received a letter three hours before the *Abraham Lincoln* left its Brooklyn pier;[1] the letter read as follows:

Pierre Aronnax
Professor at the Paris Museum
Fifth Avenue Hotel
New York

Sir:
If you would like to join the expedition on the *Abraham Lincoln*, the government of the Union will be pleased to regard you as France's representative in this undertaking. Commander Farragut has a cabin at your disposal.

Very cordially yours,
J. B. HOBSON,
Secretary of the Navy.

---

[1] Author's Note: A pier is a type of wharf expressly set aside for an individual vessel.

CHAPTER 3

As Master Wishes

THREE SECONDS BEFORE the arrival of J. B. Hobson's letter, I no more dreamed of chasing the unicorn than of trying for the Northwest Passage. Three seconds after reading this letter from the honourable Secretary of the Navy, I understood at last that my true vocation, my sole purpose in life, was to hunt down this disturbing monster and rid the world of it.

Even so, I had just returned from an arduous journey, exhausted and badly needing a rest. I wanted nothing more than to see my country again, my friends, my modest quarters by the Botanical Gardens, my dearly beloved collections! But now nothing could hold me back. I forgot everything else, and without another thought of exhaustion, friends, or collections, I accepted the American government's offer.

'Besides,' I mused, 'all roads lead home to Europe, and our unicorn may be gracious enough to take me toward the coast of France! That fine animal may even let itself be captured in European seas – as a personal favour to me – and I'll bring back to the Museum of Natural History at least half a metre of its ivory lance!'

But in the meantime I would have to look for this narwhal in the northern Pacific Ocean; which meant returning to France by way of the Antipodes.

'Conseil!' I called in an impatient voice.

Conseil was my manservant. A devoted lad who went with me on all my journeys; a gallant Flemish boy whom I genuinely liked and who returned the compliment; a born stoic, punctilious on principle, habitually hardworking, rarely startled by life's surprises, very skilful with his hands, efficient in his every duty, and despite his having a name that means 'counsel,' never giving advice – not even the unsolicited kind!

From rubbing shoulders with scientists in our little universe by the Botanical Gardens, the boy had come to know a thing or two. In

Conseil I had a seasoned specialist in biological classification, an enthusiast who could run with acrobatic agility up and down the whole ladder of branches, groups, classes, subclasses, orders, families, genera, subgenera, species and varieties. But there his science came to a halt. Classifying was everything to him, so he knew nothing else. Well versed in the theory of classification, he was poorly versed in its practical application, and I doubt that he could tell a sperm whale from a baleen whale! And yet, what a fine, gallant lad!

For the past ten years, Conseil had gone with me wherever science beckoned. Not once did he comment on the length or the hardships of a journey. Never did he object to buckling up his suitcase for any country whatever, China or the Congo, no matter how far off it was. He went here, there, and everywhere in perfect contentment. Moreover, he enjoyed excellent health that defied all ailments, owned solid muscles, but hadn't a nerve in him, not a sign of nerves – the mental type, I mean.

The lad was 30 years old, and his age to that of his employer was as 15 is to 20. Please forgive me for this underhanded way of admitting I had turned 40.

But Conseil had one flaw. He was a fanatic on formality, and he only addressed me in the third person – to the point where it got tiresome.

'Conseil!' I repeated, while feverishly beginning my preparations for departure.

To be sure, I had confidence in this devoted lad. Ordinarily, I never asked whether or not it suited him to go with me on my journeys; but this time an expedition was at issue that could drag on indefinitely, a hazardous undertaking whose purpose was to hunt an animal that could sink a frigate as easily as a walnut shell! There was good reason to stop and think, even for the world's most emotionless man. What would Conseil say?

'Conseil!' I called a third time.

Conseil appeared.

'Did master summon me?' he said, entering.

'Yes, my boy. Get my things ready, get yours ready. We're departing in two hours.'

'As master wishes,' Conseil replied serenely.

'We haven't a moment to lose. Pack as much into my trunk as you can, my travelling kit, my suits, shirts, and socks, don't bother counting, just squeeze it all in – and hurry!'

'What about master's collections?' Conseil ventured to observe.

'We'll deal with them later.'

'What! The *archaeotherium, hyracotherium, oreodonts, cheiropotamus* and master's other fossil skeletons?'

'The hotel will keep them for us.'

'What about master's live babirusa?'

'They'll feed it during our absence. Anyhow, we'll leave instructions to ship the whole menagerie to France.'

'Then we aren't returning to Paris?' Conseil asked.

'Yes, we are… certainly… ,' I replied evasively, 'but after we make a detour.'

'Whatever detour master wishes.'

'Oh, it's nothing really! A route slightly less direct, that's all. We're leaving on the *Abraham Lincoln*.'

'As master thinks best,' Conseil replied placidly.

'You see, my friend, it's an issue of the monster, the notorious narwhal. We're going to rid the seas of it! The author of a two-volume work, in quarto, on The Mysteries of the Great Ocean Depths has no excuse for not setting sail with Commander Farragut. It's a glorious mission but also a dangerous one! We don't know where it will take us! These beasts can be quite unpredictable! But we're going just the same! We have a commander who's game for anything!'

'What master does, I'll do,' Conseil replied.

'But think it over, because I don't want to hide anything from you. This is one of those voyages from which people don't always come back!'

'As master wishes.'

A quarter of an hour later, our trunks were ready. Conseil did them in a flash, and I was sure the lad hadn't missed a thing, because he classified shirts and suits as expertly as birds and mammals.

The hotel elevator dropped us off in the main vestibule on the mezzanine. I went down a short stair leading to the ground floor. I settled my bill at that huge counter that was always under siege by a considerable crowd. I left instructions for shipping my containers of stuffed animals and dried plants to Paris, France. I opened a line of credit sufficient to cover the babirusa and, Conseil at my heels, I jumped into a carriage.

For a fare of 20 francs, the vehicle went down Broadway to Union Square, took Fourth Ave. to its junction with Bowery St, turned into Katrin St and halted at Pier 34. There the Katrin ferry transferred men, horses and carriage to Brooklyn, that great New York annex located on the left bank of the East River, and in a few minutes we arrived at the wharf next to which the *Abraham Lincoln* was vomiting torrents of black smoke from its two funnels.

Our baggage was immediately carried to the deck of the frigate. I rushed aboard. I asked for Commander Farragut. One of the sailors led me to the afterdeck, where I stood in the presence of a smart-looking officer who extended his hand to me.

'Professor Pierre Aronnax?' he said to me.

'The same,' I replied. 'Commander Farragut?'

'In person. Welcome aboard, professor. Your cabin is waiting for you.'

I bowed, and letting the commander attend to getting under way, I was taken to the cabin that had been set aside for me.

The *Abraham Lincoln* had been perfectly chosen and fitted out for its new assignment. It was a high-speed frigate furnished with superheating equipment that allowed the tension of its steam to build to seven atmospheres. Under this pressure the *Abraham Lincoln* reached an average speed of 18.3 miles per hour, a considerable speed but still not enough to cope with our gigantic cetacean.

The frigate's interior accommodations complemented its nautical virtues. I was well satisfied with my cabin, which was located in the stern and opened into the officers' mess.

'We'll be quite comfortable here,' I told Conseil.

'With all due respect to master,' Conseil replied, 'as comfortable as a hermit crab inside the shell of a whelk.'

I left Conseil to the proper stowing of our luggage and climbed on deck to watch the preparations for getting under way.

Just then Commander Farragut was giving orders to cast off the last moorings holding the *Abraham Lincoln* to its Brooklyn pier. And so if I'd been delayed by a quarter of an hour or even less, the frigate would have gone without me, and I would have missed out on this unearthly, extraordinary and inconceivable expedition, whose true story might well meet with some scepticism.

But Commander Farragut didn't want to waste a single day, or even a single hour, in making for those seas where the animal had just been sighted. He summoned his engineer.

'Are we up to pressure?' he asked the man.

'Aye, sir,' the engineer replied.

'Go ahead, then!' Commander Farragut called.

At this order, which was relayed to the engine by means of a compressed-air device, the mechanics activated the start-up wheel. Steam rushed whistling into the gaping valves. Long horizontal pistons groaned and pushed the tie rods of the drive shaft. The blades of the propeller churned the waves with increasing speed, and the *Abraham Lincoln* moved out majestically amid a spectator-laden escort of some 100 ferries and tenders.[1]

The wharves of Brooklyn, and every part of New York bordering the East River, were crowded with curiosity seekers. Departing from 500,000 throats, three cheers burst forth in succession. Thousands of handkerchiefs were waving above these tightly packed masses, hailing the *Abraham Lincoln* until it reached the waters of the Hudson River, at the tip of the long peninsula that forms New York City.

The frigate then went along the New Jersey coast – the wonderful right bank of this river, all loaded down with country homes – and passed by the forts to salutes from their biggest cannons. The *Abraham Lincoln* replied by three times lowering and hoisting the American flag, whose 39 stars gleamed from the gaff of the mizzen sail; then, changing speed to take the buoy-marked channel that curved into the inner bay formed by the spit of Sandy Hook, it hugged this sand-covered strip of land where thousands of spectators acclaimed us one more time.

The escort of boats and tenders still followed the frigate and only left us when we came abreast of the lightship, whose two signal lights mark the entrance of the narrows to Upper New York Bay.

---

1 Author's Note: Tenders are small steamboats that assist the big liners.

Three o'clock then sounded. The harbour pilot went down into his dinghy and rejoined a little schooner waiting for him to leeward. The furnaces were stoked; the propeller churned the waves more swiftly; the frigate skirted the flat, yellow coast of Long Island; and at eight o'clock in the evening, after the lights of Fire Island had vanished into the northwest, we ran at full steam onto the dark waters of the Atlantic.

CHAPTER 4
Ned Land

COMMANDER FARRAGUT WAS a good seaman, worthy of the frigate he commanded. His ship and he were one. He was its very soul. On the cetacean question no doubts arose in his mind, and he didn't allow the animal's existence to be disputed aboard his vessel. He believed in it as certain pious women believe in the leviathan from the Book of Job – out of faith, not reason. The monster existed, and he had vowed to rid the seas of it. The man was a sort of Knight of Rhodes, a latter-day Sir Dieudonné of Gozo, on his way to fight an encounter with the dragon devastating the island. Either Commander Farragut would slay the narwhal, or the narwhal would slay Commander Farragut. No middle of the road for these two.

The ship's officers shared the views of their leader. They could be heard chatting, discussing, arguing, calculating the different chances of an encounter, and observing the vast expanse of the ocean. Voluntary watches from the crosstrees of the topgallant sail were self-imposed by more than one who would have cursed such toil under any other circumstances. As often as the sun swept over its daily arc, the masts were populated with sailors whose feet itched and couldn't hold still on the planking of the deck below! And the *Abraham Lincoln's* stempost hadn't even cut the suspected waters of the Pacific.

As for the crew, they only wanted to encounter the unicorn, harpoon it, haul it on board and carve it up. They surveyed the sea with scrupulous care. Besides, Commander Farragut had mentioned that a certain sum of $2,000 was waiting for the man who first sighted the animal, be he cabin boy or sailor, mate or officer. I'll let the reader decide whether eyes got proper exercise aboard the *Abraham Lincoln*.

As for me, I didn't lag behind the others and I yielded to no one my share in these daily observations. Our frigate would have had fivescore good reasons for renaming itself the *Argus*, after that mythological beast with 100 eyes! The lone rebel among us was

Conseil, who seemed utterly uninterested in the question exciting us and was out of step with the general enthusiasm on board.

As I said, Commander Farragut had carefully equipped his ship with all the gear needed to fish for a gigantic cetacean. No whaling vessel could have been better armed. We had every known mechanism, from the hand-hurled harpoon, to the blunderbuss firing barbed arrows, to the duck gun with exploding bullets. On the fo'c'sle was mounted the latest model breech-loading cannon, very heavy of barrel and narrow of bore, a weapon that would figure in the Universal Exhibition of 1867. Made in America, this valuable instrument could fire a four-kilogram conical projectile an average distance of 16 kilometres without the least bother.

So the *Abraham Lincoln* wasn't lacking in means of destruction. But it had better still. It had Ned Land, the King of Harpooners.

Gifted with uncommon manual ability, Ned Land was a Canadian who had no equal in his dangerous trade. Dexterity, coolness, bravery and cunning were virtues he possessed to a high degree, and it took a truly crafty baleen whale or an exceptionally astute sperm whale to elude the thrusts of his harpoon.

Ned Land was about 40 years old. A man of great height – over six English feet – he was powerfully built, serious in manner, not very sociable, sometimes headstrong and quite ill-tempered when crossed. His looks caught the attention, and above all the strength of his gaze, which gave a unique emphasis to his facial appearance.

Commander Farragut, to my thinking, had made a wise move in hiring on this man. With his eye and his throwing arm, he was worth the whole crew all by himself. I can do no better than to compare him with a powerful telescope that could double as a cannon always ready to fire.

To say Canadian is to say French, and as unsociable as Ned Land was, I must admit he took a definite liking to me. No doubt it was my nationality that attracted him. It was an opportunity for him to speak, and for me to hear, that old Rabelaisian dialect still used in some Canadian provinces. The harpooner's family originated in Quebec, and they were already a line of bold fishermen back in the days when this town still belonged to France.

Little by little Ned developed a taste for chatting, and I loved hearing the tales of his adventures in the polar seas. He described his fishing trips and his battles with great natural lyricism. His tales took on the form of an epic poem, and I felt I was hearing some Canadian Homer reciting his *Iliad* of the High Arctic regions.

I'm writing of this bold companion as I currently know him. Because we've become old friends, united in that permanent comradeship born and cemented during only the most frightful crises! Ah, my gallant Ned! I ask only to live 100 years more, the longer to remember you!

And now, what were Ned Land's views on this question of a marine monster? I must admit that he flatly didn't believe in the unicorn and, alone on board, he didn't share the general conviction. He avoided even dealing with the subject, for which one day I felt compelled to take him to task.

During the magnificent evening of June 25 – in other words, three weeks after our departure – the frigate lay abreast of Cabo Blanco, 30 miles to leeward of the coast of Patagonia. We had crossed the Tropic of Capricorn, and the Strait of Magellan opened less than 700 miles to the south. Before eight days were out, the *Abraham Lincoln* would plough the waves of the Pacific.

Seated on the afterdeck, Ned Land and I chatted about one thing and another, staring at that mysterious sea whose depths to this day are beyond the reach of human eyes. Quite naturally, I led our conversation around to the giant unicorn, and I weighed our expedition's various chances for success or failure. Then, seeing that Ned just let me talk without saying much himself, I pressed him more closely.

'Ned,' I asked him, 'how can you still doubt the reality of this cetacean we're after? Do you have any particular reasons for being so sceptical?'

The harpooner stared at me awhile before replying, slapped his broad forehead in one of his standard gestures, closed his eyes as if to collect himself, and finally said:

'Just maybe, Professor Aronnax.'

'But Ned, you're a professional whaler, a man familiar with all the great marine mammals – your mind should easily accept this hypothesis of an enormous cetacean, and you ought to be the last one to doubt it under these circumstances!'

'That's just where you're mistaken, professor,' Ned replied. 'The common man may still believe in fabulous comets crossing outer space, or in prehistoric monsters living at the earth's core, but astronomers and geologists don't swallow such fairy tales. It's the same with whalers. I've chased plenty of cetaceans, I've harpooned a good number, I've killed several. But no matter how powerful and well armed they were, neither their tails or their tusks could puncture the sheet–iron plates of a steamer.'

'Even so, Ned, people mention vessels that narwhal tusks have run clean through.'

'Wooden ships maybe,' the Canadian replied. 'But I've never seen the like. So till I have proof to the contrary, I'll deny that baleen whales, sperm whales or unicorns can do any such thing.'

'Listen to me, Ned—'

'No, no, professor. I'll go along with anything you want except that. Some gigantic devilfish maybe…?'

'Even less likely, Ned. The devilfish is merely a mollusc, and even this name hints at its semiliquid flesh, because it's Latin meaning, "soft one". The devilfish doesn't belong to the vertebrate branch, and even if it were 500 feet long, it would still be utterly harmless to ships like the *Scotia* or the *Abraham Lincoln*. Consequently, the feats of krakens or other monsters of that ilk must be relegated to the realm of fiction.'

'So, Mr Naturalist,' Ned Land continued in a bantering tone, 'you'll just keep on believing in the existence of some enormous cetacean…?'

'Yes, Ned, I repeat it with a conviction backed by factual logic. I believe in the existence of a mammal with a powerful constitution, belonging to the vertebrate branch like baleen whales, sperm whales, or dolphins, and armed with a tusk made of horn that has tremendous penetrating power.'

'Humph!' the harpooner put in, shaking his head with the attitude of a man who doesn't want to be convinced.

'Note well, my fine Canadian,' I went on, 'if such an animal exists, if it lives deep in the ocean, if it frequents the liquid strata located miles beneath the surface of the water, it needs to have a constitution so solid, it defies all comparison.'

'And why this powerful constitution?' Ned asked.

'Because it takes incalculable strength just to live in those deep strata and withstand their pressure.'

'Oh really?' Ned said, tipping me a wink.

'Oh really, and I can prove it to you with a few simple figures.'

'Bosh!' Ned replied. 'You can make figures do anything you want!'

'In business, Ned, but not in mathematics. Listen to me. Let's accept that the pressure of one atmosphere is represented by the pressure of a column of water 32 feet high. In reality, such a column of water wouldn't be quite so high because here we're dealing with salt water, which is denser than fresh water. Well then, when you dive under the waves, Ned, for every 32 feet of water above you, your body is tolerating the pressure of one more atmosphere, in other words, one more kilogram per each square centimetre on your body's surface. So it follows that at 320 feet down, this pressure is equal to ten atmospheres, to 100 atmospheres at 3,200 feet, and to 1,000 atmospheres at 32,000 feet, that is, at about two and a half vertical leagues down. Which is tantamount to saying that if you could reach such a depth in the ocean, each square centimetre on your body's surface would be experiencing 1,000 kilograms of pressure. Now, my gallant Ned, do you know how many square centimetres you have on your bodily surface?'

'I haven't the foggiest notion, Professor Aronnax.'

'About 17,000.'

'As many as that?'

'Yes, and since the atmosphere's pressure actually weighs slightly more than one kilogram per square centimetre, your 17,000 square centimetres are tolerating 17,568 kilograms at this very moment.'

'Without my noticing it?'

'Without your noticing it. And if you aren't crushed by so much pressure, it's because the air penetrates the interior of your body with equal pressure. When the inside and outside pressures are in perfect balance, they neutralise each other and allow you to tolerate them without discomfort. But in the water it's another story.'

'Yes, I see,' Ned replied, growing more interested. 'Because the water surrounds me but doesn't penetrate me.'

'Precisely, Ned. So at 32 feet beneath the surface of the sea, you'll undergo a pressure of 17,568 kilograms; at 320 feet, or ten times greater pressure, it's 175,680 kilograms; at 3,200 feet, or 100 times greater pressure, it's 1,756,800 kilograms; finally, at 32,000 feet, or 1,000 times greater pressure, it's 17,568,000 kilograms; in other words, you'd be squashed as flat as if you'd just been yanked from between the plates of a hydraulic press!'

'Fire and brimstone!' Ned put in.

'All right then, my fine harpooner, if vertebrates several hundred metres long and proportionate in bulk live at such depths, their surface areas make up millions of square centimetres, and the pressure they undergo must be assessed in billions of kilograms. Calculate, then, how much resistance of bone structure and strength of constitution they'd need in order to withstand such pressures!'

'They'd need to be manufactured,' Ned Land replied, 'from sheet-iron plates eight inches thick, like ironclad frigates.'

'Right, Ned, and then picture the damage such a mass could inflict if it were launched with the speed of an express train against a ship's hull.'

'Yes... indeed... maybe,' the Canadian replied, staggered by these figures but still not willing to give in.

'Well, have I convinced you?'

'You've convinced me of one thing, Mr Naturalist. That deep in the sea, such animals would need to be just as strong as you say – if they exist.'

'But if they don't exist, my stubborn harpooner, how do you explain the accident that happened to the *Scotia*?'

'It's maybe... ,' Ned said, hesitating.

'Go on!'

'Because... it just couldn't be true!' the Canadian replied, unconsciously echoing a famous catchphrase of the scientist Arago.

But this reply proved nothing, other than how bullheaded the harpooner could be. That day I pressed him no further. The *Scotia's* accident was undeniable. Its hole was real enough that it had to be plugged up, and I don't think a hole's existence can be more emphatically proven. Now then, this hole didn't make itself, and since it hadn't resulted from underwater rocks or underwater machines, it must have been caused by the perforating tool of some animal.

Now, for all the reasons put forward to this point, I believed that this animal was a member of the branch *Vertebrata*, class *Mammalia*, group *Pisciforma*, and finally, order *Cetacea*. As for the family in which it would be placed (baleen whale, sperm whale, or dolphin), the genus to which it belonged, and the species in which it would find its proper home, these questions had to be left for later. To answer them called for dissecting this unknown monster; to dissect it called for catching it; to catch it called for harpooning it – which was Ned Land's business; to harpoon it called for sighting it – which was the crew's business; and to sight it called for encountering it – which was a chancy business.

CHAPTER 5

At Random!

FOR SOME WHILE the voyage of the *Abraham Lincoln* was marked by no incident. But one circumstance arose that displayed Ned Land's marvellous skills and showed just how much confidence we could place in him.

Off the Falkland Islands on June 30, the frigate came in contact with a fleet of American whalers, and we learned that they hadn't seen the narwhal. But one of them, the captain of the *Monroe*, knew that Ned Land had shipped aboard the *Abraham Lincoln* and asked his help in hunting a baleen whale that was in sight. Anxious to see Ned Land at work, Commander Farragut authorised him to make his way aboard the *Monroe*. And the Canadian had such good luck that with a right-and-left shot, he harpooned not one whale but two, striking the first straight to the heart and catching the other after a few minutes' chase!

Assuredly, if the monster ever had to deal with Ned Land's harpoon, I wouldn't bet on the monster.

The frigate sailed along the east coast of South America with prodigious speed. By July 3 we were at the entrance to the Strait of Magellan, abreast of Cabo de las Virgenes. But Commander Farragut was unwilling to attempt this tortuous passageway and manoeuvred instead to double Cape Horn.

The crew sided with him unanimously. Indeed, were we likely to encounter the narwhal in such a cramped strait? Many of our sailors swore that the monster couldn't negotiate this passageway simply because 'he's too big for it!'

Near three o'clock in the afternoon on July 6, 15 miles south of shore, the *Abraham Lincoln* doubled that solitary islet at the tip of the South American continent, that stray rock Dutch seamen had named Cape Horn after their hometown of Hoorn. Our course was set for the northwest, and the next day our frigate's propeller finally churned the waters of the Pacific.

'Open your eyes! Open your eyes!' repeated the sailors of the *Abraham Lincoln*. And they opened amazingly wide. Eyes and spyglasses (a bit dazzled, it is true, by the vista of $2,000) didn't remain at rest for an instant. Day and night we observed the surface of the ocean, and those with nyctalopic eyes, whose ability to see in the dark increased their chances by 50 per cent, had an excellent shot at winning the prize.

As for me, I was hardly drawn by the lure of money and yet was far from the least attentive on board. Snatching only a few minutes for meals and a few hours for sleep, come rain or come shine, I no longer left the ship's deck. Sometimes bending over the fo'c'sle railings, sometimes leaning against the sternrail, I eagerly scoured that cotton-coloured wake that whitened the ocean as far as the eye could see! And how many times I shared the excitement of general staff and crew when some unpredictable whale lifted its blackish back above the waves. In an instant the frigate's deck would become densely populated. The cowls over the companionways would vomit a torrent of sailors and officers. With panting chests and anxious eyes, we each would observe the cetacean's movements. I stared; I stared until I nearly went blind from a worn-out retina, while Conseil, as stoic as ever, kept repeating to me in a calm tone:

'If master's eyes would kindly stop bulging, master will see farther!'

But what a waste of energy! The *Abraham Lincoln* would change course and race after the animal sighted, only to find an ordinary baleen whale or a common sperm whale that soon disappeared amid a chorus of curses!

However, the weather held good. Our voyage was proceeding under the most favourable conditions. By then it was the bad season in these southernmost regions, because July in this zone corresponds to our January in Europe; but the sea remained smooth and easily visible over a vast perimeter.

Ned Land still kept up the most tenacious scepticism; beyond his spells on watch, he pretended that he never even looked at the surface of the waves, at least while no whales were in sight. And yet the marvellous power of his vision could have performed yeoman service. But this stubborn Canadian spent eight hours out of every 12 reading or sleeping in his cabin. A hundred times I chided him for his unconcern.

'Bah!' he replied. 'Nothing's out there, Professor Aronnax, and if there is some animal, what chance would we have of spotting it? Can't you see we're just wandering around at random? People say they've sighted this slippery beast again in the Pacific high seas – I'm truly willing to believe it, but two months have already gone by since then, and judging by your narwhal's personality, it hates growing mouldy from hanging out too long in the same waterways! It's blessed with a terrific gift for getting around. Now, professor, you know even better than I that nature doesn't violate good sense, and she wouldn't give some naturally slow animal the ability to move swiftly if it hadn't a need to use that talent. So if the beast does exist, it's already long gone!'

I had no reply to this. Obviously we were just groping blindly. But how else could we go about it? All the same, our chances were automatically pretty limited. Yet everyone still felt confident of success, and not a sailor on board would have bet against the narwhal appearing, and soon.

On July 20 we cut the Tropic of Capricorn at longitude 105°, and by the 27th of the same month, we had cleared the equator on the 110th meridian. These bearings determined, the frigate took a more decisive westward heading and tackled the seas of the central Pacific. Commander Farragut felt, and with good reason, that it was best to stay in deep waters and keep his distance from continents or islands, whose neighbourhoods the animal always seemed to avoid – 'No doubt,' our bosun said, 'because there isn't enough water for him!' So the frigate kept well out when passing the Tuamotu, Marquesas, and Hawaiian Islands, then cut the Tropic of Cancer at longitude 132° and headed for the seas of China.

We were finally in the area of the monster's latest antics! And in all honesty, shipboard conditions became life-threatening. Hearts were pounding hideously, gearing up for futures full of incurable aneurysms. The entire crew suffered from a nervous excitement that it's beyond me to describe. Nobody ate, nobody slept. Twenty times a day some error in perception, or the optical illusions of some sailor perched in the crosstrees, would cause intolerable anguish, and this emotion, repeated twenty times over, kept us in a state of irritability so intense that a reaction was bound to follow.

And this reaction wasn't long in coming. For three months, during which each day seemed like a century, the *Abraham Lincoln* ploughed all the northerly seas of the Pacific, racing after whales sighted, abruptly veering off course, swerving sharply from one tack to another, stopping suddenly, putting on steam and reversing engines in quick succession, at the risk of stripping its gears, and it didn't leave a single point unexplored from the beaches of Japan to the coasts of America. And we found nothing! Nothing except an immenseness of deserted waves! Nothing remotely resembling a gigantic narwhal, or an underwater islet, or a derelict shipwreck, or a runaway reef, or anything the least bit unearthly!

So the reaction set in. At first, discouragement took hold of people's minds, opening the door to disbelief. A new feeling appeared on board, made up of three-tenths shame and seven-tenths fury. The crew called themselves 'out-and-out fools' for being hoodwinked by a fairy tale, then grew steadily more furious! The mountains of arguments amassed over a year collapsed all at once, and each man now wanted only to catch up on his eating and sleeping, to make up for the time he had so stupidly sacrificed.

With typical human fickleness, they jumped from one extreme to the other. Inevitably, the most enthusiastic supporters of the undertaking became its most energetic opponents. This reaction mounted upward from the bowels of the ship, from the quarters of the bunker hands to the messroom of the general staff; and for certain, if it hadn't been for Commander Farragut's characteristic stubbornness, the frigate would ultimately have put back to that cape in the south.

But this futile search couldn't drag on much longer. The *Abraham Lincoln* had done everything it could to succeed and had no reason to blame itself. Never had the crew of an American naval craft shown more patience and zeal; they weren't responsible for this failure; there was nothing to do but go home.

A request to this effect was presented to the commander. The commander stood his ground. His sailors couldn't hide their discontent, and their work suffered because of it. I'm unwilling to say that there was mutiny on board, but after a reasonable period of intransigence,

Commander Farragut, like Christopher Columbus before him, asked for a grace period of just three days more. After this three-day delay, if the monster hadn't appeared, our helmsman would give three turns of the wheel, and the *Abraham Lincoln* would chart a course toward European seas.

This promise was given on November 2. It had the immediate effect of reviving the crew's failing spirits. The ocean was observed with renewed care. Each man wanted one last look with which to sum up his experience. Spyglasses functioned with feverish energy. A supreme challenge had been issued to the giant narwhal, and the latter had no acceptable excuse for ignoring this Summons to Appear!

Two days passed. The *Abraham Lincoln* stayed at half steam. On the offchance that the animal might be found in these waterways, a thousand methods were used to spark its interest or rouse it from its apathy. Enormous sides of bacon were trailed in our wake, to the great satisfaction, I must say, of assorted sharks. While the *Abraham Lincoln* heaved to, its longboats radiated in every direction around it and didn't leave a single point of the sea unexplored. But the evening of November 4 arrived with this underwater mystery still unsolved.

At noon the next day, November 5, the agreed-upon delay expired. After a position fix, true to his promise, Commander Farragut would have to set his course for the southeast and leave the northerly regions of the Pacific decisively behind.

By then the frigate lay in latitude 31° 15' north and longitude 136° 42' east. The shores of Japan were less than 200 miles to our leeward. Night was coming on. Eight o'clock had just struck. Huge clouds covered the moon's disk, then in its first quarter. The sea undulated placidly beneath the frigate's stempost.

Just then I was in the bow, leaning over the starboard rail. Conseil, stationed beside me, stared straight ahead. Roosting in the shrouds, the crew examined the horizon, which shrank and darkened little by little. Officers were probing the increasing gloom with their night glasses. Sometimes the murky ocean sparkled beneath moonbeams that darted between the fringes of two clouds. Then all traces of light vanished into the darkness.

Observing Conseil, I discovered that, just barely, the gallant lad had fallen under the general influence. At least so I thought. Perhaps his nerves were twitching with curiosity for the first time in history.

'Come on, Conseil!' I told him. 'Here's your last chance to pocket that $2,000!'

'If master will permit my saying so,' Conseil replied, 'I never expected to win that prize, and the Union government could have promised $100,000 and been none the poorer.'

'You're right, Conseil, it turned out to be a foolish business after all, and we jumped into it too hastily. What a waste of time, what a futile expense of emotion! Six months ago we could have been back in France—'

'In master's little apartment,' Conseil answered. 'In master's museum! And by now I would have classified master's fossils. And master's babirusa would be ensconced in its cage at the zoo in the Botanical Gardens, and it would have attracted every curiosity seeker in town!'

'Quite so, Conseil, and what's more, I imagine that people will soon be poking fun at us!'

'To be sure,' Conseil replied serenely, 'I do think they'll have fun at master's expense. And must it be said…?'

'It must be said, Conseil.'

'Well then, it will serve master right!'

'How true!'

'When one has the honour of being an expert as master is, one mustn't lay himself open to—'

Conseil didn't have time to complete the compliment. In the midst of the general silence, a voice became audible. It was Ned Land's voice, and it shouted:

'Ahoy! There's the thing in question, abreast of us to leeward!'

CHAPTER 6

At Full Steam

AT THIS SHOUT the entire crew rushed toward the harpooner – commander, officers, mates, sailors, cabin boys, down to engineers leaving their machinery and stokers neglecting their furnaces. The order was given to stop, and the frigate merely coasted.

By then the darkness was profound, and as good as the Canadian's eyes were, I still wondered how he could see – and what he had seen. My heart was pounding fit to burst.

But Ned Land was not mistaken, and we all spotted the object his hand was indicating.

Two cable lengths off the *Abraham Lincoln*'s starboard quarter, the sea seemed to be lit up from underneath. This was no mere phosphorescent phenomenon, that much was unmistakable. Submerged some fathoms below the surface of the water, the monster gave off that very intense but inexplicable glow that several captains had mentioned in their reports. This magnificent radiance had to come from some force with a great illuminating capacity. The edge of its light swept over the sea in an immense, highly elongated oval, condensing at the centre into a blazing core whose unbearable glow diminished by degrees outward.

'It's only a cluster of phosphorescent particles!' exclaimed one of the officers.

'No, sir,' I answered with conviction. 'Not even angel-wing clams or salps have ever given off such a powerful light. That glow is basically electric in nature. Besides... look, look! It's shifting! It's moving back and forth! It's darting at us!'

A universal shout went up from the frigate.

'Quiet!' Commander Farragut said. 'Helm hard to leeward! Reverse engines!'

Sailors rushed to the helm, engineers to their machinery. Under reverse steam immediately, the *Abraham Lincoln* beat to port, sweeping in a semicircle.

'Right your helm! Engines forward!' Commander Farragut called.

These orders were executed, and the frigate swiftly retreated from this core of light.

My mistake. It wanted to retreat, but the unearthly animal came at us with a speed double our own.

We gasped. More stunned than afraid, we stood mute and motionless. The animal caught up with us, played with us. It made a full circle around the frigate – then doing 14 knots – and wrapped us in sheets of electricity that were like luminous dust. Then it retreated two or three miles, leaving a phosphorescent trail comparable to those swirls of steam that shoot behind the locomotive of an express train. Suddenly, all the way from the dark horizon where it had gone to gather momentum, the monster abruptly dashed toward the *Abraham Lincoln* with frightening speed, stopped sharply 20 feet from our side plates, and died out – not by diving under the water, since its glow did not recede gradually – but all at once, as if the source of this brilliant emanation had suddenly dried up. Then it reappeared on the other side of the ship, either by circling around us or by gliding under our hull. At any instant a collision could have occurred that would have been fatal to us.

Meanwhile I was astonished at the frigate's manoeuvres. It was fleeing, not fighting. Built to pursue, it was being pursued, and I commented on this to Commander Farragut. His face, ordinarily so emotionless, was stamped with indescribable astonishment.

'Professor Aronnax,' he answered me, 'I don't know what kind of fearsome creature I'm up against, and I don't want my frigate running foolish risks in all this darkness. Besides, how should we attack this unknown creature, how should we defend ourselves against it? Let's wait for daylight, and then we'll play a different role.'

'You've no further doubts, commander, as to the nature of this animal?'

'No, sir, it's apparently a gigantic narwhal, and an electric one to boot.'

'Maybe,' I added, 'it's no more approachable than an electric eel or an electric ray!'

'Right,' the commander replied. 'And if it has their power to electrocute, it's surely the most dreadful animal ever conceived by our Creator. That's why I'll keep on my guard, sir.'

The whole crew stayed on their feet all night long. No one even thought of sleeping. Unable to compete with the monster's speed, the *Abraham Lincoln* slowed down and stayed at half steam. For its part, the narwhal mimicked the frigate, simply rode with the waves, and seemed determined not to forsake the field of battle.

However, near midnight it disappeared, or to use a more appropriate expression, 'it went out,' like a huge glowworm. Had it fled from us? We were duty bound to fear so rather than hope so. But at 12:53 in the morning, a deafening hiss became audible, resembling the sound made by a waterspout expelled with tremendous intensity.

By then Commander Farragut, Ned Land, and I were on the afterdeck, peering eagerly into the profound gloom.

'Ned Land,' the commander asked, 'you've often heard whales bellowing?'

'Often, sir, but never a whale like this, whose sighting earned me $2,000.'

'Correct, the prize is rightfully yours. But tell me, isn't that the noise cetaceans make when they spurt water from their blowholes?'

'The very noise, sir, but this one's way louder. So there can be no mistake. There's definitely a whale lurking in our waters. With your permission, sir,' the harpooner added, 'tomorrow at daybreak we'll have words with it.'

'If it's in a mood to listen to you, Mr Land,' I replied in a tone far from convinced.

'Let me get within four harpoon lengths of it,' the Canadian shot back, 'and it had better listen!'

'But to get near it,' the commander went on, 'I'd have to put a whaleboat at your disposal?'

'Certainly, sir.'

'That would be gambling with the lives of my men.'

'And with my own!' the harpooner replied simply.

Near two o'clock in the morning, the core of light reappeared, no less intense, five miles to windward of the *Abraham Lincoln*. Despite the distance, despite the noise of wind and sea, we could distinctly hear the fearsome thrashings of the animal's tail, and even its panting breath. Seemingly, the moment this enormous narwhal came up to breathe at the surface of the ocean, air was sucked into its lungs like steam into the huge cylinders of a 2,000-horsepower engine.

'Hmm!' I said to myself. 'A cetacean as powerful as a whole cavalry regiment – now that's a whale of a whale!'

We stayed on the alert until daylight, getting ready for action. Whaling gear was set up along the railings. Our chief officer loaded the blunderbusses, which can launch harpoons as far as a mile, and long duck guns with exploding bullets that can mortally wound even the most powerful animals. Ned Land was content to sharpen his harpoon, a dreadful weapon in his hands.

At six o'clock day began to break, and with the dawn's early light, the narwhal's electric glow disappeared. At seven o'clock the day was well along, but a very dense morning mist shrank the horizon, and our best spyglasses were unable to pierce it. The outcome: disappointment and anger.

I hoisted myself up to the crosstrees of the mizzen sail. Some officers were already perched on the mastheads.

At eight o'clock the mist rolled ponderously over the waves, and its huge curls were lifting little by little. The horizon grew wider and clearer all at once.

Suddenly, just as on the previous evening, Ned Land's voice was audible.

'There's the thing in question, astern to port!' the harpooner shouted.

Every eye looked toward the point indicated.

There, a mile and a half from the frigate, a long blackish body emerged a metre above the waves. Quivering violently, its tail was creating a considerable eddy. Never had caudal equipment thrashed the sea with such power. An immense wake of glowing whiteness marked the animal's track, sweeping in a long curve.

Our frigate drew nearer to the cetacean. I examined it with a completely open mind. Those reports from the *Shannon* and the *Helvetia* had slightly exaggerated its dimensions, and I put its length at only 250 feet. Its girth was more difficult to judge, but all in all, the animal seemed to be wonderfully proportioned in all three dimensions.

While I was observing this phenomenal creature, two jets of steam and water sprang from its blowholes and rose to an altitude of 40 metres, which settled for me its mode of breathing. From this I finally concluded that it belonged to the branch *Vertebrata*, class *Mammalia*, subclass *Monodelphia*, group *Pisciforma*, order *Cetacea*, family... but here I couldn't make up my mind. The order *Cetacea* consists of three families, baleen whales, sperm whales, dolphins, and it's in this last group that narwhals are placed. Each of these families is divided into several genera, each genus into species, each species into varieties. So I was still missing variety, species, genus, and family, but no doubt I would complete my classifying with the aid of Heaven and Commander Farragut.

The crew were waiting impatiently for orders from their leader. The latter, after carefully observing the animal, called for his engineer. The engineer raced over.

'Sir,' the commander said, 'are you up to pressure?'

'Aye, sir,' the engineer replied.

'Fine. Stoke your furnaces and clap on full steam!'

Three cheers greeted this order. The hour of battle had sounded. A few moments later, the frigate's two funnels vomited torrents of black smoke, and its deck quaked from the trembling of its boilers.

Driven forward by its powerful propeller, the *Abraham Lincoln* headed straight for the animal. Unconcerned, the latter let us come within half a cable length; then, not bothering to dive, it got up a little speed, retreated, and was content to keep its distance.

This chase dragged on for about three-quarters of an hour without the frigate gaining two fathoms on the cetacean. At this rate, it was obvious that we would never catch up with it.

Infuriated, Commander Farragut kept twisting the thick tuft of hair that flourished below his chin.

'Ned Land!' he called.

The Canadian reported at once.

'Well, Mr Land,' the commander asked, 'do you still advise putting my longboats to sea?'

'No, sir,' Ned Land replied, 'because that beast won't be caught against its will.'

'Then what should we do?'

'Stoke up more steam, sir, if you can. As for me, with your permission I'll go perch on the bobstays under the bowsprit, and if we can get within a harpoon length, I'll harpoon the brute.'

'Go to it, Ned,' Commander Farragut replied. 'Engineer,' he called, 'keep the pressure mounting!'

Ned Land made his way to his post. The furnaces were urged into greater activity; our propeller did 43 revolutions per minute, and steam shot from the valves. Heaving the log, we verified that the *Abraham Lincoln* was going at the rate of 18.5 miles per hour.

But that damned animal also did a speed of 18.5.

For the next hour our frigate kept up this pace without gaining a fathom! This was humiliating for one of the fastest racers in the American navy. The crew were working up into a blind rage. Sailor after sailor heaved insults at the monster, which couldn't be bothered with answering back. Commander Farragut was no longer content simply to twist his goatee; he chewed on it.

The engineer was summoned once again.

'You're up to maximum pressure?' the commander asked him.

'Aye, sir,' the engineer replied.

'And your valves are charged to…?'

'To six and a half atmospheres.'

'Charge them to ten atmospheres.'

A typical American order if I ever heard one. It would have sounded just fine during some Mississippi paddle-wheeler race, to 'outstrip the competition!'

'Conseil,' I said to my gallant servant, now at my side, 'you realise that we'll probably blow ourselves skyhigh?'

'As master wishes!' Conseil replied.

All right, I admit it: I did wish to run this risk!

The valves were charged. More coal was swallowed by the furnaces. Ventilators shot torrents of air over the braziers. The *Abraham Lincoln*'s speed increased. Its masts trembled down to their blocks, and swirls of smoke could barely squeeze through the narrow funnels.

We heaved the log a second time.

'Well, helmsman?' Commander Farragut asked.

'19.3 miles per hour, sir.'

'Keep stoking the furnaces.'

The engineer did so. The pressure gauge marked ten atmospheres. But no doubt the cetacean itself had 'warmed up,' because without the least trouble, it also did 19.3.

What a chase! No, I can't describe the excitement that shook my very being. Ned Land stayed at his post, harpoon in hand. Several times the animal let us approach.

'We're overhauling it!' the Canadian would shout.

Then, just as he was about to strike, the cetacean would steal off with a swiftness I could estimate at no less than 30 miles per hour. And even at our maximum speed, it took the liberty of thumbing its nose at the frigate by running a full circle around us! A howl of fury burst from every throat!

By noon we were no farther along than at eight o'clock in the morning.

Commander Farragut then decided to use more direct methods.

'Bah!' he said. 'So that animal is faster than the *Abraham Lincoln*. All right, we'll see if it can outrun our conical shells! Mate, man the gun in the bow!'

Our fo'c'sle cannon was immediately loaded and leveled. The cannoneer fired a shot, but his shell passed some feet above the cetacean, which stayed half a mile off.

'Over to somebody with better aim!' the commander shouted. 'And $500 to the man who can pierce that infernal beast!'

Calm of eye, cool of feature, an old grey-bearded gunner – I can see him to this day – approached the cannon, put it in position, and took aim for a good while. There was a mighty explosion, mingled with cheers from the crew.

The shell reached its target; it hit the animal, but not in the usual fashion – it bounced off that rounded surface and vanished into the sea two miles out.

'Oh drat!' said the old gunner in his anger. 'That rascal must be covered with six-inch armour plate!'

'Curse the beast!' Commander Farragut shouted.

The hunt was on again, and Commander Farragut leaned over to me, saying:

'I'll chase that animal till my frigate explodes!'

'Yes,' I replied, 'and nobody would blame you!'

We could still hope that the animal would tire out and not be as insensitive to exhaustion as our steam engines. But no such luck. Hour after hour went by without it showing the least sign of weariness.

However, to the *Abraham Lincoln's* credit, it must be said that we struggled on with tireless persistence. I estimate that we covered a distance of at least 500 kilometres during this ill-fated day of November 6. But night fell and wrapped the surging ocean in its shadows.

By then I thought our expedition had come to an end, that we would never see this fantastic animal again. I was mistaken.

At 10:50 in the evening, that electric light reappeared three miles to windward of the frigate, just as clear and intense as the night before.

The narwhal seemed motionless. Was it asleep perhaps, weary from its workday, just riding with the waves? This was our chance, and Commander Farragut was determined to take full advantage of it.

He gave his orders. The *Abraham Lincoln* stayed at half steam, advancing cautiously so as not to awaken its adversary. In mid-ocean it's not unusual to encounter whales so sound asleep they can successfully be attacked, and Ned Land had harpooned more than one in its slumber. The Canadian went to resume his post on the bobstays under the bowsprit.

The frigate approached without making a sound, stopped two cable lengths from the animal and coasted. Not a soul breathed on board. A profound silence reigned over the deck. We were not 100 feet from the blazing core of light, whose glow grew stronger and dazzled the eyes.

Just then, leaning over the fo'c'sle railing, I saw Ned Land below me, one hand grasping the martingale, the other brandishing his dreadful harpoon. Barely 20 feet separated him from the motionless animal.

All at once his arm shot forward and the harpoon was launched. I heard the weapon collide resonantly, as if it had hit some hard substance.

The electric light suddenly went out, and two enormous waterspouts crashed onto the deck of the frigate, racing like a torrent from stem to stern, toppling crewmen, breaking spare masts and yardarms from their lashings.

A hideous collision occurred, and thrown over the rail with no time to catch hold of it, I was hurled into the sea.

CHAPTER 7

A Whale of Unknown Species

ALTHOUGH I WAS startled by this unexpected descent, I at least have a very clear recollection of my sensations during it.

At first I was dragged about 20 feet under. I'm a good swimmer, without claiming to equal such other authors as Byron and Edgar Allan Poe, who were master divers, and I didn't lose my head on the way down. With two vigorous kicks of the heel, I came back to the surface of the sea.

My first concern was to look for the frigate. Had the crew seen me go overboard? Was the *Abraham Lincoln* tacking about? Would Commander Farragut put a longboat to sea? Could I hope to be rescued?

The gloom was profound. I glimpsed a black mass disappearing eastward, where its running lights were fading out in the distance. It was the frigate. I felt I was done for.

'Help! Help!' I shouted, swimming desperately toward the *Abraham Lincoln*.

My clothes were weighing me down. The water glued them to my body, they were paralyzing my movements. I was sinking! I was suffocating...!

'Help!'

This was the last shout I gave. My mouth was filling with water. I struggled against being dragged into the depths....

Suddenly my clothes were seized by energetic hands, I felt myself pulled abruptly back to the surface of the sea, and yes, I heard these words pronounced in my ear:

'If master would oblige me by leaning on my shoulder, master will swim with much greater ease.'

With one hand I seised the arm of my loyal Conseil.

'You!' I said. 'You!'

'Myself,' Conseil replied, 'and at master's command.'

'That collision threw you overboard along with me?'

'Not at all. But being in master's employ, I followed master.'

The fine lad thought this only natural!

'What about the frigate?' I asked.

'The frigate?' Conseil replied, rolling over on his back. 'I think master had best not depend on it to any great extent!'

'What are you saying?'

'I'm saying that just as I jumped overboard, I heard the men at the helm shout, "Our propeller and rudder are smashed!"'

'Smashed?'

'Yes, smashed by the monster's tusk! I believe it's the sole injury the *Abraham Lincoln* has sustained. But most inconveniently for us, the ship can no longer steer.'

'Then we're done for!'

'Perhaps,' Conseil replied serenely. 'However, we still have a few hours before us, and in a few hours one can do a great many things!'

Conseil's unflappable composure cheered me up. I swam more vigorously, but hampered by clothes that were as restricting as a cloak made of lead, I was managing with only the greatest difficulty. Conseil noticed as much.

'Master will allow me to make an incision,' he said.

And he slipped an open clasp knife under my clothes, slitting them from top to bottom with one swift stroke. Then he briskly undressed me while I swam for us both.

I then did Conseil the same favour, and we continued to 'navigate' side by side.

But our circumstances were no less dreadful. Perhaps they hadn't seen us go overboard; and even if they had, the frigate – being undone by its rudder – couldn't return to leeward after us. So we could count only on its longboats.

Conseil had coolly reasoned out this hypothesis and laid his plans accordingly. An amazing character, this boy; in mid-ocean, this stoic lad seemed right at home!

So, having concluded that our sole chance for salvation lay in being picked up by the *Abraham Lincoln*'s longboats, we had to take steps to wait for them as long as possible. Consequently, I decided to divide our energies so we wouldn't both be worn out at the same time, and this was the arrangement: while one of us lay on his back, staying motionless with arms crossed and legs outstretched, the other would swim and propel his partner forward. This towing role was to last no longer than ten minutes, and by relieving each other in this way, we could stay afloat for hours, perhaps even until daybreak.

Slim chance, but hope springs eternal in the human breast! Besides, there were two of us. Lastly, I can vouch – as improbable as it seems – that even if I had wanted to destroy all my illusions, even if I had been willing to 'give in to despair,' I could not have done so!

The cetacean had rammed our frigate at about 11 o'clock in the evening. I therefore calculated on eight hours of swimming until sunrise. A strenuous task, but feasible, thanks to our relieving each other. The sea was pretty smooth and barely tired us. Sometimes I tried to peer through the dense gloom, which was broken only by the phosphorescent flickers coming from our movements. I stared at the luminous ripples breaking over my hands, shimmering sheets spattered with blotches of bluish grey. It seemed as if we'd plunged into a pool of quicksilver.

Near one o'clock in the morning, I was overcome with tremendous exhaustion. My limbs stiffened in the grip of intense cramps. Conseil had to keep me going, and attending to our self-preservation became his sole responsibility. I soon heard the poor lad gasping; his breathing became shallow and quick. I didn't think he could stand such exertions for much longer.

'Go on! Go on!' I told him.

'Leave master behind?' he replied. 'Never! I'll drown before he does!'

Just then, past the fringes of a large cloud that the wind was driving eastward, the moon appeared. The surface of the sea glistened under its rays. That kindly light rekindled our strength. I held up my head again. My eyes darted to every point of the horizon. I spotted the frigate. It was five miles from us and formed no more than a dark, barely perceptible mass. But as for longboats, not a one in sight!

I tried to call out. What was the use at such a distance! My swollen lips wouldn't let a single sound through. Conseil could still articulate a few words, and I heard him repeat at intervals:

'Help! Help!'

Ceasing all movement for an instant, we listened. And it may have been a ringing in my ear, from this organ filling with impeded blood, but it seemed to me that Conseil's shout had received an answer back.

'Did you hear that?' I muttered.

'Yes, yes!'

And Conseil hurled another desperate plea into space.

This time there could be no mistake! A human voice had answered us! Was it the voice of some poor devil left behind in mid-ocean, some other victim of that collision suffered by our ship? Or was it one of the frigate's longboats, hailing us out of the gloom?

Conseil made one final effort, and bracing his hands on my shoulders, while I offered resistance with one supreme exertion, he raised himself half out of the water, then fell back exhausted.

'What did you see?'

'I saw…,' he muttered, 'I saw… but we mustn't talk… save our strength…!'

What had he seen? Then, lord knows why, the thought of the monster came into my head for the first time…! But even so, that voice…? Gone are the days when Jonahs took refuge in the bellies of whales!

Nevertheless, Conseil kept towing me. Sometimes he looked up, stared straight ahead, and shouted a request for directions, which was answered by a voice that was getting closer and closer. I could barely hear it. I was at the end of my strength; my fingers gave out; my hands were no help to me; my mouth opened convulsively, filling with brine; its coldness ran through me; I raised my head one last time, then I collapsed….

Just then something hard banged against me. I clung to it. Then I felt myself being pulled upward, back to the surface of the water; my chest caved in, and I fainted….

For certain, I came to quickly, because someone was massaging me so vigorously it left furrows in my flesh. I half opened my eyes….

'Conseil!' I muttered.

'Did master ring for me?' Conseil replied.

Just then, in the last light of a moon settling on the horizon, I spotted a face that wasn't Conseil's but which I recognised at once.

'Ned!' I exclaimed.

'In person, sir, and still after his prize!' the Canadian replied.

'You were thrown overboard after the frigate's collision?'

'Yes, professor, but I was luckier than you, and right away I was able to set foot on this floating islet.'

'Islet?'

'Or in other words, on our gigantic narwhal.'

'Explain yourself, Ned.'

'It's just that I soon realised why my harpoon got blunted and couldn't puncture its hide.'

'Why, Ned, why?'

'Because, professor, this beast is made of boilerplate steel!'

At this point in my story, I need to get a grip on myself, reconstruct exactly what I experienced, and make doubly sure of everything I write.

The Canadian's last words caused a sudden upheaval in my brain. I swiftly hoisted myself to the summit of this half-submerged creature or object that was serving as our refuge. I tested it with my foot. Obviously it was some hard, impenetrable substance, not the soft matter that makes up the bodies of our big marine mammals.

But this hard substance could have been a bony carapace, like those that covered some prehistoric animals, and I might have left it at that and classified this monster among such amphibious reptiles as turtles or alligators.

Well, no. The blackish back supporting me was smooth and polished with no overlapping scales. On impact, it gave off a metallic sonority, and as incredible as this sounds, it seemed, I swear, to be made of riveted plates.

No doubts were possible! This animal, this monster, this natural phenomenon that had puzzled the whole scientific world, that had muddled and misled the minds of seamen in both hemispheres, was, there could be no escaping it, an even more astonishing phenomenon – a phenomenon made by the hand of man.

Even if I had discovered that some fabulous, mythological creature really existed, it wouldn't have given me such a terrific mental jolt. It's easy enough to accept that prodigious things can come from our Creator. But to find, all at once, right before your eyes, that the impossible had been mysteriously achieved by man himself: this staggers the mind!

But there was no question now. We were stretched out on the back of some kind of underwater boat that, as far as I could judge, boasted the shape of an immense steel fish. Ned Land had clear views on the issue. Conseil and I could only line up behind him.

'But then,' I said, 'does this contraption contain some sort of locomotive mechanism, and a crew to run it?'

'Apparently,' the harpooner replied. 'And yet for the three hours I've lived on this floating island, it hasn't shown a sign of life.'

'This boat hasn't moved at all?'

'No, Professor Aronnax. It just rides with the waves, but otherwise it hasn't stirred.'

'But we know that it's certainly gifted with great speed. Now then, since an engine is needed to generate that speed, and a mechanic to run that engine, I conclude: we're saved.'

'Humph!' Ned Land put in, his tone denoting reservations.

Just then, as if to take my side in the argument, a bubbling began astern of this strange submersible – whose drive mechanism was obviously a propeller – and the boat started to move. We barely had time to hang on to its topside, which emerged about 80 centimetres above water. Fortunately its speed was not excessive.

'So long as it navigates horizontally,' Ned Land muttered, 'I've no complaints. But if it gets the urge to dive, I wouldn't give $2 for my hide!'

The Canadian might have quoted a much lower price. So it was imperative to make contact with whatever beings were confined inside the plating of this machine. I searched its surface for an opening or a hatch, a 'manhole,' to use the official term; but the lines of rivets had been firmly driven into the sheet-iron joins and were straight and uniform.

Moreover, the moon then disappeared and left us in profound darkness. We had to wait for daylight to find some way of getting inside this underwater boat.

So our salvation lay totally in the hands of the mysterious helmsmen steering this submersible, and if it made a dive, we were done for! But aside from this occurring, I didn't doubt the possibility of our making contact with them. In fact, if they didn't produce their own air, they inevitably had to make periodic visits to the surface of the ocean to replenish their oxygen supply. Hence the need for some opening that put the boat's interior in contact with the atmosphere.

As for any hope of being rescued by Commander Farragut, that had to be renounced completely. We were being swept westward, and I estimate that our comparatively moderate speed reached 12 miles per hour. The propeller churned the waves with mathematical regularity, sometimes emerging above the surface and throwing phosphorescent spray to great heights.

Near four o'clock in the morning, the submersible picked up speed. We could barely cope with this dizzying rush, and the waves battered us at close range. Fortunately Ned's hands came across a big mooring ring fastened to the topside of this sheet-iron back, and we all held on for dear life.

Finally this long night was over. My imperfect memories won't let me recall my every impression of it. A single detail comes back to me. Several times, during various lulls of wind and sea, I thought I heard indistinct sounds, a sort of elusive harmony produced by distant musical chords. What was the secret behind this underwater navigating, whose explanation the whole world had sought in vain? What beings lived inside this strange boat? What mechanical force allowed it to move about with such prodigious speed?

Daylight appeared. The morning mists surrounded us, but they soon broke up. I was about to proceed with a careful examination of the hull, whose topside formed a sort of horizontal platform, when I felt it sinking little by little.

'Oh, damnation!' Ned Land shouted, stamping his foot on the resonant sheet iron. 'Open up there, you antisocial navigators!'

But it was difficult to make yourself heard above the deafening beats of the propeller. Fortunately this submerging movement stopped.

From inside the boat, there suddenly came noises of iron fastenings pushed roughly aside. One of the steel plates flew up, a man appeared, gave a bizarre yell, and instantly disappeared.

A few moments later, eight strapping fellows appeared silently, their faces like masks, and dragged us down into their fearsome machine.

CHAPTER 8
'Mobilis in Mobili'

THIS BRUTALLY EXECUTED capture was carried out with lightning speed. My companions and I had no time to collect ourselves. I don't know how they felt about being shoved inside this aquatic prison, but as for me, I was shivering all over. With whom were we dealing? Surely with some new breed of pirates, exploiting the sea after their own fashion.

The narrow hatch had barely closed over me when I was surrounded by profound darkness. Saturated with the outside light, my eyes couldn't make out a thing. I felt my naked feet clinging to the steps of an iron ladder. Forcibly seized, Ned Land and Conseil were behind me. At the foot of the ladder, a door opened and instantly closed behind us with a loud clang.

We were alone. Where? I couldn't say, could barely even imagine. All was darkness, but such utter darkness that after several minutes, my eyes were still unable to catch a single one of those hazy gleams that drift through even the blackest nights.

Meanwhile, furious at these goings on, Ned Land gave free rein to his indignation.

'Damnation!' he exclaimed. 'These people are about as hospitable as the savages of New Caledonia! All that's lacking is for them to be cannibals! I wouldn't be surprised if they were, but believe you me, they won't eat me without my kicking up a protest!'

'Calm yourself, Ned my friend,' Conseil replied serenely. 'Don't flare up so quickly! We aren't in a kettle yet!'

'In a kettle, no,' the Canadian shot back, 'but in an oven for sure. It's dark enough for one. Luckily my Bowie knife hasn't left me, and I can still see well enough to put it to use.[1] The first one of these bandits who lays a hand on me—'

'Don't be so irritable, Ned,' I then told the harpooner, 'and don't

---

[1] Author's Note: A Bowie knife is a wide-bladed dagger that Americans are forever carrying around.

ruin things for us with pointless violence. Who knows whether they might be listening to us? Instead, let's try to find out where we are!'

I started moving, groping my way. After five steps I encountered an iron wall made of riveted boilerplate. Then, turning around, I bumped into a wooden table next to which several stools had been set. The floor of this prison lay hidden beneath thick, hempen matting that deadened the sound of footsteps. Its naked walls didn't reveal any trace of a door or window. Going around the opposite way, Conseil met up with me, and we returned to the middle of this cabin, which had to be 20 feet long by ten wide. As for its height, not even Ned Land, with his great stature, was able to determine it.

Half an hour had already gone by without our situation changing, when our eyes were suddenly spirited from utter darkness into blinding light. Our prison lit up all at once; in other words, it filled with luminescent matter so intense that at first I couldn't stand the brightness of it. From its glare and whiteness, I recognised the electric glow that had played around this underwater boat like some magnificent phosphorescent phenomenon. After involuntarily closing my eyes, I reopened them and saw that this luminous force came from a frosted half globe curving out of the cabin's ceiling.

'Finally! It's light enough to see!' Ned Land exclaimed, knife in hand, staying on the defensive.

'Yes,' I replied, then ventured the opposite view. 'But as for our situation, we're still in the dark.'

'Master must learn patience,' said the emotionless Conseil.

This sudden illumination of our cabin enabled me to examine its tiniest details. It contained only a table and five stools. Its invisible door must have been hermetically sealed. Not a sound reached our ears. Everything seemed dead inside this boat. Was it in motion, or stationary on the surface of the ocean, or sinking into the depths? I couldn't tell.

But this luminous globe hadn't been turned on without good reason. Consequently, I hoped that some crewmen would soon make an appearance. If you want to consign people to oblivion, you don't light up their dungeons.

I was not mistaken. Unlocking noises became audible, a door opened, and two men appeared.

One was short and stocky, powerfully muscled, broad shouldered, robust of limbs, the head squat, the hair black and luxuriant, the moustache heavy, the eyes bright and penetrating, and his whole personality stamped with that southern-blooded zest that, in France, typifies the people of Provence. The philosopher Diderot has very aptly claimed that a man's bearing is the clue to his character, and this stocky little man was certainly a living proof of this claim. You could sense that his everyday conversation must have been packed with such vivid figures of speech as personification, symbolism and misplaced modifiers. But I was never in a position to verify this because, around me, he used only an odd and utterly incomprehensible dialect.

The second stranger deserves a more detailed description. A disciple of such character-judging anatomists as Gratiolet or Engel could have read this man's features like an open book. Without hesitation, I identified his dominant qualities – self-confidence, since his head reared like a nobleman's above the arc formed by the lines of his shoulders, and his black eyes gazed with icy assurance; calmness, since his skin, pale rather than ruddy, indicated tranquility of blood; energy, shown by the swiftly knitting muscles of his brow; and finally courage, since his deep breathing denoted tremendous reserves of vitality.

I might add that this was a man of great pride, that his calm, firm gaze seemed to reflect thinking on an elevated plane, and that the harmony of his facial expressions and bodily movements resulted in an overall effect of unquestionable candour – according to the findings of physiognomists, those analysts of facial character.

I felt 'involuntarily reassured' in his presence, and this boded well for our interview.

Whether this individual was 35 or 50 years of age, I could not precisely state. He was tall, his forehead broad, his nose straight, his mouth clearly etched, his teeth magnificent, his hands refined, tapered, and to use a word from palmistry, highly 'psychic,' in other words, worthy of serving a lofty and passionate spirit. This man was certainly the most wonderful physical specimen I had ever encountered. One unusual detail: his eyes were spaced a little far from each other and could instantly take in nearly a quarter of the horizon. This ability – as I later verified – was strengthened by a range of vision even greater than Ned Land's. When this stranger focused his gaze on an object, his eyebrow lines gathered into a frown, his heavy eyelids closed around his pupils to contract his huge field of vision, and he looked! What a look – as if he could magnify objects shrinking into the distance; as if he could probe your very soul; as if he could pierce those sheets of water so opaque to our eyes and scan the deepest seas…!

Wearing caps made of sea-otter fur, and shod in sealskin fishing boots, these two strangers were dressed in clothing made from some unique fabric that flattered the figure and allowed great freedom of movement.

The taller of the two – apparently the leader on board – examined us with the greatest care but without pronouncing a word. Then, turning to his companion, he conversed with him in a language I didn't recognise. It was a sonorous, harmonious, flexible dialect whose vowels seemed to undergo a highly varied accentuation.

The other replied with a shake of the head and added two or three utterly incomprehensible words. Then he seemed to question me directly with a long stare.

I replied in clear French that I wasn't familiar with his language; but he didn't seem to understand me, and the situation grew rather baffling.

'Still, master should tell our story,' Conseil said to me. 'Perhaps these gentlemen will grasp a few words of it!'

I tried again, telling the tale of our adventures, clearly articulating my every syllable, and not leaving out a single detail. I stated our names and titles; then, in order, I introduced Professor Aronnax, his manservant Conseil, and Mr Ned Land, harpooner.

The man with calm, gentle eyes listened to me serenely, even courteously, and paid remarkable attention. But nothing in his facial expression indicated that he understood my story. When I finished, he didn't pronounce a single word.

One resource still left was to speak English. Perhaps they would be familiar with this nearly universal language. But I only knew it, as I did the German language, well enough to read it fluently, not well enough to speak it correctly. Here, however, our overriding need was to make ourselves understood.

'Come on, it's your turn,' I told the harpooner. 'Over to you, Mr Land. Pull out of your bag of tricks the best English ever spoken by an Anglo-Saxon, and try for a more favourable result than mine.'

Ned needed no persuading and started our story all over again, most of which I could follow. Its content was the same, but the form differed. Carried away by his volatile temperament, the Canadian put great animation into it. He complained vehemently about being imprisoned in defiance of his civil rights, asked by virtue of which law he was hereby detained, invoked writs of *habeas corpus*, threatened to press charges against anyone holding him in illegal custody, ranted, gesticulated, shouted, and finally conveyed by an expressive gesture that we were dying of hunger.

This was perfectly true, but we had nearly forgotten the fact.

Much to his amazement, the harpooner seemed no more intelligible than I had been. Our visitors didn't bat an eye. Apparently they were engineers who understood the languages of neither the French physicist Arago nor the English physicist Faraday.

Thoroughly baffled after vainly exhausting our philological resources, I no longer knew what tactic to pursue, when Conseil told me:

'If master will authorise me, I'll tell the whole business in German.'

'What! You know German?' I exclaimed.

'Like most Flemish people, with all due respect to master.'

'On the contrary, my respect is due you. Go to it, my boy.'

And Conseil, in his serene voice, described for the third time the various vicissitudes of our story. But despite our narrator's fine accent and stylish turns of phrase, the German language met with no success.

Finally, as a last resort, I hauled out everything I could remember from my early schooldays, and I tried to narrate our adventures in Latin. Cicero would have plugged his ears and sent me to the scullery, but somehow I managed to pull through. With the same negative result.

This last attempt ultimately misfiring, the two strangers exchanged a few words in their incomprehensible language and withdrew, not even favouring us with one of those encouraging gestures that are used in every country in the world. The door closed again.

'This is outrageous!' Ned Land shouted, exploding for the twentieth time. 'I ask you! We speak French, English, German, and Latin to these rogues, and neither of them has the decency to even answer back!'

'Calm down, Ned,' I told the seething harpooner. 'Anger won't get us anywhere.'

'But professor,' our irascible companion went on, 'can't you see that we could die of hunger in this iron cage?'

'Bah!' Conseil put in philosophically. 'We can hold out a good while yet!'

'My friends,' I said, 'we mustn't despair. We've gotten out of tighter spots. So please do me the favour of waiting a bit before you form your views on the commander and crew of this boat.'

'My views are fully formed,' Ned Land shot back. 'They're rogues!'

'Oh good! And from what country?'

'Roguedom!'

'My gallant Ned, as yet that country isn't clearly marked on maps of the world, but I admit that the nationality of these two strangers is hard to make out! Neither English, French, nor German, that's all we can say. But I'm tempted to think that the commander and his chief officer were born in the low latitudes. There must be southern blood in them. But as to whether they're Spaniards, Turks, Arabs, or East Indians, their physical characteristics don't give me enough to go on. And as for their speech, it's utterly incomprehensible.'

'That's the nuisance in not knowing every language,' Conseil replied, 'or the drawback in not having one universal language!'

'Which would all go out the window!' Ned Land replied. 'Don't you see, these people have a language all to themselves, a language they've invented just to cause despair in decent people who ask for a little dinner! Why, in every country on earth, when you open your mouth, snap your jaws, smack your lips and teeth, isn't that the world's most understandable message? From Quebec to the Tuamotu Islands, from Paris to the Antipodes, doesn't it mean: I'm hungry, give me a bite to eat!'

'Oh,' Conseil put in, 'there are some people so unintelligent by nature...'

As he was saying these words, the door opened. A steward entered.[1] He brought us some clothes, jackets and sailor's pants, made out of a fabric whose nature I didn't recognise. I hurried to change into them, and my companions followed suit.

Meanwhile our silent steward, perhaps a deaf-mute, set the table and laid three place settings.

'There's something serious afoot,' Conseil said, 'and it bodes well.'

'Bah!' replied the rancorous harpooner. 'What the devil do you suppose they eat around here? Turtle livers, loin of shark, dogfish steaks?'

'We'll soon find out!' Conseil said.

Overlaid with silver dish covers, various platters had been neatly positioned on the table cloth, and we sat down to eat. Assuredly, we were dealing with civilised people, and if it hadn't been for this electric light flooding over us, I would have thought we were in the dining room of the Hotel Adelphi in Liverpool, or the Grand Hotel in Paris. However, I feel compelled to mention that bread and wine were totally absent. The water was fresh and clear, but it was still water – which wasn't what Ned Land had in mind. Among the foods we were served, I was able to identify various daintily dressed fish; but I couldn't make up my mind about certain otherwise excellent dishes, and I couldn't even tell whether their contents belonged to the vegetable or the animal kingdom. As for the tableware, it was elegant and in perfect taste. Each utensil, spoon, fork, knife and plate bore on its reverse a letter encircled by a Latin motto, and here is its exact duplicate:

MOBILIS IN MOBILI
N

Moving within the moving element! It was a highly appropriate motto for this underwater machine, so long as the preposition 'in' is translated as 'within' and not 'upon'. The letter 'N' was no doubt the initial of the name of that mystifying individual in command beneath the seas!

---

[1] Author's Note: A steward is a waiter on board a steamer.

Ned and Conseil had no time for such musings. They were wolfing down their food, and without further ado I did the same. By now I felt reassured about our fate, and it seemed obvious that our hosts didn't intend to let us die of starvation.

But all earthly things come to an end, all things must pass, even the hunger of people who haven't eaten for 15 hours. Our appetites appeased, we felt an urgent need for sleep. A natural reaction after that interminable night of fighting for our lives.

'Ye gods, I'll sleep soundly,' Conseil said.

'Me, I'm out like a light!' Ned Land replied.

My two companions lay down on the cabin's carpeting and were soon deep in slumber.

As for me, I gave in less readily to this intense need for sleep. Too many thoughts had piled up in my mind, too many insoluble questions had arisen, too many images were keeping my eyelids open! Where were we? What strange power was carrying us along? I felt – or at least I thought I did – the submersible sinking toward the sea's lower strata. Intense nightmares besieged me. In these mysterious marine sanctuaries, I envisioned hosts of unknown animals, and this underwater boat seemed to be a blood relation of theirs: living, breathing, just as fearsome...! Then my mind grew calmer, my imagination melted into hazy drowsiness, and I soon fell into an uneasy slumber.

CHAPTER 9

The Tantrums of Ned Land

I HAVE NO idea how long this slumber lasted; but it must have been a good while, since we were completely over our exhaustion. I was the first one to wake up. My companions weren't yet stirring and still lay in their corners like inanimate objects.

I had barely gotten up from my passably hard mattress when I felt my mind clear, my brain go on the alert. So I began a careful re-examination of our cell.

Nothing had changed in its interior arrangements. The prison was still a prison and its prisoners still prisoners. But, taking advantage of our slumber, the steward had cleared the table. Consequently, nothing indicated any forthcoming improvement in our situation, and I seriously wondered if we were doomed to spend the rest of our lives in this cage.

This prospect seemed increasingly painful to me because, even though my brain was clear of its obsessions from the night before, I was feeling an odd short-windedness in my chest. It was becoming hard for me to breathe. The heavy air was no longer sufficient for the full play of my lungs. Although our cell was large, we obviously had used up most of the oxygen it contained. In essence, over an hour's time a single human being consumes all the oxygen found in 100 liters of air, at which point that air has become charged with a nearly equal amount of carbon dioxide and is no longer fit for breathing.

So it was now urgent to renew the air in our prison, and no doubt the air in this whole underwater boat as well.

Here a question popped into my head. How did the commander of this aquatic residence go about it? Did he obtain air using chemical methods, releasing the oxygen contained in potassium chlorate by heating it, meanwhile absorbing the carbon dioxide with potassium hydroxide? If so, he would have to keep up some kind of relationship with the shore, to come by the materials needed for such an operation. Did he simply limit himself to storing the air in high-pressure tanks and then dispense it according to his crew's needs? Perhaps. Or, proceeding in a more convenient, more economical, and consequently more probable fashion, was he satisfied with merely returning to breathe at the surface of the water like a cetacean, renewing his oxygen supply every 24 hours? In any event, whatever his method was, it seemed prudent to me that he use this method without delay.

In fact, I had already resorted to speeding up my inhalations in order to extract from the cell what little oxygen it contained, when suddenly I was refreshed by a current of clean air, scented with a salty aroma. It had to be a sea breeze, life-giving and charged with iodine! I opened my mouth wide, and my lungs glutted themselves on the fresh particles. At the same time, I felt a swaying, a rolling of moderate magnitude but definitely noticeable. This boat, this sheet-iron monster, had obviously just risen to the surface of the ocean, there to breathe in good whale fashion. So the ship's mode of ventilation was finally established.

When I had absorbed a chestful of this clean air, I looked for the conduit – the 'air carrier,' if you prefer – that allowed this beneficial influx to reach us, and I soon found it. Above the door opened an air vent that let in a fresh current of oxygen, renewing the thin air in our cell.

I had gotten to this point in my observations when Ned and Conseil woke up almost simultaneously, under the influence of this reviving air purification. They rubbed their eyes, stretched their arms, and sprang to their feet.

'Did master sleep well?' Conseil asked me with his perennial good manners.

'Extremely well, my gallant lad,' I replied. 'And how about you, Mr Ned Land?'

'Like a log, professor. But I must be imagining things, because it seems like I'm breathing a sea breeze!'

A seaman couldn't be wrong on this topic, and I told the Canadian what had gone on while he slept.

'Good!' he said. 'That explains perfectly all that bellowing we heard, when our so-called narwhal lay in sight of the *Abraham Lincoln*.'

'Perfectly, Mr Land. It was catching its breath!'

'Only I've no idea what time it is, Professor Aronnax, unless maybe it's dinnertime?'

'Dinnertime, my fine harpooner? I'd say at least breakfast time, because we've certainly woken up to a new day.'

'Which indicates,' Conseil replied, 'that we've spent 24 hours in slumber.'

'That's my assessment,' I replied.

'I won't argue with you,' Ned Land answered. 'But dinner or breakfast, that steward will be plenty welcome whether he brings the one or the other.'

'The one and the other,' Conseil said.

'Well put,' the Canadian replied. 'We deserve two meals, and speaking for myself, I'll do justice to them both.'

'All right, Ned, let's wait and see!' I replied. 'It's clear that these strangers don't intend to let us die of hunger, otherwise last evening's dinner wouldn't make any sense.'

'Unless they're fattening us up!' Ned shot back.

'I object,' I replied. 'We have not fallen into the hands of cannibals.'

'Just because they don't make a habit of it,' the Canadian replied in all seriousness, 'doesn't mean they don't indulge from time to time. Who knows? Maybe these people have gone without fresh meat for a long while, and in that case three healthy, well-built specimens like the professor, his manservant, and me—'

'Get rid of those ideas, Mr Land,' I answered the harpooner. 'And above all, don't let them lead you to flare up against our hosts, which would only make our situation worse.'

'Anyhow,' the harpooner said, 'I'm as hungry as all Hades, and dinner or breakfast, not one puny meal has arrived!'

'Mr Land,' I answered, 'we have to adapt to the schedule on board, and I imagine our stomachs are running ahead of the chief cook's dinner bell.'

'Well then, we'll adjust our stomachs to the chef's timetable!' Conseil replied serenely.

'There you go again, Conseil my friend!' the impatient Canadian shot back. 'You never allow yourself any displays of bile or attacks of nerves! You're everlastingly calm! You'd say your after-meal grace even if you didn't get any food for your before-meal blessing – and you'd starve to death rather than complain!'

'What good would it do?' Conseil asked.

'Complaining doesn't have to do good, it just feels good! And if these pirates – I say pirates out of consideration for the professor's feelings, since he doesn't want us to call them cannibals – if these pirates think they're going to smother me in this cage without hearing what cusswords spice up my outbursts, they've got another think coming! Look here, Professor Aronnax, speak frankly. How long do you figure they'll keep us in this iron box?'

'To tell the truth, friend Land, I know little more about it than you do.'

'But in a nutshell, what do you suppose is going on?'

'My supposition is that sheer chance has made us privy to an important secret. Now then, if the crew of this underwater boat have a personal interest in keeping that secret, and if their personal interest is more important than the lives of three men, I believe that our very existence is in jeopardy. If such is not the case, then at the first available opportunity, this monster that has swallowed us will return us to the world inhabited by our own kind.'

'Unless they recruit us to serve on the crew,' Conseil said, 'and keep us here—'

'Till the moment,' Ned Land answered, 'when some frigate that's faster or smarter than the *Abraham Lincoln* captures this den of buccaneers, then hangs all of us by the neck from the tip of a mainmast yardarm!'

'Well thought out, Mr. Land,' I replied. 'But as yet, I don't believe we've been tendered any enlistment offers. Consequently, it's pointless to argue about what tactics we should pursue in such a case. I repeat: let's wait, let's be guided by events and let's do nothing, since right now there's nothing we can do.'

'On the contrary, professor,' the harpooner replied, not wanting to give in. 'There is something we can do.'

'Oh? And what, Mr Land?'

'Break out of here!'

'Breaking out of a prison on shore is difficult enough, but with an underwater prison, it strikes me as completely unworkable.'

'Come now, Ned my friend,' Conseil asked, 'how would you answer master's objection? I refuse to believe that an American is at the end of his tether.'

Visibly baffled, the harpooner said nothing. Under the conditions in which fate had left us, it was absolutely impossible to escape. But a Canadian's wit is half French, and Mr Ned Land made this clear in his reply.

'So, Professor Aronnax,' he went on after thinking for a few moments, 'you haven't figured out what people do when they can't escape from their prison?'

'No, my friend.'

'Easy. They fix things so they stay there.'

'Of course!' Conseil put in. 'Since we're deep in the ocean, being inside this boat is vastly preferable to being above it or below it!'

'But we fix things by kicking out all the jailers, guards and wardens,' Ned Land added.

'What's this, Ned?' I asked. 'You'd seriously consider taking over this craft?'

'Very seriously,' the Canadian replied.

'It's impossible.'

'And why is that, sir? Some promising opportunity might come up, and I don't see what could stop us from taking advantage of it. If there are only about 20 men on board this machine, I don't think they can stave off two Frenchmen and a Canadian!'

It seemed wiser to accept the harpooner's proposition than to debate it. Accordingly, I was content to reply:

'Let such circumstances come, Mr Land, and we'll see. But until then, I beg you to control your impatience. We need to act shrewdly, and your flare-ups won't give rise to any promising opportunities. So swear to me that you'll accept our situation without throwing a tantrum over it.'

'I give you my word, professor,' Ned Land replied in an unenthusiastic tone. 'No vehement phrases will leave my mouth, no vicious gestures will give my feelings away, not even when they don't feed us on time.'

'I have your word, Ned,' I answered the Canadian.

Then our conversation petered out, and each of us withdrew into his own thoughts. For my part, despite the harpooner's confident talk, I admit that I entertained no illusions. I had no faith in those promising opportunities that Ned Land mentioned. To operate with such efficiency, this underwater boat had to have a sizeable crew, so if it came to a physical contest, we would be facing an overwhelming opponent. Besides, before we could do anything, we had to be free, and that we definitely were not. I didn't see any way out of this sheet–iron, hermetically sealed cell. And if the strange commander of this boat did have a secret to keep – which seemed rather likely – he would never give us freedom of movement aboard his vessel. Now then, would he resort to violence in order to be rid of us, or would he drop us off one day on some remote coast? There lay the unknown. All these hypotheses seemed extremely plausible to me, and to hope for freedom through use of force, you had to be a harpooner.

I realised, moreover, that Ned Land's brooding was getting him madder by the minute. Little by little, I heard those aforesaid cusswords welling up in the depths of his gullet, and I saw his movements turn threatening again. He stood up, pacing in circles like a wild beast in a cage, striking the walls with his foot and fist. Meanwhile the hours passed, our hunger nagged unmercifully, and this time the steward did not appear. Which amounted to forgetting our castaway status for much too long, if they really had good intentions toward us.

Tortured by the growling of his well-built stomach, Ned Land was getting more and more riled, and despite his word of honour, I was in real dread of an explosion when he stood in the presence of one of the men on board.

For two more hours Ned Land's rage increased. The Canadian shouted and pleaded, but to no avail. The sheet-iron walls were deaf. I didn't hear a single sound inside this dead-seeming boat. The vessel hadn't stirred, because I obviously would have felt its hull vibrating under the influence of the propeller. It had undoubtedly sunk into the watery deep and no longer belonged to the outside world. All this dismal silence was terrifying.

As for our neglect, our isolation in the depths of this cell, I was afraid to guess at how long it might last. Little by little, hopes I had entertained after our interview with the ship's commander were fading away. The gentleness of the man's gaze, the generosity expressed in his facial features, the nobility of his bearing, all vanished from my memory. I saw this mystifying individual anew for what he inevitably must be: cruel and merciless. I viewed him as outside humanity, beyond all feelings of compassion, the implacable foe of his fellow man, toward whom he must have sworn an undying hate!

But even so, was the man going to let us die of starvation, locked up in this cramped prison, exposed to those horrible temptations to which people are driven by extreme hunger? This grim possibility took on a dreadful intensity in my mind, and fired by my imagination, I felt an unreasoning terror run through me. Conseil stayed calm. Ned Land bellowed.

Just then a noise was audible outside. Footsteps rang on the metal tiling. The locks were turned, the door opened, the steward appeared.

Before I could make a single movement to prevent him, the Canadian rushed at the poor man, threw him down, held him by the throat. The steward was choking in the grip of those powerful hands.

Conseil was already trying to loosen the harpooner's hands from his half-suffocated victim, and I had gone to join in the rescue, when I was abruptly nailed to the spot by these words pronounced in French:

'Calm down, Mr Land! And you, professor, kindly listen to me!'

CHAPTER 10

The Man of the Waters

IT WAS THE ship's commander who had just spoken.

At these words Ned Land stood up quickly. Nearly strangled, the steward staggered out at a signal from his superior; but such was the commander's authority aboard his vessel, not one gesture gave away the resentment that this man must have felt toward the Canadian. In silence we waited for the outcome of this scene; Conseil, in spite of himself, seemed almost fascinated, I was stunned.

Arms crossed, leaning against a corner of the table, the commander studied us with great care. Was he reluctant to speak further? Did he regret those words he had just pronounced in French? You would have thought so.

After a few moments of silence, which none of us would have dreamed of interrupting:

'Gentlemen,' he said in a calm, penetrating voice, 'I speak French, English, German and Latin with equal fluency. Hence I could have answered you as early as our initial interview, but first I wanted to make your acquaintance and then think things over. Your four versions of the same narrative, perfectly consistent by and large, established your personal identities for me. I now know that sheer chance has placed in my presence Professor Pierre Aronnax, specialist in natural history at the Paris Museum and entrusted with a scientific mission abroad, his manservant Conseil, and Ned Land, a harpooner of Canadian origin aboard the *Abraham Lincoln*, a frigate in the national navy of the United States of America.'

I bowed in agreement. The commander hadn't put a question to me. So no answer was called for. This man expressed himself with perfect ease and without a trace of an accent. His phrasing was clear, his words well chosen, his facility in elocution remarkable. And yet, to me, he didn't have 'the feel' of a fellow countryman.

He went on with the conversation as follows:

'No doubt, sir, you've felt that I waited rather too long before paying you this second visit. After discovering your identities, I wanted to weigh carefully what policy to pursue toward you. I had great difficulty deciding. Some extremely inconvenient circumstances have brought you into the presence of a man who has cut himself off from humanity. Your coming has disrupted my whole existence.'

'Unintentionally,' I said.

'Unintentionally?' the stranger replied, raising his voice a little. 'Was it unintentionally that the *Abraham Lincoln* hunted me on every sea? Was it unintentionally that you travelled aboard that frigate? Was it unintentionally that your shells bounced off my ship's hull? Was it unintentionally that Mr Ned Land hit me with his harpoon?'

I detected a controlled irritation in these words. But there was a perfectly natural reply to these charges, and I made it.

'Sir,' I said, 'you're surely unaware of the discussions that have taken place in Europe and America with yourself as the subject. You don't realise that various accidents, caused by collisions with your underwater machine, have aroused public passions on those two continents. I'll spare you the innumerable hypotheses with which we've tried to explain this inexplicable phenomenon, whose secret is yours alone. But please understand that the *Abraham Lincoln* chased you over the Pacific high seas in the belief it was hunting some powerful marine monster, which had to be purged from the ocean at all cost.'

A half smile curled the commander's lips; then, in a calmer tone:

'Professor Aronnax,' he replied, 'do you dare claim that your frigate wouldn't have chased and cannonaded an underwater boat as readily as a monster?'

This question baffled me, since Commander Farragut would certainly have shown no such hesitation. He would have seen it as his sworn duty to destroy a contrivance of this kind just as promptly as a gigantic narwhal.

'So you understand, sir,' the stranger went on, 'that I have a right to treat you as my enemy.'

I kept quiet, with good reason. What was the use of debating such a proposition, when superior force can wipe out the best arguments?

'It took me a good while to decide,' the commander went on. 'Nothing obliged me to grant you hospitality. If I were to part company with you, I'd have no personal interest in ever seeing you again. I could put you back on the platform of this ship that has served as your refuge. I could sink under the sea, and I could forget you ever existed. Wouldn't that be my right?'

'Perhaps it would be the right of a savage,' I replied. 'But not that of a civilised man.'

'Professor,' the commander replied swiftly, 'I'm not what you term a civilised man! I've severed all ties with society, for reasons that I alone have the right to appreciate. Therefore I obey none of its regulations, and I insist that you never invoke them in front of me!'

This was plain speaking. A flash of anger and scorn lit up the stranger's eyes, and I glimpsed a fearsome past in this man's life. Not only had he placed himself beyond human laws, he had rendered himself independent, out of all reach, free in the strictest sense of the word! For who would dare chase him to the depths of the sea when he thwarted all attacks on the surface? What ship could withstand a collision with his underwater *Monitor*? What armour plate, no matter how heavy, could bear the thrusts of his spur? No man among men could call him to account for his actions. God, if he believed in Him, his conscience if he had one – these were the only judges to whom he was answerable.

These thoughts swiftly crossed my mind while this strange individual fell silent, like someone completely self–absorbed. I regarded him with a mixture of fear and fascination, in the same way, no doubt, that Œdipus regarded the Sphinx.

After a fairly long silence, the commander went on with our conversation.

'So I had difficulty deciding,' he said. 'But I concluded that my personal interests could be reconciled with that natural compassion to which every human being has a right. Since fate has brought you here, you'll stay aboard my vessel. You'll be free here, and in exchange for that freedom, moreover totally related to it, I'll lay on you just one condition. Your word that you'll submit to it will be sufficient.'

'Go on, sir,' I replied. 'I assume this condition is one an honest man can accept?'

'Yes, sir. Just this. It's possible that certain unforeseen events may force me to confine you to your cabins for some hours, or even for some days as the case may be. Since I prefer never to use violence, I expect from you in such a case, even more than in any other, your unquestioning obedience. By acting in this way, I shield you from complicity, I absolve you of all responsibility, since I myself make it impossible for you to see what you aren't meant to see. Do you accept this condition?'

So things happened on board that were quite odd to say the least, things never to be seen by people not placing themselves beyond society's laws! Among all the surprises the future had in store for me, this would not be the mildest.

'We accept,' I replied. 'Only, I'll ask your permission, sir, to address a question to you, just one.'

'Go ahead, sir.'

'You said we'd be free aboard your vessel?'

'Completely.'

'Then I would ask what you mean by this freedom.'

'Why, the freedom to come, go, see, and even closely observe everything happening here – except under certain rare circumstances – in short, the freedom we ourselves enjoy, my companions and I.'

It was obvious that we did not understand each other.

'Pardon me, sir,' I went on, 'but that's merely the freedom that every prisoner has, the freedom to pace his cell! That's not enough for us.'

'Nevertheless, it will have to do!'

'What! We must give up seeing our homeland, friends and relatives ever again?'

'Yes, sir. But giving up that intolerable earthly yoke that some men call freedom is perhaps less painful than you think!'

'By thunder!' Ned Land shouted. 'I'll never promise I won't try getting out of here!'

'I didn't ask for such a promise, Mr Land,' the commander replied coldly.

'Sir,' I replied, flaring up in spite of myself, 'you're taking unfair advantage of us! This is sheer cruelty!'

'No, sir, it's an act of mercy! You're my prisoners of war! I've cared for you when, with a single word, I could plunge you back into the ocean depths! You attacked me! You've just stumbled on a secret no living man must probe, the secret of my entire existence! Do you think I'll send you back to a world that must know nothing more of me? Never! By keeping you on board, it isn't you whom I care for, it's me!'

These words indicated that the commander pursued a policy impervious to arguments.

'Then, sir,' I went on, 'you give us, quite simply, a choice between life and death?'

'Quite simply.'

'My friends,' I said, 'to a question couched in these terms, our answer can be taken for granted. But no solemn promises bind us to the commander of this vessel.'

'None, sir,' the stranger replied.

Then, in a gentler voice, he went on:

'Now, allow me to finish what I have to tell you. I've heard of you, Professor Aronnax. You, if not your companions, won't perhaps complain too much about the stroke of fate that has brought us together. Among the books that make up my favourite reading, you'll find the work you've published on the great ocean depths. I've pored over it. You've taken your studies as far as terrestrial science can go. But you don't know everything because you haven't seen everything. Let me tell you, professor, you won't regret the time you spend aboard my vessel. You're going to voyage through a land of wonders. Stunned amazement will probably be your habitual state of mind. It will be a long while before you tire of the sights constantly before your eyes. I'm going to make another underwater tour of the world – perhaps my last, who knows? – and I'll review everything I've studied in the depths of these seas that I've crossed so often, and you can be my fellow student. Starting this very day, you'll enter a new element, you'll see what no human being has ever seen before – since my men and I no longer count – and thanks to me, you're going to learn the ultimate secrets of our planet.'

I can't deny it; the commander's words had a tremendous effect on me. He had caught me on my weak side, and I momentarily forgot that not even this sublime experience was worth the loss of my freedom. Besides, I counted on the future to resolve this important question. So I was content to reply:

'Sir, even though you've cut yourself off from humanity, I can see that you haven't disowned all human feeling. We're castaways whom you've charitably taken aboard, we'll never forget that. Speaking for myself, I don't rule out that the interests of science could override even the need for freedom, which promises me that, in exchange, our encounter will provide great rewards.'

I thought the commander would offer me his hand, to seal our agreement. He did nothing of the sort. I regretted that.

'One last question,' I said, just as this inexplicable being seemed ready to withdraw.

'Ask it, professor.'

'By what name am I to call you?'

'Sir,' the commander replied, 'to you, I'm simply Captain Nemo; to me, you and your companions are simply passengers on the *Nautilus*.'

Captain Nemo called out. A steward appeared. The captain gave him his orders in that strange language I couldn't even identify. Then, turning to the Canadian and Conseil:

'A meal is waiting for you in your cabin,' he told them. 'Kindly follow this man.'

'That's an offer I can't refuse!' the harpooner replied.

After being confined for over 30 hours, he and Conseil were finally out of this cell.

'And now, Professor Aronnax, our own breakfast is ready. Allow me to lead the way.'

'Yours to command, captain.'

I followed Captain Nemo, and as soon as I passed through the doorway, I went down a kind of electrically lit passageway that resembled a gangway on a ship. After a stretch of some ten metres, a second door opened before me.

I then entered a dining room, decorated and furnished in austere good taste. Inlaid with ebony trim, tall oaken sideboards stood at both ends of this room, and sparkling on their shelves were staggered rows of earthenware, porcelain and glass of incalculable value. There silver-plated dinnerware gleamed under rays pouring from light fixtures in the ceiling, whose glare was softened and tempered by delicately painted designs.

In the centre of this room stood a table, richly spread. Captain Nemo indicated the place I was to occupy.

'Be seated,' he told me, 'and eat like the famished man you must be.'

Our breakfast consisted of several dishes whose contents were all supplied by the sea, and some foods whose nature and derivation were unknown to me. They were good, I admit, but with a peculiar flavour to which I would soon grow accustomed. These various food items seemed to be rich in phosphorous, and I thought that they, too, must have been of marine origin.

Captain Nemo stared at me. I had asked him nothing, but he read my thoughts, and on his own he answered the questions I was itching to address him.

'Most of these dishes are new to you,' he told me. 'But you can consume them without fear. They're healthy and nourishing. I renounced terrestrial foods long ago, and I'm none the worse for it. My crew are strong and full of energy, and they eat what I eat.'

'So,' I said, 'all these foods are products of the sea?'

'Yes, professor, the sea supplies all my needs. Sometimes I cast my nets in our wake, and I pull them up ready to burst. Sometimes I go hunting right in the midst of this element that has long seemed so far out of man's reach, and I corner the game that dwells in my underwater forests. Like the flocks of old Proteus, King Neptune's shepherd, my herds graze without fear on the ocean's immense prairies. There I own vast properties that I harvest myself, and which are forever sown by the hand of the Creator of All Things.'

I stared at Captain Nemo in definite astonishment, and I answered him:

'Sir, I understand perfectly how your nets can furnish excellent fish for your table; I understand less how you can chase aquatic game in your underwater forests; but how a piece of red meat, no matter how small, can figure in your menu, that I don't understand at all.'

'Nor I, sir,' Captain Nemo answered me. 'I never touch the flesh of land animals.'

'Nevertheless, this...,' I went on, pointing to a dish where some slices of loin were still left.

'What you believe to be red meat, professor, is nothing other than loin of sea turtle. Similarly, here are some dolphin livers you might mistake for stewed pork. My chef is a skillful food processor who excels at pickling and preserving these various exhibits from the ocean. Feel free to sample all of these foods. Here are some preserves of sea cucumber that a Malaysian would declare to be unrivaled in the entire world, here's cream from milk furnished by the udders of cetaceans, and sugar from the huge fucus plants in the North Sea; and finally, allow me to offer you some marmalade of sea anemone, equal to that from the tastiest fruits.'

So I sampled away, more as a curiosity seeker than an epicure, while Captain Nemo delighted me with his incredible anecdotes.

'But this sea, Professor Aronnax,' he told me, 'this prodigious, inexhaustible wet nurse of a sea not only feeds me, she dresses me as well. That fabric covering you was woven from the masses of filaments that anchor certain seashells; as the ancients were wont to do, it was dyed with purple ink from the murex snail and shaded with violet tints that I extract from a marine slug, the Mediterranean sea hare. The perfumes you'll find on the washstand in your cabin were produced from the oozings of marine plants. Your mattress was made from the ocean's softest eelgrass. Your quill pen will be whalebone, your ink a juice secreted by cuttlefish or squid. Everything comes to me from the sea, just as someday everything will return to it!'

'You love the sea, captain.'

'Yes, I love it! The sea is the be all and end all! It covers seven–tenths of the planet earth. Its breath is clean and healthy. It's an immense wilderness where a man is never lonely, because he feels life astir on every side. The sea is simply the vehicle for a prodigious, unearthly mode of existence; it's simply movement and love; it's living infinity, as one of your poets put it. And in essence, professor, nature is here made manifest by all three of her kingdoms, mineral, vegetable and animal. The last of these is amply represented by the four zoophyte groups, three classes of articulates, five classes of molluscs and three vertebrate classes: mammals, reptiles and those countless legions of fish, an infinite order of animals totaling more than 13,000 species, of which only one–tenth belong to fresh water. The sea is a vast pool of nature. Our globe began with the sea, so to speak, and who can say we won't end with it! Here lies supreme tranquility. The sea doesn't belong to tyrants. On its surface they can still exercise their iniquitous claims, battle each other, devour each other, haul every earthly horror. But 30 feet below sea level, their dominion ceases, their influence fades, their power vanishes! Ah, sir, live! Live in the heart of the seas! Here alone lies independence! Here I recognise no superiors! Here I'm free!'

Captain Nemo suddenly fell silent in the midst of this enthusiastic outpouring. Had he let himself get carried away, past the bounds of his habitual reserve? Had he said too much? For a few moments he strolled up and down, all aquiver. Then his nerves grew calmer, his facial features recovered their usual icy composure, and turning to me:

'Now, professor,' he said, 'if you'd like to inspect the *Nautilus*, I'm yours to command.'

CHAPTER 11
The Nautilus

CAPTAIN NEMO STOOD up. I followed him. Contrived at the rear of the dining room, a double door opened and I entered a room whose dimensions equalled the one I had just left.

It was a library. Tall, black-rosewood bookcases, inlaid with copperwork, held on their wide shelves a large number of uniformly bound books. These furnishings followed the contours of the room, their lower parts leading to huge couches upholstered in maroon leather and curved for maximum comfort. Light, movable reading stands, which could be pushed away or pulled near as desired, allowed books to be positioned on them for easy study. In the centre stood a huge table covered with pamphlets, among which some newspapers, long out of date, were visible. Electric light flooded this whole harmonious totality, falling from four frosted half globes set in the scrollwork of the ceiling. I stared in genuine wonderment at this room so ingeniously laid out, and I couldn't believe my eyes.

'Captain Nemo,' I told my host, who had just stretched out on a couch, 'this is a library that would do credit to more than one continental palace, and I truly marvel to think it can go with you into the deepest seas.'

'Where could one find greater silence or solitude, professor?' Captain Nemo replied. 'Did your study at the museum afford you such a perfect retreat?'

'No, sir, and I might add that it's quite a humble one next to yours. You own 6,000 or 7,000 volumes here…'

'Twelve thousand, Professor Aronnax. They're my sole remaining ties with dry land. But I was done with the shore the day my *Nautilus* submerged for the first time under the waters. That day I purchased my last volumes, my last pamphlets, my last newspapers, and ever since I've chosen to believe that humanity no longer thinks or writes. In any event, professor, these books are at your disposal, and you may use them freely.'

I thanked Captain Nemo and approached the shelves of this library. Written in every language, books on science, ethics and literature were there in abundance, but I didn't see a single work on economics – they seemed to be strictly banned on board. One odd detail: all these books were shelved indiscriminately without regard to the language in which they were written, and this jumble proved that the *Nautilus*'s captain could read fluently whatever volumes he chanced to pick up.

Among these books I noted masterpieces by the greats of ancient and modern times, in other words, all of humanity's finest achievements in history, poetry, fiction and science, from Homer to Victor Hugo, from Xenophon to Michelet, from Rabelais to Madame George Sand. But science, in particular, represented the major investment of this library: books on mechanics, ballistics, hydrography, meteorology, geography, geology, etc., held a place there no less important than works on natural history, and I realised that they made up the captain's chief reading. There I saw the complete works of Humboldt, the complete Arago, as well as works by Foucault, Henri Sainte-Claire Deville, Chasles, Milne-Edwards, Quatrefages, John Tyndall, Faraday, Berthelot, Father Secchi, Petermann, Commander Maury, Louis Agassiz, etc., plus the transactions of France's Academy of Sciences, bulletins from the various geographical societies, etc., and in a prime location, those two volumes on the great ocean depths that had perhaps earned me this comparatively charitable welcome from Captain Nemo. Among the works of Joseph Bertrand, his book entitled *The Founders of Astronomy* even gave me a definite date; and since I knew it had appeared in the course of 1865, I concluded that the fitting out of the *Nautilus* hadn't taken place before then. Accordingly, three years ago at the most, Captain Nemo had begun his underwater existence. Moreover, I hoped some books even more recent would permit me to pinpoint the date precisely; but I had plenty of time to look for them, and I didn't want to put off any longer our stroll through the wonders of the *Nautilus*.

'Sir,' I told the captain, 'thank you for placing this library at my disposal. There are scientific treasures here, and I'll take advantage of them.'

'This room isn't only a library,' Captain Nemo said, 'it's also a smoking room.'

'A smoking room?' I exclaimed. 'Then one may smoke on board?'

'Surely.'

'In that case, sir, I'm forced to believe that you've kept up relations with Havana.'

'None whatever,' the captain replied. 'Try this cigar, Professor Aronnax, and even though it doesn't come from Havana, it will satisfy you if you're a connoisseur.'

I took the cigar offered me, whose shape recalled those from Cuba; but it seemed to be made of gold leaf. I lit it at a small brazier supported by an elegant bronze stand, and I inhaled my first whiffs with the relish of a smoker who hasn't had a puff in days.

'It's excellent,' I said, 'but it's not from the tobacco plant.'

'Right,' the captain replied, 'this tobacco comes from neither Havana nor the Orient. It's a kind of nicotine-rich seaweed that the ocean supplies me, albeit sparingly. Do you still miss your Cubans, sir?'

'Captain, I scorn them from this day forward.'

'Then smoke these cigars whenever you like, without debating their origin. They bear no government seal of approval, but I imagine they're none the worse for it.'

'On the contrary.'

Just then Captain Nemo opened a door facing the one by which I had entered the library, and I passed into an immense, splendidly lit lounge.

It was a huge quadrilateral with canted corners, ten metres long, six wide, five high. A luminous ceiling, decorated with delicate arabesques, distributed a soft, clear daylight over all the wonders gathered in this museum. For a museum it truly was, in which clever hands had spared no expense to amass every natural and artistic treasure, displaying them with the helter-skelter picturesqueness that distinguishes a painter's studio.

Some thirty pictures by the masters, uniformly framed and separated by gleaming panoplies of arms, adorned walls on which were stretched tapestries of austere design. There I saw canvases of the highest value, the likes of which I had marvelled at in private European collections and art exhibitions. The various schools of the old masters were represented by a Raphael Madonna, a Virgin by Leonardo da Vinci, a nymph by Correggio, a woman by Titian, an adoration of the Magi by Veronese, an assumption of the Virgin by Murillo, a Holbein portrait, a monk by Velazquez, a martyr by Ribera, a village fair by Rubens, two Flemish landscapes by Teniers, three little genre paintings by Gerard Dow, Metsu and Paul Potter, two canvases by Gericault and Prud'hon, plus seascapes by Backhuysen and Vernet. Among the works of modern art were pictures signed by Delacroix, Ingres, Decamps, Troyon, Meissonier, Daubigny, etc., and some wonderful miniature statues in marble or bronze, modelled after antiquity's finest originals, stood on their pedestals in the corners of this magnificent museum. As the *Nautilus*'s commander had predicted, my mind was already starting to fall into that promised state of stunned amazement.

'Professor,' this strange man then said, 'you must excuse the informality with which I receive you, and the disorder reigning in this lounge.'

'Sir,' I replied, 'without prying into who you are, might I venture to identify you as an artist?'

'A collector, sir, nothing more. Formerly I loved acquiring these beautiful works created by the hand of man. I sought them greedily, ferreted them out tirelessly, and I've been able to gather some objects of great value. They're my last mementos of those shores that are now dead for me. In my eyes, your modern artists are already as old as the ancients. They've existed for 2,000 or 3,000 years, and I mix them up in my mind. The masters are ageless.'

'What about these composers?' I said, pointing to sheet music by Weber, Rossini, Mozart, Beethoven, Haydn, Meyerbeer, Hérold, Wagner, Auber, Gounod, Victor Massé, and a number of others scattered over a full size piano-organ, which occupied one of the wall panels in this lounge.

'These composers,' Captain Nemo answered me, 'are the contemporaries of Orpheus, because in the annals of the dead, all chronological differences fade; and I'm dead, professor, quite as dead as those friends of yours sleeping six feet under!'

Captain Nemo fell silent and seemed lost in reverie. I regarded him with intense excitement, silently analyzing his strange facial expression.

Leaning his elbow on the corner of a valuable mosaic table, he no longer saw me, he had forgotten my very presence.

I didn't disturb his meditations but continued to pass in review the curiosities that enriched this lounge.

After the works of art, natural rarities predominated. They consisted chiefly of plants, shells and other exhibits from the ocean that must have been Captain Nemo's own personal finds. In the middle of the lounge, a jet of water, electrically lit, fell back into a basin made from a single giant clam. The delicately festooned rim of this shell, supplied by the biggest mollusc in the class *Acephala*, measured about six metres in circumference; so it was even bigger than those fine giant clams given to King François I by the Republic of Venice, and which the Church of Saint-Sulpice in Paris has made into two gigantic holy-water fonts.

Around this basin, inside elegant glass cases fastened with copper bands, there were classified and labelled the most valuable marine exhibits ever put before the eyes of a naturalist. My professorial glee may easily be imagined.

The zoophyte branch offered some very unusual specimens from its two groups, the polyps and the echinoderms. In the first group: organ-pipe coral, gorgonian coral arranged into fan shapes, soft sponges from Syria, isis coral from the Molucca Islands, sea-pen coral, wonderful coral of the genus *Virgularia* from the waters of Norway, various coral of the genus *Umbellularia*, alcyonarian coral, then a whole series of those madrepores that my mentor Professor Milne-Edwards has so shrewdly classified into divisions and among which I noted the wonderful genus *Flabellina* as well as the genus *Oculina* from Réunion Island, plus a Neptune's chariot from the Caribbean Sea – every superb variety of coral, and in short, every species of these unusual polyparies that congregate to form entire islands that will one day turn into continents. Among the echinoderms, notable for being covered with spines: starfish, feather stars, sea lilies, free-swimming crinoids, brittle stars, sea urchins, sea cucumbers, etc., represented a complete collection of the individuals in this group.

An excitable conchologist would surely have fainted dead away before other, more numerous glass cases in which were classified specimens from the mollusc branch. There I saw a collection of incalculable value that I haven't time to describe completely. Among these exhibits I'll mention, just for the record: an elegant royal hammer shell from the Indian Ocean, whose evenly spaced white spots stood out sharply against a base of red and brown; an imperial spiny oyster, brightly coloured, bristling with thorns, a specimen rare to European museums, whose value I estimated at 20,000 francs; a common hammer shell from the seas near Queensland, very hard to come by; exotic cockles from Senegal, fragile white bivalve shells that a single breath could pop like a soap bubble; several varieties of watering-pot shell from Java, a sort of limestone tube fringed with leafy folds and much fought over by collectors; a whole series of top-shell snails – greenish yellow ones fished up from American seas, others coloured reddish brown that patronise the waters off Queensland, the former coming from the Gulf of Mexico and notable for their overlapping shells, the latter some sun-carrier shells found in the southernmost seas, finally and rarest of all, the magnificent spurred-star shell from New Zealand; then some wonderful peppery-furrow shells; several valuable species of cythera clams and venus clams; the trellis wentletrap snail from Tranquebar on India's eastern shore; a marbled turban snail gleaming with mother-of-pearl; green parrot shells from the seas of China; the virtually unknown cone snail from the genus *Coenodullus*; every variety of cowry used as money in India and Africa; a 'glory-of-the-seas,' the most valuable shell in the East Indies; finally, common periwinkles, delphinula snails, turret snails, violet snails, European cowries, volute snails, olive shells, mitre shells, helmet shells, murex snails, whelks, harp shells, spiky periwinkles, triton snails, horn shells, spindle shells, conch shells, spider conchs, limpets, glass snails, sea butterflies – every kind of delicate, fragile seashell that science has baptised with its most delightful names.

Aside and in special compartments, strings of supremely beautiful pearls were spread out, the electric light flecking them with little fiery sparks: pink pearls pulled from saltwater fan shells in the Red Sea; green pearls from the rainbow abalone; yellow, blue and black pearls, the unusual handiwork of various molluscs from every ocean and of certain mussels from rivers up north; in short, several specimens of incalculable worth that had been oozed by the rarest of shellfish. Some of these pearls were bigger than a pigeon egg; they more than equalled the one that the explorer Tavernier sold the Shah of Persia for 3,000,000 francs, and they surpassed that other pearl owned by the Imam of Muscat, which I had believed to be unrivalled in the entire world.

Consequently, to calculate the value of this collection was, I should say, impossible. Captain Nemo must have spent millions in acquiring these different specimens, and I was wondering what financial resources he tapped to satisfy his collector's fancies, when these words interrupted me:

'You're examining my shells, professor? They're indeed able to fascinate a naturalist; but for me they have an added charm, since I've collected every one of them with my own two hands, and not a sea on the globe has escaped my investigations.'

'I understand, captain, I understand your delight at strolling in the midst of this wealth. You're a man who gathers his treasure in person. No museum in Europe owns such a collection of exhibits from the ocean. But if I exhaust all my wonderment on them, I'll have nothing left for the ship that carries them! I have absolutely no wish to probe those secrets of yours! But I confess that my curiosity is aroused to the limit by this *Nautilus*, the motor power it contains, the equipment enabling it to operate, the ultra powerful force that brings it to life. I see some instruments hanging on the walls of this lounge whose purposes are unknown to me. May I learn—'

'Professor Aronnax,' Captain Nemo answered me, 'I've said you'd be free aboard my vessel, so no part of the *Nautilus* is off-limits to you. You may inspect it in detail, and I'll be delighted to act as your guide.'

'I don't know how to thank you, sir, but I won't abuse your good nature. I would only ask you about the uses intended for these instruments of physical measure—'

'Professor, these same instruments are found in my stateroom, where I'll have the pleasure of explaining their functions to you. But beforehand, come inspect the cabin set aside for you. You need to learn how you'll be lodged aboard the *Nautilus*.'

I followed Captain Nemo, who, via one of the doors cut into the lounge's canted corners, led me back down the ship's gangways. He took me to the bow, and there I found not just a cabin but an elegant stateroom with a bed, a washstand and various other furnishings.

I could only thank my host.

'Your stateroom adjoins mine,' he told me, opening a door, 'and mine leads into that lounge we've just left.'

I entered the captain's stateroom. It had an austere, almost monastic appearance. An iron bedstead, a worktable, some washstand fixtures. Subdued lighting. No luxuries. Just the bare necessities.

Captain Nemo showed me to a bench.

'Kindly be seated,' he told me.

I sat, and he began speaking as follows:

CHAPTER 12

Everything through Electricity

'Sir,' Captain Nemo said, showing me the instruments hanging on the walls of his stateroom, 'these are the devices needed to navigate the *Nautilus*. Here, as in the lounge, I always have them before my eyes, and they indicate my position and exact heading in the midst of the ocean. You're familiar with some of them, such as the thermometer, which gives the temperature inside the *Nautilus*; the barometer, which measures the heaviness of the outside air and forecasts changes in the weather; the humidistat, which indicates the degree of dryness in the atmosphere; the storm glass, whose mixture decomposes to foretell the arrival of tempests; the compass, which steers my course; the sextant, which takes the sun's altitude and tells me my latitude; chronometers, which allow me to calculate my longitude; and finally, spyglasses for both day and night, enabling me to scrutinise every point of the horizon once the *Nautilus* has risen to the surface of the waves.'

'These are the normal navigational instruments,' I replied, 'and I'm familiar with their uses. But no doubt these others answer pressing needs unique to the *Nautilus*. That dial I see there, with the needle moving across it – isn't it a pressure gauge?'

'It is indeed a pressure gauge. It's placed in contact with the water, and it indicates the outside pressure on our hull, which in turn gives me the depth at which my submersible is sitting.'

'And these are some new breed of sounding line?'

'They're thermometric sounding lines that report water temperatures in the different strata.'

'And these other instruments, whose functions I can't even guess?'

'Here, professor, I need to give you some background information,' Captain Nemo said. 'So kindly hear me out.'

He fell silent for some moments, then he said:

'There's a powerful, obedient, swift and effortless force that can be bent to any use and which reigns supreme aboard my vessel. It does everything. It lights me, it warms me, it's the soul of my mechanical equipment. This force is electricity.'

'Electricity!' I exclaimed in some surprise.

'Yes, sir.'

'But, captain, you have a tremendous speed of movement that doesn't square with the strength of electricity. Until now, its dynamic potential has remained quite limited, capable of producing only small amounts of power!'

'Professor,' Captain Nemo replied, 'my electricity isn't the run-of-the-mill variety, and with your permission, I'll leave it at that.'

'I won't insist, sir, and I'll rest content with simply being flabbergasted at your results. I would ask one question, however, which you needn't answer if it's indiscreet. The electric cells you use to generate this marvellous force must be depleted very quickly. Their zinc component, for example: how do you replace it, since you no longer stay in contact with the shore?'

'That question deserves an answer,' Captain Nemo replied. 'First off, I'll mention that at the bottom of the sea there exist veins of zinc, iron, silver and gold whose mining would quite certainly be feasible. But I've tapped none of these land-based metals, and I wanted to make demands only on the sea itself for the sources of my electricity.'

'The sea itself?'

'Yes, professor, and there was no shortage of such sources. In fact, by establishing a circuit between two wires immersed to different depths, I'd be able to obtain electricity through the diverging temperatures they experience; but I preferred to use a more practical procedure.'

'And that is?'

'You're familiar with the composition of salt water. In 1,000 grams one finds 96.5 per cent water and about 2.66 per cent sodium chloride; then small quantities of magnesium chloride, potassium chloride, magnesium bromide, sulphate of magnesia, calcium sulphate and calcium carbonate. Hence you observe that sodium chloride is encountered there in significant proportions. Now then, it's this sodium that I extract from salt water and with which I compose my electric cells.'

'Sodium?'

'Yes, sir. Mixed with mercury, it forms an amalgam that takes the place of zinc in Bunsen cells. The mercury is never depleted. Only the sodium is consumed, and the sea itself gives me that. Beyond this, I'll mention that sodium batteries have been found to generate the greater energy, and their electro-motor strength is twice that of zinc batteries.'

'Captain, I fully understand the excellence of sodium under the conditions in which you're placed. The sea contains it. Fine. But it still has to be produced, in short, extracted. And how do you accomplish this? Obviously your batteries could do the extracting; but if I'm not mistaken, the consumption of sodium needed by your electric equipment would be greater than the quantity you'd extract. It would come about, then, that in the process of producing your sodium, you'd use up more than you'd make!'

'Accordingly, professor, I don't extract it with batteries; quite simply, I utilise the heat of coal from the earth.'

'From the earth?' I said, my voice going up on the word.

'We'll say coal from the seafloor, if you prefer,' Captain Nemo replied.

'And you can mine these veins of underwater coal?'

'You'll watch me work them, Professor Aronnax. I ask only a little patience of you, since you'll have ample time to be patient. Just remember one thing: I owe everything to the ocean; it generates electricity, and electricity gives the *Nautilus* heat, light, motion and, in a word, life itself.'

'But not the air you breathe?'

'Oh, I could produce the air needed on board, but it would be pointless, since I can rise to the surface of the sea whenever I like. However, even though electricity doesn't supply me with breathable air, it at least operates the powerful pumps that store it under pressure in special tanks; which, if need be, allows me to extend my stay in the lower strata for as long as I want.'

'Captain,' I replied, 'I'll rest content with marvelling. You've obviously found what all mankind will surely find one day, the true dynamic power of electricity.'

'I'm not so certain they'll find it,' Captain Nemo replied icily. 'But be that as it may, you're already familiar with the first use I've found for this valuable force. It lights us, and with a uniformity and continuity not even possessed by sunlight. Now, look at that clock: it's electric, it runs with an accuracy rivalling the finest chronometers. I've had it divided into 24 hours like Italian clocks, since neither day nor night, sun nor moon, exist for me, but only this artificial light that I import into the depths of the seas! See, right now it's ten o'clock in the morning.'

'That's perfect.'

'Another use for electricity: that dial hanging before our eyes indicates how fast the *Nautilus* is going. An electric wire puts it in contact with the patent log; this needle shows me the actual speed of my submersible. And... hold on... just now we're proceeding at the moderate pace of 15 miles per hour.'

'It's marvellous,' I replied, 'and I truly see, captain, how right you are to use this force; it's sure to take the place of wind, water and steam.'

'But that's not all, Professor Aronnax,' Captain Nemo said, standing up. 'And if you'd care to follow me, we'll inspect the *Nautilus*'s stern.'

In essence, I was already familiar with the whole forward part of this underwater boat, and here are its exact subdivisions going from amidships to its spur: the dining room, five metres long and separated from the library by a watertight bulkhead, in other words, it couldn't be penetrated by the sea; the library, five metres long; the main lounge, ten metres long, separated from the captain's stateroom by a second watertight bulkhead; the aforesaid stateroom, five metres long; mine, two-and-a-half metres long; and finally, air tanks seven-and-a-half metres long and extending to the stempost. Total: a length of 35 metres. Doors were cut into the watertight bulkheads and were shut hermetically by means of india-rubber seals, which insured complete safety aboard the *Nautilus* in the event of a leak in any one section.

I followed Captain Nemo down gangways located for easy transit, and I arrived amidships. There I found a sort of shaft heading upward between two watertight bulkheads. An iron ladder, clamped to the wall, led to the shaft's upper end. I asked the captain what this ladder was for.

'It goes to the skiff,' he replied.

'What! You have a skiff?' I replied in some astonishment.

'Surely. An excellent longboat, light and unsinkable, which is used for excursions and fishing trips.'

'But when you want to set out, don't you have to return to the surface of the sea?'

'By no means. The skiff is attached to the topside of the *Nautilus*'s hull and is set in a cavity expressly designed to receive it. It's completely decked over, absolutely watertight, and held solidly in place by bolts. This ladder leads to a manhole cut into the *Nautilus*'s hull and corresponding to a comparable hole cut into the side of the skiff. I insert myself through this double opening into the longboat. My crew close up the hole belonging to the *Nautilus*; I close up the one belonging to the skiff, simply by screwing it into place. I undo the bolts holding the skiff to the submersible, and the longboat rises with prodigious speed to the surface of the sea. I then open the deck panelling, carefully closed until that point; I up mast and hoist sail – or I take out my oars – and I go for a spin.'

'But how do you return to the ship?'

'I don't, Professor Aronnax; the *Nautilus* returns to me.'

'At your command?'

'At my command. An electric wire connects me to the ship. I fire off a telegram, and that's that.'

'Right,' I said, tipsy from all these wonders, 'nothing to it!'

After passing the well of the companionway that led to the platform, I saw a cabin two metres long in which Conseil and Ned Land, enraptured with their meal, were busy devouring it to the last crumb. Then a door opened into the galley, three metres long and located between the vessel's huge storage lockers.

There, even more powerful and obedient than gas, electricity did most of the cooking. Arriving under the stoves, wires transmitted to platinum griddles a heat that was distributed and sustained with perfect consistency. It also heated a distilling mechanism that, via evaporation, supplied excellent drinking water. Next to this galley was a bathroom, conveniently laid out, with taps supplying hot or cold water at will.

After the galley came the crew's quarters, five metres long. But the door was closed and I couldn't see its accommodations, which might have told me the number of men it took to operate the *Nautilus*.

At the far end stood a fourth watertight bulkhead, separating the crew's quarters from the engine room. A door opened, and I stood in the compartment where Captain Nemo, indisputably a world-class engineer, had set up his locomotive equipment.

Brightly lit, the engine room measured at least 20 metres in length. It was divided, by function, into two parts: the first contained the cells for generating electricity, the second that mechanism transmitting movement to the propeller.

Right off, I detected an odour permeating the compartment that was *sui generis*. Captain Nemo noticed the negative impression it made on me.

'That,' he told me, 'is a gaseous discharge caused by our use of sodium, but it's only a mild inconvenience. In any event, every morning we sanitise the ship by ventilating it in the open air.'

Meanwhile I examined the *Nautilus*'s engine with a fascination easy to imagine.

'You observe,' Captain Nemo told me, 'that I use Bunsen cells, not Ruhmkorff cells. The latter would be ineffectual. One uses fewer Bunsen cells, but they're big and strong, and experience has proven their superiority. The electricity generated here makes its way to the stern, where electromagnets of huge size activate a special system of levers and gears that transmit movement to the propeller's shaft. The latter has a diameter of six metres, a pitch of seven-and-a-half metres, and can do up to 120 revolutions per minute.'

'And that gives you?'

'A speed of 50 miles per hour.'

There lay a mystery, but I didn't insist on exploring it. How could electricity work with such power? Where did this nearly unlimited energy originate? Was it in the extraordinary voltage obtained from some new kind of induction coil? Could its transmission have been immeasurably increased by some unknown system of levers?[1] This was the point I couldn't grasp.

'Captain Nemo,' I said, 'I'll vouch for the results and not try to explain them. I've seen the *Nautilus* at work out in front of the *Abraham Lincoln*, and I know where I stand on its speed. But it isn't enough just to move, we have to see where we're going! We must be

---

[1] Author's Note: And sure enough, there's now talk of such a discovery, in which a new set of levers generates considerable power. Did its inventor meet up with Captain Nemo?

able to steer right or left, up or down! How do you reach the lower depths, where you meet an increasing resistance that's assessed in hundreds of atmospheres? How do you rise back to the surface of the ocean? Finally, how do you keep your ship at whatever level suits you? Am I indiscreet in asking you all these things?'

'Not at all, professor,' the captain answered me after a slight hesitation, 'since you'll never leave this underwater boat. Come into the lounge. It's actually our work room, and there you'll learn the full story about the *Nautilus*!'

CHAPTER 13

Some Figures

A MOMENT LATER we were seated on a couch in the lounge, cigars between our lips. The captain placed before my eyes a working drawing that gave the ground plan, cross section and side view of the *Nautilus*. Then he began his description as follows:

'Here, Professor Aronnax, are the different dimensions of this boat now transporting you. It's a very long cylinder with conical ends. It noticeably takes the shape of a cigar, a shape already adopted in London for several projects of the same kind. The length of this cylinder from end to end is exactly 70 metres, and its maximum breadth of beam is eight metres. So it isn't quite built on the ten-to-one ratio of your high-speed steamers; but its lines are sufficiently long, and their tapering gradual enough, so that the displaced water easily slips past and poses no obstacle to the ship's movements.

'These two dimensions allow you to obtain, via a simple calculation, the surface area and volume of the *Nautilus*. Its surface area totals 1,011.45 square metres, its volume 1,507.2 cubic metres – which is tantamount to saying that when it's completely submerged, it displaces 1,500 cubic metres of water, or weighs 1,500 metric tons.

'In drawing up plans for a ship meant to navigate underwater, I wanted it, when floating on the waves, to lie nine-tenths below the surface and to emerge only one-tenth. Consequently, under these conditions it needed to displace only nine-tenths of its volume, hence 1,356.48 cubic metres; in other words, it was to weigh only that same number of metric tons. So I was obliged not to exceed this weight while building it to the aforesaid dimensions.

'The *Nautilus* is made up of two hulls, one inside the other; between them, joining them together, are iron T-bars that give this ship the utmost rigidity. In fact, thanks to this cellular arrangement, it has the resistance of a stone block, as if it were completely solid. Its plating can't give way; it's self-adhering and not dependent on the tightness of its rivets; and due to the perfect union of its materials, the solidarity of its construction allows it to defy the most violent seas.

'The two hulls are manufactured from boilerplate steel, whose relative density is 7.8 times that of water. The first hull has a thickness of no less than five centimetres and weighs 394.96 metric tons. My second hull, the outer cover, includes a keel 50 centimetres high by 25 wide, which by itself weighs 62 metric tons; this hull, the engine, the ballast, the various accessories and accommodations, plus the bulkheads and interior braces, have a combined weight of 961.52 metric tons, which when added to 394.96 metric tons, gives us the desired total of 1,356.48 metric tons. Clear?'

'Clear,' I replied.

'So,' the captain went on, 'when the *Nautilus* lies on the waves under these conditions, one-tenth of it does emerge above water. Now then, if I provide some ballast tanks equal in capacity to that one-tenth, hence able to hold 150.72 metric tons, and if I fill them with water, the boat then displaces 1,507.2 metric tons – or it weighs that much – and it would be completely submerged. That's what comes about, professor. These ballast tanks exist within easy access in the lower reaches of the *Nautilus*. I open some stopcocks, the tanks fill, the boat sinks and it's exactly flush with the surface of the water.'

'Fine, captain, but now we come to a genuine difficulty. You're able to lie flush with the surface of the ocean, that I understand. But lower down, while diving beneath that surface, isn't your submersible going to encounter a pressure, and consequently undergo an upward thrust, that must be assessed at one atmosphere per every 30 feet of water, hence at about one kilogram per each square centimetre?'

'Precisely, sir.'

'Then unless you fill up the whole *Nautilus*, I don't see how you can force it down into the heart of these liquid masses.'

'Professor,' Captain Nemo replied, 'static objects mustn't be confused with dynamic ones, or we'll be open to serious error. Comparatively little effort is spent in reaching the ocean's lower regions, because all objects have a tendency to become "sinkers." Follow my logic here.'

'I'm all ears, captain.'

'When I wanted to determine what increase in weight the *Nautilus* needed to be given in order to submerge, I had only to take note of the proportionate reduction in volume that salt water experiences in deeper and deeper strata.'

'That's obvious,' I replied.

'Now then, if water isn't absolutely incompressible, at least it compresses very little. In fact, according to the most recent calculations, this reduction is only .0000436 per atmosphere, or per every 30 feet of depth. For instance, to go 1,000 metres down, I must take into account the reduction in volume that occurs under a pressure equivalent to that from a 1,000-metre column of water, in other words, under a pressure of 100 atmospheres. In this instance the reduction would be .00436. Consequently, I'd have to increase my weight from 1,507.2 metric tons to 1,513.77. So the added weight would only be 6.57 metric tons.'

'That's all?'

'That's all, Professor Aronnax, and the calculation is easy to check. Now then, I have supplementary ballast tanks capable of shipping 100 metric tons of water. So I can descend to considerable depths. When I want to rise again and lie flush with the surface, all I have to do is expel that water; and if I desire that the *Nautilus* emerge above the waves to one-tenth of its total capacity, I empty all the ballast tanks completely.'

This logic, backed up by figures, left me without a single objection.

'I accept your calculations, captain,' I replied, 'and I'd be ill-mannered to dispute them, since your daily experience bears them out. But at this juncture, I have a hunch that we're still left with one real difficulty.'

'What's that, sir?'

'When you're at a depth of 1,000 metres, the *Nautilus*'s plating bears a pressure of 100 atmospheres. If at this point you want to empty the supplementary ballast tanks in order to lighten your boat and rise to the surface, your pumps must overcome that pressure of 100 atmospheres, which is 100 kilograms per each square centimetre. This demands a strength—'

'That electricity alone can give me,' Captain Nemo said swiftly. 'Sir, I repeat: the dynamic power of my engines is nearly infinite. The *Nautilus*'s pumps have prodigious strength, as you must have noticed when their waterspouts swept like a torrent over the *Abraham Lincoln*. Besides, I use my supplementary ballast tanks only to reach an average depth of 1,500 to 2,000 metres, and that with a view to conserving my machinery. Accordingly, when I have a mind to visit the ocean depths two or three vertical leagues beneath the surface, I use manoeuvres that are more time-consuming but no less infallible.'

'What are they, captain?' I asked.

'Here I'm naturally led into telling you how the *Nautilus* is manoeuvred.'

'I can't wait to find out.'

'In order to steer this boat to port or starboard, in short, to make turns on a horizontal plane, I use an ordinary, wide-bladed rudder that's fastened to the rear of the sternpost and worked by a wheel and tackle. But I can also move the *Nautilus* upward and downward on a vertical plane by the simple method of slanting its two fins, which are attached to its sides at its centre of flotation; these fins are flexible, able to assume any position, and can be operated from inside by means of powerful levers. If these fins stay parallel with the boat, the latter moves horizontally. If they slant, the *Nautilus* follows the angle of that slant and, under its propeller's thrust, either sinks on a diagonal as steep as it suits me, or rises on that diagonal. And similarly, if I want to return more swiftly to the surface, I throw the propeller in gear, and the water's pressure makes the *Nautilus* rise vertically, as an air balloon inflated with hydrogen lifts swiftly into the skies.'

'Bravo, captain!' I exclaimed. 'But in the midst of the waters, how can your helmsman follow the course you've given him?'

'My helmsman is stationed behind the windows of a pilothouse, which protrudes from the topside of the *Nautilus*'s hull and is fitted with biconvex glass.'

'Is glass capable of resisting such pressures?'

'Perfectly capable. Though fragile on impact, crystal can still offer considerable resistance. In 1864, during experiments on fishing by electric light in the middle of the North Sea, glass panes less than seven millimetres thick were seen to resist a pressure of 16 atmospheres, all the while letting through strong, heat-generating rays whose warmth was unevenly distributed. Now then, I use glass windows measuring no less than 21 centimetres at their centres; in other words, they've 30 times the thickness.'

'Fair enough, captain, but if we're going to see, we need light to drive away the dark, and in the midst of the murky waters, I wonder how your helmsman can—'

'Set astern of the pilothouse is a powerful electric reflector whose rays light up the sea for a distance of half a mile.'

'Oh, bravo! Bravo three times over, captain! That explains the phosphorescent glow from this so-called narwhal that so puzzled us scientists! Pertinent to this, I'll ask you if the *Nautilus*'s running afoul of the *Scotia*, which caused such a great uproar, was the result of an accidental encounter?'

'Entirely accidental, sir. I was navigating two metres beneath the surface of the water when the collision occurred. However, I could see that it had no dire consequences.'

'None, sir. But as for your encounter with the *Abraham Lincoln*...?'

'Professor, that troubled me, because it's one of the best ships in the gallant American navy, but they attacked me and I had to defend myself! All the same, I was content simply to put the frigate in a condition where it could do me no harm; it won't have any difficulty getting repairs at the nearest port.'

'Ah, commander,' I exclaimed with conviction, 'your *Nautilus* is truly a marvellous boat!'

'Yes, professor,' Captain Nemo replied with genuine excitement, 'and I love it as if it were my own flesh and blood! Aboard a conventional ship, facing the ocean's perils, danger lurks everywhere; on the surface of the sea, your chief sensation is the constant feeling of an underlying chasm, as the Dutchman Jansen so aptly put it; but below the waves aboard the *Nautilus*, your heart never fails you! There are no structural deformities to worry about, because the double hull of this boat has the rigidity of iron; no rigging to be worn out by rolling and pitching on the waves; no sails for the wind to carry off; no boilers for steam to burst open; no fires to fear, because this submersible is made of sheet iron not wood; no coal to run out of, since electricity is its mechanical force; no collisions to fear, because it navigates the watery deep all by itself; no storms to brave, because just a few metres beneath the waves, it finds absolute tranquillity! There, sir. There's the ideal ship! And if it's true that the engineer has more confidence in a craft than the builder, and the builder more than the captain himself, you can understand the utter abandon with which I place my trust in this *Nautilus*, since I'm its captain, builder and engineer all in one!'

Captain Nemo spoke with winning eloquence. The fire in his eyes and the passion in his gestures transfigured him. Yes, he loved his ship the same way a father loves his child!

But one question, perhaps indiscreet, naturally popped up, and I couldn't resist asking it.

'You're an engineer, then, Captain Nemo?'

'Yes, professor,' he answered me. 'I studied in London, Paris and New York back in the days when I was a resident of the Earth's continents.'

'But how were you able to build this wonderful *Nautilus* in secret?'

'Each part of it, Professor Aronnax, came from a different spot on the globe and reached me at a cover address. Its keel was forged by Creusot in France, its propeller shaft by Pen & Co. in London, the sheet-iron plates for its hull by Laird's in Liverpool, its propeller by Scott's in Glasgow. Its tanks were manufactured by Cail & Co. in Paris, its engine by Krupp in Prussia, its spur by the Motala workshops in Sweden, its precision instruments by Hart Bros. in New York, etc.; and each of these suppliers received my specifications under a different name.'

'But,' I went on, 'once these parts were manufactured, didn't they have to be mounted and adjusted?'

'Professor, I set up my workshops on a deserted islet in mid-ocean. There our *Nautilus* was completed by me and my workmen, in other words, by my gallant companions whom I've moulded and educated. Then, when the operation was over, we burned every trace of our stay on that islet, which if I could have, I'd have blown up.'

'From all this, may I assume that such a boat costs a fortune?'

'An iron ship, Professor Aronnax, runs 1,125 francs per metric ton. Now then, the *Nautilus* has a burden of 1,500 metric tons. Consequently, it cost 1,687,000 francs, hence 2,000,000 francs including its accommodations, and 4,000,000 francs or 5,000,000 francs with all the collections and works of art it contains.'

'One last question, Captain Nemo.'

'Ask, professor.'

'You're rich, then?'

'Infinitely rich, sir, and without any trouble, I could pay off the ten-billion-franc French national debt!'

I gaped at the bizarre individual who had just spoken these words. Was he playing on my credulity? Time would tell.

CHAPTER 14

The Black Current

THE PART OF the planet earth that the seas occupy has been assessed at 3,832,558 square myriametres, hence more than 38,000,000,000 hectares. This liquid mass totals 2,250,000,000 cubic miles and could form a sphere with a diameter of 60 leagues, whose weight would be three quintillion metric tons. To appreciate such a number, we should remember that a quintillion is to a billion what a billion is to one, in other words, there are as many billions in a quintillion as ones in a billion! Now then, this liquid mass nearly equals the total amount of water that has poured through all the earth's rivers for the past 40,000 years!

During prehistoric times, an era of fire was followed by an era of water. At first there was ocean everywhere. Then, during the Silurian period, the tops of mountains gradually appeared above the waves, islands emerged, disappeared beneath temporary floods, rose again, were fused to form continents, and finally the earth's geography settled into what we have today. Solid matter had wrested from liquid matter some 37,657,000 square miles, hence 12,916,000,000 hectares.

The outlines of the continents allow the seas to be divided into five major parts: the frozen Arctic and Antarctic Oceans, the Indian Ocean, the Atlantic Ocean and the Pacific Ocean.

The Pacific Ocean extends north to south between the two polar circles and east to west between America and Asia over an expanse of 145° of longitude. It's the most tranquil of the seas; its currents are wide and slow-moving, its tides moderate, its rainfall abundant. And this was the ocean that I was first destined to cross under these strangest of auspices.

'If you don't mind, professor,' Captain Nemo told me, 'we'll determine our exact position and fix the starting point of our voyage. It's fifteen minutes before noon. I'm going to rise to the surface of the water.'

The captain pressed an electric bell three times. The pumps began to expel water from the ballast tanks; on the pressure gauge, a needle marked the decreasing pressures that indicated the *Nautilus*'s upward progress; then the needle stopped.

'Here we are,' the captain said.

I made my way to the central companionway, which led to the platform. I climbed its metal steps, passed through the open hatches, and arrived topside on the *Nautilus*.

The platform emerged only 80 centimetres above the waves. The *Nautilus*'s bow and stern boasted that spindle-shaped outline that had caused the ship to be compared appropriately to a long cigar. I noted the slight overlap of its sheet-iron plates, which resembled the scales covering the bodies of our big land reptiles. So I had a perfectly natural explanation for why, despite the best spyglasses, this boat had always been mistaken for a marine animal.

Near the middle of the platform, the skiff was half set in the ship's hull, making a slight bulge. Fore and aft stood two cupolas of moderate height, their sides slanting and partly inset with heavy biconvex glass, one reserved for the helmsman steering the *Nautilus*, the other for the brilliance of the powerful electric beacon lighting his way.

The sea was magnificent, the skies clear. This long aquatic vehicle could barely feel the broad undulations of the ocean. A mild breeze out of the east rippled the surface of the water. Free of all mist, the horizon was ideal for taking sights.

There was nothing to be seen. Not a reef, not an islet. No more *Abraham Lincoln*. A deserted immenseness.

Raising his sextant, Captain Nemo took the altitude of the sun, which would give him his latitude. He waited for a few minutes until the orb touched the rim of the horizon. While he was taking his sights, he didn't move a muscle, and the instrument couldn't have been steadier in hands made out of marble.

'Noon,' he said. 'Professor, whenever you're ready....'

I took one last look at the sea, a little yellowish near the landing places of Japan, and I went below again to the main lounge.

There the captain fixed his position and used a chronometer to calculate his longitude, which he double-checked against his previous observations of hour angles. Then he told me:

'Professor Aronnax, we're in longitude 137° 15' west—'

'West of which meridian?' I asked quickly, hoping the Captain's reply might give me a clue to his nationality.

'Sir,' he answered me, 'I have chronometers variously set to the meridians of Paris, Greenwich and Washington, D.C. But in your honour, I'll use the one for Paris.'

This reply told me nothing. I bowed, and the commander went on:

'We're in longitude 137° 15' west of the meridian of Paris, and latitude 30° 7' north, in other words, about 300 miles from the shores of Japan. At noon on this day of November 8, we hereby begin our voyage of exploration under the waters.'

'May God be with us!' I replied.

'And now, professor,' the captain added, 'I'll leave you to your intellectual pursuits. I've set our course east-northeast at a depth of 50 metres. Here are some large-scale charts on which you'll be able to follow that course. The lounge is at your disposal, and with your permission, I'll take my leave.'

Captain Nemo bowed. I was left to myself, lost in my thoughts. They all centred on the *Nautilus*'s commander. Would I ever learn the nationality of this eccentric man who had boasted of having none? His sworn hate for humanity, a hate that perhaps was bent on some dreadful revenge – what had provoked it? Was he one of those unappreciated scholars, one of those geniuses 'embittered by the world,' as Conseil expressed it, a latter-day Galileo, or maybe one of those men of science, like America's Commander Maury, whose careers were ruined by political revolutions? I couldn't say yet. As for me, whom fate had just brought aboard his vessel, whose life he had held in the balance: he had received me coolly but hospitably. Only, he never took the hand I extended to him. He never extended his own.

For an entire hour I was deep in these musings, trying to probe this mystery that fascinated me so. Then my eyes focused on a huge world map displayed on the table, and I put my finger on the very spot where our just-determined longitude and latitude intersected.

Like the continents, the sea has its rivers. These are exclusive currents that can be identified by their temperature and colour, the most remarkable being the one called the Gulf Stream. Science has defined the global paths of five chief currents: one in the north Atlantic, a second in the south Atlantic, a third in the north Pacific, a fourth in the south Pacific and a fifth in the southern Indian Ocean. Also it's likely that a sixth current used to exist in the northern Indian Ocean, when the Caspian and Aral Seas joined up with certain large Asian lakes to form a single uniform expanse of water.

Now then, at the spot indicated on the world map, one of these sea-going rivers was rolling by, the Kuroshio of the Japanese, the Black Current: heated by perpendicular rays from the tropical sun, it leaves the Bay of Bengal, crosses the Strait of Malacca, goes up the shores of Asia, and curves into the north Pacific as far as the Aleutian Islands, carrying along trunks of camphor trees and other local items, the pure indigo of its warm waters sharply contrasting with the ocean's waves. It was this current the *Nautilus* was about to cross. I watched it on the map with my eyes, I saw it lose itself in the immenseness of the Pacific, and I felt myself swept along with it, when Ned Land and Conseil appeared in the lounge doorway.

My two gallant companions stood petrified at the sight of the wonders on display.

'Where are we?' the Canadian exclaimed. 'In the Quebec Museum?'

'Begging master's pardon,' Conseil answered, 'but this seems more like the Sommerard artefacts exhibition!'

'My friends,' I replied, signalling them to enter, 'you're in neither Canada nor France, but securely aboard the *Nautilus*, 50 metres below sea level.'

'If master says so, then so be it,' Conseil answered. 'But in all honesty, this lounge is enough to astonish even someone Flemish like myself.'

'Indulge your astonishment, my friend, and have a look, because there's plenty of work here for a classifier of your talents.'

Conseil needed no encouraging. Bending over the glass cases, the gallant lad was already muttering choice words from the naturalist's vocabulary: class *Gastropoda*, family *Buccinoidea*, genus *Cowry*, species *Cypraea madagascariensis*, etc.

Meanwhile Ned Land, less dedicated to conchology, questioned me about my interview with Captain Nemo. Had I discovered who he was, where he came from, where he was heading, how deep he was taking us? In short, a thousand questions I had no time to answer.

I told him everything I knew – or, rather, everything I didn't know – and I asked him what he had seen or heard on his part.

'Haven't seen or heard a thing!' the Canadian replied. 'I haven't even spotted the crew of this boat. By any chance, could they be electric too?'

'Electric?'

'Oh ye gods, I'm half tempted to believe it! But back to you, Professor Aronnax,' Ned Land said, still hanging on to his ideas. 'Can't you tell me how many men are on board? Ten, twenty, fifty, a hundred?'

'I'm unable to answer you, Mr Land. And trust me on this: for the time being, get rid of these notions of taking over the *Nautilus* or escaping from it. This boat is a masterpiece of modern technology, and I'd be sorry to have missed it! Many people would welcome the circumstances that have been handed us, just to walk in the midst of these wonders. So keep calm, and let's see what's happening around us.'

'See!' the harpooner exclaimed. 'There's nothing to see, nothing we'll ever see from this sheet-iron prison! We're simply running around blindfolded—'

Ned Land was just pronouncing these last words when we were suddenly plunged into darkness, utter darkness. The ceiling lights went out so quickly, my eyes literally ached, just as if we had experienced the opposite sensation of going from the deepest gloom to the brightest sunlight.

We stood stock-still, not knowing what surprise was waiting for us, whether pleasant or unpleasant. But a sliding sound became audible. You could tell that some panels were shifting over the *Nautilus*'s sides.

'It's the beginning of the end!' Ned Land said.

'... order *Hydromedusa*,' Conseil muttered.

Suddenly, through two oblong openings, daylight appeared on both sides of the lounge. The liquid masses came into view, brightly lit by the ship's electric outpourings. We were separated from the sea by two panes of glass. Initially I shuddered at the thought that these fragile partitions could break; but strong copper bands secured them, giving them nearly infinite resistance.

The sea was clearly visible for a one-mile radius around the *Nautilus*. What a sight! What pen could describe it? Who could portray the effects of this light through these translucent sheets of water, the subtlety of its progressive shadings into the ocean's upper and lower strata?

The transparency of salt water has long been recognised. Its clarity is believed to exceed that of spring water. The mineral and organic substances it holds in suspension actually increase its translucency. In certain parts of the Caribbean Sea, you can see the sandy bottom with startling distinctness as deep as 145 metres down, and the penetrating power of the sun's rays seems to give out only at a depth of 300 metres. But in this fluid setting travelled by the *Nautilus*, our electric glow was being generated in the very heart of the waves. It was no longer illuminated water, it was liquid light.

If we accept the hypotheses of the microbiologist Ehrenberg – who believes that these underwater depths are lit up by phosphorescent organisms – nature has certainly saved one of her most prodigious sights for residents of the sea, and I could judge for myself from the thousandfold play of the light. On both sides I had windows opening over these unexplored depths. The darkness in the lounge enhanced the brightness outside, and we stared as if this clear glass were the window of an immense aquarium.

The *Nautilus* seemed to be standing still. This was due to the lack of landmarks. But streaks of water, parted by the ship's spur, sometimes threaded before our eyes with extraordinary speed.

In wonderment, we leaned on our elbows before these show windows, and our stunned silence remained unbroken until Conseil said:

'You wanted to see something, Ned my friend; well, now you have something to see!'

'How unusual!' the Canadian put in, setting aside his tantrums and getaway schemes while submitting to this irresistible allure. 'A man would go an even greater distance just to stare at such a sight!'

'Ah!' I exclaimed. 'I see our captain's way of life! He's found himself a separate world that saves its most astonishing wonders just for him!'

'But where are the fish?' the Canadian ventured to observe. 'I don't see any fish!'

'Why would you care, Ned my friend?' Conseil replied. 'Since you have no knowledge of them.'

'Me? A fisherman!' Ned Land exclaimed.

And on this subject a dispute arose between the two friends, since both were knowledgeable about fish, but from totally different standpoints.

Everyone knows that fish make up the fourth and last class in the vertebrate branch. They have been quite aptly defined as:

'cold-blooded vertebrates with a double circulatory system, breathing through gills, and designed to live in water.'

They consist of two distinct series: the series of bony fish, in other words, those whose spines have vertebrae made of bone; and cartilaginous fish, in other words, those whose spines have vertebrae made of cartilage.

Possibly the Canadian was familiar with this distinction, but Conseil knew far more about it; and since he and Ned were now fast friends, he just had to show off. So he told the harpooner:

'Ned my friend, you're a slayer of fish, a highly skilled fisherman. You've caught a large number of these fascinating animals. But I'll bet you don't know how they're classified.'

'Sure I do,' the harpooner replied in all seriousness. 'They're classified into fish we eat and fish we don't eat!'

'Spoken like a true glutton,' Conseil replied. 'But tell me, are you familiar with the differences between bony fish and cartilaginous fish?'

'Just maybe, Conseil.'

'And how about the subdivisions of these two large classes?'

'I haven't the foggiest notion,' the Canadian replied.

'All right, listen and learn, Ned my friend! Bony fish are subdivided into six orders. Primo, the *acanthopterygians*, whose upper jaw is fully formed and free-moving, and whose gills take the shape of a comb. This order consists of 15 families, in other words, three-quarters of all known fish. Example: the common perch.'

'Pretty fair eating,' Ned Land replied.

'Secundo,' Conseil went on, 'the *abdominals*, whose pelvic fins hang under the abdomen to the rear of the pectorals but aren't attached to the shoulder bone, an order that's divided into five families and makes up the great majority of freshwater fish. Examples: carp, pike.'

'Ugh!' the Canadian put in with distinct scorn. 'You can keep the freshwater fish!'

'Tertio,' Conseil said, 'the *subbrachians*, whose pelvic fins are attached under the pectorals and hang directly from the shoulder bone. This order contains four families. Examples: flatfish such as sole, turbot, dab, plaice, brill, etc.'

'Excellent, really excellent!' the harpooner exclaimed, interested in fish only from an edible viewpoint.

'Quarto,' Conseil went on, unabashed, 'the *apods*, with long bodies that lack pelvic fins and are covered by a heavy, often glutinous skin, an order consisting of only one family. Examples: common eels and electric eels.'

'So-so, just so-so!' Ned Land replied.

'Quinto,' Conseil said, 'the *lophobranchians*, which have fully formed, free-moving jaws but whose gills consist of little tufts arranged in pairs along their gill arches. This order includes only one family. Examples: seahorses and dragonfish.'

'Bad, very bad!' the harpooner replied.

'Sexto and last,' Conseil said, 'the *plectognaths*, whose maxillary bone is firmly attached to the side of the intermaxillary that forms the jaw, and whose palate arch is locked to the skull by sutures that render the jaw immovable, an order lacking true pelvic fins and which consists of two families. Examples: puffers and moonfish.'

'They're an insult to a frying pan!' the Canadian exclaimed.

'Are you grasping all this, Ned my friend?' asked the scholarly Conseil.

'Not a lick of it, Conseil my friend,' the harpooner replied. 'But keep going, because you fill me with fascination.'

'As for cartilaginous fish,' Conseil went on unflappably, 'they consist of only three orders.'

'Good news,' Ned put in.

'Primo, the *cyclostomes*, whose jaws are fused into a flexible ring and whose gill openings are simply a large number of holes, an order consisting of only one family. Example: the lamprey.'

'An acquired taste,' Ned Land replied.

'Secundo, the *selacians*, with gills resembling those of the cyclostomes but whose lower jaw is free-moving. This order, which is the most important in the class, consists of two families. Examples: the ray and the shark.'

'What!' Ned Land exclaimed. 'Rays and man-eaters in the same order? Well, Conseil my friend, on behalf of the rays, I wouldn't advise you to put them in the same fish tank!'

'Tertio,' Conseil replied, 'The *sturionians*, whose gill opening is the usual single slit adorned with a gill cover, an order consisting of four genera. Example: the sturgeon.'

'Ah, Conseil my friend, you saved the best for last, in my opinion anyhow! And that's all of 'em?'

'Yes, my gallant Ned,' Conseil replied. 'And note well, even when one has grasped all this, one still knows next to nothing, because these families are subdivided into genera, subgenera, species, varieties—'

'All right, Conseil my friend,' the harpooner said, leaning toward the glass panel, 'here come a couple of your varieties now!'

'Yes! Fish!' Conseil exclaimed. 'One would think he was in front of an aquarium!'

'No,' I replied, 'because an aquarium is nothing more than a cage, and these fish are as free as birds in the air!'

'Well, Conseil my friend, identify them! Start naming them!' Ned Land exclaimed.

'Me?' Conseil replied. 'I'm unable to! That's my employer's bailiwick!'

And in truth, although the fine lad was a classifying maniac, he was no naturalist, and I doubt that he could tell a bonito from a tuna. In short, he was the exact opposite of the Canadian, who knew nothing about classification but could instantly put a name to any fish.

'A triggerfish,' I said.

'It's a Chinese triggerfish,' Ned Land replied.

'Genus *Balistes*, family *Scleroderma*, order *Plectognatha*,' Conseil muttered.

Assuredly, Ned and Conseil in combination added up to one outstanding naturalist.

The Canadian was not mistaken. Cavorting around the *Nautilus* was a school of triggerfish with flat bodies, grainy skins, armed with stings on their dorsal fins, and with four prickly rows of quills quivering on both sides of their tails. Nothing could have been more wonderful than the skin covering them: white underneath, grey above, with spots of gold sparkling in the dark eddies of the waves. Around them, rays were undulating like sheets flapping in the wind, and among these I spotted, much to my glee, a Chinese ray, yellowish on its topside, a dainty pink on its belly, and armed with three stings behind its eyes; a rare species whose very existence was still doubted in Lacépède's day, since that pioneering classifier of fish had seen one only in a portfolio of Japanese drawings.

For two hours a whole aquatic army escorted the *Nautilus*. In the midst of their leaping and cavorting, while they competed with each other in beauty, radiance and speed, I could distinguish some green wrasse, bewhiskered mullet marked with pairs of black lines, white gobies from the genus *Eleotris* with curved caudal fins and violet spots on the back, wonderful Japanese mackerel from the genus *Scomber* with blue bodies and silver heads, glittering azure goldfish whose name by itself gives their full description, several varieties of porgy or gilthead (some banded gilthead with fins variously blue and yellow, some with horizontal heraldic bars and enhanced by a black strip around their caudal area, some with colour zones and elegantly corseted in their six waistbands), trumpetfish with flutelike beaks that looked like genuine seafaring woodcocks and were sometimes a metre long, Japanese salamanders, serpentine moray eels from the genus *Echidna* that were six feet long with sharp little eyes and a huge mouth bristling with teeth; etc.

Our wonderment stayed at an all-time fever pitch. Our exclamations were endless. Ned identified the fish, Conseil classified them, and as for me, I was in ecstasy over the verve of their movements and the beauty of their forms. Never before had I been given the chance to glimpse these animals alive and at large in their native element.

Given such a complete collection from the seas of Japan and China, I won't mention every variety that passed before our dazzled eyes. More numerous than birds in the air, these fish raced right up to us, no doubt attracted by the brilliant glow of our electric beacon.

Suddenly daylight appeared in the lounge. The sheet-iron panels slid shut. The magical vision disappeared. But for a good while I kept dreaming away, until the moment my eyes focused on the instruments hanging on the wall. The compass still showed our heading as east-northeast, the pressure gauge indicated a pressure of five atmospheres (corresponding to a depth of 50 metres), and the electric log gave our speed as 15 miles per hour.

I waited for Captain Nemo. But he didn't appear. The clock marked the hour of five.

Ned Land and Conseil returned to their cabin. As for me, I repaired to my stateroom. There I found dinner ready for me. It consisted of turtle soup made from the daintiest hawksbill, a red mullet with white, slightly flaky flesh, whose liver, when separately prepared, makes delicious eating, plus loin of imperial angelfish, whose flavour struck me as even better than salmon.

I spent the evening in reading, writing and thinking. Then drowsiness overtook me, I stretched out on my eelgrass mattress, and I fell into a deep slumber, while the *Nautilus* glided through the swiftly flowing Black Current.

CHAPTER 15

An Invitation in Writing

THE NEXT DAY, November 9, I woke up only after a long, 12–hour slumber. Conseil, a creature of habit, came to ask 'how master's night went,' and to offer his services. He had left his Canadian friend sleeping like a man who had never done anything else.

I let the gallant lad babble as he pleased, without giving him much in the way of a reply. I was concerned about Captain Nemo's absence during our session the previous afternoon, and I hoped to see him again today.

Soon I had put on my clothes, which were woven from strands of seashell tissue. More than once their composition provoked comments from Conseil. I informed him that they were made from the smooth, silken filaments with which the fan mussel, a type of seashell quite abundant along Mediterranean beaches, attaches itself to rocks. In olden times, fine fabrics, stockings and gloves were made from such filaments, because they were both very soft and very warm. So the *Nautilus*'s crew could dress themselves at little cost, without needing a thing from cotton growers, sheep, or silkworms on shore.

As soon as I was dressed, I made my way to the main lounge. It was deserted.

I dove into studying the conchological treasures amassed inside the glass cases. I also investigated the huge plant albums that were filled with the rarest marine herbs, which, although they were pressed and dried, still kept their wonderful colours. Among these valuable water plants, I noted various seaweed: some *Cladostephus verticillatus*, peacock's tails, fig-leafed caulerpa, grain-bearing beauty bushes, delicate rosetangle tinted scarlet, sea colander arranged into fan shapes, mermaid's cups that looked like the caps of squat mushrooms and for years had been classified among the zoophytes; in short, a complete series of algae.

The entire day passed without my being honoured by a visit from

Captain Nemo. The panels in the lounge didn't open. Perhaps they didn't want us to get tired of these beautiful things.

The *Nautilus* kept to an east-northeasterly heading, a speed of 12 miles per hour, and a depth between 50 and 60 metres.

Next day, November 10: the same neglect, the same solitude. I didn't see a soul from the crew. Ned and Conseil spent the better part of the day with me. They were astonished at the captain's inexplicable absence. Was this eccentric man ill? Did he want to change his plans concerning us?

But after all, as Conseil noted, we enjoyed complete freedom, we were daintily and abundantly fed. Our host had kept to the terms of his agreement. We couldn't complain, and moreover the very uniqueness of our situation had such generous rewards in store for us, we had no grounds for criticism.

That day I started my diary of these adventures, which has enabled me to narrate them with the most scrupulous accuracy; and one odd detail: I wrote it on paper manufactured from marine eelgrass.

Early in the morning on November 11, fresh air poured through the *Nautilus*'s interior, informing me that we had returned to the surface of the ocean to renew our oxygen supply. I headed for the central companionway and climbed onto the platform.

It was six o'clock. I found the weather overcast, the sea grey but calm. Hardly a billow. I hoped to encounter Captain Nemo there – would he come? I saw only the helmsman imprisoned in his glass-windowed pilothouse. Seated on the ledge furnished by the hull of the skiff, I inhaled the sea's salty aroma with great pleasure.

Little by little, the mists were dispersed under the action of the sun's rays. The radiant orb cleared the eastern horizon. Under its gaze, the sea caught on fire like a trail of gunpowder. Scattered on high, the clouds were coloured in bright, wonderfully shaded hues, and numerous 'ladyfingers'[1] warned of daylong winds.

But what were mere winds to this *Nautilus*, which no storms could intimidate!

So I was marvelling at this delightful sunrise, so life-giving and cheerful, when I heard someone climbing onto the platform.

---

1 Author's Note: 'Ladyfingers' are small, thin, white clouds with ragged edges.

I was prepared to greet Captain Nemo, but it was his chief officer who appeared – whom I had already met during our first visit with the captain. He advanced over the platform, not seeming to notice my presence. A powerful spyglass to his eye, he scrutinised every point of the horizon with the utmost care. Then, his examination over, he approached the hatch and pronounced a phrase whose exact wording follows below. I remember it because, every morning, it was repeated under the same circumstances. It ran like this:

'Nautron respoc lorni virch.'

What it meant I was unable to say.

These words pronounced, the chief officer went below again. I thought the *Nautilus* was about to resume its underwater navigating. So I went down the hatch and back through the gangways to my stateroom.

Five days passed in this way with no change in our situation. Every morning I climbed onto the platform. The same phrase was pronounced by the same individual. Captain Nemo did not appear.

I was pursuing the policy that we had seen the last of him, when on November 16, while re-entering my stateroom with Ned and Conseil, I found a note addressed to me on the table.

I opened it impatiently. It was written in a script that was clear and neat but a bit 'Old English' in style, its characters reminding me of German calligraphy.

The note was worded as follows:

Professor Aronnax
Aboard the *Nautilus*
November 16, 1867

Captain Nemo invites Professor Aronnax on a hunting trip that will take place tomorrow morning in his Crespo Island forests. He hopes nothing will prevent the professor from attending, and he looks forward with pleasure to the professor's companions joining him.
 CAPTAIN NEMO,
 Commander of the *Nautilus*.

'A hunting trip!' Ned exclaimed.

'And in his forests on Crespo Island!' Conseil added.

'But does this mean the old boy goes ashore?' Ned Land went on.

'That seems to be the gist of it,' I said, rereading the letter.

'Well, we've got to accept!' the Canadian answered. 'Once we're on solid ground, we'll figure out a course of action. Besides, it wouldn't pain me to eat a couple slices of fresh venison!'

Without trying to reconcile the contradictions between Captain Nemo's professed horror of continents or islands and his invitation to go hunting in a forest, I was content to reply:

'First let's look into this Crespo Island.'

I consulted the world map; and in latitude 32° 40' north and longitude 167° 50' west, I found an islet that had been discovered in 1801 by Captain Crespo, which old Spanish charts called Rocca de la Plata, in other words, 'Silver Rock.' So we were about 1,800 miles from our starting point, and by a slight change of heading, the *Nautilus* was bringing us back toward the southeast.

I showed my companions this small, stray rock in the middle of the north Pacific.

'If Captain Nemo does sometimes go ashore,' I told them, 'at least he only picks desert islands!'

Ned Land shook his head without replying; then he and Conseil left me. After supper was served me by the mute and emotionless steward, I fell asleep; but not without some anxieties.

When I woke up the next day, November 17, I sensed that the *Nautilus* was completely motionless. I dressed hurriedly and entered the main lounge.

Captain Nemo was there waiting for me. He stood up, bowed and asked if it suited me to come along.

Since he made no allusion to his absence the past eight days, I also refrained from mentioning it, and I simply answered that my companions and I were ready to go with him.

'Only, sir,' I added, 'I'll take the liberty of addressing a question to you.'

'Address away, Professor Aronnax, and if I'm able to answer, I will.'

'Well then, captain, how is it that you've severed all ties with the shore, yet you own forests on Crespo Island?'

'Professor,' the captain answered me, 'these forests of mine don't bask in the heat and light of the sun. They aren't frequented by lions, tigers, panthers, or other quadrupeds. They're known only to me. They grow only for me. These forests aren't on land, they're actual underwater forests.'

'Underwater forests!' I exclaimed.

'Yes, professor.'

'And you're offering to take me to them?'

'Precisely.'

'On foot?'

'Without getting your feet wet.'

'While hunting?'

'While hunting.'

'Rifles in hand?'

'Rifles in hand.'

I stared at the *Nautilus*'s commander with an air anything but flattering to the man.

'Assuredly,' I said to myself, 'he's contracted some mental illness. He's had a fit that's lasted eight days and isn't over even yet. What a shame! I liked him better eccentric than insane!'

These thoughts were clearly readable on my face; but Captain Nemo remained content with inviting me to follow him, and I did so like a man resigned to the worst.

We arrived at the dining room, where we found breakfast served.

'Professor Aronnax,' the captain told me, 'I beg you to share my breakfast without formality. We can chat while we eat. Because, although I promised you a stroll in my forests, I made no pledge to arrange for your encountering a restaurant there. Accordingly, eat your breakfast like a man who'll probably eat dinner only when it's extremely late.'

I did justice to this meal. It was made up of various fish and some slices of sea cucumber, that praiseworthy zoophyte, all garnished with such highly appetizing seaweed as the *Porphyra laciniata* and the *Laurencia primafetida*. Our beverage consisted of clear water to which, following the captain's example, I added some drops of a fermented liquor extracted by the Kamchatka process from the seaweed known by name as *Rhodymenia palmata*.

At first Captain Nemo ate without pronouncing a single word. Then he told me:

'Professor, when I proposed that you go hunting in my Crespo forests, you thought I was contradicting myself. When I informed you that it was an issue of underwater forests, you thought I'd gone insane. Professor, you must never make snap judgments about your fellow man.'

'But, captain, believe me—'

'Kindly listen to me, and you'll see if you have grounds for accusing me of insanity or self-contradiction.'

'I'm all attention.'

'Professor, you know as well as I do that a man can live underwater so long as he carries with him his own supply of breathable air. For underwater work projects, the workman wears a waterproof suit with his head imprisoned in a metal capsule, while he receives air from above by means of force pumps and flow regulators.'

'That's the standard equipment for a diving suit,' I said.

'Correct, but under such conditions the man has no freedom. He's attached to a pump that sends him air through an india-rubber hose; it's an actual chain that fetters him to the shore, and if we were to be bound in this way to the *Nautilus*, we couldn't go far either.'

'Then how do you break free?' I asked.

'We use the Rouquayrol-Denayrouze device, invented by two of your fellow countrymen but refined by me for my own special uses, thereby enabling you to risk these new physiological conditions without suffering any organic disorders. It consists of a tank built from heavy sheet iron in which I store air under a pressure of 50 atmospheres. This tank is fastened to the back by means of straps, like a soldier's knapsack. Its top part forms a box where the air is regulated by a bellows mechanism and can be released only at its proper tension. In the Rouquayrol device that has been in general use, two india-rubber hoses leave this box and feed to a kind of tent that imprisons the operator's nose and mouth; one hose is for the entrance of air to be inhaled, the other for the exit of air to be exhaled, and the tongue closes off the former or the latter depending on the breather's needs. But in my case, since I face considerable pressures at the bottom of the sea, I needed to enclose my head in a copper sphere, like those found on standard diving suits, and the two hoses for inhalation and exhalation now feed to that sphere.'

'That's perfect, Captain Nemo, but the air you carry must be quickly depleted; and once it contains no more than 15 per cent oxygen, it becomes unfit for breathing.'

'Surely, but as I told you, Professor Aronnax, the *Nautilus*'s pumps enable me to store air under considerable pressure, and given this circumstance, the tank on my diving equipment can supply breathable air for nine or ten hours.'

'I've no more objections to raise,' I replied. 'I'll only ask you, captain: how can you light your way at the bottom of the ocean?'

'With the Ruhmkorff device, Professor Aronnax. If the first is carried on the back, the second is fastened to the belt. It consists of a Bunsen battery that I activate not with potassium dichromate but with sodium. An induction coil gathers the electricity generated and directs it to a specially designed lantern. In this lantern one finds a glass spiral that contains only a residue of carbon dioxide gas. When the device is operating, this gas becomes luminous and gives off a continuous whitish light. Thus provided for, I breathe and I see.'

'Captain Nemo, to my every objection you give such crushing answers, I'm afraid to entertain a single doubt. However, though I have no choice but to accept both the Rouquayrol and Ruhmkorff devices, I'd like to register some reservations about the rifle with which you'll equip me.'

'But it isn't a rifle that uses gunpowder,' the captain replied.

'Then it's an air gun?'

'Surely. How can I make gunpowder on my ship when I have no saltpetre, sulphur, or charcoal?'

'Even so,' I replied, 'to fire underwater in a medium that's 855 times denser than air, you'd have to overcome considerable resistance.'

'That doesn't necessarily follow. There are certain Fulton-style guns perfected by the Englishmen Philippe-Coles and Burley, the Frenchman Furcy, and the Italian Landi; they're equipped with a special system of airtight fastenings and can fire in underwater conditions. But I repeat: having no gunpowder, I've replaced it with air at high pressure, which is abundantly supplied me by the *Nautilus*'s pumps.'

'But this air must be swiftly depleted.'

'Well, in a pinch can't my Rouquayrol tank supply me with more? All I have to do is draw it from an ad hoc spigot. Besides, Professor Aronnax, you'll see for yourself that during these underwater hunting trips, we make no great expenditure of either air or bullets.'

'But it seems to me that in this semi-darkness, amid this liquid that's so dense in comparison to the atmosphere, a gunshot couldn't carry far and would prove fatal only with difficulty!'

'On the contrary, sir, with this rifle every shot is fatal; and as soon as the animal is hit, no matter how lightly, it falls as if struck by lightning.'

'Why?'

'Because this rifle doesn't shoot ordinary bullets but little glass capsules invented by the Austrian chemist Leniebroek, and I have a considerable supply of them. These glass capsules are covered with a strip of steel and weighted with a lead base; they're genuine little Leyden jars charged with high-voltage electricity. They go off at the slightest impact, and the animal, no matter how strong, drops dead. I might add that these capsules are no bigger than number four shot, and the chamber of any ordinary rifle could hold ten of them.'

'I'll quit debating,' I replied, getting up from the table. 'And all that's left is for me to shoulder my rifle. So where you go, I'll go.'

Captain Nemo led me to the *Nautilus*'s stern, and passing by Ned and Conseil's cabin, I summoned my two companions, who instantly followed us.

Then we arrived at a cell located within easy access of the engine room; in this cell we were to get dressed for our stroll.

CHAPTER 16

Strolling the Plains

THIS CELL, PROPERLY speaking, was the *Nautilus*'s arsenal and wardrobe. Hanging from its walls, a dozen diving outfits were waiting for anybody who wanted to take a stroll.

After seeing these, Ned Land exhibited an obvious distaste for the idea of putting one on.

'But my gallant Ned,' I told him, 'the forests of Crespo Island are simply underwater forests!'

'Oh great!' put in the disappointed harpooner, watching his dreams of fresh meat fade away. 'And you, Professor Aronnax, are you going to stick yourself inside these clothes?'

'It has to be, Mr Ned.'

'Have it your way, sir,' the harpooner replied, shrugging his shoulders. 'But speaking for myself, I'll never get into those things unless they force me!'

'No one will force you, Mr Land,' Captain Nemo said.

'And is Conseil going to risk it?' Ned asked.

'Where master goes, I go,' Conseil replied.

At the captain's summons, two crewmen came to help us put on these heavy, waterproof clothes, made from seamless india rubber and expressly designed to bear considerable pressures. They were like suits of armour that were both yielding and resistant, you might say. These clothes consisted of jacket and pants. The pants ended in bulky footwear adorned with heavy lead soles. The fabric of the jacket was reinforced with copper mail that shielded the chest, protected it from the water's pressure, and allowed the lungs to function freely; the sleeves ended in supple gloves that didn't impede hand movements.

These perfected diving suits, it was easy to see, were a far cry from such misshapen costumes as the cork breastplates, leather jumpers, seagoing tunics, barrel helmets, etc., invented and acclaimed in the 18th century.

Conseil and I were soon dressed in these diving suits, as were Captain Nemo and one of his companions – a herculean type who must have been prodigiously strong. All that remained was to encase one's head in its metal sphere. But before proceeding with this operation, I asked the captain for permission to examine the rifles set aside for us.

One of the *Nautilus*'s men presented me with a streamlined rifle whose butt was boilerplate steel, hollow inside and of fairly large dimensions. This served as a tank for the compressed air, which a trigger-operated valve could release into the metal chamber. In a groove where the butt was heaviest, a cartridge clip held some 20 electric bullets that, by means of a spring, automatically took their places in the barrel of the rifle. As soon as one shot had been fired, another was ready to go off.

'Captain Nemo,' I said, 'this is an ideal, easy-to-use weapon. I ask only to put it to the test. But how will we reach the bottom of the sea?'

'Right now, professor, the *Nautilus* is aground in ten metres of water, and we've only to depart.'

'But how will we set out?'

'You'll see.'

Captain Nemo inserted his cranium into its spherical headgear. Conseil and I did the same, but not without hearing the Canadian toss us a sarcastic 'happy hunting.' On top, the suit ended in a collar of threaded copper onto which the metal helmet was screwed. Three holes, protected by heavy glass, allowed us to see in any direction with simply a turn of the head inside the sphere. Placed on our backs, the Rouquayrol device went into operation as soon as it was in position, and for my part, I could breathe with ease.

The Ruhmkorff lamp hanging from my belt, my rifle in hand, I was ready to go forth. But in all honesty, while imprisoned in these heavy clothes and nailed to the deck by my lead soles, it was impossible for me to take a single step.

But this circumstance had been foreseen, because I felt myself propelled into a little room adjoining the wardrobe. Towed in the same way, my companions went with me. I heard a door with water-tight seals close after us, and we were surrounded by profound darkness.

After some minutes a sharp hissing reached my ears. I felt a distinct sensation of cold rising from my feet to my chest. Apparently a stopcock inside the boat was letting in water from outside, which overran us and soon filled up the room. Contrived in the *Nautilus*'s side, a second door then opened. We were lit by a subdued light. An instant later our feet were treading the bottom of the sea.

And now, how can I convey the impressions left on me by this stroll under the waters. Words are powerless to describe such wonders! When even the painter's brush can't depict the effects unique to the liquid element, how can the writer's pen hope to reproduce them?

Captain Nemo walked in front, and his companion followed us a few steps to the rear. Conseil and I stayed next to each other, as if daydreaming that through our metal carapaces, a little polite conversation might still be possible! Already I no longer felt the bulkiness of my clothes, footwear and air tank, nor the weight of the heavy sphere inside which my head was rattling like an almond in its shell. Once immersed in water, all these objects lost a part of their weight equal to the weight of the liquid they displaced, and thanks to this law of physics discovered by Archimedes, I did just fine. I was no longer an inert mass, and I had, comparatively speaking, great freedom of movement.

Lighting up the seafloor even 30 feet beneath the surface of the ocean, the sun astonished me with its power. The solar rays easily crossed this aqueous mass and dispersed its dark colours. I could easily distinguish objects 100 metres away. Farther on, the bottom was tinted with fine shades of ultramarine; then, off in the distance, it turned blue and faded in the midst of a hazy darkness. Truly, this water surrounding me was just a kind of air, denser than the atmosphere on land but almost as transparent. Above me I could see the calm surface of the ocean.

We were walking on sand that was fine-grained and smooth, not wrinkled like beach sand, which preserves the impressions left by the waves. This dazzling carpet was a real mirror, throwing back the sun's rays with startling intensity. The outcome: an immense vista of reflections that penetrated every liquid molecule. Will anyone believe me if I assert that at this 30-foot depth, I could see as if it was broad daylight?

For a quarter of an hour, I trod this blazing sand, which was strewn with tiny crumbs of seashell. Looming like a long reef, the *Nautilus*'s hull disappeared little by little, but when night fell in the midst of the waters, the ship's beacon would surely facilitate our return on board, since its rays carried with perfect distinctness. This effect is difficult to understand for anyone who has never seen light beams so sharply defined on shore. There the dust that saturates the air gives such rays the appearance of a luminous fog; but above water as well as underwater, shafts of electric light are transmitted with incomparable clarity.

Meanwhile we went ever onward, and these vast plains of sand seemed endless. My hands parted liquid curtains that closed again behind me, and my footprints faded swiftly under the water's pressure.

Soon, scarcely blurred by their distance from us, the forms of some objects took shape before my eyes. I recognised the lower slopes of some magnificent rocks carpeted by the finest zoophyte specimens, and right off, I was struck by an effect unique to this medium.

By then it was ten o'clock in the morning. The sun's rays hit the surface of the waves at a fairly oblique angle, decomposing by refraction as though passing through a prism; and when this light came in contact with flowers, rocks, buds, seashells and polyps, the edges of these objects were shaded with all seven hues of the solar spectrum. This riot of rainbow tints was a wonder, a feast for the eyes: a genuine kaleidoscope of red, green, yellow, orange, violet, indigo and blue; in short, the whole palette of a colour-happy painter! If only I had been able to share with Conseil the intense sensations rising in my brain, competing with him in exclamations of wonderment! If only I had known, like Captain Nemo and his companion, how to exchange thoughts by means of prearranged signals! So, for lack of anything better, I talked to myself: I declaimed inside this copper box that topped my head, spending more air on empty words than was perhaps advisable.

Conseil, like me, had stopped before this splendid sight. Obviously, in the presence of these zoophyte and mollusc specimens, the fine lad was classifying his head off. Polyps and echinoderms abounded on the seafloor: various isis coral, cornularian coral living in isolation, tufts of virginal genus *Oculina* formerly known by the name 'white coral,' prickly fungus coral in the shape of mushrooms, sea anemone holding on by their muscular disks, providing a literal flowerbed adorned by jellyfish from the genus *Porpita* wearing collars of azure tentacles, and starfish that spangled the sand, including veinlike feather stars from the genus *Asterophyton* that were like fine lace embroidered by the hands of water nymphs, their festoons swaying to the faint undulations caused by our walking. It filled me with real chagrin to crush underfoot the gleaming mollusc samples that littered the seafloor by the thousands: concentric comb shells, hammer shells, coquina (seashells that actually hop around), top-shell snails, red helmet shells, angel-wing conchs, sea hares, and so many other exhibits from this inexhaustible ocean. But we had to keep walking, and we went forward while overhead there scudded schools of Portuguese men-of-war that let their ultramarine tentacles drift in their wakes, medusas whose milky white or dainty pink parasols were festooned with azure tassels and shaded us from the sun's rays, plus jellyfish of the species *Pelagia panopyra* that, in the dark, would have strewn our path with phosphorescent glimmers!

All these wonders I glimpsed in the space of a quarter of a mile, barely pausing, following Captain Nemo whose gestures kept beckoning me onward. Soon the nature of the seafloor changed. The plains of sand were followed by a bed of that viscous slime Americans call 'ooze,' which is composed exclusively of seashells rich in limestone or silica. Then we crossed a prairie of algae, open-sea plants that the waters hadn't yet torn loose, whose vegetation grew in wild profusion. Soft to the foot, these densely textured lawns would have rivalled the most luxuriant carpets woven by the hand of man. But while this greenery was sprawling under our steps, it didn't neglect us overhead. The surface of the water was crisscrossed by a floating arbour of marine plants belonging to that superabundant algae family that numbers more than 2,000 known species. I saw long ribbons of fucus drifting above me, some globular, others tubular: *Laurencia*, *Cladostephus* with the slenderest foliage, *Rhodymenia palmata* resembling the fan shapes of cactus. I observed that green-coloured plants kept closer to the surface of the sea, while reds occupied a medium depth, which left blacks and browns in charge of designing gardens and flowerbeds in the ocean's lower strata.

These algae are a genuine prodigy of creation, one of the wonders of world flora. This family produces both the biggest and smallest vegetables in the world. Because, just as 40,000 near-invisible buds have been counted in one five-square-millimetre space, so also have fucus plants been gathered that were over 500 metres long!

We had been gone from the *Nautilus* for about an hour and a half. It was almost noon. I spotted this fact in the perpendicularity of the sun's rays, which were no longer refracted. The magic of these solar colours disappeared little by little, with emerald and sapphire shades vanishing from our surroundings altogether. We walked with steady steps that rang on the seafloor with astonishing intensity. The tiniest sounds were transmitted with a speed to which the ear is unaccustomed on shore. In fact, water is a better conductor of sound than air, and under the waves noises carry four times as fast.

Just then the seafloor began to slope sharply downward. The light took on a uniform hue. We reached a depth of 100 metres, by which point we were undergoing a pressure of ten atmospheres. But my diving clothes were built along such lines that I never suffered from this pressure. I felt only a certain tightness in the joints of my fingers, and even this discomfort soon disappeared. As for the exhaustion bound to accompany a two-hour stroll in such unfamiliar trappings – it was nil. Helped by the water, my movements were executed with startling ease.

Arriving at this 300-foot depth, I still detected the sun's rays, but just barely. Their intense brilliance had been followed by a reddish twilight, a midpoint between day and night. But we could see well enough to find our way, and it still wasn't necessary to activate the Ruhmkorff device.

Just then Captain Nemo stopped. He waited until I joined him, then he pointed a finger at some dark masses outlined in the shadows a short distance away.

'It's the forest of Crespo Island,' I thought; and I was not mistaken.

CHAPTER 17

An Underwater Forest

WE HAD FINALLY arrived on the outskirts of this forest, surely one of the finest in Captain Nemo's immense domains. He regarded it as his own and had laid the same claim to it that, in the first days of the world, the first men had to their forests on land. Besides, who else could dispute his ownership of this underwater property? What other, bolder pioneer would come, axe in hand, to clear away its dark underbrush?

This forest was made up of big treelike plants, and when we entered beneath their huge arches, my eyes were instantly struck by the unique arrangement of their branches – an arrangement that I had never before encountered.

None of the weeds carpeting the seafloor, none of the branches bristling from the shrubbery, crept, or leaned, or stretched on a horizontal plane. They all rose right up toward the surface of the ocean. Every filament or ribbon, no matter how thin, stood ramrod straight. Fucus plants and creepers were growing in stiff perpendicular lines, governed by the density of the element that generated them. After I parted them with my hands, these otherwise motionless plants would shoot right back to their original positions. It was the regime of verticality.

I soon grew accustomed to this bizarre arrangement, likewise to the comparative darkness surrounding us. The seafloor in this forest was strewn with sharp chunks of stone that were hard to avoid. Here the range of underwater flora seemed pretty comprehensive to me, as well as more abundant than it might have been in the arctic or tropical zones, where such exhibits are less common. But for a few minutes I kept accidentally confusing the two kingdoms, mistaking zoophytes for water plants, animals for vegetables. And who hasn't made the same blunder? Flora and fauna are so closely associated in the underwater world!

I observed that all these exhibits from the vegetable kingdom were attached to the seafloor by only the most makeshift methods. They had no roots and didn't care which solid objects secured them, sand, shells, husks, or pebbles; they didn't ask their hosts for sustenance, just a point of purchase. These plants are entirely self-propagating, and the principle of their existence lies in the water that sustains and nourishes them. In place of leaves, most of them sprouted blades of unpredictable shape, which were confined to a narrow gamut of colours consisting only of pink, crimson, green, olive, tan and brown. There I saw again, but not yet pressed and dried like the *Nautilus*'s specimens, some peacock's tails spread open like fans to stir up a cooling breeze, scarlet rosetangle, sea tangle stretching out their young and edible shoots, twisting strings of kelp from the genus *Nereocystis* that bloomed to a height of 15 metres, bouquets of mermaid's cups whose stems grew wider at the top, and a number of other open-sea plants, all without flowers. 'It's an odd anomaly in this bizarre element!' as one witty naturalist puts it. 'The animal kingdom blossoms, and the vegetable kingdom doesn't!'

These various types of shrubbery were as big as trees in the temperate zones; in the damp shade between them, there were clustered actual bushes of moving flowers, hedges of zoophytes in which there grew stony coral striped with twisting furrows, yellowish sea anemone from the genus *Caryophylia* with translucent tentacles, plus anemone with grassy tufts from the genus *Zoantharia*; and to complete the illusion, minnows flitted from branch to branch like a swarm of hummingbirds, while there rose underfoot, like a covey of snipe, yellow fish from the genus *Lepisocanthus* with bristling jaws and sharp scales, flying gurnards and pinecone fish.

Near one o'clock, Captain Nemo gave the signal to halt. Speaking for myself, I was glad to oblige, and we stretched out beneath an arbour of winged kelp, whose long thin tendrils stood up like arrows.

This short break was a delight. It lacked only the charm of conversation. But it was impossible to speak, impossible to reply. I simply nudged my big copper headpiece against Conseil's headpiece. I saw a happy gleam in the gallant lad's eyes, and to communicate his pleasure, he jiggled around inside his carapace in the world's silliest way.

After four hours of strolling, I was quite astonished not to feel any intense hunger. What kept my stomach in such a good mood I'm unable to say. But, in exchange, I experienced that irresistible desire for sleep that comes over every diver. Accordingly, my eyes soon closed behind their heavy glass windows and I fell into an uncontrollable doze, which until then I had been able to fight off only through the movements of our walking. Captain Nemo and his muscular companion were already stretched out in this clear crystal, setting us a fine naptime example.

How long I was sunk in this torpor I cannot estimate; but when I awoke, it seemed as if the sun were settling toward the horizon. Captain Nemo was already up, and I had started to stretch my limbs, when an unexpected apparition brought me sharply to my feet.

A few paces away, a monstrous, metre-high sea spider was staring at me with beady eyes, poised to spring at me. Although my diving suit was heavy enough to protect me from this animal's bites, I couldn't keep back a shudder of horror. Just then Conseil woke up, together with the *Nautilus*'s sailor. Captain Nemo alerted his companion to this hideous crustacean, which a swing of the rifle butt quickly brought down, and I watched the monster's horrible legs writhing in dreadful convulsions.

This encounter reminded me that other, more daunting animals must be lurking in these dark reaches, and my diving suit might not be adequate protection against their attacks. Such thoughts hadn't previously crossed my mind, and I was determined to keep on my guard. Meanwhile I had assumed this rest period would be the turning point in our stroll, but I was mistaken; and instead of heading back to the *Nautilus*, Captain Nemo continued his daring excursion.

The seafloor kept sinking, and its significantly steeper slope took us to greater depths. It must have been nearly three o'clock when we reached a narrow valley gouged between high, vertical walls and located 150 metres down. Thanks to the perfection of our equipment, we had thus gone 90 metres below the limit that nature had, until then, set on man's underwater excursions.

I say 150 metres, although I had no instruments for estimating this distance. But I knew that the sun's rays, even in the clearest seas, could reach no deeper. So at precisely this point the darkness became profound. Not a single object was visible past ten paces. Consequently, I had begun to grope my way when suddenly I saw the glow of an intense white light. Captain Nemo had just activated his electric device. His companion did likewise. Conseil and I followed suit. By turning a switch, I established contact between the induction coil and the glass spiral, and the sea, lit up by our four lanterns, was illuminated for a radius of 25 metres.

Captain Nemo continued to plummet into the dark depths of this forest, whose shrubbery grew ever more sparse. I observed that vegetable life was disappearing more quickly than animal life. The open-sea plants had already left behind the increasingly arid seafloor, where a prodigious number of animals were still swarming: zoophytes, articulates, molluscs and fish.

While we were walking, I thought the lights of our Ruhmkorff devices would automatically attract some inhabitants of these dark strata. But if they did approach us, at least they kept at a distance regrettable from the hunter's standpoint. Several times I saw Captain Nemo stop and take aim with his rifle; then, after sighting down its barrel for a few seconds, he would straighten up and resume his walk.

Finally, at around four o'clock, this marvellous excursion came to an end. A wall of superb rocks stood before us, imposing in its sheer mass: a pile of gigantic stone blocks, an enormous granite cliffside pitted with dark caves but not offering a single gradient we could climb up. This was the underpinning of Crespo Island. This was land.

The captain stopped suddenly. A gesture from him brought us to a halt, and however much I wanted to clear this wall, I had to stop. Here ended the domains of Captain Nemo. He had no desire to pass beyond them. Farther on lay a part of the globe he would no longer tread underfoot.

Our return journey began. Captain Nemo resumed the lead in our little band, always heading forward without hesitation. I noted that we didn't follow the same path in returning to the *Nautilus*. This new route, very steep and hence very arduous, quickly took us close to the surface of the sea. But this return to the upper strata wasn't so sudden that decompression took place too quickly, which could have led to serious organic disorders and given us those internal injuries so fatal to divers. With great promptness, the light reappeared and grew stronger; and the refraction of the sun, already low on the horizon, again ringed the edges of various objects with the entire colour spectrum.

At a depth of ten metres, we walked amid a swarm of small fish from every species, more numerous than birds in the air, more agile too; but no aquatic game worthy of a gunshot had yet been offered to our eyes.

Just then I saw the captain's weapon spring to his shoulder and track a moving object through the bushes. A shot went off, I heard a faint hissing, and an animal dropped a few paces away, literally struck by lightning.

It was a magnificent sea otter from the genus *Enhydra*, the only exclusively marine quadruped. One and a half metres long, this otter had to be worth a good high price. Its coat, chestnut brown above and silver below, would have made one of those wonderful fur pieces so much in demand in the Russian and Chinese markets; the fineness and lustre of its pelt guaranteed that it would go for at least 2,000 francs. I was full of wonderment at this unusual mammal, with its circular head adorned by short ears, its round eyes, its white whiskers like those on a cat, its webbed and clawed feet, its bushy tail. Hunted and trapped by fishermen, this valuable carnivore has become extremely rare, and it takes refuge chiefly in the northernmost parts of the Pacific, where in all likelihood its species will soon be facing extinction.

Captain Nemo's companion picked up the animal, loaded it on his shoulder, and we took to the trail again.

For an hour plains of sand unrolled before our steps. Often the seafloor rose to within two metres of the surface of the water. I could then see our images clearly mirrored on the underside of the waves, but reflected upside down: above us there appeared an identical band that duplicated our every movement and gesture; in short, a perfect likeness of the quartet near which it walked, but with heads down and feet in the air.

Another unusual effect. Heavy clouds passed above us, forming and fading swiftly. But after thinking it over, I realised that these so-called clouds were caused simply by the changing densities of the long ground swells, and I even spotted the foaming 'white caps' that their breaking crests were proliferating over the surface of the water. Lastly, I couldn't help seeing the actual shadows of large birds passing over our heads, swiftly skimming the surface of the sea.

On this occasion I witnessed one of the finest gunshots ever to thrill the marrow of a hunter. A large bird with a wide wingspan, quite clearly visible, approached and hovered over us. When it was just a few metres above the waves, Captain Nemo's companion took aim and fired. The animal dropped, electrocuted, and its descent brought it within reach of our adroit hunter, who promptly took possession of it. It was an albatross of the finest species, a wonderful specimen of these open-sea fowl.

This incident did not interrupt our walk. For two hours we were sometimes led over plains of sand, sometimes over prairies of seaweed that were quite arduous to cross. In all honesty, I was dead tired by the time I spotted a hazy glow half a mile away, cutting through the darkness of the waters. It was the *Nautilus*'s beacon. Within 20 minutes we would be on board, and there I could breathe easy again – because my tank's current air supply seemed to be quite low in oxygen. But I was reckoning without an encounter that slightly delayed our arrival.

I was lagging behind some 20 paces when I saw Captain Nemo suddenly come back toward me. With his powerful hands he sent me buckling to the ground, while his companion did the same to Conseil. At first I didn't know what to make of this sudden assault, but I was reassured to observe the captain lying motionless beside me.

I was stretched out on the seafloor directly beneath some bushes of algae, when I raised my head and spied two enormous masses hurtling by, throwing off phosphorescent glimmers.

My blood turned cold in my veins! I saw that we were under threat from a fearsome pair of sharks. They were blue sharks, dreadful man-eaters with enormous tails, dull, glassy stares and phosphorescent matter oozing from holes around their snouts. They were like monstrous fireflies that could thoroughly pulverise a man in their iron jaws! I don't know if Conseil was busy with their classification, but as for me, I looked at their silver bellies, their fearsome mouths bristling with teeth, from a viewpoint less than scientific – more as a victim than as a professor of natural history.

Luckily these voracious animals have poor eyesight. They went by without noticing us, grazing us with their brownish fins; and miraculously, we escaped a danger greater than encountering a tiger deep in the jungle.

Half an hour later, guided by its electric trail, we reached the *Nautilus*. The outside door had been left open, and Captain Nemo closed it after we re-entered the first cell. Then he pressed a button. I heard pumps operating within the ship, I felt the water lowering around me, and in a few moments the cell was completely empty. The inside door opened, and we passed into the wardrobe.

There our diving suits were removed, not without difficulty; and utterly exhausted, faint from lack of food and rest, I repaired to my stateroom, full of wonder at this startling excursion on the bottom of the sea.

CHAPTER 18

Four Thousand Leagues Under the Pacific

BY THE NEXT morning, November 18, I was fully recovered from my exhaustion of the day before, and I climbed onto the platform just as the *Nautilus*'s chief officer was pronouncing his daily phrase. It then occurred to me that these words either referred to the state of the sea, or that they meant: 'There's nothing in sight.'

And in truth, the ocean was deserted. Not a sail on the horizon. The tips of Crespo Island had disappeared during the night. The sea, absorbing every colour of the prism except its blue rays, reflected the latter in every direction and sported a wonderful indigo tint. The undulating waves regularly took on the appearance of watered silk with wide stripes.

I was marvelling at this magnificent ocean view when Captain Nemo appeared. He didn't seem to notice my presence and began a series of astronomical observations. Then, his operations finished, he went and leaned his elbows on the beacon housing, his eyes straying over the surface of the ocean.

Meanwhile some 20 of the *Nautilus*'s sailors – all energetic, well-built fellows – climbed onto the platform. They had come to pull up the nets left in our wake during the night. These seamen obviously belonged to different nationalities, although indications of European physical traits could be seen in them all. If I'm not mistaken, I recognised some Irishmen, some Frenchmen, a few Slavs and a native of either Greece or Crete. Even so, these men were frugal of speech and used among themselves only that bizarre dialect whose origin I couldn't even guess. So I had to give up any notions of questioning them.

The nets were hauled on board. They were a breed of trawl resembling those used off the Normandy coast, huge pouches held half open by a floating pole and a chain laced through the lower meshes. Trailing in this way from these iron glove makers, the resulting receptacles scoured the ocean floor and collected every marine exhibit in their path. That day they gathered up some unusual specimens from these fish-filled waterways: anglerfish whose comical movements qualify them for the epithet 'clowns,' black Commerson anglers equipped with their antennas, undulating triggerfish encircled by little red bands, bloated puffers whose venom is extremely insidious, some olive-hued lampreys, snipefish covered with silver scales, cutlass fish whose electrocuting power equals that of the electric eel and the electric ray, scaly featherbacks with brown crosswise bands, greenish codfish, several varieties of goby, etc.; finally, some fish of larger proportions: a one-metre jack with a prominent head, several fine bonito from the genus *Scomber* decked out in the colours blue and silver, and three magnificent tuna whose high speeds couldn't save them from our trawl.

I estimate that this cast of the net brought in more than 1,000 pounds of fish. It was a fine catch but not surprising. In essence, these nets stayed in our wake for several hours, incarcerating an entire aquatic world in prisons made of thread. So we were never lacking in provisions of the highest quality, which the *Nautilus*'s speed and the allure of its electric light could continually replenish.

These various exhibits from the sea were immediately lowered down the hatch in the direction of the storage lockers, some to be eaten fresh, others to be preserved.

After its fishing was finished and its air supply renewed, I thought the *Nautilus* would resume its underwater excursion, and I was getting ready to return to my stateroom, when Captain Nemo turned to me and said without further preamble:

'Look at this ocean, professor! Doesn't it have the actual gift of life? Doesn't it experience both anger and affection? Last evening it went to sleep just as we did, and there it is, waking up after a peaceful night!'

No hellos or good mornings for this gent! You would have thought this eccentric individual was simply continuing a conversation we'd already started!

'See!' he went on. 'It's waking up under the sun's caresses! It's going to relive its daily existence! What a fascinating field of study lies in watching the play of its organism. It owns a pulse and arteries, it has spasms, and I side with the scholarly Commander Maury, who discovered that it has a circulation as real as the circulation of blood in animals.'

I'm sure that Captain Nemo expected no replies from me, and it seemed pointless to pitch in with 'Ah yes,' 'Exactly,' or 'How right you are!' Rather, he was simply talking to himself, with long pauses between sentences. He was meditating out loud.

'Yes,' he said, 'the ocean owns a genuine circulation, and to start it going, the Creator of All Things has only to increase its heat, salt and microscopic animal life. In essence, heat creates the different densities that lead to currents and countercurrents. Evaporation, which is nil in the High Arctic regions and very active in equatorial zones, brings about a constant interchange of tropical and polar waters. What's more, I've detected those falling and rising currents that make up the ocean's true breathing. I've seen a molecule of salt water heat up at the surface, sink into the depths, reach maximum density at $-2°$ centigrade, then cool off, grow lighter, and rise again. At the poles you'll see the consequences of this phenomenon, and through this law of farseeing nature, you'll understand why water can freeze only at the surface!'

As the captain was finishing his sentence, I said to myself: 'The pole! Is this brazen individual claiming he'll take us even to that location?'

Meanwhile the captain fell silent and stared at the element he had studied so thoroughly and unceasingly. Then, going on:

'Salts,' he said, 'fill the sea in considerable quantities, professor, and if you removed all its dissolved saline content, you'd create a mass measuring 4,500,000 cubic leagues, which if it were spread all over the globe, would form a layer more than ten metres high. And don't think that the presence of these salts is due merely to some whim of nature. No. They make ocean water less open to evaporation and prevent winds from carrying off excessive amounts of steam, which, when condensing, would submerge the temperate zones. Salts play a leading role, the role of stabiliser for the general ecology of the globe!'

Captain Nemo stopped, straightened up, took a few steps along the platform and returned to me:

'As for those billions of tiny animals,' he went on, 'those infusoria that live by the millions in one droplet of water, 800,000 of which are needed to weigh one milligram, their role is no less important. They absorb the marine salts, they assimilate the solid elements in the water, and since they create coral and madrepores, they're the true builders of limestone continents! And so, after they've finished depriving our water drop of its mineral nutrients, the droplet gets lighter, rises to the surface, there absorbs more salts left behind through evaporation, gets heavier, sinks again, and brings those tiny animals new elements to absorb. The outcome: a double current, rising and falling, constant movement, constant life! More intense than on land, more abundant, more infinite, such life blooms in every part of this ocean, an element fatal to man, they say, but vital to myriads of animals – and to me!'

When Captain Nemo spoke in this way, he was transfigured, and he filled me with extraordinary excitement.

'There,' he added, 'out there lies true existence! And I can imagine the founding of nautical towns, clusters of underwater households that, like the *Nautilus*, would return to the surface of the sea to breathe each morning, free towns if ever there were, independent cities! Then again, who knows whether some tyrant...'

Captain Nemo finished his sentence with a vehement gesture. Then, addressing me directly, as if to drive away an ugly thought:

'Professor Aronnax,' he asked me, 'do you know the depth of the ocean floor?'

'At least, captain, I know what the major soundings tell us.'

'Could you quote them to me, so I can double-check them as the need arises?'

'Here,' I replied, 'are a few of them that stick in my memory. If I'm not mistaken, an average depth of 8,200 metres was found in the north Atlantic, and 2,500 metres in the Mediterranean. The most remarkable soundings were taken in the south Atlantic near the 35th parallel, and they gave 12,000 metres, 14,091 metres, and 15,149 metres. All in all, it's estimated that if the sea bottom were made level, its average depth would be about seven kilometres.'

'Well, professor,' Captain Nemo replied, 'we'll show you better than that, I hope. As for the average depth of this part of the Pacific, I'll inform you that it's a mere 4,000 metres.'

This said, Captain Nemo headed to the hatch and disappeared down the ladder. I followed him and went back to the main lounge.

The propeller was instantly set in motion, and the log gave our speed as 20 miles per hour.

Over the ensuing days and weeks, Captain Nemo was very frugal with his visits. I saw him only at rare intervals. His chief officer regularly fixed the positions I found reported on the chart, and in such a way that I could exactly plot the *Nautilus*'s course.

Conseil and Land spent the long hours with me. Conseil had told his friend about the wonders of our undersea stroll, and the Canadian was sorry he hadn't gone along. But I hoped an opportunity would arise for a visit to the forests of Oceania.

Almost every day the panels in the lounge were open for some hours, and our eyes never tired of probing the mysteries of the underwater world.

The *Nautilus*'s general heading was southeast, and it stayed at a depth between 100 and 150 metres. However, from Lord-knows-what whim, one day it did a diagonal dive by means of its slanting fins, reaching strata located 2,000 metres underwater. The thermometer indicated a temperature of 4.25° centigrade, which at this depth seemed to be a temperature common to all latitudes.

On November 26, at three o'clock in the morning, the *Nautilus* cleared the Tropic of Cancer at longitude 172°. On the 27th it passed in sight of the Hawaiian Islands, where the famous Captain Cook met his death on February 14, 1779. By then we had fared 4,860 leagues from our starting point. When I arrived on the platform that morning, I saw the Island of Hawaii two miles to leeward, the largest of the seven islands making up this group. I could clearly distinguish the tilled soil on its outskirts, the various mountain chains running parallel with its coastline, and its volcanoes, crowned by Mauna Kea, whose elevation is 5,000 metres above sea level. Among other specimens from these waterways, our nets brought up some peacock-tailed flabellarian coral, polyps flattened into stylish shapes and unique to this part of the ocean.

The *Nautilus* kept to its southeasterly heading. On December 1 it cut the equator at longitude 142°, and on the 4th of the same month, after a quick crossing marked by no incident, we raised the Marquesas Islands. Three miles off, in latitude 8° 57' south and longitude 139° 32' west, I spotted Martin Point on Nuku Hiva, chief member of this island group that belongs to France. I could make out only its wooded mountains on the horizon, because Captain Nemo hated to hug shore. There our nets brought up some fine fish samples: dolphinfish with azure fins, gold tails, and flesh that's unrivalled in the entire world, wrasse from the genus *Hologymnosus* that were nearly denuded of scales but exquisite in flavour, knifejaws with bony beaks, yellowish albacore that were as tasty as bonito, all fish worth classifying in the ship's pantry.

After leaving these delightful islands to the protection of the French flag, the *Nautilus* covered about 2,000 miles from December 4 to the 11th. Its navigating was marked by an encounter with an immense school of squid, unusual molluscs that are near neighbours of the cuttlefish. French fishermen give them the name 'cuckoldfish,' and they belong to the class *Cephalopoda*, family *Dibranchiata*, consisting of themselves together with cuttlefish and argonauts. The naturalists of antiquity made a special study of them, and these animals furnished many ribald figures of speech for soapbox orators in the Greek marketplace, as well as excellent dishes for the tables of rich citizens, if we're to believe Athenæus, a Greek physician predating Galen.

It was during the night of December 9–10 that the *Nautilus* encountered this army of distinctly nocturnal molluscs. They numbered in the millions. They were migrating from the temperate zones toward zones still warmer, following the itineraries of herring and sardines. We stared at them through our thick glass windows: they swam backward with tremendous speed, moving by means of their locomotive tubes, chasing fish and molluscs, eating the little ones, eaten by the big ones, and tossing in indescribable confusion the ten feet that nature has rooted in their heads like a hairpiece of pneumatic snakes. Despite its speed, the *Nautilus* navigated for several hours in the midst of this school of animals, and its nets brought up an incalculable number, among which I recognised all nine species that Professor Orbigny has classified as native to the Pacific Ocean.

During this crossing, the sea continually lavished us with the most marvellous sights. Its variety was infinite. It changed its setting and decor for the mere pleasure of our eyes, and we were called upon not simply to contemplate the works of our Creator in the midst of the liquid element, but also to probe the ocean's most daunting mysteries.

During the day of December 11, I was busy reading in the main lounge. Ned Land and Conseil were observing the luminous waters through the gaping panels. The *Nautilus* was motionless. Its ballast tanks full, it was sitting at a depth of 1,000 metres in a comparatively unpopulated region of the ocean where only larger fish put in occasional appearances.

Just then I was studying a delightful book by Jean Macé, *The Servants of the Stomach*, and savouring its ingenious teachings, when Conseil interrupted my reading.

'Would master kindly come here for an instant?' he said to me in an odd voice.

'What is it, Conseil?'

'It's something that master should see.'

I stood up, went, leaned on my elbows before the window, and I saw it.

In the broad electric daylight, an enormous black mass, quite motionless, hung suspended in the midst of the waters. I observed it carefully, trying to find out the nature of this gigantic cetacean. Then a sudden thought crossed my mind.

'A ship!' I exclaimed.

'Yes,' the Canadian replied, 'a disabled craft that's sinking straight down!'

Ned Land was not mistaken. We were in the presence of a ship whose severed shrouds still hung from their clasps. Its hull looked in good condition, and it must have gone under only a few hours before. The stumps of three masts, chopped off two feet above the deck, indicated a flooding ship that had been forced to sacrifice its masting. But it had heeled sideways, filling completely, and it was listing to port even yet. A sorry sight, this carcass lost under the waves, but sorrier still was the sight on its deck, where, lashed with ropes to prevent their being washed overboard, some human corpses still lay! I counted four of them – four men, one still standing at the helm – then a woman, halfway out of a skylight on the afterdeck, holding a child in her arms. This woman was young. Under the brilliant lighting of the *Nautilus*'s rays, I could make out her features, which the water hadn't yet decomposed. With a supreme effort, she had lifted her child above her head, and the poor little creature's arms were still twined around its mother's neck! The postures of the four seamen seemed ghastly to me, twisted from convulsive movements, as if making a last effort to break loose from the ropes that bound them to their ship. And the helmsman, standing alone, calmer, his face smooth and serious, his grizzled hair plastered to his brow, his hands clutching the wheel, seemed even yet to be guiding his wrecked three-master through the ocean depths!

What a scene! We stood dumbstruck, hearts pounding, before this shipwreck caught in the act, as if it had been photographed in its final moments, so to speak! And already I could see enormous sharks moving in, eyes ablaze, drawn by the lure of human flesh!

Meanwhile, turning, the *Nautilus* made a circle around the sinking ship, and for an instant I could read the board on its stern:

The Florida
Sunderland, England

CHAPTER 19
Vanikoro

THIS DREADFUL SIGHT was the first of a whole series of maritime catastrophes that the *Nautilus* would encounter on its run. When it plied more heavily travelled seas, we often saw wrecked hulls rotting in midwater, and farther down, cannons, shells, anchors, chains and a thousand other iron objects rusting away.

Meanwhile, continuously swept along by the *Nautilus*, where we lived in near isolation, we raised the Tuamotu Islands on December 11, that old 'dangerous group' associated with the French global navigator Commander Bougainville; it stretches from Ducie Island to Lazareff Island over an area of 500 leagues from the east-southeast to the west-northwest, between latitude 13° 30' and 23° 50' south, and between longitude 125° 30' and 151° 30' west. This island group covers a surface area of 370 square leagues, and it's made up of some 60 subgroups, among which we noted the Gambier group, which is a French protectorate. These islands are coral formations. Thanks to the work of polyps, a slow but steady upheaval will someday connect these islands to each other. Later on, this new island will be fused to its neighbouring island groups, and a fifth continent will stretch from New Zealand and New Caledonia as far as the Marquesas Islands.

The day I expounded this theory to Captain Nemo, he answered me coldly:

'The earth doesn't need new continents, but new men!'

Sailors' luck led the *Nautilus* straight to Reao Island, one of the most unusual in this group, which was discovered in 1822 by Captain Bell aboard the *Minerva*. So I was able to study the madreporic process that has created the islands in this ocean.

Madrepores, which one must guard against confusing with precious coral, clothe their tissue in a limestone crust, and their variations in structure have led my famous mentor Professor Milne-Edwards to classify them into five divisions. The tiny microscopic animals that secrete this polypary live by the billions in the depths of their cells.

Their limestone deposits build up into rocks, reefs, islets, islands. In some places, they form atolls, a circular ring surrounding a lagoon or small inner lake that gaps place in contact with the sea. Elsewhere, they take the shape of barrier reefs, such as those that exist along the coasts of New Caledonia and several of the Tuamotu Islands. In still other localities, such as Réunion Island and the island of Mauritius, they build fringing reefs, high, straight walls next to which the ocean's depth is considerable.

While cruising along only a few cable lengths from the underpinning of Reao Island, I marvelled at the gigantic piece of work accomplished by these microscopic labourers. These walls were the express achievements of *madrepores* known by the names fire coral, finger coral, star coral and stony coral. These polyps grow exclusively in the agitated strata at the surface of the sea, and so it's in the upper reaches that they begin these substructures, which sink little by little together with the secreted rubble binding them. This, at least, is the theory of Mr Charles Darwin, who thus explains the formation of atolls – a theory superior, in my view, to the one that says these madreporic edifices sit on the summits of mountains or volcanoes submerged a few feet below sea level.

I could observe these strange walls quite closely: our sounding lines indicated that they dropped perpendicularly for more than 300 metres, and our electric beams made the bright limestone positively sparkle.

In reply to a question Conseil asked me about the growth rate of these colossal barriers, I thoroughly amazed him by saying that scientists put it at an eighth of an inch per biennium.

'Therefore,' he said to me, 'to build these walls, it took…?'

'192,000 years, my gallant Conseil, which significantly extends the biblical Days of Creation. What's more, the formation of coal – in other words, the petrification of forests swallowed by floods – and the cooling of basaltic rocks likewise call for a much longer period of time. I might add that those "days" in the Bible must represent whole epochs and not literally the lapse of time between two sunrises, because according to the Bible itself, the sun doesn't date from the first day of Creation.'

When the *Nautilus* returned to the surface of the ocean, I could take in Reao Island over its whole flat, wooded expanse. Obviously its madreporic rocks had been made fertile by tornadoes and thunderstorms. One day, carried off by a hurricane from neighbouring shores, some seed fell onto these limestone beds, mixing with decomposed particles of fish and marine plants to form vegetable humus. Propelled by the waves, a coconut arrived on this new coast. Its germ took root. Its tree grew tall, catching steam off the water. A brook was born. Little by little, vegetation spread. Tiny animals – worms, insects – rode ashore on tree trunks snatched from islands to windward. Turtles came to lay their eggs. Birds nested in the young trees. In this way animal life developed, and drawn by the greenery and fertile soil, man appeared. And that's how these islands were formed, the immense achievement of microscopic animals.

Near evening Reao Island melted into the distance, and the *Nautilus* noticeably changed course. After touching the Tropic of Capricorn at longitude 135°, it headed west-northwest, going back up the whole intertropical zone. Although the summer sun lavished its rays on us, we never suffered from the heat, because 30 or 40 metres underwater, the temperature didn't go over 10° to 12° centigrade.

By December 15 we had left the alluring Society Islands in the west, likewise elegant Tahiti, queen of the Pacific. In the morning I spotted this island's lofty summits a few miles to leeward. Its waters supplied excellent fish for the tables on board: mackerel, bonito, albacore, and a few varieties of that sea serpent named the moray eel.

The *Nautilus* had cleared 8,100 miles. We logged 9,720 miles when we passed between the Tonga Islands, where crews from the Argo, Port-au-Prince, and Duke of Portland had perished, and the island group of Samoa, scene of the slaying of Captain de Langle, friend of that long-lost navigator, the Count de La Pérouse. Then we raised the Fiji Islands, where savages slaughtered sailors from the *Union*, as well as Captain Bureau, commander of the *Darling Josephine* out of Nantes, France.

Extending over an expanse of 100 leagues north to south, and over 90 leagues east to west, this island group lies between latitude 2° and 6° south, and between longitude 174° and 179° west. It consists of a number of islands, islets, and reefs, among which we noted the islands of Viti Levu, Vanua Levu, and Kadavu.

It was the Dutch navigator Tasman who discovered this group in 1643, the same year the Italian physicist Torricelli invented the barometer and King Louis XIV ascended the French throne. I'll let the reader decide which of these deeds was more beneficial to humanity. Coming later, Captain Cook in 1774, Rear Admiral d'Entrecasteaux in 1793, and finally Captain Dumont d'Urville in 1827, untangled the whole chaotic geography of this island group. The *Nautilus* drew near Wailea Bay, an unlucky place for England's Captain Dillon, who was the first to shed light on the longstanding mystery surrounding the disappearance of ships under the Count de La Pérouse.

This bay, repeatedly dredged, furnished a huge supply of excellent oysters. As the Roman playwright Seneca recommended, we opened them right at our table, then stuffed ourselves. These molluscs belonged to the species known by name as *Ostrea lamellosa*, whose members are quite common off Corsica. This Wailea oysterbank must have been extensive, and for certain, if they hadn't been controlled by numerous natural checks, these clusters of shellfish would have ended up jam-packing the bay, since as many as 2,000,000 eggs have been counted in a single individual.

And if Mr Ned Land did not repent of his gluttony at our oyster fest, it's because oysters are the only dish that never causes indigestion. In fact, it takes no less than 16 dozen of these headless molluscs to supply the 315 grams that satisfy one man's minimum daily requirement for nitrogen.

On December 25 the *Nautilus* navigated amid the island group of the New Hebrides, which the Portuguese seafarer Queirós discovered in 1606, which Commander Bougainville explored in 1768, and to which Captain Cook gave its current name in 1773. This group is chiefly made up of nine large islands and forms a 120-league strip from the north-northwest to the south-southeast, lying between latitude 2° and 15° south, and between longitude 164° and 168°. At the moment of our noon sights, we passed fairly close to the island of Aurou, which looked to me like a mass of green woods crowned by a peak of great height.

That day it was yuletide, and it struck me that Ned Land badly missed celebrating 'Christmas,' that genuine family holiday where Protestants are such zealots.

I hadn't seen Captain Nemo for over a week, when, on the morning of the 27th, he entered the main lounge, as usual acting as if he'd been gone for just five minutes. I was busy tracing the *Nautilus*'s course on the world map. The captain approached, placed a finger over a position on the chart, and pronounced just one word:

'Vanikoro.'

This name was magic! It was the name of those islets where vessels under the Count de La Pérouse had miscarried. I straightened suddenly.

'The *Nautilus* is bringing us to Vanikoro?' I asked.

'Yes, professor,' the captain replied.

'And I'll be able to visit those famous islands where the *Compass* and the *Astrolabe* came to grief?'

'If you like, professor.'

'When will we reach Vanikoro?'

'We already have, professor.'

Followed by Captain Nemo, I climbed onto the platform, and from there my eyes eagerly scanned the horizon.

In the northeast there emerged two volcanic islands of unequal size, surrounded by a coral reef whose circuit measured 40 miles. We were facing the island of Vanikoro proper, to which Captain Dumont d'Urville had given the name 'Island of the Search'; we lay right in front of the little harbour of Vana, located in latitude 16° 4' south and longitude 164° 32' east. Its shores seemed covered with greenery from its beaches to its summits inland, crowned by Mt Kapogo, which is 476 fathoms high.

After clearing the outer belt of rocks via a narrow passageway, the *Nautilus* lay inside the breakers where the sea had a depth of 30 to 40 fathoms. Under the green shade of some tropical evergreens, I spotted a few savages who looked extremely startled at our approach. In this long, blackish object advancing flush with the water, didn't they see some fearsome cetacean that they were obliged to view with distrust?

Just then Captain Nemo asked me what I knew about the shipwreck of the Count de La Pérouse.

'What everybody knows, captain,' I answered him.

'And could you kindly tell me what everybody knows?' he asked me in a gently ironic tone.

'Very easily.'

I related to him what the final deeds of Captain Dumont d'Urville had brought to light, deeds described here in this heavily condensed summary of the whole matter.

In 1785 the Count de La Pérouse and his subordinate, Captain de Langle, were sent by King Louis XVI of France on a voyage to circumnavigate the globe. They boarded two sloops of war, the *Compass* and the *Astrolabe*, which were never seen again.

In 1791, justly concerned about the fate of these two sloops of war, the French government fitted out two large cargo boats, the *Search* and the *Hope*, which left Brest on September 28 under orders from Rear Admiral Bruni d'Entrecasteaux. Two months later, testimony from a certain Commander Bowen, aboard the *Albemarle*, alleged that rubble from shipwrecked vessels had been seen on the coast of New Georgia. But d'Entrecasteaux was unaware of this news – which seemed a bit dubious anyhow – and headed toward the Admiralty Islands, which had been named in a report by one Captain Hunter as the site of the Count de La Pérouse's shipwreck.

They looked in vain. The *Hope* and the *Search* passed right by Vanikoro without stopping there; and overall, this voyage was plagued by misfortune, ultimately costing the lives of Rear Admiral d'Entrecasteaux, two of his subordinate officers and several seamen from his crew.

It was an old hand at the Pacific, the English adventurer Captain Peter Dillon, who was the first to pick up the trail left by castaways from the wrecked vessels. On May 15, 1824, his ship, the *St Patrick*, passed by Tikopia Island, one of the New Hebrides. There a native boatman pulled alongside in a dugout canoe and sold Dillon a silver sword hilt bearing the imprint of characters engraved with a cutting tool known as a burin. Furthermore, this native boatman claimed that during a stay in Vanikoro six years earlier, he had seen two Europeans belonging to ships that had run aground on the island's reefs many years before.

Dillon guessed that the ships at issue were those under the Count de La Pérouse, ships whose disappearance had shaken the entire world. He tried to reach Vanikoro, where, according to the native boatman, a good deal of rubble from the shipwreck could still be found, but winds and currents prevented his doing so.

Dillon returned to Calcutta. There he was able to interest the Asiatic Society and the East India Company in his discovery. A ship named after the *Search* was placed at his disposal, and he departed on January 23, 1827, accompanied by a French deputy.

This new *Search*, after putting in at several stops over the Pacific, dropped anchor before Vanikoro on July 7, 1827, in the same harbour of Vana where the *Nautilus* was currently floating.

There Dillon collected many relics of the shipwreck: iron utensils, anchors, eyelets from pulleys, swivel guns, an 18-pound shell, the remains of some astronomical instruments, a piece of sternrail and a bronze bell bearing the inscription 'Made by Bazin,' the foundry mark at Brest Arsenal around 1785. There could no longer be any doubt.

Finishing his investigations, Dillon stayed at the site of the casualty until the month of October. Then he left Vanikoro, headed toward New Zealand, dropped anchor at Calcutta on April 7, 1828, and returned to France, where he received a very cordial welcome from King Charles X.

But just then the renowned French explorer Captain Dumont d'Urville, unaware of Dillon's activities, had already set sail to search elsewhere for the site of the shipwreck. In essence, a whaling vessel had reported that some medals and a Cross of St. Louis had been found in the hands of savages in the Louisiade Islands and New Caledonia.

So Captain Dumont d'Urville had put to sea in command of a vessel named after the *Astrolabe*, and just two months after Dillon had left Vanikoro, Dumont d'Urville dropped anchor before Hobart. There he heard about Dillon's findings, and he further learned that a certain James Hobbs, chief officer on the *Union* out of Calcutta, had put to shore on an island located in latitude 8° 18' south and longitude 156° 30' east, and had noted the natives of those waterways making use of iron bars and red fabrics.

Pretty perplexed, Dumont d'Urville didn't know if he should give credence to these reports, which had been carried in some of the less reliable newspapers; nevertheless, he decided to start on Dillon's trail.

On February 10, 1828, the new *Astrolabe* hove before Tikopia Island, took on a guide and interpreter in the person of a deserter who had settled there, plied a course toward Vanikoro, raised it on February 12, sailed along its reefs until the 14th, and only on the 20th dropped anchor inside its barrier in the harbour of Vana.

On the 23rd, several officers circled the island and brought back some rubble of little importance. The natives, adopting a system of denial and evasion, refused to guide them to the site of the casualty. This rather shady conduct aroused the suspicion that the natives had mistreated the castaways; and in truth, the natives seemed afraid that Dumont d'Urville had come to avenge the Count de La Pérouse and his unfortunate companions.

But on the 26th, appeased with gifts and seeing that they didn't need to fear any reprisals, the natives led the chief officer, Mr Jacquinot, to the site of the shipwreck.

At this location, in three or four fathoms of water between the Paeu and Vana reefs, there lay some anchors, cannons and ingots of iron and lead, all caked with limestone concretions. A launch and whaleboat from the new *Astrolabe* were steered to this locality, and after going to exhausting lengths, their crews managed to dredge up an anchor weighing 1,800 pounds, a cast-iron eight-pounder cannon, a lead ingot and two copper swivel guns.

Questioning the natives, Captain Dumont d'Urville also learned that after La Pérouse's two ships had miscarried on the island's reefs, the count had built a smaller craft, only to go off and miscarry a second time. Where? Nobody knew.

The commander of the new *Astrolabe* then had a monument erected under a tuft of mangrove, in memory of the famous navigator and his companions. It was a simple quadrangular pyramid, set on a coral base, with no ironwork to tempt the natives' avarice.

Then Dumont d'Urville tried to depart; but his crews were run down from the fevers raging on these unsanitary shores, and quite ill himself, he was unable to weigh anchor until March 17.

Meanwhile, fearing that Dumont d'Urville wasn't abreast of Dillon's activities, the French government sent a sloop of war to Vanikoro, the Bayonnaise under Commander Legoarant de Tromelin, who had been stationed on the American west coast. Dropping anchor before Vanikoro a few months after the new *Astrolabe*'s departure, the Bayonnaise didn't find any additional evidence but verified that the savages hadn't disturbed the memorial honouring the Count de La Pérouse.

This is the substance of the account I gave Captain Nemo.

'So,' he said to me, 'the castaways built a third ship on Vanikoro Island, and to this day, nobody knows where it went and perished?'

'Nobody knows.'

Captain Nemo didn't reply but signalled me to follow him to the main lounge. The *Nautilus* sank a few metres beneath the waves and the panels opened.

I rushed to the window and saw crusts of coral: fungus coral, siphonula coral, alcyon coral, sea anemone from the genus *Caryophylia*, plus myriads of charming fish including greenfish, damselfish, sweepers, snappers and squirrelfish; underneath this coral covering I detected some rubble the old dredges hadn't been able to tear free – iron stirrups, anchors, cannons, shells, tackle from a capstan, a stempost, all objects hailing from the wrecked ships and now carpeted in moving flowers.

And as I stared at this desolate wreckage, Captain Nemo told me in a solemn voice:

'Commander La Pérouse set out on December 7, 1785, with his ships, the *Compass* and the *Astrolabe*. He dropped anchor first at Botany Bay, visited the Tonga Islands and New Caledonia, headed toward the Santa Cruz Islands, and put in at Nomuka, one of the islands in the Ha'apai group. Then his ships arrived at the unknown reefs of Vanikoro. Travelling in the lead, the *Compass* ran afoul of breakers on the southerly coast. The *Astrolabe* went to its rescue and also ran aground. The first ship was destroyed almost immediately. The second, stranded to leeward, held up for some days. The natives gave the castaways a fair enough welcome. The latter took up residence on the island and built a smaller craft with rubble from the two large ones. A few seamen stayed voluntarily in Vanikoro. The others, weak and ailing, set sail with the Count de La Pérouse. They headed to the Solomon Islands, and they perished with all hands on the westerly coast of the chief island in that group, between Cape Deception and Cape Satisfaction!'

'And how do you know all this?' I exclaimed.

'Here's what I found at the very site of that final shipwreck!'

Captain Nemo showed me a tin box, stamped with the coat of arms of France and all corroded by salt water. He opened it and I saw a bundle of papers, yellowed but still legible.

They were the actual military orders given by France's Minister of the Navy to Commander La Pérouse, with notes along the margin in the handwriting of King Louis XVI!

'Ah, what a splendid death for a seaman!' Captain Nemo then said. 'A coral grave is a tranquil grave, and may Heaven grant that my companions and I rest in no other!'

CHAPTER 20

The Torres Strait

DURING THE NIGHT of December 27–28, the *Nautilus* left the waterways of Vanikoro behind with extraordinary speed. Its heading was southwesterly, and in three days it had cleared the 750 leagues that separated La Pérouse's islands from the southeastern tip of Papua.

On January 1, 1868, bright and early, Conseil joined me on the platform.

'Will master,' the gallant lad said to me, 'allow me to wish him a happy new year?'

'Good heavens, Conseil, it's just like old times in my office at the Botanical Gardens in Paris! I accept your kind wishes and I thank you for them. Only, I'd like to know what you mean by a "happy year" under the circumstances in which we're placed. Is it a year that will bring our imprisonment to an end, or a year that will see this strange voyage continue?'

'Ye gods,' Conseil replied, 'I hardly know what to tell master. We're certainly seeing some unusual things, and for two months we've had no time for boredom. The latest wonder is always the most astonishing, and if this progression keeps up, I can't imagine what its climax will be. In my opinion, we'll never again have such an opportunity.'

'Never, Conseil.'

'Besides, Mr Nemo really lives up to his Latin name, since he couldn't be less in the way if he didn't exist.'

'True enough, Conseil.'

'Therefore, with all due respect to master, I think a "happy year" would be a year that lets us see everything—'

'Everything, Conseil? No year could be that long. But what does Ned Land think about all this?'

'Ned Land's thoughts are exactly the opposite of mine,' Conseil replied. 'He has a practical mind and a demanding stomach. He's tired of staring at fish and eating them day in and day out. This shortage of wine, bread and meat isn't suitable for an upstanding Anglo-Saxon, a man accustomed to beefsteak and unfazed by regular doses of brandy or gin!'

'For my part, Conseil, that doesn't bother me in the least, and I've adjusted very nicely to the diet on board.'

'So have I,' Conseil replied. 'Accordingly, I think as much about staying as Mr Land about making his escape. Thus, if this new year isn't a happy one for me, it will be for him, and vice versa. No matter what happens, one of us will be pleased. So, in conclusion, I wish master to have whatever his heart desires.'

'Thank you, Conseil. Only I must ask you to postpone the question of new year's gifts, and temporarily accept a hearty handshake in their place. That's all I have on me.'

'Master has never been more generous,' Conseil replied.

And with that, the gallant lad went away.

By January 2 we had fared 11,340 miles, hence 5,250 leagues, from our starting point in the seas of Japan. Before the *Nautilus*'s spur there stretched the dangerous waterways of the Coral Sea, off the northeast coast of Australia. Our boat cruised along a few miles away from that daunting shoal where Captain Cook's ships well-nigh miscarried on June 10, 1770. The craft that Cook was aboard charged into some coral rock, and if his vessel didn't go down, it was thanks to the circumstance that a piece of coral broke off in the collision and plugged the very hole it had made in the hull.

I would have been deeply interested in visiting this long, 360-league reef, against which the ever-surging sea broke with the fearsome intensity of thunderclaps. But just then the *Nautilus*'s slanting fins took us to great depths, and I could see nothing of those high coral walls. I had to rest content with the various specimens of fish brought up by our nets. Among others I noted some long-finned albacore, a species in the genus *Scomber*, as big as tuna, bluish on the flanks, and streaked with crosswise stripes that disappear when the animal dies. These fish followed us in schools and supplied our table with very dainty flesh. We also caught a large number of yellow-green gilthead, half a decimetre long and tasting like dorado, plus some flying gurnards, authentic underwater swallows that, on dark nights, alternately streak air and water with their phosphorescent glimmers. Among molluscs and zoophytes, I found in our trawl's meshes various species of alcyonarian coral, sea urchins, hammer shells, spurred-star shells, wentletrap snails, horn shells, glass snails. The local flora was represented by fine floating algae: sea tangle, and kelp from the genus *Macrocystis*, saturated with the mucilage their pores perspire, from which I selected a wonderful *Nemastoma geliniaroidea*, classifying it with the natural curiosities in the museum.

On January 4, two days after crossing the Coral Sea, we raised the coast of Papua. On this occasion Captain Nemo told me that he intended to reach the Indian Ocean via the Torres Strait. This was the extent of his remarks. Ned saw with pleasure that this course would bring us, once again, closer to European seas.

The Torres Strait is regarded as no less dangerous for its bristling reefs than for the savage inhabitants of its coasts. It separates Queensland from the huge island of Papua, also called New Guinea.

Papua is 400 leagues long by 130 leagues wide, with a surface area of 40,000 geographic leagues. It's located between latitude 0° 19' and 10° 2' south, and between longitude 128° 23' and 146° 15'. At noon, while the chief officer was taking the sun's altitude, I spotted the summits of the Arfak Mountains, rising in terraces and ending in sharp peaks.

Discovered in 1511 by the Portuguese Francisco Serrano, these shores were successively visited by Don Jorge de Meneses in 1526, by Juan de Grijalva in 1527, by the Spanish general Alvaro de Saavedra in 1528, by Inigo Ortiz in 1545, by the Dutchman Schouten in 1616, by Nicolas Sruick in 1753, by Tasman, Dampier, Fumel, Carteret, Edwards, Bougainville, Cook, McClure, and Thomas Forrest, by Rear Admiral d'Entrecasteaux in 1792, by Louis–Isidore Duperrey in 1823, and by Captain Dumont d'Urville in 1827. 'It's the heartland of the blacks who occupy all Malaysia,' Mr de Rienzi has said; and I hadn't the foggiest inkling that sailors' luck was about to bring me face to face with these daunting Andaman aborigines.

So the *Nautilus* hove before the entrance to the world's most dangerous strait, a passageway that even the boldest navigators hesitated to clear: the strait that Luis Vaez de Torres faced on returning from the South Seas in Melanesia, the strait in which sloops of war under Captain Dumont d'Urville ran aground in 1840 and nearly miscarried with all hands. And even the *Nautilus*, rising superior to every danger in the sea, was about to become intimate with its coral reefs.

The Torres Strait is about 34 leagues wide, but it's obstructed by an incalculable number of islands, islets, breakers and rocks that make it nearly impossible to navigate. Consequently, Captain Nemo took every desired precaution in crossing it. Floating flush with the water, the *Nautilus* moved ahead at a moderate pace. Like a cetacean's tail, its propeller churned the waves slowly.

Taking advantage of this situation, my two companions and I found seats on the ever-deserted platform. In front of us stood the pilothouse, and unless I'm extremely mistaken, Captain Nemo must have been inside, steering his *Nautilus* himself.

Under my eyes I had the excellent charts of the Torres Strait that had been surveyed and drawn up by the hydrographic engineer Vincendon Dumoulin and Sub-lieutenant (now Admiral) Coupvent-Desbois, who were part of Dumont d'Urville's general staff during his final voyage to circumnavigate the globe. These, along with the efforts of Captain King, are the best charts for untangling the snarl of this narrow passageway, and I consulted them with scrupulous care.

Around the *Nautilus* the sea was boiling furiously. A stream of waves, bearing from southeast to northwest at a speed of two and a half miles per hour, broke over heads of coral emerging here and there.

'That's one rough sea!' Ned Land told me.

'Abominable indeed,' I replied, 'and hardly suitable for a craft like the *Nautilus*.'

'That damned captain,' the Canadian went on, 'must really be sure of his course, because if these clumps of coral so much as brush us, they'll rip our hull into a thousand pieces!'

The situation was indeed dangerous, but as if by magic, the *Nautilus* seemed to glide right down the middle of these rampaging reefs. It didn't follow the exact course of the *Zealous* and the new *Astrolabe*, which had proved so ill-fated for Captain Dumont d'Urville. It went more to the north, hugged the Murray Islands, and returned to the southwest near Cumberland Passage. I thought it was about to charge wholeheartedly into this opening, but it went up to the northwest, through a large number of little-known islands and islets, and steered toward Tound Island and the Bad Channel.

I was already wondering if Captain Nemo, rash to the point of sheer insanity, wanted his ship to tackle the narrows where Dumont d'Urville's two sloops of war had gone aground, when he changed direction a second time and cut straight to the west, heading toward Gueboroa Island.

By then it was three o'clock in the afternoon. The current was slacking off, it was almost full tide. The *Nautilus* drew near this island, which I can see to this day with its remarkable fringe of screw pines. We hugged it from less than two miles out.

A sudden jolt threw me down. The *Nautilus* had just struck a reef, and it remained motionless, listing slightly to port.

When I stood up, I saw Captain Nemo and his chief officer on the platform. They were examining the ship's circumstances, exchanging a few words in their incomprehensible dialect.

Here is what those circumstances entailed. Two miles to starboard lay Gueboroa Island, its coastline curving north to west like an immense arm. To the south and east, heads of coral were already on display, left uncovered by the ebbing waters. We had run aground at full tide and in one of those seas whose tides are moderate, an inconvenient state of affairs for floating the *Nautilus* off. However, the ship hadn't suffered in any way, so solidly joined was its hull. But although it could neither sink nor split open, it was in serious danger of being permanently attached to these reefs, and that would have been the finish of Captain Nemo's submersible.

I was mulling this over when the captain approached, cool and calm, forever in control of himself, looking neither alarmed nor annoyed.

'An accident?' I said to him.

'No, an incident,' he answered me.

'But an incident,' I replied, 'that may oblige you to become a resident again of these shores you avoid!'

Captain Nemo gave me an odd look and gestured no. Which told me pretty clearly that nothing would ever force him to set foot on a land mass again. Then he said:

'No, Professor Aronnax, the *Nautilus* isn't consigned to perdition.

It will still carry you through the midst of the ocean's wonders. Our voyage is just beginning, and I've no desire to deprive myself so soon of the pleasure of your company.'

'Even so, Captain Nemo,' I went on, ignoring his ironic turn of phrase, 'the *Nautilus* has run aground at a moment when the sea is full. Now then, the tides aren't strong in the Pacific, and if you can't unballast the *Nautilus*, which seems impossible to me, I don't see how it will float off.'

'You're right, professor, the Pacific tides aren't strong,' Captain Nemo replied. 'But in the Torres Strait, one still finds a metre-and-a-half difference in level between high and low seas. Today is January 4, and in five days the moon will be full. Now then, I'll be quite astonished if that good-natured satellite doesn't sufficiently raise these masses of water and do me a favour for which I'll be forever grateful.'

This said, Captain Nemo went below again to the *Nautilus*'s interior, followed by his chief officer. As for our craft, it no longer stirred, staying as motionless as if these coral polyps had already walled it in with their indestructible cement.

'Well, sir?' Ned Land said to me, coming up after the captain's departure.

'Well, Ned my friend, we'll serenely wait for the tide on the 9th, because it seems the moon will have the good nature to float us away!'

'As simple as that?'

'As simple as that.'

'So our captain isn't going to drop his anchors, put his engines on the chains and do anything to haul us off?'

'Since the tide will be sufficient,' Conseil replied simply.

The Canadian stared at Conseil, then he shrugged his shoulders. The seaman in him was talking now.

'Sir,' he answered, 'you can trust me when I say this hunk of iron will never navigate again, on the seas or under them. It's only fit to be sold for its weight. So I think it's time we gave Captain Nemo the slip.'

'Ned my friend,' I replied, 'unlike you, I haven't given up on our valiant *Nautilus*, and in four days we'll know where we stand on these Pacific tides. Besides, an escape attempt might be timely if we were in sight of the coasts of England or Provence, but in the waterways of Papua it's another story. And we'll always have that as a last resort if the *Nautilus* doesn't right itself, which I'd regard as a real calamity.'

'But couldn't we at least get the lay of the land?' Ned went on. 'Here's an island. On this island there are trees. Under those trees land animals loaded with cutlets and roast beef, which I'd be happy to sink my teeth into.'

'In this instance our friend Ned is right,' Conseil said, 'and I side with his views. Couldn't master persuade his friend Captain Nemo to send the three of us ashore, if only so our feet don't lose the knack of treading on the solid parts of our planet?'

'I can ask him,' I replied, 'but he'll refuse.'

'Let master take the risk,' Conseil said, 'and we'll know where we stand on the captain's affability.'

Much to my surprise, Captain Nemo gave me the permission I asked for, and he did so with grace and alacrity, not even exacting my promise to return on board. But fleeing across the New Guinea territories would be extremely dangerous, and I wouldn't have advised Ned Land to try it. Better to be prisoners aboard the *Nautilus* than to fall into the hands of Papuan natives.

The skiff was put at our disposal for the next morning. I hardly needed to ask whether Captain Nemo would be coming along. I likewise assumed that no crewmen would be assigned to us, that Ned Land would be in sole charge of piloting the longboat. Besides, the shore lay no more than two miles off, and it would be child's play for the Canadian to guide that nimble skiff through those rows of reefs so ill-fated for big ships.

The next day, January 5, after its deck panelling was opened, the skiff was wrenched from its socket and launched to sea from the top of the platform. Two men were sufficient for this operation. The oars were inside the longboat and we had only to take our seats.

At eight o'clock, armed with rifles and axes, we pulled clear of the *Nautilus*. The sea was fairly calm. A mild breeze blew from shore. In place by the oars, Conseil and I rowed vigorously, and Ned steered us into the narrow lanes between the breakers. The skiff handled easily and sped swiftly.

Ned Land couldn't conceal his glee. He was a prisoner escaping from prison and never dreaming he would need to re-enter it.

'Meat!' he kept repeating. 'Now we'll eat red meat! Actual game! A real mess call, by thunder! I'm not saying fish aren't good for you, but we mustn't overdo 'em, and a slice of fresh venison grilled over live coals will be a nice change from our standard fare.'

'You glutton,' Conseil replied, 'you're making my mouth water!'

'It remains to be seen,' I said, 'whether these forests do contain game, and if the types of game aren't of such size that they can hunt the hunter.'

'Fine, Professor Aronnax!' replied the Canadian, whose teeth seemed to be as honed as the edge of an axe. 'But if there's no other quadruped on this island, I'll eat tiger – tiger sirloin.'

'Our friend Ned grows disturbing,' Conseil replied.

'Whatever it is,' Ned Land went on, 'any animal having four feet without feathers, or two feet with feathers, will be greeted by my very own one-gun salute.'

'Oh good!' I replied. 'The reckless Mr Land is at it again!'

'Don't worry, Professor Aronnax, just keep rowing!' the Canadian replied. 'I only need 25 minutes to serve you one of my own special creations.'

By 8:30 the *Nautilus*'s skiff had just run gently aground on a sandy strand, after successfully clearing the ring of coral that surrounds Gueboroa Island.

CHAPTER 21

Some Days Ashore

STEPPING ASHORE HAD an exhilarating effect on me. Ned Land tested the soil with his foot, as if he were laying claim to it. Yet it had been only two months since we had become, as Captain Nemo expressed it, 'passengers on the *Nautilus*,' in other words, the literal prisoners of its commander.

In a few minutes we were a gunshot away from the coast. The soil was almost entirely madreporic, but certain dry stream beds were strewn with granite rubble, proving that this island was of primordial origin. The entire horizon was hidden behind a curtain of wonderful forests. Enormous trees, sometimes as high as 200 feet, were linked to each other by garlands of tropical creepers, genuine natural hammocks that swayed in a mild breeze. There were mimosas, banyan trees, beefwood, teakwood, hibiscus, screw pines, palm trees, all mingling in wild profusion; and beneath the shade of their green canopies, at the feet of their gigantic trunks, there grew orchids, leguminous plants and ferns.

Meanwhile, ignoring all these fine specimens of Papuan flora, the Canadian passed up the decorative in favour of the functional. He spotted a coconut palm, beat down some of its fruit, broke them open, and we drank their milk and ate their meat with a pleasure that was a protest against our standard fare on the *Nautilus*.

'Excellent!' Ned Land said.

'Exquisite!' Conseil replied.

'And I don't think,' the Canadian said, 'that your Nemo would object to us stashing a cargo of coconuts aboard his vessel?'

'I imagine not,' I replied, 'but he won't want to sample them.'

'Too bad for him!' Conseil said.

'And plenty good for us!' Ned Land shot back. 'There'll be more left over!'

'A word of caution, Mr Land,' I told the harpooner, who was about to ravage another coconut palm. 'Coconuts are admirable things, but before we stuff the skiff with them, it would be wise to find out whether this island offers other substances just as useful. Some fresh vegetables would be well received in the *Nautilus*'s pantry.'

'Master is right,' Conseil replied, 'and I propose that we set aside three places in our longboat: one for fruit, another for vegetables and a third for venison, of which I still haven't glimpsed the tiniest specimen.'

'Don't give up so easily, Conseil,' the Canadian replied.

'So let's continue our excursion,' I went on, 'but keep a sharp lookout. This island seems uninhabited, but it still might harbour certain individuals who aren't so finicky about the sort of game they eat!'

'Hee hee!' Ned put in, with a meaningful movement of his jaws.

'Ned! Oh horrors!' Conseil exclaimed.

'Ye gods,' the Canadian shot back, 'I'm starting to appreciate the charms of cannibalism!'

'Ned, Ned! Don't say that!' Conseil answered. 'You a cannibal? Why, I'll no longer be safe next to you, I who share your cabin! Does this mean I'll wake up half devoured one fine day?'

'I'm awfully fond of you, Conseil my friend, but not enough to eat you when there's better food around.'

'Then I daren't delay,' Conseil replied. 'The hunt is on! We absolutely must bag some game to placate this man-eater, or one of these mornings master won't find enough pieces of his manservant to serve him.'

While exchanging this chitchat, we entered beneath the dark canopies of the forest, and for two hours we explored it in every direction.

We couldn't have been luckier in our search for edible vegetation, and some of the most useful produce in the tropical zones supplied us with a valuable foodstuff missing on board.

I mean the breadfruit tree, which is quite abundant on Gueboroa Island, and there I chiefly noted the seedless variety that in Malaysia is called 'rima.'

This tree is distinguished from other trees by a straight trunk 40 feet high. To the naturalist's eye, its gracefully rounded crown, formed of big multilobed leaves, was enough to denote the artocarpus that has been so successfully transplanted to the Mascarene Islands east of

Madagascar. From its mass of greenery, huge globular fruit stood out, a decimetre wide and furnished on the outside with creases that assumed a hexagonal pattern. It's a handy plant that nature gives to regions lacking in wheat; without needing to be cultivated, it bears fruit eight months out of the year.

Ned Land was on familiar terms with this fruit. He had already eaten it on his many voyages and knew how to cook its edible substance. So the very sight of it aroused his appetite, and he couldn't control himself.

'Sir,' he told me, 'I'll die if I don't sample a little breadfruit pasta!'

'Sample some, Ned my friend, sample all you like. We're here to conduct experiments, let's conduct them.'

'It won't take a minute,' the Canadian replied.

Equipped with a magnifying glass, he lit a fire of deadwood that was soon crackling merrily. Meanwhile Conseil and I selected the finest *artocarpus* fruit. Some still weren't ripe enough, and their thick skins covered white, slightly fibrous pulps. But a great many others were yellowish and gelatinous, just begging to be picked.

This fruit contained no pits. Conseil brought a dozen of them to Ned Land, who cut them into thick slices and placed them over a fire of live coals, all the while repeating:

'You'll see, sir, how tasty this bread is!'

'Especially since we've gone without baked goods for so long,' Conseil said.

'It's more than just bread,' the Canadian added. 'It's a dainty pastry. You've never eaten any, sir?'

'No, Ned.'

'All right, get ready for something downright delectable! If you don't come back for seconds, I'm no longer the King of Harpooners!'

After a few minutes, the parts of the fruit exposed to the fire were completely toasted. On the inside there appeared some white pasta, a sort of soft bread centre whose flavour reminded me of artichoke.

This bread was excellent, I must admit, and I ate it with great pleasure.

'Unfortunately,' I said, 'this pasta won't stay fresh, so it seems pointless to make a supply for on board.'

'By thunder, sir!' Ned Land exclaimed. 'There you go, talking like a naturalist, but meantime I'll be acting like a baker! Conseil, harvest some of this fruit to take with us when we go back.'

'And how will you prepare it?' I asked the Canadian.

'I'll make a fermented batter from its pulp that'll keep indefinitely without spoiling. When I want some, I'll just cook it in the galley on board – it'll have a slightly tart flavour, but you'll find it excellent.'

'So, Mr Ned, I see that this bread is all we need—'

'Not quite, professor,' the Canadian replied. 'We need some fruit to go with it, or at least some vegetables.'

'Then let's look for fruit and vegetables.'

When our breadfruit harvesting was done, we took to the trail to complete this 'dry-land dinner.'

We didn't search in vain, and near noontime we had an ample supply of bananas. This delicious produce from the Torrid Zones ripens all year round, and Malaysians, who give them the name 'pisang,' eat them without bothering to cook them. In addition to bananas, we gathered some enormous jackfruit with a very tangy flavour, some tasty mangoes, and some pineapples of unbelievable sise. But this foraging took up a good deal of our time, which, even so, we had no cause to regret.

Conseil kept Ned under observation. The harpooner walked in the lead, and during his stroll through this forest, he gathered with sure hands some excellent fruit that should have completed his provisions.

'So,' Conseil asked, 'you have everything you need, Ned my friend?'

'Humph!' the Canadian put in.

'What! You're complaining?'

'All this vegetation doesn't make a meal,' Ned replied. 'Just side dishes, dessert. But where's the soup course? Where's the roast?'

'Right,' I said. 'Ned promised us cutlets, which seems highly questionable to me.'

'Sir,' the Canadian replied, 'our hunting not only isn't over, it hasn't even started. Patience! We're sure to end up bumping into some animal with either feathers or fur, if not in this locality, then in another.'

'And if not today, then tomorrow, because we mustn't wander too far off,' Conseil added. 'That's why I propose that we return to the skiff.'

'What! Already!' Ned exclaimed.

'We ought to be back before nightfall,' I said.

'But what hour is it, then?' the Canadian asked.

'Two o'clock at least,' Conseil replied.

'How time flies on solid ground!' exclaimed Mr Ned Land with a sigh of regret.

'Off we go!' Conseil replied.

So we returned through the forest, and we completed our harvest by making a clean sweep of some palm cabbages that had to be picked from the crowns of their trees, some small beans that I recognised as the 'abrou' of the Malaysians, and some high-quality yams.

We were overloaded when we arrived at the skiff. However, Ned Land still found these provisions inadequate. But fortune smiled on him. Just as we were boarding, he spotted several trees 25 to 30 feet high, belonging to the palm species. As valuable as the *actocarpus*, these trees are justly ranked among the most useful produce in Malaysia.

They were sago palms, vegetation that grows without being cultivated; like mulberry trees, they reproduce by means of shoots and seeds.

Ned Land knew how to handle these trees. Taking his axe and wielding it with great vigour, he soon stretched out on the ground two or three sago palms, whose maturity was revealed by the white dust sprinkled over their palm fronds.

I watched him more as a naturalist than as a man in hunger. He began by removing from each trunk an inch-thick strip of bark that covered a network of long, hopelessly tangled fibres that were puttied with a sort of gummy flour. This flour was the starch-like sago, an edible substance chiefly consumed by the Melanesian peoples.

For the time being, Ned Land was content to chop these trunks into pieces, as if he were making firewood; later he would extract the flour by sifting it through cloth to separate it from its fibrous ligaments, let it dry out in the sun, and leave it to harden inside moulds.

Finally, at five o'clock in the afternoon, laden with all our treasures, we left the island beach and half an hour later pulled alongside the *Nautilus*. Nobody appeared on our arrival. The enormous sheet-iron cylinder seemed deserted. Our provisions loaded on board, I went below to my stateroom. There I found my supper ready. I ate and then fell asleep.

The next day, January 6: nothing new on board. Not a sound inside, not a sign of life. The skiff stayed alongside in the same place we had left it. We decided to return to Gueboroa Island. Ned Land hoped for better luck in his hunting than on the day before, and he wanted to visit a different part of the forest.

By sunrise we were off. Carried by an inbound current, the longboat reached the island in a matter of moments.

We disembarked, and thinking it best to abide by the Canadian's instincts, we followed Ned Land, whose long legs threatened to outpace us.

Ned Land went westward up the coast; then, fording some stream beds, he reached open plains that were bordered by wonderful forests. Some kingfishers lurked along the watercourses, but they didn't let us approach. Their cautious behaviour proved to me that these winged creatures knew where they stood on bipeds of our species, and I concluded that if this island wasn't inhabited, at least human beings paid it frequent visits.

After crossing a pretty lush prairie, we arrived on the outskirts of a small wood, enlivened by the singing and soaring of a large number of birds.

'Still, they're merely birds,' Conseil said.

'But some are edible,' the harpooner replied.

'Wrong, Ned my friend,' Conseil answered, 'because I see only ordinary parrots here.'

'Conseil my friend,' Ned replied in all seriousness, 'parrots are like pheasant to people with nothing else on their plates.'

'And I might add,' I said, 'that when these birds are properly cooked, they're at least worth a stab of the fork.'

Indeed, under the dense foliage of this wood, a whole host of parrots fluttered from branch to branch, needing only the proper upbringing to speak human dialects. At present they were cackling in chorus with parakeets of every colour, with solemn cockatoos that seemed to be pondering some philosophical problem, while bright red lories passed by like pieces of bunting borne on the breeze, in the midst of kalao parrots raucously on the wing, Papuan lories painted the subtlest shades of azure, and a whole variety of delightful winged creatures, none terribly edible.

However, one bird unique to these shores, which never passes beyond the boundaries of the Aru and Papuan Islands, was missing from this collection. But I was given a chance to marvel at it soon enough.

After crossing through a moderately dense thicket, we again found some plains obstructed by bushes. There I saw some magnificent birds soaring aloft, the arrangement of their long feathers causing them to head into the wind. Their undulating flight, the grace of their aerial curves, and the play of their colours allured and delighted the eye. I had no trouble identifying them.

'Birds of paradise!' I exclaimed.

'Order *Passeriforma*, division *Clystomora*,' Conseil replied.

'Partridge family?' Ned Land asked.

'I doubt it, Mr Land. Nevertheless, I'm counting on your dexterity to catch me one of these delightful representatives of tropical nature!'

'I'll give it a try, professor, though I'm handier with a harpoon than a rifle.'

Malaysians, who do a booming business in these birds with the Chinese, have various methods for catching them that we couldn't use. Sometimes they set snares on the tops of the tall trees that the bird of paradise prefers to inhabit. At other times they capture it with a tenacious glue that paralyses its movements. They will even go so far as to poison the springs where these fowl habitually drink. But in our case, all we could do was fire at them on the wing, which left us little chance of getting one. And in truth, we used up a good part of our ammunition in vain.

Near 11 o'clock in the morning, we cleared the lower slopes of the mountains that form the island's centre, and we still hadn't bagged a thing. Hunger spurred us on. The hunters had counted on consuming the proceeds of their hunting, and they had miscalculated. Luckily, and much to his surprise, Conseil pulled off a right-and-left shot and insured our breakfast. He brought down a white pigeon and a ringdove, which were briskly plucked, hung from a spit and roasted over a blazing fire of deadwood. While these fascinating animals were cooking, Ned prepared some bread from the *artocarpus*. Then the pigeon and ringdove were devoured to the bones and declared excellent. Nutmeg, on which these birds habitually gorge themselves, sweetens their flesh and makes it delicious eating.

'They taste like chicken stuffed with truffles,' Conseil said.

'All right, Ned,' I asked the Canadian, 'now what do you need?'

'Game with four paws, Professor Aronnax,' Ned Land replied. 'All these pigeons are only appetisers, snacks. So till I've bagged an animal with cutlets, I won't be happy!'

'Nor I, Ned, until I've caught a bird of paradise.'

'Then let's keep hunting,' Conseil replied, 'but while heading back to the sea. We've arrived at the foothills of these mountains, and I think we'll do better if we return to the forest regions.'

It was good advice and we took it. After an hour's walk we reached a genuine sago palm forest. A few harmless snakes fled underfoot. Birds of paradise stole off at our approach, and I was in real despair of catching one when Conseil, walking in the lead, stooped suddenly, gave a triumphant shout, and came back to me, carrying a magnificent bird of paradise.

'Oh bravo, Conseil!' I exclaimed.

'Master is too kind,' Conseil replied.

'Not at all, my boy. That was a stroke of genius, catching one of these live birds with your bare hands!'

'If master will examine it closely, he'll see that I deserve no great praise.'

'And why not, Conseil?'

'Because this bird is as drunk as a lord.'

'Drunk?'

'Yes, master, drunk from the nutmegs it was devouring under that nutmeg tree where I caught it. See, Ned my friend, see the monstrous results of intemperance!'

'Damnation!' the Canadian shot back. 'Considering the amount of gin I've had these past two months, you've got nothing to complain about!'

Meanwhile I was examining this unusual bird. Conseil was not mistaken. Tipsy from that potent juice, our bird of paradise had been reduced to helplessness. It was unable to fly. It was barely able to walk. But this didn't alarm me, and I just let it sleep off its nutmeg.

This bird belonged to the finest of the eight species credited to Papua and its neighbouring islands. It was a 'great emerald,' one of the rarest birds of paradise. It measured three decimetres long. Its head was comparatively small, and its eyes, placed near the opening of its beak, were also small. But it offered a wonderful mixture of hues: a yellow beak, brown feet and claws, hazel wings with purple tips, pale yellow head and scruff of the neck, emerald throat, the belly and chest maroon to brown. Two strands, made of a horn substance covered with down, rose over its tail, which was lengthened by long, very light feathers of wonderful fineness, and they completed the costume of this marvellous bird that the islanders have poetically named 'the sun bird.'

How I wished I could take this superb bird of paradise back to Paris, to make a gift of it to the zoo at the Botanical Gardens, which doesn't own a single live specimen.

'So it must be a rarity or something?' the Canadian asked, in the tone of a hunter who, from the viewpoint of his art, gives the game a pretty low rating.

'A great rarity, my gallant comrade, and above all very hard to capture alive. And even after they're dead, there's still a major market for these birds. So the natives have figured out how to create fake ones, like people create fake pearls or diamonds.'

'What!' Conseil exclaimed. 'They make counterfeit birds of paradise?'

'Yes, Conseil.'

'And is master familiar with how the islanders go about it?'

'Perfectly familiar. During the easterly monsoon season, birds of paradise lose the magnificent feathers around their tails that naturalists call 'below-the-wing' feathers. These feathers are gathered by the fowl forgers and skilfully fitted onto some poor previously mutilated parakeet. Then they paint over the suture, varnish the bird and ship the fruits of their unique labours to museums and collectors in Europe.'

'Good enough!' Ned Land put in. 'If it isn't the right bird, it's still the right feathers, and so long as the merchandise isn't meant to be eaten, I see no great harm!'

But if my desires were fulfilled by the capture of this bird of paradise, those of our Canadian huntsman remained unsatisfied.

Luckily, near two o'clock Ned Land brought down a magnificent wild pig of the type the natives call 'bari-outang.' This animal came in the nick of time for us to bag some real quadruped meat, and it was warmly welcomed. Ned Land proved himself quite gloriously with his gunshot. Hit by an electric bullet, the pig dropped dead on the spot.

The Canadian properly skinned and cleaned it, after removing half a dozen cutlets destined to serve as the grilled meat course of our evening meal. Then the hunt was on again, and once more would be marked by the exploits of Ned and Conseil.

In essence, beating the bushes, the two friends flushed a herd of kangaroos that fled by bounding away on their elastic paws. But these animals didn't flee so swiftly that our electric capsules couldn't catch up with them.

'Oh, professor!' shouted Ned Land, whose hunting fever had gone to his brain. 'What excellent game, especially in a stew! What a supply for the *Nautilus*! Two, three, five down! And just think how we'll devour all this meat ourselves, while those numbskulls on board won't get a shred!'

In his uncontrollable glee, I think the Canadian might have slaughtered the whole horde, if he hadn't been so busy talking! But he was content with a dozen of these fascinating marsupials, which make up the first order of aplacental mammals, as Conseil just had to tell us.

These animals were small in stature. They were a species of those 'rabbit kangaroos' that usually dwell in the hollows of trees and are tremendously fast; but although of moderate dimensions, they at least furnish a meat that's highly prized.

We were thoroughly satisfied with the results of our hunting. A gleeful Ned proposed that we return the next day to this magic island, which he planned to depopulate of its every edible quadruped. But he was reckoning without events.

By six o'clock in the evening, we were back on the beach. The skiff was aground in its usual place. The *Nautilus*, looking like a long reef, emerged from the waves two miles offshore.

Without further ado, Ned Land got down to the important business of dinner. He came wonderfully to terms with its entire cooking. Grilling over the coals, those cutlets from the 'bari-outang' soon gave off a succulent aroma that perfumed the air.

But I catch myself following in the Canadian's footsteps. Look at me – in ecstasy over freshly grilled pork! Please grant me a pardon as I've already granted one to Mr Land, and on the same grounds!

In short, dinner was excellent. Two ringdoves rounded out this extraordinary menu. Sago pasta, bread from the *artocarpus*, mangoes, half a dozen pineapples, and the fermented liquor from certain coconuts heightened our glee. I suspect that my two fine companions weren't quite as clearheaded as one could wish.

'What if we don't return to the *Nautilus* this evening?' Conseil said.

'What if we never return to it?' Ned Land added.

Just then a stone whizzed toward us, landed at our feet, and cut short the harpooner's proposition.

CHAPTER 22

The Lightning Bolts of Captain Nemo

WITHOUT STANDING UP, we stared in the direction of the forest, my hand stopping halfway to my mouth, Ned Land's completing its assignment.

'Stones don't fall from the sky,' Conseil said, 'or else they deserve to be called meteorites.'

A second well-polished stone removed a tasty ringdove leg from Conseil's hand, giving still greater relevance to his observation.

We all three stood up, rifles to our shoulders, ready to answer any attack.

'Apes maybe?' Ned Land exclaimed.

'Nearly,' Conseil replied. 'Savages.'

'Head for the skiff!' I said, moving toward the sea.

Indeed, it was essential to beat a retreat because some 20 natives, armed with bows and slings, appeared barely a hundred paces off, on the outskirts of a thicket that masked the horizon to our right.

The skiff was aground ten fathoms away from us.

The savages approached without running, but they favoured us with a show of the greatest hostility. It was raining stones and arrows.

Ned Land was unwilling to leave his provisions behind, and despite the impending danger, he clutched his pig on one side, his kangaroos on the other, and scampered off with respectable speed.

In two minutes we were on the strand. Loading provisions and weapons into the skiff, pushing it to sea, and positioning its two oars were the work of an instant. We hadn't gone two cable lengths when a hundred savages, howling and gesticulating, entered the water up to their waists. I looked to see if their appearance might draw some of the *Nautilus*'s men onto the platform. But no. Lying well out, that enormous machine still seemed completely deserted.

Twenty minutes later we boarded ship. The hatches were open. After mooring the skiff, we re-entered the *Nautilus*'s interior.

I went below to the lounge, from which some chords were wafting.

Captain Nemo was there, leaning over the organ, deep in a musical trance.

'Captain!' I said to him.

He didn't hear me.

'Captain!' I went on, touching him with my hand.

He trembled, and turning around:

'Ah, it's you, professor!' he said to me. 'Well, did you have a happy hunt? Was your herb gathering a success?'

'Yes, captain,' I replied, 'but unfortunately we've brought back a horde of bipeds whose proximity worries me.'

'What sort of bipeds?'

'Savages.'

'Savages!' Captain Nemo replied in an ironic tone. 'You set foot on one of the shores of this globe, professor, and you're surprised to find savages there? Where aren't there savages? And besides, are they any worse than men elsewhere, these people you call savages?'

'But captain—'

'Speaking for myself, sir, I've encountered them everywhere.'

'Well then,' I replied, 'if you don't want to welcome them aboard the *Nautilus*, you'd better take some precautions!'

'Easy, professor, no cause for alarm.'

'But there are a large number of these natives.'

'What's your count?'

'At least a hundred.'

'Professor Aronnax,' replied Captain Nemo, whose fingers took their places again on the organ keys, 'if every islander in Papua were to gather on that beach, the *Nautilus* would still have nothing to fear from their attacks!'

The captain's fingers then ran over the instrument's keyboard, and I noticed that he touched only its black keys, which gave his melodies a basically Scottish colour. Soon he had forgotten my presence and was lost in a reverie that I no longer tried to dispel.

I climbed onto the platform. Night had already fallen, because in this low latitude the sun sets quickly, without any twilight. I could see Gueboroa Island only dimly. But numerous fires had been kindled on the beach, attesting that the natives had no thoughts of leaving it.

For several hours I was left to myself, sometimes musing on the islanders – but no longer fearing them because the captain's unflappable confidence had won me over – and sometimes forgetting them to marvel at the splendours of this tropical night. My memories took wing toward France, in the wake of those zodiacal stars due to twinkle over it in a few hours. The moon shone in the midst of the constellations at their zenith. I then remembered that this loyal, good-natured satellite would return to this same place the day after tomorrow, to raise the tide and tear the *Nautilus* from its coral bed. Near midnight, seeing that all was quiet over the darkened waves as well as under the waterside trees, I repaired to my cabin and fell into a peaceful sleep.

The night passed without mishap. No doubt the Papuans had been frightened off by the mere sight of this monster aground in the bay, because our hatches stayed open, offering easy access to the *Nautilus*'s interior.

At six o'clock in the morning, January 8, I climbed onto the platform. The morning shadows were lifting. The island was soon on view through the dissolving mists, first its beaches, then its summits.

The islanders were still there, in greater numbers than on the day before, perhaps 500 or 600 of them. Taking advantage of the low tide, some of them had moved forward over the heads of coral to within two cable lengths of the *Nautilus*. I could easily distinguish them. They obviously were true Papuans, men of fine stock, athletic in build, forehead high and broad, nose large but not flat, teeth white. Their woolly, red-tinted hair was in sharp contrast to their bodies, which were black and glistening like those of Nubians. Beneath their pierced, distended earlobes there dangled strings of beads made from bone. Generally these savages were naked. I noted some women among them, dressed from hip to knee in grass skirts held up by belts made of vegetation. Some of the chieftains adorned their necks with crescents and with necklaces made from beads of red and white glass. Armed with bows, arrows and shields, nearly all of them carried from their shoulders a sort of net, which held those polished stones their slings hurl with such dexterity.

One of these chieftains came fairly close to the *Nautilus*, examining it with care. He must have been a 'mado' of high rank, because he paraded in a mat of banana leaves that had ragged edges and was accented with bright colours.

I could easily have picked off this islander, he stood at such close range; but I thought it best to wait for an actual show of hostility. Between Europeans and savages, it's acceptable for Europeans to shoot back but not to attack first.

During this whole time of low tide, the islanders lurked near the *Nautilus*, but they weren't boisterous. I often heard them repeat the word 'assai,' and from their gestures I understood they were inviting me to go ashore, an invitation I felt obliged to decline.

So the skiff didn't leave shipside that day, much to the displeasure of Mr Land who couldn't complete his provisions. The adroit Canadian spent his time preparing the meat and flour products he had brought from Gueboroa Island. As for the savages, they went back to shore near 11 o'clock in the morning, when the heads of coral began to disappear under the waves of the rising tide. But I saw their numbers swell considerably on the beach. It was likely that they had come from neighbouring islands or from the mainland of Papua proper. However, I didn't see one local dugout canoe.

Having nothing better to do, I decided to dredge these beautiful, clear waters, which exhibited a profusion of shells, zoophytes and open-sea plants. Besides, it was the last day the *Nautilus* would spend in these waterways, if, tomorrow, it still floated off to the open sea as Captain Nemo had promised.

So I summoned Conseil, who brought me a small, light dragnet similar to those used in oyster fishing.

'What about these savages?' Conseil asked me. 'With all due respect to master, they don't strike me as very wicked!'

'They're cannibals even so, my boy.'

'A person can be both a cannibal and a decent man,' Conseil replied, 'just as a person can be both gluttonous and honourable. The one doesn't exclude the other.'

'Fine, Conseil! And I agree that there are honourable cannibals who decently devour their prisoners. However, I'm opposed to being devoured, even in all decency, so I'll keep on my guard, especially since the *Nautilus*'s commander seems to be taking no precautions. And now let's get to work!'

For two hours our fishing proceeded energetically but without bringing up any rarities. Our dragnet was filled with Midas abalone, harp shells, obelisk snails and especially the finest hammer shells I had seen to that day. We also gathered in a few sea cucumbers, some pearl oysters and a dozen small turtles that we saved for the ship's pantry.

But just when I least expected it, I laid my hands on a wonder, a natural deformity I'd have to call it, something very seldom encountered. Conseil had just made a cast of the dragnet, and his gear had come back up loaded with a variety of fairly ordinary seashells, when suddenly he saw me plunge my arms swiftly into the net, pull out a shelled animal and give a conchological yell, in other words, the most piercing yell a human throat can produce.

'Eh? What happened to master?' Conseil asked, very startled. 'Did master get bitten?'

'No, my boy, but I'd gladly have sacrificed a finger for such a find!'

'What find?'

'This shell,' I said, displaying the subject of my triumph.

'But that's simply an olive shell of the "tent olive" species, genus *Oliva*, order *Pectinibranchia*, class *Gastropoda*, branch *Mollusca*—'

'Yes, yes, Conseil! But instead of coiling from right to left, this olive shell rolls from left to right!'

'It can't be!' Conseil exclaimed.

'Yes, my boy, it's a left-handed shell!'

'A left-handed shell!' Conseil repeated, his heart pounding.

'Look at its spiral!'

'Oh, master can trust me on this,' Conseil said, taking the valuable shell in trembling hands, 'but never have I felt such excitement!'

And there was good reason to be excited! In fact, as naturalists have ventured to observe, 'dextrality' is a well-known law of nature. In their rotational and orbital movements, stars and their satellites go from right to left. Man uses his right hand more often than his left, and consequently his various instruments and equipment (staircases, locks, watch springs, etc.) are designed to be used in a right-to-left manner. Now then, nature has generally obeyed this law in coiling her shells. They're right-handed with only rare exceptions, and when by chance a shell's spiral is left-handed, collectors will pay its weight in gold for it.

So Conseil and I were deep in the contemplation of our treasure, and I was solemnly promising myself to enrich the Paris Museum with it, when an ill-timed stone, hurled by one of the islanders, whizzed over and shattered the valuable object in Conseil's hands.

I gave a yell of despair! Conseil pounced on his rifle and aimed at a savage swinging a sling just ten metres away from him. I tried to stop him, but his shot went off and shattered a bracelet of amulets dangling from the islander's arm.

'Conseil!' I shouted. 'Conseil!'

'Eh? What? Didn't master see that this man-eater initiated the attack?'

'A shell isn't worth a human life!' I told him.

'Oh, the rascal!' Conseil exclaimed. 'I'd rather he cracked my shoulder!'

Conseil was in dead earnest, but I didn't subscribe to his views. However, the situation had changed in only a short time and we hadn't noticed. Now some 20 dugout canoes were surrounding the *Nautilus*. Hollowed from tree trunks, these dugouts were long, narrow, and well designed for speed, keeping their balance by means of two bamboo poles that floated on the surface of the water. They were manoeuvred by skilful, half-naked paddlers, and I viewed their advance with definite alarm.

It was obvious these Papuans had already entered into relations with Europeans and knew their ships. But this long, iron cylinder lying in the bay, with no masts or funnels – what were they to make of it? Nothing good, because at first they kept it at a respectful distance. However, seeing that it stayed motionless, they regained confidence little by little and tried to become more familiar with it. Now then, it was precisely this familiarity that we needed to prevent. Since our weapons made no sound when they went off, they would have only a moderate effect on these islanders, who reputedly respect nothing but noisy mechanisms. Without thunderclaps, lightning bolts would be much less frightening, although the danger lies in the flash, not the noise.

Just then the dugout canoes drew nearer to the *Nautilus*, and a cloud of arrows burst over us.

'Fire and brimstone, it's hailing!' Conseil said. 'And poisoned hail perhaps!'

'We've got to alert Captain Nemo,' I said, re-entering the hatch.

I went below to the lounge. I found no one there. I ventured a knock at the door opening into the captain's stateroom.

The word 'Enter!' answered me. I did so and found Captain Nemo busy with calculations in which there was no shortage of X and other algebraic signs.

'Am I disturbing you?' I said out of politeness.

'Correct, Professor Aronnax,' the captain answered me. 'But I imagine you have pressing reasons for looking me up?'

'Very pressing. Native dugout canoes are surrounding us, and in a few minutes we're sure to be assaulted by several hundred savages.'

'Ah!' Captain Nemo put in serenely. 'They've come in their dugouts?'

'Yes, sir.'

'Well, sir, closing the hatches should do the trick.'

'Precisely, and that's what I came to tell you—'

'Nothing easier,' Captain Nemo said.

And he pressed an electric button, transmitting an order to the crew's quarters.

'There, sir, all under control!' he told me after a few moments. 'The skiff is in place and the hatches are closed. I don't imagine you're worried that these gentlemen will stave in walls that shells from your frigate couldn't breach?'

'No, captain, but one danger still remains.'

'What's that, sir?'

'Tomorrow at about this time, we'll need to reopen the hatches to renew the *Nautilus*'s air.'

'No argument, sir, since our craft breathes in the manner favoured by cetaceans.'

'But if these Papuans are occupying the platform at that moment, I don't see how you can prevent them from entering.'

'Then, sir, you assume they'll board the ship?'

'I'm certain of it.'

'Well, sir, let them come aboard. I see no reason to prevent them. Deep down they're just poor devils, these Papuans, and I don't want my visit to Gueboroa Island to cost the life of a single one of these unfortunate people!'

On this note I was about to withdraw; but Captain Nemo detained me and invited me to take a seat next to him. He questioned me with interest on our excursions ashore and on our hunting, but seemed not to understand the Canadian's passionate craving for red meat. Then our conversation skimmed various subjects, and without being more forthcoming, Captain Nemo proved more affable.

Among other things, we came to talk of the *Nautilus*'s circumstances, aground in the same strait where Captain Dumont d'Urville had nearly miscarried. Then, pertinent to this:

'He was one of your great seamen,' the captain told me, 'one of your shrewdest navigators, that d'Urville! He was the Frenchman's Captain Cook. A man wise but unlucky! Braving the ice banks of the South Pole, the coral of Oceania, the cannibals of the Pacific, only to perish wretchedly in a train wreck! If that energetic man was able to think about his life in its last seconds, imagine what his final thoughts must have been!'

As he spoke, Captain Nemo seemed deeply moved, an emotion I felt was to his credit.

Then, chart in hand, we returned to the deeds of the French navigator: his voyages to circumnavigate the globe, his double attempt at the South Pole, which led to his discovery of the Adélie Coast and the Louis-Philippe Peninsula, finally his hydrographic surveys of the chief islands in Oceania.

'What your d'Urville did on the surface of the sea,' Captain Nemo told me, 'I've done in the ocean's interior, but more easily, more completely than he. Constantly tossed about by hurricanes, the *Zealous* and the new *Astrolabe* couldn't compare with the *Nautilus*, a quiet work room truly at rest in the midst of the waters!'

'Even so, captain,' I said, 'there is one major similarity between Dumont d'Urville's sloops of war and the *Nautilus*.'

'What's that, sir?'

'Like them, the *Nautilus* has run aground!'

'The *Nautilus* is not aground, sir,' Captain Nemo replied icily. 'The *Nautilus* was built to rest on the ocean floor, and I don't need to undertake the arduous labours, the manoeuvres d'Urville had to attempt in order to float off his sloops of war. The *Zealous* and the new *Astrolabe* wellnigh perished, but my *Nautilus* is in no danger. Tomorrow, on the day stated and at the hour stated, the tide will peacefully lift it off, and it will resume its navigating through the seas.'

'Captain,' I said, 'I don't doubt—'

'Tomorrow,' Captain Nemo added, standing up, 'tomorrow at 2:40 in the afternoon, the *Nautilus* will float off and exit the Torres Strait undamaged.'

Pronouncing these words in an extremely sharp tone, Captain Nemo gave me a curt bow. This was my dismissal, and I re-entered my stateroom.

There I found Conseil, who wanted to know the upshot of my interview with the captain.

'My boy,' I replied, 'when I expressed the belief that these Papuan natives were a threat to his *Nautilus*, the captain answered me with great irony. So I've just one thing to say to you: have faith in him and sleep in peace.'

'Master has no need for my services?'

'No, my friend. What's Ned Land up to?'

'Begging master's indulgence,' Conseil replied, 'but our friend Ned is concocting a kangaroo pie that will be the eighth wonder!'

I was left to myself; I went to bed but slept pretty poorly. I kept hearing noises from the savages, who were stamping on the platform and letting out deafening yells. The night passed in this way, without the crew ever emerging from their usual inertia. They were no more disturbed by the presence of these man-eaters than soldiers in an armoured fortress are troubled by ants running over the armour plate.

I got up at six o'clock in the morning. The hatches weren't open. So the air inside hadn't been renewed; but the air tanks were kept full for any eventuality and would function appropriately to shoot a few cubic metres of oxygen into the *Nautilus*'s thin atmosphere.

I worked in my stateroom until noon without seeing Captain Nemo even for an instant. Nobody on board seemed to be making any preparations for departure.

I still waited for a while, then I made my way to the main lounge. Its timepiece marked 2:30. In ten minutes the tide would reach its maximum elevation, and if Captain Nemo hadn't made a rash promise, the *Nautilus* would immediately break free. If not, many months might pass before it could leave its coral bed.

But some preliminary vibrations could soon be felt over the boat's hull. I heard its plating grind against the limestone roughness of that coral base.

At 2:35 Captain Nemo appeared in the lounge.

'We're about to depart,' he said.

'Ah!' I put in.

'I've given orders to open the hatches.'

'What about the Papuans?'

'What about them?' Captain Nemo replied, with a light shrug of his shoulders.

'Won't they come inside the *Nautilus*?'

'How will they manage that?'

'By jumping down the hatches you're about to open.'

'Professor Aronnax,' Captain Nemo replied serenely, 'the *Nautilus*'s hatches aren't to be entered in that fashion even when they're open.'

I gaped at the captain.

'You don't understand?' he said to me.

'Not in the least.'

'Well, come along and you'll see!'

I headed to the central companionway. There, very puzzled, Ned Land and Conseil watched the crewmen opening the hatches, while a frightful clamour and furious shouts resounded outside.

The hatch lids fell back onto the outer plating. Twenty horrible faces appeared. But when the first islander laid hands on the companionway railing, he was flung backward by some invisible power, lord knows what! He ran off, howling in terror and wildly prancing around.

Ten of his companions followed him. All ten met the same fate.

Conseil was in ecstasy. Carried away by his violent instincts, Ned Land leaped up the companionway. But as soon as his hands seized the railing, he was thrown backward in his turn.

'Damnation!' he exclaimed. 'I've been struck by a lightning bolt!'

These words explained everything to me. It wasn't just a railing that led to the platform, it was a metal cable fully charged with the ship's electricity. Anyone who touched it got a fearsome shock – and such a shock would have been fatal if Captain Nemo had thrown the full current from his equipment into this conducting cable! It could honestly be said that he had stretched between himself and his assailants a network of electricity no one could clear with impunity.

Meanwhile, crazed with terror, the unhinged Papuans beat a retreat. As for us, half laughing, we massaged and comforted poor Ned Land, who was swearing like one possessed.

But just then, lifted off by the tide's final undulations, the *Nautilus* left its coral bed at exactly that fortieth minute pinpointed by the captain. Its propeller churned the waves with lazy majesty. Gathering speed little by little, the ship navigated on the surface of the ocean, and safe and sound, it left behind the dangerous narrows of the Torres Strait.

CHAPTER 23

'Aegri Somnia'

THE FOLLOWING DAY, January 10, the *Nautilus* resumed its travels in midwater but at a remarkable speed that I estimated to be at least 35 miles per hour. The propeller was going so fast I could neither follow nor count its revolutions.

I thought about how this marvellous electric force not only gave motion, heat and light to the *Nautilus* but even protected it against outside attack, transforming it into a sacred ark no profane hand could touch without being blasted; my wonderment was boundless, and it went from the submersible itself to the engineer who had created it.

We were travelling due west and on January 11 we doubled Cape Wessel, located in longitude 135° and latitude 10° north, the western tip of the Gulf of Carpentaria. Reefs were still numerous but more widely scattered and were fixed on the chart with the greatest accuracy. The *Nautilus* easily avoided the Money breakers to port and the Victoria reefs to starboard, positioned at longitude 130° on the tenth parallel, which we went along rigorously.

On January 13, arriving in the Timor Sea, Captain Nemo raised the island of that name at longitude 122°. This island, whose surface area measures 1,625 square leagues, is governed by rajahs. These aristocrats deem themselves the sons of crocodiles, in other words, descendants with the most exalted origins to which a human being can lay claim. Accordingly, their scaly ancestors infest the island's rivers and are the subjects of special veneration. They are sheltered, nurtured, flattered, pampered and offered a ritual diet of nubile maidens; and woe to the foreigner who lifts a finger against these sacred *saurians*.

But the *Nautilus* wanted nothing to do with these nasty animals. Timor Island was visible for barely an instant at noon while the chief officer determined his position. I also caught only a glimpse of little Roti Island, part of this same group, whose women have a well-established reputation for beauty in the Malaysian marketplace.

After our position fix, the *Nautilus*'s latitude bearings were modulated to the southwest. Our prow pointed to the Indian Ocean. Where would Captain Nemo's fancies take us? Would he head up to the shores of Asia? Would he pull nearer to the beaches of Europe? Unlikely choices for a man who avoided populated areas! So would he go down south? Would he double the Cape of Good Hope, then Cape Horn, and push on to the Antarctic pole? Finally, would he return to the seas of the Pacific, where his *Nautilus* could navigate freely and easily? Time would tell.

After cruising along the Cartier, Hibernia, Seringapatam and Scott reefs, the solid element's last exertions against the liquid element, we were beyond all sight of shore by January 14. The *Nautilus* slowed down in an odd manner, and very unpredictable in its ways, it sometimes swam in the midst of the waters, sometimes drifted on their surface.

During this phase of our voyage, Captain Nemo conducted interesting experiments on the different temperatures in various strata of the sea. Under ordinary conditions, such readings are obtained using some pretty complicated instruments whose findings are dubious to say the least, whether they're thermometric sounding lines, whose glass often shatters under the water's pressure, or those devices based on the varying resistance of metals to electric currents. The results so obtained can't be adequately double-checked. By contrast, Captain Nemo would seek the sea's temperature by going himself into its depths, and when he placed his thermometer in contact with the various layers of liquid, he found the sought-for degree immediately and with certainty.

And so, by loading up its ballast tanks, or by sinking obliquely with its slanting fins, the *Nautilus* successively reached depths of 3,000, 4,000, 5,000, 7,000, 9,000, and 10,000 metres, and the ultimate conclusion from these experiments was that, in all latitudes, the sea had a permanent temperature of 4.5° centigrade at a depth of 1,000 metres.

I watched these experiments with the most intense fascination. Captain Nemo brought a real passion to them. I often wondered why he took these observations. Were they for the benefit of his fellow man? It was unlikely, because sooner or later his work would perish with him in some unknown sea! Unless he intended the results of his experiments for me. But that meant this strange voyage of mine would come to an end, and no such end was in sight.

Be that as it may, Captain Nemo also introduced me to the different data he had obtained on the relative densities of the water in our globe's chief seas. From this news I derived some personal enlightenment having nothing to do with science.

It happened the morning of January 15. The captain, with whom I was strolling on the platform, asked me if I knew how salt water differs in density from sea to sea. I said no, adding that there was a lack of rigorous scientific observations on this subject.

'I've taken such observations,' he told me, 'and I can vouch for their reliability.'

'Fine,' I replied, 'but the *Nautilus* lives in a separate world, and the secrets of its scientists don't make their way ashore.'

'You're right, professor,' he told me after a few moments of silence. 'This is a separate world. It's as alien to the earth as the planets accompanying our globe around the sun, and we'll never become familiar with the work of scientists on Saturn or Jupiter. But since fate has linked our two lives, I can reveal the results of my observations to you.'

'I'm all attention, captain.'

'You're aware, professor, that salt water is denser than fresh water, but this density isn't uniform. In essence, if I represent the density of fresh water by 1.000, then I find 1.028 for the waters of the Atlantic, 1.026 for the waters of the Pacific, 1.030 for the waters of the Mediterranean—'

Aha, I thought, so he ventures into the Mediterranean?

'—1.018 for the waters of the Ionian Sea, and 1.029 for the waters of the Adriatic.'

Assuredly, the *Nautilus* didn't avoid the heavily travelled seas of Europe, and from this insight I concluded that the ship would take us back – perhaps very soon – to more civilised shores. I expected Ned Land to greet this news with unfeigned satisfaction.

For several days our work hours were spent in all sorts of

experiments, on the degree of salinity in waters of different depths, or on their electric properties, colouration, and transparency, and in every instance Captain Nemo displayed an ingenuity equalled only by his graciousness toward me. Then I saw no more of him for some days and again lived on board in seclusion.

On January 16 the *Nautilus* seemed to have fallen asleep just a few metres beneath the surface of the water. Its electric equipment had been turned off, and the motionless propeller let it ride with the waves. I assumed that the crew were busy with interior repairs, required by the engine's strenuous mechanical action.

My companions and I then witnessed an unusual sight. The panels in the lounge were open, and since the *Nautilus*'s beacon was off, a hazy darkness reigned in the midst of the waters. Covered with heavy clouds, the stormy sky gave only the faintest light to the ocean's upper strata.

I was observing the state of the sea under these conditions, and even the largest fish were nothing more than ill-defined shadows, when the *Nautilus* was suddenly transferred into broad daylight. At first I thought the beacon had gone back on and was casting its electric light into the liquid mass. I was mistaken, and after a hasty examination I discovered my error.

The *Nautilus* had drifted into the midst of some phosphorescent strata, which, in this darkness, came off as positively dazzling. This effect was caused by myriads of tiny, luminous animals whose brightness increased when they glided over the metal hull of our submersible. In the midst of these luminous sheets of water, I then glimpsed flashes of light, like those seen inside a blazing furnace from streams of molten lead or from masses of metal brought to a white heat – flashes so intense that certain areas of the light became shadows by comparison, in a fiery setting from which every shadow should seemingly have been banished. No, this was no longer the calm emission of our usual lighting! This light throbbed with unprecedented vigour and activity! You sensed that it was alive!

In essence, it was a cluster of countless open-sea *infusoria*, of *noctiluca* an eighth of an inch wide, actual globules of transparent jelly equipped with a threadlike tentacle, up to 25,000 of which have been counted in 30 cubic centimetres of water. And the power of their light was increased by those glimmers unique to medusas, starfish, common jellyfish, angel-wing clams and other phosphorescent zoophytes, which were saturated with grease from organic matter decomposed by the sea, and perhaps with mucus secreted by fish.

For several hours the *Nautilus* drifted in this brilliant tide, and our wonderment grew when we saw huge marine animals cavorting in it, like the fire-dwelling salamanders of myth. In the midst of these flames that didn't burn, I could see swift, elegant porpoises, the tireless pranksters of the seas, and sailfish three metres long, those shrewd heralds of hurricanes, whose fearsome broadswords sometimes banged against the lounge window. Then smaller fish appeared: miscellaneous triggerfish, leather jacks, unicornfish and a hundred others that left stripes on this luminous atmosphere in their course.

Some magic lay behind this dazzling sight! Perhaps some atmospheric condition had intensified this phenomenon? Perhaps a storm had been unleashed on the surface of the waves? But only a few metres down, the *Nautilus* felt no tempest's fury, and the ship rocked peacefully in the midst of the calm waters.

And so it went, some new wonder constantly delighting us. Conseil observed and classified his zoophytes, articulates, molluscs and fish. The days passed quickly, and I no longer kept track of them. Ned, as usual, kept looking for changes of pace from our standard fare. Like actual snails, we were at home in our shell, and I can vouch that it's easy to turn into a full-fledged snail.

So this way of living began to seem simple and natural to us, and we no longer envisioned a different lifestyle on the surface of the planet earth, when something happened to remind us of our strange circumstances.

On January 18 the *Nautilus* lay in longitude 105° and latitude 15° south. The weather was threatening, the sea rough and billowy. The wind was blowing a strong gust from the east. The barometer, which had been falling for some days, forecast an approaching struggle of the elements.

I had climbed onto the platform just as the chief officer was taking his readings of hour angles. Out of habit I waited for him to pronounce his daily phrase. But that day it was replaced by a different phrase, just as incomprehensible. Almost at once I saw Captain Nemo appear, lift his spyglass and inspect the horizon.

For some minutes the captain stood motionless, rooted to the spot contained within the field of his lens. Then he lowered his spyglass and exchanged about ten words with his chief officer. The latter seemed to be in the grip of an excitement he tried in vain to control. More in command of himself, Captain Nemo remained cool. Furthermore, he seemed to be raising certain objections that his chief officer kept answering with flat assurances. At least that's what I gathered from their differences in tone and gesture.

As for me, I stared industriously in the direction under observation but without spotting a thing. Sky and water merged into a perfectly clean horizon line.

Meanwhile Captain Nemo strolled from one end of the platform to the other, not glancing at me, perhaps not even seeing me. His step was firm but less regular than usual. Sometimes he would stop, cross his arms over his chest and observe the sea. What could he be looking for over that immense expanse? By then the *Nautilus* lay hundreds of miles from the nearest coast!

The chief officer kept lifting his spyglass and stubbornly examining the horizon, walking up and down, stamping his foot, in his nervous agitation a sharp contrast to his superior.

But this mystery would inevitably be cleared up, and soon, because Captain Nemo gave orders to increase speed; at once the engine stepped up its drive power, setting the propeller in swifter rotation.

Just then the chief officer drew the captain's attention anew. The latter interrupted his strolling and aimed his spyglass at the point indicated. He observed it a good while. As for me, deeply puzzled, I went below to the lounge and brought back an excellent long-range telescope I habitually used. Leaning my elbows on the beacon housing, which jutted from the stern of the platform, I got set to scour that whole stretch of sky and sea.

But no sooner had I peered into the eyepiece than the instrument was snatched from my hands.

I spun around. Captain Nemo was standing before me, but I almost didn't recognise him. His facial features were transfigured. Gleaming with dark fire, his eyes had shrunk beneath his frowning brow. His teeth were half bared. His rigid body, clenched fists, and head drawn between his shoulders, all attested to a fierce hate breathing from every pore. He didn't move. My spyglass fell from his hand and rolled at his feet.

Had I accidentally caused these symptoms of anger? Did this incomprehensible individual think I had detected some secret forbidden to guests on the *Nautilus*?

No! I wasn't the subject of his hate because he wasn't even looking at me; his eyes stayed stubbornly focused on that inscrutable point of the horizon.

Finally Captain Nemo regained his self-control. His facial appearance, so profoundly changed, now resumed its usual calm. He addressed a few words to his chief officer in their strange language, then he turned to me:

'Professor Aronnax,' he told me in a tone of some urgency, 'I ask that you now honour one of the binding agreements between us.'

'Which one, captain?'

'You and your companions must be placed in confinement until I see fit to set you free.'

'You're in command,' I answered, gaping at him. 'But may I address a question to you?'

'You may not, sir.'

After that, I stopped objecting and started obeying, since resistance was useless.

I went below to the cabin occupied by Ned Land and Conseil, and I informed them of the captain's decision. I'll let the reader decide how this news was received by the Canadian. In any case, there was no time for explanations. Four crewmen were waiting at the door, and they led us to the cell where we had spent our first night aboard the *Nautilus*.

Ned Land tried to lodge a complaint, but the only answer he got was a door shut in his face.

'Will master tell me what this means?' Conseil asked me.

I told my companions what had happened. They were as astonished as I was, but no wiser.

Then I sank into deep speculation, and Captain Nemo's strange facial seizure kept haunting me. I was incapable of connecting two ideas in logical order, and I had strayed into the most absurd hypotheses, when I was snapped out of my mental struggles by these words from Ned Land:

'Well, look here! Lunch is served!'

Indeed, the table had been laid. Apparently Captain Nemo had given this order at the same time he commanded the *Nautilus* to pick up speed.

'Will master allow me to make him a recommendation?' Conseil asked me.

'Yes, my boy,' I replied.

'Well, master needs to eat his lunch! It's prudent, because we have no idea what the future holds.'

'You're right, Conseil.'

'Unfortunately,' Ned Land said, 'they've only given us the standard menu.'

'Ned my friend,' Conseil answered, 'what would you say if they'd given us no lunch at all?'

This dose of sanity cut the harpooner's complaints clean off.

We sat down at the table. Our meal proceeded pretty much in silence. I ate very little. Conseil, everlastingly prudent, 'force-fed' himself; and despite the menu, Ned Land didn't waste a bite. Then, lunch over, each of us propped himself in a corner.

Just then the luminous globe lighting our cell went out, leaving us in profound darkness. Ned Land soon dozed off, and to my astonishment, Conseil also fell into a heavy slumber. I was wondering what could have caused this urgent need for sleep, when I felt a dense torpor saturate my brain. I tried to keep my eyes open, but they closed in spite of me. I was in the grip of anguished hallucinations. Obviously some sleep-inducing substance had been laced into the food we'd just eaten! So imprisonment wasn't enough to conceal Captain Nemo's plans from us – sleep was needed as well!

Then I heard the hatches close. The sea's undulations, which had been creating a gentle rocking motion, now ceased. Had the *Nautilus* left the surface of the ocean? Was it re-entering the motionless strata deep in the sea?

I tried to fight off this drowsiness. It was impossible. My breathing grew weaker. I felt a mortal chill freeze my dull, nearly paralysed limbs.

Like little domes of lead, my lids fell over my eyes. I couldn't raise them. A morbid sleep, full of hallucinations, seized my whole being. Then the visions disappeared and left me in utter oblivion.

CHAPTER 24

The Coral Realm

THE NEXT DAY I woke up with my head unusually clear. Much to my surprise, I was in my stateroom. No doubt my companions had been put back in their cabin without noticing it any more than I had. Like me, they would have no idea what took place during the night, and to unravel this mystery I could count only on some future happenstance.

I then considered leaving my stateroom. Was I free or still a prisoner? Perfectly free. I opened my door, headed down the gangways, and climbed the central companionway. Hatches that had been closed the day before were now open. I arrived on the platform.

Ned Land and Conseil were there waiting for me. I questioned them. They knew nothing. Lost in a heavy sleep of which they had no memory, they were quite startled to be back in their cabin.

As for the *Nautilus*, it seemed as tranquil and mysterious as ever. It was cruising on the surface of the waves at a moderate speed. Nothing seemed to have changed on board.

Ned Land observed the sea with his penetrating eyes. It was deserted. The Canadian sighted nothing new on the horizon, neither sail nor shore. A breeze was blowing noisily from the west, and dishevelled by the wind, long billows made the submersible roll very noticeably.

After renewing its air, the *Nautilus* stayed at an average depth of 15 metres, enabling it to return quickly to the surface of the waves. And, contrary to custom, it executed such a manoeuvre several times during that day of January 19. The chief officer would then climb onto the platform, and his usual phrase would ring through the ship's interior.

As for Captain Nemo, he didn't appear. Of the other men on board, I saw only my emotionless steward, who served me with his usual mute efficiency.

Near two o'clock I was busy organizing my notes in the lounge, when the captain opened the door and appeared. I bowed to him. He gave me an almost imperceptible bow in return, without saying a word to me. I resumed my work, hoping he might give me some explanation of the previous afternoon's events. He did nothing of the sort. I stared at him. His face looked exhausted; his reddened eyes hadn't been refreshed by sleep; his facial features expressed profound sadness, real chagrin. He walked up and down, sat and stood, picked up a book at random, discarded it immediately, consulted his instruments without taking his customary notes, and seemed unable to rest easy for an instant.

Finally he came over to me and said:

'Are you a physician, Professor Aronnax?'

This inquiry was so unexpected that I stared at him a good while without replying.

'Are you a physician?' he repeated. 'Several of your scientific colleagues took their degrees in medicine, such as Gratiolet, Moquin-Tandon, and others.'

'That's right,' I said, 'I am a doctor, I used to be on call at the hospitals. I was in practice for several years before joining the museum.'

'Excellent, sir.'

My reply obviously pleased Captain Nemo. But not knowing what he was driving at, I waited for further questions, ready to reply as circumstances dictated.

'Professor Aronnax,' the captain said to me, 'would you consent to give your medical attentions to one of my men?'

'Someone is sick?'

'Yes.'

'I'm ready to go with you.'

'Come.'

I admit that my heart was pounding. Lord knows why, but I saw a definite connection between this sick crewman and yesterday's happenings, and the mystery of those events concerned me at least as much as the man's sickness.

Captain Nemo led me to the *Nautilus*'s stern and invited me into a cabin located next to the sailors' quarters.

On a bed there lay a man some 40 years old, with strongly moulded features, the very image of an Anglo-Saxon.

I bent over him. Not only was he sick, he was wounded. Swathed in blood-soaked linen, his head was resting on a folded pillow. I undid the linen bandages, while the wounded man gazed with great staring eyes and let me proceed without making a single complaint.

It was a horrible wound. The cranium had been smashed open by some blunt instrument, leaving the naked brains exposed, and the cerebral matter had suffered deep abrasions. Blood clots had formed in this dissolving mass, taking on the colour of wine dregs. Both contusion and concussion of the brain had occurred. The sick man's breathing was laboured, and muscle spasms quivered in his face. Cerebral inflammation was complete and had brought on a paralysis of movement and sensation.

I took the wounded man's pulse. It was intermittent. The body's extremities were already growing cold, and I saw that death was approaching without any possibility of my holding it in check. After dressing the poor man's wound, I redid the linen bandages around his head, and I turned to Captain Nemo.

'How did he get this wound?' I asked him.

'That's not important,' the captain replied evasively. 'The *Nautilus* suffered a collision that cracked one of the engine levers, and it struck this man. My chief officer was standing beside him. This man leaped forward to intercept the blow. A brother lays down his life for his brother, a friend for his friend, what could be simpler? That's the law for everyone on board the *Nautilus*. But what's your diagnosis of his condition?'

I hesitated to speak my mind.

'You may talk freely,' the captain told me. 'This man doesn't understand French.'

I took a last look at the wounded man, then I replied:

'This man will be dead in two hours.'

'Nothing can save him?'

'Nothing.'

Captain Nemo clenched his fists, and tears slid from his eyes, which I had thought incapable of weeping.

For a few moments more I observed the dying man, whose life was ebbing little by little. He grew still more pale under the electric light that bathed his deathbed. I looked at his intelligent head, furrowed with premature wrinkles that misfortune, perhaps misery, had etched long before. I was hoping to detect the secret of his life in the last words that might escape from his lips!

'You may go, Professor Aronnax,' Captain Nemo told me.

I left the captain in the dying man's cabin and I repaired to my stateroom, very moved by this scene. All day long I was aquiver with gruesome forebodings. That night I slept poorly, and between my fitful dreams I thought I heard a distant moaning, like a funeral dirge. Was it a prayer for the dead, murmured in that language I couldn't understand?

The next morning I climbed on deck. Captain Nemo was already there. As soon as he saw me, he came over.

'Professor,' he said to me, 'would it be convenient for you to make an underwater excursion today?'

'With my companions?' I asked.

'If they're agreeable.'

'We're yours to command, captain.'

'Then kindly put on your diving suits.'

As for the dead or dying man, he hadn't come into the picture. I rejoined Ned Land and Conseil. I informed them of Captain Nemo's proposition. Conseil was eager to accept, and this time the Canadian proved perfectly amenable to going with us.

It was eight o'clock in the morning. By 8:30 we were suited up for this new stroll and equipped with our two devices for lighting and breathing. The double door opened, and accompanied by Captain Nemo with a dozen crewmen following, we set foot on the firm seafloor where the *Nautilus* was resting, ten metres down.

A gentle slope gravitated to an uneven bottom whose depth was about 15 fathoms. This bottom was completely different from the one I had visited during my first excursion under the waters of the Pacific Ocean. Here I saw no fine-grained sand, no underwater prairies, not one open-sea forest. I immediately recognised the wondrous region in which Captain Nemo did the honours that day. It was the coral realm.

In the zoophyte branch, class *Alcyonaria*, one finds the order *Gorgonaria*, which contains three groups: sea fans, isidian polyps and coral polyps. It's in this last that precious coral belongs, an unusual substance that, at different times, has been classified in the mineral, vegetable and animal kingdoms. Medicine to the ancients, jewellery to the moderns, it wasn't decisively placed in the animal kingdom until 1694, by Peysonnel of Marseilles.

A coral is a unit of tiny animals assembled over a polypary that's brittle and stony in nature. These polyps have a unique generating mechanism that reproduces them via the budding process, and they have an individual existence while also participating in a communal life. Hence they embody a sort of natural socialism. I was familiar with the latest research on this bizarre zoophyte – which turns to stone while taking on a tree form, as some naturalists have very aptly observed – and nothing could have been more fascinating to me than to visit one of these petrified forests that nature has planted on the bottom of the sea.

We turned on our Ruhmkorff devices and went along a coral shoal in the process of forming, which, given time, will someday close off this whole part of the Indian Ocean. Our path was bordered by hopelessly tangled bushes, formed from snarls of shrubs all covered with little star-shaped, white-streaked flowers. Only, contrary to plants on shore, these tree forms become attached to rocks on the seafloor by heading from top to bottom.

Our lights produced a thousand delightful effects while playing over these brightly coloured boughs. I fancied I saw these cylindrical, membrane-filled tubes trembling beneath the water's undulations. I was tempted to gather their fresh petals, which were adorned with delicate tentacles, some newly in bloom, others barely opened, while nimble fish with fluttering fins brushed past them like flocks of birds. But if my hands came near the moving flowers of these sensitive, lively creatures, an alarm would instantly sound throughout the colony. The white petals retracted into their red sheaths, the flowers vanished before my eyes, and the bush changed into a chunk of stony nipples.

Sheer chance had placed me in the presence of the most valuable specimens of this zoophyte. This coral was the equal of those fished up from the Mediterranean off the Barbary Coast or the shores of France and Italy. With its bright colours, it lived up to those poetic names of blood flower and blood foam that the industry confers on its finest exhibits. Coral sells for as much as 500 francs per kilogram, and in this locality the liquid strata hid enough to make the fortunes of a whole host of coral fishermen. This valuable substance often merges with other polyparies, forming compact, hopelessly tangled units known as 'macciota,' and I noted some wonderful pink samples of this coral.

But as the bushes shrank, the tree forms magnified. Actual petrified thickets and long alcoves from some fantastic school of architecture kept opening up before our steps. Captain Nemo entered beneath a dark gallery whose gentle slope took us to a depth of 100 metres. The light from our glass coils produced magical effects at times, lingering on the wrinkled roughness of some natural arch, or some overhang suspended like a chandelier, which our lamps flecked with fiery sparks. Amid these shrubs of precious coral, I observed other polyps no less unusual: melita coral, rainbow coral with jointed outgrowths, then a few tufts of genus *Corallina*, some green and others red, actually a type of seaweed encrusted with limestone salts, which, after long disputes, naturalists have finally placed in the vegetable kingdom. But as one intellectual has remarked, 'Here, perhaps, is the actual point where life rises humbly out of slumbering stone, but without breaking away from its crude starting point.'

Finally, after two hours of walking, we reached a depth of about 300 metres, in other words, the lowermost limit at which coral can begin to form. But here it was no longer some isolated bush or a modest grove of low timber. It was an immense forest, huge mineral vegetation, enormous petrified trees linked by garlands of elegant hydras from the genus *Plumularia*, those tropical creepers of the sea, all decked out in shades and gleams. We passed freely under their lofty boughs, lost up in the shadows of the waves, while at our feet organ-pipe coral, stony coral, star coral, fungus coral and sea anemone from the genus *Caryophyllia* formed a carpet of flowers all strewn with dazzling gems.

What an indescribable sight! Oh, if only we could share our feelings! Why were we imprisoned behind these masks of metal and glass! Why were we forbidden to talk with each other! At least let us lead the lives of the fish that populate this liquid element, or better yet, the lives of amphibians, which can spend long hours either at sea or on shore, travelling through their double domain as their whims dictate!

Meanwhile Captain Nemo had called a halt. My companions and

I stopped walking, and turning around I saw the crewmen form a semicircle around their leader. Looking with greater care, I observed that four of them were carrying on their shoulders an object that was oblong in shape.

At this locality we stood in the centre of a huge clearing surrounded by the tall tree forms of this underwater forest. Our lamps cast a sort of brilliant twilight over the area, making inordinately long shadows on the seafloor. Past the boundaries of the clearing, the darkness deepened again, relieved only by little sparkles given off by the sharp crests of coral.

Ned Land and Conseil stood next to me. We stared, and it dawned on me that I was about to witness a strange scene. Observing the seafloor, I saw that it swelled at certain points from low bulges that were encrusted with limestone deposits and arranged with a symmetry that betrayed the hand of man.

In the middle of the clearing, on a pedestal of roughly piled rocks, there stood a cross of coral, extending long arms you would have thought were made of petrified blood.

At a signal from Captain Nemo, one of his men stepped forward and, a few feet from this cross, detached a mattock from his belt and began to dig a hole.

I finally understood! This clearing was a cemetery, this hole a grave, that oblong object the body of the man who must have died during the night! Captain Nemo and his men had come to bury their companion in this communal resting place on the inaccessible ocean floor!

No! My mind was reeling as never before! Never had ideas of such impact raced through my brain! I didn't want to see what my eyes saw!

Meanwhile the grave digging went slowly. Fish fled here and there as their retreat was disturbed. I heard the pick ringing on the limestone soil, its iron tip sometimes giving off sparks when it hit a stray piece of flint on the sea bottom. The hole grew longer, wider, and soon was deep enough to receive the body.

Then the pallbearers approached. Wrapped in white fabric made from filaments of the fan mussel, the body was lowered into its watery grave. Captain Nemo, arms crossed over his chest, knelt in a posture of prayer, as did all the friends of him who had loved them.... My two companions and I bowed reverently.

The grave was then covered over with the rubble dug from the seafloor, and it formed a low mound.

When this was done, Captain Nemo and his men stood up; then they all approached the grave, sank again on bended knee, and extended their hands in a sign of final farewell....

Then the funeral party went back up the path to the *Nautilus*, returning beneath the arches of the forest, through the thickets, along the coral bushes, going steadily higher.

Finally the ship's rays appeared. Their luminous trail guided us to the *Nautilus*. By one o'clock we had returned.

After changing clothes, I climbed onto the platform, and in the grip of dreadfully obsessive thoughts, I sat next to the beacon.

Captain Nemo rejoined me. I stood up and said to him:

'So, as I predicted, that man died during the night?'

'Yes, Professor Aronnax,' Captain Nemo replied.

'And now he rests beside his companions in that coral cemetery?'

'Yes, forgotten by the world but not by us! We dig the graves, then entrust the polyps with sealing away our dead for eternity!'

And with a sudden gesture, the captain hid his face in his clenched fists, vainly trying to hold back a sob. Then he added:

'There lies our peaceful cemetery, hundreds of feet beneath the surface of the waves!'

'At least, captain, your dead can sleep serenely there, out of the reach of sharks!'

'Yes, sir,' Captain Nemo replied solemnly, 'of sharks and men!'

SECOND PART

CHAPTER 1

The Indian Ocean

NOW WE BEGIN the second part of this voyage under the seas. The first ended in that moving scene at the coral cemetery, which left a profound impression on my mind. And so Captain Nemo would live out his life entirely in the heart of this immense sea, and even his grave lay ready in its impenetrable depths. There the last sleep of the *Nautilus*'s occupants, friends bound together in death as in life, would be disturbed by no monster of the deep! 'No man either!' the captain had added.

Always that same fierce, implacable defiance of human society!

As for me, I was no longer content with the hypotheses that satisfied Conseil. That fine lad persisted in seeing the *Nautilus*'s commander as merely one of those unappreciated scientists who repay humanity's indifference with contempt. For Conseil, the captain was still a misunderstood genius who, tired of the world's deceptions, had been driven to take refuge in this inaccessible environment where he was free to follow his instincts. But to my mind, this hypothesis explained only one side of Captain Nemo.

In fact, the mystery of that last afternoon when we were locked in prison and put to sleep, the captain's violent precaution of snatching from my grasp a spyglass poised to scour the horizon, and the fatal wound given that man during some unexplained collision suffered by the *Nautilus*, all led me down a plain trail. No! Captain Nemo wasn't content simply to avoid humanity! His fearsome submersible served not only his quest for freedom, but also, perhaps, it was used in Lord-knows-what schemes of dreadful revenge.

Right now, nothing is clear to me, I still glimpse only glimmers in the dark, and I must limit my pen, as it were, to taking dictation from events.

But nothing binds us to Captain Nemo. He believes that escaping from the *Nautilus* is impossible. We are not even constrained by our word of honour. No promises fetter us. We're simply captives, prisoners masquerading under the name 'guests' for the sake of everyday courtesy. Even so, Ned Land hasn't given up all hope of recovering his freedom. He's sure to take advantage of the first chance that comes his way. No doubt I will do likewise. And yet I will feel some regret at making off with the *Nautilus*'s secrets, so generously unveiled for us by Captain Nemo! Because, ultimately, should we detest or admire this man? Is he the persecutor or the persecuted? And in all honesty, before I leave him forever, I want to finish this underwater tour of the world, whose first stages have been so magnificent. I want to observe the full series of these wonders gathered under the seas of our globe. I want to see what no man has seen yet, even if I must pay for this insatiable curiosity with my life! What are my discoveries to date? Nothing, relatively speaking – since so far we've covered only 6,000 leagues across the Pacific!

Nevertheless, I'm well aware that the *Nautilus* is drawing near to populated shores, and if some chance for salvation becomes available to us, it would be sheer cruelty to sacrifice my companions to my passion for the unknown. I must go with them, perhaps even guide them. But will this opportunity ever arise? The human being, robbed of his free will, craves such an opportunity; but the scientist, forever inquisitive, dreads it.

That day, January 21, 1868, the chief officer went at noon to take the sun's altitude. I climbed onto the platform, lit a cigar, and watched him at work. It seemed obvious to me that this man didn't understand French, because I made several remarks in a loud voice that were bound to provoke him to some involuntary show of interest had he understood them; but he remained mute and emotionless.

While he took his sights with his sextant, one of the *Nautilus*'s sailors – that muscular man who had gone with us to Crespo Island during our first underwater excursion – came up to clean the glass panes of the beacon. I then examined the fittings of this mechanism, whose power was increased a hundredfold by biconvex lenses that were designed like those in a lighthouse and kept its rays productively focused. This electric lamp was so constructed as to yield its maximum illuminating power. In essence, its light was generated in a vacuum, insuring both its steadiness and intensity. Such a vacuum also reduced wear on the graphite points between which the luminous arc expanded.

This was an important saving for Captain Nemo, who couldn't easily renew them. But under these conditions, wear and tear were almost nonexistent.

When the *Nautilus* was ready to resume its underwater travels, I went below again to the lounge. The hatches closed once more, and our course was set due west.

We then ploughed the waves of the Indian Ocean, vast liquid plains with an area of 550,000,000 hectares, whose waters are so transparent it makes you dizzy to lean over their surface. There the *Nautilus* generally drifted at a depth between 100 and 200 metres. It behaved in this way for some days. To anyone without my grand passion for the sea, these hours would surely have seemed long and monotonous; but my daily strolls on the platform where I was revived by the life-giving ocean air, the sights in the rich waters beyond the lounge windows, the books to be read in the library, and the composition of my memoirs, took up all my time and left me without a moment of weariness or boredom.

All in all, we enjoyed a highly satisfactory state of health. The diet on board agreed with us perfectly, and for my part, I could easily have gone without those changes of pace that Ned Land, in a spirit of protest, kept taxing his ingenuity to supply us. What's more, in this constant temperature we didn't even have to worry about catching colds. Besides, the ship had a good stock of the *madrepore Dendrophylia*, known in Provence by the name sea fennel, and a poultice made from the dissolved flesh of its polyps will furnish an excellent cough medicine.

For some days we saw a large number of aquatic birds with webbed feet, known as gulls or sea mews. Some were skilfully slain, and when cooked in a certain fashion, they make a very acceptable platter of water game. Among the great wind riders – carried over long distances from every shore and resting on the waves from their exhausting flights – I spotted some magnificent albatross, birds belonging to the *Longipennes* (long-winged) family, whose discordant calls sound like the braying of an ass. The *Totipalmes* (fully webbed) family was represented by swift frigate birds, nimbly catching fish at the surface, and by numerous tropic birds of the genus Phaeton, among others the red-tailed tropic bird, the size of a pigeon, its white plumage shaded with pink tints that contrasted with its dark-hued wings.

The *Nautilus*'s nets hauled up several types of sea turtle from the *hawksbill* genus with arching backs whose scales are highly prized. Diving easily, these reptiles can remain a good while underwater by closing the fleshy valves located at the external openings of their nasal passages. When they were captured, some hawksbills were still asleep inside their carapaces, a refuge from other marine animals. The flesh of these turtles was nothing memorable, but their eggs made an excellent feast.

As for fish, they always filled us with wonderment when, staring through the open panels, we could unveil the secrets of their aquatic lives. I noted several species I hadn't previously been able to observe.

I'll mention chiefly some trunkfish unique to the Red Sea, the sea of the East Indies, and that part of the ocean washing the coasts of equinoctial America. Like turtles, armadillos, sea urchins, and crustaceans, these fish are protected by armour plate that's neither chalky nor stony but actual bone. Sometimes this armour takes the shape of a solid triangle, sometimes that of a solid quadrangle. Among the triangular type, I noticed some half a decimetre long, with brown tails, yellow fins, and wholesome, exquisitely tasty flesh; I even recommend that they be acclimatised to fresh water, a change, incidentally, that a number of saltwater fish can make with ease. I'll also mention some quadrangular trunkfish topped by four large protuberances along the back; trunkfish sprinkled with white spots on the underside of the body, which make good house pets like certain birds; boxfish armed with stings formed by extensions of their bony crusts, and whose odd grunting has earned them the nickname 'sea pigs'; then some trunkfish known as dromedaries, with tough, leathery flesh and big conical humps.

From the daily notes kept by Mr Conseil, I also retrieved certain fish from the genus *Tetradon* unique to these seas: southern puffers with red backs and white chests distinguished by three lengthwise rows of filaments, and jugfish, seven inches long, decked out in the brightest colours. Then, as specimens of other genera, blowfish resembling a dark brown egg, furrowed with white bands, and lacking tails; globefish, genuine porcupines of the sea, armed with stings and able to inflate themselves until they look like a pin cushion bristling with needles; seahorses common to every ocean; flying dragonfish with long snouts and highly distended pectoral fins shaped like wings, which enable them, if not to fly, at least to spring into the air; spatula-shaped paddlefish whose tails are covered with many scaly rings; snipefish with long jaws, excellent animals 25 centimetres long and gleaming with the most cheerful colours; bluish grey dragonets with wrinkled heads; myriads of leaping blennies with black stripes and long pectoral fins, gliding over the surface of the water with prodigious speed; delicious sailfish that can hoist their fins in a favourable current like so many unfurled sails; splendid nurseryfish on which nature has lavished yellow, azure, silver, and gold; yellow mackerel with wings made of filaments; bullheads forever spattered with mud, which make distinct hissing sounds; sea robins whose livers are thought to be poisonous; ladyfish that can flutter their eyelids; finally, archerfish with long, tubular snouts, real oceangoing flycatchers, armed with a rifle unforeseen by either Remington or Chassepot: it slays insects by shooting them with a simple drop of water.

From the eighty-ninth fish genus in Lacépède's system of classification, belonging to his second subclass of bony fish (characterised by gill covers and a bronchial membrane), I noted some scorpionfish whose heads are adorned with stings and which have only one dorsal fin; these animals are covered with small scales, or have none at all, depending on the subgenus to which they belong. The second subgenus gave us some *Didactylus* specimens three to four decimetres long, streaked with yellow, their heads having a phantasmagoric appearance. As for the first subgenus, it furnished several specimens of that bizarre fish aptly nicknamed 'toadfish,' whose big head is sometimes gouged with deep cavities, sometimes swollen with protuberances; bristling with stings and strewn with nodules, it sports hideously irregular horns; its body and tail are adorned with callosities; its stings can inflict dangerous injuries; it's repulsive and horrible.

From January 21 to the 23rd, the *Nautilus* travelled at the rate of 250 leagues in 24 hours, hence 540 miles at 22 miles per hour. If, during our trip, we were able to identify these different varieties of fish, it's because they were attracted by our electric light and tried to follow alongside; but most of them were outdistanced by our speed and soon fell behind; temporarily, however, a few managed to keep pace in the *Nautilus*'s waters.

On the morning of the 24th, in latitude 12° 5' south and longitude 94° 33', we raised Keeling Island, a madreporic upheaving planted with magnificent coconut trees, which had been visited by Mr Darwin and Captain Fitzroy. The *Nautilus* cruised along a short distance off the shore of this desert island. Our dragnets brought up many specimens of polyps and echinoderms plus some unusual shells from the branch *Mollusca*. Captain Nemo's treasures were enhanced by some valuable exhibits from the *delphinula* snail species, to which I joined some pointed star coral, a sort of parasitic polypary that often attaches itself to seashells.

Soon Keeling Island disappeared below the horizon, and our course was set to the northwest, toward the tip of the Indian peninsula.

'Civilization!' Ned Land told me that day. 'Much better than those Papuan Islands where we ran into more savages than venison! On this Indian shore, professor, there are roads and railways, English, French and Hindu villages. We wouldn't go five miles without bumping into a fellow countryman. Come on now, isn't it time for our sudden departure from Captain Nemo?'

'No, no, Ned,' I replied in a very firm tone. 'Let's ride it out, as you seafaring fellows say. The *Nautilus* is approaching populated areas. It's going back toward Europe, let it take us there. After we arrive in home waters, we can do as we see fit. Besides, I don't imagine Captain Nemo will let us go hunting on the coasts of Malabar or Coromandel as he did in the forests of New Guinea.'

'Well, sir, can't we manage without his permission?'

I didn't answer the Canadian. I wanted no arguments. Deep down, I was determined to fully exploit the good fortune that had put me on board the *Nautilus*.

After leaving Keeling Island, our pace got generally slower. It also got more unpredictable, often taking us to great depths. Several times we used our slanting fins, which internal levers could set at an oblique angle to our waterline. Thus we went as deep as two or three kilometres down but without ever verifying the lowest depths of this sea near India, which soundings of 13,000 metres have been unable to reach. As for the temperature in these lower strata, the thermometer always and invariably indicated 4° centigrade. I merely observed that in the upper layers, the water was always colder over shallows than in the open sea.

On January 25, the ocean being completely deserted, the *Nautilus* spent the day on the surface, churning the waves with its powerful propeller and making them spurt to great heights. Under these conditions, who wouldn't have mistaken it for a gigantic cetacean? I spent three-quarters of the day on the platform. I stared at the sea. Nothing on the horizon, except near four o'clock in the afternoon a long steamer to the west, running on our opposite tack. Its masting was visible for an instant, but it couldn't have seen the *Nautilus* because we were lying too low in the water. I imagine that steamboat belonged to the Peninsular & Oriental line, which provides service from the island of Ceylon to Sidney, also calling at King George Sound and Melbourne.

At five o'clock in the afternoon, just before that brief twilight that links day with night in tropical zones, Conseil and I marvelled at an unusual sight.

It was a delightful animal whose discovery, according to the ancients, is a sign of good luck. Aristotle, Athenaeus, Pliny and Oppian studied its habits and lavished on its behalf all the scientific poetry of Greece and Italy. They called it 'nautilus' and 'pompilius.' But modern science has not endorsed these designations, and this mollusc is now known by the name argonaut.

Anyone consulting Conseil would soon learn from the gallant lad that the branch *Mollusca* is divided into five classes; that the first class features the *Cephalopoda* (whose members are sometimes naked, sometimes covered with a shell), which consists of two families, the *Dibranchiata* and the *Tetrabranchiata*, which are distinguished by their number of gills; that the family *Dibranchiata* includes three genera, the argonaut, the squid, and the cuttlefish, and that the family *Tetrabranchiata* contains only one genus, the nautilus. After this catalogue, if some recalcitrant listener confuses the argonaut, which is *acetabuliferous* (in other words, a bearer of suction tubes), with the nautilus, which is *tentaculiferous* (a bearer of tentacles), it will be simply unforgivable.

Now, it was a school of argonauts then voyaging on the surface of the ocean. We could count several hundred of them. They belonged to that species of argonaut covered with protuberances and exclusive to the seas near India.

These graceful molluscs were swimming backward by means of their locomotive tubes, sucking water into these tubes and then expelling it. Six of their eight tentacles were long, thin and floated on the water, while the other two were rounded into palms and spread to the wind like light sails. I could see perfectly their undulating, spiral-shaped shells, which Cuvier aptly compared to an elegant cockleboat. It's an actual boat indeed. It transports the animal that secretes it without the animal sticking to it.

'The argonaut is free to leave its shell,' I told Conseil, 'but it never does.'

'Not unlike Captain Nemo,' Conseil replied sagely. 'Which is why he should have christened his ship the *Argonaut*.'

For about an hour the *Nautilus* cruised in the midst of this school of molluscs. Then, lord knows why, they were gripped with a sudden fear. As if at a signal, every sail was abruptly lowered; arms folded, bodies contracted, shells turned over by changing their centre of gravity, and the whole flotilla disappeared under the waves. It was instantaneous, and no squadron of ships ever manoeuvred with greater togetherness.

Just then night fell suddenly, and the waves barely surged in the breeze, spreading placidly around the *Nautilus*'s side plates.

The next day, January 26, we cut the equator on the 82nd meridian and we re-entered the northern hemisphere.

During that day a fearsome school of sharks provided us with an escort. Dreadful animals that teem in these seas and make them extremely dangerous. There were Port Jackson sharks with a brown back, a whitish belly, and 11 rows of teeth, bigeye sharks with necks marked by a large black spot encircled in white and resembling an eye, and Isabella sharks whose rounded snouts were strewn with dark speckles. Often these powerful animals rushed at the lounge window with a violence less than comforting. By this point Ned Land had lost all self-control. He wanted to rise to the surface of the waves and harpoon the monsters, especially certain smooth-hound sharks whose mouths were paved with teeth arranged like a mosaic, and some big five-metre tiger sharks that insisted on personally provoking him. But the *Nautilus* soon picked up speed and easily left astern the fastest of these man-eaters.

On January 27, at the entrance to the huge Bay of Bengal, we repeatedly encountered a gruesome sight: human corpses floating on the surface of the waves! Carried by the Ganges to the high seas, these were deceased Indian villagers who hadn't been fully devoured by vultures, the only morticians in these parts. But there was no shortage of sharks to assist them with their undertaking chores.

Near seven o'clock in the evening, the *Nautilus* lay half submerged, navigating in the midst of milky white waves. As far as the eye could see, the ocean seemed lactified. Was it an effect of the moon's rays? No, because the new moon was barely two days old and was still lost below the horizon in the sun's rays. The entire sky, although lit up by stellar radiation, seemed pitch-black in comparison with the whiteness of these waters.

Conseil couldn't believe his eyes, and he questioned me about the causes of this odd phenomenon. Luckily I was in a position to answer him.

'That's called a milk sea,' I told him, 'a vast expanse of white waves often seen along the coasts of Amboina and in these waterways.'

'But,' Conseil asked, 'could master tell me the cause of this effect, because I presume this water hasn't really changed into milk!'

'No, my boy, and this whiteness that amazes you is merely due to the presence of myriads of tiny creatures called infusoria, a sort of diminutive glowworm that's colourless and gelatinous in appearance, as thick as a strand of hair, and no longer than one-fifth of a millimetre. Some of these tiny creatures stick together over an area of several leagues.'

'Several leagues!' Conseil exclaimed.

'Yes, my boy, and don't even try to compute the number of these infusoria. You won't pull it off, because if I'm not mistaken, certain navigators have cruised through milk seas for more than 40 miles.'

I'm not sure that Conseil heeded my recommendation, because he seemed to be deep in thought, no doubt trying to calculate how many one-fifths of a millimetre are found in 40 square miles. As for me, I continued to observe this phenomenon. For several hours the *Nautilus*'s spur sliced through these whitish waves, and I watched it glide noiselessly over this soapy water, as if it were cruising through those foaming eddies that a bay's currents and countercurrents sometimes leave between each other.

Near midnight the sea suddenly resumed its usual hue, but behind us all the way to the horizon, the skies kept mirroring the whiteness of those waves and for a good while seemed imbued with the hazy glow of an aurora borealis.

CHAPTER 2

A New Proposition from Captain Nemo

ON JANUARY 28, in latitude 9° 4' north, when the *Nautilus* returned at noon to the surface of the sea, it lay in sight of land some eight miles to the west. Right off, I observed a cluster of mountains about 2,000 feet high, whose shapes were very whimsically sculpted. After our position fix, I re-entered the lounge, and when our bearings were reported on the chart, I saw that we were off the island of Ceylon, that pearl dangling from the lower lobe of the Indian peninsula.

I went looking in the library for a book about this island, one of the most fertile in the world. Sure enough, I found a volume entitled *Ceylon and the Singhalese* by H. C. Sirr, Esq. Re-entering the lounge, I first noted the bearings of Ceylon, on which antiquity lavished so many different names. It was located between latitude 5° 55' and 9° 49' north, and between longitude 79° 42' and 82° 4' east of the meridian of Greenwich; its length is 275 miles; its maximum width, 150 miles; its circumference, 900 miles; its surface area, 24,448 square miles, in other words, a little smaller than that of Ireland.

Just then Captain Nemo and his chief officer appeared.

The captain glanced at the chart. Then, turning to me:

'The island of Ceylon,' he said, 'is famous for its pearl fisheries. Would you be interested, Professor Aronnax, in visiting one of those fisheries?'

'Certainly, captain.'

'Fine. It's easily done. Only, when we see the fisheries, we'll see no fishermen. The annual harvest hasn't yet begun. No matter. I'll give orders to make for the Gulf of Mannar, and we'll arrive there late tonight.'

The captain said a few words to his chief officer who went out immediately. Soon the *Nautilus* re-entered its liquid element, and the pressure gauge indicated that it was staying at a depth of 30 feet.

With the chart under my eyes, I looked for the Gulf of Mannar. I found it by the 9th parallel off the northwestern shores of Ceylon. It was formed by the long curve of little Mannar Island. To reach it we had to go all the way up Ceylon's west coast.

'Professor,' Captain Nemo then told me, 'there are pearl fisheries in the Bay of Bengal, the seas of the East Indies, the seas of China and Japan, plus those seas south of the United States, the Gulf of Panama and the Gulf of California; but it's off Ceylon that such fishing reaps its richest rewards. No doubt we'll be arriving a little early. Fishermen gather in the Gulf of Mannar only during the month of March, and for 30 days some 300 boats concentrate on the lucrative harvest of these treasures from the sea. Each boat is manned by ten oarsmen and ten fishermen. The latter divide into two groups, dive in rotation, and descend to a depth of 12 metres with the help of a heavy stone clutched between their feet and attached by a rope to their boat.'

'You mean,' I said, 'that such primitive methods are still all that they use?'

'All,' Captain Nemo answered me, 'although these fisheries belong to the most industrialised people in the world, the English, to whom the Treaty of Amiens granted them in 1802.'

'Yet it strikes me that diving suits like yours could perform yeoman service in such work.'

'Yes, since those poor fishermen can't stay long underwater. On his voyage to Ceylon, the Englishman Percival made much of a Kaffir who stayed under five minutes without coming up to the surface, but I find that hard to believe. I know that some divers can last up to 57 seconds, and highly skilful ones to 87; but such men are rare, and when the poor fellows climb back on board, the water coming out of their noses and ears is tinted with blood. I believe the average time underwater that these fishermen can tolerate is 30 seconds, during which they hastily stuff their little nets with all the pearl oysters they can tear loose. But these fishermen generally don't live to advanced age: their vision weakens, ulcers break out on their eyes, sores form on their bodies, and some are even stricken with apoplexy on the ocean floor.'

'Yes,' I said, 'it's a sad occupation, and one that exists only to gratify the whims of fashion. But tell me, captain, how many oysters can a boat fish up in a workday?'

'About 40,000 to 50,000. It's even said that in 1814, when the English government went fishing on its own behalf, its divers worked just 20 days and brought up 76,000,000 oysters.'

'At least,' I asked, 'the fishermen are well paid, aren't they?'

'Hardly, professor. In Panama they make just $1 per week. In most places they earn only a penny for each oyster that has a pearl, and they bring up so many that have none!'

'Only one penny to those poor people who make their employers rich! That's atrocious!'

'On that note, professor,' Captain Nemo told me, 'you and your companions will visit the Mannar oysterbank, and if by chance some eager fisherman arrives early, well, we can watch him at work.'

'That suits me, captain.'

'By the way, Professor Aronnax, you aren't afraid of sharks, are you?'

'Sharks?' I exclaimed.

This struck me as a pretty needless question, to say the least.

'Well?' Captain Nemo went on.

'I admit, captain, I'm not yet on very familiar terms with that genus of fish.'

'We're used to them, the rest of us,' Captain Nemo answered. 'And in time you will be too. Anyhow, we'll be armed, and on our way we might hunt a man-eater or two. It's a fascinating sport. So, professor, I'll see you tomorrow, bright and early.'

This said in a carefree tone, Captain Nemo left the lounge.

If you're invited to hunt bears in the Swiss mountains, you might say: 'Oh good, I get to go bear hunting tomorrow!' If you're invited to hunt lions on the Atlas plains or tigers in the jungles of India, you might say: 'Ha! Now's my chance to hunt lions and tigers!' But if you're invited to hunt sharks in their native element, you might want to think it over before accepting.

As for me, I passed a hand over my brow, where beads of cold sweat were busy forming.

'Let's think this over,' I said to myself, 'and let's take our time. Hunting otters in underwater forests, as we did in the forests of Crespo Island, is an acceptable activity. But to roam the bottom of the sea when you're almost certain to meet man-eaters in the neighbourhood, that's another story! I know that in certain countries, particularly the Andaman Islands, Negroes don't hesitate to attack sharks, dagger in one hand and noose in the other; but I also know that many who face those fearsome animals don't come back alive. Besides, I'm not a Negro, and even if I were a Negro, in this instance I don't think a little hesitation on my part would be out of place.'

And there I was, fantasizing about sharks, envisioning huge jaws armed with multiple rows of teeth and capable of cutting a man in half. I could already feel a definite pain around my pelvic girdle. And how I resented the offhand manner in which the captain had extended his deplorable invitation! You would have thought it was an issue of going into the woods on some harmless fox hunt!

'Thank heavens!' I said to myself. 'Conseil will never want to come along, and that'll be my excuse for not going with the captain.'

As for Ned Land, I admit I felt less confident of his wisdom. Danger, however great, held a perennial attraction for his aggressive nature.

I went back to reading Sirr's book, but I leafed through it mechanically. Between the lines I kept seeing fearsome, wide-open jaws.

Just then Conseil and the Canadian entered with a calm, even gleeful air. Little did they know what was waiting for them.

'Ye gods, sir!' Ned Land told me. 'Your Captain Nemo – the devil take him – has just made us a very pleasant proposition!'

'Oh!' I said 'You know about—'

'With all due respect to master,' Conseil replied, 'the *Nautilus*'s commander has invited us, together with master, for a visit tomorrow to Ceylon's magnificent pearl fisheries. He did so in the most cordial terms and conducted himself like a true gentleman.'

'He didn't tell you anything else?'

'Nothing, sir,' the Canadian replied. 'He said you'd already discussed this little stroll.'

'Indeed,' I said. 'But didn't he give you any details on—'

'Not a one, Mr Naturalist. You will be going with us, right?'

'Me? Why yes, certainly, of course! I can see that you like the idea, Mr Land.'

'Yes! It will be a really unusual experience!'

'And possibly dangerous!' I added in an insinuating tone.

'Dangerous?' Ned Land replied. 'A simple trip to an oysterbank?'

Assuredly, Captain Nemo hadn't seen fit to plant the idea of sharks in the minds of my companions. For my part, I stared at them with anxious eyes, as if they were already missing a limb or two. Should I alert them? Yes, surely, but I hardly knew how to go about it.

'Would master,' Conseil said to me, 'give us some background on pearl fishing?'

'On the fishing itself?' I asked. 'Or on the occupational hazards that—'

'On the fishing,' the Canadian replied. 'Before we tackle the terrain, it helps to be familiar with it.'

'All right, sit down, my friends, and I'll teach you everything I myself have just been taught by the Englishman H. C. Sirr!'

Ned and Conseil took seats on a couch, and right off the Canadian said to me:

'Sir, just what is a pearl exactly?'

'My gallant Ned,' I replied, 'for poets a pearl is a tear from the sea; for Orientals it's a drop of solidified dew; for the ladies it's a jewel they can wear on their fingers, necks and ears that's oblong in shape, glassy in lustre, and formed from mother-of-pearl; for chemists it's a mixture of calcium phosphate and calcium carbonate with a little gelatin protein; and finally, for naturalists it's a simple festering secretion from the organ that produces mother-of-pearl in certain bivalves.'

'Branch *Mollusca*,' Conseil said, 'class *Acephala*, order *Testacea*.'

'Correct, my scholarly Conseil. Now then, those *Testacea* capable of producing pearls include rainbow abalone, turbo snails, giant clams and saltwater scallops – briefly, all those that secrete mother-of-pearl, in other words, that blue, azure, violet, or white substance lining the insides of their valves.'

'Are mussels included too?' the Canadian asked.

'Yes! The mussels of certain streams in Scotland, Wales, Ireland, Saxony, Bohemia and France.'

'Good!' the Canadian replied. 'From now on we'll pay closer attention to 'em.'

'But,' I went on, 'for secreting pearls, the ideal mollusc is the pearl oyster *Meleagrina margaritifera*, that valuable shellfish. Pearls result simply from mother-of-pearl solidifying into a globular shape. Either they stick to the oyster's shell, or they become embedded in the creature's folds. On the valves a pearl sticks fast; on the flesh it lies loose. But its nucleus is always some small, hard object, say a sterile egg or a grain of sand, around which the mother-of-pearl is deposited in thin, concentric layers over several years in succession.'

'Can one find several pearls in the same oyster?' Conseil asked.

'Yes, my boy. There are some shellfish that turn into real jewel coffers. They even mention one oyster, about which I remain dubious, that supposedly contained at least 150 sharks.'

'150 sharks!' Ned Land yelped.

'Did I say sharks?' I exclaimed hastily. 'I meant 150 pearls. Sharks wouldn't make sense.'

'Indeed,' Conseil said. 'But will master now tell us how one goes about extracting these pearls?'

'One proceeds in several ways, and often when pearls stick to the valves, fishermen even pull them loose with pliers. But usually the shellfish are spread out on mats made from the esparto grass that covers the beaches. Thus they die in the open air, and by the end of ten days they've rotted sufficiently. Next they're immersed in huge tanks of salt water, then they're opened up and washed. At this point the sorters begin their twofold task. First they remove the layers of mother-of-pearl, which are known in the industry by the names legitimate silver, bastard white, or bastard black, and these are shipped out in cases weighing 125 to 150 kilograms. Then they remove the oyster's meaty tissue, boil it and finally strain it, in order to extract even the smallest pearls.'

'Do the prices of these pearls differ depending on their size?' Conseil asked.

'Not only on their size,' I replied, 'but also according to their shape, their water – in other words, their colour – and their orient – in other words, that dappled, shimmering glow that makes them so delightful to the eye. The finest pearls are called virgin pearls, or paragons; they form in isolation within the mollusc's tissue. They're white, often opaque but sometimes of opalescent transparency, and usually spherical or pear-shaped. The spherical ones are made into bracelets; the pear-shaped ones into earrings, and since they're the most valuable, they're priced individually. The other pearls that stick to the oyster's shell are more erratically shaped and are priced by weight. Finally, classed in the lowest order, the smallest pearls are known by the name seed pearls; they're priced by the measuring cup and are used mainly in the creation of embroidery for church vestments.'

'But it must be a long, hard job, sorting out these pearls by size,' the Canadian said.

'No, my friend. That task is performed with 11 strainers, or sieves, that are pierced with different numbers of holes. Those pearls staying in the strainers with 20 to 80 holes are in the first order. Those not slipping through the sieves pierced with 100 to 800 holes are in the second order. Finally, those pearls for which one uses strainers pierced with 900 to 1,000 holes make up the seed pearls.'

'How ingenious,' Conseil said, 'to reduce dividing and classifying pearls to a mechanical operation. And could master tell us the profits brought in by harvesting these banks of pearl oysters?'

'According to Sirr's book,' I replied, 'these Ceylon fisheries are farmed annually for a total profit of 3,000,000 man-eaters.'

'Francs!' Conseil rebuked.

'Yes, francs! 3,000,000 francs!' I went on. 'But I don't think these fisheries bring in the returns they once did. Similarly, the Central American fisheries used to make an annual profit of 4,000,000 francs during the reign of King Charles V, but now they bring in only two-thirds of that amount. All in all, it's estimated that 9,000,000 francs is the current yearly return for the whole pearl-harvesting industry.'

'But,' Conseil asked, 'haven't certain famous pearls been quoted at extremely high prices?'

'Yes, my boy. They say Julius Caesar gave Servilia a pearl worth 120,000 francs in our currency.'

'I've even heard stories,' the Canadian said, 'about some lady in ancient times who drank pearls in vinegar.'

'Cleopatra,' Conseil shot back.

'It must have tasted pretty bad,' Ned Land added.

'Abominable, Ned my friend,' Conseil replied. 'But when a little glass of vinegar is worth 1,500,000 francs, its taste is a small price to pay.'

'I'm sorry I didn't marry the gal,' the Canadian said, throwing up his hands with an air of discouragement.

'Ned Land married to Cleopatra?' Conseil exclaimed.

'But I was all set to tie the knot, Conseil,' the Canadian replied in all seriousness, 'and it wasn't my fault the whole business fell through. I even bought a pearl necklace for my fiancée, Kate Tender, but she married somebody else instead. Well, that necklace cost me only $1.50, but you can absolutely trust me on this, professor, its pearls were so big, they wouldn't have gone through that strainer with 20 holes.'

'My gallant Ned,' I replied, laughing, 'those were artificial pearls, ordinary glass beads whose insides were coated with Essence of Orient.'

'Wow!' the Canadian replied. 'That Essence of Orient must sell for quite a large sum.'

'As little as zero! It comes from the scales of a European carp, it's nothing more than a silver substance that collects in the water and is preserved in ammonia. It's worthless.'

'Maybe that's why Kate Tender married somebody else,' replied Mr Land philosophically.

'But,' I said, 'getting back to pearls of great value, I don't think any sovereign ever possessed one superior to the pearl owned by Captain Nemo.'

'This one?' Conseil said, pointing to a magnificent jewel in its glass case.

'Exactly. And I'm certainly not far off when I estimate its value at 2,000,000... uh...'

'Francs!' Conseil said quickly.

'Yes,' I said, '2,000,000 francs, and no doubt all it cost our captain was the effort to pick it up.'

'Ha!' Ned Land exclaimed. 'During our stroll tomorrow, who says we won't run into one just like it?'

'Bah!' Conseil put in.

'And why not?'

'What good would a pearl worth millions do us here on the *Nautilus*?'

'Here, no,' Ned Land said. 'But elsewhere....'

'Oh! Elsewhere!' Conseil put in, shaking his head.

'In fact,' I said, 'Mr Land is right. And if we ever brought back to Europe or America a pearl worth millions, it would make the story of our adventures more authentic – and much more rewarding.'

'That's how I see it,' the Canadian said.

'But,' said Conseil, who perpetually returned to the didactic side of things, 'is this pearl fishing ever dangerous?'

'No,' I replied quickly, 'especially if one takes certain precautions.'

'What risks would you run in a job like that?' Ned Land said. 'Swallowing a few gulps of salt water?'

'Whatever you say, Ned.' Then, trying to imitate Captain Nemo's carefree tone, I asked, 'By the way, gallant Ned, are you afraid of sharks?'

'Me?' the Canadian replied. 'I'm a professional harpooner! It's my job to make a mockery of them!'

'It isn't an issue,' I said, 'of fishing for them with a swivel hook, hoisting them onto the deck of a ship, chopping off the tail with a sweep of the axe, opening the belly, ripping out the heart, and tossing it into the sea.'

'So it's an issue of...?'

'Yes, precisely.'

'In the water?'

'In the water.'

'Ye gods, just give me a good harpoon! You see, sir, these sharks are badly designed. They have to roll their bellies over to snap you up, and in the meantime...'

Ned Land had a way of pronouncing the word 'snap' that sent chills down the spine.

'Well, how about you, Conseil? What are your feelings about these man-eaters?'

'Me?' Conseil said. 'I'm afraid I must be frank with master.'

Good for you, I thought.

'If master faces these sharks,' Conseil said, 'I think his loyal manservant should face them with him!'

CHAPTER 3

A Pearl Worth Ten Million

NIGHT FELL. I went to bed. I slept pretty poorly. Man-eaters played a major role in my dreams. And I found it more or less appropriate that the French word for shark, *requin*, has its linguistic roots in the word *requiem*.

The next day at four o'clock in the morning, I was awakened by the steward whom Captain Nemo had placed expressly at my service. I got up quickly, dressed, and went into the lounge.

Captain Nemo was waiting for me.

'Professor Aronnax,' he said to me, 'are you ready to start?'

'I'm ready.'

'Kindly follow me.'

'What about my companions, captain?'

'They've been alerted and are waiting for us.'

'Aren't we going to put on our diving suits?' I asked.

'Not yet. I haven't let the *Nautilus* pull too near the coast, and we're fairly well out from the Mannar oysterbank. But I have the skiff ready, and it will take us to the exact spot where we'll disembark, which will save us a pretty long trek. It's carrying our diving equipment, and we'll suit up just before we begin our underwater exploring.'

Captain Nemo took me to the central companionway whose steps led to the platform. Ned and Conseil were there, enraptured with the 'pleasure trip' getting under way. Oars in position, five of the *Nautilus*'s sailors were waiting for us aboard the skiff, which was moored alongside. The night was still dark. Layers of clouds cloaked the sky and left only a few stars in view. My eyes flew to the side where land lay, but I saw only a blurred line covering three-quarters of the horizon from southwest to northwest. Going up Ceylon's west coast during the night, the *Nautilus* lay west of the bay, or rather that gulf formed by the mainland and Mannar Island. Under these dark waters there stretched the bank of shellfish, an inexhaustible field of pearls more than 20 miles long.

Captain Nemo, Conseil, Ned Land and I found seats in the stern of the skiff. The longboat's coxswain took the tiller; his four companions leaned into their oars; the moorings were cast off and we pulled clear.

The skiff headed southward. The oarsmen took their time. I watched their strokes vigorously catch the water, and they always waited ten seconds before rowing again, following the practice used in most navies. While the longboat coasted, drops of liquid flicked from the oars and hit the dark troughs of the waves, pitter-pattering like splashes of molten lead. Coming from well out, a mild swell made the skiff roll gently, and a few cresting billows lapped at its bow.

We were silent. What was Captain Nemo thinking? Perhaps that this approaching shore was too close for comfort, contrary to the Canadian's views in which it still seemed too far away. As for Conseil, he had come along out of simple curiosity.

Near 5:30 the first glimmers of light on the horizon defined the upper lines of the coast with greater distinctness. Fairly flat to the east, it swelled a little toward the south. Five miles still separated it from us, and its beach merged with the misty waters. Between us and the shore, the sea was deserted. Not a boat, not a diver. Profound solitude reigned over this gathering place of pearl fishermen. As Captain Nemo had commented, we were arriving in these waterways a month too soon.

At six o'clock the day broke suddenly, with that speed unique to tropical regions, which experience no real dawn or dusk. The sun's rays pierced the cloud curtain gathered on the easterly horizon, and the radiant orb rose swiftly.

I could clearly see the shore, which featured a few sparse trees here and there.

The skiff advanced toward Mannar Island, which curved to the south. Captain Nemo stood up from his thwart and studied the sea.

At his signal the anchor was lowered, but its chain barely ran because the bottom lay no more than a metre down, and this locality was one of the shallowest spots near the bank of shellfish. Instantly the skiff wheeled around under the ebb tide's outbound thrust.

'Here we are, Professor Aronnax,' Captain Nemo then said. 'You observe this confined bay? A month from now in this very place, the numerous fishing boats of the harvesters will gather, and these are the waters their divers will ransack so daringly. This bay is felicitously laid out for their type of fishing. It's sheltered from the strongest winds, and the sea is never very turbulent here, highly favourable conditions for diving work. Now let's put on our underwater suits, and we'll begin our stroll.'

I didn't reply, and while staring at these suspicious waves, I began to put on my heavy aquatic clothes, helped by the longboat's sailors. Captain Nemo and my two companions suited up as well. None of the *Nautilus*'s men were to go with us on this new excursion.

Soon we were imprisoned up to the neck in india-rubber clothing, and straps fastened the air devices onto our backs. As for the Ruhmkorff device, it didn't seem to be in the picture. Before inserting my head into its copper capsule, I commented on this to the captain.

'Our lighting equipment would be useless to us,' the captain answered me. 'We won't be going very deep, and the sun's rays will be sufficient to light our way. Besides, it's unwise to carry electric lanterns under these waves. Their brightness might unexpectedly attract certain dangerous occupants of these waterways.'

As Captain Nemo pronounced these words, I turned to Conseil and Ned Land. But my two friends had already encased their craniums in their metal headgear, and they could neither hear nor reply.

I had one question left to address to Captain Nemo.

'What about our weapons?' I asked him. 'Our rifles?'

'Rifles! What for? Don't your mountaineers attack bears dagger in hand? And isn't steel surer than lead? Here's a sturdy blade. Slip it under your belt and let's be off.'

I stared at my companions. They were armed in the same fashion, and Ned Land was also brandishing an enormous harpoon he had stowed in the skiff before leaving the *Nautilus*.

Then, following the captain's example, I let myself be crowned with my heavy copper sphere, and our air tanks immediately went into action.

An instant later, the longboat's sailors helped us overboard one after the other, and we set foot on level sand in a metre and a half of water. Captain Nemo gave us a hand signal. We followed him down a gentle slope and disappeared under the waves.

There the obsessive fears in my brain left me. I became surprisingly calm again. The ease with which I could move increased my confidence, and the many strange sights captivated my imagination.

The sun was already sending sufficient light under these waves. The tiniest objects remained visible. After ten minutes of walking, we were in five metres of water, and the terrain had become almost flat.

Like a covey of snipe over a marsh, there rose underfoot schools of unusual fish from the genus *Monopterus*, whose members have no fin but their tail. I recognised the Javanese eel, a genuine eight-decimetre serpent with a bluish grey belly, which, without the gold lines over its flanks, could easily be confused with the conger eel. From the butterfish genus, whose oval bodies are very flat, I observed several adorned in brilliant colours and sporting a dorsal fin like a sickle, edible fish that, when dried and marinated, make an excellent dish known by the name 'karawade'; then some sea poachers, fish belonging to the genus *Aspidophoroides*, whose bodies are covered with scaly armour divided into eight lengthwise sections.

Meanwhile, as the sun got progressively higher, it lit up the watery mass more and more. The seafloor changed little by little. Its fine-grained sand was followed by a genuine causeway of smooth crags covered by a carpet of molluscs and zoophytes. Among other specimens in these two branches, I noted some windowpane oysters with thin valves of unequal size, a type of ostracod unique to the Red Sea and the Indian Ocean, then orange-hued lucina with circular shells, awl-shaped auger shells, some of those Persian murex snails that supply the *Nautilus* with such wonderful dye, spiky periwinkles 15 centimetres long that rose under the waves like hands ready to grab you, turban snails with shells made of horn and bristling all over with spines, lamp shells, edible duck clams that feed the Hindu marketplace, subtly luminous jellyfish of the species *Pelagia panopyra*, and finally some wonderful *Oculina flabelliforma*, magnificent sea fans that fashion one of the most luxuriant tree forms in this ocean.

In the midst of this moving vegetation, under arbours of water plants, there raced legions of clumsy articulates, in particular some fanged frog crabs whose carapaces form a slightly rounded triangle, robber crabs exclusive to these waterways, and horrible parthenope crabs whose appearance was repulsive to the eye. One animal no less hideous, which I encountered several times, was the enormous crab that Mr Darwin observed, to which nature has given the instinct and requisite strength to eat coconuts; it scrambles up trees on the beach and sends the coconuts tumbling; they fracture in their fall and are opened by its powerful pincers. Here, under these clear waves, this crab raced around with matchless agility, while green turtles from the species frequenting the Malabar coast moved sluggishly among the crumbling rocks.

Near seven o'clock we finally surveyed the bank of shellfish, where pearl oysters reproduce by the millions. These valuable molluscs stick to rocks, where they're strongly attached by a mass of brown filaments that forbids their moving about. In this respect oysters are inferior even to mussels, to whom nature has not denied all talent for locomotion.

The shellfish Meleagrina, that womb for pearls whose valves are nearly equal in size, has the shape of a round shell with thick walls and a very rough exterior. Some of these shells were furrowed with flaky, greenish bands that radiated down from the top. These were the young oysters. The others had rugged black surfaces, measured up to 15 centimetres in width, and were ten or more years old.

Captain Nemo pointed to this prodigious heap of shellfish, and I saw that these mines were genuinely inexhaustible, since nature's creative powers are greater than man's destructive instincts. True to those instincts, Ned Land greedily stuffed the finest of these molluscs into a net he carried at his side.

But we couldn't stop. We had to follow the captain, who headed down trails seemingly known only to himself. The seafloor rose noticeably, and when I lifted my arms, sometimes they would pass above the surface of the sea. Then the level of the oysterbank would lower unpredictably. Often we went around tall, pointed rocks rising like pyramids. In their dark crevices huge crustaceans, aiming their long legs like heavy artillery, watched us with unblinking eyes, while underfoot there crept millipedes, bloodworms, aricia worms and annelid worms, whose antennas and tubular tentacles were incredibly long.

Just then a huge cave opened up in our path, hollowed from a picturesque pile of rocks whose smooth heights were completely hung with underwater flora. At first this cave looked pitch-black to me.

Inside, the sun's rays seemed to diminish by degrees. Their hazy transparency was nothing more than drowned light.

Captain Nemo went in. We followed him. My eyes soon grew accustomed to this comparative gloom. I distinguished the unpredictably contoured springings of a vault, supported by natural pillars firmly based on a granite foundation, like the weighty columns of Tuscan architecture. Why had our incomprehensible guide taken us into the depths of this underwater crypt? I would soon find out.

After going down a fairly steep slope, our feet trod the floor of a sort of circular pit. There Captain Nemo stopped, and his hand indicated an object that I hadn't yet noticed.

It was an oyster of extraordinary dimensions, a titanic giant clam, a holy-water font that could have held a whole lake, a basin more than two metres wide, hence even bigger than the one adorning the *Nautilus*'s lounge.

I approached this phenomenal mollusc. Its mass of filaments attached it to a table of granite, and there it grew by itself in the midst of the cave's calm waters. I estimated the weight of this giant clam at 300 kilograms. Hence such an oyster held 15 kilos of meat, and you'd need the stomach of King Gargantua to eat a couple dozen.

Captain Nemo was obviously familiar with this bivalve's existence. This wasn't the first time he'd paid it a visit, and I thought his sole reason for leading us to this locality was to show us a natural curiosity. I was mistaken. Captain Nemo had an explicit personal interest in checking on the current condition of this giant clam.

The mollusc's two valves were partly open. The captain approached and stuck his dagger vertically between the shells to discourage any ideas about closing; then with his hands he raised the fringed, membrane-filled tunic that made up the animal's mantle.

There, between its leaflike folds, I saw a loose pearl as big as a coconut. Its globular shape, perfect clarity, and wonderful orient made it a jewel of incalculable value. Carried away by curiosity, I stretched out my hand to take it, weigh it, fondle it! But the captain stopped me, signalled no, removed his dagger in one swift motion, and let the two valves snap shut.

I then understood Captain Nemo's intent. By leaving the pearl buried beneath the giant clam's mantle, he allowed it to grow imperceptibly.

With each passing year the mollusc's secretions added new concentric layers. The captain alone was familiar with the cave where this wonderful fruit of nature was 'ripening'; he alone reared it, so to speak, in order to transfer it one day to his dearly beloved museum. Perhaps, following the examples of oyster farmers in China and India, he had even predetermined the creation of this pearl by sticking under the mollusc's folds some piece of glass or metal that was gradually covered with mother-of-pearl. In any case, comparing this pearl to others I already knew about, and to those shimmering in the captain's collection, I estimated that it was worth at least 10,000,000 francs. It was a superb natural curiosity rather than a luxurious piece of jewellery, because I don't know of any female ear that could handle it.

Our visit to this opulent giant clam came to an end. Captain Nemo left the cave, and we climbed back up the bank of shellfish in the midst of these clear waters not yet disturbed by divers at work.

We walked by ourselves, genuine loiterers stopping or straying as our fancies dictated. For my part, I was no longer worried about those dangers my imagination had so ridiculously exaggerated. The shallows drew noticeably closer to the surface of the sea, and soon, walking in only a metre of water, my head passed well above the level of the ocean. Conseil rejoined me, and gluing his huge copper capsule to mine, his eyes gave me a friendly greeting. But this lofty plateau measured only a few fathoms, and soon we re-entered Our Element. I think I've now earned the right to dub it that.

Ten minutes later, Captain Nemo stopped suddenly. I thought he'd called a halt so that we could turn and start back. No. With a gesture he ordered us to crouch beside him at the foot of a wide crevice. His hand motioned toward a spot within the liquid mass, and I looked carefully.

Five metres away a shadow appeared and dropped to the seafloor. The alarming idea of sharks crossed my mind. But I was mistaken, and once again we didn't have to deal with monsters of the deep.

It was a man, a living man, a black Indian fisherman, a poor devil who no doubt had come to gather what he could before harvest time. I saw the bottom of his dinghy, moored a few feet above his head. He would dive and go back up in quick succession. A stone cut in the shape of a sugar loaf, which he gripped between his feet while a rope connected it to his boat, served to lower him more quickly to the ocean floor. This was the extent of his equipment. Arriving on the seafloor at a depth of about five metres, he fell to his knees and stuffed his sack with shellfish gathered at random. Then he went back up, emptied his sack, pulled up his stone, and started all over again, the whole process lasting only 30 seconds.

This diver didn't see us. A shadow cast by our crag hid us from his view. And besides, how could this poor Indian ever have guessed that human beings, creatures like himself, were near him under the waters, eavesdropping on his movements, not missing a single detail of his fishing!

So he went up and down several times. He gathered only about ten shellfish per dive, because he had to tear them from the banks where each clung with its tough mass of filaments. And how many of these oysters for which he risked his life would have no pearl in them!

I observed him with great care. His movements were systematically executed, and for half an hour no danger seemed to threaten him. So I had gotten used to the sight of this fascinating fishing when all at once, just as the Indian was kneeling on the seafloor, I saw him make a frightened gesture, stand, and gather himself to spring back to the surface of the waves.

I understood his fear. A gigantic shadow appeared above the poor diver. It was a shark of huge size, moving in diagonally, eyes ablaze, jaws wide open!

I was speechless with horror, unable to make a single movement.

With one vigorous stroke of its fins, the voracious animal shot toward the Indian, who jumped aside and avoided the shark's bite but not the thrashing of its tail, because that tail struck him across the chest and stretched him out on the seafloor.

This scene lasted barely a few seconds. The shark returned, rolled over on its back, and was getting ready to cut the Indian in half, when Captain Nemo, who was stationed beside me, suddenly stood up. Then he strode right toward the monster, dagger in hand, ready to fight it at close quarters.

Just as it was about to snap up the poor fisherman, the man-eater saw its new adversary, repositioned itself on its belly, and headed swiftly toward him.

I can see Captain Nemo's bearing to this day. Bracing himself, he waited for the fearsome man-eater with wonderful composure, and when the latter rushed at him, the captain leaped aside with prodigious quickness, avoided a collision, and sank his dagger into its belly. But that wasn't the end of the story. A dreadful battle was joined.

The shark bellowed, so to speak. Blood was pouring into the waves from its wounds. The sea was dyed red, and through this opaque liquid I could see nothing else.

Nothing else until the moment when, through a rift in the clouds, I saw the daring captain clinging to one of the animal's fins, fighting the monster at close quarters, belabouring his enemy's belly with stabs of the dagger yet unable to deliver the deciding thrust, in other words, a direct hit to the heart. In its struggles the man-eater churned the watery mass so furiously, its eddies threatened to knock me over.

I wanted to run to the captain's rescue. But I was transfixed with horror, unable to move.

I stared, wild-eyed. I saw the fight enter a new phase. The captain fell to the seafloor, toppled by the enormous mass weighing him down. Then the shark's jaws opened astoundingly wide, like a pair of industrial shears, and that would have been the finish of Captain Nemo had not Ned Land, quick as thought, rushed forward with his harpoon and driven its dreadful point into the shark's underside.

The waves were saturated with masses of blood. The waters shook with the movements of the man-eater, which thrashed about with indescribable fury. Ned Land hadn't missed his target. This was the monster's death rattle. Pierced to the heart, it was struggling with dreadful spasms whose aftershocks knocked Conseil off his feet.

Meanwhile Ned Land pulled the captain clear. Uninjured, the latter stood up, went right to the Indian, quickly cut the rope binding the man to his stone, took the fellow in his arms, and with a vigorous kick of the heel, rose to the surface of the sea.

The three of us followed him, and a few moments later, miraculously safe, we reached the fisherman's longboat.

Captain Nemo's first concern was to revive this unfortunate man. I wasn't sure he would succeed. I hoped so, since the poor devil hadn't been under very long. But that stroke from the shark's tail could have been his deathblow.

Fortunately, after vigorous massaging by Conseil and the captain, I saw the nearly drowned man regain consciousness little by little. He opened his eyes. How startled he must have felt, how frightened even, at seeing four huge, copper craniums leaning over him!

And above all, what must he have thought when Captain Nemo pulled a bag of pearls from a pocket in his diving suit and placed it in the fisherman's hands? This magnificent benefaction from the Man of the Waters to the poor Indian from Ceylon was accepted by the latter with trembling hands. His bewildered eyes indicated that he didn't know to what superhuman creatures he owed both his life and his fortune.

At the captain's signal we returned to the bank of shellfish, and retracing our steps, we walked for half an hour until we encountered the anchor connecting the seafloor with the *Nautilus*'s skiff.

Back on board, the sailors helped divest us of our heavy copper carapaces.

Captain Nemo's first words were spoken to the Canadian.

'Thank you, Mr Land,' he told him.

'Tit for tat, captain,' Ned Land replied. 'I owed it to you.'

The ghost of a smile glided across the captain's lips, and that was all.

'To the *Nautilus*,' he said.

The longboat flew over the waves. A few minutes later we encountered the shark's corpse again, floating.

From the black markings on the tips of its fins, I recognised the dreadful *Squalus melanopterus* from the seas of the East Indies, a variety in the species of sharks proper. It was more than 25 feet long; its enormous mouth occupied a third of its body. It was an adult, as could be seen from the six rows of teeth forming an isosceles triangle in its upper jaw.

Conseil looked at it with purely scientific fascination, and I'm sure he placed it, not without good reason, in the class of cartilaginous fish, order *Chondropterygia* with fixed gills, family *Selacia*, genus *Squalus*.

While I was contemplating this inert mass, suddenly a dozen of these voracious *melanoptera* appeared around our longboat; but, paying no attention to us, they pounced on the corpse and quarreled over every scrap of it.

By 8:30 we were back on board the *Nautilus*.

There I fell to thinking about the incidents that marked our excursion over the Mannar oysterbank. Two impressions inevitably stood out. One concerned Captain Nemo's matchless bravery, the other his devotion to a human being, a representative of that race from which he had fled beneath the seas. In spite of everything, this strange man hadn't yet succeeded in completely stifling his heart.

When I shared these impressions with him, he answered me in a tone touched with emotion:

'That Indian, professor, lives in the land of the oppressed, and I am to this day, and will be until my last breath, a native of that same land!'

CHAPTER 4

The Red Sea

DURING THE DAY of January 29, the island of Ceylon disappeared below the horizon, and at a speed of 20 miles per hour, the *Nautilus* glided into the labyrinthine channels that separate the Maldive and Laccadive Islands. It likewise hugged Kiltan Island, a shore of madreporic origin discovered by Vasco da Gama in 1499 and one of 19 chief islands in the island group of the Laccadives, located between latitude 10° and 14° 30' north, and between longitude 50° 72' and 69° east.

By then we had fared 16,220 miles, or 7,500 leagues, from our starting point in the seas of Japan.

The next day, January 30, when the *Nautilus* rose to the surface of the ocean, there was no more land in sight. Setting its course to the north-northwest, the ship headed toward the Gulf of Oman, carved out between Arabia and the Indian peninsula and providing access to the Persian Gulf.

This was obviously a blind alley with no possible outlet. So where was Captain Nemo taking us? I was unable to say. Which didn't satisfy the Canadian, who that day asked me where we were going.

'We're going, Mr Ned, where the captain's fancy takes us.'

'His fancy,' the Canadian replied, 'won't take us very far. The Persian Gulf has no outlet, and if we enter those waters, it won't be long before we return in our tracks.'

'All right, we'll return, Mr Land, and after the Persian Gulf, if the *Nautilus* wants to visit the Red Sea, the Strait of Bab el Mandeb is still there to let us in!'

'I don't have to tell you, sir,' Ned Land replied, 'that the Red Sea is just as landlocked as the gulf, since the Isthmus of Suez hasn't been cut all the way through yet; and even if it was, a boat as secretive as ours wouldn't risk a canal intersected with locks. So the Red Sea won't be our way back to Europe either.'

'But I didn't say we'd return to Europe.'

'What do you figure, then?'

'I figure that after visiting these unusual waterways of Arabia and Egypt, the *Nautilus* will go back down to the Indian Ocean, perhaps through Mozambique Channel, perhaps off the Mascarene Islands, and then make for the Cape of Good Hope.'

'And once we're at the Cape of Good Hope?' the Canadian asked with typical persistence.

'Well then, we'll enter that Atlantic Ocean with which we aren't yet familiar. What's wrong, Ned my friend? Are you tired of this voyage under the seas? Are you bored with the constantly changing sight of these underwater wonders? Speaking for myself, I'll be extremely distressed to see the end of a voyage so few men will ever have a chance to make.'

'But don't you realise, Professor Aronnax,' the Canadian replied, 'that soon we'll have been imprisoned for three whole months aboard this *Nautilus*?'

'No, Ned, I didn't realise it, I don't want to realise it, and I don't keep track of every day and every hour.'

'But when will it be over?'

'In its appointed time. Meanwhile there's nothing we can do about it, and our discussions are futile. My gallant Ned, if you come and tell me, "A chance to escape is available to us," then I'll discuss it with you. But that isn't the case, and in all honesty, I don't think Captain Nemo ever ventures into European seas.'

This short dialogue reveals that in my mania for the *Nautilus*, I was turning into the spitting image of its commander.

As for Ned Land, he ended our talk in his best speechifying style: 'That's all fine and dandy. But in my humble opinion, a life in jail is a life without joy.'

For four days until February 3, the *Nautilus* inspected the Gulf of Oman at various speeds and depths. It seemed to be travelling at random, as if hesitating over which course to follow, but it never crossed the Tropic of Cancer.

After leaving this gulf we raised Muscat for an instant, the most important town in the country of Oman. I marvelled at its strange appearance in the midst of the black rocks surrounding it, against which the white of its houses and forts stood out sharply. I spotted the rounded domes of its mosques, the elegant tips of its minarets and its fresh, leafy terraces. But it was only a fleeting vision, and the *Nautilus* soon sank beneath the dark waves of these waterways.

Then our ship went along at a distance of six miles from the Arabic coasts of Mahra and Hadhramaut, their undulating lines of mountains relieved by a few ancient ruins. On February 5 we finally put into the Gulf of Aden, a genuine funnel stuck into the neck of Bab el Mandeb and bottling these Indian waters in the Red Sea.

On February 6 the *Nautilus* cruised in sight of the city of Aden, perched on a promontory connected to the continent by a narrow isthmus, a sort of inaccessible Gibraltar whose fortifications the English rebuilt after capturing it in 1839. I glimpsed the octagonal minarets of this town, which used to be one of the wealthiest, busiest commercial centres along this coast, as the Arab historian Idrisi tells it.

I was convinced that when Captain Nemo reached this point, he would back out again; but I was mistaken, and much to my surprise, he did nothing of the sort.

The next day, February 7, we entered the Strait of Bab el Mandeb, whose name means 'Gate of Tears' in the Arabic language. Twenty miles wide, it's only 52 kilometres long, and with the *Nautilus* launched at full speed, clearing it was the work of barely an hour. But I didn't see a thing, not even Perim Island where the British government built fortifications to strengthen Aden's position. There were many English and French steamers ploughing this narrow passageway, liners going from Suez to Bombay, Calcutta, Melbourne, Réunion Island and Mauritius; far too much traffic for the *Nautilus* to make an appearance on the surface. So it wisely stayed in midwater.

Finally, at noon, we were ploughing the waves of the Red Sea.

The Red Sea: that great lake so famous in biblical traditions, seldom replenished by rains, fed by no important rivers, continually drained by a high rate of evaporation, its water level dropping a metre and a half every year! If it were fully landlocked like a lake, this odd gulf might dry up completely; on this score it's inferior to its neighbours, the Caspian Sea and the Dead Sea, whose levels lower only to the point where their evaporation exactly equals the amounts of water they take to their hearts.

This Red Sea is 2,600 kilometres long with an average width of 240. In the days of the Ptolemies and the Roman emperors, it was a great commercial artery for the world, and when its isthmus has been cut through, it will completely regain that bygone importance that the Suez railways have already brought back in part.

I would not even attempt to understand the whim that induced Captain Nemo to take us into this gulf. But I wholeheartedly approved of the *Nautilus*'s entering it. It adopted a medium pace, sometimes staying on the surface, sometimes diving to avoid some ship, and so I could observe both the inside and topside of this highly unusual sea.

On February 8, as early as the first hours of daylight, Mocha appeared before us: a town now in ruins, whose walls would collapse at the mere sound of a cannon, and which shelters a few leafy date trees here and there. This once-important city used to contain six public marketplaces plus 26 mosques, and its walls, protected by 14 forts, fashioned a three-kilometre girdle around it.

Then the *Nautilus* drew near the beaches of Africa, where the sea is considerably deeper. There, through the open panels and in a midwater of crystal clarity, our ship enabled us to study wonderful bushes of shining coral and huge chunks of rock wrapped in splendid green furs of algae and fucus. What an indescribable sight, and what a variety of settings and scenery where these reefs and volcanic islands levelled off by the Libyan coast! But soon the *Nautilus* hugged the eastern shore where these tree forms appeared in all their glory. This was off the coast of Tihama, and there such zoophyte displays not only flourished below sea level but they also fashioned picturesque networks that unreeled as high as ten fathoms above it; the latter were more whimsical but less colourful than the former, which kept their bloom thanks to the moist vitality of the waters.

How many delightful hours I spent in this way at the lounge window! How many new specimens of underwater flora and fauna I marvelled at beneath the light of our electric beacon! Mushroom-shaped fungus coral, some slate-coloured sea anemone including the species Thalassianthus aster among others, organ-pipe coral arranged like flutes and just begging for a puff from the god Pan, shells unique to this sea that dwell in madreporic cavities and whose bases are twisted into squat spirals, and finally a thousand samples of a polypary I hadn't observed until then: the common sponge.

First division in the polyp group, the class *Spongiaria* has been created by scientists precisely for this unusual exhibit whose usefulness is beyond dispute. The sponge is definitely not a plant, as some naturalists still believe, but an animal of the lowest order, a polypary inferior even to coral. Its animal nature isn't in doubt, and we can't accept even the views of the ancients, who regarded it as halfway between plant and animal. But I must say that naturalists are not in agreement on the structural mode of sponges. For some it's a polypary, and for others, such as Professor Milne-Edwards, it's a single, solitary individual.

The class Spongiaria contains about 300 species that are encountered in a large number of seas and even in certain streams, where they've been given the name freshwater sponges. But their waters of choice are the Red Sea and the Mediterranean near the Greek Islands or the coast of Syria. These waters witness the reproduction and growth of soft, delicate bath sponges whose prices run as high as 150 francs apiece: the yellow sponge from Syria, the horn sponge from Barbary, etc. But since I had no hope of studying these zoophytes in the seaports of the Levant, from which we were separated by the insuperable Isthmus of Suez, I had to be content with observing them in the waters of the Red Sea.

So I called Conseil to my side, while at an average depth of eight to nine metres, the *Nautilus* slowly skimmed every beautiful rock on the easterly coast.

There sponges grew in every shape, globular, stalklike, leaflike, fingerlike. With reasonable accuracy, they lived up to their nicknames of basket sponges, chalice sponges, distaff sponges, elkhorn sponges, lion's paws, peacock's tails and Neptune's gloves – designations bestowed on them by fishermen, more poetically inclined than scientists. A gelatinous, semifluid substance coated the fibrous tissue of these sponges, and from this tissue there escaped a steady trickle of water that, after carrying sustenance to each cell, was being expelled by a contracting movement. This jellylike substance disappears when the polyp dies, emitting ammonia as it rots. Finally nothing remains but the fibres, either gelatinous or made of horn, that constitute your household sponge, which takes on a russet hue and is used for various tasks depending on its degree of elasticity, permeability, or resistance to saturation.

These polyparies were sticking to rocks, shells of molluscs, and even the stalks of water plants. They adorned the smallest crevices, some sprawling, others standing or hanging like coral outgrowths. I told Conseil that sponges are fished up in two ways, either by dragnet or by hand. The latter method calls for the services of a diver, but it's preferable because it spares the polypary's tissue, leaving it with a much higher market value.

Other zoophytes swarming near the sponges consisted chiefly of a very elegant species of jellyfish; molluscs were represented by varieties of squid that, according to Professor Orbigny, are unique to the Red Sea; and reptiles by virgata turtles belonging to the genus *Chelonia*, which furnished our table with a dainty but wholesome dish.

As for fish, they were numerous and often remarkable. Here are the ones that the *Nautilus*'s nets most frequently hauled on board: rays, including spotted rays that were oval in shape and brick red in colour, their bodies strewn with erratic blue speckles and identifiable by their jagged double stings, silver-backed skates, common stingrays with stippled tails, butterfly rays that looked like huge two-metre cloaks flapping at mid-depth, toothless guitarfish that were a type of cartilaginous fish closer to the shark, trunkfish known as dromedaries that were one and a half feet long and had humps ending in backward-curving stings, serpentine moray eels with silver tails and bluish backs plus brown pectorals trimmed in grey piping, a species of butterfish called the fiatola decked out in thin gold stripes and the three colours of the French flag, Montague blennies four decimetres long, superb jacks handsomely embellished by seven black crosswise streaks with blue and yellow fins plus gold and silver scales, snooks, standard mullet with yellow heads, parrotfish, wrasse, triggerfish, gobies, etc., plus a thousand other fish common to the oceans we had already crossed.

On February 9 the *Nautilus* cruised in the widest part of the Red Sea, measuring 190 miles straight across from Suakin on the west coast to Qunfidha on the east coast.

At noon that day after our position fix, Captain Nemo climbed onto the platform, where I happened to be. I vowed not to let him go below again without at least sounding him out on his future plans.

As soon as he saw me, he came over, graciously offered me a cigar, and said to me:

'Well, professor, are you pleased with this Red Sea? Have you seen enough of its hidden wonders, its fish and zoophytes, its gardens of sponges and forests of coral? Have you glimpsed the towns built on its shores?'

'Yes, Captain Nemo,' I replied, 'and the *Nautilus* is wonderfully suited to this whole survey. Ah, it's a clever boat!'

'Yes, sir, clever, daring, and invulnerable! It fears neither the Red Sea's dreadful storms nor its currents and reefs.'

'Indeed,' I said, 'this sea is mentioned as one of the worst, and in the days of the ancients, if I'm not mistaken, it had an abominable reputation.'

'Thoroughly abominable, Professor Aronnax. The Greek and Latin historians can find nothing to say in its favour, and the Greek geographer Strabo adds that it's especially rough during the rainy season and the period of summer prevailing winds. The Arab Idrisi, referring to it by the name Gulf of Colzoum, relates that ships perished in large numbers on its sandbanks and that no one risked navigating it by night. This, he claims, is a sea subject to fearful hurricanes, strewn with inhospitable islands, and "with nothing good to offer," either on its surface or in its depths. As a matter of fact, the same views can also be found in Arrian, Agatharchides, and Artemidorus.'

'One can easily see,' I answered, 'that those historians didn't navigate aboard the *Nautilus*.'

'Indeed,' the captain replied with a smile, 'and in this respect, the moderns aren't much farther along than the ancients. It took many centuries to discover the mechanical power of steam! Who knows whether we'll see a second *Nautilus* within the next 100 years! Progress is slow, Professor Aronnax.'

'It's true,' I replied. 'Your ship is a century ahead of its time, perhaps several centuries. It would be most unfortunate if such a secret were to die with its inventor!'

Captain Nemo did not reply. After some minutes of silence:

'We were discussing,' he said, 'the views of ancient historians on the dangers of navigating this Red Sea?'

'True,' I replied. 'But weren't their fears exaggerated?'

'Yes and no, Professor Aronnax,' answered Captain Nemo, who seemed to know 'his Red Sea' by heart. 'To a modern ship, well rigged, solidly constructed, and in control of its course thanks to obedient steam, some conditions are no longer hazardous that offered all sorts of dangers to the vessels of the ancients. Picture those early navigators venturing forth in sailboats built from planks lashed together with palm-tree ropes, caulked with powdered resin and coated with dogfish grease. They didn't even have instruments for taking their bearings, they went by guesswork in the midst of currents they barely knew. Under such conditions, shipwrecks had to be numerous. But nowadays steamers providing service between Suez and the South Seas have nothing to fear from the fury of this gulf, despite the contrary winds of its monsoons. Their captains and passengers no longer prepare for departure with sacrifices to placate the gods, and after returning, they don't traipse in wreaths and gold ribbons to say thanks at the local temple.'

'Agreed,' I said. 'And steam seems to have killed off all gratitude in seamen's hearts. But since you seem to have made a special study of this sea, captain, can you tell me how it got its name?'

'Many explanations exist on the subject, Professor Aronnax. Would you like to hear the views of one chronicler in the 14th century?'

'Gladly.'

'This fanciful fellow claims the sea was given its name after the crossing of the Israelites, when the Pharaoh perished in those waves that came together again at Moses' command:

To mark that miraculous sequel, the sea turned a red without equal.

Thus no other course would do but to name it for its hue.'

'An artistic explanation, Captain Nemo,' I replied, 'but I'm unable to rest content with it. So I'll ask you for your own personal views.'

'Here they come. To my thinking, Professor Aronnax, this "Red Sea" designation must be regarded as a translation of the Hebrew word *Edrom*, and if the ancients gave it that name, it was because of the unique colour of its waters.'

'Until now, however, I've seen only clear waves, without any unique hue.'

'Surely, but as we move ahead to the far end of this gulf, you'll note its odd appearance. I recall seeing the bay of El Tur completely red, like a lake of blood.'

'And you attribute this colour to the presence of microscopic algae?'

'Yes. It's a purplish, mucilaginous substance produced by those tiny buds known by the name *trichodesmia*, 40,000 of which are needed to occupy the space of one square millimetre. Perhaps you'll encounter them when we reach El Tur.'

'Hence, Captain Nemo, this isn't the first time you've gone through the Red Sea aboard the *Nautilus*?'

'No, sir.'

'Then, since you've already mentioned the crossing of the Israelites and the catastrophe that befell the Egyptians, I would ask if you've ever discovered any traces under the waters of that great historic event?'

'No, professor, and for an excellent reason.'

'What's that?'

'It's because that same locality where Moses crossed with all his people is now so clogged with sand, camels can barely get their legs wet. You can understand that my *Nautilus* wouldn't have enough water for itself.'

'And that locality is...?' I asked.

'That locality lies a little above Suez in a sound that used to form a deep estuary when the Red Sea stretched as far as the Bitter Lakes. Now, whether or not their crossing was literally miraculous, the Israelites did cross there in returning to the Promised Land, and the Pharaoh's army did perish at precisely that locality. So I think that excavating those sands would bring to light a great many weapons and tools of Egyptian origin.'

'Obviously,' I replied. 'And for the sake of archaeology, let's hope that sooner or later such excavations do take place, once new towns are settled on the isthmus after the Suez Canal has been cut through – a canal, by the way, of little use to a ship such as the *Nautilus*!'

'Surely, but of great use to the world at large,' Captain Nemo said. 'The ancients well understood the usefulness to commerce of connecting the Red Sea with the Mediterranean, but they never dreamed of cutting a canal between the two, and instead they picked the Nile as their link.

If we can trust tradition, it was probably Egypt's King Sesostris who started digging the canal needed to join the Nile with the Red Sea. What's certain is that in 615 BC King Necho II was hard at work on a canal that was fed by Nile water and ran through the Egyptian plains opposite Arabia. This canal could be travelled in four days, and it was so wide, two triple-tiered galleys could pass through it abreast. Its construction was continued by Darius the Great, son of Hystaspes, and probably completed by King Ptolemy II. Strabo saw it used for shipping; but the weakness of its slope between its starting point, near Bubastis, and the Red Sea left it navigable only a few months out of the year. This canal served commerce until the century of Rome's Antonine emperors; it was then abandoned and covered with sand, subsequently reinstated by Arabia's Caliph Omar I, and finally filled in for good in 761 or 762 AD by Caliph Al-Mansur, in an effort to prevent supplies from reaching Mohammed ibn Abdullah, who had rebelled against him. During his Egyptian campaign, your General Napoleon Bonaparte discovered traces of this old canal in the Suez desert, and when the tide caught him by surprise, he wellnigh perished just a few hours before rejoining his regiment at Hadjaroth, the very place where Moses had pitched camp 3,300 years before him.'

'Well, captain, what the ancients hesitated to undertake, Mr de Lesseps is now finishing up; his joining of these two seas will shorten the route from Cadiz to the East Indies by 9,000 kilometres, and he'll soon change Africa into an immense island.'

'Yes, Professor Aronnax, and you have every right to be proud of your fellow countryman. Such a man brings a nation more honour than the greatest commanders! Like so many others, he began with difficulties and setbacks, but he triumphed because he has the volunteer spirit. And it's sad to think that this deed, which should have been an international deed, which would have insured that any administration went down in history, will succeed only through the efforts of one man. So all hail to Mr de Lesseps!'

'Yes, all hail to that great French citizen,' I replied, quite startled by how emphatically Captain Nemo had just spoken.

'Unfortunately,' he went on, 'I can't take you through that Suez Canal, but the day after tomorrow, you'll be able to see the long jetties of Port Said when we're in the Mediterranean.'

'In the Mediterranean!' I exclaimed.

'Yes, professor. Does that amaze you?'

'What amazes me is thinking we'll be there the day after tomorrow.'

'Oh really?'

'Yes, captain, although since I've been aboard your vessel, I should have formed the habit of not being amazed by anything!'

'But what is it that startles you?'

'The thought of how hideously fast the *Nautilus* will need to go, if it's to double the Cape of Good Hope, circle around Africa, and lie in the open Mediterranean by the day after tomorrow.'

'And who says it will circle Africa, professor? What's this talk about doubling the Cape of Good Hope?'

'But unless the *Nautilus* navigates on dry land and crosses over the isthmus—'

'Or under it, Professor Aronnax.'

'Under it?'

'Surely,' Captain Nemo replied serenely. 'Under that tongue of land, nature long ago made what man today is making on its surface.'

'What! There's a passageway?'

'Yes, an underground passageway that I've named the Arabian Tunnel. It starts below Suez and leads to the Bay of Pelusium.'

'But isn't that isthmus only composed of quicksand?'

'To a certain depth. But at merely 50 metres, one encounters a firm foundation of rock.'

'And it's by luck that you discovered this passageway?' I asked, more and more startled.

'Luck plus logic, professor, and logic even more than luck.'

'Captain, I hear you, but I can't believe my ears.'

'Oh, sir! The old saying still holds good: *Aures habent et non audient!* Not only does this passageway exist, but I've taken advantage of it on several occasions. Without it, I wouldn't have ventured today into such a blind alley as the Red Sea.'

'Is it indiscreet to ask how you discovered this tunnel?'

'Sir,' the captain answered me, 'there can be no secrets between men who will never leave each other.'

I ignored this innuendo and waited for Captain Nemo's explanation.

'Professor,' he told me, 'the simple logic of the naturalist led me to discover this passageway, and I alone am familiar with it. I'd noted that in the Red Sea and the Mediterranean there exist a number of absolutely identical species of fish: eels, butterfish, greenfish, bass, jewelfish, flying fish. Certain of this fact, I wondered if there weren't a connection between the two seas. If there were, its underground current had to go from the Red Sea to the Mediterranean simply because of their difference in level. So I caught a large number of fish in the vicinity of Suez. I slipped copper rings around their tails and tossed them back into the sea. A few months later off the coast of Syria, I recaptured a few specimens of my fish, adorned with their telltale rings. So this proved to me that some connection existed between the two seas. I searched for it with my *Nautilus*, I discovered it, I ventured into it; and soon, professor, you also will have cleared my Arabic tunnel!'

CHAPTER 5

Arabian Tunnel

THE SAME DAY, I reported to Conseil and Ned Land that part of the foregoing conversation directly concerning them. When I told them we would be lying in Mediterranean waters within two days, Conseil clapped his hands, but the Canadian shrugged his shoulders.

'An underwater tunnel!' he exclaimed. 'A connection between two seas! Who ever heard of such malarkey!'

'Ned my friend,' Conseil replied, 'had you ever heard of the *Nautilus*? No, yet here it is! So don't shrug your shoulders so blithely, and don't discount something with the feeble excuse that you've never heard of it.'

'We'll soon see!' Ned Land shot back, shaking his head. 'After all, I'd like nothing better than to believe in your captain's little passageway, and may Heaven grant it really does take us to the Mediterranean.'

The same evening, at latitude 21° 30' north, the *Nautilus* was afloat on the surface of the sea and drawing nearer to the Arab coast. I spotted Jidda, an important financial centre for Egypt, Syria, Turkey and the East Indies. I could distinguish with reasonable clarity the overall effect of its buildings, the ships made fast along its wharves, and those bigger vessels whose draught of water required them to drop anchor at the port's offshore mooring. The sun, fairly low on the horizon, struck full force on the houses in this town, accenting their whiteness. Outside the city limits, some wood or reed huts indicated the quarter where the bedouins lived.

Soon Jidda faded into the shadows of evening, and the *Nautilus* went back beneath the mildly phosphorescent waters.

The next day, February 10, several ships appeared, running on our opposite tack. The *Nautilus* resumed its underwater navigating; but at the moment of our noon sights, the sea was deserted and the ship rose again to its waterline.

With Ned and Conseil, I went to sit on the platform. The coast to the east looked like a slightly blurred mass in a damp fog.

Leaning against the sides of the skiff, we were chatting of one thing and another, when Ned Land stretched his hand toward a point in the water, saying to me:

'See anything out there, professor?'

'No, Ned,' I replied, 'but you know I don't have your eyes.'

'Take a good look,' Ned went on. 'There, ahead to starboard, almost level with the beacon! Don't you see a mass that seems to be moving around?'

'Right,' I said after observing carefully, 'I can make out something like a long, blackish object on the surface of the water.'

'A second *Nautilus*?' Conseil said.

'No,' the Canadian replied, 'unless I'm badly mistaken, that's some marine animal.'

'Are there whales in the Red Sea?' Conseil asked.

'Yes, my boy,' I replied, 'they're sometimes found here.'

'That's no whale,' continued Ned Land, whose eyes never strayed from the object they had sighted. 'We're old chums, whales and I, and I couldn't mistake their little ways.'

'Let's wait and see,' Conseil said. 'The *Nautilus* is heading that direction, and we'll soon know what we're in for.'

In fact, that blackish object was soon only a mile away from us. It looked like a huge reef stranded in midocean. What was it? I still couldn't make up my mind.

'Oh, it's moving off! It's diving!' Ned Land exclaimed. 'Damnation! What can that animal be? It doesn't have a forked tail like baleen whales or sperm whales, and its fins look like sawed-off limbs.'

'But in that case—' I put in.

'Good lord,' the Canadian went on, 'it's rolled over on its back, and it's raising its breasts in the air!'

'It's a siren!' Conseil exclaimed. 'With all due respect to master, it's an actual mermaid!'

That word 'siren' put me back on track, and I realised that the animal belonged to the order *Sirenia*: marine creatures that legends have turned into mermaids, half woman, half fish.

'No,' I told Conseil, 'that's no mermaid, it's an unusual creature of which only a few specimens are left in the Red Sea. That's a dugong.'

'Order *Sirenia*, group *Pisciforma*, subclass *Monodelphia*, class *Mammalia*, branch *Vertebrata*,' Conseil replied.

And when Conseil has spoken, there's nothing else to be said.

Meanwhile Ned Land kept staring. His eyes were gleaming with desire at the sight of that animal. His hands were ready to hurl a harpoon. You would have thought he was waiting for the right moment to jump overboard and attack the creature in its own element.

'Oh, sir,' he told me in a voice trembling with excitement, 'I've never killed anything like that!'

His whole being was concentrated in this last word.

Just then Captain Nemo appeared on the platform. He spotted the dugong. He understood the Canadian's frame of mind and addressed him directly:

'If you held a harpoon, Mr Land, wouldn't your hands be itching to put it to work?'

'Positively, sir.'

'And just for one day, would it displease you to return to your fisherman's trade and add this cetacean to the list of those you've already hunted down?'

'It wouldn't displease me one bit.'

'All right, you can try your luck!'

'Thank you, sir,' Ned Land replied, his eyes ablaze.

'Only,' the captain went on, 'I urge you to aim carefully at this animal, in your own personal interest.'

'Is the dugong dangerous to attack?' I asked, despite the Canadian's shrug of the shoulders.

'Yes, sometimes,' the captain replied. 'These animals have been known to turn on their assailants and capsize their longboats. But with Mr Land that danger isn't to be feared. His eye is sharp, his arm is sure. If I recommend that he aim carefully at this dugong, it's because the animal is justly regarded as fine game, and I know Mr Land doesn't despise a choice morsel.'

'Aha!' the Canadian put in. 'This beast offers the added luxury of being good to eat?'

'Yes, Mr Land. Its flesh is actual red meat, highly prized, and set aside throughout Malaysia for the tables of aristocrats. Accordingly, this excellent animal has been hunted so bloodthirstily that, like its manatee relatives, it has become more and more scarce.'

'In that case, captain,' Conseil said in all seriousness, 'on the offchance that this creature might be the last of its line, wouldn't it be advisable to spare its life, in the interests of science?'

'Maybe,' the Canadian answered, 'it would be better to hunt it down, in the interests of mealtime.'

'Then proceed, Mr Land,' Captain Nemo replied.

Just then, as mute and emotionless as ever, seven crewmen climbed onto the platform. One carried a harpoon and line similar to those used in whale fishing. Its deck panelling opened, the skiff was wrenched from its socket and launched to sea. Six rowers sat on the thwarts, and the coxswain took the tiller. Ned, Conseil and I found seats in the stern.

'Aren't you coming, captain?' I asked.

'No, sir, but I wish you happy hunting.'

The skiff pulled clear, and carried off by its six oars, it headed swiftly toward the dugong, which by then was floating two miles from the *Nautilus*.

Arriving within a few cable lengths of the cetacean, our longboat slowed down, and the sculls dipped noiselessly into the tranquil waters. Harpoon in hand, Ned Land went to take his stand in the skiff's bow. Harpoons used for hunting whales are usually attached to a very long rope that pays out quickly when the wounded animal drags it with him. But this rope measured no more than about ten fathoms, and its end had simply been fastened to a small barrel that, while floating, would indicate the dugong's movements beneath the waters.

I stood up and could clearly observe the Canadian's adversary. This dugong – which also boasts the name halicore – closely resembled a manatee. Its oblong body ended in a very long caudal fin and its lateral fins in actual fingers. It differs from the manatee in that its upper jaw is armed with two long, pointed teeth that form diverging tusks on either side.

This dugong that Ned Land was preparing to attack was of colossal dimensions, easily exceeding seven metres in length. It didn't stir and seemed to be sleeping on the surface of the waves, a circumstance that should have made it easier to capture.

The skiff approached cautiously to within three fathoms of the animal. The oars hung suspended above their rowlocks. I was crouching. His body leaning slightly back, Ned Land brandished his harpoon with expert hands.

Suddenly a hissing sound was audible, and the dugong disappeared. Although the harpoon had been forcefully hurled, it apparently had hit only water.

'Damnation!' exclaimed the furious Canadian. 'I missed it!'

'No,' I said, 'the animal's wounded, there's its blood; but your weapon didn't stick in its body.'

'My harpoon! Get my harpoon!' Ned Land exclaimed.

The sailors went back to their sculling, and the coxswain steered the longboat toward the floating barrel. We fished up the harpoon, and the skiff started off in pursuit of the animal.

The latter returned from time to time to breathe at the surface of the sea. Its wound hadn't weakened it because it went with tremendous speed. Driven by energetic arms, the longboat flew on its trail. Several times we got within a few fathoms of it, and the Canadian hovered in readiness to strike; but then the dugong would steal away with a sudden dive, and it proved impossible to overtake the beast.

I'll let you assess the degree of anger consuming our impatient Ned Land. He hurled at the hapless animal the most potent swearwords in the English language. For my part, I was simply distressed to see this dugong outwit our every scheme.

We chased it unflaggingly for a full hour, and I'd begun to think it would prove too difficult to capture, when the animal got the untimely idea of taking revenge on us, a notion it would soon have cause to regret. It wheeled on the skiff, to assault us in its turn.

This manoeuvre did not escape the Canadian.

'Watch out!' he said.

The coxswain pronounced a few words in his bizarre language, and no doubt he alerted his men to keep on their guard.

Arriving within 20 feet of the skiff, the dugong stopped, sharply sniffing the air with its huge nostrils, pierced not at the tip of its muzzle but on its topside. Then it gathered itself and sprang at us.

The skiff couldn't avoid the collision. Half overturned, it shipped a ton or two of water that we had to bail out. But thanks to our skilful coxswain, we were fouled on the bias rather than broadside, so we didn't capsize. Clinging to the stempost, Ned Land thrust his harpoon again and again into the gigantic animal, which imbedded its teeth in our gunwale and lifted the longboat out of the water as a lion would lift a deer. We were thrown on top of each other, and I have no idea how the venture would have ended had not the Canadian, still thirsting for the beast's blood, finally pierced it to the heart.

I heard its teeth grind on sheet iron, and the dugong disappeared, taking our harpoon along with it. But the barrel soon popped up on the surface, and a few moments later the animal's body appeared and rolled over on its back. Our skiff rejoined it, took it in tow, and headed to the *Nautilus*.

It took pulleys of great strength to hoist this dugong onto the platform. The beast weighed 5,000 kilograms. It was carved up in sight of the Canadian, who remained to watch every detail of the operation. At dinner the same day, my steward served me some slices of this flesh, skilfully dressed by the ship's cook. I found it excellent, even better than veal if not beef.

The next morning, February 11, the *Nautilus*'s pantry was enriched by more dainty game. A covey of terns alighted on the *Nautilus*. They were a species of *Sterna nilotica* unique to Egypt: beak black, head grey and stippled, eyes surrounded by white dots, back, wings, and tail greyish, belly and throat white, feet red. Also caught were a couple of dozen Nile duck, superior-tasting wildfowl whose neck and crown of the head are white speckled with black.

By then the *Nautilus* had reduced speed. It moved ahead at a saunter, so to speak. I observed that the Red Sea's water was becoming less salty the closer we got to Suez.

Near five o'clock in the afternoon, we sighted Cape Ras Mohammed to the north. This cape forms the tip of Arabia Petraea, which lies between the Gulf of Suez and the Gulf of Aqaba.

The *Nautilus* entered the Strait of Jubal, which leads to the Gulf of Suez. I could clearly make out a high mountain crowning Ras Mohammed between the two gulfs. It was Mt Horeb, that biblical Mt Sinai on whose summit Moses met God face to face, that summit the mind's eye always pictures as wreathed in lightning.

At six o'clock, sometimes afloat and sometimes submerged, the *Nautilus* passed well out from El Tur, which sat at the far end of a bay whose waters seemed to be dyed red, as Captain Nemo had already mentioned. Then night fell in the midst of a heavy silence occasionally broken by the calls of pelicans and nocturnal birds, by the sound of surf chafing against rocks, or by the distant moan of a steamer churning the waves of the gulf with noisy blades.

From eight to nine o'clock, the *Nautilus* stayed a few metres beneath the waters. According to my calculations, we had to be quite close to Suez. Through the panels in the lounge, I spotted rocky bottoms brightly lit by our electric rays. It seemed to me that the strait was getting narrower and narrower.

At 9:15 when our boat returned to the surface, I climbed onto the platform. I was quite impatient to clear Captain Nemo's tunnel, couldn't sit still, and wanted to breathe the fresh night air.

Soon, in the shadows, I spotted a pale signal light glimmering a mile away, half discoloured by mist.

'A floating lighthouse,' said someone next to me.

I turned and discovered the captain.

'That's the floating signal light of Suez,' he went on. 'It won't be long before we reach the entrance to the tunnel.'

'It can't be very easy to enter it.'

'No, sir. Accordingly, I'm in the habit of staying in the pilothouse and directing manoeuvres myself. And now if you'll kindly go below, Professor Aronnax, the *Nautilus* is about to sink beneath the waves, and it will only return to the surface after we've cleared the Arabian Tunnel.'

I followed Captain Nemo. The hatch closed, the ballast tanks filled with water, and the submersible sank some ten metres down.

Just as I was about to repair to my stateroom, the captain stopped me.

'Professor,' he said to me, 'would you like to go with me to the wheelhouse?'

'I was afraid to ask,' I replied.

'Come along, then. This way, you'll learn the full story about this combination underwater and underground navigating.'

Captain Nemo led me to the central companionway. In midstair he opened a door, went along the upper gangways, and arrived at the wheelhouse, which, as you know, stands at one end of the platform.

It was a cabin measuring six feet square and closely resembling those occupied by the helmsmen of steamboats on the Mississippi or Hudson rivers. In the centre stood an upright wheel geared to rudder cables running to the *Nautilus*'s stern. Set in the cabin's walls were four deadlights, windows of biconvex glass that enabled the man at the helm to see in every direction.

The cabin was dark; but my eyes soon grew accustomed to its darkness and I saw the pilot, a muscular man whose hands rested on the pegs of the wheel. Outside, the sea was brightly lit by the beacon shining behind the cabin at the other end of the platform.

'Now,' Captain Nemo said, 'let's look for our passageway.'

Electric wires linked the pilothouse with the engine room, and from this cabin the captain could simultaneously signal heading and speed to his *Nautilus*. He pressed a metal button and at once the propeller slowed down significantly.

I stared in silence at the high, sheer wall we were skirting just then, the firm base of the sandy mountains on the coast. For an hour we went along it in this fashion, staying only a few metres away. Captain Nemo never took his eyes off the two concentric circles of the compass hanging in the cabin. At a mere gesture from him, the helmsman would instantly change the *Nautilus*'s heading.

Standing by the port deadlight, I spotted magnificent coral substructures, zoophytes, algae and crustaceans with enormous quivering claws that stretched forth from crevices in the rock.

At 10:15 Captain Nemo himself took the helm. Dark and deep, a wide gallery opened ahead of us. The *Nautilus* was brazenly swallowed up. Strange rumblings were audible along our sides. It was the water of the Red Sea, hurled toward the Mediterranean by the tunnel's slope. Our engines tried to offer resistance by churning the waves with propeller in reverse, but the *Nautilus* went with the torrent, as swift as an arrow.

Along the narrow walls of this passageway, I saw only brilliant streaks, hard lines, fiery furrows, all scrawled by our speeding electric light. With my hand I tried to curb the pounding of my heart.

At 10:35 Captain Nemo left the steering wheel and turned to me: 'The Mediterranean,' he told me.

In less than 20 minutes, swept along by the torrent, the *Nautilus* had just cleared the Isthmus of Suez.

CHAPTER 6

The Greek Islands

AT SUNRISE THE next morning, February 12, the *Nautilus* rose to the surface of the waves.

I rushed onto the platform. The hazy silhouette of Pelusium was outlined three miles to the south. A torrent had carried us from one sea to the other. But although that tunnel was easy to descend, going back up must have been impossible.

Near seven o'clock Ned and Conseil joined me. Those two inseparable companions had slept serenely, utterly unaware of the *Nautilus*'s feat.

'Well, Mr Naturalist,' the Canadian asked in a gently mocking tone, 'and how about that Mediterranean?'

'We're floating on its surface, Ned my friend.'

'What!' Conseil put in. 'Last night…?'

'Yes, last night, in a matter of minutes, we cleared that insuperable isthmus.'

'I don't believe a word of it,' the Canadian replied.

'And you're in the wrong, Mr Land,' I went on. 'That flat coastline curving southward is the coast of Egypt.'

'Tell it to the marines, sir,' answered the stubborn Canadian.

'But if master says so,' Conseil told him, 'then so be it.'

'What's more, Ned,' I said, 'Captain Nemo himself did the honours in his tunnel, and I stood beside him in the pilothouse while he steered the *Nautilus* through that narrow passageway.'

'You hear, Ned?' Conseil said.

'And you, Ned, who have such good eyes,' I added, 'you can spot the jetties of Port Said stretching out to sea.'

The Canadian looked carefully.

'Correct,' he said. 'You're right, professor, and your captain's a superman. We're in the Mediterranean. Fine. So now let's have a chat about our little doings, if you please, but in such a way that nobody overhears.'

I could easily see what the Canadian was driving at. In any event, I thought it best to let him have his chat, and we all three went to sit next to the beacon, where we were less exposed to the damp spray from the billows.

'Now, Ned, we're all ears,' I said. 'What have you to tell us?'

'What I've got to tell you is very simple,' the Canadian replied. 'We're in Europe, and before Captain Nemo's whims take us deep into the polar seas or back to Oceania, I say we should leave this *Nautilus*.'

I confess that such discussions with the Canadian always baffled me. I didn't want to restrict my companions' freedom in any way, and yet I had no desire to leave Captain Nemo. Thanks to him and his submersible, I was finishing my undersea research by the day, and I was rewriting my book on the great ocean depths in the midst of its very element. Would I ever again have such an opportunity to observe the ocean's wonders? Absolutely not! So I couldn't entertain this idea of leaving the *Nautilus* before completing our course of inquiry.

'Ned my friend,' I said, 'answer me honestly. Are you bored with this ship? Are you sorry that fate has cast you into Captain Nemo's hands?'

The Canadian paused for a short while before replying. Then, crossing his arms:

'Honestly,' he said, 'I'm not sorry about this voyage under the seas. I'll be glad to have done it, but in order to have done it, it has to finish. That's my feeling.'

'It will finish, Ned.'

'Where and when?'

'Where? I don't know. When? I can't say. Or, rather, I suppose it will be over when these seas have nothing more to teach us. Everything that begins in this world must inevitably come to an end.'

'I think as master does,' Conseil replied, 'and it's extremely possible that after crossing every sea on the globe, Captain Nemo will bid the three of us a fond farewell.'

'Bid us a fond farewell?' the Canadian exclaimed. 'You mean beat us to a fare-thee-well!'

'Let's not exaggerate, Mr Land,' I went on. 'We have nothing to fear from the captain, but neither do I share Conseil's views. We're privy to the *Nautilus*'s secrets, and I don't expect that its commander, just to set us free, will meekly stand by while we spread those secrets all over the world.'

'But in that case what do you expect?' the Canadian asked.

'That we'll encounter advantageous conditions for escaping just as readily in six months as now.'

'Great Scott!' Ned Land put in. 'And where, if you please, will we be in six months, Mr Naturalist?'

'Perhaps here, perhaps in China. You know how quickly the *Nautilus* moves. It crosses oceans like swallows cross the air or express trains continents. It doesn't fear heavily travelled seas. Who can say it won't hug the coasts of France, England, or America, where an escape attempt could be carried out just as effectively as here.'

'Professor Aronnax,' the Canadian replied, 'your arguments are rotten to the core. You talk way off in the future: "We'll be here, we'll be there!" Me, I'm talking about right now: we are here, and we must take advantage of it!'

I was hard pressed by Ned Land's common sense, and I felt myself losing ground. I no longer knew what arguments to put forward on my behalf.

'Sir,' Ned went on, 'let's suppose that by some impossibility, Captain Nemo offered your freedom to you this very day. Would you accept?'

'I don't know,' I replied.

'And suppose he adds that this offer he's making you today won't ever be repeated, then would you accept?'

I did not reply.

'And what thinks our friend Conseil?' Ned Land asked.

'Your friend Conseil,' the fine lad replied serenely, 'has nothing to say for himself. He's a completely disinterested party on this question. Like his master, like his comrade Ned, he's a bachelor. Neither wife, parents, nor children are waiting for him back home. He's in master's employ, he thinks like master, he speaks like master, and much to his regret, he can't be counted on to form a majority. Only two persons face each other here: master on one side, Ned Land on the other. That said, your friend Conseil is listening, and he's ready to keep score.'

I couldn't help smiling as Conseil wiped himself out of existence. Deep down, the Canadian must have been overjoyed at not having to contend with him.

'Then, sir,' Ned Land said, 'since Conseil is no more, we'll have this discussion between just the two of us. I've talked, you've listened. What's your reply?'

It was obvious that the matter had to be settled, and evasions were distasteful to me.

'Ned my friend,' I said, 'here's my reply. You have right on your side and my arguments can't stand up to yours. It will never do to count on Captain Nemo's benevolence. The most ordinary good sense would forbid him to set us free. On the other hand, good sense decrees that we take advantage of our first opportunity to leave the *Nautilus*.'

'Fine, Professor Aronnax, that's wisely said.'

'But one proviso,' I said, 'just one. The opportunity must be the real thing. Our first attempt to escape must succeed, because if it misfires, we won't get a second chance, and Captain Nemo will never forgive us.'

'That's also well put,' the Canadian replied. 'But your proviso applies to any escape attempt, whether it happens in two years or two days. So this is still the question: if a promising opportunity comes up, we have to grab it.'

'Agreed. And now, Ned, will you tell me what you mean by a promising opportunity?'

'One that leads the *Nautilus* on a cloudy night within a short distance of some European coast.'

'And you'll try to get away by swimming?'

'Yes, if we're close enough to shore and the ship's afloat on the surface. No, if we're well out and the ship's navigating under the waters.'

'And in that event?'

'In that event I'll try to get hold of the skiff. I know how to handle it. We'll stick ourselves inside, undo the bolts, and rise to the surface, without the helmsman in the bow seeing a thing.'

'Fine, Ned. Stay on the lookout for such an opportunity, but don't forget, one slipup will finish us.'

'I won't forget, sir.'

'And now, Ned, would you like to know my overall thinking on your plan?'

'Gladly, Professor Aronnax.'

'Well then, I think – and I don't mean "I hope" – that your promising opportunity won't ever arise.'

'Why not?'

'Because Captain Nemo recognises that we haven't given up all hope of recovering our freedom, and he'll keep on his guard, above all in seas within sight of the coasts of Europe.'

'I'm of master's opinion,' Conseil said.

'We'll soon see,' Ned Land replied, shaking his head with a determined expression.

'And now, Ned Land,' I added, 'let's leave it at that. Not another word on any of this. The day you're ready, alert us and we're with you. I turn it all over to you.'

That's how we ended this conversation, which later was to have such serious consequences. At first, I must say, events seemed to confirm my forecasts, much to the Canadian's despair. Did Captain Nemo view us with distrust in these heavily travelled seas, or did he simply want to hide from the sight of those ships of every nation that ploughed the Mediterranean? I have no idea, but usually he stayed in midwater and well out from any coast. Either the *Nautilus* surfaced only enough to let its pilothouse emerge, or it slipped away to the lower depths, although, between the Greek Islands and Asia Minor, we didn't find bottom even at 2,000 metres down.

Accordingly, I became aware of the isle of Karpathos, one of the Sporades Islands, only when Captain Nemo placed his finger over a spot on the world map and quoted me this verse from Virgil:

Est in Carpathio Neptuni gurgite vates
Caeruleus Proteus...

It was indeed that bygone abode of Proteus, the old shepherd of King Neptune's flocks: an island located between Rhodes and Crete, which Greeks now call Karpathos, Italians Scarpanto. Through the lounge window I could see only its granite bedrock.

The next day, February 14, I decided to spend a few hours studying the fish of this island group; but for whatever reason, the panels remained hermetically sealed. After determining the *Nautilus*'s heading, I noted that it was proceeding toward the ancient island of Crete, also called Candia. At the time I had shipped aboard the *Abraham Lincoln*, this whole island was in rebellion against its tyrannical rulers, the Ottoman Empire of Turkey. But since then I had absolutely no idea what happened to this revolution, and Captain Nemo, deprived of all contact with the shore, was hardly the man to keep me informed.

So I didn't allude to this event when, that evening, I chanced to be alone with the captain in the lounge. Besides, he seemed silent and preoccupied. Then, contrary to custom, he ordered that both panels in the lounge be opened, and going from the one to the other, he carefully observed the watery mass. For what purpose? I hadn't a guess, and for my part, I spent my time studying the fish that passed before my eyes.

Among others I noted that sand goby mentioned by Aristotle and commonly known by the name sea loach, which is encountered exclusively in the salty waters next to the Nile Delta. Near them some semi-phosphorescent red porgy rolled by, a variety of gilthead that the Egyptians ranked among their sacred animals, lauding them in religious ceremonies when their arrival in the river's waters announced the fertile flood season. I also noticed some wrasse known as the tapiro, three decimetres long, bony fish with transparent scales whose bluish grey colour is mixed with red spots; they're enthusiastic eaters of marine vegetables, which gives them an exquisite flavour; hence these tapiro were much in demand by the epicures of ancient Rome, and their entrails were dressed with brains of peacock, tongue of flamingo and testes of moray to make that divine platter that so enraptured the Roman emperor Vitellius.

Another resident of these seas caught my attention and revived all my memories of antiquity. This was the remora, which travels attached to the bellies of sharks; as the ancients tell it, when these little fish cling to the undersides of a ship, they can bring it to a halt, and by so impeding Mark Antony's vessel during the Battle of Actium, one of them facilitated the victory of Augustus Caesar. From such slender threads hang the destinies of nations! I also observed some wonderful snappers belonging to the order *Lutianida*, sacred fish for the Greeks, who claimed they could drive off sea monsters from the waters they frequent; their Greek name *anthias* means 'flower,' and they live up to it in the play of their colours and in those fleeting reflections that turn their dorsal fins into watered silk; their hues are confined to a gamut of reds, from the pallor of pink to the glow of ruby. I couldn't take my eyes off these marine wonders, when I was suddenly jolted by an unexpected apparition.

In the midst of the waters, a man appeared, a diver carrying a little leather bag at his belt. It was no corpse lost in the waves. It was a living man, swimming vigorously, sometimes disappearing to breathe at the surface, then instantly diving again.

I turned to Captain Nemo, and in an agitated voice:

'A man! A castaway!' I exclaimed. 'We must rescue him at all cost!'

The captain didn't reply but went to lean against the window.

The man drew near, and gluing his face to the panel, he stared at us.

To my deep astonishment, Captain Nemo gave him a signal. The diver answered with his hand, immediately swam up to the surface of the sea, and didn't reappear.

'Don't be alarmed,' the captain told me. 'That's Nicolas from Cape Matapan, nicknamed "Il Pesce." He's well known throughout the Cyclades Islands. A bold diver! Water is his true element, and he lives in the sea more than on shore, going constantly from one island to another, even to Crete.'

'You know him, captain?'

'Why not, Professor Aronnax?'

This said, Captain Nemo went to a cabinet standing near the lounge's left panel. Next to this cabinet I saw a chest bound with hoops of iron, its lid bearing a copper plaque that displayed the *Nautilus*'s monogram with its motto *Mobilis in Mobili*.

Just then, ignoring my presence, the captain opened this cabinet, a sort of safe that contained a large number of ingots.

They were gold ingots. And they represented an enormous sum of money. Where had this precious metal come from? How had the captain amassed this gold, and what was he about to do with it?

I didn't pronounce a word. I gaped. Captain Nemo took out the ingots one by one and arranged them methodically inside the chest, filling it to the top. At which point I estimate that it held more than 1,000 kilograms of gold, in other words, close to 5,000,000 francs.

After securely fastening the chest, Captain Nemo wrote an address on its lid in characters that must have been modern Greek.

This done, the captain pressed a button whose wiring was in communication with the crew's quarters. Four men appeared and, not without difficulty, pushed the chest out of the lounge. Then I heard them hoist it up the iron companionway by means of pulleys.

Just then Captain Nemo turned to me:

'You were saying, professor?' he asked me.

'I wasn't saying a thing, captain.'

'Then, sir, with your permission, I'll bid you good evening.'

And with that, Captain Nemo left the lounge.

I re-entered my stateroom, very puzzled, as you can imagine. I tried in vain to fall asleep. I kept searching for a relationship between the appearance of the diver and that chest filled with gold. Soon, from certain rolling and pitching movements, I sensed that the *Nautilus* had left the lower strata and was back on the surface of the water.

Then I heard the sound of footsteps on the platform. I realised that the skiff was being detached and launched to sea. For an instant it bumped the *Nautilus*'s side, then all sounds ceased.

Two hours later, the same noises, the same comings and goings, were repeated. Hoisted on board, the longboat was readjusted into its socket, and the *Nautilus* plunged back beneath the waves.

So those millions had been delivered to their address. At what spot on the continent? Who was the recipient of Captain Nemo's gold?

The next day I related the night's events to Conseil and the Canadian, events that had aroused my curiosity to a fever pitch. My companions were as startled as I was.

'But where does he get those millions?' Ned Land asked.

To this no reply was possible. After breakfast I made my way to the lounge and went about my work. I wrote up my notes until five o'clock in the afternoon. Just then – was it due to some personal indisposition? – I felt extremely hot and had to take off my jacket made of fan mussel fabric. A perplexing circumstance because we weren't in the low latitudes, and besides, once the *Nautilus* was submerged, it shouldn't be subject to any rise in temperature. I looked at the pressure gauge. It marked a depth of 60 feet, a depth beyond the reach of atmospheric heat.

I kept on working, but the temperature rose to the point of becoming unbearable.

'Could there be a fire on board?' I wondered.

I was about to leave the lounge when Captain Nemo entered. He approached the thermometer, consulted it, and turned to me:

'42° centigrade,' he said.

'I've detected as much, captain,' I replied, 'and if it gets even slightly hotter, we won't be able to stand it.'

'Oh, professor, it won't get any hotter unless we want it to!'

'You mean you can control this heat?'

'No, but I can back away from the fireplace producing it.'

'So it's outside?'

'Surely. We're cruising in a current of boiling water.'

'It can't be!' I exclaimed.

'Look.'

The panels had opened, and I could see a completely white sea around the *Nautilus*. Steaming sulphurous fumes uncoiled in the midst of waves bubbling like water in a boiler. I leaned my hand against one of the windows, but the heat was so great, I had to snatch it back.

'Where are we?' I asked.

'Near the island of Santorini, professor,' the captain answered me, 'and right in the channel that separates the volcanic islets of Nea Kameni and Palea Kameni. I wanted to offer you the unusual sight of an underwater eruption.'

'I thought,' I said, 'that the formation of such new islands had come to an end.'

'Nothing ever comes to an end in these volcanic waterways,' Captain Nemo replied, 'and thanks to its underground fires, our globe is continuously under construction in these regions. According to the Latin historians Cassiodorus and Pliny, by the year 19 of the Christian era, a new island, the divine Thera, had already appeared in the very place these islets have more recently formed. Then Thera sank under the waves, only to rise and sink once more in the year 69 AD From that day to this, such plutonic construction work has been in abeyance.

But on February 3, 1866, a new islet named George Island emerged in the midst of sulphurous steam near Nea Kameni and was fused to it on the 6th of the same month. Seven days later, on February 13, the islet of Aphroessa appeared, leaving a ten-metre channel between itself and Nea Kameni. I was in these seas when that phenomenon occurred and I was able to observe its every phase. The islet of Aphroessa was circular in shape, measuring 300 feet in diameter and 30 feet in height. It was made of black, glassy lava mixed with bits of feldspar. Finally, on March 10, a smaller islet called Reka appeared next to Nea Kameni, and since then, these three islets have fused to form one single, selfsame island.'

'What about this channel we're in right now?' I asked.

'Here it is,' Captain Nemo replied, showing me a chart of the Greek Islands. 'You observe that I've entered the new islets in their place.'

'But will this channel fill up one day?'

'Very likely, Professor Aronnax, because since 1866 eight little lava islets have surged up in front of the port of St Nicolas on Palea Kameni. So it's obvious that Nea and Palea will join in days to come. In the middle of the Pacific, tiny infusoria build continents, but here they're built by volcanic phenomena. Look, sir! Look at the construction work going on under these waves.'

I returned to the window. The *Nautilus* was no longer moving. The heat had become unbearable. From the white it had recently been, the sea was turning red, a colouration caused by the presence of iron salts. Although the lounge was hermetically sealed, it was filling with an intolerable stink of sulphur, and I could see scarlet flames of such brightness, they overpowered our electric light.

I was swimming in perspiration, I was stifling, I was about to be cooked. Yes, I felt myself cooking in actual fact!

'We can't stay any longer in this boiling water,' I told the captain.

'No, it wouldn't be advisable,' replied Nemo the Emotionless.

He gave an order. The *Nautilus* tacked about and retreated from this furnace it couldn't brave with impunity. A quarter of an hour later, we were breathing fresh air on the surface of the waves.

It then occurred to me that if Ned had chosen these waterways for our escape attempt, we wouldn't have come out alive from this sea of fire.

The next day, February 16, we left this basin, which tallies depths of 3,000 metres between Rhodes and Alexandria, and passing well out from Cerigo Island after doubling Cape Matapan, the *Nautilus* left the Greek Islands behind.

CHAPTER 7

The Mediterranean in Forty–Eight Hours

THE MEDITERRANEAN, YOUR ideal blue sea: to Greeks simply 'the sea,' to Hebrews 'the great sea,' to Romans *mare nostrum*. Bordered by orange trees, aloes, cactus and maritime pine trees, perfumed with the scent of myrtle, framed by rugged mountains, saturated with clean, transparent air but continuously under construction by fires in the earth, this sea is a genuine battlefield where Neptune and Pluto still struggle for world domination. Here on these beaches and waters, says the French historian Michelet, a man is revived by one of the most invigorating climates in the world.

But as beautiful as it was, I could get only a quick look at this basin whose surface area comprises 2,000,000 square kilometres. Even Captain Nemo's personal insights were denied me, because that mystifying individual didn't appear one single time during our high-speed crossing. I estimate that the *Nautilus* covered a track of some 600 leagues under the waves of this sea, and this voyage was accomplished in just 24 hours times two. Departing from the waterways of Greece on the morning of February 16, we cleared the Strait of Gibraltar by sunrise on the 18th.

It was obvious to me that this Mediterranean, pinned in the middle of those shores he wanted to avoid, gave Captain Nemo no pleasure. Its waves and breezes brought back too many memories, if not too many regrets. Here he no longer had the ease of movement and freedom of manoeuvre that the oceans allowed him, and his *Nautilus* felt cramped so close to the coasts of both Africa and Europe.

Accordingly, our speed was 25 miles (that is, 12 four-kilometre leagues) per hour. Needless to say, Ned Land had to give up his escape plans, much to his distress. Swept along at the rate of 12 to 13 metres per second, he could hardly make use of the skiff. Leaving the *Nautilus* under these conditions would have been like jumping off a train racing at this speed, a rash move if there ever was one. Moreover, to renew our air supply, the submersible rose to the surface of the waves only at night, and relying solely on compass and log, it steered by dead reckoning.

Inside the Mediterranean, then, I could catch no more of its fast-passing scenery than a traveller might see from an express train; in other words, I could view only the distant horizons because the foregrounds flashed by like lightning. But Conseil and I were able to observe those Mediterranean fish whose powerful fins kept pace for a while in the *Nautilus*'s waters. We stayed on watch before the lounge windows, and our notes enable me to reconstruct, in a few words, the ichthyology of this sea.

Among the various fish inhabiting it, some I viewed, others I glimpsed, and the rest I missed completely because of the *Nautilus*'s speed. Kindly allow me to sort them out using this whimsical system of classification. It will at least convey the quickness of my observations.

In the midst of the watery mass, brightly lit by our electric beams, there snaked past those one-metre lampreys that are common to nearly every clime. A type of ray from the genus *Oxyrhynchus*, five feet wide, had a white belly with a spotted, ash-grey back and was carried along by the currents like a huge, wide-open shawl. Other rays passed by so quickly I couldn't tell if they deserved that name 'eagle ray' coined by the ancient Greeks, or those designations of 'rat ray,' 'bat ray,' and 'toad ray' that modern fishermen have inflicted on them. Dogfish known as topes, 12 feet long and especially feared by divers, were racing with each other. Looking like big bluish shadows, thresher sharks went by, eight feet long and gifted with an extremely acute sense of smell. Dorados from the genus *Sparus*, some measuring up to 13 decimetres, appeared in silver and azure costumes encircled with ribbons, which contrasted with the dark colour of their fins; fish sacred to the goddess Venus, their eyes set in brows of gold; a valuable species that patronises all waters fresh or salt, equally at home in rivers, lakes, and oceans, living in every clime, tolerating any temperature, their line dating back to prehistoric times on this earth yet preserving all its beauty from those far-off days. Magnificent sturgeons, nine to ten metres long and extremely fast, banged their powerful tails against the glass of our panels, showing bluish backs with small brown spots; they resemble sharks, without equalling their strength, and are encountered in every sea; in the spring they delight in swimming up the great rivers, fighting the currents of the Volga, Danube, Po, Rhine, Loire and Oder, while feeding on herring, mackerel, salmon and codfish; although they belong to the class of cartilaginous fish, they rate as a delicacy; they're eaten fresh, dried, marinated, or salt-preserved, and in olden times they were borne in triumph to the table of the Roman epicure Lucullus.

But whenever the *Nautilus* drew near the surface, those denizens of the Mediterranean I could observe most productively belonged to the 63rd genus of bony fish. These were tuna from the genus *Scomber*, blue-black on top, silver on the belly armour, their dorsal stripes giving off a golden gleam. They are said to follow ships in search of refreshing shade from the hot tropical sun, and they did just that with the *Nautilus*, as they had once done with the vessels of the Count de La Pérouse. For long hours they competed in speed with our submersible. I couldn't stop marvelling at these animals so perfectly cut out for racing, their heads small, their bodies sleek, spindle-shaped, and in some cases over three metres long, their pectoral fins gifted with remarkable strength, their caudal fins forked. Like certain flocks of birds, whose speed they equal, these tuna swim in triangle formation, which prompted the ancients to say they'd boned up on geometry and military strategy. And yet they can't escape the Provençal fishermen, who prize them as highly as did the ancient inhabitants of Turkey and Italy; and these valuable animals, as oblivious as if they were deaf and blind, leap right into the Marseilles tuna nets and perish by the thousands.

Just for the record, I'll mention those Mediterranean fish that Conseil and I barely glimpsed. There were whitish eels of the species *Gymnotus fasciatus* that passed like elusive wisps of steam, conger eels three to four metres long that were tricked out in green, blue, and yellow, three-foot hake with a liver that makes a dainty morsel, wormfish drifting like thin seaweed, sea robins that poets call lyrefish and seamen pipers and whose snouts have two jagged triangular plates shaped like old Homer's lyre, swallowfish swimming as fast as the bird they're named after, redheaded groupers whose dorsal fins are trimmed with filaments, some shad (spotted with black, grey, brown, blue, yellow, and green) that actually respond to tinkling handbells, splendid diamond-shaped turbot that were like aquatic pheasants with yellowish fins stippled in brown and the left topside mostly marbled in brown and yellow, finally schools of wonderful red mullet, real oceanic birds of paradise that ancient Romans bought for as much as 10,000 sesterces apiece, and which they killed at the table, so they could heartlessly watch it change colour from cinnabar red when alive to pallid white when dead.

And as for other fish common to the Atlantic and Mediterranean, I was unable to observe miralets, triggerfish, puffers, seahorses, jewelfish, trumpetfish, blennies, grey mullet, wrasse, smelt, flying fish, anchovies, sea bream, porgies, garfish, or any of the chief representatives of the order Pleuronecta, such as sole, flounder, plaice, dab and brill, simply because of the dizzying speed with which the *Nautilus* hustled through these opulent waters.

As for marine mammals, on passing by the mouth of the Adriatic Sea, I thought I recognised two or three sperm whales equipped with the single dorsal fin denoting the genus *Physeter*, some pilot whales from the genus *Globicephalus* exclusive to the Mediterranean, the forepart of the head striped with small distinct lines, and also a dozen seals with white bellies and black coats, known by the name monk seals and just as solemn as if they were three-metre Dominicans.

For his part, Conseil thought he spotted a turtle six feet wide and adorned with three protruding ridges that ran lengthwise. I was sorry to miss this reptile, because from Conseil's description, I believe I recognised the leatherback turtle, a pretty rare species. For my part, I noted only some loggerhead turtles with long carapaces.

As for zoophytes, for a few moments I was able to marvel at a wonderful, orange-hued hydra from the genus *Galeolaria* that clung to the glass of our port panel; it consisted of a long, lean filament that spread out into countless branches and ended in the most delicate lace ever spun by the followers of Arachne. Unfortunately I couldn't fish up this wonderful specimen, and surely no other Mediterranean zoophytes would have been offered to my gaze, if, on the evening of the 16th, the *Nautilus* hadn't slowed down in an odd fashion. This was the situation.

By then we were passing between Sicily and the coast of Tunisia. In the cramped space between Cape Bon and the Strait of Messina, the sea bottom rises almost all at once. It forms an actual ridge with only 17 metres of water remaining above it, while the depth on either side is 170 metres. Consequently, the *Nautilus* had to manoeuvre with caution so as not to bump into this underwater barrier.

I showed Conseil the position of this long reef on our chart of the Mediterranean.

'But with all due respect to master,' Conseil ventured to observe, 'it's like an actual isthmus connecting Europe to Africa.'

'Yes, my boy,' I replied, 'it cuts across the whole Strait of Sicily, and Smith's soundings prove that in the past, these two continents were genuinely connected between Cape Boeo and Cape Farina.'

'I can easily believe it,' Conseil said.

'I might add,' I went on, 'that there's a similar barrier between Gibraltar and Ceuta, and in prehistoric times it closed off the Mediterranean completely.'

'Gracious!' Conseil put in. 'Suppose one day some volcanic upheaval raises these two barriers back above the waves!'

'That's most unlikely, Conseil.'

'If master will allow me to finish, I mean that if this phenomenon occurs, it might prove distressing to Mr de Lesseps, who has gone to such pains to cut through his isthmus!'

'Agreed, but I repeat, Conseil: such a phenomenon won't occur. The intensity of these underground forces continues to diminish. Volcanoes were quite numerous in the world's early days, but they're going extinct one by one; the heat inside the earth is growing weaker, the temperature in the globe's lower strata is cooling appreciably every century, and to our globe's detriment, because its heat is its life.'

'But the sun—'

'The sun isn't enough, Conseil. Can it restore heat to a corpse?'

'Not that I've heard.'

'Well, my friend, someday the earth will be just such a cold corpse. Like the moon, which long ago lost its vital heat, our globe will become lifeless and unlivable.'

'In how many centuries?' Conseil asked.

'In hundreds of thousands of years, my boy.'

'Then we have ample time to finish our voyage,' Conseil replied, 'if Ned Land doesn't mess things up!'

Thus reassured, Conseil went back to studying the shallows that the *Nautilus* was skimming at moderate speed.

On the rocky, volcanic seafloor, there bloomed quite a collection of moving flora: sponges, sea cucumbers, jellyfish called sea gooseberries that were adorned with reddish tendrils and gave off a subtle phosphorescence, members of the genus *Beroe* that are commonly known by the name melon jellyfish and are bathed in the shimmer of the whole solar spectrum, free-swimming crinoids one metre wide that reddened the waters with their crimson hue, treelike basket stars of the greatest beauty, sea fans from the genus *Pavonacea* with long stems, numerous edible sea urchins of various species, plus green sea anemones with a greyish trunk and a brown disk lost beneath the olive-coloured tresses of their tentacles.

Conseil kept especially busy observing molluscs and articulates, and although his catalogue is a little dry, I wouldn't want to wrong the gallant lad by leaving out his personal observations.

From the branch *Mollusca*, he mentions numerous comb-shaped scallops, hooflike spiny oysters piled on top of each other, triangular coquina, three-pronged glass snails with yellow fins and transparent shells, orange snails from the genus *Pleurobranchus* that looked like eggs spotted or speckled with greenish dots, members of the genus *Aplysia* also known by the name sea hares, other sea hares from the genus *Dolabella*, plump paper-bubble shells, umbrella shells exclusive to the Mediterranean, abalone whose shell produces a mother-of-pearl much in demand, pilgrim scallops, saddle shells that diners in the French province of Languedoc are said to like better than oysters, some of those cockleshells so dear to the citizens of Marseilles, fat white venus shells that are among the clams so abundant off the coasts of North America and eaten in such quantities by New Yorkers, variously coloured comb shells with gill covers, burrowing date mussels with a peppery flavour I relish, furrowed heart cockles whose shells have riblike ridges on their arching summits, triton shells pocked with scarlet bumps, carniaira snails with backward-curving tips that make them resemble flimsy gondolas, crowned ferola snails, atlanta snails with spiral shells, grey nudibranchs from the genus *Tethys* that were spotted with white and covered by fringed mantles, nudibranchs from the suborder *Eolidea* that looked like small slugs, sea butterflies crawling on their backs, seashells from the genus *Auricula* including the oval-shaped *Auricula myosotis*, tan wentletrap snails, common periwinkles, violet snails, cineraira snails, rock borers, ear shells, cabochon snails, pandora shells, etc.

As for the articulates, in his notes Conseil has very appropriately divided them into six classes, three of which belong to the marine world. These classes are the *Crustacea*, *Cirripedia*, and *Annelida*.

Crustaceans are subdivided into nine orders, and the first of these consists of the decapods, in other words, animals whose head and thorax are usually fused, whose cheek-and-mouth mechanism is made up of several pairs of appendages, and whose thorax has four, five, or six pairs of walking legs. Conseil used the methods of our mentor Professor Milne-Edwards, who puts the decapods in three divisions: *Brachyura*, *Macrura*, and *Anomura*. These names may look a tad fierce, but they're accurate and appropriate. Among the *Brachyura*, Conseil mentions some amanthia crabs whose fronts were armed with two big diverging tips, those inachus scorpions that – lord knows why – symbolised wisdom to the ancient Greeks, spider crabs of the *massena* and *spinimane* varieties that had probably gone astray in these shallows because they usually live in the lower depths, xanthid crabs, pilumna crabs, rhomboid crabs, granular box crabs (easy on the digestion, as Conseil ventured to observe), toothless masked crabs, ebalia crabs, cymopolia crabs, woolly-handed crabs, etc. Among the *Macrura* (which are subdivided into five families: hardshells, burrowers, crayfish, prawns and ghost crabs) Conseil mentions some common spiny lobsters whose females supply a meat highly prized, slipper lobsters or common shrimp, waterside gebia shrimp, and all sorts of edible species, but he says nothing of the crayfish subdivision that includes the true lobster, because spiny lobsters are the only type in the Mediterranean. Finally, among the *Anomura*, he saw common drocina crabs dwelling inside whatever abandoned seashells they could take over, homola crabs with spiny fronts, hermit crabs, hairy porcelain crabs, etc.

There Conseil's work came to a halt. He didn't have time to finish off the class *Crustacea* through an examination of its *stomatopods, amphipods, homopods, isopods, trilobites, branchiopods, ostracods* and *entomostraceans*. And in order to complete his study of marine articulates, he needed to mention the class *Cirripedia*, which contains water fleas and carp lice, plus the class *Annelida*, which he would have divided without fail into *tubifex* worms and *dorsibranchian* worms. But having gone past the shallows of the Strait of Sicily, the *Nautilus* resumed its usual deep-water speed. From then on, no more molluscs, no more zoophytes, no more articulates. Just a few large fish sweeping by like shadows.

During the night of February 16–17, we entered the second Mediterranean basin, whose maximum depth we found at 3,000 metres. The *Nautilus*, driven downward by its propeller and slanting fins, descended to the lowest strata of this sea.

There, in place of natural wonders, the watery mass offered some thrilling and dreadful scenes to my eyes. In essence, we were then crossing that part of the whole Mediterranean so fertile in casualties. From the coast of Algiers to the beaches of Provence, how many ships have wrecked, how many vessels have vanished! Compared to the vast liquid plains of the Pacific, the Mediterranean is a mere lake, but it's an unpredictable lake with fickle waves, today kindly and affectionate to those frail single-masters drifting between a double ultramarine of sky and water, tomorrow bad-tempered and turbulent, agitated by the winds, demolishing the strongest ships beneath sudden waves that smash down with a headlong wallop.

So, in our swift cruise through these deep strata, how many vessels I saw lying on the seafloor, some already caked with coral, others clad only in a layer of rust, plus anchors, cannons, shells, iron fittings, propeller blades, parts of engines, cracked cylinders, staved-in boilers, then hulls floating in midwater, here upright, there overturned.

Some of these wrecked ships had perished in collisions, others from hitting granite reefs. I saw a few that had sunk straight down, their masting still upright, their rigging stiffened by the water. They looked like they were at anchor by some immense, open, offshore mooring where they were waiting for their departure time. When the *Nautilus* passed between them, covering them with sheets of electricity, they seemed ready to salute us with their colours and send us their serial numbers! But no, nothing but silence and death filled this field of catastrophes!

I observed that these Mediterranean depths became more and more cluttered with such gruesome wreckage as the *Nautilus* drew nearer to the Strait of Gibraltar. By then the shores of Africa and Europe were converging, and in this narrow space collisions were commonplace. There I saw numerous iron undersides, the phantasmagoric ruins of steamers, some lying down, others rearing up like fearsome animals. One of these boats made a dreadful first impression: sides torn open, funnel bent, paddle wheels stripped to the mountings, rudder separated from the sternpost and still hanging from an iron chain, the board on its stern eaten away by marine salts! How many lives were dashed in this shipwreck! How many victims were swept under the waves! Had some sailor on board lived to tell the story of this dreadful disaster, or do the waves still keep this casualty a secret? It occurred to me, Lord knows why, that this boat buried under the sea might have been the *Atlas*, lost with all hands some 20 years ago and never heard from again! Oh, what a gruesome tale these Mediterranean depths could tell, this huge boneyard where so much wealth has been lost, where so many victims have met their deaths!

Meanwhile, briskly unconcerned, the *Nautilus* ran at full propeller through the midst of these ruins. On February 18, near three o'clock in the morning, it hove before the entrance to the Strait of Gibraltar.

There are two currents here: an upper current, long known to exist, that carries the ocean's waters into the Mediterranean basin; then a lower countercurrent, the only present-day proof of its existence being logic. In essence, the Mediterranean receives a continual influx of water not only from the Atlantic but from rivers emptying into it; since local evaporation isn't enough to restore the balance, the total amount of added water should make this sea's level higher every year. Yet this isn't the case, and we're naturally forced to believe in the existence of some lower current that carries the Mediterranean's surplus through the Strait of Gibraltar and into the Atlantic basin.

And so it turned out. The *Nautilus* took full advantage of this countercurrent. It advanced swiftly through this narrow passageway.

For an instant I could glimpse the wonderful ruins of the Temple of Hercules, buried undersea, as Pliny and Avianus have mentioned, together with the flat island they stand on; and a few minutes later, we were floating on the waves of the Atlantic.

CHAPTER 8

The Bay of Vigo

THE ATLANTIC! A vast expanse of water whose surface area is 25,000,000 square miles, with a length of 9,000 miles and an average width of 2,700. A major sea nearly unknown to the ancients, except perhaps the Carthaginians, those Dutchmen of antiquity who went along the west coasts of Europe and Africa on their commercial junkets! An ocean whose parallel winding shores form an immense perimeter fed by the world's greatest rivers: the St Lawrence, Mississippi, Amazon, Plata, Orinoco, Niger, Senegal, Elbe, Loire and Rhine, which bring it waters from the most civilised countries as well as the most undeveloped areas! A magnificent plain of waves ploughed continuously by ships of every nation, shaded by every flag in the world, and ending in those two dreadful headlands so feared by navigators, Cape Horn and the Cape of Tempests!

The *Nautilus* broke these waters with the edge of its spur after doing nearly 10,000 leagues in three and a half months, a track longer than a great circle of the earth. Where were we heading now, and what did the future have in store for us?

Emerging from the Strait of Gibraltar, the *Nautilus* took to the high seas. It returned to the surface of the waves, so our daily strolls on the platform were restored to us.

I climbed onto it instantly, Ned Land and Conseil along with me. Twelve miles away, Cape St Vincent was hazily visible, the southwestern tip of the Hispanic peninsula. The wind was blowing a pretty strong gust from the south. The sea was swelling and surging. Its waves made the *Nautilus* roll and jerk violently. It was nearly impossible to stand up on the platform, which was continuously buffeted by this enormously heavy sea. After inhaling a few breaths of air, we went below once more.

I repaired to my stateroom. Conseil returned to his cabin; but the Canadian, looking rather worried, followed me. Our quick trip through the Mediterranean hadn't allowed him to put his plans into execution, and he could barely conceal his disappointment.

After the door to my stateroom was closed, he sat and stared at me silently.

'Ned my friend,' I told him, 'I know how you feel, but you mustn't blame yourself. Given the way the *Nautilus* was navigating, it would have been sheer insanity to think of escaping!'

Ned Land didn't reply. His pursed lips and frowning brow indicated that he was in the grip of his monomania.

'Look here,' I went on, 'as yet there's no cause for despair. We're going up the coast of Portugal. France and England aren't far off, and there we'll easily find refuge. Oh, I grant you, if the *Nautilus* had emerged from the Strait of Gibraltar and made for that cape in the south, if it were taking us toward those regions that have no continents, then I'd share your alarm. But we now know that Captain Nemo doesn't avoid the seas of civilization, and in a few days I think we can safely take action.'

Ned Land stared at me still more intently and finally unpursed his lips:

'We'll do it this evening,' he said.

I straightened suddenly. I admit that I was less than ready for this announcement. I wanted to reply to the Canadian, but words failed me.

'We agreed to wait for the right circumstances,' Ned Land went on. 'Now we've got those circumstances. This evening we'll be just a few miles off the coast of Spain. It'll be cloudy tonight. The wind's blowing toward shore. You gave me your promise, Professor Aronnax, and I'm counting on you.'

Since I didn't say anything, the Canadian stood up and approached me:

'We'll do it this evening at nine o'clock,' he said. 'I've alerted Conseil. By that time Captain Nemo will be locked in his room and probably in bed. Neither the mechanics or the crewmen will be able to see us. Conseil and I will go to the central companionway. As for you, Professor Aronnax, you'll stay in the library two steps away and wait for my signal. The oars, mast and sail are in the skiff. I've even managed to stow some provisions inside. I've gotten hold of a monkey wrench to unscrew the nuts bolting the skiff to the *Nautilus*'s hull. So everything's ready. I'll see you this evening.'

'The sea is rough,' I said.

'Admitted,' the Canadian replied, 'but we've got to risk it. Freedom is worth paying for. Besides, the longboat's solidly built, and a few miles with the wind behind us is no big deal. By tomorrow, who knows if this ship won't be 100 leagues out to sea? If circumstances are in our favour, between ten and 11 this evening we'll be landing on some piece of solid ground, or we'll be dead. So we're in God's hands, and I'll see you this evening!'

This said, the Canadian withdrew, leaving me close to dumbfounded. I had imagined that if it came to this, I would have time to think about it, to talk it over. My stubborn companion hadn't granted me this courtesy. But after all, what would I have said to him? Ned Land was right a hundred times over. These were near-ideal circumstances, and he was taking full advantage of them. In my selfish personal interests, could I go back on my word and be responsible for ruining the future lives of my companions? Tomorrow, might not Captain Nemo take us far away from any shore?

Just then a fairly loud hissing told me that the ballast tanks were filling, and the *Nautilus* sank beneath the waves of the Atlantic.

I stayed in my stateroom. I wanted to avoid the captain, to hide from his eyes the agitation overwhelming me. What an agonizing day I spent, torn between my desire to regain my free will and my regret at abandoning this marvellous *Nautilus*, leaving my underwater research incomplete! How could I relinquish this ocean – 'my own Atlantic,' as I liked to call it – without observing its lower strata, without wresting from it the kinds of secrets that had been revealed to me by the seas of the East Indies and the Pacific! I was putting down my novel half read, I was waking up as my dream neared its climax! How painfully the hours passed, as I sometimes envisioned myself safe on shore with my companions, or, despite my better judgement, as I sometimes wished that some unforeseen circumstances would prevent Ned Land from carrying out his plans.

Twice I went to the lounge. I wanted to consult the compass. I wanted to see if the *Nautilus*'s heading was actually taking us closer to the coast or spiriting us farther away. But no. The *Nautilus* was still in Portuguese waters. Heading north, it was cruising along the ocean's beaches.

So I had to resign myself to my fate and get ready to escape. My baggage wasn't heavy. My notes, nothing more.

As for Captain Nemo, I wondered what he would make of our escaping, what concern or perhaps what distress it might cause him, and what he would do in the twofold event of our attempt either failing or being found out! Certainly I had no complaints to register with him, on the contrary. Never was hospitality more wholehearted than his. Yet in leaving him I couldn't be accused of ingratitude. No solemn promises bound us to him. In order to keep us captive, he had counted only on the force of circumstances and not on our word of honour. But his avowed intention to imprison us forever on his ship justified our every effort.

I hadn't seen the captain since our visit to the island of Santorini. Would fate bring me into his presence before our departure? I both desired and dreaded it. I listened for footsteps in the stateroom adjoining mine. Not a sound reached my ear. His stateroom had to be deserted.

Then I began to wonder if this eccentric individual was even on board. Since that night when the skiff had left the *Nautilus* on some mysterious mission, my ideas about him had subtly changed. In spite of everything, I thought that Captain Nemo must have kept up some type of relationship with the shore. Did he himself never leave the *Nautilus*? Whole weeks had often gone by without my encountering him. What was he doing all the while? During all those times I'd thought he was convalescing in the grip of some misanthropic fit, was he instead far away from the ship, involved in some secret activity whose nature still eluded me?

All these ideas and a thousand others assaulted me at the same time. In these strange circumstances the scope for conjecture was unlimited. I felt an unbearable queasiness. This day of waiting seemed endless. The hours struck too slowly to keep up with my impatience.

As usual, dinner was served me in my stateroom. Full of anxiety, I ate little. I left the table at seven o'clock. 120 minutes – I was keeping track of them – still separated me from the moment I was to rejoin Ned Land. My agitation increased. My pulse was throbbing violently. I couldn't stand still. I walked up and down, hoping to calm my troubled mind with movement. The possibility of perishing in our reckless undertaking was the least of my worries; my heart was pounding at the thought that our plans might be discovered before we had left the *Nautilus*, at the thought of being hauled in front of Captain Nemo and finding him angered, or worse, saddened by my deserting him.

I wanted to see the lounge one last time. I went down the gangways and arrived at the museum where I had spent so many pleasant and productive hours. I stared at all its wealth, all its treasures, like a man on the eve of his eternal exile, a man departing to return no more. For so many days now, these natural wonders and artistic masterworks had been central to my life, and I was about to leave them behind forever. I wanted to plunge my eyes through the lounge window and into these Atlantic waters; but the panels were hermetically sealed, and a mantle of sheet iron separated me from this ocean with which I was still unfamiliar.

Crossing through the lounge, I arrived at the door, contrived in one of the canted corners, that opened into the captain's stateroom. Much to my astonishment, this door was ajar. I instinctively recoiled. If Captain Nemo was in his stateroom, he might see me. But, not hearing any sounds, I approached. The stateroom was deserted. I pushed the door open. I took a few steps inside. Still the same austere, monastic appearance.

Just then my eye was caught by some etchings hanging on the wall, which I hadn't noticed during my first visit. They were portraits of great men of history who had spent their lives in perpetual devotion to a great human ideal: Thaddeus Kosciusko, the hero whose dying words had been *Finis Poloniae*; Markos Botzaris, for modern Greece the reincarnation of Sparta's King Leonidas; Daniel O'Connell, Ireland's defender; George Washington, founder of the American Union; Daniele Manin, the Italian patriot; Abraham Lincoln, dead from the bullet of a believer in slavery; and finally, that martyr for the redemption of the black race, John Brown, hanging from his gallows as Victor Hugo's pencil has so terrifyingly depicted.

What was the bond between these heroic souls and the soul of Captain Nemo? From this collection of portraits could I finally unravel the mystery of his existence? Was he a fighter for oppressed peoples, a liberator of enslaved races? Had he figured in the recent political or social upheavals of this century? Was he a hero of that dreadful civil war in America, a war lamentable yet forever glorious…?

Suddenly the clock struck eight. The first stroke of its hammer on the chime snapped me out of my musings. I shuddered as if some invisible eye had plunged into my innermost thoughts, and I rushed outside the stateroom.

There my eyes fell on the compass. Our heading was still northerly. The log indicated a moderate speed, the pressure gauge a depth of about 60 feet. So circumstances were in favour of the Canadian's plans.

I stayed in my stateroom. I dressed warmly: fishing boots, otter cap, coat of fan-mussel fabric lined with sealskin. I was ready. I was waiting. Only the propeller's vibrations disturbed the deep silence reigning on board. I cocked an ear and listened. Would a sudden outburst of voices tell me that Ned Land's escape plans had just been detected? A ghastly uneasiness stole through me. I tried in vain to recover my composure.

A few minutes before nine o'clock, I glued my ear to the captain's door. Not a sound. I left my stateroom and returned to the lounge, which was deserted and plunged in near darkness.

I opened the door leading to the library. The same inadequate light, the same solitude. I went to man my post near the door opening into the well of the central companionway. I waited for Ned Land's signal.

At this point the propeller's vibrations slowed down appreciably, then they died out altogether. Why was the *Nautilus* stopping? Whether this layover would help or hinder Ned Land's schemes I couldn't have said.

The silence was further disturbed only by the pounding of my heart.

Suddenly I felt a mild jolt. I realised the *Nautilus* had come to rest on the ocean floor. My alarm increased. The Canadian's signal hadn't reached me. I longed to rejoin Ned Land and urge him to postpone his attempt. I sensed that we were no longer navigating under normal conditions.

Just then the door to the main lounge opened and Captain Nemo appeared. He saw me, and without further preamble:

'Ah, professor,' he said in an affable tone, 'I've been looking for you. Do you know your Spanish history?'

Even if he knew it by heart, a man in my disturbed, befuddled condition couldn't have quoted a syllable of his own country's history.

'Well?' Captain Nemo went on. 'Did you hear my question? Do you know the history of Spain?'

'Very little of it,' I replied.

'The most learned men,' the captain said, 'still have much to learn. Have a seat,' he added, 'and I'll tell you about an unusual episode in this body of history.'

The captain stretched out on a couch, and I mechanically took a seat near him, but half in the shadows.

'Professor,' he said, 'listen carefully. This piece of history concerns you in one definite respect, because it will answer a question you've no doubt been unable to resolve.'

'I'm listening, captain,' I said, not knowing what my partner in this dialogue was driving at, and wondering if this incident related to our escape plans.

'Professor,' Captain Nemo went on, 'if you're amenable, we'll go back in time to 1702. You're aware of the fact that in those days your King Louis XIV thought an imperial gesture would suffice to humble the Pyrenees in the dust, so he inflicted his grandson, the Duke of Anjou, on the Spaniards. Reigning more or less poorly under the name King Philip V, this aristocrat had to deal with mighty opponents abroad.

'In essence, the year before, the royal houses of Holland, Austria and England had signed a treaty of alliance at The Hague, aiming to wrest the Spanish crown from King Philip V and to place it on the head of an archduke whom they prematurely dubbed King Charles III.

'Spain had to withstand these allies. But the country had practically no army or navy. Yet it wasn't short of money, provided that its galleons, laden with gold and silver from America, could enter its ports. Now then, late in 1702 Spain was expecting a rich convoy, which France ventured to escort with a fleet of 23 vessels under the command of Admiral de Chateau-Renault, because by that time the allied navies were roving the Atlantic.

'This convoy was supposed to put into Cadiz, but after learning that the English fleet lay across those waterways, the admiral decided to make for a French port.

'The Spanish commanders in the convoy objected to this decision. They wanted to be taken to a Spanish port, if not to Cadiz, then to the Bay of Vigo, located on Spain's northwest coast and not blockaded.

'Admiral de Chateau-Renault was so indecisive as to obey this directive, and the galleons entered the Bay of Vigo.

'Unfortunately this bay forms an open, offshore mooring that's impossible to defend. So it was essential to hurry and empty the galleons before the allied fleets arrived, and there would have been ample time for this unloading, if a wretched question of trade agreements hadn't suddenly come up.

'Are you clear on the chain of events?' Captain Nemo asked me.

'Perfectly clear,' I said, not yet knowing why I was being given this history lesson.

'Then I'll continue. Here's what came to pass. The tradesmen of Cadiz had negotiated a charter whereby they were to receive all merchandise coming from the West Indies. Now then, unloading the ingots from those galleons at the port of Vigo would have been a violation of their rights. So they lodged a complaint in Madrid, and they obtained an order from the indecisive King Philip V: without unloading, the convoy would stay in custody at the offshore mooring of Vigo until the enemy fleets had retreated.

'Now then, just as this decision was being handed down, English vessels arrived in the Bay of Vigo on October 22, 1702. Despite his inferior forces, Admiral de Chateau-Renault fought courageously. But when he saw that the convoy's wealth was about to fall into enemy hands, he burned and scuttled the galleons, which went to the bottom with their immense treasures.'

Captain Nemo stopped. I admit it: I still couldn't see how this piece of history concerned me.

'Well?' I asked him.

'Well, Professor Aronnax,' Captain Nemo answered me, 'we're actually in that Bay of Vigo, and all that's left is for you to probe the mysteries of the place.'

The captain stood up and invited me to follow him. I'd had time to collect myself. I did so. The lounge was dark, but the sea's waves sparkled through the transparent windows. I stared.

Around the *Nautilus* for a half-mile radius, the waters seemed saturated with electric light. The sandy bottom was clear and bright. Dressed in diving suits, crewmen were busy clearing away half-rotted barrels and disemboweled trunks in the midst of the dingy hulks of ships. Out of these trunks and kegs spilled ingots of gold and silver, cascades of jewels, pieces of eight. The sand was heaped with them. Then, laden with these valuable spoils, the men returned to the *Nautilus*, dropped off their burdens inside, and went to resume this inexhaustible fishing for silver and gold.

I understood. This was the setting of that battle on October 22, 1702. Here, in this very place, those galleons carrying treasure to the Spanish government had gone to the bottom. Here, whenever he needed, Captain Nemo came to withdraw these millions to ballast his *Nautilus*. It was for him, for him alone, that America had yielded up its precious metals. He was the direct, sole heir to these treasures wrested from the Incas and those peoples conquered by Hernando Cortez!

'Did you know, professor,' he asked me with a smile, 'that the sea contained such wealth?'

'I know it's estimated,' I replied, 'that there are 2,000,000 metric tons of silver held in suspension in seawater.'

'Surely, but in extracting that silver, your expenses would outweigh your profits. Here, by contrast, I have only to pick up what other men have lost, and not only in this Bay of Vigo but at a thousand other sites where ships have gone down, whose positions are marked on my underwater chart. Do you understand now that I'm rich to the tune of billions?'

'I understand, Captain. Nevertheless, allow me to inform you that by harvesting this very Bay of Vigo, you're simply forestalling the efforts of a rival organization.'

'What organization?'

'A company chartered by the Spanish government to search for these sunken galleons. The company's investors were lured by the bait of enormous gains, because this scuttled treasure is estimated to be worth 500,000,000 francs.'

'It was 500,000,000 francs,' Captain Nemo replied, 'but no more!'

'Right,' I said. 'Hence a timely warning to those investors would be an act of charity. Yet who knows if it would be well received? Usually what gamblers regret the most isn't the loss of their money so much as the loss of their insane hopes. But ultimately I feel less sorry for them than for the thousands of unfortunate people who would have benefited from a fair distribution of this wealth, whereas now it will be of no help to them!'

No sooner had I voiced this regret than I felt it must have wounded Captain Nemo.

'No help!' he replied with growing animation. 'Sir, what makes you assume this wealth goes to waste when I'm the one amassing it? Do you think I toil to gather this treasure out of selfishness? Who says I don't put it to good use? Do you think I'm unaware of the suffering beings and oppressed races living on this earth, poor people to comfort, victims to avenge? Don't you understand…?'

Captain Nemo stopped on these last words, perhaps sorry that he had said too much. But I had guessed. Whatever motives had driven him to seek independence under the seas, he remained a human being before all else! His heart still throbbed for suffering humanity, and his immense philanthropy went out both to downtrodden races and to individuals!

And now I knew where Captain Nemo had delivered those millions, when the *Nautilus* navigated the waters where Crete was in rebellion against the Ottoman Empire!

CHAPTER 9

A Lost Continent

THE NEXT MORNING, February 19, I beheld the Canadian entering my stateroom. I was expecting this visit. He wore an expression of great disappointment.

'Well, sir?' he said to me.

'Well, Ned, the fates were against us yesterday.'

'Yes! That damned captain had to call a halt just as we were going to escape from his boat.'

'Yes, Ned, he had business with his bankers.'

'His bankers?'

'Or rather his bank vaults. By which I mean this ocean, where his wealth is safer than in any national treasury.'

I then related the evening's incidents to the Canadian, secretly hoping he would come around to the idea of not deserting the captain; but my narrative had no result other than Ned's voicing deep regret that he hadn't strolled across the Vigo battlefield on his own behalf.

'Anyhow,' he said, 'it's not over yet! My first harpoon missed, that's all! We'll succeed the next time, and as soon as this evening, if need be...'

'What's the *Nautilus*'s heading?' I asked.

'I've no idea,' Ned replied.

'All right, at noon we'll find out what our position is!'

The Canadian returned to Conseil's side. As soon as I was dressed, I went into the lounge. The compass wasn't encouraging. The *Nautilus*'s course was south-southwest. We were turning our backs on Europe.

I could hardly wait until our position was reported on the chart. Near 11:30 the ballast tanks emptied, and the submersible rose to the surface of the ocean. I leaped onto the platform. Ned Land was already there.

No more shore in sight. Nothing but the immenseness of the sea. A few sails were on the horizon, no doubt ships going as far as Cape

São Roque to find favourable winds for doubling the Cape of Good Hope. The sky was overcast. A squall was on the way.

Furious, Ned tried to see through the mists on the horizon. He still hoped that behind all that fog there lay those shores he longed for.

At noon the sun made a momentary appearance. Taking advantage of this rift in the clouds, the chief officer took the orb's altitude. Then the sea grew turbulent, we went below again, and the hatch closed once more.

When I consulted the chart an hour later, I saw that the *Nautilus*'s position was marked at longitude 16° 17' and latitude 33° 22', a good 150 leagues from the nearest coast. It wouldn't do to even dream of escaping, and I'll let the reader decide how promptly the Canadian threw a tantrum when I ventured to tell him our situation.

As for me, I wasn't exactly grief-stricken. I felt as if a heavy weight had been lifted from me, and I was able to resume my regular tasks in a state of comparative calm.

Near 11 o'clock in the evening, I received a most unexpected visit from Captain Nemo. He asked me very graciously if I felt exhausted from our vigil the night before. I said no.

'Then, Professor Aronnax, I propose an unusual excursion.'

'Propose away, captain.'

'So far you've visited the ocean depths only by day and under sunlight. Would you like to see these depths on a dark night?'

'Very much.'

'I warn you, this will be an exhausting stroll. We'll need to walk long hours and scale a mountain. The roads aren't terribly well kept up.'

'Everything you say, captain, just increases my curiosity. I'm ready to go with you.'

'Then come along, professor, and we'll go put on our diving suits.'

Arriving at the wardrobe, I saw that neither my companions nor any crewmen would be coming with us on this excursion. Captain Nemo hadn't even suggested my fetching Ned or Conseil.

In a few moments we had put on our equipment. Air tanks, abundantly charged, were placed on our backs, but the electric lamps were not in readiness. I commented on this to the captain.

'They'll be useless to us,' he replied.

I thought I hadn't heard him right, but I couldn't repeat my comment because the captain's head had already disappeared into its metal covering. I finished harnessing myself, I felt an alpenstock being placed in my hand, and a few minutes later, after the usual procedures, we set foot on the floor of the Atlantic, 300 metres down.

Midnight was approaching. The waters were profoundly dark, but Captain Nemo pointed to a reddish spot in the distance, a sort of wide glow shimmering about two miles from the *Nautilus*. What this fire was, what substances fed it, how and why it kept burning in the liquid mass, I couldn't say. Anyhow it lit our way, although hazily, but I soon grew accustomed to this unique gloom, and in these circumstances I understood the uselessness of the Ruhmkorff device.

Side by side, Captain Nemo and I walked directly toward this conspicuous flame. The level seafloor rose imperceptibly. We took long strides, helped by our alpenstocks; but in general our progress was slow, because our feet kept sinking into a kind of slimy mud mixed with seaweed and assorted flat stones.

As we moved forward, I heard a kind of pitter-patter above my head. Sometimes this noise increased and became a continuous crackle. I soon realised the cause. It was a heavy rainfall rattling on the surface of the waves. Instinctively I worried that I might get soaked! By water in the midst of water! I couldn't help smiling at this outlandish notion. But to tell the truth, wearing these heavy diving suits, you no longer feel the liquid element, you simply think you're in the midst of air a little denser than air on land, that's all.

After half an hour of walking, the seafloor grew rocky. Jellyfish, microscopic crustaceans, and sea-pen coral lit it faintly with their phosphorescent glimmers. I glimpsed piles of stones covered by a couple of million zoophytes and tangles of algae. My feet often slipped on this viscous seaweed carpet, and without my alpenstock I would have fallen more than once. When I turned around, I could still see the *Nautilus*'s whitish beacon, which was starting to grow pale in the distance.

Those piles of stones just mentioned were laid out on the ocean floor with a distinct but inexplicable symmetry. I spotted gigantic furrows trailing off into the distant darkness, their length incalculable. There also were other peculiarities I couldn't make sense of. It seemed to me that my heavy lead soles were crushing a litter of bones that made a dry crackling noise. So what were these vast plains we were now crossing? I wanted to ask the captain, but I still didn't grasp that sign language that allowed him to chat with his companions when they went with him on his underwater excursions.

Meanwhile the reddish light guiding us had expanded and inflamed the horizon. The presence of this furnace under the waters had me extremely puzzled. Was it some sort of electrical discharge? Was I approaching some natural phenomenon still unknown to scientists on shore? Or, rather (and this thought did cross my mind), had the hand of man intervened in that blaze? Had human beings fanned those flames? In these deep strata would I meet up with more of Captain Nemo's companions, friends he was about to visit who led lives as strange as his own? Would I find a whole colony of exiles down here, men tired of the world's woes, men who had sought and found independence in the ocean's lower depths? All these insane, inadmissible ideas dogged me, and in this frame of mind, continually excited by the series of wonders passing before my eyes, I wouldn't have been surprised to find on this sea bottom one of those underwater towns Captain Nemo dreamed about!

Our path was getting brighter and brighter. The red glow had turned white and was radiating from a mountain peak about 800 feet high. But what I saw was simply a reflection produced by the crystal waters of these strata. The furnace that was the source of this inexplicable light occupied the far side of the mountain.

In the midst of the stone mazes furrowing this Atlantic seafloor, Captain Nemo moved forward without hesitation. He knew this dark path. No doubt he had often travelled it and was incapable of losing his way. I followed him with unshakeable confidence. He seemed like some Spirit of the Sea, and as he walked ahead of me, I marvelled at his tall figure, which stood out in black against the glowing background of the horizon.

It was one o'clock in the morning. We arrived at the mountain's lower gradients. But in grappling with them, we had to venture up difficult trails through a huge thicket.

Yes, a thicket of dead trees! Trees without leaves, without sap, turned to stone by the action of the waters, and crowned here and there by gigantic pines. It was like a still-erect coalfield, its roots clutching broken soil, its boughs clearly outlined against the ceiling of the waters like thin, black, paper cutouts. Picture a forest clinging to the sides of a peak in the Harz Mountains, but a submerged forest. The trails were cluttered with algae and fucus plants, hosts of crustaceans swarming among them. I plunged on, scaling rocks, straddling fallen tree trunks, snapping marine creepers that swayed from one tree to another, startling the fish that flitted from branch to branch. Carried away, I didn't feel exhausted any more. I followed a guide who was immune to exhaustion.

What a sight! How can I describe it! How can I portray these woods and rocks in this liquid setting, their lower parts dark and sullen, their upper parts tinted red in this light whose intensity was doubled by the reflecting power of the waters! We scaled rocks that crumbled behind us, collapsing in enormous sections with the hollow rumble of an avalanche. To our right and left there were carved gloomy galleries where the eye lost its way. Huge glades opened up, seemingly cleared by the hand of man, and I sometimes wondered whether some residents of these underwater regions would suddenly appear before me.

But Captain Nemo kept climbing. I didn't want to fall behind. I followed him boldly. My alpenstock was a great help. One wrong step would have been disastrous on the narrow paths cut into the sides of these chasms, but I walked along with a firm tread and without the slightest feeling of dizziness. Sometimes I leaped over a crevasse whose depth would have made me recoil had I been in the midst of glaciers on shore; sometimes I ventured out on a wobbling tree trunk fallen across a gorge, without looking down, having eyes only for marvelling at the wild scenery of this region. There, leaning on erratically cut foundations, monumental rocks seemed to defy the laws of balance. From between their stony knees, trees sprang up like jets under fearsome pressure, supporting other trees that supported them in turn. Next, natural towers with wide, steeply carved battlements leaned at angles that, on dry land, the laws of gravity would never have authorised.

And I too could feel the difference created by the water's powerful density – despite my heavy clothing, copper headpiece and metal soles, I climbed the most impossibly steep gradients with all the nimbleness, I swear it, of a chamois or a Pyrenees mountain goat!

As for my account of this excursion under the waters, I'm well aware that it sounds incredible! I'm the chronicler of deeds seemingly impossible and yet incontestably real. This was no fantasy. This was what I saw and felt!

Two hours after leaving the *Nautilus*, we had cleared the timberline, and 100 feet above our heads stood the mountain peak, forming a dark silhouette against the brilliant glare that came from its far slope. Petrified shrubs rambled here and there in sprawling zigzags. Fish rose in a body at our feet like birds startled in tall grass. The rocky mass was gouged with impenetrable crevices, deep caves, unfathomable holes at whose far ends I could hear fearsome things moving around. My blood would curdle as I watched some enormous antenna bar my path, or saw some frightful pincer snap shut in the shadow of some cavity! A thousand specks of light glittered in the midst of the gloom. They were the eyes of gigantic crustaceans crouching in their lairs, giant lobsters rearing up like spear carriers and moving their claws with a scrap-iron clanking, titanic crabs aiming their bodies like cannons on their carriages, and hideous devilfish intertwining their tentacles like bushes of writhing snakes.

What was this astounding world that I didn't yet know? In what order did these articulates belong, these creatures for which the rocks provided a second carapace? Where had nature learned the secret of their vegetating existence, and for how many centuries had they lived in the ocean's lower strata?

But I couldn't linger. Captain Nemo, on familiar terms with these dreadful animals, no longer minded them. We arrived at a preliminary plateau where still other surprises were waiting for me. There picturesque ruins took shape, betraying the hand of man, not our Creator. They were huge stacks of stones in which you could distinguish the indistinct forms of palaces and temples, now arrayed in hosts of blossoming zoophytes, and over it all, not ivy but a heavy mantle of algae and fucus plants.

But what part of the globe could this be, this land swallowed by cataclysms? Who had set up these rocks and stones like the dolmens of prehistoric times? Where was I, where had Captain Nemo's fancies taken me?

I wanted to ask him. Unable to, I stopped him. I seized his arm. But he shook his head, pointed to the mountain's topmost peak, and seemed to tell me:

'Come on! Come with me! Come higher!'

I followed him with one last burst of energy, and in a few minutes I had scaled the peak, which crowned the whole rocky mass by some ten metres.

I looked back down the side we had just cleared. There the mountain rose only 700 to 800 feet above the plains; but on its far slope it crowned the receding bottom of this part of the Atlantic by a height twice that. My eyes scanned the distance and took in a vast area lit by intense flashes of light. In essence, this mountain was a volcano. Fifty feet below its peak, amid a shower of stones and slag, a wide crater vomited torrents of lava that were dispersed in fiery cascades into the heart of the liquid mass. So situated, this volcano was an immense torch that lit up the lower plains all the way to the horizon.

As I said, this underwater crater spewed lava, but not flames. Flames need oxygen from the air and are unable to spread underwater; but a lava flow, which contains in itself the principle of its incandescence, can rise to a white heat, overpower the liquid element, and turn it into steam on contact. Swift currents swept away all this diffuse gas, and torrents of lava slid to the foot of the mountain, like the disgorgings of a Mt Vesuvius over the city limits of a second Torre del Greco.

In fact, there beneath my eyes was a town in ruins, demolished, overwhelmed, laid low, its roofs caved in, its temples pulled down, its arches dislocated, its columns stretching over the earth; in these ruins you could still detect the solid proportions of a sort of Tuscan architecture; farther off, the remains of a gigantic aqueduct; here, the caked heights of an acropolis along with the fluid forms of a Parthenon; there, the remnants of a wharf, as if some bygone port had long ago harboured merchant vessels and triple-tiered war galleys on the shores of some lost ocean; still farther off, long rows of collapsing walls, deserted thoroughfares, a whole Pompeii buried under the waters, which Captain Nemo had resurrected before my eyes!

Where was I? Where was I? I had to find out at all cost, I wanted to speak, I wanted to rip off the copper sphere imprisoning my head.

But Captain Nemo came over and stopped me with a gesture. Then, picking up a piece of chalky stone, he advanced to a black basaltic rock and scrawled this one word:

ATLANTIS

What lightning flashed through my mind! Atlantis, that ancient land of Meropis mentioned by the historian Theopompus; Plato's Atlantis; the continent whose very existence has been denied by such philosophers and scientists as Origen, Porphyry, Iamblichus, d'Anville, Malte-Brun and Humboldt, who entered its disappearance in the ledger of myths and folk tales; the country whose reality has nevertheless been accepted by such other thinkers as Posidonius, Pliny, Ammianus Marcellinus, Tertullian, Engel, Scherer, Tournefort, Buffon and d'Avezac; I had this land right under my eyes, furnishing its own unimpeachable evidence of the catastrophe that had overtaken it! So this was the submerged region that had existed outside Europe, Asia and Libya, beyond the Pillars of Hercules, home of those powerful Atlantean people against whom ancient Greece had waged its earliest wars!

The writer whose narratives record the lofty deeds of those heroic times is Plato himself. His dialogues *Timæus* and *Critias* were drafted with the poet and legislator Solon as their inspiration, as it were.

One day Solon was conversing with some elderly wise men in the Egyptian capital of Sais, a town already 8,000 years of age, as documented by the annals engraved on the sacred walls of its temples. One of these elders related the history of another town 1,000 years older still. This original city of Athens, ninety centuries old, had been invaded and partly destroyed by the Atlanteans. These Atlanteans, he said, resided on an immense continent greater than Africa and Asia combined, taking in an area that lay between latitude 12° and 40° north. Their dominion extended even to Egypt. They tried to enforce their rule as far as Greece, but they had to retreat before the indomitable resistance of the Hellenic people. Centuries passed. A cataclysm occurred – floods, earthquakes. A single night and day were enough to obliterate this Atlantis, whose highest peaks (Madeira, the Azores, the Canaries, the Cape Verde Islands) still emerge above the waves.

These were the historical memories that Captain Nemo's scrawl sent rushing through my mind. Thus, led by the strangest of fates, I was treading underfoot one of the mountains of that continent! My hands were touching ruins many thousands of years old, contemporary with prehistoric times! I was walking in the very place where contemporaries of early man had walked! My heavy soles were crushing the skeletons of animals from the age of fable, animals that used to take cover in the shade of these trees now turned to stone!

Oh, why was I so short of time! I would have gone down the steep slopes of this mountain, crossed this entire immense continent, which surely connects Africa with America, and visited its great prehistoric cities. Under my eyes there perhaps lay the warlike town of Makhimos or the pious village of Eusebes, whose gigantic inhabitants lived for whole centuries and had the strength to raise blocks of stone that still withstood the action of the waters. One day perhaps, some volcanic phenomenon will bring these sunken ruins back to the surface of the waves! Numerous underwater volcanoes have been sighted in this part of the ocean, and many ships have felt terrific tremors when passing over these turbulent depths. A few have heard hollow noises that announced some struggle of the elements far below, others have hauled in volcanic ash hurled above the waves. As far as the equator this whole seafloor is still under construction by plutonic forces. And in some remote epoch, built up by volcanic disgorgings and successive layers of lava, who knows whether the peaks of these fire-belching mountains may reappear above the surface of the Atlantic!

As I mused in this way, trying to establish in my memory every detail of this impressive landscape, Captain Nemo was leaning his elbows on a moss-covered monument, motionless as if petrified in some mute trance. Was he dreaming of those lost generations, asking them for the secret of human destiny? Was it here that this strange man came to revive himself, basking in historical memories, reliving that bygone life, he who had no desire for our modern one? I would have given anything to know his thoughts, to share them, understand them!

We stayed in this place an entire hour, contemplating its vast plains in the lava's glow, which sometimes took on a startling intensity. Inner boilings sent quick shivers running through the mountain's crust. Noises from deep underneath, clearly transmitted by the liquid medium, reverberated with majestic amplitude.

Just then the moon appeared for an instant through the watery mass, casting a few pale rays over this submerged continent. It was only a fleeting glimmer, but its effect was indescribable. The captain stood up and took one last look at these immense plains; then his hand signalled me to follow him.

We went swiftly down the mountain. Once past the petrified forest, I could see the *Nautilus*'s beacon twinkling like a star. The captain walked straight toward it, and we were back on board just as the first glimmers of dawn were whitening the surface of the ocean.

CHAPTER 10

The Underwater Coalfields

THE NEXT DAY, February 20, I overslept. I was so exhausted from the night before, I didn't get up until 11 o'clock. I dressed quickly. I hurried to find out the *Nautilus*'s heading. The instruments indicated that it was running southward at a speed of 20 miles per hour and a depth of 100 metres.

Conseil entered. I described our nocturnal excursion to him, and since the panels were open, he could still catch a glimpse of this submerged continent.

In fact, the *Nautilus* was skimming only ten metres over the soil of these Atlantis plains. The ship scudded along like an air balloon borne by the wind over some prairie on land; but it would be more accurate to say that we sat in the lounge as if we were riding in a coach on an express train. As for the foregrounds passing before our eyes, they were fantastically carved rocks, forests of trees that had crossed over from the vegetable kingdom into the mineral kingdom, their motionless silhouettes sprawling beneath the waves. There also were stony masses buried beneath carpets of axidia and sea anemone, bristling with long, vertical water plants, then strangely contoured blocks of lava that testified to all the fury of those plutonic developments.

While this bizarre scenery was glittering under our electric beams, I told Conseil the story of the Atlanteans, who had inspired the old French scientist Jean Bailly to write so many entertaining – albeit utterly fictitious – pages. I told the lad about the wars of these heroic people. I discussed the question of Atlantis with the fervour of a man who no longer had any doubts. But Conseil was so distracted he barely heard me, and his lack of interest in any commentary on this historical topic was soon explained.

In essence, numerous fish had caught his eye, and when fish pass by, Conseil vanishes into his world of classifying and leaves real life behind. In which case I could only tag along and resume our ichthyological research.

Even so, these Atlantic fish were not noticeably different from those we had observed earlier. There were rays of gigantic size, five metres long and with muscles so powerful they could leap above the waves, sharks of various species including a 15-foot glaucous shark with sharp triangular teeth and so transparent it was almost invisible amid the waters, brown lantern sharks, prism-shaped humantin sharks armoured with protuberant hides, sturgeons resembling their relatives in the Mediterranean, trumpet-snouted pipefish a foot and a half long, yellowish brown with small grey fins and no teeth or tongue, unreeling like slim, supple snakes.

Among bony fish, Conseil noticed some blackish marlin three metres long with a sharp sword jutting from the upper jaw, bright-coloured weevers known in Aristotle's day as sea dragons and whose dorsal stingers make them quite dangerous to pick up, then dolphin-fish with brown backs striped in blue and edged in gold, handsome dorados, moonlike opahs that look like azure disks but which the sun's rays turn into spots of silver, finally eight-metre swordfish from the genus *Xiphias*, swimming in schools, sporting yellowish sickle-shaped fins and six-foot broadswords, stalwart animals, plant eaters rather than fish eaters, obeying the tiniest signals from their females like henpecked husbands.

But while observing these different specimens of marine fauna, I didn't stop examining the long plains of Atlantis. Sometimes an unpredictable irregularity in the seafloor would force the *Nautilus* to slow down, and then it would glide into the narrow channels between the hills with a cetacean's dexterity. If the labyrinth became hopelessly tangled, the submersible would rise above it like an airship, and after clearing the obstacle, it would resume its speedy course just a few metres above the ocean floor. It was an enjoyable and impressive way of navigating that did indeed recall the manoeuvres of an airship ride, with the major difference that the *Nautilus* faithfully obeyed the hands of its helmsman.

The terrain consisted mostly of thick slime mixed with petrified branches, but it changed little by little near four o'clock in the afternoon; it grew rockier and seemed to be strewn with pudding stones and a basaltic gravel called 'tuff,' together with bits of lava and sulphurous obsidian. I expected these long plains to change into mountain regions, and in fact, as the *Nautilus* was executing certain turns, I noticed that the southerly horizon was blocked by a high wall that seemed to close off every exit. Its summit obviously poked above the level of the ocean. It had to be a continent or at least an island, either one of the Canaries or one of the Cape Verde Islands. Our bearings hadn't been marked on the chart – perhaps deliberately – and I had no idea what our position was. In any case this wall seemed to signal the end of Atlantis, of which, all in all, we had crossed only a small part.

Nightfall didn't interrupt my observations. I was left to myself. Conseil had repaired to his cabin. The *Nautilus* slowed down, hovering above the muddled masses on the seafloor, sometimes grazing them as if wanting to come to rest, sometimes rising unpredictably to the surface of the waves. Then I glimpsed a few bright constellations through the crystal waters, specifically five or six of those zodiacal stars trailing from the tail end of Orion.

I would have stayed longer at my window, marvelling at these beauties of sea and sky, but the panels closed. Just then the *Nautilus* had arrived at the perpendicular face of that high wall. How the ship would manoeuvre I hadn't a guess. I repaired to my stateroom. The *Nautilus* did not stir. I fell asleep with the firm intention of waking up in just a few hours.

But it was eight o'clock the next day when I returned to the lounge. I stared at the pressure gauge. It told me that the *Nautilus* was afloat on the surface of the ocean. Furthermore, I heard the sound of footsteps on the platform. Yet there were no rolling movements to indicate the presence of waves undulating above me.

I climbed as far as the hatch. It was open. But instead of the broad daylight I was expecting, I found that I was surrounded by total darkness. Where were we? Had I been mistaken? Was it still night? No! Not one star was twinkling, and nighttime is never so utterly black.

I wasn't sure what to think, when a voice said to me:
'Is that you, professor?'
'Ah, Captain Nemo!' I replied. 'Where are we?'
'Underground, professor.'
'Underground!' I exclaimed. 'And the *Nautilus* is still floating?'

'It always floats.'

'But I don't understand!'

'Wait a little while. Our beacon is about to go on, and if you want some light on the subject, you'll be satisfied.'

I set foot on the platform and waited. The darkness was so profound I couldn't see even Captain Nemo. However, looking at the zenith directly overhead, I thought I caught sight of a feeble glimmer, a sort of twilight filtering through a circular hole. Just then the beacon suddenly went on, and its intense brightness made that hazy light vanish.

This stream of electricity dazzled my eyes, and after momentarily shutting them, I looked around. The *Nautilus* was stationary. It was floating next to an embankment shaped like a wharf. As for the water now buoying the ship, it was a lake completely encircled by an inner wall about two miles in diameter, hence six miles around. Its level – as indicated by the pressure gauge – would be the same as the outside level, because some connection had to exist between this lake and the sea. Slanting inward over their base, these high walls converged to form a vault shaped like an immense upside-down funnel that measured 500 or 600 metres in height. At its summit there gaped the circular opening through which I had detected that faint glimmer, obviously daylight.

Before more carefully examining the interior features of this enormous cavern, and before deciding if it was the work of nature or humankind, I went over to Captain Nemo.

'Where are we?' I said.

'In the very heart of an extinct volcano,' the captain answered me, 'a volcano whose interior was invaded by the sea after some convulsion in the earth. While you were sleeping, professor, the *Nautilus* entered this lagoon through a natural channel that opens ten metres below the surface of the ocean. This is our home port, secure, convenient, secret, and sheltered against winds from any direction! Along the coasts of your continents or islands, show me any offshore mooring that can equal this safe refuge for withstanding the fury of hurricanes.'

'Indeed,' I replied, 'here you're in perfect safety, Captain Nemo. Who could reach you in the heart of a volcano? But don't I see an opening at its summit?'

'Yes, its crater, a crater formerly filled with lava, steam and flames, but which now lets in this life-giving air we're breathing.'

'But which volcanic mountain is this?' I asked.

'It's one of the many islets with which this sea is strewn. For ships a mere reef, for us an immense cavern. I discovered it by chance, and chance served me well.'

'But couldn't someone enter through the mouth of its crater?'

'No more than I could exit through it. You can climb about 100 feet up the inner base of this mountain, but then the walls overhang, they lean too far in to be scaled.'

'I can see, captain, that nature is your obedient servant, any time or any place. You're safe on this lake, and nobody else can visit its waters. But what's the purpose of this refuge? The *Nautilus* doesn't need a harbour.'

'No, professor, but it needs electricity to run, batteries to generate its electricity, sodium to feed its batteries, coal to make its sodium, and coalfields from which to dig its coal. Now then, right at this spot the sea covers entire forests that sank underwater in prehistoric times; today, turned to stone, transformed into carbon fuel, they offer me inexhaustible coal mines.'

'So, captain, your men practise the trade of miners here?'

'Precisely. These mines extend under the waves like the coalfields at Newcastle. Here, dressed in diving suits, pick and mattock in hand, my men go out and dig this carbon fuel for which I don't need a single mine on land. When I burn this combustible to produce sodium, the smoke escaping from the mountain's crater gives it the appearance of a still-active volcano.'

'And will we see your companions at work?'

'No, at least not this time, because I'm eager to continue our underwater tour of the world. Accordingly, I'll rest content with drawing on my reserve stock of sodium. We'll stay here long enough to load it on board, in other words, a single workday, then we'll resume our voyage. So, Professor Aronnax, if you'd like to explore this cavern and circle its lagoon, seize the day.'

I thanked the captain and went to look for my two companions, who hadn't yet left their cabin. I invited them to follow me, not telling them where we were.

They climbed onto the platform. Conseil, whom nothing could startle, saw it as a perfectly natural thing to fall asleep under the waves and wake up under a mountain. But Ned Land had no idea in his head other than to see if this cavern offered some way out.

After breakfast near ten o'clock, we went down onto the embankment.

'So here we are, back on shore,' Conseil said.

'I'd hardly call this shore,' the Canadian replied. 'And besides, we aren't on it but under it.'

A sandy beach unfolded before us, measuring 500 feet at its widest point between the waters of the lake and the foot of the mountain's walls. Via this strand you could easily circle the lake. But the base of these high walls consisted of broken soil over which there lay picturesque piles of volcanic blocks and enormous pumice stones. All these crumbling masses were covered with an enamel polished by the action of underground fires, and they glistened under the stream of electric light from our beacon. Stirred up by our footsteps, the mica-rich dust on this beach flew into the air like a cloud of sparks.

The ground rose appreciably as it moved away from the sand flats by the waves, and we soon arrived at some long, winding gradients, genuinely steep paths that allowed us to climb little by little; but we had to tread cautiously in the midst of pudding stones that weren't cemented together, and our feet kept skidding on glassy trachyte, made of feldspar and quartz crystals.

The volcanic nature of this enormous pit was apparent all around us. I ventured to comment on it to my companions.

'Can you picture,' I asked them, 'what this funnel must have been like when it was filled with boiling lava, and the level of that incandescent liquid rose right to the mountain's mouth, like cast iron up the insides of a furnace?'

'I can picture it perfectly,' Conseil replied. 'But will master tell me why this huge smelter suspended operations, and how it is that an oven was replaced by the tranquil waters of a lake?'

'In all likelihood, Conseil, because some convulsion created an opening below the surface of the ocean, the opening that serves as a passageway for the *Nautilus*. Then the waters of the Atlantic rushed inside the mountain. There ensued a dreadful struggle between the elements of fire and water, a struggle ending in King Neptune's favour. But many centuries have passed since then, and this submerged volcano has changed into a peaceful cavern.'

'That's fine,' Ned Land answered. 'I accept the explanation, but in our personal interests, I'm sorry this opening the professor mentions wasn't made above sea level.'

'But Ned my friend,' Conseil answered, 'if it weren't an underwater passageway, the *Nautilus* couldn't enter it!'

'And I might add, Mr Land,' I said, 'that the waters wouldn't have rushed under the mountain, and the volcano would still be a volcano. So you have nothing to be sorry about.'

Our climb continued. The gradients got steeper and narrower. Sometimes they were cut across by deep pits that had to be cleared. Masses of overhanging rock had to be gotten around. You slid on your knees, you crept on your belly. But helped by the Canadian's strength and Conseil's dexterity, we overcame every obstacle.

At an elevation of about 30 metres, the nature of the terrain changed without becoming any easier. Pudding stones and trachyte gave way to black basaltic rock: here, lying in slabs all swollen with blisters; there, shaped like actual prisms and arranged into a series of columns that supported the springings of this immense vault, a wonderful sample of natural architecture. Then, among this basaltic rock, there snaked long, hardened lava flows inlaid with veins of bituminous coal and in places covered by wide carpets of sulphur. The sunshine coming through the crater had grown stronger, shedding a hazy light over all the volcanic waste forever buried in the heart of this extinct mountain.

But when we had ascended to an elevation of about 250 feet, we were stopped by insurmountable obstacles. The converging inside walls changed into overhangs, and our climb into a circular stroll. At this topmost level the vegetable kingdom began to challenge the mineral kingdom. Shrubs, and even a few trees, emerged from crevices in the walls. I recognised some spurges that let their caustic, purgative sap trickle out. There were heliotropes, very remiss at living up to their sun-worshipping reputations since no sunlight ever reached them; their clusters of flowers drooped sadly, their colours and scents were faded. Here and there chrysanthemums sprouted timidly at the feet of aloes with long, sad, sickly leaves. But between these lava flows

I spotted little violets that still gave off a subtle fragrance, and I confess that I inhaled it with delight. The soul of a flower is its scent, and those splendid water plants, flowers of the sea, have no souls!

We had arrived at the foot of a sturdy clump of dragon trees, which were splitting the rocks with exertions of their muscular roots, when Ned Land exclaimed:

'Oh, sir, a hive!'

'A hive?' I answered, with a gesture of utter disbelief.

'Yes, a hive,' the Canadian repeated, 'with bees buzzing around!'

I went closer and was forced to recognise the obvious. At the mouth of a hole cut in the trunk of a dragon tree, there swarmed thousands of these ingenious insects so common to all the Canary Islands, where their output is especially prized.

Naturally enough, the Canadian wanted to lay in a supply of honey, and it would have been ill-mannered of me to say no. He mixed sulphur with some dry leaves, set them on fire with a spark from his tinderbox, and proceeded to smoke the bees out. Little by little the buzzing died down and the disemboweled hive yielded several pounds of sweet honey. Ned Land stuffed his haversack with it.

'When I've mixed this honey with our breadfruit batter,' he told us, 'I'll be ready to serve you a delectable piece of cake.'

'But of course,' Conseil put in, 'it will be gingerbread!'

'I'm all for gingerbread,' I said, 'but let's resume this fascinating stroll.'

At certain turns in the trail we were going along, the lake appeared in its full expanse. The ship's beacon lit up that whole placid surface, which experienced neither ripples nor undulations. The *Nautilus* lay perfectly still. On its platform and on the embankment, crewmen were bustling around, black shadows that stood out clearly in the midst of the luminous air.

Just then we went around the highest ridge of these rocky foothills that supported the vault. Then I saw that bees weren't the animal kingdom's only representatives inside this volcano. Here and in the shadows, birds of prey soared and whirled, flying away from nests perched on tips of rock. There were sparrow hawks with white bellies, and screeching kestrels. With all the speed their stiltlike legs could muster, fine fat bustards scampered over the slopes. I'll let the reader decide whether the Canadian's appetite was aroused by the sight of this tasty game, and whether he regretted having no rifle in his hands. He tried to make stones do the work of bullets, and after several fruitless attempts, he managed to wound one of these magnificent bustards. To say he risked his life 20 times in order to capture this bird is simply the unadulterated truth; but he fared so well, the animal went into his sack to join the honeycombs.

By then we were forced to go back down to the beach because the ridge had become impossible. Above us, the yawning crater looked like the wide mouth of a well. From where we stood, the sky was pretty easy to see, and I watched clouds race by, dishevelled by the west wind, letting tatters of mist trail over the mountain's summit. Proof positive that those clouds kept at a moderate altitude, because this volcano didn't rise more than 1,800 feet above the level of the ocean.

Half an hour after the Canadian's latest exploits, we were back on the inner beach. There the local flora was represented by a wide carpet of samphire, a small *umbelliferous* plant that keeps quite nicely, which also boasts the names glasswort, saxifrage and sea fennel. Conseil picked a couple bunches. As for the local fauna, it included thousands of crustaceans of every type: lobsters, hermit crabs prawns, mysid shrimps, daddy longlegs, rock crabs, and a prodigious number of seashells, such as cowries, murex snails and limpets.

In this locality there gaped the mouth of a magnificent cave. My companions and I took great pleasure in stretching out on its fine-grained sand. Fire had polished the sparkling enamel of its inner walls, sprinkled all over with mica-rich dust. Ned Land tapped these walls and tried to probe their thickness. I couldn't help smiling. Our conversation then turned to his everlasting escape plans, and without going too far, I felt I could offer him this hope: Captain Nemo had gone down south only to replenish his sodium supplies. So I hoped he would now hug the coasts of Europe and America, which would allow the Canadian to try again with a greater chance of success.

We were stretched out in this delightful cave for an hour. Our conversation, lively at the outset, then languished. A definite drowsiness overcame us. Since I saw no good reason to resist the call of sleep, I fell into a heavy doze. I dreamed – one doesn't choose his dreams –

that my life had been reduced to the vegetating existence of a simple mollusc. It seemed to me that this cave made up my double-valved shell....

Suddenly Conseil's voice startled me awake.

'Get up! Get up!' shouted the fine lad.

'What is it?' I asked, in a sitting position.

'The water's coming up to us!'

I got back on my feet. Like a torrent the sea was rushing into our retreat, and since we definitely were not molluscs, we had to clear out.

In a few seconds we were safe on top of the cave.

'What happened?' Conseil asked. 'Some new phenomenon?'

'Not quite, my friends!' I replied. 'It was the tide, merely the tide, which wellnigh caught us by surprise just as it did Sir Walter Scott's hero! The ocean outside is rising, and by a perfectly natural law of balance, the level of this lake is also rising. We've gotten off with a mild dunking. Let's go change clothes on the *Nautilus*.'

Three-quarters of an hour later, we had completed our circular stroll and were back on board. Just then the crewmen finished loading the sodium supplies, and the *Nautilus* could have departed immediately.

But Captain Nemo gave no orders. Would he wait for nightfall and exit through his underwater passageway in secrecy? Perhaps.

Be that as it may, by the next day the *Nautilus* had left its home port and was navigating well out from any shore, a few metres beneath the waves of the Atlantic.

CHAPTER 11

The Sargasso Sea

THE *NAUTILUS* DIDN'T change direction. For the time being, then, we had to set aside any hope of returning to European seas. Captain Nemo kept his prow pointing south. Where was he taking us? I was afraid to guess.

That day the *Nautilus* crossed an odd part of the Atlantic Ocean. No one is unaware of the existence of that great warm-water current known by name as the Gulf Stream. After emerging from channels off Florida, it heads toward Spitzbergen. But before entering the Gulf of Mexico near latitude 44° north, this current divides into two arms; its chief arm makes for the shores of Ireland and Norway while the second flexes southward at the level of the Azores; then it hits the coast of Africa, sweeps in a long oval, and returns to the Caribbean Sea.

Now then, this second arm – more accurately, a collar – forms a ring of warm water around a section of cool, tranquil, motionless ocean called the Sargasso Sea. This is an actual lake in the open Atlantic, and the great current's waters take at least three years to circle it.

Properly speaking, the Sargasso Sea covers every submerged part of Atlantis. Certain authors have even held that the many weeds strewn over this sea were torn loose from the prairies of that ancient continent. But it's more likely that these grasses, algae and fucus plants were carried off from the beaches of Europe and America, then taken as far as this zone by the Gulf Stream. This is one of the reasons why Christopher Columbus assumed the existence of a New World. When the ships of that bold investigator arrived in the Sargasso Sea, they had great difficulty navigating in the midst of these weeds, which, much to their crews' dismay, slowed them down to a halt; and they wasted three long weeks crossing this sector.

Such was the region our *Nautilus* was visiting just then: a genuine prairie, a tightly woven carpet of algae, gulfweed and bladder wrack so dense and compact a craft's stempost couldn't tear through it without difficulty. Accordingly, not wanting to entangle his propeller in this weed-choked mass, Captain Nemo stayed at a depth some metres below the surface of the waves.

The name Sargasso comes from the Spanish word *sargazo*, meaning gulfweed. This gulfweed, the swimming gulfweed or berry carrier, is the chief substance making up this immense shoal. And here's why these water plants collect in this placid Atlantic basin, according to the expert on the subject, Commander Maury, author of *The Physical Geography of the Sea*.

The explanation he gives seems to entail a set of conditions that everybody knows: 'Now,' Maury says, 'if bits of cork or chaff, or any floating substance, be put into a basin, and a circular motion be given to the water, all the light substances will be found crowding together near the centre of the pool, where there is the least motion. Just such a basin is the Atlantic Ocean to the Gulf Stream, and the Sargasso Sea is the centre of the whirl.'

I share Maury's view, and I was able to study the phenomenon in this exclusive setting where ships rarely go. Above us, huddled among the brown weeds, there floated objects originating from all over: tree trunks ripped from the Rocky Mountains or the Andes and sent floating down the Amazon or the Mississippi, numerous pieces of wreckage, remnants of keels or undersides, bulwarks staved in and so weighed down with seashells and barnacles, they couldn't rise to the surface of the ocean. And the passing years will someday bear out Maury's other view that by collecting in this way over the centuries, these substances will be turned to stone by the action of the waters and will then form inexhaustible coalfields. Valuable reserves prepared by farseeing nature for that time when man will have exhausted his mines on the continents.

In the midst of this hopelessly tangled fabric of weeds and fucus plants, I noted some delightful pink-coloured, star-shaped alcyon coral, sea anemone trailing the long tresses of their tentacles, some green, red and blue jellyfish, and especially those big rhizostome jellyfish that Cuvier described, whose bluish parasols are trimmed with violet festoons.

We spent the whole day of February 22 in the Sargasso Sea, where fish that dote on marine plants and crustaceans find plenty to eat. The next day the ocean resumed its usual appearance.

From this moment on, for 19 days from February 23 to March 12, the *Nautilus* stayed in the middle of the Atlantic, hustling us along at a constant speed of 100 leagues every 24 hours. It was obvious that Captain Nemo wanted to carry out his underwater programme, and I had no doubt that he intended, after doubling Cape Horn, to return to the Pacific South Seas.

So Ned Land had good reason to worry. In these wide seas empty of islands, it was no longer feasible to jump ship. Nor did we have any way to counter Captain Nemo's whims. We had no choice but to acquiesce; but if we couldn't attain our end through force or cunning, I liked to think we might achieve it through persuasion. Once this voyage was over, might not Captain Nemo consent to set us free in return for our promise never to reveal his existence? Our word of honour, which we sincerely would have kept. However, this delicate question would have to be negotiated with the captain. But how would he receive our demands for freedom? At the very outset and in no uncertain terms, hadn't he declared that the secret of his life required that we be permanently imprisoned on board the *Nautilus*? Wouldn't he see my four-month silence as a tacit acceptance of this situation? Would my returning to this subject arouse suspicions that could jeopardise our escape plans, if we had promising circumstances for trying again later on? I weighed all these considerations, turned them over in my mind, submitted them to Conseil, but he was as baffled as I was. In short, although I'm not easily discouraged, I realised that my chances of ever seeing my fellow men again were shrinking by the day, especially at a time when Captain Nemo was recklessly racing toward the south Atlantic!

During those 19 days just mentioned, no unique incidents distinguished our voyage. I saw little of the captain. He was at work. In the library I often found books he had left open, especially books on natural history. He had thumbed through my work on the great ocean depths, and the margins were covered with his notes, which sometimes contradicted my theories and formulations. But the captain remained content with this method of refining my work, and he rarely discussed it with me. Sometimes I heard melancholy sounds reverberating from the organ, which he played very expressively, but only at night in the midst of the most secretive darkness, while the *Nautilus* slumbered in the wilderness of the ocean.

During this part of our voyage, we navigated on the surface of the waves for entire days. The sea was nearly deserted. A few sailing ships, laden for the East Indies, were heading toward the Cape of Good Hope. One day we were chased by the longboats of a whaling vessel, which undoubtedly viewed us as some enormous baleen whale of great value. But Captain Nemo didn't want these gallant gentlemen wasting their time and energy, so he ended the hunt by diving beneath the waters. This incident seemed to fascinate Ned Land intensely. I'm sure the Canadian was sorry that these fishermen couldn't harpoon our sheet-iron cetacean and mortally wound it.

During this period the fish Conseil and I observed differed little from those we had already studied in other latitudes. Chief among them were specimens of that dreadful *cartilaginous* genus that's divided into three subgenera numbering at least 32 species: striped sharks five metres long, the head squat and wider than the body, the caudal fin curved, the back with seven big, black, parallel lines running lengthwise; then perlon sharks, ash grey, pierced with seven gill openings, furnished with a single dorsal fin placed almost exactly in the middle of the body.

Some big dogfish also passed by, a voracious species of shark if there ever was one. With some justice, fishermen's yarns aren't to be trusted, but here's what a few of them relate. Inside the corpse of one of these animals there were found a buffalo head and a whole calf; in another, two tuna and a sailor in uniform; in yet another, a soldier with his sabre; in another, finally, a horse with its rider. In candour, none of these sounds like divinely inspired truth. But the fact remains that not a single dogfish let itself get caught in the *Nautilus*'s nets, so I can't vouch for their voracity.

Schools of elegant, playful dolphin swam alongside for entire days. They went in groups of five or six, hunting in packs like wolves over the countryside; moreover, they're just as voracious as dogfish, if I can believe a certain Copenhagen professor who says that from one dolphin's stomach, he removed 13 porpoises and 15 seals. True, it was a killer whale, belonging to the biggest known species, whose length sometimes exceeds 24 feet. The family *Delphinia* numbers ten genera, and the dolphins I saw were akin to the genus *Delphinorhynchus*, remarkable for an extremely narrow muzzle four times as long as the cranium. Measuring three metres, their bodies were black on top, underneath a pinkish white strewn with small, very scattered spots.

From these seas I'll also mention some unusual specimens of croakers, fish from the order *Acanthopterygia*, family *Scienidea*. Some authors – more artistic than scientific – claim that these fish are melodious singers, that their voices in unison put on concerts unmatched by human choristers. I don't say nay, but to my regret these croakers didn't serenade us as we passed.

Finally, to conclude, Conseil classified a large number of flying fish. Nothing could have made a more unusual sight than the marvellous timing with which dolphins hunt these fish. Whatever the range of its flight, however evasive its trajectory (even up and over the *Nautilus*), the hapless flying fish always found a dolphin to welcome it with open mouth. These were either flying gurnards or kitelike sea robins, whose lips glowed in the dark, at night scrawling fiery streaks in the air before plunging into the murky waters like so many shooting stars.

Our navigating continued under these conditions until March 13. That day the *Nautilus* was put to work in some depth-sounding experiments that fascinated me deeply.

By then we had fared nearly 13,000 leagues from our starting point in the Pacific high seas. Our position fix placed us in latitude 45° 37' south and longitude 37° 53' west. These were the same waterways where Captain Denham, aboard the *Herald*, let down 14,000 metres of sounding line without finding bottom. It was here too that Lieutenant Parker, aboard the American frigate *Congress*, was unable to reach the underwater soil at 15,149 metres.

Captain Nemo decided to take his *Nautilus* down to the lowest depths in order to double-check these different soundings. I got ready to record the results of this experiment. The panels in the lounge opened, and manoeuvres began for reaching those strata so prodigiously far removed.

It was apparently considered out of the question to dive by filling the ballast tanks. Perhaps they wouldn't sufficiently increase the *Nautilus*'s specific gravity. Moreover, in order to come back up, it would be necessary to expel the excess water, and our pumps might not have been strong enough to overcome the outside pressure.

Captain Nemo decided to make for the ocean floor by submerging on an appropriately gradual diagonal with the help of his side fins, which were set at a 45° angle to the *Nautilus*'s waterline. Then the propeller was brought to its maximum speed, and its four blades churned the waves with indescribable violence.

Under this powerful thrust the *Nautilus*'s hull quivered like a resonating chord, and the ship sank steadily under the waters. Stationed in the lounge, the captain and I watched the needle swerving swiftly over the pressure gauge. Soon we had gone below the livable zone where most fish reside. Some of these animals can thrive only at the surface of seas or rivers, but a minority can dwell at fairly great depths. Among the latter I observed a species of dogfish called the cow shark that's equipped with six respiratory slits, the telescope fish with its enormous eyes, the armoured gurnard with grey thoracic fins plus black pectoral fins and a breastplate protected by pale red slabs of bone, then finally the grenadier, living at a depth of 1,200 metres, by that point tolerating a pressure of 120 atmospheres.

I asked Captain Nemo if he had observed any fish at more considerable depths.

'Fish? Rarely!' he answered me. 'But given the current state of marine science, who are we to presume, what do we really know of these depths?'

'Just this, captain. In going toward the ocean's lower strata, we know that vegetable life disappears more quickly than animal life. We know that moving creatures can still be encountered where water plants no longer grow. We know that oysters and pilgrim scallops live in 2,000 metres of water, and that Admiral McClintock, England's hero of the polar seas, pulled in a live sea star from a depth of 2,500 metres. We know that the crew of the Royal Navy's *Bulldog* fished up a starfish from 2,620 fathoms, hence from a depth of more than one vertical league. Would you still say, Captain Nemo, that we really know nothing?'

'No, professor,' the captain replied, 'I wouldn't be so discourteous. Yet I'll ask you to explain how these creatures can live at such depths?'

'I explain it on two grounds,' I replied. 'In the first place, because vertical currents, which are caused by differences in the water's salinity and density, can produce enough motion to sustain the rudimentary lifestyles of sea lilies and starfish.'

'True,' the captain put in.

'In the second place, because oxygen is the basis of life, and we know that the amount of oxygen dissolved in salt water increases rather than decreases with depth, that the pressure in these lower strata helps to concentrate their oxygen content.'

'Oho! We know that, do we?' Captain Nemo replied in a tone of mild surprise. 'Well, professor, we have good reason to know it because it's the truth. I might add, in fact, that the air bladders of fish contain more nitrogen than oxygen when these animals are caught at the surface of the water, and conversely, more oxygen than nitrogen when they're pulled up from the lower depths. Which bears out your formulation. But let's continue our observations.'

My eyes flew back to the pressure gauge. The instrument indicated a depth of 6,000 metres. Our submergence had been going on for an hour. The *Nautilus* slid downward on its slanting fins, still sinking. These deserted waters were wonderfully clear, with a transparency impossible to convey. An hour later we were at 13,000 metres – about three and a quarter vertical leagues – and the ocean floor was nowhere in sight.

However, at 14,000 metres I saw blackish peaks rising in the midst of the waters. But these summits could have belonged to mountains as high or even higher than the Himalayas or Mt Blanc, and the extent of these depths remained incalculable.

Despite the powerful pressures it was undergoing, the *Nautilus* sank still deeper. I could feel its sheet-iron plates trembling down to their rivetted joins; metal bars arched; bulkheads groaned; the lounge windows seemed to be warping inward under the water's pressure. And this whole sturdy mechanism would surely have given way, if, as its captain had said, it weren't capable of resisting like a solid block.

While grazing these rocky slopes lost under the waters, I still spotted some seashells, tube worms, lively annelid worms from the genus *Spirorbis*, and certain starfish specimens.

But soon these last representatives of animal life vanished, and three vertical leagues down, the *Nautilus* passed below the limits of underwater existence just as an air balloon rises above the breathable zones in the sky. We reached a depth of 16,000 metres – four vertical leagues – and by then the *Nautilus*'s plating was tolerating a pressure of 1,600 atmospheres, in other words, 1,600 kilograms per each square centimetre on its surface!

'What an experience!' I exclaimed. 'Travelling these deep regions where no man has ever ventured before! Look, captain! Look at these magnificent rocks, these uninhabited caves, these last global haunts where life is no longer possible! What unheard-of scenery, and why are we reduced to preserving it only as a memory?'

'Would you like,' Captain Nemo asked me, 'to bring back more than just a memory?'

'What do you mean?'

'I mean that nothing could be easier than taking a photograph of this underwater region!'

Before I had time to express the surprise this new proposition caused me, a camera was carried into the lounge at Captain Nemo's request. The liquid setting, electrically lit, unfolded with perfect clarity through the wide-open panels. No shadows, no blurs, thanks to our artificial light. Not even sunshine could have been better for our purposes. With the thrust of its propeller curbed by the slant of its fins, the *Nautilus* stood still. The camera was aimed at the scenery on the ocean floor, and in a few seconds we had a perfect negative.

I attach a print of the positive. In it you can view these primordial rocks that have never seen the light of day, this nether granite that forms the powerful foundation of our globe, the deep caves cut into the stony mass, the outlines of incomparable distinctness whose far edges stand out in black as if from the brush of certain Flemish painters. In the distance is a mountainous horizon, a wondrously undulating line that makes up the background of this landscape. The general effect of these smooth rocks is indescribable: black, polished, without moss or other blemish, carved into strange shapes, sitting firmly on a carpet of sand that sparkled beneath our streams of electric light.

Meanwhile, his photographic operations over, Captain Nemo told me:

'Let's go back up, professor. We mustn't push our luck and expose the *Nautilus* too long to these pressures.'

'Let's go back up!' I replied.

'Hold on tight.'

Before I had time to realise why the captain made this recommendation, I was hurled to the carpet.

Its fins set vertically, its propeller thrown in gear at the captain's signal, the *Nautilus* rose with lightning speed, shooting upward like an air balloon into the sky. Vibrating resonantly, it knifed through the watery mass. Not a single detail was visible. In four minutes it had cleared the four vertical leagues separating it from the surface of the ocean, and after emerging like a flying fish, it fell back into the sea, making the waves leap to prodigious heights.

CHAPTER 12

Sperm Whales and Baleen Whales

DURING THE NIGHT of March 13–14, the *Nautilus* resumed its southward heading. Once it was abreast of Cape Horn, I thought it would strike west of the cape, make for Pacific seas, and complete its tour of the world. It did nothing of the sort and kept moving toward the southernmost regions. So where was it bound? The pole? That was insanity. I was beginning to think that the captain's recklessness more than justified Ned Land's worst fears.

For a good while the Canadian had said nothing more to me about his escape plans. He had become less sociable, almost sullen. I could see how heavily this protracted imprisonment was weighing on him. I could feel the anger building in him. Whenever he encountered the captain, his eyes would flicker with dark fire, and I was in constant dread that his natural vehemence would cause him to do something rash.

That day, March 14, he and Conseil managed to find me in my stateroom. I asked them the purpose of their visit.

'To put a simple question to you, sir,' the Canadian answered me.

'Go on, Ned.'

'How many men do you think are on board the *Nautilus*?'

'I'm unable to say, my friend.'

'It seems to me,' Ned Land went on, 'that it wouldn't take much of a crew to run a ship like this one.'

'Correct,' I replied. 'Under existing conditions some ten men at the most should be enough to operate it.'

'All right,' the Canadian said, 'then why should there be any more than that?'

'Why?' I answered.

I stared at Ned Land, whose motives were easy to guess.

'Because,' I said, 'if I can trust my hunches, if I truly understand the captain's way of life, his *Nautilus* isn't simply a ship. It's meant to be a refuge for people like its commander, people who have severed all ties with the shore.'

'Perhaps,' Conseil said, 'but in a nutshell, the *Nautilus* can hold only a certain number of men, so couldn't Master estimate their maximum?'

'How, Conseil?'

'By calculating it. Master is familiar with the ship's capacity, hence the amount of air it contains; on the other hand, Master knows how much air each man consumes in the act of breathing, and he can compare this data with the fact that the *Nautilus* must rise to the surface every 24 hours...'

Conseil didn't finish his sentence, but I could easily see what he was driving at.

'I follow you,' I said. 'But while they're simple to do, such calculations can give only a very uncertain figure.'

'No problem,' the Canadian went on insistently.

'Then here's how to calculate it,' I replied. 'In one hour each man consumes the oxygen contained in 100 litres of air, hence during 24 hours the oxygen contained in 2,400 litres. Therefore, we must look for the multiple of 2,400 litres of air that gives us the amount found in the *Nautilus*.'

'Precisely,' Conseil said.

'Now then,' I went on, 'the *Nautilus*'s capacity is 1,500 metric tons, and that of a ton is 1,000 litres, so the *Nautilus* holds 1,500,000 litres of air, which, divided by 2,400...'

I did a quick pencil calculation.

'... gives us the quotient of 625. Which is tantamount to saying that the air contained in the *Nautilus* would be exactly enough for 625 men over 24 hours.'

'625!' Ned repeated.

'But rest assured,' I added, 'that between passengers, seamen, or officers, we don't total one-tenth of that figure.'

'Which is still too many for three men!' Conseil muttered.

'So, my poor Ned, I can only counsel patience.'

'And,' Conseil replied, 'even more than patience, resignation.'

Conseil had said the true word.

'Even so,' he went on, 'Captain Nemo can't go south forever! He'll surely have to stop, if only at the Ice Bank, and he'll return to the seas of civilization! Then it will be time to resume Ned Land's plans.'

The Canadian shook his head, passed his hand over his brow, made no reply, and left us.

'With master's permission, I'll make an observation to him,' Conseil then told me. 'Our poor Ned broods about all the things he can't have. He's haunted by his former life. He seems to miss everything that's denied us. He's obsessed by his old memories and it's breaking his heart. We must understand him. What does he have to occupy him here? Nothing. He isn't a scientist like master, and he doesn't share our enthusiasm for the sea's wonders. He would risk anything just to enter a tavern in his own country!'

To be sure, the monotony of life on board must have seemed unbearable to the Canadian, who was accustomed to freedom and activity. It was a rare event that could excite him. That day, however, a development occurred that reminded him of his happy years as a harpooner.

Near 11 o'clock in the morning, while on the surface of the ocean, the *Nautilus* fell in with a herd of baleen whales. This encounter didn't surprise me, because I knew these animals were being hunted so relentlessly that they took refuge in the ocean basins of the high latitudes.

In the maritime world and in the realm of geographic exploration, whales have played a major role. This is the animal that first dragged the Basques in its wake, then Asturian Spaniards, Englishmen and Dutchmen, emboldening them against the ocean's perils, and leading them to the ends of the earth. Baleen whales like to frequent the southernmost and northernmost seas. Old legends even claim that these cetaceans led fishermen to within a mere seven leagues of the North Pole. Although this feat is fictitious, it will someday come true, because it's likely that by hunting whales in the Arctic or Antarctic regions, man will finally reach this unknown spot on the globe.

We were seated on the platform next to a tranquil sea. The month of March, since it's the equivalent of October in these latitudes, was giving us some fine autumn days. It was the Canadian – on this topic he was never mistaken – who sighted a baleen whale on the eastern horizon. If you looked carefully, you could see its blackish back alternately rise and fall above the waves, five miles from the *Nautilus*.

'Wow!' Ned Land exclaimed. 'If I were on board a whaler, there's an encounter that would be great fun! That's one big animal! Look how high its blowholes are spouting all that air and steam! Damnation! Why am I chained to this hunk of sheet iron!'

'Why, Ned!' I replied. 'You still aren't over your old fishing urges?'

'How could a whale fisherman forget his old trade, sir? Who could ever get tired of such exciting hunting?'

'You've never fished these seas, Ned?'

'Never, sir. Just the northernmost seas, equally in the Bering Strait and the Davis Strait.'

'So the southern right whale is still unknown to you. Until now it's the bowhead whale you've hunted, and it won't risk going past the warm waters of the equator.'

'Oh, professor, what are you feeding me?' the Canadian answered in a tolerably sceptical tone.

'I'm feeding you the facts.'

'By thunder! In '65, just two and a half years ago, I to whom you speak, I myself stepped onto the carcass of a whale near Greenland, and its flank still carried the marked harpoon of a whaling ship from the Bering Sea. Now I ask you, after it had been wounded west of America, how could this animal be killed in the east, unless it had cleared the equator and doubled Cape Horn or the Cape of Good Hope?'

'I agree with our friend Ned,' Conseil said, 'and I'm waiting to hear how master will reply to him.'

'Master will reply, my friends, that baleen whales are localised, according to species, within certain seas that they never leave. And if one of these animals went from the Bering Strait to the Davis Strait, it's quite simply because there's some passageway from the one sea to the other, either along the coasts of Canada or Siberia.'

'You expect us to fall for that?' the Canadian asked, tipping me a wink.

'If master says so,' Conseil replied.

'Which means,' the Canadian went on, 'since I've never fished these waterways, I don't know the whales that frequent them?'

'That's what I've been telling you, Ned.'

'All the more reason to get to know them,' Conseil answered.

'Look! Look!' the Canadian exclaimed, his voice full of excitement.

'It's approaching! It's coming toward us! It's thumbing its nose at me! It knows I can't do a blessed thing to it!'

Ned stamped his foot. Brandishing an imaginary harpoon, his hands positively trembled.

'These cetaceans,' he asked, 'are they as big as the ones in the northernmost seas?'

'Pretty nearly, Ned.'

'Because I've seen big baleen whales, sir, whales measuring up to 100 feet long! I've even heard that those rorqual whales off the Aleutian Islands sometimes get over 150 feet.'

'That strikes me as exaggerated,' I replied. 'Those animals are only members of the genus *Balaenoptera* furnished with dorsal fins, and like sperm whales, they're generally smaller than the bowhead whale.'

'Oh!' exclaimed the Canadian, whose eyes hadn't left the ocean. 'It's getting closer, it's coming into the *Nautilus*'s waters!'

Then, going on with his conversation:

'You talk about sperm whales,' he said, 'as if they were little beasts! But there are stories of gigantic sperm whales. They're shrewd cetaceans. I hear that some will cover themselves with algae and fucus plants. People mistake them for islets. They pitch camp on top, make themselves at home, light a fire—'

'Build houses,' Conseil said.

'Yes, funny man,' Ned Land replied. 'Then one fine day the animal dives and drags all its occupants down into the depths.'

'Like in the voyages of Sinbad the Sailor,' I answered, laughing. 'Oh, Mr Land, you're addicted to tall tales! What sperm whales you're handing us! I hope you don't really believe in them!'

'Mr Naturalist,' the Canadian replied in all seriousness, 'when it comes to whales, you can believe anything! (Look at that one move! Look at it stealing away!) People claim these animals can circle around the world in just 15 days.'

'I don't say nay.'

'But what you undoubtedly don't know, Professor Aronnax, is that at the beginning of the world, whales travelled even quicker.'

'Oh really, Ned! And why so?'

'Because in those days their tails moved side to side, like those on fish, in other words, their tails were straight up, thrashing the water from left to right, right to left. But spotting that they swam too fast, our Creator twisted their tails, and ever since they've been thrashing the waves up and down, at the expense of their speed.'

'Fine, Ned,' I said, then resurrected one of the Canadian's expressions. 'You expect us to fall for that?'

'Not too terribly,' Ned Land replied, 'and no more than if I told you there are whales that are 300 feet long and weigh 1,000,000 pounds.'

'That's indeed considerable,' I said. 'But you must admit that certain cetaceans do grow to significant size, since they're said to supply as much as 120 metric tons of oil.'

'That I've seen,' the Canadian said.

'I can easily believe it, Ned, just as I can believe that certain baleen whales equal 100 elephants in bulk. Imagine the impact of such a mass if it were launched at full speed!'

'Is it true,' Conseil asked, 'that they can sink ships?'

'Ships? I doubt it,' I replied. 'However, they say that in 1820, right in these southern seas, a baleen whale rushed at the *Essex* and pushed it backward at a speed of four metres per second. Its stern was flooded, and the *Essex* went down fast.'

Ned looked at me with a bantering expression.

'Speaking for myself,' he said, 'I once got walloped by a whale's tail – in my longboat, needless to say. My companions and I were launched to an altitude of six metres. But next to the Professor's whale, mine was just a baby.'

'Do these animals live a long time?' Conseil asked.

'A thousand years,' the Canadian replied without hesitation.

'And how, Ned,' I asked, 'do you know that's so?'

'Because people say so.'

'And why do people say so?'

'Because people know so.'

'No, Ned! People don't know so, they suppose so, and here's the logic with which they back up their beliefs. When fishermen first hunted whales 400 years ago, these animals grew to bigger sizes than they do today. Reasonably enough, it's assumed that today's whales are smaller because they haven't had time to reach their full growth.

That's why the Count de Buffon's encyclopedia says that cetaceans can live, and even must live, for a thousand years. You understand?'

Ned Land didn't understand. He no longer even heard me. That baleen whale kept coming closer. His eyes devoured it.

'Oh!' he exclaimed. 'It's not just one whale, it's ten, 20, a whole gam! And I can't do a thing! I'm tied hand and foot!'

'But Ned my friend,' Conseil said, 'why not ask Captain Nemo for permission to hunt—'

Before Conseil could finish his sentence, Ned Land scooted down the hatch and ran to look for the captain. A few moments later, the two of them reappeared on the platform.

Captain Nemo observed the herd of cetaceans cavorting on the waters a mile from the *Nautilus*.

'They're southern right whales,' he said. 'There goes the fortune of a whole whaling fleet.'

'Well, sir,' the Canadian asked, 'couldn't I hunt them, just so I don't forget my old harpooning trade?'

'Hunt them? What for?' Captain Nemo replied. 'Simply to destroy them? We have no use for whale oil on this ship.'

'But, sir,' the Canadian went on, 'in the Red Sea you authorised us to chase a dugong!'

'There it was an issue of obtaining fresh meat for my crew. Here it would be killing for the sake of killing. I'm well aware that's a privilege reserved for mankind, but I don't allow such murderous pastimes. When your peers, Mr Land, destroy decent, harmless creatures like the southern right whale or the bowhead whale, they commit a reprehensible offence. Thus they've already depopulated all of Baffin Bay, and they'll wipe out a whole class of useful animals. So leave these poor cetaceans alone. They have quite enough natural enemies, such as sperm whales, swordfish and sawfish, without you meddling with them.'

I'll let the reader decide what faces the Canadian made during this lecture on hunting ethics. Furnishing such arguments to a professional harpooner was a waste of words. Ned Land stared at Captain Nemo and obviously missed his meaning. But the captain was right. Thanks to the mindless, barbaric bloodthirstiness of fishermen, the last baleen whale will someday disappear from the ocean.

Ned Land whistled *Yankee Doodle* between his teeth, stuffed his hands in his pockets, and turned his back on us.

Meanwhile Captain Nemo studied the herd of cetaceans, then addressed me:

'I was right to claim that baleen whales have enough natural enemies without counting man. These specimens will soon have to deal with mighty opponents. Eight miles to leeward, Professor Aronnax, can you see those blackish specks moving about?'

'Yes, captain,' I replied.

'Those are sperm whales, dreadful animals that I've sometimes encountered in herds of 200 or 300! As for them, they're cruel, destructive beasts, and they deserve to be exterminated.'

The Canadian turned swiftly at these last words.

'Well, captain,' I said, 'on behalf of the baleen whales, there's still time—'

'It's pointless to run any risks, professor. The *Nautilus* will suffice to disperse these sperm whales. It's armed with a steel spur quite equal to Mr Land's harpoon, I imagine.'

The Canadian didn't even bother shrugging his shoulders. Attacking cetaceans with thrusts from a spur! Who ever heard of such malarkey!

'Wait and see, Professor Aronnax,' Captain Nemo said. 'We'll show you a style of hunting with which you aren't yet familiar. We'll take no pity on these ferocious cetaceans. They're merely mouth and teeth!'

Mouth and teeth! There's no better way to describe the long-skulled sperm whale, whose length sometimes exceeds 25 metres. The enormous head of this cetacean occupies about a third of its body. Better armed than a baleen whale, whose upper jaw is adorned solely with whalebone, the sperm whale is equipped with 25 huge teeth that are 20 centimetres high, have cylindrical, conical summits, and weigh two pounds each. In the top part of this enormous head, inside big cavities separated by cartilage, you'll find 300 to 400 kilograms of that valuable oil called 'spermaceti.' The sperm whale is an awkward animal, more tadpole than fish, as Professor Frédol has noted. It's poorly constructed, being 'defective,' so to speak, over the whole left side of its frame, with good eyesight only in its right eye.

Meanwhile that monstrous herd kept coming closer. It had seen the baleen whales and was preparing to attack. You could tell in advance that the sperm whales would be victorious, not only because they were better built for fighting than their harmless adversaries, but also because they could stay longer underwater before returning to breathe at the surface.

There was just time to run to the rescue of the baleen whales. The *Nautilus* proceeded to midwater. Conseil, Ned and I sat in front of the lounge windows. Captain Nemo made his way to the helmsman's side to operate his submersible as an engine of destruction. Soon I felt the beats of our propeller getting faster and we picked up speed.

The battle between sperm whales and baleen whales had already begun when the *Nautilus* arrived. It manoeuvred to cut into the herd of long-skulled predators. At first the latter showed little concern at the sight of this new monster meddling in the battle. But they soon had to sidestep its thrusts.

What a struggle! Ned Land quickly grew enthusiastic and even ended up applauding. Brandished in its captain's hands, the *Nautilus* was simply a fearsome harpoon. He hurled it at those fleshy masses and ran them clean through, leaving behind two squirming animal halves. As for those daunting strokes of the tail hitting our sides, the ship never felt them. No more than the collisions it caused. One sperm whale exterminated, it ran at another, tacked on the spot so as not to miss its prey, went ahead or astern, obeyed its rudder, dived when the cetacean sank to deeper strata, rose with it when it returned to the surface, struck it head-on or slantwise, hacked at it or tore it, and from every direction and at any speed, skewered it with its dreadful spur.

What bloodshed! What a hubbub on the surface of the waves! What sharp hisses and snorts unique to these frightened animals! Their tails churned the normally peaceful strata into actual billows.

This Homeric slaughter dragged on for an hour, and the long-skulled predators couldn't get away. Several times ten or 12 of them teamed up, trying to crush the *Nautilus* with their sheer mass. Through the windows you could see their enormous mouths paved with teeth, their fearsome eyes. Losing all self-control, Ned Land hurled threats and insults at them. You could feel them clinging to the submersible like hounds atop a wild boar in the underbrush. But by forcing the pace of its propeller, the *Nautilus* carried them off, dragged them under, or brought them back to the upper level of the waters, untroubled by their enormous weight or their powerful grip.

Finally this mass of sperm whales thinned out. The waves grew tranquil again. I felt us rising to the surface of the ocean. The hatch opened and we rushed onto the platform.

The sea was covered with mutilated corpses. A fearsome explosion couldn't have slashed, torn, or shredded these fleshy masses with greater violence. We were floating in the midst of gigantic bodies, bluish on the back, whitish on the belly, and all deformed by enormous protuberances. A few frightened sperm whales were fleeing toward the horizon. The waves were dyed red over an area of several miles, and the *Nautilus* was floating in the middle of a sea of blood.

Captain Nemo rejoined us.

'Well, Mr Land?' he said.

'Well, sir,' replied the Canadian, whose enthusiasm had subsided, 'it's a dreadful sight for sure. But I'm a hunter not a butcher, and this is plain butchery.'

'It was a slaughter of destructive animals,' the captain replied, 'and the *Nautilus* is no butcher knife.'

'I prefer my harpoon,' the Canadian answered.

'To each his own,' the captain replied, staring intently at Ned Land.

I was in dread the latter would give way to some violent outburst that might have had deplorable consequences. But his anger was diverted by the sight of a baleen whale that the *Nautilus* had pulled alongside of just then.

This animal had been unable to escape the teeth of those sperm whales. I recognised the southern right whale, its head squat, its body dark all over. Anatomically, it's distinguished from the white whale and the black right whale by the fusion of its seven cervical vertebrae, and it numbers two more ribs than its relatives. Floating on its side, its belly riddled with bites, the poor cetacean was dead. Still hanging from the tip of its mutilated fin was a little baby whale that it had been unable to rescue from the slaughter. Its open mouth let water flow through its whalebone like a murmuring surf.

Captain Nemo guided the *Nautilus* next to the animal's corpse. Two of his men climbed onto the whale's flank, and to my astonishment,

I saw them draw from its udders all the milk they held, in other words, enough to fill two or three casks.

The captain offered me a cup of this still-warm milk. I couldn't help showing my distaste for such a beverage. He assured me that this milk was excellent, no different from cow's milk.

I sampled it and agreed. So this milk was a worthwhile reserve ration for us, because in the form of salt butter or cheese, it would provide a pleasant change of pace from our standard fare.

From that day on, I noted with some uneasiness that Ned Land's attitudes toward Captain Nemo grew worse and worse, and I decided to keep a close watch on the Canadian's movements and activities.

CHAPTER 13

The Ice Bank

THE *NAUTILUS* RESUMED its unruffled southbound heading. It went along the 50th meridian with considerable speed. Would it go to the pole? I didn't think so, because every previous attempt to reach this spot on the globe had failed. Besides, the season was already quite advanced, since March 13 on Antarctic shores corresponds with September 13 in the northernmost regions, which marks the beginning of the equinoctial period.

On March 14 at latitude 55°, I spotted floating ice, plain pale bits of rubble 20 to 25 feet long, which formed reefs over which the sea burst into foam. The *Nautilus* stayed on the surface of the ocean. Having fished in the Arctic seas, Ned Land was already familiar with the sight of icebergs. Conseil and I were marvelling at them for the first time.

In the sky toward the southern horizon, there stretched a dazzling white band. English whalers have given this the name 'ice blink.' No matter how heavy the clouds may be, they can't obscure this phenomenon. It announces the presence of a pack, or shoal, of ice.

Indeed, larger blocks of ice soon appeared, their brilliance varying at the whim of the mists. Some of these masses displayed green veins, as if scrawled with undulating lines of copper sulphate. Others looked like enormous amethysts, letting the light penetrate their insides. The latter reflected the sun's rays from the thousand facets of their crystals. The former, tinted with a bright limestone sheen, would have supplied enough building material to make a whole marble town.

The farther down south we went, the more these floating islands grew in numbers and prominence. Polar birds nested on them by the thousands. These were petrels, cape pigeons, or puffins, and their calls were deafening. Mistaking the *Nautilus* for the corpse of a whale, some of them alighted on it and prodded its resonant sheet iron with pecks of their beaks.

During this navigating in the midst of the ice, Captain Nemo often stayed on the platform. He observed these deserted waterways carefully. I saw his calm eyes sometimes perk up. In these polar seas forbidden to man, did he feel right at home, the lord of these unreachable regions? Perhaps. But he didn't say. He stood still, reviving only when his pilot's instincts took over. Then, steering his *Nautilus* with consummate dexterity, he skilfully dodged the masses of ice, some of which measured several miles in length, their heights varying from 70 to 80 metres. Often the horizon seemed completely closed off. Abreast of latitude 60°, every passageway had disappeared. Searching with care, Captain Nemo soon found a narrow opening into which he brazenly slipped, well aware, however, that it would close behind him.

Guided by his skilful hands, the *Nautilus* passed by all these different masses of ice, which are classified by size and shape with a precision that enraptured Conseil: 'icebergs,' or mountains; 'ice fields,' or smooth, limitless tracts; 'drift ice,' or floating floes; 'packs,' or broken tracts, called 'patches' when they're circular and 'streams' when they form long strips.

The temperature was fairly low. Exposed to the outside air, the thermometer marked −2° to −3° centigrade. But we were warmly dressed in furs, for which seals and aquatic bears had paid the price. Evenly heated by all its electric equipment, the *Nautilus*'s interior defied the most intense cold. Moreover, to find a bearable temperature, the ship had only to sink just a few metres beneath the waves.

Two months earlier we would have enjoyed perpetual daylight in this latitude; but night already fell for three or four hours, and later it would cast six months of shadow over these circumpolar regions.

On March 15 we passed beyond the latitude of the South Shetland and South Orkney Islands. The captain told me that many tribes of seals used to inhabit these shores; but English and American whalers, in a frenzy of destruction, slaughtered all the adults, including pregnant females, and where life and activity once existed, those fishermen left behind only silence and death.

Going along the 55th meridian, the *Nautilus* cut the Antarctic Circle on March 16 near eight o'clock in the morning. Ice completely surrounded us and closed off the horizon. Nevertheless, Captain Nemo went from passageway to passageway, always proceeding south.

'But where's he going?' I asked.

'Straight ahead,' Conseil replied. 'Ultimately, when he can't go any farther, he'll stop.'

'I wouldn't bet on it!' I replied.

And in all honesty, I confess that this venturesome excursion was far from displeasing to me. I can't express the intensity of my amazement at the beauties of these new regions. The ice struck superb poses. Here, its general effect suggested an oriental town with countless minarets and mosques. There, a city in ruins, flung to the ground by convulsions in the earth. These views were varied continuously by the sun's oblique rays, or were completely swallowed up by grey mists in the middle of blizzards. Then explosions, cave-ins and great iceberg somersaults would occur all around us, altering the scenery like the changing landscape in a diorama.

If the *Nautilus* was submerged during these losses of balance, we heard the resulting noises spread under the waters with frightful intensity, and the collapse of these masses created daunting eddies down to the ocean's lower strata. The *Nautilus* then rolled and pitched like a ship left to the fury of the elements.

Often, no longer seeing any way out, I thought we were imprisoned for good, but Captain Nemo, guided by his instincts, discovered new passageways from the tiniest indications. He was never wrong when he observed slender threads of bluish water streaking through these ice fields. Accordingly, I was sure that he had already risked his *Nautilus* in the midst of the Antarctic seas.

However, during the day of March 16, these tracts of ice completely barred our path. It wasn't the Ice Bank as yet, just huge ice fields cemented together by the cold. This obstacle couldn't stop Captain Nemo, and he launched his ship against the ice fields with hideous violence. The *Nautilus* went into these brittle masses like a wedge, splitting them with dreadful cracklings. It was an old–fashioned battering ram propelled with infinite power. Hurled aloft, ice rubble fell back around us like hail. Through brute force alone, the submersible carved out a channel for itself. Carried away by its momentum, the ship sometimes mounted on top of these tracts of ice and crushed them with its weight, or at other times, when cooped up beneath the ice fields, it split them with simple pitching movements, creating wide punctures.

Violent squalls assaulted us during the daytime. Thanks to certain heavy mists, we couldn't see from one end of the platform to the other. The wind shifted abruptly to every point on the compass. The snow was piling up in such packed layers, it had to be chipped loose with blows from picks. Even in a temperature of merely −5° centigrade, every outside part of the *Nautilus* was covered with ice. A ship's rigging would have been unusable, because all its tackle would have jammed in the grooves of the pulleys. Only a craft without sails, driven by an electric motor that needed no coal, could face such high latitudes.

Under these conditions the barometer generally stayed quite low. It fell as far as 73.5 centimetres. Our compass indications no longer offered any guarantees. The deranged needles would mark contradictory directions as we approached the southern magnetic pole, which doesn't coincide with the South Pole proper. In fact, according to the astronomer Hansteen, this magnetic pole is located fairly close to latitude 70° and longitude 130°, or abiding by the observations of Louis-Isidore Duperrey, in longitude 135° and latitude 70° 30'. Hence we had to transport compasses to different parts of the ship, take many readings, and strike an average. Often we could chart our course only by guesswork, a less than satisfactory method in the midst of these winding passageways whose landmarks change continuously.

At last on March 18, after 20 futile assaults, the *Nautilus* was decisively held in check. No longer was it an ice stream, patch, or field – it was an endless, immovable barrier formed by ice mountains fused to each other.

'The Ice Bank!' the Canadian told me.

For Ned Land, as well as for every navigator before us, I knew that this was the great insurmountable obstacle. When the sun appeared for an instant near noon, Captain Nemo took a reasonably accurate sight that gave our position as longitude 51° 30' and latitude 67° 39' south. This was a position already well along in these Antarctic regions.

As for the liquid surface of the sea, there was no longer any semblance of it before our eyes. Before the *Nautilus*'s spur there lay vast broken plains, a tangle of confused chunks with all the helter-skelter unpredictability typical of a river's surface a short while before its ice breakup; but in this case the proportions were gigantic. Here and there stood sharp peaks, lean spires that rose as high as 200 feet;

farther off, a succession of steeply cut cliffs sporting a greyish tint, huge mirrors that reflected the sparse rays of a sun half drowned in mist. Beyond, a stark silence reigned in this desolate natural setting, a silence barely broken by the flapping wings of petrels or puffins. By this point everything was frozen, even sound.

So the *Nautilus* had to halt in its venturesome course among these tracts of ice.

'Sir,' Ned Land told me that day, 'if your captain goes any farther…'

'Yes?'

'He'll be a superman.'

'How so, Ned?'

'Because nobody can clear the Ice Bank. Your captain's a powerful man, but damnation, he isn't more powerful than nature. If she draws a boundary line, there you stop, like it or not!'

'Correct, Ned Land, but I still want to know what's behind this Ice Bank! Behold my greatest source of irritation – a wall!'

'Master is right,' Conseil said. 'Walls were invented simply to frustrate scientists. All walls should be banned.'

'Fine!' the Canadian put in. 'But we already know what's behind this Ice Bank.'

'What?' I asked.

'Ice, ice and more ice.'

'You may be sure of that, Ned,' I answered, 'but I'm not. That's why I want to see for myself.'

'Well, professor,' the Canadian replied, 'you can just drop that idea! You've made it to the Ice Bank, which is already far enough, but you won't get any farther, neither your Captain Nemo or his *Nautilus*. And whether he wants to or not, we'll head north again, in other words, to the land of sensible people.'

I had to agree that Ned Land was right, and until ships are built to navigate over tracts of ice, they'll have to stop at the Ice Bank.

Indeed, despite its efforts, despite the powerful methods it used to split this ice, the *Nautilus* was reduced to immobility. Ordinarily, when someone can't go any farther, he still has the option of returning in his tracks. But here it was just as impossible to turn back as to go forward, because every passageway had closed behind us, and if our submersible remained even slightly stationary, it would be frozen in without delay. Which is exactly what happened near two o'clock in the afternoon, and fresh ice kept forming over the ship's sides with astonishing speed. I had to admit that Captain Nemo's leadership had been most injudicious.

Just then I was on the platform. Observing the situation for some while, the captain said to me:

'Well, professor! What think you?'

'I think we're trapped, captain.'

'Trapped! What do you mean?'

'I mean we can't go forward, backward, or sideways. I think that's the standard definition of "trapped," at least in the civilised world.'

'So, Professor Aronnax, you think the *Nautilus* won't be able to float clear?'

'Only with the greatest difficulty, captain, since the season is already too advanced for you to depend on an ice breakup.'

'Oh, professor,' Captain Nemo replied in an ironic tone, 'you never change! You see only impediments and obstacles! I promise you, not only will the *Nautilus* float clear, it will go farther still!'

'Farther south?' I asked, gaping at the captain.

'Yes, sir, it will go to the pole.'

'To the pole!' I exclaimed, unable to keep back a movement of disbelief.

'Yes,' the captain replied coolly, 'the Antarctic pole, that unknown spot crossed by every meridian on the globe. As you know, I do whatever I like with my *Nautilus*.'

Yes, I did know that! I knew this man was daring to the point of being foolhardy. But to overcome all the obstacles around the South Pole – even more unattainable than the North Pole, which still hadn't been reached by the boldest navigators – wasn't this an absolutely insane undertaking, one that could occur only in the brain of a madman?

It then dawned on me to ask Captain Nemo if he had already discovered this pole, which no human being had ever trod underfoot.

'No, sir,' he answered me, 'but we'll discover it together. Where others have failed, I'll succeed. Never before has my *Nautilus* cruised so far into these southernmost seas, but I repeat: it will go farther still.'

'I'd like to believe you, captain,' I went on in a tone of some sarcasm. 'Oh I do believe you! Let's forge ahead! There are no obstacles for us! Let's shatter this Ice Bank! Let's blow it up, and if it still resists, let's put wings on the *Nautilus* and fly over it!'

'Over it, professor?' Captain Nemo replied serenely. 'No, not over it, but under it.'

'Under it!' I exclaimed.

A sudden insight into Captain Nemo's plans had just flashed through my mind. I understood. The marvellous talents of his *Nautilus* would be put to work once again in this superhuman undertaking!

'I can see we're starting to understand each other, professor,' Captain Nemo told me with a half smile. 'You already glimpse the potential – myself, I'd say the success – of this attempt. Manoeuvres that aren't feasible for an ordinary ship are easy for the *Nautilus*. If a continent emerges at the pole, we'll stop at that continent. But on the other hand, if open sea washes the pole, we'll go to that very place!'

'Right,' I said, carried away by the captain's logic. 'Even though the surface of the sea has solidified into ice, its lower strata are still open, thanks to that divine justice that puts the maximum density of salt water one degree above its freezing point. And if I'm not mistaken, the submerged part of this Ice Bank is in a four-to-one ratio to its emerging part.'

'Very nearly, professor. For each foot of iceberg above the sea, there are three more below. Now then, since these ice mountains don't exceed a height of 100 metres, they sink only to a depth of 300 metres. And what are 300 metres to the *Nautilus*?'

'A mere nothing, sir.'

'We could even go to greater depths and find that temperature layer common to all ocean water, and there we'd brave with impunity the $-30°$ or $-40°$ cold on the surface.'

'True, sir, very true,' I replied with growing excitement.

'Our sole difficulty,' Captain Nemo went on, 'lies in our staying submerged for several days without renewing our air supply.'

'That's all?' I answered. 'The *Nautilus* has huge air tanks; we'll fill them up and they'll supply all the oxygen we need.'

'Good thinking, Professor Aronnax,' the captain replied with a smile. 'But since I don't want to be accused of foolhardiness, I'm giving you all my objections in advance.'

'You have more?'

'Just one. If a sea exists at the South Pole, it's possible this sea may be completely frozen over, so we couldn't come up to the surface!'

'My dear sir, have you forgotten that the *Nautilus* is armed with a fearsome spur? Couldn't it be launched diagonally against those tracts of ice, which would break open from the impact?'

'Ah, professor, you're full of ideas today!'

'Besides, captain,' I added with still greater enthusiasm, 'why wouldn't we find open sea at the South Pole just as at the North Pole? The cold-temperature poles and the geographical poles don't coincide in either the northern or southern hemispheres, and until proof to the contrary, we can assume these two spots on the earth feature either a continent or an ice-free ocean.'

'I think as you do, Professor Aronnax,' Captain Nemo replied. 'I'll only point out that after raising so many objections against my plan, you're now crushing me under arguments in its favour.'

Captain Nemo was right. I was outdoing him in daring! It was I who was sweeping him to the pole. I was leading the way, I was out in front... but no, you silly fool! Captain Nemo already knew the pros and cons of this question, and it amused him to see you flying off into impossible fantasies!

Nevertheless, he didn't waste an instant. At his signal, the chief officer appeared. The two men held a quick exchange in their incomprehensible language, and either the chief officer had been alerted previously or he found the plan feasible, because he showed no surprise.

But as unemotional as he was, he couldn't have been more impeccably emotionless than Conseil when I told the fine lad our intention of pushing on to the South Pole. He greeted my announcement with the usual 'As Master wishes,' and I had to be content with that. As for Ned Land, no human shoulders ever executed a higher shrug than the pair belonging to our Canadian.

'Honestly, sir,' he told me. 'You and your Captain Nemo, I pity you both!'

'But we will go to the pole, Mr Land.'

'Maybe, but you won't come back!'

And Ned Land re-entered his cabin, 'to keep from doing something desperate,' he said as he left me.

Meanwhile preparations for this daring attempt were getting under way. The *Nautilus*'s powerful pumps forced air down into the tanks and stored it under high pressure. Near four o'clock Captain Nemo informed me that the platform hatches were about to be closed. I took a last look at the dense Ice Bank we were going to conquer. The weather was fair, the skies reasonably clear, the cold quite brisk, namely −12° centigrade; but after the wind had lulled, this temperature didn't seem too unbearable.

Equipped with picks, some ten men climbed onto the *Nautilus*'s sides and cracked loose the ice around the ship's lower plating, which was soon set free. This operation was swiftly executed because the fresh ice was still thin. We all re-entered the interior. The main ballast tanks were filled with the water that hadn't yet congealed at our line of flotation. The *Nautilus* submerged without delay.

I took a seat in the lounge with Conseil. Through the open window we stared at the lower strata of this southernmost ocean. The thermometer rose again. The needle on the pressure gauge swerved over its dial.

About 300 metres down, just as Captain Nemo had predicted, we cruised beneath the undulating surface of the Ice Bank. But the *Nautilus* sank deeper still. It reached a depth of 800 metres. At the surface this water gave a temperature of −12° centigrade, but now it gave no more than −10°. Two degrees had already been gained. Thanks to its heating equipment, the *Nautilus*'s temperature, needless to say, stayed at a much higher degree. Every manoeuvre was accomplished with extraordinary precision.

'With all due respect to master,' Conseil told me, 'we'll pass it by.'

'I fully expect to!' I replied in a tone of deep conviction.

Now in open water, the *Nautilus* took a direct course to the pole without veering from the 52nd meridian. From 67° 30' to 90°, 22 and a half degrees of latitude were left to cross, in other words, slightly more than 500 leagues. The *Nautilus* adopted an average speed of 26 miles per hour, the speed of an express train. If it kept up this pace, 40 hours would do it for reaching the pole.

For part of the night, the novelty of our circumstances kept Conseil and me at the lounge window. The sea was lit by our beacon's electric rays. But the depths were deserted. Fish didn't linger in these imprisoned waters. Here they found merely a passageway for going from the Antarctic Ocean to open sea at the pole. Our progress was swift. You could feel it in the vibrations of the long steel hull.

Near two o'clock in the morning, I went to snatch a few hours of sleep. Conseil did likewise. I didn't encounter Captain Nemo while going down the gangways. I assumed that he was keeping to the pilothouse.

The next day, March 19, at five o'clock in the morning, I was back at my post in the lounge. The electric log indicated that the *Nautilus* had reduced speed. By then it was rising to the surface, but cautiously, while slowly emptying its ballast tanks.

My heart was pounding. Would we emerge into the open and find the polar air again?

No. A jolt told me that the *Nautilus* had bumped the underbelly of the Ice Bank, still quite thick to judge from the hollowness of the accompanying noise. Indeed, we had 'struck bottom,' to use nautical terminology, but in the opposite direction and at a depth of 3,000 feet. That gave us 4,000 feet of ice overhead, of which 1,000 feet emerged above water. So the Ice Bank was higher here than we had found it on the outskirts. A circumstance less than encouraging.

Several times that day, the *Nautilus* repeated the same experiment and always it bumped against this surface that formed a ceiling above it. At certain moments the ship encountered ice at a depth of 900 metres, denoting a thickness of 1,200 metres, of which 300 metres rose above the level of the ocean. This height had tripled since the moment the *Nautilus* had dived beneath the waves.

I meticulously noted these different depths, obtaining the underwater profile of this upside-down mountain chain that stretched beneath the sea.

By evening there was still no improvement in our situation. The ice stayed between 400 and 500 metres deep. It was obviously shrinking, but what a barrier still lay between us and the surface of the ocean!

By then it was eight o'clock. The air inside the *Nautilus* should have been renewed four hours earlier, following daily practice on board. But I didn't suffer very much, although Captain Nemo hadn't yet made demands on the supplementary oxygen in his air tanks.

That night my sleep was fitful. Hope and fear besieged me by turns. I got up several times. The *Nautilus* continued groping. Near three o'clock in the morning, I observed that we encountered the Ice Bank's underbelly at a depth of only 50 metres. So only 150 feet separated us from the surface of the water. Little by little the Ice Bank was turning into an ice field again. The mountains were changing back into plains.

My eyes didn't leave the pressure gauge. We kept rising on a diagonal, going along this shiny surface that sparkled beneath our electric rays. Above and below, the Ice Bank was subsiding in long gradients. Mile after mile it was growing thinner.

Finally, at six o'clock in the morning on that memorable day of March 19, the lounge door opened. Captain Nemo appeared.

'Open sea!' he told me.

CHAPTER 14

The South Pole

I RUSHED UP onto the platform. Yes, open sea! Barely a few sparse floes, some moving icebergs; a sea stretching into the distance; hosts of birds in the air and myriads of fish under the waters, which varied from intense blue to olive green depending on the depth. The thermometer marked 3° centigrade. It was as if a comparative springtime had been locked up behind that Ice Bank, whose distant masses were outlined on the northern horizon.

'Are we at the pole?' I asked the captain, my heart pounding.

'I've no idea,' he answered me. 'At noon we'll fix our position.'

'But will the sun show through this mist?' I said, staring at the greyish sky.

'No matter how faintly it shines, it will be enough for me,' the captain replied.

To the south, ten miles from the *Nautilus*, a solitary islet rose to a height of 200 metres. We proceeded toward it, but cautiously, because this sea could have been strewn with reefs.

In an hour we had reached the islet. Two hours later we had completed a full circle around it. It measured four to five miles in circumference. A narrow channel separated it from a considerable shore, perhaps a continent whose limits we couldn't see. The existence of this shore seemed to bear out Commander Maury's hypotheses. In essence, this ingenious American has noted that between the South Pole and the 60th parallel, the sea is covered with floating ice of dimensions much greater than any found in the north Atlantic. From this fact he drew the conclusion that the Antarctic Circle must contain considerable shores, since icebergs can't form on the high seas but only along coastlines. According to his calculations, this frozen mass enclosing the southernmost pole forms a vast ice cap whose width must reach 4,000 kilometres.

Meanwhile, to avoid running aground, the *Nautilus* halted three cable lengths from a strand crowned by superb piles of rocks. The skiff was launched to sea. Two crewmen carrying instruments, the captain, Conseil and I were on board. It was ten o'clock in the morning. I hadn't seen Ned Land. No doubt, in the presence of the South Pole, the Canadian hated having to eat his words.

A few strokes of the oar brought the skiff to the sand, where it ran aground. Just as Conseil was about to jump ashore, I held him back.

'Sir,' I told Captain Nemo, 'to you belongs the honour of first setting foot on this shore.'

'Yes, sir,' the captain replied, 'and if I have no hesitation in treading this polar soil, it's because no human being until now has left a footprint here.'

So saying, he leaped lightly onto the sand. His heart must have been throbbing with intense excitement. He scaled an overhanging rock that ended in a small promontory and there, mute and motionless, with crossed arms and blazing eyes, he seemed to be laying claim to these southernmost regions. After spending five minutes in this trance, he turned to us.

'Whenever you're ready, sir,' he called to me.

I got out, Conseil at my heels, leaving the two men in the skiff.

Over an extensive area, the soil consisted of that igneous gravel called 'tuff,' reddish in colour as if made from crushed bricks. The ground was covered with slag, lava flows and pumice stones. Its volcanic origin was unmistakable. In certain localities thin smoke holes gave off a sulphurous odour, showing that the inner fires still kept their wide-ranging power. Nevertheless, when I scaled a high escarpment, I could see no volcanoes within a radius of several miles. In these Antarctic districts, as is well known, Sir James Clark Ross had found the craters of Mt Erebus and Mt Terror in fully active condition on the 167th meridian at latitude 77° 32'.

The vegetation on this desolate continent struck me as quite limited. A few lichens of the species *Usnea melanoxanthra* sprawled over the black rocks. The whole meagre flora of this region consisted of certain microscopic buds, rudimentary diatoms made up of a type of cell positioned between two quartz-rich shells, plus long purple and crimson fucus plants, buoyed by small air bladders and washed up on the coast by the surf.

The beach was strewn with molluscs: small mussels, limpets,

smooth heart-shaped cockles, and especially some sea butterflies with oblong, membrane-filled bodies whose heads are formed from two rounded lobes. I also saw myriads of those northernmost sea butterflies three centimetres long, which a baleen whale can swallow by the thousands in one gulp. The open waters at the shoreline were alive with these delightful pteropods, true butterflies of the sea.

Among other zoophytes present in these shallows, there were a few coral tree forms that, according to Sir James Clark Ross, live in these Antarctic seas at depths as great as 1,000 metres; then small alcyon coral belonging to the species *Procellaria pelagica*, also a large number of starfish unique to these climes, plus some feather stars spangling the sand.

But it was in the air that life was superabundant. There various species of birds flew and fluttered by the thousands, deafening us with their calls. Crowding the rocks, other fowl watched without fear as we passed and pressed familiarly against our feet. These were auks, as agile and supple in water, where they are sometimes mistaken for fast bonito, as they are clumsy and heavy on land. They uttered outlandish calls and participated in numerous public assemblies that featured much noise but little action.

Among other fowl I noted some sheathbills from the wading-bird family, the size of pigeons, white in colour, the beak short and conical, the eyes framed by red circles. Conseil laid in a supply of them, because when they're properly cooked, these winged creatures make a pleasant dish. In the air there passed sooty albatross with four-metre wingspans, birds aptly dubbed 'vultures of the ocean,' also gigantic petrels including several with arching wings, enthusiastic eaters of seal that are known as *quebrantahuesos*, and cape pigeons, a sort of small duck, the tops of their bodies black and white – in short, a whole series of petrels, some whitish with wings trimmed in brown, others blue and exclusive to these Antarctic seas, the former 'so oily,' I told Conseil, 'that inhabitants of the Faroe Islands simply fit the bird with a wick, then light it up.'

'With that minor addition,' Conseil replied, 'these fowl would make perfect lamps! After this, we should insist that nature equip them with wicks in advance!'

Half a mile farther on, the ground was completely riddled with penguin nests, egg-laying burrows from which numerous birds emerged. Later Captain Nemo had hundreds of them hunted because their black flesh is highly edible. They brayed like donkeys. The size of a goose with slate-coloured bodies, white undersides, and lemon-coloured neck bands, these animals let themselves be stoned to death without making any effort to get away.

Meanwhile the mists didn't clear, and by 11 o'clock the sun still hadn't made an appearance. Its absence disturbed me. Without it, no sights were possible. Then how could we tell whether we had reached the pole?

When I rejoined Captain Nemo, I found him leaning silently against a piece of rock and staring at the sky. He seemed impatient, baffled. But what could we do? This daring and powerful man couldn't control the sun as he did the sea.

Noon arrived without the orb of day appearing for a single instant. You couldn't even find its hiding place behind the curtain of mist. And soon this mist began to condense into snow.

'Until tomorrow,' the captain said simply; and we went back to the *Nautilus*, amid flurries in the air.

During our absence the nets had been spread, and I observed with fascination the fish just hauled on board. The Antarctic seas serve as a refuge for an extremely large number of migratory fish that flee from storms in the subpolar zones, in truth only to slide down the gullets of porpoises and seals. I noted some one-decimetre southern bullhead, a species of whitish cartilaginous fish overrun with bluish grey stripes and armed with stings, then some Antarctic rabbitfish three feet long, the body very slender, the skin a smooth silver white, the head rounded, the topside furnished with three fins, the snout ending in a trunk that curved back toward the mouth. I sampled its flesh but found it tasteless, despite Conseil's views, which were largely approving.

The blizzard lasted until the next day. It was impossible to stay on the platform. From the lounge, where I was writing up the incidents of this excursion to the polar continent, I could hear the calls of petrel and albatross cavorting in the midst of the turmoil. The *Nautilus* didn't stay idle, and cruising along the coast, it advanced some ten miles farther south amid the half light left by the sun as it skimmed the edge of the horizon.

The next day, March 20, it stopped snowing. The cold was a little more brisk. The thermometer marked −2° centigrade. The mist had cleared, and on that day I hoped our noon sights could be accomplished.

Since Captain Nemo hadn't yet appeared, only Conseil and I were taken ashore by the skiff. The soil's nature was still the same: volcanic. Traces of lava, slag and basaltic rock were everywhere, but I couldn't find the crater that had vomited them up. There as yonder, myriads of birds enlivened this part of the polar continent. But they had to share their dominion with huge herds of marine mammals that looked at us with gentle eyes. These were seals of various species, some stretched out on the ground, others lying on drifting ice floes, several leaving or re-entering the sea. Having never dealt with man, they didn't run off at our approach, and I counted enough of them thereabouts to provision a couple hundred ships.

'Ye gods,' Conseil said, 'it's fortunate that Ned Land didn't come with us!'

'Why so, Conseil?'

'Because that madcap hunter would kill every animal here.'

'Every animal may be overstating it, but in truth I doubt we could keep our Canadian friend from harpooning some of these magnificent cetaceans. Which would be an affront to Captain Nemo, since he hates to slay harmless beasts needlessly.'

'He's right.'

'Certainly, Conseil. But tell me, haven't you finished classifying these superb specimens of marine fauna?'

'Master is well aware,' Conseil replied, 'that I'm not seasoned in practical application. When master has told me these animals' names...'

'They're seals and walruses.'

'Two genera,' our scholarly Conseil hastened to say, 'that belong to the family *Pinnipedia*, order *Carnivora*, group *Unguiculata*, subclass *Monodelphia*, class *Mammalia*, branch *Vertebrata*.'

'Very nice, Conseil,' I replied, 'but these two genera of seals and walruses are each divided into species, and if I'm not mistaken, we now have a chance to actually look at them. Let's.'

It was eight o'clock in the morning. We had four hours to ourselves before the sun could be productively observed. I guided our steps toward a huge bay that made a crescent-shaped incision in the granite cliffs along the beach.

There, all about us, I swear that the shores and ice floes were crowded with marine mammals as far as the eye could see, and I involuntarily looked around for old Proteus, that mythological shepherd who guarded King Neptune's immense flocks. To be specific, these were seals. They formed distinct male-and-female groups, the father watching over his family, the mother suckling her little ones, the stronger youngsters emancipated a few paces away. When these mammals wanted to relocate, they moved in little jumps made by contracting their bodies, clumsily helped by their imperfectly developed flippers, which, as with their manatee relatives, form actual forearms. In the water, their ideal element, I must say these animals swim wonderfully thanks to their flexible backbones, narrow pelvises, close-cropped hair and webbed feet. Resting on shore, they assumed extremely graceful positions. Consequently, their gentle features, their sensitive expressions equal to those of the loveliest women, their soft, limpid eyes, their charming poses, led the ancients to glorify them by metamorphosing the males into sea gods and the females into mermaids.

I drew Conseil's attention to the considerable growth of the cerebral lobes found in these intelligent cetaceans. No mammal except man has more abundant cerebral matter. Accordingly, seals are quite capable of being educated; they make good pets, and together with certain other naturalists, I think these animals can be properly trained to perform yeoman service as hunting dogs for fishermen.

Most of these seals were sleeping on the rocks or the sand. Among those properly termed seals – which have no external ears, unlike sea lions whose ears protrude – I observed several varieties of the species *stenorhynchus*, three metres long, with white hair, bulldog heads, and armed with ten teeth in each jaw: four incisors in both the upper and lower, plus two big canines shaped like the fleur-de-lis. Among them slithered some sea elephants, a type of seal with a short, flexible trunk; these are the giants of the species, with a circumference of 20 feet and a length of ten metres. They didn't move as we approached.

'Are these animals dangerous?' Conseil asked me.

'Only if they're attacked,' I replied. 'But when these giant seals defend their little ones, their fury is dreadful, and it isn't rare for them to smash a fisherman's longboat to bits.'

'They're within their rights,' Conseil answered.

'I don't say nay.'

Two miles farther on, we were stopped by a promontory that screened the bay from southerly winds. It dropped straight down to the sea, and surf foamed against it. From beyond this ridge there came fearsome bellows, such as a herd of cattle might produce.

'Gracious,' Conseil put in, 'a choir of bulls?'

'No,' I said, 'a choir of walruses.'

'Are they fighting with each other?'

'Either fighting or playing.'

'With all due respect to master, this we must see.'

'Then see it we must, Conseil.'

And there we were, climbing these blackish rocks amid sudden landslides and over stones slippery with ice. More than once I took a tumble at the expense of my backside. Conseil, more cautious or more stable, barely faltered and would help me up, saying:

'If master's legs would kindly adopt a wider stance, master will keep his balance.'

Arriving at the topmost ridge of this promontory, I could see vast white plains covered with walruses. These animals were playing among themselves. They were howling not in anger but in glee.

Walruses resemble seals in the shape of their bodies and the arrangement of their limbs. But their lower jaws lack canines and incisors, and as for their upper canines, they consist of two tusks 80 centimetres long with a circumference of 33 centimetres at the socket. Made of solid ivory, without striations, harder than elephant tusks, and less prone to yellowing, these teeth are in great demand. Accordingly, walruses are the victims of a mindless hunting that soon will destroy them all, since their hunters indiscriminately slaughter pregnant females and youngsters, and over 4,000 individuals are destroyed annually.

Passing near these unusual animals, I could examine them at my leisure since they didn't stir. Their hides were rough and heavy, a tan colour leaning toward a reddish brown; their coats were short and less than abundant. Some were four metres long. More tranquil and less fearful than their northern relatives, they posted no sentinels on guard duty at the approaches to their campsite.

After examining this community of walruses, I decided to return in my tracks. It was 11 o'clock, and if Captain Nemo found conditions favourable for taking his sights, I wanted to be present at the operation. But I held no hopes that the sun would make an appearance that day. It was hidden from our eyes by clouds squeezed together on the horizon. Apparently the jealous orb didn't want to reveal this inaccessible spot on the globe to any human being.

Yet I decided to return to the *Nautilus*. We went along a steep, narrow path that ran over the cliff's summit. By 11:30 we had arrived at our landing place. The beached skiff had brought the captain ashore. I spotted him standing on a chunk of basalt. His instruments were beside him. His eyes were focused on the northern horizon, along which the sun was sweeping in its extended arc.

I found a place near him and waited without speaking. Noon arrived, and just as on the day before, the sun didn't put in an appearance.

It was sheer bad luck. Our noon sights were still lacking. If we couldn't obtain them tomorrow, we would finally have to give up any hope of fixing our position.

In essence, it was precisely March 20. Tomorrow, the 21st, was the day of the equinox; the sun would disappear below the horizon for six months not counting refraction, and after its disappearance the long polar night would begin. Following the September equinox, the sun had emerged above the northerly horizon, rising in long spirals until December 21. At that time, the summer solstice of these southernmost districts, the sun had started back down, and tomorrow it would cast its last rays.

I shared my thoughts and fears with Captain Nemo.

'You're right, Professor Aronnax,' he told me. 'If I can't take the sun's altitude tomorrow, I won't be able to try again for another six months. But precisely because sailors' luck has led me into these seas on March 21, it will be easy to get our bearings if the noonday sun does appear before our eyes.'

'Why easy, captain?'

'Because when the orb of day sweeps in such long spirals, it's difficult to measure its exact altitude above the horizon, and our instruments are open to committing serious errors.'

'Then what can you do?'

'I use only my chronometer,' Captain Nemo answered me. 'At noon tomorrow, March 21, if, after accounting for refraction, the sun's disk is cut exactly in half by the northern horizon, that will mean I'm at the South Pole.'

'Right,' I said. 'Nevertheless, it isn't mathematically exact proof, because the equinox needn't fall precisely at noon.'

'No doubt, sir, but the error will be under 100 metres, and that's close enough for us. Until tomorrow then.'

Captain Nemo went back on board. Conseil and I stayed behind until five o'clock, surveying the beach, observing and studying. The only unusual object I picked up was an auk's egg of remarkable sise, for which a collector would have paid more than 1,000 francs. Its cream-coloured tint, plus the streaks and markings that decorated it like so many hieroglyphics, made it a rare trinket. I placed it in Conseil's hands, and holding it like precious porcelain from China, that cautious, sure-footed lad got it back to the *Nautilus* in one piece.

There I put this rare egg inside one of the glass cases in the museum. I ate supper, feasting with appetite on an excellent piece of seal liver whose flavour reminded me of pork. Then I went to bed; but not without praying, like a good Hindu, for the favours of the radiant orb.

The next day, March 21, bright and early at five o'clock in the morning, I climbed onto the platform. I found Captain Nemo there.

'The weather is clearing a bit,' he told me. 'I have high hopes. After breakfast we'll make our way ashore and choose an observation post.'

This issue settled, I went to find Ned Land. I wanted to take him with me. The obstinate Canadian refused, and I could clearly see that his tight-lipped mood and his bad temper were growing by the day. Under the circumstances I ultimately wasn't sorry that he refused. In truth, there were too many seals ashore, and it would never do to expose this impulsive fisherman to such temptations.

Breakfast over, I made my way ashore. The *Nautilus* had gone a few more miles during the night. It lay well out, a good league from the coast, which was crowned by a sharp peak 400 to 500 metres high. In addition to me, the skiff carried Captain Nemo, two crewmen, and the instruments – in other words, a chronometer, a spyglass, and a barometer.

During our crossing I saw numerous baleen whales belonging to the three species unique to these southernmost seas: the bowhead whale (or 'right whale,' according to the English), which has no dorsal fin; the humpback whale from the genus *Balaenoptera* (in other words, 'winged whales'), beasts with wrinkled bellies and huge whitish fins that, genus name regardless, do not yet form wings; and the finback whale, yellowish brown, the swiftest of all cetaceans. This powerful animal is audible from far away when it sends up towering spouts of air and steam that resemble swirls of smoke. Herds of these different mammals were playing about in the tranquil waters, and I could easily see that this Antarctic polar basin now served as a refuge for those cetaceans too relentlessly pursued by hunters.

I also noted long, whitish strings of salps, a type of mollusc found in clusters, and some jellyfish of large size that swayed in the eddies of the billows.

By nine o'clock we had pulled up to shore. The sky was growing brighter. Clouds were fleeing to the south. Mists were rising from the cold surface of the water. Captain Nemo headed toward the peak, which he no doubt planned to make his observatory. It was an arduous climb over sharp lava and pumice stones in the midst of air often reeking with sulphurous fumes from the smoke holes. For a man out of practice at treading land, the captain scaled the steepest slopes with a supple agility I couldn't equal, and which would have been envied by hunters of Pyrenees mountain goats.

It took us two hours to reach the summit of this half-crystal, half-basalt peak. From there our eyes scanned a vast sea, which scrawled its boundary line firmly against the background of the northern sky. At our feet: dazzling tracts of white. Over our heads: a pale azure, clear of mists. North of us: the sun's disk, like a ball of fire already cut into by the edge of the horizon. From the heart of the waters: jets of liquid rising like hundreds of magnificent bouquets. Far off, like a sleeping cetacean: the *Nautilus*. Behind us to the south and east: an immense shore, a chaotic heap of rocks and ice whose limits we couldn't see.

Arriving at the summit of this peak, Captain Nemo carefully determined its elevation by means of his barometer, since he had to take this factor into account in his noon sights.

At 11:45 the sun, by then seen only by refraction, looked like a golden disk, dispersing its last rays over this deserted continent and down to these seas not yet ploughed by the ships of man.

Captain Nemo had brought a spyglass with a reticular eyepiece, which corrected the sun's refraction by means of a mirror, and he used it to observe the orb sinking little by little along a very extended diagonal that reached below the horizon. I held the chronometer. My heart was pounding mightily. If the lower half of the sun's disk disappeared just as the chronometer said noon, we were right at the pole.

'Noon!' I called.

'The South Pole!' Captain Nemo replied in a solemn voice, handing me the spyglass, which showed the orb of day cut into two exactly equal parts by the horizon.

I stared at the last rays wreathing this peak, while shadows were gradually climbing its gradients.

Just then, resting his hand on my shoulder, Captain Nemo said to me:

'In 1600, sir, the Dutchman Gheritk was swept by storms and currents, reaching latitude 64° south and discovering the South Shetland Islands. On January 17, 1773, the famous Captain Cook went along the 38th meridian, arriving at latitude 67° 30'; and on January 30, 1774, along the 109th meridian, he reached latitude 71° 15'. In 1819 the Russian Bellinghausen lay on the 69th parallel, and in 1821 on the 66th at longitude 111° west. In 1820 the Englishman Bransfield stopped at 65°. That same year the American Morrel, whose reports are dubious, went along the 42nd meridian, finding open sea at latitude 70° 14'. In 1825 the Englishman Powell was unable to get beyond 62°. That same year a humble seal fisherman, the Englishman Weddell, went as far as latitude 72° 14' on the 35th meridian, and as far as 74° 15' on the 36th. In 1829 the Englishman Forster, commander of the *Chanticleer*, laid claim to the Antarctic continent in latitude 63° 26' and longitude 66° 26'. On February 1, 1831, the Englishman Biscoe discovered Enderby Land at latitude 68° 50', Adelaide Land at latitude

67° on February 5, 1832, and Graham Land at latitude 64° 45' on February 21. In 1838 the Frenchman Dumont d'Urville stopped at the Ice Bank in latitude 62° 57', sighting the Louis-Philippe Peninsula; on January 21 two years later, at a new southerly position of 66° 30', he named the Adélie Coast and eight days later, the Clarie Coast at 64° 40'. In 1838 the American Wilkes advanced as far as the 69th parallel on the 100th meridian. In 1839 the Englishman Balleny discovered the Sabrina Coast at the edge of the polar circle. Lastly, on January 12, 1842, with his ships, the *Erebus* and the *Terror*, the Englishman Sir James Clark Ross found Victoria Land in latitude 70° 56' and longitude 171° 7' east; on the 23rd of that same month, he reached the 74th parallel, a position denoting the Farthest South attained until then; on the 27th he lay at 76° 8'; on the 28th at 77° 32'; on February 2 at 78° 4'; and late in 1842 he returned to 71° but couldn't get beyond it. Well now! In 1868, on this 21st day of March, I myself, Captain Nemo, have reached the South Pole at 90°, and I hereby claim this entire part of the globe, equal to one-sixth of the known continents.'

'In the name of which sovereign, captain?'

'In my own name, sir!'

So saying, Captain Nemo unfurled a black flag bearing a gold 'N' on its quartered bunting. Then, turning toward the orb of day, whose last rays were licking at the sea's horizon:

'Farewell, O sun!' he called. 'Disappear, O radiant orb! Retire beneath this open sea, and let six months of night spread their shadows over my new domains!'

CHAPTER 15

Accident or Incident?

THE NEXT DAY, March 22, at six o'clock in the morning, preparations for departure began. The last gleams of twilight were melting into night. The cold was brisk. The constellations were glittering with startling intensity. The wonderful Southern Cross, polar star of the Antarctic regions, twinkled at its zenith.

The thermometer marked −12° centigrade, and a fresh breeze left a sharp nip in the air. Ice floes were increasing over the open water. The sea was starting to congeal everywhere. Numerous blackish patches were spreading over its surface, announcing the imminent formation of fresh ice. Obviously this southernmost basin froze over during its six-month winter and became utterly inaccessible. What happened to the whales during this period? No doubt they went beneath the Ice Bank to find more feasible seas. As for seals and walruses, they were accustomed to living in the harshest climates and stayed on in these icy waterways. These animals know by instinct how to gouge holes in the ice fields and keep them continually open; they go to these holes to breathe. Once the birds have migrated northward to escape the cold, these marine mammals remain as sole lords of the polar continent.

Meanwhile the ballast tanks filled with water and the *Nautilus* sank slowly. At a depth of 1,000 feet, it stopped. Its propeller churned the waves and it headed due north at a speed of 15 miles per hour. Near the afternoon it was already cruising under the immense frozen carapace of the Ice Bank.

As a precaution, the panels in the lounge stayed closed, because the *Nautilus*'s hull could run afoul of some submerged block of ice. So I spent the day putting my notes into final form. My mind was completely wrapped up in my memories of the pole. We had reached that inaccessible spot without facing exhaustion or danger, as if our seagoing passenger carriage had glided there on railroad tracks. And now we had actually started our return journey. Did it still have comparable surprises in store for me? I felt sure it did, so inexhaustible is this series of underwater wonders! As it was, in the five and a half months since fate had brought us on board, we had cleared 14,000 leagues, and over this track longer than the earth's equator, so many fascinating or frightening incidents had beguiled our voyage: that hunting trip in the Crespo forests, our running aground in the Torres Strait, the coral cemetery, the pearl fisheries of Ceylon, the Arabic tunnel, the fires of Santorini, those millions in the Bay of Vigo, Atlantis, the South Pole! During the night all these memories crossed over from one dream to the next, not giving my brain a moment's rest.

At three o'clock in the morning, I was awakened by a violent collision. I sat up in bed, listening in the darkness, and then was suddenly hurled into the middle of my stateroom. Apparently the *Nautilus* had gone aground, then heeled over sharply.

Leaning against the walls, I dragged myself down the gangways to the lounge, whose ceiling lights were on. The furniture had been knocked over. Fortunately the glass cases were solidly secured at the base and had stood fast. Since we were no longer vertical, the starboard pictures were glued to the tapestries, while those to port had their lower edges hanging a foot away from the wall. So the *Nautilus* was lying on its starboard side, completely stationary to boot.

In its interior I heard the sound of footsteps and muffled voices. But Captain Nemo didn't appear. Just as I was about to leave the lounge, Ned Land and Conseil entered.

'What happened?' I instantly said to them.

'I came to ask master that,' Conseil replied.

'Damnation!' the Canadian exclaimed. 'I know full well what happened! The *Nautilus* has gone aground, and judging from the way it's listing, I don't think it'll pull through like that first time in the Torres Strait.'

'But,' I asked, 'are we at least back on the surface of the sea?'

'We have no idea,' Conseil replied.

'It's easy to find out,' I answered.

I consulted the pressure gauge. Much to my surprise, it indicated a depth of 360 metres.

'What's the meaning of this?' I exclaimed.

'We must confer with Captain Nemo,' Conseil said.

'But where do we find him?' Ned Land asked.

'Follow me,' I told my two companions.

We left the lounge. Nobody in the library. Nobody by the central companionway or the crew's quarters. I assumed that Captain Nemo was stationed in the pilothouse. Best to wait. The three of us returned to the lounge.

I'll skip over the Canadian's complaints. He had good grounds for an outburst. I didn't answer him back, letting him blow off all the steam he wanted.

We had been left to ourselves for 20 minutes, trying to detect the tiniest noises inside the *Nautilus*, when Captain Nemo entered. He didn't seem to see us. His facial features, usually so emotionless, revealed a certain uneasiness. He studied the compass and pressure gauge in silence, then went and put his finger on the world map at a spot in the sector depicting the southernmost seas.

I hesitated to interrupt him. But some moments later, when he turned to me, I threw back at him a phrase he had used in the Torres Strait:

'An incident, captain?'

'No, sir,' he replied, 'this time an accident.'

'Serious?'

'Perhaps.'

'Is there any immediate danger?'

'No.'

'The *Nautilus* has run aground?'

'Yes.'

'And this accident came about...?'

'Through nature's unpredictability not man's incapacity. No errors were committed in our manoeuvres. Nevertheless, we can't prevent a loss of balance from taking its toll. One may defy human laws, but no one can withstand the laws of nature.'

Captain Nemo had picked an odd time to philosophise. All in all, this reply told me nothing.

'May I learn, sir,' I asked him, 'what caused this accident?'

'An enormous block of ice, an entire mountain, has toppled over,' he answered me. 'When an iceberg is eroded at the base by warmer waters or by repeated collisions, its centre of gravity rises. Then it somersaults, it turns completely upside down. That's what happened here. When it overturned, one of these blocks hit the *Nautilus* as it was cruising under the waters. Sliding under our hull, this block then raised us with irresistible power, lifting us into less congested strata where we now lie on our side.'

'But can't we float the *Nautilus* clear by emptying its ballast tanks, to regain our balance?'

'That, sir, is being done right now. You can hear the pumps working. Look at the needle on the pressure gauge. It indicates that the *Nautilus* is rising, but this block of ice is rising with us, and until some obstacle halts its upward movement, our position won't change.'

Indeed, the *Nautilus* kept the same heel to starboard. No doubt it would straighten up once the block came to a halt. But before that happened, who knew if we might not hit the underbelly of the Ice Bank and be hideously squeezed between two frozen surfaces?

I mused on all the consequences of this situation. Captain Nemo didn't stop studying the pressure gauge. Since the toppling of this iceberg, the *Nautilus* had risen about 150 feet, but it still stayed at the same angle to the perpendicular.

Suddenly a slight movement could be felt over the hull. Obviously the *Nautilus* was straightening a bit. Objects hanging in the lounge were visibly returning to their normal positions. The walls were approaching the vertical. Nobody said a word. Hearts pounding, we could see and feel the ship righting itself. The floor was becoming horizontal beneath our feet. Ten minutes went by.

'Finally, we're upright!' I exclaimed.

'Yes,' Captain Nemo said, heading to the lounge door.

'But will we float off?' I asked him.

'Certainly,' he replied, 'since the ballast tanks aren't yet empty, and when they are, the *Nautilus* must rise to the surface of the sea.'

The captain went out, and soon I saw that at his orders, the *Nautilus* had halted its upward movement. In fact, it soon would have hit the underbelly of the Ice Bank, but it had stopped in time and was floating in midwater.

'That was a close call!' Conseil then said.

'Yes. We could have been crushed between these masses of ice, or at least imprisoned between them. And then, with no way to renew our air supply.... Yes, that was a close call!'

'If it's over with!' Ned Land muttered.

I was unwilling to get into a pointless argument with the Canadian and didn't reply. Moreover, the panels opened just then, and the outside light burst through the uncovered windows.

We were fully afloat, as I have said; but on both sides of the *Nautilus*, about ten metres away, there rose dazzling walls of ice. There also were walls above and below. Above, because the Ice Bank's underbelly spread over us like an immense ceiling. Below, because the somersaulting block, shifting little by little, had found points of purchase on both side walls and had gotten jammed between them. The *Nautilus* was imprisoned in a genuine tunnel of ice about 20 metres wide and filled with quiet water. So the ship could easily exit by going either ahead or astern, sinking a few hundred metres deeper, and then taking an open passageway beneath the Ice Bank.

The ceiling lights were off, yet the lounge was still brightly lit. This was due to the reflecting power of the walls of ice, which threw the beams of our beacon right back at us. Words cannot describe the effects produced by our galvanic rays on these huge, whimsically sculpted blocks, whose every angle, ridge, and facet gave off a different glow depending on the nature of the veins running inside the ice. It was a dazzling mine of gems, in particular sapphires and emeralds, whose jets of blue and green crisscrossed. Here and there, opaline hues of infinite subtlety raced among sparks of light that were like so many fiery diamonds, their brilliance more than any eye could stand. The power of our beacon was increased a hundredfold, like a lamp shining through the biconvex lenses of a world-class lighthouse.

'How beautiful!' Conseil exclaimed.

'Yes,' I said, 'it's a wonderful sight! Isn't it, Ned?'

'Oh damnation, yes!' Ned Land shot back. 'It's superb! I'm furious that I have to admit it. Nobody has ever seen the like. But this sight could cost us dearly. And in all honesty, I think we're looking at things God never intended for human eyes.'

Ned was right. It was too beautiful. All at once a yell from Conseil made me turn around.

'What is it?' I asked.

'Master must close his eyes! Master mustn't look!'

With that, Conseil clapped his hands over his eyes.

'But what's wrong, my boy?'

'I've been dazzled, struck blind!'

Involuntarily my eyes flew to the window, but I couldn't stand the fire devouring it.

I realised what had happened. The *Nautilus* had just started off at great speed. All the tranquil glimmers of the ice walls had then changed into blazing streaks. The sparkles from these myriads of diamonds were merging with each other. Swept along by its propeller, the *Nautilus* was travelling through a sheath of flashing light.

Then the panels in the lounge closed. We kept our hands over our eyes, which were utterly saturated with those concentric gleams that swirl before the retina when sunlight strikes it too intensely. It took some time to calm our troubled vision.

Finally we lowered our hands.

'Ye gods, I never would have believed it,' Conseil said.

'And I still don't believe it!' the Canadian shot back.

'When we return to shore, jaded from all these natural wonders,' Conseil added, 'think how we'll look down on those pitiful land masses, those puny works of man! No, the civilised world won't be good enough for us!'

Such words from the lips of this emotionless Flemish boy showed that our enthusiasm was near the boiling point. But the Canadian didn't fail to throw his dram of cold water over us.

'The civilised world!' he said, shaking his head. 'Don't worry, Conseil my friend, we're never going back to that world!'

By this point it was five o'clock in the morning. Just then there was a collision in the *Nautilus*'s bow. I realised that its spur had just bumped a block of ice. It must have been a faulty manoeuvre because this underwater tunnel was obstructed by such blocks and didn't make for easy navigating. So I had assumed that Captain Nemo, in adjusting his course, would go around each obstacle or would hug the walls and follow the windings of the tunnel. In either case our forward motion wouldn't receive an absolute check. Nevertheless, contrary to my expectations, the *Nautilus* definitely began to move backward.

'We're going astern?' Conseil said.

'Yes,' I replied. 'Apparently the tunnel has no way out at this end.'

'And so...?'

'So,' I said, 'our manoeuvres are quite simple. We'll return in our tracks and go out the southern opening. That's all.'

As I spoke, I tried to sound more confident than I really felt. Meanwhile the *Nautilus* accelerated its backward movement, and running with propeller in reverse, it swept us along at great speed.

'This'll mean a delay,' Ned said.

'What are a few hours more or less, so long as we get out.'

'Yes,' Ned Land repeated, 'so long as we get out!'

I strolled for a little while from the lounge into the library. My companions kept their seats and didn't move. Soon I threw myself down on a couch and picked up a book, which my eyes skimmed mechanically.

A quarter of an hour later, Conseil approached me, saying:

'Is it deeply fascinating, this volume master is reading?'

'Tremendously fascinating,' I replied.

'I believe it. Master is reading his own book!'

'My own book?'

Indeed, my hands were holding my own work on the great ocean depths. I hadn't even suspected. I closed the book and resumed my strolling. Ned and Conseil stood up to leave.

'Stay here, my friends,' I said, stopping them. 'Let's stay together until we're out of this blind alley.'

'As master wishes,' Conseil replied.

The hours passed. I often studied the instruments hanging on the lounge wall. The pressure gauge indicated that the *Nautilus* stayed at a constant depth of 300 metres, the compass that it kept heading south, the log that it was travelling at a speed of 20 miles per hour, an excessive speed in such a cramped area. But Captain Nemo knew that by this point there was no such thing as too fast, since minutes were now worth centuries.

At 8:25 a second collision took place. This time astern. I grew pale. My companions came over. I clutched Conseil's hand. Our eyes questioned each other, and more directly than if our thoughts had been translated into words.

Just then the captain entered the lounge. I went to him.

'Our path is barred to the south?' I asked him.
'Yes, sir. When it overturned, that iceberg closed off every exit.'
'We're boxed in?'
'Yes.'

CHAPTER 16
Shortage of Air

CONSEQUENTLY, ABOVE, BELOW, and around the *Nautilus*, there were impenetrable frozen walls. We were the Ice Bank's prisoners! The Canadian banged a table with his fearsome fist. Conseil kept still. I stared at the captain. His face had resumed its usual emotionlessness. He crossed his arms. He pondered. The *Nautilus* did not stir.

The captain then broke into speech:

'Gentlemen,' he said in a calm voice, 'there are two ways of dying under the conditions in which we're placed.'

This inexplicable individual acted like a mathematics professor working out a problem for his pupils.

'The first way,' he went on, 'is death by crushing. The second is death by asphyxiation. I don't mention the possibility of death by starvation because the *Nautilus*'s provisions will certainly last longer than we will. Therefore, let's concentrate on our chances of being crushed or asphyxiated.'

'As for asphyxiation, captain,' I replied, 'that isn't a cause for alarm, because the air tanks are full.'

'True,' Captain Nemo went on, 'but they'll supply air for only two days. Now then, we've been buried beneath the waters for 36 hours, and the *Nautilus*'s heavy atmosphere already needs renewing. In another 48 hours, our reserve air will be used up.'

'Well then, captain, let's free ourselves within 48 hours!'

'We'll try to at least, by cutting through one of these walls surrounding us.'

'Which one?' I asked.

'Borings will tell us that. I'm going to ground the *Nautilus* on the lower shelf, then my men will put on their diving suits and attack the thinnest of these ice walls.'

'Can the panels in the lounge be left open?'

'Without ill effect. We're no longer in motion.'

Captain Nemo went out. Hissing sounds soon told me that water was being admitted into the ballast tanks. The *Nautilus* slowly settled and rested on the icy bottom at a depth of 350 metres, the depth at which the lower shelf of ice lay submerged.

'My friends,' I said, 'we're in a serious predicament, but I'm counting on your courage and energy.'

'Sir,' the Canadian replied, 'this is no time to bore you with my complaints. I'm ready to do anything I can for the common good.'

'Excellent, Ned,' I said, extending my hand to the Canadian.

'I might add,' he went on, 'that I'm as handy with a pick as a harpoon. If I can be helpful to the captain, he can use me any way he wants.'

'He won't turn down your assistance. Come along, Ned.'

I led the Canadian to the room where the *Nautilus*'s men were putting on their diving suits. I informed the captain of Ned's proposition, which was promptly accepted. The Canadian got into his underwater costume and was ready as soon as his fellow workers. Each of them carried on his back a Rouquayrol device that the air tanks had supplied with a generous allowance of fresh oxygen. A considerable but necessary drain on the *Nautilus*'s reserves. As for the Ruhmkorff lamps, they were unnecessary in the midst of these brilliant waters saturated with our electric rays.

After Ned was dressed, I re-entered the lounge, whose windows had been uncovered; stationed next to Conseil, I examined the strata surrounding and supporting the *Nautilus*.

Some moments later, we saw a dozen crewmen set foot on the shelf of ice, among them Ned Land, easily recognised by his tall figure. Captain Nemo was with them.

Before digging into the ice, the captain had to obtain borings, to insure working in the best direction. Long bores were driven into the side walls; but after 15 metres, the instruments were still impeded by the thickness of those walls. It was futile to attack the ceiling since that surface was the Ice Bank itself, more than 400 metres high. Captain Nemo then bored into the lower surface. There we were separated from the sea by a ten–metre barrier. That's how thick the iceberg was. From this point on, it was an issue of cutting out a piece equal in surface area to the *Nautilus*'s waterline. This meant detaching about

6,500 cubic metres, to dig a hole through which the ship could descend below this tract of ice.

Work began immediately and was carried on with tireless tenacity. Instead of digging all around the *Nautilus*, which would have entailed even greater difficulties, Captain Nemo had an immense trench outlined on the ice, eight metres from our port quarter. Then his men simultaneously staked it off at several points around its circumference. Soon their picks were vigorously attacking this compact matter, and huge chunks were loosened from its mass. These chunks weighed less than the water, and by an unusual effect of specific gravity, each chunk took wing, as it were, to the roof of the tunnel, which thickened above by as much as it diminished below. But this hardly mattered so long as the lower surface kept growing thinner.

After two hours of energetic work, Ned Land re-entered, exhausted. He and his companions were replaced by new workmen, including Conseil and me. The *Nautilus*'s chief officer supervised us.

The water struck me as unusually cold, but I warmed up promptly while wielding my pick. My movements were quite free, although they were executed under a pressure of 30 atmospheres.

After two hours of work, reentering to snatch some food and rest, I found a noticeable difference between the clean elastic fluid supplied me by the Rouquayrol device and the *Nautilus*'s atmosphere, which was already charged with carbon dioxide. The air hadn't been renewed in 48 hours, and its life-giving qualities were considerably weakened. Meanwhile, after 12 hours had gone by, we had removed from the outlined surface area a slice of ice only one metre thick, hence about 600 cubic metres. Assuming the same work would be accomplished every twelve hours, it would still take five nights and four days to see the undertaking through to completion.

'Five nights and four days!' I told my companions. 'And we have oxygen in the air tanks for only two days.'

'Without taking into account,' Ned answered, 'that once we're out of this damned prison, we'll still be cooped up beneath the Ice Bank, without any possible contact with the open air!'

An apt remark. For who could predict the minimum time we would need to free ourselves? Before the *Nautilus* could return to the surface of the waves, couldn't we all die of asphyxiation? Were this ship and everyone on board doomed to perish in this tomb of ice? It was a dreadful state of affairs. But we faced it head-on, each one of us determined to do his duty to the end.

During the night, in line with my forecasts, a new one-metre slice was removed from this immense socket. But in the morning, wearing my diving suit, I was crossing through the liquid mass in a temperature of $-6°$ to $-7°$ centigrade, when I noted that little by little the side walls were closing in on each other. The liquid strata farthest from the trench, not warmed by the movements of workmen and tools, were showing a tendency to solidify. In the face of this imminent new danger, what would happen to our chances for salvation, and how could we prevent this liquid medium from solidifying, then cracking the *Nautilus*'s hull like glass?

I didn't tell my two companions about this new danger. There was no point in dampening the energy they were putting into our arduous rescue work. But when I returned on board, I mentioned this serious complication to Captain Nemo.

'I know,' he told me in that calm tone the most dreadful outlook couldn't change. 'It's one more danger, but I don't know any way of warding it off. Our sole chance for salvation is to work faster than the water solidifies. We've got to get there first, that's all.'

Get there first! By then I should have been used to this type of talk!

For several hours that day, I wielded my pick doggedly. The work kept me going. Besides, working meant leaving the *Nautilus*, which meant breathing the clean oxygen drawn from the air tanks and supplied by our equipment, which meant leaving the thin, foul air behind.

Near evening one more metre had been dug from the trench. When I returned on board, I was well nigh asphyxiated by the carbon dioxide saturating the air. Oh, if only we had the chemical methods that would enable us to drive out this noxious gas! There was no lack of oxygen. All this water contained a considerable amount, and after it was decomposed by our powerful batteries, this life-giving elastic fluid could have been restored to us. I had thought it all out, but to no avail because the carbon dioxide produced by our breathing permeated every part of the ship. To absorb it, we would need to fill containers with potassium hydroxide and shake them continually. But this substance was missing on board and nothing else could replace it.

That evening Captain Nemo was forced to open the spigots of his air tanks and shoot a few spouts of fresh oxygen through the *Nautilus*'s interior. Without this precaution we wouldn't have awakened the following morning.

The next day, March 26, I returned to my miner's trade, working to remove the fifth metre. The Ice Bank's side walls and underbelly had visibly thickened. Obviously they would come together before the *Nautilus* could break free. For an instant I was gripped by despair. My pick nearly slipped from my hands. What was the point of this digging if I was to die smothered and crushed by this water turning to stone, a torture undreamed of by even the wildest savages! I felt like I was lying in the jaws of a fearsome monster, jaws irresistibly closing.

Supervising our work, working himself, Captain Nemo passed near me just then. I touched him with my hand and pointed to the walls of our prison. The starboard wall had moved forward to a point less than four metres from the *Nautilus*'s hull.

The captain understood and gave me a signal to follow him. We returned on board. My diving suit removed, I went with him to the lounge.

'Professor Aronnax,' he told me, 'this calls for heroic measures, or we'll be sealed up in this solidified water as if it were cement.'

'Yes!' I said. 'But what can we do?'

'Oh,' he exclaimed, 'if only my *Nautilus* were strong enough to stand that much pressure without being crushed!'

'Well?' I asked, not catching the captain's meaning.

'Don't you understand,' he went on, 'that the congealing of this water could come to our rescue? Don't you see that by solidifying, it could burst these tracts of ice imprisoning us, just as its freezing can burst the hardest stones? Aren't you aware that this force could be the instrument of our salvation rather than our destruction?'

'Yes, captain, maybe so. But whatever resistance to crushing the *Nautilus* may have, it still couldn't stand such dreadful pressures, and it would be squashed as flat as a piece of sheet iron.'

'I know it, sir. So we can't rely on nature to rescue us, only our own efforts. We must counteract this solidification. We must hold it in check. Not only are the side walls closing in, but there aren't ten feet of water ahead or astern of the *Nautilus*. All around us, this freeze is gaining fast.'

'How long,' I asked, 'will the oxygen in the air tanks enable us to breathe on board?'

The captain looked me straight in the eye.

'After tomorrow,' he said, 'the air tanks will be empty!'

I broke out in a cold sweat. But why should I have been startled by this reply? On March 22 the *Nautilus* had dived under the open waters at the pole. It was now the 26th. We had lived off the ship's stores for five days! And all remaining breathable air had to be saved for the workmen. Even today as I write these lines, my sensations are so intense that an involuntary terror sweeps over me, and my lungs still seem short of air!

Meanwhile, motionless and silent, Captain Nemo stood lost in thought. An idea visibly crossed his mind. But he seemed to brush it aside. He told himself no. At last these words escaped his lips:

'Boiling water!' he muttered.

'Boiling water?' I exclaimed.

'Yes, sir. We're shut up in a relatively confined area. If the *Nautilus*'s pumps continually injected streams of boiling water into this space, wouldn't that raise its temperature and delay its freezing?'

'It's worth trying!' I said resolutely.

'So let's try it, professor.'

By then the thermometer gave $-7°$ centigrade outside. Captain Nemo led me to the galley where a huge distilling mechanism was at work, supplying drinking water via evaporation. The mechanism was loaded with water, and the full electric heat of our batteries was thrown into coils awash in liquid. In a few minutes the water reached $100°$ centigrade. It was sent to the pumps while new water replaced it in the process. The heat generated by our batteries was so intense that after simply going through the mechanism, water drawn cold from the sea arrived boiling hot at the body of the pump.

The steaming water was injected into the icy water outside, and after three hours had passed, the thermometer gave the exterior temperature as $-6°$ centigrade. That was one degree gained. Two hours later the thermometer gave only $-4°$.

After I monitored the operation's progress, double-checking it with many inspections, I told the captain, 'It's working.'

'I think so,' he answered me. 'We've escaped being crushed. Now we have only asphyxiation to fear.'

During the night the water temperature rose to −1° centigrade. The injections couldn't get it to go a single degree higher. But since salt water freezes only at −2°, I was finally assured that there was no danger of it solidifying.

By the next day, March 27, six metres of ice had been torn from the socket. Only four metres were left to be removed. That still meant 48 hours of work. The air couldn't be renewed in the *Nautilus*'s interior. Accordingly, that day it kept getting worse.

An unbearable heaviness weighed me down. Near three o'clock in the afternoon, this agonizing sensation affected me to an intense degree. Yawns dislocated my jaws. My lungs were gasping in their quest for that enkindling elastic fluid required for breathing, now growing scarcer and scarcer. My mind was in a daze. I lay outstretched, strength gone, nearly unconscious. My gallant Conseil felt the same symptoms, suffered the same sufferings, yet never left my side. He held my hand, he kept encouraging me, and I even heard him mutter:

'Oh, if only I didn't have to breathe, to leave more air for master!'

It brought tears to my eyes to hear him say these words.

Since conditions inside were universally unbearable, how eagerly, how happily, we put on our diving suits to take our turns working! Picks rang out on that bed of ice. Arms grew weary, hands were rubbed raw, but who cared about exhaustion, what difference were wounds? Life-sustaining air reached our lungs! We could breathe! We could breathe!

And yet nobody prolonged his underwater work beyond the time allotted him. His shift over, each man surrendered to a gasping companion the air tank that would revive him. Captain Nemo set the example and was foremost in submitting to this strict discipline. When his time was up, he yielded his equipment to another and re-entered the foul air on board, always calm, unflinching and uncomplaining.

That day the usual work was accomplished with even greater energy. Over the whole surface area, only two metres were left to be removed.

Only two metres separated us from the open sea. But the ship's air tanks were nearly empty. The little air that remained had to be saved for the workmen. Not an atom for the *Nautilus*!

When I returned on board, I felt half suffocated. What a night! I'm unable to depict it. Such sufferings are indescribable. The next day I was short-winded. Headaches and staggering fits of dizziness made me reel like a drunk. My companions were experiencing the same symptoms. Some crewmen were at their last gasp.

That day, the sixth of our imprisonment, Captain Nemo concluded that picks and mattocks were too slow to deal with the ice layer still separating us from open water – and he decided to crush this layer. The man had kept his energy and composure. He had subdued physical pain with moral strength. He could still think, plan and act.

At his orders the craft was eased off, in other words, it was raised from its icy bed by a change in its specific gravity. When it was afloat, the crew towed it, leading it right above the immense trench outlined to match the ship's waterline. Next the ballast tanks filled with water, the boat sank, and was fitted into its socket.

Just then the whole crew returned on board, and the double outside door was closed. By this point the *Nautilus* was resting on a bed of ice only one metre thick and drilled by bores in a thousand places.

The stopcocks of the ballast tanks were then opened wide, and 100 cubic metres of water rushed in, increasing the *Nautilus*'s weight by 100,000 kilograms.

We waited, we listened, we forgot our sufferings, we hoped once more. We had staked our salvation on this one last gamble.

Despite the buzzing in my head, I soon could hear vibrations under the *Nautilus*'s hull. We tilted. The ice cracked with an odd ripping sound, like paper tearing, and the *Nautilus* began settling downward.

'We're going through!' Conseil muttered in my ear.

I couldn't answer him. I clutched his hand. I squeezed it in an involuntary convulsion.

All at once, carried away by its frightful excess load, the *Nautilus* sank into the waters like a cannonball, in other words, dropping as if in a vacuum!

Our full electric power was then put on the pumps, which instantly began to expel water from the ballast tanks. After a few minutes we had checked our fall. The pressure gauge soon indicated an ascending movement. Brought to full speed, the propeller made the sheet-iron hull tremble down to its rivets, and we sped northward.

But how long would it take to navigate under the Ice Bank to the open sea? Another day? I would be dead first!

Half lying on a couch in the library, I was suffocating. My face was purple, my lips blue, my faculties in abeyance. I could no longer see or hear. I had lost all sense of time. My muscles had no power to contract.

I'm unable to estimate the hours that passed in this way. But I was aware that my death throes had begun. I realised that I was about to die...

Suddenly I regained consciousness. A few whiffs of air had entered my lungs. Had we risen to the surface of the waves? Had we cleared the Ice Bank?

No! Ned and Conseil, my two gallant friends, were sacrificing themselves to save me. A few atoms of air were still left in the depths of one Rouquayrol device. Instead of breathing it themselves, they had saved it for me, and while they were suffocating, they poured life into me drop by drop! I tried to push the device away. They held my hands, and for a few moments I could breathe luxuriously.

My eyes flew toward the clock. It was 11 in the morning. It had to be March 28. The *Nautilus* was travelling at the frightful speed of 40 miles per hour. It was writhing in the waters.

Where was Captain Nemo? Had he perished? Had his companions died with him?

Just then the pressure gauge indicated we were no more than 20 feet from the surface. Separating us from the open air was a mere tract of ice. Could we break through it?

Perhaps! In any event the *Nautilus* was going to try. In fact, I could feel it assuming an oblique position, lowering its stern and raising its spur. The admission of additional water was enough to shift its balance. Then, driven by its powerful propeller, it attacked this ice field from below like a fearsome battering ram. It split the barrier little by little, backing up, then putting on full speed against the punctured tract of ice; and finally, carried away by its supreme momentum, it lunged through and onto this frozen surface, crushing the ice beneath its weight.

The hatches were opened – or torn off, if you prefer – and waves of clean air were admitted into every part of the *Nautilus*.

CHAPTER 17

From Cape Horn to the Amazon

How I got onto the platform I'm unable to say. Perhaps the Canadian transferred me there. But I could breathe, I could inhale the life-giving sea air. Next to me my two companions were getting tipsy on the fresh oxygen particles. Poor souls who have suffered from long starvation mustn't pounce heedlessly on the first food given them. We, on the other hand, didn't have to practice such moderation: we could suck the atoms from the air by the lungful, and it was the breeze, the breeze itself, that poured into us this luxurious intoxication!

'Ahhh!' Conseil was putting in. 'What fine oxygen! Let master have no fears about breathing. There's enough for everyone.'

As for Ned Land, he didn't say a word, but his wide-open jaws would have scared off a shark. And what powerful inhalations! The Canadian 'drew' like a furnace going full blast.

Our strength returned promptly, and when I looked around, I saw that we were alone on the platform. No crewmen. Not even Captain Nemo. Those strange seamen on the *Nautilus* were content with the oxygen circulating inside. Not one of them had come up to enjoy the open air.

The first words I pronounced were words of appreciation and gratitude to my two companions. Ned and Conseil had kept me alive during the final hours of our long death throes. But no expression of thanks could repay them fully for such devotion.

'Good lord, professor,' Ned Land answered me, 'don't mention it! What did we do that's so praiseworthy? Not a thing. It was a question of simple arithmetic. Your life is worth more than ours. So we had to save it.'

'No, Ned,' I replied, 'it isn't worth more. Nobody could be better than a kind and generous man like yourself!'

'All right, all right!' the Canadian repeated in embarrassment.

'And you, my gallant Conseil, you suffered a great deal.'

'Not too much, to be candid with master. I was lacking a few throatfuls of air, but I would have gotten by. Besides, when I saw Master fainting, it left me without the slightest desire to breathe. It took my breath away, in a manner of...'

Confounded by this lapse into banality, Conseil left his sentence hanging.

'My friends,' I replied, very moved, 'we're bound to each other forever, and I'm deeply indebted to you—'

'Which I'll take advantage of,' the Canadian shot back.

'Eh?' Conseil put in.

'Yes,' Ned Land went on. 'You can repay your debt by coming with me when I leave this infernal *Nautilus*.'

'By the way,' Conseil said, 'are we going in a favourable direction?'

'Yes,' I replied, 'because we're going in the direction of the sun, and here the sun is due north.'

'Sure,' Ned Land went on, 'but it remains to be seen whether we'll make for the Atlantic or the Pacific, in other words, whether we'll end up in well-travelled or deserted seas.'

I had no reply to this, and I feared that Captain Nemo wouldn't take us homeward but rather into that huge ocean washing the shores of both Asia and America. In this way he would complete his underwater tour of the world, going back to those seas where the *Nautilus* enjoyed the greatest freedom. But if we returned to the Pacific, far from every populated shore, what would happen to Ned Land's plans?

We would soon settle this important point. The *Nautilus* travelled swiftly. Soon we had cleared the Antarctic Circle plus the promontory of Cape Horn. We were abreast of the tip of South America by March 31 at seven o'clock in the evening.

By then all our past sufferings were forgotten. The memory of that imprisonment under the ice faded from our minds. We had thoughts only of the future. Captain Nemo no longer appeared, neither in the lounge nor on the platform. The positions reported each day on the world map were put there by the chief officer, and they enabled me to determine the *Nautilus*'s exact heading. Now then, that evening it became obvious, much to my satisfaction, that we were returning north by the Atlantic route.

I shared the results of my observations with the Canadian and Conseil.

'That's good news,' the Canadian replied, 'but where's the *Nautilus* going?'

'I'm unable to say, Ned.'

'After the South Pole, does our captain want to tackle the North Pole, then go back to the Pacific by the notorious Northwest Passage?'

'I wouldn't double dare him,' Conseil replied.

'Oh well,' the Canadian said, 'we'll give him the slip long before then.'

'In any event,' Conseil added, 'he's a superman, that Captain Nemo, and we'll never regret having known him.'

'Especially once we've left him,' Ned Land shot back.

The next day, April 1, when the *Nautilus* rose to the surface of the waves a few minutes before noon, we raised land to the west. It was Tierra del Fuego, the Land of Fire, a name given it by early navigators after they saw numerous curls of smoke rising from the natives' huts. This Land of Fire forms a huge cluster of islands over 30 leagues long and 80 leagues wide, extending between latitude 53° and 56° south, and between longitude 67° 50' and 77° 15' west. Its coastline looked flat, but high mountains rose in the distance. I even thought I glimpsed Mt Sarmiento, whose elevation is 2,070 metres above sea level: a pyramid-shaped block of shale with a very sharp summit, which, depending on whether it's clear or veiled in vapour, 'predicts fair weather or foul,' as Ned Land told me.

'A first-class barometer, my friend.'

'Yes, sir, a natural barometer that didn't let me down when I navigated the narrows of the Strait of Magellan.'

Just then its peak appeared before us, standing out distinctly against the background of the skies. This forecast fair weather. And so it proved.

Going back under the waters, the *Nautilus* drew near the coast, cruising along it for only a few miles. Through the lounge windows I could see long creepers and gigantic fucus plants, bulb-bearing seaweed of which the open sea at the pole had revealed a few specimens; with their smooth, viscous filaments, they measured as much as 300 metres long; genuine cables more than an inch thick and very tough, they're often used as mooring lines for ships. Another weed, known by the name velp and boasting four-foot leaves, was crammed into the coral concretions and carpeted the ocean floor. It served as both nest and nourishment for myriads of crustaceans and molluscs, for crabs and cuttlefish. Here seals and otters could indulge in a sumptuous meal, mixing meat from fish with vegetables from the sea, like the English with their Irish stews.

The *Nautilus* passed over these lush, luxuriant depths with tremendous speed. Near evening it approached the Falkland Islands, whose rugged summits I recognised the next day. The sea was of moderate depth. So not without good reason, I assumed that these two islands, plus the many islets surrounding them, used to be part of the Magellan coastline. The Falkland Islands were probably discovered by the famous navigator John Davis, who gave them the name Davis Southern Islands. Later Sir Richard Hawkins called them the Maidenland, after the Blessed Virgin. Subsequently, at the beginning of the 18th century, they were named the Malouines by fishermen from Saint-Malo in Brittany, then finally dubbed the Falklands by the English, to whom they belong today.

In these waterways our nets brought up fine samples of algae, in particular certain fucus plants whose roots were laden with the world's best mussels. Geese and duck alighted by the dozens on the platform and soon took their places in the ship's pantry. As for fish, I specifically observed some bony fish belonging to the *goby* genus, especially some gudgeon two decimetres long, sprinkled with whitish and yellow spots.

I likewise marvelled at the numerous *medusas*, including the most beautiful of their breed, the compass jellyfish, unique to the Falkland seas. Some of these jellyfish were shaped like very smooth, semispheric parasols with russet stripes and fringes of 12 neat festoons. Others looked like upside-down baskets from which wide leaves and long red twigs were gracefully trailing. They swam with quiverings of their four leaflike arms, letting the opulent tresses of their tentacles dangle in the drift. I wanted to preserve a few specimens of these delicate zoophytes, but they were merely clouds, shadows, illusions, melting and evaporating outside their native element.

When the last tips of the Falkland Islands had disappeared below the horizon, the *Nautilus* submerged to a depth between 20 and 25 metres and went along the South American coast. Captain Nemo didn't put in an appearance.

We didn't leave these Patagonian waterways until April 3, sometimes cruising under the ocean, sometimes on its surface. The *Nautilus* passed the wide estuary formed by the mouth of the Rio de la Plata, and on April 4 we lay abreast of Uruguay, albeit 50 miles out. Keeping to its northerly heading, it followed the long windings of South America. By then we had fared 16,000 leagues since coming on board in the seas of Japan.

Near 11 o'clock in the morning, we cut the Tropic of Capricorn on the 37th meridian, passing well out from Cape Frio. Much to Ned Land's displeasure, Captain Nemo had no liking for the neighbourhood of Brazil's populous shores, because he shot by with dizzying speed. Not even the swiftest fish or birds could keep up with us, and the natural curiosities in these seas completely eluded our observation.

This speed was maintained for several days, and on the evening of April 9, we raised South America's easternmost tip, Cape São Roque. But then the *Nautilus* veered away again and went looking for the lowest depths of an underwater valley gouged between this cape and Sierra Leone on the coast of Africa. Abreast of the West Indies, this valley forks into two arms, and to the north it ends in an enormous depression 9,000 metres deep. From this locality to the Lesser Antilles, the ocean's geologic profile features a steeply cut cliff six kilometres high, and abreast of the Cape Verde Islands, there's another wall just as imposing; together these two barricades confine the whole submerged continent of Atlantis. The floor of this immense valley is made picturesque by mountains that furnish these underwater depths with scenic views. This description is based mostly on certain hand-drawn charts kept in the *Nautilus*'s library, charts obviously rendered by Captain Nemo himself from his own personal observations.

For two days we visited these deep and deserted waters by means of our slanting fins. The *Nautilus* would do long, diagonal dives that took us to every level. But on April 11 it rose suddenly, and the shore reappeared at the mouth of the Amazon River, a huge estuary whose outflow is so considerable, it desalts the sea over an area of several leagues.

We cut the Equator. Twenty miles to the west lay Guiana, French territory where we could easily have taken refuge. But the wind was blowing a strong gust, and the furious billows would not allow us to face them in a mere skiff. No doubt Ned Land understood this because he said nothing to me. For my part, I made no allusion to his escape plans because I didn't want to push him into an attempt that was certain to misfire.

I was readily compensated for this delay by fascinating research. During those two days of April 11–12, the *Nautilus* didn't leave the surface of the sea, and its trawl brought up a simply miraculous catch of zoophytes, fish, and reptiles.

Some zoophytes were dredged up by the chain of our trawl. Most were lovely sea anemone belonging to the family *Actinidia*, including among other species, the *Phyctalis protexta*, native to this part of the ocean: a small cylindrical trunk adorned with vertical lines, mottled with red spots, and crowned by a wondrous blossoming of tentacles. As for molluscs, they consisted of exhibits I had already observed: turret snails, olive shells of the 'tent olive' species with neatly intersecting lines and russet spots standing out sharply against a flesh-coloured background, fanciful spider conchs that looked like petrified scorpions, transparent glass snails, argonauts, some highly edible cuttlefish and certain species of squid that the naturalists of antiquity classified with the flying fish, which are used chiefly as bait for catching cod.

As for the fish in these waterways, I noted various species that I hadn't yet had the opportunity to study. Among cartilaginous fish: some brook lamprey, a type of eel 15 inches long, head greenish, fins violet, back bluish grey, belly a silvery brown strewn with bright spots, iris of the eye encircled in gold, unusual animals that the Amazon's current must have swept out to sea because their natural habitat is fresh water; sting rays, the snout pointed, the tail long, slender, and armed with an extensive jagged sting; small one-metre sharks with grey and whitish hides, their teeth arranged in several backward-curving rows, fish commonly known by the name carpet shark; batfish, a sort of reddish isosceles triangle half a metre long, whose pectoral fins are attached by fleshy extensions that make these fish look like bats, although an appendage made of horn, located near the nostrils, earns them the nickname of sea unicorns; lastly, a couple of species of triggerfish, the cucuyo whose stippled flanks glitter with a sparkling gold colour, and the bright purple leatherjacket whose hues glisten like a pigeon's throat.

I'll finish up this catalogue, a little dry but quite accurate, with the series of bony fish I observed: eels belonging to the genus *Apteronotus* whose snow-white snout is very blunt, the body painted a handsome black and armed with a very long, slender, fleshy whip; long sardines from the genus *Odontognathus*, like three-decimetre pike, shining with a bright silver glow; Guaranian mackerel furnished with two anal fins; black-tinted rudderfish that you catch by using torches, fish measuring two metres and boasting white, firm, plump meat that, when fresh, tastes like eel, when dried, like smoked salmon; semi-red wrasse sporting scales only at the bases of their dorsal and anal fins; grunts on which gold and silver mingle their lustre with that of ruby and topaz; yellow-tailed gilthead whose flesh is extremely dainty and whose phosphorescent properties give them away in the midst of the waters; porgies tinted orange, with slender tongues; croakers with gold caudal fins; black surgeonfish; four-eyed fish from Surinam, etc.

This 'et cetera' won't keep me from mentioning one more fish that Conseil, with good reason, will long remember.

One of our nets had hauled up a type of very flat ray that weighed some 20 kilograms; with its tail cut off, it would have formed a perfect disk. It was white underneath and reddish on top, with big round spots of deep blue encircled in black, its hide quite smooth and ending in a double-lobed fin. Laid out on the platform, it kept struggling with convulsive movements, trying to turn over, making such efforts that its final lunge was about to flip it into the sea. But Conseil, being very possessive of his fish, rushed at it, and before I could stop him, he seized it with both hands.

Instantly there he was, thrown on his back, legs in the air, his body half paralysed, and yelling:

'Oh, sir, sir! Will you help me!'

For once in his life, the poor lad didn't address me 'in the third person.'

The Canadian and I sat him up; we massaged his contracted arms, and when he regained his five senses, that eternal classifier mumbled in a broken voice:

'Class of *cartilaginous* fish, order *Chondropterygia* with fixed gills, suborder *Selacia*, family *Rajiiforma*, genus *electric ray*.'

'Yes, my friend,' I answered, 'it was an electric ray that put you in this deplorable state.'

'Oh, master can trust me on this,' Conseil shot back. 'I'll be revenged on that animal!'

'How?'

'I'll eat it.'

Which he did that same evening, but strictly as retaliation. Because, frankly, it tasted like leather.

Poor Conseil had assaulted an electric ray of the most dangerous species, the *cumana*. Living in a conducting medium such as water, this bizarre animal can electrocute other fish from several metres away, so great is the power of its electric organ, an organ whose two chief surfaces measure at least 27 square feet.

During the course of the next day, April 12, the *Nautilus* drew near the coast of Dutch Guiana, by the mouth of the Maroni River. There several groups of sea cows were living in family units. These were manatees, which belong to the order *Sirenia*, like the dugong and Steller's sea cow. Harmless and unaggressive, these fine animals were six to seven metres long and must have weighed at least 4,000 kilograms each. I told Ned Land and Conseil that farseeing nature had given these mammals a major role to play. In essence, manatees, like seals, are designed to graze the underwater prairies, destroying the clusters of weeds that obstruct the mouths of tropical rivers.

'And do you know,' I added, 'what happened since man has almost completely wiped out these beneficial races? Rotting weeds have poisoned the air, and this poisoned air causes the yellow fever that devastates these wonderful countries. This toxic vegetation has increased beneath the seas of the Torrid Zone, so the disease spreads unchecked from the mouth of the Rio de la Plata to Florida!'

And if Professor Toussenel is correct, this plague is nothing compared to the scourge that will strike our descendants once the seas are depopulated of whales and seals. By then, crowded with jellyfish, squid, and other devilfish, the oceans will have become huge centres of infection, because their waves will no longer possess 'these huge stomachs that God has entrusted with scouring the surface of the sea.'

Meanwhile, without scorning these theories, the *Nautilus*'s crew captured half a dozen manatees. In essence, it was an issue of stocking the larder with excellent red meat, even better than beef or veal. Their hunting was not a fascinating sport. The manatees let themselves be struck down without offering any resistance. Several thousand kilos of meat were hauled below, to be dried and stored.

The same day an odd fishing practice further increased the *Nautilus*'s stores, so full of game were these seas. Our trawl brought up in its meshes a number of fish whose heads were topped by little oval slabs with fleshy edges. These were suckerfish from the third family of the *subbrachian Malacopterygia*. These flat disks on their heads consist of crosswise plates of movable cartilage, between which the animals can create a vacuum, enabling them to stick to objects like suction cups.

The *remoras* I had observed in the Mediterranean were related to this species. But the creature at issue here was an *Echeneis osteochara*, unique to this sea. Right after catching them, our seamen dropped them in buckets of water.

Its fishing finished, the *Nautilus* drew nearer to the coast. In this locality a number of sea turtles were sleeping on the surface of the waves. It would have been difficult to capture these valuable reptiles, because they wake up at the slightest sound, and their solid carapaces are harpoon-proof. But our suckerfish would effect their capture with extraordinary certainty and precision. In truth, this animal is a living fishhook, promising wealth and happiness to the greenest fisherman in the business.

The *Nautilus*'s men attached to each fish's tail a ring that was big enough not to hamper its movements, and to this ring a long rope whose other end was moored on board.

Thrown into the sea, the suckerfish immediately began to play their roles, going and fastening themselves onto the breastplates of the turtles. Their tenacity was so great, they would rip apart rather than let go. They were hauled in, still sticking to the turtles that came aboard with them.

In this way we caught several loggerheads, reptiles a metre wide and weighing 200 kilos. They're extremely valuable because of their carapaces, which are covered with big slabs of horn, thin, brown, transparent, with white and yellow markings. Besides, they were excellent from an edible viewpoint, with an exquisite flavour comparable to the green turtle.

This fishing ended our stay in the waterways of the Amazon, and that evening the *Nautilus* took to the high seas once more.

CHAPTER 18

The Devilfish

FOR SOME DAYS the *Nautilus* kept veering away from the American coast. It obviously didn't want to frequent the waves of the Gulf of Mexico or the Caribbean Sea. Yet there was no shortage of water under its keel, since the average depth of these seas is 1,800 metres; but these waterways, strewn with islands and ploughed by steamers, probably didn't agree with Captain Nemo.

On April 16 we raised Martinique and Guadalupe from a distance of about 30 miles. For one instant I could see their lofty peaks.

The Canadian was quite disheartened, having counted on putting his plans into execution in the gulf, either by reaching shore or by pulling alongside one of the many boats plying a coastal trade from one island to another. An escape attempt would have been quite feasible, assuming Ned Land managed to seize the skiff without the captain's knowledge. But in midocean it was unthinkable.

The Canadian, Conseil, and I had a pretty long conversation on this subject. For six months we had been prisoners aboard the *Nautilus*. We had fared 17,000 leagues, and as Ned Land put it, there was no end in sight. So he made me a proposition I hadn't anticipated. We were to ask Captain Nemo this question straight out: did the captain mean to keep us on board his vessel permanently?

This measure was distasteful to me. To my mind it would lead nowhere. We could hope for nothing from the *Nautilus*'s commander but could depend only on ourselves. Besides, for some time now the man had been gloomier, more withdrawn, less sociable. He seemed to be avoiding me. I encountered him only at rare intervals. He used to take pleasure in explaining the underwater wonders to me; now he left me to my research and no longer entered the lounge.

What changes had come over him? From what cause? I had no reason to blame myself. Was our presence on board perhaps a burden to him? Even so, I cherished no hopes that the man would set us free.

So I begged Ned to let me think about it before taking action. If this measure proved fruitless, it could arouse the captain's suspicions, make our circumstances even more arduous, and jeopardise the Canadian's plans. I might add that I could hardly use our state of health as an argument. Except for that gruelling ordeal under the Ice Bank at the South Pole, we had never felt better, neither Ned, Conseil, nor I. The nutritious food, life-giving air, regular routine and uniform temperature kept illness at bay; and for a man who didn't miss his past existence on land, for a Captain Nemo who was at home here, who went where he wished, who took paths mysterious to others if not himself in attaining his ends, I could understand such a life. But we ourselves hadn't severed all ties with humanity. For my part, I didn't want my new and unusual research to be buried with my bones. I had now earned the right to pen the definitive book on the sea, and sooner or later I wanted that book to see the light of day.

There once more, through the panels opening into these Caribbean waters ten metres below the surface of the waves, I found so many fascinating exhibits to describe in my daily notes! Among other zoophytes there were Portuguese men-of-war known by the name *Physalia pelagica*, like big, oblong bladders with a pearly sheen, spreading their membranes to the wind, letting their blue tentacles drift like silken threads; to the eye delightful jellyfish, to the touch actual nettles that ooze a corrosive liquid. Among the articulates there were annelid worms one and a half metres long, furnished with a pink proboscis, equipped with 1,700 organs of locomotion, snaking through the waters, and as they went, throwing off every gleam in the solar spectrum. From the fish branch there were manta rays, enormous cartilaginous fish ten feet long and weighing 600 pounds, their pectoral fin triangular, their midback slightly arched, their eyes attached to the edges of the face at the front of the head; they floated like wreckage from a ship, sometimes fastening onto our windows like opaque shutters. There were American triggerfish for which nature has ground only black and white pigments, feather-shaped gobies that were long and plump with yellow fins and jutting jaws, 16-decimetre mackerel with short, sharp teeth, covered with small scales, and related to the albacore species. Next came swarms of red mullet corseted in gold stripes from head to tail, their shining fins all aquiver, genuine masterpieces of jewellery, formerly sacred to the goddess Diana, much in demand by rich Romans, and about which the old saying goes: 'He who catches them doesn't eat them!' Finally, adorned with emerald ribbons and dressed in velvet and silk, golden angelfish passed before our eyes like courtiers in the paintings of Veronese; spurred gilthead stole by with their swift thoracic fins; thread herring 15 inches long were wrapped in their phosphorescent glimmers; grey mullet thrashed the sea with their big fleshy tails; red salmon seemed to mow the waves with their slicing pectorals; and silver moonfish, worthy of their name, rose on the horizon of the waters like the whitish reflections of many moons.

How many other marvellous new specimens I still could have observed if, little by little, the *Nautilus* hadn't settled to the lower strata! Its slanting fins drew it to depths of 2,000 and 3,500 metres. There animal life was represented by nothing more than sea lilies, starfish, delightful *crinoids* with bell-shaped heads like little chalices on straight stems, top-shell snails, blood-red tooth shells, and *fissurella* snails, a large species of coastal mollusc.

By April 20 we had risen to an average level of 1,500 metres. The nearest land was the island group of the Bahamas, scattered like a batch of cobblestones over the surface of the water. There high underwater cliffs reared up, straight walls made of craggy chunks arranged like big stone foundations, among which there gaped black caves so deep our electric rays couldn't light them to the far ends.

These rocks were hung with huge weeds, immense sea tangle, gigantic *fucus* – a genuine trellis of water plants fit for a world of giants.

In discussing these colossal plants, Conseil, Ned and I were naturally led into mentioning the sea's gigantic animals. The former were obviously meant to feed the latter. However, through the windows of our almost motionless *Nautilus*, I could see nothing among these long filaments other than the chief articulates of the division *Brachyura*: long-legged spider crabs, violet crabs and sponge crabs unique to the waters of the Caribbean.

It was about 11 o'clock when Ned Land drew my attention to a fearsome commotion out in this huge seaweed.

'Well,' I said, 'these are real devilfish caverns, and I wouldn't be surprised to see some of those monsters hereabouts.'

'What!' Conseil put in. 'Squid, ordinary squid from the class *Cephalopoda*?'

'No,' I said, 'devilfish of large dimensions. But friend Land is no doubt mistaken, because I don't see a thing.'

'That's regrettable,' Conseil answered. 'I'd like to come face to face with one of those devilfish I've heard so much about, which can drag ships down into the depths. Those beasts go by the name of krake—'

'Fake is more like it,' the Canadian replied sarcastically.

'Krakens!' Conseil shot back, finishing his word without wincing at his companion's witticism.

'Nobody will ever make me believe,' Ned Land said, 'that such animals exist.'

'Why not?' Conseil replied. 'We sincerely believed in master's narwhal.'

'We were wrong, Conseil.'

'No doubt, but there are others with no doubts who believe to this day!'

'Probably, Conseil. But as for me, I'm bound and determined not to accept the existence of any such monster till I've dissected it with my own two hands.'

'Yet,' Conseil asked me, 'doesn't master believe in gigantic devilfish?'

'Yikes! Who in Hades ever believed in them?' the Canadian exclaimed.

'Many people, Ned my friend,' I said.

'No fishermen. Scientists maybe!'

'Pardon me, Ned. Fishermen and scientists!'

'Why, I to whom you speak,' Conseil said with the world's straightest face, 'I recall perfectly seeing a large boat dragged under the waves by the arms of a *cephalopod*.'

'You saw that?' the Canadian asked.

'Yes, Ned.'

'With your own two eyes?'

'With my own two eyes.'

'Where, may I ask?'

'In Saint-Malo,' Conseil returned unflappably.

'In the harbour?' Ned Land said sarcastically.

'No, in a church,' Conseil replied.

'In a church!' the Canadian exclaimed.

'Yes, Ned my friend. It had a picture that portrayed the devilfish in question.'

'Oh good!' Ned Land exclaimed with a burst of laughter. 'Mr Conseil put one over on me!'

'Actually he's right,' I said. 'I've heard about that picture. But the subject it portrays is taken from a legend, and you know how to rate legends in matters of natural history! Besides, when it's an issue of monsters, the human imagination always tends to run wild. People not only claimed these devilfish could drag ships under, but a certain Olaus Magnus tells of a *cephalopod* a mile long that looked more like an island than an animal. There's also the story of how the Bishop of Trondheim set up an altar one day on an immense rock. After he finished saying mass, this rock started moving and went back into the sea. The rock was a devilfish.'

'And that's everything we know?' the Canadian asked.

'No,' I replied, 'another bishop, Pontoppidan of Bergen, also tells of a devilfish so large a whole cavalry regiment could manoeuvre on it.'

'They sure did go on, those old time bishops!' Ned Land said.

'Finally, the naturalists of antiquity mention some monsters with mouths as big as a gulf, which were too huge to get through the Strait of Gibraltar.'

'Good work, men!' the Canadian put in.

'But in all these stories, is there any truth?' Conseil asked.

'None at all, my friends, at least in those that go beyond the bounds of credibility and fly off into fable or legend. Yet for the imaginings of these storytellers there had to be, if not a cause, at least an excuse. It can't be denied that some species of squid and other devilfish are quite large, though still smaller than cetaceans. Aristotle put the dimensions of one squid at five cubits, or 3.1 metres. Our fishermen frequently see specimens over 1.8 metres long. The museums in Trieste and Montpellier have preserved some devilfish carcasses measuring two metres. Besides, according to the calculations of naturalists, one of these animals only six feet long would have tentacles as long as 27. Which is enough to make a fearsome monster.'

'Does anybody fish for 'em nowadays?' the Canadian asked.

'If they don't fish for them, sailors at least sight them. A friend of mine, Captain Paul Bos of Le Havre, has often sworn to me that he encountered one of these monsters of colossal sise in the seas of the East Indies. But the most astonishing event, which proves that these gigantic animals undeniably exist, took place a few years ago in 1861.'

'What event was that?' Ned Land asked.

'Just this. In 1861, to the northeast of Tenerife and fairly near the latitude where we are right now, the crew of the gunboat *Alecto* spotted a monstrous squid swimming in their waters. Commander Bouguer approached the animal and attacked it with blows from harpoons and blasts from rifles, but without much success because bullets and harpoons crossed its soft flesh as if it were semi-liquid jelly. After several fruitless attempts, the crew managed to slip a noose around the mollusc's body. This noose slid as far as the caudal fins and came to a halt. Then they tried to haul the monster on board, but its weight was so considerable that when they tugged on the rope, the animal parted company with its tail; and deprived of this adornment, it disappeared beneath the waters.'

'Finally, an actual event,' Ned Land said.

'An indisputable event, my gallant Ned. Accordingly, people have proposed naming this devilfish Bouguer's Squid.'

'And how long was it?' the Canadian asked.

'Didn't it measure about six metres?' said Conseil, who was stationed at the window and examining anew the crevices in the cliff.

'Precisely,' I replied.

'Wasn't its head,' Conseil went on, 'crowned by eight tentacles that quivered in the water like a nest of snakes?'

'Precisely.'

'Weren't its eyes prominently placed and considerably enlarged?'

'Yes, Conseil.'

'And wasn't its mouth a real parrot's beak but of fearsome size?'

'Correct, Conseil.'

'Well, with all due respect to master,' Conseil replied serenely, 'if this isn't Bouguer's Squid, it's at least one of his close relatives!'

I stared at Conseil. Ned Land rushed to the window.

'What an awful animal!' he exclaimed.

I stared in my turn and couldn't keep back a movement of revulsion. Before my eyes there quivered a horrible monster worthy of a place among the most far-fetched teratological legends.

It was a squid of colossal dimensions, fully eight metres long. It was travelling backward with tremendous speed in the same direction as the *Nautilus*. It gazed with enormous, staring eyes that were tinted sea green. Its eight arms (or more accurately, feet) were rooted in its head, which has earned these animals the name *cephalopod*; its arms stretched a distance twice the length of its body and were writhing like the serpentine hair of the Furies. You could plainly see its 250 suckers, arranged over the inner sides of its tentacles and shaped like semispheric capsules. Sometimes these suckers fastened onto the lounge window by creating vacuums against it. The monster's mouth – a beak made of horn and shaped like that of a parrot – opened and closed vertically. Its tongue, also of horn substance and armed with several rows of sharp teeth, would flicker out from between these genuine shears. What a freak of nature! A bird's beak on a mollusc! Its body was spindle-shaped and swollen in the middle, a fleshy mass that must have weighed 20,000 to 25,000 kilograms. Its unstable colour would change with tremendous speed as the animal grew irritated, passing successively from bluish grey to reddish brown.

What was irritating this mollusc? No doubt the presence of the *Nautilus*, even more fearsome than itself, and which it couldn't grip with its mandibles or the suckers on its arms. And yet what monsters these devilfish are, what vitality our Creator has given them, what vigour in their movements, thanks to their owning a triple heart!

Sheer chance had placed us in the presence of this squid, and I didn't want to lose this opportunity to meticulously study such a *cephalopod* specimen. I overcame the horror that its appearance inspired in me, picked up a pencil, and began to sketch it.

'Perhaps this is the same as the *Alecto*'s,' Conseil said.

'Can't be,' the Canadian replied, 'because this one's complete while the other one lost its tail!'

'That doesn't necessarily follow,' I said. 'The arms and tails of these animals grow back through regeneration, and in seven years the tail on Bouguer's Squid has surely had time to sprout again.'

'Anyhow,' Ned shot back, 'if it isn't this fellow, maybe it's one of those!'

Indeed, other devilfish had appeared at the starboard window. I counted seven of them. They provided the *Nautilus* with an escort, and I could hear their beaks gnashing on the sheet-iron hull. We couldn't have asked for a more devoted following.

I continued sketching. These monsters kept pace in our waters with such precision, they seemed to be standing still, and I could have traced their outlines in miniature on the window. But we were moving at a moderate speed.

All at once the *Nautilus* stopped. A jolt made it tremble through its entire framework.

'Did we strike bottom?' I asked.

'In any event we're already clear,' the Canadian replied, 'because we're afloat.'

The *Nautilus* was certainly afloat, but it was no longer in motion. The blades of its propeller weren't churning the waves. A minute passed. Followed by his chief officer, Captain Nemo entered the lounge.

I hadn't seen him for a good while. He looked gloomy to me. Without speaking to us, without even seeing us perhaps, he went to the panel, stared at the devilfish, and said a few words to his chief officer.

The latter went out. Soon the panels closed. The ceiling lit up.

I went over to the captain.

'An unusual assortment of devilfish,' I told him, as carefree as a collector in front of an aquarium.

'Correct, Mr Naturalist,' he answered me, 'and we're going to fight them at close quarters.'

I gaped at the captain. I thought my hearing had gone bad.

'At close quarters?' I repeated.

'Yes, sir. Our propeller is jammed. I think the horn-covered mandibles of one of these squid are entangled in the blades. That's why we aren't moving.'

'And what are you going to do?'

'Rise to the surface and slaughter the vermin.'

'A difficult undertaking.'

'Correct. Our electric bullets are ineffective against such soft flesh, where they don't meet enough resistance to go off. But we'll attack the beasts with axes.'

'And harpoons, sir,' the Canadian said, 'if you don't turn down my help.'

'I accept it, Mr Land.'

'We'll go with you,' I said. And we followed Captain Nemo, heading to the central companionway.

There some ten men were standing by for the assault, armed with boarding axes. Conseil and I picked up two more axes. Ned Land seized a harpoon.

By then the *Nautilus* had returned to the surface of the waves. Stationed on the top steps, one of the seamen undid the bolts of the hatch. But he had scarcely unscrewed the nuts when the hatch flew up with tremendous violence, obviously pulled open by the suckers on a devilfish's arm.

Instantly one of those long arms glided like a snake into the opening, and 20 others were quivering above. With a sweep of the axe, Captain Nemo chopped off this fearsome tentacle, which slid writhing down the steps.

Just as we were crowding each other to reach the platform, two more arms lashed the air, swooped on the seaman stationed in front of Captain Nemo, and carried the fellow away with irresistible violence.

Captain Nemo gave a shout and leaped outside. We rushed after him.

What a scene! Seized by the tentacle and glued to its suckers, the unfortunate man was swinging in the air at the mercy of this enormous appendage. He gasped, he choked, he yelled: 'Help! Help!' These words, pronounced in French, left me deeply stunned! So I had a fellow countryman on board, perhaps several! I'll hear his harrowing plea the rest of my life!

The poor fellow was done for. Who could tear him from such a powerful grip? Even so, Captain Nemo rushed at the devilfish and with a sweep of the axe hewed one more of its arms. His chief officer struggled furiously with other monsters crawling up the *Nautilus*'s sides. The crew battled with flailing axes. The Canadian, Conseil and I sank our weapons into these fleshy masses. An intense, musky odour filled the air. It was horrible.

For an instant I thought the poor man entwined by the devilfish might be torn loose from its powerful suction. Seven arms out of eight had been chopped off. Brandishing its victim like a feather, one lone tentacle was writhing in the air. But just as Captain Nemo and his chief officer rushed at it, the animal shot off a spout of blackish liquid, secreted by a pouch located in its abdomen. It blinded us. When this cloud had dispersed, the squid was gone, and so was my poor fellow countryman!

What rage then drove us against these monsters! We lost all self-control. Ten or 12 devilfish had overrun the *Nautilus*'s platform and sides. We piled helter-skelter into the thick of these sawed-off snakes, which darted over the platform amid waves of blood and sepia ink. It seemed as if these viscous tentacles grew back like the many heads of Hydra. At every thrust Ned Land's harpoon would plunge into a squid's sea-green eye and burst it. But my daring companion was suddenly toppled by the tentacles of a monster he could not avoid.

Oh, my heart nearly exploded with excitement and horror! The squid's fearsome beak was wide open over Ned Land. The poor man was about to be cut in half. I ran to his rescue. But Captain Nemo got there first. His axe disappeared between the two enormous mandibles, and the Canadian, miraculously saved, stood and plunged his harpoon all the way into the devilfish's triple heart.

'Tit for tat,' Captain Nemo told the Canadian. 'I owed it to myself!'

Ned bowed without answering him.

This struggle had lasted a quarter of an hour. Defeated, mutilated, battered to death, the monsters finally yielded to us and disappeared beneath the waves.

Red with blood, motionless by the beacon, Captain Nemo stared at the sea that had swallowed one of his companions and large tears streamed from his eyes.

CHAPTER 19

The Gulf Stream

THIS DREADFUL SCENE on April 20 none of us will ever be able to forget. I wrote it up in a state of intense excitement. Later I reviewed my narrative. I read it to Conseil and the Canadian. They found it accurate in detail but deficient in impact. To convey such sights, it would take the pen of our most famous poet, Victor Hugo, author of *The Toilers of the Sea*.

As I said, Captain Nemo wept while staring at the waves. His grief was immense. This was the second companion he had lost since we had come aboard. And what a way to die! Smashed, strangled, crushed by the fearsome arms of a devilfish, ground between its iron mandibles, this friend would never rest with his companions in the placid waters of their coral cemetrey!

As for me, what had harrowed my heart in the thick of this struggle was the despairing yell given by this unfortunate man. Forgetting his regulation language, this poor Frenchman had reverted to speaking his own mother tongue to fling out one supreme plea! Among the *Nautilus*'s crew, allied body and soul with Captain Nemo and likewise fleeing from human contact, I had found a fellow countryman! Was he the only representative of France in this mysterious alliance, obviously made up of individuals from different nationalities? This was just one more of those insoluble problems that kept welling up in my mind!

Captain Nemo re-entered his stateroom, and I saw no more of him for a good while. But how sad, despairing and irresolute he must have felt, to judge from this ship whose soul he was, which reflected his every mood! The *Nautilus* no longer kept to a fixed heading. It drifted back and forth, riding with the waves like a corpse. Its propeller had been disentangled but was barely put to use. It was navigating at random. It couldn't tear itself away from the setting of this last struggle, from this sea that had devoured one of its own!

Ten days went by in this way. It was only on May 1 that the *Nautilus* openly resumed its northbound course, after raising the Bahamas at the mouth of Old Bahama Channel. We then went with the current of the sea's greatest river, which has its own banks, fish, and temperature. I mean the Gulf Stream.

It is indeed a river that runs independently through the middle of the Atlantic, its waters never mixing with the ocean's waters. It's a salty river, saltier than the sea surrounding it. Its average depth is 3,000 feet, its average width 60 miles. In certain localities its current moves at a speed of four kilometres per hour. The unchanging volume of its waters is greater than that of all the world's rivers combined.

As discovered by Commander Maury, the true source of the Gulf Stream, its starting point, if you prefer, is located in the Bay of Biscay. There its waters, still weak in temperature and colour, begin to form. It goes down south, skirts equatorial Africa, warms its waves in the rays of the Torrid Zone, crosses the Atlantic, reaches Cape São Roque on the coast of Brazil, and forks into two branches, one going to the Caribbean Sea for further saturation with heat particles. Then, entrusted with restoring the balance between hot and cold temperatures and with mixing tropical and northern waters, the Gulf Stream begins to play its stabilizing role. Attaining a white heat in the Gulf of Mexico, it heads north up the American coast, advances as far as Newfoundland, swerves away under the thrust of a cold current from the Davis Strait, and resumes its ocean course by going along a great circle of the earth on a rhumb line; it then divides into two arms near the 43rd parallel; one, helped by the northeast trade winds, returns to the Bay of Biscay and the Azores; the other washes the shores of Ireland and Norway with lukewarm water, goes beyond Spitzbergen, where its temperature falls to 4° centigrade, and fashions the open sea at the pole.

It was on this oceanic river that the *Nautilus* was then navigating. Leaving Old Bahama Channel, which is 14 leagues wide by 350 metres deep, the Gulf Stream moves at the rate of eight kilometres per hour. Its speed steadily decreases as it advances northward, and we must pray that this steadiness continues, because, as experts agree, if its speed and direction were to change, the climates of Europe would undergo disturbances whose consequences are incalculable.

Near noon I was on the platform with Conseil. I shared with him the relevant details on the Gulf Stream. When my explanation was over, I invited him to dip his hands into its current.

Conseil did so, and he was quite astonished to experience no sensation of either hot or cold.

'That comes,' I told him, 'from the water temperature of the Gulf Stream, which, as it leaves the Gulf of Mexico, is barely different from your blood temperature. This Gulf Stream is a huge heat generator that enables the coasts of Europe to be decked in eternal greenery. And if Commander Maury is correct, were one to harness the full warmth of this current, it would supply enough heat to keep molten a river of iron solder as big as the Amazon or the Missouri.'

Just then the Gulf Stream's speed was 2.25 metres per second. So distinct is its current from the surrounding sea, its confined waters stand out against the ocean and operate on a different level from the colder waters. Murky as well, and very rich in saline material, their pure indigo contrasts with the green waves surrounding them. Moreover, their line of demarcation is so clear that abreast of the Carolinas, the *Nautilus*'s spur cut the waves of the Gulf Stream while its propeller was still churning those belonging to the ocean.

This current swept along with it a whole host of moving creatures. Argonauts, so common in the Mediterranean, voyaged here in schools of large numbers. Among cartilaginous fish, the most remarkable were rays whose ultra slender tails made up nearly a third of the body, which was shaped like a huge diamond 25 feet long; then little one-metre sharks, the head large, the snout short and rounded, the teeth sharp and arranged in several rows, the body seemingly covered with scales.

Among bony fish, I noted grizzled wrasse unique to these seas, deep-water gilthead whose iris has a fiery gleam, one-metre croakers whose large mouths bristle with small teeth and which let out thin cries, black rudderfish like those I've already discussed, blue dorados accented with gold and silver, rainbow-hued parrotfish that can rival the loveliest tropical birds in colouring, banded blennies with triangular heads, bluish flounder without scales, toadfish covered with a crosswise yellow band in the shape of a T, swarms of little freckled gobies stippled with brown spots, lungfish with silver heads and yellow tails, various specimens of salmon, mullet with slim figures and a softly glowing radiance that Lacépède dedicated to the memory of his wife, and finally the American cavalla, a handsome fish decorated by every honorary order, bedisened with their every ribbon, frequenting the shores of this great nation where ribbons and orders are held in such low esteem.

I might add that during the night, the Gulf Stream's phosphorescent waters rivalled the electric glow of our beacon, especially in the stormy weather that frequently threatened us.

On May 8, while abreast of North Carolina, we were across from Cape Hatteras once more. There the Gulf Stream is 75 miles wide and 210 metres deep. The *Nautilus* continued to wander at random. Seemingly, all supervision had been jettisoned. Under these conditions I admit that we could easily have gotten away. In fact, the populous shores offered ready refuge everywhere. The sea was ploughed continuously by the many steamers providing service between the Gulf of Mexico and New York or Boston, and it was crossed night and day by little schooners engaged in coastal trade over various points on the American shore. We could hope to be picked up. So it was a promising opportunity, despite the 30 miles that separated the *Nautilus* from these Union coasts.

But one distressing circumstance totally thwarted the Canadian's plans. The weather was thoroughly foul. We were approaching waterways where storms are commonplace, the very homeland of tornadoes and cyclones specifically engendered by the Gulf Stream's current. To face a frequently raging sea in a frail skiff was a race to certain disaster. Ned Land conceded this himself. So he champed at the bit, in the grip of an intense homesickness that could be cured only by our escape.

'Sir,' he told me that day, 'it's got to stop. I want to get to the bottom of this. Your Nemo's veering away from shore and heading up north. But believe you me, I had my fill at the South Pole and I'm not going with him to the North Pole.'

'What can we do, Ned, since it isn't feasible to escape right now?'

'I keep coming back to my idea. We've got to talk to the captain. When we were in your own country's seas, you didn't say a word. Now that we're in mine, I intend to speak up. Before a few days are out, I figure the *Nautilus* will lie abreast of Nova Scotia, and from there to Newfoundland is the mouth of a large gulf, and the St Lawrence empties into that gulf, and the St Lawrence is my own river, the river running by Quebec, my hometown – and when I think about all this, my gorge rises and my hair stands on end! Honestly, sir, I'd rather jump overboard! I can't stay here any longer! I'm suffocating!'

The Canadian was obviously at the end of his patience. His vigorous nature couldn't adapt to this protracted imprisonment. His facial appearance was changing by the day. His moods grew gloomier and gloomier. I had a sense of what he was suffering because I also was gripped by homesickness. Nearly seven months had gone by without our having any news from shore. Moreover, Captain Nemo's reclusiveness, his changed disposition, and especially his total silence since the battle with the devilfish all made me see things in a different light. I no longer felt the enthusiasm of our first days on board. You needed to be Flemish like Conseil to accept these circumstances, living in a habitat designed for cetaceans and other denizens of the deep. Truly, if that gallant lad had owned gills instead of lungs, I think he would have made an outstanding fish!

'Well, sir?' Ned Land went on, seeing that I hadn't replied.

'Well, Ned, you want me to ask Captain Nemo what he intends to do with us?'

'Yes, sir.'

'Even though he has already made that clear?'

'Yes. I want it settled once and for all. Speak just for me, strictly on my behalf, if you want.'

'But I rarely encounter him. He positively avoids me.'

'All the more reason you should go look him up.'

'I'll confer with him, Ned.'

'When?' the Canadian asked insistently.

'When I encounter him.'

'Professor Aronnax, would you like me to go find him myself?'

'No, let me do it. Tomorrow—'

'Today,' Ned Land said.

'So be it. I'll see him today,' I answered the Canadian, who, if he took action himself, would certainly have ruined everything.

I was left to myself. His request granted, I decided to dispose of it immediately. I like things over and done with.

I re-entered my stateroom. From there I could hear movements inside Captain Nemo's quarters. I couldn't pass up this chance for an encounter. I knocked on his door. I received no reply. I knocked again, then tried the knob. The door opened.

I entered. The captain was there. He was bending over his worktable and hadn't heard me. Determined not to leave without questioning him, I drew closer. He looked up sharply, with a frowning brow, and said in a pretty stern tone:

'Oh, it's you! What do you want?'

'To speak with you, captain.'

'But I'm busy, sir, I'm at work. I give you the freedom to enjoy your privacy, can't I have the same for myself?'

This reception was less than encouraging. But I was determined to give as good as I got.

'Sir,' I said coolly, 'I need to speak with you on a matter that simply can't wait.'

'Whatever could that be, sir?' he replied sarcastically. 'Have you made some discovery that has escaped me? Has the sea yielded up some novel secret to you?'

We were miles apart. But before I could reply, he showed me a manuscript open on the table and told me in a more serious tone:

'Here, Professor Aronnax, is a manuscript written in several languages. It contains a summary of my research under the sea, and God willing, it won't perish with me. Signed with my name, complete with my life story, this manuscript will be enclosed in a small, unsinkable contrivance. The last surviving man on the *Nautilus* will throw this contrivance into the sea, and it will go wherever the waves carry it.'

The man's name! His life story written by himself! So the secret of his existence might someday be unveiled? But just then I saw this announcement only as a lead-in to my topic.

'Captain,' I replied, 'I'm all praise for this idea you're putting into effect. The fruits of your research must not be lost. But the methods you're using strike me as primitive. Who knows where the winds will take that contrivance, into whose hands it may fall? Can't you find something better? Can't you or one of your men—'

'Never, sir,' the captain said, swiftly interrupting me.

'But my companions and I would be willing to safeguard this manuscript, and if you give us back our freedom—'

'Your freedom!' Captain Nemo put in, standing up.

'Yes, sir, and that's the subject on which I wanted to confer with you. For seven months we've been aboard your vessel, and I ask you today, in the name of my companions as well as myself, if you intend to keep us here forever.'

'Professor Aronnax,' Captain Nemo said, 'I'll answer you today just as I did seven months ago: whomever boards the *Nautilus* must never leave it.'

'What you're inflicting on us is outright slavery!'

'Call it anything you like.'

'But every slave has the right to recover his freedom! By any worthwhile, available means!'

'Who has denied you that right?' Captain Nemo replied. 'Did I ever try to bind you with your word of honour?'

The captain stared at me, crossing his arms.

'Sir,' I told him, 'to take up this subject a second time would be distasteful to both of us. So let's finish what we've started. I repeat: it isn't just for myself that I raise this issue. To me, research is a relief, a potent diversion, an enticement, a passion that can make me forget everything else. Like you, I'm a man neglected and unknown, living in the faint hope that someday I can pass on to future generations the fruits of my labours – figuratively speaking, by means of some contrivance left to the luck of winds and waves. In short, I can admire you and comfortably go with you while playing a role I only partly understand; but I still catch glimpses of other aspects of your life that are surrounded by involvements and secrets that, alone on board, my companions and I can't share. And even when our hearts could beat with yours, moved by some of your griefs or stirred by your deeds of courage and genius, we've had to stifle even the slightest token of that sympathy that arises at the sight of something fine and good, whether it comes from friend or enemy. All right then! It's this feeling of being alien to your deepest concerns that makes our situation unacceptable, impossible, even impossible for me but especially for Ned Land. Every man, by virtue of his very humanity, deserves fair treatment. Have you considered how a love of freedom and hatred of slavery could lead to plans of vengeance in a temperament like the Canadian's, what he might think, attempt, endeavour…?'

I fell silent. Captain Nemo stood up.

'Ned Land can think, attempt, or endeavour anything he wants, what difference is it to me? I didn't go looking for him! I don't keep him on board for my pleasure! As for you, Professor Aronnax, you're a man able to understand anything, even silence. I have nothing more to say to you. Let this first time you've come to discuss this subject also be the last, because a second time I won't even listen.'

I withdrew. From that day forward our position was very strained. I reported this conversation to my two companions.

'Now we know,' Ned said, 'that we can't expect a thing from this man. The *Nautilus* is nearing Long Island. We'll escape, no matter what the weather.'

But the skies became more and more threatening. There were conspicuous signs of a hurricane on the way. The atmosphere was turning white and milky. Slender sheaves of cirrus clouds were followed on the horizon by layers of nimbocumulus. Other low clouds fled swiftly. The sea grew towering, inflated by long swells. Every bird had disappeared except a few petrels, friends of the storms. The barometer fell significantly, indicating a tremendous tension in the surrounding haze. The mixture in our stormglass decomposed under the influence of the electricity charging the air. A struggle of the elements was approaching.

The storm burst during the daytime of May 13, just as the *Nautilus* was cruising abreast of Long Island, a few miles from the narrows to Upper New York Bay. I'm able to describe this struggle of the elements because Captain Nemo didn't flee into the ocean depths; instead, from some inexplicable whim, he decided to brave it out on the surface.

The wind was blowing from the southwest, initially a stiff breeze, in other words, with a speed of 15 metres per second, which built to 25 metres near three o'clock in the afternoon. This is the figure for major storms.

Unshaken by these squalls, Captain Nemo stationed himself on the platform. He was lashed around the waist to withstand the monstrous breakers foaming over the deck. I hoisted and attached myself to the same place, dividing my wonderment between the storm and this incomparable man who faced it head-on.

The raging sea was swept with huge tattered clouds drenched by the waves. I saw no more of the small intervening billows that form in the troughs of the big crests. Just long, soot-coloured undulations with crests so compact they didn't foam. They kept growing taller. They were spurring each other on. The *Nautilus*, sometimes lying on its side, sometimes standing on end like a mast, rolled and pitched frightfully.

Near five o'clock a torrential rain fell, but it lulled neither wind nor sea. The hurricane was unleashed at a speed of 45 metres per second, hence almost 40 leagues per hour. Under these conditions houses topple, roof tiles puncture doors, iron railings snap in two, and 24-pounder cannons relocate. And yet in the midst of this turmoil, the *Nautilus* lived up to that saying of an expert engineer: 'A well-constructed hull can defy any sea!' This submersible was no resisting rock that waves could demolish; it was a steel spindle, obediently in motion, without rigging or masting, and able to brave their fury with impunity.

Meanwhile I was carefully examining these unleashed breakers. They measured up to 15 metres in height over a length of 150 to 175 metres, and the speed of their propagation (half that of the wind) was 15 metres per second. Their volume and power increased with the depth of the waters. I then understood the role played by these waves, which trap air in their flanks and release it in the depths of the sea where its oxygen brings life. Their utmost pressure – it has been calculated – can build to 3,000 kilograms on every square foot of surface they strike. It was such waves in the Hebrides that repositioned a stone block weighing 84,000 pounds. It was their relatives in the tidal wave on December 23, 1854, that toppled part of the Japanese city of Tokyo, then went that same day at 700 kilometres per hour to break on the beaches of America.

After nightfall the storm grew in intensity. As in the 1860 cyclone on Réunion Island, the barometer fell to 710 millimetres. At the close of day, I saw a big ship passing on the horizon, struggling painfully. It lay to at half steam in an effort to hold steady on the waves. It must have been a steamer on one of those lines out of New York to Liverpool or Le Havre. It soon vanished into the shadows.

At ten o'clock in the evening, the skies caught on fire. The air was streaked with violent flashes of lightning. I couldn't stand this brightness, but Captain Nemo stared straight at it, as if to inhale the spirit of the storm. A dreadful noise filled the air, a complicated noise made up of the roar of crashing breakers, the howl of the wind, claps of thunder. The wind shifted to every point of the horizon, and the cyclone left the east to return there after passing through north, west and south, moving in the opposite direction of revolving storms in the southern hemisphere.

Oh, that Gulf Stream! It truly lives up to its nickname, the Lord of Storms! All by itself it creates these fearsome cyclones through the difference in temperature between its currents and the superimposed layers of air.

The rain was followed by a downpour of fire. Droplets of water changed into exploding tufts. You would have thought Captain Nemo was courting a death worthy of himself, seeking to be struck by lightning. In one hideous pitching movement, the *Nautilus* reared its steel spur into the air like a lightning rod, and I saw long sparks shoot down it.

Shattered, at the end of my strength, I slid flat on my belly to the hatch. I opened it and went below to the lounge. By then the storm had reached its maximum intensity. It was impossible to stand upright inside the *Nautilus*.

Captain Nemo re-entered near midnight. I could hear the ballast tanks filling little by little, and the *Nautilus* sank gently beneath the surface of the waves.

Through the lounge's open windows, I saw large, frightened fish passing like phantoms in the fiery waters. Some were struck by lightning right before my eyes!

The *Nautilus* kept descending. I thought it would find calm again at 15 metres down. No. The upper strata were too violently agitated. It needed to sink to 50 metres, searching for a resting place in the bowels of the sea.

But once there, what tranquillity we found, what silence, what peace all around us! Who would have known that a dreadful hurricane was then unleashed on the surface of this ocean?

CHAPTER 20

In Latitude 47° 24' and Longitude 17° 28'

IN THE AFTERMATH of this storm, we were thrown back to the east. Away went any hope of escaping to the landing places of New York or the St Lawrence. In despair, poor Ned went into seclusion like Captain Nemo. Conseil and I no longer left each other.

As I said, the *Nautilus* veered to the east. To be more accurate, I should have said to the northeast. Sometimes on the surface of the waves, sometimes beneath them, the ship wandered for days amid these mists so feared by navigators. These are caused chiefly by melting ice, which keeps the air extremely damp. How many ships have perished in these waterways as they tried to get directions from the hazy lights on the coast! How many casualties have been caused by these opaque mists! How many collisions have occurred with these reefs, where the breaking surf is covered by the noise of the wind! How many vessels have rammed each other, despite their running lights, despite the warnings given by their bosun's pipes and alarm bells!

So the floor of this sea had the appearance of a battlefield where every ship defeated by the ocean still lay, some already old and encrusted, others newer and reflecting our beacon light on their ironwork and copper undersides. Among these vessels, how many went down with all hands, with their crews and hosts of immigrants, at these trouble spots so prominent in the statistics: Cape Race, St Paul Island, the Strait of Belle Isle, the St Lawrence estuary! And in only a few years, how many victims have been furnished to the obituary notices by the Royal Mail, Inman and Montreal lines; by vessels named the *Solway*, the *Isis*, the *Paramatta*, the *Hungarian*, the *Canadian*, the *Anglo-Saxon*, the *Humboldt*, and the *United States*, all run aground; by the *Arctic* and the *Lyonnais*, sunk in collisions; by the *President*, the *Pacific*, and the *City of Glasgow*, lost for reasons unknown; in the midst of their gloomy rubble, the *Nautilus* navigated as if passing the dead in review!

By May 15 we were off the southern tip of the Grand Banks of Newfoundland. These banks are the result of marine sedimentation, an extensive accumulation of organic waste brought either from the equator by the Gulf Stream's current, or from the North Pole by the countercurrent of cold water that skirts the American coast. Here, too, erratically drifting chunks collect from the ice breakup. Here a huge boneyard forms from fish, molluscs and zoophytes dying over it by the billions.

The sea is of no great depth at the Grand Banks. A few hundred fathoms at best. But to the south there is a deep, suddenly occurring depression, a 3,000-metre pit. Here the Gulf Stream widens. Its waters come to full bloom. It loses its speed and temperature, but it turns into a sea.

Among the fish that the *Nautilus* startled on its way, I'll mention a one-metre lumpfish, blackish on top with orange on the belly and rare among its brethren in that it practices monogamy, a good-sized eelpout, a type of emerald moray whose flavour is excellent, wolf-fish with big eyes in a head somewhat resembling a canine's, viviparous blennies whose eggs hatch inside their bodies like those of snakes, bloated gobio (or black gudgeon) measuring two decimetres, grenadiers with long tails and gleaming with a silvery glow, speedy fish venturing far from their High Arctic seas.

Our nets also hauled in a bold, daring, vigorous and muscular fish armed with prickles on its head and stings on its fins, a real scorpion measuring two to three metres, the ruthless enemy of cod, blennies and salmon; it was the bullhead of the northerly seas, a fish with red fins and a brown body covered with nodules. The *Nautilus*'s fishermen had some trouble getting a grip on this animal, which, thanks to the formation of its gill covers, can protect its respiratory organs from any parching contact with the air and can live out of water for a good while.

And I'll mention – for the record – some little banded blennies that follow ships into the northernmost seas, sharp-snouted carp exclusive to the north Atlantic, scorpionfish, and lastly the *gadoid* family, chiefly the *cod* species, which I detected in their waters of choice over these inexhaustible Grand Banks.

Because Newfoundland is simply an underwater peak, you could call these cod mountain fish. While the *Nautilus* was clearing a path through their tight ranks, Conseil couldn't refrain from making this comment:

'Mercy, look at these cod!' he said. 'Why, I thought cod were flat, like dab or sole!'

'Innocent boy!' I exclaimed. 'Cod are flat only at the grocery store, where they're cut open and spread out on display. But in the water they're like mullet, spindle-shaped and perfectly built for speed.'

'I can easily believe master,' Conseil replied. 'But what crowds of them! What swarms!'

'Bah! My friend, there'd be many more without their enemies, scorpionfish and human beings! Do you know how many eggs have been counted in a single female?'

'I'll go all out,' Conseil replied. '500,000.'

'11,000,000, my friend.'

'11,000,000! I refuse to accept that until I count them myself.'

'So count them, Conseil. But it would be less work to believe me. Besides, Frenchmen, Englishmen, Americans, Danes and Norwegians catch these cod by the thousands. They're eaten in prodigious quantities, and without the astonishing fertility of these fish, the seas would soon be depopulated of them. Accordingly, in England and America alone, 5,000 ships manned by 75,000 seamen go after cod. Each ship brings back an average catch of 4,400 fish, making 22,000,000. Off the coast of Norway, the total is the same.'

'Fine,' Conseil replied, 'I'll take master's word for it. I won't count them.'

'Count what?'

'Those 11,000,000 eggs. But I'll make one comment.'

'What's that?'

'If all their eggs hatched, just four codfish could feed England, America and Norway.'

As we skimmed the depths of the Grand Banks, I could see perfectly those long fishing lines, each armed with 200 hooks, that every boat dangled by the dozens. The lower end of each line dragged the bottom by means of a small grappling iron, and at the surface it was secured to the buoy-rope of a cork float. The *Nautilus* had to manoeuvre shrewdly in the midst of this underwater spiderweb.

But the ship didn't stay long in these heavily travelled waterways. It went up to about latitude 42°. This brought it abreast of St John's in Newfoundland and Heart's Content, where the Atlantic Cable reaches its end point.

Instead of continuing north, the *Nautilus* took an easterly heading, as if to go along this plateau on which the telegraph cable rests, where multiple soundings have given the contours of the terrain with the utmost accuracy.

It was on May 17, about 500 miles from Heart's Content and 2,800 metres down, that I spotted this cable lying on the seafloor. Conseil, whom I hadn't alerted, mistook it at first for a gigantic sea snake and was gearing up to classify it in his best manner. But I enlightened the fine lad and let him down gently by giving him various details on the laying of this cable.

The first cable was put down during the years 1857–1858; but after transmitting about 400 telegrams, it went dead. In 1863 engineers built a new cable that measured 3,400 kilometres, weighed 4,500 metric tons, and was shipped aboard the *Great Eastern*. This attempt also failed.

Now then, on May 25 while submerged to a depth of 3,836 metres, the *Nautilus* lay in precisely the locality where this second cable suffered the rupture that ruined the undertaking. It happened 638 miles from the coast of Ireland. At around two o'clock in the afternoon, all contact with Europe broke off. The electricians on board decided to cut the cable before fishing it up, and by 11 o'clock that evening they had retrieved the damaged part. They repaired the joint and its splice; then the cable was resubmerged. But a few days later it snapped again and couldn't be recovered from the ocean depths.

These Americans refused to give up. The daring Cyrus Field, who had risked his whole fortune to promote this undertaking, called for a new bond issue. It sold out immediately. Another cable was put down under better conditions. Its sheaves of conducting wire were insulated within a gutta-percha covering, which was protected by a padding of textile material enclosed in a metal sheath. The *Great Eastern* put back to sea on July 13, 1866.

The operation proceeded apace. Yet there was one hitch. As they gradually unrolled this third cable, the electricians observed on several occasions that someone had recently driven nails into it, trying to damage its core. Captain Anderson, his officers, and the engineers put their heads together, then posted a warning that if the culprit were detected, he would be thrown overboard without a trial. After that, these villainous attempts were not repeated.

By July 23 the *Great Eastern* was lying no farther than 800 kilometres from Newfoundland when it received telegraphed news from Ireland of an armistice signed between Prussia and Austria after the Battle of Sadova. Through the mists on the 27th, it sighted the port of Heart's Content. The undertaking had ended happily, and in its first dispatch, young America addressed old Europe with these wise words so rarely understood: 'Glory to God in the highest, and peace on earth to men of good will.'

I didn't expect to find this electric cable in mint condition, as it looked on leaving its place of manufacture. The long snake was covered with seashell rubble and bristling with *foraminifera*; a crust of caked gravel protected it from any molluscs that might bore into it. It rested serenely, sheltered from the sea's motions, under a pressure favourable to the transmission of that electric spark that goes from America to Europe in 32/100 of a second. This cable will no doubt last indefinitely because, as observers note, its gutta-percha casing is improved by a stay in salt water.

Besides, on this well-chosen plateau, the cable never lies at depths that could cause a break. The *Nautilus* followed it to its lowest reaches, located 4,431 metres down, and even there it rested without any stress or strain. Then we returned to the locality where the 1863 accident had taken place.

There the ocean floor formed a valley 120 kilometres wide, into which you could fit Mt Blanc without its summit poking above the surface of the waves. This valley is closed off to the east by a sheer wall 2,000 metres high. We arrived there on May 28, and the *Nautilus* lay no farther than 150 kilometres from Ireland.

Would Captain Nemo head up north and beach us on the British Isles? No. Much to my surprise, he went back down south and returned to European seas. As we swung around the Emerald Isle, I spotted Cape Clear for an instant, plus the lighthouse on Fastnet Rock that guides all those thousands of ships setting out from Glasgow or Liverpool.

An important question then popped into my head. Would the *Nautilus* dare to tackle the English Channel? Ned Land (who promptly reappeared after we hugged shore) never stopped questioning me. What could I answer him? Captain Nemo remained invisible. After giving the Canadian a glimpse of American shores, was he about to show me the coast of France?

But the *Nautilus* kept gravitating southward. On May 30, in sight of Land's End, it passed between the lowermost tip of England and the Scilly Islands, which it left behind to starboard.

If it was going to enter the English Channel, it clearly needed to head east. It did not.

All day long on May 31, the *Nautilus* swept around the sea in a series of circles that had me deeply puzzled. It seemed to be searching for a locality that it had some trouble finding. At noon Captain Nemo himself came to take our bearings. He didn't address a word to me. He looked gloomier than ever. What was filling him with such sadness? Was it our proximity to these European shores? Was he reliving his memories of that country he had left behind? If so, what did he feel? Remorse or regret? For a good while these thoughts occupied my mind, and I had a hunch that fate would soon give away the captain's secrets.

The next day, June 1, the *Nautilus* kept to the same tack. It was obviously trying to locate some precise spot in the ocean. Just as on the day before, Captain Nemo came to take the altitude of the sun. The sea was smooth, the skies clear. Eight miles to the east, a big steamship was visible on the horizon line. No flag was flapping from the gaff of its fore-and-aft sail, and I couldn't tell its nationality.

A few minutes before the sun passed its zenith, Captain Nemo raised his sextant and took his sights with the utmost precision. The absolute calm of the waves facilitated this operation. The *Nautilus* lay motionless, neither rolling nor pitching.

I was on the platform just then. After determining our position, the captain pronounced only these words:

'It's right here!'

He went down the hatch. Had he seen that vessel change course and seemingly head toward us? I'm unable to say.

I returned to the lounge. The hatch closed, and I heard water hissing in the ballast tanks. The *Nautilus* began to sink on a vertical line, because its propeller was in check and no longer furnished any forward motion.

Some minutes later it stopped at a depth of 833 metres and came to rest on the seafloor.

The ceiling lights in the lounge then went out, the panels opened, and through the windows I saw, for a half-mile radius, the sea brightly lit by the beacon's rays.

I looked to port and saw nothing but the immenseness of these tranquil waters.

To starboard, a prominent bulge on the sea bottom caught my attention. You would have thought it was some ruin enshrouded in a crust of whitened seashells, as if under a mantle of snow. Carefully examining this mass, I could identify the swollen outlines of a ship shorn of its masts, which must have sunk bow first. This casualty certainly dated from some far–off time. To be so caked with the limestone of these waters, this wreckage must have spent many a year on the ocean floor.

What ship was this? Why had the *Nautilus* come to visit its grave? Was it something other than a maritime accident that had dragged this craft under the waters?

I wasn't sure what to think, but next to me I heard Captain Nemo's voice slowly say:

'Originally this ship was christened the *Marseillais*. It carried 74 cannons and was launched in 1762. On August 13, 1778, commanded by La Poype-Vertrieux, it fought valiantly against the *Preston*. On July 4, 1779, as a member of the squadron under Admiral d'Estaing, it assisted in the capture of the island of Grenada. On September 5, 1781, under the Count de Grasse, it took part in the Battle of Chesapeake Bay. In 1794 the new Republic of France changed the name of this ship. On April 16 of that same year, it joined the squadron at Brest under Rear Admiral Villaret de Joyeuse, who was entrusted with escorting a convoy of wheat coming from America under the command of Admiral Van Stabel. In this second year of the French Revolutionary Calendar, on the 11th and 12th days in the Month of Pasture, this squadron fought an encounter with English vessels. Sir, today is June 1, 1868, or the 13th day in the Month of Pasture.

Seventy–four years ago to the day, at this very spot in latitude 47° 24' and longitude 17° 28', this ship sank after a heroic battle; its three masts gone, water in its hold, a third of its crew out of action, it preferred to go to the bottom with its 356 seamen rather than surrender; and with its flag nailed up on the afterdeck, it disappeared beneath the waves to shouts of "Long live the Republic!"'

'This is the *Avenger*!' I exclaimed.

'Yes, sir! The *Avenger*! A splendid name!' Captain Nemo murmured, crossing his arms.

CHAPTER 21

A Mass Execution

THE WAY HE said this, the unexpectedness of this scene, first the biography of this patriotic ship, then the excitement with which this eccentric individual pronounced these last words – the name *Avenger* whose significance could not escape me – all this, taken together, had a profound impact on my mind. My eyes never left the captain. Hands outstretched toward the sea, he contemplated the proud wreck with blazing eyes. Perhaps I would never learn who he was, where he came from or where he was heading, but more and more I could see a distinction between the man and the scientist. It was no ordinary misanthropy that kept Captain Nemo and his companions sequestered inside the *Nautilus*'s plating, but a hate so monstrous or so sublime that the passing years could never weaken it.

Did this hate also hunger for vengeance? Time would soon tell.

Meanwhile the *Nautilus* rose slowly to the surface of the sea, and I watched the *Avenger*'s murky shape disappearing little by little. Soon a gentle rolling told me that we were afloat in the open air.

Just then a hollow explosion was audible. I looked at the captain. The captain did not stir.

'Captain?' I said.

He didn't reply.

I left him and climbed onto the platform. Conseil and the Canadian were already there.

'What caused that explosion?' I asked.

'A cannon going off,' Ned Land replied.

I stared in the direction of the ship I had spotted. It was heading toward the *Nautilus*, and you could tell it had put on steam. Six miles separated it from us.

'What sort of craft is it, Ned?'

'From its rigging and its low masts,' the Canadian replied, 'I bet it's a warship. Here's hoping it pulls up and sinks this damned *Nautilus*!'

'Ned my friend,' Conseil replied, 'what harm could it do the

Nautilus? Will it attack us under the waves? Will it cannonade us at the bottom of the sea?'

'Tell me, Ned,' I asked, 'can you make out the nationality of that craft?'

Creasing his brow, lowering his lids, and puckering the corners of his eyes, the Canadian focused the full power of his gaze on the ship for a short while.

'No, sir,' he replied. 'I can't make out what nation it's from. It's flying no flag. But I'll swear it's a warship, because there's a long pennant streaming from the peak of its mainmast.'

For a quarter of an hour, we continued to watch the craft bearing down on us. But it was inconceivable to me that it had discovered the *Nautilus* at such a distance, still less that it knew what this underwater machine really was.

Soon the Canadian announced that the craft was a big battleship, a double-decker ironclad complete with ram. Dark, dense smoke burst from its two funnels. Its furled sails merged with the lines of its yardarms. The gaff of its fore-and-aft sail flew no flag. Its distance still kept us from distinguishing the colours of its pennant, which was fluttering like a thin ribbon.

It was coming on fast. If Captain Nemo let it approach, a chance for salvation might be available to us.

'Sir,' Ned Land told me, 'if that boat gets within a mile of us, I'm jumping overboard, and I suggest you follow suit.'

I didn't reply to the Canadian's proposition but kept watching the ship, which was looming larger on the horizon. Whether it was English, French, American, or Russian, it would surely welcome us aboard if we could just get to it.

'Master may recall,' Conseil then said, 'that we have some experience with swimming. He can rely on me to tow him to that vessel, if he's agreeable to going with our friend Ned.'

Before I could reply, white smoke streamed from the battleship's bow. Then, a few seconds later, the waters splashed astern of the *Nautilus*, disturbed by the fall of a heavy object. Soon after, an explosion struck my ears.

'What's this? They're firing at us!' I exclaimed.

'Good lads!' the Canadian muttered.

'That means they don't see us as castaways clinging to some wreckage!'

'With all due respect to master – gracious!' Conseil put in, shaking off the water that had sprayed over him from another shell. 'With all due respect to master, they've discovered the narwhal and they're cannonading the same.'

'But it must be clear to them,' I exclaimed, 'that they're dealing with human beings.'

'Maybe that's why!' Ned Land replied, staring hard at me.

The full truth dawned on me. Undoubtedly people now knew where they stood on the existence of this so-called monster. Undoubtedly the latter's encounter with the *Abraham Lincoln*, when the Canadian hit it with his harpoon, had led Commander Farragut to recognise the narwhal as actually an underwater boat, more dangerous than any unearthly cetacean!

Yes, this had to be the case, and undoubtedly they were now chasing this dreadful engine of destruction on every sea!

Dreadful indeed, if, as we could assume, Captain Nemo had been using the *Nautilus* in works of vengeance! That night in the middle of the Indian Ocean, when he imprisoned us in the cell, hadn't he attacked some ship? That man now buried in the coral cemetery, wasn't he the victim of some collision caused by the *Nautilus*? Yes, I repeat: this had to be the case. One part of Captain Nemo's secret life had been unveiled. And now, even though his identity was still unknown, at least the nations allied against him knew they were no longer hunting some fairy-tale monster, but a man who had sworn an implacable hate toward them!

This whole fearsome sequence of events appeared in my mind's eye. Instead of encountering friends on this approaching ship, we would find only pitiless enemies.

Meanwhile shells fell around us in increasing numbers. Some, meeting the liquid surface, would ricochet and vanish into the sea at considerable distances. But none of them reached the *Nautilus*.

By then the ironclad was no more than three miles off. Despite its violent cannonade, Captain Nemo hadn't appeared on the platform. And yet if one of those conical shells had scored a routine hit on the *Nautilus*'s hull, it could have been fatal to him.

The Canadian then told me:

'Sir, we've got to do everything we can to get out of this jam! Let's signal them! Damnation! Maybe they'll realise we're decent people!'

Ned Land pulled out his handkerchief to wave it in the air. But he had barely unfolded it when he was felled by an iron fist, and despite his great strength, he tumbled to the deck.

'Scum!' the captain shouted. 'Do you want to be nailed to the *Nautilus*'s spur before it charges that ship?'

Dreadful to hear, Captain Nemo was even more dreadful to see. His face was pale from some spasm of his heart, which must have stopped beating for an instant. His pupils were hideously contracted. His voice was no longer speaking, it was bellowing. Bending from the waist, he shook the Canadian by the shoulders.

Then, dropping Ned and turning to the battleship, whose shells were showering around him:

'O ship of an accursed nation, you know who I am!' he shouted in his powerful voice. 'And I don't need your colours to recognise you! Look! I'll show you mine!'

And in the bow of the platform, Captain Nemo unfurled a black flag, like the one he had left planted at the South Pole.

Just then a shell hit the *Nautilus*'s hull obliquely, failed to breach it, ricocheted near the captain, and vanished into the sea.

Captain Nemo shrugged his shoulders. Then, addressing me:

'Go below!' he told me in a curt tone. 'You and your companions, go below!'

'Sir,' I exclaimed, 'are you going to attack this ship?'

'Sir, I'm going to sink it.'

'You wouldn't!'

'I will,' Captain Nemo replied icily. 'You're ill-advised to pass judgement on me, sir. Fate has shown you what you weren't meant to see. The attack has come. Our reply will be dreadful. Get back inside!'

'From what country is that ship?'

'You don't know? Fine, so much the better! At least its nationality will remain a secret to you. Go below!'

The Canadian, Conseil, and I could only obey. Some 15 of the *Nautilus*'s seamen surrounded their captain and stared with a feeling of implacable hate at the ship bearing down on them. You could feel the same spirit of vengeance enkindling their every soul.

I went below just as another projectile scraped the *Nautilus*'s hull, and I heard the captain exclaim:

'Shoot, you demented vessel! Shower your futile shells! You won't escape the *Nautilus*'s spur! But this isn't the place where you'll perish! I don't want your wreckage mingling with that of the *Avenger*!'

I repaired to my stateroom. The captain and his chief officer stayed on the platform. The propeller was set in motion. The *Nautilus* swiftly retreated, putting us outside the range of the vessel's shells. But the chase continued, and Captain Nemo was content to keep his distance.

Near four o'clock in the afternoon, unable to control the impatience and uneasiness devouring me, I went back to the central companionway. The hatch was open. I ventured onto the platform. The captain was still strolling there, his steps agitated. He stared at the ship, which stayed to his leeward five or six miles off. He was circling it like a wild beast, drawing it eastward, letting it chase after him. Yet he didn't attack. Was he, perhaps, still undecided?

I tried to intervene one last time. But I had barely queried Captain Nemo when the latter silenced me:

'I'm the law, I'm the tribunal! I'm the oppressed, and there are my oppressors! Thanks to them, I've witnessed the destruction of everything I loved, cherished, and venerated – homeland, wife, children, father, and mother! There lies everything I hate! Not another word out of you!'

I took a last look at the battleship, which was putting on steam. Then I rejoined Ned and Conseil.

'We'll escape!' I exclaimed.

'Good,' Ned put in. 'Where's that ship from?'

'I've no idea. But wherever it's from, it will sink before nightfall. In any event, it's better to perish with it than be accomplices in some act of revenge whose merits we can't gauge.'

'That's my feeling,' Ned Land replied coolly. 'Let's wait for nightfall.'

Night fell. A profound silence reigned on board. The compass indicated that the *Nautilus* hadn't changed direction. I could hear the beat of its propeller, churning the waves with steady speed. Staying on the surface of the water, it rolled gently, sometimes to one side, sometimes to the other.

My companions and I had decided to escape as soon as the vessel came close enough for us to be heard – or seen, because the moon would wax full in three days and was shining brightly. Once we were aboard that ship, if we couldn't ward off the blow that threatened it, at least we could do everything that circumstances permitted. Several times I thought the *Nautilus* was about to attack. But it was content to let its adversary approach, and then it would quickly resume its retreating ways.

Part of the night passed without incident. We kept watch for an opportunity to take action. We talked little, being too keyed up. Ned Land was all for jumping overboard. I forced him to wait. As I saw it, the *Nautilus* would attack the double-decker on the surface of the waves, and then it would be not only possible but easy to escape.

At three o'clock in the morning, full of uneasiness, I climbed onto the platform. Captain Nemo hadn't left it. He stood in the bow next to his flag, which a mild breeze was unfurling above his head. His eyes never left that vessel. The extraordinary intensity of his gaze seemed to attract it, beguile it, and draw it more surely than if he had it in tow!

The moon then passed its zenith. Jupiter was rising in the east. In the midst of this placid natural setting, sky and ocean competed with each other in tranquillity, and the sea offered the orb of night the loveliest mirror ever to reflect its image.

And when I compared this deep calm of the elements with all the fury seething inside the plating of this barely perceptible *Nautilus*, I shivered all over.

The vessel was two miles off. It drew nearer, always moving toward the phosphorescent glow that signalled the *Nautilus*'s presence. I saw its green and red running lights, plus the white lantern hanging from the large stay of its foremast. Hazy flickerings were reflected on its rigging and indicated that its furnaces were pushed to the limit. Showers of sparks and cinders of flaming coal escaped from its funnels, spangling the air with stars.

I stood there until six o'clock in the morning, Captain Nemo never seeming to notice me. The vessel lay a mile and a half off, and with the first glimmers of daylight, it resumed its cannonade. The time couldn't be far away when the *Nautilus* would attack its adversary, and my companions and I would leave forever this man I dared not judge.

I was about to go below to alert them, when the chief officer climbed onto the platform. Several seamen were with him. Captain Nemo didn't see them, or didn't want to see them. They carried out certain procedures that, on the *Nautilus*, you could call 'clearing the decks for action.' They were quite simple. The manropes that formed a handrail around the platform were lowered. Likewise the pilothouse and the beacon housing were withdrawn into the hull until they lay exactly flush with it. The surface of this long sheet-iron cigar no longer offered a single protrusion that could hamper its manoeuvres.

I returned to the lounge. The *Nautilus* still emerged above the surface. A few morning gleams infiltrated the liquid strata. Beneath the undulations of the billows, the windows were enlivened by the blushing of the rising sun. That dreadful day of June 2 had dawned.

At seven o'clock the log told me that the *Nautilus* had reduced speed. I realised that it was letting the warship approach. Moreover, the explosions grew more intensely audible. Shells furrowed the water around us, drilling through it with an odd hissing sound.

'My friends,' I said, 'it's time. Let's shake hands, and may God be with us!'

Ned Land was determined, Conseil calm, I myself nervous and barely in control.

We went into the library. Just as I pushed open the door leading to the well of the central companionway, I heard the hatch close sharply overhead.

The Canadian leaped up the steps, but I stopped him. A well-known hissing told me that water was entering the ship's ballast tanks. Indeed, in a few moments the *Nautilus* had submerged some metres below the surface of the waves.

I understood this manoeuvre. It was too late to take action. The *Nautilus* wasn't going to strike the double-decker where it was clad in impenetrable iron armour, but below its waterline, where the metal carapace no longer protected its planking.

We were prisoners once more, unwilling spectators at the performance of this gruesome drama. But we barely had time to think. Taking refuge in my stateroom, we stared at each other without pronouncing a word. My mind was in a total daze. My mental processes came to a dead stop. I hovered in that painful state that predominates during the period of anticipation before some frightful explosion. I waited, I listened, I lived only through my sense of hearing!

Meanwhile the *Nautilus*'s speed had increased appreciably. So it was gathering momentum. Its entire hull was vibrating.

Suddenly I let out a yell. There had been a collision, but it was comparatively mild. I could feel the penetrating force of the steel spur. I could hear scratchings and scrapings. Carried away with its driving power, the *Nautilus* had passed through the vessel's mass like a sailmaker's needle through canvas!

I couldn't hold still. Frantic, going insane, I leaped out of my stateroom and rushed into the lounge.

Captain Nemo was there. Mute, gloomy, implacable, he was staring through the port panel.

An enormous mass was sinking beneath the waters, and the *Nautilus*, missing none of its death throes, was descending into the depths with it. Ten metres away, I could see its gaping hull, into which water was rushing with a sound of thunder, then its double rows of cannons and railings. Its deck was covered with dark, quivering shadows.

The water was rising. Those poor men leaped up into the shrouds, clung to the masts, writhed beneath the waters. It was a human anthill that an invading sea had caught by surprise!

Paralysed, rigid with anguish, my hair standing on end, my eyes popping out of my head, short of breath, suffocating, speechless, I stared – I too! I was glued to the window by an irresistible allure!

The enormous vessel settled slowly. Following it down, the *Nautilus* kept watch on its every movement. Suddenly there was an eruption. The air compressed inside the craft sent its decks flying, as if the powder stores had been ignited. The thrust of the waters was so great, the *Nautilus* swerved away.

The poor ship then sank more swiftly. Its mastheads appeared, laden with victims, then its crosstrees bending under clusters of men, finally the peak of its mainmast. Then the dark mass disappeared, and with it a crew of corpses dragged under by fearsome eddies....

I turned to Captain Nemo. This dreadful executioner, this true archangel of hate, was still staring. When it was all over, Captain Nemo headed to the door of his stateroom, opened it, and entered. I followed him with my eyes.

On the rear panelling, beneath the portraits of his heroes, I saw the portrait of a still-youthful woman with two little children. Captain Nemo stared at them for a few moments, stretched out his arms to them, sank to his knees, and melted into sobs.

CHAPTER 22

The Last Words of Captain Nemo

THE PANELS CLOSED over this frightful view, but the lights didn't go on in the lounge. Inside the *Nautilus* all was gloom and silence. It left this place of devastation with prodigious speed, 100 feet beneath the waters. Where was it going? North or south? Where would the man flee after this horrible act of revenge?

I re-entered my stateroom, where Ned and Conseil were waiting silently. Captain Nemo filled me with insurmountable horror. Whatever he had once suffered at the hands of humanity, he had no right to mete out such punishment. He had made me, if not an accomplice, at least an eyewitness to his vengeance! Even this was intolerable.

At 11 o'clock the electric lights came back on. I went into the lounge. It was deserted. I consulted the various instruments. The *Nautilus* was fleeing northward at a speed of 25 miles per hour, sometimes on the surface of the sea, sometimes 30 feet beneath it.

After our position had been marked on the chart, I saw that we were passing into the mouth of the English Channel, that our heading would take us to the northernmost seas with incomparable speed.

I could barely glimpse the swift passing of longnose sharks, hammerhead sharks, spotted dogfish that frequent these waters, big eagle rays, swarms of seahorse looking like knights on a chessboard, eels quivering like fireworks serpents, armies of crab that fled obliquely by crossing their pincers over their carapaces, finally schools of porpoise that held contests of speed with the *Nautilus*. But by this point observing, studying and classifying were out of the question.

By evening we had cleared 200 leagues up the Atlantic. Shadows gathered and gloom overran the sea until the moon came up.

I repaired to my stateroom. I couldn't sleep. I was assaulted by nightmares. That horrible scene of destruction kept repeating in my mind's eye.

From that day forward, who knows where the *Nautilus* took us in the north Atlantic basin? Always at incalculable speed! Always amid the High Arctic mists! Did it call at the capes of Spitzbergen or the shores of Novaya Zemlya? Did it visit such uncharted seas as the White Sea, the Kara Sea, the Gulf of Ob, the Lyakhov Islands, or those unknown beaches on the Siberian coast? I'm unable to say. I lost track of the passing hours. Time was in abeyance on the ship's clocks. As happens in the polar regions, it seemed that night and day no longer followed their normal sequence. I felt myself being drawn into that strange domain where the overwrought imagination of Edgar Allan Poe was at home. Like his fabled Arthur Gordon Pym, I expected any moment to see that 'shrouded human figure, very far larger in its proportions than any dweller among men,' thrown across the cataract that protects the outskirts of the pole!

I estimate – but perhaps I'm mistaken – that the *Nautilus*'s haphazard course continued for 15 or 20 days, and I'm not sure how long this would have gone on without the catastrophe that ended our voyage. As for Captain Nemo, he was no longer in the picture. As for his chief officer, the same applied. Not one crewman was visible for a single instant. The *Nautilus* cruised beneath the waters almost continuously. When it rose briefly to the surface to renew our air, the hatches opened and closed as if automated. No more positions were reported on the world map. I didn't know where we were.

I'll also mention that the Canadian, at the end of his strength and patience, made no further appearances. Conseil couldn't coax a single word out of him and feared that, in a fit of delirium while under the sway of a ghastly homesickness, Ned would kill himself. So he kept a devoted watch on his friend every instant.

You can appreciate that under these conditions, our situation had become untenable.

One morning – whose date I'm unable to specify – I was slumbering near the first hours of daylight, a painful, sickly slumber. Waking up, I saw Ned Land leaning over me, and I heard him tell me in a low voice:

'We're going to escape!'

I sat up.

'When?' I asked.

'Tonight. There doesn't seem to be any supervision left on the *Nautilus*. You'd think a total daze was reigning on board. Will you be ready, sir?'

'Yes. Where are we?'

'In sight of land. I saw it through the mists just this morning, 20 miles to the east.'

'What land is it?'

'I've no idea, but whatever it is, there we'll take refuge.'

'Yes, Ned! We'll escape tonight even if the sea swallows us up!'

'The sea's rough, the wind's blowing hard, but a 20-mile run in the *Nautilus*'s nimble longboat doesn't scare me. Unknown to the crew, I've stowed some food and flasks of water inside.'

'I'm with you.'

'What's more,' the Canadian added, 'if they catch me, I'll defend myself, I'll fight to the death.'

'Then we'll die together, Ned my friend.'

My mind was made up. The Canadian left me. I went out on the platform, where I could barely stand upright against the jolts of the billows. The skies were threatening, but land lay inside those dense mists, and we had to escape. Not a single day, or even a single hour, could we afford to lose.

I returned to the lounge, dreading yet desiring an encounter with Captain Nemo, wanting yet not wanting to see him. What would I say to him? How could I hide the involuntary horror he inspired in me? No! It was best not to meet him face to face! Best to try and forget him! And yet...!

How long that day seemed, the last I would spend aboard the *Nautilus*! I was left to myself. Ned Land and Conseil avoided speaking to me, afraid they would give themselves away.

At six o'clock I ate supper, but I had no appetite. Despite my revulsion, I forced it down, wanting to keep my strength up.

At 6:30 Ned Land entered my stateroom. He told me:

'We won't see each other again before we go. At ten o'clock the moon won't be up yet. We'll take advantage of the darkness. Come to the skiff. Conseil and I will be inside waiting for you.'

The Canadian left without giving me time to answer him.

I wanted to verify the *Nautilus*'s heading. I made my way to the lounge. We were racing north-northeast with frightful speed, 50 metres down.

I took one last look at the natural wonders and artistic treasures amassed in the museum, this unrivalled collection doomed to perish someday in the depths of the seas, together with its curator. I wanted to establish one supreme impression in my mind. I stayed there an hour, basking in the aura of the ceiling lights, passing in review the treasures shining in their glass cases. Then I returned to my stateroom.

There I dressed in sturdy seafaring clothes. I gathered my notes and packed them tenderly about my person. My heart was pounding mightily. I couldn't curb its pulsations. My anxiety and agitation would certainly have given me away if Captain Nemo had seen me.

What was he doing just then? I listened at the door to his stateroom. I heard the sound of footsteps. Captain Nemo was inside. He hadn't gone to bed. With his every movement I imagined he would appear and ask me why I wanted to escape! I felt in a perpetual state of alarm. My imagination magnified this sensation. The feeling became so acute, I wondered whether it wouldn't be better to enter the captain's stateroom, dare him face to face, brave it out with word and deed!

It was an insane idea. Fortunately I controlled myself and stretched out on the bed to soothe my bodily agitation. My nerves calmed a little, but with my brain so aroused, I did a swift review of my whole existence aboard the *Nautilus*, every pleasant or unpleasant incident that had crossed my path since I went overboard from the *Abraham Lincoln*: the underwater hunting trip, the Torres Strait, our running aground, the savages of Papua, the coral cemetery, the Suez passageway, the island of Santorini, the Cretan diver, the Bay of Vigo, Atlantis, the Ice Bank, the South Pole, our imprisonment in the ice, the battle with the devilfish, the storm in the Gulf Stream, the *Avenger*, and that horrible scene of the vessel sinking with its crew...! All these events passed before my eyes like backdrops unrolling upstage in a theatre. In this strange setting Captain Nemo then grew fantastically. His features were accentuated, taking on superhuman proportions. He was no longer my equal, he was the Man of the Waters, the Spirit of the Seas.

By then it was 9:30. I held my head in both hands to keep it from bursting. I closed my eyes. I no longer wanted to think. A half hour still to wait! A half hour of nightmares that could drive me insane!

Just then I heard indistinct chords from the organ, melancholy harmonies from some undefinable hymn, actual pleadings from a soul trying to sever its earthly ties. I listened with all my senses at once, barely breathing, immersed like Captain Nemo in this musical trance that was drawing him beyond the bounds of this world.

Then a sudden thought terrified me. Captain Nemo had left his stateroom. He was in the same lounge I had to cross in order to escape. There I would encounter him one last time. He would see me, perhaps speak to me! One gesture from him could obliterate me, a single word shackle me to his vessel!

Even so, ten o'clock was about to strike. It was time to leave my stateroom and rejoin my companions.

I dared not hesitate, even if Captain Nemo stood before me. I opened the door cautiously, but as it swung on its hinges, it seemed to make a frightful noise. This noise existed, perhaps, only in my imagination!

I crept forward through the *Nautilus*'s dark gangways, pausing after each step to curb the pounding of my heart.

I arrived at the corner door of the lounge. I opened it gently. The lounge was plunged in profound darkness. Chords from the organ were reverberating faintly. Captain Nemo was there. He didn't see me. Even in broad daylight I doubt that he would have noticed me, so completely was he immersed in his trance.

I inched over the carpet, avoiding the tiniest bump whose noise might give me away. It took me five minutes to reach the door at the far end, which led into the library.

I was about to open it when a gasp from Captain Nemo nailed me to the spot. I realised that he was standing up. I even got a glimpse of him because some rays of light from the library had filtered into the lounge. He was coming toward me, arms crossed, silent, not walking but gliding like a ghost. His chest was heaving, swelling with sobs. And I heard him murmur these words, the last of his to reach my ears:

'O almighty God! Enough! Enough!'

Was it a vow of repentance that had just escaped from this man's conscience...?

Frantic, I rushed into the library. I climbed the central companionway, and going along the upper gangway, I arrived at the skiff. I went through the opening that had already given access to my two companions.

'Let's go, let's go!' I exclaimed.

'Right away!' the Canadian replied.

First, Ned Land closed and bolted the opening cut into the *Nautilus*'s sheet iron, using the monkey wrench he had with him. After likewise closing the opening in the skiff, the Canadian began to unscrew the nuts still bolting us to the underwater boat.

Suddenly a noise from the ship's interior became audible. Voices were answering each other hurriedly. What was it? Had they spotted our escape? I felt Ned Land sliding a dagger into my hand.

'Yes,' I muttered, 'we know how to die!'

The Canadian paused in his work. But one word 20 times repeated, one dreadful word, told me the reason for the agitation spreading aboard the *Nautilus*. We weren't the cause of the crew's concern.

'Maelstrom! Maelstrom!' they were shouting.

The Maelstrom! Could a more frightening name have rung in our ears under more frightening circumstances? Were we lying in the dangerous waterways off the Norwegian coast? Was the *Nautilus* being dragged into this whirlpool just as the skiff was about to detach from its plating?

As you know, at the turn of the tide, the waters confined between the Faroe and Lofoten Islands rush out with irresistible violence. They form a vortex from which no ship has ever been able to escape. Monstrous waves race together from every point of the horizon. They form a whirlpool aptly called 'the ocean's navel,' whose attracting power extends a distance of 15 kilometres. It can suck down not only ships but whales, and even polar bears from the northernmost regions.

This was where the *Nautilus* had been sent accidentally – or perhaps deliberately – by its captain. It was sweeping around in a spiral whose radius kept growing smaller and smaller. The skiff, still attached to the ship's plating, was likewise carried around at dizzying speed. I could feel us whirling. I was experiencing that accompanying nausea that follows such continuous spinning motions. We were in dread, in the last stages of sheer horror, our blood frozen in our veins, our nerves numb, drenched in cold sweat as if from the throes of dying! And what a noise around our frail skiff! What roars echoing from several miles away! What crashes from the waters breaking against sharp rocks on the seafloor, where the hardest objects are smashed, where tree trunks are worn down and worked into 'a shaggy fur,' as Norwegians express it!

What a predicament! We were rocking frightfully. The *Nautilus* defended itself like a human being. Its steel muscles were cracking. Sometimes it stood on end, the three of us along with it!

'We've got to hold on tight,' Ned said, 'and screw the nuts down again! If we can stay attached to the *Nautilus*, we can still make it…!'

He hadn't finished speaking when a cracking sound occurred. The nuts gave way, and ripped out of its socket, the skiff was hurled like a stone from a sling into the midst of the vortex.

My head struck against an iron timber, and with this violent shock I lost consciousness.

CHAPTER 23

Conclusion

WE COME TO the conclusion of this voyage under the seas. What happened that night, how the skiff escaped from the Maelstrom's fearsome eddies, how Ned Land, Conseil and I got out of that whirlpool, I'm unable to say. But when I regained consciousness, I was lying in a fisherman's hut on one of the Lofoten Islands. My two companions, safe and sound, were at my bedside clasping my hands. We embraced each other heartily.

Just now we can't even dream of returning to France. Travel between upper Norway and the south is limited. So I have to wait for the arrival of a steamboat that provides bimonthly service from North Cape.

So it is here, among these gallant people who have taken us in, that I'm reviewing my narrative of these adventures. It is accurate. Not a fact has been omitted, not a detail has been exaggerated. It's the faithful record of this inconceivable expedition into an element now beyond human reach, but where progress will someday make great inroads.

Will anyone believe me? I don't know. Ultimately it's unimportant. What I can now assert is that I've earned the right to speak of these seas, beneath which in less than ten months, I've cleared 20,000 leagues in this underwater tour of the world that has shown me so many wonders across the Pacific, the Indian Ocean, the Red Sea, the Mediterranean, the Atlantic, the southernmost and northernmost seas!

But what happened to the *Nautilus*? Did it withstand the Maelstrom's clutches? Is Captain Nemo alive? Is he still under the ocean pursuing his frightful programme of revenge, or did he stop after that latest mass execution? Will the waves someday deliver that manuscript that contains his full life story? Will I finally learn the man's name? Will the nationality of the stricken warship tell us the nationality of Captain Nemo?

I hope so. I likewise hope that his powerful submersible has defeated the sea inside its most dreadful whirlpool, that the *Nautilus* has survived where so many ships have perished! If this is the case and Captain Nemo still inhabits the ocean – his adopted country – may the hate be appeased in that fierce heart! May the contemplation of so many wonders extinguish the spirit of vengeance in him! May the executioner pass away, and the scientist continue his peaceful exploration of the seas! If his destiny is strange, it's also sublime. Haven't I encompassed it myself? Didn't I lead ten months of this otherworldly existence? Thus to that question asked 6,000 years ago in the Book of Ecclesiastes – 'Who can fathom the soundless depths?' – two men out of all humanity have now earned the right to reply. Captain Nemo and I.

AROUND THE WORLD IN 80 DAYS

AROUND THE WORLD IN 80 DAYS

JULES VERNE

This edition published in 2021 by Arcturus Publishing Limited
26/27 Bickels Yard, 151–153 Bermondsey Street,
London SE1 3HA

Copyright © Arcturus Holdings Limited

All rights reserved. No part of this publication may be reproduced, stored in a retrieval system, or transmitted, in any form or by any means, electronic, mechanical, photocopying, recording or otherwise, without prior written permission in accordance with the provisions of the Copyright Act 1956 (as amended). Any person or persons who do any unauthorised act in relation to this publication may be liable to criminal prosecution and civil claims for damages.

Cover design: Peter Ridley
Cover illustration: Peter Gray

AD007670UK

Printed in the UK

Contents

Introduction   9

1   *In which Phileas Fogg and Passepartout accept each other, the one as master, the other as man*   11

2   *In which Passepartout is convinced that he has at last found his ideal*   17

3   *In which a conversation takes place which seems likely to cost Phileas Fogg dear*   21

4   *In which Phileas Fogg astounds Passepartout, his servant*   29

5   *In which a new species of funds, unknown to the moneyed men, appears on 'Change*   33

6   *In which Fix, the detective, betrays a very natural impatience*   37

7   *Which once more demonstrates the uselessness of passports as aids to detectives*   43

8   *In which Passepartout talks rather more, perhaps, than is prudent*   47

9   *In which the Red Sea and the Indian Ocean prove propitious to the designs of Phileas Fogg*   53

10   *In which Passepartout is only too glad to get off with the loss of his shoes*   59

11   *In which Phileas Fogg secures a curious means of conveyance at a fabulous price*   65

12	*In which Phileas Fogg and his companions venture across the Indian forests, and what ensued*	75
13	*In which Passepartout receives a new proof that fortune favours the brave*	83
14	*In which Phileas Fogg descends the whole length of the beautiful valley of the Ganges without ever thinking of seeing it*	91
15	*In which the bag of banknotes disgorges some thousands of pounds more*	99
16	*In which Fix does not seem to understand in the least what is said to him*	107
17	*Showing what happened on the voyage from Singapore to Hong Kong*	113
18	*In which Phileas Fogg, Passepartout, and Fix go each about his business*	121
19	*In which Passepartout takes too great interest in his master, and what comes of it*	127
20	*In which Fix comes face to face with Phileas Fogg*	135
21	*In which the master of the 'Tankadere' runs great risk of losing a reward of two hundred pounds*	143
22	*In which Passepartout finds out that, even at the Antipodes, it is convenient to have some money in one's pocket*	153
23	*In which Passepartout's nose becomes outrageously long*	161

24	*During which Mr. Fogg and party cross the Pacific Ocean*	169
25	*In which a slight glimpse is had of San Francisco*	177
26	*In which Phileas Fogg and party travel by the Pacific Railroad*	185
27	*In which Passepartout undergoes, at a speed of twenty miles an hour, a course of Mormon history*	191
28	*In which Passepartout does not succeed in making anybody listen to reason*	199
29	*In which certain incidents are narrated which are only to be met with on American railroads*	209
30	*In which Phileas Fogg simply does his duty*	217
31	*In which Fix, the detective, considerably furthers the interests of Phileas Fogg*	225
32	*In which Phileas Fogg engages in a direct struggle with bad fortune*	233
33	*In which Phileas Fogg shows himself equal to the occasion*	239
34	*In which Phileas Fogg at last reaches London*	249
35	*In which Phileas Fogg does not have to repeat his orders to Passepartout twice*	253
36	*In which Phileas Fogg's name is once more at a premium on 'Change*	259
37	*In which it is shown that Phileas Fogg gained nothing by his tour around the world, unless it were happiness*	265

Introduction

The great early pioneer of science fiction, Jules Verne was celebrated for his *Voyages Extraordinaires*. His heroes travelled around the world, to the moon and, in this volume, to the centre of the earth. It is therefore fitting that the author began life – on 8 February 1828 – in the busy, bustling French harbour city of Nantes.

Drawn to a life of adventure, at twelve Verne was beaten by his father when found hiding on a ship bound for India. After this bitter experience, the future writer famously resolved to travel only in his imagination.

The troubled relationship with his father marked much of Verne's early literary career. Upon learning that his son was writing, rather than studying law, the elder Verne withdrew all support. For over a decade, the author worked as a stockbroker, while attempting to interest publishers in his work. Verne's fortunes changed when he met Pierre-Jules Hetzel. An editor and publisher, in 1863 he published Verne's first novel, *Five Weeks in a Balloon* (*Cinq Semaines en Ballon*). *Journey to the Centre of the Earth* (*Voyage au centre de la Terre*), published the following year, proved to be one of the author's most enduring works. Verne came to be celebrated the world over for such classic novels as *Twenty Thousand Leagues Under the Sea* (1870) and *Around the World in Eighty Days* (1873). He died on 24 March 1905.

CHAPTER 1

In which Phileas Fogg and Passepartout accept each other, the one as master, the other as man

Mr. Phileas Fogg lived, in 1872, at No. 7, Savile Row, Burlington Gardens, the house in which Sheridan died in 1814. He was one of the most noticeable members of the Reform Club, though he seemed always to avoid attracting attention; an enigmatical personage, about whom little was known, except that he was a polished man of the world. People said that he resembled Byron – at least that his head was Byronic; but he was a bearded, tranquil Byron, who might live on a thousand years without growing old.

Certainly an Englishman, it was more doubtful whether Phileas Fogg was a Londoner. He was never seen on 'Change, nor at the Bank, nor in the counting-rooms of the 'City'; no ships ever came into London docks of which he was the owner; he had no public employment; he had never been entered at any of the Inns of Court, either at the Temple, or Lincoln's Inn, or Gray's Inn; nor had his voice ever resounded in the Court of Chancery, or in the Exchequer, or the Queen's Bench, or the Ecclesiastical Courts. He certainly was not a manufacturer; nor was he a merchant or a gentleman farmer.

His name was strange to the scientific and learned societies, and he never was known to take part in the sage deliberations of the Royal Institution or the London Institution, the Artisan's Association, or the Institution of Arts and Sciences. He belonged, in fact, to none of the numerous societies which swarm in the English capital, from the Harmonic to that of the Entomologists, founded mainly for the purpose of abolishing pernicious insects.

Phileas Fogg was a member of the Reform, and that was all.

The way in which he got admission to this exclusive club was simple enough.

He was recommended by the Barings, with whom he had an open credit. His cheques were regularly paid at sight from his account current, which was always flush.

Was Phileas Fogg rich? Undoubtedly. But those who knew him best could not imagine how he had made his fortune, and Mr. Fogg was the last person to whom to apply for the information. He was not lavish, nor, on the contrary, avaricious; for, whenever he knew that money was needed for a noble, useful, or benevolent purpose, he supplied it quietly and sometimes anonymously. He was, in short, the least communicative of men. He talked very little, and seemed all the more mysterious for his taciturn manner. His daily habits were quite open to observation; but whatever he did was so exactly the same thing that he had always done before, that the wits of the curious were fairly puzzled.

Had he travelled? It was likely, for no one seemed to know the world more familiarly; there was no spot so secluded that he did not appear to have an intimate acquaintance with it. He often corrected, with a few clear words, the thousand conjectures advanced by members of the club as to lost and unheard-of travellers, pointing out the true probabilities, and seeming as if gifted with a sort of second sight, so often did events justify his predictions. He must have travelled everywhere, at least in the spirit.

It was at least certain that Phileas Fogg had not absented himself from London for many years. Those who were honoured by a better acquaintance with him than the rest, declared that nobody could pretend to have ever seen him anywhere else. His sole pastimes were reading the papers and playing whist. He often won at this game, which, as a silent one, harmonised with his nature; but his winnings never went into his purse, being reserved as a fund for his charities. Mr. Fogg played, not to win, but for the sake of playing. The game was in his eyes a contest, a struggle with a difficulty, yet a motionless, unwearying struggle, congenial to his tastes.

Phileas Fogg was not known to have either wife or children, which may happen to the most honest people; either relatives or near friends, which is certainly more unusual. He lived alone in his house in Savile Row, whither none penetrated. A single domestic sufficed to serve him. He breakfasted and dined at the club, at hours mathematically fixed, in the same room, at the same table, never taking his meals with other members, much less bringing a guest with him; and went home at exactly midnight, only to retire at once to bed. He never used the cosy chambers which the Reform provides for its favoured members. He passed ten hours out of the twenty-four in Savile Row, either in sleeping or making his toilet. When he chose to take a walk it was with a regular step in the entrance hall with its mosaic flooring, or in the circular gallery with its dome supported by twenty red porphyry Ionic columns, and illumined by blue painted windows. When he breakfasted or dined all the resources of the club – its kitchens and pantries, its buttery and dairy – aided to crowd his table with their most succulent stores; he was served by the gravest waiters, in dress coats, and shoes with swan-skin soles, who proffered the viands in special porcelain, and on the finest linen; club decanters, of a lost mould, contained his sherry, his port, and his cinnamon-spiced claret; while his beverages were refreshingly cooled with ice, brought at great cost from the American lakes.

If to live in this style is to be eccentric, it must be confessed that there is something good in eccentricity.

The mansion in Savile Row, though not sumptuous, was exceedingly comfortable. The habits of its occupant were such as to demand but little from the sole domestic, but Phileas Fogg required him to be almost superhumanly prompt and regular. On this very 2nd of October he had dismissed James Forster, because that luckless youth had brought him shaving-water at eighty-four degrees Fahrenheit instead of eighty-six; and he was awaiting his successor, who was due at the house between eleven and half-past.

Phileas Fogg was seated squarely in his armchair, his feet close together like those of a grenadier on parade, his hands resting on his knees, his body straight, his head erect; he was steadily watching a complicated clock which indicated the hours, the minutes, the seconds, the days, the months, and the years. At exactly half-past eleven Mr. Fogg would, according to his daily habit, quit Savile Row, and repair to the Reform.

A rap at this moment sounded on the door of the cosy apartment where Phileas Fogg was seated, and James Forster, the dismissed servant, appeared.

'The new servant,' said he.

A young man of thirty advanced and bowed.

'You are a Frenchman, I believe,' asked Phileas Fogg, 'and your name is John?'

'Jean, if monsieur pleases,' replied the newcomer, 'Jean Passepartout, a surname which has clung to me because I have a natural aptness for going out of one business into another. I believe I'm honest, monsieur, but, to be outspoken, I've had several trades. I've been an itinerant singer, a circus-rider, when I used to vault like Leotard, and dance on a rope like Blondin. Then I got to be a professor of gymnastics, so as to make better use of my talents; and then I was a sergeant fireman at Paris, and assisted at many a big fire. But I quitted France five years ago, and, wishing to taste the sweets of domestic life, took service as a valet here in England. Finding myself out of place, and hearing that Monsieur Phileas Fogg was the most exact and settled gentleman in the United Kingdom, I have come to monsieur in the hope of living with him a tranquil life, and forgetting even the name of Passepartout.'

'Passepartout suits me,' responded Mr. Fogg. 'You are well recommended to me; I hear a good report of you. You know my conditions?'

'Yes, monsieur.'

'Good! What time is it?'

'Twenty-two minutes after eleven,' returned Passepartout, drawing an enormous silver watch from the depths of his pocket.

'You are too slow,' said Mr. Fogg.

'Pardon me, monsieur, it is impossible – '

'You are four minutes too slow. No matter; it's enough to mention the error. Now from this moment, twenty-nine minutes after eleven, a.m., this Wednesday, 2nd October, you are in my service.'

Phileas Fogg got up, took his hat in his left hand, put it

on his head with an automatic motion, and went off without a word.

Passepartout heard the street door shut once; it was his new master going out. He heard it shut again; it was his predecessor, James Forster, departing in his turn. Passepartout remained alone in the house in Savile Row.

CHAPTER 2

In which Passepartout is convinced that he has at last found his ideal

'Faith,' muttered Passepartout, somewhat flurried, 'I've seen people at Madame Tussaud's as lively as my new master!'

Madame Tussaud's 'people,' let it be said, are of wax, and are much visited in London; speech is all that is wanting to make them human.

During his brief interview with Mr. Fogg, Passepartout had been carefully observing him. He appeared to be a man about forty years of age, with fine, handsome features, and a tall, well-shaped figure; his hair and whiskers were light, his forehead compact and unwrinkled, his face rather pale, his teeth magnificent. His countenance possessed in the highest degree what physiognomists call 'repose in action,' a quality of those who act rather than talk. Calm and phlegmatic, with a clear eye, Mr. Fogg seemed a perfect type of that English composure which Angelica Kauffmann has so skilfully represented on canvas. Seen in the various phases of his daily life, he gave the idea of being perfectly well-balanced, as exactly regulated as a Leroy chronometer. Phileas Fogg was, indeed, exactitude personified, and this was betrayed even in the expression of his very hands and feet; for in men, as well as in animals, the limbs themselves are expressive of the passions.

He was so exact that he was never in a hurry, was always ready, and was economical alike of his steps and his motions. He never took one step too many, and always went to his destination by the shortest cut; he made no superfluous gestures, and was never seen to be moved or agitated. He was the most deliberate person in the world, yet always reached his destination at the exact moment.

He lived alone, and, so to speak, outside of every social relation; and as he knew that in this world account must be taken of friction, and that friction retards, he never rubbed against anybody.

As for Passepartout, he was a true Parisian of Paris. Since he had abandoned his own country for England, taking service as a valet, he had in vain searched for a master after his own heart. Passepartout was by no means one of those pert dunces depicted by Moliere with a bold gaze and a nose held high in the air; he was an honest fellow, with a pleasant face, lips a trifle protruding, soft-mannered and serviceable, with a good round head, such as one likes to see on the shoulders of a friend. His eyes were blue, his complexion rubicund, his figure almost portly and well-built, his body muscular, and his physical powers fully developed by the exercises of his younger days. His brown hair was somewhat tumbled; for, while the ancient sculptors are said to have known eighteen methods of arranging Minerva's tresses, Passepartout was familiar with but one of dressing his own: three strokes of a large-tooth comb completed his toilet.

It would be rash to predict how Passepartout's lively nature would agree with Mr. Fogg. It was impossible to tell whether the new servant would turn out as absolutely methodical as

CHAPTER 2

his master required; experience alone could solve the question. Passepartout had been a sort of vagrant in his early years, and now yearned for repose; but so far he had failed to find it, though he had already served in ten English houses. But he could not take root in any of these; with chagrin, he found his masters invariably whimsical and irregular, constantly running about the country, or on the look-out for adventure. His last master, young Lord Longferry, Member of Parliament, after passing his nights in the Haymarket taverns, was too often brought home in the morning on policemen's shoulders. Passepartout, desirous of respecting the gentleman whom he served, ventured a mild remonstrance on such conduct; which, being ill-received, he took his leave. Hearing that Mr. Phileas Fogg was looking for a servant, and that his life was one of unbroken regularity, that he neither travelled nor stayed from home overnight, he felt sure that this would be the place he was after. He presented himself, and was accepted, as has been seen.

At half-past eleven, then, Passepartout found himself alone in the house in Savile Row. He began its inspection without delay, scouring it from cellar to garret. So clean, well-arranged, solemn a mansion pleased him; it seemed to him like a sñail's shell, lighted and warmed by gas, which sufficed for both these purposes. When Passepartout reached the second story he recognised at once the room which he was to inhabit, and he was well satisfied with it. Electric bells and speaking-tubes afforded communication with the lower stories; while on the mantel stood an electric clock, precisely like that in Mr. Fogg's bedchamber, both beating the same second at the same instant. 'That's good, that'll do,' said Passepartout to himself.

He suddenly observed, hung over the clock, a card which,

upon inspection, proved to be a programme of the daily routine of the house. It comprised all that was required of the servant, from eight in the morning, exactly at which hour Phileas Fogg rose, till half-past eleven, when he left the house for the Reform Club – all the details of service, the tea and toast at twenty-three minutes past eight, the shaving-water at thirty-seven minutes past nine, and the toilet at twenty minutes before ten. Everything was regulated and foreseen that was to be done from half-past eleven a.m. till midnight, the hour at which the methodical gentleman retired.

Mr. Fogg's wardrobe was amply supplied and in the best taste. Each pair of trousers, coat, and vest bore a number, indicating the time of year and season at which they were in turn to be laid out for wearing; and the same system was applied to the master's shoes. In short, the house in Savile Row, which must have been a very temple of disorder and unrest under the illustrious but dissipated Sheridan, was cosiness, comfort, and method idealised. There was no study, nor were there books, which would have been quite useless to Mr. Fogg; for at the Reform two libraries, one of general literature and the other of law and politics, were at his service. A moderate-sized safe stood in his bedroom, constructed so as to defy fire as well as burglars; but Passepartout found neither arms nor hunting weapons anywhere; everything betrayed the most tranquil and peaceable habits.

Having scrutinised the house from top to bottom, he rubbed his hands, a broad smile overspread his features, and he said joyfully, 'This is just what I wanted! Ah, we shall get on together, Mr. Fogg and I! What a domestic and regular gentleman! A real machine; well, I don't mind serving a machine.'

CHAPTER 3

In which a conversation takes place which seems likely to cost Phileas Fogg dear

Phileas Fogg, having shut the door of his house at half-past eleven, and having put his right foot before his left five hundred and seventy-five times, and his left foot before his right five hundred and seventy-six times, reached the Reform Club, an imposing edifice in Pall Mall, which could not have cost less than three millions. He repaired at once to the dining-room, the nine windows of which open upon a tasteful garden, where the trees were already gilded with an autumn colouring; and took his place at the habitual table, the cover of which had already been laid for him. His breakfast consisted of a side-dish, a broiled fish with Reading sauce, a scarlet slice of roast beef garnished with mushrooms, a rhubarb and gooseberry tart, and a morsel of Cheshire cheese, the whole being washed down with several cups of tea, for which the Reform is famous. He rose at thirteen minutes to one, and directed his steps towards the large hall, a sumptuous apartment adorned with lavishly-framed paintings. A flunkey handed him an uncut *Times*, which he proceeded to cut with a skill which betrayed familiarity with this delicate operation.

The perusal of this paper absorbed Phileas Fogg until a quarter before four, whilst the *Standard*, his next task, occupied him till the dinner hour. Dinner passed as breakfast had done, and Mr. Fogg re-appeared in the reading-room and sat down to the Pall Mall at twenty minutes before six. Half an hour later several members of the Reform came in and drew up to the fireplace, where a coal fire was steadily burning. They were Mr. Fogg's usual partners at whist: Andrew Stuart, an engineer; John Sullivan and Samuel Fallentin, bankers; Thomas Flanagan, a brewer; and Gauthier Ralph, one of the Directors of the Bank of England – all rich and highly respectable personages, even in a club which comprises the princes of English trade and finance.

'Well, Ralph,' said Thomas Flanagan, 'what about that robbery?'

'Oh,' replied Stuart, 'the Bank will lose the money.'

'On the contrary,' broke in Ralph, 'I hope we may put our hands on the robber. Skilful detectives have been sent to all the principal ports of America and the Continent, and he'll be a clever fellow if he slips through their fingers.'

'But have you got the robber's description?' asked Stuart.

'In the first place, he is no robber at all,' returned Ralph, positively.

'What! a fellow who makes off with fifty-five thousand pounds, no robber?'

'No.'

'Perhaps he's a manufacturer, then.'

'The *Daily Telegraph* says that he is a gentleman.'

It was Phileas Fogg, whose head now emerged from behind his newspapers, who made this remark. He bowed to his friends, and entered into the conversation. The affair which formed its subject, and which was town talk, had occurred three days before at the Bank of England. A package of banknotes, to the value of fifty-five thousand pounds, had been taken from the principal cashier's table, that functionary being at the moment engaged in registering the receipt of three shillings and sixpence. Of course, he could not have his eyes everywhere. Let it be observed that the Bank of England reposes a touching confidence in the honesty of the public. There are neither guards nor gratings to protect its treasures; gold, silver, banknotes are freely exposed, at the mercy of the first comer. A keen observer of English customs relates that, being in one of the rooms of the Bank one day, he had the curiosity to examine a gold ingot weighing some seven or eight pounds. He took it up, scrutinised it, passed it to his neighbour, he to the next man, and so on until the ingot, going from hand to hand, was transferred to the end of a dark entry; nor did it return to its place for half an hour. Meanwhile, the cashier had not so much as raised his head. But in the present instance things had not gone so smoothly. The package of notes not being found when five o'clock sounded from the ponderous clock in the 'drawing office,' the amount was passed to the account of profit and loss. As soon as the robbery was discovered, picked detectives hastened off to Liverpool, Glasgow, Havre, Suez, Brindisi, New York, and other ports, inspired by the proffered reward of two thousand pounds, and five per cent. on the sum that might be recovered. Detectives were also charged with narrowly watching those who arrived at or left London by rail, and a judicial examination was at once entered upon.

There were real grounds for supposing, as the Daily Telegraph said, that the thief did not belong to a professional band. On the day of the robbery a well-dressed gentleman of polished manners, and with a well-to-do air, had been observed going to and fro in the paying room where the crime was committed. A description of him was easily procured and sent to the detectives; and some hopeful spirits, of whom Ralph was one, did not despair of his apprehension. The papers and clubs were full of the affair, and everywhere people were discussing the probabilities of a successful pursuit; and the Reform Club was especially agitated, several of its members being Bank officials.

Ralph would not concede that the work of the detectives was likely to be in vain, for he thought that the prize offered would greatly stimulate their zeal and activity. But Stuart was far from sharing this confidence; and, as they placed themselves at the whist-table, they continued to argue the matter. Stuart and Flanagan played together, while Phileas Fogg had Fallentin for his partner. As the game proceeded the conversation ceased, excepting between the rubbers, when it revived again.

'I maintain,' said Stuart, 'that the chances are in favour of the thief, who must be a shrewd fellow.'

'Well, but where can he fly to?' asked Ralph. 'No country is safe for him.'

'Pshaw!'

'Where could he go, then?'

'Oh, I don't know that. The world is big enough.'

'It was once,' said Phileas Fogg, in a low tone. 'Cut, sir,' he added, handing the cards to Thomas Flanagan.

The discussion fell during the rubber, after which Stuart took up its thread.

'What do you mean by "once"? Has the world grown smaller?'

'Certainly,' returned Ralph. 'I agree with Mr. Fogg. The world has grown smaller, since a man can now go round it ten times more quickly than a hundred years ago. And that is why the search for this thief will be more likely to succeed.'

'And also why the thief can get away more easily.'

'Be so good as to play, Mr. Stuart,' said Phileas Fogg.

But the incredulous Stuart was not convinced, and when the hand was finished, said eagerly: 'You have a strange way, Ralph, of proving that the world has grown smaller. So, because you can go round it in three months – '

'In eighty days,' interrupted Phileas Fogg.

'That is true, gentlemen,' added John Sullivan. 'Only eighty days, now that the section between Rothal and Allahabad, on the Great Indian Peninsula Railway, has been opened. Here is the estimate made by the Daily Telegraph:

From London to Suez via Mont Cenis and Brindisi, by rail and steamboats	*7 days*
From Suez to Bombay, by steamer	*13 "*
From Bombay to Calcutta, by rail	*3 "*
From Calcutta to Hong Kong, by steamer	*13 "*
From Hong Kong to Yokohama, by steamer	*6 "*
From Yokohama to San Francisco, by steamer	*22 "*
From San Francisco to New York, by rail	*7 "*
From New York to London, by steamer and rail	*9 "*
Total	*80 days.*

'Yes, in eighty days!' exclaimed Stuart, who in his excitement made a false deal. 'But that doesn't take into account bad weather, contrary winds, shipwrecks, railway accidents, and so on.'

'All included,' returned Phileas Fogg, continuing to play despite the discussion.

'But suppose the Hindoos or Indians pull up the rails,' replied Stuart; 'suppose they stop the trains, pillage the luggage-vans, and scalp the passengers!'

'All included,' calmly retorted Fogg; adding, as he threw down the cards, 'Two trumps.'

Stuart, whose turn it was to deal, gathered them up, and went on: 'You are right, theoretically, Mr. Fogg, but practically—'

'Practically also, Mr. Stuart.'

'I'd like to see you do it in eighty days.'

'It depends on you. Shall we go?'

'Heaven preserve me! But I would wager four thousand pounds that such a journey, made under these conditions, is impossible.'

'Quite possible, on the contrary,' returned Mr. Fogg.

'Well, make it, then!'

'The journey round the world in eighty days?'

'Yes.'

'I should like nothing better.'

'When?'

'At once. Only I warn you that I shall do it at your expense.'

'It's absurd!' cried Stuart, who was beginning to be annoyed at the persistency of his friend. 'Come, let's go on with the game.'

'Deal over again, then,' said Phileas Fogg. 'There's a false deal.'

Stuart took up the pack with a feverish hand; then suddenly put them down again.

'Well, Mr. Fogg,' said he, 'it shall be so: I will wager the four thousand on it.'

'Calm yourself, my dear Stuart,' said Fallentin. 'It's only a joke.'

'When I say I'll wager,' returned Stuart, 'I mean it.'

'All right,' said Mr. Fogg; and, turning to the others, he continued: 'I have a deposit of twenty thousand at Baring's which I will willingly risk upon it.'

'Twenty thousand pounds!' cried Sullivan. 'Twenty thousand pounds, which you would lose by a single accidental delay!'

'The unforeseen does not exist,' quietly replied Phileas Fogg.

'But, Mr. Fogg, eighty days are only the estimate of the least possible time in which the journey can be made.'

'A well-used minimum suffices for everything.'

'But, in order not to exceed it, you must jump mathematically from the trains upon the steamers, and from the steamers upon the trains again.'

'I will jump – mathematically.'

'You are joking.'

'A true Englishman doesn't joke when he is talking about so serious a thing as a wager,' replied Phileas Fogg, solemnly. 'I will bet twenty thousand pounds against anyone who wishes that I will make the tour of the world in eighty days or less; in nineteen hundred and twenty hours, or a hundred and fifteen thousand two hundred minutes. Do you accept?'

'We accept,' replied Messrs. Stuart, Fallentin, Sullivan, Flanagan, and Ralph, after consulting each other.

'Good,' said Mr. Fogg. 'The train leaves for Dover at a quarter before nine. I will take it.'

'This very evening?' asked Stuart.

'This very evening,' returned Phileas Fogg. He took out and consulted a pocket almanac, and added, 'As today is Wednesday, the 2nd of October, I shall be due in London in this very room of the Reform Club, on Saturday, the 21st of

December, at a quarter before nine p.m.; or else the twenty thousand pounds, now deposited in my name at Baring's, will belong to you, in fact and in right, gentlemen. Here is a cheque for the amount.'

A memorandum of the wager was at once drawn up and signed by the six parties, during which Phileas Fogg preserved a stoical composure. He certainly did not bet to win, and had only staked the twenty thousand pounds, half of his fortune, because he foresaw that he might have to expend the other half to carry out this difficult, not to say unattainable, project. As for his antagonists, they seemed much agitated; not so much by the value of their stake, as because they had some scruples about betting under conditions so difficult to their friend.

The clock struck seven, and the party offered to suspend the game so that Mr. Fogg might make his preparations for departure.

'I am quite ready now,' was his tranquil response. 'Diamonds are trumps: be so good as to play, gentlemen.'

CHAPTER 4

In which Phileas Fogg astounds Passepartout, his servant

Having won twenty guineas at whist, and taken leave of his friends, Phileas Fogg, at twenty-five minutes past seven, left the Reform Club.

Passepartout, who had conscientiously studied the programme of his duties, was more than surprised to see his master guilty of the inexactness of appearing at this unaccustomed hour; for, according to rule, he was not due in Savile Row until precisely midnight.

Mr. Fogg repaired to his bedroom, and called out, 'Passepartout!'

Passepartout did not reply. It could not be he who was called; it was not the right hour.

'Passepartout!' repeated Mr. Fogg, without raising his voice.

Passepartout made his appearance.

'I've called you twice,' observed his master.

'But it is not midnight,' responded the other, showing his watch.

'I know it; I don't blame you. We start for Dover and Calais in ten minutes.'

A puzzled grin overspread Passepartout's round face;

clearly he had not comprehended his master.

'Monsieur is going to leave home?'

'Yes,' returned Phileas Fogg. 'We are going round the world.'

Passepartout opened wide his eyes, raised his eyebrows, held up his hands, and seemed about to collapse, so overcome was he with stupefied astonishment.

'Round the world!' he murmured.

'In eighty days,' responded Mr. Fogg. 'So we haven't a moment to lose.'

'But the trunks?' gasped Passepartout, unconsciously swaying his head from right to left.

'We'll have no trunks; only a carpet-bag, with two shirts and three pairs of stockings for me, and the same for you. We'll buy our clothes on the way. Bring down my mackintosh and travelling-cloak, and some stout shoes, though we shall do little walking. Make haste!'

Passepartout tried to reply, but could not. He went out, mounted to his own room, fell into a chair, and muttered: 'That's good, that is! And I, who wanted to remain quiet!'

He mechanically set about making the preparations for departure. Around the world in eighty days! Was his master a fool? No. Was this a joke, then? They were going to Dover; good! To Calais; good again! After all, Passepartout, who had been away from France five years, would not be sorry to set foot on his native soil again. Perhaps they would go as far as Paris, and it would do his eyes good to see Paris once more. But surely a gentleman so chary of his steps would stop there; no doubt – but, then, it was none the less true that he was going away, this so domestic person hitherto!

By eight o'clock Passepartout had packed the modest carpet-bag, containing the wardrobes of his master and

CHAPTER 4

himself; then, still troubled in mind, he carefully shut the door of his room, and descended to Mr. Fogg.

Mr. Fogg was quite ready. Under his arm might have been observed a red-bound copy of Bradshaw's *Continental Railway Steam Transit and General Guide*, with its timetables showing the arrival and departure of steamers and railways. He took the carpet-bag, opened it, and slipped into it a goodly roll of Bank of England notes, which would pass wherever he might go.

'You have forgotten nothing?' asked he.

'Nothing, monsieur.'

'My mackintosh and cloak?'

'Here they are.'

'Good! Take this carpet-bag,' handing it to Passepartout. 'Take good care of it, for there are twenty thousand pounds in it.'

Passepartout nearly dropped the bag, as if the twenty thousand pounds were in gold, and weighed him down.

Master and man then descended, the street-door was double-locked, and at the end of Savile Row they took a cab and drove rapidly to Charing Cross. The cab stopped before the railway station at twenty minutes past eight. Passepartout jumped off the box and followed his master, who, after paying the cabman, was about to enter the station, when a poor beggar-woman, with a child in her arms, her naked feet smeared with mud, her head covered with a wretched bonnet, from which hung a tattered feather, and her shoulders shrouded in a ragged shawl, approached, and mournfully asked for alms.

Mr. Fogg took out the twenty guineas he had just won at whist, and handed them to the beggar, saying, 'Here, my good woman. I'm glad that I met you;' and passed on.

Passepartout had a moist sensation about the eyes; his master's action touched his susceptible heart.

Two first-class tickets for Paris having been speedily purchased, Mr. Fogg was crossing the station to the train, when he perceived his five friends of the Reform.

'Well, gentlemen,' said he, 'I'm off, you see; and, if you will examine my passport when I get back, you will be able to judge whether I have accomplished the journey agreed upon.'

'Oh, that would be quite unnecessary, Mr. Fogg,' said Ralph politely. 'We will trust your word, as a gentleman of honour.'

'You do not forget when you are due in London again?' asked Stuart.

'In eighty days; on Saturday, the 21st of December, 1872, at a quarter before nine p.m. Good-bye, gentlemen.'

Phileas Fogg and his servant seated themselves in a first-class carriage at twenty minutes before nine; five minutes later the whistle screamed, and the train slowly glided out of the station.

The night was dark, and a fine, steady rain was falling. Phileas Fogg, snugly ensconced in his corner, did not open his lips. Passepartout, not yet recovered from his stupefaction, clung mechanically to the carpet-bag, with its enormous treasure.

Just as the train was whirling through Sydenham, Passepartout suddenly uttered a cry of despair.

'What's the matter?' asked Mr. Fogg.

'Alas! In my hurry – I – I forgot – '

'What?'

'To turn off the gas in my room!'

'Very well, young man,' returned Mr. Fogg, coolly; 'it will burn – at your expense.'

CHAPTER 5

In which a new species of funds, unknown to the moneyed men, appears on 'Change

Phileas Fogg rightly suspected that his departure from London would create a lively sensation at the West End. The news of the bet spread through the Reform Club, and afforded an exciting topic of conversation to its members. From the club it soon got into the papers throughout England. The boasted 'tour of the world' was talked about, disputed, argued with as much warmth as if the subject were another Alabama claim. Some took sides with Phileas Fogg, but the large majority shook their heads and declared against him; it was absurd, impossible, they declared, that the tour of the world could be made, except theoretically and on paper, in this minimum of time, and with the existing means of travelling. The *Times*, *Standard*, *Morning Post*, and *Daily News*, and twenty other highly respectable newspapers scouted Mr. Fogg's project as madness; the *Daily Telegraph* alone hesitatingly supported him. People in general thought him a lunatic, and blamed his Reform Club friends for having accepted a wager which betrayed the mental aberration of its proposer.

Articles no less passionate than logical appeared on the

question, for geography is one of the pet subjects of the English; and the columns devoted to Phileas Fogg's venture were eagerly devoured by all classes of readers. At first some rash individuals, principally of the gentler sex, espoused his cause, which became still more popular when the *Illustrated London News* came out with his portrait, copied from a photograph in the Reform Club. A few readers of the *Daily Telegraph* even dared to say, 'Why not, after all? Stranger things have come to pass.'

At last a long article appeared, on the 7th of October, in the bulletin of the Royal Geographical Society, which treated the question from every point of view, and demonstrated the utter folly of the enterprise.

Everything, it said, was against the travellers, every obstacle imposed alike by man and by nature. A miraculous agreement of the times of departure and arrival, which was impossible, was absolutely necessary to his success. He might, perhaps, reckon on the arrival of trains at the designated hours, in Europe, where the distances were relatively moderate; but when he calculated upon crossing India in three days, and the United States in seven, could he rely beyond misgiving upon accomplishing his task? There were accidents to machinery, the liability of trains to run off the line, collisions, bad weather, the blocking up by snow – were not all these against Phileas Fogg? Would he not find himself, when travelling by steamer in winter, at the mercy of the winds and fogs? Is it uncommon for the best ocean steamers to be two or three days behind time? But a single delay would suffice to fatally break the chain of communication; should Phileas Fogg once miss, even by an hour; a steamer, he would have to wait for the next, and that would irrevocably render his attempt vain.

CHAPTER 5

This article made a great deal of noise, and, being copied into all the papers, seriously depressed the advocates of the rash tourist.

Everybody knows that England is the world of betting men, who are of a higher class than mere gamblers; to bet is in the English temperament. Not only the members of the Reform, but the general public, made heavy wagers for or against Phileas Fogg, who was set down in the betting books as if he were a race-horse. Bonds were issued, and made their appearance on 'Change; 'Phileas Fogg bonds' were offered at par or at a premium, and a great business was done in them. But five days after the article in the bulletin of the Geographical Society appeared, the demand began to subside: 'Phileas Fogg' declined. They were offered by packages, at first of five, then of ten, until at last nobody would take less than twenty, fifty, a hundred!

Lord Albemarle, an elderly paralytic gentleman, was now the only advocate of Phileas Fogg left. This noble lord, who was fastened to his chair, would have given his fortune to be able to make the tour of the world, if it took ten years; and he bet five thousand pounds on Phileas Fogg. When the folly as well as the uselessness of the adventure was pointed out to him, he contented himself with replying, 'If the thing is feasible, the first to do it ought to be an Englishman.'

The Fogg party dwindled more and more, everybody was going against him, and the bets stood a hundred and fifty and two hundred to one; and a week after his departure an incident occurred which deprived him of backers at any price.

The commissioner of police was sitting in his office at nine o'clock one evening, when the following telegraphic dispatch was put into his hands:

Suez to London.
Rowan, Commissioner of Police, Scotland Yard:
I've found the bank robber, Phileas Fogg. Send with out delay warrant of arrest to Bombay.
Fix, Detective.

The effect of this dispatch was instantaneous. The polished gentleman disappeared to give place to the bank robber. His photograph, which was hung with those of the rest of the members at the Reform Club, was minutely examined, and it betrayed, feature by feature, the description of the robber which had been provided to the police. The mysterious habits of Phileas Fogg were recalled; his solitary ways, his sudden departure; and it seemed clear that, in undertaking a tour round the world on the pretext of a wager, he had had no other end in view than to elude the detectives, and throw them off his track.

CHAPTER 6

In which Fix, the detective, betrays a very natural impatience

The circumstances under which this telegraphic dispatch about Phileas Fogg was sent were as follows:

The steamer *Mongolia*, belonging to the Peninsular and Oriental Company, built of iron, of two thousand eight hundred tons burden, and five hundred horse-power, was due at eleven o'clock a.m. on Wednesday, the 9th of October, at Suez. The *Mongolia* plied regularly between Brindisi and Bombay via the Suez Canal, and was one of the fastest steamers belonging to the company, always making more than ten knots an hour between Brindisi and Suez, and nine and a half between Suez and Bombay.

Two men were promenading up and down the wharves, among the crowd of natives and strangers who were sojourning at this once straggling village – now, thanks to the enterprise of M. Lesseps, a fast-growing town. One was the British consul at Suez, who, despite the prophecies of the English Government, and the unfavourable predictions of Stephenson, was in the habit of seeing, from his office window, English ships daily passing to and fro on the great canal, by which the old roundabout route from England to India by the Cape of Good Hope was abridged by at least a half. The other was a small, slight-built personage, with a nervous, intelligent face, and bright eyes peering out from under eyebrows which he was incessantly twitching. He was just now manifesting unmistakable signs of impatience, nervously pacing up and down, and unable to stand still for a moment. This was Fix, one of the detectives who had been dispatched from England in search of the bank robber; it was his task to narrowly watch every passenger who arrived at Suez, and to follow up all who seemed to be suspicious characters, or bore a resemblance to the description of the criminal, which he had received two days before from the police headquarters at London. The detective was evidently inspired by the hope of obtaining the splendid reward which would be the prize of success, and awaited with a feverish impatience, easy to understand, the arrival of the steamer *Mongolia*.

'So you say, consul,' asked he for the twentieth time, 'that this steamer is never behind time?'

'No, Mr. Fix,' replied the consul. 'She was bespoken yesterday at Port Said, and the rest of the way is of no account to such a craft. I repeat that the *Mongolia* has been in advance of the time required by the company's regulations, and gained the prize awarded for excess of speed.'

'Does she come directly from Brindisi?'

'Directly from Brindisi; she takes on the Indian mails there, and she left there Saturday at five p.m. Have patience, Mr. Fix; she will not be late. But really, I don't see how, from the description you have, you will be able to recognise your man, even if he is on board the *Mongolia*.'

'A man rather feels the presence of these fellows, consul, than recognises them. You must have a scent for them, and a scent is like a sixth sense which combines hearing, seeing, and smelling. I've arrested more than one of these gentlemen in my time, and, if my thief is on board, I'll answer for it; he'll not slip through my fingers.'

'I hope so, Mr. Fix, for it was a heavy robbery.'

'A magnificent robbery, consul; fifty-five thousand pounds! We don't often have such windfalls. Burglars are getting to be so contemptible nowadays! A fellow gets hung for a handful of shillings!'

'Mr. Fix,' said the consul, 'I like your way of talking, and hope you'll succeed; but I fear you will find it far from easy. Don't you see, the description which you have there has a singular resemblance to an honest man?'

'Consul,' remarked the detective, dogmatically, 'great robbers always resemble honest folks. Fellows who have rascally faces have only one course to take, and that is to remain honest; otherwise they would be arrested off-hand. The artistic thing is, to unmask honest countenances; it's no light task, I admit, but a real art.'

Mr. Fix evidently was not wanting in a tinge of self-conceit.

Little by little the scene on the quay became more animated; sailors of various nations, merchants, ship-brokers, porters, fellahs, bustled to and fro as if the steamer were immediately expected. The weather was clear, and slightly chilly. The minarets of the town loomed above the houses in the pale rays of the sun. A jetty pier, some two thousand yards along, extended into the roadstead. A number of fishing-smacks and coasting boats, some retaining the fantastic fashion of ancient galleys, were discernible on the Red Sea.

As he passed among the busy crowd, Fix, according to habit, scrutinised the passers-by with a keen, rapid glance.

It was now half-past ten.

'The steamer doesn't come!' he exclaimed, as the port clock struck.

'She can't be far off now,' returned his companion.

'How long will she stop at Suez?'

'Four hours; long enough to get in her coal. It is thirteen hundred and ten miles from Suez to Aden, at the other end of the Red Sea, and she has to take in a fresh coal supply.'

'And does she go from Suez directly to Bombay?'

'Without putting in anywhere.'

'Good!' said Fix. 'If the robber is on board he will no doubt get off at Suez, so as to reach the Dutch or French colonies in Asia by some other route. He ought to know that he would not be safe an hour in India, which is English soil.'

'Unless,' objected the consul, 'he is exceptionally shrewd. An English criminal, you know, is always better concealed in London than anywhere else.'

This observation furnished the detective food for thought, and meanwhile the consul went away to his office. Fix, left alone, was more impatient than ever, having a presentiment that the robber was on board the *Mongolia*. If he had indeed left London intending to reach the New World, he would naturally take the route via India, which was less watched and more difficult to watch than that of the Atlantic. But Fix's reflections were soon interrupted by a succession of sharp whistles, which announced the arrival of the *Mongolia*. The porters and fellahs rushed down the quay, and a dozen boats pushed off from the shore to go and meet the steamer. Soon her gigantic hull appeared passing along between the banks, and eleven o'clock struck as she anchored in the road. She brought an unusual number of passengers, some of whom remained on deck to scan the picturesque panorama of the town, while the greater part disembarked in the boats, and landed on the quay.

CHAPTER 6

Fix took up a position, and carefully examined each face and figure which made its appearance. Presently one of the passengers, after vigorously pushing his way through the importunate crowd of porters, came up to him and politely asked if he could point out the English consulate, at the same time showing a passport which he wished to have visaed. Fix instinctively took the passport, and with a rapid glance read the description of its bearer. An involuntary motion of surprise nearly escaped him, for the description in the passport was identical with that of the bank robber which he had received from Scotland Yard.

'Is this your passport?' asked he.

'No, it's my master's.'

'And your master is – '

'He stayed on board.'

'But he must go to the consul's in person, so as to establish his identity.'

'Oh, is that necessary?'

'Quite indispensable.'

'And where is the consulate?'

'There, on the corner of the square,' said Fix, pointing to a house two hundred steps off.

'I'll go and fetch my master, who won't be much pleased, however, to be disturbed.'

The passenger bowed to Fix, and returned to the steamer.

CHAPTER 7

Which once more demonstrates the uselessness of passports as aids to detectives

The detective passed down the quay, and rapidly made his way to the consul's office, where he was at once admitted to the presence of that official.

'Consul,' said he, without preamble, 'I have strong reasons for believing that my man is a passenger on the *Mongolia*.' And he narrated what had just passed concerning the passport.

'Well, Mr. Fix,' replied the consul, 'I shall not be sorry to see the rascal's face; but perhaps he won't come here – that is, if he is the person you suppose him to be. A robber doesn't quite like to leave traces of his flight behind him; and, besides, he is not obliged to have his passport countersigned.'

'If he is as shrewd as I think he is, consul, he will come.'

'To have his passport visaed?'

'Yes. Passports are only good for annoying honest folks, and aiding in the flight of rogues. I assure you it will be quite the thing for him to do; but I hope you will not visa the passport.'

'Why not? If the passport is genuine I have no right to refuse.'

'Still, I must keep this man here until I can get a warrant to arrest him from London.'

'Ah, that's your look-out. But I cannot – '

The consul did not finish his sentence, for as he spoke a knock was heard at the door, and two strangers entered, one of whom was the servant whom Fix had met on the quay. The other, who was his master, held out his passport with the request that the consul would do him the favour to visa it. The consul took the document and carefully read it, whilst Fix observed, or rather devoured, the stranger with his eyes from a corner of the room.

'You are Mr. Phileas Fogg?' said the consul, after reading the passport.

'I am.'

'And this man is your servant?'

'He is: a Frenchman, named Passepartout.'

'You are from London?'

'Yes.'

'And you are going – '

'To Bombay.'

'Very good, sir. You know that a visa is useless, and that no passport is required?'

'I know it, sir,' replied Phileas Fogg; 'but I wish to prove, by your visa, that I came by Suez.'

'Very well, sir.'

The consul proceeded to sign and date the passport, after which he added his official seal. Mr. Fogg paid the customary fee, coldly bowed, and went out, followed by his servant.

'Well?' queried the detective.

'Well, he looks and acts like a perfectly honest man,' replied the consul.

'Possibly; but that is not the question. Do you think, consul, that this phlegmatic gentleman resembles, feature by feature, the robber whose description I have received?'

'I concede that; but then, you know, all descriptions – '

'I'll make certain of it,' interrupted Fix. 'The servant seems to me less mysterious than the master; besides, he's a Frenchman, and can't help talking. Excuse me for a little while, consul.'

Fix started off in search of Passepartout.

Meanwhile Mr. Fogg, after leaving the consulate, repaired to the quay, gave some orders to Passepartout, went off to the *Mongolia* in a boat, and descended to his cabin. He took up his note-book, which contained the following memoranda:

'Left London, Wednesday, October 2nd, at 8.45 p.m.

'Reached Paris, Thursday, October 3rd, at 7.20 a.m.

'Left Paris, Thursday, at 8.40 a.m.

'Reached Turin by Mont Cenis, Friday, October 4th, at 6.35 a.m.

'Left Turin, Friday, at 7.20 a.m.

'Arrived at Brindisi, Saturday, October 5th, at 4 p.m.

'Sailed on the *Mongolia*, Saturday, at 5 p.m.

'Reached Suez, Wednesday, October 9th, at 11 a.m.

'Total of hours spent, 158+; or, in days, six days and a half.'

These dates were inscribed in an itinerary divided into columns, indicating the month, the day of the month, and the day for the stipulated and actual arrivals at each principal point Paris, Brindisi, Suez, Bombay, Calcutta, Singapore, Hong Kong, Yokohama, San Francisco, New York, and London – from the 2nd of October to the 21st of December; and giving a space for setting down the gain made or the loss suffered on arrival at each locality. This methodical record thus contained an account of everything needed, and Mr. Fogg always knew whether he was behind-hand or in advance of his time. On this Friday, October 9th, he noted his arrival at Suez, and observed that he had as yet neither gained nor lost. He sat down quietly to breakfast in his cabin, never once thinking of inspecting the town, being one of those Englishmen who are wont to see foreign countries through the eyes of their domestics.

CHAPTER 8

In which Passepartout talks rather more, perhaps, than is prudent

Fix soon rejoined Passepartout, who was lounging and looking about on the quay, as if he did not feel that he, at least, was obliged not to see anything.

'Well, my friend,' said the detective, coming up with him, 'is your passport visaed?'

'Ah, it's you, is it, monsieur?' responded Passepartout. 'Thanks, yes, the passport is all right.'

'And you are looking about you?'

'Yes; but we travel so fast that I seem to be journeying in a dream. So this is Suez?'

'Yes.'

'In Egypt?'

'Certainly, in Egypt.'

'And in Africa?'

'In Africa.'

'In Africa!' repeated Passepartout. 'Just think, monsieur, I had no idea that we should go farther than Paris; and all that I saw of Paris was between twenty minutes past seven and twenty minutes before nine in the morning, between the

Northern and the Lyons stations, through the windows of a car, and in a driving rain! How I regret not having seen once more Pere la Chaise and the circus in the Champs Elysees!'

'You are in a great hurry, then?'

'I am not, but my master is. By the way, I must buy some shoes and shirts. We came away without trunks, only with a carpet-bag.'

'I will show you an excellent shop for getting what you want.'

'Really, monsieur, you are very kind.'

And they walked off together, Passepartout chatting volubly as they went along.

'Above all,' said he; 'don't let me lose the steamer.'

'You have plenty of time; it's only twelve o'clock.'

Passepartout pulled out his big watch. 'Twelve!' he exclaimed; 'why, it's only eight minutes before ten.'

'Your watch is slow.'

'My watch? A family watch, monsieur, which has come down from my great-grandfather! It doesn't vary five minutes in the year. It's a perfect chronometer, look you.'

'I see how it is,' said Fix. 'You have kept London time, which is two hours behind that of Suez. You ought to regulate your watch at noon in each country.'

'I regulate my watch? Never!'

'Well, then, it will not agree with the sun.'

'So much the worse for the sun, monsieur. The sun will be wrong, then!'

And the worthy fellow returned the watch to its fob with a defiant gesture. After a few minutes silence, Fix resumed: 'You left London hastily, then?'

'I rather think so! Last Friday at eight o'clock in the evening, Monsieur Fogg came home from his club, and three-quarters of an hour afterwards we were off.'

'But where is your master going?'

'Always straight ahead. He is going round the world.'

'Round the world?' cried Fix.

'Yes, and in eighty days! He says it is on a wager; but, between us, I don't believe a word of it. That wouldn't be common sense. There's something else in the wind.'

'Ah! Mr. Fogg is a character, is he?'

'I should say he was.'

'Is he rich?'

'No doubt, for he is carrying an enormous sum in brand new banknotes with him. And he doesn't spare the money on the way, either: he has offered a large reward to the engineer of the *Mongolia* if he gets us to Bombay well in advance of time.'

'And you have known your master a long time?'

'Why, no; I entered his service the very day we left London.'

The effect of these replies upon the already suspicious and excited detective may be imagined. The hasty departure from London soon after the robbery; the large sum carried by Mr. Fogg; his eagerness to reach distant countries; the pretext of an eccentric and foolhardy bet – all confirmed Fix in his theory. He continued to pump poor Passepartout, and learned that he really knew little or nothing of his master, who lived a solitary existence in London, was said to be rich, though no one knew whence came his riches, and was mysterious and impenetrable in his affairs and habits. Fix felt sure that Phileas Fogg would not land at Suez, but was really going on to Bombay.

'Is Bombay far from here?' asked Passepartout.

'Pretty far. It is a ten days' voyage by sea.'

'And in what country is Bombay?'

'India.'

'In Asia?'

'Certainly.'

'The deuce! I was going to tell you there's one thing that worries me – my burner!'

'What burner?'

'My gas-burner, which I forgot to turn off, and which is at this moment burning at my expense. I have calculated, monsieur, that I lose two shillings every four and twenty hours, exactly sixpence more than I earn; and you will understand that the longer our journey – '

Did Fix pay any attention to Passepartout's trouble about the gas? It is not probable. He was not listening, but was cogitating a project. Passepartout and he had now reached the shop, where Fix left his companion to make his purchases, after recommending him not to miss the steamer, and hurried back to the consulate. Now that he was fully convinced, Fix had quite recovered his equanimity.

'Consul,' said he, 'I have no longer any doubt. I have spotted my man. He passes himself off as an odd stick who is going round the world in eighty days.'

'Then he's a sharp fellow,' returned the consul, 'and counts on returning to London after putting the police of the two countries off his track.'

'We'll see about that,' replied Fix.

'But are you not mistaken?'

'I am not mistaken.'

'Why was this robber so anxious to prove, by the visa, that he had passed through Suez?'

'Why? I have no idea; but listen to me.'

He reported in a few words the most important parts of his conversation with Passepartout.

'In short,' said the consul, 'appearances are wholly against this man. And what are you going to do?'

'Send a dispatch to London for a warrant of arrest to be dispatched instantly to Bombay, take passage on board the *Mongolia*, follow my rogue to India, and there, on English ground, arrest him politely, with my warrant in my hand, and my hand on his shoulder.'

Having uttered these words with a cool, careless air, the detective took leave of the consul, and repaired to the telegraph office, whence he sent the dispatch which we have seen to the London police office. A quarter of an hour later found Fix, with a small bag in his hand, proceeding on board the *Mongolia*; and, ere many moments longer, the noble steamer rode out at full steam upon the waters of the Red Sea.

CHAPTER 9

In which the Red Sea and the Indian Ocean prove propitious to the designs of Phileas Fogg

The distance between Suez and Aden is precisely thirteen hundred and ten miles, and the regulations of the company allow the steamers one hundred and thirty-eight hours in which to traverse it. The *Mongolia*, thanks to the vigorous exertions of the engineer, seemed likely, so rapid was her speed, to reach her destination considerably within that time. The greater part of the passengers from Brindisi were bound for India some for Bombay, others for Calcutta by way of Bombay, the nearest route thither, now that a railway crosses the Indian peninsula. Among the passengers was a number of officials and military officers of various grades, the latter being either attached to the regular British forces or commanding the Sepoy troops, and receiving high salaries ever since the central government has assumed the powers of the East India Company: for the sub-lieutenants get 280 pounds, brigadiers, 2,400 pounds, and generals of divisions, 4,000 pounds. What with the military men, a number of rich young Englishmen on their travels, and the hospitable efforts of the purser, the time passed quickly on the *Mongolia*. The best of fare was spread upon the cabin tables at breakfast, lunch, dinner, and the eight o'clock supper, and the ladies scrupulously changed their toilets twice a day; and the hours were whirled away, when the sea was tranquil, with music, dancing, and games.

But the Red Sea is full of caprice, and often boisterous, like most long and narrow gulfs. When the wind came from the African or Asian coast the *Mongolia*, with her long hull, rolled fearfully. Then the ladies speedily disappeared below; the pianos were silent; singing and dancing suddenly ceased. Yet the good ship ploughed straight on, unretarded by wind or wave, towards the straits of Bab-el-Mandeb. What was Phileas Fogg doing all this time? It might be thought that, in his anxiety, he would be constantly watching the changes of the wind, the disorderly raging of the billows – every chance, in short, which might force the *Mongolia* to slacken her speed, and thus interrupt his journey. But, if he thought of these possibilities, he did not betray the fact by any outward sign.

Always the same impassible member of the Reform Club, whom no incident could surprise, as unvarying as the ship's chronometers, and seldom having the curiosity even to go upon the deck, he passed through the memorable scenes of the Red Sea with cold indifference; did not care to recognise the historic towns and villages which, along its borders, raised their picturesque outlines against the sky; and betrayed no fear of the dangers of the Arabic Gulf, which the old historians always spoke of with horror, and upon which the ancient navigators never ventured without propitiating the gods by ample sacrifices. How did this eccentric personage pass his time on the *Mongolia*? He made his four hearty meals every day, regardless of the most persistent rolling and pitching on the part of the steamer; and he played whist indefatigably, for he had found partners as enthusiastic in the game as himself. A tax-collector, on the way to his post at Goa; the Rev. Decimus Smith, returning to his parish at Bombay; and a brigadier-general of the English army, who was about to rejoin his brigade at Benares, made up the party, and, with Mr. Fogg, played whist by the hour together in absorbing silence.

As for Passepartout, he, too, had escaped sea-sickness, and took his meals conscientiously in the forward cabin. He rather enjoyed the voyage, for he was well fed and well lodged, took a great interest in the scenes through which they were passing, and consoled himself with the delusion that his master's whim would end at Bombay. He was pleased, on the day after leaving Suez, to find on deck the obliging person with whom he had walked and chatted on the quays.

'If I am not mistaken,' said he, approaching this person, with his most amiable smile, 'you are the gentleman who so kindly volunteered to guide me at Suez?'

'Ah! I quite recognise you. You are the servant of the strange Englishman – '

'Just so, monsieur – '

'Fix.'

'Monsieur Fix,' resumed Passepartout, 'I'm charmed to find you on board. Where are you bound?'

'Like you, to Bombay.'

'That's capital! Have you made this trip before?'

'Several times. I am one of the agents of the Peninsular Company.'

'Then you know India?'

'Why yes,' replied Fix, who spoke cautiously.

'A curious place, this India?'

'Oh, very curious. Mosques, minarets, temples, fakirs,

pagodas, tigers, snakes, elephants! I hope you will have ample time to see the sights.'

'I hope so, Monsieur Fix. You see, a man of sound sense ought not to spend his life jumping from a steamer upon a railway train, and from a railway train upon a steamer again, pretending to make the tour of the world in eighty days! No; all these gymnastics, you may be sure, will cease at Bombay.'

'And Mr. Fogg is getting on well?' asked Fix, in the most natural tone in the world.

'Quite well, and I too. I eat like a famished ogre; it's the sea air.'

'But I never see your master on deck.'

'Never; he hasn't the least curiosity.'

'Do you know, Mr. Passepartout, that this pretended tour in eighty days may conceal some secret errand – perhaps a diplomatic mission?'

'Faith, Monsieur Fix, I assure you I know nothing about it, nor would I give half a crown to find out.'

After this meeting, Passepartout and Fix got into the habit of chatting together, the latter making it a point to gain the worthy man's confidence. He frequently offered him a glass of whiskey or pale ale in the steamer bar-room, which Passepartout never failed to accept with graceful alacrity, mentally pronouncing Fix the best of good fellows.

Meanwhile the *Mongolia* was pushing forward rapidly; on the 13th, Mocha, surrounded by its ruined walls whereon date-trees were growing, was sighted, and on the mountains beyond were espied vast coffee-fields. Passepartout was ravished to behold this celebrated place, and thought that, with its circular walls and dismantled fort, it looked like an immense coffee-cup and saucer. The following night they passed through the Strait of Bab-el-Mandeb, which means in

Arabic The Bridge of Tears, and the next day they put in at Steamer Point, north-west of Aden harbour, to take in coal. This matter of fuelling steamers is a serious one at such distances from the coal-mines; it costs the Peninsular Company some eight hundred thousand pounds a year. In these distant seas, coal is worth three or four pounds sterling a ton.

The *Mongolia* had still sixteen hundred and fifty miles to traverse before reaching Bombay, and was obliged to remain four hours at Steamer Point to coal up. But this delay, as it was foreseen, did not affect Phileas Fogg's programme; besides, the *Mongolia*, instead of reaching Aden on the morning of the 15th, when she was due, arrived there on the evening of the 14th, a gain of fifteen hours.

Mr. Fogg and his servant went ashore at Aden to have the passport again visaed; Fix, unobserved, followed them. The visa procured, Mr. Fogg returned on board to resume his former habits; while Passepartout, according to custom, sauntered about among the mixed population of Somalis, Banyans, Parsees, Jews, Arabs, and Europeans who comprise the twenty-five thousand inhabitants of Aden. He gazed with wonder upon the fortifications which make this place the Gibraltar of the Indian Ocean, and the vast cisterns where the English engineers were still at work, two thousand years after the engineers of Solomon.

'Very curious, very curious,' said Passepartout to himself, on returning to the steamer. 'I see that it is by no means useless to travel, if a man wants to see something new.' At six p.m. the *Mongolia* slowly moved out of the roadstead, and was soon once more on the Indian Ocean. She had a hundred and sixty-eight hours in which to reach Bombay, and the sea was favourable, the wind being in the north-west, and all sails aiding the engine. The steamer rolled but little, the ladies, in fresh toilets, reappeared on deck, and the singing and dancing were resumed. The trip was being accomplished most successfully, and Passepartout was enchanted with the congenial companion which chance had secured him in the person of the delightful Fix. On Sunday, October 20th, towards noon, they came in sight of the Indian coast: two hours later the pilot came on board. A range of hills lay against the sky in the horizon, and soon the rows of palms which adorn Bombay came distinctly into view. The steamer entered the road formed by the islands in the bay, and at half-past four she hauled up at the quays of Bombay.

Phileas Fogg was in the act of finishing the thirty-third rubber of the voyage, and his partner and himself having, by a bold stroke, captured all thirteen of the tricks, concluded this fine campaign with a brilliant victory.

The *Mongolia* was due at Bombay on the 22nd; she arrived on the 20th. This was a gain to Phileas Fogg of two days since his departure from London, and he calmly entered the fact in the itinerary, in the column of gains.

CHAPTER 10

In which Passepartout is only too glad to get off with the loss of his shoes

Everybody knows that the great reversed triangle of land, with its base in the north and its apex in the south, which is called India, embraces fourteen hundred thousand square miles, upon which is spread unequally a population of one hundred and eighty millions of souls. The British Crown exercises a real and despotic dominion over the larger portion of this vast country, and has a governor-general stationed at Calcutta, governors at Madras, Bombay, and in Bengal, and a lieutenant-governor at Agra.

But British India, properly so called, only embraces seven hundred thousand square miles, and a population of from one hundred to one hundred and ten millions of inhabitants. A considerable portion of India is still free from British authority; and there are certain ferocious rajahs in the interior who are absolutely independent. The celebrated East India Company was all-powerful from 1756, when the English first gained a foothold on the spot where now stands the city of Madras, down to the time of the great Sepoy insurrection. It gradually annexed province after province, purchasing them of the native chiefs, whom it seldom paid, and appointed the governor-general and his subordinates, civil and military. But the East India Company has now passed away, leaving the British possessions in India directly under the control of the Crown. The aspect of the country, as well as the manners and distinctions of race, is daily changing.

Formerly one was obliged to travel in India by the old cumbrous methods of going on foot or on horseback, in palanquins or unwieldy coaches; now fast steamboats ply on the Indus and the Ganges, and a great railway, with branch lines joining the main line at many points on its route, traverses the peninsula from Bombay to Calcutta in three days. This railway does not run in a direct line across India. The distance between Bombay and Calcutta, as the bird flies, is only from one thousand to eleven hundred miles; but the deflections of the road increase this distance by more than a third.

The general route of the Great Indian Peninsula Railway is as follows: Leaving Bombay, it passes through Salcette, crossing to the continent opposite Tannah, goes over the chain of the Western Ghauts, runs thence north-east as far as Burhampoor, skirts the nearly independent territory of Bundelcund, ascends to Allahabad, turns thence eastwardly, meeting the Ganges at Benares, then departs from the river a little, and, descending south-eastward by Burdivan and the French town of Chandernagor, has its terminus at Calcutta.

The passengers of the *Mongolia* went ashore at half-past four p.m.; at exactly eight the train would start for Calcutta.

Mr. Fogg, after bidding good-bye to his whist partners, left the steamer, gave his servant several errands to do, urged it upon him to be at the station promptly at eight, and, with his regular step, which beat to the second, like an astronomical clock, directed his steps to the passport office. As for the wonders of Bombay – its famous city hall, its splendid library, its forts and docks, its bazaars, mosques, synagogues, its Armenian churches, and the noble pagoda on Malabar Hill, with its two polygonal towers – he cared not a straw to see them. He would not deign to examine even the masterpieces of Elephanta, or the mysterious hypogea, concealed south-east from the docks, or those fine remains of Buddhist architecture, the Kanherian grottoes of the island of Salcette.

Having transacted his business at the passport office, Phileas Fogg repaired quietly to the railway station, where he ordered dinner. Among the dishes served up to him, the landlord especially recommended a certain giblet of 'native rabbit,' on which he prided himself.

Mr. Fogg accordingly tasted the dish, but, despite its spiced sauce, found it far from palatable. He rang for the landlord, and, on his appearance, said, fixing his clear eyes upon him, 'Is this rabbit, sir?'

'Yes, my lord,' the rogue boldly replied, 'rabbit from the jungles.'

'And this rabbit did not mew when he was killed?'

'Mew, my lord! What, a rabbit mew! I swear to you – '

'Be so good, landlord, as not to swear, but remember this: cats were formerly considered, in India, as sacred animals. That was a good time.'

'For the cats, my lord?'

'Perhaps for the travellers as well!'

After which Mr. Fogg quietly continued his dinner. Fix had gone on shore shortly after Mr. Fogg, and his first destination was the headquarters of the Bombay police. He made himself known as a London detective, told his business at Bombay, and the position of affairs relative to the supposed robber, and nervously asked if a warrant had arrived from

London. It had not reached the office; indeed, there had not yet been time for it to arrive. Fix was sorely disappointed, and tried to obtain an order of arrest from the director of the Bombay police. This the director refused, as the matter concerned the London office, which alone could legally deliver the warrant. Fix did not insist, and was fain to resign himself to await the arrival of the important document; but he was determined not to lose sight of the mysterious rogue as long as he stayed in Bombay. He did not doubt for a moment, any more than Passepartout, that Phileas Fogg would remain there, at least until it was time for the warrant to arrive.

Passepartout, however, had no sooner heard his master's orders on leaving the *Mongolia* than he saw at once that they were to leave Bombay as they had done Suez and Paris, and that the journey would be extended at least as far as Calcutta, and perhaps beyond that place. He began to ask himself if this bet that Mr. Fogg talked about was not really in good earnest, and whether his fate was not in truth forcing him, despite his love of repose, around the world in eighty days!

Having purchased the usual quota of shirts and shoes, he took a leisurely promenade about the streets, where crowds of people of many nationalities – Europeans, Persians with pointed caps, Banyas with round turbans, Sindes with square bonnets, Parsees with black mitres, and long-robed Armenians – were collected. It happened to be the day of a Parsee festival. These descendants of the sect of Zoroaster – the most thrifty, civilised, intelligent, and austere of the East Indians, among whom are counted the richest native merchants of Bombay – were celebrating a sort of religious carnival, with processions and shows, in the midst of which Indian dancing-girls, clothed in rose-coloured gauze, looped up with gold and silver, danced airily, but with perfect modesty, to the sound of viols and the clanging of tambourines. It is needless to say that Passepartout watched these curious ceremonies with staring eyes and gaping mouth, and that his countenance was that of the greenest booby imaginable.

Unhappily for his master, as well as himself, his curiosity drew him unconsciously farther off than he intended to go. At last, having seen the Parsee carnival wind away in the distance, he was turning his steps towards the station, when he happened to espy the splendid pagoda on Malabar Hill, and was seized with an irresistible desire to see its interior. He was quite ignorant that it is forbidden to Christians to enter certain Indian temples, and that even the faithful must not go in without first leaving their shoes outside the door. It may be said here that the wise policy of the British Government severely punishes a disregard of the practices of the native religions.

Passepartout, however, thinking no harm, went in like a simple tourist, and was soon lost in admiration of the splendid Brahmin ornamentation which everywhere met his eyes, when of a sudden he found himself sprawling on the sacred flagging. He looked up to behold three enraged priests, who forthwith fell upon him; tore off his shoes, and began to beat him with loud, savage exclamations. The agile Frenchman was soon upon his feet again, and lost no time in knocking down two of his long-gowned adversaries with his fists and a vigorous application of his toes; then, rushing out of the pagoda as fast as his legs could carry him, he soon escaped the third priest by mingling with the crowd in the streets.

At five minutes before eight, Passepartout, hatless, shoeless, and having in the squabble lost his package of shirts and shoes, rushed breathlessly into the station.

Fix, who had followed Mr. Fogg to the station, and saw that he was really going to leave Bombay, was there, upon the platform. He had resolved to follow the supposed robber to Calcutta, and farther, if necessary. Passepartout did not observe the detective, who stood in an obscure corner; but Fix heard him relate his adventures in a few words to Mr. Fogg.

'I hope that this will not happen again,' said Phileas Fogg coldly, as he got into the train. Poor Passepartout, quite crestfallen, followed his master without a word. Fix was on the point of entering another carriage, when an idea struck him which induced him to alter his plan.

'No, I'll stay,' muttered he. 'An offence has been committed on Indian soil. I've got my man.'

Just then the locomotive gave a sharp screech, and the train passed out into the darkness of the night.

CHAPTER 11

In which Phileas Fogg secures a curious means of conveyance at a fabulous price

The train had started punctually. Among the passengers were a number of officers, Government officials, and opium and indigo merchants, whose business called them to the eastern coast. Passepartout rode in the same carriage with his master, and a third passenger occupied a seat opposite to them. This was Sir Francis Cromarty, one of Mr. Fogg's whist partners on the *Mongolia*, now on his way to join his corps at Benares. Sir Francis was a tall, fair man of fifty, who had greatly distinguished himself in the last Sepoy revolt. He made India his home, only paying brief visits to England at rare intervals; and was almost as familiar as a native with the customs, history, and character of India and its people. But Phileas Fogg, who was not travelling, but only describing a circumference, took no pains to inquire into these subjects; he was a solid body, traversing an orbit around the terrestrial globe, according to the laws of rational mechanics. He was at this moment calculating in his mind the number of hours spent since his departure from London, and, had it been in his nature to make a useless demonstration, would have rubbed his hands for satisfaction. Sir Francis Cromarty had observed the oddity of his travelling companion – although the only opportunity he had for studying him had been while he was dealing the cards, and between two rubbers – and questioned himself whether a human heart really beat beneath this cold exterior, and whether Phileas Fogg had any sense of the beauties of nature. The brigadier-general was free to mentally confess that, of all the eccentric persons he had ever met, none was comparable to this product of the exact sciences.

Phileas Fogg had not concealed from Sir Francis his design of going round the world, nor the circumstances under which he set out; and the general only saw in the wager a useless eccentricity and a lack of sound common sense. In the way this strange gentleman was going on, he would leave the world without having done any good to himself or anybody else.

An hour after leaving Bombay the train had passed the viaducts and the Island of Salcette, and had got into the open country. At Callyan they reached the junction of the branch line which descends towards south-eastern India by Kandallah and Pounah; and, passing Pauwell, they entered the defiles of the mountains, with their basalt bases, and their summits crowned with thick and verdant forests. Phileas Fogg and Sir Francis Cromarty exchanged a few words from time to time, and now Sir Francis, reviving the conversation, observed, 'Some years ago, Mr. Fogg, you would have met with a delay at this point which would probably have lost you your wager.'

'How so, Sir Francis?'

'Because the railway stopped at the base of these mountains, which the passengers were obliged to cross in palanquins or on ponies to Kandallah, on the other side.'

'Such a delay would not have deranged my plans in the

least,' said Mr. Fogg. 'I have constantly foreseen the likelihood of certain obstacles.'

'But, Mr. Fogg,' pursued Sir Francis, 'you run the risk of having some difficulty about this worthy fellow's adventure at the pagoda.' Passepartout, his feet comfortably wrapped in his travelling-blanket, was sound asleep and did not dream that anybody was talking about him. 'The Government is very severe upon that kind of offence. It takes particular care that the religious customs of the Indians should be respected, and if your servant were caught – '

'Very well, Sir Francis,' replied Mr. Fogg; 'if he had been caught he would have been condemned and punished, and then would have quietly returned to Europe. I don't see how this affair could have delayed his master.'

The conversation fell again. During the night the train left the mountains behind, and passed Nassik, and the next day proceeded over the flat, well-cultivated country of the Khandeish, with its straggling villages, above which rose the minarets of the pagodas. This fertile territory is watered by numerous small rivers and limpid streams, mostly tributaries of the Godavery.

Passepartout, on waking and looking out, could not realise that he was actually crossing India in a railway train. The locomotive, guided by an English engineer and fed with English coal, threw out its smoke upon cotton, coffee, nutmeg, clove, and pepper plantations, while the steam curled in spirals around groups of palm-trees, in the midst of which were seen picturesque bungalows, viharis (sort of abandoned monasteries), and marvellous temples enriched by the exhaustless ornamentation of Indian architecture. Then they came upon vast tracts extending to the horizon, with jungles inhabited by snakes and tigers, which fled at the noise of the train; succeeded by forests penetrated by the railway, and still haunted by elephants which, with pensive eyes, gazed at the train as it passed. The travellers crossed, beyond Milligaum, the fatal country so often stained with blood by the sectaries of the goddess Kali. Not far off rose Ellora, with its graceful pagodas, and the famous Aurungabad, capital of the ferocious Aureng-Zeb, now the chief town of one of the detached provinces of the kingdom of the Nizam. It was thereabouts that Feringhea, the Thuggee chief, king of the stranglers, held his sway. These ruffians, united by a secret bond, strangled victims of every age in honour of the goddess Death, without ever shedding blood; there was a period when this part of the country could scarcely be travelled over without corpses being found in every direction. The English Government has succeeded in greatly diminishing these murders, though the Thuggees still exist, and pursue the exercise of their horrible rites.

At half-past twelve the train stopped at Burhampoor where Passepartout was able to purchase some Indian slippers, ornamented with false pearls, in which, with evident vanity, he proceeded to encase his feet. The travellers made a hasty breakfast and started off for Assurghur, after skirting for a little the banks of the small river Tapty, which empties into the Gulf of Cambray, near Surat.

Passepartout was now plunged into absorbing reverie. Up to his arrival at Bombay, he had entertained hopes that their journey would end there; but, now that they were plainly whirling across India at full speed, a sudden change had come over the spirit of his dreams. His old vagabond nature returned to him; the fantastic ideas of his youth once more took possession of him. He came to regard his master's project as intended in good earnest, believed in the reality of the bet, and therefore in the tour of the world and the necessity of making it without fail within the designated period. Already he began to worry about possible delays, and accidents which might happen on the way. He recognised himself as being personally interested in the wager, and trembled at the thought that he might have been the means of losing it by his unpardonable folly of the night before. Being much less cool-headed than Mr. Fogg, he was much more restless, counting and recounting the days passed over, uttering maledictions when the train stopped, and accusing it of sluggishness, and mentally blaming Mr. Fogg for not having bribed the engineer. The worthy fellow was ignorant that, while it was possible by such means to hasten the rate of a steamer, it could not be done on the railway.

The train entered the defiles of the Sutpour Mountains, which separate the Khandeish from Bundelcund, towards evening. The next day Sir Francis Cromarty asked Passepartout what time it was; to which, on consulting his watch, he replied that it was three in the morning. This famous timepiece, always regulated on the Greenwich meridian, which was now some seventy-seven degrees westward, was at least four hours slow. Sir Francis corrected Passepartout's time, whereupon the latter made the same remark that he had done to Fix; and upon the general insisting that the watch should be regulated in each new meridian, since he was constantly going eastward, that is in the face of the sun, and therefore the days were shorter by four minutes for each degree gone over, Passepartout obstinately refused to alter his watch, which he kept at London time. It was an innocent delusion which could harm no one.

The train stopped, at eight o'clock, in the midst of a glade some fifteen miles beyond Rothal, where there were several bungalows, and workmen's cabins. The conductor, passing along the carriages, shouted, 'Passengers will get out here!'

Phileas Fogg looked at Sir Francis Cromarty for an explanation; but the general could not tell what meant a halt in the midst of this forest of dates and acacias.

Passepartout, not less surprised, rushed out and speedily returned, crying: 'Monsieur, no more railway!'

'What do you mean?' asked Sir Francis.

'I mean to say that the train isn't going on.'

The general at once stepped out, while Phileas Fogg calmly followed him, and they proceeded together to the conductor.

'Where are we?' asked Sir Francis.

'At the hamlet of Kholby.'

'Do we stop here?'

'Certainly. The railway isn't finished.'

'What! not finished?'

'No. There's still a matter of fifty miles to be laid from here to Allahabad, where the line begins again.'

'But the papers announced the opening of the railway throughout.'

'What would you have, officer? The papers were mistaken.'

'Yet you sell tickets from Bombay to Calcutta,' retorted Sir Francis, who was growing warm.

'No doubt,' replied the conductor; 'but the passengers know that they must provide means of transportation for themselves from Kholby to Allahabad.'

Sir Francis was furious. Passepartout would willingly have knocked the conductor down, and did not dare to look at his master.

'Sir Francis,' said Mr. Fogg quietly, 'we will, if you please, look about for some means of conveyance to Allahabad.'

'Mr. Fogg, this is a delay greatly to your disadvantage.'

'No, Sir Francis; it was foreseen.'

'What! You knew that the way – '

'Not at all; but I knew that some obstacle or other would sooner or later arise on my route. Nothing, therefore, is lost. I have two days, which I have already gained, to sacrifice. A steamer leaves Calcutta for Hong Kong at noon, on the 25th. This is the 22nd, and we shall reach Calcutta in time.'

There was nothing to say to so confident a response.

It was but too true that the railway came to a termination at this point. The papers were like some watches, which have a way of getting too fast, and had been premature in their announcement of the completion of the line. The greater part of the travellers were aware of this interruption, and, leaving the train, they began to engage such vehicles as the village could provide four-wheeled palkigharis, waggons drawn by zebus, carriages that looked like perambulating pagodas, palanquins, ponies, and what not.

Mr. Fogg and Sir Francis Cromarty, after searching the village from end to end, came back without having found anything.

'I shall go afoot,' said Phileas Fogg.

Passepartout, who had now rejoined his master, made a wry grimace, as he thought of his magnificent, but too frail Indian shoes. Happily he too had been looking about him, and, after a moment's hesitation, said, 'Monsieur, I think I have found a means of conveyance.'

'What?'

'An elephant! An elephant that belongs to an Indian who lives but a hundred steps from here.'

'Let's go and see the elephant,' replied Mr. Fogg.

They soon reached a small hut, near which, enclosed within some high palings, was the animal in question. An Indian came out of the hut, and, at their request, conducted them within the enclosure. The elephant, which its owner had reared, not for a beast of burden, but for warlike purposes, was half domesticated. The Indian had begun already, by often irritating him, and feeding him every three months on sugar and butter, to impart to him a ferocity not in his nature, this method being often employed by those who train the Indian elephants for battle. Happily, however, for Mr. Fogg, the animal's instruction in this direction had not gone far, and the elephant still preserved his natural gentleness. Kiouni – this was the name of the beast – could doubtless travel rapidly for a long time, and, in default of any other means of conveyance, Mr. Fogg resolved to hire him. But elephants are far from cheap in India, where they are becoming scarce, the males, which alone are suitable for circus shows, are much sought, especially as but few of them are domesticated. When therefore Mr. Fogg proposed to the Indian to hire Kiouni, he refused point-blank. Mr. Fogg persisted, offering the excessive sum of ten pounds an hour for the loan of the beast to Allahabad. Refused. Twenty pounds? Refused also. Forty pounds? Still refused. Passepartout jumped at each advance; but the Indian declined to be tempted. Yet the offer was an alluring one, for, supposing it took the elephant fifteen hours to reach Allahabad, his owner would receive no less than six hundred pounds sterling.

Phileas Fogg, without getting in the least flurried, then proposed to purchase the animal outright, and at first offered a thousand pounds for him. The Indian, perhaps thinking he was going to make a great bargain, still refused.

Sir Francis Cromarty took Mr. Fogg aside, and begged him to reflect before he went any further; to which that gentleman replied that he was not in the habit of acting rashly, that a bet of twenty thousand pounds was at stake, that the elephant was absolutely necessary to him, and that he would secure him if he had to pay twenty times his value. Returning to the Indian, whose small, sharp eyes, glistening with avarice, betrayed that with him it was only a question of how great a price he could obtain. Mr. Fogg offered first twelve hundred, then fifteen hundred, eighteen hundred, two thousand pounds. Passepartout, usually so rubicund, was fairly white with suspense.

At two thousand pounds the Indian yielded.

'What a price, good heavens!' cried Passepartout, 'for an elephant.'

It only remained now to find a guide, which was comparatively easy. A young Parsee, with an intelligent face, offered his services, which Mr. Fogg accepted, promising so generous a reward as to materially stimulate his zeal. The elephant was led out and equipped. The Parsee, who was an accomplished elephant driver, covered his back with a sort of saddle-cloth, and attached to each of his flanks some curiously uncomfortable howdahs. Phileas Fogg paid the Indian with some banknotes which he extracted from the famous carpet-bag, a proceeding that seemed to deprive poor Passepartout of his vitals. Then he offered to carry Sir Francis to Allahabad, which the brigadier gratefully accepted, as one traveller the more would not be likely to fatigue the gigantic beast. Provisions were purchased at Kholby, and, while Sir Francis and Mr. Fogg took the howdahs on either side, Passepartout got astride the saddle-cloth between them. The Parsee perched himself on the elephant's neck, and at nine o'clock they set out from the village, the animal marching off through the dense forest of palms by the shortest cut.

CHAPTER 12

In which Phileas Fogg and his companions venture across the Indian forests, and what ensued

In order to shorten the journey, the guide passed to the left of the line where the railway was still in process of being built. This line, owing to the capricious turnings of the Vindhia Mountains, did not pursue a straight course. The Parsee, who was quite familiar with the roads and paths in the district, declared that they would gain twenty miles by striking directly through the forest.

Phileas Fogg and Sir Francis Cromarty, plunged to the neck in the peculiar howdahs provided for them, were horribly jostled by the swift trotting of the elephant, spurred on as he was by the skilful Parsee; but they endured the discomfort with true British phlegm, talking little, and scarcely able to catch a glimpse of each other. As for Passepartout, who was mounted on the beast's back, and received the direct force of each concussion as he trod along, he was very careful, in accordance with his master's advice, to keep his tongue from between his teeth, as it would otherwise have been bitten off short. The worthy fellow bounced from the elephant's neck to his rump, and vaulted like a clown on a spring-board; yet he laughed in the midst of his bouncing, and from time to time took a piece of sugar out of his pocket, and inserted it in Kiouni's trunk, who received it without in the least slackening his regular trot.

After two hours the guide stopped the elephant, and gave him an hour for rest, during which Kiouni, after quenching his thirst at a neighbouring spring, set to devouring the branches and shrubs round about him. Neither Sir Francis nor Mr. Fogg regretted the delay, and both descended with a feeling of relief. 'Why, he's made of iron!' exclaimed the general, gazing admiringly on Kiouni.

'Of forged iron,' replied Passepartout, as he set about preparing a hasty breakfast.

At noon the Parsee gave the signal of departure. The country soon presented a very savage aspect. Copses of dates and dwarf-palms succeeded the dense forests; then vast, dry plains, dotted with scanty shrubs, and sown with great blocks of syenite. All this portion of Bundelcund, which is little frequented by travellers, is inhabited by a fanatical population, hardened in the most horrible practices of the Hindoo faith. The English have not been able to secure complete dominion over this territory, which is subjected to the influence of rajahs, whom it is almost impossible to reach in their inaccessible mountain fastnesses. The travellers several times saw bands of ferocious Indians, who, when they perceived the elephant striding across-country, made angry and threatening motions. The Parsee avoided them as much as possible. Few animals were observed on the route; even the monkeys hurried from their path with contortions and grimaces which convulsed Passepartout with laughter.

In the midst of his gaiety, however, one thought troubled the worthy servant. What would Mr. Fogg do with the elephant when he got to Allahabad? Would he carry him on with him?

Impossible! The cost of transporting him would make him ruinously expensive. Would he sell him, or set him free? The estimable beast certainly deserved some consideration. Should Mr. Fogg choose to make him, Passepartout, a present of Kiouni, he would be very much embarrassed; and these thoughts did not cease worrying him for a long time.

The principal chain of the Vindhias was crossed by eight in the evening, and another halt was made on the northern slope, in a ruined bungalow. They had gone nearly twenty-five miles that day, and an equal distance still separated them from the station of Allahabad.

The night was cold. The Parsee lit a fire in the bungalow with a few dry branches, and the warmth was very grateful, provisions purchased at Kholby sufficed for supper, and the travellers ate ravenously. The conversation, beginning with a few disconnected phrases, soon gave place to loud and steady snores. The guide watched Kiouni, who slept standing, bolstering himself against the trunk of a large tree. Nothing occurred during the night to disturb the slumberers, although occasional growls from panthers and chatterings of monkeys broke the silence; the more formidable beasts made no cries or hostile demonstration against the occupants of the bungalow. Sir Francis slept heavily, like an honest soldier overcome with fatigue. Passepartout was wrapped in uneasy dreams of the bouncing of the day before. As for Mr. Fogg, he slumbered as peacefully as if he had been in his serene mansion in Savile Row.

The journey was resumed at six in the morning; the guide hoped to reach Allahabad by evening. In that case, Mr. Fogg would only lose a part of the forty-eight hours saved since the beginning of the tour. Kiouni, resuming his rapid gait, soon descended the lower spurs of the Vindhias, and towards noon they passed by the village of Kallenger, on the Cani, one of the branches of the Ganges. The guide avoided inhabited places, thinking it safer to keep the open country, which lies along the first depressions of the basin of the great river. Allahabad was now only twelve miles to the north-east. They stopped under a clump of bananas, the fruit of which, as healthy as bread and as succulent as cream, was amply partaken of and appreciated.

At two o'clock the guide entered a thick forest which extended several miles; he preferred to travel under cover of the woods. They had not as yet had any unpleasant encounters, and the journey seemed on the point of being successfully accomplished, when the elephant, becoming restless, suddenly stopped.

It was then four o'clock.

'What's the matter?' asked Sir Francis, putting out his head.

'I don't know, officer,' replied the Parsee, listening attentively to a confused murmur which came through the thick branches.

The murmur soon became more distinct; it now seemed like a distant concert of human voices accompanied by brass instruments. Passepartout was all eyes and ears. Mr. Fogg patiently waited without a word. The Parsee jumped to the ground, fastened the elephant to a tree, and plunged into the thicket. He soon returned, saying:

'A procession of Brahmins is coming this way. We must prevent their seeing us, if possible.'

The guide unloosed the elephant and led him into a thicket, at the same time asking the travellers not to stir. He held himself ready to bestride the animal at a moment's notice, should flight become necessary; but he evidently thought that the procession of the faithful would pass without perceiving them amid the thick foliage, in which they were wholly concealed.

The discordant tones of the voices and instruments drew nearer, and now droning songs mingled with the sound of the tambourines and cymbals. The head of the procession soon appeared beneath the trees, a hundred paces away; and the strange figures who performed the religious ceremony were easily distinguished through the branches. First came the priests, with mitres on their heads, and clothed in long lace robes. They were surrounded by men, women, and children, who sang a kind of lugubrious psalm, interrupted at regular intervals by the tambourines and cymbals; while behind them was drawn a car with large wheels, the spokes of which represented serpents entwined with each other. Upon the car, which was drawn by four richly caparisoned zebus, stood a hideous statue with four arms, the body coloured a dull red, with haggard eyes, dishevelled hair, protruding tongue, and lips tinted with betel. It stood upright upon the figure of a prostrate and headless giant.

Sir Francis, recognising the statue, whispered, 'The goddess Kali; the goddess of love and death.'

'Of death, perhaps,' muttered back Passepartout, 'but of love – that ugly old hag? Never!'

The Parsee made a motion to keep silence.

A group of old fakirs were capering and making a wild ado round the statue; these were striped with ochre, and covered with cuts whence their blood issued drop by drop – stupid fanatics, who, in the great Indian ceremonies, still throw themselves under the wheels of Juggernaut. Some Brahmins, clad in all the sumptuousness of Oriental apparel, and leading a woman who faltered at every step, followed.

This woman was young, and as fair as a European. Her head and neck, shoulders, ears, arms, hands, and toes were loaded down with jewels and gems with bracelets, earrings, and rings; while a tunic bordered with gold, and covered with a light muslin robe, betrayed the outline of her form.

The guards who followed the young woman presented a violent contrast to her, armed as they were with naked sabres hung at their waists, and long damascened pistols, and bearing a corpse on a palanquin. It was the body of an old man, gorgeously arrayed in the habiliments of a rajah, wearing, as in life, a turban embroidered with pearls, a robe of tissue of silk and gold, a scarf of cashmere sewed with diamonds, and the magnificent weapons of a Hindoo prince. Next came the musicians and a rearguard of capering fakirs, whose cries sometimes drowned the noise of the instruments; these closed the procession.

Sir Francis watched the procession with a sad countenance, and, turning to the guide, said, 'A suttee.'

The Parsee nodded, and put his finger to his lips. The procession slowly wound under the trees, and soon its last ranks disappeared in the depths of the wood. The songs gradually died away; occasionally cries were heard in the distance, until at last all was silence again.

Phileas Fogg had heard what Sir Francis said, and, as soon as the procession had disappeared, asked: 'What is a suttee?'

'A suttee,' returned the general, 'is a human sacrifice, but a voluntary one. The woman you have just seen will be burned to-morrow at the dawn of day.'

'Oh, the scoundrels!' cried Passepartout, who could not repress his indignation.

'And the corpse?' asked Mr. Fogg.

'Is that of the prince, her husband,' said the guide; 'an

independent rajah of Bundelcund.'

'Is it possible,' resumed Phileas Fogg, his voice betraying not the least emotion, 'that these barbarous customs still exist in India, and that the English have been unable to put a stop to them?'

'These sacrifices do not occur in the larger portion of India,' replied Sir Francis; 'but we have no power over these savage territories, and especially here in Bundelcund. The whole district north of the Vindhias is the theatre of incessant murders and pillage.'

'The poor wretch!' exclaimed Passepartout, 'to be burned alive!'

'Yes,' returned Sir Francis, 'burned alive. And, if she were not, you cannot conceive what treatment she would be obliged to submit to from her relatives. They would shave off her hair, feed her on a scanty allowance of rice, treat her with contempt; she would be looked upon as an unclean creature, and would die in some corner, like a scurvy dog. The prospect of so frightful an existence drives these poor creatures to the sacrifice much more than love or religious fanaticism. Sometimes, however, the sacrifice is really voluntary, and it requires the active interference of the Government to prevent it. Several years ago, when I was living at Bombay, a young widow asked permission of the governor to be burned along with her husband's body; but, as you may imagine, he refused. The woman left the town, took refuge with an independent rajah, and there carried out her self-devoted purpose.'

While Sir Francis was speaking, the guide shook his head several times, and now said: 'The sacrifice which will take place to-morrow at dawn is not a voluntary one.'

'How do you know?'

'Everybody knows about this affair in Bundelcund.'

'But the wretched creature did not seem to be making any resistance,' observed Sir Francis.

'That was because they had intoxicated her with fumes of hemp and opium.'

'But where are they taking her?'

'To the pagoda of Pillaji, two miles from here; she will pass the night there.'

'And the sacrifice will take place – '

'To-morrow, at the first light of dawn.'

The guide now led the elephant out of the thicket, and leaped upon his neck. Just at the moment that he was about to urge Kiouni forward with a peculiar whistle, Mr. Fogg stopped him, and, turning to Sir Francis Cromarty, said, 'Suppose we save this woman.'

'Save the woman, Mr. Fogg!'

'I have yet twelve hours to spare; I can devote them to that.'

'Why, you are a man of heart!'

'Sometimes,' replied Phileas Fogg, quietly; 'when I have the time.'

CHAPTER 13

In which Passepartout receives a new proof that fortune favours the brave

The project was a bold one, full of difficulty, perhaps impracticable. Mr. Fogg was going to risk life, or at least liberty, and therefore the success of his tour. But he did not hesitate, and he found in Sir Francis Cromarty an enthusiastic ally.

As for Passepartout, he was ready for anything that might be proposed. His master's idea charmed him; he perceived a heart, a soul, under that icy exterior. He began to love Phileas Fogg.

There remained the guide: what course would he adopt? Would he not take part with the Indians? In default of his assistance, it was necessary to be assured of his neutrality.

Sir Francis frankly put the question to him.

'Officers,' replied the guide, 'I am a Parsee, and this woman is a Parsee. Command me as you will.'

'Excellent!' said Mr. Fogg.

'However,' resumed the guide, 'it is certain, not only that we shall risk our lives, but horrible tortures, if we are taken.'

'That is foreseen,' replied Mr. Fogg. 'I think we must wait till night before acting.'

'I think so,' said the guide.

The worthy Indian then gave some account of the victim, who, he said, was a celebrated beauty of the Parsee race, and the daughter of a wealthy Bombay merchant. She had received a thoroughly English education in that city, and, from her manners and intelligence, would be thought an European. Her name was Aouda. Left an orphan, she was married against her will to the old rajah of Bundelcund; and, knowing the fate that awaited her, she escaped, was retaken, and devoted by the rajah's relatives, who had an interest in her death, to the sacrifice from which it seemed she could not escape.

The Parsee's narrative only confirmed Mr. Fogg and his companions in their generous design. It was decided that the guide should direct the elephant towards the pagoda of Pillaji, which he accordingly approached as quickly as possible. They halted, half an hour afterwards, in a copse, some five hundred feet from the pagoda, where they were well concealed; but they could hear the groans and cries of the fakirs distinctly.

They then discussed the means of getting at the victim. The guide was familiar with the pagoda of Pillaji, in which, as he declared, the young woman was imprisoned. Could they enter any of its doors while the whole party of Indians was plunged in a drunken sleep, or was it safer to attempt to make a hole in the walls? This could only be determined at the moment and the place themselves; but it was certain that the abduction must be made that night, and not when, at break of day, the victim was led to her funeral pyre. Then no human intervention could save her.

As soon as night fell, about six o'clock, they decided to make a reconnaissance around the pagoda. The cries of the fakirs were just ceasing; the Indians were in the act of plunging themselves into the drunkenness caused by liquid opium mingled with hemp, and it might be possible to slip between them to the temple itself.

The Parsee, leading the others, noiselessly crept through the wood, and in ten minutes they found themselves on the banks of a small stream, whence, by the light of the rosin torches, they perceived a pyre of wood, on the top of which lay the embalmed body of the rajah, which was to be burned with his wife. The pagoda, whose minarets loomed above the trees in the deepening dusk, stood a hundred steps away.

'Come!' whispered the guide.

He slipped more cautiously than ever through the brush, followed by his companions; the silence around was only broken by the low murmuring of the wind among the branches.

Soon the Parsee stopped on the borders of the glade, which was lit up by the torches. The ground was covered by groups of the Indians, motionless in their drunken sleep; it seemed a battlefield strewn with the dead. Men, women, and children lay together.

In the background, among the trees, the pagoda of Pillaji loomed distinctly. Much to the guide's disappointment, the guards of the rajah, lighted by torches, were watching at the doors and marching to and fro with naked sabres; probably the priests, too, were watching within.

The Parsee, now convinced that it was impossible to force an entrance to the temple, advanced no farther, but led his companions back again. Phileas Fogg and Sir Francis Cromarty also saw that nothing could be attempted in that direction. They stopped, and engaged in a whispered colloquy.

'It is only eight now,' said the brigadier, 'and these guards may also go to sleep.'

'It is not impossible,' returned the Parsee.

They lay down at the foot of a tree, and waited.

The time seemed long; the guide ever and anon left them to take an observation on the edge of the wood, but the guards watched steadily by the glare of the torches, and a dim light crept through the windows of the pagoda.

They waited till midnight; but no change took place among the guards, and it became apparent that their yielding to sleep could not be counted on. The other plan must be carried out; an opening in the walls of the pagoda must be made. It remained to ascertain whether the priests were watching by the side of their victim as assiduously as were the soldiers at the door.

After a last consultation, the guide announced that he was ready for the attempt, and advanced, followed by the others. They took a roundabout way, so as to get at the pagoda on the rear. They reached the walls about half-past twelve, without having met anyone; here there was no guard, nor were there either windows or doors.

The night was dark. The moon, on the wane, scarcely left the horizon, and was covered with heavy clouds; the height of the trees deepened the darkness.

It was not enough to reach the walls; an opening in them must be accomplished, and to attain this purpose the party only had their pocket-knives. Happily the temple walls were built of brick and wood, which could be penetrated with little difficulty; after one brick had been taken out, the rest would yield easily.

They set noiselessly to work, and the Parsee on one side and Passepartout on the other began to loosen the bricks so as to make an aperture two feet wide. They were getting on rapidly, when suddenly a cry was heard in the interior of the temple, followed almost instantly by other cries replying from the outside. Passepartout and the guide stopped. Had they been heard? Was the alarm being given? Common prudence urged them to retire, and they did so, followed by Phileas Fogg and Sir Francis. They again hid themselves in the wood, and waited till the disturbance, whatever it might be, ceased, holding themselves ready to resume their attempt without delay. But, awkwardly enough, the guards now appeared at the rear of the temple, and there installed themselves, in readiness to prevent a surprise.

It would be difficult to describe the disappointment of the party, thus interrupted in their work. They could not now reach the victim; how, then, could they save her? Sir Francis shook his fists, Passepartout was beside himself, and the guide gnashed his teeth with rage. The tranquil Fogg waited, without betraying any emotion.

'We have nothing to do but to go away,' whispered Sir Francis.

'Nothing but to go away,' echoed the guide.

'Stop,' said Fogg. 'I am only due at Allahabad tomorrow before noon.'

'But what can you hope to do?' asked Sir Francis. 'In a few hours it will be daylight, and – '

'The chance which now seems lost may present itself at the last moment.'

Sir Francis would have liked to read Phileas Fogg's eyes. What was this cool Englishman thinking of? Was he planning to make a rush for the young woman at the very moment of the sacrifice, and boldly snatch her from her executioners?

This would be utter folly, and it was hard to admit that Fogg was such a fool. Sir Francis consented, however, to remain to the end of this terrible drama. The guide led them to the rear of the glade, where they were able to observe the sleeping groups.

Meanwhile Passepartout, who had perched himself on the lower branches of a tree, was resolving an idea which had at first struck him like a flash, and which was now firmly lodged in his brain.

He had commenced by saying to himself, 'What folly!' and then he repeated, 'Why not, after all? It's a chance, – perhaps the only one; and with such sots!' Thinking thus, he slipped, with the suppleness of a serpent, to the lowest branches, the ends of which bent almost to the ground.

The hours passed, and the lighter shades now announced the approach of day, though it was not yet light. This was the moment. The slumbering multitude became animated, the tambourines sounded, songs and cries arose; the hour of the sacrifice had come. The doors of the pagoda swung open, and a bright light escaped from its interior, in the midst of which Mr. Fogg and Sir Francis espied the victim. She seemed, having shaken off the stupor of intoxication, to be striving to escape from her executioner. Sir Francis's heart throbbed; and, convulsively seizing Mr. Fogg's hand, found in it an open knife. Just at this moment the crowd began to move. The young woman had again fallen into a stupor caused by the fumes of hemp, and passed among the fakirs, who escorted her with their wild, religious cries.

Phileas Fogg and his companions, mingling in the rear ranks of the crowd, followed; and in two minutes they reached the banks of the stream, and stopped fifty paces from the pyre, upon which still lay the rajah's corpse. In the semi-obscurity they saw the victim, quite senseless, stretched out beside her husband's body. Then a torch was brought, and the wood, heavily soaked with oil, instantly took fire.

At this moment Sir Francis and the guide seized Phileas Fogg, who, in an instant of mad generosity, was about to rush upon the pyre. But he had quickly pushed them aside, when the whole scene suddenly changed. A cry of terror arose. The whole multitude prostrated themselves, terror-stricken, on the ground.

The old rajah was not dead, then, since he rose of a sudden, like a spectre, took up his wife in his arms, and descended from the pyre in the midst of the clouds of smoke, which only heightened his ghostly appearance.

Fakirs and soldiers and priests, seized with instant terror, lay there, with their faces on the ground, not daring to lift their eyes and behold such a prodigy.

The inanimate victim was borne along by the vigorous arms which supported her, and which she did not seem in the least to burden. Mr. Fogg and Sir Francis stood erect, the Parsee bowed his head, and Passepartout was, no doubt, scarcely less stupefied.

The resuscitated rajah approached Sir Francis and Mr. Fogg, and, in an abrupt tone, said, 'Let us be off!'

It was Passepartout himself, who had slipped upon the pyre in the midst of the smoke and, profiting by the still overhanging darkness, had delivered the young woman from death! It was Passepartout who, playing his part with a happy audacity, had passed through the crowd amid the general terror.

A moment after all four of the party had disappeared in the woods, and the elephant was bearing them away at a rapid pace. But the cries and noise, and a ball which whizzed through Phileas Fogg's hat, apprised them that the trick had been discovered.

The old rajah's body, indeed, now appeared upon the burning pyre; and the priests, recovered from their terror, perceived that an abduction had taken place. They hastened into the forest, followed by the soldiers, who fired a volley after the fugitives; but the latter rapidly increased the distance between them, and ere long found themselves beyond the reach of the bullets and arrows.

CHAPTER 14

In which Phileas Fogg descends the whole length of the beautiful valley of the Ganges without ever thinking of seeing it

The rash exploit had been accomplished; and for an hour Passepartout laughed gaily at his success. Sir Francis pressed the worthy fellow's hand, and his master said, 'Well done!' which, from him, was high commendation; to which Passepartout replied that all the credit of the affair belonged to Mr. Fogg. As for him, he had only been struck with a 'queer' idea; and he laughed to think that for a few moments he, Passepartout, the ex-gymnast, ex-sergeant fireman, had been the spouse of a charming woman, a venerable, embalmed rajah! As for the young Indian woman, she had been unconscious throughout of what was passing, and now, wrapped up in a travelling-blanket, was reposing in one of the howdahs.

The elephant, thanks to the skilful guidance of the Parsee, was advancing rapidly through the still darksome forest, and, an hour after leaving the pagoda, had crossed a vast plain. They made a halt at seven o'clock, the young woman being still in a state of complete prostration. The guide made her drink a little brandy and water, but the drowsiness which stupefied her could not yet be shaken off. Sir Francis, who was familiar with the effects of the intoxication produced by the fumes of hemp, reassured his companions on her account. But he was more disturbed at the prospect of her future fate. He told Phileas Fogg that, should Aouda remain in India, she would inevitably fall again into the hands of her executioners. These fanatics were scattered throughout the county, and would, despite the English police, recover their victim at Madras, Bombay, or Calcutta. She would only be safe by quitting India for ever.

Phileas Fogg replied that he would reflect upon the matter.

The station at Allahabad was reached about ten o'clock, and, the interrupted line of railway being resumed, would enable them to reach Calcutta in less than twenty-four hours. Phileas Fogg would thus be able to arrive in time to take the steamer which left Calcutta the next day, October 25th, at noon, for Hong Kong.

The young woman was placed in one of the waiting-rooms of the station, whilst Passepartout was charged with purchasing for her various articles of toilet, a dress, shawl, and some furs; for which his master gave him unlimited credit. Passepartout started off forthwith, and found himself in the streets of Allahabad, that is, the City of God, one of the most venerated in India, being built at the junction of the two sacred rivers, Ganges and Jumna, the waters of which attract pilgrims from every part of the peninsula. The Ganges, according to the legends of the Ramayana, rises in heaven, whence, owing to Brahma's agency, it descends to the earth.

Passepartout made it a point, as he made his purchases, to take a good look at the city. It was formerly defended by a noble fort, which has since become a state prison; its commerce has dwindled away, and Passepartout in vain looked about him for such a bazaar as he used to frequent in Regent Street. At last he came upon an elderly, crusty Jew, who sold second-hand articles, and from whom he purchased a dress of Scotch stuff, a large mantle, and a fine otter-skin pelisse, for which he did not hesitate to pay seventy-five pounds. He then returned triumphantly to the station.

The influence to which the priests of Pillaji had subjected Aouda began gradually to yield, and she became more herself, so that her fine eyes resumed all their soft Indian expression.

When the poet-king, Ucaf Uddaul, celebrates the charms of the queen of Ahmehnagara, he speaks thus:

'Her shining tresses, divided in two parts, encircle the harmonious contour of her white and delicate cheeks, brilliant in their glow and freshness. Her ebony brows have the form and charm of the bow of Kama, the god of love, and beneath her long silken lashes the purest reflections and a celestial light swim, as in the sacred lakes of Himalaya, in the black pupils of her great clear eyes. Her teeth, fine, equal, and white, glitter between her smiling lips like dewdrops in a passion-flower's half-enveloped breast. Her delicately formed ears, her vermilion hands, her little feet, curved and tender as the lotus-bud, glitter with the brilliancy of the loveliest pearls of Ceylon, the most dazzling diamonds of Golconda. Her narrow and supple waist, which a hand may clasp around, sets forth the outline of her rounded figure and the beauty of her bosom, where youth in its flower displays the wealth of its treasures; and beneath the silken folds of her tunic she seems to have been modelled in pure silver by the godlike hand of Vicvarcarma, the immortal sculptor.'

It is enough to say, without applying this poetical rhapsody to Aouda, that she was a charming woman, in all the European acceptation of the phrase. She spoke English with great purity, and the guide had not exaggerated in saying that the young Parsee had been transformed by her bringing up.

The train was about to start from Allahabad, and Mr. Fogg proceeded to pay the guide the price agreed upon for his service, and not a farthing more; which astonished Passepartout, who remembered all that his master owed to the guide's devotion. He had, indeed, risked his life in the adventure at Pillaji, and, if he should be caught afterwards by the Indians, he would with difficulty escape their vengeance. Kiouni, also, must be disposed of. What should be done with the elephant, which had been so dearly purchased? Phileas Fogg had already determined this question.

'Parsee,' said he to the guide, 'you have been serviceable and devoted. I have paid for your service, but not for your devotion. Would you like to have this elephant? He is yours.'

The guide's eyes glistened.

'Your honour is giving me a fortune!' cried he.

'Take him, guide,' returned Mr. Fogg, 'and I shall still be your debtor.'

'Good!' exclaimed Passepartout. 'Take him, friend. Kiouni is a brave and faithful beast.' And, going up to the elephant, he gave him several lumps of sugar, saying, 'Here, Kiouni, here, here.'

The elephant grunted out his satisfaction, and, clasping Passepartout around the waist with his trunk, lifted him as high as his head. Passepartout, not in the least alarmed, caressed the animal, which replaced him gently on the ground.

Soon after, Phileas Fogg, Sir Francis Cromarty, and Passepartout, installed in a carriage with Aouda, who had the best seat, were whirling at full speed towards Benares. It was a run of eighty miles, and was accomplished in two hours.

CHAPTER 14

During the journey, the young woman fully recovered her senses. What was her astonishment to find herself in this carriage, on the railway, dressed in European habiliments, and with travellers who were quite strangers to her! Her companions first set about fully reviving her with a little liquor, and then Sir Francis narrated to her what had passed, dwelling upon the courage with which Phileas Fogg had not hesitated to risk his life to save her, and recounting the happy sequel of the venture, the result of Passepartout's rash idea. Mr. Fogg said nothing; while Passepartout, abashed, kept repeating that 'it wasn't worth telling.'

Aouda pathetically thanked her deliverers, rather with tears than words; her fine eyes interpreted her gratitude better than her lips. Then, as her thoughts strayed back to the scene of the sacrifice, and recalled the dangers which still menaced her, she shuddered with terror.

Phileas Fogg understood what was passing in Aouda's mind, and offered, in order to reassure her, to escort her to Hong Kong, where she might remain safely until the affair was hushed up – an offer which she eagerly and gratefully accepted. She had, it seems, a Parsee relation, who was one of the principal merchants of Hong Kong, which is wholly an English city, though on an island on the Chinese coast.

At half-past twelve the train stopped at Benares. The Brahmin legends assert that this city is built on the site of the ancient Casi, which, like Mahomet's tomb, was once suspended between heaven and earth; though the Benares of to-day, which the Orientalists call the Athens of India, stands quite unpoetically on the solid earth, Passepartout caught glimpses of its brick houses and clay huts, giving an aspect of desolation to the place, as the train entered it.

Benares was Sir Francis Cromarty's destination, the troops

he was rejoining being encamped some miles northward of the city. He bade adieu to Phileas Fogg, wishing him all success, and expressing the hope that he would come that way again in a less original but more profitable fashion. Mr. Fogg lightly pressed him by the hand. The parting of Aouda, who did not forget what she owed to Sir Francis, betrayed more warmth; and, as for Passepartout, he received a hearty shake of the hand from the gallant general.

The railway, on leaving Benares, passed for a while along the valley of the Ganges. Through the windows of their carriage the travellers had glimpses of the diversified landscape of Behar, with its mountains clothed in verdure, its fields of barley, wheat, and corn, its jungles peopled with green alligators, its neat villages, and its still thickly-leaved forests. Elephants were bathing in the waters of the sacred river, and groups of Indians, despite the advanced season and chilly air, were performing solemnly their pious ablutions. These were fervent Brahmins, the bitterest foes of Buddhism, their deities being Vishnu, the solar god, Shiva, the divine impersonation of natural forces, and Brahma, the supreme ruler of priests and legislators. What would these divinities think of India, anglicised as it is to-day, with steamers whistling and scudding along the Ganges, frightening the gulls which float upon its surface, the turtles swarming along its banks, and the faithful dwelling upon its borders?

The panorama passed before their eyes like a flash, save when the steam concealed it fitfully from the view; the travellers could scarcely discern the fort of Chupenie, twenty miles south-westward from Benares, the ancient stronghold of the rajahs of Behar; or Ghazipur and its famous rose-water factories; or the tomb of Lord Cornwallis, rising on the left bank of the Ganges; the fortified town of Buxar, or Patna, a large manufacturing and trading-place, where is held the principal opium market of India; or Monghir, a more than European town, for it is as English as Manchester or Birmingham, with its iron foundries, edgetool factories, and high chimneys puffing clouds of black smoke heavenward.

Night came on; the train passed on at full speed, in the midst of the roaring of the tigers, bears, and wolves which fled before the locomotive; and the marvels of Bengal, Golconda ruined Gour, Murshedabad, the ancient capital, Burdwan, Hugly, and the French town of Chandernagor, where Passepartout would have been proud to see his country's flag flying, were hidden from their view in the darkness.

Calcutta was reached at seven in the morning, and the packet left for Hong Kong at noon; so that Phileas Fogg had five hours before him.

According to his journal, he was due at Calcutta on the 25th of October, and that was the exact date of his actual arrival. He was therefore neither behind-hand nor ahead of time. The two days gained between London and Bombay had been lost, as has been seen, in the journey across India. But it is not to be supposed that Phileas Fogg regretted them.

CHAPTER 15

In which the bag of banknotes disgorges some thousands of pounds more

The train entered the station, and Passepartout jumping out first, was followed by Mr. Fogg, who assisted his fair companion to descend. Phileas Fogg intended to proceed at once to the Hong Kong steamer, in order to get Aouda comfortably settled for the voyage. He was unwilling to leave her while they were still on dangerous ground.

Just as he was leaving the station a policeman came up to him, and said, 'Mr. Phileas Fogg?'

'I am he.'

'Is this man your servant?' added the policeman, pointing to Passepartout.

'Yes.'

'Be so good, both of you, as to follow me.'

Mr. Fogg betrayed no surprise whatever. The policeman was a representative of the law, and law is sacred to an Englishman. Passepartout tried to reason about the matter, but the policeman tapped him with his stick, and Mr. Fogg made him a signal to obey.

'May this young lady go with us?' asked he.

'She may,' replied the policeman.

Mr. Fogg, Aouda, and Passepartout were conducted to a palkigahri, a sort of four-wheeled carriage, drawn by two horses, in which they took their places and were driven away. No one spoke during the twenty minutes which elapsed before they reached their destination. They first passed through the 'black town,' with its narrow streets, its miserable, dirty huts, and squalid population; then through the 'European town,' which presented a relief in its bright brick mansions, shaded by coconut-trees and bristling with masts, where, although it was early morning, elegantly dressed horsemen and handsome equipages were passing back and forth.

The carriage stopped before a modest-looking house, which, however, did not have the appearance of a private mansion. The policeman having requested his prisoners – for so, truly, they might be called – to descend, conducted them into a room with barred windows, and said: 'You will appear before Judge Obadiah at half-past eight.'

He then retired, and closed the door.

'Why, we are prisoners!' exclaimed Passepartout, falling into a chair.

Aouda, with an emotion she tried to conceal, said to Mr. Fogg: 'Sir, you must leave me to my fate! It is on my account that you receive this treatment, it is for having saved me!'

Phileas Fogg contented himself with saying that it was impossible. It was quite unlikely that he should be arrested for preventing a suttee. The complainants would not dare present themselves with such a charge. There was some mistake. Moreover, he would not, in any event, abandon Aouda, but would escort her to Hong Kong.

'But the steamer leaves at noon!' observed Passepartout, nervously.

CHAPTER 15

'We shall be on board by noon,' replied his master, placidly.

It was said so positively that Passepartout could not help muttering to himself, 'Parbleu that's certain! Before noon we shall be on board.' But he was by no means reassured.

At half-past eight the door opened, the policeman appeared, and, requesting them to follow him, led the way to an adjoining hall. It was evidently a court-room, and a crowd of Europeans and natives already occupied the rear of the apartment.

Mr. Fogg and his two companions took their places on a bench opposite the desks of the magistrate and his clerk. Immediately after, Judge Obadiah, a fat, round man, followed by the clerk, entered. He proceeded to take down a wig which was hanging on a nail, and put it hurriedly on his head.

'The first case,' said he. Then, putting his hand to his head, he exclaimed, 'Heh! This is not my wig!'

'No, your worship,' returned the clerk, 'it is mine.'

'My dear Mr. Oysterpuff, how can a judge give a wise sentence in a clerk's wig?'

The wigs were exchanged.

Passepartout was getting nervous, for the hands on the face of the big clock over the judge seemed to go around with terrible rapidity.

'The first case,' repeated Judge Obadiah.

'Phileas Fogg?' demanded Oysterpuff.

'I am here,' replied Mr. Fogg.

'Passepartout?'

'Present,' responded Passepartout.

'Good,' said the judge. 'You have been looked for, prisoners, for two days on the trains from Bombay.'

'But of what are we accused?' asked Passepartout, impatiently.

'You are about to be informed.'

'I am an English subject, sir,' said Mr. Fogg, 'and I have the right – '

'Have you been ill-treated?'

'Not at all.'

'Very well; let the complainants come in.'

A door was swung open by order of the judge, and three Indian priests entered.

'That's it,' muttered Passepartout; 'these are the rogues who were going to burn our young lady.'

The priests took their places in front of the judge, and the clerk proceeded to read in a loud voice a complaint of sacrilege against Phileas Fogg and his servant, who were accused of having violated a place held consecrated by the Brahmin religion.

'You hear the charge?' asked the judge.

'Yes, sir,' replied Mr. Fogg, consulting his watch, 'and I admit it.'

'You admit it?'

'I admit it, and I wish to hear these priests admit, in their turn, what they were going to do at the pagoda of Pillaji.'

The priests looked at each other; they did not seem to understand what was said.

'Yes,' cried Passepartout, warmly; 'at the pagoda of Pillaji, where they were on the point of burning their victim.'

The judge stared with astonishment, and the priests were stupefied.

'What victim?' said Judge Obadiah. 'Burn whom? In Bombay itself?'

'Bombay?' cried Passepartout.

'Certainly. We are not talking of the pagoda of Pillaji, but of the pagoda of Malabar Hill, at Bombay.'

'And as a proof,' added the clerk, 'here are the desecrator's very shoes, which he left behind him.'

Whereupon he placed a pair of shoes on his desk.

'My shoes!' cried Passepartout, in his surprise permitting this imprudent exclamation to escape him.

The confusion of master and man, who had quite forgotten the affair at Bombay, for which they were now detained at Calcutta, may be imagined.

Fix the detective, had foreseen the advantage which Passepartout's escapade gave him, and, delaying his departure for twelve hours, had consulted the priests of Malabar Hill. Knowing that the English authorities dealt very severely with this kind of misdemeanour, he promised them a goodly sum in damages, and sent them forward to Calcutta by the next train. Owing to the delay caused by the rescue of the young widow, Fix and the priests reached the Indian capital before Mr. Fogg and his servant, the magistrates having been already warned by a dispatch to arrest them should they arrive. Fix's disappointment when he learned that Phileas Fogg had not made his appearance in Calcutta may be imagined. He made up his mind that the robber had stopped somewhere on the route and taken refuge in the southern provinces. For twenty-four hours Fix watched the station with feverish anxiety; at last he was rewarded by seeing Mr. Fogg and Passepartout arrive, accompanied by a young woman, whose presence he was wholly at a loss to explain. He hastened for a policeman; and this was how the party came to be arrested and brought before Judge Obadiah.

Had Passepartout been a little less preoccupied, he would have espied the detective ensconced in a corner of the courtroom, watching the proceedings with an interest easily understood; for the warrant had failed to reach him at Calcutta, as it had done at Bombay and Suez.

Judge Obadiah had unfortunately caught Passepartout's rash exclamation, which the poor fellow would have given the world to recall.

'The facts are admitted?' asked the judge.

'Admitted,' replied Mr. Fogg, coldly.

'Inasmuch,' resumed the judge, 'as the English law protects equally and sternly the religions of the Indian people, and as the man Passepartout has admitted that he violated the sacred pagoda of Malabar Hill, at Bombay, on the 20th of October, I condemn the said Passepartout to imprisonment for fifteen days and a fine of three hundred pounds.'

'Three hundred pounds!' cried Passepartout, startled at the largeness of the sum.

'Silence!' shouted the constable.

'And inasmuch,' continued the judge, 'as it is not proved that the act was not done by the connivance of the master with the servant, and as the master in any case must be held responsible for the acts of his paid servant, I condemn Phileas Fogg to a week's imprisonment and a fine of one hundred and fifty pounds.'

Fix rubbed his hands softly with satisfaction; if Phileas Fogg could be detained in Calcutta a week, it would be more than time for the warrant to arrive. Passepartout was stupefied. This sentence ruined his master. A wager of twenty thousand pounds lost, because he, like a precious fool, had gone into that abominable pagoda!

Phileas Fogg, as self-composed as if the judgment did not in the least concern him, did not even lift his eyebrows while it was being pronounced. Just as the clerk was calling the next case, he rose, and said, 'I offer bail.'

'You have that right,' returned the judge.

Fix's blood ran cold, but he resumed his composure when

he heard the judge announce that the bail required for each prisoner would be one thousand pounds.

'I will pay it at once,' said Mr. Fogg, taking a roll of bank-bills from the carpet-bag, which Passepartout had by him, and placing them on the clerk's desk.

'This sum will be restored to you upon your release from prison,' said the judge. 'Meanwhile, you are liberated on bail.'

'Come!' said Phileas Fogg to his servant.

'But let them at least give me back my shoes!' cried Passepartout angrily.

'Ah, these are pretty dear shoes!' he muttered, as they were handed to him. 'More than a thousand pounds apiece; besides, they pinch my feet.'

Mr. Fogg, offering his arm to Aouda, then departed, followed by the crestfallen Passepartout. Fix still nourished hopes that the robber would not, after all, leave the two thousand pounds behind him, but would decide to serve out his week in jail, and issued forth on Mr. Fogg's traces. That gentleman took a carriage, and the party were soon landed on one of the quays.

The *Rangoon* was moored half a mile off in the harbour, its signal of departure hoisted at the mast-head. Eleven o'clock was striking; Mr. Fogg was an hour in advance of time. Fix saw them leave the carriage and push off in a boat for the steamer, and stamped his feet with disappointment.

'The rascal is off, after all!' he exclaimed. 'Two thousand pounds sacrificed! He's as prodigal as a thief! I'll follow him to the end of the world if necessary; but, at the rate he is going on, the stolen money will soon be exhausted.'

The detective was not far wrong in making this conjecture. Since leaving London, what with travelling expenses, bribes, the purchase of the elephant, bails, and fines, Mr. Fogg had already spent more than five thousand pounds on the way, and the percentage of the sum recovered from the bank robber promised to the detectives, was rapidly diminishing.

CHAPTER 16

In which Fix does not seem to understand in the least what is said to him

The *Rangoon* – one of the Peninsular and Oriental Company's boats plying in the Chinese and Japanese seas – was a screw steamer, built of iron, weighing about seventeen hundred and seventy tons, and with engines of four hundred horse-power. She was as fast, but not as well fitted up, as the *Mongolia*, and Aouda was not as comfortably provided for on board of her as Phileas Fogg could have wished. However, the trip from Calcutta to Hong Kong only comprised some three thousand five hundred miles, occupying from ten to twelve days, and the young woman was not difficult to please.

During the first days of the journey Aouda became better acquainted with her protector, and constantly gave evidence of her deep gratitude for what he had done. The phlegmatic gentleman listened to her, apparently at least, with coldness, neither his voice nor his manner betraying the slightest emotion; but he seemed to be always on the watch that nothing should be wanting to Aouda's comfort. He visited her regularly each day at certain hours, not so much to talk himself, as to sit and hear her talk. He treated her with the strictest politeness, but with the precision of an automaton, the movements of which had been arranged for this purpose. Aouda did not quite know what to make of him, though Passepartout had given her some hints of his master's eccentricity, and made her smile by telling her of the wager which was sending him round the world. After all, she owed Phileas Fogg her life, and she always regarded him through the exalting medium of her gratitude.

Aouda confirmed the Parsee guide's narrative of her touching history. She did, indeed, belong to the highest of the native races of India. Many of the Parsee merchants have made great fortunes there by dealing in cotton; and one of them, Sir Jametsee Jeejeebhoy, was made a baronet by the English government. Aouda was a relative of this great man, and it was his cousin, Jeejeeh, whom she hoped to join at Hong Kong. Whether she would find a protector in him she could not tell; but Mr. Fogg essayed to calm her anxieties, and to assure her that everything would be mathematically – he used the very word – arranged. Aouda fastened her great eyes, 'clear as the sacred lakes of the Himalaya,' upon him; but the intractable Fogg, as reserved as ever, did not seem at all inclined to throw himself into this lake.

The first few days of the voyage passed prosperously, amid favourable weather and propitious winds, and they soon came in sight of the great Andaman, the principal of the islands in the Bay of Bengal, with its picturesque Saddle Peak, two thousand four hundred feet high, looming above the waters. The steamer passed along near the shores, but the savage Papuans, who are in the lowest scale of humanity, but are not, as has been asserted, cannibals, did not make their appearance.

The panorama of the islands, as they steamed by them, was superb. Vast forests of palms, arecs, bamboo, teakwood, of the gigantic mimosa, and tree-like ferns covered the foreground, while behind, the graceful outlines of the mountains were traced against the sky; and along the coasts swarmed by thousands the precious swallows whose nests furnish a luxurious dish to the tables of the Celestial Empire. The varied landscape afforded by the Andaman Islands was soon passed, however, and the *Rangoon* rapidly approached the Straits of Malacca, which gave access to the China seas.

What was detective Fix, so unluckily drawn on from country to country, doing all this while? He had managed to embark on the *Rangoon* at Calcutta without being seen by Passepartout, after leaving orders that, if the warrant should arrive, it should be forwarded to him at Hong Kong; and he hoped to conceal his presence to the end of the voyage. It would have been difficult to explain why he was on board without awakening Passepartout's suspicions, who thought him still at Bombay. But necessity impelled him, nevertheless, to renew his acquaintance with the worthy servant, as will be seen.

All the detective's hopes and wishes were now centred on Hong Kong; for the steamer's stay at Singapore would be too brief to enable him to take any steps there. The arrest must be made at Hong Kong, or the robber would probably escape him for ever. Hong Kong was the last English ground on which he would set foot; beyond, China, Japan, America offered to Fogg an almost certain refuge. If the warrant should at last make its appearance at Hong Kong, Fix could arrest him and give him into the hands of the local police, and there would be no further trouble. But beyond Hong Kong, a simple warrant would be of no avail; an extradition warrant would be necessary, and that would result in delays and obstacles, of which the rascal would take advantage to elude justice.

Fix thought over these probabilities during the long hours which he spent in his cabin, and kept repeating to himself, 'Now, either the warrant will be at Hong Kong, in which case I shall arrest my man, or it will not be there; and this time it is absolutely necessary that I should delay his departure. I have failed at Bombay, and I have failed at Calcutta; if I fail at Hong Kong, my reputation is lost: Cost what it may, I must succeed! But how shall I prevent his departure, if that should turn out to be my last resource?'

Fix made up his mind that, if worst came to worst, he would make a confidant of Passepartout, and tell him what kind of a fellow his master really was. That Passepartout was not Fogg's accomplice, he was very certain. The servant, enlightened by his disclosure, and afraid of being himself implicated in the crime, would doubtless become an ally of the detective. But this method was a dangerous one, only to be employed when everything else had failed. A word from Passepartout to his master would ruin all. The detective was therefore in a sore strait. But suddenly a new idea struck him. The presence of Aouda on the *Rangoon*, in company with Phileas Fogg, gave him new material for reflection.

Who was this woman? What combination of events had made her Fogg's travelling companion? They had evidently met somewhere between Bombay and Calcutta; but where? Had they met accidentally, or had Fogg gone into the interior purposely in quest of this charming damsel? Fix was fairly puzzled. He asked himself whether there had not been a wicked elopement; and this idea so impressed itself upon his mind that he determined to make use of the supposed intrigue. Whether the young woman were married or not, he would be able to create such difficulties for Mr. Fogg at Hong Kong that he could not escape by paying any amount of money.

But could he even wait till they reached Hong Kong? Fogg had an abominable way of jumping from one boat to another, and, before anything could be effected, might get full under way again for Yokohama.

Fix decided that he must warn the English authorities, and signal the *Rangoon* before her arrival. This was easy to do, since the steamer stopped at Singapore, whence there is a telegraphic wire to Hong Kong. He finally resolved, moreover, before acting more positively, to question Passepartout. It would not be difficult to make him talk; and, as there was no time to lose, Fix prepared to make himself known.

It was now the 30th of October, and on the following day the *Rangoon* was due at Singapore.

Fix emerged from his cabin and went on deck. Passepartout was promenading up and down in the forward part of the steamer. The detective rushed forward with every appearance of extreme surprise, and exclaimed, 'You here, on the *Rangoon*?'

'What, Monsieur Fix, are you on board?' returned the really astonished Passepartout, recognising his crony of the *Mongolia*. 'Why, I left you at Bombay, and here you are, on the way to Hong Kong! Are you going round the world too?'

'No, no,' replied Fix; 'I shall stop at Hong Kong – at least for some days.'

'Hum!' said Passepartout, who seemed for an instant perplexed. 'But how is it I have not seen you on board since we left Calcutta?'

'Oh, a trifle of sea-sickness – I've been staying in my berth. The Gulf of Bengal does not agree with me as well as the Indian Ocean. And how is Mr. Fogg?'

'As well and as punctual as ever, not a day behind time! But, Monsieur Fix, you don't know that we have a young lady with us.'

'A young lady?' replied the detective, not seeming to comprehend what was said.

Passepartout thereupon recounted Aouda's history, the affair at the Bombay pagoda, the purchase of the elephant for two thousand pounds, the rescue, the arrest, and sentence of the Calcutta court, and the restoration of Mr. Fogg and himself to liberty on bail. Fix, who was familiar with the last events, seemed to be equally ignorant of all that Passepartout related; and the later was charmed to find so interested a listener.

'But does your master propose to carry this young woman to Europe?'

'Not at all. We are simply going to place her under the protection of one of her relatives, a rich merchant at Hong Kong.'

'Nothing to be done there,' said Fix to himself, concealing his disappointment. 'A glass of gin, Mr. Passepartout?'

'Willingly, Monsieur Fix. We must at least have a friendly glass on board the *Rangoon*.'

CHAPTER 17

Showing what happened on the voyage from Singapore to Hong Kong

The detective and Passepartout met often on deck after this interview, though Fix was reserved, and did not attempt to induce his companion to divulge any more facts concerning Mr. Fogg. He caught a glimpse of that mysterious gentleman once or twice; but Mr. Fogg usually confined himself to the cabin, where he kept Aouda company, or, according to his inveterate habit, took a hand at whist.

Passepartout began very seriously to conjecture what strange chance kept Fix still on the route that his master was pursuing. It was really worth considering why this certainly very amiable and complacent person, whom he had first met at Suez, had then encountered on board the *Mongolia*, who disembarked at Bombay, which he announced as his destination, and now turned up so unexpectedly on the *Rangoon*, was following Mr. Fogg's tracks step by step. What was Fix's object? Passepartout was ready to wager his Indian shoes – which he religiously preserved – that Fix would also leave Hong Kong at the same time with them, and probably on the same steamer.

Passepartout might have cudgelled his brain for a century without hitting upon the real object which the detective had in view. He never could have imagined that Phileas Fogg was being tracked as a robber around the globe. But, as it is in human nature to attempt the solution of every mystery, Passepartout suddenly discovered an explanation of Fix's movements, which was in truth far from unreasonable. Fix, he thought, could only be an agent of Mr. Fogg's friends at the Reform Club, sent to follow him up, and to ascertain that he really went round the world as had been agreed upon.

'It's clear!' repeated the worthy servant to himself, proud of his shrewdness. 'He's a spy sent to keep us in view! That isn't quite the thing, either, to be spying Mr. Fogg, who is so honourable a man! Ah, gentlemen of the Reform, this shall cost you dear!'

Passepartout, enchanted with his discovery, resolved to say nothing to his master, lest he should be justly offended at this mistrust on the part of his adversaries. But he determined to chaff Fix, when he had the chance, with mysterious allusions, which, however, need not betray his real suspicions.

During the afternoon of Wednesday, 30th October, the *Rangoon* entered the Strait of Malacca, which separates the peninsula of that name from Sumatra. The mountainous and craggy islets intercepted the beauties of this noble island from the view of the travellers. The *Rangoon* weighed anchor at Singapore the next day at four a.m., to receive coal, having gained half a day on the prescribed time of her arrival. Phileas Fogg noted this gain in his journal, and then, accompanied by Aouda, who betrayed a desire for a walk on shore, disembarked.

Fix, who suspected Mr. Fogg's every movement, followed them cautiously, without being himself perceived; while

Passepartout, laughing in his sleeve at Fix's manoeuvres, went about his usual errands.

The island of Singapore is not imposing in aspect, for there are no mountains; yet its appearance is not without attractions. It is a park checkered by pleasant highways and avenues. A handsome carriage, drawn by a sleek pair of New Holland horses, carried Phileas Fogg and Aouda into the midst of rows of palms with brilliant foliage, and of clove-trees, whereof the cloves form the heart of a half-open flower. Pepper plants replaced the prickly hedges of European fields; sago-bushes, large ferns with gorgeous branches, varied the aspect of this tropical clime; while nutmeg-trees in full foliage filled the air with a penetrating perfume. Agile and grinning bands of monkeys skipped about in the trees, nor were tigers wanting in the jungles.

After a drive of two hours through the country, Aouda and Mr. Fogg returned to the town, which is a vast collection of heavy-looking, irregular houses, surrounded by charming gardens rich in tropical fruits and plants; and at ten o'clock they re-embarked, closely followed by the detective, who had kept them constantly in sight.

Passepartout, who had been purchasing several dozen mangoes – a fruit as large as good-sized apples, of a dark-brown colour outside and a bright red within, and whose white pulp, melting in the mouth, affords gourmands a delicious sensation – was waiting for them on deck. He was only too glad to offer some mangoes to Aouda, who thanked him very gracefully for them.

At eleven o'clock the *Rangoon* rode out of Singapore harbour, and in a few hours the high mountains of Malacca, with their forests, inhabited by the most beautifully-furred tigers in the world, were lost to view. Singapore is distant some thirteen hundred miles from the island of Hong Kong, which is a little English colony near the Chinese coast. Phileas Fogg hoped to accomplish the journey in six days, so as to be in time for the steamer which would leave on the 6th of November for Yokohama, the principal Japanese port.

The *Rangoon* had a large quota of passengers, many of whom disembarked at Singapore, among them a number of Indians, Ceylonese, Chinamen, Malays, and Portuguese, mostly second-class travellers.

The weather, which had hitherto been fine, changed with the last quarter of the moon. The sea rolled heavily, and the wind at intervals rose almost to a storm, but happily blew from the south-west, and thus aided the steamer's progress. The captain as often as possible put up his sails, and under the double action of steam and sail the vessel made rapid progress along the coasts of Anam and Cochin China. Owing to the defective construction of the *Rangoon*, however, unusual precautions became necessary in unfavourable weather; but the loss of time which resulted from this cause, while it nearly drove Passepartout out of his senses, did not seem to affect his master in the least. Passepartout blamed the captain, the engineer, and the crew, and consigned all who were connected with the ship to the land where the pepper grows. Perhaps the thought of the gas, which was remorselessly burning at his expense in Savile Row, had something to do with his hot impatience.

'You are in a great hurry, then,' said Fix to him one day, 'to reach Hong Kong?'

'A very great hurry!'

'Mr. Fogg, I suppose, is anxious to catch the steamer for Yokohama?'

'Terribly anxious.'

CHAPTER 17

'You believe in this journey around the world, then?'

'Absolutely. Don't you, Mr. Fix?'

'I? I don't believe a word of it.'

'You're a sly dog!' said Passepartout, winking at him.

This expression rather disturbed Fix, without his knowing why. Had the Frenchman guessed his real purpose? He knew not what to think. But how could Passepartout have discovered that he was a detective? Yet, in speaking as he did, the man evidently meant more than he expressed.

Passepartout went still further the next day; he could not hold his tongue.

'Mr. Fix,' said he, in a bantering tone, 'shall we be so unfortunate as to lose you when we get to Hong Kong?'

'Why,' responded Fix, a little embarrassed, 'I don't know; perhaps – '

'Ah, if you would only go on with us! An agent of the Peninsular Company, you know, can't stop on the way! You were only going to Bombay, and here you are in China. America is not far off, and from America to Europe is only a step.'

Fix looked intently at his companion, whose countenance was as serene as possible, and laughed with him. But Passepartout persisted in chaffing him by asking him if he made much by his present occupation.

'Yes, and no,' returned Fix; 'there is good and bad luck in such things. But you must understand that I don't travel at my own expense.'

'Oh, I am quite sure of that!' cried Passepartout, laughing heartily.

Fix, fairly puzzled, descended to his cabin and gave himself up to his reflections. He was evidently suspected; somehow or other the Frenchman had found out that he was a detective.

But had he told his master? What part was he playing in all this: was he an accomplice or not? Was the game, then, up? Fix spent several hours turning these things over in his mind, sometimes thinking that all was lost, then persuading himself that Fogg was ignorant of his presence, and then undecided what course it was best to take.

Nevertheless, he preserved his coolness of mind, and at last resolved to deal plainly with Passepartout. If he did not find it practicable to arrest Fogg at Hong Kong, and if Fogg made preparations to leave that last foothold of English territory, he, Fix, would tell Passepartout all. Either the servant was the accomplice of his master, and in this case the master knew of his operations, and he should fail; or else the servant knew nothing about the robbery, and then his interest would be to abandon the robber.

Such was the situation between Fix and Passepartout. Meanwhile Phileas Fogg moved about above them in the most majestic and unconscious indifference. He was passing methodically in his orbit around the world, regardless of the lesser stars which gravitated around him. Yet there was near by what the astronomers would call a disturbing star, which might have produced an agitation in this gentleman's heart. But no! the charms of Aouda failed to act, to Passepartout's great surprise; and the disturbances, if they existed, would have been more difficult to calculate than those of Uranus which led to the discovery of Neptune.

It was every day an increasing wonder to Passepartout, who read in Aouda's eyes the depths of her gratitude to his master. Phileas Fogg, though brave and gallant, must be, he thought, quite heartless. As to the sentiment which this journey might have awakened in him, there was clearly no trace of such a thing; while poor Passepartout existed in perpetual reveries.

One day he was leaning on the railing of the engine-room, and was observing the engine, when a sudden pitch of the steamer threw the screw out of the water. The steam came hissing out of the valves; and this made Passepartout indignant.

'The valves are not sufficiently charged!' he exclaimed. 'We are not going. Oh, these English! If this was an American craft, we should blow up, perhaps, but we should at all events go faster!'

CHAPTER 18

In which Phileas Fogg, Passepartout, and Fix go each about his business

The weather was bad during the latter days of the voyage. The wind, obstinately remaining in the north-west, blew a gale, and retarded the steamer. The *Rangoon* rolled heavily and the passengers became impatient of the long, monstrous waves which the wind raised before their path. A sort of tempest arose on the 3rd of November, the squall knocking the vessel about with fury, and the waves running high. The *Rangoon* reefed all her sails, and even the rigging proved too much, whistling and shaking amid the squall. The steamer was forced to proceed slowly, and the captain estimated that she would reach Hong Kong twenty hours behind time, and more if the storm lasted.

Phileas Fogg gazed at the tempestuous sea, which seemed to be struggling especially to delay him, with his habitual tranquillity. He never changed countenance for an instant, though a delay of twenty hours, by making him too late for the Yokohama boat, would almost inevitably cause the loss of the wager. But this man of nerve manifested neither impatience nor annoyance; it seemed as if the storm were a part of his programme, and had been foreseen. Aouda was amazed to find him as calm as he had been from the first time she saw him.

Fix did not look at the state of things in the same light. The storm greatly pleased him. His satisfaction would have been complete had the *Rangoon* been forced to retreat before the violence of wind and waves. Each delay filled him with hope, for it became more and more probable that Fogg would be obliged to remain some days at Hong Kong; and now the heavens themselves became his allies, with the gusts and squalls. It mattered not that they made him sea-sick – he made no account of this inconvenience; and, whilst his body was writhing under their effects, his spirit bounded with hopeful exultation.

Passepartout was enraged beyond expression by the unpropitious weather. Everything had gone so well till now! Earth and sea had seemed to be at his master's service; steamers and railways obeyed him; wind and steam united to speed his journey. Had the hour of adversity come? Passepartout was as much excited as if the twenty thousand pounds were to come from his own pocket. The storm exasperated him, the gale made him furious, and he longed to lash the obstinate sea into obedience. Poor fellow! Fix carefully concealed from him his own satisfaction, for, had he betrayed it, Passepartout could scarcely have restrained himself from personal violence.

Passepartout remained on deck as long as the tempest lasted, being unable to remain quiet below, and taking it into his head to aid the progress of the ship by lending a hand with the crew. He overwhelmed the captain, officers, and sailors, who could not help laughing at his impatience, with all sorts of questions. He wanted to know exactly how long the storm was going to last; whereupon he was referred to the barometer, which seemed to have no intention of rising.

Passepartout shook it, but with no perceptible effect; for neither shaking nor maledictions could prevail upon it to change its mind.

On the 4th, however, the sea became more calm, and the storm lessened its violence; the wind veered southward, and was once more favourable. Passepartout cleared up with the weather. Some of the sails were unfurled, and the *Rangoon* resumed its most rapid speed. The time lost could not, however, be regained. Land was not signalled until five o'clock on the morning of the 6th; the steamer was due on the 5th. Phileas Fogg was twenty-four hours behind-hand, and the Yokohama steamer would, of course, be missed.

The pilot went on board at six, and took his place on the bridge, to guide the *Rangoon* through the channels to the port of Hong Kong. Passepartout longed to ask him if the steamer had left for Yokohama; but he dared not, for he wished to preserve the spark of hope, which still remained till the last moment. He had confided his anxiety to Fix who – the sly rascal! – tried to console him by saying that Mr. Fogg would be in time if he took the next boat; but this only put Passepartout in a passion.

Mr. Fogg, bolder than his servant, did not hesitate to approach the pilot, and tranquilly ask him if he knew when a steamer would leave Hong Kong for Yokohama.

'At high tide to-morrow morning,' answered the pilot.

'Ah!' said Mr. Fogg, without betraying any astonishment.

Passepartout, who heard what passed, would willingly have embraced the pilot, while Fix would have been glad to twist his neck.

'What is the steamer's name?' asked Mr. Fogg.

'The *Carnatic*.'

'Ought she not to have gone yesterday?'

'Yes, sir; but they had to repair one of her boilers, and so her departure was postponed till to-morrow.'

'Thank you,' returned Mr. Fogg, descending mathematically to the saloon.

Passepartout clasped the pilot's hand and shook it heartily in his delight, exclaiming, 'Pilot, you are the best of good fellows!'

The pilot probably does not know to this day why his responses won him this enthusiastic greeting. He remounted the bridge, and guided the steamer through the flotilla of junks, tankas, and fishing boats which crowd the harbour of Hong Kong.

At one o'clock the *Rangoon* was at the quay, and the passengers were going ashore.

Chance had strangely favoured Phileas Fogg, for had not the *Carnatic* been forced to lie over for repairing her boilers, she would have left on the 6th of November, and the passengers for Japan would have been obliged to await for a week the sailing of the next steamer. Mr. Fogg was, it is true, twenty-four hours behind his time; but this could not seriously imperil the remainder of his tour.

The steamer which crossed the Pacific from Yokohama to San Francisco made a direct connection with that from Hong Kong, and it could not sail until the latter reached Yokohama; and if Mr. Fogg was twenty-four hours late on reaching Yokohama, this time would no doubt be easily regained in the voyage of twenty-two days across the Pacific. He found himself, then, about twenty-four hours behind-hand, thirty-five days after leaving London.

The *Carnatic* was announced to leave Hong Kong at five the next morning. Mr. Fogg had sixteen hours in which to attend to his business there, which was to deposit Aouda safely with her wealthy relative.

On landing, he conducted her to a palanquin, in which they repaired to the Club Hotel. A room was engaged for the young woman, and Mr. Fogg, after seeing that she wanted for nothing, set out in search of her cousin Jeejeeh. He instructed Passepartout to remain at the hotel until his return, that Aouda might not be left entirely alone.

Mr. Fogg repaired to the Exchange, where, he did not doubt, every one would know so wealthy and considerable a personage as the Parsee merchant. Meeting a broker, he made the inquiry, to learn that Jeejeeh had left China two years before, and, retiring from business with an immense fortune, had taken up his residence in Europe – in Holland the broker thought, with the merchants of which country he had principally traded. Phileas Fogg returned to the hotel, begged a moment's conversation with Aouda, and without more ado, apprised her that Jeejeeh was no longer at Hong Kong, but probably in Holland.

Aouda at first said nothing. She passed her hand across her forehead, and reflected a few moments. Then, in her sweet, soft voice, she said: 'What ought I to do, Mr. Fogg?'

'It is very simple,' responded the gentleman. 'Go on to Europe.'

'But I cannot intrude – '

'You do not intrude, nor do you in the least embarrass my project. Passepartout!'

'Monsieur.'

'Go to the *Carnatic*, and engage three cabins.'

Passepartout, delighted that the young woman, who was very gracious to him, was going to continue the journey with them, went off at a brisk gait to obey his master's order.

CHAPTER 19

In which Passepartout takes too great interest in his master, and what comes of it

Hong Kong is an island which came into the possession of the English by the Treaty of Nankin, after the war of 1842; and the colonising genius of the English has created upon it an important city and an excellent port. The island is situated at the mouth of the Canton River, and is separated by about sixty miles from the Portuguese town of Macao, on the opposite coast. Hong Kong has beaten Macao in the struggle for the Chinese trade, and now the greater part of the transportation of Chinese goods finds its depot at the former place. Docks, hospitals, wharves, a Gothic cathedral, a government house, macadamised streets, give to Hong Kong the appearance of a town in Kent or Surrey transferred by some strange magic to the antipodes.

Passepartout wandered, with his hands in his pockets, towards the Victoria port, gazing as he went at the curious palanquins and other modes of conveyance, and the groups of Chinese, Japanese, and Europeans who passed to and fro in the streets. Hong Kong seemed to him not unlike Bombay, Calcutta, and Singapore, since, like them, it betrayed everywhere the evidence of English supremacy. At the Victoria port he found a confused mass of ships of all nations: English, French, American, and Dutch, men-of-war and trading vessels, Japanese and Chinese junks, sempas, tankas, and flower-boats, which formed so many floating parterres. Passepartout noticed in the crowd a number of the natives who seemed very old and were dressed in yellow. On going into a barber's to get shaved he learned that these ancient men were all at least eighty years old, at which age they are permitted to wear yellow, which is the Imperial colour. Passepartout, without exactly knowing why, thought this very funny.

On reaching the quay where they were to embark on the *Carnatic*, he was not astonished to find Fix walking up and down. The detective seemed very much disturbed and disappointed.

'This is bad,' muttered Passepartout, 'for the gentlemen of the Reform Club!' He accosted Fix with a merry smile, as if he had not perceived that gentleman's chagrin. The detective had, indeed, good reasons to inveigh against the bad luck which pursued him. The warrant had not come! It was certainly on the way, but as certainly it could not now reach Hong Kong for several days; and, this being the last English territory on Mr. Fogg's route, the robber would escape, unless he could manage to detain him.

'Well, Monsieur Fix,' said Passepartout, 'have you decided to go with us so far as America?'

'Yes,' returned Fix, through his set teeth.

'Good!' exclaimed Passepartout, laughing heartily. 'I knew you could not persuade yourself to separate from us. Come and engage your berth.'

They entered the steamer office and secured cabins for four persons. The clerk, as he gave them the tickets, informed them that, the repairs on the *Carnatic* having been completed, the steamer would leave that very evening, and not next morning, as had been announced.

'That will suit my master all the better,' said Passepartout. 'I will go and let him know.'

Fix now decided to make a bold move; he resolved to tell Passepartout all. It seemed to be the only possible means of keeping Phileas Fogg several days longer at Hong Kong. He accordingly invited his companion into a tavern which caught his eye on the quay. On entering, they found themselves in a large room handsomely decorated, at the end of which was a large camp-bed furnished with cushions. Several persons lay upon this bed in a deep sleep. At the small tables which were arranged about the room some thirty customers were drinking English beer, porter, gin, and brandy; smoking, the while, long red clay pipes stuffed with little balls of opium mingled with essence of rose. From time to time one of the smokers, overcome with the narcotic, would slip under the table, whereupon the waiters, taking him by the head and feet, carried and laid him upon the bed. The bed already supported twenty of these stupefied sots.

Fix and Passepartout saw that they were in a smoking-house haunted by those wretched, cadaverous, idiotic creatures to whom the English merchants sell every year the miserable drug called opium, to the amount of one million four hundred thousand pounds – thousands devoted to one of the most despicable vices which afflict humanity! The Chinese government has in vain attempted to deal with the evil by stringent laws. It passed gradually from the rich, to whom it was at first exclusively reserved, to the lower classes, and then its ravages could not be arrested. Opium is smoked everywhere, at all times, by men and women, in the Celestial

Empire; and, once accustomed to it, the victims cannot dispense with it, except by suffering horrible bodily contortions and agonies. A great smoker can smoke as many as eight pipes a day; but he dies in five years. It was in one of these dens that Fix and Passepartout, in search of a friendly glass, found themselves. Passepartout had no money, but willingly accepted Fix's invitation in the hope of returning the obligation at some future time.

They ordered two bottles of port, to which the Frenchman did ample justice, whilst Fix observed him with close attention. They chatted about the journey, and Passepartout was especially merry at the idea that Fix was going to continue it with them. When the bottles were empty, however, he rose to go and tell his master of the change in the time of the sailing of the *Carnatic*.

Fix caught him by the arm, and said, 'Wait a moment.'

'What for, Mr. Fix?'

'I want to have a serious talk with you.'

'A serious talk!' cried Passepartout, drinking up the little wine that was left in the bottom of his glass. 'Well, we'll talk about it to-morrow; I haven't time now.'

'Stay! What I have to say concerns your master.'

Passepartout, at this, looked attentively at his companion. Fix's face seemed to have a singular expression. He resumed his seat.

'What is it that you have to say?'

Fix placed his hand upon Passepartout's arm, and, lowering his voice, said, 'You have guessed who I am?'

'Parbleu!' said Passepartout, smiling.

'Then I'm going to tell you everything – '

'Now that I know everything, my friend! Ah! that's very good. But go on, go on. First, though, let me tell you that those gentlemen have put themselves to a useless expense.'

'Useless!' said Fix. 'You speak confidently. It's clear that you don't know how large the sum is.'

'Of course I do,' returned Passepartout. 'Twenty thousand pounds.'

'Fifty-five thousand!' answered Fix, pressing his companion's hand.

'What!' cried the Frenchman. 'Has Monsieur Fogg dared – fifty-five thousand pounds! Well, there's all the more reason for not losing an instant,' he continued, getting up hastily.

Fix pushed Passepartout back in his chair, and resumed: 'Fifty-five thousand pounds; and if I succeed, I get two thousand pounds. If you'll help me, I'll let you have five hundred of them.'

'Help you?' cried Passepartout, whose eyes were standing wide open.

'Yes; help me keep Mr. Fogg here for two or three days.'

'Why, what are you saying? Those gentlemen are not satisfied with following my master and suspecting his honour, but they must try to put obstacles in his way! I blush for them!'

'What do you mean?'

'I mean that it is a piece of shameful trickery. They might as well waylay Mr. Fogg and put his money in their pockets!'

'That's just what we count on doing.'

'It's a conspiracy, then,' cried Passepartout, who became more and more excited as the liquor mounted in his head, for he drank without perceiving it. 'A real conspiracy! And gentlemen, too. Bah!'

Fix began to be puzzled.

'Members of the Reform Club!' continued Passepartout. 'You must know, Monsieur Fix, that my master is an honest man, and that, when he makes a wager, he tries to win it fairly!'

'But who do you think I am?' asked Fix, looking at him intently.

'Parbleu! An agent of the members of the Reform Club, sent out here to interrupt my master's journey. But, though I found you out some time ago, I've taken good care to say nothing about it to Mr. Fogg.'

'He knows nothing, then?'

'Nothing,' replied Passepartout, again emptying his glass.

The detective passed his hand across his forehead, hesitating before he spoke again. What should he do? Passepartout's mistake seemed sincere, but it made his design more difficult. It was evident that the servant was not the master's accomplice, as Fix had been inclined to suspect.

'Well,' said the detective to himself, 'as he is not an accomplice, he will help me.'

He had no time to lose: Fogg must be detained at Hong Kong, so he resolved to make a clean breast of it.

'Listen to me,' said Fix abruptly. 'I am not, as you think, an agent of the members of the Reform Club – '

'Bah!' retorted Passepartout, with an air of raillery.

'I am a police detective, sent out here by the London office.'

'You, a detective?'

'I will prove it. Here is my commission.'

Passepartout was speechless with astonishment when Fix displayed this document, the genuineness of which could not be doubted.

'Mr. Fogg's wager,' resumed Fix, 'is only a pretext, of which you and the gentlemen of the Reform are dupes. He had a motive for securing your innocent complicity.'

'But why?'

'Listen. On the 28th of last September a robbery of fifty-five thousand pounds was committed at the Bank of England by a person whose description was fortunately secured. Here is his description; it answers exactly to that of Mr. Phileas Fogg.'

'What nonsense!' cried Passepartout, striking the table with his fist. 'My master is the most honourable of men!'

'How can you tell? You know scarcely anything about him. You went into his service the day he came away; and he came away on a foolish pretext, without trunks, and carrying a large amount in banknotes. And yet you are bold enough to assert that he is an honest man!'

'Yes, yes,' repeated the poor fellow, mechanically.

'Would you like to be arrested as his accomplice?'

Passepartout, overcome by what he had heard, held his head between his hands, and did not dare to look at the detective. Phileas Fogg, the saviour of Aouda, that brave and generous man, a robber! And yet how many presumptions there were against him! Passepartout essayed to reject the suspicions which forced themselves upon his mind; he did not wish to believe that his master was guilty.

'Well, what do you want of me?' said he, at last, with an effort.

'See here,' replied Fix; 'I have tracked Mr. Fogg to this place, but as yet I have failed to receive the warrant of arrest for which I sent to London. You must help me to keep him here in Hong Kong – '

'I! But I – '

'I will share with you the two thousand pounds reward offered by the Bank of England.'

'Never!' replied Passepartout, who tried to rise, but fell

back, exhausted in mind and body.

'Mr. Fix,' he stammered, 'even should what you say be true – if my master is really the robber you are seeking for – which I deny – I have been, am, in his service; I have seen his generosity and goodness; and I will never betray him – not for all the gold in the world. I come from a village where they don't eat that kind of bread!'

'You refuse?'

'I refuse.'

'Consider that I've said nothing,' said Fix; 'and let us drink.'

'Yes; let us drink!'

Passepartout felt himself yielding more and more to the effects of the liquor. Fix, seeing that he must, at all hazards, be separated from his master, wished to entirely overcome him. Some pipes full of opium lay upon the table. Fix slipped one into Passepartout's hand. He took it, put it between his lips, lit it, drew several puffs, and his head, becoming heavy under the influence of the narcotic, fell upon the table.

'At last!' said Fix, seeing Passepartout unconscious. 'Mr. Fogg will not be informed of the *Carnatic*'s departure; and, if he is, he will have to go without this cursed Frenchman!'

And, after paying his bill, Fix left the tavern.

CHAPTER 20

In which Fix comes face to face with Phileas Fogg

While these events were passing at the opium-house, Mr. Fogg, unconscious of the danger he was in of losing the steamer, was quietly escorting Aouda about the streets of the English quarter, making the necessary purchases for the long voyage before them. It was all very well for an Englishman like Mr. Fogg to make the tour of the world with a carpet-bag; a lady could not be expected to travel comfortably under such conditions. He acquitted his task with characteristic serenity, and invariably replied to the remonstrances of his fair companion, who was confused by his patience and generosity:

'It is in the interest of my journey – a part of my programme.'

The purchases made, they returned to the hotel, where they dined at a sumptuously served table-d'hote; after which Aouda, shaking hands with her protector after the English fashion, retired to her room for rest. Mr. Fogg absorbed himself throughout the evening in the perusal of The *Times* and *Illustrated London News*.

Had he been capable of being astonished at anything, it would have been not to see his servant return at bedtime. But, knowing that the steamer was not to leave for Yokohama until the next morning, he did not disturb himself about the matter. When Passepartout did not appear the next morning to answer his master's bell, Mr. Fogg, not betraying the least vexation, contented himself with taking his carpet-bag, calling Aouda, and sending for a palanquin.

It was then eight o'clock; at half-past nine, it being then high tide, the *Carnatic* would leave the harbour. Mr. Fogg and Aouda got into the palanquin, their luggage being brought after on a wheelbarrow, and half an hour later stepped upon the quay whence they were to embark. Mr. Fogg then learned that the *Carnatic* had sailed the evening before. He had expected to find not only the steamer, but his domestic, and was forced to give up both; but no sign of disappointment appeared on his face, and he merely remarked to Aouda, 'It is an accident, madam; nothing more.'

At this moment a man who had been observing him attentively approached. It was Fix, who, bowing, addressed Mr. Fogg: 'Were you not, like me, sir, a passenger by the *Rangoon*, which arrived yesterday?'

'I was, sir,' replied Mr. Fogg coldly. 'But I have not the honour – '

'Pardon me; I thought I should find your servant here.'

'Do you know where he is, sir?' asked Aouda anxiously.

'What!' responded Fix, feigning surprise. 'Is he not with you?'

'No,' said Aouda. 'He has not made his appearance since yesterday. Could he have gone on board the *Carnatic* without us?'

'Without you, madam?' answered the detective. 'Excuse me, did you intend to sail in the *Carnatic*?'

'Yes, sir.'

'So did I, madam, and I am excessively disappointed. The *Carnatic*, its repairs being completed, left Hong Kong twelve hours before the stated time, without any notice being given; and we must now wait a week for another steamer.'

As he said 'a week' Fix felt his heart leap for joy. Fogg detained at Hong Kong for a week! There would be time for the warrant to arrive, and fortune at last favoured the representative of the law. His horror may be imagined when he heard Mr. Fogg say, in his placid voice, 'But there are other vessels besides the *Carnatic*, it seems to me, in the harbour of Hong Kong.'

And, offering his arm to Aouda, he directed his steps toward the docks in search of some craft about to start. Fix, stupefied, followed; it seemed as if he were attached to Mr. Fogg by an invisible thread. Chance, however, appeared really to have abandoned the man it had hitherto served so well. For three hours Phileas Fogg wandered about the docks, with the determination, if necessary, to charter a vessel to carry him to Yokohama; but he could only find vessels which were loading or unloading, and which could not therefore set sail. Fix began to hope again.

But Mr. Fogg, far from being discouraged, was continuing his search, resolved not to stop if he had to resort to Macao, when he was accosted by a sailor on one of the wharves.

'Is your honour looking for a boat?'

'Have you a boat ready to sail?'

'Yes, your honour; a pilot-boat – No. 43 – the best in the harbour.'

'Does she go fast?'

'Between eight and nine knots the hour. Will you look at her?'

'Yes.'

'Your honour will be satisfied with her. Is it for a sea excursion?'

'No; for a voyage.'

'A voyage?'

'Yes, will you agree to take me to Yokohama?'

The sailor leaned on the railing, opened his eyes wide, and said, 'Is your honour joking?'

'No. I have missed the *Carnatic*, and I must get to Yokohama by the 14th at the latest, to take the boat for San Francisco.'

'I am sorry,' said the sailor; 'but it is impossible.'

'I offer you a hundred pounds per day, and an additional reward of two hundred pounds if I reach Yokohama in time.'

'Are you in earnest?'

'Very much so.'

The pilot walked away a little distance, and gazed out to sea, evidently struggling between the anxiety to gain a large sum and the fear of venturing so far. Fix was in mortal suspense.

Mr. Fogg turned to Aouda and asked her, 'You would not be afraid, would you, madam?'

'Not with you, Mr. Fogg,' was her answer.

The pilot now returned, shuffling his hat in his hands.

'Well, pilot?' said Mr. Fogg.

'Well, your honour,' replied he, 'I could not risk myself, my men, or my little boat of scarcely twenty tons on so long a voyage at this time of year. Besides, we could not reach Yokohama in time, for it is sixteen hundred and sixty miles from Hong Kong.'

'Only sixteen hundred,' said Mr. Fogg.

'It's the same thing.'

Fix breathed more freely.

CHAPTER 20

'But,' added the pilot, 'it might be arranged another way.'
Fix ceased to breathe at all.

'How?' asked Mr. Fogg.

'By going to Nagasaki, at the extreme south of Japan, or even to Shanghai, which is only eight hundred miles from here. In going to Shanghai we should not be forced to sail wide of the Chinese coast, which would be a great advantage, as the currents run northward, and would aid us.'

'Pilot,' said Mr. Fogg, 'I must take the American steamer at Yokohama, and not at Shanghai or Nagasaki.'

'Why not?' returned the pilot. 'The San Francisco steamer does not start from Yokohama. It puts in at Yokohama and Nagasaki, but it starts from Shanghai.'

'You are sure of that?'

'Perfectly.'

'And when does the boat leave Shanghai?'

'On the 11th, at seven in the evening. We have, therefore, four days before us, that is ninety-six hours; and in that time, if we had good luck and a south-west wind, and the sea was calm, we could make those eight hundred miles to Shanghai.'

'And you could go – '

'In an hour; as soon as provisions could be got aboard and the sails put up.'

'It is a bargain. Are you the master of the boat?'

'Yes; John Bunsby, master of the *Tankadere*.'

'Would you like some earnest-money?'

'If it would not put your honour out – '

'Here are two hundred pounds on account sir,' added Phileas Fogg, turning to Fix, 'if you would like to take advantage – '

'Thanks, sir; I was about to ask the favour.'

'Very well. In half an hour we shall go on board.'

'But poor Passepartout?' urged Aouda, who was much disturbed by the servant's disappearance.

'I shall do all I can to find him,' replied Phileas Fogg.

While Fix, in a feverish, nervous state, repaired to the pilot-boat, the others directed their course to the police-station at Hong Kong. Phileas Fogg there gave Passepartout's description, and left a sum of money to be spent in the search for him. The same formalities having been gone through at the French consulate, and the palanquin having stopped at the hotel for the luggage, which had been sent back there, they returned to the wharf.

It was now three o'clock; and pilot-boat No. 43, with its crew on board, and its provisions stored away, was ready for departure.

The *Tankadere* was a neat little craft of twenty tons, as gracefully built as if she were a racing yacht. Her shining copper sheathing, her galvanised iron-work, her deck, white as ivory, betrayed the pride taken by John Bunsby in making her presentable. Her two masts leaned a trifle backward; she carried brigantine, foresail, storm-jib, and standing-jib, and was well rigged for running before the wind; and she seemed capable of brisk speed, which, indeed, she had already proved by gaining several prizes in pilot-boat races. The crew of the *Tankadere* was composed of John Bunsby, the master, and four hardy mariners, who were familiar with the Chinese seas. John Bunsby, himself, a man of forty-five or thereabouts, vigorous, sunburnt, with a sprightly expression of the eye, and energetic and self-reliant countenance, would have inspired confidence in the most timid.

Phileas Fogg and Aouda went on board, where they found Fix already installed. Below deck was a square cabin, of which the walls bulged out in the form of cots, above a circular divan; in the centre was a table provided with a swinging lamp. The accommodation was confined, but neat.

'I am sorry to have nothing better to offer you,' said Mr. Fogg to Fix, who bowed without responding.

The detective had a feeling akin to humiliation in profiting by the kindness of Mr. Fogg.

'It's certain,' thought he, 'though rascal as he is, he is a polite one!'

The sails and the English flag were hoisted at ten minutes past three. Mr. Fogg and Aouda, who were seated on deck, cast a last glance at the quay, in the hope of espying Passepartout. Fix was not without his fears lest chance should direct the steps of the unfortunate servant, whom he had so badly treated, in this direction; in which case an explanation the reverse of satisfactory to the detective must have ensued. But the Frenchman did not appear, and, without doubt, was still lying under the stupefying influence of the opium.

John Bunsby, master, at length gave the order to start, and the *Tankadere*, taking the wind under her brigantine, foresail, and standing-jib, bounded briskly forward over the waves.

CHAPTER 21

In which the master of the 'Tankadere' runs great risk of losing a reward of two hundred pounds

This voyage of eight hundred miles was a perilous venture on a craft of twenty tons, and at that season of the year. The Chinese seas are usually boisterous, subject to terrible gales of wind, and especially during the equinoxes; and it was now early November.

It would clearly have been to the master's advantage to carry his passengers to Yokohama, since he was paid a certain sum per day; but he would have been rash to attempt such a voyage, and it was imprudent even to attempt to reach Shanghai. But John Bunsby believed in the *Tankadere*, which rode on the waves like a seagull; and perhaps he was not wrong.

Late in the day they passed through the capricious channels of Hong Kong, and the *Tankadere*, impelled by favourable winds, conducted herself admirably.

'I do not need, pilot,' said Phileas Fogg, when they got into the open sea, 'to advise you to use all possible speed.'

'Trust me, your honour. We are carrying all the sail the wind will let us. The poles would add nothing, and are only used when we are going into port.'

'It's your trade, not mine, pilot, and I confide in you.'

Phileas Fogg, with body erect and legs wide apart, standing like a sailor, gazed without staggering at the swelling waters. The young woman, who was seated aft, was profoundly affected as she looked out upon the ocean, darkening now with the twilight, on which she had ventured in so frail a vessel. Above her head rustled the white sails, which seemed like great white wings. The boat, carried forward by the wind, seemed to be flying in the air.

Night came. The moon was entering her first quarter, and her insufficient light would soon die out in the mist on the horizon. Clouds were rising from the east, and already overcast a part of the heavens.

The pilot had hung out his lights, which was very necessary in these seas crowded with vessels bound landward; for collisions are not uncommon occurrences, and, at the speed she was going, the least shock would shatter the gallant little craft.

Fix, seated in the bow, gave himself up to meditation. He kept apart from his fellow-travellers, knowing Mr. Fogg's taciturn tastes; besides, he did not quite like to talk to the man whose favours he had accepted. He was thinking, too, of the future. It seemed certain that Fogg would not stop at Yokohama, but would at once take the boat for San Francisco; and the vast extent of America would ensure him impunity and safety. Fogg's plan appeared to him the simplest in the world. Instead of sailing directly from England to the United States, like a common villain, he had traversed three quarters of the globe, so as to gain the American continent more surely; and there, after throwing the police off his track, he would quietly enjoy himself with the fortune stolen from the bank. But, once in the United States, what should he, Fix, do?

Should he abandon this man? No, a hundred times no! Until he had secured his extradition, he would not lose sight of him for an hour. It was his duty, and he would fulfil it to the end. At all events, there was one thing to be thankful for; Passepartout was not with his master; and it was above all important, after the confidences Fix had imparted to him, that the servant should never have speech with his master.

Phileas Fogg was also thinking of Passepartout, who had so strangely disappeared. Looking at the matter from every point of view, it did not seem to him impossible that, by some mistake, the man might have embarked on the *Carnatic* at the last moment; and this was also Aouda's opinion, who regretted very much the loss of the worthy fellow to whom she owed so much. They might then find him at Yokohama; for, if the *Carnatic* was carrying him thither, it would be easy to ascertain if he had been on board.

A brisk breeze arose about ten o'clock; but, though it might have been prudent to take in a reef, the pilot, after carefully examining the heavens, let the craft remain rigged as before. The *Tankadere* bore sail admirably, as she drew a great deal of water, and everything was prepared for high speed in case of a gale.

Mr. Fogg and Aouda descended into the cabin at midnight, having been already preceded by Fix, who had lain down on one of the cots. The pilot and crew remained on deck all night.

At sunrise the next day, which was 8th November, the boat had made more than one hundred miles. The log indicated a mean speed of between eight and nine miles. The *Tankadere* still carried all sail, and was accomplishing her greatest capacity of speed. If the wind held as it was, the chances would be in her favour. During the day she kept along the coast, where the currents were favourable; the coast, irregular in profile, and visible sometimes across the clearings, was at most five miles distant. The sea was less boisterous, since the wind came off land – a fortunate circumstance for the boat, which would suffer, owing to its small tonnage, by a heavy surge on the sea.

The breeze subsided a little towards noon, and set in from the south-west. The pilot put up his poles, but took them down again within two hours, as the wind freshened up anew.

Mr. Fogg and Aouda, happily unaffected by the roughness of the sea, ate with a good appetite, Fix being invited to share their repast, which he accepted with secret chagrin. To travel at this man's expense and live upon his provisions was not palatable to him. Still, he was obliged to eat, and so he ate.

When the meal was over, he took Mr. Fogg apart, and said, 'sir' – this 'sir' scorched his lips, and he had to control himself to avoid collaring this 'gentleman' – 'sir, you have been very kind to give me a passage on this boat. But, though my means will not admit of my expending them as freely as you, I must ask to pay my share – '

'Let us not speak of that, sir,' replied Mr. Fogg.

'But, if I insist – '

'No, sir,' repeated Mr. Fogg, in a tone which did not admit of a reply. 'This enters into my general expenses.'

Fix, as he bowed, had a stifled feeling, and, going forward, where he ensconced himself, did not open his mouth for the rest of the day.

Meanwhile they were progressing famously, and John Bunsby was in high hope. He several times assured Mr. Fogg that they would reach Shanghai in time; to which that gentleman responded that he counted upon it. The crew set to work in good earnest, inspired by the reward to be gained. There was not a sheet which was not tightened, not a sail which was not vigorously hoisted; not a lurch could be charged to the man at the helm. They worked as desperately as if they were contesting in a Royal yacht regatta.

By evening, the log showed that two hundred and twenty miles had been accomplished from Hong Kong, and Mr. Fogg might hope that he would be able to reach Yokohama without recording any delay in his journal; in which case, the many misadventures which had overtaken him since he left London would not seriously affect his journey.

The *Tankadere* entered the Straits of Fo-Kien, which separate the island of Formosa from the Chinese coast, in the small hours of the night, and crossed the Tropic of Cancer. The sea was very rough in the straits, full of eddies formed by the counter-currents, and the chopping waves broke her course, whilst it became very difficult to stand on deck.

At daybreak the wind began to blow hard again, and the heavens seemed to predict a gale. The barometer announced a speedy change, the mercury rising and falling capriciously; the sea also, in the south-east, raised long surges which indicated a tempest. The sun had set the evening before in a red mist, in the midst of the phosphorescent scintillations of the ocean.

John Bunsby long examined the threatening aspect of the heavens, muttering indistinctly between his teeth. At last he said in a low voice to Mr. Fogg, 'Shall I speak out to your honour?'

'Of course.'

'Well, we are going to have a squall.'

'Is the wind north or south?' asked Mr. Fogg quietly.

'South. Look! a typhoon is coming up.'

'Glad it's a typhoon from the south, for it will carry us forward.'

'Oh, if you take it that way,' said John Bunsby, 'I've nothing more to say.' John Bunsby's suspicions were confirmed. At a less advanced season of the year the typhoon, according to a famous meteorologist, would have passed away like a luminous cascade of electric flame; but in the winter equinox it was to be feared that it would burst upon them with great violence.

The pilot took his precautions in advance. He reefed all sail, the pole-masts were dispensed with; all hands went forward to the bows. A single triangular sail, of strong canvas, was hoisted as a storm-jib, so as to hold the wind from behind. Then they waited.

John Bunsby had requested his passengers to go below; but this imprisonment in so narrow a space, with little air, and the boat bouncing in the gale, was far from pleasant. Neither Mr. Fogg, Fix, nor Aouda consented to leave the deck.

The storm of rain and wind descended upon them towards eight o'clock. With but its bit of sail, the *Tankadere* was lifted like a feather by a wind, an idea of whose violence can scarcely be given. To compare her speed to four times that of a locomotive going on full steam would be below the truth.

The boat scudded thus northward during the whole day, borne on by monstrous waves, preserving always, fortunately, a speed equal to theirs. Twenty times she seemed almost to be submerged by these mountains of water which rose behind her; but the adroit management of the pilot saved her. The passengers were often bathed in spray, but they submitted to it philosophically. Fix cursed it, no doubt; but Aouda, with her eyes fastened upon her protector, whose coolness amazed her, showed herself worthy of him, and bravely weathered the storm. As for Phileas Fogg, it seemed just as if the typhoon were a part of his programme.

Up to this time the *Tankadere* had always held her course to the north; but towards evening the wind, veering three quarters, bore down from the north-west. The boat, now lying in the trough of the waves, shook and rolled terribly; the sea struck her with fearful violence. At night the tempest increased in violence. John Bunsby saw the approach of darkness and the rising of the storm with dark misgivings. He thought awhile, and then asked his crew if it was not time to slacken speed. After a consultation he approached Mr. Fogg, and said, 'I think, your honour, that we should do well to make for one of the ports on the coast.'

'I think so too.'

'Ah!' said the pilot. 'But which one?'

'I know of but one,' returned Mr. Fogg tranquilly.

'And that is – '

'Shanghai.'

The pilot, at first, did not seem to comprehend; he could scarcely realise so much determination and tenacity. Then he cried, 'Well – yes! Your honour is right. To Shanghai!'

So the *Tankadere* kept steadily on her northward track.

The night was really terrible; it would be a miracle if the craft did not founder. Twice it could have been all over with her if the crew had not been constantly on the watch. Aouda was exhausted, but did not utter a complaint. More than once Mr. Fogg rushed to protect her from the violence of the waves.

Day reappeared. The tempest still raged with undiminished fury; but the wind now returned to the south-east. It was a favourable change, and the *Tankadere* again bounded forward on this mountainous sea, though the waves crossed each other, and imparted shocks and counter-shocks which would have crushed a craft less solidly built. From time to time the coast was visible through the broken mist, but no vessel was in sight. The *Tankadere* was alone upon the sea.

There were some signs of a calm at noon, and these became more distinct as the sun descended toward the horizon. The tempest had been as brief as terrific. The passengers, thoroughly exhausted, could now eat a little, and take some repose.

The night was comparatively quiet. Some of the sails were again hoisted, and the speed of the boat was very good. The next morning at dawn they espied the coast, and John Bunsby was able to assert that they were not one hundred miles from Shanghai. A hundred miles, and only one day to traverse them! That very evening Mr. Fogg was due at Shanghai, if he did not wish to miss the steamer to Yokohama. Had there been no storm, during which several hours were lost, they would be at this moment within thirty miles of their destination.

The wind grew decidedly calmer, and happily the sea fell with it. All sails were now hoisted, and at noon the *Tankadere* was within forty-five miles of Shanghai. There remained yet six hours in which to accomplish that distance. All on board feared that it could not be done, and every one – Phileas Fogg, no doubt, excepted – felt his heart beat with impatience. The boat must keep up an average of nine miles an hour, and the wind was becoming calmer every moment! It was a capricious breeze, coming from the coast, and after it passed the sea became smooth. Still, the *Tankadere* was so light, and her fine sails caught the fickle zephyrs so well, that, with the aid of the currents John Bunsby found himself at six o'clock not more than ten miles from the mouth of

Shanghai River. Shanghai itself is situated at least twelve miles up the stream. At seven they were still three miles from Shanghai. The pilot swore an angry oath; the reward of two hundred pounds was evidently on the point of escaping him. He looked at Mr. Fogg. Mr. Fogg was perfectly tranquil; and yet his whole fortune was at this moment at stake.

At this moment, also, a long black funnel, crowned with wreaths of smoke, appeared on the edge of the waters. It was the American steamer, leaving for Yokohama at the appointed time.

'Confound her!' cried John Bunsby, pushing back the rudder with a desperate jerk.

'Signal her!' said Phileas Fogg quietly.

A small brass cannon stood on the forward deck of the *Tankadere*, for making signals in the fogs. It was loaded to the muzzle; but just as the pilot was about to apply a red-hot coal to the touchhole, Mr. Fogg said, 'Hoist your flag!'

The flag was run up at half-mast, and, this being the signal of distress, it was hoped that the American steamer, perceiving it, would change her course a little, so as to succour the pilot-boat.

'Fire!' said Mr. Fogg. And the booming of the little cannon resounded in the air.

CHAPTER 22

In which Passepartout finds out that, even at the Antipodes, it is convenient to have some money in one's pocket

The *Carnatic*, setting sail from Hong Kong at half-past six on the 7th of November, directed her course at full steam towards Japan. She carried a large cargo and a well-filled cabin of passengers. Two state-rooms in the rear were, however, unoccupied – those which had been engaged by Phileas Fogg.

The next day a passenger with a half-stupefied eye, staggering gait, and disordered hair, was seen to emerge from the second cabin, and to totter to a seat on deck.

It was Passepartout; and what had happened to him was as follows: Shortly after Fix left the opium den, two waiters had lifted the unconscious Passepartout, and had carried him to the bed reserved for the smokers. Three hours later, pursued even in his dreams by a fixed idea, the poor fellow awoke, and struggled against the stupefying influence of the narcotic. The thought of a duty unfulfilled shook off his torpor, and he hurried from the abode of drunkenness. Staggering and holding himself up by keeping against the walls, falling down and creeping up again, and irresistibly impelled by a kind of instinct, he kept crying out, 'The *Carnatic*! The *Carnatic*!'

The steamer lay puffing alongside the quay, on the point of starting. Passepartout had but few steps to go; and, rushing upon the plank, he crossed it, and fell unconscious on the deck, just as the *Carnatic* was moving off. Several sailors, who were evidently accustomed to this sort of scene, carried the poor Frenchman down into the second cabin, and Passepartout did not wake until they were one hundred and fifty miles away from China. Thus he found himself the next morning on the deck of the *Carnatic*, and eagerly inhaling the exhilarating sea-breeze. The pure air sobered him. He began to collect his sense, which he found a difficult task; but at last he recalled the events of the evening before, Fix's revelation, and the opium-house.

'It is evident,' said he to himself, 'that I have been abominably drunk! What will Mr. Fogg say? At least I have not missed the steamer, which is the most important thing.'

Then, as Fix occurred to him: 'As for that rascal, I hope we are well rid of him, and that he has not dared, as he proposed, to follow us on board the *Carnatic*. A detective on the track of Mr. Fogg, accused of robbing the Bank of England! Pshaw! Mr. Fogg is no more a robber than I am a murderer.'

Should he divulge Fix's real errand to his master? Would it do to tell the part the detective was playing? Would it not be better to wait until Mr. Fogg reached London again, and then impart to him that an agent of the metropolitan police had been following him round the world, and have a good laugh over it? No doubt; at least, it was worth considering. The first thing to do was to find Mr. Fogg, and apologise for his singular behaviour.

Passepartout got up and proceeded, as well as he could

with the rolling of the steamer, to the after-deck. He saw no one who resembled either his master or Aouda. 'Good!' muttered he; 'Aouda has not got up yet, and Mr. Fogg has probably found some partners at whist.'

He descended to the saloon. Mr. Fogg was not there. Passepartout had only, however, to ask the purser the number of his master's state-room. The purser replied that he did not know any passenger by the name of Fogg.

'I beg your pardon,' said Passepartout persistently. 'He is a tall gentleman, quiet, and not very talkative, and has with him a young lady – '

'There is no young lady on board,' interrupted the purser. 'Here is a list of the passengers; you may see for yourself.'

Passepartout scanned the list, but his master's name was not upon it. All at once an idea struck him.

'Ah! Am I on the *Carnatic*?'

'Yes.'

'On the way to Yokohama?'

'Certainly.'

Passepartout had for an instant feared that he was on the wrong boat; but, though he was really on the *Carnatic*, his master was not there.

He fell thunderstruck on a seat. He saw it all now. He remembered that the time of sailing had been changed, that he should have informed his master of that fact, and that he had not done so. It was his fault, then, that Mr. Fogg and Aouda had missed the steamer. Yes, but it was still more the fault of the traitor who, in order to separate him from his master, and detain the latter at Hong Kong, had inveigled him into getting drunk! He now saw the detective's trick; and at this moment Mr. Fogg was certainly ruined, his bet was lost, and he himself perhaps arrested and imprisoned! At this thought Passepartout tore his hair. Ah, if Fix ever came within his reach, what a settling of accounts there would be!

After his first depression, Passepartout became calmer, and began to study his situation. It was certainly not an enviable one. He found himself on the way to Japan, and what should he do when he got there? His pocket was empty; he had not a solitary shilling, not so much as a penny. His passage had fortunately been paid for in advance; and he had five or six days in which to decide upon his future course. He fell to at meals with an appetite, and ate for Mr. Fogg, Aouda, and himself. He helped himself as generously as if Japan were a desert, where nothing to eat was to be looked for.

At dawn on the 13th the *Carnatic* entered the port of Yokohama. This is an important port of call in the Pacific, where all the mail-steamers, and those carrying travellers between North America, China, Japan, and the Oriental islands put in. It is situated in the bay of Yeddo, and at but a short distance from that second capital of the Japanese Empire, and the residence of the Tycoon, the civil Emperor, before the Mikado, the spiritual Emperor, absorbed his office in his own. The *Carnatic* anchored at the quay near the custom-house, in the midst of a crowd of ships bearing the flags of all nations.

Passepartout went timidly ashore on this so curious territory of the Sons of the Sun. He had nothing better to do than, taking chance for his guide, to wander aimlessly through the streets of Yokohama. He found himself at first in a thoroughly European quarter, the houses having low fronts, and being adorned with verandas, beneath which he caught glimpses of neat peristyles. This quarter occupied, with its streets, squares, docks, and warehouses, all the space between the 'promontory of the Treaty' and the river. Here, as at Hong Kong and Calcutta, were mixed crowds of all races, Americans and English, Chinamen and Dutchmen, mostly merchants ready to buy or sell anything. The Frenchman felt himself as much alone among them as if he had dropped down in the midst of Hottentots.

He had, at least, one resource, – to call on the French and English consuls at Yokohama for assistance. But he shrank from telling the story of his adventures, intimately connected as it was with that of his master; and, before doing so, he determined to exhaust all other means of aid. As chance did not favour him in the European quarter, he penetrated that inhabited by the native Japanese, determined, if necessary, to push on to Yeddo.

The Japanese quarter of Yokohama is called Benten, after the goddess of the sea, who is worshipped on the islands round about. There Passepartout beheld beautiful fir and cedar groves, sacred gates of a singular architecture, bridges half hid in the midst of bamboos and reeds, temples shaded by immense cedar-trees, holy retreats where were sheltered Buddhist priests and sectaries of Confucius, and interminable streets, where a perfect harvest of rose-tinted and red-cheeked children, who looked as if they had been cut out of Japanese screens, and who were playing in the midst of short-legged poodles and yellowish cats, might have been gathered.

The streets were crowded with people. Priests were passing in processions, beating their dreary tambourines; police and custom-house officers with pointed hats encrusted with lac and carrying two sabres hung to their waists; soldiers, clad in blue cotton with white stripes, and bearing guns; the Mikado's guards, enveloped in silken doubles, hauberks and coats of mail; and numbers of military folk of all ranks – for the military profession is as much respected in Japan as it is despised in China – went hither and thither in groups and pairs. Passepartout saw, too, begging friars, long-robed pilgrims, and simple civilians, with their warped and jet-black hair, big heads, long busts, slender legs, short stature, and complexions varying from copper-colour to a dead white, but never yellow, like the Chinese, from whom the Japanese widely differ. He did not fail to observe the curious equipages – carriages and palanquins, barrows supplied with sails, and litters made of bamboo; nor the women – whom he thought not especially handsome – who took little steps with their little feet, whereon they wore canvas shoes, straw sandals, and clogs of worked wood, and who displayed tight-looking eyes, flat chests, teeth fashionably blackened, and gowns crossed with silken scarfs, tied in an enormous knot behind an ornament which the modern Parisian ladies seem to have borrowed from the dames of Japan.

Passepartout wandered for several hours in the midst of this motley crowd, looking in at the windows of the rich and curious shops, the jewellery establishments glittering with quaint Japanese ornaments, the restaurants decked with streamers and banners, the tea-houses, where the odorous beverage was being drunk with saki, a liquor concocted from the fermentation of rice, and the comfortable smoking-houses, where they were puffing, not opium, which is almost unknown in Japan, but a very fine, stringy tobacco. He went on till he found himself in the fields, in the midst of vast rice plantations. There he saw dazzling camellias expanding themselves, with flowers which were giving forth their last colours and perfumes, not on bushes, but on trees, and within bamboo enclosures, cherry, plum, and apple trees, which the Japanese cultivate rather for their blossoms than their fruit, and which queerly-fashioned, grinning scarecrows protected from the sparrows, pigeons, ravens, and other voracious birds. On the branches of the cedars were perched large eagles; amid the foliage of the weeping willows were herons, solemnly standing on one leg; and on every hand were crows, ducks, hawks, wild birds, and a multitude of cranes, which the Japanese consider sacred, and which to their minds symbolise long life and prosperity.

As he was strolling along, Passepartout espied some violets among the shrubs.

'Good!' said he; 'I'll have some supper.'

But, on smelling them, he found that they were odourless.

'No chance there,' thought he.

The worthy fellow had certainly taken good care to eat as hearty a breakfast as possible before leaving the *Carnatic*; but, as he had been walking about all day, the demands of hunger were becoming importunate. He observed that the butchers stalls contained neither mutton, goat, nor pork; and, knowing also that it is a sacrilege to kill cattle, which are preserved solely for farming, he made up his mind that meat was far from plentiful in Yokohama – nor was he mistaken; and, in default of butcher's meat, he could have wished for a quarter of wild boar or deer, a partridge, or some quails, some game or fish, which, with rice, the Japanese eat almost exclusively. But he found it necessary to keep up a stout heart, and to postpone the meal he craved till the following morning. Night came, and Passepartout re-entered the native quarter, where he wandered through the streets, lit by vari-coloured lanterns, looking on at the dancers, who were executing skilful steps and boundings, and the astrologers who stood in the open air with their telescopes. Then he came to the harbour, which was lit up by the resin torches of the fishermen, who were fishing from their boats.

The streets at last became quiet, and the patrol, the officers of which, in their splendid costumes, and surrounded by their suites, Passepartout thought seemed like ambassadors, succeeded the bustling crowd. Each time a company passed, Passepartout chuckled, and said to himself: 'Good! Another Japanese embassy departing for Europe!'

CHAPTER 23

In which Passepartout's nose becomes outrageously long

The next morning poor, jaded, famished Passepartout said to himself that he must get something to eat at all hazards, and the sooner he did so the better. He might, indeed, sell his watch; but he would have starved first. Now or never he must use the strong, if not melodious voice which nature had bestowed upon him. He knew several French and English songs, and resolved to try them upon the Japanese, who must be lovers of music, since they were for ever pounding on their cymbals, tam-tams, and tambourines, and could not but appreciate European talent.

It was, perhaps, rather early in the morning to get up a concert, and the audience prematurely aroused from their slumbers, might not possibly pay their entertainer with coin bearing the Mikado's features. Passepartout therefore decided to wait several hours; and, as he was sauntering along, it occurred to him that he would seem rather too well dressed for a wandering artist. The idea struck him to change his garments for clothes more in harmony with his project; by which he might also get a little money to satisfy the immediate cravings of hunger. The resolution taken, it remained to carry it out.

It was only after a long search that Passepartout discovered a native dealer in old clothes, to whom he applied for an exchange. The man liked the European costume, and ere long Passepartout issued from his shop accoutred in an old Japanese coat, and a sort of one-sided turban, faded with long use. A few small pieces of silver, moreover, jingled in his pocket.

'Good!' thought he. 'I will imagine I am at the Carnival!'

His first care, after being thus 'Japanesed,' was to enter a tea-house of modest appearance, and, upon half a bird and a little rice, to breakfast like a man for whom dinner was as yet a problem to be solved.

'Now,' thought he, when he had eaten heartily, 'I mustn't lose my head. I can't sell this costume again for one still more Japanese. I must consider how to leave this country of the Sun, of which I shall not retain the most delightful of memories, as quickly as possible.'

It occurred to him to visit the steamers which were about to leave for America. He would offer himself as a cook or servant, in payment of his passage and meals. Once at San Francisco, he would find some means of going on. The difficulty was, how to traverse the four thousand seven hundred miles of the Pacific which lay between Japan and the New World.

Passepartout was not the man to let an idea go begging, and directed his steps towards the docks. But, as he approached them, his project, which at first had seemed so simple, began to grow more and more formidable to his mind. What need would they have of a cook or servant on an American steamer, and what confidence would they put in him, dressed as he was? What references could he give?

As he was reflecting in this wise, his eyes fell upon an immense placard which a sort of clown was carrying through the streets. This placard, which was in English, read as follows:

ACROBATIC JAPANESE TROUPE,

HONOURABLE WILLIAM BATULCAR, PROPRIETOR,

LAST REPRESENTATIONS,

PRIOR TO THEIR DEPARTURE TO THE UNITED STATES, OF THE LONG NOSES! LONG NOSES!

UNDER THE DIRECT PATRONAGE OF THE GOD TINGOU!

GREAT ATTRACTION!

'The United States!' said Passepartout; 'that's just what I want!'

He followed the clown, and soon found himself once more in the Japanese quarter. A quarter of an hour later he stopped before a large cabin, adorned with several clusters of streamers, the exterior walls of which were designed to represent, in violent colours and without perspective, a company of jugglers.

This was the Honourable William Batulcar's establishment. That gentleman was a sort of Barnum, the director of a troupe of mountebanks, jugglers, clowns, acrobats, equilibrists, and gymnasts, who, according to the placard, was giving his last performances before leaving the Empire of the Sun for the States of the Union.

Passepartout entered and asked for Mr. Batulcar, who straightway appeared in person.

'What do you want?' said he to Passepartout, whom he at first took for a native.

'Would you like a servant, sir?' asked Passepartout.

'A servant!' cried Mr. Batulcar, caressing the thick grey beard which hung from his chin. 'I already have two who are obedient and faithful, have never left me, and serve me for their nourishment and here they are,' added he, holding out his two robust arms, furrowed with veins as large as the strings of a bass-viol.

'So I can be of no use to you?'

'None.'

'The devil! I should so like to cross the Pacific with you!'

'Ah!' said the Honourable Mr. Batulcar. 'You are no more a Japanese than I am a monkey! Who are you dressed up in that way?'

'A man dresses as he can.'

'That's true. You are a Frenchman, aren't you?'

'Yes; a Parisian of Paris.'

'Then you ought to know how to make grimaces?'

'Why,' replied Passepartout, a little vexed that his nationality should cause this question, 'we Frenchmen know how to make grimaces, it is true but not any better than the Americans do.'

'True. Well, if I can't take you as a servant, I can as a clown. You see, my friend, in France they exhibit foreign clowns, and in foreign parts French clowns.'

'Ah!'

'You are pretty strong, eh?'

'Especially after a good meal.'

'And you can sing?'

'Yes,' returned Passepartout, who had formerly been wont to sing in the streets.

'But can you sing standing on your head, with a top spinning on your left foot, and a sabre balanced on your right?'

'Humph! I think so,' replied Passepartout, recalling the exercises of his younger days.

'Well, that's enough,' said the Honourable William Batulcar.

CHAPTER 23

The engagement was concluded there and then.

Passepartout had at last found something to do. He was engaged to act in the celebrated Japanese troupe. It was not a very dignified position, but within a week he would be on his way to San Francisco.

The performance, so noisily announced by the Honourable Mr. Batulcar, was to commence at three o'clock, and soon the deafening instruments of a Japanese orchestra resounded at the door. Passepartout, though he had not been able to study or rehearse a part, was designated to lend the aid of his sturdy shoulders in the great exhibition of the 'human pyramid,' executed by the Long Noses of the god Tingou. This 'great attraction' was to close the performance.

Before three o'clock the large shed was invaded by the spectators, comprising Europeans and natives, Chinese and Japanese, men, women and children, who precipitated themselves upon the narrow benches and into the boxes opposite the stage. The musicians took up a position inside, and were vigorously performing on their gongs, tam-tams, flutes, bones, tambourines, and immense drums.

The performance was much like all acrobatic displays; but it must be confessed that the Japanese are the first equilibrists in the world.

One, with a fan and some bits of paper, performed the graceful trick of the butterflies and the flowers; another traced in the air, with the odorous smoke of his pipe, a series of blue words, which composed a compliment to the audience; while a third juggled with some lighted candles, which he extinguished successively as they passed his lips, and relit again without interrupting for an instant his juggling. Another reproduced the most singular combinations with a spinning-top; in his hands the revolving tops seemed to be animated with a life of their own in their interminable whirling; they ran over pipe-stems, the edges of sabres, wires and even hairs stretched across the stage; they turned around on the edges of large glasses, crossed bamboo ladders, dispersed into all the corners, and produced strange musical effects by the combination of their various pitches of tone. The jugglers tossed them in the air, threw them like shuttlecocks with wooden battledores, and yet they kept on spinning; they put them into their pockets, and took them out still whirling as before.

It is useless to describe the astonishing performances of the acrobats and gymnasts. The turning on ladders, poles, balls, barrels, &c., was executed with wonderful precision.

But the principal attraction was the exhibition of the Long Noses, a show to which Europe is as yet a stranger.

The Long Noses form a peculiar company, under the direct patronage of the god Tingou. Attired after the fashion of the Middle Ages, they bore upon their shoulders a splendid pair of wings; but what especially distinguished them was the long noses which were fastened to their faces, and the uses which they made of them. These noses were made of bamboo, and were five, six, and even ten feet long, some straight, others curved, some ribboned, and some having imitation warts upon them. It was upon these appendages, fixed tightly on their real noses, that they performed their gymnastic exercises. A dozen of these sectaries of Tingou lay flat upon their backs, while others, dressed to represent lightning-rods, came and frolicked on their noses, jumping from one to another, and performing the most skilful leapings and somersaults.

As a last scene, a 'human pyramid' had been announced, in which fifty Long Noses were to represent the Car of Juggernaut. But, instead of forming a pyramid by mounting each other's shoulders, the artists were to group themselves on top of the noses. It happened that the performer who had hitherto formed the base of the Car had quitted the troupe, and as, to fill this part, only strength and adroitness were necessary, Passepartout had been chosen to take his place.

The poor fellow really felt sad when – melancholy reminiscence of his youth! – he donned his costume, adorned with vari-coloured wings, and fastened to his natural feature a false nose six feet long. But he cheered up when he thought that this nose was winning him something to eat.

He went upon the stage, and took his place beside the rest who were to compose the base of the Car of Juggernaut. They all stretched themselves on the floor, their noses pointing to the ceiling. A second group of artists disposed themselves on these long appendages, then a third above these, then a fourth, until a human monument reaching to the very cornices of the theatre soon arose on top of the noses. This elicited loud applause, in the midst of which the orchestra was just striking up a deafening air, when the pyramid tottered, the balance was lost, one of the lower noses vanished from the pyramid, and the human monument was shattered like a castle built of cards!

It was Passepartout's fault. Abandoning his position, clearing the footlights without the aid of his wings, and, clambering up to the right-hand gallery, he fell at the feet of one of the spectators, crying, 'Ah, my master! my master!'

'You here?'

'Myself.'

'Very well; then let us go to the steamer, young man!'

Mr. Fogg, Aouda, and Passepartout passed through the lobby of the theatre to the outside, where they encountered the Honourable Mr. Batulcar, furious with rage. He demanded damages for the 'breakage' of the pyramid; and Phileas Fogg appeased him by giving him a handful of banknotes.

At half-past six, the very hour of departure, Mr. Fogg and Aouda, followed by Passepartout, who in his hurry had retained his wings, and nose six feet long, stepped upon the American steamer.

CHAPTER 24

During which Mr. Fogg and party cross the Pacific Ocean

What happened when the pilot-boat came in sight of Shanghai will be easily guessed. The signals made by the *Tankadere* had been seen by the captain of the Yokohama steamer, who, espying the flag at half-mast, had directed his course towards the little craft. Phileas Fogg, after paying the stipulated price of his passage to John Busby, and rewarding that worthy with the additional sum of five hundred and fifty pounds, ascended the steamer with Aouda and Fix; and they started at once for Nagasaki and Yokohama.

They reached their destination on the morning of the 14th of November. Phileas Fogg lost no time in going on board the *Carnatic*, where he learned, to Aouda's great delight – and perhaps to his own, though he betrayed no emotion – that Passepartout, a Frenchman, had really arrived on her the day before.

The San Francisco steamer was announced to leave that very evening, and it became necessary to find Passepartout, if possible, without delay. Mr. Fogg applied in vain to the French and English consuls, and, after wandering through the streets a long time, began to despair of finding his missing servant. Chance, or perhaps a kind of presentiment, at last led him into the Honourable Mr. Batulcar's theatre. He certainly would not have recognised Passepartout in the eccentric mountebank's costume; but the latter, lying on his back, perceived his master in the gallery. He could not help starting, which so changed the position of his nose as to bring the 'pyramid' pell-mell upon the stage.

All this Passepartout learned from Aouda, who recounted to him what had taken place on the voyage from Hong Kong to Shanghai on the *Tankadere*, in company with one Mr. Fix.

Passepartout did not change countenance on hearing this name. He thought that the time had not yet arrived to divulge to his master what had taken place between the detective and himself; and, in the account he gave of his absence, he simply excused himself for having been overtaken by drunkenness, in smoking opium at a tavern in Hong Kong.

Mr. Fogg heard this narrative coldly, without a word; and then furnished his man with funds necessary to obtain clothing more in harmony with his position. Within an hour the Frenchman had cut off his nose and parted with his wings, and retained nothing about him which recalled the sectary of the god Tingou.

The steamer which was about to depart from Yokohama to San Francisco belonged to the Pacific Mail Steamship Company, and was named the *General Grant*. She was a large paddle-wheel steamer of two thousand five hundred tons; well equipped and very fast. The massive walking-beam rose and fell above the deck; at one end a piston-rod worked up and down; and at the other was a connecting-rod which, in changing the rectilinear motion to a circular one, was directly connected with the shaft of the paddles. The *General Grant* was rigged with three masts, giving a large capacity for sails, and thus materially aiding the steam power. By making twelve miles an hour, she would cross the ocean in twenty-one days. Phileas Fogg was therefore justified in hoping that he would reach San Francisco by the 2nd of December, New York by the 11th, and London on the 20th – thus gaining several hours on the fatal date of the 21st of December.

There was a full complement of passengers on board, among them English, many Americans, a large number of coolies on their way to California, and several East Indian officers, who were spending their vacation in making the tour of the world. Nothing of moment happened on the voyage; the steamer, sustained on its large paddles, rolled but little, and the Pacific almost justified its name. Mr. Fogg was as calm and taciturn as ever. His young companion felt herself more and more attached to him by other ties than gratitude; his silent but generous nature impressed her more than she thought; and it was almost unconsciously that she yielded to emotions which did not seem to have the least effect upon her protector. Aouda took the keenest interest in his plans, and became impatient at any incident which seemed likely to retard his journey.

She often chatted with Passepartout, who did not fail to perceive the state of the lady's heart; and, being the most faithful of domestics, he never exhausted his eulogies of Phileas Fogg's honesty, generosity, and devotion. He took pains to calm Aouda's doubts of a successful termination of the journey, telling her that the most difficult part of it had passed, that now they were beyond the fantastic countries of Japan and China, and were fairly on their way to civilised places again. A railway train from San Francisco to New York, and a transatlantic steamer from New York to Liverpool, would doubtless bring them to the end of this impossible journey round the world within the period agreed upon.

On the ninth day after leaving Yokohama, Phileas Fogg had traversed exactly one half of the terrestrial globe. The *General Grant* passed, on the 23rd of November, the one hundred and eightieth meridian, and was at the very antipodes of London. Mr. Fogg had, it is true, exhausted fifty-two of the eighty days in which he was to complete the tour, and there were only twenty-eight left. But, though he was only half-way by the difference of meridians, he had really gone over two-thirds of the whole journey; for he had been obliged to make long circuits from London to Aden, from Aden to Bombay, from Calcutta to Singapore, and from Singapore to Yokohama. Could he have followed without deviation the fiftieth parallel, which is that of London, the whole distance would only have been about twelve thousand miles; whereas he would be forced, by the irregular methods of locomotion, to traverse twenty-six thousand, of which he had, on the 23rd of November, accomplished seventeen thousand five hundred. And now the course was a straight one, and Fix was no longer there to put obstacles in their way!

It happened also, on the 23rd of November, that Passepartout made a joyful discovery. It will be remembered that the obstinate fellow had insisted on keeping his famous family watch at London time, and on regarding that of the countries he had passed through as quite false and unreliable. Now, on this day, though he had not changed the hands, he found that his watch exactly agreed with the ship's chronometers. His triumph was hilarious. He would have liked to know what Fix would say if he were aboard!

'The rogue told me a lot of stories,' repeated Passepartout, 'about the meridians, the sun, and the moon! Moon, indeed! moonshine more likely! If one listened to that sort of people, a pretty sort of time one would keep! I was sure that the sun would some day regulate itself by my watch!'

Passepartout was ignorant that, if the face of his watch had been divided into twenty-four hours, like the Italian clocks, he would have no reason for exultation; for the hands of his watch would then, instead of as now indicating nine o'clock in the morning, indicate nine o'clock in the evening, that is, the twenty-first hour after midnight precisely the difference between London time and that of the one hundred and eightieth meridian. But if Fix had been able to explain this purely physical effect, Passepartout would not have admitted, even if he had comprehended it. Moreover, if the detective had been on board at that moment, Passepartout would have joined issue with him on a quite different subject, and in an entirely different manner.

Where was Fix at that moment?

He was actually on board the *General Grant*.

On reaching Yokohama, the detective, leaving Mr. Fogg, whom he expected to meet again during the day, had repaired at once to the English consulate, where he at last found the warrant of arrest. It had followed him from Bombay, and had come by the *Carnatic*, on which steamer he himself was supposed to be. Fix's disappointment may be imagined when he reflected that the warrant was now useless. Mr. Fogg had left English ground, and it was now necessary to procure his extradition!

'Well,' thought Fix, after a moment of anger, 'my warrant is not good here, but it will be in England. The rogue evidently intends to return to his own country, thinking he has thrown the police off his track. Good! I will follow him across the Atlantic. As for the money, heaven grant there may be some left! But the fellow has already spent in travelling, rewards, trials, bail, elephants, and all sorts of charges, more than five thousand pounds. Yet, after all, the Bank is rich!'

His course decided on, he went on board the *General Grant*, and was there when Mr. Fogg and Aouda arrived. To his utter amazement, he recognised Passepartout, despite his theatrical disguise. He quickly concealed himself in his cabin, to avoid an awkward explanation, and hoped – thanks to the number of passengers – to remain unperceived by Mr. Fogg's servant.

On that very day, however, he met Passepartout face to face on the forward deck. The latter, without a word, made a rush for him, grasped him by the throat, and, much to the amusement of a group of Americans, who immediately began to bet on him, administered to the detective a perfect volley of blows, which proved the great superiority of French over English pugilistic skill.

When Passepartout had finished, he found himself relieved and comforted. Fix got up in a somewhat rumpled condition, and, looking at his adversary, coldly said, 'Have you done?'

'For this time – yes.'

'Then let me have a word with you.'

'But I – '

'In your master's interests.'

Passepartout seemed to be vanquished by Fix's coolness, for he quietly followed him, and they sat down aside from the rest of the passengers.

'You have given me a thrashing,' said Fix. 'Good, I expected it. Now, listen to me. Up to this time I have been Mr. Fogg's adversary. I am now in his game.'

'Aha!' cried Passepartout; 'you are convinced he is an honest man?'

'No,' replied Fix coldly, 'I think him a rascal. Sh! don't

budge, and let me speak. As long as Mr. Fogg was on English ground, it was for my interest to detain him there until my warrant of arrest arrived. I did everything I could to keep him back. I sent the Bombay priests after him, I got you intoxicated at Hong Kong, I separated you from him, and I made him miss the Yokohama steamer.'

Passepartout listened, with closed fists.

'Now,' resumed Fix, 'Mr. Fogg seems to be going back to England. Well, I will follow him there. But hereafter I will do as much to keep obstacles out of his way as I have done up to this time to put them in his path. I've changed my game, you see, and simply because it was for my interest to change it. Your interest is the same as mine; for it is only in England that you will ascertain whether you are in the service of a criminal or an honest man.'

Passepartout listened very attentively to Fix, and was convinced that he spoke with entire good faith.

'Are we friends?' asked the detective.

'Friends? – no,' replied Passepartout; 'but allies, perhaps. At the least sign of treason, however, I'll twist your neck for you.'

'Agreed,' said the detective quietly.

Eleven days later, on the 3rd of December, the *General Grant* entered the bay of the Golden Gate, and reached San Francisco.

Mr. Fogg had neither gained nor lost a single day.

CHAPTER 25

In which a slight glimpse is had of San Francisco

It was seven in the morning when Mr. Fogg, Aouda, and Passepartout set foot upon the American continent, if this name can be given to the floating quay upon which they disembarked. These quays, rising and falling with the tide, thus facilitate the loading and unloading of vessels. Alongside them were clippers of all sizes, steamers of all nationalities, and the steamboats, with several decks rising one above the other, which ply on the Sacramento and its tributaries. There were also heaped up the products of a commerce which extends to Mexico, Chili, Peru, Brazil, Europe, Asia, and all the Pacific islands.

Passepartout, in his joy on reaching at last the American continent, thought he would manifest it by executing a perilous vault in fine style; but, tumbling upon some worm-eaten planks, he fell through them. Put out of countenance by the manner in which he thus 'set foot' upon the New World, he uttered a loud cry, which so frightened the innumerable cormorants and pelicans that are always perched upon these movable quays, that they flew noisily away.

Mr. Fogg, on reaching shore, proceeded to find out at what

hour the first train left for New York, and learned that this was at six o'clock p.m.; he had, therefore, an entire day to spend in the Californian capital. Taking a carriage at a charge of three dollars, he and Aouda entered it, while Passepartout mounted the box beside the driver, and they set out for the International Hotel.

From his exalted position Passepartout observed with much curiosity the wide streets, the low, evenly ranged houses, the Anglo-Saxon Gothic churches, the great docks, the palatial wooden and brick warehouses, the numerous conveyances, omnibuses, horse-cars, and upon the sidewalks, not only Americans and Europeans, but Chinese and Indians. Passepartout was surprised at all he saw. San Francisco was no longer the legendary city of 1849 – a city of banditti, assassins, and incendiaries, who had flocked hither in crowds in pursuit of plunder; a paradise of outlaws, where they gambled with gold-dust, a revolver in one hand and a bowie-knife in the other: it was now a great commercial emporium.

The lofty tower of its City Hall overlooked the whole panorama of the streets and avenues, which cut each other at right-angles, and in the midst of which appeared pleasant, verdant squares, while beyond appeared the Chinese quarter, seemingly imported from the Celestial Empire in a toy-box. Sombreros and red shirts and plumed Indians were rarely to be seen; but there were silk hats and black coats everywhere worn by a multitude of nervously active, gentlemanly-looking men. Some of the streets – especially Montgomery Street, which is to San Francisco what Regent Street is to London, the Boulevard des Italiens to Paris, and Broadway to New York – were lined with splendid and spacious stores, which exposed in their windows the products of the entire world.

When Passepartout reached the International Hotel, it did not seem to him as if he had left England at all.

The ground floor of the hotel was occupied by a large bar, a sort of restaurant freely open to all passers-by, who might partake of dried beef, oyster soup, biscuits, and cheese, without taking out their purses. Payment was made only for the ale, porter, or sherry which was drunk. This seemed 'very American' to Passepartout. The hotel refreshment-rooms were comfortable, and Mr. Fogg and Aouda, installing themselves at a table, were abundantly served on diminutive plates by negroes of darkest hue.

After breakfast, Mr. Fogg, accompanied by Aouda, started for the English consulate to have his passport visaed. As he was going out, he met Passepartout, who asked him if it would not be well, before taking the train, to purchase some dozens of Enfield rifles and Colt's revolvers. He had been listening to stories of attacks upon the trains by the Sioux and Pawnees. Mr. Fogg thought it a useless precaution, but told him to do as he thought best, and went on to the consulate.

He had not proceeded two hundred steps, however, when, 'by the greatest chance in the world,' he met Fix. The detective seemed wholly taken by surprise. What! Had Mr. Fogg and himself crossed the Pacific together, and not met on the steamer! At least Fix felt honoured to behold once more the gentleman to whom he owed so much, and, as his business recalled him to Europe, he should be delighted to continue the journey in such pleasant company.

Mr. Fogg replied that the honour would be his; and the detective – who was determined not to lose sight of him – begged permission to accompany them in their walk about San Francisco – a request which Mr. Fogg readily granted.

They soon found themselves in Montgomery Street, where a great crowd was collected; the side-walks, street, horsecar rails, the shop-doors, the windows of the houses, and even the roofs, were full of people. Men were going about carrying large posters, and flags and streamers were floating in the wind; while loud cries were heard on every hand.

'Hurrah for Camerfield!'

'Hurrah for Mandiboy!'

It was a political meeting; at least so Fix conjectured, who said to Mr. Fogg, 'Perhaps we had better not mingle with the crowd. There may be danger in it.'

'Yes,' returned Mr. Fogg; 'and blows, even if they are political are still blows.'

Fix smiled at this remark; and, in order to be able to see without being jostled about, the party took up a position on the top of a flight of steps situated at the upper end of Montgomery Street. Opposite them, on the other side of the street, between a coal wharf and a petroleum warehouse, a large platform had been erected in the open air, towards which the current of the crowd seemed to be directed.

For what purpose was this meeting? What was the occasion of this excited assemblage? Phileas Fogg could not imagine. Was it to nominate some high official – a governor or member of Congress? It was not improbable, so agitated was the multitude before them.

Just at this moment there was an unusual stir in the human mass. All the hands were raised in the air. Some, tightly closed, seemed to disappear suddenly in the midst of the cries – an energetic way, no doubt, of casting a vote. The crowd swayed back, the banners and flags wavered, disappeared an instant, then reappeared in tatters. The undulations of the human surge reached the steps, while all the heads floundered on the surface like a sea agitated by a squall. Many of the black hats disappeared, and the greater part of the crowd seemed to have diminished in height.

'It is evidently a meeting,' said Fix, 'and its object must be an exciting one. I should not wonder if it were about the Alabama, despite the fact that that question is settled.'

'Perhaps,' replied Mr. Fogg, simply.

'At least, there are two champions in presence of each other, the Honourable Mr. Camerfield and the Honourable Mr. Mandiboy.'

Aouda, leaning upon Mr. Fogg's arm, observed the tumultuous scene with surprise, while Fix asked a man near him what the cause of it all was. Before the man could reply, a fresh agitation arose; hurrahs and excited shouts were heard; the staffs of the banners began to be used as offensive weapons; and fists flew about in every direction. Thumps were exchanged from the tops of the carriages and omnibuses which had been blocked up in the crowd. Boots and shoes went whirling through the air, and Mr. Fogg thought he even heard the crack of revolvers mingling in the din, the rout approached the stairway, and flowed over the lower step. One of the parties had evidently been repulsed; but the mere lookers-on could not tell whether Mandiboy or Camerfield had gained the upper hand.

'It would be prudent for us to retire,' said Fix, who was anxious that Mr. Fogg should not receive any injury, at least until they got back to London. 'If there is any question about England in all this, and we were recognised, I fear it would go hard with us.'

'An English subject – ' began Mr. Fogg.

He did not finish his sentence; for a terrific hubbub now arose on the terrace behind the flight of steps where they stood, and there were frantic shouts of, 'Hurrah for Mandiboy! Hip, hip, hurrah!'

It was a band of voters coming to the rescue of their allies, and taking the Camerfield forces in flank. Mr. Fogg, Aouda, and Fix found themselves between two fires; it was too late to escape. The torrent of men, armed with loaded canes and sticks, was irresistible. Phileas Fogg and Fix were roughly hustled in their attempts to protect their fair companion; the former, as cool as ever, tried to defend himself with the weapons which nature has placed at the end of every Englishman's arm, but in vain. A big brawny fellow with a red beard, flushed face, and broad shoulders, who seemed to be the chief of the band, raised his clenched fist to strike Mr. Fogg, whom he would have given a crushing blow, had not Fix rushed in and received it in his stead. An enormous bruise immediately made its appearance under the detective's silk hat, which was completely smashed in.

'Yankee!' exclaimed Mr. Fogg, darting a contemptuous look at the ruffian.

'Englishman!' returned the other. 'We will meet again!'

'When you please.'

'What is your name?'

'Phileas Fogg. And yours?'

'Colonel Stamp Proctor.'

The human tide now swept by, after overturning Fix, who speedily got upon his feet again, though with tattered clothes. Happily, he was not seriously hurt. His travelling overcoat was divided into two unequal parts, and his trousers resembled those of certain Indians, which fit less compactly than they are easy to put on. Aouda had escaped unharmed, and Fix alone bore marks of the fray in his black and blue bruise.

'Thanks,' said Mr. Fogg to the detective, as soon as they were out of the crowd.

'No thanks are necessary,' replied. Fix; 'but let us go.'

'Where?'

'To a tailor's.'

Such a visit was, indeed, opportune. The clothing of both Mr. Fogg and Fix was in rags, as if they had themselves been actively engaged in the contest between Camerfield and Mandiboy. An hour after, they were once more suitably attired, and with Aouda returned to the International Hotel.

Passepartout was waiting for his master, armed with half a dozen six-barrelled revolvers. When he perceived Fix, he knit his brows; but Aouda having, in a few words, told him of their adventure, his countenance resumed its placid expression. Fix evidently was no longer an enemy, but an ally; he was faithfully keeping his word.

Dinner over, the coach which was to convey the passengers and their luggage to the station drew up to the door. As he was getting in, Mr. Fogg said to Fix, 'You have not seen this Colonel Proctor again?'

'No.'

'I will come back to America to find him,' said Phileas Fogg calmly. 'It would not be right for an Englishman to permit himself to be treated in that way, without retaliating.'

The detective smiled, but did not reply. It was clear that Mr. Fogg was one of those Englishmen who, while they do not tolerate duelling at home, fight abroad when their honour is attacked.

At a quarter before six the travellers reached the station, and found the train ready to depart. As he was about to enter it, Mr. Fogg called a porter, and said to him: 'My friend, was there not some trouble to-day in San Francisco?'

'It was a political meeting, sir,' replied the porter.

'But I thought there was a great deal of disturbance in the streets.'

'It was only a meeting assembled for an election.'

'The election of a general-in-chief, no doubt?' asked Mr. Fogg.

'No, sir; of a justice of the peace.'

Phileas Fogg got into the train, which started off at full speed.

CHAPTER 26

In which Phileas Fogg and party travel by the Pacific Railroad

'From ocean to ocean' – so say the Americans; and these four words compose the general designation of the 'great trunk line' which crosses the entire width of the United States. The Pacific Railroad is, however, really divided into two distinct lines: the Central Pacific, between San Francisco and Ogden, and the Union Pacific, between Ogden and Omaha. Five main lines connect Omaha with New York.

New York and San Francisco are thus united by an uninterrupted metal ribbon, which measures no less than three thousand seven hundred and eighty-six miles. Between Omaha and the Pacific the railway crosses a territory which is still infested by Indians and wild beasts, and a large tract which the Mormons, after they were driven from Illinois in 1845, began to colonise.

The journey from New York to San Francisco consumed, formerly, under the most favourable conditions, at least six months. It is now accomplished in seven days.

It was in 1862 that, in spite of the Southern Members of Congress, who wished a more southerly route, it was decided to lay the road between the forty-first and forty-second parallels. President Lincoln himself fixed the end of the line at Omaha, in Nebraska. The work was at once commenced, and pursued with true American energy; nor did the rapidity with which it went on injuriously affect its good execution. The road grew, on the prairies, a mile and a half a day. A locomotive, running on the rails laid down the evening before, brought the rails to be laid on the morrow, and advanced upon them as fast as they were put in position.

The Pacific Railroad is joined by several branches in Iowa, Kansas, Colorado, and Oregon. On leaving Omaha, it passes along the left bank of the Platte River as far as the junction of its northern branch, follows its southern branch, crosses the Laramie territory and the Wahsatch Mountains, turns the Great Salt Lake, and reaches Salt Lake City, the Mormon capital, plunges into the Tuilla Valley, across the American Desert, Cedar and Humboldt Mountains, the Sierra Nevada, and descends, via Sacramento, to the Pacific – its grade, even on the Rocky Mountains, never exceeding one hundred and twelve feet to the mile.

Such was the road to be traversed in seven days, which would enable Phileas Fogg – at least, so he hoped – to take the Atlantic steamer at New York on the 11th for Liverpool.

The car which he occupied was a sort of long omnibus on eight wheels, and with no compartments in the interior. It was supplied with two rows of seats, perpendicular to the direction of the train on either side of an aisle which conducted to the front and rear platforms. These platforms were found throughout the train, and the passengers were able to pass from one end of the train to the other. It was supplied with saloon cars, balcony cars, restaurants, and smoking-cars; theatre cars alone were wanting, and they will have these some day.

Book and news dealers, sellers of edibles, drinkables, and cigars, who seemed to have plenty of customers, were continually circulating in the aisles.

The train left Oakland station at six o'clock. It was already night, cold and cheerless, the heavens being overcast with clouds which seemed to threaten snow. The train did not proceed rapidly; counting the stoppages, it did not run more than twenty miles an hour, which was a sufficient speed, however, to enable it to reach Omaha within its designated time.

There was but little conversation in the car, and soon many of the passengers were overcome with sleep. Passepartout found himself beside the detective; but he did not talk to him. After recent events, their relations with each other had grown somewhat cold; there could no longer be mutual sympathy or intimacy between them. Fix's manner had not changed; but Passepartout was very reserved, and ready to strangle his former friend on the slightest provocation.

Snow began to fall an hour after they started, a fine snow, however, which happily could not obstruct the train; nothing could be seen from the windows but a vast, white sheet, against which the smoke of the locomotive had a greyish aspect.

At eight o'clock a steward entered the car and announced that the time for going to bed had arrived; and in a few minutes the car was transformed into a dormitory. The backs of the seats were thrown back, bedsteads carefully packed were rolled out by an ingenious system, berths were suddenly improvised, and each traveller had soon at his disposition a comfortable bed, protected from curious eyes by thick curtains. The sheets were clean and the pillows soft. It only remained to go to bed and sleep which everybody did – while the train sped on across the State of California.

The country between San Francisco and Sacramento is not very hilly. The Central Pacific, taking Sacramento for its starting-point, extends eastward to meet the road from Omaha. The line from San Francisco to Sacramento runs in a north-easterly direction, along the American River, which empties into San Pablo Bay. The one hundred and twenty miles between these cities were accomplished in six hours, and towards midnight, while fast asleep, the travellers passed through Sacramento; so that they saw nothing of that important place, the seat of the State government, with its fine quays, its broad streets, its noble hotels, squares, and churches.

The train, on leaving Sacramento, and passing the junction, Roclin, Auburn, and Colfax, entered the range of the Sierra Nevada. 'Cisco was reached at seven in the morning; and an hour later the dormitory was transformed into an ordinary car, and the travellers could observe the picturesque beauties of the mountain region through which they were steaming. The railway track wound in and out among the passes, now approaching the mountain-sides, now suspended over precipices, avoiding abrupt angles by bold curves, plunging into narrow defiles, which seemed to have no outlet. The locomotive, its great funnel emitting a weird light, with its sharp bell, and its cow-catcher extended like a spur, mingled its shrieks and bellowings with the noise of torrents and cascades, and twined its smoke among the branches of the gigantic pines.

There were few or no bridges or tunnels on the route. The railway turned around the sides of the mountains, and did not attempt to violate nature by taking the shortest cut from one point to another.

The train entered the State of Nevada through the Carson Valley about nine o'clock, going always northeasterly; and at midday reached Reno, where there was a delay of twenty minutes for breakfast.

From this point the road, running along Humboldt River, passed northward for several miles by its banks; then it turned eastward, and kept by the river until it reached the Humboldt Range, nearly at the extreme eastern limit of Nevada.

Having breakfasted, Mr. Fogg and his companions resumed their places in the car, and observed the varied landscape which unfolded itself as they passed along the vast prairies, the mountains lining the horizon, and the creeks, with their frothy, foaming streams. Sometimes a great herd of buffaloes, massing together in the distance, seemed like a moveable dam. These innumerable multitudes of ruminating beasts often form an insurmountable obstacle to the passage of the trains; thousands of them have been seen passing over the track for hours together, in compact ranks. The locomotive is then forced to stop and wait till the road is once more clear.

This happened, indeed, to the train in which Mr. Fogg was travelling. About twelve o'clock a troop of ten or twelve thousand head of buffalo encumbered the track. The locomotive, slackening its speed, tried to clear the way with its cow-catcher; but the mass of animals was too great. The buffaloes marched along with a tranquil gait, uttering now and then deafening bellowings. There was no use of interrupting them, for, having taken a particular direction, nothing can moderate and change their course; it is a torrent of living flesh which no dam could contain.

The travellers gazed on this curious spectacle from the platforms; but Phileas Fogg, who had the most reason of all to be in a hurry, remained in his seat, and waited philosophically until it should please the buffaloes to get out of the way.

Passepartout was furious at the delay they occasioned, and longed to discharge his arsenal of revolvers upon them.

'What a country!' cried he. 'Mere cattle stop the trains, and go by in a procession, just as if they were not impeding travel! Parbleu! I should like to know if Mr. Fogg foresaw this mishap in his programme! And here's an engineer who doesn't dare to run the locomotive into this herd of beasts!'

The engineer did not try to overcome the obstacle, and he was wise. He would have crushed the first buffaloes, no doubt, with the cow-catcher; but the locomotive, however powerful, would soon have been checked, the train would inevitably have been thrown off the track, and would then have been helpless.

The best course was to wait patiently, and regain the lost time by greater speed when the obstacle was removed. The procession of buffaloes lasted three full hours, and it was night before the track was clear. The last ranks of the herd were now passing over the rails, while the first had already disappeared below the southern horizon.

It was eight o'clock when the train passed through the defiles of the Humboldt Range, and half-past nine when it penetrated Utah, the region of the Great Salt Lake, the singular colony of the Mormons.

CHAPTER 27

In which Passepartout undergoes, at a speed of twenty miles an hour, a course of Mormon history

During the night of the 5th of December, the train ran south-easterly for about fifty miles; then rose an equal distance in a north-easterly direction, towards the Great Salt Lake.

Passepartout, about nine o'clock, went out upon the platform to take the air. The weather was cold, the heavens grey, but it was not snowing. The sun's disc, enlarged by the mist, seemed an enormous ring of gold, and Passepartout was amusing himself by calculating its value in pounds sterling, when he was diverted from this interesting study by a strange-looking personage who made his appearance on the platform.

This personage, who had taken the train at Elko, was tall and dark, with black moustache, black stockings, a black silk hat, a black waistcoat, black trousers, a white cravat, and dogskin gloves. He might have been taken for a clergyman. He went from one end of the train to the other, and affixed to the door of each car a notice written in manuscript.

Passepartout approached and read one of these notices, which stated that Elder William Hitch, Mormon missionary, taking advantage of his presence on train No. 48, would deliver a lecture on Mormonism in car No. 117, from eleven to twelve o'clock; and that he invited all who were desirous of being instructed concerning the mysteries of the religion of the 'Latter Day Saints' to attend.

'I'll go,' said Passepartout to himself. He knew nothing of Mormonism except the custom of polygamy, which is its foundation.

The news quickly spread through the train, which contained about one hundred passengers, thirty of whom, at most, attracted by the notice, ensconced themselves in car No. 117. Passepartout took one of the front seats. Neither Mr. Fogg nor Fix cared to attend.

At the appointed hour Elder William Hitch rose, and, in an irritated voice, as if he had already been contradicted, said, 'I tell you that Joe Smith is a martyr, that his brother Hiram is a martyr, and that the persecutions of the United States Government against the prophets will also make a martyr of Brigham Young. Who dares to say the contrary?'

No one ventured to gainsay the missionary, whose excited tone contrasted curiously with his naturally calm visage. No doubt his anger arose from the hardships to which the Mormons were actually subjected. The government had just succeeded, with some difficulty, in reducing these independent fanatics to its rule. It had made itself master of Utah, and subjected that territory to the laws of the Union, after imprisoning Brigham Young on a charge of rebellion and polygamy. The disciples of the prophet had since redoubled their efforts, and resisted, by words at least, the authority of Congress. Elder Hitch, as is seen, was trying to make proselytes on the very railway trains.

Then, emphasising his words with his loud voice and

frequent gestures, he related the history of the Mormons from Biblical times: how that, in Israel, a Mormon prophet of the tribe of Joseph published the annals of the new religion, and bequeathed them to his son Mormon; how, many centuries later, a translation of this precious book, which was written in Egyptian, was made by Joseph Smith, junior, a Vermont farmer, who revealed himself as a mystical prophet in 1825; and how, in short, the celestial messenger appeared to him in an illuminated forest, and gave him the annals of the Lord.

Several of the audience, not being much interested in the missionary's narrative, here left the car; but Elder Hitch, continuing his lecture, related how Smith, junior, with his father, two brothers, and a few disciples, founded the church of the 'Latter Day Saints,' which, adopted not only in America, but in England, Norway and Sweden, and Germany, counts many artisans, as well as men engaged in the liberal professions, among its members; how a colony was established in Ohio, a temple erected there at a cost of two hundred thousand dollars, and a town built at Kirkland; how Smith became an enterprising banker, and received from a simple mummy showman a papyrus scroll written by Abraham and several famous Egyptians.

The Elder's story became somewhat wearisome, and his audience grew gradually less, until it was reduced to twenty passengers. But this did not disconcert the enthusiast, who proceeded with the story of Joseph Smith's bankruptcy in 1837, and how his ruined creditors gave him a coat of tar and feathers; his reappearance some years afterwards, more honourable and honoured than ever, at Independence, Missouri, the chief of a flourishing colony of three thousand disciples, and his pursuit thence by outraged Gentiles, and retirement into the Far West.

Ten hearers only were now left, among them honest Passepartout, who was listening with all his ears. Thus he learned that, after long persecutions, Smith reappeared in Illinois, and in 1839 founded a community at Nauvoo, on the Mississippi, numbering twenty-five thousand souls, of which he became mayor, chief justice, and general-in-chief; that he announced himself, in 1843, as a candidate for the Presidency of the United States; and that finally, being drawn into ambuscade at Carthage, he was thrown into prison, and assassinated by a band of men disguised in masks.

Passepartout was now the only person left in the car, and the Elder, looking him full in the face, reminded him that, two years after the assassination of Joseph Smith, the inspired prophet, Brigham Young, his successor, left Nauvoo for the banks of the Great Salt Lake, where, in the midst of that fertile region, directly on the route of the emigrants who crossed Utah on their way to California, the new colony, thanks to the polygamy practised by the Mormons, had flourished beyond expectations.

'And this,' added Elder William Hitch, 'this is why the jealousy of Congress has been aroused against us! Why have the soldiers of the Union invaded the soil of Utah? Why has Brigham Young, our chief, been imprisoned, in contempt of all justice? Shall we yield to force? Never! Driven from Vermont, driven from Illinois, driven from Ohio, driven from Missouri, driven from Utah, we shall yet find some independent territory on which to plant our tents. And you, my brother,' continued the Elder, fixing his angry eyes upon his single auditor, 'will you not plant yours there, too, under the shadow of our flag?'

'No!' replied Passepartout courageously, in his turn retiring from the car, and leaving the Elder to preach to vacancy.

During the lecture the train had been making good progress, and towards half-past twelve it reached the northwest border of the Great Salt Lake. Thence the passengers could observe the vast extent of this interior sea, which is also called the Dead Sea, and into which flows an American Jordan. It is a picturesque expanse, framed in lofty crags in large strata, encrusted with white salt – a superb sheet of water, which was formerly of larger extent than now, its shores having encroached with the lapse of time, and thus at once reduced its breadth and increased its depth.

The Salt Lake, seventy miles long and thirty-five wide, is situated three miles eight hundred feet above the sea. Quite different from Lake Asphaltite, whose depression is twelve hundred feet below the sea, it contains considerable salt, and one quarter of the weight of its water is solid matter, its specific weight being 1,170, and, after being distilled, 1,000. Fishes are, of course, unable to live in it, and those which descend through the Jordan, the Weber, and other streams soon perish.

The country around the lake was well cultivated, for the Mormons are mostly farmers; while ranches and pens for domesticated animals, fields of wheat, corn, and other cereals, luxuriant prairies, hedges of wild rose, clumps of acacias and milk-wort, would have been seen six months later. Now the ground was covered with a thin powdering of snow.

The train reached Ogden at two o'clock, where it rested for six hours, Mr. Fogg and his party had time to pay a visit to Salt Lake City, connected with Ogden by a branch road; and they spent two hours in this strikingly American town, built on the pattern of other cities of the Union, like a checker-board, 'with the sombre sadness of right-angles,' as Victor Hugo expresses it. The founder of the City of the Saints could not escape from the taste for symmetry which distinguishes the Anglo-Saxons. In this strange country, where the people are certainly not up to the level of their institutions, everything is done 'squarely' – cities, houses, and follies.

The travellers, then, were promenading, at three o'clock, about the streets of the town built between the banks of the Jordan and the spurs of the Wahsatch Range. They saw few or no churches, but the prophet's mansion, the court-house, and the arsenal, blue-brick houses with verandas and porches, surrounded by gardens bordered with acacias, palms, and locusts. A clay and pebble wall, built in 1853, surrounded the town; and in the principal street were the market and several hotels adorned with pavilions. The place did not seem thickly populated. The streets were almost deserted, except in the vicinity of the temple, which they only reached after having traversed several quarters surrounded by palisades. There were many women, which was easily accounted for by the 'peculiar institution' of the Mormons; but it must not be supposed that all the Mormons are polygamists. They are free to marry or not, as they please; but it is worth noting that it is mainly the female citizens of Utah who are anxious to marry, as, according to the Mormon religion, maiden ladies are not admitted to the possession of its highest joys. These poor creatures seemed to be neither well off nor happy. Some – the more well-to-do, no doubt – wore short, open, black silk dresses, under a hood or modest shawl; others were habited in Indian fashion.

Passepartout could not behold without a certain fright these women, charged, in groups, with conferring happiness on a single Mormon. His common sense pitied, above all, the husband. It seemed to him a terrible thing to have to guide so many wives at once across the vicissitudes of life, and to conduct them, as it were, in a body to the Mormon paradise with the prospect of seeing them in the company of the glorious Smith, who doubtless was the chief ornament of that delightful place, to all eternity. He felt decidedly repelled from such a vocation, and he imagined – perhaps he was mistaken – that the fair ones of Salt Lake City cast rather alarming glances on his person. Happily, his stay there was but brief. At four the party found themselves again at the station, took their places in the train, and the whistle sounded for starting. Just at the moment, however, that the locomotive wheels began to move, cries of 'Stop! stop!' were heard.

Trains, like time and tide, stop for no one. The gentleman who uttered the cries was evidently a belated Mormon. He was breathless with running. Happily for him, the station had neither gates nor barriers. He rushed along the track, jumped on the rear platform of the train, and fell, exhausted, into one of the seats.

Passepartout, who had been anxiously watching this amateur gymnast, approached him with lively interest, and learned that he had taken flight after an unpleasant domestic scene.

When the Mormon had recovered his breath, Passepartout ventured to ask him politely how many wives he had; for, from the manner in which he had decamped, it might be thought that he had twenty at least.

'One, sir,' replied the Mormon, raising his arms heavenward – 'one, and that was enough!'

CHAPTER 28

In which Passepartout does not succeed in making anybody listen to reason

The train, on leaving Great Salt Lake at Ogden, passed northward for an hour as far as Weber River, having completed nearly nine hundred miles from San Francisco. From this point it took an easterly direction towards the jagged Wahsatch Mountains. It was in the section included between this range and the Rocky Mountains that the American engineers found the most formidable difficulties in laying the road, and that the government granted a subsidy of forty-eight thousand dollars per mile, instead of sixteen thousand allowed for the work done on the plains. But the engineers, instead of violating nature, avoided its difficulties by winding around, instead of penetrating the rocks. One tunnel only, fourteen thousand feet in length, was pierced in order to arrive at the great basin.

The track up to this time had reached its highest elevation at the Great Salt Lake. From this point it described a long curve, descending towards Bitter Creek Valley, to rise again to the dividing ridge of the waters between the Atlantic and the Pacific. There were many creeks in this mountainous region, and it was necessary to cross Muddy Creek, Green Creek, and others, upon culverts.

Passepartout grew more and more impatient as they went on, while Fix longed to get out of this difficult region, and was more anxious than Phileas Fogg himself to be beyond the danger of delays and accidents, and set foot on English soil.

At ten o'clock at night the train stopped at Fort Bridger station, and twenty minutes later entered Wyoming Territory, following the valley of Bitter Creek throughout. The next day, 7th December, they stopped for a quarter of an hour at Green River station. Snow had fallen abundantly during the night, but, being mixed with rain, it had half melted, and did not interrupt their progress. The bad weather, however, annoyed Passepartout; for the accumulation of snow, by blocking the wheels of the cars, would certainly have been fatal to Mr. Fogg's tour.

'What an idea!' he said to himself. 'Why did my master make this journey in winter? Couldn't he have waited for the good season to increase his chances?'

While the worthy Frenchman was absorbed in the state of the sky and the depression of the temperature, Aouda was experiencing fears from a totally different cause.

Several passengers had got off at Green River, and were walking up and down the platforms; and among these Aouda recognised Colonel Stamp Proctor, the same who had so grossly insulted Phileas Fogg at the San Francisco meeting. Not wishing to be recognised, the young woman drew back from the window, feeling much alarm at her discovery. She was attached to the man who, however coldly, gave her daily evidences of the most absolute devotion. She did not comprehend, perhaps, the depth of the sentiment with which her protector inspired her, which she called gratitude, but which, though she was unconscious of it, was really more than that. Her heart sank within her when she recognised the man whom Mr. Fogg desired, sooner or later, to call to account for his conduct. Chance alone, it was clear, had brought Colonel Proctor on this train; but there he was, and it was necessary, at all hazards, that Phileas Fogg should not perceive his adversary.

Aouda seized a moment when Mr. Fogg was asleep to tell Fix and Passepartout whom she had seen.

'That Proctor on this train!' cried Fix. 'Well, reassure yourself, madam; before he settles with Mr. Fogg; he has got to deal with me! It seems to me that I was the more insulted of the two.'

'And, besides,' added Passepartout, 'I'll take charge of him, colonel as he is.'

'Mr. Fix,' resumed Aouda, 'Mr. Fogg will allow no one to avenge him. He said that he would come back to America to find this man. Should he perceive Colonel Proctor, we could not prevent a collision which might have terrible results. He must not see him.'

'You are right, madam,' replied Fix; 'a meeting between them might ruin all. Whether he were victorious or beaten, Mr. Fogg would be delayed, and – '

'And,' added Passepartout, 'that would play the game of the gentlemen of the Reform Club. In four days we shall be in New York. Well, if my master does not leave this car during those four days, we may hope that chance will not bring him face to face with this confounded American. We must, if possible, prevent his stirring out of it.'

The conversation dropped. Mr. Fogg had just woke up, and was looking out of the window. Soon after Passepartout, without being heard by his master or Aouda, whispered to the detective, 'Would you really fight for him?'

'I would do anything,' replied Fix, in a tone which betrayed determined will, 'to get him back living to Europe!'

Passepartout felt something like a shudder shoot through his frame, but his confidence in his master remained unbroken.

Was there any means of detaining Mr. Fogg in the car, to avoid a meeting between him and the colonel? It ought not to be a difficult task, since that gentleman was naturally sedentary and little curious. The detective, at least, seemed to have found a way; for, after a few moments, he said to Mr. Fogg, 'These are long and slow hours, sir, that we are passing on the railway.'

'Yes,' replied Mr. Fogg; 'but they pass.'

'You were in the habit of playing whist,' resumed Fix, 'on the steamers.'

'Yes; but it would be difficult to do so here. I have neither cards nor partners.'

'Oh, but we can easily buy some cards, for they are sold on all the American trains. And as for partners, if madam plays – '

'Certainly, sir,' Aouda quickly replied; 'I understand whist. It is part of an English education.'

'I myself have some pretensions to playing a good game. Well, here are three of us, and a dummy – '

'As you please, sir,' replied Phileas Fogg, heartily glad to resume his favourite pastime even on the railway.

Passepartout was dispatched in search of the steward, and soon returned with two packs of cards, some pins, counters, and a shelf covered with cloth.

The game commenced. Aouda understood whist sufficiently well, and even received some compliments on her playing from Mr. Fogg. As for the detective, he was simply an adept, and worthy of being matched against his present opponent.

'Now,' thought Passepartout, 'we've got him. He won't budge.'

At eleven in the morning the train had reached the dividing ridge of the waters at Bridger Pass, seven thousand five hundred and twenty-four feet above the level of the sea, one of the highest points attained by the track in crossing the Rocky Mountains. After going about two hundred miles, the travellers at last found themselves on one of those vast plains which extend to the Atlantic, and which nature has made so propitious for laying the iron road.

On the declivity of the Atlantic basin the first streams, branches of the North Platte River, already appeared. The whole northern and eastern horizon was bounded by the immense semi-circular curtain which is formed by the southern portion of the Rocky Mountains, the highest being Laramie Peak. Between this and the railway extended vast plains, plentifully irrigated. On the right rose the lower spurs of the mountainous mass which extends southward to the sources of the Arkansas River, one of the great tributaries of the Missouri.

At half-past twelve the travellers caught sight for an instant of Fort Halleck, which commands that section; and in a few more hours the Rocky Mountains were crossed. There was reason to hope, then, that no accident would mark the journey through this difficult country. The snow had ceased falling, and the air became crisp and cold. Large birds, frightened by the locomotive, rose and flew off in the distance. No wild beast appeared on the plain. It was a desert in its vast nakedness.

After a comfortable breakfast, served in the car, Mr. Fogg and his partners had just resumed whist, when a violent whistling was heard, and the train stopped. Passepartout put his head out of the door, but saw nothing to cause the delay; no station was in view.

Aouda and Fix feared that Mr. Fogg might take it into his head to get out; but that gentleman contented himself with saying to his servant, 'See what is the matter.'

Passepartout rushed out of the car. Thirty or forty passengers had already descended, amongst them Colonel Stamp Proctor.

The train had stopped before a red signal which blocked the way. The engineer and conductor were talking excitedly with a signal-man, whom the station-master at Medicine Bow, the next stopping place, had sent on before. The passengers drew around and took part in the discussion, in which Colonel Proctor, with his insolent manner, was conspicuous.

Passepartout, joining the group, heard the signal-man say, 'No! you can't pass. The bridge at Medicine Bow is shaky, and would not bear the weight of the train.'

This was a suspension-bridge thrown over some rapids, about a mile from the place where they now were. According to the signal-man, it was in a ruinous condition, several of the iron wires being broken; and it was impossible to risk the passage. He did not in any way exaggerate the condition of the bridge. It may be taken for granted that, rash as the Americans usually are, when they are prudent there is good reason for it.

Passepartout, not daring to apprise his master of what he heard, listened with set teeth, immovable as a statue.

'Hum!' cried Colonel Proctor; 'but we are not going to stay here, I imagine, and take root in the snow?'

'Colonel,' replied the conductor, 'we have telegraphed to Omaha for a train, but it is not likely that it will reach Medicine Bow in less than six hours.'

'Six hours!' cried Passepartout.

'Certainly,' returned the conductor, 'besides, it will take us as long as that to reach Medicine Bow on foot.'

'But it is only a mile from here,' said one of the passengers.

'Yes, but it's on the other side of the river.'

'And can't we cross that in a boat?' asked the colonel.

'That's impossible. The creek is swelled by the rains. It is a rapid, and we shall have to make a circuit of ten miles to the north to find a ford.'

The colonel launched a volley of oaths, denouncing the railway company and the conductor; and Passepartout, who was furious, was not disinclined to make common cause with him. Here was an obstacle, indeed, which all his master's banknotes could not remove.

There was a general disappointment among the passengers, who, without reckoning the delay, saw themselves compelled to trudge fifteen miles over a plain covered with snow. They grumbled and protested, and would certainly have thus attracted Phileas Fogg's attention if he had not been completely absorbed in his game.

Passepartout found that he could not avoid telling his master what had occurred, and, with hanging head, he was turning towards the car, when the engineer, a true Yankee, named Forster called out, 'Gentlemen, perhaps there is a way, after all, to get over.'

'On the bridge?' asked a passenger.

'On the bridge.'

'With our train?'

'With our train.'

Passepartout stopped short, and eagerly listened to the engineer.

'But the bridge is unsafe,' urged the conductor.

'No matter,' replied Forster; 'I think that by putting on the very highest speed we might have a chance of getting over.'

'The devil!' muttered Passepartout.

But a number of the passengers were at once attracted by the engineer's proposal, and Colonel Proctor was especially delighted, and found the plan a very feasible one. He told stories about engineers leaping their trains over rivers without bridges, by putting on full steam; and many of those present avowed themselves of the engineer's mind.

'We have fifty chances out of a hundred of getting over,' said one.

'Eighty! ninety!'

Passepartout was astounded, and, though ready to attempt anything to get over Medicine Creek, thought the experiment proposed a little too American. 'Besides,' thought he, 'there's a still more simple way, and it does not even occur to any of these people! Sir,' said he aloud to one of the passengers, 'the engineer's plan seems to me a little dangerous, but – '

'Eighty chances!' replied the passenger, turning his back on him.

'I know it,' said Passepartout, turning to another passenger, 'but a simple idea – '

'Ideas are no use,' returned the American, shrugging his shoulders, 'as the engineer assures us that we can pass.'

'Doubtless,' urged Passepartout, 'we can pass, but perhaps it would be more prudent – '

'What! Prudent!' cried Colonel Proctor, whom this word seemed to excite prodigiously. 'At full speed, don't you see, at full speed!'

'I know – I see,' repeated Passepartout; 'but it would be, if not more prudent, since that word displeases you, at least more natural – '

'Who! What! What's the matter with this fellow?' cried several.

The poor fellow did not know to whom to address himself.

'Are you afraid?' asked Colonel Proctor.

'I afraid? Very well; I will show these people that a Frenchman can be as American as they!'

'All aboard!' cried the conductor.

'Yes, all aboard!' repeated Passepartout, and immediately. 'But they can't prevent me from thinking that it would be more natural for us to cross the bridge on foot, and let the train come after!'

But no one heard this sage reflection, nor would anyone have acknowledged its justice. The passengers resumed their places in the cars. Passepartout took his seat without telling what had passed. The whist-players were quite absorbed in their game.

The locomotive whistled vigorously; the engineer, reversing the steam, backed the train for nearly a mile – retiring, like a jumper, in order to take a longer leap. Then, with another whistle, he began to move forward; the train increased its speed, and soon its rapidity became frightful; a prolonged screech issued from the locomotive; the piston worked up and down twenty strokes to the second. They perceived that the whole train, rushing on at the rate of a hundred miles an hour, hardly bore upon the rails at all.

And they passed over! It was like a flash. No one saw the bridge. The train leaped, so to speak, from one bank to the other, and the engineer could not stop it until it had gone five miles beyond the station. But scarcely had the train passed the river, when the bridge, completely ruined, fell with a crash into the rapids of Medicine Bow.

CHAPTER 29

In which certain incidents are narrated which are only to be met with on American railroads

The train pursued its course, that evening, without interruption, passing Fort Saunders, crossing Cheyne Pass, and reaching Evans Pass. The road here attained the highest elevation of the journey, eight thousand and ninety-two feet above the level of the sea. The travellers had now only to descend to the Atlantic by limitless plains, levelled by nature. A branch of the 'grand trunk' led off southward to Denver, the capital of Colorado. The country round about is rich in gold and silver, and more than fifty thousand inhabitants are already settled there.

Thirteen hundred and eighty-two miles had been passed over from San Francisco, in three days and three nights; four days and nights more would probably bring them to New York. Phileas Fogg was not as yet behind-hand.

During the night Camp Walbach was passed on the left; Lodge Pole Creek ran parallel with the road, marking the boundary between the territories of Wyoming and Colorado. They entered Nebraska at eleven, passed near Sedgwick, and touched at Julesburg, on the southern branch of the Platte River.

It was here that the Union Pacific Railroad was inaugurated on the 23rd of October, 1867, by the chief engineer, General Dodge. Two powerful locomotives, carrying nine cars of invited guests, amongst whom was Thomas C. Durant, vice-president of the road, stopped at this point; cheers were given, the Sioux and Pawnees performed an imitation Indian battle, fireworks were let off, and the first number of the Railway Pioneer was printed by a press brought on the train. Thus was celebrated the inauguration of this great railroad, a mighty instrument of progress and civilisation, thrown across the desert, and destined to link together cities and towns which do not yet exist. The whistle of the locomotive, more powerful than Amphion's lyre, was about to bid them rise from American soil.

Fort McPherson was left behind at eight in the morning, and three hundred and fifty-seven miles had yet to be traversed before reaching Omaha. The road followed the capricious windings of the southern branch of the Platte River, on its left bank. At nine the train stopped at the important town of North Platte, built between the two arms of the river, which rejoin each other around it and form a single artery, a large tributary, whose waters empty into the Missouri a little above Omaha.

The one hundred and first meridian was passed.

Mr. Fogg and his partners had resumed their game; no one – not even the dummy – complained of the length of the trip. Fix had begun by winning several guineas, which he seemed likely to lose; but he showed himself a not less eager whist-player than Mr. Fogg. During the morning, chance distinctly favoured that gentleman. Trumps and honours were showered upon his hands.

Once, having resolved on a bold stroke, he was on the

CHAPTER 29

point of playing a spade, when a voice behind him said, 'I should play a diamond.'

Mr. Fogg, Aouda, and Fix raised their heads, and beheld Colonel Proctor.

Stamp Proctor and Phileas Fogg recognised each other at once.

'Ah! it's you, is it, Englishman?' cried the colonel; 'it's you who are going to play a spade!'

'And who plays it,' replied Phileas Fogg coolly, throwing down the ten of spades.

'Well, it pleases me to have it diamonds,' replied Colonel Proctor, in an insolent tone.

He made a movement as if to seize the card which had just been played, adding, 'You don't understand anything about whist.'

'Perhaps I do, as well as another,' said Phileas Fogg, rising.

'You have only to try, son of John Bull,' replied the colonel.

Aouda turned pale, and her blood ran cold. She seized Mr. Fogg's arm and gently pulled him back. Passepartout was ready to pounce upon the American, who was staring insolently at his opponent. But Fix got up, and, going to Colonel Proctor said, 'You forget that it is I with whom you have to deal, sir; for it was I whom you not only insulted, but struck!'

'Mr. Fix,' said Mr. Fogg, 'pardon me, but this affair is mine, and mine only. The colonel has again insulted me, by insisting that I should not play a spade, and he shall give me satisfaction for it.'

'When and where you will,' replied the American, 'and with whatever weapon you choose.'

Aouda in vain attempted to retain Mr. Fogg; as vainly did the detective endeavour to make the quarrel his. Passepartout wished to throw the colonel out of the window, but a sign from his master checked him. Phileas Fogg left the car, and the American followed him upon the platform. 'Sir,' said Mr. Fogg to his adversary, 'I am in a great hurry to get back to Europe, and any delay whatever will be greatly to my disadvantage.'

'Well, what's that to me?' replied Colonel Proctor.

'Sir,' said Mr. Fogg, very politely, 'after our meeting at San Francisco, I determined to return to America and find you as soon as I had completed the business which called me to England.'

'Really!'

'Will you appoint a meeting for six months hence?'

'Why not ten years hence?'

'I say six months,' returned Phileas Fogg; 'and I shall be at the place of meeting promptly.'

'All this is an evasion,' cried Stamp Proctor. 'Now or never!'

'Very good. You are going to New York?'

'No.'

'To Chicago?'

'No.'

'To Omaha?'

'What difference is it to you? Do you know Plum Creek?'

'No,' replied Mr. Fogg.

'It's the next station. The train will be there in an hour, and will stop there ten minutes. In ten minutes several revolver-shots could be exchanged.'

'Very well,' said Mr. Fogg. 'I will stop at Plum Creek.'

'And I guess you'll stay there too,' added the American insolently.

'Who knows?' replied Mr. Fogg, returning to the car as coolly as usual. He began to reassure Aouda, telling her that blusterers were never to be feared, and begged Fix to be his second at the approaching duel, a request which the detective could not refuse. Mr. Fogg resumed the interrupted game with perfect calmness.

At eleven o'clock the locomotive's whistle announced that they were approaching Plum Creek station. Mr. Fogg rose, and, followed by Fix, went out upon the platform. Passepartout accompanied him, carrying a pair of revolvers. Aouda remained in the car, as pale as death.

The door of the next car opened, and Colonel Proctor appeared on the platform, attended by a Yankee of his own stamp as his second. But just as the combatants were about to step from the train, the conductor hurried up, and shouted, 'You can't get off, gentlemen!'

'Why not?' asked the colonel.

'We are twenty minutes late, and we shall not stop.'

'But I am going to fight a duel with this gentleman.'

'I am sorry,' said the conductor; 'but we shall be off at once. There's the bell ringing now.'

The train started.

'I'm really very sorry, gentlemen,' said the conductor. 'Under any other circumstances I should have been happy to oblige you. But, after all, as you have not had time to fight here, why not fight as we go along?'

'That wouldn't be convenient, perhaps, for this gentleman,' said the colonel, in a jeering tone.

'It would be perfectly so,' replied Phileas Fogg.

'Well, we are really in America,' thought Passepartout, 'and the conductor is a gentleman of the first order!'

So muttering, he followed his master.

The two combatants, their seconds, and the conductor passed through the cars to the rear of the train. The last car was only occupied by a dozen passengers, whom the conductor politely asked if they would not be so kind as to leave it vacant for a few moments, as two gentlemen had an affair of honour to settle. The passengers granted the request with alacrity, and straightway disappeared on the platform.

The car, which was some fifty feet long, was very convenient for their purpose. The adversaries might march on each other in the aisle, and fire at their ease. Never was duel more easily arranged. Mr. Fogg and Colonel Proctor, each provided with two six-barrelled revolvers, entered the car. The seconds, remaining outside, shut them in. They were to begin firing at the first whistle of the locomotive. After an interval of two minutes, what remained of the two gentlemen would be taken from the car.

Nothing could be more simple. Indeed, it was all so simple that Fix and Passepartout felt their hearts beating as if they would crack. They were listening for the whistle agreed upon, when suddenly savage cries resounded in the air, accompanied by reports which certainly did not issue from the car where the duellists were. The reports continued in front and the whole length of the train. Cries of terror proceeded from the interior of the cars.

Colonel Proctor and Mr. Fogg, revolvers in hand, hastily quitted their prison, and rushed forward where the noise was most clamorous. They then perceived that the train was attacked by a band of Sioux.

This was not the first attempt of these daring Indians, for more than once they had waylaid trains on the road. A hundred of them had, according to their habit, jumped upon the steps without stopping the train, with the ease of a clown mounting a horse at full gallop.

The Sioux were armed with guns, from which came the

reports, to which the passengers, who were almost all armed, responded by revolver-shots.

The Indians had first mounted the engine, and half stunned the engineer and stoker with blows from their muskets. A Sioux chief, wishing to stop the train, but not knowing how to work the regulator, had opened wide instead of closing the steam-valve, and the locomotive was plunging forward with terrific velocity.

The Sioux had at the same time invaded the cars, skipping like enraged monkeys over the roofs, thrusting open the doors, and fighting hand to hand with the passengers. Penetrating the baggage-car, they pillaged it, throwing the trunks out of the train. The cries and shots were constant. The travellers defended themselves bravely; some of the cars were barricaded, and sustained a siege, like moving forts, carried along at a speed of a hundred miles an hour.

Aouda behaved courageously from the first. She defended herself like a true heroine with a revolver, which she shot through the broken windows whenever a savage made his appearance. Twenty Sioux had fallen mortally wounded to the ground, and the wheels crushed those who fell upon the rails as if they had been worms. Several passengers, shot or stunned, lay on the seats.

It was necessary to put an end to the struggle, which had lasted for ten minutes, and which would result in the triumph of the Sioux if the train was not stopped. Fort Kearney station, where there was a garrison, was only two miles distant; but, that once passed, the Sioux would be masters of the train between Fort Kearney and the station beyond.

The conductor was fighting beside Mr. Fogg, when he was shot and fell. At the same moment he cried, 'Unless the train is stopped in five minutes, we are lost!'

'It shall be stopped,' said Phileas Fogg, preparing to rush from the car.

'Stay, monsieur,' cried Passepartout; 'I will go.'

Mr. Fogg had not time to stop the brave fellow, who, opening a door unperceived by the Indians, succeeded in slipping under the car; and while the struggle continued and the balls whizzed across each other over his head, he made use of his old acrobatic experience, and with amazing agility worked his way under the cars, holding on to the chains, aiding himself by the brakes and edges of the sashes, creeping from one car to another with marvellous skill, and thus gaining the forward end of the train.

There, suspended by one hand between the baggage-car and the tender, with the other he loosened the safety chains; but, owing to the traction, he would never have succeeded in unscrewing the yoking-bar, had not a violent concussion jolted this bar out. The train, now detached from the engine, remained a little behind, whilst the locomotive rushed forward with increased speed.

Carried on by the force already acquired, the train still moved for several minutes; but the brakes were worked and at last they stopped, less than a hundred feet from Kearney station.

The soldiers of the fort, attracted by the shots, hurried up; the Sioux had not expected them, and decamped in a body before the train entirely stopped.

But when the passengers counted each other on the station platform several were found missing; among others the courageous Frenchman, whose devotion had just saved them.

CHAPTER 30

In which Phileas Fogg simply does his duty

Three passengers including Passepartout had disappeared. Had they been killed in the struggle? Were they taken prisoners by the Sioux? It was impossible to tell.

There were many wounded, but none mortally. Colonel Proctor was one of the most seriously hurt; he had fought bravely, and a ball had entered his groin. He was carried into the station with the other wounded passengers, to receive such attention as could be of avail.

Aouda was safe; and Phileas Fogg, who had been in the thickest of the fight, had not received a scratch. Fix was slightly wounded in the arm. But Passepartout was not to be found, and tears coursed down Aouda's cheeks.

All the passengers had got out of the train, the wheels of which were stained with blood. From the tyres and spokes hung ragged pieces of flesh. As far as the eye could reach on the white plain behind, red trails were visible. The last Sioux were disappearing in the south, along the banks of Republican River.

Mr. Fogg, with folded arms, remained motionless. He had a serious decision to make. Aouda, standing near him, looked at him without speaking, and he understood her look. If his servant was a prisoner, ought he not to risk everything to rescue him from the Indians? 'I will find him, living or dead,' said he quietly to Aouda.

'Ah, Mr. – Mr. Fogg!' cried she, clasping his hands and covering them with tears.

'Living,' added Mr. Fogg, 'if we do not lose a moment.'

Phileas Fogg, by this resolution, inevitably sacrificed himself; he pronounced his own doom. The delay of a single day would make him lose the steamer at New York, and his bet would be certainly lost. But as he thought, 'It is my duty,' he did not hesitate.

The commanding officer of Fort Kearney was there. A hundred of his soldiers had placed themselves in a position to defend the station, should the Sioux attack it.

'Sir,' said Mr. Fogg to the captain, 'three passengers have disappeared.'

'Dead?' asked the captain.

'Dead or prisoners; that is the uncertainty which must be solved. Do you propose to pursue the Sioux?'

'That's a serious thing to do, sir,' returned the captain. 'These Indians may retreat beyond the Arkansas, and I cannot leave the fort unprotected.'

'The lives of three men are in question, sir,' said Phileas Fogg.

'Doubtless; but can I risk the lives of fifty men to save three?'

'I don't know whether you can, sir; but you ought to do so.'

'Nobody here,' returned the other, 'has a right to teach me my duty.'

'Very well,' said Mr. Fogg, coldly. 'I will go alone.'

'You, sir!' cried Fix, coming up; 'you go alone in pursuit of the Indians?'

'Would you have me leave this poor fellow to perish – him to whom every one present owes his life? I shall go.'

'No, sir, you shall not go alone,' cried the captain, touched in spite of himself. 'No! you are a brave man. Thirty volunteers!' he added, turning to the soldiers.

The whole company started forward at once. The captain had only to pick his men. Thirty were chosen, and an old sergeant placed at their head.

'Thanks, captain,' said Mr. Fogg.

'Will you let me go with you?' asked Fix.

'Do as you please, sir. But if you wish to do me a favour, you will remain with Aouda. In case anything should happen to me – '

A sudden pallor overspread the detective's face. Separate himself from the man whom he had so persistently followed step by step! Leave him to wander about in this desert! Fix gazed attentively at Mr. Fogg, and, despite his suspicions and of the struggle which was going on within him, he lowered his eyes before that calm and frank look.

'I will stay,' said he.

A few moments after, Mr. Fogg pressed the young woman's hand, and, having confided to her his precious carpet-bag, went off with the sergeant and his little squad. But, before going, he had said to the soldiers, 'My friends, I will divide five thousand dollars among you, if we save the prisoners.'

It was then a little past noon.

Aouda retired to a waiting-room, and there she waited alone, thinking of the simple and noble generosity, the tranquil courage of Phileas Fogg. He had sacrificed his fortune, and was now risking his life, all without hesitation, from duty, in silence.

Fix did not have the same thoughts, and could scarcely conceal his agitation. He walked feverishly up and down the platform, but soon resumed his outward composure. He now saw the folly of which he had been guilty in letting Fogg go alone. What! This man, whom he had just followed around the world, was permitted now to separate himself from him! He began to accuse and abuse himself, and, as if he were director of police, administered to himself a sound lecture for his greenness.

'I have been an idiot!' he thought, 'and this man will see it. He has gone, and won't come back! But how is it that I, Fix, who have in my pocket a warrant for his arrest, have been so fascinated by him? Decidedly, I am nothing but an ass!'

So reasoned the detective, while the hours crept by all too slowly. He did not know what to do. Sometimes he was tempted to tell Aouda all; but he could not doubt how the young woman would receive his confidences. What course should he take? He thought of pursuing Fogg across the vast white plains; it did not seem impossible that he might overtake him. Footsteps were easily printed on the snow! But soon, under a new sheet, every imprint would be effaced.

Fix became discouraged. He felt a sort of insurmountable longing to abandon the game altogether. He could now leave Fort Kearney station, and pursue his journey homeward in peace.

Towards two o'clock in the afternoon, while it was snowing hard, long whistles were heard approaching from the east. A great shadow, preceded by a wild light, slowly advanced, appearing still larger through the mist, which gave it a fantastic aspect. No train was expected from the east, neither had there been time for the succour asked for by telegraph to arrive;

the train from Omaha to San Francisco was not due till the next day. The mystery was soon explained.

The locomotive, which was slowly approaching with deafening whistles, was that which, having been detached from the train, had continued its route with such terrific rapidity, carrying off the unconscious engineer and stoker. It had run several miles, when, the fire becoming low for want of fuel, the steam had slackened; and it had finally stopped an hour after, some twenty miles beyond Fort Kearney. Neither the engineer nor the stoker was dead, and, after remaining for some time in their swoon, had come to themselves. The train had then stopped. The engineer, when he found himself in the desert, and the locomotive without cars, understood what had happened. He could not imagine how the locomotive had become separated from the train; but he did not doubt that the train left behind was in distress.

He did not hesitate what to do. It would be prudent to continue on to Omaha, for it would be dangerous to return to the train, which the Indians might still be engaged in pillaging. Nevertheless, he began to rebuild the fire in the furnace; the pressure again mounted, and the locomotive returned, running backwards to Fort Kearney. This it was which was whistling in the mist.

The travellers were glad to see the locomotive resume its place at the head of the train. They could now continue the journey so terribly interrupted.

Aouda, on seeing the locomotive come up, hurried out of the station, and asked the conductor, 'Are you going to start?'

'At once, madam.'

'But the prisoners, our unfortunate fellow-travellers – '

'I cannot interrupt the trip,' replied the conductor. 'We are already three hours behind time.'

'And when will another train pass here from San Francisco?'

'To-morrow evening, madam.'

'To-morrow evening! But then it will be too late! We must wait – '

'It is impossible,' responded the conductor. 'If you wish to go, please get in.'

'I will not go,' said Aouda.

Fix had heard this conversation. A little while before, when there was no prospect of proceeding on the journey, he had made up his mind to leave Fort Kearney; but now that the train was there, ready to start, and he had only to take his seat in the car, an irresistible influence held him back. The station platform burned his feet, and he could not stir. The conflict in his mind again began; anger and failure stifled him. He wished to struggle on to the end.

Meanwhile the passengers and some of the wounded, among them Colonel Proctor, whose injuries were serious, had taken their places in the train. The buzzing of the overheated boiler was heard, and the steam was escaping from the valves. The engineer whistled, the train started, and soon disappeared, mingling its white smoke with the eddies of the densely falling snow.

The detective had remained behind.

Several hours passed. The weather was dismal, and it was very cold. Fix sat motionless on a bench in the station; he might have been thought asleep. Aouda, despite the storm, kept coming out of the waiting-room, going to the end of the platform, and peering through the tempest of snow, as if to pierce the mist which narrowed the horizon around her, and to hear, if possible, some welcome sound. She heard and saw nothing. Then she would return, chilled through, to issue out again after the lapse of a few moments, but always in vain.

Evening came, and the little band had not returned. Where could they be? Had they found the Indians, and were they having a conflict with them, or were they still wandering amid the mist? The commander of the fort was anxious, though he tried to conceal his apprehensions. As night approached, the snow fell less plentifully, but it became intensely cold. Absolute silence rested on the plains. Neither flight of bird nor passing of beast troubled the perfect calm.

Throughout the night Aouda, full of sad forebodings, her heart stifled with anguish, wandered about on the verge of the plains. Her imagination carried her far off, and showed her innumerable dangers. What she suffered through the long hours it would be impossible to describe.

Fix remained stationary in the same place, but did not sleep. Once a man approached and spoke to him, and the detective merely replied by shaking his head.

Thus the night passed. At dawn, the half-extinguished disc of the sun rose above a misty horizon; but it was now possible to recognise objects two miles off. Phileas Fogg and the squad had gone southward; in the south all was still vacancy. It was then seven o'clock.

The captain, who was really alarmed, did not know what course to take.

Should he send another detachment to the rescue of the first? Should he sacrifice more men, with so few chances of saving those already sacrificed? His hesitation did not last long, however. Calling one of his lieutenants, he was on the point of ordering a reconnaissance, when gunshots were heard. Was it a signal? The soldiers rushed out of the fort, and half a mile off they perceived a little band returning in good order.

Mr. Fogg was marching at their head, and just behind him were Passepartout and the other two travellers, rescued from the Sioux.

They had met and fought the Indians ten miles south of Fort Kearney. Shortly before the detachment arrived, Passepartout and his companions had begun to struggle with their captors, three of whom the Frenchman had felled with his fists, when his master and the soldiers hastened up to their relief.

All were welcomed with joyful cries. Phileas Fogg distributed the reward he had promised to the soldiers, while Passepartout, not without reason, muttered to himself, 'It must certainly be confessed that I cost my master dear!'

Fix, without saying a word, looked at Mr. Fogg, and it would have been difficult to analyse the thoughts which struggled within him. As for Aouda, she took her protector's hand and pressed it in her own, too much moved to speak.

Meanwhile, Passepartout was looking about for the train; he thought he should find it there, ready to start for Omaha, and he hoped that the time lost might be regained.

'The train! the train!' cried he.

'Gone,' replied Fix.

'And when does the next train pass here?' said Phileas Fogg.

'Not till this evening.'

'Ah!' returned the impassible gentleman quietly.

CHAPTER 31

In which Fix, the detective, considerably furthers the interests of Phileas Fogg

Phileas Fogg found himself twenty hours behind time. Passepartout, the involuntary cause of this delay, was desperate. He had ruined his master!

At this moment the detective approached Mr. Fogg, and, looking him intently in the face, said:

'Seriously, sir, are you in great haste?'

'Quite seriously.'

'I have a purpose in asking,' resumed Fix. 'Is it absolutely necessary that you should be in New York on the 11th, before nine o'clock in the evening, the time that the steamer leaves for Liverpool?'

'It is absolutely necessary.'

'And, if your journey had not been interrupted by these Indians, you would have reached New York on the morning of the 11th?'

'Yes; with eleven hours to spare before the steamer left.'

'Good! you are therefore twenty hours behind. Twelve from twenty leaves eight. You must regain eight hours. Do you wish to try to do so?'

'On foot?' asked Mr. Fogg.

'No; on a sledge,' replied Fix. 'On a sledge with sails. A man has proposed such a method to me.'

It was the man who had spoken to Fix during the night, and whose offer he had refused.

Phileas Fogg did not reply at once; but Fix, having pointed out the man, who was walking up and down in front of the station, Mr. Fogg went up to him. An instant after, Mr. Fogg and the American, whose name was Mudge, entered a hut built just below the fort.

There Mr. Fogg examined a curious vehicle, a kind of frame on two long beams, a little raised in front like the runners of a sledge, and upon which there was room for five or six persons. A high mast was fixed on the frame, held firmly by metallic lashings, to which was attached a large brigantine sail. This mast held an iron stay upon which to hoist a jib-sail. Behind, a sort of rudder served to guide the vehicle. It was, in short, a sledge rigged like a sloop. During the winter, when the trains are blocked up by the snow, these sledges make extremely rapid journeys across the frozen plains from one station to another. Provided with more sails than a cutter, and with the wind behind them, they slip over the surface of the prairies with a speed equal if not superior to that of the express trains.

Mr. Fogg readily made a bargain with the owner of this land-craft. The wind was favourable, being fresh, and blowing from the west. The snow had hardened, and Mudge was very confident of being able to transport Mr. Fogg in a few hours to Omaha. Thence the trains eastward run frequently to Chicago and New York. It was not impossible that the lost time might yet be recovered; and such an opportunity was not to be rejected.

Not wishing to expose Aouda to the discomforts of travelling in the open air, Mr. Fogg proposed to leave her with Passepartout at Fort Kearney, the servant taking upon himself to escort her to Europe by a better route and under more favourable conditions. But Aouda refused to separate from Mr. Fogg, and Passepartout was delighted with her decision; for nothing could induce him to leave his master while Fix was with him.

It would be difficult to guess the detective's thoughts. Was this conviction shaken by Phileas Fogg's return, or did he still regard him as an exceedingly shrewd rascal, who, his journey round the world completed, would think himself absolutely safe in England? Perhaps Fix's opinion of Phileas Fogg was somewhat modified; but he was nevertheless resolved to do his duty, and to hasten the return of the whole party to England as much as possible.

At eight o'clock the sledge was ready to start. The passengers took their places on it, and wrapped themselves up closely in their travelling-cloaks. The two great sails were hoisted, and under the pressure of the wind the sledge slid over the hardened snow with a velocity of forty miles an hour.

The distance between Fort Kearney and Omaha, as the birds fly, is at most two hundred miles. If the wind held good, the distance might be traversed in five hours; if no accident happened the sledge might reach Omaha by one o'clock.

What a journey! The travellers, huddled close together, could not speak for the cold, intensified by the rapidity at which they were going. The sledge sped on as lightly as a boat over the waves. When the breeze came skimming the earth the sledge seemed to be lifted off the ground by its sails. Mudge, who was at the rudder, kept in a straight line, and by a turn of his hand checked the lurches which the vehicle had a tendency to make. All the sails were up, and the jib was so arranged as not to screen the brigantine. A top-mast was hoisted, and another jib, held out to the wind, added its force to the other sails. Although the speed could not be exactly estimated, the sledge could not be going at less than forty miles an hour.

'If nothing breaks,' said Mudge, 'we shall get there!'

Mr. Fogg had made it for Mudge's interest to reach Omaha within the time agreed on, by the offer of a handsome reward.

The prairie, across which the sledge was moving in a straight line, was as flat as a sea. It seemed like a vast frozen lake. The railroad which ran through this section ascended from the south-west to the north-west by Great Island, Columbus, an important Nebraska town, Schuyler, and Fremont, to Omaha. It followed throughout the right bank of the Platte River. The sledge, shortening this route, took a chord of the arc described by the railway. Mudge was not afraid of being stopped by the Platte River, because it was frozen. The road, then, was quite clear of obstacles, and Phileas Fogg had but two things to fear – an accident to the sledge, and a change or calm in the wind.

But the breeze, far from lessening its force, blew as if to bend the mast, which, however, the metallic lashings held firmly. These lashings, like the chords of a stringed instrument, resounded as if vibrated by a violin bow. The sledge slid along in the midst of a plaintively intense melody.

'Those chords give the fifth and the octave,' said Mr. Fogg.

These were the only words he uttered during the journey. Aouda, cosily packed in furs and cloaks, was sheltered as much as possible from the attacks of the freezing wind. As for Passepartout, his face was as red as the sun's disc when it sets in the mist, and he laboriously inhaled the biting air.

With his natural buoyancy of spirits, he began to hope again. They would reach New York on the evening, if not on the morning, of the 11th, and there was still some chances that it would be before the steamer sailed for Liverpool.

Passepartout even felt a strong desire to grasp his ally, Fix, by the hand. He remembered that it was the detective who procured the sledge, the only means of reaching Omaha in time; but, checked by some presentiment, he kept his usual reserve. One thing, however, Passepartout would never forget, and that was the sacrifice which Mr. Fogg had made, without hesitation, to rescue him from the Sioux. Mr. Fogg had risked his fortune and his life. No! His servant would never forget that!

While each of the party was absorbed in reflections so different, the sledge flew past over the vast carpet of snow. The creeks it passed over were not perceived. Fields and streams disappeared under the uniform whiteness. The plain was absolutely deserted. Between the Union Pacific road and the branch which unites Kearney with Saint Joseph it formed a great uninhabited island. Neither village, station, nor fort appeared. From time to time they sped by some phantom-like tree, whose white skeleton twisted and rattled in the wind. Sometimes flocks of wild birds rose, or bands of gaunt, famished, ferocious prairie-wolves ran howling after the sledge. Passepartout, revolver in hand, held himself ready to fire on those which came too near. Had an accident then happened to the sledge, the travellers, attacked by these beasts, would have been in the most terrible danger; but it held on its even course, soon gained on the wolves, and ere long left the howling band at a safe distance behind.

About noon Mudge perceived by certain landmarks that he was crossing the Platte River. He said nothing, but he felt certain that he was now within twenty miles of Omaha. In less than an hour he left the rudder and furled his sails, whilst the sledge, carried forward by the great impetus the wind had given it, went on half a mile further with its sails unspread.

It stopped at last, and Mudge, pointing to a mass of roofs white with snow, said: 'We have got there!'

Arrived! Arrived at the station which is in daily communication, by numerous trains, with the Atlantic seaboard!

Passepartout and Fix jumped off, stretched their stiffened limbs, and aided Mr. Fogg and the young woman to descend from the sledge. Phileas Fogg generously rewarded Mudge, whose hand Passepartout warmly grasped, and the party directed their steps to the Omaha railway station.

The Pacific Railroad proper finds its terminus at this important Nebraska town. Omaha is connected with Chicago by the Chicago and Rock Island Railroad, which runs directly east, and passes fifty stations.

A train was ready to start when Mr. Fogg and his party reached the station, and they only had time to get into the cars. They had seen nothing of Omaha; but Passepartout confessed to himself that this was not to be regretted, as they were not travelling to see the sights.

The train passed rapidly across the State of Iowa, by Council Bluffs, Des Moines, and Iowa City. During the night it crossed the Mississippi at Davenport, and by Rock Island entered Illinois. The next day, which was the 10th, at four o'clock in the evening, it reached Chicago, already risen from its ruins, and more proudly seated than ever on the borders of its beautiful Lake Michigan.

Nine hundred miles separated Chicago from New York; but trains are not wanting at Chicago. Mr. Fogg passed at once from one to the other, and the locomotive of the Pittsburgh, Fort Wayne, and Chicago Railway left at full speed, as if it fully comprehended that that gentleman had no time to lose. It traversed Indiana, Ohio, Pennsylvania, and New Jersey like a flash, rushing through towns with antique names, some of which had streets and car-tracks, but as yet no houses. At last the Hudson came into view; and, at a quarter-past eleven in the evening of the 11th, the train stopped in the station on the right bank of the river, before the very pier of the Cunard line.

The *China*, for Liverpool, had started three-quarters of an hour before!

CHAPTER 32

In which Phileas Fogg engages in a direct struggle with bad fortune

The *China*, in leaving, seemed to have carried off Phileas Fogg's last hope. None of the other steamers were able to serve his projects. The *Pereire*, of the French Transatlantic Company, whose admirable steamers are equal to any in speed and comfort, did not leave until the 14th; the Hamburg boats did not go directly to Liverpool or London, but to Havre; and the additional trip from Havre to Southampton would render Phileas Fogg's last efforts of no avail. The *Inman* steamer did not depart till the next day, and could not cross the Atlantic in time to save the wager.

Mr. Fogg learned all this in consulting his Bradshaw, which gave him the daily movements of the trans-Atlantic steamers.

Passepartout was crushed; it overwhelmed him to lose the boat by three-quarters of an hour. It was his fault, for, instead of helping his master, he had not ceased putting obstacles in his path! And when he recalled all the incidents of the tour, when he counted up the sums expended in pure loss and on his own account, when he thought that the immense stake, added to the heavy charges of this useless journey, would completely ruin Mr. Fogg, he overwhelmed himself with bitter self-accusations. Mr. Fogg, however, did not reproach him; and, on leaving the Cunard pier, only said: 'We will consult about what is best to-morrow. Come.'

The party crossed the Hudson in the Jersey City ferryboat, and drove in a carriage to the St. Nicholas Hotel, on Broadway. Rooms were engaged, and the night passed, briefly to Phileas Fogg, who slept profoundly, but very long to Aouda and the others, whose agitation did not permit them to rest.

The next day was the 12th of December. From seven in the morning of the 12th to a quarter before nine in the evening of the 21st there were nine days, thirteen hours, and forty-five minutes. If Phileas Fogg had left in the *China*, one of the fastest steamers on the Atlantic, he would have reached Liverpool, and then London, within the period agreed upon.

Mr. Fogg left the hotel alone, after giving Passepartout instructions to await his return, and inform Aouda to be ready at an instant's notice. He proceeded to the banks of the Hudson, and looked about among the vessels moored or anchored in the river, for any that were about to depart. Several had departure signals, and were preparing to put to sea at morning tide; for in this immense and admirable port there is not one day in a hundred that vessels do not set out for every quarter of the globe. But they were mostly sailing vessels, of which, of course, Phileas Fogg could make no use.

He seemed about to give up all hope, when he espied, anchored at the Battery, a cable's length off at most, a trading vessel, with a screw, well-shaped, whose funnel, puffing a cloud of smoke, indicated that she was getting ready for departure.

Phileas Fogg hailed a boat, got into it, and soon found himself on board the *Henrietta*, iron-hulled, wood-built above. He ascended to the deck, and asked for the captain, who forthwith presented himself. He was a man of fifty, a sort of sea-wolf, with big eyes, a complexion of oxidised copper, red hair and thick neck, and a growling voice.

'The captain?' asked Mr. Fogg.

'I am the captain.'

'I am Phileas Fogg, of London.'

'And I am Andrew Speedy, of Cardiff.'

'You are going to put to sea?'

'In an hour.'

'You are bound for – '

'Bordeaux.'

'And your cargo?'

'No freight. Going in ballast.'

'Have you any passengers?'

'No passengers. Never have passengers. Too much in the way.'

'Is your vessel a swift one?'

'Between eleven and twelve knots. The *Henrietta*, well known.'

'Will you carry me and three other persons to Liverpool?'

'To Liverpool? Why not to China?'

'I said Liverpool.'

'No!'

'No?'

'No. I am setting out for Bordeaux, and shall go to Bordeaux.'

'Money is no object?'

'None.'

The captain spoke in a tone which did not admit of a reply.

'But the owners of the *Henrietta* – ' resumed Phileas Fogg.

'The owners are myself,' replied the captain. 'The vessel belongs to me.'

'I will freight it for you.'

'No.'

'I will buy it off you.'

'No.'

Phileas Fogg did not betray the least disappointment; but the situation was a grave one. It was not at New York as at Hong Kong, nor with the captain of the *Henrietta* as with the captain of the *Tankadere*. Up to this time money had smoothed away every obstacle. Now money failed.

Still, some means must be found to cross the Atlantic on a boat, unless by balloon – which would have been venturesome, besides not being capable of being put in practice. It seemed that Phileas Fogg had an idea, for he said to the captain, 'Well, will you carry me to Bordeaux?'

'No, not if you paid me two hundred dollars.'

'I offer you two thousand.'

'Apiece?'

'Apiece.'

'And there are four of you?'

'Four.'

Captain Speedy began to scratch his head. There were eight thousand dollars to gain, without changing his route; for which it was well worth conquering the repugnance he had for all kinds of passengers. Besides, passengers at two thousand dollars are no longer passengers, but valuable merchandise. 'I start at nine o'clock,' said Captain Speedy, simply. 'Are you and your party ready?'

'We will be on board at nine o'clock,' replied, no less simply, Mr. Fogg.

It was half-past eight. To disembark from the *Henrietta*, jump into a hack, hurry to the St. Nicholas, and return with Aouda, Passepartout, and even the inseparable Fix was the work of a brief time, and was performed by Mr. Fogg with the coolness which never abandoned him. They were on board when the *Henrietta* made ready to weigh anchor.

When Passepartout heard what this last voyage was going to cost, he uttered a prolonged 'Oh!' which extended throughout his vocal gamut.

As for Fix, he said to himself that the Bank of England would certainly not come out of this affair well indemnified. When they reached England, even if Mr. Fogg did not throw some handfuls of bank-bills into the sea, more than seven thousand pounds would have been spent!

CHAPTER 33

In which Phileas Fogg shows himself equal to the occasion

An hour after, the *Henrietta* passed the lighthouse which marks the entrance of the Hudson, turned the point of Sandy Hook, and put to sea. During the day she skirted Long Island, passed Fire Island, and directed her course rapidly eastward.

At noon the next day, a man mounted the bridge to ascertain the vessel's position. It might be thought that this was Captain Speedy. Not the least in the world. It was Phileas Fogg, Esquire. As for Captain Speedy, he was shut up in his cabin under lock and key, and was uttering loud cries, which signified an anger at once pardonable and excessive.

What had happened was very simple. Phileas Fogg wished to go to Liverpool, but the captain would not carry him there. Then Phileas Fogg had taken passage for Bordeaux, and, during the thirty hours he had been on board, had so shrewdly managed with his banknotes that the sailors and stokers, who were only an occasional crew, and were not on the best terms with the captain, went over to him in a body. This was why Phileas Fogg was in command instead of Captain Speedy; why the captain was a prisoner in his cabin; and why, in short, the *Henrietta* was directing her course towards

Liverpool. It was very clear, to see Mr. Fogg manage the craft, that he had been a sailor.

How the adventure ended will be seen anon. Aouda was anxious, though she said nothing. As for Passepartout, he thought Mr. Fogg's manoeuvre simply glorious. The captain had said 'between eleven and twelve knots,' and the *Henrietta* confirmed his prediction.

If, then – for there were 'ifs' still – the sea did not become too boisterous, if the wind did not veer round to the east, if no accident happened to the boat or its machinery, the *Henrietta* might cross the three thousand miles from New York to Liverpool in the nine days, between the 12th and the 21st of December. It is true that, once arrived, the affair on board the *Henrietta*, added to that of the Bank of England, might create more difficulties for Mr. Fogg than he imagined or could desire.

During the first days, they went along smoothly enough. The sea was not very unpropitious, the wind seemed stationary in the north-east, the sails were hoisted, and the *Henrietta* ploughed across the waves like a real trans-Atlantic steamer.

Passepartout was delighted. His master's last exploit, the consequences of which he ignored, enchanted him. Never had the crew seen so jolly and dexterous a fellow. He formed warm friendships with the sailors, and amazed them with his acrobatic feats. He thought they managed the vessel like gentlemen, and that the stokers fired up like heroes. His loquacious good-humour infected everyone. He had forgotten the past, its vexations and delays. He only thought of the end, so nearly accomplished; and sometimes he boiled over with impatience, as if heated by the furnaces of the *Henrietta*. Often, also, the worthy fellow revolved around Fix, looking at him with a keen, distrustful eye; but he did not speak to him, for their old intimacy no longer existed.

Fix, it must be confessed, understood nothing of what was going on. The conquest of the *Henrietta*, the bribery of the crew, Fogg managing the boat like a skilled seaman, amazed and confused him. He did not know what to think. For, after all, a man who began by stealing fifty-five thousand pounds might end by stealing a vessel; and Fix was not unnaturally inclined to conclude that the *Henrietta* under Fogg's command, was not going to Liverpool at all, but to some part of the world where the robber, turned into a pirate, would quietly put himself in safety. The conjecture was at least a plausible one, and the detective began to seriously regret that he had embarked on the affair.

As for Captain Speedy, he continued to howl and growl in his cabin; and Passepartout, whose duty it was to carry him his meals, courageous as he was, took the greatest precautions. Mr. Fogg did not seem even to know that there was a captain on board.

On the 13th they passed the edge of the Banks of Newfoundland, a dangerous locality; during the winter, especially, there are frequent fogs and heavy gales of wind. Ever since the evening before the barometer, suddenly falling, had indicated an approaching change in the atmosphere; and during the night the temperature varied, the cold became sharper, and the wind veered to the south-east.

This was a misfortune. Mr. Fogg, in order not to deviate from his course, furled his sails and increased the force of the steam; but the vessel's speed slackened, owing to the state of the sea, the long waves of which broke against the stern. She pitched violently, and this retarded her progress. The breeze little by little swelled into a tempest, and it was to be feared that the *Henrietta* might not be able to maintain herself upright on the waves.

Passepartout's visage darkened with the skies, and for two days the poor fellow experienced constant fright. But Phileas Fogg was a bold mariner, and knew how to maintain headway against the sea; and he kept on his course, without even decreasing his steam. The *Henrietta*, when she could not rise upon the waves, crossed them, swamping her deck, but passing safely. Sometimes the screw rose out of the water, beating its protruding end, when a mountain of water raised the stern above the waves; but the craft always kept straight ahead.

The wind, however, did not grow as boisterous as might have been feared; it was not one of those tempests which burst, and rush on with a speed of ninety miles an hour. It continued fresh, but, unhappily, it remained obstinately in the south-east, rendering the sails useless.

The 16th of December was the seventy-fifth day since Phileas Fogg's departure from London, and the *Henrietta* had not yet been seriously delayed. Half of the voyage was almost accomplished, and the worst localities had been passed. In summer, success would have been well-nigh certain. In winter, they were at the mercy of the bad season. Passepartout said nothing; but he cherished hope in secret, and comforted himself with the reflection that, if the wind failed them, they might still count on the steam.

On this day the engineer came on deck, went up to Mr. Fogg, and began to speak earnestly with him. Without knowing why it was a presentiment, perhaps Passepartout became vaguely uneasy. He would have given one of his ears to hear with the other what the engineer was saying. He finally managed to catch a few words, and was sure he heard his master say, 'You are certain of what you tell me?'

'Certain, sir,' replied the engineer. 'You must remember that, since we started, we have kept up hot fires in all our furnaces, and, though we had coal enough to go on short steam from New York to Bordeaux, we haven't enough to go with all steam from New York to Liverpool.'

'I will consider,' replied Mr. Fogg.

Passepartout understood it all; he was seized with mortal anxiety. The coal was giving out! 'Ah, if my master can get over that,' muttered he, 'he'll be a famous man!' He could not help imparting to Fix what he had overheard.

'Then you believe that we really are going to Liverpool?'

'Of course.'

'Ass!' replied the detective, shrugging his shoulders and turning on his heel.

Passepartout was on the point of vigorously resenting the epithet, the reason of which he could not for the life of him comprehend; but he reflected that the unfortunate Fix was probably very much disappointed and humiliated in his self-esteem, after having so awkwardly followed a false scent around the world, and refrained.

And now what course would Phileas Fogg adopt? It was difficult to imagine. Nevertheless he seemed to have decided upon one, for that evening he sent for the engineer, and said to him, 'Feed all the fires until the coal is exhausted.'

A few moments after, the funnel of the *Henrietta* vomited forth torrents of smoke. The vessel continued to proceed with all steam on; but on the 18th, the engineer, as he had predicted, announced that the coal would give out in the course of the day.

'Do not let the fires go down,' replied Mr. Fogg. 'Keep them up to the last. Let the valves be filled.'

Towards noon Phileas Fogg, having ascertained their position, called Passepartout, and ordered him to go for Captain Speedy. It was as if the honest fellow had been commanded to unchain a tiger. He went to the poop, saying to himself, 'He will be like a madman!'

In a few moments, with cries and oaths, a bomb appeared on the poop-deck. The bomb was Captain Speedy. It was clear that he was on the point of bursting. 'Where are we?' were the first words his anger permitted him to utter. Had the poor man been an apoplectic, he could never have recovered from his paroxysm of wrath.

'Where are we?' he repeated, with purple face.

'Seven hundred and seven miles from Liverpool,' replied Mr. Fogg, with imperturbable calmness.

'Pirate!' cried Captain Speedy.

'I have sent for you, sir – '

'Pickaroon!'

' – sir,' continued Mr. Fogg, 'to ask you to sell me your vessel.'

'No! By all the devils, no!'

'But I shall be obliged to burn her.'

'Burn the *Henrietta*!'

'Yes; at least the upper part of her. The coal has given out.'

'Burn my vessel!' cried Captain Speedy, who could scarcely pronounce the words. 'A vessel worth fifty thousand dollars!'

'Here are sixty thousand,' replied Phileas Fogg, handing the captain a roll of bank-bills. This had a prodigious effect on Andrew Speedy. An American can scarcely remain unmoved at the sight of sixty thousand dollars. The captain forgot in an instant his anger, his imprisonment, and all his grudges against his passenger. The *Henrietta* was twenty years old; it was a great bargain. The bomb would not go off after all. Mr. Fogg had taken away the match.

'And I shall still have the iron hull,' said the captain in a softer tone.

'The iron hull and the engine. Is it agreed?'

'Agreed.'

And Andrew Speedy, seizing the banknotes, counted them and consigned them to his pocket.

During this colloquy, Passepartout was as white as a sheet, and Fix seemed on the point of having an apoplectic fit. Nearly twenty thousand pounds had been expended, and Fogg left the hull and engine to the captain, that is, near the whole value of the craft! It was true, however, that fifty-five thousand pounds had been stolen from the Bank.

When Andrew Speedy had pocketed the money, Mr. Fogg said to him, 'Don't let this astonish you, sir. You must know that I shall lose twenty thousand pounds, unless I arrive in London by a quarter before nine on the evening of the 21st of December. I missed the steamer at New York, and as you refused to take me to Liverpool – '

'And I did well!' cried Andrew Speedy; 'for I have gained at least forty thousand dollars by it!' He added, more sedately, 'Do you know one thing, Captain – '

'Fogg.'

'Captain Fogg, you've got something of the Yankee about you.'

And, having paid his passenger what he considered a high compliment, he was going away, when Mr. Fogg said, 'The vessel now belongs to me?'

'Certainly, from the keel to the truck of the masts – all the wood, that is.'

'Very well. Have the interior seats, bunks, and frames pulled down, and burn them.'

It was necessary to have dry wood to keep the steam up

to the adequate pressure, and on that day the poop, cabins, bunks, and the spare deck were sacrificed. On the next day, the 19th of December, the masts, rafts, and spars were burned; the crew worked lustily, keeping up the fires. Passepartout hewed, cut, and sawed away with all his might. There was a perfect rage for demolition.

The railings, fittings, the greater part of the deck, and top sides disappeared on the 20th, and the *Henrietta* was now only a flat hulk. But on this day they sighted the Irish coast and Fastnet Light. By ten in the evening they were passing Queenstown. Phileas Fogg had only twenty-four hours more in which to get to London; that length of time was necessary to reach Liverpool, with all steam on. And the steam was about to give out altogether!

'Sir,' said Captain Speedy, who was now deeply interested in Mr. Fogg's project, 'I really commiserate you. Everything is against you. We are only opposite Queenstown.'

'Ah,' said Mr. Fogg, 'is that place where we see the lights Queenstown?'

'Yes.'

'Can we enter the harbour?'

'Not under three hours. Only at high tide.'

'Stay,' replied Mr. Fogg calmly, without betraying in his features that by a supreme inspiration he was about to attempt once more to conquer ill-fortune.

Queenstown is the Irish port at which the trans-Atlantic steamers stop to put off the mails. These mails are carried to Dublin by express trains always held in readiness to start; from Dublin they are sent on to Liverpool by the most rapid boats, and thus gain twelve hours on the Atlantic steamers.

Phileas Fogg counted on gaining twelve hours in the same way. Instead of arriving at Liverpool the next evening by the

Henrietta, he would be there by noon, and would therefore have time to reach London before a quarter before nine in the evening.

The *Henrietta* entered Queenstown Harbour at one o'clock in the morning, it then being high tide; and Phileas Fogg, after being grasped heartily by the hand by Captain Speedy, left that gentleman on the levelled hulk of his craft, which was still worth half what he had sold it for.

The party went on shore at once. Fix was greatly tempted to arrest Mr. Fogg on the spot; but he did not. Why? What struggle was going on within him? Had he changed his mind about 'his man'? Did he understand that he had made a grave mistake? He did not, however, abandon Mr. Fogg. They all got upon the train, which was just ready to start, at half-past one; at dawn of day they were in Dublin; and they lost no time in embarking on a steamer which, disdaining to rise upon the waves, invariably cut through them.

Phileas Fogg at last disembarked on the Liverpool quay, at twenty minutes before twelve, 21st December. He was only six hours distant from London.

But at this moment Fix came up, put his hand upon Mr. Fogg's shoulder, and, showing his warrant, said, 'You are really Phileas Fogg?'

'I am.'

'I arrest you in the Queen's name!'

CHAPTER 34

In which Phileas Fogg at last reaches London

Phileas Fogg was in prison. He had been shut up in the Custom House, and he was to be transferred to London the next day.

Passepartout, when he saw his master arrested, would have fallen upon Fix had he not been held back by some policemen. Aouda was thunderstruck at the suddenness of an event which she could not understand. Passepartout explained to her how it was that the honest and courageous Fogg was arrested as a robber. The young woman's heart revolted against so heinous a charge, and when she saw that she could attempt to do nothing to save her protector, she wept bitterly.

As for Fix, he had arrested Mr. Fogg because it was his duty, whether Mr. Fogg were guilty or not.

The thought then struck Passepartout, that he was the cause of this new misfortune! Had he not concealed Fix's errand from his master? When Fix revealed his true character and purpose, why had he not told Mr. Fogg? If the latter had been warned, he would no doubt have given Fix proof of his innocence, and satisfied him of his mistake; at least, Fix would not have continued his journey at the expense and on the heels of his master, only to arrest him the moment he set foot on English soil. Passepartout wept till he was blind, and felt like blowing his brains out.

Aouda and he had remained, despite the cold, under the portico of the Custom House. Neither wished to leave the place; both were anxious to see Mr. Fogg again.

That gentleman was really ruined, and that at the moment when he was about to attain his end. This arrest was fatal. Having arrived at Liverpool at twenty minutes before twelve on the 21st of December, he had till a quarter before nine that evening to reach the Reform Club, that is, nine hours and a quarter; the journey from Liverpool to London was six hours.

If anyone, at this moment, had entered the Custom House, he would have found Mr. Fogg seated, motionless, calm, and without apparent anger, upon a wooden bench. He was not, it is true, resigned; but this last blow failed to force him into an outward betrayal of any emotion. Was he being devoured by one of those secret rages, all the more terrible because contained, and which only burst forth, with an irresistible force, at the last moment? No one could tell. There he sat, calmly waiting – for what? Did he still cherish hope? Did he still believe, now that the door of this prison was closed upon him, that he would succeed?

However that may have been, Mr. Fogg carefully put his watch upon the table, and observed its advancing hands. Not a word escaped his lips, but his look was singularly set and stern. The situation, in any event, was a terrible one, and might be thus stated: if Phileas Fogg was honest he was ruined; if he was a knave, he was caught.

Did escape occur to him? Did he examine to see if there were any practicable outlet from his prison? Did he think of escaping from it? Possibly; for once he walked slowly around the room. But the door was locked, and the window heavily barred with iron rods. He sat down again, and drew his journal from his pocket. On the line where these words were written, '21st December, Saturday, Liverpool,' he added, '80th day, 11.40 a.m.,' and waited.

The Custom House clock struck one. Mr. Fogg observed that his watch was two hours too fast.

Two hours! Admitting that he was at this moment taking an express train, he could reach London and the Reform Club by a quarter before nine, p.m. His forehead slightly wrinkled.

At thirty-three minutes past two he heard a singular noise outside, then a hasty opening of doors. Passepartout's voice was audible, and immediately after that of Fix. Phileas Fogg's eyes brightened for an instant.

The door swung open, and he saw Passepartout, Aouda, and Fix, who hurried towards him.

Fix was out of breath, and his hair was in disorder. He could not speak. 'Sir,' he stammered, 'sir – forgive me – most – unfortunate resemblance – robber arrested three days ago – you are free!'

Phileas Fogg was free! He walked to the detective, looked him steadily in the face, and with the only rapid motion he had ever made in his life, or which he ever would make, drew back his arms, and with the precision of a machine knocked Fix down.

'Well hit!' cried Passepartout, 'Parbleu! that's what you might call a good application of English fists!'

Fix, who found himself on the floor, did not utter a word. He had only received his deserts. Mr. Fogg, Aouda, and Passepartout left the Custom House without delay, got into a cab, and in a few moments descended at the station.

Phileas Fogg asked if there was an express train about to leave for London. It was forty minutes past two. The express train had left thirty-five minutes before. Phileas Fogg then ordered a special train.

There were several rapid locomotives on hand; but the railway arrangements did not permit the special train to leave until three o'clock.

At that hour Phileas Fogg, having stimulated the engineer by the offer of a generous reward, at last set out towards London with Aouda and his faithful servant.

It was necessary to make the journey in five hours and a half; and this would have been easy on a clear road throughout. But there were forced delays, and when Mr. Fogg stepped from the train at the terminus, all the clocks in London were striking ten minutes before nine.

Having made the tour of the world, he was behind-hand five minutes. He had lost the wager!

CHAPTER 35

In which Phileas Fogg does not have to repeat his orders to Passepartout twice

The dwellers in Savile Row would have been surprised the next day, if they had been told that Phileas Fogg had returned home. His doors and windows were still closed, no appearance of change was visible.

After leaving the station, Mr. Fogg gave Passepartout instructions to purchase some provisions, and quietly went to his domicile.

He bore his misfortune with his habitual tranquillity. Ruined! And by the blundering of the detective! After having steadily traversed that long journey, overcome a hundred obstacles, braved many dangers, and still found time to do some good on his way, to fail near the goal by a sudden event which he could not have foreseen, and against which he was unarmed; it was terrible! But a few pounds were left of the large sum he had carried with him. There only remained of his fortune the twenty thousand pounds deposited at Barings, and this amount he owed to his friends of the Reform Club. So great had been the expense of his tour that, even had he won, it would not have enriched him; and it is probable that he had not sought to enrich himself, being a man who rather laid wagers for honour's sake than for the stake proposed. But this wager totally ruined him.

Mr. Fogg's course, however, was fully decided upon; he knew what remained for him to do.

A room in the house in Savile Row was set apart for Aouda, who was overwhelmed with grief at her protector's misfortune. From the words which Mr. Fogg dropped, she saw that he was meditating some serious project.

Knowing that Englishmen governed by a fixed idea sometimes resort to the desperate expedient of suicide, Passepartout kept a narrow watch upon his master, though he carefully concealed the appearance of so doing.

First of all, the worthy fellow had gone up to his room, and had extinguished the gas burner, which had been burning for eighty days. He had found in the letter-box a bill from the gas company, and he thought it more than time to put a stop to this expense, which he had been doomed to bear.

The night passed. Mr. Fogg went to bed, but did he sleep? Aouda did not once close her eyes. Passepartout watched all night, like a faithful dog, at his master's door.

Mr. Fogg called him in the morning, and told him to get Aouda's breakfast, and a cup of tea and a chop for himself. He desired Aouda to excuse him from breakfast and dinner, as his time would be absorbed all day in putting his affairs to rights. In the evening he would ask permission to have a few moment's conversation with the young lady.

Passepartout, having received his orders, had nothing to do but obey them. He looked at his imperturbable master, and could scarcely bring his mind to leave him. His heart was full, and his conscience tortured by remorse; for he accused himself more bitterly than ever of being the cause of the irretrievable disaster. Yes! if he had warned Mr. Fogg, and had betrayed Fix's projects to him, his master would certainly not have given the detective passage to Liverpool, and then –

Passepartout could hold in no longer.

'My master! Mr. Fogg!' he cried, 'why do you not curse me? It was my fault that – '

'I blame no one,' returned Phileas Fogg, with perfect calmness. 'Go!'

Passepartout left the room, and went to find Aouda, to whom he delivered his master's message.

'Madam,' he added, 'I can do nothing myself – nothing! I have no influence over my master; but you, perhaps – '

'What influence could I have?' replied Aouda. 'Mr. Fogg is influenced by no one. Has he ever understood that my gratitude to him is overflowing? Has he ever read my heart? My friend, he must not be left alone an instant! You say he is going to speak with me this evening?'

'Yes, madam; probably to arrange for your protection and comfort in England.'

'We shall see,' replied Aouda, becoming suddenly pensive.

Throughout this day (Sunday) the house in Savile Row was as if uninhabited, and Phileas Fogg, for the first time since he had lived in that house, did not set out for his club when Westminster clock struck half-past eleven.

Why should he present himself at the Reform? His friends no longer expected him there. As Phileas Fogg had not appeared in the saloon on the evening before (Saturday, the 21st of December, at a quarter before nine), he had lost his wager. It was not even necessary that he should go to his bankers for the twenty thousand pounds; for his antagonists already had his cheque in their hands, and they had only to fill it out and send it to the Barings to have the amount transferred to their credit.

Mr. Fogg, therefore, had no reason for going out, and so he remained at home. He shut himself up in his room, and busied himself putting his affairs in order. Passepartout continually ascended and descended the stairs. The hours were long for him. He listened at his master's door, and looked through the keyhole, as if he had a perfect right so to do, and as if he feared that something terrible might happen at any moment. Sometimes he thought of Fix, but no longer in anger. Fix, like all the world, had been mistaken in Phileas Fogg, and had only done his duty in tracking and arresting him; while he, Passepartout. . . . This thought haunted him, and he never ceased cursing his miserable folly.

Finding himself too wretched to remain alone, he knocked at Aouda's door, went into her room, seated himself, without speaking, in a corner, and looked ruefully at the young woman. Aouda was still pensive.

About half-past seven in the evening Mr. Fogg sent to know if Aouda would receive him, and in a few moments he found himself alone with her.

Phileas Fogg took a chair, and sat down near the fireplace, opposite Aouda. No emotion was visible on his face. Fogg returned was exactly the Fogg who had gone away; there was the same calm, the same impassibility.

He sat several minutes without speaking; then, bending his eyes on Aouda, 'Madam,' said he, 'will you pardon me for bringing you to England?'

'I, Mr. Fogg!' replied Aouda, checking the pulsations of her heart.

'Please let me finish,' returned Mr. Fogg. 'When I decided to bring you far away from the country which was so unsafe for you, I was rich, and counted on putting a portion of my fortune at your disposal; then your existence would have been free and happy. But now I am ruined.'

'I know it, Mr. Fogg,' replied Aouda; 'and I ask you in my turn, will you forgive me for having followed you, and – who knows? – for having, perhaps, delayed you, and thus contributed to your ruin?'

'Madam, you could not remain in India, and your safety could only be assured by bringing you to such a distance that your persecutors could not take you.'

'So, Mr. Fogg,' resumed Aouda, 'not content with rescuing me from a terrible death, you thought yourself bound to secure my comfort in a foreign land?'

'Yes, madam; but circumstances have been against me. Still, I beg to place the little I have left at your service.'

'But what will become of you, Mr. Fogg?'

'As for me, madam,' replied the gentleman, coldly, 'I have need of nothing.'

'But how do you look upon the fate, sir, which awaits you?'

'As I am in the habit of doing.'

'At least,' said Aouda, 'want should not overtake a man like you. Your friends – '

'I have no friends, madam.'

'Your relatives – '

'I have no longer any relatives.'

'I pity you, then, Mr. Fogg, for solitude is a sad thing, with no heart to which to confide your griefs. They say, though, that misery itself, shared by two sympathetic souls, may be borne with patience.'

'They say so, madam.'

'Mr. Fogg,' said Aouda, rising and seizing his hand, 'do

you wish at once a kinswoman and friend? Will you have me for your wife?'

Mr. Fogg, at this, rose in his turn. There was an unwonted light in his eyes, and a slight trembling of his lips. Aouda looked into his face. The sincerity, rectitude, firmness, and sweetness of this soft glance of a noble woman, who could dare all to save him to whom she owed all, at first astonished, then penetrated him. He shut his eyes for an instant, as if to avoid her look. When he opened them again, 'I love you!' he said, simply. 'Yes, by all that is holiest, I love you, and I am entirely yours!'

'Ah!' cried Aouda, pressing his hand to her heart.

Passepartout was summoned and appeared immediately. Mr. Fogg still held Aouda's hand in his own; Passepartout understood, and his big, round face became as radiant as the tropical sun at its zenith.

Mr. Fogg asked him if it was not too late to notify the Reverend Samuel Wilson, of Marylebone parish, that evening.

Passepartout smiled his most genial smile, and said, 'Never too late.'

It was five minutes past eight.

'Will it be for to-morrow, Monday?'

'For to-morrow, Monday,' said Mr. Fogg, turning to Aouda.

'Yes; for to-morrow, Monday,' she replied.

Passepartout hurried off as fast as his legs could carry him.

CHAPTER 36

In which Phileas Fogg's name is once more at a premium on 'Change

It is time to relate what a change took place in English public opinion when it transpired that the real bankrobber, a certain James Strand, had been arrested, on the 17th day of December, at Edinburgh. Three days before, Phileas Fogg had been a criminal, who was being desperately followed up by the police; now he was an honourable gentleman, mathematically pursuing his eccentric journey round the world.

The papers resumed their discussion about the wager; all those who had laid bets, for or against him, revived their interest, as if by magic; the 'Phileas Fogg bonds' again became negotiable, and many new wagers were made. Phileas Fogg's name was once more at a premium on 'Change.

His five friends of the Reform Club passed these three days in a state of feverish suspense. Would Phileas Fogg, whom they had forgotten, reappear before their eyes! Where was he at this moment? The 17th of December, the day of James Strand's arrest, was the seventy-sixth since Phileas Fogg's departure, and no news of him had been received. Was he dead? Had he abandoned the effort, or was he continuing his journey along the route agreed upon? And would he appear on Saturday, the 21st of December, at a quarter before nine in the evening, on the threshold of the Reform Club saloon?

The anxiety in which, for three days, London society existed, cannot be described. Telegrams were sent to America and Asia for news of Phileas Fogg. Messengers were dispatched to the house in Savile Row morning and evening. No news. The police were ignorant what had become of the detective, Fix, who had so unfortunately followed up a false scent. Bets increased, nevertheless, in number and value. Phileas Fogg, like a racehorse, was drawing near his last turning-point. The bonds were quoted, no longer at a hundred below par, but at twenty, at ten, and at five; and paralytic old Lord Albemarle bet even in his favour.

A great crowd was collected in Pall Mall and the neighbouring streets on Saturday evening; it seemed like a multitude of brokers permanently established around the Reform Club. Circulation was impeded, and everywhere disputes, discussions, and financial transactions were going on. The police had great difficulty in keeping back the crowd, and as the hour when Phileas Fogg was due approached, the excitement rose to its highest pitch.

The five antagonists of Phileas Fogg had met in the great saloon of the club. John Sullivan and Samuel Fallentin, the bankers, Andrew Stuart, the engineer, Gauthier Ralph, the director of the Bank of England, and Thomas Flanagan, the brewer, one and all waited anxiously.

When the clock indicated twenty minutes past eight, Andrew Stuart got up, saying, 'Gentlemen, in twenty minutes the time agreed upon between Mr. Fogg and ourselves will have expired.'

'What time did the last train arrive from Liverpool?' asked Thomas Flanagan.

'At twenty-three minutes past seven,' replied Gauthier Ralph; 'and the next does not arrive till ten minutes after twelve.'

'Well, gentlemen,' resumed Andrew Stuart, 'if Phileas Fogg had come in the 7:23 train, he would have got here by this time. We can, therefore, regard the bet as won.'

'Wait; don't let us be too hasty,' replied Samuel Fallentin. 'You know that Mr. Fogg is very eccentric. His punctuality is well known; he never arrives too soon, or too late; and I should not be surprised if he appeared before us at the last minute.'

'Why,' said Andrew Stuart nervously, 'if I should see him, I should not believe it was he.'

'The fact is,' resumed Thomas Flanagan, 'Mr. Fogg's project was absurdly foolish. Whatever his punctuality, he could not prevent the delays which were certain to occur; and a delay of only two or three days would be fatal to his tour.'

'Observe, too,' added John Sullivan, 'that we have received no intelligence from him, though there are telegraphic lines all along his route.'

'He has lost, gentleman,' said Andrew Stuart, 'he has a hundred times lost! You know, besides, that the *China* the only steamer he could have taken from New York to get here in time arrived yesterday. I have seen a list of the passengers, and the name of Phileas Fogg is not among them. Even if we admit that fortune has favoured him, he can scarcely have reached America. I think he will be at least twenty days behind-hand, and that Lord Albemarle will lose a cool five thousand.'

'It is clear,' replied Gauthier Ralph; 'and we have nothing

to do but to present Mr. Fogg's cheque at Barings to-morrow.'

At this moment, the hands of the club clock pointed to twenty minutes to nine.

'Five minutes more,' said Andrew Stuart.

The five gentlemen looked at each other. Their anxiety was becoming intense; but, not wishing to betray it, they readily assented to Mr. Fallentin's proposal of a rubber.

'I wouldn't give up my four thousand of the bet,' said Andrew Stuart, as he took his seat, 'for three thousand nine hundred and ninety-nine.'

The clock indicated eighteen minutes to nine.

The players took up their cards, but could not keep their eyes off the clock. Certainly, however secure they felt, minutes had never seemed so long to them!

'Seventeen minutes to nine,' said Thomas Flanagan, as he cut the cards which Ralph handed to him.

Then there was a moment of silence. The great saloon was perfectly quiet; but the murmurs of the crowd outside were heard, with now and then a shrill cry. The pendulum beat the seconds, which each player eagerly counted, as he listened, with mathematical regularity.

'Sixteen minutes to nine!' said John Sullivan, in a voice which betrayed his emotion.

One minute more, and the wager would be won. Andrew Stuart and his partners suspended their game. They left their cards, and counted the seconds.

At the fortieth second, nothing. At the fiftieth, still nothing.

At the fifty-fifth, a loud cry was heard in the street, followed by applause, hurrahs, and some fierce growls.

The players rose from their seats.

At the fifty-seventh second the door of the saloon opened; and the pendulum had not beat the sixtieth second when

Phileas Fogg appeared, followed by an excited crowd who had forced their way through the club doors, and in his calm voice, said, 'Here I am, gentlemen!'

CHAPTER 37

In which it is shown that Phileas Fogg gained nothing by his tour around the world, unless it were happiness

Yes; Phileas Fogg in person.

The reader will remember that at five minutes past eight in the evening – about five and twenty hours after the arrival of the travellers in London – Passepartout had been sent by his master to engage the services of the Reverend Samuel Wilson in a certain marriage ceremony, which was to take place the next day.

Passepartout went on his errand enchanted. He soon reached the clergyman's house, but found him not at home. Passepartout waited a good twenty minutes, and when he left the reverend gentleman, it was thirty-five minutes past eight. But in what a state he was! With his hair in disorder, and without his hat, he ran along the street as never man was seen to run before, overturning passers-by, rushing over the sidewalk like a waterspout.

In three minutes he was in Savile Row again, and staggered back into Mr. Fogg's room.

He could not speak.

'What is the matter?' asked Mr. Fogg.

'My master!' gasped Passepartout – 'marriage – impossible – '

'Impossible?'

'Impossible – for to-morrow.'

'Why so?'

'Because to-morrow – is Sunday!'

'Monday,' replied Mr. Fogg.

'No – to-day is Saturday.'

'Saturday? Impossible!'

'Yes, yes, yes, yes!' cried Passepartout. 'You have made a mistake of one day! We arrived twenty-four hours ahead of time; but there are only ten minutes left!'

Passepartout had seized his master by the collar, and was dragging him along with irresistible force.

Phileas Fogg, thus kidnapped, without having time to think, left his house, jumped into a cab, promised a hundred pounds to the cabman, and, having run over two dogs and overturned five carriages, reached the Reform Club.

The clock indicated a quarter before nine when he appeared in the great saloon.

Phileas Fogg had accomplished the journey round the world in eighty days!

Phileas Fogg had won his wager of twenty thousand pounds!

How was it that a man so exact and fastidious could have made this error of a day? How came he to think that he had arrived in London on Saturday, the twenty-first day of December, when it was really Friday, the twentieth, the seventy-ninth day only from his departure?

The cause of the error is very simple.

Phileas Fogg had, without suspecting it, gained one day on his journey, and this merely because he had travelled constantly eastward; he would, on the contrary, have lost a day had he gone in the opposite direction, that is, westward.

In journeying eastward he had gone towards the sun, and the days therefore diminished for him as many times four minutes as he crossed degrees in this direction. There are three hundred and sixty degrees on the circumference of the earth; and these three hundred and sixty degrees, multiplied by four minutes, gives precisely twenty-four hours – that is, the day unconsciously gained. In other words, while Phileas Fogg, going eastward, saw the sun pass the meridian eighty times, his friends in London only saw it pass the meridian seventy-nine times. This is why they awaited him at the Reform Club on Saturday, and not Sunday, as Mr. Fogg thought.

And Passepartout's famous family watch, which had always kept London time, would have betrayed this fact, if it had marked the days as well as the hours and the minutes!

Phileas Fogg, then, had won the twenty thousand pounds; but, as he had spent nearly nineteen thousand on the way, the pecuniary gain was small. His object was, however, to be victorious, and not to win money. He divided the one thousand pounds that remained between Passepartout and the unfortunate Fix, against whom he cherished no grudge. He deducted, however, from Passepartout's share the cost of the gas which had burned in his room for nineteen hundred and twenty hours, for the sake of regularity.

That evening, Mr. Fogg, as tranquil and phlegmatic as ever, said to Aouda: 'Is our marriage still agreeable to you?'

'Mr. Fogg,' replied she, 'it is for me to ask that question. You were ruined, but now you are rich again.'

'Pardon me, madam; my fortune belongs to you. If you had not suggested our marriage, my servant would not have gone to the Reverend Samuel Wilson's, I should not have been apprised of my error, and – '

'Dear Mr. Fogg!' said the young woman.

'Dear Aouda!' replied Phileas Fogg.

It need not be said that the marriage took place forty-eight hours after, and that Passepartout, glowing and dazzling, gave the bride away. Had he not saved her, and was he not entitled to this honour?

The next day, as soon as it was light, Passepartout rapped vigorously at his master's door. Mr. Fogg opened it, and asked, 'What's the matter, Passepartout?'

'What is it, sir? Why, I've just this instant found out – '

'What?'

'That we might have made the tour of the world in only seventy-eight days.'

'No doubt,' returned Mr. Fogg, 'by not crossing India. But if I had not crossed India, I should not have saved Aouda; she would not have been my wife, and – '

Mr. Fogg quietly shut the door.

Phileas Fogg had won his wager, and had made his journey around the world in eighty days. To do this he had employed every means of conveyance – steamers, railways, carriages, yachts, trading-vessels, sledges, elephants. The eccentric gentleman had throughout displayed all his marvellous qualities of coolness and exactitude. But what then? What had he really gained by all this trouble? What had he brought back from this long and weary journey?

Nothing, say you? Perhaps so; nothing but a charming woman, who, strange as it may appear, made him the happiest of men!

Truly, would you not for less than that make the tour around the world?

AROUND THE MOON

AROUND THE MOON

JULES VERNE

This edition published in 2021 by Arcturus Publishing Limited
26/27 Bickels Yard, 151–153 Bermondsey Street,
London SE1 3HA

Copyright © Arcturus Holdings Limited

All rights reserved. No part of this publication may be reproduced, stored in a retrieval system, or transmitted, in any form or by any means, electronic, mechanical, photocopying, recording or otherwise, without prior written permission in accordance with the provisions of the Copyright Act 1956 (as amended). Any person or persons who do any unauthorised act in relation to this publication may be liable to criminal prosecution and civil claims for damages.

Cover design: Peter Ridley
Cover illustration: Peter Gray

AD008687UK

Printed in the UK

MIX
Paper from responsible sources
FSC® C018072

CONTENTS

Introduction 6
Preliminary Chapter 9

Chapter I: *From 10 P.M. To 10 46' 40"* 15
Chapter II: *The First Half Hour* 22
Chapter III: *They Make Themselves at Home and
                Feel Quite Comfortable* 43
Chapter IV: *A Chapter for the Cornell Girls* 55
Chapter V: *The Colds of Space* 65
Chapter VI: *Instructive Conversation* 77
Chapter VII: *A High Old Time* 88
Chapter VIII: *The Neutral Point* 102
Chapter IX: *A Little off the Track* 114
Chapter X: *The Observers Of The Moon* 123
Chapter XI: *Fact and Fancy* 131
Chapter XII: *A Bird's Eye View of the Lunar Mountains* 140
Chapter XIII: *Lunar Landscapes* 154
Chapter XIV: *A Night of Fifteen Days* 169
Chapter XV: *Glimpses at the Invisible* 186
Chapter XVI: *The Southern Hemisphere* 204
Chapter XVII: *Tycho* 214
Chapter XVIII: *Puzzling Questions* 227
Chapter XIX: *In Every Fight, the Impossible Wins* 244
Chapter XX: *Off the Pacific Coast* 259
Chapter XXI: *News for Marston!* 268
Chapter XXII: *On the Wings of the Wind* 285
Chapter XXIII: *The Club Men Go A Fishing* 293
Chapter XXIV: *Farewell to the Baltimore Gun Club* 308

Introduction

Deservedly known as the 'Father of Science Fiction', Jules Verne wrote of adventures to unexplored regions of the world and wonderful inventions. On many occasions, his technological marvels, such as the submarine and space travel, predicted scientific advances that were years, or even decades, in the future.

Born on 8 February 1828 in the port city of Nantes, France, Verne saw vessels come and go, wondering what adventures they were going on. As a young boy, he dreamed of having his own adventures at sea, and at the age of 12 he smuggled himself onto a ship bound for India, only to be discovered and beaten for his disobedience. His relationship with his father, Pierre Verne, was a troubled one. Pierre, hoping to see his son follow in his footsteps, sent him to Paris to study law.

However, the appeal of writing proved too strong. Jules spent much of his time writing plays rather than studying law, and despite graduating in 1849, showed little inclination to pursue a legal career. Encouraged by the writer, Alexandre Dumas, Verne decided to remain in Paris and write plays instead. His first production in 1850, *Blindman's Bluff*, was a lukewarm start to his ten-year playwriting career. When he found the love of his life, the divorcée Honorine de Viane Morel in 1856, Verne sought financial stability and found work as a stockbroker to maintain his marriage.

But the writing never stopped, and he would soon ignite his adventures off-stage with one of literature's greatest partnerships: Jules Verne and his publisher Pierre-Jules Hertzel were an exceptional duo. Recognising the untapped potential in his author's seemingly crazy, futuristic ideas, Hertzel's masterful editing and knowledgeable suggestions kept his stories grounded and accessible enough for audiences to digest when Verne's original manuscripts would have been too far-fetched.

When writing his 1863 adventure novel, *Five Weeks in a Balloon*, Verne had no experience in a balloon, let alone using one to cross the Atlantic. He researched Edgar Allan Poe's story 'The Unparalleled Adventure of One Hans Pfaall' as well as travel magazines to familiarise himself with the experience. He continued to venture into the unknown, generating exciting titles including *Journey to the Centre of the Earth* (1864), and *Around the World in Eighty Days* (1872).

From the Earth to the Moon (1865) examined a subject that had fascinated humanity for centuries – could we really visit the moon? How would we get there? The Baltimore Gun Club, left in idleness following the end of the American Civil War, sets out to create a gun powerful enough to launch men into space. The novel presents a plausible, scientific approach that is surprisingly similar to the rockets used to launch the Apollo 11 mission nearly a century later – an endeavour that saw men land on the moon in reality, not just fiction.

To the disappointment of some, the story did not include the actual journey around the moon itself. This would have to wait until the sequel, *Around the Moon* (1869). The three friends Barbicane, Nicholl and Ardan face several dangers as they attempt to complete a mission of scientific observation. What they saw proved startlingly close to what we now know to be the reality. Verne described the moon as devoid of life with a surface temperature at night of –218 degrees Fahrenheit (–139 degrees Celsius); its real temperature at night is approximately –280 degrees Fahrenheit (–173 degrees Celsius). It was an extraordinary work of imagination that nevertheless drew heavily on the scientific knowledge of the day.

One of his most visionary novels, *Paris in the Twentieth Century*, featured skyscrapers, bullet trains, calculators, and gas-fuelled cars, but was not published until 1994 due to Hertzel's belief that the subject matter was too subversive. While Verne was fascinated with the progress of technology, he was also sceptical about its overpowering effect on mankind. This was most apparent in his nautical masterpiece, *Twenty Thousand Leagues Under the Sea* (1869).

Jules Verne died on 24 March 1905 after suffering from diabetes. A prolific writer throughout his life, the success of his tales and their worldwide appeal made him the second most translated writer of all time. He may have not been a scientist, but the innovations in his work have influenced many writers and scientists, paving the way for one of literature's most exciting and thought-provoking genres – science fiction.

PRELIMINARY CHAPTER

Resuming the First Part of the Work and Serving as an Introduction to the Second

A FEW YEARS ago the world was suddenly astounded by hearing of an experiment of a most novel and daring nature, altogether unprecedented in the annals of science. The BALTIMORE GUN CLUB, a society of artillerymen started in America during the great Civil War, had conceived the idea of nothing less than establishing direct communication with the Moon by means of a projectile! President Barbican, the originator of the enterprise, was strongly encouraged in its feasibility by the astronomers of Cambridge Observatory, and took upon himself to provide all the means necessary to secure its success. Having realized by means of a public subscription the sum of nearly five and a half millions of dollars, he immediately set himself to work at the necessary gigantic labours.

In accordance with the Cambridge men's note, the cannon intended to discharge the projectile was to be planted in some country not further than 28° north or south from the equator, so that it might be aimed vertically at the Moon in the zenith. The bullet was to be animated with an initial velocity of 12,000 yards to the second. It was to be fired off on the night of December 1st, at thirteen minutes and twenty seconds before eleven o'clock, precisely. Four days afterwards it was to hit the Moon, at the very moment that she reached her *perigee*, that is to say, her nearest point to the Earth, about 228,000 miles distant.

The leading members of the Club, namely President Barbican, Secretary Marston, Major Elphinstone and General Morgan, forming the executive committee, held several meetings to discuss the shape and material of the bullet, the nature and position of the cannon, and the quantity and quality of the powder. The decision soon arrived at was as follows: 1st – The bullet was to be a hollow aluminium shell, its diameter nine feet, its walls a foot in thickness, and its weight 19,250 pounds; 2nd – The cannon was to be a columbiad 900 feet in length, a well of that depth forming the vertical mould in which it was to be cast, and 3rd – The powder was to be 400 thousand pounds of gun cotton, which, by developing more than 200 thousand millions of cubic feet of gas under the projectile, would easily send it as far as our satellite.

These questions settled, Barbican, aided by Murphy, the Chief Engineer of the Cold Spring Iron Works, selected a spot in Florida, near the 27th degree north latitude, called Stony Hill, where after the performance of many wonderful feats in mining engineering, the Columbiad was successfully cast.

Things had reached this state when an incident occurred which excited the general interest a hundred fold.

A Frenchman from Paris, Michel Ardan by name, eccentric, but keen and shrewd as well as daring, demanded, by the Atlantic telegraph, permission to be enclosed in the bullet so that he might be carried to the Moon, where he was curious to make certain investigations. Received in America with great enthusiasm, Ardan held a great meeting, triumphantly carried his point, reconciled Barbican to his mortal foe, a certain Captain M'Nicholl, and even, by way of clinching the reconciliation, induced both the newly made friends to join him in his contemplated trip to the Moon.

The bullet, so modified as to become a hollow conical cylinder with plenty of room inside, was further provided with powerful water-springs and readily-ruptured partitions below the floor, intended to deaden the dreadful concussion sure to accompany the start. It was supplied with provisions for a year, water for a few months, and gas for nearly two weeks. A self-acting apparatus, of ingenious construction, kept the confined atmosphere sweet and healthy by manufacturing pure oxygen and absorbing carbonic acid. Finally, the Gun Club had constructed, at enormous expense, a gigantic telescope, which, from the summit of Long's Peak, could pursue the Projectile as it winged its way through the regions of space. Everything at last was ready.

On December 1st, at the appointed moment, in the midst of an immense concourse of spectators, the departure took place, and, for the first time in the world's history, three human beings quitted our terrestrial globe with some possibility in their favour of finally reaching a point of destination in the inter-planetary spaces. They expected to accomplish their journey in 97 hours, 13 minutes and 20 seconds, consequently reaching the Lunar surface precisely at midnight on December 5-6, the exact moment when the Moon would be full.

Unfortunately, the instantaneous explosion of such a vast quantity of gun-cotton, by giving rise to a violent commotion in the atmosphere, generated so much vapour and mist as to render the Moon invisible for several nights to the innumerable watchers in the Western Hemisphere, who vainly tried to catch sight of her.

In the meantime, J.T. Marston, the Secretary of the Gun Club, and a most devoted friend of Barbican's, had started for Long's Peak, Colorado, on the summit of which the immense telescope, already alluded to, had been erected; it was of the reflecting kind, and possessed power sufficient to bring the Moon within a distance of five miles. While Marston was prosecuting his long journey with all possible speed, Professor Belfast, who had charge of the telescope, was endeavouring to catch a glimpse of the Projectile, but for a long time with no success. The hazy, cloudy weather lasted for more than a week, to the great disgust of the public at large. People even began to fear that further observation would have to be deferred to the 3rd of the following month, January, as during the latter half of December the waning Moon could not possibly give light enough to render the Projectile visible.

At last, however, to the unbounded satisfaction of all, a violent tempest suddenly cleared the sky, and on the 13th of December, shortly after midnight, the Moon, verging towards her last quarter, revealed herself sharp and bright on the dark background of the starry firmament.

That same morning, a few hours before Marston's arrival at the summit of Long's Peak, a very remarkable telegram had been dispatched by Professor Belfast to the Smithsonian Institute, Washington. It announced:

That on December 13th, at 2 o'clock in the morning, the Projectile shot from Stony Hill had been perceived by Professor Belfast and his assistants; that, deflected a little from its course by some unknown cause, it had not reached its mark, though it had approached near enough to be affected by the Lunar attraction; and that, its rectilineal motion having become circular, it should henceforth continue to describe a regular orbit around the Moon, of which in fact it had become the Satellite. The dispatch went on further to state:

That the *elements* of the new heavenly body had not yet been calculated, as at least three different observations, taken at different times, were necessary to determine them. The distance of the Projectile from the Lunar surface, however, might be set down roughly at roughly 2,833 miles.

The dispatch concluded with the following hypotheses, positively pronounced to be the only two possible: Either, 1, The Lunar attraction would finally prevail, in which case the travellers would reach their destination; or 2, The Projectile, kept whirling forever in an immutable orbit, would go on revolving around the Moon till time should be no more.

In either alternative, what should be the lot of the daring adventurers? They had, it is true, abundant provisions to last them for some time, but even supposing that they did reach the Moon and thereby completely establish the practicability of their daring enterprise, how were they ever to get back? *Could* they ever get back? or ever even be heard from? Questions of this nature, freely discussed by the ablest pens of the day, kept the public mind in a very restless and excited condition.

We must be pardoned here for making a little remark which, however, astronomers and other scientific men of sanguine temperament would do well to ponder over. An observer cannot be too cautious in announcing to the public his discovery when it is of a nature purely speculative. Nobody is obliged to discover a planet, or a comet, or even a satellite, but, before announcing to the world that you have made such a discovery, first make sure that such is really the fact. Because, you know, should it afterwards come out that you have done nothing of the kind, you make yourself a butt for the stupid jokes of the lowest newspaper scribblers. Belfast had never thought of this. Impelled by his irrepressible rage for discovery – the *furor inveniendi* ascribed to all astronomers by Aurelius Priscus – he had therefore been guilty of an indiscretion highly un-scientific when his famous telegram, launched to the world at large from the summit of the Rocky Mountains, pronounced so dogmatically on the only possible issues of the great enterprise.

The truth was that his telegram contained *two* very important errors: 1. Error of *observation*, as facts afterwards proved; the Projectile *was* not seen on the 13th and *could* not have been on that day, so that the little black spot which Belfast professed to have seen was most certainly not the Projectile; 2. Error of *theory* regarding the final fate of the Projectile, since to make it become the Moon's satellite was flying in the face of one of the great fundamental laws of Theoretical Mechanics.

Only one, therefore, the first, of the hypotheses so positively announced, was capable of realization. The travellers – that is to say if they still lived – might so combine and unite their own efforts with those of the Lunar attraction as actually to succeed at last in reaching the Moon's surface.

Now the travellers, those daring but cool-headed men who knew very well what they were about, *did* still live, they *had* survived the frightful concussion of the start, and it is to the faithful record of their wonderful trip in the bullet-car, with all its singular and dramatic details, that the present volume is devoted. The story may destroy many illusions, prejudices and conjectures; but it will at least give correct ideas of the strange incidents to which such an enterprise is exposed, and it will certainly bring out in strong colours the effects of Barbican's scientific conceptions, M'Nicholl's mechanical resources, and Ardan's daring, eccentric, but brilliant and effective combinations.

Besides, it will show that J.T. Marston, their faithful friend and a man every way worthy of the friendship of such men, was only losing his time while mirroring the Moon in the speculum of the gigantic telescope on that lofty peak of the mountains.

CHAPTER I
From 10 P.M. to 10 46' 40"

THE MOMENT THAT the great clock belonging to the works at Stony Hill had struck ten, Barbican, Ardan and M'Nicholl began to take their last farewells of the numerous friends surrounding them. The two dogs intended to accompany them had been already deposited in the Projectile. The three travellers approached the mouth of the enormous cannon, seated themselves in the flying car, and once more took leave for the last time of the vast throng standing in silence around them. The windlass creaked, the car started, and the three daring men disappeared in the yawning gulf.

The trap-hole giving them ready access to the interior of the Projectile, the car soon came back empty; the great windlass was presently rolled away; the tackle and scaffolding were removed, and in a short space of time the great mouth of the Columbiad was completely rid of all obstructions.

M'Nicholl took upon himself to fasten the door of the trap on the inside by means of a powerful combination of screws and bolts of his own invention. He also covered up very carefully the glass lights with strong iron plates of extreme solidity and tightly fitting joints.

Ardan's first care was to turn on the gas, which he found burning rather low; but he lit no more than one burner, being desirous to economize as much as possible their store of light and heat, which, as he well knew, could not at the very utmost last them longer than a few weeks.

Under the cheerful blaze, the interior of the Projectile looked like a comfortable little chamber, with its circular sofa, nicely padded walls, and dome shaped ceiling.

All the articles that it contained, arms, instruments, utensils, etc., were solidly fastened to the projections of the wadding, so as to sustain the least injury possible from the first terrible shock. In fact, all precautions possible, humanly speaking, had been taken to counteract this, the first, and possibly one of the very greatest dangers to which the courageous adventurers would be exposed.

Ardan expressed himself to be quite pleased with the appearance of things in general.

'It's a prison, to be sure,' said he 'but not one of your ordinary prisons that always keep in the one spot. For my part, as long as I can have the privilege of looking out of the window, I am willing to lease it for a hundred years. Ah! Barbican, that brings out one of your stony smiles. You think our lease may last longer than that! Our tenement may become our coffin, eh? Be it so. I prefer it anyway to Mahomet's; it may indeed float in the air, but it won't be motionless as a milestone!'

Barbican, having made sure by personal inspection that everything was in perfect order, consulted his chronometer, which he had carefully set a short time before with Chief Engineer Murphy's, who had been charged to fire off the Projectile.

'Friends,' he said, 'it is now twenty minutes past ten. At 10 46' 40", precisely, Murphy will send the electric current into the gun-cotton. We have, therefore, twenty-six minutes more to remain on earth.'

'Twenty-six minutes and twenty seconds,' observed Captain M'Nicholl, who always aimed at mathematical precision.

'Twenty-six minutes!' cried Ardan, gaily. 'An age, a cycle, according to the use you make of them. In twenty-six minutes how much can be done! The weightiest questions of warfare, politics, morality, can be discussed, even decided, in twenty-six minutes. Twenty-six minutes well spent are infinitely more valuable than twenty-six lifetimes wasted! A few seconds even, employed by a Pascal, or a Newton, or a Barbican, or any other profoundly intellectual being whose thoughts wander through eternity—'

'As mad as Marston! Every bit!' muttered the Captain, half audibly.

'What do you conclude from this rigmarole of yours?' interrupted Barbican.

'I conclude that we have twenty-six good minutes still left—'

'Only twenty-four minutes, ten seconds,' interrupted the Captain, watch in hand.

'Well, twenty-four minutes, Captain,' Ardan went on; 'now even in twenty-four minutes, I maintain—'

'Ardan,' interrupted Barbican, 'after a very little while we shall have plenty of time for philosophical disputations. Just now let us think of something far more pressing.'

'More pressing! what do you mean? are we not fully prepared?'

'Yes, fully prepared, as far at least as we have been able to foresee. But we may still, I think, possibly increase the number of precautions to be taken against the terrible shock that we are so soon to experience.'

'What? Have you any doubts whatever of the effectiveness of your brilliant and extremely original idea? Don't you think that the layers of water, regularly disposed in easily-ruptured partitions beneath this floor, will afford us sufficient protection by their elasticity?'

'I hope so, indeed, my dear friend, but I am by no means confident.'

'He hopes! He is by no means confident! Listen to that, Mac! Pretty time to tell us so! Let me out of here!'

'Too late!' observed the Captain quietly. 'The trap-hole alone would take ten or fifteen minutes to open.'

'Oh then I suppose I must make the best of it,' said Ardan, laughing. 'All aboard, gentlemen! The train starts in twenty minutes!'

'In nineteen minutes and eighteen seconds,' said the Captain, who never took his eye off the chronometer.

The three travellers looked at each other for a little while, during which even Ardan appeared to become serious. After another careful glance at the several objects lying around them, Barbican said, quietly:

'Everything is in its place, except ourselves. What we have now to do is to decide on the position we must take in order to neutralize the shock as much as possible. We must be particularly careful to guard against a rush of blood to the head.'

'Correct!' said the Captain.

'Suppose we stood on our heads, like the circus tumblers!' cried Ardan, ready to suit the action to the word.

'Better than that,' said Barbican; 'we can lie on our side. Keep clearly in mind, dear friends, that at the instant of departure it makes very little difference to us whether we are inside the bullet or in front of it. There is, no doubt, *some* difference,' he added, seeing the great eyes made by his friends, 'but it is exceedingly little.'

'Thank heaven for the *some*!' interrupted Ardan, fervently.

'Don't you approve of my suggestion, Captain?' asked Barbican.

'Certainly,' was the hasty reply. 'That is to say, absolutely. Seventeen minutes twenty-seven seconds!'

'Mac isn't a human being at all!' cried Ardan, admiringly. 'He is a repeating chronometer, horizontal escapement, London-made lever, capped, jewelled—'

His companions let him run on while they busied themselves in making their last arrangements, with the greatest coolness and most systematic method. In fact, I don't think of anything just now to compare them to except a couple of old travellers who, having to pass the night in the train, are trying to make themselves as comfortable as possible for their long journey. In your profound astonishment, you may naturally ask me of what strange material can the hearts of these Americans be made, who can view without the slightest semblance of a flutter the approach of the most appalling dangers? In your curiosity I fully participate, but, I'm sorry to say, I can't gratify it. It is one of those things that I could never find out.

Three mattresses, thick and well wadded, spread on the disc forming the false bottom of the Projectile, were arranged in lines whose parallelism was simply perfect. But Ardan would never think of occupying his until the very last moment. Walking up and down, with the restless nervousness of a wild beast in a cage, he kept up a continuous fire of talk; at one moment with his friends, at another with the dogs, addressing the latter by the euphonious and suggestive names of Diana and Satellite.

'Ho, pets!' he would exclaim as he patted them gently, 'you must not forget the noble part you are to play up there. You must be models of canine deportment. The eyes of the whole Selenitic world will be upon you. You are the standard bearers of your race. From you they will receive their first impression regarding its merits. Let it be a favourable one. Compel those Selenites to acknowledge, in spite of themselves, that the terrestrial race of canines is far superior to that of the very best Moon dog among them!'

'Dogs in the Moon!' sneered M'Nicholl, 'I like that!'

'Plenty of dogs!' cried Ardan, 'and horses too, and cows, and sheep, and no end of chickens!'

'A hundred dollars to one there isn't a single chicken within the whole Lunar realm, not excluding even the invisible side!' cried the Captain, in an authoritative tone, but never taking his eye off the chronometer.

'I take that bet, my son,' coolly replied Ardan, shaking the Captain's hand by way of ratifying the wager; 'and this reminds me, by the way, Mac, that you have lost three bets already, to the pretty little tune of six thousand dollars.'

'And paid them, too!' cried the captain, monotonously; 'ten, thirty-six, six!'

'Yes, and in a quarter of an hour you will have to pay nine thousand dollars more; four thousand because the Columbiad will not burst, and five thousand because the Projectile will rise more than six miles from the Earth.'

'I have the money ready,' answered the Captain, touching his breeches pocket. 'When I lose I pay. Not sooner. Ten, thirty-eight, ten!'

'Captain, you're a man of method, if there ever was one. I think, however, that you made a mistake in your wagers.'

'How so?' asked the Captain listlessly, his eye still on the dial.

'Because, by Jove, if you win there will be no more of you left to take the money than there will be of Barbican to pay it!'

'Friend Ardan,' quietly observed Barbican, 'my stakes are deposited in the *Wall Street Bank*, of New York, with orders to pay them over to the Captain's heirs, in case the Captain himself should fail to put in an appearance at the proper time.'

'Oh! you rhinoceroses, you pachyderms, you granite men!' cried Ardan, gasping with surprise; 'you machines with iron heads, and iron hearts! I may admire you, but I'm blessed if I understand you!'

'Ten, forty-two, ten!' repeated M'Nicholl, as mechanically as if it was the chronometer itself that spoke.

'Four minutes and a half more,' said Barbican.

'Oh! four and a half little minutes!' went on Ardan. 'Only think of it! We are shut up in a bullet that lies in the chamber of a cannon nine hundred feet long. Underneath this bullet is piled a charge of 400 thousand pounds of gun-cotton, equivalent to 1600 thousand pounds of ordinary gunpowder! And at this very instant our friend Murphy, chronometer in hand, eye on dial, finger on discharger, is counting the last seconds and getting ready to launch us into the limitless regions of planetary—'

'Ardan, dear friend,' interrupted Barbican, in a grave tone, 'a serious moment is now at hand. Let us meet it with some interior recollection. Give me your hands, my dear friends.'

'Certainly,' said Ardan, with tears in his voice, and already at the other extreme of his apparent levity.

CHAPTER I

The three brave men united in one last, silent, but warm and impulsively affectionate pressure.

'And now, great God, our Creator, protect us! In Thee we trust!' prayed Barbican, the others joining him with folded hands and bowed heads.

'Ten, forty-six!' whispered the Captain, as he and Ardan quietly took their places on the mattresses.

Only forty seconds more!

Barbican rapidly extinguishes the gas and lies down beside his companions.

The deathlike silence now reigning in the Projectile is interrupted only by the sharp ticking of the chronometer as it beats the seconds.

Suddenly, a dreadful shock is felt, and the Projectile, shot up by the instantaneous development of 200,000 millions of cubic feet of gas, is flying into space with inconceivable rapidity!

CHAPTER II
The First Half Hour

WHAT HAD TAKEN place within the Projectile? What effect had been produced by the frightful concussion? Had Barbican's ingenuity been attended with a fortunate result? Had the shock been sufficiently deadened by the springs, the buffers, the water layers, and the partitions so readily ruptured? Had their combined effect succeeded in counteracting the tremendous violence of a velocity of 12,000 yards a second, actually sufficient to carry them from London to New York in six minutes? These, and a hundred other questions of a similar nature were asked that night by the millions who had been watching the explosion from the base of Stony Hill. Themselves they forgot altogether for the moment; they forgot everything in their absorbing anxiety regarding the fate of the daring travellers. Had one among them, our friend Marston, for instance, been favoured with a glimpse at the interior of the projectile, what would he have seen?

Nothing at all at first, on account of the darkness; except that the walls had solidly resisted the frightful shock. Not a crack, nor a bend, nor a dent could be perceived; not even the slightest injury had the admirably constructed piece of mechanical workmanship endured. It had not yielded an inch to the enormous pressure, and, far from melting and falling back to earth, as had been so seriously apprehended, in showers of blazing aluminium, it was still as strong in every respect as it had been on the very day that it left the Cold Spring Iron Works, glittering like a silver dollar.

Of real damage there was actually none, and even the disorder into which things had been thrown in the interior by the violent shock was comparatively slight. A few small objects lying around loose had been furiously hurled against the ceiling, but the others appeared not to have suffered the slightest injury. The straps that fastened them up were unfrayed, and the fixtures that held them down were uncracked.

The partitions beneath the disc having been ruptured, and the water having escaped, the false floor had been dashed with tremendous violence against the bottom of the Projectile, and on this disc at this moment three human bodies could be seen lying perfectly still and motionless.

Were they three corpses? Had the Projectile suddenly become a great metallic coffin bearing its ghastly contents through the air with the rapidity of a lightning flash?

In a very few minutes after the shock, one of the bodies stirred a little, the arms moved, the eyes opened, the head rose and tried to look around; finally, with some difficulty, the body managed to get on its knees. It was the Frenchman! He held his head tightly squeezed between his hands for some time as if to keep it from splitting. Then he felt himself rapidly all over, cleared his throat with a vigorous 'hem!' listened to the sound critically for an instant, and then said to himself in a relieved tone, but in his native tongue:

'One man all right! Call the roll for the others!'

He tried to rise, but the effort was too great for his strength. He fell back again, his brain swimming, his eyes bursting, his head splitting. His state very much resembled that of a young man waking up in the morning after his first tremendous 'spree.'

'Br–rr!' he muttered to himself, still talking French; 'this reminds me of one of my wild nights long ago in the *Quartier Latin*, only decidedly more so!'

Lying quietly on his back for a while, he could soon feel that the circulation of his blood, so suddenly and violently arrested by the terrific shock, was gradually recovering its regular flow; his heart grew more normal in its action; his head became clearer, and the pain less distracting.

'Time to call that roll,' he at last exclaimed in a voice with some pretensions to firmness; 'Barbican! M'Nicholl!'

He listens anxiously for a reply. None comes. A snow-wrapt grave at midnight is not more silent. In vain does he try to catch even the faintest sound of breathing, though he listens intently enough to hear the beating of their hearts; but he hears only his own.

'Call that roll again!' he mutters in a voice far less assured than before; 'Barbican! M'Nicholl!'

The same fearful unearthly stillness.

'The thing is getting decidedly monotonous!' he exclaimed, still speaking French. Then rapidly recovering his consciousness as the full horror of the situation began to break on his mind, he went on muttering audibly: 'Have they really hopped the twig? Bah! Fudge! what has not been able to knock the life out of one little Frenchman can't have killed two Americans! They're all right! But first and foremost, let us enlighten the situation!'

So saying, he contrived without much difficulty to get on his feet. Balancing himself then for a moment, he began groping about for the gas. But he stopped suddenly.

'Hold on a minute!' he cried; 'before lighting this match, let us see if the gas has been escaping. Setting fire to a mixture of air and hydrogen would make a pretty how-do-you-do! Such an explosion would infallibly burst the Projectile, which so far seems all right, though I'm blest if I can tell whether we're moving or not.'

He began sniffing and smelling to discover if possible the odour of escaped gas. He could not detect the slightest sign of anything of the kind. This gave him great courage. He knew of course that his senses were not yet in good order, still he thought he might trust them so far as to be certain that the gas had not escaped and that consequently all the other receptacles were uninjured.

At the touch of the match, the gas burst into light and burned with a steady flame. Ardan immediately bent anxiously over the prostrate bodies of his friends. They lay on each other like inert masses, M'Nicholl stretched across Barbican.

Ardan first lifted up the Captain, laid him on the sofa, opened his clenched hands, rubbed them, and slapped the palms vigorously. Then he went all over the body carefully, kneading it, rubbing it, and gently patting it. In such intelligent efforts to restore suspended circulation, he seemed perfectly at home, and after a few minutes his patience was rewarded by seeing the Captain's pallid face gradually recover its natural colour, and by feeling his heart gradually beat with a firm pulsation.

At last M'Nicholl opened his eyes, stared at Ardan for an instant, pressed his hand, looked around searchingly and anxiously, and at last whispered in a faint voice:

'How's Barbican?'

'Barbican is all right, Captain,' answered Ardan quietly, but still speaking French. 'I'll attend to him in a jiffy. He had to wait for his turn. I began with you because you were the top man. We'll see in a minute what we can do for dear old Barby (*ce cher Barbican*)!'

In less than thirty seconds more, the Captain not only was able to sit up himself, but he even insisted on helping Ardan to lift Barbican, and deposit him gently on the sofa.

The poor President had evidently suffered more from the concussion than either of his companions. As they took off his coat they were at first terribly shocked at the sight of a great patch of blood staining his shirt bosom, but they were inexpressibly relieved at finding that it proceeded from a slight contusion of the shoulder, little more than skin deep.

Every approved operation that Ardan had performed for the Captain, both now repeated for Barbican, but for a long time with nothing like a favourable result.

Ardan at first tried to encourage the Captain by whispers of a lively and hopeful nature, but not yet understanding why M'Nicholl did not deign to make a single reply, he grew reserved by degrees and at last would not speak a single word. He worked at Barbican, however, just as before.

M'Nicholl interrupted himself every moment to lay his ear on the breast of the unconscious man. At first he had shaken his head quite despondingly, but by degrees he found himself more and more encouraged to persist.

'He breathes!' he whispered at last.

'Yes, he has been breathing for some time,' replied Ardan, quietly, still unconsciously speaking French. 'A little more rubbing and pulling and pounding will make him as spry as a young grasshopper.'

They worked at him, in fact, so vigorously, intelligently and perseveringly, that, after what they considered a long hour's labour, they had the delight of seeing the pale face assume a healthy hue, the inert limbs give signs of returning animation, and the breathing become strong and regular.

At last, Barbican suddenly opened his eyes, started into an upright position on the sofa, took his friends by the hands, and, in a voice showing complete consciousness, demanded eagerly:

'Ardan, M'Nicholl, are we moving?'

His friends looked at each other, a little amused, but more perplexed. In their anxiety regarding their own and their friend's recovery, they had never thought of asking such a question. His words recalled them at once to a full sense of their situation.

'Moving? Blessed if I can tell!' said Ardan, still speaking French.

'We may be lying fifty feet deep in a Florida marsh, for all I know,' observed M'Nicholl.

'Or, likely as not, in the bottom of the Gulf of Mexico,' suggested Ardan, still in French.

'Suppose we find out,' observed Barbican, jumping up to try, his voice as clear and his step as firm as ever.

But trying is one thing, and finding out another. Having no means of comparing themselves with external objects, they could not possibly tell whether they were moving, or at an absolute standstill. Though our Earth is whirling us continually around the Sun at the tremendous speed of 500 miles a minute, its inhabitants are totally unconscious of the slightest motion. It was the same with our travellers. Through their own personal consciousness they could tell absolutely nothing. Were they shooting through space like a meteor? They could not tell. Had they fallen back and buried themselves deep in the sandy soil of Florida, or, still more likely, hundreds of fathoms deep beneath the waters of the Gulf of Mexico? They could not form the slightest idea.

Listening evidently could do no good. The profound silence proved nothing. The padded walls of the Projectile were too thick to admit any sound whether of wind, water, or human beings. Barbican, however, was soon struck forcibly by one circumstance. He felt himself to be very uncomfortably warm, and his friend's faces looked very hot and flushed. Hastily removing the cover that protected the thermometer, he closely inspected it, and in an instant uttered a joyous exclamation.

'Hurrah!' he cried. 'We're moving! There's no mistake about it. The thermometer marks 113 degrees Fahrenheit. Such a stifling heat could not come from the gas. It comes from the exterior walls of our projectile, which atmospheric friction must have made almost red hot. But this heat must soon diminish, because we are already far beyond the regions of the atmosphere, so that instead of smothering we shall be shortly in danger of freezing.'

'What?' asked Ardan, much bewildered. 'We are already far beyond the limits of the terrestrial atmosphere! Why do you think so?'

M'Nicholl was still too much flustered to venture a word.

'If you want me to answer your question satisfactorily, my dear Ardan,' replied Barbican, with a quiet smile, 'you will have the kindness to put your questions in English.'

'What do you mean, Barbican!' asked Ardan, hardly believing his ears.

'Hurrah!' cried M'Nicholl, in the tone of a man who has suddenly made a welcome but most unexpected discovery.

'I don't know exactly how it is with the Captain,' continued Barbican, with the utmost tranquillity, 'but for my part the study of the languages never was my strong point, and though I always admired the French, and even understood it pretty well, I never could converse in it without giving myself more trouble than I always find it convenient to assume.'

'You don't mean to say that I have been talking French to you all this time!' cried Ardan, horror-stricken.

'The most elegant French I ever heard, backed by the purest Parisian accent,' replied Barbican, highly amused; 'Don't you think so, Captain?' he added, turning to M'Nicholl, whose countenance still showed the most comical traces of bewilderment.

'Well, I swan to man!' cried the Captain, who always swore a little when his feelings got beyond his control; 'Ardan, the Boss has got the rig on both of us this time, but rough as it is on you it is a darned sight more so on me. Be hanged if I did not think you were talking English the whole time, and I put the whole blame for not understanding you on the disordered state of my brain!'

Ardan only stared, and scratched his head, but Barbican actually – no, not *laughed*, that serene nature could not *laugh*. His cast-iron features puckered into a smile of the richest drollery, and his eyes twinkled with the wickedest fun; but no undignified giggle escaped the portal of those majestic lips.

'It *sounds* like French, I'd say to myself,' continued the Captain, 'but I *know* it's English, and by and by, when this whirring goes out of my head, I shall easily understand it.'

Ardan now looked as if he was beginning to see the joke.

'The most puzzling part of the thing to me,' went on M'Nicholl, giving his experience with the utmost gravity, 'was why English sounded so like *French*. If it was simple incomprehensible gibberish,

I could readily blame the state of my ears for it. But the idea that my bothered ears could turn a mere confused, muzzled, buzzing reverberation into a sweet, harmonious, articulate, though unintelligible, human language, made me sure that I was fast becoming crazy, if I was not so already.'

'Ha! ha! ha!' roared Ardan, laughing till the tears came. 'Now I understand why the poor Captain made me no reply all the time, and looked at me with such a hapless woe-begone expression of countenance. The fact is, Barbican, that shock was too much both for M'Nicholl and myself. You are the only man among us whose head is fire-proof, blast-proof, and powder-proof. I really believe a burglar would have greater difficulty in blowing your head-piece open than in bursting one of those famous American safes your papers make such a fuss about. A wonderful head, the Boss's, isn't it M'Nicholl?'

'Yes,' said the Captain, as slowly as if every word were a gem of the profoundest thought, 'the Boss has a fearful and a wonderful head!'

'But now to business!' cried the versatile Ardan, 'Why do you think, Barbican, that we are at present beyond the limits of the terrestrial atmosphere?'

'For a very simple reason,' said Barbican, pointing to the chronometer; 'it is now more than seven minutes after 11. We must, therefore, have been in motion more than twenty minutes. Consequently, unless our initial velocity has been very much diminished by the friction, we must have long before this completely cleared the fifty miles of atmosphere enveloping the earth.'

'Correct,' said the Captain, cool as a cucumber, because once more in complete possession of all his senses; 'but how much do you think the initial velocity to have been diminished by the friction?'

'By a third, according to my calculations,' replied Barbican, 'which I think are right. Supposing our initial velocity, therefore, to have been 12,000 yards per second, by the time we quitted the atmosphere it must have been reduced to 8,000 yards per second. At that rate, we must have gone by this time—'

'Then, Mac, my boy, you've lost your two bets!' interrupted Ardan. 'The Columbiad has not burst, four thousand dollars; the Projectile has risen at least six miles, five thousand dollars; come, Captain, bleed!'

'Let me first be sure we're right,' said the Captain, quietly. 'I don't deny, you see, that friend Barbican's arguments are quite right, and, therefore, that I have lost my nine thousand dollars. But there is another view of the case possible, which might annul the bet.'

'What other view?' asked Barbican, quickly.

'Suppose,' said the Captain, very drily, 'that the powder had not caught, and that we were still lying quietly at the bottom of the Columbiad!'

'By Jove!' laughed Ardan, 'there's an idea truly worthy of my own nondescript brain! We must surely have changed heads during that concussion! No matter, there is some sense left in us yet. Come now, Captain, consider a little, if you can. Weren't we both half-killed by the shock? Didn't I rescue you from certain death with these two hands? Don't you see Barbican's shoulder still bleeding by the violence of the shock?'

'Correct, friend Michael, correct in every particular,' replied the Captain, 'But one little question.'

'Out with it!'

'Friend Michael, you say we're moving?'

'Yes.'

'In consequence of the explosion?'

'Certainly!'

'Which must have been attended with a tremendous report?'

'Of course!'

'Did you hear that report, friend Michael?'

'N–o,' replied Ardan, a little disconcerted at the question. 'Well, no; I can't say that I did hear any report.'

'Did you, friend Barbican?'

'No,' replied Barbican, promptly. 'I heard no report whatever.'

His answer was ready, but his look was quite as disconcerted as Ardan's.

'Well, friend Barbican and friend Michael,' said the Captain, very drily as he leered wickedly at both, 'put that and that together and tell me what you make of it.'

'It's a fact!' exclaimed Barbican, puzzled, but not bewildered. 'Why did we not hear that report?'

'Too hard for me,' said Ardan. 'Give it up!'

The three friends gazed at each other for a while with countenances expressive of much perplexity. Barbican appeared to be the least self-possessed of the party. It was a complete turning of the tables from the state of things a few moments ago. The problem was certainly simple enough, but for that very reason the more inexplicable. If they were moving the explosion must have taken place; but if the explosion had taken place, why had they not heard the report?

Barbican's decision soon put an end to speculation.

'Conjecture being useless,' said he, 'let us have recourse to facts. First, let us see where we are. Drop the deadlights!'

This operation, simple enough in itself and being immediately undertaken by the whole three, was easily accomplished. The screws fastening the bolts by which the external plates of the deadlights were solidly pinned, readily yielded to the pressure of a powerful wrench. The bolts were then driven outwards, and the holes which had contained them were immediately filled with solid plugs of India rubber. The bolts once driven out, the external plates dropped by their own weight, turning on a hinge, like portholes, and the strong plate-glass forming the light immediately showed itself. A second light exactly similar, could be cleared away on the opposite side of the Projectile; a third, on the summit of the dome, and a fourth, in the centre of the bottom. The travellers could thus take observations in four different directions, having an opportunity of gazing at the firmament through the side lights, and at the Earth and the Moon through the lower and the upper lights of the Projectile.

Ardan and the Captain had commenced examining the floor, previous to operating on the bottom light. But Barbican was the first to get through his work at one of the side lights, and M'Nicholl and Ardan soon heard him shouting:

'No, my friends!' he exclaimed, in tones of decided emotion; 'we have *not* fallen back to Earth; nor are we lying in the bottom of the Gulf of Mexico. No! We are driving through space! Look at the stars glittering all around! Brighter, but smaller than we have ever seen them before! We have left the Earth and the Earth's atmosphere far behind us!'

'Hurrah! Hurrah!' cried M'Nicholl and Ardan, feeling as if electric shocks were coursing through them, though they could see nothing, looking down from the side light, but the blackest and profoundest obscurity.

Barbican soon convinced them that this pitchy blackness proved that they were not, and could not be, reposing on the surface of the Earth, where at that moment, everything was illuminated by the bright moonlight; also that they had passed the different layers of the atmosphere, where the diffused and refracted rays would be also sure to reveal themselves through the lights of the Projectile. They were, therefore, certainly moving. No doubt was longer possible.

'It's a fact!' observed the Captain, now quite convinced. 'Then I've lost!'

'Let me congratulate you!' cried Ardan, shaking his hand.

'Here is your nine thousand dollars, friend Barbican,' said the Captain, taking a roll of greenbacks of high denomination out of his porte-monnaie.

'You want a receipt, don't you, Captain?' asked Barbican, counting the money.

'Yes, I should prefer one, if it is not too much trouble,' answered M'Nicholl; 'it saves dispute.'

Coolly and mechanically, as if seated at his desk, in his office, Barbican opened his memorandum book, wrote a receipt on a blank page, dated, signed and sealed it, and then handed it to the Captain, who put it away carefully among the other papers of his portfolio.

Ardan, taking off his hat, made a profound bow to both of his companions, without saying a word. Such formality, under such extraordinary circumstances, actually paralysed his tongue for the moment. No wonder that he could not understand those Americans. Even Indians would have surprised him by an exhibition of such stoicism. After indulging in silent wonder for a minute or two, he joined his companions who were now busy looking out at the starry sky.

'Where is the Moon?' he asked. 'How is it that we cannot see her?'

'The fact of our not seeing her,' answered Barbican, 'gives me very great satisfaction in one respect; it shows that our Projectile was shot so rapidly out of the Columbiad that it had not time to be impressed with the slightest revolving motion – for us a most fortunate matter. As for the rest – see, there is *Cassiopeia*, a little to the left is *Andromeda*, further down is the great square of *Pegasus*, and to the southwest *Fomalhaut* can be easily seen swallowing the *Cascade*. All this shows we are looking west and consequently cannot see the Moon, which is approaching the zenith from the east. Open the other light – But hold on! Look here! What can this be?'

The three travellers, looking westwardly in the direction of *Alpherat*, saw a brilliant object rapidly approaching them. At a distance, it looked like a dusky moon, but the side turned towards the Earth blazed with a bright light, which every moment became more intense. It came towards them with prodigious velocity and, what was worse, its path lay so directly in the course of the Projectile that a collision seemed inevitable. As it moved onward, from west to east, they could easily see that it rotated on its axis, like all heavenly bodies; in fact, it somewhat resembled a Moon on a small scale, describing its regular orbit around the Earth.

'*Mille tonerres!*' cried Ardan, greatly excited; 'what is that? Can it be another projectile?' M'Nicholl, wiping his spectacles, looked again, but made no reply. Barbican looked puzzled and uneasy. A collision was quite possible, and the results, even if not frightful in the highest degree, must be extremely deplorable. The Projectile, if not absolutely dashed to pieces, would be diverted from its own course and dragged along in a new one in obedience to the irresistible attraction of this furious asteroid.

Barbican fully realized that either alternative involved the complete failure of their enterprise. He kept perfectly still, but, never losing his presence of mind, he curiously looked on the approaching object with a gladiatorial eye, as if seeking to detect some unguarded point in his terrible adversary. The Captain was equally silent; he looked like a man who had fully made up his mind to regard every possible contingency with the most stoical indifference. But Ardan's tongue, more fluent than ever, rattled away incessantly.

'Look! Look!' he exclaimed, in tones so perfectly expressive of his rapidly alternating feelings as to render the medium of words totally unnecessary. 'How rapidly the cursed thing is nearing us! Plague take your ugly phiz, the more I know you, the less I like you! Every second she doubles in size! Come, Madame Projectile! Stir your stumps a little livelier, old lady! He's making for you as straight as an arrow! We're going right in his way, or he's coming in ours, I can't say which. It's taking a mean advantage of us either way. As for ourselves – what can *we* do! Before such a monster as that we are as helpless as three men in a little skiff shooting down the rapids to the brink of Niagara! Now for it!'

Nearer and nearer it came, but without noise, without sparks, without a trail, though its lower part was brighter than ever. Its path lying little above them, the nearer it came the more the collision seemed inevitable. Imagine yourself caught on a narrow railroad bridge at midnight with an express train approaching at full speed, its reflector already dazzling you with its light, the roar of the cars rattling in your ears, and you may conceive the feelings of the travellers. At last it was so near that the travellers started back in affright, with eyes shut, hair on end, and fully believing their last hour had come. Even then Ardan had his *mot*.

'We can neither switch off, down brakes, nor clap on more steam! Hard luck!'

In an instant all was over. The velocity of the Projectile was fortunately great enough to carry it barely above the dangerous point; and in a flash the terrible bolide disappeared rapidly several hundred yards beneath the affrighted travellers.

'Good bye! And may you never come back!' cried Ardan, hardly able to breathe. 'It's perfectly outrageous! Not room enough in infinite space to let an unpretending bullet like ours move about a little without incurring the risk of being run over by such a monster as that! What is it anyhow? Do you know, Barbican?'

'I do,' was the reply.

'Of course, you do! What is it that he don't know? Eh, Captain?'

'It is a simple bolide, but one of such enormous dimensions that the Earth's attraction has made it a satellite.'

'What!' cried Ardan, 'another satellite besides the Moon? I hope there are no more of them!'

'They are pretty numerous,' replied Barbican; 'but they are so small and they move with such enormous velocity that they are very seldom seen. Petit, the Director of the Observatory of Toulouse, who these last years has devoted much time and care to the observation of bolides, has calculated that the very one we have just encountered moves with such astonishing swiftness that it accomplishes its revolution around the Earth in about 3 hours and 20 minutes!'

'Whew!' whistled Ardan, 'where should we be now if it had struck us!'

'You don't mean to say, Barbican,' observed M'Nicholl, 'that Petit has seen this very one?'

'So it appears,' replied Barbican.

'And do all astronomers admit its existence?' asked the Captain.

'Well, some of them have their doubts,' replied Barbican –

'If the unbelievers had been here a minute or two ago,' interrupted Ardan, 'they would never express a doubt again.'

'If Petit's calculation is right,' continued Barbican, 'I can even form a very good idea as to our distance from the Earth.'

'It seems to me Barbican can do what he pleases here or elsewhere,' observed Ardan to the Captain.

'Let us see, Barbican,' asked M'Nicholl; 'where has Petit's calculation placed us?'

'The bolide's distance being known,' replied Barbican, 'at the moment we met it we were a little more than 5 thousand miles from the Earth's surface.'

'Five thousand miles already!' cried Ardan, 'why we have only just started!'

'Let us see about that,' quietly observed the Captain, looking at his chronometer, and calculating with his pencil. 'It is now 10 minutes past eleven; we have therefore been 23 minutes on the road. Supposing our initial velocity of 10,000 yards or nearly seven miles a second, to have been kept up, we should by this time be about 9,000 miles from the Earth; but by allowing for friction and gravity, we can hardly be more than 5,500 miles. Yes, friend Barbican, Petit does not seem to be very wrong in his calculations.'

But Barbican hardly heard the observation. He had not yet answered the puzzling question that had already presented itself to them for solution; and until he had done so he could not attend to anything else.

'That's all very well and good, Captain,' he replied in an absorbed manner, 'but we have not yet been able to account for a very strange phenomenon. Why didn't we hear the report?'

No one replying, the conversation came to a stand-still, and Barbican, still absorbed in his reflections, began clearing the second light of its external shutter. In a few minutes the plate dropped, and the Moon beams, flowing in, filled the interior of the Projectile with her brilliant light. The Captain immediately put out the gas, from motives of economy as well as because its glare somewhat interfered with the observation of the interplanetary regions.

The Lunar disc struck the travellers as glittering with a splendour and purity of light that they had never witnessed before. The beams, no longer strained through the misty atmosphere of the Earth, streamed copiously in through the glass and coated the interior walls of the Projectile with a brilliant silvery plating. The intense blackness of the sky enhanced the dazzling radiance of the Moon. Even the stars blazed with a new and unequalled splendour, and, in the absence of a refracting atmosphere, they flamed as bright in the close proximity of the Moon as in any other part of the sky.

You can easily conceive the interest with which these bold travellers gazed on the Starry Queen, the final object of their daring journey. She was now insensibly approaching the zenith, the mathematical point which she was to reach four days later. They presented their telescopes, but her mountains, plains, craters and general characteristics hardly came out a particle more sharply than if they had been viewed from the Earth. Still, her light, unobstructed by air or vapour, shimmered with a lustre actually transplendent. Her disc shone like a mirror of polished platins. The travellers remained for some time absorbed in the silent contemplation of the glorious scene.

'How they're gazing at her this very moment from Stony Hill!' said the Captain at last to break the silence.

'By Jove!' cried Ardan; 'It's true! Captain you're right. We were near forgetting our dear old Mother, the Earth. What ungrateful children! Let me feast my eyes once more on the blessed old creature!'

Barbican, to satisfy his companion's desire, immediately commenced to clear away the disc which covered the floor of the Projectile and prevented them from getting at the lower light. This disc, though it had been dashed to the bottom of the Projectile with great violence, was still as strong as ever, and, being made in compartments fastened by screws, to dismount it was no easy matter. Barbican, however, with the help of the others, soon had it all taken apart, and put away the pieces carefully, to serve again in case of need. A round hole about a foot and a half in diameter appeared, bored through the floor of the Projectile. It was closed by a circular pane of plate-glass, which was about six inches thick, fastened by a ring of copper. Below, on the outside, the glass was protected by an aluminium plate, kept in its place by strong bolts and nuts. The latter being unscrewed, the bolts slipped out by their own weight, the shutter fell, and a new communication was established between the interior and the exterior.

Ardan knelt down, applied his eye to the light, and tried to look out. At first everything was quite dark and gloomy.

'I see no Earth!' he exclaimed at last.

'Don't you see a fine ribbon of light?' asked Barbican, 'right beneath us? A thin, pale, silvery crescent?'

'Of course I do. Can that be the Earth?'

'*Terra Mater* herself, friend Ardan. That fine fillet of light, now hardly visible on her eastern border, will disappear altogether as soon as the Moon is full. Then, lying as she will be between the Sun and the Moon, her illuminated face will be turned away from us altogether, and for several days she will be involved in impenetrable darkness.'

'And that's the Earth!' repeated Ardan, hardly able to believe his eyes, as he continued to gaze on the slight thread of silvery white light, somewhat resembling the appearance of the 'Young May Moon' a few hours after sunset.

Barbican's explanation was quite correct. The Earth, in reference to the Moon or the Projectile, was in her last phase, or octant as it is called, and showed a sharp-horned, attenuated, but brilliant crescent strongly relieved by the black background of the sky. Its light, rendered a little bluish by the density of the atmospheric envelopes, was not quite as brilliant as the Moon's. But the Earth's crescent, compared to the Lunar, was of dimensions much greater, being fully 4 times larger. You would have called it a vast, beautiful, but very thin bow extending over the sky. A few points, brighter than the rest, particularly in its concave part, revealed the presence of lofty mountains, probably the Himalayahs. But they disappeared every now and then under thick vapoury spots, which are never seen on the Lunar disc. They were the thin concentric cloud rings that surround the terrestrial sphere.

However, the travellers' eyes were soon able to trace the rest of the Earth's surface not only with facility, but even to follow its outline with absolute delight. This was in consequence of two different phenomena, one of which they could easily account for; but the other they could not explain without Barbican's assistance. No wonder. Never before had mortal eye beheld such a sight. Let us take each in its turn.

We all know that the ashy light by means of which we perceive what is called the *Old Moon in the Young Moon's arms* is due to the Earth-shine, or the reflection of the solar rays from the Earth to the Moon. By a phenomenon exactly identical, the travellers could now see that portion of the Earth's surface which was unillumined by the Sun; only, as, in consequence of the different areas of the respective surfaces, the *Earthlight* is thirteen times more intense than the *Moonlight*, the dark portion of the Earth's disc appeared considerably more adumbrated than the *Old Moon*.

But the other phenomenon had burst on them so suddenly that they uttered a cry loud enough to wake up Barbican from his problem. They had discovered a true starry ring! Around the Earth's outline, a ring, of internally well defined thickness, but somewhat hazy on the outside, could easily be traced by its surpassing brilliancy. Neither the *Pleiades*, the *Northern Crown*, the *Magellanic Clouds* nor the great nebulas of *Orion*, or of *Argo*, no sparkling cluster, no corona, no group of glittering star-dust that the travellers had ever gazed at, presented such attractions as the diamond ring they now saw encompassing the Earth, just as the brass meridian encompasses a terrestrial globe. The resplendency of its light enchanted them, its pure softness delighted them, its perfect regularity astonished them. What was it? they asked Barbican. In a few words he explained it. The beautiful luminous ring was simply an optical illusion, produced by the refraction of the terrestrial atmosphere. All the stars in the neighbourhood of the Earth, and many actually behind it, had their rays refracted, diffused, radiated, and finally converged to a focus by the atmosphere, as if by a double convex lens of gigantic power.

Whilst the travellers were profoundly absorbed in the contemplation of this wondrous sight, a sparkling shower of shooting stars suddenly flashed over the Earth's dark surface, making it for a moment as bright as the external ring. Hundreds of bolides, catching fire from contact with the atmosphere, streaked the darkness with their luminous trails, overspreading it occasionally with sheets of electric flame. The Earth was just then in her perihelion, and we all know that the months of November and December are so highly favourable to the appearance of these meteoric showers that at the famous display of November, 1866, astronomers counted as many as 8,000 between midnight and four o'clock.

Barbican explained the whole matter in a few words. The Earth, when nearest to the sun, occasionally plunges into a group of countless meteors travelling like comets, in eccentric orbits around the grand centre of our solar system. The atmosphere strikes the rapidly moving bodies with such violence as to set them on fire and render them visible to us in beautiful star showers. But to this simple explanation of the famous November meteors Ardan would not listen. He preferred believing that Mother Earth, feeling that her three daring children were still looking at her, though five thousand miles away, shot off her best rocket-signals to show that she still thought of them and would never let them out of her watchful eye.

For hours they continued to gaze with indescribable interest on the faintly luminous mass so easily distinguishable among the other heavenly bodies. Jupiter blazed on their right, Mars flashed his ruddy light on their left, Saturn with his rings looked like a round white spot on a black wall; even Venus they could see almost directly under them, easily recognizing her by her soft, sweetly scintillant light. But no planet or constellation possessed any attraction for the travellers, as long as their eyes could trace that shadowy, crescent-edged, diamond-girdled, meteor-furrowed spheroid, the theatre of their existence, the home of so many undying desires, the mysterious cradle of their race!

Meantime the Projectile cleaved its way upwards, rapidly, unswervingly, though with a gradually retarding velocity. As the Earth sensibly grew darker, and the travellers' eyes grew dimmer, an irresistible somnolency slowly stole over their weary frames. The extraordinary excitement they had gone through during the last four or five hours, was naturally followed by a profound reaction.

'Captain, you're nodding,' said Ardan at last, after a longer silence than usual; 'the fact is, Barbican is the only wake man of the party, because he is puzzling over his problem. *Dum vivimus vivamus*! As we are asleep let us be asleep!'

So saying he threw himself on the mattress, and his companions immediately followed the example.

They had been lying hardly a quarter of an hour, when Barbican started up with a cry so loud and sudden as instantly to awaken his companions.

The bright moonlight showed them the President sitting up in his bed, his eye blazing, his arms waving, as he shouted in a tone reminding them of the day they had found him in St. Helena wood.

'*Eureka!* I've got it! I know it!'

'What have you got?' cried Ardan, bouncing up and seizing him by the right hand.

'What do you know?' cried the Captain, stretching over and seizing him by the left.

'The reason why we did not hear the report!'

'Well, why did not we hear it!' asked both rapidly in the same breath.

'Because we were shot up 30 times faster than sound can travel!'

CHAPTER III
They Make Themselves at Home and Feel Quite Comfortable

THIS CURIOUS EXPLANATION given, and its soundness immediately recognized, the three friends were soon fast wrapped in the arms of Morpheus. Where in fact could they have found a spot more favourable for undisturbed repose? On land, where the dwellings, whether in populous city or lonely country, continually experience every shock that thrills the Earth's crust? At sea, where between waves or winds or paddles or screws or machinery, everything is tremor, quiver or jar? In the air, where the balloon is incessantly twirling, oscillating, on account of the ever varying strata of different densities, and even occasionally threatening to spill you out? The Projectile alone, floating grandly through the absolute void, in the midst of the profoundest silence, could offer to its inmates the possibility of enjoying slumber the most complete, repose the most profound.

There is no telling how long our three daring travellers would have continued to enjoy their sleep, if it had not been suddenly terminated by an unexpected noise about seven o'clock in the morning of December 2nd, eight hours after their departure.

This noise was most decidedly of barking.

'The dogs! It's the dogs!' cried Ardan, springing up at a bound.

'They must be hungry!' observed the Captain.

'We have forgotten the poor creatures!' cried Barbican.

'Where can they have gone to?' asked Ardan, looking for them in all directions.

At last they found one of them hiding under the sofa. Thunderstruck and perfectly bewildered by the terrible shock, the poor animal had kept close in its hiding place, never daring to utter a sound, until at last the pangs of hunger had proved too strong even for its fright.

They readily recognized the amiable Diana, but they could not allure the shivering, whining animal from her retreat without a good deal of coaxing. Ardan talked to her in his most honeyed and seductive accents, while trying to pull her out by the neck.

'Come out to your friends, charming Diana,' he went on, 'come out, my beauty, destined for a lofty niche in the temple of canine glory! Come out, worthy scion of a race deemed worthy by the Egyptians to be a companion of the great god, Anubis, by the Christians, to be a friend of the good Saint Roch! Come out and partake of a glory before which the stars of Montargis and of St. Bernard shall henceforward pale their ineffectual fire! Come out, my lady, and let me think o'er the countless multiplication of thy species, so that, while sailing through the interplanetary spaces, we may indulge in endless flights of fancy on the number and variety of thy descendants who will ere long render the Selenitic atmosphere vocal with canine ululation!'

Diana, whether flattered or not, allowed herself to be dragged out, still uttering short, plaintive whines. A hasty examination satisfying her friends that she was more frightened than hurt and more hungry than either, they continued their search for her companion.

'Satellite! Satellite! Step this way, sir!' cried Ardan. But no Satellite appeared and, what was worse, not the slightest sound indicated his presence. At last he was discovered on a ledge in the upper portion of the Projectile, whither he had been shot by the terrible concussion. Less fortunate than his female companion, the poor fellow had received a frightful shock and his life was evidently in great danger.

'The acclimatization project looks shaky!' cried Ardan, handing the animal very carefully and tenderly to the others. Poor Satellite's head had been crushed against the roof, but, though recovery seemed hopeless, they laid the body on a soft cushion, and soon had the satisfaction of hearing it give vent to a slight sigh.

'Good!' said Ardan, 'while there's life there's hope. You must not die yet, old boy. We shall nurse you. We know our duty and shall not shirk the responsibility. I should rather lose the right arm off my body than be the cause of your death, poor Satellite! Try a little water?'

The suffering creature swallowed the cool draught with evident avidity, then sunk into a deep slumber.

The friends, sitting around and having nothing more to do, looked out of the window and began once more to watch the Earth and the Moon with great attention. The glittering crescent of the Earth was evidently narrower than it had been the preceding evening, but its volume was still enormous when compared to the Lunar crescent, which was now rapidly assuming the proportions of a perfect circle.

'By Jove,' suddenly exclaimed Ardan, 'why didn't we start at the moment of Full Earth? – that is when our globe and the Sun were in opposition?'

'Why *should* we!' growled M'Nicholl.

'Because in that case we should be now looking at the great continents and the great seas in a new light – the former glittering under the solar rays, the latter darker and somewhat shaded, as we see them on certain maps. How I should like to get a glimpse at those poles of the Earth, on which the eye of man has never yet lighted!'

'True,' replied Barbican, 'but if the Earth had been Full, the Moon would have been New, that is to say, invisible to us on account of solar irradiation. Of the two it is much preferable to be able to keep the point of arrival in view rather than the point of departure.'

'You're right, Barbican,' observed the Captain; 'besides, once we're in the Moon, the long Lunar night will give us plenty of time to gaze our full at yonder great celestial body, our former home, and still swarming with our fellow beings.'

'Our fellow beings no longer, dear boy!' cried Ardan. 'We inhabit a new world peopled by ourselves alone, the Projectile! Ardan is Barbican's fellow being, and Barbican M'Nicholl's. Beyond us, outside us, humanity ends, and we are now the only inhabitants of this microcosm, and so we shall continue till the moment when we become Selenites pure and simple.'

'Which shall be in about eighty-eight hours from now,' replied the Captain.

'Which is as much as to say—?' asked Ardan.

'That it is half past eight,' replied M'Nicholl.

'My regular hour for breakfast,' exclaimed Ardan, 'and I don't see the shadow of a reason for changing it now.'

The proposition was most acceptable, especially to the Captain, who frequently boasted that, whether on land or water, on mountain summits or in the depths of mines, he had never missed a meal in all his life. In escaping from the Earth, our travellers felt that they had by no means escaped from the laws of humanity, and their stomachs now called on them lustily to fill the aching void. Ardan, as a Frenchman, claimed the post of chief cook, an important office, but his companions yielded it with alacrity. The gas furnished the requisite heat, and the provision chest supplied the materials for their first repast. They commenced with three plates of excellent soup, extracted from *Liebig's* precious tablets, prepared from the best beef that ever roamed over the Pampas.

To this succeeded several tenderloin beefsteaks, which, though reduced to a small bulk by the hydraulic engines of the *American Dessicating Company*, were pronounced to be fully as tender, juicy and savory as if they had just left the gridiron of a London Club House. Ardan even swore that they were 'bleeding,' and the others were too busy to contradict him.

Preserved vegetables of various kinds, 'fresher than nature,' according to Ardan, gave an agreeable variety to the entertainment, and these were followed by several cups of magnificent tea, unanimously allowed to be the best they had ever tasted. It was an odoriferous young hyson gathered that very year, and presented to the Emperor of Russia by the famous rebel chief Yakub Kushbegi, and of which Alexander had expressed himself as very happy in being able to send a few boxes to his friend, the distinguished President of the Baltimore Gun Club. To crown the meal, Ardan unearthed an exquisite bottle of *Chambertin*, and, in glasses sparkling with the richest juice of the *Cote d'or*, the travellers drank to the speedy union of the Earth and her satellite.

And, as if his work among the generous vineyards of Burgundy had not been enough to show his interest in the matter, even the Sun wished to join the party. Precisely at this moment, the Projectile beginning to leave the conical shadow cast by the Earth, the rays of the glorious King of Day struck its lower surface, not obliquely, but perpendicularly, on account of the slight obliquity of the Moon's orbit with that of the Earth.

'The Sun,' cried Ardan.

'Of course,' said Barbican, looking at his watch, 'he's exactly up to time.'

'How is it that we see him only through the bottom light of our Projectile?' asked Ardan.

'A moment's reflection must tell you,' replied Barbican, 'that when we started last night, the Sun was almost directly below us; therefore, as we continue to move in a straight line, he must still be in our rear.'

'That's clear enough,' said the Captain, 'but another consideration, I'm free to say, rather perplexes me. Since our Earth lies between us and the Sun, why don't we see the sunlight forming a great ring around the globe, in other words, instead of the full Sun that we plainly see there below, why do we not witness an annular eclipse?'

'Your cool, clear head has not yet quite recovered from the shock, my dear Captain;' replied Barbican, with a smile. 'For two reasons we can't see the ring eclipse: on account of the angle the Moon's orbit makes with the Earth, the three bodies are not at present in a direct line; we, therefore, see the Sun a little to the west of the earth; secondly, even if they were exactly in a straight line, we should still be far from the point whence an annular eclipse would be visible.'

'That's true,' said Ardan; 'the cone of the Earth's shadow must extend far beyond the Moon.'

'Nearly four times as far,' said Barbican; 'still, as the Moon's orbit and the Earth's do not lie in exactly the same plane, a Lunar eclipse can occur only when the nodes coincide with the period of the Full Moon, which is generally twice, never more than three times in a year. If we had started about four days before the occurrence of a Lunar eclipse, we should travel all the time in the dark. This would have been obnoxious for many reasons.'

'One, for instance?'

'An evident one is that, though at the present moment we are moving through a vacuum, our Projectile, steeped in the solar rays, revels in their light and heat. Hence great saving in gas, an important point in our household economy.'

In effect, the solar rays, tempered by no genial medium like our atmosphere, soon began to glare and glow with such intensity, that the Projectile under their influence, felt like suddenly passing from winter to summer. Between the Moon overhead and the Sun beneath it was actually inundated with fiery rays.

'One feels good here,' cried the Captain, rubbing his hands.

'A little too good,' cried Ardan. 'It's already like a hot-house. With a little garden clay, I could raise you a splendid crop of peas in twenty-four hours. I hope in heaven the walls of our Projectile won't melt like wax!'

'Don't be alarmed, dear friend,' observed Barbican, quietly. 'The

CHAPTER III

Projectile has seen the worst as far as heat is concerned; when tearing through the atmosphere, she endured a temperature with which what she is liable to at present stands no comparison. In fact, I should not be astonished if, in the eyes of our friends at Stony Hill, it had resembled for a moment or two a red-hot meteor.'

'Poor Marston must have looked on us as roasted alive!' observed Ardan.

'What could have saved us I'm sure I can't tell,' replied Barbican. 'I must acknowledge that against such a danger, I had made no provision whatever.'

'I knew all about it,' said the Captain, 'and on the strength of it, I had laid my fifth wager.'

'Probably,' laughed Ardan, 'there was not time enough to get grilled in: I have heard of men who dipped their fingers into molten iron with impunity.'

Whilst Ardan and the Captain were arguing the point, Barbican began busying himself in making everything as comfortable as if, instead of a four days' journey, one of four years was contemplated. The reader, no doubt, remembers that the floor of the Projectile contained about 50 square feet; that the chamber was nine feet high; that space was economized as much as possible, nothing but the most absolute necessities being admitted, of which each was kept strictly in its own place; therefore, the travellers had room enough to move around in with a certain liberty. The thick glass window in the floor was quite as solid as any other part of it; but the Sun, streaming in from below, lit up the Projectile strangely, producing some very singular and startling effects of light appearing to come in by the wrong way.

The first thing now to be done was to see after the water cask and the provision chest. They were not injured in the slightest respect, thanks to the means taken to counteract the shock. The provisions were in good condition, and abundant enough to supply the travellers for a whole year – Barbican having taken care to be on the safe side, in case the Projectile might land in a deserted region of the Moon. As for the water and the other liquors, the travellers had enough only for two months. Relying on the latest observations of astronomers, they had convinced themselves that the Moon's atmosphere, being heavy, dense and thick in the deep valleys, springs and streams of water could hardly fail to show themselves there. During the journey, therefore, and for the first year of their installation on the Lunar continent, the daring travellers would be pretty safe from all danger of hunger or thirst.

The air supply proved also to be quite satisfactory. The *Reiset* and *Regnault* apparatus for producing oxygen contained a supply of chlorate of potash sufficient for two months. As the productive material had to be maintained at a temperature of between 7 and 8 hundred degrees Fahr., a steady consumption of gas was required; but here too the supply far exceeded the demand. The whole arrangement worked charmingly, requiring only an odd glance now and then. The high temperature changing the chlorate into a chloride, the oxygen was disengaged gradually but abundantly, every eighteen pounds of chlorate of potash, furnishing the seven pounds of oxygen necessary for the daily consumption of the inmates of the Projectile.

Still – as the reader need hardly be reminded – it was not sufficient to renew the exhausted oxygen; the complete purification of the air required the absorption of the carbonic acid, exhaled from the lungs. For nearly 12 hours the atmosphere had been gradually becoming more and more charged with this deleterious gas, produced from the combustion of the blood by the inspired oxygen. The Captain soon saw this, by noticing with what difficulty Diana was panting. She even appeared to be smothering, for the carbonic acid – as in the famous *Grotto del Cane* on the banks of Lake Agnano, near Naples – was collecting like water on the floor of the Projectile, on account of its great specific gravity. It already threatened the poor dog's life, though not yet endangering that of

CHAPTER III — 51

her masters. The Captain, seeing this state of things, hastily laid on the floor one or two cups containing caustic potash and water, and stirred the mixture gently: this substance, having a powerful affinity for carbonic acid, greedily absorbed it, and after a few moments the air was completely purified.

The others had begun by this time to check off the state of the instruments. The thermometer and the barometer were all right, except one self-recorder of which the glass had got broken. An excellent aneroid barometer, taken safe and sound out of its wadded box, was carefully hung on a hook in the wall. It marked not only the pressure of the air in the Projectile, but also the quantity of the watery vapour that it contained. The needle, oscillating a little beyond thirty, pointed pretty steadily at '*Fair*.'

The mariner's compasses were also found to be quite free from injury. It is, of course, hardly necessary to say that the needles pointed in no particular direction, the magnetic pole of the Earth being unable at such a distance to exercise any appreciable influence on them. But when brought to the Moon, it was expected that these compasses, once more subjected to the influence of the current, would attest certain phenomena. In any case, it would be interesting to verify if the Earth and her satellite were similarly affected by the magnetic forces.

A hypsometer, or instrument for ascertaining the heights of the Lunar mountains by the barometric pressure under which water boils, a sextant to measure the altitude of the Sun, a theodolite for taking horizontal or vertical angles, telescopes, of indispensable necessity when the travellers should approach the Moon, – all these instruments, carefully examined, were found to be still in perfect working order, notwithstanding the violence of the terrible shock at the start.

As to the picks, spades, and other tools that had been carefully selected by the Captain; also the bags of various kinds of grain and the bundles of various kinds of shrubs, which Ardan expected to transplant to the Lunar plains – they were all still safe in their places around the upper corners of the Projectile.

Some other articles were also up there which evidently possessed great interest for the Frenchman. What they were nobody else seemed to know, and he seemed to be in no hurry to tell. Every now and then, he would climb up, by means of iron pins fixed in the wall, to inspect his treasures; whatever they were, he arranged them and rearranged them with evident pleasure, and as he rapidly passed a careful hand through certain mysterious boxes, he joyfully sang in the falsest possible of false voices the lively piece from *Nicolo*:

> *Le temps est beau, la route est belle,*
> *La promenade est un plaisir.*

> [The day is bright, our hearts are light.
> How sweet to rove through wood and dell.]

or the well known air in *Mignon*:

> *Legères hirondelles,*
> *Oiseaux bénis de Dieu,*
> *Ouvrez-ouvrez vos ailes,*
> *Envolez-vous! adieu!*

> [Farewell, happy Swallows, farewell!
> With summer for ever to dwell
> Ye leave our northern strand
> For the genial southern land
> Balmy with breezes bland.
> Return? Ah, who can tell?
> Farewell, happy Swallows, farewell!]

Barbican was much gratified to find that his rockets and other fireworks had not received the least injury. He relied upon them for the performance of a very important service as soon as the Projectile, having passed the point of neutral attraction between the Earth and the Moon, would begin to fall with accelerated velocity towards the Lunar surface. This descent, though – thanks to the respective volumes of the attracting bodies – six times less rapid than it would have been on the surface of the Earth, would still be violent enough to dash the Projectile into a thousand pieces. But Barbican confidently expected by means of his powerful rockets to offer very considerable obstruction to the violence of this fall, if not to counteract its terrible effects altogether.

The inspection having thus given general satisfaction, the travellers once more set themselves to watching external space through the lights in the sides and the floor of the Projectile.

Everything still appeared to be in the same state as before. Nothing was changed. The vast arch of the celestial dome glittered with stars, and constellations blazed with a light clear and pure enough to throw an astronomer into an ecstasy of admiration. Below them shone the Sun, like the mouth of a white-hot furnace, his dazzling disc defined sharply on the pitch-black back-ground of the sky. Above them the Moon, reflecting back his rays from her glowing surface, appeared to stand motionless in the midst of the starry host.

A little to the east of the Sun, they could see a pretty large dark spot, like a hole in the sky, the broad silver fringe on one edge fading off into a faint glimmering mist on the other – it was the Earth. Here and there in all directions, nebulous masses gleamed like large flakes of star dust, in which, from nadir to zenith, the eye could trace without a break that vast ring of impalpable star powder, the famous *Milky Way*, through the midst of which the beams of our glorious Sun struggle with the dusky pallor of a star of only the fourth magnitude.

Our observers were never weary of gazing on this magnificent and novel spectacle, of the grandeur of which, it is hardly necessary to say, no description can give an adequate idea. What profound reflections it suggested to their understandings! What vivid emotions it enkindled in their imaginations! Barbican, desirous of commenting the story of the journey while still influenced by these inspiring impressions, noted carefully hour by hour every fact that signalized the beginning of his enterprise. He wrote out his notes very carefully and systematically, his round full hand, as business-like as ever, never betraying the slightest emotion.

The Captain was quite as busy, but in a different way. Pulling out his tablets, he reviewed his calculations regarding the motion of projectiles, their velocities, ranges and paths, their retardations and their accelerations, jotting down the figures with a rapidity wonderful to behold. Ardan neither wrote nor calculated, but kept up an incessant fire of small talk, now with Barbican, who hardly ever answered him, now with M'Nicholl, who never heard him, occasionally with Diana, who never understood him, but oftenest with himself, because, as he said, he liked not only to talk to a sensible man but also to hear what a sensible man had to say. He never stood still for a moment, but kept 'bobbing around' with the effervescent briskness of a bee, at one time roosting at the top of the ladder, at another peering through the floor light, now to the right, then to the left, always humming scraps from the *Opera Bouffe*, but never changing the air. In the small space which was then a whole world to the travellers, he represented to the life the animation and loquacity of the French, and I need hardly say he played his part to perfection.

The eventful day, or, to speak more correctly, the space of twelve hours which with us forms a day, ended for our travellers with an abundant supper, exquisitely cooked. It was highly enjoyed.

No incident had yet occurred of a nature calculated to shake their confidence. Apprehending none therefore, full of hope rather and already certain of success, they were soon lost in a peaceful slumber, whilst the Projectile, moving rapidly, though with a velocity uniformly retarding, still cleaved its way through the pathless regions of the empyrean.

CHAPTER IV
A Chapter for the Cornell Girls

No incident worth recording occurred during the night, if night indeed it could be called. In reality there was now no night or even day in the Projectile, or rather, strictly speaking, it was always *night* on the upper end of the bullet, and always *day* on the lower. Whenever, therefore, the words *night* and *day* occur in our story, the reader will readily understand them as referring to those spaces of time that are so called in our Earthly almanacs, and were so measured by the travellers' chronometers.

The repose of our friends must indeed have been undisturbed, if absolute freedom from sound or jar of any kind could secure tranquillity. In spite of its immense velocity, the Projectile still seemed to be perfectly motionless. Not the slightest sign of movement could be detected. Change of locality, though ever so rapid, can never reveal itself to our senses when it takes place in a vacuum, or when the enveloping atmosphere travels at the same rate as the moving body. Though we are incessantly whirled around the Sun at the rate of about seventy thousand miles an hour, which of us is conscious of the slightest motion? In such a case, as far as sensation is concerned, motion and repose are absolutely identical. Neither has any effect one way or another on a material body. Is such a body in motion? It remains in motion until some obstacle stops it. Is it at rest? It remains at rest until some superior force compels it to change its position. This indifference of bodies to motion or rest is what physicists call *inertia*.

Barbican and his companions, therefore, shut up in the Projectile, could readily imagine themselves to be completely motionless. Had they been outside, the effect would have been precisely the same. No rush of air, no jarring sensation would betray the slightest movement. But for the sight of the Moon gradually growing larger above them, and of the Earth gradually growing smaller beneath them, they could safely swear that they were fast anchored in an ocean of deathlike immobility.

Towards the morning of next day (December 3), they were awakened by a joyful, but quite unexpected sound.

'Cock-a-doodle! doo!' accompanied by a decided flapping of wings.

The Frenchman, on his feet in one instant and on the top of the ladder in another, attempted to shut the lid of a half open box, speaking in an angry but suppressed voice:

'Stop this hullabaloo, won't you? Do you want me to fail in my great combination!'

'Hello?' cried Barbican and M'Nicholl, starting up and rubbing their eyes.

'What noise was that?' asked Barbican.

'Seems to me I heard the crowing of a cock,' observed the Captain.

'I never thought your ears could be so easily deceived, Captain,' cried Ardan, quickly, 'Let us try it again,' and, flapping his ribs with his arms, he gave vent to a crow so loud and natural that the lustiest chanticleer that ever saluted the orb of day might be proud of it.

The Captain roared right out, and even Barbican snickered, but as they saw that their companion evidently wanted to conceal something, they immediately assumed straight faces and pretended to think no more about the matter.

'Barbican,' said Ardan, coming down the ladder and evidently anxious to change the conversation, 'have you any idea of what I was thinking about all night?'

'Not the slightest.'

'I was thinking of the promptness of the reply you received last year from the authorities of Cambridge University, when you asked them about the feasibility of sending a bullet to the Moon. You know very well by this time what a perfect ignoramus I am in Mathematics. I own I have been often puzzled when thinking on what grounds they could form such a positive opinion, in a case where I am certain that the calculation must be an exceedingly delicate matter.'

'The feasibility, you mean to say,' replied Barbican, 'not exactly of sending a bullet to the Moon, but of sending it to the neutral point between the Earth and the Moon, which lies at about nine-tenths of the journey, where the two attractions counteract each other. Because that point once passed, the Projectile would reach the Moon's surface by virtue of its own weight.'

'Well, reaching that neutral point be it;' replied Ardan, 'but, once more, I should like to know how they have been able to come at the necessary initial velocity of 12,000 yards a second?'

'Nothing simpler,' answered Barbican.

'Could you have done it yourself?' asked the Frenchman.

'Without the slightest difficulty. The Captain and myself could have readily solved the problem, only the reply from the University saved us the trouble.'

'Well, Barbican, dear boy,' observed Ardan, 'all I've got to say is, you might chop the head off my body, beginning with my feet, before you could make me go through such a calculation.'

'Simply because you don't understand Algebra,' replied Barbican, quietly.

'Oh! that's all very well!' cried Ardan, with an ironical smile. 'You great $x+y$ men think you settle everything by uttering the word *Algebra*!'

'Ardan,' asked Barbican, 'do you think people could beat iron without a hammer, or turn up furrows without a plough?'

'Hardly.'

'Well, Algebra is an instrument or utensil just as much as a hammer or a plough, and a very good instrument too if you know how to make use of it.'

'You're in earnest?'

'Quite so.'

'And you can handle the instrument right before my eyes?'

'Certainly, if it interests you so much.'

'You can show me how they got at the initial velocity of our Projectile?'

'With the greatest pleasure. By taking into proper consideration all the elements of the problem, viz.: (1) the distance between the centres of the Earth and the Moon, (2) the Earth's radius, (3) its volume, and (4) the Moon's volume, I can easily calculate what must be the initial velocity, and that too by a very simple formula.'

'Let us have the formula.'

'In one moment; only I can't give you the curve really described by the Projectile as it moves between the Earth and the Moon; this is to be obtained by allowing for their combined movement around the Sun. I will consider the Earth and the Sun to be motionless, that being sufficient for our present purpose.'

'Why so?'

'Because to give you that exact curve would be to solve a point in the "Problem of the Three Bodies," which Integral Calculus has not yet reached.'

'What!' cried Ardan, in a mocking tone, 'is there really anything that Mathematics can't do?'

'Yes,' said Barbican, 'there is still a great deal that Mathematics can't even attempt.'

'So far, so good;' resumed Ardan. 'Now then what is this Integral Calculus of yours?'

'It is a branch of Mathematics that has for its object the summation of a certain infinite series of indefinitely small terms: but for the solution of which, we must generally know the function of which a given function is the differential coefficient. In other words,' continued Barbican, 'in it we return from the differential coefficient, to the function from which it was deduced.'

'Clear as mud!' cried Ardan, with a hearty laugh.

'Now then, let me have a bit of paper and a pencil,' added Barbican, 'and in half an hour you shall have your formula; meantime you can easily find something interesting to do.'

In a few seconds Barbican was profoundly absorbed in his problem, while M'Nicholl was watching out of the window, and Ardan was busily employed in preparing breakfast.

The morning meal was not quite ready, when Barbican, raising his head, showed Ardan a page covered with algebraic signs at the end of which stood the following formula: –

$$\frac{1}{2}\left(v'^2 - v^2\right) = gr\left\{\frac{r}{x} - 1 + \frac{m'}{m}\left(\frac{r}{d-x} - \frac{r}{d-r}\right)\right\}$$

'Which means?' asked Ardan.

'It means,' said the Captain, now taking part in the discussion, 'that the half of v prime squared minus v squared equals gr multiplied by r over x minus one plus m prime over m multiplied by r over d minus x minus r over d minus r... that is—'

'That is,' interrupted Ardan, in a roar of laughter, 'x straddles on y, making for z and jumping over p! Do *you* mean to say you understand the terrible jargon, Captain?'

'Nothing is clearer, Ardan.'

'You too, Captain! Then of course I must give in gracefully, and declare that the sun at noon-day is not more palpably evident than the sense of Barbican's formula.'

'You asked for Algebra, you know,' observed Barbican.

'Rock crystal is nothing to it!'

'The fact is, Barbican,' said the Captain, who had been looking over the paper, 'you have worked the thing out very well. You have the integral equation of the living forces, and I have no doubt it will give us the result sought for.'

'Yes, but I should like to understand it, you know,' cried Ardan: 'I would give ten years of the Captain's life to understand it!'

'Listen then,' said Barbican. 'Half of v prime squared less v squared, is the formula giving us the half variation of the living force.'

'Mac pretends he understands all that!'

'You need not be a *Solomon* to do it,' said the Captain. 'All these signs that you appear to consider so cabalistic form a language the clearest, the shortest, and the most logical, for all those who can read it.'

'You pretend, Captain, that, by means of these hieroglyphics, far more incomprehensible than the sacred Ibis of the Egyptians, you can discover the velocity at which the Projectile should start?'

'Most undoubtedly,' replied the Captain, 'and, by the same formula I can even tell you the rate of our velocity at any particular point of our journey.'

'You can?'

'I can.'

'Then you're just as deep a one as our President.'

'No, Ardan; not at all. The really difficult part of the question Barbican has done. That is, to make out such an equation as takes into account all the conditions of the problem. After that, it's a simple affair of Arithmetic, requiring only a knowledge of the four rules to work it out.'

'Very simple,' observed Ardan, who always got muddled at any kind of a difficult sum in addition.

'Captain,' said Barbican, '*you* could have found the formulas too, if you tried.'

'I don't know about that,' was the Captain's reply, 'but I do know that this formula is wonderfully come at.'

'Now, Ardan, listen a moment,' said Barbican, 'and you will see what sense there is in all these letters.'

'I listen,' sighed Ardan with the resignation of a martyr.

'd is the distance from the centre of the Earth to the centre of the Moon, for it is from the centres that we must calculate the attractions.'

'That I comprehend.'

'r is the radius of the Earth.'

'That I comprehend.'

'm is the mass or volume of the Earth; m prime that of the Moon. We must take the mass of the two attracting bodies into consideration, since attraction is in direct proportion to their masses.'

'That I comprehend.'

'g is the gravity or the velocity acquired at the end of a second by a body falling towards the centre of the Earth. Clear?'

'That I comprehend.'

'Now I represent by x the varying distance that separates the Projectile from the centre of the Earth, and by v prime its velocity at that distance.'

'That I comprehend.'

'Finally, v is its velocity when quitting our atmosphere.'

'Yes,' chimed in the Captain, 'it is for this point, you see, that the velocity had to be calculated, because we know already that the initial velocity is exactly the three halves of the velocity when the Projectile quits the atmosphere.'

'That I don't comprehend,' cried the Frenchman, energetically.

'It's simple enough, however,' said Barbican.

'Not so simple as a simpleton,' replied the Frenchman.

'The Captain merely means,' said Barbican, 'that at the instant the Projectile quitted the terrestrial atmosphere it had already lost a third of its initial velocity.'

'So much as a third?'

'Yes, by friction against the atmospheric layers: the quicker its motion, the greater resistance it encountered.'

'That of course I admit, but your v squared and your v prime squared rattle in my head like nails in a box!'

'The usual effect of Algebra on one who is a stranger to it; to finish you, our next step is to express numerically the value of these several symbols. Now some of them are already known, and some are to be calculated.'

'Hand the latter over to me,' said the Captain.

'First,' continued Barbican: 'r, the Earth's radius is, in the latitude of Florida, about 3,921 miles. d, the distance from the centre of the Earth to the centre of the Moon is 56 terrestrial radii, which the Captain calculates to be...?'

'To be,' cried M'Nicholl working rapidly with his pencil, '219,572 miles, the moment the Moon is in her *perigee*, or nearest point to the Earth.'

'Very well,' continued Barbican. 'Now m prime over m, that is the ratio of the Moon's mass to that of the Earth is about the $\frac{1}{81}$. g gravity being at Florida about 32¼ feet, of course $g \times r$ must be – how much, Captain?'

'38,465 miles,' replied M'Nicholl.

'Now then?' asked Ardan.

'Now then,' replied Barbican, 'the expression having numerical values, I am trying to find v, that is to say, the initial velocity which the Projectile must possess in order to reach the point where the two attractions neutralize each other. Here the velocity being null, v prime becomes zero, and x the required distance of this neutral point must be represented by the nine-tenths of d, the distance between the two centres.'

'I have a vague kind of idea that it must be so,' said Ardan.

'I shall, therefore, have the following result;' continued Barbican, figuring up; 'x being nine-tenths of d, and v prime being zero, my formula becomes: –

$$v^2 = gr\left\{1 - \frac{10r}{d} - \frac{1}{81}\left(\frac{10r}{d} - \frac{r}{d-r}\right)\right\}"$$

The Captain read it off rapidly.

'Right! that's correct!' he cried.

'You think so?' asked Barbican.

'As true as Euclid!' exclaimed M'Nicholl.

'Wonderful fellows,' murmured the Frenchman, smiling with admiration.

'You understand now, Ardan, don't you?' asked Barbican.

'Don't I though?' exclaimed Ardan, 'why my head is splitting with it!'

'Therefore,' continued Barbican,

$$"2v^2 = 2gr\left\{1 - \frac{10r}{d} - \frac{1}{81}\left(\frac{10r}{d} - \frac{r}{d-r}\right)\right\}"$$

'And now,' exclaimed M'Nicholl, sharpening his pencil; 'in order to obtain the velocity of the Projectile when leaving the atmosphere, we have only to make a slight calculation.'

The Captain, who before clerking on a Mississippi steamboat had been professor of Mathematics in an Indiana university, felt quite at home at the work. He rained figures from his pencil with a velocity that would have made Marston stare. Page after page was filled with his multiplications and divisions, while Barbican looked quietly on, and Ardan impatiently stroked his head and ears to keep down a rising head-ache.

'Well?' at last asked Barbican, seeing the Captain stop and throw a somewhat hasty glance over his work.

'Well,' answered M'Nicholl slowly but confidently, 'the calculation is made, I think correctly; and v, that is, the velocity of the Projectile when quitting the atmosphere, sufficient to carry it to the neutral point, should be at least...'

'How much?' asked Barbican, eagerly.

'Should be at least 11,972 yards the first second.'

'What!' cried Barbican, jumping off his seat. 'How much did you say?'

'11,972 yards the first second it quits the atmosphere.'

'Oh, malediction!' cried Barbican, with a gesture of terrible despair.

'What's the matter?' asked Ardan, very much surprised.

'Enough is the matter!' answered Barbican excitedly. 'This

velocity having been diminished by a third, our initial velocity should have been at least...'

'17,958 yards the first second!' cried M'Nicholl, rapidly flourishing his pencil.

'But the Cambridge Observatory having declared that 12,000 yards the first second were sufficient, our Projectile started with no greater velocity!'

'Well?' asked M'Nicholl.

'Well, such a velocity will never do!'

"How??'

'How!' cried the Captain and Ardan in one voice.

'We can never reach the neutral point!'

'Thunder and lightning'

'Fire and Fury!'

'We can't get even halfway!'

'Heaven and Earth!'

'*Mille noms d'un boulet!*' cried Ardan, wildly gesticulating.

'And we shall fall back to the Earth!'

'Oh!'

'Ah!'

They could say no more. This fearful revelation took them like a stroke of apoplexy.

CHAPTER V
The Colds of Space

How could they imagine that the Observatory men had committed such a blunder? Barbican would not believe it possible. He made the Captain go over his calculation again and again; but no flaw was to be found in it. He himself carefully examined it, figure after figure, but he could find nothing wrong. They both took up the formula and subjected it to the strongest tests; but it was invulnerable. There was no denying the fact. The Cambridge professors had undoubtedly blundered in saying that an initial velocity of 12,000 yards a second would be enough to carry them to the neutral point. A velocity of nearly 18,000 yards would be the very lowest required for such a purpose. They had simply forgotten to allow a third for friction.

The three friends kept profound silence for some time. Breakfast now was the last thing thought of. Barbican, with teeth grating, fingers clutching, and eye-brows closely contracting, gazed grimly through the window. The Captain, as a last resource, once more examined his calculations, earnestly hoping to find a figure wrong. Ardan could neither sit, stand nor lie still for a second, though he tried all three. His silence, of course, did not last long.

'Ha! ha! ha!' he laughed bitterly. 'Precious scientific men! Villainous old hombogues! The whole set not worth a straw! I hope to gracious, since we must fall, that we shall drop down plumb on Cambridge Observatory, and not leave a single one of the miserable old women, called professors, alive in the premises!'

A certain expression in Ardan's angry exclamation had struck the Captain like a shot, and set his temples throbbing violently.

'*Must* fall!' he exclaimed, starting up suddenly. 'Let us see about that! It is now seven o'clock in the morning. We must have, therefore, been at least thirty-two hours on the road, and more than half of our passage is already made. If we are going to fall at all, we must be falling now! I'm certain we're not, but, Barbican, you have to find it out!'

Barbican caught the idea like lightning, and, seizing a compass, he began through the floor window to measure the visual angle of the distant Earth. The apparent immobility of the Projectile allowed him to do this with great exactness. Then laying aside the instrument, and wiping off the thick drops of sweat that bedewed his forehead, he began jotting down some figures on a piece of paper. The Captain looked on with keen interest; he knew very well that Barbican was calculating their distance from the Earth by the apparent measure of the terrestrial diameter, and he eyed him anxiously.

Pretty soon his friends saw a colour stealing into Barbican's pale face, and a triumphant light glittering in his eye.

'No, my brave boys!' he exclaimed at last throwing down his pencil, 'we're not falling! Far from it, we are at present more than 150 thousand miles from the Earth!'

'Hurrah! Bravo!' cried M'Nicholl and Ardan, in a breath.

'We have passed the point where we should have stopped if we had had no more initial velocity than the Cambridge men allowed us!'

'Hurrah! hurrah!'

'Bravo, Bravissimo!'

'And we're still going up!'

'Glory, glory, hallelujah!' sang M'Nicholl, in the highest excitement.

'*Vive ce cher Barbican!*' cried Ardan, bursting into French as usual whenever his feelings had the better of him.

'Of course we're marching on!' continued M'Nicholl, 'and I know the reason why, too. Those 400,000 pounds of gun-cotton gave us greater initial velocity than we had expected!'

'You're right, Captain!' added Barbican; 'besides, you must not forget that, by getting rid of the water, the Projectile was relieved of considerable weight!'

'Correct again!' cried the Captain. 'I had not thought of that!'

'Therefore, my brave boys,' continued Barbican, with some excitement; 'away with melancholy! We're all right!'

'Yes; everything is lovely and the goose hangs high!' cried the Captain, who on grand occasions was not above a little slang.

'Talking of goose reminds me of breakfast,' cried Ardan; 'I assure you, my fright has not taken away my appetite!'

'Yes,' continued Barbican. 'Captain, you're quite right. Our initial velocity very fortunately was much greater than what our Cambridge friends had calculated for us!'

'Hang our Cambridge friends and their calculations!' cried Ardan, with some asperity; 'as usual with your scientific men they've more brass than brains! If we're not now bed-fellows with the oysters in the Gulf of Mexico, no thanks to our kind Cambridge friends. But talking of oysters, let me remind you again that breakfast is ready.'

The meal was a most joyous one. They ate much, they talked more, but they laughed most. The little incident of Algebra had certainly very much enlivened the situation.

'Now, my boys,' Ardan went on, 'all things thus turning out quite comfortable, I would just ask you why we should not succeed? We are fairly started. No breakers ahead that I can see. No rock on our road. It is freer than the ships on the raging ocean, aye, freer than the balloons in the blustering air. But the ship arrives at her destination; the balloon, borne on the wings of the wind, rises to as high an altitude as can be endured; why then should not our Projectile reach the Moon?'

'It *will* reach the Moon!' nodded Barbican.

'We shall reach the Moon or know for what!' cried M'Nicholl, enthusiastically.

'The great American nation must not be disappointed!' continued Ardan. 'They are the only people on Earth capable of originating such an enterprise! They are the only people capable of producing a Barbican!'

'Hurrah!' cried M'Nicholl.

'That point settled,' continued the Frenchman, 'another question comes up to which I have not yet called your attention. When we get to the Moon, what shall we do there? How are we going to amuse ourselves? I'm afraid our life there will be awfully slow!'

His companions emphatically disclaimed the possibility of such a thing.

'You may deny it, but I know better, and knowing better, I have laid in my stores accordingly. You have but to choose. I possess a varied assortment. Chess, draughts, cards, dominoes – everything in fact, but a billiard table?'

'What!' exclaimed Barbican; 'cumbered yourself with such gimcracks?'

'Such gimcracks are not only good to amuse ourselves with, but are eminently calculated also to win us the friendship of the Selenites.'

'Friend Michael,' said Barbican, 'if the Moon is inhabited at all, her inhabitants must have appeared several thousand years before the advent of Man on our Earth, for there seems to be very little doubt that Luna is considerably older than Terra in her present state. Therefore, Selenites, if their brain is organized like our own, must have by this time invented all that we are possessed of, and even much which we are still to invent in the course of ages. The probability is that, instead of their learning from us, we shall have much to learn from them.'

'What!' asked Ardan, 'you think they have artists like Phidias, Michael Angelo and Raphael?'

'Certainly.'

'And poets like Homer, Virgil, Dante, Shakespeare, Goethe and Hugo?'

'Not a doubt of it.'

'And philosophers like Plato, Aristotle, Descartes, Bacon, Kant?'

'Why not?'

'And scientists like Euclid, Archimedes, Copernicus, Newton, Pascal?'

'I should think so.'

'And famous actors, and singers, and composers, and – and photographers?'

'I could almost swear to it.'

'Then, dear boy, since they have gone ahead as far as we and even farther, why have not those great Selenites tried to start a communication with the Earth? Why have they not fired a projectile from the regions lunar to the regions terrestrial?'

'Who says they have not done so?' asked Barbican, coolly.

'Attempting such a communication,' observed the Captain, 'would certainly be much easier for them than for us, principally for two reasons. First, attraction on the Moon's surface being six times less than on the Earth's, a projectile could be sent off more rapidly; second, because, as this projectile need be sent only 24 instead of 240 thousand miles, they could do it with a quantity of powder ten times less than what we should require for the same purpose.'

'Then I ask again,' said the Frenchman; 'why haven't they made such an attempt?'

'And I reply again,' answered Barbican. 'How do you know that they have not made such an attempt?'

'Made it? When?'

'Thousands of years ago, before the invention of writing, before even the appearance of Man on the Earth.'

'But the bullet?' asked Ardan, triumphantly; 'Where's the bullet? Produce the bullet!'

'Friend Michael,' answered Barbican, with a quiet smile, 'you appear to forget that the ⅚ of the surface of our Earth is water. 5

to 1, therefore, that the bullet is more likely to be lying this moment at the bottom of the Atlantic or the Pacific than anywhere else on the surface of our globe. Besides, it may have sunk into some weak point of the surface, at the early epoch when the crust of the Earth had not acquired sufficient solidity.'

'Captain,' said Ardan, turning with a smile to M'Nicholl; 'no use in trying to catch Barby; slippery as an eel, he has an answer for everything. Still I have a theory on the subject myself, which I think it no harm to ventilate. It is this: The Selenites have never sent us any projectile at all, simply because they had no gunpowder: being older and wiser than we, they were never such fools as to invent any. – But, what's that? Diana howling for her breakfast! Good! Like genuine scientific men, while squabbling over nonsense, we let the poor animals die of hunger. Excuse us, Diana; it is not the first time the little suffer from the senseless disputes of the great.'

So saying he laid before the animal a very toothsome pie, and contemplated with evident pleasure her very successful efforts towards its hasty and complete disappearance.

'Looking at Diana,' he went on, 'makes me almost wish we had made a Noah's Ark of our Projectile by introducing into it a pair of all the domestic animals!'

'Not room enough,' observed Barbican.

'No doubt,' remarked the Captain, 'the ox, the cow, the horse, the goat, all the ruminating animals would be very useful in the Lunar continent. But we couldn't turn our Projectile into a stable, you know.'

'Still, we might have made room for a pair of poor little donkeys!' observed Ardan; 'how I love the poor beasts. Fellow feeling, you will say. No doubt, but there really is no animal I pity more. They are the most ill-treated brutes in all creation. They are not only banged during life; they are banged worse after death!'

'Hey! How do you make that out?' asked his companions, surprised.

'Because we make their skins into drum heads!' replied Ardan, with an air, as if answering a conundrum.

Barbican and M'Nicholl could hardly help laughing at the absurd reply of their lively companion, but their hilarity was soon stopped by the expression his face assumed as he bent over Satellite's body, where it lay stretched on the sofa.

'What's the matter now?' asked Barbican.

'Satellite's attack is over,' replied Ardan.

'Good!' said M'Nicholl, misunderstanding him.

'Yes, I suppose it is good for the poor fellow,' observed Ardan, in melancholy accents. 'Life with one's skull broken is hardly an enviable possession. Our grand acclimatization project is knocked sky high, in more senses than one!'

There was no doubt of the poor dog's death. The expression of Ardan's countenance, as he looked at his friends, was of a very rueful order.

'Well,' said the practical Barbican, 'there's no help for that now; the next thing to be done is to get rid of the body. We can't keep it here with us forty-eight hours longer.'

'Of course not,' replied the Captain, 'nor need we; our lights, being provided with hinges, can be lifted back. What is to prevent us from opening one of them, and flinging the body out through it!'

The President of the Gun Club reflected a few minutes; then he spoke:

'Yes, it can be done; but we must take the most careful precautions.'

'Why so?' asked Ardan.

'For two simple reasons;' replied Barbican; 'the first refers to the air enclosed in the Projectile, and of which we must be very careful to lose only the least possible quantity.'

'But as we manufacture air ourselves!' objected Ardan.

'We manufacture air only partly, friend Michael,' replied Barbican. 'We manufacture only oxygen; we can't supply nitrogen – By the bye, Ardan, won't you watch the apparatus carefully every now and then to see that the oxygen is not generated too freely. Very serious consequences would attend an immoderate supply of oxygen – No, we can't manufacture nitrogen, which is so absolutely necessary for our air and which might escape readily through the open windows.'

'What! the few seconds we should require for flinging out poor Satellite?'

'A very few seconds indeed they should be,' said Barbican, very gravely.

'Your second reason?' asked Ardan.

'The second reason is, that we must not allow the external cold, which must be exceedingly great, to penetrate into our Projectile and freeze us alive.'

'But the Sun, you know—'

'Yes, the Sun heats our Projectile, but it does not heat the vacuum through which we are now floating. Where there is no air there can neither be heat nor light; just as wherever the rays of the Sun do not arrive directly, it must be both cold and dark. The temperature around us, if there be anything that can be called temperature, is produced solely by stellar radiation. I need not say how low that is in the scale, or that it would be the temperature to which our Earth should fall, if the Sun were suddenly extinguished.'

'Little fear of that for a few more million years,' said M'Nicholl.

'Who can tell?' asked Ardan. 'Besides, even admitting that the Sun will not soon be extinguished, what is to prevent the Earth from shooting away from him?'

'Let friend Michael speak,' said Barbican, with a smile, to the Captain; 'we may learn something.'

'Certainly you may,' continued the Frenchman, 'if you have room for anything new. Were we not struck by a comet's tail in 1861?'

'So it was said, anyhow,' observed the Captain. 'I well remember what nonsense there was in the papers about the "phosphorescent auroral glare"'.

'Well,' continued the Frenchman, 'suppose the comet of 1861 influenced the Earth by an attraction superior to the Sun's. What would be the consequence? Would not the Earth follow the attracting body, become its satellite, and thus at last be dragged off to such a distance that the Sun's rays could no longer excite heat on her surface?'

'Well, that might possibly occur,' said Barbican slowly, 'but even then I question if the consequences would be so terrible as you seem to apprehend.'

'Why not?'

'Because the cold and the heat might still manage to be nearly equalized on our globe. It has been calculated that, had the Earth been carried off by the comet of '61, when arrived at her greatest distance, she would have experienced a temperature hardly sixteen times greater than the heat we receive from the Moon, which, as everybody knows, produces no appreciable effect, even when concentrated to a focus by the most powerful lenses.'

'Well then,' exclaimed Ardan, 'at such a temperature—'

'Wait a moment,' replied Barbican. 'Have you never heard of the principle of compensation? Listen to another calculation. Had the Earth been dragged along with the comet, it has been calculated that at her perihelion, or nearest point to the Sun, she would have to endure a heat 28,000 times greater than our mean summer temperature. But this heat, fully capable of turning the rocks into glass and the oceans into vapour, before proceeding to such extremity, must have first formed a thick interposing ring of clouds, and thus considerably modified the excessive temperature. Therefore, between the extreme cold of the aphelion and the excessive heat of the perihelion, by the great law of compensation, it is probable that the mean temperature would be tolerably endurable.'

'At how many degrees is the temperature of the interplanetary space estimated?' asked M'Nicholl.

'Some time ago,' replied Barbican, 'this temperature was considered to be very low indeed – millions and millions of degrees below zero. But Fourrier of Auxerre, a distinguished member of the *Académie des Sciences*, whose *Mémoires* on the temperature of the Planetary spaces appeared about 1827, reduced these figures to considerably diminished proportions. According to his careful estimation, the temperature of space is not much lower than 70 or 80 degrees Fahr. below zero.'

'No more?' asked Ardan.

'No more,' answered Barbican, 'though I must acknowledge we have only his word for it, as the *Mémoire* in which he had recorded all the elements of that important determination, has been lost somewhere, and is no longer to be found.'

'I don't attach the slightest importance to his, or to any man's words, unless they are sustained by reliable evidence,' exclaimed M'Nicholl. 'Besides, if I'm not very much mistaken, Pouillet – another countryman of yours, Ardan, and an Academician as well as Fourrier – esteems the temperature of interplanetary spaces to be at least 256° Fahr. below zero. This we can easily verify for ourselves this moment by actual experiment.'

'Not just now exactly,' observed Barbican, 'for the solar rays, striking our Projectile directly, would give us a very elevated instead of a very low temperature. But once arrived at the Moon, during those nights fifteen days long, which each of her faces experiences alternately, we shall have plenty of time to make an experiment with every condition in our favour. To be sure, our Satellite is at present moving in a vacuum.'

'A vacuum?' asked Ardan; 'a perfect vacuum?'

'Well, a perfect vacuum as far as air is concerned.'

'But is the air replaced by nothing?'

'Oh yes,' replied Barbican. 'By ether.'

'Ah, ether! and what, pray, is ether?'

'Ether, friend Michael, is an elastic gas consisting of imponderable atoms, which, as we are told by works on molecular physics, are, in proportion to their size, as far apart as the celestial bodies are from each other in space. This distance is less than the 1/3000000 x 1/1000', or the one trillionth of a foot. The vibrations of the molecules of this ether produce the sensations of light and heat, by making 430 trillions of undulations per second, each undulation being hardly more than the one ten-millionth of an inch in width.'

'Trillions per second! ten-millionths of an inch in width!' cried Ardan. 'These oscillations have been very neatly counted and ticketed, and checked off! Ah, friend Barbican,' continued the Frenchman, shaking his head, 'these numbers are just tremendous guesses, frightening the ear but revealing nothing to the intelligence.'

'To get ideas, however, we must calculate—'

'No, no!' interrupted Ardan: 'not calculate, but compare. A trillion tells you nothing – Comparison, everything. For instance, you say, the volume of *Uranus* is 76 times greater than the Earth's; *Saturn's* 900 times greater; *Jupiter's* 1,300 times greater; the Sun's 1,300 thousand times greater – You may tell me all that till I'm tired hearing it, and I shall still be almost as ignorant as ever. For my part I prefer to be told one of those simple comparisons that I find in the old almanacs: The Sun is a globe two feet in diameter; *Jupiter*, a good sized orange; *Saturn*, a smaller orange; *Neptune*, a plum; *Uranus*, a good sized cherry; the Earth, a pea; *Venus*, also a pea but somewhat smaller; *Mars*, a large pin's head; *Mercury*, a mustard seed; *Juno, Ceres, Vesta, Pallas*, and the other asteroids so many grains of sand. Be told something like that, and you have got at least the tail of an idea!'

This learned burst of Ardan's had the natural effect of making his hearers forget what they had been arguing about, and they therefore proceeded at once to dispose of Satellite's body. It was a simple matter enough – no more than to fling it out of the Projectile into space, just as the sailors get rid of a dead body by throwing it into the sea. Only in this operation they had to act, as Barbican recommended, with the utmost care and dispatch, so as to lose as little as possible of the internal air, which, by its great elasticity, would violently strive to escape. The bolts of the floor-light, which was more than a foot in diameter, were carefully unscrewed, while Ardan, a good deal affected, prepared to launch his dog's body into space. The glass, worked by a powerful lever which enabled it to overcome the pressure of the enclosed air, turned quickly on its hinges, and poor Satellite was dropped out. The whole operation was so well managed that very little air escaped, and ever afterwards Barbican employed the same means to rid the Projectile of all the litter and other useless matter by which it was occasionally encumbered.

The evening of this third of December wore away without further incident. As soon as Barbican had announced that the Projectile was still winging its way, though with retarded velocity, towards the lunar disc, the travellers quietly retired to rest.

CHAPTER VI
Instructive Conversation

ON THE FOURTH of December, the Projectile chronometers marked five o'clock in the morning, just as the travellers woke up from a pleasant slumber. They had now been 54 hours on their journey. As to lapse of *time*, they had passed not much more than half of the number of hours during which their trip was to last; but, as to lapse of *space*, they had already accomplished very nearly the seven-tenths of their passage. This difference between time and distance was due to the regular retardation of their velocity.

They looked at the earth through the floor-light, but it was little more than visible – a black spot drowned in the solar rays. No longer any sign of a crescent, no longer any sign of ashy light. Next day, towards midnight, the Earth was to be *new*, at the precise moment when the Moon was to be *full*. Overhead, they could see the Queen of Night coming nearer and nearer to the line followed by the Projectile, and evidently approaching the point where both should meet at the appointed moment. All around, the black vault of heaven was dotted with luminous points which seemed to move somewhat, though, of course, in their extreme distance their relative size underwent no change. The Sun and the stars looked exactly as they had appeared when observed from the Earth. The Moon indeed had become considerably enlarged in size, but the travellers' telescopes were still too weak to enable them to make any important observation regarding the nature of her surface, or that might determine her topographical or geological features.

Naturally, therefore, the time slipped away in endless conversation. The Moon, of course, was the chief topic. Each one contributed his share of peculiar information, or peculiar ignorance, as the case might be. Barbican and M'Nicholl always treated the subject gravely, as became learned scientists, but Ardan preferred to look on things with the eye of fancy. The Projectile, its situation, its direction, the incidents possible to occur, the precautions necessary to take in order to break the fall on the Moon's surface – these and many other subjects furnished endless food for constant debate and inexhaustible conjectures.

For instance, at breakfast that morning, a question of Ardan's regarding the Projectile drew from Barbican an answer curious enough to be reported.

'Suppose, on the night that we were shot up from Stony Hill,' said Ardan, 'suppose the Projectile had encountered some obstacle powerful enough to stop it – what would be the consequence of the sudden halt?'

'But,' replied Barbican, 'I don't understand what obstacle it could have met powerful enough to stop it.'

'Suppose some obstacle, for the sake of argument,' said Ardan.

'Suppose what can't be supposed,' replied the matter-of-fact Barbican, 'what cannot possibly be supposed, unless indeed the original impulse proved too weak. In that case, the velocity would have decreased by degrees, but the Projectile itself would not have suddenly stopped.'

'Suppose it had struck against some body in space.'

'What body, for instance?'

'Well, that enormous bolide which we met.'

'Oh!' hastily observed the Captain, 'the Projectile would have been dashed into a thousand pieces and we along with it.'

'Better than that,' observed Barbican; 'we should have been burned alive.'

'Burned alive!' laughed Ardan. 'What a pity we missed so interesting an experiment! How I should have liked to find out how it felt!'

'You would not have much time to record your observations, friend Michael, I assure you,' observed Barbican. 'The case is plain enough. Heat and motion are convertible terms. What do we mean by heating water? Simply giving increased, in fact, violent motion to its molecules.'

'Well!' exclaimed the Frenchman, 'that's an ingenious theory any how!'

'Not only ingenious but correct, my dear friend, for it completely explains all the phenomena of caloric. Heat is nothing but molecular movement, the violent oscillation of the particles of a body. When you apply the brakes to the train, the train stops. But what has become of its motion? It turns into heat and makes the brakes hot. Why do people grease the axles? To hinder them from getting too hot, which they assuredly would become if friction was allowed to obstruct the motion. You understand, don't you?'

'Don't I though?' replied Ardan, apparently in earnest. 'Let me show you how thoroughly. When I have been running hard and long, I feel myself perspiring like a bull and hot as a furnace. Why am I then forced to stop? Simply because my motion has been transformed into heat! Of course, I understand all about it!'

Barbican smiled a moment at this comical illustration of his theory and then went on:

'Accordingly, in case of a collision it would have been all over instantly with our Projectile. You have seen what becomes of the bullet that strikes the iron target. It is flattened out of all shape; sometimes it is even melted into a thin film. Its motion has been turned into heat. Therefore, I maintain that if our Projectile had struck that bolide, its velocity, suddenly checked, would have given rise to a heat capable of completely volatilizing it in less than a second.'

'Not a doubt of it!' said the Captain. 'President,' he added after a moment, 'haven't they calculated what would be the result, if the Earth were suddenly brought to a stand-still in her journey, through her orbit?'

'It has been calculated,' answered Barbican, 'that in such a case so much heat would be developed as would instantly reduce her to vapour.'

'Hm!' exclaimed Ardan; 'a remarkably simple way for putting an end to the world!'

'And supposing the Earth to fall into the Sun?' asked the Captain.

'Such a fall,' answered Barbican, 'according to the calculations of Tyndall and Thomson, would develop an amount of heat equal to that produced by sixteen hundred globes of burning coal, each globe equal in size to the earth itself. Furthermore such a fall would supply the Sun with at least as much heat as he expends in a hundred years!'

'A hundred years! Good! Nothing like accuracy!' cried Ardan. 'Such infallible calculators as Messrs. Tyndall and Thomson I can easily excuse for any airs they may give themselves. They must be of an order much higher than that of ordinary mortals like us!'

'I would not answer myself for the accuracy of such intricate problems,' quietly observed Barbican; 'but there is no doubt whatever regarding one fact: motion suddenly interrupted always develops heat. And this has given rise to another theory regarding the maintenance of the Sun's temperature at a constant point. An incessant rain of bolides falling on his surface compensates sufficiently for the heat that he is continually giving forth. It has been calculated—'

'Good Lord deliver us!' cried Ardan, putting his hands to his ears: 'here comes Tyndall and Thomson again!'

'It has been calculated,' continued Barbican, not heeding the interruption, 'that the shock of every bolide drawn to the Sun's surface by gravity, must produce there an amount of heat equal to that of the combustion of four thousand blocks of coal, each the same size as the falling bolide.'

'I'll wager another cent that our bold savants calculated the heat of the Sun himself,' cried Ardan, with an incredulous laugh.

'That is precisely what they have done,' answered Barbican

referring to his memorandum book; 'the heat emitted by the Sun,' he continued, 'is exactly that which would be produced by the combustion of a layer of coal enveloping the Sun's surface, like an atmosphere, 17 miles in thickness.'

'Well done! and such heat would be capable of—?'

'Of melting in an hour a stratum of ice 2,400 feet thick, or, according to another calculation, of raising a globe of ice-cold water, 3 times the size of our Earth, to the boiling point in an hour.'

'Why not calculate the exact fraction of a second it would take to cook a couple of eggs?' laughed Ardan. 'I should as soon believe in one calculation as in the other. – But – by the by – why does not such extreme heat cook us all up like so many beefsteaks?'

'For two very good and sufficient reasons,' answered Barbican. 'In the first place, the terrestrial atmosphere absorbs the $4/10$ of the solar heat. In the second, the quantity of solar heat intercepted by the Earth is only about the two billionth part of all that is radiated.'

'How fortunate to have such a handy thing as an atmosphere around us,' cried the Frenchman; 'it not only enables us to breathe, but it actually keeps us from sizzling up like griskins.'

'Yes,' said the Captain, 'but unfortunately we can't say so much for the Moon.'

'Oh pshaw!' cried Ardan, always full of confidence. 'It's all right there too! The Moon is either inhabited or she is not. If she is, the inhabitants must breathe. If she is not, there must be oxygen enough left for we, us and co., even if we should have to go after it to the bottom of the ravines, where, by its gravity, it must have accumulated! So much the better! we shall not have to climb those thundering mountains!'

So saying, he jumped up and began to gaze with considerable interest on the lunar disc, which just then was glittering with dazzling brightness.

'By Jove!' he exclaimed at length; 'it must be pretty hot up there!'

'I should think so,' observed the Captain; 'especially when you remember that the day up there lasts 360 hours!'

'Yes,' observed Barbican, 'but remember on the other hand that the nights are just as long, and, as the heat escapes by radiation, the mean temperature cannot be much greater than that of interplanetary space.'

'A high old place for living in!' cried Ardan. 'No matter! I wish we were there now! Wouldn't it be jolly, dear boys, to have old Mother Earth for our Moon, to see her always on our sky, never rising, never setting, never undergoing any change except from New Earth to Last Quarter! Would not it be fun to trace the shape of our great Oceans and Continents, and to say: "there is the Mediterranean! there is China! there is the gulf of Mexico! there is the white line of the Rocky Mountains where old Marston is watching for us with his big telescope!" Then we should see every line, and brightness, and shadow fade away by degrees, as she came nearer and nearer to the Sun, until at last she sat completely lost in his dazzling rays! But – by the way – Barbican, are there any eclipses in the Moon?'

'O yes; solar eclipses' replied Barbican, 'must always occur whenever the centres of the three heavenly bodies are in the same line, the Earth occupying the middle place. However, such eclipses must always be annular, as the Earth, projected like a screen on the solar disc, allows more than half of the Sun to be still visible.'

'How is that?' asked M'Nicholl, 'no total eclipses in the Moon? Surely the cone of the Earth's shadow must extend far enough to envelop her surface?'

'It does reach her, in one sense,' replied Barbican, 'but it does not in another. Remember the great refraction of the solar rays that must be produced by the Earth's atmosphere. It is easy to show that this refraction prevents the Sun from ever being totally invisible. See here!' he continued, pulling out his tablets, 'Let a represent the horizontal parallax, and b the half of the Sun's apparent diameter—'

CHAPTER VI

'Ouch!' cried the Frenchman, making a wry face, 'here comes Mr. x square riding to the mischief on a pair of double zeros again! Talk English, or Yankee, or Dutch, or Greek, and I'm your man! Even a little Arabic I can digest! But hang me, if I can endure your Algebra!'

'Well then, talking Yankee,' replied Barbican with a smile, 'the mean distance of the Moon from the Earth being sixty terrestrial radii, the length of the conic shadow, in consequence of atmospheric refraction, is reduced to less than forty-two radii. Consequently, at the moment of an eclipse, the Moon is far beyond the reach of the real shadow, so that she can see not only the border rays of the Sun, but even those proceeding from his very centre.'

'Oh then,' cried Ardan with a loud laugh, 'we have an eclipse of the Sun at the moment when the Sun is quite visible! Isn't that very like a bull, Mr. Philosopher Barbican?'

'Yet it is perfectly true notwithstanding,' answered Barbican. 'At such a moment the Sun is not eclipsed, because we can see him: and then again he is eclipsed because we see him only by means of a few of his rays, and even these have lost nearly all their brightness in their passage through the terrestrial atmosphere!'

'Barbican is right, friend Michael,' observed the Captain slowly: 'the same phenomenon occurs on earth every morning at sunrise, when refraction shows us

'the Sun new ris'n
Looking through the horizontal misty air,
Shorn of his beams."

'He must be right,' said Ardan, who, to do him justice, though quick at seeing a reason, was quicker to acknowledge its justice: 'yes, he must be right, because I begin to understand at last very clearly what he really meant. However, we can judge for ourselves when we get there. – But, apropos of nothing, tell me, Barbican, what do you think of the Moon being an ancient comet, which had come so far within the sphere of the Earth's attraction as to be kept there and turned into a satellite?'

'Well, that *is* an original idea!' said Barbican with a smile.

'My ideas generally are of that category,' observed Ardan with an affectation of dry pomposity.

'Not this time, however, friend Michael,' observed M'Nicholl.

'Oh! I'm a plagiarist, am I?' asked the Frenchman, pretending to be irritated.

'Well, something very like it,' observed M'Nicholl quietly. 'Apollonius Rhodius, as I read one evening in the Philadelphia Library, speaks of the Arcadians of Greece having a tradition that their ancestors were so ancient that they inhabited the Earth long before the Moon had ever become our satellite. They therefore called them Προσεληνοι or *Ante-lunarians*. Now starting with some such wild notion as this, certain scientists have looked on the Moon as an ancient comet brought close enough to the Earth to be retained in its orbit by terrestrial attraction.'

'Why may not there be something plausible in such a hypothesis?' asked Ardan with some curiosity.

'There is nothing whatever in it,' replied Barbican decidedly: 'a simple proof is the fact that the Moon does not retain the slightest trace of the vaporous envelope by which comets are always surrounded.'

'Lost her tail you mean,' said Ardan. 'Pooh! Easy to account for that! It might have got cut off by coming too close to the Sun!'

'It might, friend Michael, but an amputation by such means is not very likely.'

'No? Why not?'

'Because – because – By Jove, I can't say, because I don't know,' cried Barbican with a quiet smile on his countenance.

'Oh what a lot of volumes,' cried Ardan, 'could be made out of what we don't know!'

'At present, for instance,' observed M'Nicholl, 'I don't know what o'clock it is.'

'Three o'clock!' said Barbican, glancing at his chronometer.

'No!' cried Ardan in surprise. 'Bless us! How rapidly the time passes when we are engaged in scientific conversation! Ouf! I'm getting decidedly too learned! I feel as if I had swallowed a library!'

'I feel,' observed M'Nicholl, 'as if I had been listening to a lecture on Astronomy in the *Star* course.'

'Better stir around a little more,' said the Frenchman; 'fatigue of body is the best antidote to such severe mental labour as ours. I'll run up the ladder a bit.' So saying, he paid another visit to the upper portion of the Projectile and remained there awhile whistling *Malbrouk*, whilst his companions amused themselves in looking through the floor window.

Ardan was coming down the ladder, when his whistling was cut short by a sudden exclamation of surprise.

'What's the matter?' asked Barbican quickly, as he looked up and saw the Frenchman pointing to something outside the Projectile.

Approaching the window, Barbican saw with much surprise a sort of flattened bag floating in space and only a few yards off. It seemed perfectly motionless, and, consequently, the travellers knew that it must be animated by the same ascensional movement as themselves.

'What on earth can such a consarn be, Barbican?' asked Ardan, who every now and then liked to ventilate his stock of American slang. 'Is it one of those particles of meteoric matter you were speaking of just now, caught within the sphere of our Projectile's attraction and accompanying us to the Moon?'

'What I am surprised at,' observed the Captain, 'is that though the specific gravity of that body is far inferior to that of our Projectile, it moves with exactly the same velocity.'

'Captain,' said Barbican, after a moment's reflection, 'I know no more what that object is than you do, but I can understand very well why it keeps abreast with the Projectile.'

'Very well then, why?'

'Because, my dear Captain, we are moving through a vacuum, and because all bodies fall or move – the same thing – with equal velocity through a vacuum, no matter what may be their shape or their specific gravity. It is the air alone that makes a difference of weight. Produce an artificial vacuum in a glass tube and you will see that all objects whatever falling through, whether bits of feather or grains of shot, move with precisely the same rapidity. Up here, in space, like cause and like effect.'

'Correct,' assented M'Nicholl. 'Everything therefore that we shall throw out of the Projectile is bound to accompany us to the Moon.'

'Well, we *were* smart!' cried Ardan suddenly.

'How so, friend Michael?' asked Barbican.

'Why not have packed the Projectile with ever so many useful objects, books, instruments, tools, et cetera, and fling them out into space once we were fairly started! They would have all followed us safely! Nothing would have been lost! And – now I think on it – why not fling ourselves out through the window? Shouldn't we be as safe out there as that bolide? What fun it would be to feel ourselves sustained and upborne in the ether, more highly favoured even than the birds, who must keep on flapping their wings continually to prevent themselves from falling!'

'Very true, my dear boy,' observed Barbican; 'but how could we breathe?'

'It's a fact,' exclaimed the Frenchman. 'Hang the air for spoiling our fun! So we must remain shut up in our Projectile?'

'Not a doubt of it!'

'Oh Thunder!' roared Ardan, suddenly striking his forehead.

'What ails you?' asked the Captain, somewhat surprised.

'Now I know what that bolide of ours is! Why didn't we think of it before? It is no asteroid! It is no particle of meteoric matter! Nor is it a piece of a shattered planet!'

'What is it then?' asked both of his companions in one voice.

'It is nothing more or less than the body of the dog that we threw out yesterday!'

So in fact it was. That shapeless, unrecognizable mass, melted, expunged, flat as a bladder under an unexhausted receiver, drained of its air, was poor Satellite's body, flying like a rocket through space, and rising higher and higher in close company with the rapidly ascending Projectile!

CHAPTER VII
A High Old Time

A new phenomenon, therefore, strange but logical, startling but admitting of easy explanation, was now presented to their view, affording a fresh subject for lively discussion. Not that they disputed much about it. They soon agreed on a principle from which they readily deducted the following general law: *Every object thrown out of the Projectile should partake of the Projectile's motion: it should therefore follow the same path, and never cease to move until the Projectile itself came to a stand-still.*

But, in sober truth, they were at anything but a loss of subjects of warm discussion. As the end of their journey began to approach, their senses became keener and their sensations vivider. Steeled against surprise, they looked for the unexpected, the strange, the startling; and the only thing at which they would have wondered would be to be five minutes without having something new to wonder at. Their excited imaginations flew far ahead of the Projectile, whose velocity, by the way, began to be retarded very decidedly by this time, though, of course, the travellers had as yet no means to become aware of it. The Moon's size on the sky was meantime getting larger and larger; her apparent distance was growing shorter and shorter, until at last they could almost imagine that by putting their hands out they could nearly touch her.

Next morning, December 5th, all were up and dressed at a very early hour. This was to be the last day of their journey, if all calculations were correct. That very night, at 12 o'clock, within nineteen hours at furthest, at the very moment of Full Moon, they were to reach her resplendent surface. At that hour was to be completed the most extraordinary journey ever undertaken by man in ancient or modern times. Naturally enough, therefore, they found themselves unable to sleep after four o'clock in the morning; peering upwards through the windows now visibly glittering under the rays of the Moon, they spent some very exciting hours in gazing at her slowly enlarging disc, and shouting at her with confident and joyful hurrahs.

The majestic Queen of the Stars had now risen so high in the spangled heavens that she could hardly rise higher. In a few degrees more she would reach the exact point of space where her junction with the Projectile was to be effected. According to his own observations, Barbican calculated that they should strike her in the northern hemisphere, where her plains, or *seas* as they are called, are immense, and her mountains are comparatively rare. This, of course, would be so much the more favourable, if, as was to be apprehended, the lunar atmosphere was confined exclusively to the low lands.

'Besides,' as Ardan observed, 'a plain is a more suitable landing place than a mountain. A Selenite deposited on the top of Mount Everest or even on Mont Blanc, could hardly be considered, in strict language, to have arrived on Earth.'

'Not to talk,' added M'Nicholl, 'of the comfort of the thing! When you land on a plain, there you are. When you land on a peak or on a steep mountain side, where are you? Tumbling over an embankment with the train going forty miles an hour, would be nothing to it.'

'Therefore, Captain Barbican,' cried the Frenchman, 'as we should like to appear before the Selenites in full skins, please land us in the snug though unromantic North. We shall have time enough to break our necks in the South.'

Barbican made no reply to his companions, because a new reflection had begun to trouble him, to talk about which would have done no good. There was certainly something wrong. The Projectile was evidently heading towards the northern hemisphere of the Moon. What did this prove? Clearly, a deviation resulting from some cause. The bullet, lodged, aimed, and fired with the most careful mathematical precision, had been calculated to reach the very centre of the Moon's disc. Clearly it was not going to the centre now. What could have produced the deviation? This Barbican could not tell; nor could he even determine its extent, having no points of sight by which to make his observations. For the present he tried to console himself with the hope that the deviation of the Projectile would be followed by no worse consequence than carrying them towards the northern border of the Moon, where for several reasons it would be comparatively easier to alight. Carefully avoiding, therefore, the use of any expression which might needlessly alarm his companions, he continued to observe the Moon as carefully as he could, hoping every moment to find some grounds for believing that the deviation from the centre was only a slight one. He almost shuddered at the thought of what would be their situation, if the bullet, missing its aim, should pass the Moon, and plunge into the interplanetary space beyond it.

As he continued to gaze, the Moon, instead of presenting the usual flatness of her disc, began decidedly to show a surface somewhat convex. Had the Sun been shining on her obliquely, the shadows would have certainly thrown the great mountains into strong relief. The eye could then bury itself deep in the yawning chasms of the craters, and easily follow the cracks, streaks, and ridges which stripe, flecker, and bar the immensity of her plains. But for the present all relief was lost in the dazzling glare. The Captain could hardly distinguish even those dark spots that impart to the full Moon some resemblance to the human face.

'Face!' cried Ardan: 'well, a very fanciful eye may detect a face, though, for the sake of Apollo's beauteous sister, I regret to say, a terribly pockmarked one!'

The travellers, now evidently approaching the end of their journey, observed the rapidly increasing world above them with newer and greater curiosity every moment. Their fancies enkindled at the sight of the new and strange scenes dimly presented to their view. In imagination they climbed to the summit of this lofty peak. They let themselves down to the abyss of that yawning crater. Here they imagined they saw vast seas hardly kept in their basins by a rarefied atmosphere; there they thought they could trace mighty rivers bearing to vast oceans the tribute of the snowy mountains. In the first promptings of their eager curiosity, they peered greedily into her cavernous depths, and almost expected, amidst the death-like hush of inaudible nature, to surprise some sound from the mystic orb floating up there in eternal silence through a boundless ocean of never ending vacuum.

This last day of their journey left their memories stored with thrilling recollections. They took careful note of the slightest details. As they neared their destination, they felt themselves invaded by a vague, undefined restlessness. But this restlessness would have given way to decided uneasiness, if they had known at what a slow rate they were travelling. They would have surely concluded that their present velocity would never be able to take them as far as the neutral point, not to talk of passing it. The reason of such considerable retardation was, that by this time the Projectile had reached such a great distance from the Earth that it had hardly any weight. But even this weight, such as it was, was to be diminished still further, and finally, to vanish altogether as soon as the bullet reached the neutral point, where the two attractions, terrestrial and lunar, should counteract each other with new and surprising effects.

Notwithstanding the absorbing nature of his observations, Ardan never forgot to prepare breakfast with his usual punctuality. It was eaten readily and relished heartily. Nothing could be more exquisite than his calf's foot jelly liquefied and prepared by gas heat, except perhaps his meat biscuits of preserved Texas beef and Southdown mutton. A bottle of Château Yquem and another of

Clos de Vougeot, both of superlative excellence in quality and flavour, crowned the repast. Their vicinity to the Moon and their incessant glancing at her surface did not prevent the travellers from touching each other's glasses merrily and often. Ardan took occasion to remark that the lunar vineyards – if any existed – must be magnificent, considering the intense solar heat they continually experienced. Not that he counted on them too confidently, for he told his friends that to provide for the worst he had supplied himself with a few cases of the best vintages of Médoc and the Côte d'Or, of which the bottles, then under discussion, might be taken as very favourable specimens.

The Reiset and Regnault apparatus for purifying the air worked splendidly, and maintained the atmosphere in a perfectly sanitary condition. Not an atom of carbonic acid could resist the caustic potash; and as for the oxygen, according to M'Nicholl's expression, 'it was A prime number one!'

The small quantity of watery vapour enclosed in the Projectile did no more harm than serving to temper the dryness of the air: many a splendid *salon* in New York, London, or Paris, and many an auditorium, even of theatre, opera house or Academy of Music, could be considered its inferior in what concerned its hygienic condition.

To keep it in perfect working order, the apparatus should be carefully attended to. This, Ardan looked on as his own peculiar occupation. He was never tired regulating the tubes, trying the taps, and testing the heat of the gas by the pyrometer. So far everything had worked satisfactorily, and the travellers, following the example of their friend Marston on a previous occasion, began to get so stout that their own mothers would not know them in another month, should their imprisonment last so long. Ardan said they all looked so sleek and thriving that he was reminded forcibly of a nice lot of pigs fattening in a pen for a country fair. But how long was this good fortune of theirs going to last?

Whenever they took their eyes off the Moon, they could not help noticing that they were still attended outside by the spectre of Satellite's corpse and by the other refuse of the Projectile. An occasional melancholy howl also attested Diana's recognition of her companion's unhappy fate. The travellers saw with surprise that these waifs still seemed perfectly motionless in space, and kept their respective distances apart as mathematically as if they had been fastened with nails to a stone wall.

'I tell you what, dear boys;' observed Ardan, commenting on this curious phenomenon; 'if the concussion had been a little too violent for one of us that night, his survivors would have been seriously embarrassed in trying to get rid of his remains. With no earth to cover him up, no sea to plunge him into, his corpse would never disappear from view, but would pursue us day and night, grim and ghastly like an avenging ghost!'

'Ugh!' said the Captain, shuddering at the idea.

'But, by the bye, Barbican!' cried the Frenchman, dropping the subject with his usual abruptness; 'you have forgotten something else! Why didn't you bring a scaphander and an air pump? I could then venture out of the Projectile as readily and as safely as the diver leaves his boat and walks about on the bottom of the river! What fun to float in the midst of that mysterious ether! to steep myself, aye, actually to revel in the pure rays of the glorious sun! I should have ventured out on the very point of the Projectile, and there I should have danced and postured and kicked and bobbed and capered in a style that Taglioni never dreamed of!'

'Shouldn't I like to see you!' cried the Captain grimly, smiling at the idea.

'You would not see him long!' observed Barbican quietly. 'The air confined in his body, freed from external pressure, would burst him like a shell, or like a balloon that suddenly rises to too great a height in the air! A scaphander would have been a fatal gift. Don't regret its absence, friend Michael; never forget this axiom: *As long as we are floating in empty space, the only spot where safety is possible is inside the Projectile!'*

The words 'possible' and 'impossible' always grated on Ardan's ears. If he had been a lexicographer, he would have rigidly excluded them from his dictionary, both as meaningless and useless. He was preparing an answer for Barbican, when he was cut out by a sudden observation from M'Nicholl.

'See here, friends!' cried the Captain; 'this going to the Moon is all very well, but how shall we get back?'

His listeners looked at each other with a surprised and perplexed air. The question, though a very natural one, now appeared to have presented itself to their consideration absolutely for the first time.

'What do you mean by such a question, Captain?' asked Barbican in a grave judicial tone.

'Mac, my boy,' said Ardan seriously, 'don't it strike you as a little out of order to ask how you are to return when you have not got there yet?'

'I don't ask the question with any idea of backing out,' observed the Captain quietly; 'as a matter of purely scientific inquiry, I repeat my question: how are we to return?'

'I don't know,' replied Barbican promptly.

'For my part,' said Ardan; 'if I had known how to get back, I should have never come at all!'

'Well! of all the answers!' said the Captain, lifting his hands and shaking his head.

'The best under the circumstances;' observed Barbican; 'and I shall further observe that such a question as yours at present is both useless and uncalled for. On some future occasion, when we shall consider it advisable to return, the question will be in order, and we shall discuss it with all the attention it deserves. Though the Columbiad is at Stony Hill, the Projectile will still be in the Moon.'

'Much we shall gain by that! A bullet without a gun!'

'The gun we can make and the powder too!' replied Barbican confidently. 'Metal and sulphur and charcoal and saltpetre are likely enough to be present in sufficient quantities beneath the Moon's surface. Besides, to return is a problem of comparatively easy solution: we should have to overcome the lunar attraction only – a slight matter – the rest of the business would be readily done by gravity.'

'Enough said on the subject!' exclaimed Ardan curtly; 'how to get back is indefinitely postponed! How to communicate with our friends on the Earth, is another matter, and, as it seems to me, an extremely easy one.'

'Let us hear the very easy means by which you propose to communicate with our friends on Earth,' asked the Captain, with a sneer, for he was by this time a little out of humour.

'By means of bolides ejected from the lunar volcanoes,' replied the Frenchman without an instant's hesitation.

'Well said, friend Ardan,' exclaimed Barbican. 'I am quite disposed to acknowledge the feasibility of your plan. Laplace has calculated that a force five times greater than that of an ordinary cannon would be sufficient to send a bolide from the Moon to the Earth. Now there is no cannon that can vie in force with even the smallest volcano.'

'Hurrah!' cried Ardan, delighted at his success; 'just imagine the pleasure of sending our letters postage free! But – oh! what a splendid idea! – Dolts that we were for not thinking of it sooner!'

'Let us have the splendid idea!' cried the Captain, with some of his old acrimony.

'Why didn't we fasten a wire to the Projectile?' asked Ardan, triumphantly, 'It would have enabled us to exchange telegrams with the Earth!'

'Ho! ho! ho!' roared the Captain, rapidly recovering his good humour; 'decidedly the best joke of the season! Ha! ha! ha! Of course you have calculated the weight of a wire 240 thousand miles long?'

'No matter about its weight!' cried the Frenchman impetuously; 'we should have laughed at its weight! We could have tripled the charge of the Columbiad; we could have quadrupled it! – aye, quintupled it, if necessary!' he added in tones evidently increasing in loudness and violence.

'Yes, friend Michael,' observed Barbican; 'but there is a slight and unfortunately a fatal defect in your project. The Earth, by its rotation, would have wrapped our wire around herself, like thread around a spool, and dragged us back almost with the speed of lightning!'

'By the Nine gods of Porsena!' cried Ardan, 'something is wrong with my head to-day! My brain is out of joint, and I am making as nice a mess of things as my friend Marston was ever capable of! By the bye – talking of Marston – if we never return to the Earth, what is to prevent him from following us to the Moon?'

'Nothing!' replied Barbican; 'he is a faithful friend and a reliable comrade. Besides, what is easier? Is not the Columbiad still at Stony Hill? Cannot gun-cotton be readily manufactured on any occasion? Will not the Moon again pass through the zenith of Florida? Eighteen years from now, will she not occupy exactly the same spot that she does to-day?'

'Certainly!' cried Ardan, with increasing enthusiasm, 'Marston will come! and Elphinstone of the torpedo! and the gallant Bloomsbury, and Billsby the brave, and all our friends of the Baltimore Gun Club! And we shall receive them with all the honours! And then we shall establish projectile trains between the Earth and the Moon! Hurrah for J.T. Marston!'

'Hurrah for Secretary Marston!' cried the Captain, with an enthusiasm almost equal to Ardan's.

'Hurrah for my dear friend Marston!' cried Barbican, hardly less excited than his comrades.

Our old acquaintance, Marston, of course could not have heard the joyous acclamations that welcomed his name, but at that moment he certainly must have felt his ears most unaccountably tingling. What was he doing at the time? He was rattling along the banks of the Kansas River, as fast as an express train could take him, on the road to Long's Peak, where, by means of the great Telescope, he expected to find some traces of the Projectile that contained his friends. He never forgot them for a moment, but of course he little dreamed that his name at that very time was exciting their vividest recollections and their warmest applause.

In fact, their recollections were rather too vivid, and their applause decidedly too warm. Was not the animation that prevailed among the guests of the Projectile of a very unusual character, and was it not becoming more and more violent every moment? Could the wine have caused it? No; though not teetotallers, they never drank to excess. Could the Moon's proximity, shedding her subtle, mysterious influence over their nervous systems, have stimulated them to a degree that was threatening to border on frenzy? Their faces were as red as if they were standing before a hot fire; their breathing was loud, and their lungs heaved like a smith's bellows; their eyes blazed like burning coals; their voices sounded as loud and harsh as that of a stump speaker trying to make himself heard by an inattentive or hostile crowd; their words popped from their lips like corks from Champagne bottles; their gesticulating became wilder and in fact more alarming – considering the little room left in the Projectile for muscular displays of any kind.

But the most extraordinary part of the whole phenomenon was that neither of them, not even Barbican, had the slightest consciousness of any strange or unusual ebullition of spirits either on his own part or on that of the others.

'See here, gentlemen!' said the Captain in a quick imperious manner – the roughness of his old life on the Mississippi would still break out – 'See here, gentlemen! It seems I'm not to know if we are to return from the Moon. Well! – Pass that for the present! But there is one thing I *must* know!'

'Hear! hear the Captain!' cried Barbican, stamping with his foot, like an excited fencing master. 'There is one thing he *must* know!'

'I want to know what we're going to do when we get there!'

'He wants to know what we're going to do when we get there! A sensible question! Answer it, Ardan!'

'Answer it yourself, Barbican! You know more about the Moon than I do! You know more about it than all the Nasmyths that ever lived!'

'I'm blessed if I know anything at all about it!' cried Barbican, with a joyous laugh. 'Ha, ha, ha! The first eastern shore Marylander or any other simpleton you meet in Baltimore, knows as much about the Moon as I do! Why we're going there, I can't tell! What we're going to do when we get there, can't tell either! Ardan knows all about it! He can tell! He's taking us there!'

'Certainly I can tell! should I have offered to take you there without a good object in view?' cried Ardan, husky with continual roaring. 'Answer me that!'

'No conundrums!' cried the Captain, in a voice sourer and rougher than ever; 'tell us if you can in plain English, what the demon we have come here for!'

'I'll tell you if I feel like it,' cried Ardan, folding his arms with an aspect of great dignity; 'and I'll not tell you if I don't feel like it!'

'What's that?' cried Barbican. 'You'll not give us an answer when we ask you a reasonable question?'

'Never!' cried Ardan, with great determination. 'I'll never answer a question reasonable or unreasonable, unless it is asked in a proper manner!'

'None of your French airs here!' exclaimed M'Nicholl, by this time almost completely out of himself between anger and excitement. 'I don't know where I am; I don't know where I'm going; I don't know why I'm going; *you* know all about it, Ardan, or at least you think you do! Well then, give me a plain answer to a plain question, or by the Thirty-eight States of our glorious Union, I shall know what for!'

'Listen, Ardan!' cried Barbican, grappling with the Frenchman, and with some difficulty restraining him from flying at M'Nicholl's throat; 'You ought to tell him! It is only your duty! One day you found us both in St. Helena woods, where we had no more idea of going to the Moon than of sailing to the South Pole! There you twisted us both around your finger, and induced us to follow you blindly on the most formidable journey ever undertaken by man! And now you refuse to tell us what it was all for!'

'I don't refuse, dear old Barbican! To you, at least, I can't refuse anything!' cried Ardan, seizing his friend's hands and wringing them violently. Then letting them go and suddenly starting back, 'you wish to know,' he continued in resounding tones, 'why we have followed out the grandest idea that ever set a human brain on fire! Why we have undertaken a journey that for length, danger, and novelty, for fascinating, soul-stirring and delirious sensations, for all that can attract man's burning heart, and satisfy the intensest cravings of his intellect, far surpasses the vividest realities of Dante's passionate dream! Well, I will tell you! It is to annex another World to the New One! It is to take possession of the Moon in the name of the United States of America! It is to add a thirty-ninth State to the glorious Union! It is to colonize the lunar regions, to cultivate them, to people them, to transport to them some of our wonders of art, science, and industry! It is to civilize the Selenites, unless they are more civilized already than we are ourselves! It is to make them all good Republicans, if they are not so already!'

'Provided, of course, that there are Selenites in existence!' sneered the Captain, now sourer than ever, and in his unaccountable excitement doubly irritating.

'Who says there are no Selenites?' cried Ardan fiercely, with fists clenched and brows contracted.

'I do!' cried M'Nicholl stoutly; 'I deny the existence of anything of the kind, and I denounce every one that maintains any such whim as a visionary, if not a fool!'

Ardan's reply to this taunt was a desperate facer, which, however, Barbican managed to stop while on its way towards the Captain's nose. M'Nicholl, seeing himself struck at, immediately assumed such a posture of defence as showed him to be no novice at the business. A battle seemed unavoidable; but even at this trying moment Barbican showed himself equal to the emergency.

'Stop, you crazy fellows! you ninnyhammers! you overgrown babies!' he exclaimed, seizing his companions by the collar, and violently swinging them around with his vast strength until they stood back to back; 'what are you going to fight about? Suppose there are Lunarians in the Moon! Is that a reason why there should be Lunatics in the Projectile! But, Ardan, why do you insist on Lunarians? Are we so shiftless that we can't do without them when we get to the Moon?'

'I don't insist on them!' cried Ardan, who submitted to Barbican like a child. 'Hang the Lunarians! Certainly, we can do without them! What do I care for them? Down with them!'

'Yes, down with the Lunarians!' cried M'Nicholl as spitefully as if he had even the slightest belief in their existence.

'We shall take possession of the Moon ourselves!' cried Ardan. 'Lunarians or no Lunarians!'

'We three shall constitute a Republic!' cried M'Nicholl.

'I shall be the House!' cried Ardan.

'And I the Senate!' answered the Captain.

'And Barbican our first President!' shrieked the Frenchman.

'Our first and last!' roared M'Nicholl.

'No objections to a third term!' yelled Ardan.

'He's welcome to any number of terms he pleases!' vociferated M'Nicholl.

'Hurrah for President Barbican of the Lunatic – I mean of the Lunar Republic!' screamed Ardan.

'Long may he wave, and may his shadow never grow less!' shouted Captain M'Nicholl, his eyes almost out of their sockets.

Then with voices reminding you of sand fiercely blown against the window panes, the *President* and the *Senate* chanted the immortal *Yankee Doodle*, whilst the *House* delivered itself of the *Marseillaise*, in a style which even the wildest Jacobins in Robespierre's day could hardly have surpassed.

But long before either song was ended, all three broke out into a dance, wild, insensate, furious, delirious, paroxysmatical. No Orphic festivals on Mount Cithaeron ever raged more wildly. No Bacchic revels on Mount Parnassus were ever more corybantic. Diana, demented by the maddening example, joined in the orgie, howling and barking frantically in her turn, and wildly jumping as high as the ceiling of the Projectile. Then came new accessions to the infernal din. Wings suddenly began to flutter, cocks to crow, hens to cluck; and five or six chickens, managing to escape out of their coop, flew backwards and forwards blindly, with frightened screams, dashing against each other and against the walls of the Projectile, and altogether getting up as demoniacal a hullabaloo as could be made by ten thousand bats that you suddenly disturbed in a cavern where they had slept through the winter.

Then the three companions, no longer able to withstand the overpowering influence of the mysterious force that mastered them, intoxicated, more than drunk, burned by the air that scorched their organs of respiration, dropped at last, and lay flat, motionless, senseless as dabs of clay, on the floor of the Projectile.

CHAPTER VIII

The Neutral Point

WHAT HAD TAKEN place? Whence proceeded this strange intoxication whose consequences might have proved so disastrous? A little forgetfulness on Ardan's part had done the whole mischief, but fortunately M'Nicholl was able to remedy it in time.

After a regular fainting spell several minutes long, the Captain was the first man to return to consciousness and the full recovery of his intellectual faculties. His first feelings were far from pleasant. His stomach gnawed him as if he had not eaten for a week, though he had taken breakfast only a few hours before; his eyes were dim, his brain throbbing, and his limbs shaking. In short, he presented every symptom usually seen in a man dying of starvation. Picking himself up with much care and difficulty, he roared out to Ardan for something to eat. Seeing that the Frenchman was unable or unwilling to respond, he concluded to help himself, by beginning first of all to prepare a little tea. To do this, fire was necessary; so, to light his lamp, he struck a match.

But what was his surprise at seeing the sulphur tip of the match blazing with a light so bright and dazzling that his eyes could hardly bear it! Touching it to the gas burner, a stream of light flashed forth equal in its intensity to the flame of an electric lamp. Then he understood it all in an instant. The dazzling glare, his maddened brain, his gnawing stomach – all were now clear as the noon-day Sun.

'The oxygen!' he cried, and, suddenly stooping down and examining the tap of the air apparatus, he saw that it had been only half turned off. Consequently the air was gradually getting more and more impregnated with this powerful gas, colourless, odourless, tasteless, infinitely precious, but, unless when strongly diluted with nitrogen, capable of producing fatal disorders in the human system. Ardan, startled by M'Nicholl's question about the means of returning from the Moon, had turned the cock only half off.

The Captain instantly stopped the escape of the oxygen, but not one moment too soon. It had completely saturated the atmosphere. A few minutes more and it would have killed the travellers, not like carbonic acid, by smothering them, but by burning them up, as a strong draught burns up the coals in a stove.

It took nearly an hour for the air to become pure enough to allow the lungs their natural play. Slowly and by degrees, the travellers recovered from their intoxication; they had actually to sleep off the fumes of the oxygen as a drunkard has to sleep off the effects of his brandy. When Ardan learned that he was responsible for the whole trouble, do you think the information disconcerted him? Not a bit of it. On the contrary, he was rather proud of having done something startling, to break the monotony of the journey; and to put a little life, as he said, into old Barbican and the grim Captain, so as to get a little fun out of such grave philosophers.

After laughing heartily at the comical figure cut by his two friends capering like crazy students at the *Closerie des Lilas*, he went on moralizing on the incident:

'For my part, I'm not a bit sorry for having partaken of this fuddling gas. It gives me an idea, dear boys. Would it not be worth some enterprising fellow's while to establish a sanatorium provided with oxygen chambers, where people of a debilitated state of health could enjoy a few hours of intensely active existence! There's money in it, as you Americans say. Just suppose balls or parties given in halls where the air would be provided with an extra supply of this enrapturing gas! Or, theatres where the atmosphere would be maintained in a highly oxygenated condition. What passion, what fire in the actors! What enthusiasm in the spectators! And, carrying the idea a little further, if, instead of an assembly or an audience, we should oxygenize towns, cities, a whole country – what activity would be infused into the whole people! What new life would electrify a stagnant community! Out of an old used-up nation we could perhaps make a brand-new one, and, for my part, I know more than one state in old Europe where this oxygen experiment might be attended with a decided advantage, or where, at all events, it could do no harm!'

The Frenchman spoke so glibly and gesticulated so earnestly that M'Nicholl once more gravely examined the stop-cock; but Barbican damped his enthusiasm by a single observation.

'Friend Michael,' said he, 'your new and interesting idea we shall discuss at a more favourable opportunity. At present we want to know where all these cocks and hens have come from.'

'These cocks and hens?'

'Yes.'

Ardan threw a glance of comical bewilderment on half a dozen or so of splendid barn-yard fowls that were now beginning to recover from the effects of the oxygen. For an instant he could not utter a word; then, shrugging his shoulders, he muttered in a low voice:

'Catastrophe prematurely exploded!'

'What are you going to do with these chickens?' persisted Barbican.

'Acclimatize them in the Moon, by Jove! what else?' was the ready reply.

'Why conceal them then?'

'A hoax, a poor hoax, dear President, which proves a miserable failure! I intended to let them loose on the Lunar Continent at the first favourable opportunity. I often had a good laugh to myself, thinking of your astonishment and the Captain's at seeing a lot of American poultry scratching for worms on a Lunar dunghill!'

'Ah! wag, jester, incorrigible *farceur*!' cried Barbican with a smile; 'you want no nitrous oxide to put a bee in your bonnet! He is always as bad as you and I were for a short time, M'Nicholl, under the laughing gas! He's never had a sensible moment in his life!'

'I can't say the same of you,' replied Ardan; 'you had at least one sensible moment in all your lives, and that was about an hour ago!'

Their incessant chattering did not prevent the friends from at once repairing the disorder of the interior of the Projectile. Cocks and hens were put back in their cages. But while doing so, the friends were astonished to find that the birds, though good sized creatures, and now pretty fat and plump, hardly felt heavier in their hands than if they had been so many sparrows. This drew their interested attention to a new phenomenon.

From the moment they had left the Earth, their own weight, and that of the Projectile and the objects therein contained, had been undergoing a progressive diminution. They might never be able to ascertain this fact with regard to the Projectile, but the moment was now rapidly approaching when the loss of weight would become perfectly sensible, both regarding themselves and the tools and instruments surrounding them. Of course, it is quite clear, that this decrease could not be indicated by an ordinary scales, as the weight to balance the object would have lost precisely as much as the object itself. But a spring balance, for instance, in which the tension of the coil is independent of attraction, would have readily given the exact equivalent of the loss.

Attraction or weight, according to Newton's well known law, acting in direct proportion to the mass of the attracting body and in inverse proportion to the square of the distance, this consequence clearly follows: Had the Earth been alone in space, or had the other heavenly bodies been suddenly annihilated, the further from the Earth the Projectile would be, the less weight it would have. However, it would never *entirely* lose its weight, as the terrestrial attraction would have always made itself felt at no matter what distance. But as the Earth is not the only celestial body possessing attraction, it is evident that there may be a point in space where the respective attractions may be entirely annihilated by mutual counteraction. Of this phenomenon the present instance was a case in point. In a short time, the Projectile and its contents would for a few moments be absolutely and completely deprived of all weight whatsoever.

The path described by the Projectile was evidently a line from the Earth to the Moon averaging somewhat less than 240,000 miles in length. According as the distance between the Projectile and the Earth was increasing, the terrestrial attraction was diminishing in the ratio of the square of the distance, and the lunar attraction was augmenting in the same proportion.

As before observed, the point was not now far off where, the two attractions counteracting each other, the bullet would actually weigh nothing at all. If the masses of the Earth and the Moon had been equal, this should evidently be found half way between the two bodies. But by making allowance for the difference of the respective masses, it was easy to calculate that this point would be situated at the $9/10$ of the total distance, or, in round numbers, at something less than 216,000 miles from the Earth.

At this point, a body that possessed no energy or principle of movement within itself, would remain forever, relatively motionless, suspended like Mahomet's coffin, being equally attracted by the two orbs and nothing impelling it in one direction rather than in the other.

Now the Projectile at this moment was nearing this point; if it reached it, what would be the consequence?

To this question three answers presented themselves, all possible under the circumstances, but very different in their results.

1. Suppose the Projectile to possess velocity enough to pass the neutral point. In such case, it would undoubtedly proceed onward to the Moon, being drawn thither by Lunar attraction.

2. Suppose it lacked the requisite velocity for reaching the neutral point. In such a case it would just as certainly fall back to the Earth, in obedience to the law of Terrestrial attraction.

3. Suppose it to be animated by just sufficient velocity to reach the neutral point, but not to pass it. In that case, the Projectile would remain forever in the same spot, perfectly motionless as far as regards the Earth and the Moon, though of course following them both in their annual orbits round the Sun.

Such was now the state of things, which Barbican tried to explain to his friends, who, it need hardly be said, listened to his remarks with the most intense interest. How were they to know, they asked him, the precise instant at which the Projectile would reach the neutral point? That would be an easy matter, he assured them. It would be at the very moment when both themselves and all the other objects contained in the Projectile would be completely free from every operation of the law of gravity; in other words, when everything would cease to have weight.

This gradual diminution of the action of gravity, the travellers had been for some time noticing, but they had not yet witnessed its total cessation. But that very morning, about an hour before noon, as the Captain was making some little experiment in Chemistry, he happened by accident to overturn a glass full of water. What was his surprise at seeing that neither the glass nor the water fell to the floor! Both remained suspended in the air almost completely motionless.

'The prettiest experiment I ever saw!' cried Ardan; 'let us have more of it!'

And seizing the bottles, the arms, and the other objects in the Projectile, he arranged them around each other in the air with some regard to symmetry and proportion. The different articles, keeping strictly each in its own place, formed a very attractive group wonderful to behold. Diana, placed in the apex of the pyramid, would remind you of those marvellous suspensions in the air performed by Houdin, Herman, and a few other first class wizards. Only being kept in her place without being hampered by invisible strings, the animal rather seemed to enjoy the exhibition, though in all probability she was hardly conscious of any thing unusual in her appearance.

Our travellers had been fully prepared for such a phenomenon, yet it struck them with as much surprise as if they had never uttered a scientific reason to account for it. They saw that, no longer subject to the ordinary laws of nature, they were now entering the realms of the marvellous. They felt that their bodies were absolutely without weight. Their arms, fully extended, no longer sought their sides. Their heads oscillated unsteadily on their shoulders. Their feet no longer rested on the floor. In their efforts to hold themselves straight, they looked like drunken men trying to maintain the perpendicular. We have all read stories of some men deprived of the power of reflecting light and of others who could not cast a shadow. But here reality, no fantastic story, showed you men who, through the counteraction of attractive forces, could tell no difference between light substances and heavy substances, and who absolutely had no weight whatever themselves!

'Let us take graceful attitudes!' cried Ardan, 'and imagine we are playing *tableaux*! Let us, for instance, form a grand historical group of the three great goddesses of the nineteenth century. Barbican will represent Minerva or *Science*; the Captain, Bellona or *War*; while I, as Madre Natura, the newly born goddess of *Progress*, floating gracefully over you both, extend my hands so, fondly patronizing the one, but grandly ordering off the other, to the regions of eternal night! More on your toe, Captain! Your right foot a little higher! Look at Barbican's admirable pose! Now then, prepare to receive orders for a new tableau! Form group *à la Jardin Mabille!* Presto! Change!'

In an instant, our travellers, changing attitudes, formed the new group with tolerable success. Even Barbican, who had been to Paris in his youth, yielding for a moment to the humour of the thing, acted the *naif Anglais* to the life. The Captain was frisky enough to remind you of a middle-aged Frenchman from the provinces, on a hasty visit to the capital for a few days' fun. Ardan was in raptures.

'Oh! if Raphael could only see us!' he exclaimed in a kind of ecstasy. 'He would paint such a picture as would throw all his other masterpieces in the shade!'

'Knock spots out of the best of them by fifty per cent!' cried the Captain, gesticulating well enough *à l'étudiant*, but rather mixing his metaphors.

'He should be pretty quick in getting through the job,' observed Barbican, the first as usual to recover tranquillity. 'As soon as the Projectile will have passed the neutral point – in half an hour at longest – lunar attraction will draw us to the Moon.'

'We shall have to crawl on the ceiling then like flies,' said Ardan.

'Not at all,' said the Captain; 'the Projectile, having its centre of gravity very low, will turn upside down by degrees.'

'Upside down!' cried Ardan. 'That will be a nice mess! everything higgledy-piggledy!'

'No danger, friend Michael,' said M'Nicholl; 'there shall be no disorder whatever; nothing will quit its place; the movement of the Projectile will be effected by such slow degrees as to be imperceptible.'

'Yes,' added Barbican, 'as soon as we shall have passed the neutral point, the base of the Projectile, its heaviest part, will swing around gradually until it faces the Moon. Before this phenomenon, however, can take place, we must of course cross the line.'

'Cross the line!' cried the Frenchman; 'then let us imitate the sailors when they do the same thing in the Atlantic Ocean! Splice the main brace!'

A slight effort carried him sailing over to the side of the Projectile. Opening a cupboard and taking out a bottle and a few glasses, he placed them on a tray. Then setting the tray itself in the air as on a table in front of his companions, he filled the glasses, passed them around, and, in a lively speech interrupted with many a joyous hurrah, congratulated his companions on their glorious achievement in being the first that ever crossed the lunar line.

This counteracting influence of the attractions lasted nearly an hour. By that time the travellers could keep themselves on the floor without much effort. Barbican also made his companions remark that the conical point of the Projectile diverged a little from the direct line to the Moon, while by an inverse movement, as they could notice through the window of the floor, the base was gradually turning away from the Earth. The Lunar attraction was evidently getting the better of the Terrestrial. The fall towards the Moon, though still almost insensible, was certainly beginning.

It could not be more than the eightieth part of an inch in the first second. But by degrees, as the attractive force would increase, the fall would be more decided, and the Projectile, overbalanced by its base, and presenting its cone to the Earth, would descend with accelerated velocity to the Lunar surface. The object of their daring attempt would then be successfully attained. No further obstacle, therefore, being likely to stand in the way of the complete success of the enterprise, the Captain and the Frenchman cordially shook hands with Barbican, all kept congratulating each other on their good fortune as long as the bottle lasted.

They could not talk enough about the wonderful phenomenon lately witnessed; the chief point, the neutralization of the law of gravity, particularly, supplied them with an inexhaustible subject. The Frenchman, as usual, as enthusiastic in his fancy, as he was fanciful in his enthusiasm, got off some characteristic remarks.

'What a fine thing it would be, my boys,' he exclaimed, 'if on Earth we could be so fortunate as we have been here, and get rid of that weight that keeps us down like lead, that rivets us to it like an adamantine chain! Then should we prisoners become free! Adieu forever to all weariness of arms or feet! At present, in order to fly over the surface of the Earth by the simple exertion of our muscles or even to sustain ourselves in the air, we require a muscular force fifty times greater than we possess; but if attraction did not exist, the simplest act of the will, our slightest whim even, would be sufficient to transport us to whatever part of space we wished to visit.'

'Ardan, you had better invent something to kill attraction,' observed M'Nicholl drily; 'you can do it if you try. Jackson and Morton have killed pain by sulphuric ether. Suppose you try your hand on attraction!'

'It would be worth a trial!' cried Ardan, so full of his subject as not to notice the Captain's jeering tone; 'attraction once destroyed, there is an end forever to all loads, packs and burdens! How the poor omnibus horses would rejoice! Adieu forever to all cranes, derricks, capstans, jack-screws, and even hotel-elevators! We could dispense with all ladders, door steps, and even stair-cases!'

'And with all houses too,' interrupted Barbican; 'or, at least, we *should* dispense with them because we could not have them. If there was no weight, you could neither make a wall of bricks nor cover your house with a roof. Even your hat would not stay on your head. The cars would not stay on the railway nor the boats on the water. What do I say? We could not have any water. Even the Ocean would leave its bed and float away into space. Nay, the atmosphere itself would leave us, being detained in its place by terrestrial attraction and by nothing else.'

'Too true, Mr. President,' replied Ardan after a pause. 'It's a fact. I acknowledge the corn, as Marston says. But how you positive fellows do knock holes into our pretty little creations of fancy!'

'Don't feel so bad about it, Ardan;' observed M'Nicholl; 'though there may be no orb from which gravity is excluded altogether, we shall soon land in one, where it is much less powerful than on the Earth.'

'You mean the Moon!'

'Yes, the Moon. Her mass being $1/89$ of the Earth's, her attractive power should be in the same proportion; that is, a boy 10 years old, whose weight on Earth is about 90 lbs., would weigh on the

Moon only about 1 pound, if nothing else were to be taken into consideration. But when standing on the surface of the Moon, he is relatively 4 times nearer to the centre than when he is standing on the surface of the Earth. His weight, therefore, having to be increased by the square of the distance, must be sixteen times greater. Now 16 times $1/89$ being less than $1/5$, it is clear that my weight of 150 pounds will be cut down to nearly 30 as soon as we reach the Moon's surface.'

'And mine?' asked Ardan.

'Yours will hardly reach 25 pounds, I should think,' was the reply.

'Shall my muscular strength diminish in the same proportion?' was the next question.

'On the contrary, it will be relatively so much the more increased that you can take a stride 15 feet in width as easily as you can now take one of ordinary length.'

'We shall be all Samsons, then, in the Moon!' cried Ardan.

'Especially,' replied M'Nicholl, 'if the stature of the Selenites is in proportion to the mass of their globe.'

'If so, what should be their height?'

'A tall man would hardly be twelve inches in his boots!'

'They must be veritable Lilliputians then!' cried Ardan; 'and we are all to be Gullivers! The old myth of the Giants realized! Perhaps the Titans that played such famous parts in the prehistoric period of our Earth, were adventurers like ourselves, casually arrived from some great planet!'

'Not from such planets as *Mercury, Venus* or *Mars* anyhow, friend Michael,' observed Barbican. 'But the inhabitants of *Jupiter, Saturn, Uranus,* or *Neptune*, if they bear the same proportion to their planet that we do ours, must certainly be regular Brobdignagians.'

'Let us keep severely away from all planets of the latter class then,' said Ardan. 'I never liked to play the part of Lilliputian myself. But how about the Sun, Barbican? I always had a hankering after the Sun!'

'The Sun's volume is about 1 $\frac{1}{3}$ million times greater than that of the Earth, but his density being only about ¼, the attraction on his surface is hardly 30 times greater than that of our globe. Still, every proportion observed, the inhabitants of the Sun can't be much less than 150 or 160 feet in height.'

'*Mille tonnerres!*' cried Ardan, 'I should be there like Ulysses among the Cyclops! I'll tell you what it is, Barbican; if we ever decide on going to the Sun, we must provide ourselves before hand with a few of your Rodman's Columbiads to frighten off the Solarians!'

'Your Columbiads would not do great execution there,' observed M'Nicholl; 'your bullet would be hardly out of the barrel when it would drop to the surface like a heavy stone pushed off the wall of a house.'

'Oh! I like that!' laughed the incredulous Ardan.

'A little calculation, however, shows the Captain's remark to be perfectly just,' said Barbican. 'Rodman's ordinary 15 inch Columbiad requires a charge of 100 pounds of mammoth powder to throw a ball of 500 pounds weight. What could such a charge do with a ball weighing 30 times as much or 15,000 pounds? Reflect on the enormous weight everything must have on the surface of the Sun! Your hat, for instance, would weigh 20 or 30 pounds. Your cigar nearly a pound. In short, your own weight on the Sun's surface would be so great, more than two tons, that if you ever fell you should never be able to pick yourself up again!'

'Yes,' added the Captain, 'and whenever you wanted to eat or drink you should rig up a set of powerful machinery to hoist the eatables and drinkables into your mouth.'

'Enough of the Sun to-day, boys!' cried Ardan, shrugging his shoulders; 'I don't contemplate going there at present. Let us be satisfied with the Moon! There, at least, we shall be of some account!'

CHAPTER IX
A Little off the Track

BARBICAN'S MIND WAS now completely at rest at least on one subject. The original force of the discharge had been great enough to send the Projectile beyond the neutral line. Therefore, there was no longer any danger of its falling back to the Earth. Therefore, there was no longer any danger of its resting eternally motionless on the point of the counteracting attractions. The next subject to engage his attention was the question: would the Projectile, under the influence of lunar attraction, succeed in reaching its destination?

The only way in which it *could* succeed was by falling through a space of nearly 24,000 miles and then striking the Moon's surface. A most terrific fall! Even taking the lunar attraction to be only the one-sixth of the Earth's, such a fall was simply bewildering to think of. The greatest height to which a balloon ever ascended was seven miles (Glaisher, 1862). Imagine a fall from even that distance! Then imagine a fall from a height of four thousand miles!

Yet it was for a fall of this appalling kind on the surface of the Moon that the travellers had now to prepare themselves. Instead of avoiding it, however, they eagerly desired it and would be very much disappointed if they missed it. They had taken the best precautions they could devise to guard against the terrific shock. These were mainly of two kinds: one was intended to counteract as much as possible the fearful results to be expected the instant the Projectile touched the lunar surface; the other, to retard the velocity of the fall itself, and thereby to render it less violent.

The best arrangement of the first kind was certainly Barbican's water-contrivance for counteracting the shock at starting, which has been so fully described in our former volume. (See *Baltimore Gun Club*, page 353.) But unfortunately it could be no longer employed. Even if the partitions were in working order, the water – two thousand pounds in weight had been required – was no longer to be had. The little still left in the tanks was of no account for such a purpose. Besides, they had not a single drop of the precious liquid to spare, for they were as yet anything but sanguine regarding the facility of finding water on the Moon's surface.

Fortunately, however, as the gentle reader may remember, Barbican, besides using water to break the concussion, had provided the movable disc with stout pillars containing a strong buffing apparatus, intended to protect it from striking the bottom too violently after the destruction of the different partitions. These buffers were still good, and, gravity being as yet almost imperceptible, to put them once more in order and adjust them to the disc was not a difficult task.

The travellers set to work at once and soon accomplished it. The different pieces were put together readily – a mere matter of bolts and screws, with plenty of tools to manage them. In a short time the repaired disc rested on its steel buffers, like a table on its legs, or rather like a sofa seat on its springs. The new arrangement was attended with at least one disadvantage. The bottom light being covered up, a convenient view of the Moon's surface could not be had as soon as they should begin to fall in a perpendicular descent. This, however, was only a slight matter, as the side lights would permit the adventurers to enjoy quite as favourable a view of the vast regions of the Moon as is afforded to balloon travellers when looking down on the Earth over the sides of their car.

The disc arrangement was completed in about an hour, but it was not till past twelve o'clock before things were restored to their usual order. Barbican then tried to make fresh observations regarding the inclination of the Projectile; but to his very decided chagrin he found that it had not yet turned over sufficiently to commence the perpendicular fall: on the contrary, it even seemed to be following a curve rather parallel with that of the lunar disc.

The Queen of the Stars now glittered with a light more dazzling than ever, whilst from an opposite part of the sky the glorious King of Day flooded her with his fires.

The situation began to look a little serious.

'Shall we ever get there!' asked the Captain.

'Let us be prepared for getting there, any how,' was Barbican's dubious reply.

'You're a pretty pair of suspenders,' said Ardan cheerily (he meant of course doubting hesitators, but his fluent command of English sometimes led him into such solecisms). 'Certainly we shall get there – and perhaps a little sooner than will be good for us.'

This reply sharply recalled Barbican to the task he had undertaken, and he now went to work seriously, trying to combine arrangements to break the fall. The reader may perhaps remember Ardan's reply to the Captain on the day of the famous meeting in Tampa.

'Your fall would be violent enough,' the Captain had urged, 'to splinter you like glass into a thousand fragments.'

'And what shall prevent me,' had been Ardan's ready reply, 'from breaking my fall by means of counteracting rockets suitably disposed, and let off at the proper time?'

The practical utility of this idea had at once impressed Barbican. It could hardly be doubted that powerful rockets, fastened on the outside to the bottom of the Projectile, could, when discharged, considerably retard the velocity of the fall by their sturdy recoil. They could burn in a vacuum by means of oxygen furnished by themselves, as powder burns in the chamber of a gun, or as the volcanoes of the Moon continue their action regardless of the absence of a lunar atmosphere.

Barbican had therefore provided himself with rockets enclosed in strong steel gun barrels, grooved on the outside so that they could be screwed into corresponding holes already made with much care in the bottom of the Projectile. They were just long enough, when flush with the floor inside, to project outside by about six inches. They were twenty in number, and formed two concentric circles around the dead light. Small holes in the disc gave admission to the wires by which each of the rockets was to be discharged externally by electricity. The whole effect was therefore to be confined to the outside. The mixtures having been already carefully deposited in each barrel, nothing further need be done than to take away the metallic plugs which had been screwed into the bottom of the Projectile, and replace them by the rockets, every one of which was found to fit its grooved chamber with rigid exactness.

This evidently should have been all done before the disc had been finally laid on its springs. But as this had to be lifted up again in order to reach the bottom of the Projectile, more work was to be done than was strictly necessary. Though the labour was not very hard, considering that gravity had as yet scarcely made itself felt, M'Nicholl and Ardan were not sorry to have their little joke at Barbican's expense. The Frenchman began humming

'*Aliquandoque bonus dormitat Homerus,*'

to a tune from *Orphée aux Enfers*, and the Captain said something about the Philadelphia Highway Commissioners who pave a street one day, and tear it up the next to lay the gas pipes. But his friends' humour was all lost on Barbican, who was so wrapped up in his work that he probably never heard a word they said.

Towards three o'clock every preparation was made, every possible precaution taken, and now our bold adventurers had nothing more to do than watch and wait.

The Projectile was certainly approaching the Moon. It had by this time turned over considerably under the influence of attraction, but its own original motion still followed a decidedly oblique direction. The consequence of these two forces might possibly be a tangent, line approaching the edge of the Moon's disc. One thing was certain: the Projectile had not yet commenced to fall directly towards her surface; its base, in which its centre of gravity lay, was still turned away considerably from the perpendicular.

Barbican's countenance soon showed perplexity and even alarm. His Projectile was proving intractable to the laws of gravitation. The *unknown* was opening out dimly before him, the great boundless unknown of the starry plains. In his pride and confidence as a scientist, he had flattered himself with having sounded the consequence of every possible hypothesis regarding the Projectile's ultimate fate: the return to the Earth; the arrival at the Moon; and the motionless dead stop at the neutral point. But here, a new and incomprehensible fourth hypothesis, big with the terrors of the mystic infinite, rose up before his disturbed mind, like a grim and hollow ghost. After a few seconds, however, he looked at it straight in the face without wincing. His companions showed themselves just as firm. Whether it was science that emboldened Barbican, his phlegmatic stoicism that propped up the Captain, or his enthusiastic vivacity that cheered the irrepressible Ardan, I cannot exactly say. But certainly they were all soon talking over the matter as calmly as you or I would discuss the advisability of taking a sail on the lake some beautiful evening in July.

Their first remarks were decidedly peculiar and quite characteristic. Other men would have asked themselves where the Projectile was taking them to. Do you think such a question ever occurred to them? Not a bit of it. They simply began asking each other what could have been the cause of this new and strange state of things.

'Off the track, it appears,' observed Ardan. 'How's that?'

'My opinion is,' answered the Captain, 'that the Projectile was not aimed true. Every possible precaution had been taken, I am well aware, but we all know that an inch, a line, even the tenth part of a hair's breadth wrong at the start would have sent us thousands of miles off our course by this time.'

'What have you to say to that, Barbican?' asked Ardan.

'I don't think there was any error at the start,' was the confident reply; 'not even so much as a line! We took too many tests proving the absolute perpendicularity of the Columbiad, to entertain the slightest doubt on that subject. Its direction towards the zenith being incontestable, I don't see why we should not reach the Moon when she comes to the zenith.'

'Perhaps we're behind time,' suggested Ardan.

'What have you to say to that, Barbican?' asked the Captain. 'You know the Cambridge men said the journey had to be done in 97 hours 13 minutes and 20 seconds. That's as much as to say that if we're not up to time we shall miss the Moon.'

'Correct,' said Barbican. 'But we *can't* be behind time. We started, you know, on December 1st, at 13 minutes and 20 seconds before 11 o'clock, and we were to arrive four days later at midnight precisely. To-day is December 5th Gentlemen, please examine your watches. It is now half past three in the afternoon. Eight hours and a half are sufficient to take us to our journey's end. Why should we not arrive there?'

'How about being ahead of time?' asked the Captain.

'Just so!' said Ardan. 'You know we have discovered the initial velocity to have been greater than was expected.'

'Not at all! not at all!' cried Barbican 'A slight excess of velocity would have done no harm whatever had the direction of the Projectile been perfectly true. No. There must have been a digression. We must have been switched off!'

'Switched off? By what?' asked both his listeners in one breath.

'I can't tell,' said Barbican curtly.

'Well!' said Ardan; 'if Barbican can't tell, there is an end to all further talk on the subject. We're switched off – that's enough for me. What has done it? I don't care. Where are we going to? I don't care. What is the use of pestering our brains about it? We shall soon find out. We are floating around in space, and we shall end by hauling up somewhere or other.'

But in this indifference Barbican was far from participating. Not that he was not prepared to meet the future with a bold and manly heart. It was his inability to answer his own question that rendered him uneasy. What *had* switched them off? He would have given worlds for an answer, but his brain sorely puzzled sought one in vain.

In the mean time, the Projectile continued to turn its side rather than its base towards the Moon; that is, to assume a lateral rather than a direct movement, and this movement was fully participated in by the multitude of the objects that had been thrown outside. Barbican could even convince himself by sighting several points on the lunar surface, by this time hardly more than fifteen or eighteen thousand miles distant, that the velocity of the Projectile instead of accelerating was becoming more and more uniform. This was another proof that there was no perpendicular fall. However, though the original impulsive force was still superior to the Moon's attraction, the travellers were evidently approaching the lunar disc, and there was every reason to hope that they would at last reach a point where, the lunar attraction at last having the best of it, a decided fall should be the result.

The three friends, it need hardly be said, continued to make their observations with redoubled interest, if redoubled interest were possible. But with all their care they could as yet determine nothing regarding the topographical details of our radiant satellite. Her surface still reflected the solar rays too dazzlingly to show the relief necessary for satisfactory observation.

Our travellers kept steadily on the watch looking out of the side lights, till eight o'clock in the evening, by which time the Moon had grown so large in their eyes that she covered up fully half the sky. At this time the Projectile itself must have looked like a streak of light, reflecting, as it did, the Sun's brilliancy on the one side and the Moon's splendour on the other.

Barbican now took a careful observation and calculated that they could not be much more than 2,000 miles from the object of their journey. The velocity of the Projectile he calculated to be about 650 feet per second or 450 miles an hour. They had therefore still plenty of time to reach the Moon in about four hours. But though the bottom of the Projectile continued to turn towards the lunar surface in obedience to the law of centripetal force, the centrifugal force was still evidently strong enough to change the path which it followed into some kind of curve, the exact nature of which would be exceedingly difficult to calculate.

The careful observations that Barbican continued to take did not however prevent him from endeavouring to solve his difficult problem. What *had* switched them off? The hours passed on, but brought no result. That the adventurers were approaching the Moon was evident, but it was just as evident that they should never reach her. The nearest point the Projectile could ever possibly attain would only be the result of two opposite forces, the attractive and the repulsive, which, as was now clear, influenced its motion. Therefore, to land in the Moon was an utter impossibility, and any such idea was to be given up at once and for ever.

'*Quand même*! What of it!' cried Ardan; after some moments' silence. 'We're not to land in the Moon! Well! let us do the next best thing – pass close enough to discover her secrets!'

But M'Nicholl could not accept the situation so coolly. On the contrary, he decidedly lost his temper, as is occasionally the case with even phlegmatic men. He muttered an oath or two, but in a voice hardly loud enough to reach Barbican's ear. At last, impatient of further restraint, he burst out:

'Who the deuce cares for her secrets? To the hangman with her secrets! We started to land in the Moon! That's what's got to be done! That I want or nothing! Confound the darned thing, I say, whatever it was, whether on the Earth or off it, that shoved us off the track!'

'On the Earth or off it!' cried Barbican, striking his head suddenly; 'now I see it! You're right, Captain! Confound the bolide that we met the first night of our journey!'

'Hey?' cried Ardan.

'What do you mean?' asked M'Nicholl.

'I mean,' replied Barbican, with a voice now perfectly calm, and in a tone of quiet conviction, 'that our deviation is due altogether to that wandering meteor.'

'Why, it did not even graze us!' cried Ardan.

'No matter for that,' replied Barbican. 'Its mass, compared to ours, was enormous, and its attraction was undoubtedly sufficiently great to influence our deviation.'

'Hardly enough to be appreciable,' urged M'Nicholl.

'Right again, Captain,' observed Barbican. 'But just remember an observation of your own made this very afternoon: an inch, a line, even the tenth part of a hair's breadth wrong at the beginning, in a journey of 240 thousand miles, would be sufficient to make us miss the Moon!

CHAPTER X
The Observers of the Moon

BARBICAN'S HAPPY CONJECTURE had probably hit the nail on the head. The divergency even of a second may amount to millions of miles if you only have your lines long enough. The Projectile had certainly gone off its direct course; whatever the cause, the fact was undoubted. It was a great pity. The daring attempt must end in a failure due altogether to a fortuitous accident, against which no human foresight could have possibly taken precaution. Unless in case of the occurrence of some other most improbable accident, reaching the Moon was evidently now impossible. To failure, therefore, our travellers had to make up their minds.

But was nothing to be gained by the trip? Though missing actual contact with the Moon, might they not pass near enough to solve several problems in physics and geology over which scientists had been for a long time puzzling their brains in vain? Even this would be some compensation for all their trouble, courage, and intelligence. As to what was to be their own fate, to what doom were themselves to be reserved – they never appeared to think of such a thing. They knew very well that in the midst of those infinite solitudes they should soon find themselves without air. The slight supply that kept them from smothering could not possibly last more than five or six days longer. Five or six days! What of that? *Quand même*! as Ardan often exclaimed. Five or six days were centuries to our bold adventurers! At present every second was a year in events, and infinitely too precious to be squandered away in mere preparations for possible contingencies. The Moon could never be reached, but was it not possible that her surface could be carefully observed? This they set themselves at once to find out.

The distance now separating them from our Satellite they estimated at about 400 miles. Therefore relatively to their power of discovering the details of her disc, they were still farther off from the Moon than some of our modern astronomers are to-day, when provided with their powerful telescopes.

We know, for example, that Lord Rosse's great telescope at Parsonstown, possessing a power of magnifying 6,000 times, brings the Moon to within 40 miles of us; not to speak of Barbican's great telescope on the summit of Long's Peak, by which the Moon, magnified 48,000 times, was brought within 5 miles of the Earth, where it therefore could reveal with sufficient distinctness every object above 40 feet in diameter.

Therefore our adventurers, though at such a comparatively small distance, could not make out the topographical details of the Moon with any satisfaction by their unaided vision. The eye indeed could easily enough catch the rugged outline of these vast depressions improperly called 'Seas,' but it could do very little more. Its powers of adjustability seemed to fail before the strange and bewildering scene. The prominence of the mountains vanished, not only through the foreshortening, but also in the dazzling radiation produced by the direct reflection of the solar rays. After a short time therefore, completely foiled by the blinding glare, the eye turned itself unwillingly away, as if from a furnace of molten silver.

The spherical surface, however, had long since begun to reveal its convexity. The Moon was gradually assuming the appearance of a gigantic egg with the smaller end turned towards the Earth. In the earlier days of her formation, while still in a state of mobility, she had been probably a perfect sphere in shape, but, under the influence of terrestrial gravity operating for uncounted ages, she was drawn at last so much towards the centre of attraction as to resemble somewhat a prolate spheriod. By becoming a satellite, she had lost the native perfect regularity of her outline; her centre of gravity had shifted from her real centre; and as a result of this arrangement, some scientists have drawn the conclusion that the Moon's air and water have been attracted to that portion of her surface which is always invisible to the inhabitants of the Earth.

The convexity of her outline, this bulging prominence of her surface, however, did not last long. The travellers were getting too near to notice it. They were beginning to survey the Moon as balloonists survey the Earth. The Projectile was now moving with great rapidity – with nothing like its initial velocity, but still eight or nine times faster than an express train. Its line of movement, however, being oblique instead of direct, was so deceptive as to induce Ardan to flatter himself that they might still reach the lunar surface. He could never persuade himself to believe that they should get so near their aim and still miss it. No; nothing might, could, would or should induce him to believe it, he repeated again and again. But Barbican's pitiless logic left him no reply.

'No, dear friend, no. We can reach the Moon only by a fall, and we don't fall. Centripetal force keeps us at least for a while under the lunar influence, but centrifugal force drives us away irresistibly.'

These words were uttered in a tone that killed Ardan's last and fondest hope.

The portion of the Moon they were now approaching was her northern hemisphere, found usually in the lower part of lunar maps. The lens of a telescope, as is well known, gives only the inverted image of the object; therefore, when an upright image is required, an additional glass must be used. But as every additional glass is an additional obstruction to the light, the object glass of a Lunar telescope is employed without a corrector; light is thereby saved, and in viewing the Moon, as in viewing a map, it evidently makes very little difference whether we see her inverted or not. Maps of the Moon therefore, being drawn from the image formed by the telescope, show the north in the lower part, and *vice versa*. Of this kind was the *Mappa Selenographica*, by Beer and Maedler, so often previously alluded to and now carefully consulted by Barbican. The northern hemisphere, towards which they were now rapidly approaching, presented a strong contrast with the southern, by its vast plains and great depressions, checkered here and there by very remarkable isolated mountains.[1]

At midnight the Moon was full. This was the precise moment at which the travellers would have landed had not that unlucky bolide drawn them off the track. The Moon was therefore strictly up to time, arriving at the instant rigidly determined by the Cambridge Observatory. She occupied the exact point, to a mathematical nicety, where our 28th parallel crossed the perigee. An observer posted in the bottom of the Columbiad at Stony Hill, would have found himself at this moment precisely under the Moon. The axis of the enormous gun, continued upwards vertically, would have struck the orb of night exactly in her centre.

It is hardly necessary to tell our readers that, during this memorable night of the 5th and 6th of December, the travellers had no desire to close their eyes. Could they do so, even if they had desired? No! All their faculties, thoughts, and desires, were concentrated in one single word: 'Look!' Representatives of the Earth, and of all humanity past and present, they felt that it was with their eyes that the race of man contemplated the lunar regions and penetrated the secrets of our satellite! A certain indescribable emotion therefore, combined with an undefined sense of responsibility, held possession of their hearts, as they moved silently from window to window.

Their observations, recorded by Barbican, were vigorously remade, revised, and re-determined, by the others. To make them, they had telescopes which they now began to employ with great advantage. To regulate and investigate them, they had the best maps of the day.

1   In our Map of the Moon, prepared expressly for this work, we have so far improved on Beer and Maedler as to give her surface as it appears to the naked eye: that is, the north is in the north; only we must always remember that the west is and must be on the *right hand*.

Whilst occupied in this silent work, they could not help throwing a short retrospective glance on the former Observers of the Moon.

The first of these was Galileo. His slight telescope magnified only thirty times, still, in the spots flecking the lunar surface, like the eyes checkering a peacock's tail, he was the first to discover mountains and even to measure their heights. These, considering the difficulties under which he laboured, were wonderfully accurate, but unfortunately he made no map embodying his observations.

A few years afterwards, Hevel of Dantzic, (1611–1688) a Polish astronomer – more generally known as Hevelius, his works being all written in Latin – undertook to correct Galileo's measurements. But as his method could be strictly accurate only twice a month – the periods of the first and second quadratures – his rectifications could be hardly called successful.

Still it is to the labours of this eminent astronomer, carried on uninterruptedly for fifty years in his own observatory, that we owe the first map of the Moon. It was published in 1647 under the name of *Selenographia*. He represented the circular mountains by open spots somewhat round in shape, and by shaded figures he indicated the vast plains, or, as he called them, the *seas*, that occupied so much of her surface. These he designated by names taken from our Earth. His map shows you a *Mount Sinai* the midst of an *Arabia*, an *Ætna* in the centre of a *Sicily*, *Alps*, *Apennines*, *Carpathians*, a *Mediterranean*, a *Palus Mæolis*, a *Pontus Euxinus*, and a *Caspian Sea*. But these names seem to have been given capriciously and at random, for they never recall any resemblance existing between themselves and their namesakes on our globe. In the wide open spot, for instance, connected on the south with vast continents and terminating in a point, it would be no easy matter to recognize the reversed image of the *Indian Peninsula*, the *Bay of Bengal*, and *Cochin China*. Naturally, therefore, these names were nearly all soon dropped; but another system of nomenclature, proposed by an astronomer better acquainted with the human heart, met with a success that has lasted to the present day.

This was Father Riccioli, a Jesuit, and (1598-1671) a contemporary of Hevelius. In his *Astronomia Reformata*, (1665), he published a rough and incorrect map of the Moon, compiled from observations made by Grimaldi of Ferrara; but in designating the mountains, he named them after eminent astronomers, and this idea of his has been carefully carried out by map makers of later times.

A third map of the Moon was published at Rome in 1666 by Dominico Cassini of Nice (1625–1712), the famous discoverer of Saturn's satellites. Though somewhat incorrect regarding measurements, it was superior to Riccioli's in execution, and for a long time it was considered a standard work. Copies of this map are still to be found, but Cassini's original copper-plate, preserved for a long time at the *Imprimerie Royale* in Paris, was at last sold to a brazier, by no less a personage than the Director of the establishment himself, who, according to Arago, wanted to get rid of what he considered useless lumber!

La Hire (1640–1718), professor of astronomy in the *Collège de France*, and an accomplished draughtsman, drew a map of the Moon which was thirteen feet in diameter. This map could be seen long afterwards in the library of St. Genevieve, Paris, but it was never engraved.

About 1760, Mayer, a famous German astronomer and the director of the observatory of Göttingen, began the publication of a magnificent map of the Moon, drawn after lunar measurements all rigorously verified by himself. Unfortunately his death in 1762 interrupted a work which would have surpassed in accuracy every previous effort of the kind.

Next appears Schroeter of Erfurt (1745–1816), a fine observer (he first discovered the Lunar *Rills*), but a poor draughtsman: his maps are therefore of little value. Lohrman of Dresden published in 1838 an excellent map of the Moon, 15 inches in diameter, accompanied by descriptive text and several charts of particular portions on a larger scale.

But this and all other maps were thrown completely into the shade by Beer and Maedler's famous *Mappa Selenographica*, so often alluded to in the course of this work. This map, projected orthographically – that is, one in which all the rays proceeding from the surface to the eye are supposed to be parallel to each other – gives a reproduction of the lunar disc exactly as it appears. The representation of the mountains and plains is therefore correct only in the central portion; elsewhere, north, south, east, or west, the features, being foreshortened, are crowded together, and cannot be compared in measurement with those in the centre. It is more than three feet square; for convenient reference it is divided into four parts, each having a very full index; in short, this map is in all respects a master piece of lunar cartography.[2]

After Beer and Maedler, we should allude to Julius Schmitt's (of Athens) excellent selenographic reliefs: to Doctor Draper's, and to Father Secchi's successful application of photography to lunar representation; to De La Rue's (of London) magnificent stereographs of the Moon, to be had at every optician's; to the clear and correct map prepared by Lecouturier and Chapuis in 1860; to the many beautiful pictures of the Moon in various phases of illumination obtained by the Messrs. Bond of Harvard University; to Rutherford's (of New York) unparalleled lunar photographs; and finally to Nasmyth and Carpenter's wonderful work on the Moon, illustrated by photographs of her surface in detail, prepared from models at which they had been labouring for more than a quarter of the century.

Of all these maps, pictures, and projections, Barbican had provided himself with only two – Beer and Maedler's in German,

---

2 In our Map the *Mappa Selenographica* is copied as closely and as fully as is necessary for understanding the details of the story. For further information the reader is referred to Nasmyth's late magnificent work: the MOON.

and Lecouturier and Chapuis' in French. These he considered quite sufficient for all purposes, and certainly they considerably simplified his labours as an observer.

His best optical instruments were several excellent marine telescopes, manufactured especially under his direction. Magnifying the object a hundred times, on the surface of the Earth they would have brought the Moon to within a distance of somewhat less than 2400 miles. But at the point to which our travellers had arrived towards three o'clock in the morning, and which could hardly be more than 12 or 1,300 miles from the Moon, these telescopes, ranging through a medium disturbed by no atmosphere, easily brought the lunar surface to within less than 13 miles' distance from the eyes of our adventurers.

Therefore they should now see objects in the Moon as clearly as people can see the opposite bank of a river that is about 12 miles wide.

CHAPTER XI
Fact and Fancy

'Have you ever seen the Moon?' said a teacher ironically one day in class to one of his pupils.

'No, sir;' was the pert reply; 'but I think I can safely say I've heard it spoken about.'

Though saying what he considered a smart thing, the pupil was probably perfectly right. Like the immense majority of his fellow beings, he had looked at the Moon, heard her talked of, written poetry about her, but, in the strict sense of the term, he had probably never seen her – that is – scanned her, examined her, surveyed her, inspected her, reconnoitred her – even with an opera glass! Not one in a thousand, not one in ten thousand, has ever examined even the map of our only Satellite. To guard our beloved and intelligent reader against this reproach, we have prepared an excellent reduction of Beer and Maedler's *Mappa*, on which, for the better understanding of what is to follow, we hope he will occasionally cast a gracious eye.

When you look at any map of the Moon, you are struck first of all with one peculiarity. Contrary to the arrangement prevailing in Mars and on our Earth, the continents occupy principally the southern hemisphere of the lunar orb. Then these continents are far from presenting such sharp and regular outlines as distinguish the Indian Peninsula, Africa, and South America. On the contrary, their coasts, angular, jagged, and deeply indented, abound in bays and peninsulas. They remind you of the coast of Norway, or of the islands in the Sound, where the land seems to be cut up into endless divisions. If navigation ever existed on the Moon's surface, it must have been of a singularly difficult and dangerous nature, and we can scarcely say which of the two should be more pitied

– the sailors who had to steer through these dangerous and complicated passes, or the map-makers who had to designate them on their charts.

You will also remark that the southern pole of the Moon is much more *continental* than the northern. Around the latter, there exists only a slight fringe of lands separated from the other continents by vast 'seas.' This word 'seas' – a term employed by the first lunar map constructors – is still retained to designate those vast depressions on the Moon's surface, once perhaps covered with water, though they are now only enormous plains. In the south, the continents cover nearly the whole hemisphere. It is therefore possible that the Selenites have planted their flag on at least one of their poles, whereas the Parrys and Franklins of England, the Kanes and the Wilkeses of America, the Dumont d'Urvilles and the Lamberts of France, have so far met with obstacles completely insurmountable, while in search of those unknown points of our terrestrial globe.

The islands – the next feature on the Moon's surface – are exceedingly numerous. Generally oblong or circular in shape and almost as regular in outline as if drawn with a compass, they form vast archipelagoes like the famous group lying between Greece and Asia Minor, which mythology has made the scene of her earliest and most charming legends. As we gaze at them, the names of Naxos, Tenedos, Milo, and Carpathos rise up before our mind's eye, and we begin looking around for the Trojan fleet and Jason's Argo. This, at least, was Ardan's idea, and at first his eyes would see nothing on the map but a Grecian archipelago. But his companions, sound practical men, and therefore totally devoid of sentiment, were reminded by these rugged coasts of the beetling cliffs of New Brunswick and Nova Scotia; so that, where the Frenchman saw the tracks of ancient heroes, the Americans saw only commodious shipping points and favourable sites for trading posts – all, of course, in the purest interest of lunar commerce and industry.

To end our hasty sketch of the continental portion of the Moon, we must say a few words regarding her orthography or mountain systems. With a fair telescope you can distinguish very readily her mountain chains, her isolated mountains, her circuses or ring formations, and her rills, cracks and radiating streaks. The character of the whole lunar relief is comprised in these divisions. It is a surface prodigiously reticulated, upheaved and depressed, apparently without the slightest order or system. It is a vast Switzerland, an enormous Norway, where everything is the result of direct plutonic action. This surface, so rugged, craggy and wrinkled, seems to be the result of successive contractions of the crust, at an early period of the planet's existence. The examination of the lunar disc is therefore highly favourable for the study of the great geological phenomena of our own globe. As certain astronomers have remarked, the Moon's surface, though older than the Earth's, has remained younger. That is, it has undergone less change. No water has broken through its rugged elevations, filled up its scowling cavities, and by incessant action tended continuously to the production of a general level. No atmosphere, by its disintegrating, decomposing influence has softened off the rugged features of the plutonic mountains. Volcanic action alone, unaffected by either aqueous or atmospheric forces, can here be seen in all its glory. In other words the Moon looks now as our Earth did endless ages ago, when 'she was void and empty and when darkness sat upon the face of the deep;' eons of ages ago, long before the tides of the ocean and the winds of the atmosphere had begun to strew her rough surface with sand and clay, rock and coal, forest and meadow, gradually preparing it, according to the laws of our beneficent Creator, to be at last the pleasant though the temporary abode of Man!

Having wandered over vast continents, your eye is attracted by the 'seas' of dimensions still vaster. Not only their shape, situation, and look, remind us of our own oceans, but, again like them, they occupy the greater part of the Moon's surface. The 'seas,' or, more correctly, plains, excited our travellers' curiosity to a very high degree, and they set themselves at once to examine their nature.

The astronomer who first gave names to those 'seas' in all probability was a Frenchman. Hevelius, however, respected them, even Riccioli did not disturb them, and so they have come down to us. Ardan laughed heartily at the fancies which they called up, and said the whole thing reminded him of one of those 'maps of matrimony' that he had once seen or read of in the works of Scudéry or Cyrano de Bergerac.

'However,' he added, 'I must say that this map has much more reality in it than could be found in the sentimental maps of the 17th century. In fact, I have no difficulty whatever in calling it the *Map of Life!* very neatly divided into two parts, the east and the west, the masculine and the feminine. The women on the right, and the men on the left!'

At such observations, Ardan's companions only shrugged their shoulders. A map of the Moon in their eyes was a map of the Moon, no more, no less; their romantic friend might view it as he pleased. Nevertheless, their romantic friend was not altogether wrong. Judge a little for yourselves.

What is the first 'sea' you find in the hemisphere on the left? The *Mare Imbrium* or the Rainy Sea, a fit emblem of our human life, beaten by many a pitiless storm. In a corresponding part of the southern hemisphere you see *Mare Nubium*, the Cloudy Sea, in which our poor human reason so often gets befogged. Close to this lies *Mare Humorum*, the Sea of Humours, where we sail about, the sport of each fitful breeze, 'everything by starts and nothing long.' Around all, embracing all, lies *Oceanus Procellarum*, the Ocean of Tempests, where, engaged in one continuous struggle with the gusty whirlwinds, excited by our own passions or those of others, so few of us escape shipwreck. And, when disgusted by the difficulties of life, its deceptions, its treacheries and all the other miseries 'that flesh is heir to,' where do we too often fly to avoid them? To the *Sinus Iridium* or the *Sinus Roris*, that is Rainbow Gulf and Dewy Gulf whose glittering lights, alas! give forth no real illumination to guide our stumbling feet, whose sun-tipped pinnacles have less substance than a dream, whose enchanting waters all evaporate before we can lift a cup-full to our parched lips! Showers, storms, fogs, rainbows – is not the whole mortal life of man comprised in these four words?

Now turn to the hemisphere on the right, the women's side, and you also discover 'seas,' more numerous indeed, but of smaller dimensions and with gentler names, as more befitting the feminine temperament. First comes *Mare Serenitatis*, the Sea of Serenity, so expressive of the calm, tranquil soul of an innocent maiden. Near it is *Lacus Somniorum*, the Lake of Dreams, in which she loves to gaze at her gilded and rosy future. In the southern division is seen *Mare Nectaris*, the Sea of Nectar, over whose soft heaving billows she is gently wafted by Love's caressing winds, 'Youth on the prow and Pleasure at the helm.' Not far off is *Mare Fecunditatis*, the Sea of Fertility, in which she becomes the happy mother of rejoicing children. A little north is *Mare Crisium*, the Sea of Crises where her life and happiness are sometimes exposed to sudden, and unexpected dangers which fortunately, however, seldom end fatally. Far to the left, near the men's side, is *Mare Vapourum*, the Sea of Vapours, into which, though it is rather small, and full of sunken rocks, she sometimes allows herself to wander, moody, and pouting, and not exactly knowing where she wants to go or what she wants to do. Between the two last expands the great *Mare Tranquillitatis*, the Sea of Tranquillity, into whose quiet depths are at last absorbed all her simulated passions, all her futile aspirations, all her unglutted desires, and whose unruffled waters are gliding on forever in noiseless current towards *Lacus Mortis*, the Lake of Death, whose misty shores

'In ruthless, vast, and gloomy woods are girt.'

So at least Ardan mused as he stooped over Beer and Maedler's map. Did not these strange successive names somewhat justify his flights of fancy? Surely they had a wonderful variety of meaning. Was it by accident or by forethought deep that the two hemispheres of the Moon had been thus so strangely divided, yet, as man to woman, though divided still united, and thus forming even in the cold regions of space a perfect image of our terrestrial existence? Who can say that our romantic French friend was altogether wrong in thus explaining the astute fancies of the old astronomers?

His companions, however, it need hardly be said, never saw the 'seas' in that light. They looked on them not with sentimental but with geographical eyes. They studied this new world and tried to get it by heart, working at it like a school boy at his lessons. They began by measuring its angles and diameters.

To their practical, common sense vision *Mare Nubium*, the Cloudy Sea, was an immense depression of the surface, sprinkled here and there with a few circular mountains. Covering a great portion of that part of the southern hemisphere which lies east of the centre, it occupied a space of about 270 thousand square miles, its central point lying in 15° south latitude and 20° east longitude. Northeast from this lay *Oceanus Procellarum*, the Ocean of Tempests, the most extensive of all the plains on the lunar disc, embracing a surface of about half a million of square miles, its centre being in 10° north and 45° east. From its bosom those wonderful mountains *Kepler* and *Aristarchus* lifted their vast ramparts glittering with innumerable streaks radiating in all directions.

To the north, in the direction of *Mare Frigoris*, extends *Mare Imbrium*, the Sea of Rains, its central point in 35° north and 20° east. It is somewhat circular in shape, and it covers a space of about 300 thousand square miles. South of *Oceanus Procellarum* and separated from *Mare Nubium* by a goodly number of ring mountains, lies the little basin of *Mare Humorum*, the Sea of Humours, containing only about 66 thousand square miles, its central point having a latitude of 25° south and a longitude of 40° east.

On the shores of these great seas three 'Gulfs' are easily found: *Sinus Aestuum*, the Gulf of the Tides, northeast of the centre; *Sinus Iridium*, the Gulf of the Rainbows, northeast of the *Mare Imbrium*; and *Sinus Roris*, the Dewy Gulf, a little further northeast. All seem to be small plains enclosed between chains of lofty mountains.

The western hemisphere, dedicated to the ladies, according to Ardan, and therefore naturally more capricious, was remarkable for 'seas' of smaller dimensions, but much more numerous. These were principally: *Mare Serenitatis*, the Sea of Serenity, 25° north and 20° west, comprising a surface of about 130 thousand square miles; *Mare Crisium*, the Sea of Crises, a round, well defined, dark depression towards the northwestern edge, 17° north 55° west, embracing a surface of 60 thousand square miles, a regular Caspian Sea in fact, only that the plateau in which it lies buried is surrounded by a girdle of much higher mountains. Then towards the equator, with a latitude of 5° north and a longitude of 25° west, appears *Mare Tranquillitatis*, the Sea of Tranquillity, occupying about 180 thousand square miles. This communicates on the south with *Mare Nectaris*, the Sea of Nectar, embracing an extent of about 42 thousand square miles, with a mean latitude of 15° south and a longitude of 35° west. Southwest from *Mare Tranquillitatis*, lies *Mare Fecunditatis*, the Sea of Fertility, the greatest in this hemisphere, as it occupies an extent of more than 300 thousand square miles, its latitude being 3° south and its longitude 50° west. For away to the north, on the borders of the *Mare Frigoris*, or Icy Sea, is seen the small *Mare Humboldtianum*, or Humboldt Sea, with a surface of about 10 thousand square miles. Corresponding to this in the southern hemisphere lies the *Mare Australe*, or South Sea, whose surface, as it extends along the western rim, is rather difficult to calculate. Finally, right in the centre of the lunar disc, where the equator intersects the first meridian, can be seen *Sinus Medii*, the Central Gulf, the common property therefore of all the hemispheres, the northern and southern, as well as of the eastern and western.

Into these great divisions the surface of our satellite resolved itself before the eyes of Barbican and M'Nicholl. Adding up the various measurements, they found that the surface of her visible hemisphere was about 7½ millions of square miles, of which about the two thirds comprised the volcanoes, the mountain chains, the rings, the islands – in short, the land portion of the lunar surface; the other third comprised the 'seas,' the 'lakes,' the 'marshes,' the 'bays' or 'gulfs,' and the other divisions usually assigned to water.

To all this deeply interesting information, though the fruit of observation the closest, aided and confirmed by calculation the profoundest, Ardan listened with the utmost indifference. In fact, even his French politeness could not suppress two or three decided yawns, which of course the mathematicians were too absorbed to notice.

In their enthusiasm they tried to make him understand that though the Moon is 13½ times smaller than our Earth, she can show more than 50 thousand craters, which astronomers have already counted and designated by specific names.

'To conclude this portion of our investigation therefore,' cried Barbican, clearing his throat, and occupying Aldan's right ear, – 'the Moon's surface is a honey combed, perforated, punctured—'

'A fistulous, a rugose, salebrous—' cut in the Captain, close on the left.

– 'And highly cribriform superficies—' cried Barbican.

– 'A sieve, a riddle, a colander—' shouted the Captain.

– 'A skimming dish, a buckwheat cake, a lump of green cheese—' went on Barbican.

– In fact, there is no knowing how far they would have proceeded with their designations, comparisons, and scientific expressions, had not Ardan, driven to extremities by Barbican's last profanity, suddenly jumped up, broken away from his companions, and clapped a forcible extinguisher on their eloquence by putting his hands on their lips and keeping them there awhile. Then striking a grand attitude, he looked towards the Moon and burst out in accents of thrilling indignation:

'Pardon, O beautiful Diana of the Ephesians! Pardon, O Phoebe, thou pearl-faced goddess of night beloved of Greece! O Isis, thou sympathetic queen of Nile-washed cities! O Astarte, thou favourite deity of the Syrian hills! O Artemis, thou symbolical daughter of Jupiter and Latona, that is of light and darkness! O brilliant sister of the radiant Apollo! enshrined in the enchanting strains of Virgil and Homer, which I only half learned at college, and therefore unfortunately forget just now! Otherwise what pleasure I should have had in hurling them at the heads of Barbican, M'Nicholl, and every other barbarous iconoclast of the nineteenth century!—'

Here he stopped short, for two reasons: first he was out of breath; secondly, he saw that the irrepressible scientists had been too busy making observations of their own to hear a single word of what he had uttered, and were probably totally unconscious that he had spoken at all. In a few seconds his breath came back in full blast, but the idea of talking when only deaf men were listening was so disconcerting as to leave him actually unable to get off another syllable.

CHAPTER XII

A Bird's Eye View of the Lunar Mountains

I AM RATHER inclined to believe myself that not one word of Ardan's rhapsody had been ever heard by Barbican or M'Nicholl. Long before he had spoken his last words, they had once more become mute as statues, and now were both eagerly watching, pencil in hand, spyglass to eye, the northern lunar hemisphere towards which they were rapidly but indirectly approaching. They had fully made up their minds by this time that they were leaving far behind them the central point which they would have probably reached half an hour ago if they had not been shunted off their course by that inopportune bolide.

About half past twelve o'clock, Barbican broke the dead silence by saying that after a careful calculation they were now only about 875 miles from the Moon's surface, a distance two hundred miles less in length than the lunar radius, and which was still to be diminished as they advanced further north. They were at that moment ten degrees north of the equator, almost directly over the ridge lying between the *Mare Serenitatis* and the *Mare Tranquillitatis*. From this latitude all the way up to the north pole the travellers enjoyed a most satisfactory view of the Moon in all directions and under the most favourable conditions. By means of their spyglasses, magnifying a hundred times, they cut down this distance of 875 miles to about 9. The great telescope of the Rocky Mountains, by its enormous magnifying power of 48,000, brought the Moon, it is true, within a distance of 5 miles, or nearly twice as near; but this advantage of nearness was considerably more than counter-balanced by a want of clearness, resulting from the haziness and refractiveness of the terrestrial atmosphere, not to mention those fatal defects in the reflector that the art of man has not yet succeeded in remedying. Accordingly, our travellers, armed with excellent telescopes – of just power enough to be no injury to clearness, – and posted on unequalled vantage ground, began already to distinguish certain details that had probably never been noticed before by terrestrial observers. Even Ardan, by this time quite recovered from his fit of sentiment and probably infected a little by the scientific enthusiasm of his companions, began to observe and note and observe and note, alternately, with all the *sangfroid* of a veteran astronomer.

'Friends,' said Barbican, again interrupting a silence that had lasted perhaps ten minutes, 'whither we are going I can't say; if we shall ever revisit the Earth, I can't tell. Still, it is our duty so to act in all respects as if these labours of ours were one day to be of service to our fellow-creatures. Let us keep our souls free from every distraction. We are now astronomers. We see now what no mortal eye has ever gazed on before. This Projectile is simply a work room of the great Cambridge Observatory lifted into space. Let us take observations!'

With these words, he set to work with a renewed ardour, in which his companions fully participated. The consequence was that they soon had several of the outline maps covered with the best sketches they could make of the Moon's various aspects thus presented under such favourable circumstances. They could now remark not only that they were passing the tenth degree of north latitude, but that the Projectile followed almost directly the twentieth degree of east longitude.

'One thing always puzzled me when examining maps of the Moon,' observed Ardan, 'and I can't say that I see it yet as clearly as if I had thought over the matter. It is this. I could understand, when looking through a lens at an object, why we get only its reversed image – a simple law of optics explains *that*. Therefore, in a map of the Moon, as the bottom means the north and the top the south, why does not the right mean the west and the left the east? I suppose I could have made this out by a little thought, but thinking, that is reflection, not being my forte, it is the last thing I ever care to do. Barbican, throw me a word or two on the subject.'

'I can see what troubles you,' answered Barbican, 'but I can also see that one moment's reflection would have put an end to your perplexity. On ordinary maps of the Earth's surface when the north is the top, the right hand must be the east, the left hand the west, and so on. That is simply because we look *down* from *above*. And such a map seen through a lens will appear reversed in all respects. But in looking at the Moon, that is *up* from *down*, we change our position so far that our right hand points west and our left east. Consequently, in our reversed map, though the north becomes south, the right remains east, and—'

'Enough said! I see it at a glance! Thank you, Barbican. Why did not they make you a professor of astronomy? Your hint will save me a world of trouble.'[3]

Aided by the *Mappa Selenographica*, the travellers could easily recognize the different portions of the Moon over which they were now moving. An occasional glance at our reduction of this map, given as a frontispiece, will enable the gentle reader to follow the travellers on the line in which they moved and to understand the remarks and observations in which they occasionally indulged.

'Where are we now?' asked Ardan.

'Over the northern shores of the *Mare Nubium*,' replied Barbican. 'But we are still too far off to see with any certainty what they are like. What is the *Mare* itself? A sea, according to the early astronomers? a plain of solid sand, according to later authority? or an immense forest, according to De la Rue of London, so far the Moon's most successful photographer? This gentleman's authority, Ardan, would have given you decided support in your

---

[3] We must again remind our readers that, in our map, though every thing is set down as it appears to the eye not as it is reversed by the telescope, still, for the reason made so clear by Barbican, the right hand side must be the west and the left the east.

famous dispute with the Captain at the meeting near Tampa, for he says very decidedly that the Moon has an atmosphere, very low to be sure but very dense. This, however, we must find out for ourselves; and in the meantime let us affirm nothing until we have good grounds for positive assertion.'

Mare Nubium, though not very clearly outlined on the maps, is easily recognized by lying directly east of the regions about the centre. It would appear as if this vast plain were sprinkled with immense lava blocks shot forth from the great volcanoes on the right, *Ptolemaeus*, *Alphonse*, *Alpetragius* and *Arzachel*. But the Projectile advanced so rapidly that these mountains soon disappeared, and the travellers were not long before they could distinguish the great peaks that closed the 'Sea' on its northern boundary. Here a radiating mountain showed a summit so dazzling with the reflection of the solar rays that Ardan could not help crying out:

'It looks like one of the carbon points of an electric light projected on a screen! What do you call it, Barbican?'

'*Copernicus*,' replied the President. 'Let us examine old *Copernicus*!'

This grand crater is deservedly considered one of the greatest of the lunar wonders. It lifts its giant ramparts to upwards of 12,000 feet above the level of the lunar surface. Being quite visible from the Earth and well situated for observation, it is a favourite object for astronomical study; this is particularly the case during the phase existing between Last Quarter and the New Moon, when its vast shadows, projected boldly from the east towards the west, allow its prodigious dimensions to be measured.

After *Tycho*, which is situated in the southern hemisphere, *Copernicus* forms the most important radiating mountain in the lunar disc. It looms up, single and isolated, like a gigantic light-house, on the peninsula separating *Mare Nubium* from *Oceanus Procellarum* on one side and from *Mare*

Imbrium on the other; thus illuminating with its splendid radiation three 'Seas' at a time. The wonderful complexity of its bright streaks diverging on all sides from its centre presented a scene alike splendid and unique. These streaks, the travellers thought, could be traced further north than in any other direction: they fancied they could detect them even in the *Mare Imbrium*, but this of course might be owing to the point from which they made their observations. At one o'clock in the morning, the Projectile, flying through space, was exactly over this magnificent mountain.

In spite of the brilliant sunlight that was blazing around them, the travellers could easily recognize the peculiar features of *Copernicus*. It belongs to those ring mountains of the first class called Circuses. Like *Kepler* and *Aristarchus*, who rule over *Oceanus Procellarum*, *Copernicus*, when viewed through our telescopes, sometimes glistens so brightly through the ashy light of the Moon that it has been frequently taken for a volcano in full activity. Whatever it may have been once, however, it is certainly nothing more now than, like all the other mountains on the visible side of the Moon, an extinct volcano, only with a crater of such exceeding grandeur and sublimity as to throw utterly into the shade everything like it on our Earth. The crater of Etna is at most little more than a mile across. The crater of *Copernicus* has a diameter of at least 50 miles. Within it, the travellers could easily discover by their glasses an immense number of terraced ridges, probably landslips, alternating with stratifications resulting from successive eruptions. Here and there, but particularly in the southern side, they caught glimpses of shadows of such intense blackness, projected across the plateau and lying there like pitch spots, that they could not tell them from yawning chasms of incalculable depth. Outside the crater the shadows were almost as deep, whilst on the plains all around, particularly in the west, so many small craters could be detected that the eye in vain attempted to count them.

'Many circular mountains of this kind,' observed Barbican, 'can be seen on the lunar surface, but *Copernicus*, though not one of the greatest, is one of the most remarkable on account of those diverging streaks of bright light that you see radiating from its summit. By looking steadily into its crater, you can see more cones than mortal eye ever lit on before. They are so numerous as to render the interior plateau quite rugged, and were formerly so many openings giving vent to fire and volcanic matter. A curious and very common arrangement of this internal plateau of lunar craters is its lying at a lower level than the external plains, quite the contrary to a terrestrial crater, which generally has its bottom much higher than the level of the surrounding country. It follows therefore that the deep lying curve of the bottom of these ring mountains would give a sphere with a diameter somewhat smaller than the Moon's.'

'What can be the cause of this peculiarity?' asked M'Nicholl.

'I can't tell;' answered Barbican, 'but, as a conjecture, I should say that it is probably to the comparatively smaller area of the Moon and the more violent character of her volcanic action that the extremely rugged character of her surface is mainly due.'

'Why, it's the *Campi Phlegraei* or the Fire Fields of Naples over again!' cried Ardan suddenly. 'There's *Monte Barbaro*, there's the *Solfatara*, there is the crater of *Astroni*, and there is the *Monte Nuovo*, as plain as the hand on my body!'

'The great resemblance between the region you speak of and the general surface of the Moon has been often remarked;' observed Barbican, 'but it is even still more striking in the neighbourhood of *Theophilus* on the borders of *Mare Nectaris*.'

'That's *Mare Nectaris*, the gray spot over there on the southwest, isn't it?' asked M'Nicholl; 'is there any likelihood of our getting a better view of it?'

'Not the slightest,' answered Barbican, 'unless we go round the Moon and return this way, like a satellite describing its orbit.'

By this time they had arrived at a point vertical to the mountain centre. *Copernicus's* vast ramparts formed a perfect circle or rather a pair of concentric circles. All around the mountain extended a dark greyish plain of savage aspect, on which the peak shadows projected themselves in sharp relief. In the gloomy bottom of the crater, whose dimensions are vast enough to swallow Mont Blanc body and bones, could be distinguished a magnificent group of cones, at least half a mile in height and glittering like piles of crystal. Towards the north several breaches could be seen in the ramparts, due probably to a caving in of immense masses accumulated on the summit of the precipitous walls.

As already observed, the surrounding plains were dotted with numberless craters mostly of small dimensions, except *Gay Lussac* on the north, whose crater was about 12 miles in diameter. Towards the southwest and the immediate east, the plain appeared to be very flat, no protuberance, no prominence of any kind lifting itself above the general dead level. Towards the north, on the contrary, as far as where the peninsula jutted on *Oceanus Procellarum*, the plain looked like a sea of lava wildly lashed for a while by a furious hurricane and then, when its waves and breakers and driving ridges were at their wildest, suddenly frozen into solidity. Over this rugged, rumpled, wrinkled surface and in all directions, ran the wonderful streaks whose radiating point appeared to be the summit of *Copernicus*. Many of them appeared to be ten miles wide and hundreds of miles in length.

The travellers disputed for some time on the origin of these strange radii, but could hardly be said to have arrived at any conclusion more satisfactory than that already reached by some terrestrial observers.

To M'Nicholl's question:

'Why can't these streaks be simply prolonged mountain crests reflecting the sun's rays more vividly by their superior altitude and comparative smoothness?'

Barbican readily replied:

'These streaks *can't* be mountain crests, because, if they were, under certain conditions of solar illumination they should project *shadows* – a thing which they have never been known to do under any circumstances whatever. In fact, it is only during the period of the full Moon that these streaks are seen at all; as soon as the sun's rays become oblique, they disappear altogether – a proof that their appearance is due altogether to peculiar advantages in their surface for the reflection of light.'

'Dear boys, will you allow me to give my little guess on the subject?' asked Ardan.

His companions were profuse in expressing their desire to hear it.

'Well then,' he resumed, 'seeing that these bright streaks invariably start from a certain point to radiate in all directions, why not suppose them to be streams of lava issuing from the crater and flowing down the mountain side until they cooled?'

'Such a supposition or something like it has been put forth by Herschel,' replied Barbican; 'but your own sense will convince you that it is quite untenable when you consider that lava, however hot and liquid it may be at the commencement of its journey, cannot flow on for hundreds of miles, up hills, across ravines, and over plains, all the time in streams of almost exactly equal width.'

'That theory of yours holds no more water than mine, Ardan,' observed M'Nicholl.

'Correct, Captain,' replied the Frenchman; 'Barbican has a trick of knocking the bottom out of every weaker vessel. But let us hear what he has to say on the subject himself. What is your theory. Barbican?'

'My theory,' said Barbican, 'is pretty much the same as that lately presented by an English astronomer, Nasmyth, who has devoted much study and reflection to lunar matters. Of course, I only formulate my theory, I don't affirm it. These streaks are cracks, made in the Moon's surface by cooling or by shrinkage, through which volcanic matter has been forced up by internal pressure. The sinking ice of a frozen lake, when meeting with some sharp pointed rock, cracks in a radiating manner: every one of its fissures then admits the water, which immediately spreads laterally over the ice pretty much as the lava spreads itself over the lunar surface. This theory accounts for the radiating nature of the streaks, their great and nearly equal thickness, their immense length, their inability to cast a shadow, and their invisibility at any time except at or near the Full Moon. Still it is nothing but a theory, and I don't deny that serious objections may be brought against it.'

'Do you know, dear boys,' cried Ardan, led off as usual by the slightest fancy, 'do you know what I am thinking of when I look down on the great rugged plains spread out beneath us?'

'I can't say, I'm sure,' replied Barbican, somewhat piqued at the little attention he had secured for his theory.

'Well, what are you thinking of?' asked M'Nicholl.

'Spillikins!' answered Ardan triumphantly.

'Spillikins?' cried his companions, somewhat surprised.

'Yes, Spillikins! These rocks, these blocks, these peaks, these streaks, these cones, these cracks, these ramparts, these escarpments, – what are they but a set of spillikins, though I acknowledge on a grand scale? I wish I had a little hook to pull them one by one!'

'Oh, do be serious, Ardan!' cried Barbican, a little impatiently.

'Certainly,' replied Ardan. 'Let us be serious, Captain, since seriousness best befits the subject in hand. What do you think of another comparison? Does not this plain look like an immense battle field piled with the bleaching bones of myriads who had slaughtered each other to a man at the bidding of some mighty Caesar? What do you think of that lofty comparison, hey?'

'It is quite on a par with the other,' muttered Barbican.

'He's hard to please, Captain,' continued Ardan, 'but let us try him again! Does not this plain look like –?'

'My worthy friend,' interrupted Barbican, quietly, but in a tone to discourage further discussion, 'what you think the plain *looks like* is of very slight import, as long as you know no more than a child what it really *is*!'

'Bravo, Barbican! well put!' cried the irrepressible Frenchman. 'Shall I ever realize the absurdity of my entering into an argument with a scientist!'

But this time the Projectile, though advancing northward with a pretty uniform velocity, had neither gained nor lost in its nearness to the lunar disc. Each moment altering the character of the fleeting landscape beneath them, the travellers, as may well be imagined, never thought of taking an instant's repose. At about half past one, looking to their right on the west, they saw the summits of another mountain; Barbican, consulting his map, recognized *Eratosthenes*.

This was a ring mountain, about 33 miles in diameter, having, like *Copernicus*, a crater of immense profundity containing central cones. Whilst they were directing their glasses towards its gloomy depths, Barbican mentioned to his friends Kepler's strange idea regarding the formation of these ring mountains. 'They must have been constructed,' he said, 'by mortal hands.'

'With what object?' asked the Captain.

'A very natural one,' answered Barbican. 'The Selenites must have undertaken the immense labour of digging these enormous pits at places of refuge in which they could protect themselves against the fierce solar rays that beat against them for 15 days in succession!'

'Not a bad idea, that of the Selenites!' exclaimed Ardan.

'An absurd idea!' cried M'Nicholl. 'But probably Kepler never knew the real dimensions of these craters. Barbican knows the trouble and time required to dig a well in Stony Hill only nine hundred feet deep. To dig out a single lunar crater would take hundreds and hundreds of years, and even then they should be giants who would attempt it!'

'Why so?' asked Ardan. 'In the Moon, where gravity is six times less than on the Earth, the labour of the Selenites can't be compared with that of men like us.'

'But suppose a Selenite to be six times smaller than a man like us!' urged M'Nicholl.

'And suppose a Selenite never had an existence at all!' interposed Barbican with his usual success in putting an end to the argument. 'But never mind the Selenites now. Observe *Eratosthenes* as long as you have the opportunity.'

'Which will not be very long,' said M'Nicholl. 'He is already sinking out of view too far to the right to be carefully observed.'

'What are those peaks beyond him?' asked Ardan.

'The *Apennines*,' answered Barbican; 'and those on the left are the *Carpathians*.'

'I have seen very few mountain chains or ranges in the Moon,' remarked Ardan, after some minutes' observation.

'Mountains chains are not numerous in the Moon,' replied Barbican, 'and in that respect her oreographic system presents a decided contrast with that of the Earth. With us the ranges are many, the craters few; in the Moon the ranges are few and the craters innumerable.'

Barbican might have spoken of another curious feature regarding the mountain ranges: namely, that they are chiefly confined to the northern hemisphere, where the craters are fewest and the 'seas' the most extensive.

For the benefit of those interested, and to be done at once with this part of the subject, we give in the following little table a list of the chief lunar mountain chains, with their latitude, and respective heights in English feet.

	Name	Degrees of Latitude	Height
Southern Hemishpere.	Altai Mountains	17° to 28	13,000ft.
	Cordilleras	10 to 20	12,000
	Pyrenees	8 to 18	12,000
	Riphean	5 to 10	2,600
Northern Hemishpere.	Haemus	10 to 20	6,300
	Carpathian	15 to 19	6,000
	Apennines	14 to 27	18,000
	Taurus	25 to 34	8,500
	Hercynian	17 to 29	3,400
	Caucasus	33 to 40	17,000
	Alps	42 to 30	10,000

Of these different chains, the most important is that of the *Apennines*, about 450 miles long, a length, however, far inferior to that of many of the great mountain ranges of our globe. They skirt the western shores of the *Mare Imbrium*, over which they rise in immense cliffs, 18 or 20 thousand feet in height, steep as a wall and casting over the plain intensely black shadows at least 90 miles long. Of Mt. *Huyghens*, the highest in the group, the travellers were just barely able to distinguish the sharp angular summit in the far west. To the east, however, the *Carpathians*, extending from the 18th to 30th degrees of east longitude, lay directly under their eyes and could be examined in all the peculiarities of their distribution.

Barbican proposed a hypothesis regarding the formation of those mountains, which his companions thought at least as good as any other. Looking carefully over the *Carpathians* and catching occasional glimpses of semi-circular formations and half domes, he concluded that the chain must have formerly been a succession of vast craters. Then had come some mighty internal discharge, or rather the subsidence to which *Mare Imbrium* is due, for it immediately broke off or swallowed up one half of those mountains, leaving the other half steep as a wall on one side and sloping gently on the other to the level of the surrounding plains. The *Carpathians* were therefore pretty nearly in the same condition as the crater mountains *Ptolemy*, *Alpetragius* and *Arzachel* would find themselves in, if some terrible cataclysm, by tearing away their eastern ramparts, had turned them into a chain of mountains whose towering cliffs would nod threateningly over the western shores of *Mare Nubium*. The mean height of the *Carpathians* is about 6,000 feet, the altitude of certain points in the Pyrenees such as the *Port of Pineda*, or *Roland's Breach*, in the shadow of *Mont Perdu*. The northern slopes of the *Carpathians* sink rapidly towards the shores of the vast *Mare Imbrium*.

Towards two o'clock in the morning, Barbican calculated the Projectile to be on the 20th northern parallel, and therefore almost immediately over the little ring mountain called *Pytheas*, about 4,600 feet in height. The distance of the travellers from the Moon at this point could not be more than about 750 miles, reduced to about 7 by means of their excellent telescopes.

Mare Imbrium, the Sea of Rains here revealed itself in all its vastness to the eyes of the travellers, though it must be acknowledged that the immense depression so called, did not afford them a very clear idea regarding its exact boundaries. Right ahead of them rose *Lambert* about a mile in height; and further on, more to the left, in the direction of *Oceanus Procellarum*, *Euler* revealed itself by its glittering radiations. This mountain, of about the same height as *Lambert*, had been the object of very interesting calculations on the part of Schroeter of Erfurt. This keen observer, desirous of inquiring into the probable origin of the lunar mountains, had proposed to himself the following question: Does the volume of the crater appear to be equal to that of the surrounding ramparts? His calculations showing him that this was generally the case, he naturally concluded that these ramparts must therefore have been the product of a single eruption, for successive eruptions of volcanic matter would have disturbed this correlation. *Euler* alone, he found, to be an exception to this general law, as the volume of its crater appeared to be twice as great as that of the mass surrounding it. It must therefore have been formed by several eruptions in succession, but in that case what had become of the ejected matter?

Theories of this nature and all manner of scientific questions were, of course, perfectly permissible to terrestrial astronomers labouring under the disadvantage of imperfect instruments. But Barbican could not think of wasting his time in any speculation of the kind, and now, seeing that his Projectile perceptibly approached the lunar disc, though he despaired of ever reaching it, he was more sanguine than ever of being soon able to discover positively and unquestionably some of the secrets of its formation.

CHAPTER XIII
Lunar Landscapes

AT HALF PAST two in the morning of December 6th, the travellers crossed the 30th northern parallel, at a distance from the lunar surface of 625 miles, reduced to about 6 by their spy-glasses. Barbican could not yet see the least probability of their landing at any point of the disc. The velocity of the Projectile was decidedly slow, but for that reason extremely puzzling. Barbican could not account for it. At such a proximity to the Moon, the velocity, one would think, should be very great indeed to be able to counteract the lunar attraction. Why did it not fall? Barbican could not tell; his companions were equally in the dark. Ardan said he gave it up. Besides they had no time to spend in investigating it. The lunar panorama was unrolling all its splendours beneath them, and they could not bear to lose one of its slightest details.

The lunar disc being brought within a distance of about six miles by the spy-glasses, it is a fair question to ask, what *could* an aeronaut at such an elevation from our Earth discover on its surface? At present that question can hardly be answered, the most remarkable balloon ascensions never having passed an altitude of five miles under circumstances favourable for observers. Here, however, is an account, carefully transcribed from notes taken on the spot, of what Barbican and his companions *did* see from their peculiar post of observation.

Varieties of colour, in the first place, appeared here and there upon the disc. Selenographers are not quite agreed as to the nature of these colours. Not that such colours are without variety or too faint to be easily distinguished. Schmidt of Athens even says that if our oceans on earth were all evaporated, an observer in the Moon would hardly find the seas and continents of our globe even so well outlined as those of the Moon are to the eye of a terrestrial observer. According to him, the shade of colour distinguishing those vast plains known as 'seas' is a dark gray dashed with green and brown, – a colour presented also by a few of the great craters.

This opinion of Schmidt's, shared by Beer and Maedler, Barbican's observations now convinced him to be far better founded than that of certain astronomers who admit of no colour at all being visible on the Moon's surface but grey. In certain spots the greenish tint was quite decided, particularly in *Mare Serenitatis* and *Mare Humorum,* the very localities where Schmidt had most noticed it. Barbican also remarked that several large craters, of the class that had no interior cones, reflected a kind of bluish tinge, somewhat like that given forth by a freshly polished steel plate. These tints, he now saw enough to convince him, proceeded really from the lunar surface, and were not due, as certain astronomers asserted, either to the imperfections of the spy-glasses, or to the interference of the terrestrial atmosphere. His singular opportunity for correct observation allowed him to entertain no doubt whatever on the subject. Hampered by no atmosphere, he was free from all liability to optical illusion. Satisfied therefore as to the reality of these tints, he considered such knowledge a positive gain to science. But that greenish tint – to what was it due? To a dense tropical vegetation maintained by a low atmosphere, a mile or so in thickness? Possibly. But this was another question that could not be answered at present.

Further on he could detect here and there traces of a decidedly ruddy tint. Such a shade he knew had been already detected in the *Palus Somnii*, near *Mare Crisium*, and in the circular area of *Lichtenberg*, near the *Hercynian Mountains*, on the eastern edge of the Moon. To what cause was this tint to be attributed? To the actual colour of the surface itself? Or to that of the lava covering it here and there? Or to the colour resulting from the mixture of other colours seen at a distance too great to allow of their being distinguished separately? Impossible to tell.

Barbican and his companions succeeded no better at a new problem that soon engaged their undivided attention. It deserves some detail.

Having passed *Lambert*, being just over *Timocharis*, all were attentively gazing at the magnificent crater of *Archimedes* with a diameter of 52 miles across and ramparts more than 5,000 feet in height, when Ardan startled his companions by suddenly exclaiming:

'Hello! Cultivated fields as I am a living man!'

'What do you mean by your cultivated fields?' asked M'Nicholl sourly, wiping his glasses and shrugging his shoulders.

'Certainly cultivated fields!' replied Ardan. 'Don't you see the furrows? They're certainly plain enough. They are white too from glistening in the sun, but they are quite different from the radiating streaks of *Copernicus*. Why, their sides are perfectly parallel!'

'Where are those furrows?' asked M'Nicholl, putting his glasses to his eye and adjusting the focus.

'You can see them in all directions,' answered Ardan; 'but two are particularly visible: one running north from *Archimedes*, the other south towards the *Apennines*.'

M'Nicholl's face, as he gazed, gradually assumed a grin which soon developed into a snicker, if not a positive laugh, as he observed to Ardan:

'Your Selenites must be Brobdignagians, their oxen Leviathans, and their ploughs bigger than Marston's famous cannon, if these are furrows!'

'How's that, Barbican?' asked Ardan doubtfully, but unwilling to submit to M'Nicholl.

'They're not furrows, dear friend,' said Barbican, 'and can't be, either, simply on account of their immense size. They are what the German astronomers called *Rillen*; the French, *rainures*, and the English, *grooves, canals, clefts, cracks, chasms*, or *fissures*.'

'You have a good stock of names for them anyhow,' observed Ardan, 'if that does any good.'

'The number of names given them,' answered Barbican, 'shows how little is really known about them. They have been observed in all the level portion of the Moon's surface. Small as they appear to us, a little calculation must convince you that they are in some places hundreds of miles in length, a mile in width and probably in many points several miles in depth. Their width and depth, however, vary, though their sides, so far as observed, are always rigorously parallel. Let us take a good look at them.'

Putting the glass to his eye, Barbican examined the clefts for some time with close attention. He saw that their banks were sharp edged and extremely steep. In many places they were of such geometrical regularity that he readily excused Gruithuysen's idea of deeming them to be gigantic earthworks thrown up by the Selenite engineers. Some of them were as straight as if laid out with a line, others were curved a little here and there, though still maintaining the strict parallelism of their sides. These crossed each other; those entered craters and came out at the other side. Here, they furrowed annular plateaus, such as *Posidonius* or *Petavius*. There, they wrinkled whole seas, for instance, *Mare Serenitatis*.

These curious peculiarities of the lunar surface had interested the astronomic mind to a very high degree at their first discovery, and have proved to be very perplexing problems ever since. The first observers do not seem to have noticed them. Neither Hevelius, nor Cassini, nor La Hire, nor Herschel, makes a single remark regarding their nature.

It was Schroeter, in 1789, who called the attention of scientists to them for the first time. He had only 11 to show, but Lohrmann soon recorded 75 more. Pastorff, Gruithuysen, and particularly Beer and Maedler were still more successful, but Julius Schmidt, the famous astronomer of Athens, has raised their number up to 425, and has even published their names in a catalogue. But counting them is one thing, determining their nature is another. They are not fortifications, certainly: and cannot be ancient beds of dried up rivers, for two very good and sufficient reasons: first, water, even under the most favourable circumstances on the Moon's surface, could have never ploughed up such vast channels; secondly, these chasms often traverse lofty craters through and through, like an immense railroad cutting.

At these details, Ardan's imagination became unusually excited and of course it was not without some result. It even happened that he hit on an idea that had already suggested itself to Schmidt of Athens.

'Why not consider them,' he asked, 'to be the simple phenomena of vegetation?'

'What do you mean?' asked Barbican.

'Rows of sugar cane?' suggested M'Nicholl with a snicker.

'Not exactly, my worthy Captain,' answered Ardan quietly, 'though you were perhaps nearer to the mark than you expected. I don't mean exactly rows of sugar cane, but I do mean vast avenues of trees – poplars, for instance – planted regularly on each side of a great high road.'

'Still harping on vegetation!' said the Captain. 'Ardan, what a splendid historian was spoiled in you! The less you know about your facts, the readier you are to account for them.'

'*Ma foi*,' said Ardan simply, 'I do only what the greatest of your scientific men do – that is, guess. There is this difference however between us – I call my guesses, guesses, mere conjecture; – they dignify theirs as profound theories or as astounding discoveries!'

'Often the case, friend Ardan, too often the case,' said Barbican.

'In the question under consideration, however,' continued the Frenchman, 'my conjecture has this advantage over some others: it explains why these rills appear and seem to disappear at regular intervals.'

'Let us hear the explanation,' said the Captain.

'They become invisible when the trees lose their leaves, and they reappear when they resume them.'

'His explanation is not without ingenuity,' observed Barbican to M'Nicholl, 'but, my dear friend,' turning to Ardan, 'it is hardly admissible.'

'Probably not,' said Ardan, 'but why not?'

'Because as the Sun is nearly always vertical to the lunar equator, the Moon can have no change of seasons worth mentioning; therefore her vegetation can present none of the phenomena that you speak of.'

This was perfectly true. The slight obliquity of the Moon's axis, only 1½°, keeps the Sun in the same altitude the whole year around. In the equatorial regions he is always vertical, and in the polar he is never higher than the horizon. Therefore, there can be no change of seasons; according to the latitude, it is a perpetual winter, spring, summer, or autumn the whole year round. This state of things is almost precisely similar to that which prevails in Jupiter, who also stands nearly upright in his orbit, the inclination of his axis being only about 3°.

But how to account for the *grooves*? A very hard nut to crack. They must certainly be a later formation than the craters and the rings, for they are often found breaking right through the circular ramparts. Probably the latest of all lunar features, the results of the last geological epochs, they are due altogether to expansion or shrinkage acting on a large scale and brought about by the great forces of nature, operating after a manner altogether unknown on our earth. Such at least was Barbican's idea.

'My friends,' he quietly observed, 'without meaning to put forward any pretentious claims to originality, but by simply turning to account some advantages that have never before befallen contemplative mortal eye, why not construct a little hypothesis of our own regarding the nature of these grooves and the causes that gave them birth? Look at that great chasm just below us, somewhat to the right. It is at least fifty or sixty miles long and runs along the base of the *Apennines* in a line almost perfectly straight. Does not its parallelism with the mountain chain suggest a causative relation? See that other mighty *rill*, at least a hundred and fifty miles long, starting directly north of it and pursuing so true a course that it cleaves *Archimedes* almost cleanly into two. The nearer it lies to the mountain, as you perceive, the greater its width; as it recedes in either direction it grows narrower. Does not everything point out to one great cause of their origin? They are simple crevasses, like those so often noticed on Alpine glaciers, only that these tremendous cracks in the surface are produced by the shrinkage of the crust consequent on cooling. Can we point out some analogies to this on the Earth? Certainly. The defile of the Jordan, terminating in the awful depression of the Dead Sea, no doubt occurs to you on the moment. But the *Yosemite Valley*, as I saw it ten years ago, is an apter comparison. There I stood on the brink of a tremendous chasm with perpendicular walls, a mile in width, a mile in depth and eight miles in length. Judge if I was astounded! But how should we feel it, when travelling on the lunar surface, we should suddenly find ourselves on the brink of a yawning chasm two miles wide, fifty miles long, and so fathomless in sheer vertical depth as to leave its black profundities absolutely invisible in spite of the dazzling sunlight!'

'I feel my flesh already crawling even in the anticipation!' cried Ardan.

'I shan't regret it much if we never get to the Moon,' growled M'Nicholl; 'I never hankered after it anyhow!'

By this time the Projectile had reached the fortieth degree of lunar latitude, and could hardly be further than five hundred miles from the surface, a distance reduced to about 5 miles by the travellers' glasses. Away to their left appeared *Helicon*, a ring mountain about 1,600 feet high; and still further to the left the eye could catch a glimpse of the cliffs enclosing a semi-elliptical portion of *Mare Imbrium*, called the *Sinus Iridium*, or Bay of the Rainbows.

In order to allow astronomers to make complete observations on the lunar surface, the terrestrial atmosphere should possess a transparency seventy times greater than its present power of transmission. But in the void through which the Projectile was now floating, no fluid whatever interposed between the eye of the observer and the object observed. Besides, the travellers now found themselves at a distance that had never before been reached by the most powerful telescopes, including even Lord Rosse's and the great instrument on the Rocky Mountains. Barbican was therefore in a condition singularly favourable to resolve the great question concerning the Moon's inhabitableness. Nevertheless, the solution still escaped him. He could discover nothing around him but a dreary waste of immense plains, and towards the north, beneath him, bare mountains of the aridest character.

Not the slightest vestige of man's work could be detected over the vast expanse. Not the slightest sign of a ruin spoke of his ever having been there. Nothing betrayed the slightest trace of the development of animal life, even in an inferior degree. No movement. Not the least glimpse of vegetation. Of the three great kingdoms that hold dominion on the surface of the globe, the mineral, the vegetable and the animal, one alone was represented on the lunar sphere: the mineral, the whole mineral, and nothing but the mineral.

'Why!' exclaimed Ardan, with a disconcerted look, after a long and searching examination, 'I can't find anybody. Everything is as motionless as a street in Pompeii at 4 o'clock in the morning!'

'Good comparison, friend Ardan;' observed M'Nicholl. 'Lava, slag, volcanic eminences, vitreous matter glistening like ice, piles of scoria, pitch black shadows, dazzling streaks, like rivers of light breaking over jagged rocks – these are now beneath my eye – these alone I can detect – not a man – not an animal – not a tree. The great American Desert is a land of milk and honey in comparison with the joyless orb over which we are now moving. However, even yet we can predicate nothing positive. The atmosphere may have taken refuge in the depths of the chasms, in the interior of the craters, or even on the opposite side of the Moon, for all we know!'

'Still we must remember,' observed Barbican, 'that even the sharpest eye cannot detect a man at a distance greater than four miles and a-half, and our glasses have not yet brought us nearer than five.'

'Which means to say,' observed Ardan, 'that though we can't see the Selenites, they can see our Projectile!'

But matters had not improved much when, towards four o'clock in the morning, the travellers found themselves on the 50th parallel, and at a distance of only about 375 miles from the lunar surface. Still no trace of the least movement, or even of the lowest form of life.

'What peaked mountain is that which we have just passed on our right?' asked Ardan. 'It is quite remarkable, standing as it does in almost solitary grandeur in the barren plain.'

'That is *Pico*,' answered Barbican. 'It is at least 8,000 feet high and is well known to terrestrial astronomers as well by its peculiar shadow as on account of its comparative isolation. See the collection of perfectly formed little craters nestling around its base.'

'Barbican,' asked M'Nicholl suddenly, 'what peak is that which lies almost directly south of *Pico*? I see it plainly, but I can't find it on my map.'

'I have remarked that pyramidal peak myself,' replied Barbican; 'but I can assure you that so far it has received no name as yet, although it is likely enough to have been distinguished by the terrestrial astronomers. It can't be less than 4,000 feet in height.'

'I propose we called it *Barbican*!' cried Ardan enthusiastically.

'Agreed!' answered M'Nicholl, 'unless we can find a higher one.'

'We must be before-hand with Schmidt of Athens!' exclaimed Ardan. 'He will leave nothing unnamed that his telescope can catch a glimpse of.'

'Passed unanimously!' cried M'Nicholl.

'And officially recorded!' added the Frenchman, making the proper entry on his map.

'*Salve, Mt. Barbican!*' then cried both gentlemen, rising and taking off their hats respectfully to the distant peak.

'Look to the west!' interrupted Barbican, watching, as usual, while his companions were talking, and probably perfectly unconscious of what they were saying; 'directly to the west! Now tell me what you see!'

'I see a vast valley!' answered M'Nicholl.

'Straight as an arrow!' added Ardan.

'Running through lofty mountains!' cried M'Nicholl.

'Cut through with a pair of saws and scooped out with a chisel!' cried Ardan.

'See the shadows of those peaks!' cried M'Nicholl catching fire at the sight. 'Black, long, and sharp as if cast by cathedral spires!'

'Oh! ye crags and peaks!' burst forth Ardan; 'how I should like to catch even a faint echo of the chorus you could chant, if a wild storm roared over your beetling summits! The pine forests of Norwegian mountains howling in midwinter would not be an accordeon in comparison!'

'Wonderful instance of subsidence on a grand scale!' exclaimed the Captain, hastily relapsing into science.

'Not at all!' cried the Frenchman, still true to his colours; 'no subsidence there! A comet simply came too close and left its mark as it flew past.'

'Fanciful exclamations, dear friends,' observed Barbican; 'but I'm not surprised at your excitement. Yonder is the famous *Valley of the Alps*, a standing enigma to all selenographers. How it could have been formed, no one can tell. Even wilder guesses than yours,

Ardan, have been hazarded on the subject. All we can state positively at present regarding this wonderful formation, is what I have just recorded in my note-book: the *Valley of the Alps* is about 5 mile wide and 70 or 80 long: it is remarkably flat and free from *debris*, though the mountains on each side rise like walls to the height of at least 10,000 feet. – Over the whole surface of our Earth I know of no natural phenomenon that can be at all compared with it.'

'Another wonder almost in front of us!' cried Ardan. 'I see a vast lake black as pitch and round as a crater; it is surrounded by such lofty mountains that their shadows reach clear across, rendering the interior quite invisible!'

'That's *Plato*;' said M'Nicholl; 'I know it well; it's the darkest spot on the Moon: many a night I gazed at it from my little observatory in Broad Street, Philadelphia.'

'Right, Captain,' said Barbican; 'the crater *Plato*, is, indeed, generally considered the blackest spot on the Moon, but I am inclined to consider the spots *Grimaldi* and *Riccioli* on the extreme eastern edge to be somewhat darker. If you take my glass, Ardan, which is of somewhat greater power than yours, you will distinctly see the bottom of the crater. The reflective power of its plateau probably proceeds from the exceedingly great number of small craters that you can detect there.'

'I think I see something like them now,' said Ardan. 'But I am sorry the Projectile's course will not give us a vertical view.'

'Can't be helped!' said Barbican; 'we must go where it takes us. The day may come when man can steer the projectile or the balloon in which he is shut up, in any way he pleases, but that day has not come yet!'

Towards five in the morning, the northern limit of *Mare Imbrium* was finally passed, and *Mare Frigoris* spread its frost-coloured plains far to the right and left. On the east the travellers could easily see the ring-mountain *Condamine*, about

4,000 feet high, while a little ahead on the right they could plainly distinguish *Fontenelle* with an altitude nearly twice as great. *Mare Frigoris* was soon passed, and the whole lunar surface beneath the travellers, as far as they could see in all directions, now bristled with mountains, crags, and peaks. Indeed, at the 70th parallel the 'Seas' or plains seem to have come to an end. The spy-glasses now brought the surface to within about three miles, a distance less than that between the hotel at Chamouni and the summit of Mont Blanc. To the left, they had no difficulty in distinguishing the ramparts of *Philolaus*, about 12,000 feet high, but though the crater had a diameter of nearly thirty miles, the black shadows prevented the slightest sign of its interior from being seen. The Sun was now sinking very low, and the illuminated surface of the Moon was reduced to a narrow rim.

By this time, too, the bird's eye view to which the observations had so far principally confined, decidedly altered its character. They could now look back at the lunar mountains that they had been just sailing over – a view somewhat like that enjoyed by a tourist standing on the summit of Mt. St. Gothard as he sees the sun setting behind the peaks of the Bernese Oberland. The lunar landscapes however, though seen under these new and ever varying conditions, 'hardly gained much by the change,' according to Ardan's expression. On the contrary, they looked, if possible, more dreary and inhospitable than before.

The Moon having no atmosphere, the benefit of this gaseous envelope in softening off and nicely shading the approaches of light and darkness, heat and cold, is never felt on her surface. There, no twilight ever softly ushers in the brilliant sun, or sweetly heralds the near approach of night's dark shadow. Night follows day, and day night, with the startling suddenness of a match struck or a lamp extinguished in a cavern. Nor can it present any gradual transition from either extreme of temperature. Hot jumps to cold, and cold jumps to hot. A moment after a glacial midnight, it is a roasting noon. Without an instant's warning the temperature falls from 212° Fahrenheit to the icy winter of interstellar space. The surface is all dazzling glare, or pitchy gloom. Wherever the direct rays of the sun do not fall, darkness reigns supreme. What we call diffused light on Earth, the grateful result of refraction, the luminous matter held in suspension by the air, the mother of our dawns and our dusks, of our blushing mornings and our dewy eyes, of our shades, our penumbras, our tints and all the other magical effects of *chiaro-oscuro* – this diffused light has absolutely no existence on the surface of the Moon. Nothing is there to break the inexorable contrast between intense white and intense black. At mid-day, let a Selenite shade his eyes and look at the sky: it will appear to him as black as pitch, while the stars still sparkle before him as vividly as they do to us on the coldest and darkest night in winter.

From this you can judge of the impression made on our travellers by those strange lunar landscapes. Even their decided novelty and very strange character produced any thing but a pleasing effect on the organs of sight. With all their enthusiasm, the travellers felt their eyes 'get out of gear,' as Ardan said, like those of a man blind from his birth and suddenly restored to sight. They could not adjust them so as to be able to realize the different plains of vision. All things seemed in a heap. Foreground and background were indistinguishably commingled. No painter could ever transfer a lunar landscape to his canvas.

'Landscape,' Ardan said; 'what do you mean by a landscape? Can you call a bottle of ink intensely black, spilled over a sheet of paper intensely white, a landscape?'

At the eightieth degree, when the Projectile was hardly 100 miles distant from the Moon, the aspect of things underwent no improvement. On the contrary, the nearer the travellers approached the lunar surface, the drearier, the more inhospitable, and the more *unearthly*, everything seem to look. Still when five o'clock in the morning brought our travellers to within 50 miles of *Mount Gioja* – which their spy-glasses rendered as visible as if it was only about half a mile off, Ardan could not control himself.

'Why, we're there' he exclaimed; 'we can touch her with our hands! Open the windows and let me out! Don't mind letting me go by myself. It is not very inviting quarters I admit. But as we are come to the jumping off place, I want to see the whole thing through. Open the lower window and let me out. I can take care of myself!'

'That's what's more than any other man can do,' said M'Nicholl drily, 'who wants to take a jump of 50 miles!'

'Better not try it, friend Ardan,' said Barbican grimly: 'think of Satellite! The Moon is no more attainable by your body than by our Projectile. You are far more comfortable in here than when floating about in empty space like a bolide.'

Ardan, unwilling to quarrel with his companions, appeared to give in; but he secretly consoled himself by a hope which he had been entertaining for some time, and which now looked like assuming the appearance of a certainty. The Projectile had been lately approaching the Moon's surface so rapidly that it at last seemed actually impossible not to finally touch it somewhere in the neighbourhood of the north pole, whose dazzling ridges now presented themselves in sharp and strong relief against the black sky. Therefore he kept silent, but quietly bided his time.

The Projectile moved on, evidently getting nearer and nearer to the lunar surface. The Moon now appeared to the travellers as she does to us towards the beginning of her Second Quarter, that is as a bright crescent instead of a hemisphere. On one side, glaring dazzling light; on the other, cavernous pitchy darkness. The line separating both was broken into a thousand bits of protuberances and concavities, dented, notched, and jagged.

At six o'clock the travellers found themselves exactly over the north pole. They were quietly gazing at the rapidly shifting features of the wondrous view unrolling itself beneath them, and were silently wondering what was to come next, when, suddenly, the Projectile passed the dividing line. The Sun and Moon instantly vanished from view. The next moment, without the slightest warning the travellers found themselves plunged in an ocean of the most appalling darkness!

CHAPTER XIV
A Night of Fifteen Days

THE PROJECTILE BEING not quite 30 miles from the Moon's north pole when the startling phenomenon, recorded in our last chapter, took place, a few seconds were quite sufficient to launch it at once from the brightest day into the unknown realms of night. The transition was so abrupt, so unexpected, without the slightest shading off, from dazzling effulgence to Cimmerian gloom, that the Moon seemed to have been suddenly extinguished like a lamp when the gas is turned off.

'Where's the Moon?' cried Ardan in amazement.

'It appears as if she had been wiped out of creation!' cried M'Nicholl.

Barbican said nothing, but observed carefully. Not a particle, however, could he see of the disc that had glittered so resplendently before his eyes a few moments ago. Not a shadow, not a gleam, not the slightest vestige could he trace of its existence. The darkness being profound, the dazzling splendour of the stars only gave a deeper blackness to the pitchy sky. No wonder. The travellers found themselves now in a night that had plenty of time not only to become black itself, but to steep everything connected with it in palpable blackness. This was the night 354¼ hours long, during which the invisible face of the Moon is turned away from the Sun. In this black darkness the Projectile now fully participated. Having plunged into the Moon's shadow, it was as effectually cut off from the action of the solar rays as was every point on the invisible lunar surface itself.

The travellers being no longer able to see each other, it was proposed to light the gas, though such an unexpected demand on a commodity at once so scarce and so valuable was certainly disquieting. The gas, it will be remembered, had been intended for heating alone, not illumination, of which both Sun and Moon had promised a never ending supply. But here both Sun and Moon, in a single instant vanished from before their eyes and left them in Stygian darkness.

'It's all the Sun's fault!' cried Ardan, angrily trying to throw the blame on something, and, like every angry man in such circumstances, bound to be rather nonsensical.

'Put the saddle on the right horse, Ardan,' said M'Nicholl patronizingly, always delighted at an opportunity of counting a point off the Frenchman. 'You mean it's all the Moon's fault, don't you, in setting herself like a screen between us and the Sun?'

'No, I don't!' cried Ardan, not at all soothed by his friend's patronizing tone, and sticking like a man to his first assertion right or wrong. 'I know what I say! It will be all the Sun's fault if we use up our gas!'

'Nonsense!' said M'Nicholl. 'It's the Moon, who by her interposition has cut off the Sun's light.'

'The Sun had no business to allow it to be cut off,' said Ardan, still angry and therefore decidedly loose in his assertions.

Before M'Nicholl could reply, Barbican interposed, and his even voice was soon heard pouring balm on the troubled waters.

'Dear friends,' he observed, 'a little reflection on either side would convince you that our present situation is neither the Moon's fault nor the Sun's fault. If anything is to be blamed for it, it is our Projectile which, instead of rigidly following its allotted course, has awkwardly contrived to deviate from it. However, strict justice must acquit even the Projectile. It only obeyed a great law of nature in shifting its course as soon as it came within the sphere of that inopportune bolide's influence.'

'All right!' said Ardan, as usual in the best of humour after Barbican had laid down the law. 'I have no doubt it is exactly as you say; and, now that all is settled, suppose we take breakfast.

After such a hard night spent in work, a little refreshment would not be out of place!'

Such a proposition being too reasonable even for M'Nicholl to oppose, Ardan turned on the gas, and had everything ready for the meal in a few minutes. But, this time, breakfast was consumed in absolute silence. No toasts were offered, no hurrahs were uttered. A painful uneasiness had seized the hearts of the daring travellers. The darkness into which they were so suddenly plunged, told decidedly on their spirits. They felt almost as if they had been suddenly deprived of their sight. That thick, dismal savage blackness, which Victor Hugo's pen is so fond of occasionally revelling in, surrounded them on all sides and crushed them like an iron shroud.

It was felt worse than ever when, breakfast being over, Ardan carefully turned off the gas, and everything within the Projectile was as dark as without. However, though they could not see each other's faces, they could hear each other's voices, and therefore they soon began to talk. The most natural subject of conversation was this terrible night 354 hours long, which the laws of nature have imposed on the Lunar inhabitants. Barbican undertook to give his friends some explanation regarding the cause of the startling phenomenon, and the consequences resulting from it.

'Yes, startling is the word for it,' observed Barbican, replying to a remark of Ardan's; 'and still more so when we reflect that not only are both lunar hemispheres deprived, by turns, of sun light for nearly 15 days, but that also the particular hemisphere over which we are at this moment floating is all that long night completely deprived of earth-light. In other words, it is only one side of the Moon's disc that ever receives any light from the Earth. From nearly every portion of one side of the Moon, the Earth is always as completely absent as the Sun is from us at midnight. Suppose an analogous case existed on the Earth; suppose, for instance, that neither in Europe, Asia or North America was the

Moon ever visible – that, in fact, it was to be seen only at our antipodes. With what astonishment should we contemplate her for the first time on our arrival in Australia or New Zealand!'

'Every man of us would pack off to Australia to see her!' cried Ardan.

'Yes,' said M'Nicholl sententiously; 'for a visit to the South Sea a Turk would willingly forego Mecca; and a Bostonian would prefer Sidney even to Paris.'

'Well,' resumed Barbican, 'this interesting marvel is reserved for the Selenite that inhabits the side of the Moon which is always turned away from our globe.'

'And which,' added the Captain, 'we should have had the unspeakable satisfaction of contemplating if we had only arrived at the period when the Sun and the Earth are not at the same side of the Moon – that is, 15 days sooner or later than now.'

'For my part, however,' continued Barbican, not heeding these interruptions, 'I must confess that, notwithstanding the magnificent splendour of the spectacle when viewed for the first time by the Selenite who inhabits the dark side of the Moon, I should prefer to be a resident on the illuminated side. The former, when his long, blazing, roasting, dazzling day is over, has a night 354 hours long, whose darkness, like that, just now surrounding us, is ever unrelieved save by the cold cheerless rays of the stars. But the latter has hardly seen his fiery sun sinking on one horizon when he beholds rising on the opposite one an orb, milder, paler, and colder indeed than the Sun, but fully as large as thirteen of our full Moons, and therefore shedding thirteen times as much light. This would be our Earth. It would pass through all its phases too, exactly like our Satellite. The Selenites would have their New Earth, Full Earth, and Last Quarter. At midnight, grandly illuminated, it would shine with the greatest glory. But that is almost as much as can be said for it. Its futile heat would but poorly compensate for its superior radiance. All the calorie accumulated in the lunar soil during the 354 hours day would have by this time radiated completely into space. An intensity of cold would prevail, in comparison to which a Greenland winter is tropical. The temperature of interstellar space, 250° below zero, would be reached. Our Selenite, heartily tired of the cold pale Earth, would gladly see her sink towards the horizon, waning as she sank, till at last she appeared no more than half full. Then suddenly a faint rim of the solar orb reveals itself on the edge of the opposite sky. Slowly, more than 14 times more slowly than with us, does the Sun lift himself above the lunar horizon. In half an hour, only half his disc is revealed, but that is more than enough to flood the lunar landscape with a dazzling intensity of light, of which we have no counterpart on Earth. No atmosphere refracts it, no hazy screen softens it, no enveloping vapour absorbs it, no obstructing medium colours it. It breaks on the eye, harsh, white, dazzling, blinding, like the electric light seen a few yards off. As the hours wear away, the more blasting becomes the glare; and the higher he rises in the black sky, but slowly, slowly. It takes him seven of our days to reach the meridian. By that time the heat has increased from an arctic temperature to double the boiling water point, from 250° below zero to 500° above it, or the point at which tin melts. Subjected to these extremes, the glassy rocks crack, shiver and crumble away; enormous land slides occur; peaks topple over; and tons of debris, crashing down the mountains, are swallowed up forever in the yawing chasms of the bottomless craters.'

'Bravo!' cried Ardan, clapping his hands softly: 'our President is sublime! He reminds me of the overture of *Guillaume Tell*!'

'Souvenir de Marston!' growled M'Nicholl.

'These phenomena,' continued Barbican, heedless of interruption and his voice betraying a slight glow of excitement, 'these phenomena going on without interruption from month to month, from year to year, from age to age, from *eon* to *eon*, have finally convinced me that – what?' he asked his hearers, interrupting himself suddenly.

– 'That the existence at the present time—' answered M'Nicholl.

– 'Of either animal or vegetable life—' interrupted Ardan.

– 'In the Moon is hardly possible!' cried both in one voice.

'Besides?' asked Barbican: 'even if there *is* any life—?'

– 'That to live on the dark side would be much more inconvenient than on the light side!' cried M'Nicholl promptly.

– 'That there is no choice between them!' cried Ardan just as ready. 'For my part, I should think a residence on Mt. Erebus or in Grinnell Land a terrestrial paradise in comparison to either. The *Earth shine* might illuminate the light side of the Moon a little during the long night, but for any practical advantage towards heat or life, it would be perfectly useless!'

'But there is another serious difference between the two sides,' said Barbican, 'in addition to those enumerated. The dark side is actually more troubled with excessive variations of temperature than the light one.'

'That assertion of our worthy President,' interrupted Ardan, 'with all possible respect for his superior knowledge, I am disposed to question.'

'It's as clear as day!' said Barbican.

'As clear as mud, you mean, Mr. President;' interrupted Ardan, 'the temperature of the light side is excited by two objects at the same time, the Earth and the Sun, whereas—'

– 'I beg your pardon, Ardan—' said Barbican.

– 'Granted, dear boy – granted with the utmost pleasure!' interrupted the Frenchman.

'I shall probably have to direct my observations altogether to you, Captain,' continued Barbican; 'friend Michael interrupts me so often that I'm afraid he can hardly understand my remarks.'

'I always admired your candor, Barbican,' said Ardan; 'it's a noble quality, a grand quality!'

'Don't mention it,' replied Barbican, turning towards M'Nicholl, still in the dark, and addressing him exclusively; 'You see, my dear

Captain, the period at which the Moon's invisible side receives at once its light and heat is exactly the period of her *conjunction*, that is to say, when she is lying between the Earth and the Sun. In comparison therefore with the place which she had occupied at her *opposition*, or when her visible side was fully illuminated, she is nearer to the Sun by double her distance from the Earth, or nearly 480 thousand miles. Therefore, my dear Captain, you can see how when the invisible side of the Moon is turned towards the Sun, she is nearly half a million of miles nearer to him than she had been before. Therefore, her heat should be so much the greater.'

'I see it at a glance,' said the Captain.

'Whereas—' continued Barbican.

'One moment!' cried Ardan.

'Another interruption!' exclaimed Barbican; 'What is the meaning of it, Sir?'

'I ask my honourable friend the privilege of the floor for one moment,' cried Ardan.

'What for?'

'To continue the explanation.'

'Why so?'

'To show that I can understand as well as interrupt!'

'You have the floor!' exclaimed Barbican, in a voice no longer showing any traces of ill humour.

'I expected no less from the honourable gentleman's well known courtesy,' replied Ardan. Then changing his manner and imitating to the life Barbican's voice, articulation, and gestures, he continued: 'Whereas, you see, my dear Captain, the period at which the Moon's visible side receives at once its light and heat, is exactly the period of her *opposition*, that is to say, when she is lying on one side of the Earth and the Sun at the other. In comparison therefore with the point which she had occupied in *conjunction*, or when her invisible side was fully illuminated, she is farther from the Sun by double her distance from the Earth, or nearly 480,000 miles. Therefore, my dear Captain, you can readily see how when the Moon's invisible side is turned *from* the Sun, she is nearly half a million miles further from him than she had been before. Therefore her heat should be so much the less.'

'Well done, friend Ardan!' cried Barbican, clapping his hands with pleasure. 'Yes, Captain, he understood it as well as either of us the whole time. Intelligence, not indifference, caused him to interrupt. Wonderful fellow!'

'That's the kind of a man I am!' replied Ardan, not without some degree of complacency. Then he added simply: 'Barbican, my friend, if I understand your explanations so readily, attribute it all to their astonishing lucidity. If I have any faculty, it is that of being able to scent common sense at the first glimmer. Your sentences are so steeped in it that I catch their full meaning long before you end them – hence my apparent inattention. But we're not yet done with the visible face of the Moon: it seems to me you have not yet enumerated all the advantages in which it surpasses the other side.'

'Another of these advantages,' continued Barbican, 'is that it is from the visible side alone that eclipses of the Sun can be seen. This is self-evident, the interposition of the Earth being possible only between this visible face and the Sun. Furthermore, such eclipses of the Sun would be of a far more imposing character than anything of the kind to be witnessed from our Earth. This is chiefly for two reasons: first, when we, terrestrians, see the Sun eclipsed, we notice that, the discs of the two orbs being of about the same apparent size, one cannot hide the other except for a short time; second, as the two bodies are moving in opposite directions, the total duration of the eclipse, even under the most favourable circumstances, can't last longer than 7 minutes. Whereas to a Selenite who sees the Earth eclipse the Sun, not only does the Earth's disc appear four times larger than the Sun's, but also, as his day is 14 times longer than ours, the two heavenly bodies must remain several hours in contact. Besides, notwithstanding the apparent superiority of the Earth's disc, the refracting power of the atmosphere will never allow the Sun to be eclipsed altogether. Even when completely screened by the Earth, he would form a beautiful circle around her of yellow, red, and crimson light, in which she would appear to float like a vast sphere of jet in a glowing sea of gold, rubies, sparkling carbuncles and garnets.'

'It seems to me,' said M'Nicholl, 'that, taking everything into consideration, the invisible side has been rather shabbily treated.'

'I know I should not stay there very long,' said Ardan; 'the desire of seeing such a splendid sight as that eclipse would be enough to bring me to the visible side as soon as possible.'

'Yes, I have no doubt of that, friend Michael,' pursued Barbican; 'but to see the eclipse it would not be necessary to quit the dark hemisphere altogether. You are, of course, aware that in consequence of her librations, or noddings, or wobblings, the Moon presents to the eyes of the Earth a little more than the exact half of her disc. She has two motions, one on her path around the Earth, and the other a shifting around on her own axis by which she endeavours to keep the same side always turned towards our sphere. This she cannot always do, as while one motion, the latter, is strictly uniform, the other being eccentric, sometimes accelerating her and sometimes retarding, she has not time to shift herself around completely and with perfect correspondence of movement. At her perigee, for instance, she moves forward quicker than she can shift, so that we detect a portion of her western border before she has time to conceal it. Similarly, at her apogee, when her rate of motion is comparatively slow, she shifts a little too quickly for her velocity, and therefore cannot help revealing a certain portion of her eastern border. She shows altogether about 8 degrees of the dark side, about 4 at the east and 4 at the west, so that, out of her 360 degrees, about 188, in other words, a little more than 57 per cent, about $4/7$ of the entire surface, becomes visible to human eyes. Consequently a Selenite could catch an occasional glimpse of our Earth, without altogether quitting the dark side.'

'No matter for that!' cried Ardan; 'if we ever become Selenites we must inhabit the visible side. My weak point is light, and that I must have when it can be got.'

'Unless, as perhaps in this case, you might be paying too dear for it,' observed M'Nicholl. 'How would you like to pay for your light by the loss of the atmosphere, which, according to some philosophers, is piled away on the dark side?'

'Ah! In that case I should consider a little before committing myself,' replied Ardan, 'I should like to hear your opinion regarding such a notion, Barbican. Hey! Do your hear? Have astronomers any valid reasons for supposing the atmosphere to have fled to the dark side of the Moon?'

'Defer that question till some other time, Ardan,' whispered M'Nicholl; 'Barbican is just now thinking out something that interests him far more deeply than any empty speculation of astronomers. If you are near the window, look out through it towards the Moon. Can you see anything?'

'I can feel the window with my hand; but for all I can see, I might as well be over head and ears in a hogshead of ink.'

The two friends kept up a desultory conversation, but Barbican did not hear them. One fact, in particular, troubled him, and he sought in vain to account for it. Having come so near the Moon – about 30 miles – why had not the Projectile gone all the way? Had its velocity been very great, the tendency to fall could certainly be counteracted. But the velocity being undeniably very moderate, how explain such a decided resistance to Lunar attraction? Had the Projectile come within the sphere of some strange unknown influence? Did the neighbourhood of some mysterious body retain it firmly imbedded in ether? That it would never reach the Moon, was now beyond all doubt; but where was it going? Nearer to her or further off? Or was it rushing resistlessly into infinity on the wings of that pitchy night? Who could tell, know, calculate – who could even guess, amid the horror of this gloomy blackness? Questions, like these, left Barbican no rest; in vain he tried to grapple with them; he felt like a child before them, baffled and almost despairing.

In fact, what could be more tantalizing? Just outside their windows, only a few leagues off, perhaps only a few miles, lay the radiant planet of the night, but in every respect as far off from the eyes of himself and his companions as if she was hiding at the other side of Jupiter! And to their ears she was no nearer. Earthquakes of the old Titanic type might at that very moment be upheaving her surface with resistless force, crashing mountain against mountain as fiercely as wave meets wave around the storm-lashed cliffs of Cape Horn. But not the faintest far off murmur even of such a mighty tumult could break the dead brooding silence that surrounded the travellers. Nay, the Moon, realizing the weird fancy of the Arabian poet, who calls her a 'giant stiffening into granite, but struggling madly against his doom,' might shriek, in a spasm of agony, loudly enough to be heard in Sirius. But our travellers could not hear it. Their ears no sound could now reach. They could no more detect the rending of a continent than the falling of a feather. Air, the propagator and transmitter of sound, was absent from her surface. Her cries, her struggles, her groans, were all smothered beneath the impenetrable tomb of eternal silence!

These were some of the fanciful ideas by which Ardan tried to amuse his companions in the present unsatisfactory state of affairs. His efforts, however well meant, were not successful. M'Nicholl's growls were more savage than usual, and even Barbican's patience was decidedly giving way. The loss of the other face they could have easily borne – with most of its details they had been already familiar. But, no, it must be the dark face that now escaped their observation! The very one that for numberless reasons they were actually dying to see! They looked out of the windows once more at the black Moon beneath them.

There it lay below them, a round black spot, hiding the sweet faces of the stars, but otherwise no more distinguishable by the travellers than if they were lying in the depths of the Mammoth Cave of Kentucky. And just think. Only fifteen days before, that dark face had been splendidly illuminated by the solar beams, every crater lustrous, every peak sparkling, every streak glistening under the vertical ray. In fifteen days later, a day light the most brilliant would have replaced a midnight the most Cimmerian. But in fifteen days later, where would the Projectile be? In what direction would it have been drawn by the forces innumerable of attractions incalculable? To such a question as this, even Ardan would reply only by an ominous shake of the head.

We know already that our travellers, as well as astronomers generally, judging from that portion of the dark side occasionally revealed by the Moon's librations, were *pretty certain* that there is no great difference between her two sides, as far as regards their physical constitutions. This portion, about the seventh part, shows plains and mountains, circles and craters, all of precisely the same nature as those already laid down on the chart. Judging therefore from analogy, the other three-sevenths are, in all probability a world in every respect exactly like the visible face – that is, arid, desert, dead. But our travellers also knew that *pretty certain* is far from *quite certain*, and that arguing merely from analogy may enable you to give a good guess, but can never lead you to an undoubted conclusion. What if the atmosphere had really withdrawn to this dark face? And if air, why not water? Would not this be enough to infuse life into the whole continent? Why should not vegetation flourish on its plains, fish in its seas, animals in its forests, and man in every one of its zones that were capable of sustaining life? To these interesting questions, what a satisfaction it would be to able to answer positively one way or another!

For thousands of difficult problems a mere glimpse at this hemisphere would be enough to furnish a satisfactory reply. How glorious it would be to contemplate a realm on which the eye of man has never yet rested!

Great, therefore, as you may readily conceive, was the depression of our travellers' spirits, as they pursued their way, enveloped in a veil of darkness the most profound. Still even then Ardan, as usual, formed somewhat of an exception. Finding it impossible to see a particle of the Lunar surface, he gave it up for good, and tried to console himself by gazing at the stars, which now fairly blazed in the spangled heavens. And certainly never before had astronomer enjoyed an opportunity for gazing at the heavenly bodies under such peculiar advantages. How Fraye of Paris, Chacornac of Lyons, and Father Secchi of Rome would have envied him!

For, candidly and truly speaking, never before had mortal eye revelled on such a scene of starry splendour. The black sky sparkled with lustrous fires, like the ceiling of a vast hall of ebony encrusted with flashing diamonds. Ardan's eye could take in the whole extent in an easy sweep from the *Southern Cross* to the *Little Bear*, thus embracing within one glance not only the two polar stars of the present day, but also *Campus* and *Vega*, which, by reason of the *precession of the Equinoxes*, are to be our polar stars 12,000 years hence. His imagination, as if intoxicated, reeled wildly through these sublime infinitudes and got lost in them. He forgot all about himself and all about his companions. He forgot even the strangeness of the fate that had sent them wandering through these forbidden regions, like a bewildered comet that had lost its way. With what a soft sweet light every star glowed! No matter what its magnitude, the stream that flowed from it looked calm and holy. No twinkling, no scintillation, no nictitation, disturbed their pure and lambent gleam. No atmosphere here interposed its layers of humidity or of unequal density to interrupt the stately majesty of their effulgence. The longer he gazed upon them, the more absorbing became their attraction.

He felt that they were great kindly eyes looking down even yet with benevolence and protection on himself and his companions now driving wildly through space, and lost in the pathless depths of the black ocean of infinity!

He soon became aware that his friends, following his example, had interested themselves in gazing at the stars, and were now just as absorbed as himself in the contemplation of the transcendent spectacle. For a long time all three continued to feast their eyes on all the glories of the starry firmament; but, strange to say, the part that seemed to possess the strangest and weirdest fascination for their wandering glances was the spot where the vast disc of the Moon showed like an enormous round hole, black and soundless, and apparently deep enough to permit a glance into the darkest mysteries of the infinite.

A disagreeable sensation, however, against which they had been for some time struggling, at last put an end to their contemplations, and compelled them to think of themselves. This was nothing less than a pretty sharp cold, at first somewhat endurable, but which soon covered the inside surface of the window panes with a thick coating of ice. The fact was that, the Sun's direct rays having no longer an opportunity of warming up the Projectile, the latter began to lose rapidly by radiation whatever heat it had stored away within its walls. The consequence was a very decided falling of the thermometer, and so thick a condensation of the internal moisture on the window glasses as to soon render all external observations extremely difficult, if not actually impossible.

The Captain, as the oldest man in the party, claimed the privilege of saying he could stand it no longer. Striking a light, he consulted the thermometer and cried out:

'Seventeen degrees below zero, centigrade! that is certainly low enough to make an old fellow like me feel rather chilly!'

'Just one degree and a half above zero, Fahrenheit!' observed Barbican; 'I really had no idea that it was so cold.'

His teeth actually chattered so much that he could hardly articulate; still he, as well as the others, disliked to entrench on their short supply of gas.

'One feature of our journey that I particularly admire,' said Ardan, trying to laugh with freezing lips, 'is that we can't complain of monotony. At one time we are frying with the heat and blinded with the light, like Indians caught on a burning prairie; at another, we are freezing in the pitchy darkness of a hyperborean winter, like Sir John Franklin's merry men in the Bay of Boothia. *Madame La Nature*, you don't forget your devotees; on the contrary, you overwhelm us with your attentions!'

'Our external temperature may be reckoned at how much?' asked the Captain, making a desperate effort to keep up the conversation.

'The temperature outside our Projectile must be precisely the same as that of interstellar space in general,' answered Barbican.

'Is not this precisely the moment then,' interposed Ardan, quickly, 'for making an experiment which we could never have made as long as we were in the sunshine?'

'That's so!' exclaimed Barbican; 'now or never! I'm glad you thought of it, Ardan. We are just now in the position to find out the temperature of space by actual experiment, and so see whose calculations are right, Fourier's or Pouillet's.'

'Let's see,' asked Ardan, 'who was Fourier, and who was Pouillet?'

'Baron Fourier, of the French Academy, wrote a famous treatise on *Heat*, which I remember reading twenty years ago in Penington's book store,' promptly responded the Captain; 'Pouillet was an eminent professor of Physics at the Sorbonne, where he died, last year, I think.'

'Thank you, Captain,' said Ardan; 'the cold does not injure your memory, though it is decidedly on the advance. See how thick the ice is already on the window panes! Let it only keep on and we shall soon have our breaths falling around us in flakes of snow.'

'Let us prepare a thermometer,' said Barbican, who had already set himself to work in a business-like manner.

A thermometer of the usual kind, as may be readily supposed, would be of no use whatever in the experiment that was now about to be made. In an ordinary thermometer Mercury freezes hard when exposed to a temperature of 40° below zero. But Barbican had provided himself with a *Minimum, self-recording* thermometer, of a peculiar nature, invented by Wolferdin, a friend of Arago's, which could correctly register exceedingly low degrees of temperature. Before beginning the experiment, this instrument was tested by comparison with one of the usual kind, and then Barbican hesitated a few moments regarding the best means of employing it.

'How shall we start this experiment?' asked the Captain.

'Nothing simpler,' answered Ardan, always ready to reply; 'you just open your windows, and fling out your thermometer. It follows your Projectile, as a calf follows her mother. In a quarter of an hour you put out your hand—'

'Put out your hand!' interrupted Barbican.

'Put out your hand—' continued Ardan, quietly.

'You do nothing of the kind,' again interrupted Barbican; 'that is, unless you prefer, instead of a hand, to pull back a frozen stump, shapeless, colourless and lifeless!'

'I prefer a hand,' said Ardan, surprised and interested.

'Yes,' continued Barbican, 'the instant your hand left the Projectile, it would experience the same terrible sensations as is produced by cauterizing it with an iron bar white hot. For heat, whether rushing rapidly out of our bodies or rapidly entering them, is identically the same force and does the same amount of damage. Besides I am by no means certain that we are still followed by the objects that we flung out of the Projectile.'

'Why not?' asked M'Nicholl; 'we saw them all outside not long ago.'

'But we can't see them outside now,' answered Barbican; 'that may be accounted for, I know, by the darkness, but it may be also by the fact of their not being there at all. In a case like this, we can't rely on uncertainties. Therefore, to make sure of not losing our thermometer, we shall fasten it with a string and easily pull it in whenever we like.'

This advice being adopted, the window was opened quickly, and the instrument was thrown out at once by M'Nicholl, who held it fastened by a short stout cord so that it could be pulled in immediately. The window had hardly been open for longer than a second, yet that second had been enough to admit a terrible icy chill into the interior of the Projectile.

'Ten thousand ice-bergs!' cried Ardan, shivering all over; 'it's cold enough to freeze a white bear!'

Barbican waited quietly for half an hour; that time he considered quite long enough to enable the instrument to acquire the temperature of the interstellar space. Then he gave the signal, and it was instantly pulled in.

It took him a few moments to calculate the quantity of mercury that had escaped into the little diaphragm attached to the lower part of the instrument; then he said:

'A hundred and forty degrees, centigrade, below zero!'

'Two hundred and twenty degrees, Fahrenheit, below zero!' cried M'Nicholl; 'no wonder that we should feel a little chilly!'

'Pouillet is right, then,' said Barbican, 'and Fourier wrong.'

'Another victory for Sorbonne over the Academy!' cried Ardan. '*Vive la Sorbonne!* Not that I'm a bit proud of finding myself in the midst of a temperature so very *distingué* – though it is more than three times colder than Hayes ever felt it at Humboldt Glacier or Nevenoff at Yakoutsk. If Madame the Moon becomes as cold as this every time that her surface is withdrawn from the sunlight for fourteen days, I don't think, boys, that her hospitality is much to hanker after!'

CHAPTER XV
Glimpses at the Invisible

IN SPITE OF the dreadful condition in which the three friends now found themselves, and the still more dreadful future that awaited them, it must be acknowledged that Ardan bravely kept up his spirits. And his companions were just as cheerful. Their philosophy was quite simple and perfectly intelligible. What they could bear, they bore without murmuring. When it became unbearable, they only complained, if complaining would do any good. Imprisoned in an iron shroud, flying through profound darkness into the infinite abysses of space, nearly a quarter million of miles distant from all human aid, freezing with the icy cold, their little stock not only of gas but of *air* rapidly running lower and lower, a near future of the most impenetrable obscurity looming up before them, they never once thought of wasting time in asking such useless questions as where they were going, or what fate was about to befall them. Knowing that no good could possibly result from inaction or despair, they carefully kept their wits about them, making their experiments and recording their observations as calmly and as deliberately as if they were working at home in the quiet retirement of their own cabinets.

Any other course of action, however, would have been perfectly absurd on their part, and this no one knew better than themselves. Even if desirous to act otherwise, what could they have done? As powerless over the Projectile as a baby over a locomotive, they could neither clap brakes to its movement nor switch off its direction. A sailor can turn his ship's head at pleasure; an aeronaut has little trouble, by means of his ballast and his throttle-valve, in giving a vertical movement to his balloon. But nothing of this kind could our travellers attempt. No helm, or ballast, or throttle-valve could avail them now. Nothing in the world could be done to prevent things from following their own course to the bitter end.

If these three men would permit themselves to hazard an expression at all on the subject, which they didn't, each could have done it by his own favourite motto, so admirably expressive of his individual nature. '*Donnez tête baissée!*' (Go it baldheaded!) showed Ardan's uncalculating impetuosity and his Celtic blood. '*Fata quocunque vocant!*' (To its logical consequence!) revealed Barbican's imperturbable stoicism, culture hardening rather than loosening the original British phlegm. Whilst M'Nicholl's 'Screw down the valve and let her rip!' betrayed at once his unconquerable Yankee coolness and his old experiences as a Western steamboat captain.

Where were they now, at eight o'clock in the morning of the day called in America the sixth of December? Near the Moon, very certainly; near enough, in fact, for them to perceive easily in the dark the great round screen which she formed between themselves and the Projectile on one side, and the Earth, Sun, and stars on the other. But as to the exact distance at which she lay from them – they had no possible means of calculating it. The Projectile, impelled and maintained by forces inexplicable and even incomprehensible, had come within less than thirty miles from the Moon's north pole. But during those two hours of immersion in the dark shadow, had this distance been increased or diminished? There was evidently no stand-point whereby to estimate either the Projectile's direction or its velocity. Perhaps, moving rapidly away from the Moon, it would be soon out of her shadow altogether. Perhaps, on the contrary, gradually approaching her surface, it might come into contact at any moment with some sharp invisible peak of the Lunar mountains – a catastrophe sure to put a sudden end to the trip, and the travellers too.

An excited discussion on this subject soon sprang up, in which all naturally took part. Ardan's imagination as usual getting the better of his reason, he maintained very warmly that the Projectile, caught and retained by the Moon's attraction, could not help falling on her surface, just as an aerolite cannot help falling on our Earth.

'Softly, dear boy, softly,' replied Barbican; 'aerolites *can* help falling on the Earth, and the proof is, that few of them *do* fall – most of them don't. Therefore, even granting that we had already assumed the nature of an aerolite, it does not necessarily follow that we should fall on the Moon.'

'But,' objected Ardan, 'if we approach only near enough, I don't see how we can help—'

'You don't see, it may be,' said Barbican, 'but you can see, if you only reflect a moment. Have you not often seen the November meteors, for instance, streaking the skies, thousands at a time?'

'Yes; on several occasions I was so fortunate.'

'Well, did you ever see any of them strike the Earth's surface?' asked Barbican.

'I can't say I ever did,' was the candid reply, 'but—'

'Well, these shooting stars,' continued Barbican, 'or rather these wandering particles of matter, shine only from being inflamed by the friction of the atmosphere. Therefore they can never be at a greater distance from the Earth than 30 or 40 miles at furthest, and yet they seldom fall on it. So with our Projectile. It may go very close to the Moon without falling into it.'

'But our roving Projectile must pull up somewhere in the long run,' replied Ardan, 'and I should like to know where that somewhere can be, if not in the Moon.'

'Softly again, dear boy,' said Barbican; 'how do you know that our Projectile must pull up somewhere?'

'It's self-evident,' replied Ardan; 'it can't keep moving for ever.'

'Whether it can or it can't depends altogether on which one of two mathematical curves it has followed in describing its course. According to the velocity with which it was endowed at a certain moment, it must follow either the one or the other; but this velocity I do not consider myself just now able to calculate.'

'Exactly so,' chimed in M'Nicholl; 'it must describe and keep on describing either a parabola or a hyperbola.'

'Precisely,' said Barbican; 'at a certain velocity it would take a parabolic curve; with a velocity considerably greater it should describe a hyperbolic curve.'

'I always did like nice corpulent words,' said Ardan, trying to laugh; 'bloated and unwieldy, they express in a neat handy way exactly what you mean. Of course, I know all about the high – high – those high curves, and those low curves. No matter. Explain them to me all the same. Consider me most deplorably ignorant on the nature of these curves.'

'Well,' said the Captain, a little bumptiously, 'a parabola is a curve of the second order, formed by the intersection of a cone by a plane parallel to one of its sides.'

'You don't say so!' cried Ardan, with mouth agape. 'Do tell!'

'It is pretty nearly the path taken by a shell shot from a mortar.'

'Well now!' observed Ardan, apparently much surprised; 'who'd have thought it? Now for the high – high – bully old curve!'

'The hyperbola,' continued the Captain, not minding Ardan's antics, 'the hyperbola is a curve of the second order, formed from the intersection of a cone by a plane parallel to its axis, or rather parallel to its two *generatrices*, constituting two separate branches, extending indefinitely in both directions.'

'Oh, what an accomplished scientist I'm going to turn out, if only left long enough at your feet, illustrious *maestro*!' cried Ardan, with effusion. 'Only figure it to yourselves, boys; before the Captain's lucid explanations, I fully expected to hear something about the high curves and the low curves in the back of an Ancient Thomas! Oh, Michael, Michael, why didn't you know the Captain earlier?'

But the Captain was now too deeply interested in a hot discussion with Barbican to notice that the Frenchman was only funning him. Which of the two curves had been the one most probably taken by the Projectile? Barbican maintained it was the parabolic; M'Nicholl insisted that it was the hyperbolic. Their tempers were not improved by the severe cold, and both became rather excited in the dispute. They drew so many lines on the table, and crossed them so often with others, that nothing was left at last but a great blot. They covered bits of paper with x's and y's, which they read out like so many classic passages, shouting them, declaiming them, drawing attention to the strong points by gesticulation so forcible and voice so loud that neither of the disputants could hear a word that the other said. Possibly the very great difference in temperature between the external air in contact with their skin and the blood coursing through their veins, had given rise to magnetic currents as potential in their effects as a superabundant supply of oxygen. At all events, the language they soon began to employ in the enforcement of their arguments fairly made the Frenchman's hair stand on end.

'You probably forget the important difference between a *directrix* and an *axis*,' hotly observed Barbican.

'I know what an *abscissa* is, any how!' cried the Captain. 'Can you say as much?'

'Did you ever understand what is meant by a *double ordinate*?' asked Barbican, trying to keep cool.

'More than you ever did about a *transverse* and a *conjugate*!' replied the Captain, with much asperity.

'Any one not convinced at a glance that this *eccentricity* is equal to *unity*, must be blind as a bat!' exclaimed Barbican, fast losing his ordinary urbanity.

'*Less* than *unity*, you mean! If you want spectacles, here are mine!' shouted the Captain, angrily tearing them off and offering them to his adversary.

'Dear boys!' interposed Ardan—

– 'The *eccentricity* is *equal* to *unity*!' cried Barbican.

– 'The *eccentricity* is *less* than *unity*!' screamed M'Nicholl.

'Talking of eccentricity—' put in Ardan.

– 'Therefore it's a *parabola*, and must be!' cried Barbican, triumphantly.

– 'Therefore it's *hyperbola* and nothing shorter!' was the Captain's quite as confident reply.

'For gracious sake!—' resumed Ardan.

'Then produce your *asymptote*!' exclaimed Barbican, with an angry sneer.

'Let us see the *symmetrical point*!' roared the Captain, quite savagely.

'Dear boys! old fellows!—' cried Ardan, as loud as his lungs would let him.

'It's useless to argue with a Mississippi steamboat Captain,' ejaculated Barbican; 'he never gives in till he blows up!'

'Never try to convince a Yankee schoolmaster,' replied M'Nicholl; 'he has one book by heart and don't believe in any other!'

'Here, friend Michael, get me a cord, won't you? It's the only way to convince him!' cried Barbican, hastily turning to the Frenchman.

'Hand me over that ruler, Ardan!' yelled the Captain. 'The heavy one! It's the only way now left to bring him to reason!'

'Look here, Barbican and M'Nicholl!' cried Ardan, at last making himself heard, and keeping a tight hold both on the cord and the ruler. 'This thing has gone far enough! Come. Stop your talk, and answer me a few questions. What do you want of this cord, Barbican?'

'To describe a parabolic curve!'

'And what are you going to do with the ruler, M'Nicholl!'

'To help draw a true hyperbola!'

'Promise me, Barbican, that you're not going to lasso the Captain!'

'Lasso the Captain! Ha! ha! ha!'

'You promise, M'Nicholl, that you're not going to brain the President!'

'I brain the President! Ho! ho! ho!'

'I want merely to convince him that it is a parabola!'

'I only want to make it clear as day that it is hyperbola!'

'Does it make any real difference whether it is one or the other?' yelled Ardan.

'The greatest possible difference – in the Eye of Science.'

'A radical and incontrovertible difference – in the Eye of Science!'

'Oh! Hang the Eye of Science – will either curve take us to the Moon?'

'No!'

'Will either take us back to the Earth?'

'No!'

'Will either take us anywhere that you know of?'

'No!'

'Why not?'

'Because they are both *open* curves, and therefore can never end!'

'Is it of the slightest possible importance which of the two curves controls the Projectile?'

'Not the slightest – except in the Eye of Science!'

'Then let the Eye of Science and her parabolas and hyperbolas, and conjugates, and asymptotes, and the rest of the confounded nonsensical farrago, all go to pot! What's the use of bothering your heads about them here! Have you not enough to trouble you otherwise? A nice pair of scientists you are? "Stanislow" scientists, probably. Do *real* scientists lose their tempers for a trifle? Am I ever to see my ideal of a true scientific man in the flesh? Barbican came very near realizing my idea perfectly; but I see that Science just has as little effect as Culture in driving the Old Adam out of us! The idea of the only simpleton in the lot having to lecture the others on propriety of deportment! I thought they were going to tear each other's eyes out! Ha! Ha! Ha! It's *impayable*! Give me that cord, Michael! Hand me the heavy ruler, Ardan! It's the only way to bring him to reason! Ho! Ho! Ho! It's too good! I shall never get over it!' and he laughed till his sides ached and his cheeks streamed.

His laughter was so contagious, and his merriment so genuine, that there was really no resisting it, and the next few minutes witnessed nothing but laughing, and handshaking and rib-punching in the Projectile – though Heaven knows there was very little for the poor fellows to be merry about. As they could neither reach the Moon nor return to the Earth, what *was* to befall them? The immediate outlook was the very reverse of exhilarating. If they did not die of hunger, if they did not die of thirst, the reason would simply be that, in a few days, as soon as their gas was exhausted, they would die for want of air, unless indeed the icy cold had killed them beforehand!

By this time, in fact, the temperature had become so exceedingly cold that a further encroachment on their little stock of gas could be put off no longer. The light, of course, they could manage to do without; but a little heat was absolutely necessary to prevent them from freezing to death. Fortunately, however, the caloric developed by the Reiset and Regnault process for purifying the air, raised the internal temperature of the Projectile a little, so that, with an expenditure of gas much less than they had expected, our travellers were able to maintain it at a degree capable of sustaining human life.

By this time, also, all observations through the windows had become exceedingly difficult. The internal moisture condensed so thick and congealed so hard on the glass that nothing short of continued friction could keep up its transparency. But this friction, however labourious they might regard it at other times, they thought very little of just now, when observation had become far more interesting and important than ever.

If the Moon had any atmosphere, our travellers were near enough now to strike any meteor that might be rushing through it. If the Projectile itself were floating in it, as was possible, would not such a good conductor of sound convey to their ears the reflexion of some lunar echo, the roar of some storm raging among the mountains, the rattling of some plunging avalanche, or the detonations of some eructating volcano? And suppose some lunar Etna or Vesuvius was flashing out its fires, was it not even possible that their eye could catch a glimpse of the lurid gleam? One or two facts of this kind, well attested, would singularly elucidate the vexatious question of a lunar atmosphere, which is still so far from being decided. Full of such thoughts and intensely interested in them, Barbican, M'Nicholl and Ardan, patient as astronomers at a transit of Venus, watched steadily at their windows, and allowed nothing worth noticing to escape their searching gaze.

Ardan's patience first gave out. He showed it by an observation natural enough, for that matter, to a mind unaccustomed to long stretches of careful thought:

'This darkness is absolutely killing! If we ever take this trip again, it must be about the time of the New Moon!'

'There I agree with you, Ardan,' observed the Captain. 'That would be just the time to start. The Moon herself, I grant, would be lost in the solar rays and therefore invisible all the time of our trip, but in compensation, we should have the Full Earth in full view. Besides – and this is your chief point, no doubt, Ardan – if we should happen to be drawn round the Moon, just as we are at the present moment, we should enjoy the inestimable advantage of beholding her invisible side magnificently illuminated!'

'My idea exactly, Captain,' said Ardan. 'What is your opinion on this point, Barbican?'

'My opinion is as follows:' answered Barbican, gravely. 'If we ever repeat this journey, we shall start precisely at the same time and under precisely the same circumstances. You forget that our only object is to reach the Moon. Now suppose we had really landed there, as we expected to do yesterday, would it not have been much more agreeable to behold the lunar continents enjoying the full light of day than to find them plunged in the dismal obscurity of night? Would not our first installation of discovery have been under circumstances decidedly extremely favourable? Your silence shows that you agree with me. As to the invisible side, once landed, we should have the power to visit it when we pleased, and therefore we could always choose whatever time would best suit our purpose. Therefore, if we wanted to land in the Moon, the period of the Full Moon was the best period to select. The period was well chosen, the time was well calculated, the force was well applied, the Projectile was well aimed, but missing our way spoiled everything.'

'That's sound logic, no doubt,' said Ardan; 'still I can't help thinking that all for want of a little light we are losing, probably forever, a splendid opportunity of seeing the Moon's invisible side. How about the other planets, Barbican? Do you think that their inhabitants are as ignorant regarding their satellites as we are regarding ours?'

'On that subject,' observed M'Nicholl, 'I could venture an answer myself, though, of course, without pretending to speak dogmatically on any such open question. The satellites of the other planets, by their comparative proximity, must be much easier to study than our Moon. The Saturnians, the Uranians, the Jovians, cannot have had very serious difficulty in effecting some communication with their satellites. Jupiter's four moons, for instance, though on an average actually 2½ times farther from their planet's centre than the Moon is from us, are comparatively four times nearer to him on account of his radius being eleven times greater than the Earth's. With Saturn's eight moons, the case is almost precisely similar. Their average distance is nearly three times greater than that of our Moon; but as Saturn's diameter is about 9 times greater than the Earth's, his bodyguards are really between 3 and 4 times nearer to their principal than ours is to us. As to Uranus, his first satellite, *Ariel*, half as far from him as our Moon is from the Earth, is comparatively, though not actually, eight times nearer.'

'Therefore,' said Barbican, now taking up the subject, 'an experiment analogous to ours, starting from either of these three planets, would have encountered fewer difficulties. But the whole question resolves itself into this. *If* the Jovians and the rest have been able to quit their planets, they have probably succeeded in discovering the invisible sides of their satellites. But if they have *not* been able to do so, why, they're not a bit wiser than ourselves – But what's the matter with the Projectile? It's certainly shifting!'

Shifting it certainly was. While the path it described as it swung blindly through the darkness, could not be laid down by any chart for want of a starting point, Barbican and his companions soon became aware of a decided modification of its relative position with regard to the Moon's surface. Instead of its side, as heretofore, it now presented its base to the Moon's disc, and its axis had become rigidly vertical to the lunar horizon. Of this new feature in their journey, Barbican had assured himself by the most undoubted proof towards four o'clock in the morning. What was the cause? Gravity, of course. The heavier portion of the Projectile gravitated towards the Moon's centre exactly as if they were falling towards her surface.

But *were* they falling? Were they at last, contrary to all expectations, about to reach the goal that they had been so ardently wishing for? No! A sight-point, just discovered by M'Nicholl, very soon convinced Barbican that the Projectile was as far as ever from approaching the Moon, but was moving around it in a curve pretty near concentric.

M'Nicholl's discovery, a luminous gleam flickering on the distant verge of the black disc, at once engrossed the complete attention of our travellers and set them to divining its course. It could not possibly be confounded with a star. Its glare was reddish, like that of a distant furnace on a dark night; it kept steadily increasing in size and brightness, thus showing beyond a doubt how the Projectile was moving – in the direction of the luminous point, and *not* vertically falling towards the Moon's surface.

'It's a volcano!' cried the Captain, in great excitement; 'a volcano in full blast! An outlet of the Moon's internal fires! Therefore she can't be a burnt out cinder!'

'It certainly looks like a volcano,' replied Barbican, carefully investigating this new and puzzling phenomenon with his night-glass. 'If it is not one, in fact, what can it be?'

'To maintain combustion,' commenced Ardan syllogistically and sententiously, 'air is necessary. An undoubted case of combustion lies before us. Therefore, this part of the Moon *must* have an atmosphere!'

'Perhaps so,' observed Barbican, 'but not necessarily so. The volcano, by decomposing certain substances, gunpowder for instance, may be able to furnish its own oxygen, and thus explode in a vacuum. That blaze, in fact, seems to me to possess the intensity and the blinding glare of objects burning in pure oxygen. Let us therefore be not over hasty in jumping at the conclusion of the existence of a lunar atmosphere.'

This fire mountain was situated, according to the most plausible conjecture, somewhere in the neighbourhood of the 45th degree, south latitude, of the Moon's invisible side. For a little while the travellers indulged the fond hope that they were directly approaching it, but, to their great disappointment, the path described by the Projectile lay in a different direction. Its nature therefore they had no opportunity of ascertaining. It began to disappear behind the dark horizon within less than half an hour after the time that M'Nicholl had signalled it. Still, the fact of the uncontested existence of such a phenomenon was a grand one, and of considerable importance in selenographic investigations. It proved that heat had not altogether disappeared from the lunar world; and the existence of heat once settled, who can say positively that the vegetable kingdom and even the animal kingdom have not likewise resisted so far every influence tending to destroy them? If terrestrial astronomers could only be convinced, by undoubted evidence, of the existence of this active volcano on the Moon's surface, they would certainly admit of very considerable modifications in the present doubts regarding her inhabitability.

Thoughts of this kind continued to occupy the minds of our travellers even for some time after the little spark of light had been extinguished in the black gloom. But they said very little; even Ardan was silent, and continued to look out of the window. Barbican surrendered himself up to a reverie regarding the mysterious destinies of the lunar world. Was its present condition a foreshadowing of what our Earth is to become? M'Nicholl, too, was lost in speculation. Was the Moon older or younger than the Earth in the order of Creation? Had she ever been a beautiful world of life, and colour, and magnificent variety? If so, had her inhabitants—

Great Mercy, what a cry from Ardan! It sounded human, so seldom do we hear a shriek so expressive at once of surprise and horror and even terror! It brought back his startled companions to their senses in a second. Nor did they ask him for the cause of his alarm. It was only too clear. Right in their very path, a blazing ball of fire had suddenly risen up before their eyes, the pitchy darkness all round it rendering its glare still more blinding. Its phosphoric coruscation filled the Projectile with white streams of lurid light, tinging the contents with a pallor indescribably ghastly. The travellers' faces in particular, gleamed with that peculiar livid and cadaverous tinge, blue and yellow, which magicians so readily produce by burning table salt in alcohol.

'*Sacré!*' cried Ardan who always spoke his own language when much excited. 'What a pair of beauties you are! Say, Barbican! What thundering thing is coming at us now?'

'Another bolide,' answered Barbican, his eye as calm as ever, though a faint tremor was quite perceptible in his voice.

'A bolide? Burning *in vacuo*? You are joking!'

'I was never more in earnest,' was the President's quiet reply, as he looked through his closed fingers.

He knew exactly what he was saying. The dazzling glitter did not deceive *him*. Such a meteor seen from the Earth could not appear much brighter than the Full Moon, but here in the midst of the black ether and unsoftened by the veil of the atmosphere, it was absolutely blinding. These wandering bodies carry in themselves the principle of their incandescence. Oxygen is by no means necessary for their combustion. Some of them indeed often take fire as they rush through the layers of our atmosphere, and generally burn out before they strike the Earth. But others, on the contrary, and the greater number too, follow a track through space far more distant from the Earth than the fifty miles supposed to limit our atmosphere. In October, 1844, one of these meteors had appeared in the sky at an altitude calculated to be at least 320 miles; and in August, 1841, another had vanished when it had reached the height of 450 miles. A few even of those seen from the Earth must have been several miles in diameter. The velocity with which some of them have been calculated to move, from east to west, in a direction contrary to that of the Earth, is astounding enough to exceed belief – about fifty miles in a second. Our Earth does not move quite 20 miles in a second, though it goes a thousand times quicker than the fastest locomotive.

Barbican calculated like lightning that the present object of their alarm was only about 250 miles distant from them, and could not be less than a mile and a quarter in diameter. It was coming on at the rate of more than a mile a second or about 75 miles a minute. It lay right in the path of the Projectile, and in a very few seconds indeed a terrible collision was inevitable. The enormous rate at which it grew in size, showed the terrible velocity at which it was approaching.

You can hardly imagine the situation of our poor travellers at the sight of this frightful apparition. I shall certainly not attempt to describe it. In spite of their singular courage, wonderful coolness, extraordinary fortitude, they were now breathless, motionless, almost helpless; their muscles were tightened to their utmost tension; their eyes stared out of their sockets; their faces were petrified with horror. No wonder. Their Projectile, whose course they were powerless as children to guide, was making straight for this fiery mass, whose glare in a few seconds had become more blinding than the open vent of a reverberating furnace. Their own Projectile was carrying them headlong into a bottomless abyss of fire!

Still, even in this moment of horror, their presence of mind, or at least their consciousness, never abandoned them. Barbican had grasped each of his friends by the hand, and all three tried as well as they could to watch through half-closed eyelids the white-hot asteroid's rapid approach. They could utter no word, they could breathe no prayer. They gave themselves up for lost – in the agony of terror that partially interrupted the ordinary functions of their brains, this was absolutely all they could do! Hardly three minutes had elapsed since Ardan had caught the first glimpse of it – three ages of agony! Now it was on them! In a second – in less than a second, the terrible fireball had burst like a shell! Thousands of glittering fragments were flying around them in all directions – but with no more noise than is made by so many light flakes of thistle-down floating about some warm afternoon in summer. The blinding, blasting steely white glare of the explosion almost bereft the travellers of the use of their eyesight forever, but no more report reached their ears than if it had taken place at the bottom of the Gulf of Mexico. In an atmosphere like ours, such a crash would have burst the ear-membranes of ten thousand elephants!

In the middle of the commotion another loud cry was suddenly heard. It was the Captain who called this time. His companions rushed to his window and all looked out together in the same direction.

What a sight met their eyes! What pen can describe it? What pencil can reproduce the magnificence of its colouring? It was a Vesuvius at his best and wildest, at the moment just after the old cone has fallen in. Millions of luminous fragments streaked the sky with their blazing fires. All sizes and shapes of light, all colours and shades of colours, were inextricably mingled together. Irradiations in gold, scintillations in crimson, splendours in emerald, lucidities in ultramarine – a dazzling girandola of every tint and of every hue. Of the enormous fireball, an instant ago such an object of dread, nothing now remained but these glittering pieces, shooting about in all directions, each one an asteroid in its turn. Some flew out straight and gleaming like a steel sword; others rushed here and there irregularly like chips struck off a red-hot rock; and others left long trails of glittering cosmical dust behind them like the nebulous tail of Donati's comet.

These incandescent blocks crossed each other, struck each other, crushed each other into still smaller fragments, one of which, grazing the Projectile, jarred it so violently that the very window at which the travellers were standing, was cracked by the shock. Our friends felt, in fact, as if they were the objective point at which endless volleys of blazing shells were aimed, any of them powerful enough, if it only hit them fair, to make as short work of the Projectile as you could of an egg-shell. They had many hairbreadth escapes, but fortunately the cracking of the glass proved to be the only serious damage of which they could complain.

This extraordinary illumination lasted altogether only a few seconds; every one of its details was of a most singular and exciting nature – but one of its greatest wonders was yet to come. The ether, saturated with luminous matter, developed an intensity of blazing brightness unequalled by the lime light, the magnesium light, the electric light, or any other dazzling source of illumination with which we are acquainted on earth. It flashed out of these asteroids in all directions, and downwards, of course, as well as elsewhere. At one particular instant, it was so very vivid that Ardan, who happened to be looking downwards, cried out, as if in transport:

'Oh!! The Moon! Visible at last!'

And the three companions, thrilling with indescribable emotion, shot a hasty glance through the openings of the coruscating field beneath them. Did they really catch a glimpse of the mysterious invisible disc that the eye of man had never before lit upon? For a second or so they gazed with enraptured fascination at all they could see. What did they see, what could they see at a distance so uncertain that Barbican has never been able even to guess at it? Not much. Ardan was reminded of the night he had stood on the battlements of Dover Castle, a few years before, when the fitful flashes of a thunder storm gave him occasional and very uncertain glimpses of the French coast at the opposite side of the strait. Misty strips long and narrow, extending over one portion of the disc – probably cloud-scuds sustained by a highly rarefied atmosphere – permitted only a very dreamy idea of lofty mountains stretching beneath them in shapeless proportions, of smaller reliefs, circuses, yawning craters, and the other capricious, sponge-like formations so common on the visible side. Elsewhere the watchers became aware for an instant of immense spaces, certainly not arid plains, but seas, real oceans, vast and calm, reflecting from their placid depths the dazzling fireworks of the weird and wildly flashing meteors. Farther on, but very darkly as if behind a screen, shadowy continents revealed themselves, their surfaces flecked with black cloudy masses, probably great forests, with here and there a –

Nothing more! In less than a second the illumination had come to an end, involving everything in the Moon's direction once more in pitchy darkness.

But had the impression made on the travellers' eyes been a mere vision or the result of a reality? an optical delusion or the shadow of a solid fact? Could an observation so rapid, so fleeting, so superficial, be really regarded as a genuine scientific affirmation? Could such a feeble glimmer of the invisible disc justify them in pronouncing a decided opinion on the inhabitability of the Moon? To such questions as these, rising spontaneously and simultaneously in the minds of our travellers, they could not reply at the moment; they could not reply to them long afterwards; even to this day they can give them no satisfactory answer. All they could do at the moment, they did. To every sight and sound they kept their eyes and ears open, and, by observing the most perfect silence, they sought to render their impressions too vivid to admit of deception.

There was now, however, nothing to be heard, and very little more to be seen. The few coruscations that flashed over the sky, gradually became fewer and dimmer; the asteroids sought paths further and further apart, and finally disappeared altogether. The ether resumed its original blackness. The stars, eclipsed for a moment, blazed out again on the firmament, and the invisible disc, that had flashed into view for an instant, once more relapsed forever into the impenetrable depths of night.

CHAPTER XVI
The Southern Hemisphere

EXCEEDINGLY NARROW AND exceedingly fortunate had been the escape of the Projectile. And from a danger too the most unlikely and the most unexpected. Who would have ever dreamed of even the possibility of such an encounter? And was all danger over? The sight of one of these erratic bolides certainly justified the gravest apprehensions of our travellers regarding the existence of others. Worse than the sunken reefs of the Southern Seas or the snags of the Mississippi, how could the Projectile be expected to avoid them? Drifting along blindly through the boundless ethereal ocean, *her* inmates, even if they saw the danger, were totally powerless to turn her aside. Like a ship without a rudder, like a runaway horse, like a collapsed balloon, like an iceberg in an Atlantic storm, like a boat in the Niagara rapids, she moved on sullenly, recklessly, mechanically, mayhap into the very jaws of the most frightful danger, the bright intelligences within no more able to modify her motions even by a finger's breadth than they were able to affect Mercury's movements around the Sun.

But did our friends complain of the new perils now looming up before them? They never thought of such a thing. On the contrary, they only considered themselves (after the lapse of a few minutes to calm their nerves) extremely lucky in having witnessed this fresh glory of exuberant nature, this transcendent display of fireworks which not only cast into absolute insignificance anything of the kind they had ever seen on Earth, but had actually enabled them by its dazzling illumination to gaze for a second or two at the Moon's mysterious invisible disc. This glorious momentary glance, worth a whole lifetime of ordinary existence, had revealed to mortal ken her continents, her oceans, her forests. But did it also convince them of the existence of an atmosphere on her surface whose vivifying molecules would render *life* possible? This question they had again to leave unanswered – it will hardly ever be answered in a way quite satisfactory to human curiosity. Still, infinite was their satisfaction at having hovered even for an instant on the very verge of such a great problem's solution.

It was now half-past three in the afternoon. The Projectile still pursued its curving but otherwise unknown path over the Moon's invisible face. Had this path been disturbed by that dangerous meteor? There was every reason to fear so – though, disturbance or no disturbance, the curve it described should still be one strictly in accordance with the laws of Mechanical Philosophy. Whether it was a parabola or a hyperbola, however, or whether it was disturbed or not, made very little difference as, in any case, the Projectile was bound to quit pretty soon the cone of the shadow, at a point directly opposite to where it had entered it. This cone could not possibly be of very great extent, considering the very slight ratio borne by the Moon's diameter when compared with the Sun's. Still, to all appearances, the Projectile seemed to be quite as deeply immersed in the shadow as ever, and there was apparently not the slightest sign of such a state of things coming soon to an end. At what rate was the Projectile now moving? Hard to say, but certainly not slowly, certainly rapidly enough to be out of the shadow by this time, if describing a curve rigidly parabolic. Was the curve therefore *not* parabolic? Another puzzling problem and sadly bewildering to poor Barbican, who had now almost lost his reason by attempting to clear up questions that were proving altogether too profound for his overworked brains.

Not that he ever thought of taking rest. Not that his companions thought of taking rest. Far from it. With senses as high-strung as ever, they still watched carefully for every new fact, every unexpected incident that might throw some light on the sidereal investigations. Even their dinner, or what was called so, consisted of only a few bits of bread and meat, distributed by Ardan at five o'clock, and swallowed mechanically. They did not even turn on the gas full head to see what they were eating; each man stood solidly at his window, the glass of which they had enough to do in keeping free from the rapidly condensing moisture.

At about half-past five, however, M'Nicholl, who had been gazing for some time with his telescope in a particular direction, called the attention of his companions to some bright specks of light barely discernible in that part of the horizon towards which the Projectile was evidently moving. His words were hardly uttered when his companions announced the same discovery. They could soon all see the glittering specks not only becoming more and more numerous, but also gradually assuming the shape of an extremely slender, but extremely brilliant crescent. Rapidly more brilliant and more decided in shape the profile gradually grew, till it soon resembled the first faint sketch of the New Moon that we catch of evenings in the western sky, or rather the first glimpse we get of her limb as it slowly moves out of eclipse. But it was inconceivably brighter than either, and was furthermore strangely relieved by the pitchy blackness both of sky and Moon. In fact, it soon became so brilliant as to dispel in a moment all doubt as to its particular nature. No meteor could present such a perfect shape; no volcano, such dazzling splendour.

'The Sun!' cried Barbican.

'The Sun?' asked M'Nicholl and Ardan in some astonishment.

'Yes, dear friends; it is the Sun himself that you now see; these summits that you behold him gilding are the mountains that lie on the Moon's southern rim. We are rapidly nearing her south pole.'

'After doubling her north pole!' cried Ardan; 'why, we must be circumnavigating her!'

'Exactly; sailing all around her.'

'Hurrah! Then we're all right at last! There's nothing more to fear from your hyperbolas or parabolas or any other of your open curves!'

'Nothing more, certainly, from an open curve, but every thing from a closed one.'

'A closed curve! What is it called? And what is the trouble?'

'An eclipse it is called; and the trouble is that, instead of flying off into the boundless regions of space, our Projectile will probably describe an elliptical orbit around the Moon—'

– 'What!' cried M'Nicholl, in amazement, 'and be her satellite for ever!'

'All right and proper,' said Ardan; 'why shouldn't she have one of her own?'

'Only, my dear friend,' said Barbican to Ardan, 'this change of curve involves no change in the doom of the Projectile. We are as infallibly lost by an ellipse as by a parabola.'

'Well, there was one thing I never could reconcile myself to in the whole arrangement,' replied Ardan cheerfully; 'and that was destruction by an open curve. Safe from that, I could say, "Fate, do your worst!" Besides, I don't believe in the infallibility of your ellipsic. It may prove just as unreliable as the hyperbola. And it is no harm to hope that it may!'

From present appearances there was very little to justify Ardan's hope. Barbican's theory of the elliptic orbit was unfortunately too well grounded to allow a single reasonable doubt to be expressed regarding the Projectile's fate. It was to gravitate for ever around the Moon – a sub-satellite. It was a new born individual in the astral universe, a microcosm, a little world in itself, containing, however, only three inhabitants and even these destined to perish pretty soon for want of air. Our travellers, therefore, had no particular reason for rejoicing over the new destiny reserved for the Projectile in obedience to the inexorable laws of the centripetal and centrifugal forces. They were soon, it is true, to have the opportunity of beholding once more the illuminated face of the Moon. They might even live long enough to catch a last glimpse of the distant Earth bathed in the glory of the solar rays. They might even have strength enough left to be able to chant one solemn final eternal adieu to their dear old Mother World, upon whose features their mortal eyes should never again rest in love and longing! Then, what was their Projectile to become? An inert, lifeless, extinct mass, not a particle better than the most defunct asteroid that wanders blindly through the fields of ether. A gloomy fate to look forward to. Yet, instead of grieving over the inevitable, our bold travellers actually felt thrilled with delight at the prospect of even a momentary deliverance from those gloomy depths of darkness and of once more finding themselves, even if only for a few hours, in the cheerful precincts illuminated by the genial light of the blessed Sun!

The ring of light, in the meantime, becoming brighter and brighter, Barbican was not long in discovering and pointing out to his companions the different mountains that lay around the Moon's south pole.

'There is *Leibnitz* on your right,' said he, 'and on your left you can easily see the peaks of *Doerfel*. Belonging rather to the Moon's dark side than to her Earth side, they are visible to terrestrial astronomers only when she is in her highest northern latitudes. Those faint peaks beyond them that you can catch with such difficulty must be those of *Newton* and *Curtius*.'

'How in the world can you tell?' asked Ardan.

'They are the highest mountains in the circumpolar regions,' replied Barbican. 'They have been measured with the greatest care; *Newton* is 23,000 feet high.'

'More or less!' laughed Ardan. 'What Delphic oracle says so?'

'Dear friend,' replied Barbican quietly, 'the visible mountains of the Moon have been measured so carefully and so accurately that I should hardly hesitate in affirming their altitude to be as well known as that of Mont Blanc, or, at least, as those of the chief peaks in the Himalayahs or the Rocky Mountain Range.'

'I should like to know how people set about it,' observed Ardan incredulously.

'There are several well known methods of approaching this problem,' replied Barbican; 'and as these methods, though founded on different principles, bring us constantly to the same result, we may pretty safely conclude that our calculations are right. We have no time, just now to draw diagrams, but, if I express myself clearly, you will no doubt easily catch the general principle.'

'Go ahead!' answered Ardan. 'Anything but Algebra.'

'We want no Algebra now,' said Barbican, 'It can't enable us to find principles, though it certainly enables us to apply them. Well. The Sun at a certain altitude shines on one side of a mountain and flings a shadow on the other. The length of this shadow is easily found by means of a telescope, whose object glass is provided with a micrometer. This consists simply of two parallel spider threads, one of which is stationary and the other movable. The Moon's real diameter being known and occupying a certain space on the object glass, the exact space occupied by the shadow can be easily ascertained by means of the movable thread. This space, compared with the Moon's space, will give us the length of the shadow. Now, as under the same circumstances a certain height can cast only a certain shadow, of course a knowledge of the one must give you that of the other, and *vice versa*. This method, stated roughly, was that followed by Galileo, and, in our own day, by Beer and Maedler, with extraordinary success.'

'I certainly see some sense in this method,' said Ardan, 'if they took extraordinary pains to observe correctly. The least carelessness would set them wrong, not only by feet but by miles. We have time enough, however, to listen to another method before we get into the full blaze of the glorious old Sol.'

'The other method,' interrupted M'Nicholl laying down his telescope to rest his eyes, and now joining in the conversation to give himself something to do, 'is called that of the *tangent rays*. A solar ray, barely passing the edge of the Moon's surface, is caught on the peak of a mountain the rest of which lies in shadow. The distance between this starry peak and the line separating the light from the darkness, we measure carefully by means of our telescope. Then—'

'I see it at a glance!' interrupted Ardan with lighting eye; 'the ray, being a tangent, of course makes right angles with the radius, which is known: consequently we have two sides and one angle – quite enough to find the other parts of the triangle. Very ingenious – but now, that I think of it – is not this method absolutely impracticable for every mountain except those in the immediate neighbourhood of the light and shadow line?'

'That's a defect easily remedied by patience,' explained Barbican – the Captain, who did not like being interrupted, having withdrawn to his telescope – 'As this line is continually changing, in course of time all the mountains must come near it. A third method – to measure the mountain profile directly by means of the micrometer – is evidently applicable only to altitudes lying exactly on the lunar rim.'

'That is clear enough,' said Ardan, 'and another point is also very clear. In Full Moon no measurement is possible. When no shadows are made, none can be measured. Measurements, right or wrong, are possible only when the solar rays strike the Moon's surface obliquely with regard to the observer. Am I right, Signor Barbicani, maestro illustrissimo?'

'Perfectly right,' replied Barbican. 'You are an apt pupil.'

'Say that again,' said Ardan. 'I want Mac to hear it.'

Barbican humoured him by repeating the observation, but M'Nicholl would only notice it by a grunt of doubtful meaning.

'Was Galileo tolerably successful in his calculations?' asked Ardan, resuming the conversation.

Before answering this question, Barbican unrolled the map of the Moon, which a faint light like that of day-break now enabled him to examine. He then went on: 'Galileo was wonderfully successful – considering that the telescope which he employed was a poor instrument of his own construction, magnifying only thirty times. He gave the lunar mountains a height of about 26,000 feet – an altitude cut down by Hevelius, but almost doubled by Riccioli. Herschel was the first to come pretty close to the truth, but Beer and Maedler, whose *Mappa Selenographica* now lies before us, have left really nothing more to be done for lunar astronomy – except, of course, to pay a personal visit to the Moon – which we have tried to do, but I fear with a very poor prospect of success.'

'Cheer up! cheer up!' cried Ardan. 'It's not all over yet by long odds. Who can say what is still in store for us? Another bolide may shunt us off our ellipse and even send us to the Moon's surface.'

Then seeing Barbican shake his head ominously and his countenance become more and more depressed, this true friend tried to brighten him up a bit by feigning to take deep interest in a subject that to him was absolutely the driest in the world.

'Meer and Baedler – I mean Beer and Maedler,' he went on, 'must have measured at least forty or fifty mountains to their satisfaction.'

'Forty or fifty!' exclaimed Barbican. 'They measured no fewer than a thousand and ninety-five lunar mountains and crater summits with a perfect success. Six of these reach an altitude of upwards of 18,000 feet, and twenty-two are more than 15,000 feet high.'

'Which is the highest in the lot?' asked Ardan, keenly relishing Barbican's earnestness.

'*Doerfel* in the southern hemisphere, the peak of which I have just pointed out, is the highest of the lunar mountains so far measured,' replied Barbican. 'It is nearly 25,000 feet high.'

'Indeed! Five thousand feet lower than Mount Everest – still for a lunar mountain, it is quite a respectable altitude.'

'Respectable! Why it's an enormous altitude, my dear friend, if you compare it with the Moon's diameter. The Earth's diameter being more than 3½ times greater than the Moon's, if the Earth's mountains bore the same ratio to those of the Moon, Everest should be more than sixteen miles high, whereas it is not quite six.'

'How do the general heights of the Himalayas compare with those of the highest lunar mountains?' asked Ardan, wondering what would be his next question.

'Fifteen peaks in the eastern or higher division of the Himalayas, are higher than the loftiest lunar peaks,' replied Barbican. 'Even in the western, or lower section of the Himalayas, some of the peaks exceed *Doerfel*.'

'Which are the chief lunar mountains that exceed Mont Blanc in altitude?' asked Ardan, bravely suppressing a yawn.

'The following dozen, ranged, if my memory does not fail me, in the exact order of their respective heights,' replied Barbican, never wearied in answering such questions: '*Newton, Curtius, Casatus, Rheita, Short, Huyghens, Biancanus, Tycho, Kircher, Clavius, Endymion*, and *Catharina*.'

'Now those not quite up to Mont Blanc?' asked Ardan, hardly knowing what to say.

'Here they are, about half a dozen of them: *Moretus, Theophilus, Harpalus, Eratosthenes, Werner*, and *Piccolomini*,' answered Barbican as ready as a schoolboy reciting his lesson, and pointing them out on the map as quickly as a compositor distributing his type.

'The next in rank?' asked Ardan, astounded at his friend's wonderful memory.

'The next in rank,' replied Barbican promptly, 'are those about the size of the Matterhorn, that is to say about 2¾ miles in height. They are *Macrobius, Delambre*, and *Conon*. Come,' he added, seeing Ardan hesitating and at a loss what other question to ask, 'don't you want to know what lunar mountains are about the same height as the Peak of Tenerife? or as Ætna? or as Mount Washington? You need not be afraid of puzzling me. I studied up the subject thoroughly, and therefore know all about it.'

'Oh! I could listen to you with delight all day long!' cried Ardan, enthusiastically, though with some embarrassment, for he felt a twinge of conscience in acting so falsely towards his beloved friend. 'The fact is,' he went on, 'such a rational conversation as the present, on such an absorbing subject, with such a perfect master—'

'The Sun!' cried M'Nicholl starting up and cheering. 'He's cleared the disc completely, and he's now himself again! Long life to him! Hurrah!'

'Hurrah!' cried the others quite as enthusiastically (Ardan did not seem a bit desirous to finish his sentence).

They tossed their maps aside and hastened to the window.

CHAPTER XVII
Tycho

It was now exactly six o'clock in the evening. The Sun, completely clear of all contact with the lunar disc, steeped the whole Projectile in his golden rays. The travellers, vertically over the Moon's south pole, were, as Barbican soon ascertained, about 30 miles distant from it, the exact distance they had been from the north pole – a proof that the elliptic curve still maintained itself with mathematical rigour.

For some time, the travellers' whole attention was concentrated on the glorious Sun. His light was inexpressibly cheering; and his heat, soon penetrating the walls of the Projectile, infused a new and sweet life into their chilled and exhausted frames. The ice rapidly disappeared, and the windows soon resumed their former perfect transparency.

'Oh! how good the pleasant sunlight is!' cried the Captain, sinking on a seat in a quiet ecstasy of enjoyment. 'How I pity Ardan's poor friends the Selenites during that night so long and so icy! How impatient they must be to see the Sun back again!'

'Yes,' said Ardan, also sitting down the better to bask in the vivifying rays, 'his light no doubt brings them to life and keeps them alive. Without light or heat during all that dreary winter, they must freeze stiff like the frogs or become torpid like the bears. I can't imagine how they could get through it otherwise.'

'I'm glad *we're* through it anyhow,' observed M'Nicholl. 'I may at once acknowledge that I felt perfectly miserable as long as it lasted. I can now easily understand how the combined cold and darkness killed Doctor Kane's Esquimaux dogs. It was near killing me. I was so miserable that at last I could neither talk myself nor bear to hear others talk.'

'My own case exactly,' said Barbican – 'that is,' he added hastily, correcting himself, 'I tried to talk because I found Ardan so interested, but in spite of all we said, and saw, and had to think of, Byron's terrible dream would continually rise up before me:

> 'The bright Sun was extinguished, and the Stars
> Wandered all darkling in the eternal space,
> Rayless and pathless, and the icy Earth
> Swung blind and blackening in the Moonless air.
> Morn came and went, and came and brought no day!
> And men forgot their passions in the dread
> Of this their desolation, and all hearts
> Were chilled into a selfish prayer for *light*!'

As he pronounced these words in accents at once monotonous and melancholy, Ardan, fully appreciative, quietly gesticulated in perfect cadence with the rhythm. Then the three men remained completely silent for several minutes. Buried in recollection, or lost in thought, or magnetized by the bright Sun, they seemed to be half asleep while steeping their limbs in his vitalizing beams.

Barbican was the first to dissolve the reverie by jumping up. His sharp eye had noticed that the base of the Projectile, instead of keeping rigidly perpendicular to the lunar surface, turned away a little, so as to render the elliptical orbit somewhat elongated. This he made his companions immediately observe, and also called their attention to the fact that from this point they could easily have seen the Earth had it been Full, but that now, drowned in the Sun's beams, it was quite invisible. A more attractive spectacle, however, soon engaged their undivided attention – that of the Moon's southern regions, now brought within about the third of a mile by their telescopes. Immediately resuming their posts by the windows, they carefully noted every feature presented by the fantastic panorama that stretched itself out in endless lengths beneath their wondering eyes.

Mount *Leibnitz* and Mount *Doerfel* form two separate groups developed in the regions of the extreme south. The first extends westwardly from the pole to the 84th parallel; the second, on the southeastern border, starting from the pole, reaches the neighbourhood of the 65th. In the entangled valleys of their clustered peaks, appeared the dazzling sheets of white, noted by Father Secchi, but their peculiar nature Barbican could now examine with a greater prospect of certainty than the illustrious Roman astronomer had ever enjoyed.

'They're beds of snow,' he said at last in a decided tone.

'Snow!' exclaimed M'Nicholl.

'Yes, snow, or rather glaciers heavily coated with glittering ice. See how vividly they reflect the Sun's rays. Consolidated beds of lava could never shine with such dazzling uniformity. Therefore there must be both water and air on the Moon's surface. Not much – perhaps very little if you insist on it – but the fact that there is some can now no longer be questioned.'

This assertion of Barbican's, made so positively by a man who never decided unless when thoroughly convinced, was a great triumph for Ardan, who, as the gracious reader doubtless remembers, had had a famous dispute with M'Nicholl on that very subject at Tampa.[1] His eyes brightened and a smile of pleasure played around his lips, but, with a great effort at self-restraint, he kept perfectly silent and would not permit himself even to look in the direction of the Captain. As for M'Nicholl, he was apparently too much absorbed in *Doerfel* and *Leibnitz* to mind anything else.

These mountains rose from plains of moderate extent, bounded by an indefinite succession of walled hollows and ring ramparts. They are the only chains met in this region of ridge-brimmed craters and circles; distinguished by no particular feature, they project a few pointed peaks here and there, some of which exceed

---

1 BALTIMORE GUN CLUB, pp. 295 *et seq.*

four miles and a half in height. This altitude, however, foreshortened as it was by the vertical position of the Projectile, could not be noticed just then, even if correct observation had been permitted by the dazzling surface.

Once more again before the travellers' eyes the Moon's disc revealed itself in all the old familiar features so characteristic of lunar landscapes – no blending of tones, no softening of colours, no graduation of shadows, every line glaring in white or black by reason of the total absence of refracted light. And yet the wonderfully peculiar character of this desolate world imparted to it a weird attraction as strangely fascinating as ever.

Over this chaotic region the travellers were now sweeping, as if borne on the wings of a storm; the peaks defiled beneath them; the yawning chasms revealed their ruin-strewn floors; the fissured cracks untwisted themselves; the ramparts showed all their sides; the mysterious holes presented their impenetrable depths; the clustered mountain summits and rings rapidly decomposed themselves: but in a moment again all had become more inextricably entangled than ever. Everything appeared to be the finished handiwork of volcanic agency, in the utmost purity and highest perfection. None of the mollifying effects of air or water could here be noticed. No smooth-capped mountains, no gently winding river channels, no vast prairie-lands of deposited sediment, no traces of vegetation, no signs of agriculture, no vestiges of a great city. Nothing but vast beds of glistering lava, now rough like immense piles of scoriae and clinker, now smooth like crystal mirrors, and reflecting the Sun's rays with the same intolerable glare. Not the faintest speck of life. A world absolutely and completely dead, fixed, still, motionless – save when a gigantic land-slide, breaking off the vertical wall of a crater, plunged down into the soundless depths, with all the fury too of a crashing avalanche, with all the speed of a Niagara, but, in the total absence of atmosphere, noiseless as a feather, as a snow flake, as a grain of impalpable dust.

Careful observations, taken by Barbican and repeated by his companions, soon satisfied them that the ridgy outline of the mountains on the Moon's border, though perhaps due to different forces from those acting in the centre, still presented a character generally uniform. The same bulwark-surrounded hollows, the same abrupt projections of surface. Yet a different arrangement, as Barbican pointed out to his companions, might be naturally expected. In the central portion of the disc, the Moon's crust, before solidification, must have been subjected to two attractions – that of the Moon herself and that of the Earth – acting, however, in contrary directions and therefore, in a certain sense, serving to neutralize each other. Towards the border of her disc, on the contrary, the terrestrial attraction, having acted in a direction perpendicular to that of the lunar, should have exerted greater power, and therefore given a different shape to the general contour. But no remarkable difference had so far been perceived by terrestrial observers; and none could now be detected by our travellers. Therefore the Moon must have found in herself alone the principle of her shape and of her superficial development – that is, she owed nothing to external influences. 'Arago was perfectly right, therefore,' concluded Barbican, 'in the remarkable opinion to which he gave expression thirty years ago:

'No external action whatever has contributed to the formation of the Moon's diversified surface."

'But don't you think, Barbican,' asked the Captain, 'that every force, internal or external, that might modify the Moon's shape, has ceased long ago?'

'I am rather inclined to that opinion,' said Barbican; 'it is not, however, a new one. Descartes maintained that as the Earth is an extinct Sun, so is the Moon an extinct Earth. My own opinion at present is that the Moon is now the image of death, but I can't say if she has ever been the abode of life.'

'The abode of life!' cried Ardan, who had great repugnance in accepting the idea that the Moon was no better than a heap of cinders and ashes; 'why, look there! If those are not as neat a set of the ruins of an abandoned city as ever I saw, I should like to know what they are!'

He pointed to some very remarkable rocky formations in the neighbourhood of *Short*, a ring mountain rising to an altitude considerably higher than that of Mont Blanc. Even Barbican and M'Nicholl could detect some regularity and semblance of order in the arrangement of these rocks, but this, of course, they looked on as a mere freak of nature, like the Lurlei Rock, the Giant's Causeway, or the Old Man of the Franconia Mountains. Ardan, however, would not accept such an easy mode of getting rid of a difficulty.

'See the ruins on that bluff,' he exclaimed; 'those steep sides must have been washed by a great river in the prehistoric times. That was the fortress. Farther down lay the city. There are the dismantled ramparts; why, there's the very coping of a portico still intact! Don't you see three broken pillars lying beside their pedestals? There! a little to the left of those arches that evidently once bore the pipes of an aqueduct! You don't see them? Well, look a little to the right, and there is something that you can see! As I'm a living man I have no difficulty in discerning the gigantic butments of a great bridge that formerly spanned that immense river!'

Did he really see all this? To this day he affirms stoutly that he did, and even greater wonders besides. His companions, however, without denying that he had good grounds for his assertion on this subject or questioning the general accuracy of his observations, content themselves with saying that the reason why they had failed to discover the wonderful city, was that Ardan's telescope was of a strange and peculiar construction. Being somewhat short-sighted, he had had it manufactured expressly for his own use, but it was of such singular power that his companions could not use it without hurting their eyes.

But, whether the ruins were real or not, the moments were evidently too precious to be lost in idle discussion. The great city of the Selenites soon disappeared on the remote horizon, and, what was of far greater importance, the distance of the Projectile from the Moon's disc began to increase so sensibly that the smaller details of the surface were soon lost in a confused mass, and it was only the lofty heights, the wide craters, the great ring mountains, and the vast plains that still continued to give sharp, distinctive outlines.

A little to their left, the travellers could now plainly distinguish one of the most remarkable of the Moon's craters, *Newton*, so well known to all lunar astronomers. Its ramparts, forming a perfect circle, rise to such a height, at least 22,000 feet, as to seem insurmountable.

'You can, no doubt, notice for yourselves,' said Barbican, 'that the external height of this mountain is far from being equal to the depth of its crater. The enormous pit, in fact, seems to be a soundless sea of pitchy black, the bottom of which the Sun's rays have never reached. There, as Humboldt says, reigns eternal darkness, so absolute that Earth-shine or even Sunlight is never able to dispel it. Had Michael's friends the old mythologists ever known anything about it, they would doubtless have made it the entrance to the infernal regions. On the whole surface of our Earth, there is no mountain even remotely resembling it. It is a perfect type of the lunar crater. Like most of them, it shows that the peculiar formation of the Moon's surface is due, first, to the cooling of the lunar crust; secondly, to the cracking from internal pressure; and, thirdly, to the violent volcanic action in consequence. This must have been of a far fiercer nature than it has ever been with us. The matter was ejected to a vast height till great mountains were formed; and still the action went on, until at last the floor of the crater sank to a depth far lower than the level of the external plain.'

'You may be right,' said Ardan by way of reply; 'as for me, I'm looking out for another city. But I'm sorry to say that our Projectile is increasing its distance so fast that, even if one lay at my feet at this moment, I doubt very much if I could see it a bit better than either you or the Captain.'

Newton was soon passed, and the Projectile followed a course that took it directly over the ring mountain *Moretus*. A little to the west the travellers could easily distinguish the summits of *Blancanus*, 7,000 feet high, and, towards seven o'clock in the evening, they were approaching the neighbourhood of *Clavius*.

This walled-plain, one of the most remarkable on the Moon, lies 55° S. by 15° E. Its height is estimated at 16,000 feet, but it is considered to be about a hundred and fifty miles in diameter. Of this vast crater, the travellers now at a distance of 250 miles, reduced to 2½ by their telescopes, had a magnificent bird's-eye view.

'Our terrestrial volcanoes,' said Barbican, 'as you can now readily judge for yourselves, are no more than molehills when compared with those of the Moon. Measure the old craters formed by the early eruptions of Vesuvius and Ætna, and you will find them little more than three miles in diameter. The crater of Cantal in central France is only about six miles in width; the famous valley in Ceylon, called the *Crater*, though not at all due to volcanic action, is 44 miles across and is considered to be the greatest in the world. But even this is very little in comparison to the diameter of *Clavius* lying beneath us at the present moment.'

'How much is its diameter?' asked the Captain.

'At least one hundred and forty-two miles,' replied Barbican; 'it is probably the greatest in the Moon, but many others measure more than a hundred miles across.'

'Dear boys,' said Ardan, half to himself, half to the others, 'only imagine the delicious state of things on the surface of the gentle Moon when these craters, brimming over with hissing lava, were vomiting forth, all at the same time, showers of melted stones, clouds of blinding smoke, and sheets of blasting flame! What an intensely overpowering spectacle was here presented once, but now, how are the mighty fallen! Our Moon, as at present beheld, seems to be nothing more than the skinny spectre left after a brilliant display of fireworks, when the spluttering crackers, the glittering wheels, the hissing serpents, the revolving suns, and the dazzling stars, are all "played out", and nothing remains to tell of the gorgeous spectacle but a few blackened sticks and half a dozen half burned bits of pasteboard. I should like to hear one of you trying to explain the cause, the reason, the principle, the philosophy of such tremendous cataclysms!'

Barbican's only reply was a series of nods, for in truth he had not heard a single word of Ardan's philosophic explosion. His ears were with his eyes, and these were obstinately bent on the gigantic ramparts of *Clavius*, formed of concentric mountain ridges, which were actually leagues in depth. On the floor of the vast cavity, could be seen hundreds of smaller craters, mottling it like a skimming dish, and pierced here and there by sharp peaks, one of which could hardly be less than 15,000 feet high.

All around, the plain was desolate in the extreme. You could not conceive how anything could be barrener than these serrated outlines, or gloomier than these shattered mountains – until you looked at the plain that encircled them. Ardan hardly exaggerated when he called it the scene of a battle fought thousands of years ago but still white with the hideous bones of overthrown peaks, slaughtered mountains and mutilated precipices!

'Hills amid the air encountered hills,
Hurled to and fro in jaculation dire,'

murmured M'Nicholl, who could quote you Milton quite as readily as the Bible.

'This must have been the spot,' muttered Barbican to himself, 'where the brittle shell of the cooling sphere, being thicker than usual, offered greater resistance to an eruption of the red-hot nucleus. Hence these piled up buttresses, and these orderless heaps of consolidated lava and ejected scoriæ.'

The Projectile advanced, but the scene of desolation seemed to remain unchanged. Craters, ring mountains, pitted plateaus dotted with shapeless wrecks, succeeded each other without interruption. For level plain, for dark 'sea,' for smooth plateau, the eye here sought in vain. It was a Swiss Greenland, an Icelandic Norway, a Sahara of shattered crust studded with countless hills of glassy lava.

At last, in the very centre of this blistered region, right too at its very culmination, the travellers came on the brightest and most remarkable mountain of the Moon. In the dazzling *Tycho* they found it an easy matter to recognize the famous lunar point, which the world will for ever designate by the name of the distinguished astronomer of Denmark.

This brilliant luminosity of the southern hemisphere, no one that ever gazes at the Full Moon in a cloudless sky, can help noticing. Ardan, who had always particularly admired it, now hailed it as an old friend, and almost exhausted breath, imagination and vocabulary in the epithets with which he greeted this cynosure of the lunar mountains.

'Hail!' he cried, 'thou blazing focus of glittering streaks, thou coruscating nucleus of irradiation, thou starting point of rays divergent, thou egress of meteoric flashes! Hub of the silver wheel that ever rolls in silent majesty over the starry plains of Night! Paragon of jewels enchased in a carcanet of dazzling brilliants! Eye of the universe, beaming with heavenly resplendescence!

'Who shall say what thou art? Diana's nimbus? The golden clasp of her floating robes? The blazing head of the great bolt that rivets the lunar hemispheres in union inseverable? Or cans't thou have been some errant bolide, which missing its way, butted blindly against the lunar face, and there stuck fast, like a Minie ball mashed against a cast-iron target? Alas! nobody knows. Not even Barbican is able to penetrate thy mystery. But one thing *I* know. Thy dazzling glare so sore my eyes hath made that longer on thy light to gaze I do not dare. Captain, have you any smoked glass?'

In spite of this anti-climax, Ardan's companions could hardly consider his utterings either as ridiculous or over enthusiastic. They could easily excuse his excitement on the subject. And so could we, if we only remember that *Tycho*, though nearly a quarter of a million miles distant, is such a luminous point on the lunar disc, that almost any moonlit night it can be easily perceived by the unaided terrestrial eye. What then must have been its splendour in the eyes of our travellers whose telescopes brought it actually four thousand times nearer! No wonder that with smoked glasses, they endeavoured to soften off its effulgent glare! Then in hushed silence, or at most uttering at intervals a few interjections expressive of their intense admiration, they remained for some time completely engrossed in the overwhelming spectacle. For the time being, every sentiment, impression, thought, feeling on their part, was concentrated in the eye, just as at other times under violent excitement every throb of our life is concentrated in the heart.

Tycho belongs to the system of lunar craters that is called *radiating*, like *Aristarchus* or *Copernicus*, which had been already seen and highly admired by our travellers at their first approach to the Moon. But it is decidedly the most remarkable and conspicuous of them all. It occupies the great focus of disruption, whence it sends out great streaks thousands of miles in length; and it gives the most unmistakable evidence of the terribly eruptive nature of those forces that once shattered the Moon's solidified shell in this portion of the lunar surface.

Situated in the southern latitude of 43° by an eastern longitude of 12°, *Tycho's* crater, somewhat elliptical in shape, is 54 miles in diameter and upwards of 16,000 feet in depth. Its lofty ramparts are buttressed by other mountains, Mont Blancs in size, all grouped around it, and all streaked with the great divergent fissures that radiate from it as a centre.

Of what this incomparable mountain really is, with all these lines of projections converging towards it and with all these prominent points of relief protruding within its crater, photography has, so far, been able to give us only a very unsatisfactory idea. The reason too is very simple: it is only at Full Moon that *Tycho* reveals himself in all his splendour. The shadows therefore vanishing, the perspective foreshortenings disappear and the views become little better than a dead blank. This is the more to be regretted as this wonderful region is well worthy of being represented with the greatest possible photographic accuracy. It is a vast agglomeration of holes, craters, ring formations, a complicated intersection of crests – in short, a distracting volcanic network flung over the blistered soil. The ebullitions of the central eruption still evidently preserve their original form. As they first appeared, so they lie. Crystallizing as they cooled, they have stereotyped in imperishable characters the aspect formerly presented by the whole Moon's surface under the influences of recent plutonic upheaval.

Our travellers were far more fortunate than the photographers. The distance separating them from the peaks of *Tycho's* concentric terraces was not so considerable as to conceal the principal details from a very satisfactory view. They could easily distinguish the annular ramparts of the external circumvallation, the mountains buttressing the gigantic walls internally as well as externally, the vast esplanades descending irregularly and abruptly to the sunken plains all around. They could even detect a difference of a few hundred feet in altitude in favour of the western or right hand side over the eastern. They could also see that these dividing ridges were actually inaccessible and completely unsurmountable, at least by ordinary terrestrial efforts. No system of castrametation ever devised by Polybius or Vauban could bear the slightest comparison with such vast fortifications, A city built on the floor of the circular cavity could be no more reached by the outside Lunarians than if it had been built in the planet Mars.

This idea set Ardan off again. 'Yes,' said he, 'such a city would be at once completely inaccessible, and still not inconveniently situated in a plateau full of aspects decidedly picturesque. Even in the depths of this immense crater, Nature, as you can see, has left no flat and empty void. You can easily trace its special oreography, its various mountain systems which turn it into a regular world on a small scale. Notice its cones, its central hills, its valleys, its substructures already cut and dry and therefore quietly prepared to receive the masterpieces of Selenite architecture. Down there to the left is a lovely spot for a Saint Peter's; to the right, a magnificent site for a Forum; here a Louvre could be built capable of entrancing Michael Angelo himself; there a citadel could be raised to which even Gibraltar would be a molehill! In the middle rises a sharp peak which can hardly be less than a mile in height – a grand pedestal for the statue of some Selenite Vincent de Paul or George Washington. And around them all is a mighty mountain-ring at least 3 miles high, but which, to an eye looking from the centre of our vast city, could not appear to be more than five or six hundred feet. Enormous circus, where mighty Rome herself in her palmiest days, though increased tenfold, would have no reason to complain for want of room!'

He stopped for a few seconds, perhaps to take breath, and then resumed:

'Oh what an abode of serene happiness could be constructed within this shadow-fringed ring of the mighty mountains! O blessed refuge, unassailable by aught of human ills! What a calm unruffled life could be enjoyed within thy hallowed precincts, even by those cynics, those haters of humanity, those disgusted reconstructors of society, those misanthropes and misogynists old and young, who are continually writing whining verses in odd corners of the newspapers!'

'Right at last, Ardan, my boy!' cried M'Nicholl, quietly rubbing the glass of his spectacles; 'I should like to see the whole lot of them carted in there without a moment's delay!'

'It couldn't hold the half of them!' observed Barbican drily.

CHAPTER XVIII
Puzzling Questions

It was not until the Projectile had passed a little beyond *Tycho's* immense concavity that Barbican and his friends had a good opportunity for observing the brilliant streaks sent so wonderfully flying in all directions from this celebrated mountain as a common centre. They examined them for some time with the closest attention.

What could be the nature of this radiating aureola? By what geological phenomena could this blazing coma have been possibly produced? Such questions were the most natural things in the world for Barbican and his companions to propound to themselves, as indeed they have been to every astronomer from the beginning of time, and probably will be to the end.

What *did* they see? What you can see, what anybody can see on a clear night when the Moon is full – only our friends had all the advantages of a closer view. From *Tycho*, as a focus, radiated in all directions, as from the head of a peeled orange, more than a hundred luminous streaks or channels, edges raised, middle depressed – or perhaps *vice versa*, owing to an optical illusion – some at least twelve miles wide, some fully thirty. In certain directions they ran for a distance of at least six hundred miles, and seemed – especially towards the west, northwest, and north – to cover half the southern hemisphere. One of these flashes extended as far as *Neander* on the 40th meridian; another, curving around so as to furrow the *Mare Nectaris*, came to an end on the chain of the *Pyrenees*, after a course of perhaps a little more than seven hundred miles. On the east, some of them barred with luminous network the *Mare Nubium* and even the *Mare Humorum*.

The most puzzling feature of these glittering streaks was that they ran their course directly onward, apparently neither obstructed by valley, crater, or mountain ridge however high. They all started, as said before, from one common focus, *Tycho's* crater. From this they certainly all seemed to emanate. Could they be rivers of lava once vomited from that centre by resistless volcanic agency and afterwards crystallized into glassy rock? This idea of Herschel's, Barbican had no hesitation in qualifying as exceedingly absurd. Rivers running in perfectly straight lines, across plains, and *up* as well as *down* mountains!

'Other astronomers,' he continued, 'have looked on these streaks as a peculiar kind of *moraines*, that is, long lines of erratic blocks belched forth with mighty power at the period of *Tycho's* own upheaval.'

'How do you like that theory, Barbican,' asked the Captain.

'It's not a particle better than Herschel's,' was the reply; 'no volcanic action could project rocks to a distance of six or seven hundred miles, not to talk of laying them down so regularly that we can't detect a break in them.'

'Happy thought!' cried Ardan suddenly; 'it seems to me that I can tell the cause of these radiating streaks!'

'Let us hear it,' said Barbican.

'Certainly,' was Ardan's reply; 'these streaks are all only the parts of what we call a 'star,' as made by a stone striking ice; or by a ball, a pane of glass.'

'Not bad,' smiled Barbican approvingly; 'only where is the hand that flung the stone or threw the ball?'

'The hand is hardly necessary,' replied Ardan, by no means disconcerted; 'but as for the ball, what do you say to a comet?'

Here M'Nicholl laughed so loud that Ardan was seriously irritated. However, before he could say anything cutting enough to make the Captain mind his manners, Barbican had quickly resumed:

'Dear friend, let the comets alone, I beg of you; the old astronomers fled to them on all occasions and made them explain every difficulty—'

– 'The comets were all used up long ago—' interrupted M'Nicholl.

– 'Yes,' went on Barbican, as serenely as a judge, 'comets, they said, had fallen on the surface in meteoric showers and crushed in the crater cavities; comets had dried up the water; comets had whisked off the atmosphere; comets had done everything. All pure assumption! In your case, however, friend Michael, no comet whatever is necessary. The shock that gave rise to your great "star" may have come from the interior rather than the exterior. A violent contraction of the lunar crust in the process of cooling may have given birth to your gigantic "star" formation.'

'I accept the amendment,' said Ardan, now in the best of humor and looking triumphantly at M'Nicholl.

'An English scientist,' continued Barbican, 'Nasmyth by name, is decidedly of your opinion, especially ever since a little experiment of his own has confirmed him in it. He filled a glass globe with water, hermetically sealed it, and then plunged it into a hot bath. The enclosed water, expanding at a greater rate than the glass, burst the latter, but, in doing so, it made a vast number of cracks all diverging in every direction from the focus of disruption. Something like this he conceives to have taken place around *Tycho*. As the crust cooled, it cracked. The lava from the interior, oozing out, spread itself on both sides of the cracks. This certainly explains pretty satisfactorily why those flat glistening streaks are of much greater width than the fissures through which the lava had at first made its way to the surface.'

'Well done for an Englishman!' cried Ardan in great spirits.

'He's no Englishman,' said M'Nicholl, glad to have an opportunity of coming off with some credit. 'He is the famous Scotch engineer who invented the steam hammer, the steam ram, and discovered the "willow leaves" in the Sun's disc.'

'Better and better,' said Ardan – 'but, powers of Vulcan! What makes it so hot? I'm actually roasting!'

This observation was hardly necessary to make his companions conscious that by this time they felt extremely uncomfortable. The heat had become quite oppressive. Between the natural caloric of the Sun and the reflected caloric of the Moon, the Projectile was fast turning into a regular bake oven. This transition from intense cold to intense heat was already about quite as much as they could bear.

'What shall we do, Barbican?' asked Ardan, seeing that for some time no one else appeared inclined to say a word.

'Nothing, at least yet awhile, friend Ardan,' replied Barbican, 'I have been watching the thermometer carefully for the last few minutes, and, though we are at present at 38° centigrade, or 100° Fahrenheit, I have noticed that the mercury is slowly falling. You can also easily remark for yourself that the floor of the Projectile is turning away more and more from the lunar surface. From this I conclude quite confidently, and I see that the Captain agrees with me, that all danger of death from intense heat, though decidedly alarming ten minutes ago, is over for the present and, for some time at least, it may be dismissed from further consideration.'

'I'm not very sorry for it,' said Ardan cheerfully; 'neither to be baked like a pie in an oven nor roasted like a fat goose before a fire is the kind of death I should like to die of.'

'Yet from such a death you would suffer no more than your friends the Selenites are exposed to every day of their lives,' said the Captain, evidently determined on getting up an argument.

'I understand the full bearing of your allusion, my dear Captain,' replied Ardan quickly, but not at all in a tone showing that he was disposed to second M'Nicholl's expectations.

He was, in fact, fast losing all his old habits of positivism. Latterly he had seen much, but he had reflected more. The deeper he had reflected, the more inclined he had become to accept the conclusion that the less he knew. Hence he had decided that if M'Nicholl wanted an argument it should not be with him. All speculative disputes he should henceforth avoid; he would listen with pleasure to all that could be urged on each side; he might even skirmish a little here and there as the spirit moved him; but a regular pitched battle on a subject purely speculative he was fully determined never again to enter into.

'Yes, dear Captain,' he continued, 'that pointed arrow of yours has by no means missed its mark, but I can't deny that my faith is beginning to be what you call a little "shaky" in the existence of my friends the Selenites. However, I should like to have your square opinion on the matter. Barbican's also. We have witnessed many strange lunar phenomena lately, closer and clearer than mortal eye ever rested on them before. Has what we have seen confirmed any theory of yours or confounded any hypothesis? Have you seen enough to induce you to adopt decided conclusions? I will put the question formally. Do you, or do you not, think that the Moon resembles the Earth in being the abode of animals and intelligent beings? Come, answer, *messieurs*. Yes, or no?'

'I think we can answer your question categorically,' replied Barbican, 'if you modify its form a little.'

'Put the question any way you please,' said Ardan; 'only you answer it! I'm not particular about the form.'

'Good,' said Barbican; 'the question, being a double one, demands a double answer. First: *Is the Moon inhabitable?* Second: *Has the Moon ever been inhabited?*'

'That's the way to go about it,' said the Captain. 'Now then, Ardan, what do *you* say to the first question? Yes, or no?'

'I really can't say anything,' replied Ardan. 'In the presence of such distinguished scientists, I'm only a listener, a "mere looker on in Vienna" as the Divine Williams has it. However, for the sake of argument, suppose I reply in the affirmative, and say that *the Moon is inhabitable.*'

'If you do, I shall most unhesitatingly contradict you,' said Barbican, feeling just then in splendid humour for carrying on an argument, not, of course, for the sake of contradicting or conquering or crushing or showing off or for any other vulgar weakness of lower minds, but for the noble and indeed the only motive that should impel a philosopher – that of *enlightening* and *convincing*, 'In taking the negative side, however, or saying that the Moon is not inhabitable, I shall not be satisfied with merely negative arguments. Many words, however, are not required. Look at her present condition: her atmosphere dwindled away to the lowest ebb; her "seas" dried up or very nearly so; her waters reduced to next to nothing; her vegetation, if existing at all, existing only on the scantiest scale; her transitions from intense heat to intense cold, as we ourselves can testify, sudden in the extreme; her nights and her days each nearly 360 hours long. With all this positively against her and nothing at all that we know of positively for her, I have very little hesitation in saying that the Moon appears to me to be absolutely uninhabitable. She seems to me not only unpropitious to the development of the animal kingdom but actually incapable of sustaining life at all – that is, in the sense that we usually attach to such a term.'

'That saving clause is well introduced, friend Barbican,' said M'Nicholl, who, seeing no chance of demolishing Ardan, had not yet made up his mind as to having another little bout with the President. 'For surely you would not venture to assert that the Moon is uninhabitable by a race of beings having an organization different from ours?'

'That question too, Captain,' replied Barbican, 'though a much more difficult one, I shall try to answer. First, however, let us see, Captain, if we agree on some fundamental points. How do we detect the existence of life? Is it not by *movement*? Is not *motion* its result, no matter what may be its organization?'

'Well,' said the Captain in a drawling way, 'I guess we may grant that.'

'Then, dear friends,' resumed Barbican, 'I must remind you that, though we have had the privilege of observing the lunar continents at a distance of not more than one-third of a mile, we have never yet caught sight of the first thing moving on her surface. The presence of humanity, even of the lowest type, would have revealed itself in some form or other, by boundaries, by buildings, even by ruins. Now what *have* we seen? Everywhere and always, the geological works of *nature*; nowhere and never, the orderly labours of *man*. Therefore, if any representatives of animal life exist in the Moon, they must have taken refuge in those bottomless abysses where our eyes were unable to track them. And even this I can't admit. They could not always remain in these cavities. If there is any atmosphere at all in the Moon, it must be found in her immense low-lying plains. Over those plains her inhabitants must have often passed, and on those plains they must in some way or other have left some mark, some trace, some vestige of their existence, were it even only a road. But you both know well that nowhere are any such traces visible: therefore, they don't exist; therefore, no lunar inhabitants exist – except, of course, such a race of beings, if we can imagine any such, as could exist without revealing their existence by *movement*.'

'That is to say,' broke in Ardan, to give what he conceived a sharper point to Barbican's cogent arguments, 'such a race of beings as could exist without existing!'

'Precisely,' said Barbican: 'Life without movement, and no life at all, are equivalent expressions.'

'Captain,' said Ardan, with all the gravity he could assume, 'have you anything more to say before the Moderator of our little Debating Society gives his opinion on the arguments regarding the question before the house?'

'No more at present,' said the Captain, biding his time.

'Then,' resumed Ardan, rising with much dignity, 'the Committee on Lunar Explorations, appointed by the Honourable Baltimore Gun Club, solemnly assembled in the Projectile belonging to the aforesaid learned and respectable Society, having carefully weighed all the arguments advanced on each side of the question, and having also carefully considered all the new facts bearing on the case that have lately come under the personal notice of said Committee, unanimously decides negatively on the question now before the chair for investigation – namely, 'Is the Moon inhabitable?' Barbican, as chairman of the Committee, I empower you to duly record our solemn decision – *No, the Moon is not inhabitable.*'

Barbican, opening his note-book, made the proper entry among the minutes of the meeting of December 6th.

'Now then, gentlemen,' continued Ardan, 'if you are ready for the second question, the necessary complement of the first, we may as well approach it at once. I propound it for discussion in the following form: *Has the Moon ever been inhabited?* Captain, the Committee would be delighted to hear your remarks on the subject.'

'Gentlemen,' began the Captain in reply, 'I had formed my opinion regarding the ancient inhabitability of our Satellite long before I ever dreamed of testing my theory by anything like our present journey. I will now add that all our observations, so far made, have only served to confirm me in my opinion. I now venture to assert, not only with every kind of probability in my favour but also on what I consider most excellent arguments, that the Moon was once inhabited by a race of beings possessing an organization similar to our own, that she once produced animals anatomically resembling our terrestrial animals, and that all these living organizations, human and animal, have had their day, that that day vanished ages and ages ago, and that, consequently, *Life*, extinguished forever, can never again reveal its existence there under any form.'

'Is the Chair,' asked Ardan, 'to infer from the honourable gentleman's observations that he considers the Moon to be a world much older than the Earth?'

'Not exactly that,' replied the Captain without hesitation; 'I rather mean to say that the Moon is a world that grew old more rapidly than the Earth; that it came to maturity earlier; that it ripened quicker, and was stricken with old age sooner. Owing to the difference of the volumes of the two worlds, the organizing forces of matter must have been comparatively much more violent in the interior of the Moon than in the interior of the Earth. The present condition of its surface, as we see it lying there beneath us at this moment, places this assertion beyond all possibility of doubt. Wrinkled, pitted, knotted, furrowed, scarred, nothing that we can show on Earth resembles it. Moon and Earth were called into existence by the Creator probably at the same period of time. In the first stages of their existence, they do not seem to have been anything better than masses of gas. Acted upon by various forces and various influences, all of course directed by an omnipotent intelligence, these gases by degrees became liquid, and the liquids grew condensed into solids until solidity could retain its shape. But the two heavenly bodies, though starting at the same time, developed at a very different ratio. Most undoubtedly, our globe was still gaseous or at most only liquid, at the period when the Moon, already hardened by cooling, began to become inhabitable.'

'*Most undoubtedly* is good!' observed Ardan admiringly.

'At this period,' continued the learned Captain, 'an atmosphere surrounded her. The waters, shut in by this gaseous envelope, could no longer evaporate. Under the combined influences of air, water, light, and solar heat as well as internal heat, vegetation began to overspread the continents by this time ready to receive it, and most undoubtedly – I mean – a – incontestably – it was at this epoch that *life* manifested itself on the lunar surface. I say *incontestably* advisedly, for Nature never exhausts herself in producing useless things, and therefore a world, so wonderfully inhabitable, *must* of necessity have had inhabitants.'

'I like *of necessity* too,' said Ardan, who could never keep still; 'I always did, when I felt my arguments to be what you call a little shaky.'

'But, my dear Captain,' here observed Barbican, 'have you taken into consideration some of the peculiarities of our Satellite which are decidedly opposed to the development of vegetable and animal existence? Those nights and days, for instance, 354 hours long?'

'I have considered them all,' answered the brave Captain. 'Days and nights of such an enormous length would at the present time, I grant, give rise to variations in temperature altogether intolerable to any ordinary organization. But things were quite different in the era alluded to. At that time, the atmosphere enveloped the Moon in a gaseous mantle, and the vapours took the shape of clouds. By the screen thus formed by the hand of nature, the heat of the solar rays was tempered and the nocturnal radiation retarded. Light too, as well as heat, could be modified, tempered, and *genialized* if I may use the expression, by the air. This produced a healthy counterpoise of forces, which, now that the atmosphere has completely disappeared, of course exists no longer. Besides – friend Ardan, you will excuse me for telling you something new, something that will surprise you—'

– 'Surprise me, my dear boy, fire away surprising me!' cried Ardan. 'I like dearly to be surprised. All I regret is that you scientists have surprised me so much already that I shall never have a good, hearty, genuine surprise again!'

– 'I am most firmly convinced,' continued the Captain, hardly waiting for Ardan to finish, 'that, at the period of the Moon's occupancy by living creatures, her days and nights were by no means 354 hours long.'

'Well! if anything could surprise me,' said Ardan quickly, 'such an assertion as that most certainly would. On what does the honourable gentleman base his *most firm conviction*?'

'We know,' replied the Captain, 'that the reason of the Moon's present long day and night is the exact equality of the periods of her rotation on her axis and of her revolution around the Earth. When she has turned once around the Earth, she has turned once around herself. Consequently, her back is turned to the Sun during one-half of the month; and her face during the other half. Now, I don't believe that this state of things existed at the period referred to.'

'The gentleman does not believe!' exclaimed Ardan. 'The Chair must be excused for reminding the honourable gentleman that it can not accept his incredulity as a sound and valid argument. These two movements have certainly equal periods now; why not always?'

'For the simple reason that this equality of periods is due altogether to the influence of terrestrial attraction,' replied the ready Captain. 'This attraction at present, I grant, is so great that it actually disables the Moon from revolving on herself; consequently she must always keep the same face turned towards the Earth. But who can assert that this attraction was powerful enough to exert the same influence at the epoch when the Earth herself was only a fluid substance? In fact, who can even assert that the Moon has always been the Earth's satellite?'

'Ah, who indeed?' exclaimed Ardan. 'And who can assert that the Moon did not exist long before the Earth was called into being at all? In fact, who can assert that the Earth itself is not a great piece broken off the Moon? Nothing like asking absurd questions! I've often found them passing for the best kind of arguments!'

'Friend Ardan,' interposed Barbican, who noticed that the Captain was a little too disconcerted to give a ready reply; 'Friend Ardan, I must say you are not quite wrong in showing how certain methods of reasoning, legitimate enough in themselves, may be easily abused by being carried too far. I think, however, that the Captain might maintain his position without having recourse to speculations altogether too gigantic for ordinary intellect. By simply admitting the insufficiency of the primordeal attraction to preserve a perfect balance between the movements of the lunar rotation and revolution, we can easily see how the nights and days could once succeed each other on the Moon exactly as they do at present on the Earth.'

'Nothing can be clearer!' resumed the brave Captain, once more rushing to the charge. 'Besides, even without this alternation of days and nights, life on the lunar surface was quite possible.'

'Of course it was possible,' said Ardan; 'everything is possible except what contradicts itself. It is possible too that every possibility is a fact; therefore, it *is* a fact. However,' he added, not wishing to press the Captain's weak points too closely, 'let all these logical niceties pass for the present. Now that you have established the existence of your humanity in the Moon, the Chair would respectfully ask how it has all so completely disappeared?'

'It disappeared completely thousands, perhaps millions, of years ago,' replied the unabashed Captain. 'It perished from the physical impossibility of living any longer in a world where the atmosphere had become by degrees too rare to be able to perform its functions as the great resuscitating medium of dependent existences. What took place on the Moon is only what is to take place some day or other on the Earth, when it is sufficiently cooled off.'

'Cooled off?'

'Yes,' replied the Captain as confidently and with as little hesitation as if he was explaining some of the details of his great machine-shop in Philadelphia; 'You see, according as the internal fire near the surface was extinguished or was withdrawn towards the centre, the lunar shell naturally cooled off. The logical consequences, of course, then gradually took place: extinction of organized beings; and then extinction of vegetation. The atmosphere, in the meantime, became thinner and thinner – partly drawn off with the water evaporated by the terrestrial attraction, and partly sinking with the solid water into the crust-cracks caused by cooling. With the disappearance of air capable of respiration, and of water capable of motion, the Moon, of course, became uninhabitable. From that day it became the abode of death, as completely as it is at the present moment.'

'That is the fate in store for our Earth?'

'In all probability.'

'And when is it to befall us?'

'Just as soon as the crust becomes cold enough to be uninhabitable.'

'Perhaps your philosophership has taken the trouble to calculate how many years it will take our unfortunate *Terra Mater* to cool off?'

'Well; I have.'

'And you can rely on your figures?'

'Implicitly.'

'Why not tell it at once then to a fellow that's dying of impatience to know all about it? Captain, the Chair considers you one of the most tantalizing creatures in existence!'

'If you only listen, you will hear,' replied M'Nicholl quietly. 'By careful observations, extended through a series of many years, men have been able to discover the average loss of temperature endured by the Earth in a century. Taking this as the ground work of their calculations, they have ascertained that our Earth shall become an uninhabitable planet in about—'

'Don't cut her life too short! Be merciful!' cried Ardan in a pleading tone half in earnest. 'Come, a good long day, your Honour! A good long day!'

'The planet that we call the Earth,' continued the Captain, as grave as a judge, 'will become uninhabitable to human beings, after a lapse of 400 thousand years from the present time.'

'Hurrah!' cried Ardan, much relieved. '*Vive la Science!* Henceforward, what miscreant will persist in saying that the

Savants are good for nothing? Proudly pointing to this calculation, can't they exclaim to all defamers: 'Silence, croakers! Our services are invaluable! Haven't we insured the Earth for 400 thousand years?' Again I say *vive la Science!*'

'Ardan,' began the Captain with some asperity, 'the foundations on which Science has raised—'

'I'm half converted already,' interrupted Ardan in a cheery tone; 'I do really believe that Science is not altogether unmitigated homebogue! *Vive*—'

– 'But what has all this to do with the question under discussion?' interrupted Barbican, desirous to keep his friends from losing their tempers in idle disputation.

'True!' said Ardan. 'The Chair, thankful for being called to order, would respectfully remind the house that the question before it is: *Has the Moon been inhabited?* Affirmative has been heard. Negative is called on to reply. Mr. Barbican has the *parole.*'

But Mr. Barbican was unwilling just then to enter too deeply into such an exceedingly difficult subject. 'The probabilities,' he contented himself with saying, 'would appear to be in favour of the Captain's speculations. But we must never forget that they *are* speculations – nothing more. Not the slightest evidence has yet been produced that the Moon is anything else than "a dead and useless waste of extinct volcanoes." No signs of cities, no signs of buildings, not even of ruins, none of anything that could be reasonably ascribed to the labours of intelligent creatures. No sign of change of any kind has been established. As for the agreement between the Moon's rotation and her revolution, which compels her to keep the same face constantly turned towards the Earth, we don't know that it has not existed from the beginning. As for what is called the effect of volcanic agency upon her surface, we don't know that her peculiar blistered appearance may not have been brought about altogether by the bubbling and spitting that blisters molten iron when cooling and contracting. Some close observers have even ventured to account for her craters by saying they were due to pelting showers of meteoric rain. Then again as to her atmosphere – why should she have lost her atmosphere? Why should it sink into craters? Atmosphere is gas, great in volume, small in matter; where would there be room for it? Solidified by the intense cold? Possibly in the night time. But would not the heat of the long day be great enough to thaw it back again? The same trouble attends the alleged disappearance of the water. Swallowed up in the cavernous cracks, it is said. But why are there cracks? Cooling is not always attended by cracking. Water cools without cracking; cannon balls cool without cracking. Too much stress has been laid on the great difference between the *nucleus* and the *crust*: it is really impossible to say where one ends and the other begins. In fact, no theory explains satisfactorily anything regarding the present state of the Moon's surface. In fact, from the day that Galileo compared her clustering craters to "eyes on a peacock's tail" to the present time, we must acknowledge that we know nothing more than we can actually see, not one particle more of the Moon's history than our telescopes reveal to our corporal eyes!'

'In the lucid opinion of the honourable and learned gentleman who spoke last,' said Ardan, 'the Chair is compelled to concur. Therefore, as to the second question before the house for deliberation, *Has the Moon been ever inhabited?* the Chair gets out of its difficulty, as a Scotch jury does when it has not evidence enough either way, by returning a solemn verdict of *Not Proven!*'

'And with this conclusion,' said Barbican, hastily rising, 'of a subject on which, to tell the truth, we are unable as yet to throw any light worth speaking of, let us be satisfied for the present. Another question of greater moment to us just now is: where are we? It seems to me that we are increasing our distance from the Moon very decidedly and very rapidly.'

It was easy to see that he was quite right in this observation. The Projectile, still following a northerly course and therefore approaching the lunar equator, was certainly getting farther and farther from the Moon. Even at 30° S., only ten degrees farther north than the latitude of *Tycho*, the travellers had considerable difficulty, comparatively, in observing the details of *Pitatus*, a walled mountain on the south shores of the *Mare Nubium*. In the 'sea' itself, over which they now floated, they could see very little, but far to the left, on the 20th parallel, they could discern the vast crater of *Bullialdus*, 9,000 feet deep. On the right, they had just caught a glimpse of *Purbach*, a depressed valley almost square in shape with a round crater in the centre, when Ardan suddenly cried out:

'A Railroad!'

And, sure enough, right under them, a little northeast of *Purbach*, the travellers easily distinguished a long line straight and black, really not unlike a railroad cutting through a low hilly country.

This, Barbican explained, was of course no railway, but a steep cliff, at least 1,000 feet high, casting a very deep shadow, and probably the result of the caving in of the surface on the eastern edge.

Then they saw the immense crater of *Arzachel* and in its midst a cone mountain shining with dazzling splendour. A little north of this, they could detect the outlines of another crater, *Alphonse*, at least 70 miles in diameter. Close to it they could easily distinguish the immense crater or, as some observers call it, Ramparted Plain, *Ptolemy*, so well known to lunar astronomers, occupying, as it does, such a favourable position near the centre of the Moon, and having a diameter fully, in one direction at least, 120 miles long.

The travellers were now in about the same latitude as that at which they had at first approached the Moon, and it was here that they began most unquestionably to leave her. They looked and looked, readjusting their glasses, but the details were becoming more and more difficult to catch. The reliefs grew more and more blurred and the outlines dimmer and dimmer. Even the great mountain profiles began to fade away, the dazzling colours to grow duller, the jet black shadows greyer, and the general effect mistier.

At last, the distance had become so great that, of this lunar world so wonderful, so fantastic, so weird, so mysterious, our travellers by degrees lost even the consciousness, and their sensations, lately so vivid, grew fainter and fainter, until finally they resembled those of a man who is suddenly awakened from a peculiarly strange and impressive dream.

CHAPTER XIX

In Every Fight, the Impossible Wins

No matter what we have been accustomed to, it is sad to bid it farewell forever. The glimpse of the Moon's wondrous world imparted to Barbican and his companions had been, like that of the Promised Land to Moses on Mount Pisgah, only a distant and a dark one, yet it was with inexpressibly mournful eyes that, silent and thoughtful, they now watched her fading away slowly from their view, the conviction impressing itself deeper and deeper in their souls that, slight as their acquaintance had been, it was never to be renewed again. All doubt on the subject was removed by the position gradually, but decidedly, assumed by the Projectile. Its base was turning away slowly and steadily from the Moon, and pointing surely and unmistakably towards the Earth.

Barbican had been long carefully noticing this modification, but without being able to explain it. That the Projectile should withdraw a long distance from the Moon and still be her satellite, he could understand; but, being her satellite, why not present towards her its heaviest segment, as the Moon does towards the Earth? That was the point which he could not readily clear up.

By carefully noting its path, he thought he could see that the Projectile, though now decidedly leaving the Moon, still followed a curve exactly analogous to that by which it had approached her. It must therefore be describing a very elongated ellipse, which might possibly extend even to the neutral point where the lunar and terrestrial attractions were mutually overcome.

With this surmise of Barbican's, his companions appeared rather disposed to agree, though, of course, it gave rise to new questions.

'Suppose we reach this dead point,' asked Ardan; 'what then is to become of us?'

'Can't tell!' was Barbican's unsatisfactory reply.

'But you can form a few hypotheses?'

'Yes, two!'

'Let us have them.'

'The velocity will be either sufficient to carry us past the dead point, or it will not: sufficient, we shall keep on, just as we are now, gravitating forever around the Moon—'

– 'Hypothesis number two will have at least one point in its favour,' interrupted as usual the incorrigible Ardan; 'it can't be worse than hypothesis number one!'

– 'Insufficient,' continued Barbican, laying down the law, 'we shall rest forever motionless on the dead point of the mutually neutralizing attractions.'

'A pleasant prospect!' observed Ardan: 'from the worst possible to no better! Isn't it, Barbican?'

'Nothing to say,' was Barbican's only reply.

'Have you nothing to say either, Captain?' asked Ardan, beginning to be a little vexed at the apparent apathy of his companions.

'Nothing whatever,' replied M'Nicholl, giving point to his words by a despairing shake of his head.

'You don't mean surely that we're going to sit here, like bumps on a log, doing nothing until it will be too late to attempt anything?'

'Nothing whatever can be done,' said Barbican gloomily. 'It is vain to struggle against the impossible.'

'Impossible! Where did you get that word? I thought the American schoolboys had cut it out of their dictionaries!'

'That must have been since my time,' said Barbican smiling grimly.

'It still sticks in a few old copies anyhow,' drawled M'Nicholl drily, as he carefully wiped his glasses.

'Well! it has no business *here*!' said Ardan. 'What! A pair of live Yankees and a Frenchman, of the nineteenth century too, recoil before an old fashioned word that hardly scared our grandfathers!'

'What can we do?'

'Correct the movement that's now running away with us!'

'Correct it?'

'Certainly, correct it! or modify it! or clap brakes on it! or take some advantage of it that will be in our favour! What matters the exact term so you comprehend me?'

'Easy talking!'

'As easy doing!'

'Doing what? Doing how?'

'The what, and the how, is your business, not mine! What kind of an artillery man is he who can't master his bullets? The gunner who cannot command his own gun should be rammed into it head foremost himself and blown from its mouth! A nice pair of savants *you* are! There you sit as helpless as a couple of babies, after having inveigled me—'

'Inveigled!!' cried Barbican and M'Nicholl starting to their feet in an instant; 'WHAT!!!'

'Come, come!' went on Ardan, not giving his indignant friends time to utter a syllable; 'I don't want any recrimination! I'm not the one to complain! I'll even let up a little if you consider the expression too strong! I'll even withdraw it altogether, and assert that the trip delights me! that the Projectile is a thing after my own heart! that I was never in better spirits than at the present moment! I don't complain, I only appeal to your own good sense, and call upon you with all my voice to do everything possible, so that we may go *somewhere*, since it appears we can't get to the Moon!'

'But that's exactly what we want to do ourselves, friend Ardan,' said Barbican, endeavouring to give an example of calmness to the impatient M'Nicholl; 'the only trouble is that we have not the means to do it.'

'Can't we modify the Projectile's movement?'

'No.'

'Nor diminish its velocity?'

'No.'

'Not even by lightening it, as a heavily laden ship is lightened, by throwing cargo overboard?'

'What can we throw overboard? We have no ballast like balloon-men.'

'I should like to know,' interrupted M'Nicholl, 'what would be the good of throwing anything at all overboard. Any one with a particle of common sense in his head, can see that the lightened Projectile should only move the quicker!'

'Slower, you mean,' said Ardan.

'Quicker, I mean,' replied the Captain.

'Neither quicker nor slower, dear friends,' interposed Barbican, desirous to stop a quarrel; 'we are floating, you know, in an absolute void, where specific gravity never counts.'

'Well then, my friends,' said Ardan in a resigned tone that he evidently endeavoured to render calm, 'since the worst is come to the worst, there is but one thing left for us to do!'

'What's that?' said the Captain, getting ready to combat some new piece of nonsense.

'To take our breakfast!' said the Frenchman curtly.

It was a resource he had often fallen back on in difficult conjunctures. Nor did it fail him now.

Though it was not a project that claimed to affect either the velocity or the direction of the Projectile, still, as it was eminently practicable and not only unattended by no inconvenience on the one hand but evidently fraught with many advantages on the other, it met with decided and instantaneous success. It was rather an early hour for breakfast, two o'clock in the morning, yet the meal was keenly relished. Ardan served it up in charming style and crowned the dessert with a few bottles of a wine especially selected for the occasion from his own private stock. It was a *Tokay Imperial* of 1863, the genuine *Essenz*, from Prince Esterhazy's own wine cellar, and the best brain stimulant and brain clearer in the world, as every connoisseur knows.

It was near four o'clock in the morning when our travellers, now well fortified physically and morally, once more resumed their observations with renewed courage and determination, and with a system of recording really perfect in its arrangements.

Around the Projectile, they could still see floating most of the objects that had been dropped out of the window. This convinced them that, during their revolution around the Moon, they had not passed through any atmosphere; had anything of the kind been encountered, it would have revealed its presence by its retarding effect on the different objects that now followed close in the wake of the Projectile. One or two that were missing had been probably struck and carried off by a fragment of the exploded bolide.

Of the Earth nothing as yet could be seen. She was only one day Old, having been New the previous evening, and two days were still to elapse before her crescent would be sufficiently cleared of the solar rays to be capable of performing her ordinary duty of serving as a time-piece for the Selenites. For, as the reflecting reader need hardly be reminded, since she rotates with perfect regularity on her axis, she can make such rotations visible to the Selenites by bringing some particular point on her surface once every twenty-four hours directly over the same lunar meridian.

Towards the Moon, the view though far less distinct, was still almost as dazzling as ever. The radiant Queen of Night still glittered in all her splendour in the midst of the starry host, whose pure white light seemed to borrow only additional purity and silvery whiteness from the gorgeous contrast. On her disc, the 'seas' were already beginning to assume the ashy tint so well known to us on Earth, but the rest of her surface sparkled with all its former radiation, *Tycho* glowing like a sun in the midst of the general resplendescence.

Barbican attempted in vain to obtain even a tolerable approximation of the velocity at which the Projectile was now moving. He had to content himself with the knowledge that it was diminishing at a uniform rate – of which indeed a little reflection on a well known law of Dynamics readily convinced him. He had not much difficulty even in explaining the matter to his friends.

'Once admitting,' said he, 'the Projectile to describe an orbit round the Moon, that orbit must of necessity be an ellipse. Every moving body circulating regularly around another, describes an ellipse. Science has proved this incontestably. The satellites describe ellipses around the planets, the planets around the Sun, the Sun himself describes an ellipse around the unknown star that serves as a pivot for our whole solar system. How can our Baltimore Gun Club Projectile then escape the universal law?

'Now what is the consequence of this law? If the orbit were a *circle*, the satellite would always preserve the same distance from its primary, and its velocity should therefore be constant. But the orbit being an *ellipse*, and the attracting body always occupying one of the foci, the satellite must evidently lie nearer to this focus in one part of its orbit than in another. The Earth when nearest to the Sun, is in her *perihelion*; when most distant, in her *aphelion*. The Moon, with regard to the Earth, is similarly in her *perigee*, and her *apogee*. Analogous expressions denoting the relations of the Projectile towards the Moon, would be *periselene* and *aposelene*. At its *aposelene* the Projectile's velocity would have reached its minimum; at the *periselene*, its maximum. As it is to the former point that we are now moving, clearly the velocity must keep on diminishing until that point is reached. Then, *if it does not die out altogether*, it must spring up again, and even accelerate as it reapproaches the Moon. Now the great trouble is this: If the *Aposelenetic* point should coincide with the point of lunar attraction, our velocity must certainly become *nil*, and the Projectile must remain relatively motionless forever!'

'What do you mean by "relatively motionless"?' asked M'Nicholl, who was carefully studying the situation.

'I mean, of course, not absolutely motionless,' answered Barbican; 'absolute immobility is, as you are well aware, altogether impossible, but motionless with regard to the Earth and the—'

'By Mahomet's jackass!' interrupted Ardan hastily, 'I must say we're a precious set of *imbéciles*!'

'I don't deny it, dear friend,' said Barbican quietly, notwithstanding the unceremonious interruption; 'but why do you say so just now?'

'Because though we are possessed of the power of retarding the velocity that takes us from the Moon, we have never thought of employing it!'

'What do you mean?'

'Do you forget the rockets?'

'It's a fact!' cried M'Nicholl. 'How have we forgotten them?'

'I'm sure I can't tell,' answered Barbican, 'unless, perhaps, because we had too many other things to think about. Your thought, my dear friend, is a most happy one, and, of course, we shall utilize it.'

'When? How soon?'

'At the first favourable opportunity, not sooner. For you can see for yourselves, dear friends,' he went on explaining, 'that with the present obliquity of the Projectile with regard to the lunar disc, a discharge of our rockets would be more likely to send us away from the Moon than towards her. Of course, you are both still desirous of reaching the Moon?'

'Most emphatically so!'

'Then by reserving our rockets for the last chance, we may possibly get there after all. In consequence of some force, to me utterly inexplicable, the Projectile still seems disposed to turn its base towards the Earth. In fact, it is likely enough that at the neutral point its cone will point vertically to the Moon. That being the moment when its velocity will most probably be *nil*, it will also be the moment for us to discharge our rockets, and the possibility is that we may force a direct fall on the lunar disc.'

'Good!' cried Ardan, clapping hands.

'Why didn't we execute this grand manoeuvre the first time we reached the neutral point?' asked M'Nicholl a little crustily.

'It would be useless,' answered Barbican; 'the Projectile's velocity at that time, as you no doubt remember, not only did not need rockets, but was actually too great to be affected by them.'

'True!' chimed in Ardan; 'a wind of four miles an hour is very little use to a steamer going ten.'

'That assertion,' cried M'Nicholl, 'I am rather dis—'

– 'Dear friends,' interposed Barbican, his pale face beaming and his clear voice ringing with the new excitement; 'let us just now waste no time in mere words. We have one more chance, perhaps a great one. Let us not throw it away! We have been on the brink of despair—'

– 'Beyond it!' cried Ardan.

– 'But I now begin to see a possibility, nay, a very decided probability, of our being able to attain the great end at last!'

'Bravo!' cried Ardan.

'Hurrah!' cried M'Nicholl.

'Yes! my brave boys!' cried Barbican as enthusiastically as his companions; 'all's not over yet by a long shot!'

What had brought about this great revulsion in the spirits of our bold adventurers? The breakfast? Prince Esterhazy's Tokay? The latter, most probably. What had become of the resolutions they had discussed so ably and passed so decidedly a few hours before? *Was the Moon inhabited? No! Was the Moon habitable? No!* Yet in the face of all this – or rather as coolly as if such subjects had never been alluded to – here were the reckless scientists actually thinking of nothing but how to work heaven and earth in order to get there!

One question more remained to be answered before they played their last trump, namely: 'At what precise moment would the Projectile reach the neutral point?'

To this Barbican had very little trouble in finding an answer. The time spent in proceeding from the south pole to the dead point being evidently equal to the time previously spent in proceeding from the dead point to the north pole – to ascertain the former, he had only to calculate the latter. This was easily done. To refer to his notes, to check off the different rates of velocity at which they had readied the different parallels, and to turn these rates into time, required only a very few minutes careful calculation. The Projectile then was to reach the point of neutral attraction at one o'clock in the morning of December 8th. At the present time, it was five o'clock in the morning of the 7th; therefore, if nothing unforeseen should occur in the meantime, their great and final effort was to be made about twenty hours later.

The rockets, so often alluded to as an idea of Ardan's and already fully described, had been originally provided to break the violence of the Projectile's fall on the lunar surface; but now the dauntless travellers were about to employ them for a purpose precisely the reverse. In any case, having been put in proper order for immediate use, nothing more now remained to be done till the moment should come for firing them off.

'Now then, friends,' said M'Nicholl, rubbing his eyes but hardly able to keep them open, 'I'm not over fond of talking, but this time I think I may offer a slight proposition.'

'We shall be most happy to entertain it, my dear Captain,' said Barbican.

'I propose we lie down and take a good nap.'

'Good gracious!' protested Ardan; 'What next?'

'We have not had a blessed wink for forty hours,' continued the Captain; 'a little sleep would recuperate us wonderfully.'

'No sleep now!' exclaimed Ardan.

'Every man to his taste!' said M'Nicholl; 'mine at present is certainly to turn in!' and suiting the action to the word, he coiled himself on the sofa, and in a few minutes his deep regular breathing showed his slumber to be as tranquil as an infant's.

Barbican looked at him in a kindly way, but only for a very short time; his eyes grew so filmy that he could not keep them open any longer. 'The Captain,' he said, 'may not be without his little faults, but for good practical sense he is worth a ship-load like you and me, Ardan. By Jove, I'm going to imitate him, and, friend Michael, you might do worse!'

In a short time he was as unconscious as the Captain.

Ardan gazed on the pair for a few minutes, and then began to feel quite lonely. Even his animals were fast asleep. He tried to look out, but observing without having anybody to listen to your observations, is dull work. He looked again at the sleeping pair, and then he gave in.

'It can't be denied,' he muttered, slowly nodding his head, 'that even your practical men sometimes stumble on a good idea.'

Then curling up his long legs, and folding his arms under his head, his restless brain was soon forming fantastic shapes for itself in the mysterious land of dreams.

But his slumbers were too much disturbed to last long. After an uneasy, restless, unrefreshing attempt at repose, he sat up at about half-past seven o'clock, and began stretching himself, when he found his companions already awake and discussing the situation in whispers.

The Projectile, they were remarking, was still pursuing its way from the Moon, and turning its conical point more and more in her direction. This latter phenomenon, though as puzzling as ever, Barbican regarded with decided pleasure: the more directly the conical summit pointed to the Moon at the exact moment, the more directly towards her surface would the rockets communicate their reactionary motion.

Nearly seventeen hours, however, were still to elapse before that moment, that all important moment, would arrive.

The time began to drag. The excitement produced by the Moon's vicinity had died out. Our travellers, though as daring and as confident as ever, could not help feeling a certain sinking of heart at the approach of the moment for deciding either alternative of their doom in this world – their fall to the Moon, or their eternal imprisonment in a changeless orbit. Barbican and M'Nicholl tried to kill time by revising their calculations and putting their notes in order; Ardan, by feverishly walking back and forth from window to window, and stopping for a second or two to throw a nervous glance at the cold, silent and impassive Moon.

Now and then reminiscences of our lower world would flit across their brains. Visions of the famous Gun Club rose up before them the oftenest, with their dear friend Marston always the central figure. What was his bustling, honest, good-natured, impetuous heart at now? Most probably he was standing bravely at his post on the Rocky Mountains, his eye glued to the great Telescope, his whole soul peering through its tube. Had he seen the Projectile before it vanished behind the Moon's north pole? Could he have caught a glimpse of it at its reappearance? If so, could he have concluded it to be the satellite of a satellite! Could Belfast have announced to the world such a startling piece of intelligence? Was that all the Earth was ever to know of their great enterprise? What were the speculations of the Scientific World upon the subject? etc., etc.

In listless questions and desultory conversation of this kind the day slowly wore away, without the occurrence of any incident whatever to relieve its weary monotony. Midnight arrived, December the seventh was dead. As Ardan said: '*Le Sept Decembre est mort; vive le Huit!*' In one hour more, the neutral point would be reached. At what velocity was the Projectile now moving? Barbican could not exactly tell, but he felt quite certain that no serious error had slipped into his calculations. At one o'clock that night, *nil* the velocity was to be, and *nil* it would be!

CHAPTER XIX

Another phenomenon, in any case, was to mark the arrival of the exact moment. At the dead point, the two attractions, terrestrial and lunar, would again exactly counterbalance each other. For a few seconds, objects would no longer possess the slightest weight. This curious circumstance, which had so much surprised and amused the travellers at its first occurrence, was now to appear again as soon as the conditions should become identical. During these few seconds then would come the moment for striking the decisive blow.

They could soon notice the gradual approach of this important instant. Objects began to weigh sensibly lighter. The conical point of the Projectile had become almost directly under the centre of the lunar surface. This gladdened the hearts of the bold adventurers. The recoil of the rockets losing none of its power by oblique action, the chances pronounced decidedly in their favour. Now, only supposing the Projectile's velocity to be absolutely annihilated at the dead point, the slightest force directing it towards the Moon would be *certain* to cause it finally to fall on her surface.

Supposing! – but supposing the contrary!

– Even these brave adventurers had not the courage to suppose the contrary!

'Five minutes to one o'clock,' said M'Nicholl, his eyes never quitting his watch.

'Ready?' asked Barbican of Ardan.

'Ay, ay, sir!' was Ardan's reply, as he made sure that the electric apparatus to discharge the rockets was in perfect working order.

'Wait till I give the word,' said Barbican, pulling out his chronometer.

The moment was now evidently close at hand. The objects lying around had no weight. The travellers felt their bodies to be as buoyant as a hydrogen balloon. Barbican let go his chronometer, but it kept its place as firmly in empty space before his eyes as if it had been nailed to the wall!

'One o'clock!' cried Barbican in a solemn tone.

Ardan instantly touched the discharging key of the little electric battery. A dull, dead, distant report was immediately heard, communicated probably by the vibration of the Projectile to the internal air. But Ardan saw through the window a long thin flash, which vanished in a second. At the same moment, the three friends became instantaneously conscious of a slight shock experienced by the Projectile.

They looked at each other, speechless, breathless, for about as long as it would take you to count five: the silence so intense that they could easily hear the pulsation of their hearts. Ardan was the first to break it.

'Are we falling or are we not?' he asked in a loud whisper.

'We're not!' answered M'Nicholl, also hardly speaking above his breath. 'The base of the Projectile is still turned away as far as ever from the Moon!'

Barbican, who had been looking out of the window, now turned hastily towards his companions. His face frightened them. He was deadly pale; his eyes stared, and his lips were painfully contracted.

'We *are* falling!' he shrieked huskily.

'Towards the Moon?' exclaimed his companions.

'No!' was the terrible reply. 'Towards the Earth!'

'*Sacré!*' cried Ardan, as usually letting off his excitement in French.

'Fire and fury!' cried M'Nicholl, completely startled out of his habitual *sang froid*.

'Thunder and lightning!' swore the usually serene Barbican, now completely stunned by the blow. 'I had never expected this!'

Ardan was the first to recover from the deadening shock: his levity came to his relief.

'First impressions are always right,' he muttered philosophically. 'The moment I set eyes on the confounded thing, it reminded me of the Bastille; it is now proving its likeness to a worse place: easy enough to get into, but no redemption out of it!'

There was no longer any doubt possible on the subject. The terrible fall had begun. The Projectile had retained velocity enough not only to carry it beyond the dead point, but it was even able to completely overcome the feeble resistance offered by the rockets. It was all clear now. The same velocity that had carried the Projectile beyond the neutral point on its way to the Moon, was still swaying it on its return to the Earth. A well known law of motion required that, in the path which it was now about to describe, *it should repass, on its return through all the points through which it had already passed during its departure.*

No wonder that our friends were struck almost senseless when the fearful fall they were now about to encounter, flashed upon them in all its horror. They were to fall a clear distance of nearly 200 thousand miles! To lighten or counteract such a descent, the most powerful springs, checks, rockets, screens, deadeners, even if the whole Earth were engaged in their construction – would produce no more effect than so many spiderwebs. According to a simple law in Ballistics, *the Projectile was to strike the Earth with a velocity equal to that by which it had been animated when issuing from the mouth of the Columbiad* – a velocity of at least seven miles a second!

To have even a faint idea of this enormous velocity, let us make a little comparison. A body falling from the summit of a steeple a hundred and fifty feet high, dashes against the pavement with a velocity of fifty five miles an hour. Falling from the summit of St. Peter's, it strikes the earth at the rate of 300 miles an hour, or five times quicker than the rapidest express train. Falling from the neutral point, the Projectile should strike the Earth with a velocity of more than 25,000 miles an hour!

'We are lost!' said M'Nicholl gloomily, his philosophy yielding to despair.

'One consolation, boys!' cried Ardan, genial to the last. 'We shall die together!'

'If we die,' said Barbican calmly, but with a kind of suppressed enthusiasm, 'it will be only to remove to a more extended sphere of our investigations. In the other world, we can pursue our inquiries under far more favourable auspices. There the wonders of our great Creator, clothed in brighter light, shall be brought within a shorter range. We shall require no machine, nor projectile, nor material contrivance of any kind to be enabled to contemplate them in all their grandeur and to appreciate them fully and intelligently. Our souls, enlightened by the emanations of the Eternal Wisdom, shall revel forever in the blessed rays of Eternal Knowledge!'

'A grand view to take of it, dear friend Barbican;' replied Ardan, 'and a consoling one too. The privilege of roaming at will through God's great universe should make ample amends for missing the Moon!'

M'Nicholl fixed his eyes on Barbican admiringly, feebly muttering with hardly moving lips:

'Grit to the marrow! Grit to the marrow!'

Barbican, head bowed in reverence, arms folded across his breast, meekly and uncomplainingly uttered with sublime resignation:

'Thy will be done!'

'Amen!' answered his companions, in a loud and fervent whisper.

They were soon falling through the boundless regions of space with inconceivable rapidity!

CHAPTER XX
Off the Pacific Coast

'WELL, LIEUTENANT, HOW goes the sounding?'

'Pretty lively, Captain; we're nearly through;' replied the Lieutenant. 'But it's a tremendous depth so near land. We can't be more than 250 miles from the California coast.'

'The depression certainly is far deeper than I had expected,' observed Captain Bloomsbury. 'We have probably lit on a submarine valley channelled out by the Japanese Current.'

'The Japanese Current, Captain?'

'Certainly; that branch of it which breaks on the western shores of North America and then flows southeast towards the Isthmus of Panama.'

'That may account for it, Captain,' replied young Brownson; 'at least, I hope it does, for then we may expect the valley to get shallower as we leave the land. So far, there's no sign of a Telegraphic Plateau in this quarter of the globe.'

'Probably not, Brownson. How is the line now?'

'We have paid out 3,500 fathoms already, Captain, but, judging from the rate the reel goes at, we are still some distance from bottom.'

As he spoke, he pointed to a tall derrick temporarily rigged up at the stern of the vessel for the purpose of working the sounding apparatus, and surrounded by a group of busy men. Through a block pulley strongly lashed to the derrick, a stout cord of the best Italian hemp, wound off a large reel placed amidships, was now running rapidly and with a slight whirring noise.

'I hope it's not the "cup-lead" you are using, Brownson?' said the Captain, after a few minutes observation.

'Oh no, Captain, certainly not,' replied the Lieutenant. 'It's only Brooke's apparatus that is of any use in such depths.'

'Clever fellow that Brooke,' observed the Captain; 'served with him under Maury. His detachment of the weight is really the starting point for every new improvement in sounding gear. The English, the French, and even our own, are nothing but modifications of that fundamental principle. Exceedingly clever fellow!'

'Bottom!' sang out one of the men standing near the derrick and watching the operations.

The Captain and the Lieutenant immediately advanced to question him.

'What's the depth, Coleman?' asked the Lieutenant.

'21,762 feet,' was the prompt reply, which Brownson immediately inscribed in his note-book, handing a duplicate to the Captain.

'All right, Lieutenant,' observed the Captain, after a moment's inspection of the figures. 'While I enter it in the log, you haul the line aboard. To do so, I need hardly remind you, is a task involving care and patience. In spite of all our gallant little donkey engine can do, it's a six hours job at least. Meanwhile, the Chief Engineer had better give orders for firing up, so that we may be ready to start as soon as you're through. It's now close on to four bells, and with your permission I shall turn in. Let me be called at three. Good night!'

'Goodnight, Captain!' replied Brownson, who spent the next two hours pacing backward and forward on the quarter deck, watching the hauling in of the sounding line, and occasionally casting a glance towards all quarters of the sky.

It was a glorious night. The innumerable stars glittered with the brilliancy of the purest gems. The ship, hove to in order to take the soundings, swung gently on the faintly heaving ocean breast. You felt you were in a tropical clime, for, though no breath fanned your cheek, your senses easily detected the delicious odour of a distant garden of sweet roses. The sea sparkled with phosphorescence. Not a sound was heard except the panting of the hard-worked little donkey-engine and the whirr of the line as it came up taut and dripping from the ocean depths. The lamp, hanging from the mast, threw a bright glare on deck, presenting the strongest contrast with the black shadows, firm and motionless as marble. The 11th day of December was now near its last hour.

The steamer was the *Susquehanna*, a screw, of the United States Navy, 4,000 in tonnage, and carrying 20 guns. She had been detached to take soundings between the Pacific coast and the Sandwich Islands, the initiatory movement towards laying down an Ocean Cable, which the *Pacific Cable Company* contemplated finally extending to China. She lay just now a few hundred miles directly south of San Diego, an old Spanish town in southwestern California, and the point which is expected to be the terminus of the great *Texas and Pacific Railroad*.

The Captain, John Bloomsbury by name, but better known as 'High-Low Jack' from his great love of that game – the only one he was ever known to play – was a near relation of our old friend Colonel Bloomsbury of the Baltimore Gun Club. Of a good Kentucky family, and educated at Annapolis, he had passed his meridian without ever being heard of, when suddenly the news that he had run the gauntlet in a little gunboat past the terrible batteries of Island Number Ten, amidst a perfect storm of shell, grape and canister discharged at less than a hundred yards distance, burst on the American nation on the sixth of April, 1862, and inscribed his name at once in deep characters on the list of the giants of the Great War. But war had never been his vocation. With the return of peace, he had sought and obtained employment on the Western Coast Survey, where every thing he did he looked on as a labour of love. The Sounding Expedition he had particularly coveted, and, once entered upon it, he discharged his duties with characteristic energy.

He could not have had more favourable weather than the present for a successful performance of the nice and delicate investigations of sounding. His vessel had even been fortunate enough to have lain altogether out of the track of the terrible wind storm already alluded to, which, starting from somewhere southwest of the Sierra Madre, had swept away every vestige of mist from the summits of the Rocky Mountains and, by revealing the Moon in all her splendour, had enabled Belfast to send the famous despatch announcing that he had seen the Projectile. Every feature of the expedition was, in fact, advancing so favourably that the Captain expected to be able, in a month or two, to submit to the *P.C. Company* a most satisfactory report of his labours.

Cyrus W. Field, the life and soul of the whole enterprise, flushed with honours still in full bloom (the Atlantic Telegraph Cable having been just laid), could congratulate himself with good reason on having found a treasure in the Captain. High-Low Jack was the congenial spirit by whose active and intelligent aid he promised himself the pleasure of seeing before long the whole Pacific Ocean covered with a vast reticulation of electric cables. The practical part, therefore, being in such safe hands, Mr. Field could remain with a quiet conscience in Washington, New York or London, seeing after the financial part of the grand undertaking, worthy of the Nineteenth Century, worthy of the Great Republic, and eminently worthy of the illustrious CYRUS W. himself!

As already mentioned, the *Susquehanna* lay a few hundred miles south of San Diego, or, to be more accurate, in 27° 7' North Latitude and 118° 37' West Longitude (Greenwich).

It was now a little past midnight. The Moon, in her last quarter, was just beginning to peep over the eastern horizon. Lieutenant Brownson, leaving the quarter deck, had gone to the forecastle, where he found a crowd of officers talking together earnestly and directing their glasses towards her disc. Even here, out on the ocean, the Queen of the night, was as great an object of attraction as on the North American Continent generally, where, that very night and that very hour, at least 40 million pairs of eyes were anxiously gazing at her. Apparently forgetful that even the very best of their glasses could no more see the Projectile than angulate Sirius, the officers held them fast to their eyes for five minutes at a time, and then took them away only to talk with remarkable fluency on what they had not discovered.

'Any sign of them yet, gentlemen?' asked Brownson gaily as he joined the group. 'It's now pretty near time for them to put in an appearance. They're gone ten days I should think.'

'They're there, Lieutenant! not a doubt of it!' cried a young midshipman, fresh from Annapolis, and of course 'throughly posted' in the latest revelations of Astronomy. 'I feel as certain of their being there as I am of our being here on the forecastle of the *Susquehanna*!'

'I must agree with you of course, Mr. Midshipman,' replied Brownson with a slight smile; 'I have no grounds whatever for contradicting you.'

'Neither have I,' observed another officer, the surgeon of the vessel. 'The Projectile was to have reached the Moon when at her full, which was at midnight on the 5th. To-day was the 11th. This gives them six days of clear light – time enough in all conscience not only to land safely but to install themselves quite comfortably in their new home. In fact, I see them there already—'

'In my mind's eye, Horatio!' laughed one of the group. 'Though the Doc wears glasses, he can see more than any ten men on board.'

– 'Already' – pursued the Doctor, heedless of the interruption. '*Scene*, a stony valley near a Selenite stream; the Projectile on the right, half buried in volcanic *scoriae*, but apparently not much the worse for the wear; ring mountains, craters, sharp peaks, etc. all around; old MAC discovered taking observations with his levelling staff; BARBICAN perched on the summit of a sharp pointed rock, writing up his note-book; ARDAN, eye-glass on nose, hat under arm, legs apart, puffing at his *Imperador*, like a—'

– 'A locomotive!' interrupted the young Midshipman, his excitable imagination so far getting the better of him as to make him forget his manners. He had just finished Locke's famous MOON HOAX, and his brain was still full of its pictures. 'In the background,' he went on, 'can be seen thousands of *Vespertiliones-Homines* or *Man-Bats*, in all the various attitudes of curiosity, alarm, or consternation; some of them peeping around the rocks, some fluttering from peak to peak, all gibbering a language more or less resembling the notes of birds. *Enter* LUNATICO, King of the Selenites—'

'Excuse us, Mr. Midshipman,' interrupted Brownson with an easy smile, 'Locke's authority may have great weight among the young Middies at Annapolis, but it does not rank very high at present in the estimation of practical scientists.' This rebuff administered to the conceited little Midshipman, a rebuff which the Doctor particularly relished, Brownson continued: 'Gentlemen, we certainly know nothing whatever regarding our friends' fate; guessing gives no information. How we ever are to hear from the Moon until we are connected with it by a lunar cable, I can't even imagine. The probability is that we shall never—'

'Excuse me, Lieutenant,' interrupted the unrebuffed little Midshipman; 'Can't Barbican write?'

A shout of derisive comments greeted this question.

'Certainly he can write, and send his letter by the Pony Express!' cried one.

'A Postal Card would be cheaper!' cried another.

'The *New York Herald* will send a reporter after it!' was the exclamation of a third.

'Keep cool, just keep cool, gentlemen,' persisted the little Midshipman, not in the least abashed by the uproarious hilarity excited by his remarks. 'I asked if Barbican couldn't write. In that question I see nothing whatever to laugh at. Can't a man write without being obliged to send his letters?'

'This is all nonsense,' said the Doctor. 'What's the use of a man writing to you if he can't send you what he writes?'

'What's the use of his sending it to you if he can have it read without that trouble?' answered the little Midshipman in a confident tone. 'Is there not a telescope at Long's Peak? Doesn't it bring the Moon within a few miles of the Rocky Mountains, and enable us to see on her surface, objects as small as nine feet in diameter? Well! What's to prevent Barbican and his friends from constructing a gigantic alphabet? If they write words of even a few hundred yards and sentences a mile or two long, what is to prevent us from reading them? Catch the idea now, eh?'

They did catch the idea, and heartily applauded the little Middy for his smartness. Even the Doctor saw a certain kind of merit in it, and Brownson acknowledged it to be quite feasible. In fact, expanding on it, the Lieutenant assured his hearers that, by means of large parabolic reflectors, luminous groups of rays could be dispatched from the Earth, of sufficient brightness to establish direct communication even with Venus or Mars, where these rays would be quite as visible as the planet Neptune is from the Earth. He even added that those brilliant points of light, which have been quite frequently observed in Mars and Venus, are perhaps signals made to the Earth by the inhabitants of these planets. He concluded, however, by observing that, though we might by these means succeed in obtaining news from the Moon, we could not possibly send any intelligence back in return, unless indeed the Selenites had at their disposal optical instruments at least as good as ours.

All agreed that this was very true, and, as is generally the case when one keeps all the talk to himself, the conversation now assumed so serious a turn that for some time it was hardly worth recording.

At last the Chief Engineer, excited by some remark that had been made, observed with much earnestness:

'You may say what you please, gentlemen, but I would willingly give my last dollar to know what has become of those brave men! Have they done anything? Have they seen anything? I hope they have. But I should dearly like to know. Ever so little success would warrant a repetition of the great experiment. The Columbiad is still to the good in Florida, as it will be for many a long day. There are millions of men to day as curious as I am upon the subject. Therefore it will be only a question of mere powder and bullets if a cargo of visitors is not sent to the Moon every time she passes our zenith.

'Marston would be one of the first of them,' observed Brownson, lighting his cigar.

'Oh, he would have plenty of company!' cried the Midshipman. 'I should be delighted to go if he'd only take me.'

'No doubt you would, Mr. Midshipman,' said Brownson, 'the wise men, you know, are not all dead yet.'

'Nor the fools either, Lieutenant,' growled old Frisby, the fourth officer, getting tired of the conversation.

'There is no question at all about it,' observed another; 'every time a Projectile started, it would take off as many as it could carry.'

'I wish it would only start often enough to improve the breed!' growled old Frisby.

'I have no doubt whatever,' added the Chief Engineer, 'that the thing would get so fashionable at last that half the inhabitants of the Earth would take a trip to the Moon.'

'I should limit that privilege strictly to some of our friends in Washington,' said old Frisby, whose temper had been soured probably by a neglect to recognize his long services; 'and most of them I should by all means insist on sending to the Moon. Every month I would ram a whole raft of them into the Columbiad, with a charge under them strong enough to blow them all to the – But – Hey! – what in creation's that?'

Whilst the officer was speaking, his companions had suddenly caught a sound in the air which reminded them immediately of the whistling scream of a Lancaster shell. At first they thought the steam was escaping somewhere, but, looking upwards, they saw that the strange noise proceeded from a ball of dazzling brightness, directly over their heads, and evidently falling towards them with tremendous velocity. Too frightened to say a word, they could only see that in its light the whole ship blazed like fireworks, and the whole sea glittered like a silver lake. Quicker than tongue can utter, or mind can conceive, it flashed before their eyes for a second, an enormous bolide set on fire by friction with the atmosphere, and gleaming in its white heat like a stream of molten iron gushing straight from the furnace. For a second only did they catch its flash before their eyes; then striking the bowsprit of the vessel, which it shivered into a thousand pieces, it vanished in the sea in an instant with a hiss, a scream, and a roar, all equally indescribable. For some time the utmost confusion reigned on deck. With eyes too dazzled to see, ears still ringing with the frightful combination of unearthly sounds, faces splashed with floods of sea water, and noses stifled with clouds of scalding steam, the crew of the *Susquehanna* could hardly realize that their marvellous escape by a few feet from instant and certain destruction was an accomplished fact, not a frightful dream. They were still engaged in trying to open their eyes and to get the hot water out of their ears, when they suddenly heard the trumpet voice of Captain Bloomsbury crying, as he stood half dressed on the head of the cabin stairs:

'What's up, gentlemen? In heaven's name, what's up?'

The little Midshipman had been knocked flat by the concussion and stunned by the uproar. But before any body else could reply, his voice was heard, clear and sharp, piercing the din like an arrow:

'It's THEY, Captain! Didn't I tell you so?'

CHAPTER XXI
News for Marston!

IN A FEW minutes, consciousness had restored order on board the *Susquehanna*, but the excitement was as great as ever. They had escaped by a hairsbreadth the terrible fate of being both burned and drowned without a moment's warning, without a single soul being left alive to tell the fatal tale; but on this neither officer nor man appeared to bestow the slightest thought. They were wholly engrossed with the terrible catastrophe that had befallen the famous adventurers. What was the loss of the *Susquehanna* and all it contained, in comparison to the loss experienced by the world at large in the terrible tragic *dénouement* just witnessed? The worst had now come to the worst. At last the long agony was over forever. Those three gallant men, who had not only conceived but had actually executed the grandest and most daring enterprise of ancient or modern times, had paid by the most fearful of deaths, for their sublime devotion to science and their unselfish desire to extend the bounds of human knowledge! Before such a reflection as this, all other considerations were at once reduced to proportions of the most absolute insignificance.

But was the death of the adventurers so very certain after all? Hope is hard to kill. Consciousness had brought reflection, reflection doubt, and doubt had resuscitated hope.

'It's they!' had exclaimed the little Midshipman, and the cry had thrilled every heart on board as with an electric shock. Everybody had instantly understood it. Everybody had felt it to be true. Nothing could be more certain than that the meteor which had just flashed before their eyes was the famous projectile of the Baltimore Gun Club. Nothing could be truer than that it contained the three world renowned men and that it now lay in the black depths of the Pacific Ocean.

But here opinions began to diverge. Some courageous breasts soon refused to accept the prevalent idea.

'They're killed by the shock!' cried the crowd.

'Killed?' exclaimed the hopeful ones; 'Not a bit of it! The water here is deep enough to break a fall twice as great.'

'They're smothered for want of air!' exclaimed the crowd.

'Their stock may not be run out yet!' was the ready reply. 'Their air apparatus is still on hand.'

'They're burned to a cinder!' shrieked the crowd.

'They had not time to be burned!' answered the Band of Hope. 'The Projectile did not get hot till it reached the atmosphere, through which it tore in a few seconds.'

'If they're neither burned nor smothered nor killed by the shock, they're sure to be drowned!' persisted the crowd, with redoubled lamentations.

'Fish 'em up first!' cried the Hopeful Band. 'Come! Let's lose no time! Let's fish 'em up at once!'

The cries of Hope prevailed. The unanimous opinion of a council of the officers hastily summoned together by the Captain was to go to work and fish up the Projectile with the least possible delay. But was such an operation possible? asked a doubter. Yes! was the overwhelming reply; difficult, no doubt, but still quite possible. Certainly, however, such an attempt was not immediately possible as the *Susquehanna* had no machinery strong enough or suitable enough for a piece of work involving such a nicety of detailed operations, not to speak of its exceeding difficulty. The next unanimous decision, therefore, was to start the vessel at once for the nearest port, whence they could instantly telegraph the Projectile's arrival to the Baltimore Gun Club.

But what *was* the nearest port? A serious question, to answer which in a satisfactory manner the Captain had to carefully examine his sailing charts. The neighbouring shores of the California Peninsula, low and sandy, were absolutely destitute of good harbours. San Diego, about a day's sail directly north, possessed an excellent harbour, but, not yet having telegraphic communication with the rest of the Union, it was of course not to be thought of. San Pedro Bay was too open to be approached in winter. The Santa Barbara Channel was liable to the same objection, not to mention the trouble often caused by kelp and wintry fogs. The bay of San Luis Obispo was still worse in every respect; having no islands to act as a breakwater, landing there in winter was often impossible. The harbour of the picturesque old town of Monterey was safe enough, but some uncertainty regarding sure telegraphic communications with San Francisco, decided the council not to venture it. Half Moon Bay, a little to the north, would be just as risky, and in moments like the present when every minute was worth a day, no risk involving the slightest loss of time could be ventured.

Evidently, therefore, the most advisable plan was to sail directly for the bay of San Francisco, the Golden Gate, the finest harbour on the Pacific Coast and one of the safest in the world. Here telegraphic communication with all parts of the Union was assured beyond a doubt. San Francisco, about 750 miles distant, the *Susquehanna* could probably make in three days; with a little increased pressure, possibly in two days and a-half. The sooner then she started, the better.

The fires were soon in full blast. The vessel could get under weigh at once. In fact, nothing delayed immediate departure but the consideration that two miles of sounding line were still to be hauled up from the ocean depths. But the Captain, after a moment's thought, unwilling that any more time should be lost, determined to cut it. Then marking its position by fastening its end to a buoy, he could haul it up at his leisure on his return.

'Besides,' said he, 'the buoy will show us the precise spot where the Projectile fell.'

'As for that, Captain,' observed Brownson, 'the exact spot has been carefully recorded already: 27° 7' north latitude by 41° 37' west longitude, reckoning from the meridian of Washington.'

'All right, Lieutenant,' said the Captain curtly. 'Cut the line!'

A large cone-shaped metal buoy, strengthened still further by a couple of stout spars to which it was securely lashed, was soon rigged up on deck, whence, being hoisted overboard, the whole apparatus was carefully lowered to the surface of the sea. By means of a ring in the small end of the buoy, the latter was then solidly attached to the part of the sounding line that still remained in the water, and all possible precautions were taken to diminish the danger of friction, caused by the contrary currents, tidal waves, and the ordinary heaving swells of ocean.

It was now a little after three o'clock in the morning. The Chief Engineer announced everything to be in perfect readiness for starting. The Captain gave the signal, directing the pilot to steer straight for San Francisco, north-north by west. The waters under the stern began to boil and foam; the ship very soon felt and yielded to the power that animated her; and in a few minutes she was making at least twelve knots an hour. Her sailing powers were somewhat higher than this, but it was necessary to be careful in the neighbourhood of such a dangerous coast as that of California.

Seven hundred and fifty miles of smooth waters presented no very difficult task to a fast traveller like the *Susquehanna*, yet it was not till two days and a-half afterwards that she sighted the Golden Gate. As usual, the coast was foggy; neither Point Lobos nor Point Boneta could be seen. But Captain Bloomsbury, well acquainted with every portion of this coast, ran as close along the southern shore as he dared, the fog-gun at Point Boneta safely directing his course. Here expecting to be able to gain a few hours time by signalling to the outer telegraph station on Point Lobos, he had caused to be painted on a sail in large black letters: 'THE MOONMEN ARE BACK!' but the officers in attendance, though their fog-horn could be easily heard – the distance not being quite two miles – were unfortunately not able to see it. Perhaps they did see it, but feared a hoax.

Giving the Fort Point a good wide berth, the *Susquehanna* found the fog gradually clearing away, and by half-past three the passengers, looking under it, enjoyed the glorious view of the Contra Costa mountains east of San Francisco, which had obtained for this entrance the famous and well deserved appellation of the Golden Gate. In another half hour, they had doubled Black Point, and were lying safely at anchor between the islands of Alcatraz and Yerba Buena. In less than five minutes afterwards the Captain was quickly lowered into his gig, and eight stout pairs of arms were pulling him rapidly to shore.

The usual crowd of idlers had collected that evening on the summit of Telegraph Hill to enjoy the magnificent view, which for variety, extent, beauty and grandeur, is probably unsurpassed on earth. Of course, the inevitable reporter, hot after an item, was not absent. The *Susquehanna* had hardly crossed the bar, when they caught sight of her. A government vessel entering the bay at full speed, is something to look at even in San Francisco. Even during the war, it would be considered rather unusual. But they soon remarked that her bowsprit was completely broken off. *Very* unusual. Something decidedly is the matter. See! The vessel is hardly anchored when the Captain leaves her and makes for Megg's Wharf at North Point as hard as ever his men can pull! Something *must* be the matter – and down the steep hill they all rush as fast as ever their legs can carry them to the landing at Megg's Wharf.

The Captain could hardly force his way through the dense throng, but he made no attempt whatever to gratify their ill dissembled curiosity.

'Carriage!' he cried, in a voice seldom heard outside the din of battle.

In a moment seventeen able-bodied cabmen were trying to tear him limb from limb.

'To the telegraph office! Like lightning!' were his stifled mutterings, as he struggled in the arms of the Irish giant who had at last succeeded in securing him.

'To the telegraph office!' cried most of the crowd, running after him like fox hounds, but the more knowing ones immediately began questioning the boatmen in the Captain's gig. These honest fellows, nothing loth to tell all that they knew and more that they invented, soon had the satisfaction of finding themselves the centre-point of a wonder stricken audience, greedily swallowing up every item of the extraordinary news and still hungrily gaping for more.

By this time, however, an important dispatch was flying east, bearing four different addresses: To the Secretary of the U.S. Navy, Washington; To Colonel Joseph Wilcox, Vice-President *pro tem.*, Baltimore Gun Club, Md; To J.T. Marston, Esq. Long's Peak, Grand County, Colourado; and To Professor Wenlock, Sub-Director of the Cambridge Observatory, Mass.

This dispatch read as follows:

> 'In latitude twenty-seven degrees seven minutes north and longitude forty-one degrees thirty-seven minutes west shortly after one o'clock on the morning of twelfth instant Columbiad Projectile fell in Pacific – send instructions –
>
> BLOOMSBURY,
>
> *Captain*, SUSQUEHANNA.'

In five minutes more all San Francisco had the news. An hour later, the newspaper boys were shrieking it through the great cities of the States. Before bed-time every man, woman, and child in the country had heard it and gone into ecstasies over it. Owing to the difference in longitude, the people of Europe could not hear it till after midnight. But next morning the astounding issue of the great American enterprise fell on them like a thunder clap.

We must, of course, decline all attempts at describing the effects of this most unexpected intelligence on the world at large.

The Secretary of the Navy immediately telegraphed directions to the *Susquehanna* to keep a full head of steam up night and day so as to be ready to give instant execution to orders received at any moment.

The Observatory authorities at Cambridge held a special meeting that very evening, where, with all the serene calmness so characteristic of learned societies, they discussed the scientific points of the question in all its bearings. But, before committing themselves to any decided opinion, they unanimously resolved to wait for the development of further details.

At the rooms of the Gun Club in Baltimore there was a terrible time. The kind reader no doubt remembers the nature of the dispatch sent one day previously by Professor Belfast from the Long's Peak observatory, announcing that the Projectile had been seen but that it had become the Moon's satellite, destined to revolve around her forever and ever till time should be no more. The reader is also kindly aware by this time that such dispatch was not supported by the slightest foundations in fact. The learned Professor, in a moment of temporary cerebral excitation, to which even the greatest scientist is just as liable as the rest of us, had taken some little meteor or, still more probably, some little fly-speck in the telescope for the Projectile. The worst of it was that he had not only boldly proclaimed his alleged discovery to the world at large but he had even explained all about it with the well known easy pomposity that 'Science' sometimes ventures to assume. The consequences of all this may be readily guessed. The Baltimore Gun Club had split up immediately into two violently opposed parties. Those gentlemen who regularly conned the scientific magazines, took every word of the learned Professor's dispatch for gospel – or rather for something of far higher value, and more strictly in accordance with the highly advanced scientific developments of the day. But the others, who never read anything but the daily papers and who could not bear the idea of losing Barbican, laughed the whole thing to scorn. Belfast, they said, had seen as much of the Projectile as he had of the 'Open Polar Sea,' and the rest of the dispatch was mere twaddle, though asserted with all the sternness of a religious dogma and enveloped in the usual scientific slang.

The meeting held in the Club House, 24 Monument Square, Baltimore, on the evening of the 13th, had been therefore disorderly in the highest degree. Long before the appointed hour, the great hall was densely packed and the greatest uproar prevailed. Vice-President Wilcox took the chair, and all was comparatively quiet until Colonel Bloomsbury, the Honourary Secretary in Marston's absence, commenced to read Belfast's dispatch. Then the scene, according to the account given in the next day's *Sun*, from whose columns we condense our report, actually 'beggared description.' Roars, yells, cheers, counter-cheers, clappings, hissings, stampings, squallings, whistlings, barkings, mewings, cock crowings, all of the most fearful and demoniacal character, turned the immense hall into a regular pandemonium. In vain did President Wilcox fire off his detonating bell, with a report on ordinary occasions as loud as the roar of a small piece of ordnance. In the dreadful noise then prevailing it was no more heard than the fizz of a lucifer match.

Some cries, however, made themselves occasionally heard in the pauses of the din. 'Read! Read!' 'Dry up!' 'Sit down!' 'Give him an egg!' 'Fair play!' 'Hurrah for Barbican!' 'Down with his enemies!' 'Free Speech!' 'Belfast won't bite you!' 'He'd like to bite Barbican, but his teeth aren't sharp enough!' 'Barbican's a martyr to science, let's hear his fate!' 'Martyr be hanged; the Old Man is to the good yet!' 'Belfast is the grandest name in Science!' 'Groans for the grandest name!' (Awful groans.) 'Three cheers for Old Man Barbican!' (The exceptional strength alone of the walls saved the building, from being blown out by an explosion in which at least 5,000 pairs of lungs participated.)

'Three cheers for M'Nicholl and the Frenchman!' This was followed by another burst of cheering so hearty, vigorous and long continued that the scientific party, or *Belfasters* as they were now called, seeing that further prolongation of the meet was perfectly useless, moved to adjourn. It was carried unanimously. President Wilcox left the chair, the meeting broke up in the wildest disorder – the scientists rather crest fallen, but the Barbican men quite jubilant for having been so successful in preventing the reading of that detested dispatch.

Little sleeping was done that night in Baltimore, and less business next day. Even in the public schools so little work was done by the children that S.T. Wallace, Esq., President of the Education Board, advised an anticipation of the usual Christmas recess by a week. Every one talked of the Projectile; nothing was heard at the corners but discussions regarding its probable fate. All Baltimore was immediately rent into two parties, the *Belfasters* and the *Barbicanites*. The latter was the most enthusiastic and noisy, the former decidedly the most numerous and influential.

Science, or rather pseudo-science, always exerts a mysterious attraction of an exceedingly powerful nature over the generality – that is, the more ignorant portion of the human race. Assert the most absurd nonsense, call it a scientific truth, and back it up with strange words which, like *potentiality*, etc., sound as if they had a meaning but in reality have none, and nine out of every ten men who read your book will believe you. Acquire a remarkable name in one branch of human knowledge, and presto! you are infallible in all. Who can contradict you, if you only wrap up your assertions in specious phrases that not one man in a million attempts to ascertain the real meaning of? We like so much to be saved the trouble of thinking, that it is far easier and more comfortable to be led than to contradict, to fall in quietly with the great flock of sheep that jump blindly after their leader than to remain apart, making one's self ridiculous by foolishly attempting to argue. Real argument, in fact, is very difficult, for several reasons: first, you must understand your subject *well*, which is hardly likely; secondly, your opponent must also understand it well, which is even less likely; thirdly, you must listen patiently to his arguments, which is still less likely; and fourthly, he must listen to yours, the least likely of all. If a quack advertises a panacea for all human ills at a dollar a bottle, a hundred will buy the bottle, for one that will try how many are killed by it. What would the investigator gain by charging the quack with murder? Nobody would believe him, because nobody would take the trouble to follow his arguments. His adversary, first in the field, had gained the popular ear, and remained the unassailable master of the situation. Our love of 'Science' rests upon our admiration of intellect, only unfortunately the intellect is too often that of other people, not our own.

The very sound of Belfast's phrases, for instance, 'satellite,' 'lunar attraction,' 'immutable path of its orbit,' etc, convinced the greater part of the 'intelligent' community that he who used them so flippantly must be an exceedingly great man. Therefore, he had completely proved his case. Therefore, the great majority of the ladies and gentlemen that regularly attend the scientific lectures of the Peabody Institute, pronounced Barbican's fate and that of his companions to be sealed. Next morning's newspapers contained lengthy obituary notices of the Great Balloon-attics as the witty man of the *New York Herald* phrased it, some of which might be considered quite complimentary. These, all industriously copied into the evening papers, the people were carefully reading over again, some with honest regret, some deriving a great moral lesson from an attempt exceedingly reprehensible in every point of view, but most, we are sorry to acknowledge, with a feeling of ill concealed pleasure. Had not they always said how it was to end? Was there anything more absurd ever conceived? Scientific men too! Hang such science! If you want a real scientific man, no wind bag, no sham, take Belfast! *He* knows what he's talking about! No taking *him* in! Didn't he by means of the Monster Telescope, see the Projectile, as large as life, whirling round and round the Moon? Anyway, what else could have happened? Wasn't it what anybody's common sense expected? Don't you remember a conversation we had with you one day? etc., etc.

The *Barbicanites* were very doleful, but they never though of giving in. They would die sooner. When pressed for a scientific reply to a scientific argument, they denied that there was any argument to reply to. What! Had not Belfast seen the Projectile? No! Was not the Great Telescope then good for anything? Yes, but not for everything! Did not Belfast know his business? No! Did they mean to say that he had seen nothing at all? Well, not exactly that, but those scientific gentlemen can seldom be trusted; in their rage for discovery, they make a mountain out of a molehill, or, what is worse, they start a theory and then distort facts to support it. Answers of this kind either led directly to a fight, or the *Belfasters* moved away thoroughly disgusted with the ignorance of their opponents, who could not see a chain of reasoning as bright as the noonday sun.

Things were in this feverish state on the evening of the 14th, when, all at once, Bloomsbury's dispatch arrived in Baltimore. I need not say that it dropped like a spark in a keg of gun powder. The first question all asked was: Is it genuine or bogus? real or got up by the stockbrokers? But a few flashes backwards and forwards over the wires soon settled that point. The stunning effects of the new blow were hardly over when the *Barbicanites* began to perceive that the wonderful intelligence was decidedly in their favour. Was it not a distinct contradiction of the whole story told by their opponents? If Barbican and his friends were lying at the bottom of the Pacific, they were certainly not circumgyrating around the Moon. If it was the Projectile that had broken off the bowsprit of the *Susquehanna*, it could not certainly be the Projectile that Belfast had seen only the day previous doing the duty of a satellite. Did not the truth of one incident render the other an absolute impossibility? If Bloomsbury was right, was not Belfast an ass? Hurrah!

The new revelation did not improve poor Barbican's fate a bit — no matter for that! Did not the *party* gain by it? What would the *Belfasters* say now? Would not they hold down their heads in confusion and disgrace?

The *Belfasters*, with a versatility highly creditable to human nature, did nothing of the kind. Rapidly adopting the very line of tactics they had just been so severely censuring, they simply denied the whole thing. What! the truth of the Bloomsbury dispatch? Yes, every word of it! Had not Bloomsbury seen the Projectile? No! Were not his eyes good for anything? Yes, but not for everything! Did not the Captain know his business? No! Did they mean to say that the bowsprit of the *Susquehanna* had not been broken off? Well, not exactly that, but those naval gentlemen are not always to be trusted; after a pleasant little supper, they often see the wrong light-house, or, what is worse, in their desire to shield their negligence from censure, they dodge the blame by trying to show that the accident was unavoidable. The *Susquehanna's* bowsprit had been snapped off, in all probability, by some sudden squall, or, what was still more likely, some little aerolite had struck it and frightened the crew into fits. When answers of this kind did not lead to blows, the case was an exceptional one indeed. The contestants were so numerous and so excited that the police at last began to think of letting them fight it out without any interference. Marshal O'Kane, though ably assisted by his 12 officers and 500 patrolmen, had a terrible time of it. The most respectable men in Baltimore, with eyes blackened, noses bleeding, and collars torn, saw the inside of a prison that night for the first time in all their lives. Men that even the Great War had left the warmest of friends, now abused each other like fishwomen. The prison could not hold the half of those arrested. They were all, however, discharged next morning, for the simple reason that the Mayor and the aldermen had been themselves engaged in so many pugilistic combats during the night that they were altogether disabled from attending to their magisterial duties next day.

Our readers, however, may be quite assured that, even in the wildest whirl of the tremendous excitement around them, all the members of the Baltimore Gun Club did not lose their heads. In spite of the determined opposition of the *Belfasters* who would not allow the Bloomsbury dispatch to be read at the special meeting called that evening, a few succeeded in adjourning to a committee-room, where Joseph Wilcox, Esq., presiding, our old friends Colonel Bloomsbury, Major Elphinstone, Tom Hunter, Billsby the brave, General Morgan, Chief Engineer John Murphy, and about as many more as were sufficient to form a quorum, declared themselves to be in regular session, and proceeded quietly to debate on the nature of Captain Bloomsbury's dispatch.

Was it of a nature to justify immediate action or not? Decided unanimously in the affirmative. Why so? Because, whether actually true or untrue, the incident it announced was not impossible. Had it indeed announced the Projectile to have fallen in California or in South America, there would have been good valid reasons to question its accuracy. But by taking into consideration the Moon's distance, and the time elapsed between the moment of the start and that of the presumed fall (about 10 days), and also the Earth's revolution in the meantime, it was soon calculated that the point at which the Projectile should strike our globe, if it struck it at all, would be somewhere about 27° north latitude, and 42° west longitude – the very identical spot given in the Captain's dispatch! This certainly was a strong point in its favour, especially as there was positively nothing valid whatever to urge against it.

A decided resolution was therefore immediately taken. Everything that man could do was to be done at once, in order to fish up their brave associates from the depths of the Pacific. That very night, in fact, whilst the streets of Baltimore were still resounding with the yells of contending *Belfasters* and *Barbicanites*, a committee of four, Morgan, Hunter, Murphy, and Elphinstone, were speeding over the Alleghanies in a special train, placed at their disposal by the *Baltimore and Ohio Railroad Company*, and fast enough to land them in Chicago pretty early on the following evening.

Here a fresh locomotive and a Pullman car taking charge of them, they were whirled off to Omaha, reaching that busy locality at about supper time on the evening of December 16th. The Pacific Train, as it was called though at that time running no further west than Julesburg, instead of waiting for the regular hour of starting, fired up that very night, and was soon pulling the famous Baltimore Club men up the slopes of the Nebraska at the rate of forty miles an hour. They were awakened before light next morning by the guard, who told them that Julesburg, which they were just entering, was the last point so far reached by the rails. But their regret at this circumstance was most unexpectedly and joyfully interrupted by finding their hands warmly clasped and their names cheerily cried out by their old and beloved friend, J.T. Marston, the illustrious Secretary of the Baltimore Gun Club.

At the close of the first volume of our entertaining and veracious history, we left this most devoted friend and admirer of Barbican established firmly at his post on the summit of Long's Peak, beside the Great Telescope, watching the skies, night and day, for some traces of his departed friends. There, as the gracious Reader will also remember, he had come a little too late to catch that sight of the Projectile which Belfast had at first reported so confidently, but of which the Professor by degrees had begun to entertain the most serious doubts.

In these doubts, however, Marston, strange to say, would not permit himself for one moment to share. Belfast might shake his head as much as he pleased; he, Marston, was no fickle reed to be shaken by every wind; he firmly believed the Projectile to be there before him, actually in sight, if he could only see it. All the long night of the 13th, and even for several hours of the 14th, he never quitted the telescope for a single instant. The midnight sky was in magnificent order; not a speck dimmed its azure of an intensely dark tint. The stars blazed out like fires; the Moon refused none of her secrets to the scientists who were gazing at her so intently that night from the platform on the summit of Long's Peak. But no black spot crawling over her resplendent surface rewarded their eager gaze. Marston indeed would occasionally utter a joyful cry announcing some discovery, but in a moment after he was confessing with groans that it was all a false alarm. Towards morning, Belfast gave up in despair and went to take a sleep; but no sleep for Marston. Though he was now quite alone, the assistants having also retired, he kept on talking incessantly to himself, expressing the most unbounded confidence in the safety of his friends, and the absolute certainty of their return. It was not until some hours after the Sun had risen and the Moon had disappeared behind the snowy peaks of the west, that he at last withdrew his weary eye from the glass through which every image formed by the great reflector was to be viewed. The countenance he turned on Belfast, who had now come back, was rueful in the extreme. It was the image of grief and despair.

'Did you see nothing whatever during the night, Professor?' he asked of Belfast, though he knew very well the answer he was to get.

'Nothing whatever.'

'But you saw them once, didn't you?'

'Them! Who?'

'Our friends.'

'Oh! the Projectile – well – I think I must have made some oversight.'

'Don't say that! Did not Mr. M'Connell see it also?'

'No. He only wrote out what I dictated.'

'Why, you must have seen it! I have seen it myself!'

'You shall never see it again! It's shot off into space.'

'You're as wrong now as you thought you were right yesterday.'

'I'm sorry to say I was wrong yesterday; but I have every reason to believe I'm right to-day.'

'We shall see! Wait till to-night!'

'To-night! Too late! As far as the Projectile is concerned, night is now no better than day.'

The learned Professor was quite right, but in a way which he did not exactly expect. That very evening, after a weary day, apparently a month long, during which Marston sought in vain for a few hours' repose, just as all hands, well wrapped up in warm furs, were getting ready to assume their posts once more near the mouth of the gigantic Telescope, Mr. M'Connell hastily presented himself with a dispatch for Belfast.

The Professor was listlessly breaking the envelope, when he uttered a sharp cry of surprise.

'Hey!' cried Marston quickly. 'What's up now?'

'Oh!! The Pro – pro – projectile!!'

'What of it? What? Oh what?? Speak!!'

'IT'S BACK!!'

Marston uttered a wild yell of mingled horror, surprise, and joy, jumped a little into the air, and then fell flat and motionless on the platform. Had Belfast shot him with a ten pound weight, right between the two eyes, he could not have knocked him flatter or stiffer. Having neither slept all night, nor eaten all day, the poor fellow's system had become so weak that such unexpected news was really more than he could bear. Besides, as one of the Cambridge men of the party, a young medical student, remarked: the thin, cold air of these high mountains was extremely enervating.

The astronomers, all exceedingly alarmed, did what they could to recover their friend from his fit, but it was nearly ten minutes before they had the satisfaction of seeing his limbs moving with a slight quiver and his breast beginning to heave. At last the colour came back to his face and his eyes opened. He stared around for a few seconds at his friends, evidently unconscious, but his senses were not long in returning.

'Say!' he uttered at last in a faint voice.

'Well!' replied Belfast.

'Where is that infernal Pro – pro – jectile?'

'In the Pacific Ocean.'

'What??'

He was on his feet in an instant.

'Say that again!'

'In the Pacific Ocean.'

'Hurrah! All right! Old Barbican's not made into mincemeat yet! No, sirree! Let's start!'

'Where for?'

'San Francisco!'

'When?'

'This instant!'

'In the dark?'

'We shall soon have the light of the Moon! Curse her! it's the least she can do after all the trouble she has given us!'

CHAPTER XXII
On the Wings of the Wind

LEAVING M'CONNELL AND a few other Cambridge men to take charge of the Great Telescope, Marston and Belfast in little more than an hour after the receipt of the exciting dispatch, were scudding down the slopes of Long's Peak by the only possible route – the inclined railroad. This mode of travelling, however, highly satisfactory as far as it went, ceased altogether at the mountain foot, at the point where the Dale River formed a junction with Cache la Poudre Creek. But Marston, having already mapped out the whole journey with some care and forethought, was ready for almost every emergency. Instinctively feeling that the first act of the Baltimore Gun Club would be to send a Committee to San Francisco to investigate matters, he had determined to meet this deputation on the route, and his only trouble now was to determine at what point he would be most likely to catch them. His great start, he knew perfectly well, could not put him more than a day in advance of them: they having the advantage of a railroad nearly all the way, whilst himself and Belfast could not help losing much time in struggling through ravines, canyons, mountain precipices, and densely tangled forests, not to mention the possibility of a brush or two with prowling Indians, before they could strike the line of the Pacific Railroad, along which he knew the Club men to be approaching. After a few hours rest at La Porte, a little settlement lately started in the valley, early in the morning they took the stage that passed through from Denver to Cheyenne, a town at that time hardly a year old but already flourishing, with a busy population of several thousand inhabitants.

Losing not a moment at Cheyenne, where they arrived much sooner than they had anticipated, they took places in Wells, Fargo and Co.'s *Overland Stage Mail* bound east, and were soon flying towards Julesburg at the rate of twelve miles an hour. Here Marston was anxious to meet the Club men, as at this point the Pacific Railroad divided into two branches – one bearing north, the other south of the Great Salt Lake – and he feared they might take the wrong one.

But he arrived in Julesburg fully 10 hours before the Committee, so that himself and Belfast had not only ample time to rest a little after their rapid flight from Long's Peak, but also to make every possible preparation for the terrible journey of more than fifteen hundred miles that still lay before them.

This journey, undertaken at a most unseasonable period of the year, and over one of the most terrible deserts in the world, would require a volume for itself. Constantly presenting the sharpest points of contrast between the most savage features of wild barbaric nature on the one hand, and the most touching traits of the sweetest humanity on the other, the story of our Club men's adventures, if only well told, could hardly fail to be highly interesting. But instead of a volume, we can give it only a chapter, and that a short one.

From Julesburg, the last station on the eastern end of the Pacific Railroad, to Cisco, the last station on its western end, the distance is probably about fifteen hundred miles, about as far as Constantinople is from London, or Moscow from Paris. This enormous stretch of country had to be travelled all the way by, at the best, a six horse stage tearing along night and day at a uniform rate, road or no road, of ten miles an hour. But this was the least of the trouble. Bands of hostile Indians were a constant source of watchfulness and trouble, against which even a most liberal stock of rifles and revolvers were not always a reassurance. Whirlwinds of dust often overwhelmed the travellers so completely that they could hardly tell day from night, whilst blasts of icy chill, sweeping down from the snowy peaks of the Rocky Mountains, often made them imagine themselves in the midst of the horrors of an Arctic winter.

The predominant scenery gave no pleasure to the eye or exhilaration to the mind. It was of the dreariest description. Days and days passed with hardly a house to be seen, or a tree or a blade of grass. I might even add, or a mountain or a river, for the one was too often a heap of agglomerated sand and clay cut into unsightly chasms by the rain, and the other generally degenerated into a mere stagnant swamp, its shallowness and dryness increasing regularly with its length. The only houses were log ranches, called Relays, hardly visible in their sandy surroundings, and separate from each other by a mean distance of ten miles. The only trees were either stunted cedars, so far apart, as to be often denominated Lone Trees; and, besides wormwood, the only plant was the sage plant, about two feet high, gray, dry, crisp, and emitting a sharp pungent odour by no means pleasant.

In fact, Barbican and his companions had seen nothing drearier or savager in the dreariest and savagest of lunar landscapes than the scenes occasionally presented to Marston and his friends in their headlong journey on the track of the great Pacific Railroad. Here, bowlders, high, square, straight and plumb as an immense hotel, blocked up your way; there, lay an endless level, flat as the palm of your hand, over which your eye might roam in vain in search of something green like a meadow, yellow like a cornfield, or black like ploughed ground – a mere boundless waste of dirty white from the stunted wormwood, often rendered misty with the clouds of smarting alkali dust.

Occasionally, however, this savage scenery decidedly changed its character. Now, a lovely glen would smile before our travellers, traversed by tinkling streams, waving with sweet grasses, dotted with little groves, alive with hares, antelopes, and even elks, but apparently never yet trodden by the foot of man. Now, our Club men felt like travelling on clouds, as they careered along the great plateau west of the Black Hills, fully 8,000 feet above the level of the sea, though even there the grass was as green and fresh as if it grew in some sequestered valley of Pennsylvania. Again,

> 'In this untravelled world whose margin fades
> For ever and for ever as they moved,'

they would find themselves in an immense, tawny, treeless plain, outlined by mountains so distant as to resemble fantastic cloud piles. Here for days they would have to skirt the coasts of a Lake, vast, unruffled, unrippled, apparently of metallic consistency, from whose sapphire depths rose pyramidal islands to a height of fully three thousand feet above the surface.

In a few days all would change. No more sand wastes, salt water flats, or clouds of blinding alkali dust. The travellers' road, at the foot of black precipitous cliffs, would wind along the brink of a roaring torrent, whose devious course would lead them into the heart of the Sierras, where misty peaks solemnly sentinelled the nestling vales still smiling in genial summer verdure. Across these they were often whirled through immense forests of varied character, here dense enough to obscure the track, there swaying in the sweet sunlight and vocal with joyous birds of bright and gorgeous plumage. Then tropical vegetation would completely hide the trail, crystal lakes would obstruct it, cascades shooting down from perpendicular rocks would obliterate it, mountain passes barricaded by basaltic columns would render it uncertain, and on one occasion it was completely covered up by a fall of snow to a depth of more than twenty feet.

But nothing could oppose serious delay to our travellers. Their motto was ever 'onward!' and what they lost in one hour by some mishap they endeavoured to recover on the next by redoubled speed. They felt that they would be no friends of Barbican's if they were discouraged by impossibilities. Besides, what would have been real impossibilities at another time, several concurrent circumstances now rendered comparatively easy.

The surveys, the gradings, the cuttings, and the other preliminary labours in the great Pacific Railroad, gave them incalculable aid. Horses, help, carriages, provisions were always in abundance. Their object being well known, they had the best wishes of every hand on the road. People remained up for them all hours of the night, no matter at what station they were expected. The warmest and most comfortable of meals were always ready for them, for which no charge would be taken on any account. In Utah, a deputation of Mormons galloped alongside them for forty miles to help them over some points of the road that had been often found difficult. The season was the finest known for many years. In short, as an old Californian said as he saw them shooting over the rickety bridge that crossed the Bear River at Corinne: 'they had everything in their favour – *luck* as well as *pluck*!'

The rate at which they performed this terrible ride across the Continent and the progress they made each day, some readers may consider worthy of a few more items for the sake of future reference. Discarding the ordinary overland mail stage as altogether too slow for their purpose, they hired at Julesburg a strong, well built carriage, large enough to hold them all comfortably; but this they had to replace twice before they came to their journey's end. Their team always consisted of the best six horses that could be found, and their driver was the famous Hank Monk of California, who, happening to be in Julesburg about that time, volunteered to see them safely landed in Cisco on the summit of the Sierra Nevada. They were enabled to change horses as near as possible every hour, by telegraphing ahead in the morning, during the day, and often far into the hours of night.

Starting from Julesburg early in the morning of the 17th, their first resting place for a few hours at night was Granite Canyon, twenty miles west of Cheyenne, and just at the foot of the pass over the Black Hills. On the 18th, night-fall found them entering St. Mary's, at the further end of the pass between Rattle Snake

Hills and Elk Mountain. It was after 5 o'clock and already dark on the 19th, when the travellers, hurrying with all speed through the gloomy gorge of slate formation leading to the banks of the Green River, found the ford too deep to be ventured before morning. The 20th was a clear cold day very favourable for brisk locomotion, and the bright sun had not quite disappeared behind the Wahsatch Mountains when the Club men, having crossed the Bear River, began to leave the lofty plateau of the Rocky Mountains by the great inclined plane marked by the lines of the Echo and the Weber Rivers on their way to the valley of the Great American Desert.

Quitting Castle Rock early on the morning of the 21st, they soon came in sight of the Great Salt Lake, along the northern shores of which they sped all day, taking shelter after night-fall at Terrace, in a miserable log cabin surrounded by piles of drifting sand. The 22nd was a terrible day. The sand was blinding, the alkali dust choking, the ride for five or six hours was up considerable grade; still they had accomplished their 150 miles before resting for the night at Elko, even at this period a flourishing little village on the banks of the Humboldt. After another smothering ride on the 23rd, they rested, at Winnemucca, another flourishing village, situated at the precise point in the desert where the Little Humboldt joins Humboldt River, without, however, making the channel fuller or wider. The 24th was decidedly the hardest day, their course lying through the worst part of the terrible Nevada desert. But a glimpse of the Sierras looming in the western horizon gave them courage and strength enough to reach Wadsworth, at their foot, a little before midnight. Our travellers had now but one day's journey more to make before reaching the railroad at Cisco, but, this being a very steep ascent nearly all the way up, each mile cost almost twice as much time and exertion.

At last, late in the evening of Christmas Day, amidst the most enthusiastic cheers of all the inhabitants of Cisco, who welcomed them with a splendid pine brand procession, Marston and his friends, thoroughly used up, feet swelled, limbs bruised, bones aching, stomachs seasick, eyes bleared, ears ringing, and brains on fire for want of rest, took their places in the State Car waiting for them, and started without a moment's delay for Sacramento, about a hundred miles distant. How delicious was the change to our poor travellers! Washed, refreshed, and lying at full length on luxurious sofas, their sensations, as the locomotive spun them down the ringing grooves of the steep Sierras, can be more easily imagined than described. They were all fast asleep when the train entered Sacramento, but the Mayor and the other city authorities who had waited up to receive them, had them carried carefully, so as not to disturb their slumbers, on board the *Yo Semite*, a fine steamer belonging to the California Navigation Company, which landed them safely at San Francisco about noon on the 26th, after accomplishing the extraordinary winter journey of 1,500 miles over land in little more than nine days, only about 200 miles being done by steam.

Half-past two P.M. found our travellers bathed, dressed, shaved, dined, and ready to receive company in the grand parlour of the *Occidental Hotel*. Captain Bloomsbury was the first to call.

Marston hobbled eagerly towards him and asked:

'What have you done towards fishing them up, Captain?'

'A good deal, Mr. Marston; indeed almost everything is ready.'

'Is that really the case, Captain?' asked all, very agreeably surprised.

'Yes, gentlemen, I am most happy to state that I am quite in earnest.'

'Can we start to-morrow?' asked General Morgan. 'We have not a moment to spare, you know.'

'We can start at noon to-morrow at latest,' replied the Captain, 'if the foundry men do a little extra work to-night.'

'We must start this very day, Captain Bloomsbury,' cried Marston resolutely; 'Barbican has been lying two weeks and thirteen hours in the depths of the Pacific! If he is still alive, no thanks to Marston! He must by this time have given me up! The grappling irons must be got on board at once, Captain, and let us start this evening!'

At half-past four that very evening, a shot from the Fort and a lowering of the Stars and Stripes from its flagstaff saluted the *Susquehanna*, as she steamed proudly out of the Golden Gate at the lively rate of fifteen knots an hour.

CHAPTER XXIII
The Club Men Go A Fishing

CAPTAIN BLOOMSBURY WAS perfectly right when he said that almost everything was ready for the commencement of the great work which the Club men had to accomplish. Considering how much was required, this was certainly saying a great deal; but here also, as on many other occasions, fortune had singularly favoured the Club men.

San Francisco Bay, as everybody knows, though one of the finest and safest harbours in the world, is not without some danger from hidden rocks. One of these in particular, the Anita Rock as it was called, lying right in mid channel, had become so notorious for the wrecks of which it was the cause, that, after much time spent in the consideration of the subject, the authorities had at last determined to blow it up. This undertaking having been very satisfactorily accomplished by means of *dynamite* or giant powder, another improvement in the harbour had been also undertaken with great success. The wrecks of many vessels lay scattered here and there pretty numerously, some, like that of the *Flying Dragon*, in spots so shallow that they could be easily seen at low water, but others sunk at least twenty fathoms deep, like that of the *Caroline*, which had gone down in 1851, not far from Blossom Rock, with a treasure on board of 20,000 ounces of gold. The attempt to clear away these wrecks had also turned out very well; even sufficient treasure had been recovered to repay all the expense, though the preparations for the purpose by the contractors, M'Gowan and Co. had been made on the most extensive scale, and in accordance with the latest improvements in the apparatus for submarine operations.

Buoys, made of huge canvas sacks, coated with India rubber, and guarded by a net work of strong cordage, had been manufactured and provided by the *New York Submarine Company*. These buoys, when inflated and working in pairs, had a lifting capacity of 30 tons a pair. Reservoirs of air, provided with powerful compression pumps, always accompanied the buoys. To attach the latter, in a collapsed condition, with strong chains to the sides of the vessels which were to be lifted, a diving apparatus was necessary. This also the *New York Company* had provided, and it was so perfect in its way that, by means of peculiar appliances of easy management, the diver could walk about on the bottom, take his own bearings, ascend to the surface at pleasure, and open his helmet without assistance. A few sets likewise of Rouquayrol and Denayrouze's famous submarine armour had been provided. These would prove of invaluable advantage in all operations performed at great sea depths, as its distinctive feature, 'the regulator,' could maintain, what is not done by any other diving armour, a constant equality of pressure on the lungs between the external and the internal air.

But perhaps the most useful article of all was a new form of diving bell called the *Nautilus*, a kind of submarine boat, capable of lateral as well as vertical movement at the will of its occupants. Constructed with double sides, the intervening chambers could be filled either with water or air according as descent or ascent was required. A proper supply of water enabled the machine to descend to depths impossible to be reached otherwise; this water could then be expelled by an ingenious contrivance, which, replacing it with air, enabled the diver to rise towards the surface as fast as he pleased.

All these and many other portions of the submarine apparatus which had been employed that very year for clearing the channel, lifting the wrecks and recovering the treasure, lay now at San Francisco, unused fortunately on account of the season of the year, and therefore they could be readily obtained for the asking. They had even been generously offered to Captain Bloomsbury, who, in obedience to a telegram from Washington, had kept his crew busily employed for nearly two weeks night and day in transferring them all safely on board the *Susquehanna*.

Marston was the first to make a careful inspection of every article intended for the operation.

'Do you consider these buoys powerful enough to lift the Projectile, Captain?' he asked next morning, as the vessel was briskly heading southward, at a distance of ten or twelve miles from the coast on their left.

'You can easily calculate that problem yourself, Mr. Marston,' replied the Captain. 'It presents no difficulty. The Projectile weighs about 20 thousand pounds, or 10 tons?'

'Correct!'

'Well, a pair of these buoys when inflated can raise a weight of 30 tons.'

'So far so good. But how do you propose attaching them to the Projectile?'

'We simply let them descend in a state of collapse; the diver, going down with them, will have no difficulty in making a fast connection. As soon as they are inflated the Projectile will come up like a cork.'

'Can the divers readily reach such depths?'

'That remains to be seen Mr. Marston.'

'Captain,' said Morgan, now joining the party, 'you are a worthy member of our Gun Club. You have done wonders. Heaven grant it may not be all in vain! Who knows if our poor friends are still alive?'

'Hush!' cried Marston quickly. 'Have more sense than to ask such questions. Is Barbican alive! Am *I* alive? They're all alive, I tell you, only we must be quick about reaching them before the air gives out. That's what's the matter! Air! Provisions, water – abundance! But air – oh! that's their weak point! Quick, Captain, quick – They're throwing the reel – I must see her rate!' So saying, he hurried off to the stern, followed by General Morgan. Chief

Engineer Murphy and the Captain of the *Susquehanna* were thus left for awhile together.

These two men had a long talk on the object of their journey and the likelihood of anything satisfactory being accomplished. The man of the sea candidly acknowledged his apprehensions. He had done everything in his power towards collecting suitable machinery for fishing up the Projectile, but he had done it all, he said, more as a matter of duty than because he believed that any good could result from it; in fact, he never expected to see the bold adventurers again either living or dead. Murphy, who well understood not only what machinery was capable of effecting, but also what it would surely fail in, at first expressed the greatest confidence in the prosperous issue of the undertaking. But when he learned, as he now did for the first time, that the ocean bed on which the Projectile was lying could be hardly less than 20,000 feet below the surface, he assumed a countenance as grave as the Captain's, and at once confessed that, unless their usual luck stood by them, his poor friends had not the slightest possible chance of ever being fished up from the depths of the Pacific.

The conversation maintained among the officers and the others on board the *Susquehanna*, was pretty much of the same nature. It is almost needless to say that all heads – except Belfast's, whose scientific mind rejected the Projectile theory with the most serene contempt – were filled with the same idea, all hearts throbbed with the same emotion. Wouldn't it be glorious to fish them up alive and well? What were they doing just now? Doing? *Doing!* Their bodies most probably were lying in a shapeless pile on the floor of the Projectile, like a heap of clothes, the uppermost man being the last smothered; or perhaps floating about in the water inside the Projectile, like dead gold fish in an aquarium; or perhaps burned to a cinder, like papers in a 'champion' safe after a great fire; or, who knows? perhaps at that very moment the poor fellows were making their last and almost superhuman struggles to burst their watery prison and ascend once more into the cheerful regions of light and air! Alas! How vain must such puny efforts prove! Plunged into ocean depths of three or four miles beneath the surface, subjected to an inconceivable pressure of millions and millions of tons of sea water, their metallic shroud was utterly unassailable from within, and utterly unapproachable from without!

Early on the morning of December 29th, the Captain calculating from his log that they must now be very near the spot where they had witnessed the extraordinary phenomenon, the *Susquehanna* hove to. Having to wait till noon to find his exact position, he ordered the steamer to take a short circular course of a few hours' duration, in hope of sighting the buoy. But though at least a hundred telescopes scanned the calm ocean breast for many miles in all directions, it was nowhere to be seen.

Precisely at noon, aided by his officers and in the presence of Marston, Belfast, and the Gun Club Committee, the Captain took his observations. After a moment or two of the most profound interest, it was a great gratification to all to learn that the *Susquehanna* was on the right parallel, and only about 15 miles west of the precise spot where the Projectile had disappeared beneath the waves. The steamer started at once in the direction indicated, and a minute or two before one o'clock the Captain said they were 'there.' No sign of the buoy could yet be seen in any direction; it had probably been drifted southward by the Mexican coast current which slowly glides along these shores from December to April.

'At last!' cried Marston, with a sigh of great relief.

'Shall we commence at once?' asked the Captain.

'Without losing the twenty thousandth part of a second!' answered Marston; 'life or death depends upon our dispatch!'

The *Susquehanna* again hove to, and this time all possible precautions were taken to keep her in a state of perfect immobility

– an operation easily accomplished in these pacific latitudes, where cloud and wind and water are often as motionless as if all life had died out of the world. In fact, as the boats were quietly lowered, preparatory for beginning the operations, the mirror like calmness of sea, sky, and ship so impressed the Doctor, who was of a poetical turn of mind, that he could not help exclaiming to the little Midshipman, who was standing nearest:

'Coleridge realized, with variations:

The breeze drops down, the sail drops down,
All's still as still can be;
If we speak, it is only to break
The silence of the sea.
Still are the clouds, still are the shrouds,
No life, no breath, no motion;
Idle are all as a painted ship
Upon a painted ocean!'

Chief Engineer Murphy now took command. Before letting down the buoys, the first thing evidently to be done was to find out, if possible, the precise point where the Projectile lay. For this purpose, the *Nautilus* was clearly the only part of the machinery that could be employed with advantage. Its chambers were accordingly soon filled with water, its air reservoirs were also soon completely charged, and the *Nautilus* itself, suspended by chains from the end of a yard, lay quietly on the ocean surface, its manhole on the top remaining open for the reception of those who were willing to encounter the dangers that awaited it in the fearful depths of the Pacific. Every one looking on was well aware that, after a few hundred feet below the surface, the pressure would grow more and more enormous, until at last it became quite doubtful if any line could bear the tremendous strain. It was even possible that at a certain depth the walls of the *Nautilus* might be crushed in like an eggshell, and the whole machine made as flat as two leaves of paper pasted together.

CHAPTER XXIII

Perfectly conscious of the nature of the tremendous risk they were about to run, Marston, Morgan, and Murphy quietly bade their friends a short farewell and were lowered into the manhole. The *Nautilus* having room enough for four, Belfast had been expected to be of the party but, feeling a little sea sick, the Professor backed out at the last moment, to the great joy of Mr. Watkins, the famous reporter of the *N.Y. Herald*, who was immediately allowed to take his place.

Every provision against immediate danger had been made. By means of preconcerted signals, the inmates could have themselves drawn up, let down, or carried laterally in whatever direction they pleased. By barometers and other instruments they could readily ascertain the pressure of the air and water, also how far they had descended and at what rate they were moving. The Captain, from his bridge, carefully superintended every detail of the operation. All signals he insisted on attending to himself personally, transmitting them instantly by his bell to the engineer below. The whole power of the steam engine had been brought to bear on the windlass; the chains could withstand an enormous strain. The wheels had been carefully oiled and tested beforehand; the signalling apparatus had been subjected to the rigidest examination; and every portion of the machinery had been proved to be in admirable working order.

The chances of immediate and unforeseen danger, it is true, had been somewhat diminished by all these precautions. The risk, nevertheless, was fearful. The slightest accident or even carelessness might easily lead to the most disastrous consequence.

Five minutes after two o'clock, the manhole being closed, the lamps lit, and everything pronounced all right, the signal for the descent was given, and the *Nautilus* immediately disappeared beneath the waters. A double anxiety now possessed all on board the *Susquehanna*: the prisoners in the *Nautilus* were in danger as well as the prisoners in the Projectile. Marston and his friends, however, were anything but disquieted on their own account, and, pencil in hand and noses flattened on the glass plates, they examined carefully everything they could see in the liquid masses through which they were descending.

For the first five hundred feet, the descent was accomplished with little trouble. The *Nautilus* sank rather slowly, at a uniform rate of a foot to the second. It had not been two minutes under water when the light of day completely disappeared. But for this the occupants were fully prepared, having provided themselves with powerful lamps, whose brilliant light, radiating from polished reflectors, gave them an opportunity of seeing clearly around it for a distance of eight or ten feet in all directions. Owing to the superlatively excellent construction of the *Nautilus*, also on account of the *scaphanders*, or suits of diving armour, with which Marston and his friends had clothed themselves, the disagreeable sensations to which divers are ordinarily exposed, were hardly felt at all in the beginning of the descent.

Marston was about to congratulate his companions on the favourable auspices inaugurating their trip, when Murphy, consulting the instrument, discovered to his great surprise that the *Nautilus* was not making its time. In reply to their signal 'faster!' the downward movement increased a little, but it soon relaxed again. Instead of less than two minutes, as at the beginning, it now took twelve minutes to make a hundred feet. They had gone only seven hundred feet in thirty-seven minutes. In spite of repeated signalling, their progress during the next hour was even still more alarming, one hundred feet taking exactly 59 minutes. To shorten detail, it required two hours more to make another hundred feet; and then the *Nautilus*, after taking ten minutes to crawl an inch further, came to a perfect stand still. The pressure of the water had evidently now become too enormous to allow further descent.

The Clubmen's distress was very great; Marston's, in particular, was indescribable. In vain, catching at straws, he signalled 'eastwards!' 'westwards!' 'northwards!' or 'southwards!' the *Nautilus* moved readily every way but downwards.

'Oh! what shall we do?' he cried in despair; 'Barbican, must we really give you up though separated from us by the short distance of only a few miles?'

At last, nothing better being to be done, the unwilling signal 'heave upwards!' was given, and the hauling up commenced. It was done very slowly, and with the greatest care. A sudden jerk might snap the chains; an incautious twist might put a kink on the air tube; besides, it was well known that the sudden removal of heavy pressure resulting from rapid ascent, is attended by very disagreeable sensations, which have sometimes even proved fatal.

It was near midnight when the Clubmen were lifted out of the manhole. Their faces were pale, their eyes bloodshot, their figures stooped. Even the *Herald* Reporter seemed to have got enough of exploring. But Marston was as confident as ever, and tried to be as brisk.

He had hardly swallowed the refreshment so positively enjoined in the circumstances, when he abruptly addressed the Captain:

'What's the weight of your heaviest cannon balls?'

'Thirty pounds, Mr. Marston.'

'Can't you attach thirty of them to the *Nautilus* and sink us again?'

'Certainly, Mr. Marston, if you wish it. It shall be the first thing done to-morrow.'

'To-night, Captain! At once! Barbican has not an instant to lose.'

'At once then be it, Mr. Marston. Just as you say.'

The new sinkers were soon attached to the *Nautilus*, which disappeared once more with all its former occupants inside, except the *Herald* Reporter, who had fallen asleep over his notes, or at least seemed to be. He had probably made up his mind as to the likelihood of the *Nautilus* ever getting back again.

The second descent was quicker than the first, but just as futile. At 1,152 feet, the Nautilus positively refused to go a single inch further. Marston looked like a man in a stupor. He made no objection to the signal given by the others to return; he even helped to cut the ropes by which the cannon balls had been attached. Not a single word was spoken by the party, as they slowly rose to the surface. Marston seemed to be struggling against despair. For the first time, the impossibility of the great enterprise seemed to dawn upon him. He and his friends had undertaken a great fight with the mighty Ocean, which now played with them as a giant with a pigmy. To reach the bottom was evidently completely out of their power; and what was infinitely worse, there was nothing to be gained by reaching it. The Projectile was not on the bottom; it could not even have got to the bottom. Marston said it all in a few words to the Captain, as the Clubmen stepped on deck a few hours later:

'Barbican is floating midway in the depths of the Pacific, like Mahomet in his coffin!'

Blindly yielding, however, to the melancholy hope that is born of despair, Marston and his friends renewed the search next day, the 30th, but they were all too worn out with watching and excitement to be able to continue it longer than a few hours. After a night's rest, it was renewed the day following, the 31st, with some vigour, and a good part of the ocean lying between Guadalupe and Benito islands was carefully investigated to a depth of seven or eight hundred feet. No traces whatever of the Projectile. Several California steamers, plying between San Francisco and Panama, passed the *Susquehanna* within hailing distance. But to every question, the invariable reply one melancholy burden bore:

'No luck!'

All hands were now in despair. Marston could neither eat nor drink. He never even spoke the whole day, except on two occasions. Once, when somebody heard him muttering:

'He's now seventeen days in the ocean!'

The second time he spoke, the words seemed to be forced out of him. Belfast admitted, for the sake of argument, that the Projectile had fallen into the ocean, but he strongly denounced the absurd idea of its occupants being still alive. 'Under such circumstances,' went on the learned Professor, 'further prolongation of vital energy would be simply impossible. Want of air, want of food, want of courage—'

'No, sir!' interrupted Marston quite savagely. 'Want of air, of meat, of drink, as much as you like! But when you speak of Barbican's want of courage, you don't know what you are talking about! No holy martyr ever died at the stake with a loftier courage than my noble friend Barbican!'

That night he asked the Captain if he would not sail down as far as Cape San Lucas. Bloomsbury saw that further search was all labour lost, but he respected such heroic grief too highly to give a positive refusal. He consented to devote the following day, New Year's, to an exploring expedition as far as Magdalena Bay, making the most diligent inquiries in all directions.

But New Year's was just as barren of results as any of its predecessors, and, a little before sunset, Captain Bloomsbury, regardless of further entreaties and unwilling to risk further delay, gave orders to 'bout ship and return to San Francisco.

The *Susquehanna* was slowly turning around in obedience to her wheel, as if reluctant to abandon forever a search in which humanity at large was interested, when the look-out man, stationed in the forecastle, suddenly sang out:

'A buoy to the nor'east, not far from shore!'

All telescopes were instantly turned in the direction indicated. The buoy, or whatever object it was, could be readily distinguished. It certainly did look like one of those buoys used to mark out the channel that ships follow when entering a harbour. But as the vessel slowly approached it, a small flag, flapping in the dying wind – a strange feature in a buoy – was seen to surmount its cone, which a nearer approach showed to be emerging four or five feet from the water. And for a buoy too it was exceedingly bright and shiny, reflecting the red rays of the setting sun as strongly as if its surface was crystal or polished metal!

'Call Mr. Marston on deck at once!' cried the Captain, his voice betraying unwonted excitement as he put the glass again to his eye.

Marston, thoroughly worn out by his incessant anxiety during the day, had been just carried below by his friends, and they were now trying to make him take a little refreshment and repose. But the Captain's order brought them all on deck like a flash.

They found the whole crew gazing in one direction, and, though speaking in little more than whispers, evidently in a state of extraordinary excitement.

What could all this mean? Was there any ground for hope? The thought sent a pang of delight through Marston's wildly beating heart that almost choked him.

The Captain beckoned to the Club men to take a place on the bridge beside himself. They instantly obeyed, all quietly yielding them a passage.

The vessel was now only about a quarter of a mile distant from the object and therefore near enough to allow it to be distinguished without the aid of a glass.

What! The flag bore the well known Stars and Stripes!

An electric shudder of glad surprise shot through the assembled crowd. They still spoke, however, in whispers, hardly daring to utter their thoughts aloud.

The silence was suddenly startled by a howl of mingled ecstasy and rage from Marston.

He would have fallen off the bridge, had not the others held him firmly. Then he burst into a laugh loud and long, and quite as formidable as his howl.

Then he tore away from his friends, and began beating himself over the head.

'Oh!' he cried in accents between a yell and a groan, 'what chuckleheads we are! What numskulls! What jackasses! What double-treble-barrelled gibbering idiots!' Then he fell to beating himself over the head again.

'What's the matter, Marston, for heaven's sake!' cried his friends, vainly trying to hold him.

'Speak for yourself!' cried others, Belfast among the number.

'No exception, Belfast! You're as bad as the rest of us! We're all a set of unmitigated, demoralized, dog-goned old lunatics! Ha! Ha! Ha!'

'Speak plainly, Marston! Tell us what you mean!'

'I mean,' roared the terrible Secretary, 'that we are no better than a lot of cabbage heads, dead beats, and frauds, calling ourselves scientists! O Barbican, how you must blush for us! If we were schoolboys, we should all be skinned alive for our ignorance! Do you forget, you herd of ignoramuses, that the Projectile weighs only ten tons?'

'We don't forget it! We know it well! What of it?'

'This of it: it can't sink in water without displacing its own volume in water; its own volume in water weighs thirty tons! Consequently, it can't sink; more consequently, it hasn't sunk; and, most consequently, there it is before us, bobbing up and down all the time under our very noses! O Barbican, how can we ever venture to look at you straight in the face again!'

Marston's extravagant manner of showing it did not prevent him from being perfectly right. With all their knowledge of physics, not a single one of those scientific gentlemen had remembered the great fundamental law that governs sinking or floating bodies. Thanks to its slight specific gravity, the Projectile, after reaching unknown depths of ocean through the terrific momentum of its fall, had been at last arrested in its course and even obliged to return to the surface.

By this time, all the passengers of the *Susquehanna* could easily recognize the object of such weary longings and desperate searches, floating quietly a short distance before them in the last rays of the declining day!

The boats were out in an instant. Marston and his friends took the Captain's gig. The rowers pulled with a will towards the rapidly nearing Projectile. What did it contain? The living or the dead? The living certainly! as Marston whispered to those around him; otherwise how could they have ever run up that flag?

The boats approached in perfect silence, all hearts throbbing with the intensity of newly awakened hope, all eyes eagerly watching for some sign to confirm it. No part of the windows appeared over the water, but the trap hole had been thrown open, and through it came the pole that bore the American flag. Marston made for the trap hole and, as it was only a few feet above the surface, he had no difficulty in looking in.

At that moment, a joyful shout of triumph rose from the interior, and the whole boat's crew heard a dry drawling voice with a nasal twang exclaiming:

'Queen! How is that for high?'

It was instantly answered by another voice, shriller, louder, quicker, more joyous and triumphant in tone, but slightly tinged with a foreign accent:

'King! My brave Mac! How is that for high?'

The deep, clear, calm voice that spoke next thrilled the listeners outside with an emotion that we shall not attempt to portray. Except that their ears could detect in it the faintest possible emotion of triumph, it was in all respects as cool, resolute, and self-possessed as ever:

'Ace! Dear friends, how is that for high?'

They were quietly enjoying a little game of High-Low-Jack!

How they must have been startled by the wild cheers that suddenly rang around their ocean-prison! How madly were these cheers re-echoed from the decks of the *Susquehanna*! Who can describe the welcome that greeted these long lost, long beloved, long despaired of Sons of Earth, now so suddenly and unexpectedly rescued from destruction, and restored once more to the wonderstricken eyes of admiring humanity? Who can describe the scenes of joy and exuberant happiness, and deep felt gratitude, and roaring rollicking merriment, that were witnessed on board the steamer that night and during the next three days!

As for Marston, it need hardly be said that he was simply ecstatic, but it may interest both the psychologist and the philologist to learn that the expression *How is that for high?* struck him at once as with a kind of frenzy. It became immediately such a favourite tongue morsel of his that ever since he has been employing it on all occasions, appropriate or otherwise. Thanks to his exertions in its behalf all over the country, the phrase is now the most popular of the day, well known and relished in every part of the Union. If we can judge from its present hold on the popular ear it will continue to live and flourish for many a long day to come; it may even be accepted as the popular expression of triumph in those dim, distant, future years when the memory not only of the wonderful occasion of its formation but also of the illustrious men themselves who originated it, has been consigned forever to the dark tomb of oblivion!

CHAPTER XXIV
Farewell to the Baltimore Gun Club

THE INTENSE INTEREST of our extraordinary but most veracious history having reached its culmination at the end of the last chapter, our absorbing chronicle might with every propriety have been then and there concluded; but we can't part from our gracious and most indulgent reader before giving him a few more details which may be instructive perhaps, if not amusing.

No doubt he kindly remembers the world-wide sympathy with which our three famous travellers had started on their memorable trip to the Moon. If so, he may be able to form some idea of the enthusiasm universally excited by the news of their safe return. Would not the millions of spectators that had thronged Florida to witness their departure, now rush to the other extremity of the Union to welcome them back? Could those innumerable Europeans, Africans and Asiatics, who had visited the United States simply to have a look at M'Nicholl, Ardan and Barbican, ever think of quitting the country without having seen those wonderful men again? Certainly not! Nay, more – the reception and the welcome that those heroes would everywhere be greeted with, should be on a scale fully commensurate with the grandeur of their own gigantic enterprise. The Sons of Earth who had fearlessly quitted this terrestrial globe and who had succeeded in returning after accomplishing a journey inconceivably wonderful, well deserved to be received with every extremity of pride, pomp and glorious circumstance that the world is capable of displaying.

To catch a glimpse of these demi-gods, to hear the sound of their voices, perhaps even to touch their hands – these were the only emotions with which the great heart of the country at large was now throbbing.

To gratify this natural yearning of humanity, to afford not only to every foreigner but to every native in the land an opportunity of beholding the three heroes who had reflected such indelible glory on the American name, and to do it all in a manner eminently worthy of the great American Nation, instantly became the desire of the American People.

To desire a thing, and to have it, are synonymous terms with the great people of the American Republic.

A little thinking simplified the matter considerably: as all the people could not go to the heroes, the heroes should go to all the people.

So decided, so done.

It was nearly two months before Barbican and his friends could get back to Baltimore. The winter travelling over the Rocky Mountains had been very difficult on account of the heavy snows, and, even when they found themselves in the level country, though they tried to travel as privately as possible, and for the present positively declined all public receptions, they were compelled to spend some time in the houses of the warm friends near whom they passed in the course of their long journey.

The rough notes of their Moon adventures – the only ones that they could furnish just then – circulating like wild fire and devoured with universal avidity, only imparted a keener whet to the public desire to feast their eyes on such men. These notes were telegraphed free to every newspaper in the country, but the longest and best account of the '*Journey to the Moon*' appeared in the columns of the *New York Herald*, owing to the fact that Watkins the reporter had had the adventurers all to himself during the whole of the three days' trip of the *Susquehanna* back to San Francisco. In a week after their return, every man, woman, and child in the United States knew by heart some of the main facts and incidents in the famous journey; but, of course, it is needless to say that they knew nothing at all about the finer points and the highly interesting minor details of the astounding story. These are now all laid before the highly favoured reader for the first time. I presume it is unnecessary to add that they are worthy of his most implicit confidence, having been industriously and conscientiously compiled from the daily journals of the three travellers, revised, corrected, and digested very carefully by Barbican himself.

It was, of course, too early at this period for the critics to pass a decided opinion on the nature of the information furnished by our travellers. Besides, the Moon is an exceedingly difficult subject. Very few newspaper men in the country are capable of offering a single opinion regarding her that is worth reading. This is probably also the reason why half-scientists talk so much dogmatic nonsense about her.

Enough, however, had appeared in the notes to warrant the general opinion that Barbican's explorations had set at rest forever several pet theories lately started regarding the nature of our satellite. He and his friends had seen her with their own eyes, and under such favourable circumstances as to be altogether exceptional. Regarding her formation, her origin, her inhabitability, they could easily tell what system *should* be rejected and what *might* be admitted. Her past, her present, and her future, had been alike laid bare before their eyes. How can you object to the positive assertion of a conscientious man who has passed within a few hundred miles of *Tycho*, the culminating point in the strangest of all the strange systems of lunar oreography? What reply can you make to a man who has sounded the dark abysses of the *Plato* crater? How can you dare to contradict those men whom the vicissitudes of their daring journey had swept over the dark, Invisible Face of the Moon, never before revealed to human eye? It was now confessedly the privilege and the right of these men to set limits to that selenographic science which had till now been making itself so very busy in reconstructing the lunar world. They could now say, authoritatively, like Cuvier lecturing over a fossil skeleton: 'Once the Moon was this, a habitable world, and inhabitable long before our Earth! And now the Moon is that, an uninhabitable world, and uninhabitable ages and ages ago!'

We must not even dream of undertaking a description of the grand *fête* by which the return of the illustrious members of the Gun Club was to be adequately celebrated, and the natural curiosity of their countrymen to see them was to be reasonably gratified. It was one worthy in every way of its recipients, worthy of the Gun Club, worthy of the Great Republic, and, best of all, every man, woman, and child in the United States could take part in it. It required at least three months to prepare it: but this was not to be regretted as its leading idea could not be properly carried out during the severe colds of winter.

All the great railroads of the Union had been closely united by temporary rails, a uniform gauge had been everywhere adopted, and every other necessary arrangement had been made to enable a splendid palace car, expressly manufactured for the occasion by Pullman himself, to visit every chief point in the United States without ever breaking connection. Through the principal street in each city, or streets if one was not large enough, rails had been laid so as to admit the passage of the triumphal car. In many cities, as a precaution against unfavourable weather, these streets had been arched over with glass, thus becoming grand arcades, many of which have been allowed to remain so to the present day. The houses lining these streets, hung with tapestry, decorated with flowers, waving with banners, were all to be illuminated at night time in a style at once both the most brilliant and the most tasteful. On the sidewalks, tables had been laid, often miles and miles long, at the public expense; these were to be covered with every kind of eatables, exquisitely cooked, in the greatest profusion, and free to everyone for twelve hours before the arrival of the illustrious guests and also for twelve hours after their departure. The idea mainly aimed at was that, at the grand national banquet about to take place, every inhabitant of the United States, without exception, could consider Barbican and his companions as his own particular guests for the time being, thus giving them a welcome the heartiest and most unanimous that the world has ever yet witnessed.

Evergreens were to deck the lamp-posts; triumphal arches to span the streets; fountains, squirting *eau de cologne*, to perfume and cool the air; bands, stationed at proper intervals, to play the most inspiring music; and boys and girls from public and private schools, dressed in picturesque attire, to sing songs of joy and glory. The people, seated at the banquetting tables, were to rise and cheer and toast the heroes as they passed; the military companies, in splendid uniforms, were to salute them with presented arms; while the bells pealed from the church towers, the great guns roared from the armouries, *feux de joie* resounded from the ships in the harbor, until the day's wildest whirl of excitement was continued far into the night by a general illumination and a surpassing display of fireworks. Right in the very heart of the city, the slowly moving triumphal car was always to halt long enough to allow the Club men to join the cheering citizens at their meal, which was to be breakfast, dinner or supper according to that part of the day at which the halt was made.

The number of champagne bottles drunk on these occasions, or of the speeches made, or of the jokes told, or of the toasts offered, or of the hands shaken, of course, I cannot now weary my kind reader by detailing, though I have the whole account lying before me in black and white, written out day by day in Barbican's own bold hand. Yet I should like to give a few extracts from this wonderful journal. It is a perfect model of accuracy and system. Whether detailing his own doings or those of the innumerable people he met, Caesar himself never wrote anything more lucid or more pointed. But nothing sets the extraordinary nature of this great man in a better light than the firm, commanding, masterly character of the handwriting in which these records are made. The elegant penmanship all through might easily pass for copper plate engraving – except on one page, dated '*Boston, after dinner,*' where, candour compels me to acknowledge, the 'Solid Men' appear to have succeeded in rendering his iron nerves the least bit wabbly.

The palace car had been so constructed that, by turning a few cranks and pulling out a few bolts, it was transformed at once into a highly decorated and extremely comfortable open barouche. Marston took the seat usually occupied by the driver: Ardan and M'Nicholl sat immediately under him, face to face with Barbican, who, in order that everyone might be able to distinguish him, was to keep all the back seat for himself, the post of honour.

On Monday morning, the fifth of May, a month generally the pleasantest in the United States, the grand national banquet commenced in Baltimore, and lasted twenty-four hours. The Gun Club insisted on paying all the expenses of the day, and the city compromised by being allowed to celebrate in whatever way it pleased the reception of the Club men on their return.

They started on their trip that same day in the midst of one of the grandest ovations possible to conceive. They stopped for a little while at Wilmington, but they took dinner in Philadelphia, where the splendour of Broad Street (at present the finest boulevard in the world, being 113 feet wide and five miles long) can be more easily alluded to than even partially described.

The house fronts glittered with flowers, flags, pictures, tapestries, and other decorations; the chimneys and roofs swarmed with men and boys cheerfully risking their necks every moment to get one glance at the 'Moon men'; every window was a brilliant bouquet of beautiful ladies waving their scented handkerchiefs and showering their sweetest smiles; the elevated tables on the sidewalks, groaning with an abundance of excellent and varied food, were lined with men, women, and children, who, however occupied in eating and drinking, never forgot to salute the heroes, cheering them lustily as they slowly moved along; the spacious street itself, just paved from end to end with smooth Belgian blocks, was a living moving panorama of soldiers, temperance men, free masons, and other societies, radiant in gorgeous uniforms, brilliant in flashing banners, and simply perfect in the rhythmic cadence of their tread, wings of delicious music seeming to bear them onward in their proud and stately march.

A vast awning, spanning the street from ridge to ridge, had been so prepared and arranged that, in case of rain or too strong a glare from the summer sun, it could be opened out wholly or partially in the space of a very few minutes. There was not, however, the slightest occasion for using it, the weather being exceedingly fine, almost paradisiacal, as Marston loved to phrase it.

The 'Moon men' supped and spent the night in New York, where they were received with even greater enthusiasm than at Philadelphia. But no detailed description can be given of their majestic progress from city to city through all portions of the mighty Republic. It is enough to say that they visited every important town from Portland to San Francisco, from Salt Lake City to New Orleans, from Mobile to Charleston, and from Saint Louis to Baltimore; that, in every section of the great country, preparations for their reception were equally as enthusiastic, their arrival was welcomed with equal *furore*, and their departure accompanied with an equal amount of affectionate and touching sympathy.

The *New York Herald* reporter, Mr. Watkins, followed them closely everywhere in a palace car of his own, and kept the public fully enlightened regarding every incident worth regarding along the route, almost as soon as it happened. He was enabled to do this by means of a portable telegraphic machine of new and most ingenious construction. Though its motive power was electricity, it could dispense with the ordinary instruments and even with wires altogether, yet it managed to transmit messages to most parts of the world with an accuracy that, considering how seldom it failed, is almost miraculous. The principle actuating it, though guessed at by many shrewd scientists, is still a profound secret and will probably remain so for some time longer, the *Herald* having purchased the right to its sole and exclusive use for fifteen years, at an enormous cost.

Who shall say that the apotheosis of our three heroes was not worthy of them, or that, had they lived in the old prehistoric times, they would not have taken the loftiest places among the demi-gods?

As the tremendous whirl of excitement began slowly to die away, the more thoughtful heads of the Great Republic began asking each other a few questions:

Can this wonderful journey, unprecedented in the annals of wonderful journeys, ever lead to any practical result?

Shall we ever live to see direct communication established with the Moon?

Will any Air Line of space navigation ever undertake to start a system of locomotion between the different members of the solar system?

Have we any reasonable grounds for ever expecting to see trains running between planet and planet, as from Mars to Jupiter and, possibly afterwards, from star to star, as from Polaris to Sirius?

Even to-day these are exceedingly puzzling questions, and, with all our much vaunted scientific progress, such as 'no fellow can make out.' But if we only reflect a moment on the audacious go-a-headiveness of the Yankee branch of the Anglo Saxon race, we shall easily conclude that the American people will never rest quietly until they have pushed to its last result and to every logical consequence the astounding step so daringly conceived and so wonderfully carried out by their great countryman Barbican.

In fact, within a very few months after the return of the Club men from the Continental Banquet, as it was called in the papers, the country was flooded by a number of little books, like Insurance pamphlets, thrust into every letter box and pushed under every door, announcing the formation of a new company called *The Grand Interstellar Communication Society*. The Capital was to be 100 million dollars, at a thousand dollars a share: J.P. BARBICAN, ESQ., P.G.C. was to be President; Colonel JOSHUA D. M'NICHOLL, Vice-President; Hon. J.T. MARSTON, Secretary; Chevalier MICHAEL ARDAN, General Manager; JOHN MURPHY, ESQ., Chief Engineer; H. PHILLIPS COLEMAN, ESQ. (Philadelphia lawyer), Legal Adviser; and the Astrological Adviser was to be Professor HENRY of Washington. (Belfast's blunder had injured him so much in public estimation, his former partisans having become his most merciless revilers, that it was considered advisable to omit his name altogether even in the list of the Directors.)

From the very beginning, the moneyed public looked on the G.I.C.S, with decided favour, and its shares were bought up pretty freely. Conducted on strictly honourable principles, keeping carefully aloof from all such damaging connection as the *Credit Mobilier*, and having its books always thrown open for public inspection, its reputation even to-day is excellent and continually improving in the popular estimation. Holding out no utopian inducements to catch the unwary, and making no wheedling promises to blind the guileless, it states its great objects with all their great advantages, without at the same time suppressing its enormous and perhaps insuperable difficulties. People know exactly what to think of it, and, whether it ever meets with perfect success or proves a complete failure, no one in the country will ever think of casting a slur on the bright name of its peerless President, J.P. Barbican.

For a few years this great man devoted every faculty of his mind to the furthering of the Company's objects. But in the midst of his labours, the rapid approach of the CENTENNIAL surprised him. After a long and careful consultation on the subject, the Directors and Stockholders of the G.I.C.S. advised him to suspend all further labours in their behalf for a few years, in order that he might be freer to devote the full energies of his giant intellect towards celebrating the first hundredth anniversary of his country's Independence – as all true Americans would wish to see it celebrated – in a manner every way worthy of the GREAT REPUBLIC OF THE WEST!

Obeying orders instantly and with the single-idea'd, unselfish enthusiasm of his nature, he threw himself at once heart and soul into the great enterprise. Though possessing no official prominence – this he absolutely insists upon – he is well known to be the great fountain head whence emanate all the life, order, dispatch, simplicity, economy, and wonderful harmony which, so far, have so eminently characterized the magnificent project. With all operations for raising the necessary funds – further than by giving some sound practical advice – he positively refused to connect himself (this may be the reason why subscriptions to the Centennial stock are so slow in coming in), but in the proper apportionment of expenses and the strict surveillance of the mechanical, engineering, and architectural departments, his services have proved invaluable. His experience in the vast operations at Stony Hill has given him great skill in the difficult art of managing men. His voice is seldom heard at the meetings, but when it is, people seem to take a pleasure in readily submitting to its dictates.

In wet weather or dry, in hot weather or cold, he may still be seen every day at Fairmount Park, Philadelphia, leisurely strolling from building to building, picking his steps quietly through the bustling crowds of busy workmen, never speaking a word, not even to Marston his faithful shadow, often pencilling something in his pocket book, stopping occasionally to look apparently nowhere, but never, you may be sure, allowing a single detail in the restless panorama around him to escape the piercing shaft of his eagle glance.

He is evidently determined on rendering the great CENTENNIAL of his country a still greater and more wonderful success than even his own world-famous and never to be forgotten JOURNEY through the boundless fields of ether, and ALL AROUND THE MOON!

FROM THE EARTH TO THE MOON

FROM THE EARTH TO THE MOON

JULES VERNE

This edition published in 2021 by Arcturus Publishing Limited
26/27 Bickels Yard, 151–153 Bermondsey Street,
London SE1 3HA

Copyright © Arcturus Holdings Limited

All rights reserved. No part of this publication may be reproduced, stored in a retrieval system, or transmitted, in any form or by any means, electronic, mechanical, photocopying, recording or otherwise, without prior written permission in accordance with the provisions of the Copyright Act 1956 (as amended). Any person or persons who do any unauthorised act in relation to this publication may be liable to criminal prosecution and civil claims for damages.

Cover design: Peter Ridley
Cover illustration: Peter Gray

AD010124UK

Printed in the UK

CONTENTS

Introduction 7

Chapter I: *The Gun Club* 9
Chapter II: *President Barbicane's Communication* 17
Chapter III: *Effect of the President's Communication* 27
Chapter IV: *Reply from the Observatory of Cambridge* 31
Chapter V: *The Romance of the Moon* 39
Chapter VI: *Permissive Limits of Ignorance and Belief in
              the United States* 45
Chapter VII: *The Hymn of the Cannon-Ball* 51
Chapter VIII: *History of the Cannon* 59
Chapter IX: *The Question of the Powders* 65
Chapter X: *One Enemy v. Twenty-Five Millions of Friends* 73
Chapter XI: *Florida and Texas* 79
Chapter XII: *Urbi et Orbi* 85
Chapter XIII: *Stones Hill* 93
Chapter XIV: *Pickaxe and Trowel* 99
Chapter XV: *The Fete of the Casting* 105
Chapter XVI: *The Columbiad* 111
Chapter XVII: *A Telegraphic Dispatch* 117
Chapter XVIII: *The Passenger of the Atlanta* 119
Chapter XIX: *A Monster Meeting* 127
Chapter XX: *Attack and Riposte* 135
Chapter XXI: *How a Frenchman Manages an Affair* 147
Chapter XXII: *The New Citizen of the United States* 157

Chapter XXIII: *The Projectile-Vehicle* 163

Chapter XXIV: *The Telescope of the Rocky Mountains* 167

Chapter XXV: *Final Details* 171

Chapter XXVI: *Fire!* 177

Chapter XXVII: *Foul Weather* 183

Chapter XXVIII: *A New Star* 187

Introduction

Deservedly known as the 'Father of Science Fiction,' Jules Verne wrote of wonderful inventions and of adventures to the unexplored regions of the world. On many occasions, his technological marvels, such as the submarine and space travel, predicted scientific advances that were years, or even decades, in the future.

Born on 8 February 1828 in the port city of Nantes, France, Verne always saw vessels come and go, wondering what adventures they were going on. As a young boy, he dreamed of one day having his own adventures at sea and, at just 12 years old, he smuggled himself onto a ship bound for India – only to be discovered and beaten for his disobedience. His relationship with his father, Pierre Verne, was a troubled one. Pierre, hoping to see his son follow in his footsteps, sent him to Paris to study law.

However, the appeal of writing proved too strong. He spent much of his time writing plays rather than studying law and, despite graduating in 1849, he showed little inclination to pursue a legal career. Encouraged by the writer, Alexandre Dumas, Verne decided to remain in Paris and write plays instead. His first production in 1850, *Broken Straws*, was a lukewarm start to his ten year playwright career. Finding the love of his life, the divorced Honorine de Viane Morel, in 1856, Verne saw the need for financial stability and found work as a stockbroker to maintain his marriage. But the writing never stopped, and Verne would soon ignite his adventures off-stage with one of literature's greatest partnerships.

Verne and his publisher Pierre-Jules Hertzel were an exceptional duo. Recognising the untapped potential in Verne's seemingly crazy, futuristic ideas, Hertzel's masterful editing and knowledgeable suggestions kept his stories grounded and accessible enough for audiences to digest when Verne's original manuscripts would have been too far-fetched.

Equal respect and talent culminated in Verne's 1863 adventure novel, *Five Weeks in a Balloon*. With no experience in a balloon, let alone using one to cross the Atlantic, Verne researched Edgar Allan Poe's 'The Unparalleled Adventure of One Hans Pfaall' and travel magazines to familiarise himself with the experience. Verne continued to venture into the unknown, penning well-known titles such as *Journey to the Centre of the Earth* (1864), and *Around the World in Eighty Days* (1872).

From the Earth to the Moon (1865) examined a subject that had fascinated humanity for centuries – could we really visit the moon? How would we get there? The Baltimore Gun Club, left idle after the end of the American Civil War, sets out to create a gun powerful enough to launch men into space. Verne presented a plausible, scientific approach that was surprisingly similar to the rockets used for the Apollo 11 mission nearly a century later that saw men land on the moon in reality, not just fiction. He continued the story in Around the Moon (1869) which depicted the actual flight around the moon and the many dangers the pioneering astronauts faced.

One of his most visionary novels, *Paris in the Twentieth Century*, featuring skyscrapers, bullet trains, calculators, and gas-fuelled cars, was not published until 1994 due to Hertzel's belief that the subject matter was too subversive. While Verne was fascinated with the progress of technology, he was also sceptical about its overpowering effect on mankind. This was most apparent in his nautical masterpiece, *Twenty Thousand Leagues Under the Sea* (1869).

Jules Verne died on 24 March 1905 from diabetes. A prolific writer throughout his life, the success of Verne's tales and worldwide appeal made him the second most translated writer of all time. He may have not been a scientist, but his work's innovations have influenced many writers and scientists, paving the way for one of literature's most exciting and thought-provoking genres – science fiction.

CHAPTER I

The Gun Club

DURING THE WAR of the Rebellion, a new and influential club was established in the city of Baltimore in the State of Maryland. It is well known with what energy the taste for military matters became developed among that nation of ship-owners, shopkeepers, and mechanics. Simple tradesmen jumped their counters to become extemporised captains, colonels, and generals, without having ever passed the School of Instruction at West Point; nevertheless; they quickly rivalled their compeers of the old continent, and, like them, carried off victories by dint of lavish expenditure in ammunition, money, and men.

But the point in which the Americans singularly distanced the Europeans was in the science of *gunnery*. Not, indeed, that their weapons retained a higher degree of perfection than theirs, but that they exhibited unheard-of dimensions, and consequently attained hitherto unheard-of ranges. In point of grazing, plunging, oblique, or enfilading, or point-blank firing, the English, French, and Prussians have nothing to learn; but their cannon, howitzers, and mortars are mere pocket-pistols compared with the formidable engines of the American artillery.

This fact need surprise no one. The Yankees, the first mechanicians in the world, are engineers – just as the Italians are musicians and the Germans metaphysicians – by right of birth. Nothing is more natural, therefore, than to perceive them applying their audacious ingenuity to the science of gunnery. Witness the marvels of Parrott, Dahlgren, and Rodman. The Armstrong, Palliser, and Beaulieu guns were compelled to bow before their transatlantic rivals.

Now when an American has an idea, he directly seeks a second American to share it. If there be three, they elect a president and two secretaries. Given *four*, they name a keeper of records, and the office is ready for work; *five*, they convene a general meeting, and the club is fully constituted. So things were managed in Baltimore. The inventor of a new cannon associated himself with the caster and the borer. Thus was formed the nucleus of the 'Gun Club'. In a single month after its formation it numbered 1,833 effective members and 30,565 corresponding members.

One condition was imposed as a *sine qua non* upon every candidate for admission into the association, and that was the condition of having designed, or (more or less) perfected a cannon; or, in default of a cannon, at least a firearm of some description. It may, however, be mentioned that mere inventors of revolvers, fire-shooting carbines, and similar small arms, met with little consideration. Artillerists always commanded the chief place of favour.

The estimation in which these gentlemen were held, according to one of the most scientific exponents of the Gun Club, was 'proportional to the masses of their guns, and in the direct ratio of the square of the distances attained by their projectiles'.

The Gun Club once founded, it is easy to conceive the

result of the inventive genius of the Americans. Their military weapons attained colossal proportions, and their projectiles, exceeding the prescribed limits, unfortunately occasionally cut in two some unoffending pedestrians. These inventions, in fact, left far in the rear the timid instruments of European artillery.

It is but fair to add that these Yankees, brave as they have ever proved themselves to be, did not confine themselves to theories and formulae, but that they paid heavily, *in propria persona*, for their inventions. Among them were to be counted officers of all ranks, from lieutenants to generals; military men of every age, from those who were just making their *début* in the profession of arms up to those who had grown old in the gun-carriage. Many had found their rest on the field of battle whose names figured in the 'Book of Honour' of the Gun Club; and of those who made good their return the greater proportion bore the marks of their indisputable valour. Crutches, wooden legs, artificial arms, steel hooks, caoutchouc jaws, silver craniums, platinum noses, were all to be found in the collection; and it was calculated by the great statistician Pitcairn that throughout the Gun Club there was not quite one arm between four persons and two legs between six.

Nevertheless, these valiant artillerists took no particular account of these little facts, and felt justly proud when the despatches of a battle returned the number of victims at ten-fold the quantity of projectiles expended.

One day, however – sad and melancholy day! – peace was signed between the survivors of the war; the thunder of the guns gradually ceased, the mortars were silent, the howitzers were muzzled for an indefinite period, the cannon, with muzzles depressed, were returned into the arsenal, the shot were repiled, all bloody reminiscences were effaced; the cotton-plants grew luxuriantly in the well-manured fields, all mourning garments were laid aside, together with grief; and the Gun Club was relegated to profound inactivity.

Some few of the more advanced and inveterate theorists set themselves again to work upon calculations regarding the laws of projectiles. They reverted invariably to gigantic shells and howitzers of unparalleled calibre. Still in default of practical experience what was the value of mere theories? Consequently, the clubrooms became deserted, the servants dozed in the antechambers, the newspapers grew mouldy on the tables, sounds of snoring came from dark corners, and the members of the Gun Club, erstwhile so noisy in their seances, were reduced to silence by this disastrous peace and gave themselves up wholly to dreams of a Platonic kind of artillery.

'This is horrible!' said Tom Hunter one evening, while rapidly carbonising his wooden legs in the fireplace of the smoking-room; 'nothing to do! nothing to look forward to! what a loathsome existence! When again shall the guns arouse us in the morning with their delightful reports?'

'Those days are gone by,' said jolly Bilsby, trying to extend his missing arms. 'It was delightful once upon a time! One invented a gun, and hardly was it cast, when one hastened to try it in the face of the enemy! Then one returned to camp with a word of encouragement from Sherman or a friendly shake of the hand from McClellan. But now the generals are gone back to their counters; and in place of projectiles, they despatch bales of cotton. By Jove, the future of gunnery in America is lost!'

'Ay! and no war in prospect!' continued the famous James T. Maston, scratching with his steel hook his gutta-percha cranium. 'Not a cloud on the horizon! and that too at such a critical period in the progress of the science of artillery! Yes, gentlemen! I who address you have myself this very morning perfected a model (plan, section, elevation, etc.) of a mortar destined to change all the conditions of warfare!'

'No! is it possible?' replied Tom Hunter, his thoughts reverting involuntarily to a former invention of the Hon. J. T. Maston, by which, at its first trial, he had succeeded in killing three hundred and thirty-seven people.

'Fact!' replied he. 'Still, what is the use of so many studies worked out, so many difficulties vanquished? It's mere waste of time! The New World seems to have made up its mind to live in peace; and our bellicose *Tribune* predicts some approaching catastrophes arising out of this scandalous increase of population.'

'Nevertheless,' replied Colonel Blomsberry, 'they are always struggling in Europe to maintain the principle of nationalities.'

'Well?'

'Well, there might be some field for enterprise down there; and if they would accept our services—'

'What are you dreaming of?' screamed Bilsby; 'work at gunnery for the benefit of foreigners?'

'That would be better than doing nothing here,' returned the colonel.

'Quite so,' said J. T. Maston; 'but still we need not dream of that expedient.'

'And why not?' demanded the colonel.

'Because their ideas of progress in the Old World are contrary to our American habits of thought. Those fellows believe that one can't become a general without having served first as an ensign; which is as much as to say that one can't point a gun without having first cast it oneself!'

'Ridiculous!' replied Tom Hunter, whittling with his bowie-knife the arms of his easy chair; 'but if that be the case there, all that is left for us is to plant tobacco and distil whale-oil.'

'What!' roared J. T. Maston, 'shall we not employ these remaining years of our life in perfecting firearms? Shall there never be a fresh opportunity of trying the ranges of projectiles? Shall the air never again be lighted with the glare of our guns? No international difficulty ever arise to enable us to declare war against some transatlantic power? Shall not the French sink one of our steamers, or the English, in defiance of the rights of nations, hang a few of our countrymen?'

'No such luck,' replied Colonel Blomsberry; 'nothing of the kind is likely to happen; and even if it did, we should not profit by it. American susceptibility is fast declining, and we are all going to the dogs.'

'It is too true,' replied J. T. Maston, with fresh violence; 'there are a thousand grounds for fighting, and yet we don't fight. We save up our arms and legs for the benefit of nations who don't know what to do with them! But stop – without going out of one's way to find a cause for war – did not North America once belong to the English?'

'Undoubtedly,' replied Tom Hunter, stamping his crutch with fury.

'Well, then,' replied J. T. Maston, 'why should not England in her turn belong to the Americans?'

'It would be but just and fair,' returned Colonel Blomsberry.

'Go and propose it to the President of the United States,' cried J. T. Maston, 'and see how he will receive you.'

'Bah!' growled Bilsby between the four teeth which the war had left him; 'that will never do!'

'By Jove!' cried J. T. Maston, 'he mustn't count on my vote at the next election!'

'Nor on ours,' replied unanimously all the bellicose invalids.

'Meanwhile,' replied J. T. Maston, 'allow me to say that, if I cannot get an opportunity to try my new mortars on a real field of battle, I shall say goodbye to the members of the Gun Club, and go and bury myself in the prairies of Arkansas!'

'In that case we will accompany you,' cried the others.

Matters were in this unfortunate condition, and the club was threatened with approaching dissolution, when an unexpected circumstance occurred to prevent so deplorable a catastrophe.

On the morrow after this conversation every member of the association received a sealed circular couched in the following terms:

BALTIMORE, October 3. The president of the Gun Club has the honour to inform his colleagues that, at the meeting of the 5th instant, he will bring before them a communication of an extremely interesting nature. He requests, therefore, that they will make it convenient to attend in accordance with the present invitation. Very cordially, IMPEY BARBICANE, P.G.C.

CHAPTER II

President Barbicane's Communication

ON THE 5TH of October, at eight P.M., a dense crowd pressed toward the saloons of the Gun Club at No. 21 Union Square. All the members of the association resident in Baltimore attended the invitation of their president. As regards the corresponding members, notices were delivered by hundreds throughout the streets of the city, and, large as was the great hall, it was quite inadequate to accommodate the crowd of *savants*. They overflowed into the adjoining rooms, down the narrow passages, into the outer courtyards. There they ran against the vulgar herd who pressed up to the doors, each struggling to reach the front ranks, all eager to learn the nature of the important communication of President Barbicane; all pushing, squeezing, crushing with that perfect freedom of action which is so peculiar to the masses when educated in ideas of 'self-government'.

On that evening a stranger who might have chanced to be in Baltimore could not have gained admission for love or money into the great hall. That was reserved exclusively for resident or corresponding members; no one else could possibly have obtained a place; and the city magnates, municipal councillors, and 'select men' were compelled to mingle with the mere townspeople in order to catch stray bits of news from the interior.

Nevertheless the vast hall presented a curious spectacle. Its immense area was singularly adapted to the purpose. Lofty pillars formed of cannon, superposed upon huge mortars as a base, supported the fine ironwork of the arches, a perfect piece of cast-iron lacework. Trophies of blunderbuses, matchlocks, arquebuses, carbines, all kinds of firearms, ancient and modern, were picturesquely interlaced against the walls. The gas lit up in full glare myriads of revolvers grouped in the form of lustres, while groups of pistols, and candelabra formed of muskets bound together, completed this magnificent display of brilliance. Models of cannon, bronze castings, sights covered with dents, plates battered by the shots of the Gun Club, assortments of rammers and sponges, chaplets of shells, wreaths of projectiles, garlands of howitzers – in short, all the apparatus of the artillerist, enchanted the eye by this wonderful arrangement and induced a kind of belief that their real purpose was ornamental rather than deadly.

At the further end of the saloon the president, assisted by four secretaries, occupied a large platform. His chair, supported by a carved gun-carriage, was modelled upon the ponderous proportions of a 32-inch mortar. It was pointed at an angle of ninety degrees, and suspended upon truncheons, so that the president could balance himself upon it as upon a rocking-chair, a very agreeable fact in the very hot weather. Upon the table (a huge iron plate supported upon six carronades) stood an inkstand of exquisite elegance, made of a beautifully chased Spanish piece, and a sonnette, which, when required, could give forth a report equal to that of a revolver. During violent debates this novel kind of bell scarcely sufficed to drown the clamour of these excitable artillerists.

In front of the table benches arranged in zigzag form, like the circumvallations of a retrenchment, formed a succession of bastions and curtains set apart for the use of the members of the club; and on this especial evening one might say, 'All the world was on the ramparts.' The president was sufficiently well known, however, for all to be assured that he would not put his colleagues to discomfort without some very strong motive.

Impey Barbicane was a man of forty years of age, calm, cold, austere; of a singularly serious and self-contained demeanour, punctual as a chronometer, of imperturbable temper and immovable character; by no means chivalrous, yet adventurous withal, and always bringing practical ideas to bear upon the very rashest enterprises; an essentially New Englander, a Northern colonist, a descendant of the old anti-Stuart Roundheads, and the implacable enemy of the gentlemen of the South, those ancient cavaliers of the mother country. In a word, he was a Yankee to the backbone.

Barbicane had made a large fortune as a timber merchant. Being nominated director of artillery during the war, he proved himself fertile in invention. Bold in his conceptions, he contributed powerfully to the progress of that arm and gave an immense impetus to experimental researches.

He was personage of the middle height, having, by a rare exception in the Gun Club, all his limbs complete. His strongly marked features seemed drawn by square and rule; and if it be true that, in order to judge a man's character one must look at his profile, Barbicane, so examined, exhibited the most certain indications of energy, audacity, and *sang-froid*.

At this moment he was sitting in his armchair, silent, absorbed, lost in reflection, sheltered under his high-crowned hat – a kind of black cylinder which always seems firmly screwed upon the head of an American.

Just when the deep-toned clock in the great hall struck eight, Barbicane, as if he had been set in motion by a spring, raised himself up. A profound silence ensued, and the speaker, in a somewhat emphatic tone of voice, commenced as follows:

'My brave colleagues, too long already a paralysing peace has plunged the members of the Gun Club in deplorable inactivity. After a period of years full of incidents we have been compelled to abandon our labours, and to stop short on the road of progress. I do not hesitate to state, boldly, that any war which would recall us to arms would be welcome!' (*Tremendous applause!*) 'But war, gentlemen, is impossible under existing circumstances; and, however we may desire it, many years may elapse before our cannon shall again thunder in the field of battle. We must make up our minds, then, to seek in another train of ideas some field for the activity which we all pine for.'

The meeting felt that the president was now approaching the critical point, and redoubled their attention accordingly.

'For some months past, my brave colleagues,' continued Barbicane, 'I have been asking myself whether, while confining ourselves to our own particular objects, we could not enter upon some grand experiment worthy of the nineteenth century; and whether the progress of artillery science would not enable us to carry it out to a successful issue. I have been considering, working, calculating; and the result of my studies is the conviction that we are safe to succeed in an enterprise which to any other country would appear wholly impracticable. This project, the result of long elaboration, is the object of my present communication. It is worthy of yourselves, worthy of the antecedents of the Gun Club; and it cannot fail to make some noise in the world.'

A thrill of excitement ran through the meeting.

Barbicane, having by a rapid movement firmly fixed his hat upon his head, calmly continued his harangue:

'There is no one among you, my brave colleagues, who has not seen the moon, or, at least, heard speak of it. Don't be surprised if I am about to discourse to you regarding the Queen of the Night. It is perhaps reserved for us to become the Columbuses of this unknown world. Only enter into my plans, and second me with all your power, and I will lead you to its conquest, and its name shall be added to those of the thirty-six states which compose this Great Union.'

'Three cheers for the moon!' roared the Gun Club, with one voice.

'The moon, gentlemen, has been carefully studied,' continued Barbicane; 'her mass, density, and weight; her constitution, motions, distance, as well as her place in the solar system, have all been exactly determined. Selenographic charts have been constructed with a perfection which equals, if it does not even surpass, that of our terrestrial maps.

Photography has given us proofs of the incomparable beauty of our satellite; all is known regarding the moon which mathematical science, astronomy, geology, and optics can learn about her. But up to the present moment no direct communication has been established with her.'

A violent movement of interest and surprise here greeted this remark of the speaker.

'Permit me,' he continued, 'to recount to you briefly how certain ardent spirits, starting on imaginary journeys, have penetrated the secrets of our satellite. In the seventeenth century a certain David Fabricius boasted of having seen with his own eyes the inhabitants of the moon. In 1649 a Frenchman, one Jean Baudoin, published a 'Journey performed from the Earth to the Moon by Domingo Gonzalez', a Spanish adventurer. At the same period Cyrano de Bergerac published that celebrated 'Journeys in the Moon' which met with such success in France. Somewhat later another Frenchman, named Fontenelle, wrote 'The Plurality of Worlds', a *chef-d'œuvre* of its time. About 1835 a small treatise, translated from the *New York American*, related how Sir John Herschel, having been despatched to the Cape of Good Hope for the purpose of making there some astronomical calculations, had, by means of a telescope brought to perfection by means of internal lighting, reduced the apparent distance of the moon to eighty yards! He then distinctly perceived caverns frequented by hippopotami, green mountains bordered by golden lace-work, sheep with horns of ivory, a white species of deer and inhabitants with membranous wings, like bats. This *brochure*, the work of an American named Locke, had a great sale. But, to bring this rapid sketch to a close, I will only add that a certain Hans Pfaal, of Rotterdam, launching himself in a balloon filled with a gas extracted from nitrogen, thirty-seven times lighter than hydrogen, reached the moon after a passage of nineteen hours. This journey, like all previous ones, was purely imaginary; still, it was the work of a popular American author – I mean Edgar Poe!'

'Cheers for Edgar Poe!' roared the assemblage, electrified by their president's words.

'I have now enumerated,' said Barbicane, 'the experiments which I call purely paper ones, and wholly insufficient to establish serious relations with the Queen of the Night. Nevertheless, I am bound to add that some practical geniuses have attempted to establish actual communication with her. Thus, a few days ago, a German geometrician proposed to send a scientific expedition to the steppes of Siberia. There, on those vast plains, they were to describe enormous geometric figures, drawn in characters of reflecting luminosity, among which was the proposition regarding the 'square of the hypothenuse', commonly called the '*Ass's Bridge*' by the French. 'Every intelligent being,' said the geometrician, 'must understand the scientific meaning of that figure. The Selenites, do they exist, will respond by a similar figure; and, a communication being thus once established, it will be easy to form an alphabet which shall enable us to converse with the inhabitants of the moon.' So spoke the German geometrician; but his project was never put into practice, and up to the present day there is no bond in existence between the Earth and her satellite. It is reserved for the practical genius of Americans to establish a communication with the sidereal world. The means of arriving thither are simple, easy, certain, infallible – and that is the purpose of my present proposal.'

A storm of acclamations greeted these words. There was not a single person in the whole audience who was not overcome, carried away, lifted out of himself by the speaker's words!

Long-continued applause resounded from all sides.

As soon as the excitement had partially subsided, Barbicane resumed his speech in a somewhat graver voice.

'You know,' said he, 'what progress artillery science has made during the last few years, and what a degree of perfection firearms of every kind have reached. Moreover, you are well aware that, in general terms, the resisting power of cannon and the expansive force of gunpowder are practically unlimited. Well! starting from this principle, I ask myself whether, supposing sufficient apparatus could be obtained constructed upon the conditions of ascertained resistance, it might not be possible to project a shot up to the moon?'

At these words a murmur of amazement escaped from a thousand panting chests; then succeeded a moment of perfect silence, resembling that profound stillness which precedes the bursting of a thunderstorm. In point of fact, a thunderstorm did peal forth, but it was the thunder of applause, or cries, and of uproar which made the very hall tremble. The president attempted to speak, but could not. It was fully ten minutes before he could make himself heard.

'Suffer me to finish,' he calmly continued. 'I have looked at the question in all its bearings, I have resolutely attacked it, and by incontrovertible calculations I find that a projectile endowed with an initial velocity of 12,000 yards per second, and aimed at the moon, must necessarily reach it. I have the honour, my brave colleagues, to propose a trial of this little experiment.'

CHAPTER III

Effect of the President's Communication

IT IS IMPOSSIBLE to describe the effect produced by the last words of the honourable president – the cries, the shouts, the succession of roars, hurrahs, and all the varied vociferations which the American language is capable of supplying. It was a scene of indescribable confusion and uproar. They shouted, they clapped, they stamped on the floor of the hall. All the weapons in the museum discharged at once could not have more violently set in motion the waves of sound. One need not be surprised at this. There are some cannoneers nearly as noisy as their own guns.

Barbicane remained calm in the midst of this enthusiastic clamour; perhaps he was desirous of addressing a few more words to his colleagues, for by his gestures he demanded silence, and his powerful alarum was worn out by its violent reports. No attention, however, was paid to his request. He was presently torn from his seat and passed from the hands of his faithful colleagues into the arms of a no less excited crowd.

Nothing can astound an American. It has often been asserted that the word 'impossible' is not a French one. People have evidently been deceived by the dictionary. In America, all is easy, all is simple; and as for mechanical difficulties, they are overcome before they arise. Between Barbicane's proposition and its realisation no true Yankee would have allowed even the semblance of a difficulty to be possible. A thing with them is no sooner said than done.

The triumphal progress of the president continued throughout the evening. It was a regular torchlight procession. Irish, Germans, French, Scotch, all the heterogeneous units which make up the population of Maryland shouted in their respective vernaculars; and the 'vivas', 'hurrahs', and 'bravos' were intermingled in inexpressible enthusiasm.

Just at this crisis, as though she comprehended all this agitation regarding herself, the moon shone forth with serene splendour, eclipsing by her intense illumination all the surrounding lights. The Yankees all turned their gaze toward her resplendent orb, kissed their hands, called her by all kinds of endearing names. Between eight o'clock and midnight one optician in Jones'-Fall Street made his fortune by the sale of opera-glasses.

Midnight arrived, and the enthusiasm showed no signs of diminution. It spread equally among all classes of citizens – men of science, shopkeepers, merchants, porters, chair-men, as well as 'greenhorns', were stirred in their innermost fibres. A national enterprise was at stake. The whole city, high and low, the quays bordering the Patapsco, the ships lying in the basins, disgorged a crowd drunk with joy, gin, and whisky. Every one chattered, argued, discussed, disputed, applauded, from the gentleman lounging upon the barroom settee with his tumbler of sherry-cobbler before him down to the waterman who got drunk upon his 'knock-me-down' in the dingy taverns of Fell Point.

About two A.M., however, the excitement began to

subside. President Barbicane reached his house, bruised, crushed, and squeezed almost to a mummy. Hercules could not have resisted a similar outbreak of enthusiasm. The crowd gradually deserted the squares and streets. The four railways from Philadelphia and Washington, Harrisburg and Wheeling, which converge at Baltimore, whirled away the heterogeneous population to the four corners of the United States, and the city subsided into comparative tranquillity.

On the following day, thanks to the telegraphic wires, five hundred newspapers and journals, daily, weekly, monthly, or bi-monthly, all took up the question. They examined it under all its different aspects, physical, meteorological, economical, or moral, up to its bearings on politics or civilisation. They debated whether the moon was a finished world, or whether it was destined to undergo any further transformation. Did it resemble the earth at the period when the latter was destitute as yet of an atmosphere? What kind of spectacle would its hidden hemisphere present to our terrestrial spheroid? Granting that the question at present was simply that of sending a projectile up to the moon, every one must see that that involved the commencement of a series of experiments. All must hope that some day America would penetrate the deepest secrets of that mysterious orb; and some even seemed to fear lest its conquest should not sensibly derange the equilibrium of Europe.

The project once under discussion, not a single paragraph suggested a doubt of its realisation. All the papers, pamphlets, reports – all the journals published by the scientific, literary, and religious societies enlarged upon its advantages; and the

Society of Natural History of Boston, the Society of Science and Art of Albany, the Geographical and Statistical Society of New York, the Philosophical Society of Philadelphia, and the Smithsonian of Washington sent innumerable letters of congratulation to the Gun Club, together with offers of immediate assistance and money.

From that day forward Impey Barbicane became one of the greatest citizens of the United States, a kind of Washington of science. A single trait of feeling, taken from many others, will serve to show the point which this homage of a whole people to a single individual attained.

Some few days after this memorable meeting of the Gun Club, the manager of an English company announced, at the Baltimore theatre, the production of 'Much ado about Nothing'. But the populace, seeing in that title an allusion damaging to Barbicane's project, broke into the auditorium, smashed the benches, and compelled the unlucky director to alter his playbill. Being a sensible man, he bowed to the public will and replaced the offending comedy by 'As you like it'; and for many weeks he realised fabulous profits.

CHAPTER IV

Reply from the Observatory of Cambridge

BARBICANE, HOWEVER, LOST not one moment amid all the enthusiasm of which he had become the object. His first care was to reassemble his colleagues in the board-room of the Gun Club. There, after some discussion, it was agreed to consult the astronomers regarding the astronomical part of the enterprise. Their reply once ascertained, they could then discuss the mechanical means, and nothing should be wanting to ensure the success of this great experiment.

A note couched in precise terms, containing special interrogatories, was then drawn up and addressed to the Observatory of Cambridge in Massachusetts. This city, where the first university of the United States was founded, is justly celebrated for its astronomical staff. There are to be found assembled all the most eminent men of science. Here is to be seen at work that powerful telescope which enabled Bond to resolve the nebula of Andromeda, and Clarke to discover the satellite of Sirius. This celebrated institution fully justified on all points the confidence reposed in it by the Gun Club. So, after two days, the reply so impatiently awaited was placed in the hands of President Barbicane.

It was couched in the following terms:

> *The Director of the Cambridge Observatory to the President of the Gun Club at Baltimore.*

CAMBRIDGE, October 7. On the receipt of your favour of the 6th instant, addressed to the Observatory of Cambridge in the name of the members of the Baltimore Gun Club, our staff was immediately called together, and it was judged expedient to reply as follows:

The questions which have been proposed to it are these:

'1. Is it possible to transmit a projectile up to the moon?

'2. What is the exact distance which separates the earth from its satellite?

'3. What will be the period of transit of the projectile when endowed with sufficient initial velocity? and, consequently, at what moment ought it to be discharged in order that it may touch the moon at a particular point?

'4. At what precise moment will the moon present herself in the most favourable position to be reached by the projectile?

'5. What point in the heavens ought the cannon to be aimed at which is intended to discharge the projectile?

'6. What place will the moon occupy in the heavens at the moment of the projectile's departure?'

Regarding the *first* question, 'Is it possible to transmit a projectile up to the moon?'

Answer. – Yes; provided it possess an initial velocity of

CHAPTER IV

12,000 yards per second; calculations prove that to be sufficient. In proportion as we recede from the earth the action of gravitation diminishes in the inverse ratio of the square of the distance; that is to say, *at three times a given distance the action is nine times less.* Consequently, the weight of a shot will decrease, and will become reduced to *zero* at the instant that the attraction of the moon exactly counterpoises that of the earth; that is to say at 47/52 of its passage. At that instant the projectile will have no weight whatever; and, if it passes that point, it will fall into the moon by the sole effect of the lunar attraction. The *theoretical possibility* of the experiment is therefore absolutely demonstrated; its *success* must depend upon the power of the engine employed.

As to the *second* question, 'What is the exact distance which separates the earth from its satellite?'

Answer. – The moon does not describe a *circle* round the earth, but rather an *ellipse*, of which our earth occupies one of the *foci*; the consequence, therefore, is, that at certain times it approaches nearer to, and at others it recedes farther from, the earth; in astronomical language, it is at one time in *apogee*, at another in *perigee*. Now the difference between its greatest and its least distance is too considerable to be left out of consideration. In point of fact, in its apogee the moon is 247,552 miles, and in its perigee, 218,657 miles only distant; a fact which makes a difference of 28,895 miles, or more than one-ninth of the entire distance. The perigee distance, therefore, is that which ought to serve as the basis of all calculations.

To the *third* question: –

Answer. – If the shot should preserve continuously its initial velocity of 12,000 yards per second, it would require little more than nine hours to reach its destination; but, inasmuch as that initial velocity will be continually decreasing, it will occupy 300,000 seconds, that is 83hrs. 20m. in reaching the point where the attraction of the earth and moon will be *in equilibrio*. From this point it will fall into the moon in 50,000 seconds, or 13hrs. 53m. 20sec. It will be desirable, therefore, to discharge it 97hrs. 13m. 20sec. before the arrival of the moon at the point aimed at.

Regarding question *four*, 'At what precise moment will the moon present herself in the most favourable position, etc.?'

Answer. – After what has been said above, it will be necessary, first of all, to choose the period when the moon will be in perigee, and *also* the moment when she will be crossing the zenith, which latter event will further diminish the entire distance by a length equal to the radius of the earth, *i. e.* 3,919 miles; the result of which will be that the final passage remaining to be accomplished will be 214,976 miles. But although the moon passes her perigee every month, she does not reach the zenith always *at exactly the same moment*. She does not appear under these two conditions simultaneously, except at long intervals of time. It will be necessary, therefore, to wait for the moment when her passage in perigee shall coincide with that in the zenith. Now, by a fortunate circumstance, on the 4th of December in the ensuing year the moon *will* present these two conditions. At midnight she will be in perigee, that is, at her shortest distance from the earth, and at the same moment she will be crossing the zenith.

On the *fifth* question, 'At what point in the heavens ought the cannon to be aimed?'

Answer. – The preceding remarks being admitted, the cannon ought to be pointed to the zenith of the place. Its fire, therefore, will be perpendicular to the plane of the horizon; and the projectile will soonest pass beyond the range of the terrestrial attraction. But, in order that the moon should reach the zenith of a given place, it is necessary that the place should not exceed in latitude the declination of the luminary; in other words, it must be comprised within the degrees 0° and 28° of lat. N. or S. In every other spot the fire must necessarily be oblique, which would seriously militate against the success of the experiment.

As to the *sixth* question, 'What place will the moon occupy in the heavens at the moment of the projectile's departure?'

Answer. – At the moment when the projectile shall be discharged into space, the moon, which travels daily forward 13° 10' 35", will be distant from the zenith point by four times that quantity, *i. e.* by 52° 41' 20", a space which corresponds to the path which she will describe during the entire journey of the projectile. But, inasmuch as it is equally necessary to take into account the deviation which the rotary motion of the earth will impart to the shot, and as the shot cannot reach the moon until after a deviation equal to 16 radii of the earth, which, calculated upon the moon's orbit, are equal to about eleven degrees, it becomes necessary to add these eleven degrees to those which express the retardation of the moon just mentioned: that is to say, in round numbers, about sixty-four degrees. Consequently, at the moment of firing the visual radius applied to the moon will describe, with the vertical line of the place, an angle of sixty-four degrees.

These are our answers to the questions proposed to the Observatory of Cambridge by the members of the Gun Club: –

To sum up –

1st. The cannon ought to be planted in a country situated between 0° and 28° of N. or S. lat.

2nd. It ought to be pointed directly toward the zenith of the place.

3rd. The projectile ought to be propelled with an initial velocity of 12,000 yards per second.

4th. It ought to be discharged at 10hrs. 46m. 40sec. of the 1st of December of the ensuing year.

5th. It will meet the moon four days after its discharge, precisely at midnight on the 4th of December, at the moment of its transit across the zenith.

The members of the Gun Club ought, therefore, without delay, to commence the works necessary for such an experiment, and to be prepared to set to work at the moment determined upon; for, if they should suffer this 4th of December to go by, they will not find the moon again under the same conditions of perigee and of zenith until eighteen years and eleven days afterward.

The staff of the Cambridge Observatory place themselves entirely at their disposal in respect of all questions of theoretical astronomy; and herewith add their congratulations to those of all the rest of America. For the Astronomical Staff, J. M. BELFAST, *Director of the Observatory of Cambridge.*

CHAPTER V

The Romance of the Moon

AN OBSERVER ENDUED with an infinite range of vision, and placed in that unknown centre around which the entire world revolves, might have beheld myriads of atoms filling all space during the chaotic epoch of the universe. Little by little, as ages went on, a change took place; a general law of attraction manifested itself, to which the hitherto errant atoms became obedient: these atoms combined together chemically according to their affinities, formed themselves into molecules, and composed those nebulous masses with which the depths of the heavens are strewed. These masses became immediately endued with a rotary motion around their own central point. This centre, formed of indefinite molecules, began to revolve around its own axis during its gradual condensation; then, following the immutable laws of mechanics, in proportion as its bulk diminished by condensation, its rotary motion became accelerated, and these two effects continuing, the result was the formation of one principal star, the centre of the nebulous mass.

By attentively watching, the observer would then have perceived the other molecules of the mass, following the example of this central star, become likewise condensed by gradually accelerated rotation, and gravitating round it in the shape of innumerable stars. Thus was formed the *Nebulæ*, of which astronomers have reckoned up nearly 5,000.

Among these 5,000 nebulæ there is one which has received the name of the Milky Way, and which contains eighteen millions of stars, each of which has become the centre of a solar world.

If the observer had then specially directed his attention to one of the more humble and less brilliant of these stellar bodies, a star of the fourth class, that which is arrogantly called the sun, all the phenomena to which the formation of the universe is to be ascribed would have been successively fulfilled before his eyes. In fact, he would have perceived this sun, as yet in the gaseous state, and composed of moving molecules, revolving round its axis in order to accomplish its work of concentration. This motion, faithful to the laws of mechanics, would have been accelerated with the diminution of its volume; and a moment would have arrived when the centrifugal force would have overpowered the centripetal, which causes the molecules all to tend toward the centre.

Another phenomenon would now have passed before the observer's eye, and the molecules situated on the plane of the equator, escaping like a stone from a sling of which the cord had suddenly snapped, would have formed around the sun sundry concentric rings resembling that of Saturn. In their turn, again, these rings of cosmical matter, excited by a rotary motion about the central mass, would have been broken up and decomposed into secondary nebulosities, that is to say, into planets. Similarly he would have observed these planets throw off one or more rings each, which became the origin of the secondary bodies which we call satellites.

Thus, then, advancing from atom to molecule, from molecule to nebulous mass, from that to principal star, from star to sun, from sun to planet, and hence to satellite, we have the whole series of transformations undergone by the heavenly bodies during the first days of the world.

Now, of those attendant bodies which the sun maintains in their elliptical orbits by the great law of gravitation, some few in turn possess satellites. Uranus has eight, Saturn eight, Jupiter four, Neptune possibly three, and the Earth one. This last, one of the least important of the entire solar system, we call the moon; and it is she whom the daring genius of the Americans professed their intention of conquering.

The moon, by her comparative proximity, and the constantly varying appearances produced by her several phases, has always occupied a considerable share of the attention of the inhabitants of the earth.

From the time of Thales of Miletus, in the fifth century B.C., down to that of Copernicus in the fifteenth and Tycho Brahé in the sixteenth century A.D., observations have been from time to time carried on with more or less correctness, until in the present day the altitudes of the lunar mountains have been determined with exactitude. Galileo explained the phenomena of the lunar light produced during certain of her phases by the existence of mountains, to which he assigned a mean altitude of 27,000 feet. After him Hévelius, an astronomer of Dantzic, reduced the highest elevations to 15,000 feet; but the calculations of Riccioli brought them up again to 21,000 feet.

At the close of the eighteenth century Herschel, armed with a powerful telescope, considerably reduced the preceding measurements. He assigned a height of 11,400 feet to the maximum elevations, and reduced the mean of the different altitudes to little more than 2,400 feet. But Herschel's calculations were in their turn corrected by the observations of Halley, Nasmyth, Bianchini, Gruithuysen, and others; but it was reserved for the labours of Beer and Maedler finally to solve the question. They succeeded in measuring 1,905 different elevations, of which six exceed 15,000 feet, and twenty-two exceed 14,400 feet. The highest summit of all towers to a height of 22,606 feet above the surface of the lunar disc. At the same period the examination of the moon was completed. She appeared completely riddled with craters, and her essentially volcanic character was apparent at each observation. By the absence of refraction in the rays of the planets occulted by her we conclude that she is absolutely devoid of an atmosphere. The absence of air entails the absence of water. It became, therefore, manifest that the Selenites, to support life under such conditions, must possess a special organisation of their own, must differ remarkably from the inhabitants of the earth.

At length, thanks to modern art, instruments of still higher perfection searched the moon without intermission, not leaving a single point of her surface unexplored; and notwithstanding that her diameter measures 2,150 miles, her surface equals the one-fifteenth part of that of our globe, and her bulk the one-forty-ninth part of that of the terrestrial spheroid – not one of her secrets was able to escape the eyes of the astronomers; and these skilful men of science carried to an even greater degree their prodigious observations.

Thus they remarked that, during full moon, the disc appeared scored in certain parts with white lines; and, during the phases, with black. On prosecuting the study of these with still greater precision, they succeeded in obtaining an exact account of the nature of these lines. They were long and narrow furrows sunk between parallel ridges, bordering generally upon the edges of the craters. Their length varied between ten and 100 miles, and their width was about 1,600 yards. Astronomers called them chasms, but they could not get any further. Whether these chasms were the dried-up beds of ancient rivers or not they were unable thoroughly to ascertain.

The Americans, among others, hoped one day or other to determine this geological question. They also undertook to examine the true nature of that system of parallel ramparts discovered on the moon's surface by Gruithuysen, a learned professor of Munich, who considered them to be 'a system of fortifications thrown up by the Selenitic engineers'. These two points, yet obscure, as well as others, no doubt, could not be definitely settled except by direct communication with the moon.

Regarding the degree of intensity of its light, there was nothing more to learn on this point. It was known that it is 300,000 times weaker than that of the sun, and that its heat has no appreciable effect upon the thermometer. As to the phenomenon known as the 'ashy light', it is explained naturally by the effect of the transmission of the solar rays from the earth to the moon, which give the appearance of completeness to the lunar disc, while it presents itself under the crescent form during its first and last phases.

Such was the state of knowledge acquired regarding the earth's satellite, which the Gun Club undertook to perfect in all its aspects, cosmographic, geological, political, and moral.

CHAPTER VI

Permissive Limits of Ignorance and Belief in the United States

THE IMMEDIATE RESULT of Barbicane's proposition was to place upon the orders of the day all the astronomical facts relative to the Queen of the Night. Everybody set to work to study assiduously. One would have thought that the moon had just appeared for the first time, and that no one had ever before caught a glimpse of her in the heavens. The papers revived all the old anecdotes in which the 'sun of the wolves' played a part; they recalled the influences which the ignorance of past ages ascribed to her; in short, all America was seized with selenomania, or had become moon-mad.

The scientific journals, for their part, dealt more especially with the questions which touched upon the enterprise of the Gun Club. The letter of the Observatory of Cambridge was published by them, and commented upon with unreserved approval.

Until that time most people had been ignorant of the mode in which the distance which separates the moon from the earth is calculated. They took advantage of this fact to explain to them that this distance was obtained by measuring the parallax of the moon. The term parallax proving 'caviare to the general', they further explained that it meant the angle formed by the inclination of two straight lines drawn from either extremity of the earth's radius to the moon. On doubts being expressed as to the correctness of this method, they immediately proved that not only was the mean distance 234,347 miles, but that astronomers could not possibly be in error in their estimate by more than seventy miles either way.

To those who were not familiar with the motions of the moon, they demonstrated that she possesses two distinct motions, the first being that of rotation upon her axis, the second being that of revolution round the earth, accomplishing both together in an equal period of time, that is to say, in twenty-seven and one-third days.

The motion of rotation is that which produces day and night on the surface of the moon; save that there is only one day and one night in the lunar month, each lasting three hundred and fifty-four and one-third hours. But, happily for her, the face turned toward the terrestrial globe is illuminated by it with an intensity equal to that of fourteen moons. As to the other face, always invisible to us, it has of necessity three hundred and fifty-four hours of absolute night, tempered only by that 'pale glimmer which falls upon it from the stars'.

Some well-intentioned, but rather obstinate persons, could not at first comprehend how, if the moon displays invariably the same face to the earth during her revolution, she can describe one turn round herself. To such they answered, 'Go into your dining-room, and walk round the table in such a way as to always keep your face turned toward the centre; by the time you will have achieved one complete round you will have completed one turn around yourself, since your eye will have traversed successively every point of the room. Well, then, the room is the heavens, the table is the earth, and the moon is yourself.' And they would go away delighted.

So, then the moon displays invariably the same face to the earth; nevertheless, to be quite exact, it is necessary to add that, in consequence of certain fluctuations of north and south, and of west and east, termed her libration, she permits rather more than half, that is to say, five-sevenths, to be seen.

As soon as the ignoramuses came to understand as much as the director of the observatory himself knew, they began to worry themselves regarding her revolution round the earth, whereupon twenty scientific reviews immediately came to the rescue. They pointed out to them that the firmament, with its infinitude of stars, may be considered as one vast dial-plate, upon which the moon travels, indicating the true time to all the inhabitants of the earth; that it is during this movement that the Queen of Night exhibits her different phases; that the moon is *full* when she is in *opposition* with the sun, that is when the three bodies are on the same straight line, the earth occupying the centre; that she is *new* when she is in *conjunction* with the sun, that is, when she is between it and the earth; and, lastly that she is in her *first* or *last* quarter, when she makes with the sun and the earth an angle of which she herself occupies the apex.

Regarding the altitude which the moon attains above the horizon, the letter of the Cambridge Observatory had said all that was to be said in this respect. Every one knew that this altitude varies according to the latitude of the observer. But the only zones of the globe in which the moon passes the zenith, that is, the point directly over the head of the spectator, are of necessity comprised between the twenty-eighth parallels and the equator. Hence the importance of the advice to try the experiment upon some point of that part of the globe, in order that the projectile might be discharged perpendicularly, and so the soonest escape the action of gravitation. This was an essential condition to the success of the enterprise, and continued actively to engage the public attention.

Regarding the path described by the moon in her revolution round the earth, the Cambridge Observatory had demonstrated that this path is a re-entering curve, not a perfect circle, but an ellipse, of which the earth occupies one of the *foci*. It was also well understood that it is farthest removed from the earth during its *apogee*, and approaches most nearly to it at its *perigee*.

Such was then the extent of knowledge possessed by every American on the subject, and of which no one could decently profess ignorance. Still, while these principles were being rapidly disseminated many errors and illusory fears proved less easy to eradicate.

For instance, some worthy persons maintained that the moon was an ancient comet which, in describing its elongated orbit round the sun, happened to pass near the earth, and became confined within her circle of attraction. These drawing-room astronomers professed to explain the charred aspect of the moon – a disaster which they attributed to the intensity of the solar heat; only, on being reminded that comets have an atmosphere, and that the moon has little or none, they were fairly at a loss for a reply.

Others again, belonging to the doubting class, expressed certain fears as to the position of the moon. They had heard it said that, according to observations made in the time of the Caliphs, her revolution had become accelerated in a certain degree. Hence they concluded, logically enough, that an acceleration of motion ought to be accompanied by a corresponding diminution in the distance separating the two bodies; and that, supposing the double effect to be continued to infinity, the moon would end by one day falling into the earth. However, they became reassured as to the fate of future generations on being apprised that, according to the calculations of Laplace, this acceleration of motion is confined within very restricted limits, and that a proportional diminution of speed will be certain to succeed it. So, then, the stability of the solar system would not be deranged in ages to come.

There remains but the third class, the superstitious. These worthies were not content merely to rest in ignorance; they must know all about things which had no existence whatever, and as to the moon, they had long known all about her. One set regarded her disc as a polished mirror, by means of which people could see each other from different points of the earth and interchange their thoughts. Another set pretended that out of one thousand new moons that had been observed, nine hundred and fifty had been attended with remarkable disturbances, such as cataclysms, revolutions, earthquakes, the deluge, etc. Then they believed in some mysterious influence exercised by her over human destinies – that every Selenite was attached to some inhabitant of the earth by a tie of sympathy; they maintained that the entire vital system is subject to her control, etc. But in time the majority renounced these vulgar errors, and espoused the true side of the question. As for the Yankees, they had no other ambition than to take possession of this new continent of the sky, and to plant upon the summit of its highest elevation the star-spangled banner of the United States of America.

CHAPTER VII

The Hymn of the Cannon-Ball

THE OBSERVATORY OF Cambridge in its memorable letter had treated the question from a purely astronomical point of view. The mechanical part still remained.

President Barbicane had, without loss of time, nominated a working committee of the Gun Club. The duty of this committee was to resolve the three grand questions of the cannon, the projectile, and the powder. It was composed of four members of great technical knowledge, Barbicane (with a casting vote in case of equality), General Morgan, Major Elphinstone, and J. T. Maston, to whom were confided the functions of secretary. On the 8th of October the committee met at the house of President Barbicane, 3 Republican Street. The meeting was opened by the president himself.

'Gentlemen,' said he, 'we have to resolve one of the most important problems in the whole of the noble science of gunnery. It might appear, perhaps, the most logical course to devote our first meeting to the discussion of the engine to be employed. Nevertheless, after mature consideration, it has appeared to me that the question of the projectile must take precedence of that of the cannon, and that the dimensions of the latter must necessarily depend on those of the former.'

'Suffer me to say a word,' here broke in J. T. Maston. Permission having been granted, 'Gentlemen,' said he with an inspired accent, 'our president is right in placing the question of the projectile above all others. The ball we are about to discharge at the moon is our ambassador to her, and I wish to consider it from a moral point of view. The cannon-ball, gentlemen, to my mind, is the most magnificent manifestation of human power. If Providence has created the stars and the planets, man has called the cannon-ball into existence. Let Providence claim the swiftness of electricity and of light, of the stars, the comets, and the planets, of wind and sound – we claim to have invented the swiftness of the cannon-ball, a hundred times superior to that of the swiftest horses or railway train. How glorious will be the moment when, infinitely exceeding all hitherto attained velocities, we shall launch our new projectile with the rapidity of seven miles a second! Shall it not, gentlemen – shall it not be received up there with the honours due to a terrestrial ambassador?'

Overcome with emotion, the orator sat down and applied himself to a huge plate of sandwiches before him.

'And now,' said Barbicane, 'let us quit the domain of poetry and come direct to the question.'

'By all means,' replied the members, each with his mouth full of sandwich.

'The problem before us,' continued the president, 'is how to communicate to a projectile a velocity of 12,000 yards per second. Let us at present examine the velocities hitherto attained. General Morgan will be able to enlighten us on this point.'

'And the more easily,' replied the general, 'that during the war I was a member of the committee of experiments. I may say, then, that the 100-pounder Dahlgrens, which carried a distance of 5,000 yards, impressed upon their projectile an initial velocity of 500 yards a second. The Rodman Columbiad threw a shot weighing half a ton a distance of six miles, with a velocity of 800 yards per second – a result which Armstrong and Palisser have never obtained in England.'

'This,' replied Barbicane, 'is, I believe, the maximum velocity ever attained?'

'It is so,' replied the general.

'Ah!' groaned J. T. Maston, 'if my mortar had not burst—'

'Yes,' quietly replied Barbicane, 'but it did burst. We must take, then, for our starting point, this velocity of 800 yards. We must increase it twenty-fold. Now, reserving for another discussion the means of producing this velocity, I will call your attention to the dimensions which it will be proper to assign to the shot. You understand that we have nothing to do here with projectiles weighing at most but half a ton.'

'Why not?' demanded the major.

'Because the shot,' quickly replied J. T. Maston, 'must be big enough to attract the attention of the inhabitants of the moon, if there are any?'

'Yes,' replied Barbicane, 'and for another reason more important still.'

'What mean you?' asked the major.

'I mean that it is not enough to discharge a projectile, and then take no further notice of it; we must follow it throughout its course, up to the moment when it shall reach its goal.'

'What?' shouted the general and the major in great surprise.

'Undoubtedly,' replied Barbicane composedly, 'or our experiment would produce no result.'

'But then,' replied the major, 'you will have to give this projectile enormous dimensions.'

'No! Be so good as to listen. You know that optical instruments have acquired great perfection; with certain instruments we have succeeded in obtaining enlargements of 6,000 times and reducing the moon to within forty miles' distance. Now, at this distance, any objects sixty feet square would be perfectly visible.

'If, then, the penetrative power of telescopes has not been further increased, it is because that power detracts from their light; and the moon, which is but a reflecting mirror, does not give back sufficient light to enable us to perceive objects of lesser magnitude.'

'Well, then, what do you propose to do?' asked the general. 'Would you give your projectile a diameter of sixty feet?'

'Not so.'

'Do you intend, then, to increase the luminous power of the moon?'

'Exactly so. If I can succeed in diminishing the density of the atmosphere through which the moon's light has to travel I shall have rendered her light more intense. To effect that object it will be enough to establish a telescope on some elevated mountain. That is what we will do.'

'I give it up,' answered the major. 'You have such a way

of simplifying things. And what enlargement do you expect to obtain in this way?'

'One of 48,000 times, which should bring the moon within an apparent distance of five miles; and, in order to be visible, objects need not have a diameter of more than nine feet.'

'So, then,' cried J. T. Maston, 'our projectile need not be more than nine feet in diameter.'

'Let me observe, however,' interrupted Major Elphinstone, 'this will involve a weight such as—'

'My dear major,' replied Barbicane, 'before discussing its weight permit me to enumerate some of the marvels which our ancestors have achieved in this respect. I don't mean to pretend that the science of gunnery has not advanced, but it is as well to bear in mind that during the middle ages they obtained results more surprising, I will venture to say, than ours. For instance, during the siege of Constantinople by Mahomet II, in 1453, stone shot of 1,900 pounds weight were employed. At Malta, in the time of the knights, there was a gun of the fortress of St. Elmo which threw a projectile weighing 2,500 pounds. And, now, what is the extent of what we have seen ourselves? Armstrong guns discharging shot of 500 pounds, and the Rodman guns projectiles of half a ton! It seems, then, that if projectiles have gained in range, they have lost far more in weight. Now, if we turn our efforts in that direction, we ought to arrive, with the progress of science, at ten times the weight of the shot of Mahomet II and the Knights of Malta.'

'Clearly,' replied the major; 'but what metal do you calculate upon employing?'

'Simply cast iron,' said General Morgan.

'But,' interrupted the major, 'since the weight of a shot is proportionate to its volume, an iron ball of nine feet in diameter would be of tremendous weight.'

'Yes, if it were solid, not if it were hollow.'

'Hollow? then it would be a shell?'

'Yes, a shell,' replied Barbicane; 'decidely it must be. A solid shot of 108 inches would weigh more than 200,000 pounds, a weight evidently far too great. Still, as we must reserve a certain stability for our projectile, I propose to give it a weight of 20,000 pounds.'

'What, then, will be the thickness of the sides?' asked the major.

'If we follow the usual proportion,' replied Morgan, 'a diameter of 108 inches would require sides of two feet thickness, or less.'

'That would be too much,' replied Barbicane; 'for you will observe that the question is not that of a shot intended to pierce an iron plate; it will suffice to give it sides strong enough to resist the pressure of the gas. The problem, therefore, is this – what thickness ought a cast-iron shell to have in order not to weigh more than 20,000 pounds? Our clever secretary will soon enlighten us upon this point.'

'Nothing easier,' replied the worthy secretary of the committee; and, rapidly tracing a few algebraical formulae upon paper, among which n^2 and x^2 frequently appeared, he presently said:

'The sides will require a thickness of less than two inches.'

'Will that be enough?' asked the major doubtfully.

'Clearly not!' replied the president.

'What is to be done, then?' said Elphinstone, with a puzzled air.

'Employ another metal instead of iron.'

'Copper?' said Morgan.

'No! that would be too heavy. I have better than that to offer.'

'What then?' asked the major.

'Aluminium!' replied Barbicane.

'Aluminium?' cried his three colleagues in chorus.

'Unquestionably, my friends. This valuable metal possesses the whiteness of silver, the indestructibility of gold, the tenacity of iron, the fusibility of copper, the lightness of glass. It is easily wrought, is very widely distributed, forming the base of most of the rocks, is three times lighter than iron, and seems to have been created for the express purpose of furnishing us with the material for our projectile.'

'But, my dear president,' said the major, 'is not the cost price of aluminium extremely high?'

'It was so at its first discovery, but it has fallen now to nine dollars a pound.'

'But still, nine dollars a pound!' replied the major, who was not willing readily to give in; 'even that is an enormous price.'

'Undoubtedly, my dear major; but not beyond our reach.'

'What will the projectile weigh then?' asked Morgan.

'Here is the result of my calculations,' replied Barbicane. 'A shot of 108 inches in diameter, and twelve inches in thickness, would weigh, in cast-iron, 67,440 pounds; cast in aluminium, its weight will be reduced to 19,250 pounds.'

'Capital!' cried the major; 'but do you know that, at nine dollars a pound, this projectile will cost—'

'One hundred and seventy-three thousand and fifty dollars ($173,050). I know it quite well. But fear not, my friends; the money will not be wanting for our enterprise. I will answer for it. Now what say you to aluminium, gentlemen?'

'Adopted!' replied the three members of the committee. So ended the first meeting. The question of the projectile was definitely settled.

CHAPTER VIII

History of the Cannon

THE RESOLUTIONS PASSED at the last meeting produced a great effect out of doors. Timid people took fright at the idea of a shot weighing 20,000 pounds being launched into space; they asked what cannon could ever transmit a sufficient velocity to such a mighty mass. The minutes of the second meeting were destined triumphantly to answer such questions. The following evening the discussion was renewed.

'My dear colleagues,' said Barbicane, without further preamble, 'the subject now before us is the construction of the engine, its length, its composition, and its weight. It is probable that we shall end by giving it gigantic dimensions; but however great may be the difficulties in the way, our mechanical genius will readily surmount them. Be good enough, then, to give me your attention, and do not hesitate to make objections at the close. I have no fear of them. The problem before us is how to communicate an initial force of 12,000 yards per second to a shell of 108 inches in diameter, weighing 20,000 pounds. Now when a projectile is launched into space, what happens to it? It is acted upon by three independent forces: the resistance of the air, the attraction of the earth, and the force of impulsion with which it is endowed. Let us examine these three forces. The resistance of the air is of little importance. The atmosphere of the earth does not exceed forty miles. Now, with the given rapidity, the projectile will have traversed this in five seconds, and the period is too brief for the resistance of the medium to be regarded otherwise than as insignificant. Proceeding, then, to the attraction of the earth, that is, the weight of the shell, we know that this weight will diminish in the inverse ratio of the square of the distance. When a body left to itself falls to the surface of the earth, it falls five feet in the first second; and if the same body were removed 257,542 miles further off, in other words, to the distance of the moon, its fall would be reduced to about half a line in the first second. That is almost equivalent to a state of perfect rest. Our business, then, is to overcome progressively this action of gravitation. The mode of accomplishing that is by the force of impulsion.'

'There's the difficulty,' broke in the major.

'True,' replied the president; 'but we will overcome that, for the force of impulsion will depend on the length of the engine and the powder employed, the latter being limited only by the resisting power of the former. Our business, then, to-day is with the dimensions of the cannon.'

'Now, up to the present time,' said Barbicane, 'our longest guns have not exceeded twenty-five feet in length. We shall therefore astonish the world by the dimensions we shall be obliged to adopt. It must evidently be, then, a gun of great range, since the length of the piece will increase the detention of the gas accumulated behind the projectile; but there is no advantage in passing certain limits.'

'Quite so,' said the major. 'What is the rule in such a case?'

'Ordinarily the length of a gun is twenty to twenty-five times the diameter of the shot, and its weight two hundred and thirty-five to two hundred and forty times that of the shot.'

'That is not enough,' cried J. T. Maston impetuously.

'I agree with you, my good friend; and, in fact, following this proportion for a projectile nine feet in diameter, weighing 30,000 pounds, the gun would only have a length of two hundred and twenty-five feet, and a weight of 7,200,000 pounds.'

'Ridiculous!' rejoined Maston. 'As well take a pistol.'

'I think so too,' replied Barbicane; 'that is why I propose to quadruple that length, and to construct a gun of nine hundred feet.'

The general and the major offered some objections; nevertheless, the proposition, actively supported by the secretary, was definitely adopted.

'But,' said Elphinstone, 'what thickness must we give it?'

'A thickness of six feet,' replied Barbicane.

'You surely don't think of mounting a mass like that upon a carriage?' asked the major.

'It would be a superb idea, though,' said Maston.

'But impracticable,' replied Barbicane. 'No, I think of sinking this engine in the earth alone, binding it with hoops of wrought iron, and finally surrounding it with a thick mass of masonry of stone and cement. The piece once cast, it must be bored with great precision, so as to preclude any possible windage. So there will be no loss whatever of gas, and all the expansive force of the powder will be employed in the propulsion.'

'One simple question,' said Elphinstone: 'is our gun to be rifled?'

'No, certainly not,' replied Barbicane; 'we require an enormous initial velocity; and you are well aware that a shot quits a rifled gun less rapidly than it does a smooth-bore.'

'True,' rejoined the major.

The committee here adjourned for a few minutes to tea and sandwiches.

On the discussion being renewed, 'Gentlemen,' said Barbicane, 'we must now take into consideration the metal to be employed. Our cannon must be possessed of great tenacity, great hardness, be infusible by heat, indissoluble, and inoxidable by the corrosive action of acids.'

'There is no doubt about that,' replied the major; 'and as we shall have to employ an immense quantity of metal, we shall not be at a loss for choice.'

'Well, then,' said Morgan, 'I propose the best alloy hitherto known, which consists of one hundred parts of copper, twelve of tin, and six of brass.'

'I admit,' replied the president, 'that this composition has yielded excellent results, but in the present case it would be too expensive, and very difficult to work. I think, then, that we ought to adopt a material excellent in its way and of low price, such as cast iron. What is your advice, major?'

'I quite agree with you,' replied Elphinstone.

'In fact,' continued Barbicane, 'cast iron costs ten times less than bronze; it is easy to cast, it runs readily from the moulds of sand, it is easy of manipulation, it is at once economical of money and of time. In addition, it is excellent as a material, and I well remember that during the war, at the siege of Atlanta, some iron guns fired one thousand rounds at intervals of twenty minutes without injury.'

'Cast iron is very brittle, though,' replied Morgan.

'Yes, but it possesses great resistance. I will now ask our worthy secretary to calculate the weight of a cast-iron gun with a bore of nine feet and a thickness of six feet of metal.'

'In a moment,' replied Maston. Then, dashing off some algebraical formulae with marvellous facility, in a minute or two he declared the following result:

'The cannon will weigh 68,040 tons. And, at two cents a pound, it will cost—'

'Two million, five hundred and ten thousand, seven hundred and one dollars.'

Maston, the major, and the general regarded Barbicane with uneasy looks.

'Well, gentlemen,' replied the president, 'I repeat what I said yesterday. Make yourselves easy; the millions will not be wanting.'

With this assurance of their president the committee separated, after having fixed their third meeting for the following evening.

CHAPTER IX

The Question of the Powders

THERE REMAINED FOR consideration merely the question of powders. The public awaited with interest its final decision. The size of the projectile, the length of the cannon being settled, what would be the quantity of powder necessary to produce impulsion?

It is generally asserted that gunpowder was invented in the fourteenth century by the monk Schwartz, who paid for his grand discovery with his life. It is, however, pretty well proved that this story ought to be ranked among the legends of the middle ages. Gunpowder was not invented by any one; it was the lineal successor of the Greek fire, which, like itself, was composed of sulphur and saltpeter. Few persons are acquainted with the mechanical power of gunpowder. Now this is precisely what is necessary to be understood in order to comprehend the importance of the question submitted to the committee.

A litre of gunpowder weighs about two pounds; during combustion it produces 400 litres of gas. This gas, on being liberated and acted upon by temperature raised to 2,400 degrees, occupies a space of 4,000 litres: consequently the volume of powder is to the volume of gas produced by its combustion as 1 to 4,000. One may judge, therefore, of the tremendous pressure on this gas when compressed within a space 4,000 times too confined. All this was, of course, well known to the members of the committee when they met on the following evening.

The first speaker on this occasion was Major Elphinstone, who had been the director of the gunpowder factories during the war.

'Gentlemen,' said this distinguished chemist, 'I begin with some figures which will serve as the basis of our calculation. The old 24-pounder shot required for its discharge sixteen pounds of powder.'

'You are certain of this amount?' broke in Barbicane.

'Quite certain,' replied the major. 'The Armstrong cannon employs only seventy-five pounds of powder for a projectile of eight hundred pounds, and the Rodman Columbiad uses only one hundred and sixty pounds of powder to send its half ton shot a distance of six miles. These facts cannot be called in question, for I myself raised the point during the depositions taken before the committee of artillery.'

'Quite true,' said the general.

'Well,' replied the major, 'these figures go to prove that the quantity of powder is not increased with the weight of the shot; that is to say, if a 24-pounder shot requires sixteen pounds of powder; in other words, if in ordinary guns we employ a quantity of powder equal to two-thirds of the weight of the projectile, this proportion is not constant. Calculate, and you will see that in place of three hundred and thirty-three pounds of powder, the quantity is reduced to no more than one hundred and sixty pounds.'

'What are you aiming at?' asked the president.

'If you push your theory to extremes, my dear major,' said

J. T. Maston, 'you will get to this, that as soon as your shot becomes sufficiently heavy you will not require any powder at all.'

'Our friend Maston is always at his jokes, even in serious matters,' cried the major; 'but let him make his mind easy, I am going presently to propose gunpowder enough to satisfy his artillerist's propensities. I only keep to statistical facts when I say that, during the war, and for the very largest guns, the weight of the powder was reduced, as the result of experience, to a tenth part of the weight of the shot.'

'Perfectly correct,' said Morgan; 'but before deciding the quantity of powder necessary to give the impulse, I think it would be as well—'

'We shall have to employ a large-grained powder,' continued the major; 'its combustion is more rapid than that of the small.'

'No doubt about that,' replied Morgan; 'but it is very destructive, and ends by enlarging the bore of the pieces.'

'Granted; but that which is injurious to a gun destined to perform long service is not so to our Columbiad. We shall run no danger of an explosion; and it is necessary that our powder should take fire instantaneously in order that its mechanical effect may be complete.'

'We must have,' said Maston, 'several touch-holes, so as to fire it at different points at the same time.'

'Certainly,' replied Elphinstone; 'but that will render the working of the piece more difficult. I return then to my large-grained powder, which removes those difficulties. In his Columbiad charges Rodman employed a powder as large as chestnuts, made of willow charcoal, simply dried in cast-iron pans. This powder was hard and glittering, left no trace upon the hand, contained hydrogen and oxygen in large proportion, took fire instantaneously, and, though very destructive, did not sensibly injure the mouth-piece.'

Up to this point Barbicane had kept aloof from the discussion; he left the others to speak while he himself listened; he had evidently got an idea. He now simply said, 'Well, my friends, what quantity of powder do you propose?'

The three members looked at one another.

'Two hundred thousand pounds,' at last said Morgan.

'Five hundred thousand,' added the major.

'Eight hundred thousand,' screamed Maston.

A moment of silence followed this triple proposal; it was at last broken by the president.

'Gentlemen,' he quietly said, 'I start from this principle, that the resistance of a gun, constructed under the given conditions, is unlimited. I shall surprise our friend Maston, then, by stigmatising his calculations as timid; and I propose to double his 800,000 pounds of powder.'

'Sixteen hundred thousand pounds?' shouted Maston, leaping from his seat.

'Just so.'

'We shall have to come then to my ideal of a cannon half a mile long; for you see 1,600,000 pounds will occupy a space of about 20,000 cubic feet; and since the contents of your cannon do not exceed 54,000 cubic feet, it would be half full; and the bore will not be more than long enough for the gas to communicate to the projectile sufficient impulse.'

'Nevertheless,' said the president, 'I hold to that quantity of powder. Now, 1,600,000 pounds of powder will create 6,000,000,000 litres of gas. Six thousand millions! You quite understand?'

'What is to be done then?' said the general.

'The thing is very simple; we must reduce this enormous quantity of powder, while preserving to it its mechanical power.'

'Good; but by what means?'

'I am going to tell you,' replied Barbicane quietly.

'Nothing is more easy than to reduce this mass to one quarter of its bulk. You know that curious cellular matter which constitutes the elementary tissues of vegetable? This substance is found quite pure in many bodies, especially in cotton, which is nothing more than the down of the seeds of the cotton plant. Now cotton, combined with cold nitric acid, become transformed into a substance eminently insoluble, combustible, and explosive. It was first discovered in 1832, by Braconnot, a French chemist, who called it xyloidine. In 1838 another Frenchman, Pelouze, investigated its different properties, and finally, in 1846, Schonbein, professor of chemistry at Bale, proposed its employment for purposes of war. This powder, now called pyroxyle, or fulminating cotton, is prepared with great facility by simply plunging cotton for fifteen minutes in nitric acid, then washing it in water, then drying it, and it is ready for use.'

'Nothing could be more simple,' said Morgan.

'Moreover, pyroxyle is unaltered by moisture – a valuable property to us, inasmuch as it would take several days to charge the cannon. It ignites at 170 degrees in place of 240, and its combustion is so rapid that one may set light to it on the top of the ordinary powder, without the latter having time to ignite.'

'Perfect!' exclaimed the major.

'Only it is more expensive.'

'What matter?' cried J. T. Maston.

'Finally, it imparts to projectiles a velocity four times superior to that of gunpowder. I will even add, that if we mix it with one-eighth of its own weight of nitrate of potassium, its expansive force is again considerably augmented.'

'Will that be necessary?' asked the major.

'I think not,' replied Barbicane. 'So, then, in place of 1,600,000 pounds of powder, we shall have but 400,000 pounds of fulminating cotton; and since we can, without danger, compress 500 pounds of cotton into twenty-seven cubic feet, the whole quantity will not occupy a height of more than 180 feet within the bore of the Columbiad. In this way the shot will have more than 700 feet of bore to traverse under a force of 6,000,000,000 litres of gas before taking its flight toward the moon.'

At this juncture J. T. Maston could not repress his emotion; he flung himself into the arms of his friend with the violence of a projectile, and Barbicane would have been stove in if he had not been boom-proof.

This incident terminated the third meeting of the committee.

Barbicane and his bold colleagues, to whom nothing seemed impossible, had succeeding in solving the complex problems of projectile, cannon, and powder. Their plan was drawn up, and it only remained to put it into execution.

'A mere matter of detail, a bagatelle,' said J. T. Maston.

CHAPTER X

One Enemy v. Twenty-Five Millions of Friends

THE AMERICAN PUBLIC took a lively interest in the smallest details of the enterprise of the Gun Club. It followed day by day the discussion of the committee. The most simple preparations for the great experiment, the questions of figures which it involved, the mechanical difficulties to be resolved – in one word, the entire plan of work – roused the popular excitement to the highest pitch.

The purely scientific attraction was suddenly intensified by the following incident:

We have seen what legions of admirers and friends Barbicane's project had rallied round its author. There was, however, one single individual alone in all the States of the Union who protested against the attempt of the Gun Club. He attacked it furiously on every opportunity, and human nature is such that Barbicane felt more keenly the opposition of that one man than he did the applause of all the others. He was well aware of the motive of this antipathy, the origin of this solitary enmity, the cause of its personality and old standing, and in what rivalry of self-love it had its rise.

This persevering enemy the president of the Gun Club had never seen. Fortunate that it was so, for a meeting between the two men would certainly have been attended with serious consequences. This rival was a man of science, like Barbicane himself, of a fiery, daring, and violent disposition; a pure Yankee. His name was Captain Nicholl; he lived at Philadelphia.

Most people are aware of the curious struggle which arose during the Federal war between the guns and armour of iron-plated ships. The result was the entire reconstruction of the navy of both the continents; as the one grew heavier, the other became thicker in proportion. The *Merrimac*, the *Monitor*, the *Tennessee*, the *Weehawken* discharged enormous projectiles themselves, after having been armour-clad against the projectiles of others. In fact they did to others that which they would not they should do to them – that grand principle of immortality upon which rests the whole art of war.

Now if Barbicane was a great founder of shot, Nicholl was a great forger of plates; the one cast night and day at Baltimore, the other forged day and night at Philadelphia. As soon as ever Barbicane invented a new shot, Nicholl invented a new plate; each followed a current of ideas essentially opposed to the other. Happily for these citizens, so useful to their country, a distance of from fifty to sixty miles separated them from one another, and they had never yet met. Which of these two inventors had the advantage over the other it was difficult to decide from the results obtained. By last accounts, however, it would seem that the armour-plate would in the end have to give way to the shot; nevertheless, there were competent judges who had their doubts on the point.

At the last experiment the cylindro-conical projectiles of Barbicane stuck like so many pins in the Nicholl plates. On that day the Philadelphia iron-forger then believed himself victorious, and could not evince contempt enough for his rival; but when the other afterward substituted for conical shot simple 600-pound shells, at very moderate velocity, the captain was obliged to give in. In fact, these projectiles knocked his best metal plate to shivers.

Matters were at this stage, and victory seemed to rest with the shot, when the war came to an end on the very day when Nicholl had completed a new armour-plate of wrought steel. It was a masterpiece of its kind, and bid defiance to all the projectiles of the world. The captain had it conveyed to the Polygon at Washington, challenging the president of the Gun Club to break it. Barbicane, peace having been declared, declined to try the experiment.

Nicholl, now furious, offered to expose his plate to the shock of any shot, solid, hollow, round, or conical. Refused by the president, who did not choose to compromise his last success.

Nicholl, disgusted by this obstinacy, tried to tempt Barbicane by offering him every chance. He proposed to fix the plate within two hundred yards of the gun. Barbicane still obstinate in refusal. A hundred yards? Not even seventy-five!

'At fifty then!' roared the captain through the newspapers. 'At twenty-five yards! and I'll stand behind!'

Barbicane returned for answer that, even if Captain Nicholl would be so good as to stand in front, he would not fire any more.

Nicholl could not contain himself at this reply; threw out hints of cowardice; that a man who refused to fire a cannon-shot was pretty near being afraid of it; that artillerists who fight at six miles' distance are substituting mathematical formulae for individual courage.

To these insinuations Barbicane returned no answer; perhaps he never heard of them, so absorbed was he in the calculations for his great enterprise.

When his famous communication was made to the Gun Club, the captain's wrath passed all bounds; with his intense jealousy was mingled a feeling of absolute impotence. How was he to invent anything to beat this 900-feet Columbiad? What armour-plate could ever resist a projectile of 30,000 pounds weight? Overwhelmed at first under this violent shock, he by and by recovered himself, and resolved to crush the proposal by weight of his arguments.

He then violently attacked the labours of the Gun Club, published a number of letters in the newspapers, endeavoured to prove Barbicane ignorant of the first principles of gunnery. He maintained that it was absolutely impossible to impress upon any body whatever a velocity of 12,000 yards per second; that even with such a velocity a projectile of such a weight could not transcend the limits of the earth's atmosphere. Further still, even regarding the velocity to be acquired, and granting it to be sufficient, the shell could not resist the pressure of the gas developed by the ignition of 1,600,000 pounds of powder; and supposing it to resist that pressure, it would be less able to support that temperature; it would melt on quitting the Columbiad, and fall back in a red-hot shower upon the heads of the imprudent spectators.

Barbicane continued his work without regarding these attacks.

Nicholl then took up the question in its other aspects. Without touching upon its uselessness in all points of view, he regarded the experiment as fraught with extreme danger, both to the citizens, who might sanction by their presence so reprehensible a spectacle, and also to the towns in the neighbourhood of this deplorable cannon. He also observed that if the projectile did not succeed in reaching its destination (a result absolutely impossible), it must inevitably fall back upon the earth, and that the shock of such a mass, multiplied by the square of its velocity, would seriously endanger every point of the globe. Under the circumstances, therefore, and without interfering with the rights of free citizens, it was a case for the intervention of government, which ought not to endanger the safety of all for the pleasure of one individual.

In spite of all his arguments, however, Captain Nicholl remained alone in his opinion. Nobody listened to him, and he did not succeed in alienating a single admirer from the president of the Gun Club. The latter did not even take the pains to refute the arguments of his rival.

Nicholl, driven into his last entrenchments, and not able to fight personally in the cause, resolved to fight with money. He published, therefore, in the Richmond *Inquirer* a series of wagers, conceived in these terms, and on an increasing scale:

> No. 1 ($1,000). – That the necessary funds for the experiment of the Gun Club will not be forthcoming.

No. 2 ($2,000). – That the operation of casting a cannon of 900 feet is impracticable, and cannot possibly succeed.

No. 3 ($3,000). – That is it impossible to load the Columbiad, and that the pyroxyle will take fire spontaneously under the pressure of the projectile.

No. 4 ($4,000). – That the Columbiad will burst at the first fire.

No. 5 ($5,000). – That the shot will not travel farther than six miles, and that it will fall back again a few seconds after its discharge.

It was an important sum, therefore, which the captain risked in his invincible obstinacy. He had no less than $15,000 at stake.

Notwithstanding the importance of the challenge, on the 19th of May he received a sealed packet containing the following superbly laconic reply:

'BALTIMORE, October 19.
'Done.
'BARBICANE.'

CHAPTER XI

Florida and Texas

ONE QUESTION REMAINED yet to be decided; it was necessary to choose a favourable spot for the experiment. According to the advice of the Observatory of Cambridge, the gun must be fired perpendicularly to the plane of the horizon, that is to say, toward the zenith. Now the moon does not traverse the zenith, except in places situated between 0° and 28° of latitude. It became, then, necessary to determine exactly that spot on the globe where the immense Columbiad should be cast.

On the 20th of October, at a general meeting of the Gun Club, Barbicane produced a magnificent map of the United States. 'Gentlemen,' said he, in opening the discussion, 'I presume that we are all agreed that this experiment cannot and ought not to be tried anywhere but within the limits of the soil of the Union. Now, by good fortune, certain frontiers of the United States extend downward as far as the 28th parallel of the north latitude. If you will cast your eye over this map, you will see that we have at our disposal the whole of the southern portion of Texas and Florida.'

It was finally agreed, then, that the Columbiad must be cast on the soil of either Texas or Florida. The result, however, of this decision was to create a rivalry entirely without precedent between the different towns of these two States.

The 28th parallel, on reaching the American coast, traverses the peninsula of Florida, dividing it into two nearly equal portions. Then, plunging into the Gulf of Mexico, it subtends the arc formed by the coast of Alabama, Mississippi, and Louisiana; then skirting Texas, off which it cuts an angle, it continues its course over Mexico, crosses the Sonora, Old California, and loses itself in the Pacific Ocean. It was, therefore, only those portions of Texas and Florida which were situated below this parallel which came within the prescribed conditions of latitude.

Florida, in its southern part, reckons no cities of importance; it is simply studded with forts raised against the roving Indians. One solitary town, Tampa Town, was able to put in a claim in favour of its situation.

In Texas, on the contrary, the towns are much more numerous and important. Corpus Christi, in the county of Nueces, and all the cities situated on the Rio Bravo, Laredo, Comalites, San Ignacio on the Web, Rio Grande City on the Starr, Edinburgh in the Hidalgo, Santa Rita, Elpanda, Brownsville in the Cameron, formed an imposing league against the pretensions of Florida. So, scarcely was the decision known, when the Texan and Floridan deputies arrived at Baltimore in an incredibly short space of time. From that very moment President Barbicane and the influential members of the Gun Club were besieged day and night by formidable claims. If seven cities of Greece contended for the honour of having given birth to a Homer, here were two entire States threatening to come to blows about the question of a cannon.

The rival parties promenaded the streets with arms in their hands; and at every occasion of their meeting a collision was to be apprehended which might have been attended with disastrous results. Happily the prudence and address of President Barbicane averted the danger. These personal demonstrations found a division in the newspapers of the different States. The New York *Herald* and the *Tribune* supported Texas, while the *Times* and the *American Review* espoused the cause of the Floridan deputies. The members of the Gun Club could not decide to which to give the preference.

Texas produced its array of twenty-six counties; Florida replied that twelve counties were better than twenty-six in a country only one-sixth part of the size.

Texas plumed itself upon its 330,000 natives; Florida, with a far smaller territory, boasted of being much more densely populated with 56,000.

The Texans, through the columns of the *Herald*, claimed that some regard should be had to a State which grew the best cotton in all America, produced the best green oak for the service of the navy, and contained the finest oil, besides iron mines, in which the yield was fifty per cent of pure metal.

To this the *American Review* replied that the soil of Florida, although not equally rich, afforded the best conditions for the moulding and casting of the Columbiad, consisting as it did of sand and argillaceous earth.

'That may be all very well,' replied the Texans; 'but you must first get to this country. Now the communications with Florida are difficult, while the coast of Texas offers the bay of Galveston, which possesses a circumference of fourteen leagues, and is capable of containing the navies of the entire world!'

'A pretty notion truly,' replied the papers in the interest of Florida, 'that of Galveston bay *below the 29th parallel!* Have we not got the bay of Espiritu Santo, opening precisely upon *the 28th degree*, and by which ships can reach Tampa Town by direct route?'

'A fine bay; half choked with sand!'

'Choked yourselves!' returned the others.

Thus the war went on for several days, when Florida endeavoured to draw her adversary away on to fresh ground; and one morning the *Times* hinted that, the enterprise being essentially American, it ought not to be attempted upon other than purely American territory.

To these words Texas retorted, 'American! are we not as much so as you? Were not Texas and Florida both incorporated into the Union in 1845?'

'Undoubtedly,' replied the *Times*; 'but we have belonged to the Americans ever since 1820.'

'Yes!' returned the *Tribune*; 'after having been Spaniards or English for two hundred years, you were sold to the United States for five million dollars!'

'Well! and why need we blush for that? Was not Louisiana bought from Napoleon in 1803 at the price of sixteen million dollars?'

'Scandalous!' roared the Texas deputies. 'A wretched little strip of country like Florida to dare to compare itself to Texas, who, in place of selling herself, asserted her own independence, drove out the Mexicans in March 2, 1846, and declared herself a federal republic after the victory gained by Samuel Houston, on the banks of the San Jacinto, over the troops of Santa Anna! – a country, in fine, which voluntarily annexed itself to the United States of America!'

'Yes; because it was afraid of the Mexicans!' replied Florida.

'Afraid!' From this moment the state of things became intolerable. A sanguinary encounter seemed daily imminent between the two parties in the streets of Baltimore. It became necessary to keep an eye upon the deputies.

President Barbicane knew not which way to look. Notes, documents, letters full of menaces showered down upon his house. Which side ought he to take? As regarded the appropriation of the soil, the facility of communication, the rapidity of transport, the claims of both States were evenly balanced. As for political prepossessions, they had nothing to do with the question.

This dead block had existed for some little time, when Barbicane resolved to get rid of it all at once. He called a meeting of his colleagues, and laid before them a proposition which, it will be seen, was profoundly sagacious.

'On carefully considering,' he said, 'what is going on now between Florida and Texas, it is clear that the same difficulties will recur with all the towns of the favoured State. The rivalry will descend from State to city, and so on downward. Now Texas possesses eleven towns within the prescribed conditions, which will further dispute the honour and create us new enemies, while Florida has only one. I go in, therefore, for Florida and Tampa Town.'

This decision, on being made known, utterly crushed the

Texan deputies. Seized with an indescribable fury, they addressed threatening letters to the different members of the Gun Club by name. The magistrates had but one course to take, and they took it. They chartered a special train, forced the Texans into it whether they would or no; and they quitted the city with a speed of thirty miles an hour.

Quickly, however, as they were despatched, they found time to hurl one last and bitter sarcasm at their adversaries.

Alluding to the extent of Florida, a mere peninsula confined between two seas, they pretended that it could never sustain the shock of the discharge, and that it would 'bust up' at the very first shot.

'Very well, let it bust up!' replied the Floridans, with a brevity of the days of ancient Sparta.

CHAPTER XII

Urbi et Orbi

THE ASTRONOMICAL, MECHANICAL, and topographical difficulties resolved, finally came the question of finance. The sum required was far too great for any individual, or even any single State, to provide the requisite millions.

President Barbicane undertook, despite of the matter being a purely American affair, to render it one of universal interest, and to request the financial co-operation of all peoples. It was, he maintained, the right and duty of the whole earth to interfere in the affairs of its satellite. The subscription opened at Baltimore extended properly to the whole world – *urbi et orbi*.

This subscription was successful beyond all expectation; notwithstanding that it was a question not of lending but of giving the money. It was a purely disinterested operation in the strictest sense of the term, and offered not the slightest chance of profit.

The effect, however, of Barbicane's communication was not confined to the frontiers of the United States; it crossed the Atlantic and Pacific, invading simultaneously Asia and Europe, Africa and Oceania. The observatories of the Union placed themselves in immediate communication with those of foreign countries. Some, such as those of Paris, Petersburg, Berlin, Stockholm, Hamburg, Malta, Lisbon, Benares, Madras, and others, transmitted their good wishes; the rest maintained a prudent silence, quietly awaiting the result. As for the observatory at Greenwich, seconded as it was by the twenty-two astronomical establishments of Great Britain, it spoke plainly enough. It boldly denied the possibility of success, and pronounced in favour of the theories of Captain Nicholl. But this was nothing more than mere English jealousy.

On the 8th of October President Barbicane published a manifesto full of enthusiasm, in which he made an appeal to 'all persons of good will upon the face of the earth'. This document, translated into all languages, met with immense success.

Subscription lists were opened in all the principal cities of the Union, with a central office at the Baltimore Bank, 9 Baltimore Street.

In addition, subscriptions were received at the following banks in the different states of the two continents:

At Vienna, with S. M. de Rothschild.
At Petersburg, Stieglitz and Co.
At Paris, The Credit Mobilier.
At Stockholm, Tottie and Arfuredson.
At London, N. M. Rothschild and Son.
At Turin, Ardouin and Co.
At Berlin, Mendelssohn.
At Geneva, Lombard, Odier and Co.
At Constantinople, The Ottoman Bank.
At Brussels, J. Lambert.
At Madrid, Daniel Weisweller.
At Amsterdam, Netherlands Credit Co.

At Rome, Torlonia and Co.

At Lisbon, Lecesne.

At Copenhagen, Private Bank.

At Rio de Janeiro, Private Bank.

At Montevideo, Private Bank.

At Valparaiso and Lima, Thomas la Chambre and Co.

At Mexico, Martin Daran and Co.

Three days after the manifesto of President Barbicane $4,000,000 were paid into the different towns of the Union. With such a balance the Gun Club might begin operations at once. But some days later advices were received to the effect that foreign subscriptions were being eagerly taken up. Certain countries distinguished themselves by their liberality; others untied their purse-strings with less facility – a matter of temperament. Figures are, however, more eloquent than words, and here is the official statement of the sums which were paid in to the credit of the Gun Club at the close of the subscription.

Russia paid in as her contingent the enormous sum of 368,733 roubles. No one need be surprised at this, who bears in mind the scientific taste of the Russians, and the impetus which they have given to astronomical studies – thanks to their numerous observatories.

France began by deriding the pretensions of the Americans. The moon served as a pretext for a thousand stale puns and a score of ballads, in which bad taste contested the palm with ignorance. But as formerly the French paid before singing, so now they paid after having had their laugh, and they subscribed for a sum of 1,253,930 francs. At that price they had a right to enjoy themselves a little.

Austria showed herself generous in the midst of her financial crisis. Her public contributions amounted to the sum of 216,000 florins – a perfect godsend.

Fifty-two thousand rix-dollars were the remittance of Sweden and Norway; the amount is large for the country, but it would undoubtedly have been considerably increased had the subscription been opened in Christiana simultaneously with that at Stockholm. For some reason or other the Norwegians do not like to send their money to Sweden.

Prussia, by a remittance of 250,000 thalers, testified her high approval of the enterprise.

Turkey behaved generously; but she had a personal interest in the matter. The moon, in fact, regulates the cycle of her years and her fast of Ramadan. She could not do less than give 1,372,640 piastres; and she gave them with an eagerness which denoted, however, some pressure on the part of the government.

Belgium distinguished herself among the second-rate states by a grant of 513,000 francs – about two centimes per head of her population.

Holland and her colonies interested themselves to the extent of 110,000 florins, only demanding an allowance of five per cent discount for paying ready money.

Denmark, a little contracted in territory, gave nevertheless 9,000 ducats, proving her love for scientific experiments.

The Germanic Confederation pledged itself to 34,285 florins. It was impossible to ask for more; besides, they would not have given it.

Though very much crippled, Italy found 200,000 lire in the pockets of her people. If she had had Venetia she would have done better; but she had not.

The States of the Church thought that they could not send less than 7,040 Roman crowns; and Portugal carried her devotion to science as far as 30,000 cruzados. It was the widow's mite – eighty-six piastres; but self-constituted empires are always rather short of money.

Two hundred and fifty-seven francs, this was the modest contribution of Switzerland to the American work. One must freely admit that she did not see the practical side of the matter. It did not seem to her that the mere despatch of a shot to the moon could possibly establish any relation of affairs with her; and it did not seem prudent to her to embark her capital in so hazardous an enterprise. After all, perhaps she was right.

As to Spain, she could not scrape together more than 110 reals. She gave as an excuse that she had her railways to finish. The truth is, that science is not favourably regarded in that country, it is still in a backward state; and moreover, certain Spaniards, not by any means the least educated, did not form a correct estimate of the bulk of the projectile compared with that of the moon. They feared that it would disturb the established order of things. In that case it were better to keep aloof; which they did to the tune of some reals.

There remained but England; and we know the contemptuous antipathy with which she received Barbicane's proposition. The English have but one soul for the whole twenty-six millions of inhabitants which Great Britain contains. They hinted that the enterprise of the Gun Club was contrary to the 'principle of non-intervention'. And they did not subscribe a single farthing.

At this intimation the Gun Club merely shrugged its shoulders and returned to its great work. When South America, that is to say, Peru, Chile, Brazil, the provinces of La Plata and Colombia, had poured forth their quota into their hands, the sum of $300,000, it found itself in possession of a considerable capital, of which the following is a statement:

United States subscriptions... $4,000,000

Foreign subscriptions....... $1,446,675

– – – – –

Total................ $5,446,675

Such was the sum which the public poured into the treasury of the Gun Club.

Let no one be surprised at the vastness of the amount. The work of casting, boring, masonry, the transport of workmen, their establishment in an almost uninhabited country, the construction of furnaces and workshops, the plant, the powder, the projectile, and incipient expenses, would, according to the estimates, absorb nearly the whole. Certain cannon-shots in the Federal war cost one thousand dollars apiece. This one of President Barbicane, unique in the annals of gunnery, might well cost five thousand times more.

On the 20th of October a contract was entered into with the manufactory at Coldspring, near New York, which during the war had furnished the largest Parrott, cast-iron guns. It was stipulated between the contracting parties that the manufactory of Coldspring should engage to transport to Tampa Town, in southern Florida, the necessary materials for casting the Columbiad. The work was bound to be completed at latest by the 15th of October following, and the cannon delivered in good condition under penalty of a forfeit of one hundred dollars a day to the moment when the moon should again present herself under the same conditions – that is to say, in eighteen years and eleven days.

The engagement of the workmen, their pay, and all the necessary details of the work, devolved upon the Coldspring Company.

This contract, executed in duplicate, was signed by Barbicane, president of the Gun Club, of the one part, and T. Murchison director of the Coldspring manufactory, of the other, who thus executed the deed on behalf of their respective principals.

CHAPTER XIII

Stones Hill

WHEN THE DECISION was arrived at by the Gun Club, to the disparagement of Texas, every one in America, where reading is a universal acquirement, set to work to study the geography of Florida. Never before had there been such a sale for works like 'Bertram's Travels in Florida', 'Roman's Natural History of East and West Florida', 'William's Territory of Florida', and 'Cleland on the Cultivation of the Sugar-Cane in Florida'. It became necessary to issue fresh editions of these works.

Barbicane had something better to do than to read. He desired to see things with his own eyes, and to mark the exact position of the proposed gun. So, without a moment's loss of time, he placed at the disposal of the Cambridge Observatory the funds necessary for the construction of a telescope, and entered into negotiations with the house of Breadwill and Co., of Albany, for the construction of an aluminium projectile of the required size. He then quitted Baltimore, accompanied by J. T. Maston, Major Elphinstone, and the manager of the Coldspring factory.

On the following day, the four fellow-travellers arrived at New Orleans. There they immediately embarked on board the *Tampico*, a despatch-boat belonging to the Federal navy, which the government had placed at their disposal; and, getting up steam, the banks of Louisiana speedily disappeared from sight.

The passage was not long. Two days after starting, the *Tampico*, having made four hundred and eighty miles, came in sight of the coast of Florida. On a nearer approach Barbicane found himself in view of a low, flat country of somewhat barren aspect. After coasting along a series of creeks abounding in lobsters and oysters, the *Tampico* entered the bay of Espiritu Santo, where she finally anchored in a small natural harbour, formed by the *embouchure* of the River Hillisborough, at seven P.M., on the 22nd of October.

Our four passengers disembarked at once. 'Gentlemen,' said Barbicane, 'we have no time to lose; tomorrow we must obtain horses, and proceed to reconnoitre the country.'

Barbicane had scarcely set his foot on shore when three thousand of the inhabitants of Tampa Town came forth to meet him, an honour due to the president who had signalised their country by his choice.

Declining, however, every kind of ovation, Barbicane ensconced himself in a room of the Franklin Hotel.

On the morrow some of the small horses of the Spanish breed, full of vigour and of fire, stood snorting under his windows; but instead of four steeds, here were fifty, together with their riders. Barbicane descended with his three fellow-travellers; and much astonished were they all to find themselves in the midst of such a cavalcade. He remarked that every horseman carried a carbine slung across his shoulders and pistols in his holsters.

On expressing his surprise at these preparations, he was speedily enlightened by a young Floridan, who quietly said:

'Sir, there are Seminoles there.'

CHAPTER XIII

'What do you mean by Seminoles?'

'Savages who scour the prairies. We thought it best, therefore, to escort you on your road.'

'Pooh!' cried J. T. Maston, mounting his steed.

'All right,' said the Floridan; 'but it is true enough, nevertheless.'

'Gentlemen,' answered Barbicane, 'I thank you for your kind attention; but it is time to be off.'

It was five A.M. when Barbicane and his party, quitting Tampa Town, made their way along the coast in the direction of Alifia Creek. This little river falls into Hillisborough Bay twelve miles above Tampa Town. Barbicane and his escort coasted along its right bank to the eastward. Soon the waves of the bay disappeared behind a bend of rising ground, and the Floridan 'champagne' alone offered itself to view.

Florida, discovered on Palm Sunday, in 1512, by Juan Ponce de Leon, was originally named *Pascha Florida*. It little deserved that designation, with its dry and parched coasts. But after some few miles of tract the nature of the soil gradually changes and the country shows itself worthy of the name. Cultivated plains soon appear, where are united all the productions of the northern and tropical floras, terminating in prairies abounding with pineapples and yams, tobacco, rice, cotton-plants, and sugar-canes, which extend beyond reach of sight, flinging their riches broadcast with careless prodigality.

Barbicane appeared highly pleased on observing the progressive elevation of the land; and in answer to a question of J. T. Maston, replied:

'My worthy friend, we cannot do better than sink our Columbiad in these high grounds.'

'To get nearer the moon, perhaps?' said the secretary of the Gun Club.

'Not exactly,' replied Barbicane, smiling; 'do you not see that among these elevated plateaus we shall have a much easier work of it? No struggles with the water-springs, which will save us long expensive tubings; and we shall be working in daylight instead of down a deep and narrow well. Our business, then, is to open our trenches upon ground some hundreds of yards above the level of the sea.'

'You are right, sir,' struck in Murchison, the engineer; 'and, if I mistake not, we shall ere long find a suitable spot for our purpose.'

'I wish we were at the first stroke of the pickaxe,' said the president.

'And I wish we were at the *last*,' cried J. T. Maston.

About ten A.M. the little band had crossed a dozen miles. To fertile plains succeeded a region of forests. There perfumes of the most varied kinds mingled together in tropical profusion. These almost impenetrable forests were composed of pomegranates, orange-trees, citrons, figs, olives, apricots, bananas, huge vines, whose blossoms and fruits rivalled each other in colour and perfume. Beneath the odorous shade of these magnificent trees fluttered and warbled a little world of brilliantly plumaged birds.

J. T. Maston and the major could not repress their admiration on finding themselves in the presence of the glorious beauties of this wealth of nature. President Barbicane, however, less sensitive to these wonders, was in haste to press forward; the very luxuriance of the country was displeasing to him. They hastened onward, therefore, and were compelled to ford several rivers, not without danger, for they were infested with huge alligators from fifteen to eighteen feet long. Maston courageously menaced them with his steel hook, but he only succeeded in frightening some pelicans and teal, while tall flamingos stared stupidly at the party.

At length these denizens of the swamps disappeared in their turn; smaller trees became thinly scattered among less dense thickets – a few isolated groups detached in the midst of endless plains over which ranged herds of startled deer.

'At last,' cried Barbicane, rising in his stirrups, 'here we are at the region of pines!'

'Yes! and of savages too,' replied the major.

In fact, some Seminoles had just come in sight upon the horizon; they rode violently backward and forward on their fleet horses, brandishing their spears or discharging their guns with a dull report. These hostile demonstrations, however, had no effect upon Barbicane and his companions.

They were then occupying the centre of a rocky plain, which the sun scorched with its parching rays. This was formed by a considerable elevation of the soil, which seemed to offer to the members of the Gun Club all the conditions requisite for the construction of their Columbiad.

'Halt!' said Barbicane, reining up. 'Has this place any local appellation?'

'It is called Stones Hill,' replied one of the Floridans.

Barbicane, without saying a word, dismounted, seized his

instruments, and began to note his position with extreme exactness. The little band, drawn up in the rear, watched his proceedings in profound silence.

At this moment the sun passed the meridian. Barbicane, after a few moments, rapidly wrote down the result of his observations, and said:

'This spot is situated eighteen hundred feet above the level of the sea, in 27° 7' N. lat. and 5° 7' W. long. of the meridian of Washington. It appears to me by its rocky and barren character to offer all the conditions requisite for our experiment. On that plain will be raised our magazines, workshops, furnaces, and workmen's huts; and here, from this very spot,' said he, stamping his foot on the summit of Stones Hill, 'hence shall our projectile take its flight into the regions of the Solar World.'

CHAPTER XIV

Pickaxe And Trowel

THE SAME EVENING Barbicane and his companions returned to Tampa Town; and Murchison, the engineer, re-embarked on board the *Tampico* for New Orleans. His object was to enlist an army of workmen, and to collect together the greater part of the materials. The members of the Gun Club remained at Tampa Town, for the purpose of setting on foot the preliminary works by the aid of the people of the country.

Eight days after its departure, the *Tampico* returned into the bay of Espiritu Santo, with a whole flotilla of steamboats. Murchison had succeeded in assembling together fifteen hundred artisans. Attracted by the high pay and considerable bounties offered by the Gun Club, he had enlisted a choice legion of stokers, iron-founders, lime-burners, miners, brick-makers, and artisans of every trade, without distinction of colour. As many of these people brought their families with them, their departure resembled a perfect emigration.

On the 31st of October, at ten o'clock in the morning, the troop disembarked on the quays of Tampa Town; and one may imagine the activity which pervaded that little town, whose population was thus doubled in a single day.

During the first few days they were busy discharging the cargo brought by the flotilla, the machines, and the rations, as well as a large number of huts constructed of iron plates, separately pieced and numbered. At the same period

Barbicane laid the first sleepers of a railway fifteen miles in length, intended to unite Stones Hill with Tampa Town. On the first of November Barbicane quitted Tampa Town with a detachment of workmen; and on the following day the whole town of huts was erected round Stones Hill. This they enclosed with palisades; and in respect of energy and activity, it might have been mistaken for one of the great cities of the Union. Everything was placed under a complete system of discipline, and the works were commenced in most perfect order.

The nature of the soil having been carefully examined, by means of repeated borings, the work of excavation was fixed for the 4th of November.

On that day Barbicane called together his foremen and addressed them as follows: 'You are well aware, my friends, of the object with which I have assembled you together in this wild part of Florida. Our business is to construct a cannon measuring nine feet in its interior diameter, six feet thick, and with a stone revetment of nineteen and a half feet in thickness. We have, therefore, a well of sixty feet in diameter to dig down to a depth of nine hundred feet. This great work must be completed within eight months, so that you have 2,543,400 cubic feet of earth to excavate in 255 days; that is to say, in round numbers, 10,000 cubic feet per day. That which would present no difficulty to a thousand navvies working in open country will be of course more troublesome in a comparatively confined space. However, the thing must be done, and I reckon for its accomplishment upon your courage as much as upon your skill.'

CHAPTER XIV

At eight o'clock the next morning the first stroke of the pickaxe was struck upon the soil of Florida; and from that moment that prince of tools was never inactive for one moment in the hands of the excavators. The gangs relieved each other every three hours.

On the 4th of November fifty workmen commenced digging, in the very centre of the enclosed space on the summit of Stones Hill, a circular hole sixty feet in diameter. The pickaxe first struck upon a kind of black earth, six inches in thickness, which was speedily disposed of. To this earth succeeded two feet of fine sand, which was carefully laid aside as being valuable for serving the casting of the inner mould. After the sand appeared some compact white clay, resembling the chalk of Great Britain, which extended down to a depth of four feet. Then the iron of the picks struck upon the hard bed of the soil; a kind of rock formed of petrified shells, very dry, very solid, and which the picks could with difficulty penetrate. At this point the excavation exhibited a depth of six and a half feet and the work of the masonry was begun.

At the bottom of the excavation they constructed a wheel of oak, a kind of circle strongly bolted together, and of immense strength. The centre of this wooden disc was hollowed out to a diameter equal to the exterior diameter of the Columbiad. Upon this wheel rested the first layers of the masonry, the stones of which were bound together by hydraulic cement, with irresistible tenacity. The workmen, after laying the stones from the circumference to the centre, were thus enclosed within a kind of well twenty-one feet in diameter. When this work was accomplished, the miners resumed their picks and cut away the rock from underneath the wheel itself, taking care to support it as they advanced upon blocks of great thickness. At every two feet which the hole gained in depth they successively withdrew the blocks. The wheel then sank little by little, and with it the massive ring of masonry, on the upper bed of which the masons laboured incessantly, always reserving some vent holes to permit the escape of gas during the operation of the casting.

This kind of work required on the part of the workmen extreme nicety and minute attention. More than one, in digging underneath the wheel, was dangerously injured by the splinters of stone. But their ardour never relaxed, night or day. By day they worked under the rays of the scorching sun; by night, under the gleam of the electric light. The sounds of the picks against the rock, the bursting of mines, the grinding of the machines, the wreaths of smoke scattered through the air, traced around Stones Hill a circle of terror which the herds of buffaloes and the war parties of the Seminoles never ventured to pass. Nevertheless, the works advanced regularly, as the steam-cranes actively removed the rubbish. Of unexpected obstacles there was little account; and with regard to foreseen difficulties, they were speedily disposed of.

At the expiration of the first month the well had attained the depth assigned for that lapse of time, namely, 112 feet. This depth was doubled in December, and trebled in January.

During the month of February the workmen had to contend with a sheet of water which made its way right across the outer soil. It became necessary to employ very powerful pumps and compressed-air engines to drain it off, so as to close up the orifice from whence it issued; just as one stops a leak on board ship. They at last succeeded in getting the upper hand of these untoward streams; only, in consequence of the loosening of the soil, the wheel partly gave way, and a slight partial settlement ensued. This accident cost the life of several workmen.

No fresh occurrence thenceforward arrested the progress of the operation; and on the 10th of June, twenty days before the expiration of the period fixed by Barbicane, the well, lined throughout with its facing of stone, had attained the depth of 900 feet. At the bottom the masonry rested upon a massive block measuring thirty feet in thickness, while on the upper portion it was level with the surrounding soil.

President Barbicane and the members of the Gun Club warmly congratulated their engineer Murchison; the cyclopean work had been accomplished with extraordinary rapidity.

During these eight months Barbicane never quitted Stones Hill for a single instant. Keeping ever close by the work of excavation, he busied himself incessantly with the welfare and health of his workpeople, and was singularly fortunate in warding off the epidemics common to large communities of men, and so disastrous in those regions of the globe which are exposed to the influences of tropical climates.

Many workmen, it is true, paid with their lives for the rashness inherent in these dangerous labours; but these mishaps are impossible to be avoided, and they are classed among the details with which the Americans trouble themselves but little. They have in fact more regard for human nature in general than for the individual in particular.

Nevertheless, Barbicane professed opposite principles to these, and put them in force at every opportunity. So, thanks to his care, his intelligence, his useful intervention in all difficulties, his prodigious and humane sagacity, the average of accidents did not exceed that of transatlantic countries, noted for their excessive precautions – France, for instance, among others, where they reckon about one accident for every two hundred thousand francs of work.

CHAPTER XV

The Fete of the Casting

DURING THE EIGHT months which were employed in the work of excavation the preparatory works of the casting had been carried on simultaneously with extreme rapidity. A stranger arriving at Stones Hill would have been surprised at the spectacle offered to his view.

At 600 yards from the well, and circularly arranged around it as a central point, rose 1,200 reverberating ovens, each six feet in diameter, and separated from each other by an interval of three feet. The circumference occupied by these 1,200 ovens presented a length of two miles. Being all constructed on the same plan, each with its high quadrangular chimney, they produced a most singular effect.

It will be remembered that on their third meeting the committee had decided to use cast iron for the Columbiad, and in particular the white description. This metal, in fact, is the most tenacious, the most ductile, and the most malleable, and consequently suitable for all moulding operations; and when smelted with pit coal, is of superior quality for all engineering works requiring great resisting power, such as cannon, steam boilers, hydraulic presses, and the like.

Cast iron, however, if subjected to only one single fusion, is rarely sufficiently homogeneous; and it requires a second fusion completely to refine it by dispossessing it of its last earthly deposits. So long before being forwarded to Tampa

Town, the iron ore, molten in the great furnaces of Coldspring, and brought into contact with coal and silicium heated to a high temperature, was carburised and transformed into cast iron. After this first operation, the metal was sent on to Stones Hill. They had, however, to deal with 136,000,000 pounds of iron, a quantity far too costly to send by railway. The cost of transport would have been double that of material. It appeared preferable to freight vessels at New York, and to load them with the iron in bars. This, however, required not less than sixty-eight vessels of 1,000 tons, a veritable fleet, which, quitting New York on the 3rd of May, on the 10th of the same month ascended the Bay of Espiritu Santo, and discharged their cargoes, without dues, in the port at Tampa Town. Thence the iron was transported by rail to Stones Hill, and about the middle of January this enormous mass of metal was delivered at its destination.

It will easily be understood that 1,200 furnaces were not too many to melt simultaneously these 60,000 tons of iron. Each of these furnaces contained nearly 140,000 pounds weight of metal. They were all built after the model of those which served for the casting of the Rodman gun; they were trapezoidal in shape, with a high elliptical arch. These furnaces, constructed of fireproof brick, were especially adapted for burning pit coal, with a flat bottom upon which the iron bars were laid. This bottom, inclined at an angle of 25 degrees, allowed the metal to flow into the receiving troughs; and the 1,200 converging trenches carried the molten metal down to the central well.

The day following that on which the works of the masonry and boring had been completed, Barbicane set to work upon the central mould. His object now was to raise within the centre of the well, and with a coincident axis, a cylinder 900 feet high, and nine feet in diameter, which should exactly fill up the space reserved for the bore of the Columbiad. This cylinder was composed of a mixture of clay and sand, with the addition of a little hay and straw. The space left between the mould and the masonry was intended to be filled up by the molten metal, which would thus form the walls six feet in thickness. This cylinder, in order to maintain its equilibrium, had to be bound by iron bands, and firmly fixed at certain intervals by cross-clamps fastened into the stone lining; after the castings these would be buried in the block of metal, leaving no external projection.

This operation was completed on the 8th of July, and the run of the metal was fixed for the following day.

'This *fete* of the casting will be a grand ceremony,' said J. T. Maston to his friend Barbicane.

'Undoubtedly,' said Barbicane; 'but it will not be a public *fete*.'

'What! will you not open the gates of the enclosure to all comers?'

'I must be very careful, Maston. The casting of the Columbiad is an extremely delicate, not to say a dangerous operation, and I should prefer its being done privately. At the discharge of the projectile, a *fete* if you like – till then, no!'

The president was right. The operation involved unforeseen dangers, which a great influx of spectators would have hindered him from averting. It was necessary to preserve complete freedom of movement. No one was admitted within the enclosure except a delegation of members of the Gun Club, who had made the voyage to Tampa Town. Among these was the brisk Bilsby, Tom Hunter, Colonel Blomsberry, Major Elphinstone, General Morgan, and the rest of the lot to whom the casting of the Columbiad was a matter of personal interest. J. T. Maston became their cicerone. He omitted no point of detail; he conducted them throughout the magazines, workshops, through the midst of the engines, and compelled them to visit the whole 1,200 furnaces one after the other. At the end of the twelve-hundredth visit they were pretty well knocked up.

The casting was to take place at twelve o'clock precisely. The previous evening each furnace had been charged with 114,000 pounds weight of metal in bars disposed cross-ways to each other, so as to allow the hot air to circulate freely between them. At daybreak the 1,200 chimneys vomited their torrents of flame into the air, and the ground was agitated with dull tremblings. As many pounds of metal as there were to cast, so many pounds of coal were there to burn. Thus there were 68,000 tons of coal which projected in the face of the sun a thick curtain of smoke. The heat soon became insupportable within the circle of furnaces, the rumbling of which resembled the rolling of thunder. The powerful ventilators added their continuous blasts and saturated with oxygen the glowing plates. The operation, to be successful, required to be conducted with great rapidity. On a signal given by a cannon-shot each furnace was to give vent to the molten iron and completely to empty itself. These arrangements made, foremen and workmen waited the preconcerted moment with an impatience mingled with a certain amount of emotion. Not a soul remained within the enclosure. Each superintendent took his post by the aperture of the run.

Barbicane and his colleagues, perched on a neighbouring eminence, assisted at the operation. In front of them was a piece of artillery ready to give fire on the signal from the engineer. Some minutes before midday the first driblets of metal began to flow; the reservoirs filled little by little; and, by the time that the whole melting was completely accomplished, it was kept in abeyance for a few minutes in order to facilitate the separation of foreign substances.

Twelve o'clock struck! A gunshot suddenly pealed forth and shot its flame into the air. Twelve hundred melting-troughs were simultaneously opened and twelve hundred fiery serpents crept toward the central well, unrolling their incandescent curves. There, down they plunged with a terrific noise into a depth of 900 feet. It was an exciting and a magnificent spectacle. The ground trembled, while these molten waves, launching into the sky their wreaths of smoke, evaporated the moisture of the mould and hurled it upward through the vent-holes of the stone lining in the form of dense vapour-clouds. These artificial clouds unrolled their thick spirals to a height of 1,000 yards into the air. A savage, wandering somewhere beyond the limits of the horizon, might have believed that some new crater was forming in the bosom of Florida, although there was neither any eruption, nor typhoon, nor storm, nor struggle of the elements, nor any of those terrible phenomena which nature is capable of producing. No, it was man alone who had produced these reddish vapours, these gigantic flames worthy of a volcano itself, these tremendous vibrations resembling the shock of an earthquake, these reverberations rivalling those of hurricanes and storms; and it was his hand which precipitated into an abyss, dug by himself, a whole Niagara of molten metal!

CHAPTER XVI

The Columbiad

HAD THE CASTING succeeded? They were reduced to mere conjecture. There was indeed every reason to expect success, since the mould had absorbed the entire mass of the molten metal; still some considerable time must elapse before they could arrive at any certainty upon the matter.

The patience of the members of the Gun Club was sorely tried during this period of time. But they could do nothing. J. T. Maston escaped roasting by a miracle. Fifteen days after the casting an immense column of smoke was still rising in the open sky and the ground burned the soles of the feet within a radius of two hundred feet round the summit of Stones Hill. It was impossible to approach nearer. All they could do was to wait with what patience they might.

'Here we are at the 10th of August,' exclaimed J. T. Maston one morning, 'only four months to the 1st of December! We shall never be ready in time!' Barbicane said nothing, but his silence covered serious irritation.

However, daily observations revealed a certain change going on in the state of the ground. About the 15th of August the vapours ejected had sensibly diminished in intensity and thickness. Some days afterward the earth exhaled only a slight puff of smoke, the last breath of the monster enclosed within its circle of stone. Little by little the belt of heat contracted, until on the 22nd of August,

Barbicane, his colleagues, and the engineer were enabled to set foot on the iron sheet which lay level upon the summit of Stones Hill.

'At last!' exclaimed the president of the Gun Club, with an immense sigh of relief.

The work was resumed the same day. They proceeded at once to extract the interior mould, for the purpose of clearing out the boring of the piece. Pickaxes and boring irons were set to work without intermission. The clayey and sandy soils had acquired extreme hardness under the action of the heat; but, by the aid of the machines, the rubbish on being dug out was rapidly carted away on railway wagons; and such was the ardour of the work, so persuasive the arguments of Barbicane's dollars, that by the 3rd of September all traces of the mould had entirely disappeared.

Immediately the operation of boring was commenced; and by the aid of powerful machines, a few weeks later, the inner surface of the immense tube had been rendered perfectly cylindrical, and the bore of the piece had acquired a thorough polish.

At length, on the 22nd of September, less than a twelvemonth after Barbicane's original proposition, the enormous weapon, accurately bored, and exactly vertically pointed, was ready for work. There was only the moon now to wait for; and they were pretty sure that she would not fail in the rendezvous.

The ecstasy of J. T. Maston knew no bounds, and he narrowly escaped a frightful fall while staring down the tube. But for the strong hand of Colonel Blomsberry, the worthy secretary, like a modern Erostratus, would have found his death in the depths of the Columbiad.

The cannon was then finished; there was no possible doubt as to its perfect completion. So, on the 6th of October, Captain Nicholl opened an account between himself and President Barbicane, in which he debited himself to the latter in the sum of two thousand dollars. One may believe that the captain's wrath was increased to its highest point, and must have made him seriously ill. However, he had still three bets of three, four, and five thousand dollars, respectively; and if he gained two out of these, his position would not be very bad. But the money question did not enter into his calculations; it was the success of his rival in casting a cannon against which iron plates sixty feet thick would have been ineffectual, that dealt him a terrible blow.

After the 23rd of September the enclosure of Stones Hill was thrown open to the public; and it will be easily imagined what was the concourse of visitors to this spot! There was an incessant flow of people to and from Tampa Town and the place, which resembled a procession, or rather, in fact, a pilgrimage.

It was already clear to be seen that, on the day of the experiment itself, the aggregate of spectators would be counted by millions; for they were already arriving from all parts of the earth upon this narrow strip of promontory. Europe was emigrating to America.

Up to that time, however, it must be confessed, the curiosity of the numerous comers was but scantily gratified. Most had counted upon witnessing the spectacle of the casting, and they were treated to nothing but smoke. This was sorry food for hungry eyes; but Barbicane would admit no one to that operation. Then ensued grumbling, discontent, murmurs; they blamed the president, taxed him with dictatorial conduct. His proceedings were declared 'un-American'. There was very nearly a riot round Stones Hill; but Barbicane remained inflexible. When, however, the Columbiad was entirely finished, this state of closed doors could no longer be maintained; besides, it would have been bad taste, and even imprudence, to affront the public feeling. Barbicane, therefore, opened the enclosure to all comers; but, true to his practical disposition, he determined to coin money out of the public curiosity.

It was something, indeed, to be enabled to contemplate this immense Columbiad; but to descend into its depths, this seemed to the Americans the *ne plus ultra* of earthly felicity. Consequently, there was not one curious spectator who was not willing to give himself the treat of visiting the interior of this great metallic abyss. Baskets suspended from steam-cranes permitted them to satisfy their curiosity. There was a perfect mania. Women, children, old men, all made it a point of duty to penetrate the mysteries of the colossal gun. The fare for the descent was fixed at five dollars per head; and despite this high charge, during the two months which preceded the experiment, the influx of visitors enabled the Gun Club to pocket nearly five hundred thousand dollars!

It is needless to say that the first visitors of the Columbiad were the members of the Gun Club. This privilege was justly reserved for that illustrious body. The ceremony took place on the 25th of September. A basket of honour took down the president, J. T. Maston, Major Elphinstone, General Morgan, Colonel Blomsberry, and other members of the club, to the number of ten in all. How hot it was at the bottom of that long tube of metal! They were half suffocated. But what delight! What ecstasy! A table had been laid with six covers on the massive stone which formed the bottom of the Columbiad, and lighted by a jet of electric light resembling that of day itself. Numerous exquisite dishes, which seemed to descend from heaven, were placed successively before the guests, and the richest wines of France flowed in profusion during this splendid repast, served nine hundred feet beneath the surface of the earth!

The festival was animated, not to say somewhat noisy. Toasts flew backward and forward. They drank to the earth and to her satellite, to the Gun Club, the Union, the Moon, Diana, Phoebe, Selene, the 'peaceful courier of the night!' All the hurrahs, carried upward upon the sonorous waves of the immense acoustic tube, arrived with the sound of thunder at its mouth; and the multitude ranged round Stones Hill heartily united their shouts with those of the ten revellers hidden from view at the bottom of the gigantic Columbiad.

J. T. Maston was no longer master of himself. Whether he shouted or gesticulated, ate or drank most, would be a difficult matter to determine. At all events, he would not have given his place up for an empire, 'not even if the cannon – loaded, primed, and fired at that very moment – were to blow him in pieces into the planetary world'.

CHAPTER XVII

A Telegraphic Dispatch

THE GREAT WORKS undertaken by the Gun Club had now virtually come to an end; and two months still remained before the day for the discharge of the shot to the moon. To the general impatience these two months appeared as long as years! Hitherto the smallest details of the operation had been daily chronicled by the journals, which the public devoured with eager eyes.

Just at this moment a circumstance, the most unexpected, the most extraordinary and incredible, occurred to rouse afresh their panting spirits, and to throw every mind into a state of the most violent excitement.

One day, the 30th of September, at 3:47 P.M., a telegram, transmitted by cable from Valentia (Ireland) to Newfoundland and the American mainland, arrived at the address of President Barbicane.

The president tore open the envelope, read the dispatch, and, despite his remarkable powers of self-control, his lips turned pale and his eyes grew dim, on reading the twenty words of this telegram.

Here is the text of the dispatch, which figures now in the archives of the Gun Club:

FRANCE, PARIS,
30 September, 4 A.M.

Barbicane, Tampa Town, Florida, United States. Substitute for your spherical shell a cylindro-conical projectile. I shall go inside. Shall arrive by steamer *Atlanta*.

MICHEL ARDAN.

CHAPTER XVIII

The Passenger of the Atlanta

IF THIS ASTOUNDING news, instead of flying through the electric wires, had simply arrived by post in the ordinary sealed envelope, Barbicane would not have hesitated a moment. He would have held his tongue about it, both as a measure of prudence, and in order not to have to reconsider his plans. This telegram might be a cover for some jest, especially as it came from a Frenchman. What human being would ever have conceived the idea of such a journey? and, if such a person really existed, he must be an idiot, whom one would shut up in a lunatic ward, rather than within the walls of the projectile.

The contents of the dispatch, however, speedily became known; for the telegraphic officials possessed but little discretion, and Michel Ardan's proposition ran at once throughout the several States of the Union. Barbicane had, therefore, no further motives for keeping silence. Consequently, he called together such of his colleagues as were at the moment in Tampa Town, and without any expression of his own opinions simply read to them the laconic text itself. It was received with every possible variety of expressions of doubt, incredulity, and derision from every one, with the exception of J. T. Maston, who exclaimed, 'It is a grand idea, however!'

When Barbicane originally proposed to send a shot to the moon every one looked upon the enterprise as simple and practicable enough – a mere question of gunnery; but when a person, professing to be a reasonable being, offered to take passage within the projectile, the whole thing became a farce, or, in plainer language, a humbug.

One question, however, remained. Did such a being exist? This telegram flashed across the depths of the Atlantic, the designation of the vessel on board which he was to take his passage, the date assigned for his speedy arrival, all combined to impart a certain character of reality to the proposal. They must get some clearer notion of the matter. Scattered groups of inquirers at length condensed themselves into a compact crowd, which made straight for the residence of President Barbicane. That worthy individual was keeping quiet with the intention of watching events as they arose. But he had forgotten to take into account the public impatience; and it was with no pleasant countenance that he watched the population of Tampa Town gathering under his windows. The murmurs and vociferations below presently obliged him to appear. He came forward, therefore, and on silence being procured, a citizen put point-blank to him the following question: 'Is the person mentioned in the telegram, under the name of Michel Ardan, on his way here? Yes or no.'

'Gentlemen,' replied Barbicane, 'I know no more than you do.'

'We must know,' roared the impatient voices.

'Time will show,' calmly replied the president.

'Time has no business to keep a whole country in suspense,' replied the orator. 'Have you altered the plans of the projectile according to the request of the telegram?'

CHAPTER XVIII

'Not yet, gentlemen; but you are right! we must have better information to go by. The telegraph must complete its information.'

'To the telegraph!' roared the crowd.

Barbicane descended; and heading the immense assemblage, led the way to the telegraph office. A few minutes later a telegram was dispatched to the secretary of the underwriters at Liverpool, requesting answers to the following queries:

'About the ship *Atlanta* – when did she leave Europe? Had she on board a Frenchman named Michel Ardan?'

Two hours afterward Barbicane received information too exact to leave room for the smallest remaining doubt.

'The steamer *Atlanta* from Liverpool put to sea on the 2nd of October, bound for Tampa Town, having on board a Frenchman borne on the list of passengers by the name of Michel Ardan.'

That very evening he wrote to the house of Breadwill and Co., requesting them to suspend the casting of the projectile until the receipt of further orders. On the 10th of October, at nine A.M., the semaphores of the Bahama Canal signalled a thick smoke on the horizon. Two hours later a large steamer exchanged signals with them. The name of the *Atlanta* flew at once over Tampa Town. At four o'clock the English vessel entered the Bay of Espiritu Santo. At five it crossed the passage of Hillisborough Bay at full steam. At six she cast anchor at Port Tampa. The anchor had scarcely caught the sandy bottom when five hundred boats surrounded the *Atlanta*, and the steamer was taken by assault. Barbicane was the first to set foot on deck, and in a voice of which he vainly tried to conceal the emotion, called 'Michel Ardan'.

'Here!' replied an individual perched on the poop.

Barbicane, with arms crossed, looked fixedly at the passenger of the *Atlanta*.

He was a man of about forty-two years of age, of large build, but slightly round-shouldered. His massive head momentarily shook a shock of reddish hair, which resembled a lion's mane. His face was short with a broad forehead, and furnished with a moustache as bristly as a cat's, and little patches of yellowish whiskers upon full cheeks. Round, wildish eyes, slightly near-sighted, completed a physiognomy essentially feline. His nose was firmly shaped, his mouth particularly sweet in expression, high forehead, intelligent and furrowed with wrinkles like a newly-ploughed field. The body was powerfully developed and firmly fixed upon long legs. Muscular arms, and a general air of decision gave him the appearance of a hardy, jolly companion. He was dressed in a suit of ample dimensions, loose neckerchief, open shirt-collar, disclosing a robust neck; his cuffs were invariably unbuttoned, through which appeared a pair of red hands.

On the bridge of the steamer, in the midst of the crowd, he bustled to and fro, never still for a moment, 'dragging his anchors', as the sailors say, gesticulating, making free with everybody, biting his nails with nervous avidity. He was one of those originals which nature sometimes invents in the freak of a moment, and of which she then breaks the mould.

Among other peculiarities, this curiosity gave himself out for a sublime ignoramus, 'like Shakespeare', and professed supreme contempt for all scientific men. Those 'fellows', as he called them, 'are only fit to mark the points, while we play the game'. He was, in fact, a thorough Bohemian, adventurous, but not an adventurer; a harebrained fellow, a kind of Icarus, only possessing relays of wings. For the rest, he was ever in scrapes, ending invariably by falling on his feet, like those little figures which they sell for children's toys. In a few words, his motto was 'I have my opinions', and the love of the impossible constituted his ruling passion.

Such was the passenger of the *Atlanta*, always excitable, as if boiling under the action of some internal fire by the character of his physical organisation. If ever two individuals offered a striking contrast to each other, these were certainly Michel Ardan and the Yankee Barbicane; both, moreover, being equally enterprising and daring, each in his own way.

The scrutiny which the president of the Gun Club had instituted regarding this new rival was quickly interrupted by the shouts and hurrahs of the crowd. The cries became at last so uproarious, and the popular enthusiasm assumed so personal a form, that Michel Ardan, after having shaken hands some thousands of times, at the imminent risk of leaving his fingers behind him, was fain at last to make a bolt for his cabin.

Barbicane followed him without uttering a word.

'You are Barbicane, I suppose?' said Michel Ardan, in a tone of voice in which he would have addressed a friend of twenty years' standing.

'Yes,' replied the president of the Gun Club.

'All right! how d'ye do, Barbicane? how are you getting on – pretty well? that's right.'

'So,' said Barbicane without further preliminary, 'you are quite determined to go.'

'Quite decided.'

'Nothing will stop you?'

'Nothing. Have you modified your projectile according to my telegram?'

'I waited for your arrival. But,' asked Barbicane again, 'have you carefully reflected?'

'Reflected? have I any time to spare? I find an opportunity of making a tour in the moon, and I mean to profit by it. There is the whole gist of the matter.'

Barbicane looked hard at this man who spoke so lightly of his project with such complete absence of anxiety. 'But, at least,' said he, 'you have some plans, some means of carrying your project into execution?'

'Excellent, my dear Barbicane; only permit me to offer one remark: my wish is to tell my story once for all, to everybody, and then have done with it; then there will be no need for recapitulation. So, if you have no objection, assemble your friends, colleagues, the whole town, all Florida, all America if you like, and to-morrow I shall be ready to explain my plans and answer any objections whatever that may be advanced. You may rest assured I shall wait without stirring. Will that suit you?'

'All right,' replied Barbicane.

So saying, the president left the cabin and informed the crowd of the proposal of Michel Ardan. His words were received with clappings of hands and shouts of joy. They had removed all difficulties. To-morrow every one would contemplate at his ease this European hero. However, some of the spectators, more infatuated than the rest, would not leave the deck of the *Atlanta*. They passed the night on board. Among others J. T. Maston got his hook fixed in the combing of the poop, and it pretty nearly required the capstan to get it out again.

'He is a hero! a hero!' he cried, a theme of which he was never tired of ringing the changes; 'and we are only like weak, silly women, compared with this European!'

As to the president, after having suggested to the visitors it was time to retire, he re-entered the passenger's cabin, and remained there till the bell of the steamer made it midnight.

But then the two rivals in popularity shook hands heartily and parted on terms of intimate friendship.

CHAPTER XIX

A Monster Meeting

ON THE FOLLOWING day Barbicane, fearing that indiscreet questions might be put to Michel Ardan, was desirous of reducing the number of the audience to a few of the initiated, his own colleagues for instance. He might as well have tried to check the Falls of Niagara! he was compelled, therefore, to give up the idea, and let his new friend run the chances of a public conference. The place chosen for this monster meeting was a vast plain situated in the rear of the town. In a few hours, thanks to the help of the shipping in port, an immense roofing of canvas was stretched over the parched prairie, and protected it from the burning rays of the sun. There three hundred thousand people braved for many hours the stifling heat while awaiting the arrival of the Frenchman. Of this crowd of spectators a first set could both see and hear; a second set saw badly and heard nothing at all; and as for the third, it could neither see nor hear anything at all. At three o'clock Michel Ardan made his appearance, accompanied by the principal members of the Gun Club. He was supported on his right by President Barbicane, and on his left by J. T. Maston, more radiant than the midday sun, and nearly as ruddy. Ardan mounted a platform, from the top of which his view extended over a sea of black hats.

He exhibited not the slightest embarrassment; he was just as gay, familiar, and pleasant as if he were at home. To the hurrahs which greeted him he replied by a graceful bow; then, waving his hands to request silence, he spoke in perfectly correct English as follows:

'Gentlemen, despite the very hot weather I request your patience for a short time while I offer some explanations regarding the projects which seem to have so interested you. I am neither an orator nor a man of science, and I had no idea of addressing you in public; but my friend Barbicane has told me that you would like to hear me, and I am quite at your service. Listen to me, therefore, with your six hundred thousand ears, and please excuse the faults of the speaker. Now pray do not forget that you see before you a perfect ignoramus whose ignorance goes so far that he cannot even understand the difficulties! It seemed to him that it was a matter quite simple, natural, and easy to take one's place in a projectile and start for the moon! That journey must be undertaken sooner or later; and, as for the mode of locomotion adopted, it follows simply the law of progress. Man began by walking on all-fours; then, one fine day, on two feet; then in a carriage; then in a stage-coach; and lastly by railway. Well, the projectile is the vehicle of the future, and the planets themselves are nothing else! Now some of you, gentlemen, may imagine that the velocity we propose to impart to it is extravagant. It is nothing of the kind. All the stars exceed it in rapidity, and the earth herself is at this moment carrying us round the sun at three times as rapid a rate, and yet she is a mere lounger on the way compared with many others of the planets! And her velocity is constantly decreasing. Is it not evident, then, I ask you, that there will some day appear velocities far greater than these, of which light or electricity will probably be the mechanical agent?

'Yes, gentlemen,' continued the orator, 'in spite of the opinions of certain narrow-minded people, who would shut up the human race upon this globe, as within some magic circle which it must never outstep, we shall one day travel to the moon, the planets, and the stars, with the same facility, rapidity, and certainty as we now make the voyage from Liverpool to New York! Distance is but a relative expression, and must end by being reduced to zero.'

The assembly, strongly predisposed as they were in favour of the French hero, were slightly staggered at this bold theory. Michel Ardan perceived the fact.

'Gentlemen,' he continued with a pleasant smile, 'you do not seem quite convinced. Very good! Let us reason the matter out. Do you know how long it would take for an express train to reach the moon? Three hundred days; no more! And what is that? The distance is no more than nine times the circumference of the earth; and there are no sailors or travellers, of even moderate activity, who have not made longer journeys than that in their lifetime. And now consider that I shall be only ninety-seven hours on my journey. Ah! I see you are reckoning that the moon is a long way off from the earth, and that one must think twice before making the experiment. What would you say, then, if we were talking of going to Neptune, which revolves at a distance of more than two thousand, seven hundred and twenty millions of miles from the sun! And yet what is that compared with the distance of the fixed stars, some of which, such as Arcturus, are billions of miles distant from us? And then you talk of the distance which separates the planets from the sun! And there are people who affirm that such a thing as distance exists. Absurdity, folly, idiotic nonsense! Would you know what I think of our own solar universe? Shall I tell you my theory? It is very simple! In my opinion the solar system is a solid homogeneous body; the planets which compose it are in actual contact with each other; and whatever space exists between them is nothing more than the space which separates the molecules of the densest metal, such as silver, iron, or platinum! I have the right, therefore, to affirm, and I repeat, with the conviction which must penetrate all your minds, "Distance is but an empty name; distance does not really exist!"'

'Hurrah!' cried one voice (need it be said it was that of J. T. Maston). 'Distance does not exist!' And overcome by the energy of his movements, he nearly fell from the platform to the ground. He just escaped a severe fall, which would have proved to him that distance was by no means an empty name.

'Gentlemen,' resumed the orator, 'I repeat that the distance between the earth and her satellite is a mere trifle, and undeserving of serious consideration. I am convinced that before twenty years are over one-half of our earth will have paid a visit to the moon. Now, my worthy friends, if you have any question to put to me, you will, I fear, sadly embarrass a poor man like myself; still I will do my best to answer you.'

CHAPTER XIX

Up to this point the president of the Gun Club had been satisfied with the turn which the discussion had assumed. It became now, however, desirable to divert Ardan from questions of a practical nature, with which he was doubtless far less conversant. Barbicane, therefore, hastened to get in a word, and began by asking his new friend whether he thought that the moon and the planets were inhabited.

'You put before me a great problem, my worthy president,' replied the orator, smiling. 'Still, men of great intelligence, such as Plutarch, Swedenborg, Bernardin de St. Pierre, and others have, if I mistake not, pronounced in the affirmative. Looking at the question from the natural philosopher's point of view, I should say that nothing useless existed in the world; and, replying to your question by another, I should venture to assert, that if these worlds are habitable, they either are, have been, or will be inhabited.'

'No one could answer more logically or fairly,' replied the president. 'The question then reverts to this: are these worlds habitable? For my own part I believe they are.'

'For myself, I feel certain of it,' said Michel Ardan.

'Nevertheless,' retorted one of the audience, 'there are many arguments against the habitability of the worlds. The conditions of life must evidently be greatly modified upon the majority of them. To mention only the planets, we should be either broiled alive in some, or frozen to death in others, according as they are more or less removed from the sun.'

'I regret,' replied Michel Ardan, 'that I have not the honour of personally knowing my contradictor, for I would have attempted to answer him. His objection has its merits, I admit; but I think we may successfully combat it, as well as all others which affect the habitability of other worlds. If I were a natural philosopher, I would tell him that if less of caloric were set in motion upon the planets which are nearest to the sun, and more, on the contrary, upon those which are farthest removed from it, this simple fact would alone suffice to equalise the heat, and to render the temperature of those worlds supportable by beings organised like ourselves. If I were a naturalist, I would tell him that, according to some illustrious men of science, nature has furnished us with instances upon the earth of animals existing under very varying conditions of life; that fish respire in a medium fatal to other animals; that amphibious creatures possess a double existence very difficult of explanation; that certain denizens of the seas maintain life at enormous depths, and there support a pressure equal to that of fifty or sixty atmospheres without being crushed; that several aquatic insects, insensible to temperature, are met with equally among boiling springs and in the frozen plains of the Polar Sea; in fine, that we cannot help recognising in nature a diversity of means of operation oftentimes incomprehensible, but not the less real. If I were a chemist, I would tell him that the aerolites, bodies evidently formed exteriorly of our terrestrial globe, have, upon analysis, revealed indisputable traces of carbon, a substance which owes its origin solely to organised beings, and which, according to the experiments of Reichenbach, must necessarily itself have been endued with animation. And lastly, were I a theologian, I would tell him that the scheme of the Divine Redemption, according to St. Paul, seems to be applicable, not merely to the earth, but to all the celestial worlds. But, unfortunately, I am neither theologian, nor chemist, nor naturalist, nor philosopher; therefore, in my absolute ignorance of the great laws which govern the universe, I confine myself to saying in reply, "I do not know whether the worlds are inhabited or not: and since I do not know, I am going to see!"'

Whether Michel Ardan's antagonist hazarded any further arguments or not it is impossible to say, for the uproarious shouts of the crowd would not allow any expression of opinion to gain a hearing. On silence being restored, the triumphant orator contented himself with adding the following remarks:

'Gentlemen, you will observe that I have but slightly touched upon this great question. There is another altogether different line of argument in favour of the habitability of the stars, which I omit for the present. I only desire to call attention to one point. To those who maintain that the planets are *not* inhabited one may reply: you might be perfectly in the right, if you could only show that the earth is the best possible world, in spite of what Voltaire has said. She has but *one* satellite, while Jupiter, Uranus, Saturn, Neptune have each several, an advantage by no means to be despised. But that which renders our own globe so uncomfortable is the inclination of its axis to the plane of its orbit. Hence the inequality of days and nights; hence the disagreeable diversity of the seasons. On the surface of our unhappy spheroid we are always either too hot or too cold; we are frozen in winter, broiled in summer; it is the planet of rheumatism, coughs, bronchitis; while on the surface of Jupiter, for example, where the axis is but slightly inclined, the inhabitants may enjoy uniform temperatures. It possesses zones of perpetual springs, summers, autumns, and winters; every Jovian may choose for himself what climate he likes, and there spend the whole of his life in security from all variations of temperature. You will, I am sure, readily admit this superiority of Jupiter over our own planet, to say nothing of his years, which each equal twelve of ours! Under such auspices and such marvellous conditions of existence, it appears to me that the inhabitants of so fortunate a world must be in every respect superior to ourselves. All we require, in order to attain such perfection, is the mere trifle of having an axis of rotation less inclined to the plane of its orbit!'

'Hurrah!' roared an energetic voice, 'let us unite our efforts, invent the necessary machines, and rectify the earth's axis!'

A thunder of applause followed this proposal, the author of which was, of course, no other than J. T. Maston. And, in all probability, if the truth must be told, if the Yankees could only have found a point of application for it, they would have constructed a lever capable of raising the earth and rectifying its axis. It was just this deficiency which baffled these daring mechanicians.

CHAPTER XX

Attack and Riposte

As soon as the excitement had subsided, the following words were heard uttered in a strong and determined voice:

'Now that the speaker has favoured us with so much imagination, would he be so good as to return to his subject, and give us a little practical view of the question?'

All eyes were directed toward the person who spoke. He was a little dried-up man, of an active figure, with an American 'goatee' beard. Profiting by the different movements in the crowd, he had managed by degrees to gain the front row of spectators. There, with arms crossed and stern gaze, he watched the hero of the meeting. After having put his question he remained silent, and appeared to take no notice of the thousands of looks directed toward himself, nor of the murmur of disapprobation excited by his words. Meeting at first with no reply, he repeated his question with marked emphasis, adding, 'We are here to talk about the *moon* and not about the *earth*.'

'You are right, sir,' replied Michel Ardan; 'the discussion has become irregular. We will return to the moon.'

'Sir,' said the unknown, 'you pretend that our satellite is inhabited. Very good, but if Selenites do exist, that race of beings assuredly must live without breathing, for – I warn you for your own sake – there is not the smallest particle of air on the surface of the moon.'

At this remark Ardan pushed up his shock of red hair; he saw that he was on the point of being involved in a struggle with this person upon the very gist of the whole question. He looked sternly at him in his turn and said:

'Oh! so there is no air in the moon? And pray, if you are so good, who ventures to affirm that?'

'The men of science.'

'Really?'

'Really.'

'Sir,' replied Michel, 'pleasantry apart, I have a profound respect for men of science who do possess science, but a profound contempt for men of science who do not.'

'Do you know any who belong to the latter category?'

'Decidedly. In France there are some who maintain that, mathematically, a bird cannot possibly fly; and others who demonstrate theoretically that fishes were never made to live in water.'

'I have nothing to do with persons of that description, and I can quote, in support of my statement, names which you cannot refuse deference to.'

'Then, sir, you will sadly embarrass a poor ignorant, who, besides, asks nothing better than to learn.'

'Why, then, do you introduce scientific questions if you have never studied them?' asked the unknown somewhat coarsely.

'For the reason that "he is always brave who never suspects danger". I know nothing, it is true; but it is precisely my very weakness which constitutes my strength.'

'Your weakness amounts to folly,' retorted the unknown in a passion.

'All the better,' replied our Frenchman, 'if it carries me up to the moon.'

Barbicane and his colleagues devoured with their eyes the intruder who had so boldly placed himself in antagonism to their enterprise. Nobody knew him, and the president, uneasy as to the result of so free a discussion, watched his new friend with some anxiety. The meeting began to be somewhat fidgety also, for the contest directed their attention to the dangers, if not the actual impossibilities, of the proposed expedition.

'Sir,' replied Ardan's antagonist, 'there are many and incontrovertible reasons which prove the absence of an atmosphere in the moon. I might say that, *a priori*, if one ever did exist, it must have been absorbed by the earth; but I prefer to bring forward indisputable facts.'

'Bring them forward then, sir, as many as you please.'

'You know,' said the stranger, 'that when any luminous rays cross a medium such as the air, they are deflected out of the straight line; in other words, they undergo refraction. Well! When stars are occulted by the moon, their rays, on grazing the edge of her disc, exhibit not the least deviation, nor offer the slightest indication of refraction. It follows, therefore, that the moon cannot be surrounded by an atmosphere.

'In point of fact,' replied Ardan, 'this is your chief, if not your *only* argument; and a really scientific man might be puzzled to answer it. For myself, I will simply say that it is defective, because it assumes that the angular diameter of the moon has been completely determined, which is not the case. But let us proceed. Tell me, my dear sir, do you admit the existence of volcanoes on the moon's surface?'

'Extinct, yes! In activity, no!'

'These volcanoes, however, were at one time in a state of activity?'

'True, but, as they furnish themselves the oxygen necessary for combustion, the mere fact of their eruption does not prove the presence of an atmosphere.'

'Proceed again, then; and let us set aside this class of arguments in order to come to direct observations. In 1715 the astronomers Louville and Halley, watching the eclipse of the 3rd of May, remarked some very extraordinary scintillations. These jets of light, rapid in nature, and of frequent recurrence, they attributed to thunderstorms generated in the lunar atmosphere.'

'In 1715,' replied the unknown, 'the astronomers Louville and Halley mistook for lunar phenomena some which were purely terrestrial, such as meteoric or other bodies which are generated in our own atmosphere. This was the scientific explanation at the time of the facts; and that is my answer now.'

'On again, then,' replied Ardan; 'Herschel, in 1787, observed a great number of luminous points on the moon's surface, did he not?'

'Yes! but without offering any solution of them. Herschel himself never inferred from them the necessity of a lunar atmosphere. And I may add that Beer and Maedler, the two great authorities upon the moon, are quite agreed as to the entire absence of air on its surface.'

A movement was here manifest among the assemblage, who appeared to be growing excited by the arguments of this singular personage.

'Let us proceed,' replied Ardan, with perfect coolness, 'and come to one important fact. A skilful French astronomer, M. Laussedat, in watching the eclipse of July 18, 1860, probed that the horns of the lunar crescent were rounded and truncated. Now, this appearance could only have been produced by a deviation of the solar rays in traversing the atmosphere of the moon. There is no other possible explanation of the facts.'

'But is this established as a fact?'

'Absolutely certain!'

A counter-movement here took place in favour of the hero of the meeting, whose opponent was now reduced to silence. Ardan resumed the conversation; and without exhibiting any exultation at the advantage he had gained, simply said:

'You see, then, my dear sir, we must not pronounce with absolute positiveness against the existence of an atmosphere in the moon. That atmosphere is, probably, of extreme rarity; nevertheless at the present day science generally admits that it exists.'

'Not in the mountains, at all events,' returned the unknown, unwilling to give in.

'No! but at the bottom of the valleys, and not exceeding a few hundred feet in height.'

'In any case you will do well to take every precaution, for the air will be terribly rarefied.'

'My good sir, there will always be enough for a solitary individual; besides, once arrived up there, I shall do my best to economise, and not to breathe except on grand occasions!'

A tremendous roar of laughter rang in the ears of the mysterious interlocutor, who glared fiercely round upon the assembly.

'Then,' continued Ardan, with a careless air, 'since we are in accord regarding the presence of a certain atmosphere, we are forced to admit the presence of a certain quantity of water. This is a happy consequence for me. Moreover, my amiable contradictor, permit me to submit to you one further observation. We only know *one* side of the moon's disc; and if there is but little air on the face presented to us, it is possible that there is plenty on the one turned away from us.'

'And for what reason?'

'Because the moon, under the action of the earth's attraction, has assumed the form of an egg, which we look at from the smaller end. Hence it follows, by Hausen's calculations, that its centre of gravity is situated in the other hemisphere. Hence it results that the great mass of air and water must have been drawn away to the other face of our satellite during the first days of its creation.'

'Pure fancies!' cried the unknown.

'No! Pure theories! which are based upon the laws of mechanics, and it seems difficult to me to refute them. I appeal then to this meeting, and I put it to them whether life, such as exists upon the earth, is possible on the surface of the moon?'

Three hundred thousand auditors at once applauded the proposition. Ardan's opponent tried to get in another word, but he could not obtain a hearing. Cries and menaces fell upon him like hail.

'Enough! enough!' cried some.

'Drive the intruder off!' shouted others.

'Turn him out!' roared the exasperated crowd.

But he, holding firmly on to the platform, did not budge an inch, and let the storm pass on, which would soon have assumed formidable proportions, if Michel Ardan had not quieted it by a gesture. He was too chivalrous to abandon his opponent in an apparent extremity.

'You wished to say a few more words?' he asked, in a pleasant voice.

'Yes, a thousand; or rather, no, only one! If you persevere in your enterprise, you must be a—'

'Very rash person! How can you treat me as such? me, who have demanded a cylindro-conical projectile, in order to prevent turning round and round on my way like a squirrel?'

'But, unhappy man, the dreadful recoil will smash you to pieces at your starting.'

'My dear contradictor, you have just put your finger upon the true and only difficulty; nevertheless, I have too good an opinion of the industrial genius of the Americans not to believe that they will succeed in overcoming it.'

'But the heat developed by the rapidity of the projectile in crossing the strata of air?'

'Oh! the walls are thick, and I shall soon have crossed the atmosphere.'

'But victuals and water?'

'I have calculated for a twelvemonth's supply, and I shall be only four days on the journey.'

'But for air to breathe on the road?'

'I shall make it by a chemical process.'

'But your fall on the moon, supposing you ever reach it?'

'It will be six times less dangerous than a sudden fall upon the earth, because the weight will be only one-sixth as great on the surface of the moon.'

'Still it will be enough to smash you like glass!'

'What is to prevent my retarding the shock by means of rockets conveniently placed, and lighted at the right moment?'

'But after all, supposing all difficulties surmounted, all obstacles removed, supposing everything combined to favour you, and granting that you may arrive safe and sound in the moon, how will you come back?'

'I am not coming back!'

At this reply, almost sublime in its very simplicity, the assembly became silent. But its silence was more eloquent than could have been its cries of enthusiasm. The unknown profited by the opportunity and once more protested:

'You will inevitably kill yourself!' he cried; 'and your death will be that of a madman, useless even to science!'

'Go on, my dear unknown, for truly your prophecies are most agreeable!'

'It really is too much!' cried Michel Ardan's adversary. 'I do not know why I should continue so frivolous a discussion! Please yourself about this insane expedition! We need not trouble ourselves about you!'

'Pray don't stand upon ceremony!'

'No! another person is responsible for your act.'

'Who, may I ask?' demanded Michel Ardan in an imperious tone.

'The ignoramus who organised this equally absurd and impossible experiment!'

The attack was direct. Barbicane, ever since the interference of the unknown, had been making fearful efforts of self-control; now, however, seeing himself directly attacked, he could restrain himself no longer. He rose suddenly, and was rushing upon the enemy who thus braved him to the face, when all at once he found himself separated from him.

The platform was lifted by a hundred strong arms, and the president of the Gun Club shared with Michel Ardan triumphal honours. The shield was heavy, but the bearers came in continuous relays, disputing, struggling, even fighting among themselves in their eagerness to lend their shoulders to this demonstration.

However, the unknown had not profited by the tumult to quit his post. Besides, he could not have done it in the midst of that compact crowd. There he held on in the front row with crossed arms, glaring at President Barbicane.

The shouts of the immense crowd continued at their highest pitch throughout this triumphant march. Michel Ardan took it all with evident pleasure. His face gleamed with delight. Several times the platform seemed seized with pitching and rolling like a weather-beaten ship. But the two heroes of the meeting had good sea-legs. They never stumbled; and their vessel arrived without dues at the port of Tampa Town.

Michel Ardan managed fortunately to escape from the last embraces of his vigorous admirers. He made for the Hotel Franklin, quickly gained his chamber, and slid under the bedclothes, while an army of a hundred thousand men kept watch under his windows.

During this time a scene, short, grave, and decisive, took place between the mysterious personage and the president of the Gun Club.

Barbicane, free at last, had gone straight at his adversary.

'Come!' he said shortly.

The other followed him on the quay; and the two presently found themselves alone at the entrance of an open wharf on Jones' Fall.

The two enemies, still mutually unknown, gazed at each other.

'Who are you?' asked Barbicane.

'Captain Nicholl!'

'So I suspected. Hitherto chance has never thrown you in my way.'

'I am come for that purpose.'

'You have insulted me.'

'Publicly!'

'And you will answer to me for this insult?'

'At this very moment.'

'No! I desire that all that passes between us shall be secret. Their is a wood situated three miles from Tampa, the wood of Skersnaw. Do you know it?'

'I know it.'

'Will you be so good as to enter it to-morrow morning

at five o'clock, on one side?'

'Yes! if you will enter at the other side at the same hour.'

'And you will not forget your rifle?' said Barbicane.

'No more than you will forget yours?' replied Nicholl.

These words having been coldly spoken, the president of the Gun Club and the captain parted. Barbicane returned to his lodging; but instead of snatching a few hours of repose, he passed the night in endeavouring to discover a means of evading the recoil of the projectile, and resolving the difficult problem proposed by Michel Ardan during the discussion at the meeting.

CHAPTER XXI

How a Frenchman Manages an Affair

WHILE THE CONTRACT of this duel was being discussed by the president and the captain – this dreadful, savage duel, in which each adversary became a man-hunter – Michel Ardan was resting from the fatigues of his triumph. Resting is hardly an appropriate expression, for American beds rival marble or granite tables for hardness.

Ardan was sleeping, then, badly enough, tossing about between the cloths which served him for sheets, and he was dreaming of making a more comfortable couch in his projectile when a frightful noise disturbed his dreams. Thundering blows shook his door. They seemed to be caused by some iron instrument. A great deal of loud talking was distinguishable in this racket, which was rather too early in the morning. 'Open the door,' some one shrieked, 'for heaven's sake!' Ardan saw no reason for complying with a demand so roughly expressed. However, he got up and opened the door just as it was giving way before the blows of this determined visitor. The secretary of the Gun Club burst into the room. A bomb could not have made more noise or have entered the room with less ceremony.

'Last night,' cried J. T. Maston, *ex abrupto*, 'our president was publicly insulted during the meeting. He provoked his adversary, who is none other than Captain Nicholl! They are fighting this morning in the wood of Skersnaw. I heard all the particulars from the mouth of Barbicane himself. If he is killed, then our scheme is at an end. We must prevent this duel; and one man alone has enough influence over Barbicane to stop him, and that man is Michel Ardan.'

While J. T. Maston was speaking, Michel Ardan, without interrupting him, had hastily put on his clothes; and, in less than two minutes, the two friends were making for the suburbs of Tampa Town with rapid strides.

It was during this walk that Maston told Ardan the state of the case. He told him the real causes of the hostility between Barbicane and Nicholl; how it was of old date, and why, thanks to unknown friends, the president and the captain had, as yet, never met face to face. He added that it arose simply from a rivalry between iron plates and shot, and, finally, that the scene at the meeting was only the long-wished-for opportunity for Nicholl to pay off an old grudge.

Nothing is more dreadful than private duels in America. The two adversaries attack each other like wild beasts. Then it is that they might well covet those wonderful properties of the Indians of the prairies – their quick intelligence, their ingenious cunning, their scent of the enemy. A single mistake, a moment's hesitation, a single false step may cause death. On these occasions Yankees are often accompanied by their dogs, and keep up the struggle for hours.

'What demons you are!' cried Michel Ardan, when his companion had depicted this scene to him with much energy.

'Yes, we are,' replied J. T. modestly; 'but we had better make haste.'

CHAPTER XXI

Though Michel Ardan and he had crossed the plains still wet with dew, and had taken the shortest route over creeks and ricefields, they could not reach Skersnaw in under five hours and a half.

Barbicane must have passed the border half an hour ago.

There was an old bushman working there, occupied in selling faggots from trees that had been levelled by his axe.

Maston ran toward him, saying, 'Have you seen a man go into the wood, armed with a rifle? Barbicane, the president, my best friend?'

The worthy secretary of the Gun Club thought that his president must be known by all the world. But the bushman did not seem to understand him.

'A hunter?' said Ardan.

'A hunter? Yes,' replied the bushman.

'Long ago?'

'About an hour.'

'Too late!' cried Maston.

'Have you heard any gunshots?' asked Ardan.

'No!'

'Not one?'

'Not one! that hunter did not look as if he knew how to hunt!'

'What is to be done?' said Maston.

'We must go into the wood, at the risk of getting a ball which is not intended for us.'

'Ah!' cried Maston, in a tone which could not be mistaken, 'I would rather have twenty balls in my own head than one in Barbicane's.'

'Forward, then,' said Ardan, pressing his companion's hand.

A few moments later the two friends had disappeared in the copse. It was a dense thicket, in which rose huge cypresses, sycamores, tulip-trees, olives, tamarinds, oaks, and magnolias. These different trees had interwoven their branches into an inextricable maze, through which the eye could not penetrate. Michel Ardan and Maston walked side by side in silence through the tall grass, cutting themselves a path through the strong creepers, casting curious glances on the bushes, and momentarily expecting to hear the sound of rifles. As for the traces which Barbicane ought to have left of his passage through the wood, there was not a vestige of them visible: so they followed the barely perceptible paths along which Indians had tracked some enemy, and which the dense foliage darkly overshadowed.

After an hour spent in vain pursuit the two stopped in intensified anxiety.

'It must be all over,' said Maston, discouraged. 'A man like Barbicane would not dodge with his enemy, or ensnare him, would not even manoeuvre! He is too open, too brave. He has gone straight ahead, right into the danger, and doubtless far enough from the bushman for the wind to prevent his hearing the report of the rifles.'

'But surely,' replied Michel Ardan, 'since we entered the wood we should have heard!'

'And what if we came too late?' cried Maston in tones of despair.

For once Ardan had no reply to make, he and Maston resuming their walk in silence. From time to time, indeed,

CHAPTER XXI

they raised great shouts, calling alternately Barbicane and Nicholl, neither of whom, however, answered their cries. Only the birds, awakened by the sound, flew past them and disappeared among the branches, while some frightened deer fled precipitately before them.

For another hour their search was continued. The greater part of the wood had been explored. There was nothing to reveal the presence of the combatants. The information of the bushman was after all doubtful, and Ardan was about to propose their abandoning this useless pursuit, when all at once Maston stopped.

'Hush!' said he, 'there is some one down there!'

'Some one?' repeated Michel Ardan.

'Yes; a man! He seems motionless. His rifle is not in his hands. What can he be doing?'

'But can you recognise him?' asked Ardan, whose short sight was of little use to him in such circumstances.

'Yes! yes! He is turning toward us,' answered Maston.

'And it is?'

'Captain Nicholl!'

'Nicholl?' cried Michel Ardan, feeling a terrible pang of grief.

'Nicholl unarmed! He has, then, no longer any fear of his adversary!'

'Let us go to him,' said Michel Ardan, 'and find out the truth.'

But he and his companion had barely taken fifty steps, when they paused to examine the captain more attentively. They expected to find a bloodthirsty man, happy in his revenge.

On seeing him, they remained stupefied.

A net, composed of very fine meshes, hung between two enormous tulip-trees, and in the midst of this snare, with its wings entangled, was a poor little bird, uttering pitiful cries, while it vainly struggled to escape. The bird-catcher who had laid this snare was no human being, but a venomous spider, peculiar to that country, as large as a pigeon's egg, and armed with enormous claws. The hideous creature, instead of rushing on its prey, had beaten a sudden retreat and taken refuge in the upper branches of the tulip-tree, for a formidable enemy menaced its stronghold.

Here, then, was Nicholl, his gun on the ground, forgetful of danger, trying if possible to save the victim from its cobweb prison. At last it was accomplished, and the little bird flew joyfully away and disappeared.

Nicholl lovingly watched its flight, when he heard these words pronounced by a voice full of emotion:

'You are indeed a brave man.'

He turned. Michel Ardan was before him, repeating in a different tone:

'And a kind-hearted one!'

'Michel Ardan!' cried the captain. 'Why are you here?'

'To press your hand, Nicholl, and to prevent you from either killing Barbicane or being killed by him.'

'Barbicane!' returned the captain. 'I have been looking for him for the last two hours in vain. Where is he hiding?'

'Nicholl!' said Michel Ardan, 'this is not courteous! we ought always to treat an adversary with respect; rest assureed if Barbicane is still alive we shall find him all the more easily;

because if he has not, like you, been amusing himself with freeing oppressed birds, he must be looking for *you*. When we have found him, Michel Ardan tells you this, there will be no duel between you.'

'Between President Barbicane and myself,' gravely replied Nicholl, 'there is a rivalry which the death of one of us—'

'Pooh, pooh!' said Ardan. 'Brave fellows like you indeed! you shall not fight!'

'I will fight, sir!'

'No!'

'Captain,' said J. T. Maston, with much feeling, 'I am a friend of the president's, his *alter ego*, his second self; if you really must kill some one, *shoot me!* it will do just as well!'

'Sir,' Nicholl replied, seizing his rifle convulsively, 'these jokes—'

'Our friend Maston is not joking,' replied Ardan. 'I fully understand his idea of being killed himself in order to save his friend. But neither he nor Barbicane will fall before the balls of Captain Nicholl. Indeed I have so attractive a proposal to make to the two rivals, that both will be eager to accept it.'

'What is it?' asked Nicholl with manifest incredulity.

'Patience!' exclaimed Ardan. 'I can only reveal it in the presence of Barbicane.'

'Let us go in search of him then!' cried the captain.

The three men started off at once; the captain having discharged his rifle threw it over his shoulder, and advanced in silence. Another half hour passed, and the pursuit was still fruitless. Maston was oppressed by sinister forebodings.

He looked fiercely at Nicholl, asking himself whether the captain's vengeance had already been satisfied, and the unfortunate Barbicane, shot, was perhaps lying dead on some bloody track. The same thought seemed to occur to Ardan; and both were casting inquiring glances on Nicholl, when suddenly Maston paused.

The motionless figure of a man leaning against a gigantic catalpa twenty feet off appeared, half-veiled by the foliage.

'It is he!' said Maston.

Barbicane never moved. Ardan looked at the captain, but he did not wince. Ardan went forward crying:

'Barbicane! Barbicane!'

No answer! Ardan rushed toward his friend; but in the act of seizing his arms, he stopped short and uttered a cry of surprise.

Barbicane, pencil in hand, was tracing geometrical figures in a memorandum book, while his unloaded rifle lay beside him on the ground.

Absorbed in his studies, Barbicane, in his turn forgetful of the duel, had seen and heard nothing.

When Ardan took his hand, he looked up and stared at his visitor in astonishment.

'Ah, it is you!' he cried at last. 'I have found it, my friend, I have found it!'

'What?'

'My plan!'

'What plan?'

'The plan for countering the effect of the shock at the departure of the projectile!'

'Indeed?' said Michel Ardan, looking at the captain out of the corner of his eye.

'Yes! water! simply water, which will act as a spring – ah! Maston,' cried Barbicane, 'you here also?'

'Himself,' replied Ardan; 'and permit me to introduce to you at the same time the worthy Captain Nicholl!'

'Nicholl!' cried Barbicane, who jumped up at once. 'Pardon me, captain, I had quite forgotten – I am ready!'

Michel Ardan interfered, without giving the two enemies time to say anything more.

'Thank heaven!' said he. 'It is a happy thing that brave men like you two did not meet sooner! we should now have been mourning for one or other of you. But, thanks to Providence, which has interfered, there is now no further cause for alarm. When one forgets one's anger in mechanics or in cobwebs, it is a sign that the anger is not dangerous.'

Michel Ardan then told the president how the captain had been found occupied.

'I put it to you now,' said he in conclusion, 'are two such good fellows as you are made on purpose to smash each other's skulls with shot?'

There was in 'the situation' somewhat of the ridiculous, something quite unexpected; Michel Ardan saw this, and determined to effect a reconciliation.

'My good friends,' said he, with his most bewitching smile, 'this is nothing but a misunderstanding. Nothing more! well! to prove that it is all over between you, accept frankly the proposal I am going to make to you.'

'Make it,' said Nicholl.

'Our friend Barbicane believes that his projectile will go straight to the moon?'

'Yes, certainly,' replied the president.

'And our friend Nicholl is persuaded it will fall back upon the earth?'

'I am certain of it,' cried the captain.

'Good!' said Ardan. 'I cannot pretend to make you agree; but I suggest this: go with me, and so see whether we are stopped on our journey.'

'What?' exclaimed J. T. Maston, stupefied.

The two rivals, on this sudden proposal, looked steadily at each other. Barbicane waited for the captain's answer. Nicholl watched for the decision of the president.

'Well?' said Michel. 'There is now no fear of the shock!'

'Done!' cried Barbicane.

But quickly as he pronounced the word, he was not before Nicholl.

'Hurrah! bravo! hip! hip! hurrah!' cried Michel, giving a hand to each of the late adversaries. 'Now that it is all settled, my friends, allow me to treat you after French fashion. Let us be off to breakfast!'

CHAPTER XXII

The New Citizen of the United States

THAT SAME DAY all America heard of the affair of Captain Nicholl and President Barbicane, as well as its singular *denouement*. From that day forth, Michel Ardan had not one moment's rest. Deputations from all corners of the Union harassed him without cessation or intermission. He was compelled to receive them all, whether he would or no. How many hands he shook, how many people he was 'hail-fellow-well-met' with, it is impossible to guess! Such a triumphal result would have intoxicated any other man; but he managed to keep himself in a state of delightful *semi*-tipsiness.

Among the deputations of all kinds which assailed him, that of 'The Lunatics' were careful not to forget what they owed to the future conqueror of the moon. One day, certain of these poor people, so numerous in America, came to call upon him, and requested permission to return with him to their native country.

'Singular hallucination!' said he to Barbicane, after having dismissed the deputation with promises to convey numbers of messages to friends in the moon. 'Do you believe in the influence of the moon upon distempers?'

'Scarcely!'

'No more do I, despite some remarkable recorded facts of history. For instance, during an epidemic in 1693, a large number of persons died at the very moment of an eclipse.

The celebrated Bacon always fainted during an eclipse. Charles VI relapsed six times into madness during the year 1399, sometimes during the new, sometimes during the full moon. Gall observed that insane persons underwent an accession of their disorder twice in every month, at the epochs of new and full moon. In fact, numerous observations made upon fevers, somnambulisms, and other human maladies, seem to prove that the moon does exercise some mysterious influence upon man.'

'But the how and the wherefore?' asked Barbicane.

'Well, I can only give you the answer which Arago borrowed from Plutarch, which is nineteen centuries old. "Perhaps the stories are not true!"'

In the height of his triumph, Michel Ardan had to encounter all the annoyances incidental to a man of celebrity. Managers of entertainments wanted to exhibit him. Barnum offered him a million dollars to make a tour of the United States in his show. As for his photographs, they were sold of all size, and his portrait taken in every imaginable posture. More than half a million copies were disposed of in an incredibly short space of time.

But it was not only the men who paid him homage, but the women as well. He might have married well a hundred times over, if he had been willing to settle in life. The old maids, in particular, of forty years and upward, and dry in proportion, devoured his photographs day and night. They would have married him by hundreds, even if he had imposed upon them the condition of accompanying him into space. He had, however, no intention of transplanting a race of Franco-Americans upon the surface of the moon.

He therefore declined all offers.

As soon as he could withdraw from these somewhat embarrassing demonstrations, he went, accompanied by his friends, to pay a visit to the Columbiad. He was highly gratified by his inspection, and made the descent to the bottom of the tube of this gigantic machine which was presently to launch him to the regions of the moon. It is necessary here to mention a proposal of J. T. Maston's. When the secretary of the Gun Club found that Barbicane and Nicholl accepted the proposal of Michel Ardan, he determined to join them, and make one of a smug party of four. So one day he determined to be admitted as one of the travellers. Barbicane, pained at having to refuse him, gave him clearly to understand that the projectile could not possibly contain so many passengers. Maston, in despair, went in search of Michel Ardan, who counselled him to resign himself to the situation, adding one or two arguments *ad hominem*.

'You see, old fellow,' he said, 'you must not take what I say in bad part; but really, between ourselves, you are in too incomplete a condition to appear in the moon!'

'Incomplete?' shrieked the valiant invalid.

'Yes, my dear fellow! imagine our meeting some of the inhabitants up there! Would you like to give them such a melancholy notion of what goes on down here? to teach them what war is, to inform them that we employ our time chiefly in devouring each other, in smashing arms and legs, and that too on a globe which is capable of supporting a hundred billions of inhabitants, and which actually does contain nearly two hundred millions? Why, my worthy friend, we should have to turn you out of doors!'

'But still, if you arrive there in pieces, you will be as incomplete as I am.'

'Unquestionably,' replied Michel Ardan; 'but we shall not.'

In fact, a preparatory experiment, tried on the 18th of October, had yielded the best results and caused the most well-grounded hopes of success. Barbicane, desirous of obtaining some notion of the effect of the shock at the moment of the projectile's departure, had procured a 38-inch mortar from the arsenal of Pensacola. He had this placed on the bank of Hillisborough Roads, in order that the shell might fall back into the sea, and the shock be thereby destroyed. His object was to ascertain the extent of the shock of departure, and not that of the return.

A hollow projectile had been prepared for this curious experiment. A thick padding fastened upon a kind of elastic network, made of the best steel, lined the inside of the walls. It was a veritable *nest* most carefully wadded.

'What a pity I can't find room in there,' said J. T. Maston, regretting that his height did not allow of his trying the adventure.

Within this shell were shut up a large cat, and a squirrel belonging to J. T. Maston, and of which he was particularly fond. They were desirous, however, of ascertaining how this little animal, least of all others subject to giddiness, would endure this experimental voyage.

The mortar was charged with 160 pounds of powder, and

the shell placed in the chamber. On being fired, the projectile rose with great velocity, described a majestic parabola, attained a height of about a thousand feet, and with a graceful curve descended in the midst of the vessels that lay there at anchor.

Without a moment's loss of time a small boat put off in the direction of its fall; some divers plunged into the water and attached ropes to the handles of the shell, which was quickly dragged on board. Five minutes did not elapse between the moment of enclosing the animals and that of unscrewing the coverlid of their prison.

Ardan, Barbicane, Maston, and Nicholl were present on board the boat, and assisted at the operation with an interest which may readily be comprehended. Hardly had the shell been opened when the cat leaped out, slightly bruised, but full of life, and exhibiting no signs whatever of having made an aerial expedition. No trace, however, of the squirrel could be discovered. The truth at last became apparent – the cat had eaten its fellow-traveller!

J. T. Maston grieved much for the loss of his poor squirrel, and proposed to add its case to that of other martyrs to science.

After this experiment all hesitation, all fear disappeared. Besides, Barbicane's plans would ensure greater perfection for his projectile, and go far to annihilate altogether the effects of the shock. Nothing now remained but to go!

Two days later Michel Ardan received a message from the President of the United States, an honour of which he showed himself especially sensible.

After the example of his illustrious fellow-countryman, the Marquis de la Fayette, the government had decreed to him the title of 'Citizen of the United States of America'.

CHAPTER XXIII

The Projectile-Vehicle

ON THE COMPLETION of the Columbiad the public interest centred in the projectile itself, the vehicle which was destined to carry the three hardy adventurers into space.

The new plans had been sent to Breadwill and Co., of Albany, with the request for their speedy execution. The projectile was consequently cast on the 2nd of November, and immediately forwarded by the Eastern Railway to Stones Hill, which it reached without accident on the 10th of that month, where Michel Ardan, Barbicane, and Nicholl were waiting impatiently for it.

The projectile had now to be filled to the depth of three feet with a bed of water, intended to support a water-tight wooden disc, which worked easily within the walls of the projectile. It was upon this kind of raft that the travellers were to take their place. This body of water was divided by horizontal partitions, which the shock of the departure would have to break in succession. Then each sheet of the water, from the lowest to the highest, running off into escape tubes toward the top of the projectile, constituted a kind of spring; and the wooden disc, supplied with extremely powerful plugs, could not strike the lowest plate except after breaking successively the different partitions. Undoubtedly the travellers would still have to encounter a violent recoil after the complete escapement of the water; but the first shock would be almost entirely destroyed by this powerful spring. The upper parts of the walls were lined with a thick padding of leather, fastened upon springs of the best steel, behind which the escape tubes were completely concealed; thus all imaginable precautions had been taken for averting the first shock; and if they did get crushed, they must, as Michel Ardan said, be made of very bad materials.

The entrance into this metallic tower was by a narrow aperture contrived in the wall of the cone. This was hermetically closed by a plate of aluminium, fastened internally by powerful screw-pressure. The travellers could therefore quit their prison at pleasure, as soon as they should reach the moon.

Light and view were given by means of four thick lenticular glass scuttles, two pierced in the circular wall itself, the third in the bottom, the fourth in the top. These scuttles then were protected against the shock of departure by plates let into solid grooves, which could easily be opened outward by unscrewing them from the inside. Reservoirs firmly fixed contained water and the necessary provisions; and fire and light were procurable by means of gas, contained in a special reservoir under a pressure of several atmospheres. They had only to turn a tap, and for six hours the gas would light and warm this comfortable vehicle.

There now remained only the question of air; for allowing for the consumption of air by Barbicane, his two companions, and two dogs which he proposed taking with him, it was necessary to renew the air of the projectile. Now air consists principally of twenty-one parts of oxygen and seventy-nine of nitrogen. The lungs absorb the oxygen, which is indispensable for the support of life, and reject the nitrogen. The air expired loses nearly five per cent of the former and contains nearly an equal volume of carbonic acid, produced by the combustion of the elements of the blood. In an air-tight enclosure, then, after a certain time, all the oxygen of the air will be replaced by the carbonic acid – a gas fatal to life. There were two things to be done then – first, to replace the absorbed oxygen; secondly, to destroy the expired carbonic acid; both easy enough to do, by means of chlorate of potassium and caustic potash. The former is a salt which appears under the form of white crystals; when raised to a temperature of 400 degrees it is transformed into chlorure of potassium, and the oxygen which it contains is entirely liberated. Now twenty-eight pounds of chlorate of potassium produces seven pounds of oxygen, or 2,400 litres – the quantity necessary for the travellers during twenty-four hours.

Caustic potash has a great affinity for carbonic acid; and it is sufficient to shake it in order for it to seize upon the acid and form bicarbonate of potassium. By these two means they would be enabled to restore to the vitiated air its life-supporting properties.

It is necessary, however, to add that the experiments had hitherto been made *in anima vili*. Whatever its scientific accuracy was, they were at present ignorant how it would answer with human beings. The honour of putting it to the proof was energetically claimed by J. T. Maston.

'Since I am not to go,' said the brave artillerist, 'I may at least live for a week in the projectile.'

It would have been hard to refuse him; so they consented to his wish. A sufficient quantity of chlorate of potassium and of caustic potash was placed at his disposal, together with provisions for eight days. And having shaken hands with his friends, on the 12th of November, at six o'clock A.M., after strictly informing them not to open his prison before the 20th, at six o'clock P.M., he slid down the projectile, the plate of which was at once hermetically sealed. What did he do with himself during that week? They could get no information. The thickness of the walls of the projectile prevented any sound reaching from the inside to the outside. On the 20th of November, at six P.M. exactly, the plate was opened. The friends of J. T. Maston had been all along in a state of much anxiety; but they were promptly reassured on hearing a jolly voice shouting a boisterous hurrah.

Presently afterward the secretary of the Gun Club appeared at the top of the cone in a triumphant attitude. He had grown fat!

CHAPTER XXIV

The Telescope of the Rocky Mountains

ON THE 20TH of October in the preceding year, after the close of the subscription, the president of the Gun Club had credited the Observatory of Cambridge with the necessary sums for the construction of a gigantic optical instrument. This instrument was designed for the purpose of rendering visible on the surface of the moon any object exceeding nine feet in diameter.

At the period when the Gun Club essayed their great experiment, such instruments had reached a high degree of perfection, and produced some magnificent results. Two telescopes in particular, at this time, were possessed of remarkable power and of gigantic dimensions. The first, constructed by Herschel, was thirty-six feet in length, and had an object-glass of four feet six inches; it possessed a magnifying power of 6,000. The second was raised in Ireland, in Parsonstown Park, and belongs to Lord Rosse. The length of this tube is forty-eight feet, and the diameter of its object-glass six feet; it magnifies 6,400 times, and required an immense erection of brick work and masonry for the purpose of working it, its weight being twelve and a half tons.

Still, despite these colossal dimensions, the actual enlargements scarcely exceeded 6,000 times in round numbers; consequently, the moon was brought within no nearer an apparent distance than thirty-nine miles; and objects of less than sixty feet in diameter, unless they were of very considerable length, were still imperceptible.

In the present case, dealing with a projectile nine feet in diameter and fifteen feet long, it became necessary to bring the moon within an apparent distance of five miles at most; and for that purpose to establish a magnifying power of 48,000 times.

Such was the question proposed to the Observatory of Cambridge. There was no lack of funds; the difficulty was purely one of construction.

After considerable discussion as to the best form and principle of the proposed instrument the work was finally commenced. According to the calculations of the Observatory of Cambridge, the tube of the new reflector would require to be 280 feet in length, and the object-glass sixteen feet in diameter. Colossal as these dimensions may appear, they were diminutive in comparison with the 10,000 foot telescope proposed by the astronomer Hooke only a few years ago!

Regarding the choice of locality, that matter was promptly determined. The object was to select some lofty mountain, and there are not many of these in the United States. In fact there are but two chains of moderate elevation, between which runs the magnificent Mississippi, the 'king of rivers' as these Republican Yankees delight to call it.

Eastwards rise the Appalachians, the very highest point of which, in New Hampshire, does not exceed the very moderate altitude of 5,600 feet.

On the west, however, rise the Rocky Mountains, that immense range which, commencing at the Straits of

Magellan, follows the western coast of Southern America under the name of the Andes or the Cordilleras, until it crosses the Isthmus of Panama, and runs up the whole of North America to the very borders of the Polar Sea. The highest elevation of this range still does not exceed 10,700 feet. With this elevation, nevertheless, the Gun Club were compelled to be content, inasmuch as they had determined that both telescope and Columbiad should be erected within the limits of the Union. All the necessary apparatus was consequently sent on to the summit of Long's Peak, in the territory of Missouri.

Neither pen nor language can describe the difficulties of all kinds which the American engineers had to surmount, of the prodigies of daring and skill which they accomplished. They had to raise enormous stones, massive pieces of wrought iron, heavy corner-clamps and huge portions of cylinder, with an object-glass weighing nearly 30,000 pounds, above the line of perpetual snow for more than 10,000 feet in height, after crossing desert prairies, impenetrable forests, fearful rapids, far from all centres of population, and in the midst of savage regions, in which every detail of life becomes an almost insoluble problem. And yet, notwithstanding these innumerable obstacles, American genius triumphed. In less than a year after the commencement of the works, toward the close of September, the gigantic reflector rose into the air to a height of 280 feet. It was raised by means of an enormous iron crane; an ingenious mechanism allowed it to be easily worked toward all the points of the heavens, and to follow the stars from the one horizon to the other during their journey through the heavens.

It had cost $400,000. The first time it was directed toward the moon the observers evinced both curiosity and anxiety. What were they about to discover in the field of this telescope which magnified objects 48,000 times? Would they perceive peoples, herds of lunar animals, towns, lakes, seas? No! there was nothing which science had not already discovered! and on all the points of its disc the volcanic nature of the moon became determinable with the utmost precision.

But the telescope of the Rocky Mountains, before doing its duty to the Gun Club, rendered immense services to astronomy. Thanks to its penetrative power, the depths of the heavens were sounded to the utmost extent; the apparent diameter of a great number of stars was accurately measured; and Mr. Clark, of the Cambridge staff, resolved the Crab nebula in Taurus, which the reflector of Lord Rosse had never been able to decompose.

CHAPTER XXV

Final Details

IT WAS THE 22nd of November; the departure was to take place in ten days. One operation alone remained to be accomplished to bring all to a happy termination; an operation delicate and perilous, requiring infinite precautions, and against the success of which Captain Nicholl had laid his third bet. It was, in fact, nothing less than the loading of the Columbiad, and the introduction into it of 400,000 pounds of gun-cotton. Nicholl had thought, not perhaps without reason, that the handling of such formidable quantities of pyroxyle would, in all probability, involve a grave catastrophe; and at any rate, that this immense mass of eminently inflammable matter would inevitably ignite when submitted to the pressure of the projectile.

There were indeed dangers accruing as before from the carelessness of the Americans, but Barbicane had set his heart on success, and took all possible precautions. In the first place, he was very careful as to the transportation of the gun-cotton to Stones Hill. He had it conveyed in small quantities, carefully packed in sealed cases. These were brought by rail from Tampa Town to the camp, and from thence were taken to the Columbiad by barefooted workmen, who deposited them in their places by means of cranes placed at the orifice of the cannon. No steam-engine was permitted to work, and every fire was extinguished within two miles of the works.

Even in November they feared to work by day, lest the sun's rays acting on the gun-cotton might lead to unhappy results. This led to their working at night, by light produced in a vacuum by means of Ruhmkorff's apparatus, which threw an artificial brightness into the depths of the Columbiad. There the cartridges were arranged with the utmost regularity, connected by a metallic thread, destined to communicate to them all simultaneously the electric spark, by which means this mass of gun-cotton was eventually to be ignited.

By the 28th of November eight hundred cartridges had been placed in the bottom of the Columbiad. So far the operation had been successful! But what confusion, what anxieties, what struggles were undergone by President Barbicane! In vain had he refused admission to Stones Hill; every day the inquisitive neighbours scaled the palisades, some even carrying their imprudence to the point of smoking while surrounded by bales of gun-cotton. Barbicane was in a perpetual state of alarm. J. T. Maston seconded him to the best of his ability, by giving vigorous chase to the intruders, and carefully picking up the still lighted cigar ends which the Yankees threw about. A somewhat difficult task! seeing that more than 300,000 persons were gathered round the enclosure. Michel Ardan had volunteered to superintend the transport of the cartridges to the mouth of the Columbiad; but the president, having surprised him with an enormous cigar in his mouth, while he was hunting out the rash spectators to whom he himself offered so dangerous an example, saw that he could not trust this fearless smoker, and was therefore obliged to mount a special guard over him.

At last, Providence being propitious, this wonderful loading came to a happy termination, Captain Nicholl's third bet being thus lost. It remained now to introduce the projectile into the Columbiad, and to place it on its soft bed of gun-cotton.

But before doing this, all those things necessary for the journey had to be carefully arranged in the projectile vehicle. These necessaries were numerous; and had Ardan been allowed to follow his own wishes, there would have been no space remaining for the travellers. It is impossible to conceive of half the things this charming Frenchman wished to convey to the moon. A veritable stock of useless trifles! But Barbicane interfered and refused admission to anything not absolutely needed. Several thermometers, barometers, and telescopes were packed in the instrument case.

The travellers being desirous of examining the moon carefully during their voyage, in order to facilitate their studies, they took with them Beer and Maedller's excellent *Mappa Selenographica*, a masterpiece of patience and observation, which they hoped would enable them to identify those physical features in the moon, with which they were acquainted. This map reproduced with scrupulous fidelity the smallest details of the lunar surface which faces the earth; the mountains, valleys, craters, peaks, and ridges were all represented, with their exact dimensions, relative positions, and names; from the mountains Doerfel and Leibnitz on the eastern side of the disc, to the *Mare frigoris* of the North Pole.

They took also three rifles and three fowling-pieces, and a large quantity of balls, shot, and powder.

'We cannot tell whom we shall have to deal with,' said Michel Ardan. 'Men or beasts may possibly object to our visit. It is only wise to take all precautions.'

These defensive weapons were accompanied by pickaxes, crowbars, saws, and other useful implements, not to mention clothing adapted to every temperature, from that of polar regions to that of the torrid zone.

Ardan wished to convey a number of animals of different sorts, not indeed a pair of every known species, as he could not see the necessity of acclimatising serpents, tigers, alligators, or any other noxious beasts in the moon. 'Nevertheless,' he said to Barbicane, 'some valuable and useful beasts, bullocks, cows, horses, and donkeys, would bear the journey very well, and would also be very useful to us.'

'I dare say, my dear Ardan,' replied the president, 'but our projectile-vehicle is no Noah's ark, from which it differs both in dimensions and object. Let us confine ourselves to possibilities.'

After a prolonged discussion, it was agreed that the travellers should restrict themselves to a sporting-dog belonging to Nicholl, and to a large Newfoundland. Several packets of seeds were also included among the necessaries. Michel Ardan, indeed, was anxious to add some sacks full of earth to sow them in; as it was, he took a dozen shrubs carefully wrapped up in straw to plant in the moon.

The important question of provisions still remained; it being necessary to provide against the possibility of their finding the moon absolutely barren. Barbicane managed so successfully, that he supplied them with sufficient rations for a year. These consisted of preserved meats and vegetables, reduced by strong hydraulic pressure to the smallest possible dimensions. They were also supplied with brandy, and took water enough for two months, being confident, from astronomical observations, that there was no lack of water on the moon's surface. As to provisions, doubtless the inhabitants of the *earth* would find nourishment somewhere in the *moon*. Ardan never questioned this; indeed, had he done so, he would never have undertaken the journey.

'Besides,' he said one day to his friends, 'we shall not be completely abandoned by our terrestrial friends; they will take care not to forget us.'

'No, indeed!' replied J. T. Maston.

'Nothing would be simpler,' replied Ardan; 'the Columbiad will be always there. Well! whenever the moon is in a favourable condition as to the zenith, if not to the perigee, that is to say about once a year, could you not send us a shell packed with provisions, which we might expect on some appointed day?'

'Hurrah! hurrah!' cried J. T. Maston; 'what an ingenious fellow! what a splendid idea! Indeed, my good friends, we shall not forget you!'

'I shall reckon upon you! Then, you see, we shall receive news regularly from the earth, and we shall indeed be stupid if we hit upon no plan for communicating with our good friends here!'

These words inspired such confidence, that Michel Ardan carried all the Gun Club with him in his enthusiasm. What he said seemed so simple and so easy, so sure of success, that none could be so sordidly attached to this earth as to hesitate to follow the three travellers on their lunar expedition.

All being ready at last, it remained to place the projectile in the Columbiad, an operation abundantly accompanied by dangers and difficulties.

The enormous shell was conveyed to the summit of Stones Hill. There, powerful cranes raised it, and held it suspended over the mouth of the cylinder.

It was a fearful moment! What if the chains should break under its enormous weight? The sudden fall of such a body would inevitably cause the gun-cotton to explode!

Fortunately this did not happen; and some hours later the projectile-vehicle descended gently into the heart of the cannon and rested on its couch of pyroxyle, a veritable bed of explosive eider-down. Its pressure had no result, other than the more effectual ramming down of the charge in the Columbiad.

'I have lost,' said the captain, who forthwith paid President Barbicane the sum of three thousand dollars.

Barbicane did not wish to accept the money from one of his fellow-travellers, but gave way at last before the determination of Nicholl, who wished before leaving the earth to fulfil all his engagements.

'Now,' said Michel Ardan, 'I have only one thing more to wish for you, my brave captain.'

'What is that?' asked Nicholl.

'It is that you may lose your two other bets! Then we shall be sure not to be stopped on our journey!'

CHAPTER XXVI

Fire!

THE FIRST OF December had arrived! the fatal day! for, if the projectile were not discharged that very night at 10h. 48m. 40s. P.M., more than eighteen years must roll by before the moon would again present herself under the same conditions of zenith and perigee.

The weather was magnificent. Despite the approach of winter, the sun shone brightly, and bathed in its radiant light that earth which three of its denizens were about to abandon for a new world.

How many persons lost their rest on the night which preceded this long-expected day! All hearts beat with disquietude, save only the heart of Michel Ardan. That imperturbable personage came and went with his habitual business-like air, while nothing whatever denoted that any unusual matter preoccupied his mind.

After dawn, an innumerable multitude covered the prairie which extends, as far as the eye can reach, round Stones Hill. Every quarter of an hour the railway brought fresh accessions of sightseers; and, according to the statement of the Tampa Town *Observer*, not less than five millions of spectators thronged the soil of Florida.

For a whole month previously, the mass of these persons had bivouacked round the enclosure, and laid the foundations for a town which was afterward called 'Ardan's Town'.

The whole plain was covered with huts, cottages, and tents. Every nation under the sun was represented there; and every language might be heard spoken at the same time. It was a perfect Babel re-enacted. All the various classes of American society were mingled together in terms of absolute equality. Bankers, farmers, sailors, cotton-planters, brokers, merchants, watermen, magistrates, elbowed each other in the most free-and-easy way. Louisiana Creoles fraternised with farmers from Indiana; Kentucky and Tennessee gentlemen and haughty Virginians conversed with trappers and the half-savages of the lakes and butchers from Cincinnati. Broad-brimmed white hats and Panamas, blue-cotton trousers, light-coloured stockings, cambric frills, were all here displayed; while upon shirt-fronts, wristbands, and neckties, upon every finger, even upon the very ears, they wore an assortment of rings, shirt-pins, brooches, and trinkets, of which the value only equalled the execrable taste. Women, children, and servants, in equally expensive dress, surrounded their husbands, fathers, or masters, who resembled the patriarchs of tribes in the midst of their immense households.

At meal-times all fell to work upon the dishes peculiar to the Southern States, and consumed with an appetite that threatened speedy exhaustion of the victualling powers of Florida, fricasseed frogs, stuffed monkey, fish chowder, underdone 'possum, and raccoon steaks. And as for the liquors which accompanied this indigestible repast! The shouts, the vociferations that resounded through the bars and taverns decorated with glasses, tankards, and bottles of marvellous shape, mortars for pounding sugar, and bundles of straws! 'Mint-julep' roars one of the barmen; 'Claret sangaree!' shouts another; 'Cocktail!' 'Brandy-smash!' 'Real mint-julep in the new style!' All these cries intermingled produced a bewildering and deafening hubbub.

But on this day, 1st of December, such sounds were rare. No one thought of eating or drinking, and at four P.M. there were vast numbers of spectators who had not even taken their customary lunch! And, a still more significant fact, even the national passion for play seemed quelled for the time under the general excitement of the hour.

Up till nightfall, a dull, noiseless agitation, such as precedes great catastrophes, ran through the anxious multitude. An indescribable uneasiness pervaded all minds, an indefinable sensation which oppressed the heart. Every one wished it was over.

However, about seven o'clock, the heavy silence was dissipated. The moon rose above the horizon. Millions of hurrahs hailed her appearance. She was punctual to the rendezvous, and shouts of welcome greeted her on all sides, as her pale beams shone gracefully in the clear heavens. At this moment the three intrepid travellers appeared. This was the signal for renewed cries of still greater intensity. Instantly the vast assemblage, as with one accord, struck up the national hymn of the United States, and 'Yankee Doodle', sung by five million of hearty throats, rose like a roaring tempest to the farthest limits of the atmosphere. Then a profound silence reigned throughout the crowd.

The Frenchman and the two Americans had by this time entered the enclosure reserved in the centre of the multitude.

They were accompanied by the members of the Gun Club, and by deputations sent from all the European Observatories. Barbicane, cool and collected, was giving his final directions. Nicholl, with compressed lips, his arms crossed behind his back, walked with a firm and measured step. Michel Ardan, always easy, dressed in thorough traveller's costume, leathern gaiters on his legs, pouch by his side, in loose velvet suit, cigar in mouth, was full of inexhaustible gayety, laughing, joking, playing pranks with J. T. Maston. In one word, he was the thorough 'Frenchman' (and worse, a 'Parisian') to the last moment.

Ten o'clock struck! The moment had arrived for taking their places in the projectile! The necessary operations for the descent, and the subsequent removal of the cranes and scaffolding that inclined over the mouth of the Columbiad, required a certain period of time.

Barbicane had regulated his chronometer to the tenth part of a second by that of Murchison the engineer, who was charged with the duty of firing the gun by means of an electric spark. Thus the travellers enclosed within the projectile were enabled to follow with their eyes the impassive needle which marked the precise moment of their departure.

The moment had arrived for saying 'goodbye!' The scene was a touching one. Despite his feverish gayety, even Michel Ardan was touched. J. T. Maston had found in his own dry eyes one ancient tear, which he had doubtless reserved for the occasion. He dropped it on the forehead of his dear president.

'Can I not go?' he said, 'there is still time!'

'Impossible, old fellow!' replied Barbicane. A few moments later, the three fellow-travellers had ensconced themselves in the projectile, and screwed down the plate which covered the entrance-aperture. The mouth of the Columbiad, now completely disencumbered, was open entirely to the sky.

The moon advanced upward in a heaven of the purest clearness, outshining in her passage the twinkling light of the stars. She passed over the constellation of the Twins, and was now nearing the halfway point between the horizon and the zenith. A terrible silence weighed upon the entire scene! Not a breath of wind upon the earth! not a sound of breathing from the countless chests of the spectators! Their hearts seemed afraid to beat! All eyes were fixed upon the yawning mouth of the Columbiad.

Murchison followed with his eye the hand of his chronometer. It wanted scarce forty seconds to the moment of departure, but each second seemed to last an age! At the twentieth there was a general shudder, as it occurred to the minds of that vast assemblage that the bold travellers shut up within the projectile were also counting those terrible seconds. Some few cries here and there escaped the crowd.

'Thirty-five! – thirty-six! – thirty-seven! – thirty-eight! – thirty-nine! – forty! FIRE!!!'

Instantly Murchison pressed with his finger the key of the electric battery, restored the current of the fluid, and discharged the spark into the breech of the Columbiad.

An appalling unearthly report followed instantly, such as can be compared to nothing whatever known, not even to the roar of thunder, or the blast of volcanic explosions! No words can convey the slightest idea of the terrific sound! An immense spout of fire shot up from the bowels of the earth as from a crater. The earth heaved up, and with great difficulty some few spectators obtained a momentary glimpse of the projectile victoriously cleaving the air in the midst of the fiery vapours!

CHAPTER XXVII

Foul Weather

AT THE MOMENT when that pyramid of fire rose to a prodigious height into the air, the glare of flame lit up the whole of Florida; and for a moment day superseded night over a considerable extent of the country. This immense canopy of fire was perceived at a distance of one hundred miles out at sea, and more than one ship's captain entered in his log the appearance of this gigantic meteor.

The discharge of the Columbiad was accompanied by a perfect earthquake. Florida was shaken to its very depths. The gases of the powder, expanded by heat, forced back the atmospheric strata with tremendous violence, and this artificial hurricane rushed like a water-spout through the air.

Not a single spectator remained on his feet! Men, women, children, all lay prostrate like ears of corn under a tempest. There ensued a terrible tumult; a large number of persons were seriously injured. J. T. Maston, who, despite all dictates of prudence, had kept in advance of the mass, was pitched back 120 feet, shooting like a projectile over the heads of his fellow-citizens. Three hundred thousand persons remained deaf for a time, and as though struck stupefied.

As soon as the first effects were over, the injured, the deaf, and lastly, the crowd in general, woke up with frenzied cries. 'Hurrah for Ardan! Hurrah for Barbicane! Hurrah for Nicholl!' rose to the skies. Thousands of persons, noses in air, armed with telescopes and race-glasses, were questioning space, forgetting all contusions and emotions in the one idea of watching for the projectile. They looked in vain! It was no longer to be seen, and they were obliged to wait for telegrams from Long's Peak. The director of the Cambridge Observatory was at his post on the Rocky Mountains; and to him, as a skilful and persevering astronomer, all observations had been confided.

But an unforeseen phenomenon came in to subject the public impatience to a severe trial.

The weather, hitherto so fine, suddenly changed; the sky became heavy with clouds. It could not have been otherwise after the terrible derangement of the atmospheric strata, and the dispersion of the enormous quantity of vapour arising from the combustion of 200,000 pounds of pyroxyle!

On the morrow the horizon was covered with clouds – a thick and impenetrable curtain between earth and sky, which unhappily extended as far as the Rocky Mountains. It was a fatality! But since man had chosen so to disturb the atmosphere, he was bound to accept the consequences of his experiment.

Supposing, now, that the experiment had succeeded, the travellers having started on the 1st of December, at 10h. 46m. 40s. P.M., were due on the 4th at 0h. P.M. at their destination. So that up to that time it would have been very difficult after all to have observed, under such conditions, a body so small as the shell. Therefore they waited with what patience they might.

From the 4th to the 6th of December inclusive, the weather remaining much the same in America, the great European instruments of Herschel, Rosse, and Foucault, were constantly directed toward the moon, for the weather was then magnificent; but the comparative weakness of their glasses prevented any trustworthy observations being made.

On the 7th the sky seemed to lighten. They were in hopes now, but their hope was of but short duration, and at night again thick clouds hid the starry vault from all eyes.

Matters were now becoming serious, when on the 9th the sun reappeared for an instant, as if for the purpose of teasing the Americans. It was received with hisses; and wounded, no doubt, by such a reception, showed itself very sparing of its rays.

On the 10th, no change! J. T. Maston went nearly mad, and great fears were entertained regarding the brain of this worthy individual, which had hitherto been so well preserved within his gutta-percha cranium.

But on the 11th one of those inexplicable tempests peculiar to those intertropical regions was let loose in the atmosphere. A terrific east wind swept away the groups of clouds which had been so long gathering, and at night the semi-disc of the orb of night rode majestically amid the soft constellations of the sky.

CHAPTER XXVIII

A New Star

THAT VERY NIGHT, the startling news so impatiently awaited, burst like a thunderbolt over the United States of the Union, and thence, darting across the ocean, ran through all the telegraphic wires of the globe. The projectile had been detected, thanks to the gigantic reflector of Long's Peak! Here is the note received by the director of the Observatory of Cambridge. It contains the scientific conclusion regarding this great experiment of the Gun Club.

> LONG'S PEAK, December 12. To the Officers of the Observatory of Cambridge. The projectile discharged by the Columbiad at Stones Hill has been detected by Messrs. Belfast and J. T. Maston, 12th of December, at 8:47 P.M., the moon having entered her last quarter. This projectile has not arrived at its destination. It has passed by the side; but sufficiently near to be retained by the lunar attraction.
>
> The rectilinear movement has thus become changed into a circular motion of extreme velocity, and it is now pursuing an elliptical orbit round the moon, of which it has become a true satellite.
>
> The elements of this new star we have as yet been unable to determine; we do not yet know the velocity of its

> passage. The distance which separates it from the surface of the moon may be estimated at about 2,833 miles.
>
> However, two hypotheses come here into our consideration.
>
> 1. Either the attraction of the moon will end by drawing them into itself, and the travellers will attain their destination; or,
>
> 2. The projectile, following an immutable law, will continue to gravitate round the moon till the end of time.
>
> At some future time, our observations will be able to determine this point, but till then the experiment of the Gun Club can have no other result than to have provided our solar system with a new star. J. BELFAST.

To how many questions did this unexpected *denouement* give rise? What mysterious results was the future reserving for the investigation of science? At all events, the names of Nicholl, Barbicane, and Michel Ardan were certain to be immortalised in the annals of astronomy!

When the dispatch from Long's Peak had once become known, there was but one universal feeling of surprise and alarm. Was it possible to go to the aid of these bold travellers? No! for they had placed themselves beyond the pale of humanity, by crossing the limits imposed by the Creator on his earthly creatures. They had air enough for *two* months; they had victuals enough for *twelve; but after that?* There was only one man who would not admit that the situation was desperate – he alone had confidence; and that was their devoted friend J. T. Maston.

Besides, he never let them get out of sight. His home was henceforth the post at Long's Peak; his horizon, the mirror of that immense reflector. As soon as the moon rose above the horizon, he immediately caught her in the field of the telescope; he never let her go for an instant out of his sight, and followed her assiduously in her course through the stellar spaces. He watched with untiring patience the passage of the projectile across her silvery disc, and really the worthy man remained in perpetual communication with his three friends, whom he did not despair of seeing again some day.

'Those three men,' said he, 'have carried into space all the resources of art, science, and industry. With that, one can do anything; and you will see that, some day, they will come out all right.'

JOURNEY TO THE CENTRE OF THE EARTH

JOURNEY TO THE CENTRE OF THE EARTH

JULES VERNE

This edition published in 2021 by Arcturus Publishing Limited
26/27 Bickels Yard, 151–153 Bermondsey Street,
London SE1 3HA

Copyright © Arcturus Holdings Limited

All rights reserved. No part of this publication may be reproduced, stored in a retrieval system, or transmitted, in any form or by any means, electronic, mechanical, photocopying, recording or otherwise, without prior written permission in accordance with the provisions of the Copyright Act 1956 (as amended). Any person or persons who do any unauthorised act in relation to this publication may be liable to criminal prosecution and civil claims for damages.

Cover design: Peter Ridley

AD001541UK

Printed in the UK

Introduction

The great early pioneer of science fiction, Jules Verne was celebrated for his *Voyages Extraordinaires*. His heroes travelled around the world, to the moon and, in this volume, to the centre of the earth. It is therefore fitting that the author began life – on 8 February 1828 – in the busy, bustling French harbour city of Nantes.

Drawn to a life of adventure, at twelve Verne was beaten by his father when found hiding on a ship bound for India. After this bitter experience, the future writer famously resolved to travel only in his imagination.

The troubled relationship with his father marked much of Verne's early literary career. Upon learning that his son was writing, rather than studying law, the elder Verne withdrew all support. For over a decade, the author worked as a stockbroker, while attempting to interest publishers in his work. Verne's fortunes changed when he met Pierre-Jules Hetzel. An editor and publisher, in 1863 he published Verne's first novel, *Five Weeks in a Balloon (Cinq Semaines en Ballon)*. *Journey to the Centre of the Earth (Voyage au centre de la Terre)*, published the following year, proved to be one of the author's most enduring works. Verne came to be celebrated the world over for such classic novels as *Twenty Thousand Leagues Under the Sea* (1870) and *Around the World in Eighty Days* (1873). He died on 24 March 1905.

Editor's Note

The text published here is a modernization of the Rev F A Malleson's 1876 translation of Verne's *Voyage au centre de la Terre*, the main purpose of this reworking of Malleson being to update it in terms of style and vocabulary. While Verne's *Voyage* has been constantly at the editor's elbow to allow him where necessary to check the original French before settling on a rewording of Malleson's text, this book is by no means a new translation but simply an updating of an out-of-date English version which no longer did justice to Verne. However, since Verne's book itself was published in the mid-1860s, it would have been inappropriate to have fully altered the language of the 19th-century English translation to the idiom of the 21st century. The editor hopes he has struck the right balance between the modern and the slightly old-fashioned.

From a scientific point of view, there are some errors of fact in Verne's book, and Malleson helpfully provided a number of footnotes correcting these mistakes. However, since they have no relevance to the story, and in some cases have been overtaken by advances in scientific knowledge, these notes have for the most part been dropped from the present book. What Verne wrote was a novel, not a textbook, and nothing stands or falls on the accuracy of his science. The same is true for his historical accuracy: for example, it may be rather implausible that the British scientist Sir Humphry Davy would have visited Otto Lidenbrock in 1825 (see page 33) when Lidenbrock would only have been 12 years old (he is stated to be 50 in 1863) in order to discuss matters of science with him, but the implausibility in no way affects the story. Verne's purpose is simply to establish Lidenbrock as a respected authority in his field.

The reader will find a great deal of geological and mineralogical terminology in this book. This is hardly surprising, as it is supposedly written about the underground explorations of an eminent geologist and mineralogist by a nephew who is himself competent in these sciences. In order to enjoy the story, however, one does not need to know more about feldspar, syenite, porphyry, trachite or tufa than is explained in the story itself, and the present editor felt it unnecessary to add notes on these or other minerals mentioned. Similarly, no attempt has been made to check whether what Verne wrote about geological periods such as the Tertiary and the Quaternary conforms to modern scientific knowledge or usage.

On the other hand, the editor, aware that a 21st-century reader is likely to be less well versed in Latin and Greek literature and mythology than the readership Verne and Malleson had in mind, has added a number of notes where, for example, quotations in Latin or allusions to Greek myths might not be understood, to the detriment of the story.

The chapter headings are Malleson's, not Verne's (hence, for example, the quotation from Shakespeare used as the heading for Chapter 24). Similarly, as will be seen from the notes, Malleson included in his translation other quotations from English literature that have no basis in the French text. Most of those have been left as Malleson wrote them, since there seemed to be no good reason to remove or replace them.

GEORGE DAVIDSON

CHAPTER 1

THE PROFESSOR AND HIS FAMILY

On the 24th of May, 1863, a Sunday, my uncle, Professor Lidenbrock, came rushing back to his little house, No. 19 in the Königstrasse, one of the oldest streets in the oldest part of the city of Hamburg.

Martha, our maid, must have thought that she was running well behind time, as the dinner was only just beginning to bubble on the kitchen stove.

'Well, now,' I said to myself, 'if my uncle, that most impatient of men, is hungry, what a fuss he'll make!'

'Professor Lidenbrock back so soon!' cried poor Martha in great alarm, half opening the dining-room door.

'Yes, Martha, but it's quite all right for the dinner not to be ready, because it's not two o'clock yet. Saint Michael's clock has only just struck half past one.'

'Then why has the master come home so soon?'

'He'll probably tell us that himself.'

'Here he is, Mr Axel. I'm going to hide while you try to reason with him.'

And Martha retreated to the safety of her culinary laboratory.

I was left alone. But how could a man of my wavering character reason successfully with so irascible a person as the Professor? With this in mind, I was preparing to retreat to my own little room upstairs when the front door creaked on its hinges; heavy feet made the whole flight of stairs shake, and the master of the house, passing rapidly through the dining-room, dashed into his study.

However, during his rapid passage through the house, he had flung his stick into a corner, his broad-brimmed hat on to the table and these commanding words at his nephew:

'Axel, follow me!'

I had scarcely had time to move when the Professor was again shouting impatiently to me:

'What? Not here yet?'

And I rushed into my formidable master's study.

Otto Lidenbrock was not a bad man, I freely admit that, but unless he changes as he grows older, which is not likely, he'll have a reputation as a fearful eccentric by the time he dies.

He was a professor at the Johannaeum, and delivered a course of lectures on mineralogy, during which lectures he regularly got into a terrible temper at least once or twice. Not that he was at all concerned about his students' attendance, or about the degree of attention with which they listened to him, or about any success of theirs which might eventually crown his labours. Such little matters of detail never troubled him much. His teaching was, as German philosophy calls it, 'subjective'; it was to benefit himself, not others. He was a learned egotist. He was a well of scientific knowledge, but the pulley rather creaked when you wanted to draw anything out. In a word, he was a learned miser.

Germany has not a few professors of this sort.

It was my uncle's misfortune that he was not gifted with a smooth, flowing articulation – not an affliction when he was talking at home, of course, but certainly when speaking in public. And it is a lack much to be deplored in a public speaker. The fact is, that during the course of his lectures at the Johannaeum, the Professor often came to a complete stop. He would struggle with some wilful word that would not pass his struggling lips, a word that refused to be uttered, swelled up in his mouth, and then at last broke out in the unasked-for form of a most unscientific oath: hence his fury.

Now in mineralogy there are many half-Greek, half-Latin terms which are very hard to articulate and which would be very trying even to a poet. I don't wish to say a word against so respectable a science; far be it from me. But in the august presence of rhombohedral crystals, retinasphaltic resins, gehlenites, Fassaites, molybdenites of lead, tungstates of manganese and titanite of zirconium, why, even the most fluent of tongues may be allowed a slip now and then.

It therefore happened that this minor fault of my uncle's came to be pretty well known around the town, and people took an unfair advantage of it. The students waited for him to arrive at difficult passages, and when he began to stumble, loud was their laughter – which is not in good taste, not even in Germans. And if there was always a full audience for the Lidenbrock lectures, who knows how many came only to have a laugh at my uncle's expense?

Nevertheless, my uncle was a man of deep learning – a fact I am most anxious to assert and reassert. Sometimes he might irretrievably damage a specimen by his excessive ardour in handling it, but nevertheless in him were united the genius of a true geologist with the keen eye of the mineralogist. Armed with his hammer, his steel chisel, his magnetic needles, his blowpipe and his bottle of nitric acid, he was a powerful man of science. He would refer any mineral to its proper place among the six hundred elementary substances now known, according to the way it fractured, its appearance, its hardness, its fusibility, its sound, its smell and its taste.

The name of Lidenbrock was therefore spoken of with honour in colleges and learned societies. Humphry Davy, Humboldt, Captain Sir John Franklin and General Sabine never failed to call upon him on their way through Hamburg. Becquerel, Ebelman, Brewster, Dumas, Milne-Edwards and Saint-Claire-Deville frequently consulted him on the most difficult problems in chemistry, a science which was indebted to him for many discoveries, as in 1853 there had been published in Leipzig an imposing folio by Otto Lidenbrock, entitled 'A Treatise on Transcendental Crystallography', with plates (a work which, however, failed to cover its costs).

In addition, let me add that my uncle was the curator of the museum of mineralogy created by Mr Struve, the Russian ambassador, a most valuable collection, famous across the whole of Europe.

Such was the gentleman who addressed me in that impatient manner. Imagine a tall, spare man, with an iron constitution and a fair complexion which took a good ten years off the fifty he had to admit to. His restless eyes were constantly moving behind his full-sized spectacles. His long, thin nose was like a knife blade. Some people were heard to remark that that organ of his was magnetized and could attract iron filings. But this was merely a mischievous story; the only thing it attracted was snuff, which it seemed to draw to itself in great quantities.

When I have added, to complete my portrait, that my uncle walked in mathematically exact strides of one yard, and that while walking he kept his fists firmly closed, a sure sign of an irritable temperament, I think I'll have said enough to disenchant anyone who might by mistake have desired much of his company.

He lived in his own little house in Königstrasse, a structure half brick and half wood, with a gable cut into steps. It looked out on to one of those winding canals which intersect each other in the middle of the ancient quarter of Hamburg which the great fire of 1842 had fortunately spared.

It's true that the old house stood slightly off the perpendicular, and bulged out a little towards the street. Its roof sloped slightly to one side, just like a student in the 'League of Virtue'[1] wore his cap down over one ear, and its lines lacked balance, but nonetheless it stood firm, thanks to an old elm which buttressed it at the front and which often in spring pushed its fresh blossoms through the windows.

My uncle was tolerably well off for a German professor. The house was his own, and everything in it. The living contents were his goddaughter Gräuben (a young girl of seventeen who came from Virland[2]), Martha and myself. As his nephew and an orphan, I had become his laboratory assistant.

I freely admit that I was extremely fond of geology and all its kindred sciences. The blood of a mineralogist was in my veins, and I was always happy among my specimens.

In a word, a man could live happily enough in the little old house in the

Königstrasse, in spite of the restless impatience of its master, for although he was a little too excitable, he was very fond of me.

But the man had no idea of patience. Nature herself was too slow for him. In April, after he had planted the terracotta pots in his sitting-room with mignonette and convolvulus seedlings, he would go and give them a little pull by their leaves to make them grow faster.

In dealing with such an odd individual, there was nothing for it but prompt obedience. I therefore rushed after him to his study.

CHAPTER 2

A MYSTERY TO BE SOLVED AT ANY PRICE

That study of his was a veritable museum. Specimens of every substance known to mineralogy lay there, placed in perfect order and correctly named in accordance with the three great divisions of inflammable, metallic and lithoid minerals.

How well I knew all these bits of science! Many a time, instead of enjoying the company of boys my own age, I had preferred dusting these graphites, anthracites, coals, lignites and peats! There were bitumens, resins and organic salts to be protected from the slightest speck of dust; there were metals from iron to gold, metals whose market value meant nothing in their absolute equality as scientific specimens; and there were stones too, enough to completely rebuild the house in Königstrasse, even with an extra room, which would have suited me admirably.

But on entering this study now, I was thinking of none of these wonders. My uncle alone filled my thoughts. He had flung himself into a velvet easy-chair, and was holding a book which he was studying with intense wonder.

'What a book! What a book!' he kept repeating.

These exclamations brought to my mind the fact that my uncle was liable to occasional fits of bibliomania, but no old book had any value in his eyes unless it had the virtue of being unfindable or, at the very least, unreadable.

'Well? Well? Can't you see? I discovered this priceless treasure this morning while I was rummaging about in old Hevelius the Jew's shop.'

'Oh, that's wonderful!' I replied, with forced enthusiasm.

What was the point of all this fuss about an old quarto bound in rough calfskin, a yellowish tome with a faded bookmark hanging from it?

But there was no end yet to the Professor's exclamations of admiration.

'Look,' he went on, both asking the questions and supplying the answers. 'Isn't it a beauty? Yes, it's absolutely splendid! Did you ever see such a binding? Doesn't the book open easily? Yes, it lies flat open at any page. But does it shut equally well? Yes, because the binding and the leaves are flush, all in a straight line, with no gaps or openings anywhere. And look at its spine, not a single crack in it after seven hundred years! Why, Bozerian, Closs or Purgold[3] would have been proud of such a binding!'

While making these comments, my uncle kept opening and shutting the old tome. I just had to ask about its contents, although I really hadn't the slightest interest in what it was about.

'And what's the title of this marvellous work?' I asked with an affected eagerness which he must have been absolutely blind not to see through.

'This work,' replied my uncle, with renewed enthusiasm, 'this work is the *Heims-Kringla* of Snorre Turleson, the famous twelfth-century Icelandic writer! It's the chronicle of the Norwegian princes who ruled in Iceland.'

'Indeed?' I cried, keeping up the pretence of enthusiasm. 'And of course, it's a German translation?'

'What?' replied the Professor sharply. 'A translation? What would I be doing with a translation? Who cares about a translation? This is the Icelandic original, in the magnificent idiomatic vernacular, which is both rich and simple and admits of an infinite variety of grammatical combinations and verbal modifications.'

'Like German,' I ventured.

'Yes,' replied my uncle, shrugging his shoulders, 'but, in addition to all that, Icelandic has three genders like Greek and declensions of proper nouns like Latin.'

'Ah!' I said, shaken a little out of my indifference, 'and is the type good?'

'Type! What do you mean by talking about type, you clown? Type? Do you imagine it's a printed book, you ignorant fool? It's a manuscript, a runic manuscript.'

'Runic?'

'Yes. Do you want me to explain what that is?'

'Of course not,' I replied in a tone of wounded pride. But my uncle continued nevertheless, and told me, whether I liked it or not, many things I had no interest in knowing.

'Runic characters were in use in Iceland in times past. They were invented, it is said, by Odin himself. Just look at them, you impious young man. Admire these letters, the creation of the mind of a god!'

Well, not knowing what to say, I was going to prostrate myself before this wonderful book, a way of answering equally pleasing to gods and kings and which has the advantage of never causing them any embarrassment, when a little incident happened which diverted our conversation down a different path.

This was the appearance of a dirty piece of parchment, which slipped out of the book and fell on the floor.

My uncle pounced on this scrap with understandable eagerness. An old document, enclosed from time immemorial within the folds of this old book, had for him immeasurable value.

'What can this be?' he exclaimed.

And he carefully spread out on the table a piece of parchment, about five inches by three, on which were some lines of mysterious characters.

Here is the exact facsimile. I think it is important for these strange signs to be publicly known, for they were to lead Professor Lidenbrock and his nephew to undertake the strangest expedition of the nineteenth century.

[runic inscription]

The Professor studied this series of characters for a few moments; then, raising his spectacles, he stated:

'These are runic letters, they're exactly like those of Snorre Turleson's manuscript. But what on earth does it mean?'

Since runic letters seemed to my mind to be an invention of the learned to mystify the rest of us poor souls, I was not sorry to see that my uncle was himself utterly mystified. At least, so it seemed to me, judging from his fingers, which were beginning to work uncontrollably.

'But it's definitely Old Icelandic,' he muttered between clenched teeth.

And Professor Lidenbrock must have known that, for he was acknowledged to be quite a polyglot. Not that he was fluent in the two thousand languages and four thousand dialects which are spoken across the world, but he did nevertheless know his fair share of them.

Faced with this difficulty, I could see he was going to give way to all the impetuosity of his character, and I was expecting a violent outburst, when the little clock over the fireplace struck two o'clock.

At that moment Martha opened the study door, saying:

'The soup is ready!'

'The Devil take your soup,' shouted my uncle, 'and the person who made it, and those who will eat it!' Martha fled. I followed close behind, and, hardly knowing how I got there, I found myself seated in my usual place.

I waited for a few moments. No Professor came. Never within my memory had he missed the important ceremony of dinner. And what a good dinner it was, too! There was parsley soup, a ham omelette garnished with sorrel and nutmeg, and a fillet of veal with compote of prunes; for dessert, sugared fruit; and the whole thing washed down with a good Moselle.

All this my uncle was going to sacrifice for a bit of old parchment. As an affectionate nephew, I considered it my duty to eat for him as well as for myself, which I did most conscientiously.

'I've never known such a thing,' said Martha. 'Professor Lidenbrock not eating!'

'Who'd have believed it?' I said.

'It means something serious is going to happen,' said the old servant, shaking her head.

In my opinion, it meant nothing more serious than the awful scene that would arise when my uncle discovered that his dinner had been eaten. I had just got to the last of the fruit when a loud voice tore me away from the pleasures of my dessert. I bounded out of the dining-room into the study.

CHAPTER 3

THE RUNIC WRITING EXERCISES THE PROFESSOR'S MIND

'It's undoubtedly runic,' said the Professor, frowning, 'but there's a secret in it, and I mean to discover what it is. Otherwise . . .'

A violent gesture completed his sentence.

'Sit there,' he added, gesturing towards the table with his fist. 'Sit down there, and write.'

I was seated and ready in an instant.

'Now I'll dictate to you every letter of our alphabet which corresponds to each of these Icelandic characters. We'll see what that will give us. But, by St Michael, don't you dare make a mistake!'

The dictation began. I concentrated hard on my task. Every letter was called out to me one after the other, with the following incomprehensible result:

mm.rnlls	esreuel	seecJde
sgtssmf	unteief	niedrke
kt,samn	atrateS	Saodrrn
emtnaeI	nuaect	rrilSa
Atvaar	.nscrc	ieaabs
ccdrmi	eeutul	frantu
dt,iac	oseibo	KediiY

When this work was completed, my uncle snatched the paper from me and examined it attentively for a long time.

'What does it all mean?' he kept repeating.

I swear to you I couldn't have enlightened him. But he didn't ask me anyway, and went on talking to himself.

'This is what is called a cryptogram,' he said, 'in which the letters have been deliberately mixed up to hide the meaning, and which if properly arranged would form an intelligible sentence. Just think, there may lie concealed here the clue to some great discovery!'

As for myself, I was of the opinion that it meant nothing at all, though, of course, I was careful not to say so.

Then the Professor took the book and the parchment, and compared the one with the other.

'These two writings are not by the same hand,' he said. 'The cryptogram is of a later date than the book, an undoubted proof of which I can see immediately. The first letter is a double *m*,[4] a letter which is not to be found in Turleson's book, and which was only added to the alphabet in the fourteenth century. Therefore there are at least two hundred years between the manuscript and the document.'

I won't deny that this seemed a perfectly logical conclusion to me.

'I am therefore led to think,' continued my uncle, 'that someone who possessed this book wrote these mysterious letters. But who was that possessor? Is his name nowhere to be found in the manuscript?'

My uncle raised his spectacles, picked up a strong magnifying glass and carefully examined the blank pages of the book. On the back of the second page, the half-title page, he noticed a sort of stain which looked like an ink blot. But examining it very closely, he thought he could make out some half-effaced letters. My uncle at once latched on to this as the main area of interest, and he worked on that blot until, with the help of his magnifying glass, he managed in the end to make out the following runic characters, which he read out to me with no hesitation:

ᛅᚱᚾᛂ ᛋᛆᚴᚿᚢᛋᛋᛂᛘᛘ

'Arne Saknussemm!' he cried in triumph. 'Why, that's the name of another Icelander, a sixteenth-century scholar and celebrated alchemist!'

I looked at my uncle admiringly.

'Those alchemists,' he went on, 'Avicenna, Bacon, Llull, Paracelsus, were the real, indeed the only, scientists of their time. They made discoveries which still rightly astonish us. Is it not possible that this Saknussemm has concealed in his cryptogram some surprising invention? It must be so. It is so!'

The Professor's imagination caught fire at this hypothesis.

'No doubt,' I ventured to reply, 'but why would he have hidden so marvellous a discovery in this way?'

'Why? Why? How should I know? Didn't Galileo do the same with regard to Saturn? We shall see. I'll get to the secret of this document, and I'll neither sleep nor eat until I have.'

My comment on this was a half-suppressed 'Oh dear!'

'Nor will you, Axel,' he added.

'Oh, good Lord!' I said to myself. 'It's a good thing I ate enough for two today!'

'First of all we must find out what language this cipher is written in. That can't be difficult.'

At these words I looked up quickly. My uncle went on with his soliloquy.

'There's nothing easier. In this document there are a hundred and thirty-two letters, seventy-nine consonants and fifty-three vowels. This is the proportion found in southern languages, whilst northern tongues are much richer in consonants; therefore this is in a southern language.'

These were sensible conclusions, I thought.

'But what language is it?'

Here I expected a display of learning, but what I got instead was profound analysis.

'This Saknussemm,' he went on, 'was a well-educated man. Now, since he was not writing in his own mother tongue, he would naturally select the one which was currently adopted by the leading spirits of the sixteenth century. I mean Latin. If I'm mistaken, I can try Spanish, French, Italian, Greek or Hebrew. But the scholars of the sixteenth century generally wrote in Latin. I therefore have the right to say, *a priori*, that this will be Latin.'

I almost jumped up from my chair. My memories as a Latin scholar revolted against the notion that these barbarous words could belong to the sweet language of Virgil.

'Yes, it is Latin,' my uncle went on. 'But it's a confused and mixed-up Latin.'

'Fine, then,' I thought. 'If you can bring order out of that confusion, my dear Uncle, you're a clever man indeed.'

'Let's examine this carefully,' he said again, picking up the sheet I had been writing on. 'Here is a series of one hundred and thirty-two letters in apparent disorder. There are words consisting of consonants alone, such as 'mm.rrlls'; others, on the other hand, in which vowels predominate, as for instance the fifth, 'unteief', or the last but one, 'oseibo'. Now this arrangement has evidently not been planned; it has arisen *mathematically* in obedience to some unknown rule which has governed the ordering of these letters. It seems certain to me that the original sentence was written properly, and then scrambled according to a rule which we have yet to discover. Whoever possesses the key to this cipher will read it fluently. But what is that key? Axel, have you got it?'

I said not a word, and for a very good reason. My eyes were fixed on a charming picture hanging on the wall, the portrait of Gräuben. My uncle's ward was at that time at Altona, staying with a relative, and in her absence I was very sad, for I may confess to you now, the pretty Virland girl and the professor's nephew loved each other with a patience and a calmness that were so very German. We had become engaged without my uncle's knowledge; he was too much taken up with geology to be able to understand feelings like ours. Gräuben was a lovely blue-eyed blonde, a rather serious girl but that did not stop her from loving me deeply. As for me, I adored her, if there is such a word in the German language. So it was that the picture of my pretty Virland girl instantly carried me away from the real world to a world of daydreams and memories.

Once again I could see the faithful companion of my labours and my leisure. Every day she helped me arrange my uncle's precious specimens; she and I labelled them together. Miss Gräuben was an accomplished mineralogist; she could have taught scientists a few things. She was fond of investigating abstruse scientific questions. What pleasant hours we'd spent in study together, and how often had I envied the very stones which she handled with her delightful fingers.

Then, during our leisure hours, we would go out together and walk along the shady paths beside the Alster, and wander happily side by side up to the old windmill which looked so splendid at the head of the lake. On the way we would chat hand in hand; I would tell her amusing tales which would make her laugh heartily. Then we would reach the banks of the Elbe, and after having said good-bye to the swans swimming gracefully among the white water-lilies, we would come back to the quay on the steamer.

That is just where I was in my daydreaming when my uncle thumped the table with his fist, dragging me violently back to the realities of life.

'Right,' he said, 'the very first thought that would come into anyone's head if they wanted to scramble the letters of a sentence would be to write the words vertically instead of horizontally.'

'That's an idea,' I said to myself.

'Now we must see what the effect of that would be, Axel. Write down any sentence you like on this piece of paper, only instead of arranging the letters in the usual way, one after the other, place them in succession in vertical columns, so as to group them together in five or six vertical lines.'

I understood what I was to do, and immediately produced the following literary masterpiece:

```
I y y l u
l o l e b
o u i G e
v , t r n
e m t ä !
```

'Good,' said the professor, without reading what I had written, 'now write those words in a horizontal line.'

I did as I was told, with the following result:

Iyylu loleb ouiGe v,trn emtä!

'Excellent!' said my uncle, grabbing the paper out of my hands. 'This is beginning to look just like an ancient document: the vowels and the consonants are grouped together in equal confusion, and there are even capitals in the middle of words, and commas too, just like in Saknussemm's parchment.'

I considered my uncle's remarks highly ingenious.

'Now,' said my uncle, looking straight at me, 'to read the sentence which you've just written, and with which I am wholly unacquainted, all I have to do is take the first letter of each word, then the second, then the third, and so on.'

And my uncle, to his great astonishment, and even more to mine, read out:

'I love you, my little Gräuben!'

'What's this?' exclaimed the Professor.

Yes, indeed, without realizing what I was doing, like an awkward and unlucky lover I had compromised myself by writing this unfortunate sentence.

'Ah! You're in love with Gräuben, are you?' he said, sounding just like a guardian should.

'Er, yes! Er, no!' I stammered.

'You love Gräuben,' he went on once or twice, as if in a dream. 'Well, let's apply the procedure I've suggested to the document in question.'

My uncle, becoming absorbed once again in his contemplations, had already forgotten my imprudent words. I say 'imprudent', because the great mind of so learned a man had of course no room for love affairs. Fortunately the important business of the document was more pressing.

As the very moment for the crucial experiment arrived, the Professor's eyes flashed through his spectacles. There was a quivering in his fingers as he grasped the old parchment. He was deeply moved. At last, he gave a preliminary cough, and with profound gravity, calling out in succession the first letter, then the second letter of each word, and so on, he dictated the following series of letters to me:

mmessunkaSenrA.icefdoK.segnittamurtnecertser
rette,rotaivsadua,ednecsedsadnelacartniiiluJsira
tracSarbmutabiledmekmeretarcsilucoYsleffenSnI

I must confess I felt extremely excited when we reached the end. These letters that my uncle had called out, one at a time, conveyed no meaning to my mind, so I was waiting for the Professor to pompously unfold the magnificent but hidden Latin of this mysterious sentence.

But who could have foreseen what was going to happen? A violent thump made the furniture rattle and spilt some ink, and my pen dropped from between my fingers.

'That's not it,' shouted my uncle. 'It doesn't make any sense at all.'

Then shooting across the study like a cannonball and going down the stairs like an avalanche, he rushed out into the Königstrasse and ran off.

CHAPTER 4

THE ENEMY TO BE STARVED INTO SUBMISSION

'Has he gone?' called Martha, running out of her kitchen at the noise of the violent slamming of doors that had shaken the whole house.

'Oh, yes,' I replied, 'completely gone.'

'But what about his dinner?' said the old servant.

'He's not having any.'

'And his supper?'

'He's not having any.'

'What?' cried Martha, clasping her hands.

'No, my dear Martha, he will eat nothing more. No one in the house is to eat anything at all. Uncle Lidenbrock has put us all on a strict diet until he has succeeded in deciphering an undecipherable scrawl.'

'Oh, Heavens! Are we all to die of hunger, then?'

I couldn't bring myself to admit that, with so absolute a ruler as my uncle, such a fate was inevitable.

The old servant, visibly disturbed, returned to her kitchen, moaning pitifully.

Alone once more, I thought of going and telling Gräuben all about it. But how could I leave the house? The Professor might return at any moment. And supposing he called for me? Supposing he wanted to start work on this word-puzzle again, a puzzle which would have taxed even old Oedipus[5]. And if I wasn't there to answer his call, who knows what might happen?

The wisest course was to remain where I was. A mineralogist in Besançon had just sent us a collection of siliceous geodes, which I had to classify. So I set to work, sorting and labelling all these hollow specimens and arranging them in a glass case. Inside each hollow geode was a nest of little crystals.

But this work didn't occupy my whole attention. The business with that old document kept going round and round in my brain. My head was throbbing with excitement and I felt vaguely uneasy. I was gripped by a feeling of impending disaster.

An hour later, my geodes were all arranged on the shelves. Then I flopped into the old velvet armchair, with my head back and my arms hanging over the sides. I lit my long curved pipe, the bowl of which was carved in the likeness of a reclining water-nymph; then I amused myself watching the tobacco turn into carbon, a process which was also slowly turning my nymph into a negress. Now and then I listened for those well-known footsteps on the stairs. But there wasn't a sound. Where could my uncle be? I imagined him running along under the magnificent trees which line the road to Altona, gesticulating wildly, shooting at the walls with his cane, thrashing the long grass, cutting the heads off the thistles and disturbing the peace of the solitary storks.

Would he return in triumph or discouragement? Which of the two would get the upper hand, him or the secret? Sitting pondering such questions, without thinking I picked up the sheet of paper on which I had written the incomprehensible succession of letters, and I repeated to myself 'What does it all mean?'

I tried to group the letters so as to form words. Quite impossible! Whether I put them together in twos, threes, fives or sixes, I got nothing but nonsense. Certainly, the fourteenth, fifteenth and sixteenth letters made the English word 'ice'; the eighty-fourth letter and the next two made 'sir'; and in the middle of the document, in the second and third lines, I noticed the Latin words 'rota', 'mutabile', 'ira', 'nec' and 'atra'.

'Right,' I thought, 'these words seem to justify my uncle's idea about the language of the document. In the last line I could see the word 'luco', which means a sacred wood. In the same line there was the word 'tabiled', which looked like Hebrew, and also the French words 'mer', 'arc' and 'mere'.

It was enough to drive a poor fellow crazy. Four different languages in this ridiculous sentence! What connection could there possibly be between such words as 'ice', 'sir', 'anger', 'cruel', 'sacred wood', 'changeable', 'mother', 'bow' and 'sea'? The first and the last might have something to do with each other; it was not at all surprising that in a document written in Iceland there should be a mention of a sea of ice. But it was quite another thing to get to the meaning of this cryptogram from so small a clue.

So I was struggling with an insurmountable difficulty. My brain was overheating, my eyes were blinking over that sheet of paper; its hundred and thirty-two letters seemed to flutter and fly round me like those silvery drops which float in the air around your head when there's a sudden violent rush of blood to the brain. I was prey to some kind of hallucination; I was suffocating; I needed air. Absent-mindedly I fanned myself with the bit of paper, the back and front of which alternately passed before my eyes. Imagine my surprise when, in one of those rapid movements, just as the back of the paper was turned towards me, I thought I could make out perfectly readable words such as the Latin words 'craterem' and 'terrestre'.

Suddenly, the penny dropped! These mere hints gave me the first glimpse of the truth – I had discovered the key to the cipher! To read the document, it would not even be necessary to read it through the paper. It could be spelt out with ease just as it was, just as it had been dictated to me. All those ingenious professorial combinations were coming to fruition. He was right about the arrangement of the letters. He was right about the language. He had been within a hair's-breadth of reading this Latin sentence from beginning to end; but the crossing of that hair's-breadth, chance had given to me!

Was I excited? I certainly was. My eyes were blurring so much, I could hardly see. I had spread out the paper on the table. I would only have to glance over it to know the whole secret.

At last I became calmer. I made myself walk twice round the room quietly to settle my nerves, and then I sat down again in the huge, deep armchair.

I took a deep breath, and then said to myself 'Now, let's read it.'

I leaned over the table, placed my finger on every letter in turn, and without a pause, without a moment's hesitation, I read out the whole sentence.

What amazement, and what terror, overwhelmed me! It was as if I had received a sudden mortal blow. What? Had what I had read really, actually been done? A mortal man had had the audacity to penetrate . . .

'Oh, no!' I cried, jumping up. 'No! No! No! My uncle must never know about such an incredible journey. He'd insist on doing it too. He's such a determined geologist, ropes couldn't hold him back! He'd start out in spite of everything and everybody, and he'd take me with him, and we'd never get back again. No, never! Never!'

My agitation was beyond all description.

'No! No! I won't let it happen,' I declared emphatically. 'And since it's in my power to prevent knowledge of it reaching the mind of my tyrant, I'll do it. By dint of turning this document round and round, he too might discover the key. I'll destroy it.'

There was a little fire left in the hearth. I picked up not only the piece of paper but Saknussemm's parchment as well. Feverishly, I was just about to fling it all on to the coals and utterly destroy this dangerous secret when the study door opened and in walked my uncle.

CHAPTER 5

FAMINE, THEN VICTORY, FOLLOWED BY DISMAY

I only just had time to put the wretched document back on the table.

Professor Lidenbrock seemed to be completely preoccupied. His obsession was giving him no rest. Evidently he had gone deeply into the matter, with careful thought and analysis. He had brought all the resources of his mind to bear upon it during his walk, and he had come back to apply some new combination to the cypher.

He sat in his armchair, and pen in hand he began to write what looked very much like algebraic formulae. My eyes followed his trembling hands, I noted every movement. Might not some unexpected result come of this? I too trembled, but quite unnecessarily since the true key was in my hands and no other key would unlock the secret.

For three long hours my uncle worked on without a word, without even looking up, rubbing out what he had written, beginning again, then rubbing it all out again, and so on a hundred times.

I knew very well that if he succeeded in writing down these letters in every possible relative position, he would eventually create the correct sentence. But I also knew that twenty letters alone could form two quintillion, four hundred and thirty-two quadrillion, nine hundred and two trillion, eight billion, a hundred and seventy-six million, six hundred and forty thousand combinations. Now, there were a hundred and thirty-two letters in this sentence, and these hundred and thirty-two letters would give a number of different sentences, each made up of at least a hundred and thirty-three letters, a number almost larger than one could imagine.

So I felt reassured as far as this heroic method of solving the problem was concerned.

Time passed. Night came; the noises in the street ceased. My uncle, bent over his task, didn't notice a thing, not even Martha half-opening the door; and he didn't hear a sound, not even the voice of that worthy woman saying:

'Will Sir not have any supper tonight?'

And poor Martha had to go away unanswered. As for me, after a long struggle against it, I was overcome by sleep and dropped off at the end of the sofa, while Uncle Lidenbrock went on calculating and then rubbing out his calculations.

When I awoke the next morning, that indefatigable worker was still at his post. His red eyes, his pale complexion, his hair tangled between his feverish fingers, the red spots on his cheeks, all revealed his desperate struggle with this impossible task and the weariness of spirit and mental exertions he must have undergone all through that unhappy night.

To be honest, I pitied him. In spite of reproaching him, which I considered I had every right to do, I was beginning to feel sorry for him to some extent. The poor man was so entirely taken up with this one idea that he had even forgotten how to get angry. The full strength of his feelings was concentrated on one thing alone, and as the usual vent for his feelings was closed, I was afraid that the extreme tension might lead to an explosion sooner or later.

With one action, with just one word, I might have loosened the vice of steel that was crushing his brain, but that word I would not speak.

Yet I wasn't a hard-hearted person. Why did I stay silent at such a time of crisis? Why was I so insensible to my uncle's interests?

'No, no,' I repeated to myself. 'I'll say nothing. He would insist on going; nothing on earth could stop him. His imagination is a volcano, and he would risk his life to do something that other geologists have never done. I'll say nothing. I'll keep the secret which mere chance has revealed to me. To reveal it would be to kill Professor Lidenbrock! Let him discover it by himself if he can. I will never have it laid at my door that I led him to his destruction.'

So resolved, I folded my arms and waited. But I hadn't reckoned on one little incident which transpired a few hours later.

When Martha wanted to go to the market, she found the door locked. The big key was gone. Who could have taken it out? Undoubtedly, it was my uncle, when he had returned the night before from his hasty walk.

Had he done it on purpose? Or was it a mistake? Did he want us to suffer starvation? That would be going too far! What? Were Martha and I to be the victims of a state of affairs in which we had not the slightest interest? It was true that, a few years before this, while my uncle was working at his great classification of minerals, he went forty-eight hours without eating, and the whole household was obliged to share in this scientific fast. I remember that, for my part, I got severe stomach cramps, which hardly suited the constitution of a hungry, growing boy.

Now it seemed that there was going to be no breakfast, just as there had been no supper the night before. But I made up my mind to be a hero, and not to give in to the pangs of hunger. Martha took it very seriously, and, poor woman, was very upset. As for me, being unable to leave the house distressed me much more, and for a reason you may well understand. A caged lover's feelings may easily be imagined.

My uncle went on working, his imagination rambling through the ideal world of combinations. He was far away from the real world, and far away from worldly needs.

About noon, I began to feel real pangs of hunger. Martha had, without thinking anything about it, used up all the food in the larder the night before, so now there was nothing left in the house. Still I held out; I made it a point of honour.

The clock struck two. This was getting ridiculous; no, worse than that – unbearable. I began to tell myself that I was exaggerating the importance of the document; that my uncle would surely not believe what it said; that he would take it as mere nonsense; that if it came to the worst, we would restrain him and keep him at home if he thought of setting out on the expedition; that, after all, he might himself discover the key to the cipher, and that there would then have been no point to my involuntary abstinence.

These seemed excellent reasons to me, though I would have rejected them indignantly the previous night. I even went as far as to condemn myself for my stupidity in having waited so long, and I finally resolved to let my uncle in on the secret.

I was wondering how to approach the subject, not wanting to do so too suddenly, when the Professor jumped up, put his hat on and was about to go out.

Surely he was not leaving the house and shutting us in again? Oh, no! I wasn't having that.

'Uncle!' I cried.

He seemed not to hear me.

'Uncle Lidenbrock!' I cried, raising my voice.

'Eh?' he answered, like a man suddenly waking up.

'Uncle, the key!'

'What key? The door key?'

'No, no!' I cried. 'The key to the document.'

The Professor stared at me over his spectacles. No doubt he saw something unusual in my expression, because he took hold of my arm and wordlessly questioned me with his eyes. Never was a question more forcefully put.

I nodded my head.

He shook his pityingly, as if he was dealing with a lunatic. I made a more affirmative gesture.

His eyes flashed, his hand became threatening.

This silent conversation in such circumstances would have held the attention of the most indifferent spectator. And the fact really was that I dared not speak now, for fear that my uncle might smother me in his first joyful embraces. But he became so insistent that I was at last obliged to answer.

'Yes, that key. Chance . . .'

'What are you saying?' he shouted with an intensity of emotion that is hard to describe.

'There, read that!' I said, handing him the sheet of paper I had written on.

'But there's nothing there,' he answered, crumpling up the paper.

'No, nothing – until you read it backwards.'

I hadn't finished my sentence when the Professor gave a cry, or rather a roar. He had seen the light! He was transformed!

'Ah, you clever man, Saknussemm!' he cried. 'First you wrote your sentence backwards.'

And snatching up the paper, with vision blurred with tears and a voice choked with emotion, he read the whole document from the last letter to the first.

This is how it went:

In Sneffels Yoculis craterem kem delibat
umbra Scartaris Julii intra calendas descende,
audas viator, et terrestre centrum attinges.
Kod feci. Arne Saknussemm.

Which rather bad Latin may be translated as follows:

Descend into the crater of the jokul of Sneffels,
which the shadow of Scartaris touches before the calends[6] of July,
and you, bold traveller, will reach the centre of the Earth;
which I, Arne Saknussemm, have done.

On reading this, my uncle jumped as if he had touched a Leyden jar[7]. His courage, his joy and his certainty were magnificent to behold. He walked up and down, he held his head in his hands, he pushed the chairs around, he piled up his books; incredible as it may seem, he even juggled with his precious flint geodes; he punched this and he thumped that. Finally, he calmed down and sank back exhausted into his armchair.

'What time is it?' he asked after a few moments of silence.

'Three o'clock,' I replied.

'Is it really? Dinner-time went by quickly, and I didn't notice. I'm dying of hunger. Come on, and after dinner . . .'

'Well?'

'After dinner, pack my trunk.'

'What?' I cried.

'And yours!' replied the merciless Professor, going into the dining-room.

CHAPTER 6

EXCITING DISCUSSIONS ABOUT A UNIQUE UNDERTAKING

At these words, a shiver ran through me. But I controlled myself. I even resolved to put a good face on it. Only scientific arguments could stop Professor Lidenbrock. And there were good arguments against the practicability of such a journey. To penetrate as far as the centre of the Earth? What nonsense! But I kept my battery of arguments in reserve for a suitable opportunity, and gave my whole attention to the meal.

There would be no point in telling you here of my uncle's anger and oaths when he found himself faced with an empty table. Explanations were given, and Martha was set free again. She ran to the market, and managed so well that an hour later my hunger was assuaged, and I was able to go back to contemplating the gravity of the situation.

Throughout dinner my uncle was almost merry. He indulged in some of those learned jokes which never do anybody any harm. But when dessert was over, he beckoned me into his study.

I obeyed. He sat down at one end of his desk, and I sat down at the other.

'Axel,' he said in a kindly voice, 'you're a very clever young man. You've done me a great service, just when, weary of the struggle, I was about to give up. Who knows where I would have ended up. I'll never forget this. And you shall have your share in the glory to which your discovery will lead.'

'Right!' I thought. 'He's in a good mood. Now's the time to discuss that very glory.'

'Most of all,' my uncle went on, 'I must insist on absolute secrecy, you understand? There are not a few people in the world of science who envy me my success, and many of them would be ready to undertake this journey. Our return must be the first news they have of it.'

'Do you really think there are many people bold enough?' I said.

'Certainly. Who would hesitate to gain such fame? If that document became public knowledge, a whole army of geologists would be ready to hasten in the footsteps of Arne Saknussemm.'

'I'm not so sure of that, Uncle,' I replied, 'because we've no proof of the authenticity of this document.'

'What! Given the book we found it in?'

'All right. I'll admit that Saknussemm may have written these lines. But does it follow that he really accomplished such a journey? May it not be that this old parchment is simply intended as a joke?'

I almost regretted having uttered this last word. I said it in an unguarded moment. The Professor's shaggy brows formed into a frown, and for a moment I feared for my safety. Luckily no harm came of it. A vague smile formed on the lips of my stern companion, and he replied:

'That is what we shall see.'

'Oh!' I said, rather put out. 'But do let me go through all the possible objections against this document.'

'Speak, my boy, don't be afraid. You are quite at liberty to express your opinions. You're no longer only my nephew, but my colleague. Please go on.'

'Well, in the first place, I'd like to know what Jokul, Sneffels and Scartaris are. I've never heard these names before.'

'Nothing easier. Not long ago I received a map from my friend, Augustus Petermann, in Leipzig. It couldn't have come at a better time. Take down the third atlas in the second shelf in the large bookcase, series Z, shelf 4.'

I got up, and with the help of such precise instructions couldn't fail to find the required atlas. My uncle opened it, and said:

'Here is one of the best maps of Iceland, Handersen's, and I think this will provide the answer to all your questions.'

I bent over the map.

'Look at this volcanic island,' said the Professor. 'Notice that all the volcanoes are called 'jokuls', a word which means glacier in Icelandic, and that given the northerly latitude of Iceland nearly all the active volcanoes discharge through beds of ice. Hence this term 'jokul' is applied to all the volcanic mountains in Iceland.'

'Fine,' I said, 'but what about Sneffels?'

I was hoping that this question would be unanswerable, but I was mistaken. My uncle replied:

'Follow my finger along the west coast of Iceland. Do you see Reykjavik, the capital? You do? Well, move up past the innumerable fjords that indent those sea-beaten shores, and stop at the sixty-fifth degree of latitude. What do you see there?'

'I can see a peninsula that looks like a thigh bone with the knee bone at the end of it.'

'A very reasonable description, my boy. Now, do you see anything on that knee bone?'

'Yes, a mountain rising out of the sea.'

'Right. That's Snæfell.'

'That's Snæfell?'

'Yes. It's a mountain five thousand feet high, and one of the most remarkable in the world if its crater does lead down to the centre of the Earth.'

'But that's impossible,' I said, shrugging my shoulders, furious at such a ridiculous supposition.

'Impossible?' said the Professor severely. 'Why, may I ask?'

'Because the crater would obviously be filled with lava and burning rocks, and therefore . . .'

'But suppose it's an extinct volcano?'

'Extinct?'

'Yes. The number of active volcanoes on the surface of the globe is at the present time only about three hundred. But there's a very much larger number of extinct ones. Snæfell is one of them. In the historic period, there has only been one eruption of this volcano, in 1219. From then on, it has quietened down more and more, and now it is no longer counted among active volcanoes.'

To such definite statements, I could make no reply. I therefore took refuge in other mysterious passages in the document.

'What's the meaning of this word 'Scartaris', and what have the calends of July got to do with it?'

My uncle took a few minutes to consider. For one brief moment I felt a ray of hope, but it was quickly extinguished, as in a minute he replied with these words:

'What is darkness to you is daylight to me. This shows the care and ingenuity with which Saknussemm has indicated his discovery. Sneffels, or Snæfell, has several craters. It was therefore necessary to point out which of these leads to the centre of the world. What did the Icelandic sage do? He observed that at the approach of the calends of July, that is to say in the last days of June, one of the peaks, called Scartaris, threw its shadow down the mouth of that particular crater, and he committed that fact to his document. Could there possibly have been a more exact guide? As soon as we have arrived at the summit of Snæfell, we need have no hesitation over the proper path to take.'

There was no doubt about it, my uncle had answered every one of my objections. I saw that his position with regard to the old parchment was impregnable. I therefore stopped pressing him on that part of the subject, and since the most important thing was to convince him, I moved on to scientific objections, which in my opinion were far more serious.

'All right, then,' I said. 'I'm forced to admit that Saknussemm's sentence is clear and leaves no room for doubt. I will even allow that the document bears every mark and evidence of authenticity. That learned philosopher did get to the bottom of Sneffels, he has seen the shadow of Scartaris touch the edge of the crater before the calends of July, he may even have heard legends told in his day about that crater reaching to the centre of the world; but as for reaching it himself, as for making the journey, and returning, if he ever went, I say no – he never, ever did that.'

'And what reason do you have for saying that?' said my uncle in a mocking tone.

'All the theories of science declare such a feat to be impracticable.'

'The theories say that, do they?' replied the Professor in an affable tone. 'Oh, those nasty theories! Those theories will really hold us back, won't they?'

I could see that he was just laughing at me, but I continued all the same.

'Yes. It's perfectly well known that the internal temperature of the Earth rises by one degree for every 70 feet you go down from the surface. Now, admitting this proportion to be constant, and the radius of the Earth being fifteen hundred leagues[8], there must be a temperature of more than 200,000 degrees at the centre of the Earth. Therefore, all the substances that compose the body of this Earth must exist there in a state of incandescent gas, for the metals that most resist the action of heat, gold and platinum, and the hardest of rocks could never be solid or even liquid at such a temperature. I have therefore a perfectly good reason for asking if it is possible to penetrate through such a medium.'

'So, Axel, it's the heat that's bothering you?'

'Of course it is. Were we to reach a depth of even 25 miles, we would have arrived at the limit of the terrestrial crust, because there the temperature would be more than 1,300 degrees.'

'And you're afraid of being melted?'

'I'll leave it to you to answer that question,' I replied, rather sullenly.

'This is my answer,' replied Professor Lidenbrock, putting on one of his grandest airs. 'Neither you nor anybody else knows with any certainty what is going on in the interior of the Earth, since not a twelve-thousandth part of its radius is known. Science is always improvable, and every new theory is soon driven out by a yet newer one. Was it not always believed until Fourier that the temperature of interplanetary space decreased indefinitely? And is it not now known that the greatest cold of the ethereal regions is never lower than 40 or 50 degrees below zero? Why should it not be the same with the internal heat? Why should it not be the case that, at a certain depth, it reaches an impassable limit instead of rising to such a point as to melt the most solid metals?'

Since my uncle was now talking hypotheses, there was of course nothing to be said.

'Well, I will tell you that true men of science, amongst them Poisson, have demonstrated that if a heat of 200,000 degrees existed in the interior of the globe, the fiery gases arising from the fused matter would acquire a force that the crust of the Earth would be unable to resist, and that it would explode like the plates of a bursting boiler.'

'That's Poisson's opinion, Uncle, nothing more.'

'Granted. But it is likewise the opinion of other distinguished geologists that the interior of the globe is neither gas nor water, nor any of the heaviest minerals known, for in none of these cases would the Earth weigh what it does.'

'Oh, you can prove anything with figures!'

'But it's the same with facts! Is it not known that the number of volcanoes has decreased since the first days of creation? And if there is central heat, may we not therefore conclude that it too is decreasing?'

'My dear Uncle, if you're entering the realms of speculation, there's nothing more to be said.'

'But I have to tell you that the greatest names have come round to supporting my views. Do you remember a visit paid to me by the celebrated chemist, Humphry Davy, in 1825?'

'Not at all, since I wasn't born until nineteen years after that.'

'Well, Humphry Davy did call on me on his way through Hamburg. We spent a long time discussing, amongst other problems, the hypothesis of the liquid structure of the nucleus of the Earth. We agreed that it couldn't be in a liquid state for a reason which science has never been able to confute.'

'What is that reason?' I said, rather astonished.

'Because this liquid mass would be subject, like the ocean, to lunar attraction, and therefore twice every day there would be internal tides which, by pushing up the terrestrial crust, would cause regular earthquakes!'

'Yet it's evident that the surface of the globe has been subject to the action of fire,' I replied, 'and it is quite reasonable to suppose that the external crust cooled down first, whilst the heat took refuge down at the centre.'

'You would be wrong in that assumption,' replied my uncle. 'The Earth has been heated by combustion on its surface, and that's all. Its surface was composed of a great many metals, such as potassium and sodium, which have the peculiar property of igniting when they come into contact with air and water. These metals ignited when the atmospheric vapour fell on the ground as rain, and by and by, when the water penetrated into the fissures of the crust of the Earth, it caused fresh combustion with explosions and eruptions. This was what caused the numerous volcanoes when the Earth was formed.'

'That's a very clever hypothesis!' I exclaimed, somewhat in spite of myself.

'And one which Humphry Davy demonstrated to me by a simple experiment. He formed a small ball of the metals I have mentioned, making a very fair representation of our globe. Whenever he caused a fine spray of rain to fall on its surface, it swelled up, oxidized and formed tiny mountains. A crater broke open at one of its summits, an eruption took place, and transmitted such heat to the whole of the ball that it could not be held in one's hand.'

In truth, I was beginning to be swayed by the Professor's arguments, to which he was giving additional weight by his usual ardour and fervent enthusiasm.

'You see, Axel,' he added, 'the state of the nucleus of the Earth has given rise to various hypotheses among geologists. There is no proof at all of this internal heat, and my opinion is that there is no such thing, that there cannot *be* such a thing. In any case, we shall see for ourselves, and, like Arne Saknussemm, we'll know exactly what the truth is concerning this important question.'

'Very well, we shall see,' I replied, carried away by his contagious enthusiasm. 'Yes, we shall see. That is, if it's possible to see anything there.'

'And why not? May we not depend on electrical phenomena to give us light? May we not even expect light from the atmosphere, the pressure of which may cause it to be luminous as we near the centre?'

'Well, yes,' I said. 'That too is possible.'

'It is certain,' exclaimed my uncle in a tone of triumph. 'But not a word, do you hear? Not a word about this whole subject. We don't want anyone to get the idea of discovering the centre of the Earth before we do.'

CHAPTER 7

A WOMAN'S COURAGE

So ended this memorable session. That conversation threw me into a fever. I came out of my uncle's study quite stunned, so much so that it was as if there was not enough air in all the streets of Hamburg to put me right again. I therefore made for the banks of the Elbe, close to the quay for the steamer that plies between the town and the Harburg railway line.

Was I convinced of the truth of what I had heard? Had I not simply given way under the pressure of Professor Lidenbrock's forceful personality? Was I to believe that he was really in earnest in his intention to penetrate to the centre of this massive globe? Had I been listening to the mad speculations of a lunatic or to the scientific conclusions of a lofty genius? Where did truth end? Where did error begin?

I was all adrift amongst a thousand contradictory hypotheses, and I couldn't grasp any one of them firmly.

But I remembered that I had been convinced, although my enthusiasm now was beginning to cool. I felt a desire to make a start at once, and not to lose time and courage by calm reflection. I had at that moment quite enough courage to simply pack my case and set off.

But I have to confess that in another hour this unnatural excitement abated, my nervous tension lessened, and from the depths of the Earth I climbed back to the surface again.

'It's absolutely crazy!' I shouted out. 'There's no sense in it. No sensible young man should consider such a proposal for a moment. Nothing of that is real. I've had a bad night, it's all a bad dream.'

By this time, I had walked along the banks of the Elbe and crossed the town. After passing the port as well, I reached the Altona road. Something led me there, some intuition that was soon to be justified, for I shortly caught sight of my little Gräuben returning with her light step to Hamburg.

'Gräuben!' I shouted while still some way away.

The young girl stopped, rather frightened perhaps to hear someone call her name on the public highway. In ten strides, I was beside her.

'Axel!' she exclaimed in surprise. 'What, then? Have you come to meet me? Is that why you're here?'

But when she looked at me, Gräuben couldn't fail to see my uneasiness and distress.

'What's the matter with you?' she said, holding out her hand.

'What's the matter with me, Gräuben? You have no idea!' I said.

In two seconds and three sentences my pretty Virland girl was fully informed of what was going on. For a time she was silent. Was her heart beating like mine? I don't know, but I do know that her hand wasn't trembling in mine. We walked on a hundred yards without speaking.

At last she said, 'Axel.'

'My darling Gräuben.'

'That will be a wonderful journey!'

These words made me jump.

'Yes, Axel, it's a journey worthy of the nephew of a scientist. It's a good thing for a man to gain fame by some great undertaking.'

'What, Gräuben, aren't you going to try to dissuade me from setting out on such an expedition?'

'No, my dear Axel, and I would willingly go with you, except that a poor girl would only be in your way.'

'Are you serious?'

'Quite serious.'

Oh, women, girls, the female mind, how hard it is to understand you! When you're not the most timid of creatures, you're the bravest. Reason has no influence over you. What was she saying? Was this child encouraging me to undertake such an expedition? Would she really not be afraid to take part in it herself? And she was urging *me* to do it, me, the one she loved!

I was disconcerted and, to tell you the truth, I was ashamed.

'We'll see whether you'll say the same thing tomorrow, Gräuben.'

'Tomorrow, dear Axel, I will say exactly what I have said today.'

Gräuben and I continued on our way, hand in hand but in silence. The emotional turmoil of the day had exhausted me.

After all, I thought, the calends of July are a long way off, and between now and then many things could happen that would cure my uncle of his desire to travel underground.

It was night when we arrived at the house in Königstrasse. I expected to find the house quiet, my uncle in bed as usual, and Martha giving the dining-room a last touch with the feather duster.

But I hadn't taken into account the Professor's impatience. I found him shouting and getting himself all worked up amidst a crowd of porters who were all depositing various loads in the hallway. Our old servant was at her wits' end.

'Come on, Axel, you miserable wretch!' shouted my uncle as soon as he saw me. 'Your cases aren't packed, and my papers aren't in order. I can't find the key of my carpet bag. And I haven't got my gaiters.'

I stood thunderstruck. My voice failed. My lips could scarcely utter the words:

'Are we really going?'

'Of course we are! I never dreamed that you would go out for a walk instead of getting a move on with your preparations.'

'So we're really going?' I asked again, my hopes fading.

'Yes, the day after tomorrow, early.'

I couldn't listen to any more. I fled to my little room for refuge.

All hope was now gone. My uncle had spent the whole afternoon buying some of the tools and apparatus required for this desperate undertaking. The hallway was packed with rope ladders, knotted cords, torches, flasks, grappling irons, alpenstocks, pickaxes, iron-tipped sticks, enough for ten men to carry.

I spent a terrible night. Next morning I was called early. I had quite decided not to open the door, but how could I resist the sweet voice which was always music to my ears, saying, 'Axel dear'?

I came out of my room. I thought my pale countenance and my red and sleepless eyes would have some effect on Gräuben's sympathies and change her mind.

'Oh, Axel, my dear,' she said, 'I see you're better. A night's rest has done you good.'

'Done me good?' I exclaimed.

I rushed to the mirror. Well, in fact I did look better than I'd expected. I could hardly believe my own eyes.

'Axel,' she said, 'I've had a long talk with my guardian. He's a dedicated scientist and a man of immense courage, and you must remember that his blood flows in your veins. He has told me of his plans and his hopes, and why and how he hopes to attain his objective. I have no doubt he will succeed. My dear Axel, it's a wonderful thing to devote yourself to science! What honours await Professor Lidenbrock, and they will reflect on his companion too. When you return, Axel, you will be a man, his equal, free to speak and to act independently, and free to . . .'

The dear girl could only finish this sentence with a blush. Her words revived me. But I refused to believe we would be starting so soon. I dragged Gräuben into the Professor's study.

'Uncle, is it true we're going?'

'Why do you doubt it?'

'Well, I'm not doubting it,' I said, not wanting to annoy him, 'but what need is there for all this hurry?'

'Time! Time that's flying by with a speed that nothing can change.'

'But it's only the 16th of May, and the end of June is . . .'

'You ignoramus! Do you think you can get to Iceland in a couple of days? If you hadn't gone off and left me, like a fool, I would have taken you to the office of Liffender & Co. of Copenhagen and then you would have learned that there's only one sailing every month from Copenhagen to Reykjavik, on the 22nd.'

'Well?'

'Well, if we waited for the 22nd of June, we would be too late to see the shadow of Scartaris touch the crater of Snæfell. So we must get to Copenhagen as fast as we can in order to secure our passage. Go and pack!'

There was nothing I could say to this. I went up to my room. Gräuben followed me. She set to to pack everything I would need on my trip. She was no more affected than if I had been starting out on a little trip to Lübeck or Heligoland. Her little hands moved without haste. She talked quietly. She kept giving me sensible reasons for our expedition. She charmed me, and yet I was angry with her. Now and then I felt like exploding into a temper, but she took no notice and went on as methodically as ever.

Finally the last strap was buckled. I went downstairs again. All that day the suppliers of scientific instruments, guns and electrical equipment kept coming and going. Martha was being driven distracted.

'Is the Professor mad?' she asked.

I nodded my head.

'And is he going to take you with him?'

I nodded again.

'Where to?'

I pointed down towards the floor.

'Down into the cellar?' exclaimed the old servant.

'No,' I said. 'Lower than that.'

Night came. But I didn't notice time passing.

'Tomorrow morning, at six o'clock sharp,' said my uncle. 'That's when we're setting off.'

At ten o'clock I fell on my bed, a mere lump of inert matter. All through the night terror gripped me. I dreamed of abysses. I was a prey to delirium. I felt myself held by the Professor's sinewy hand, dragged along, hurled down, shattered into little bits. I dropped down unfathomable precipices with the accelerating velocity of bodies falling through space. My life became one unending fall. I awoke at five, trembling and weary, with my nerves shattered. I went downstairs. My uncle was already at the table, gobbling down his breakfast. I stared at him with horror and disgust. But my dear Gräuben was there, so I said nothing. But I couldn't eat a thing.

At half-past five there was a rattle of wheels outside. A large carriage had arrived to take us to the Altona railway station. It was soon piled up with my uncle's trunks and cases.

'Where's your case?' he cried.

'It's ready,' I replied in a faltering voice.

'Then hurry up and bring it down, or we'll miss the train.'

It was now clearly impossible to continue to struggle against fate. I went up to my room again and let my case slide down the stairs, following quickly after it.

At that moment, my uncle was solemnly handing over control of the household to Gräuben. My pretty Virland girl was as calm and collected as ever. She kissed her guardian, but couldn't hold back a tear as she touched my cheek with her gentle lips.

'Gräuben!' I murmured.

'Go, my dear Axel, go! I'm your fiancée now, and when you come back I will be your wife.'

I hugged her in my arms and took my seat in the carriage. Martha and the young girl, standing at the door, waved their last farewell. Then the horses, urged on by the driver's whistling, swept off at a gallop on the road to Altona.

CHAPTER 8

SERIOUS PREPARATIONS FOR A VERTICAL DESCENT

Altona, which is just a suburb of Hamburg, is the terminus of the Kiel railway, which was to take us to the coast at the Belts[9]. In twenty minutes we were in Holstein.

At half-past six the carriage stopped outside the station. My uncle's numerous voluminous trunks were unloaded, moved, labelled, weighed and put into the luggage vans, and at seven we were seated face to face in our compartment. The whistle blew and the engine pulled away. We were off.

Was I resigned to my fate? No, not yet. Nevertheless the cool morning air and the rapidly changing scenes along the way to some extent drew me out of my sad thoughts.

As for the Professor's thoughts, they were running far ahead of the express train. We were alone in the carriage, but we sat in silence. My uncle checked all his pockets and his travelling bag with the minutest care. I could see that he hadn't overlooked the slightest detail.

Amongst other documents, there was a carefully folded sheet of paper bearing the heading of the Danish consulate and signed by Mr Christiensen, the Danish consul in Hamburg and a friend of the Professor's. This we would hoped would provide us with the means in Copenhagen of getting a recommendation to the Governor of Iceland[10].

I also caught sight of the famous document, carefully hidden in a secret pocket in my uncle's wallet. I cursed it, and then began to study the countryside. It was an interminable succession of uninteresting loamy and fertile flats, a very easy country to build railways on, and particularly suitable for the laying-down of these direct, level lines so dear to railway companies.

I had no time to get tired of the monotony, for in three hours we stopped at Kiel, close to the sea.

The luggage being labelled for Copenhagen, we had no need to concern ourselves with it, but nonetheless the Professor kept a careful eye on every item until all were safe on board. There they disappeared into the hold.

My uncle, in his haste, had so well calculated the connection times between the train and the steamer that we had a whole day to spare. The steamer *Ellenora* was not leaving until that night. This caused nine hours of feverish over-excitement in which the impatient irascible traveller (my uncle) consigned to hell the railway directors and the steamboat companies and the governments which allowed such intolerable delays. I was forced to back him up when he argued with the captain of the *Ellenora* on this very subject. He wanted to get him to stoke the boilers at once. The captain told him to clear off.

In Kiel, as elsewhere, a day passes eventually. What with walking along the verdant shores of the bay on which the little town stands, exploring the thick woods which make the town look like a nest hidden in a tangle of branches, admiring the villas, each with its own little bath-house, and by rushing about and grumbling, at last ten o'clock came.

The smoke from the *Ellenora*'s funnel rose up into the sky in thick curls and the bridge shook with the throbbing of the boiler. We were on board, and for a time possessors of two berths, one above the other, in the only saloon cabin on the ship.

At a quarter past ten, the ship cast off and started on its journey over the dark waters of the Great Belt.

The night was dark. There was a sharp breeze and a rough sea. Through the thick darkness, a few lights appeared on the shore. Later on, I don't know when, a dazzling light from some lighthouse threw a bright stream of fire across the waves. And this is all I can remember of this first crossing of ours.

At seven in the morning, we landed at Korsör, a small town on the west coast of Zealand. There we transferred from the boat to another railway line, which took us across a country every bit as flat as Holstein.

Three hours' travelling brought us to the capital of Denmark. My uncle hadn't shut his eyes all night. In his impatience, I do believe he had been trying to make the train go faster with his feet!

At last he caught a glimpse of the sea.

'The Sound[11]!' he shouted.

On our left was a huge building that looked like a hospital.

'That's a lunatic asylum,' said one of our travelling companions.

'Great!' I thought. 'Just the place to end our days in. But big as it is, that asylum isn't big enough to hold the complete madness of Professor Lidenbrock!'

At ten in the morning, we at last set foot in Copenhagen. The luggage was loaded on to a carriage and, with us too, taken to the Phoenix Hotel in Breda Street. This took half an hour, because the station is outside the town. Then my uncle, after a quick wash, dragged me after him. The porter at the hotel could speak German and English, but the Professor, as a polyglot, questioned him in good Danish, and it was in the same language that we were given directions to the Museum of Northern Antiquities.

The museum was a curious establishment, a collection of wonders – stone weapons, metal goblets and jewellery – by means of which one might reconstruct the ancient history of the country. Professor Thomsen, the curator, was a learned scholar and a friend of the Danish consul in Hamburg.

My uncle had a cordial letter of introduction to him. As a general rule, one scholar greets another with a certain coolness. But here it was different. Professor Thomsen greeted Professor Lidenbrock warmly like an old friend, and the Professor's nephew as well. I need hardly say that we kept our secret from the worthy curator: we were simply visiting Iceland out of harmless curiosity.

Professor Thomsen put himself entirely at our disposal, and with him we visited the harbour with the object of finding the vessel that was due to sail the soonest.

I was still hoping there would be no way of getting to Iceland, but no such luck. A small Danish schooner, the *Valkyrie*, was due to set sail for Reykjavik on the 2nd of June. The captain, a Mr Bjarne, was on board. His passenger-to-be was so overjoyed that he shook his hand so hard he almost broke it. The worthy fellow was rather surprised at this intensity. To him it seemed a very simple thing to go to Iceland, as that was his business, but to my uncle it was sublime. The worthy captain took advantage of this enthusiasm to charge us double for the trip, but we didn't bother ourselves over such trifles.

'You must be on board on Tuesday, at seven in the morning,' said Captain Bjarne, having pocketed the cash.

Then we thanked Professor Thomsen for his kindness and returned to the Phoenix Hotel.

'That's fine, that's fine,' my uncle kept saying. 'How lucky we are to have found this boat ready to sail. Now let's have some breakfast and wander round the town.'

First we went to Kongens-nye-Torw, an irregularly-shaped square in which there are two innocent-looking guns which wouldn't frighten anyone. Close by, at No. 5, there was a French restaurant owned by a chef by the name of Vincent, where we got an ample breakfast that cost us four marks each.

Then I took a childish pleasure in exploring the city. My uncle let me drag him around with me, but he took no notice of anything: not the insignificant king's palace; nor the pretty seventeenth-century bridge which spans the canal in front of the museum; nor that immense monument to Thorwaldsen, decorated with a horrible mural painting and containing within it a collection of the sculptor's works; nor, in a beautiful park, the chocolate-box Rosenberg Castle; nor the beautiful renaissance edifice of the Exchange, nor its spire composed of the twisted tails of four bronze dragons; nor the huge windmill on the ramparts, whose huge arms billowed in the sea breeze like the sails of a ship.

What delightful walks we would have had together, my pretty Virland girl and I, along the harbour where the double-decked ships and the frigates slept peacefully beside the red roofs of the warehouses, by the green banks along the strait, through the deep shades of the trees amongst which the fort is half concealed, where the guns are thrusting out their black throats between branches of alder and willow.

But, alas, Gräuben was far away, and I had no hope of ever seeing her again.

But if my uncle felt no attraction to these romantic scenes, he was very much struck by the sight of a certain church spire situated on the island of Amager, which forms the south-west[12] part of Copenhagen.

I was ordered to head in that direction. We embarked on a small steamer which plies the canals, and in a few minutes it pulled alongside the Dockyard quay.

After making our way through a few narrow streets where some convicts in yellow and grey trousers were at work under the supervision of warders, we arrived at the Vor Frelsers Kirk. There was nothing remarkable about the church, but there was a reason why its tall spire had attracted the Professor's attention. Starting from the top of the tower, an external staircase wound around the spire, circling upwards in spirals.

'Let's go right to the top,' said my uncle.

'I'll get dizzy,' I said.

'All the more reason why we should go up. We've got to get used to it.'

'But . . .'

'Come on, I tell you. Don't waste time.'

I had no option but to obey. A caretaker who lived at the other end of the street gave us the key, and our ascent began.

My uncle went ahead, treading carefully. I followed him rather anxiously, because I was very prone to dizziness. I had neither the sense of balance of an eagle nor the nerves of one.

As long as we were protected by being on the inside of the winding staircase up the tower, all went well enough; but after we had toiled up a hundred and fifty steps, fresh air hit me in the face, and we found ourselves on the platform at the top of the tower. There the outside staircase began its spirals, protected only by a thin iron rail, and the narrowing steps seemed to lead on up into infinite space!

'I'll never be able to do it,' I said.

'Come on, don't be a coward,' said my uncle, not showing a shred of pity.

I had no option but to follow him, clutching at every step. The cold air made me giddy; I felt the spire rocking with every gust of wind; my legs were turning to jelly. Soon I was crawling on my knees, then on my stomach. I closed my eyes; I seemed to be lost in space.

At last I reached the top, assisted by my uncle dragging me up by the collar.

'Look down!' he cried. 'Take a good look down! You must have a lesson in abysses.'

I opened my eyes. I saw houses squashed flat as if they had all fallen from the sky; they seemed to be drowning in a smoky fog. Above my head ragged clouds were drifting past, and by an optical illusion they seemed stationary, while the steeple, the ball and I were all scudding along at a fantastic speed. Far away to one side was green countryside, while on the other the sea sparkled, bathed in sunlight. The Sound stretched away to Elsinore, dotted with a few white sails like seagulls' wings; and in the misty east and away to the north-east lay outstretched the faintly-shadowed shores of Sweden. All this immensity of space whirled and swirled before my eyes.

But I was forced to get up, to stand up, to look. My first lesson in dizziness lasted an hour. When I got permission to come down and feel the solid street pavements beneath my feet I was aching all over.

'We'll do the same again tomorrow,' said the Professor.

And so it was. For five days in a row, I was made to undergo this anti-vertigo exercise. And whether I wanted to or not, I made definite progress in the art of 'looking down from high places'.

CHAPTER 9

ICELAND! BUT WHAT NEXT?

The day of our departure arrived. The day before that, our kind friend Professor Thomsen had brought us letters of introduction to Count Trampe, the Governor of Iceland, Mr Pictursson, the bishop's suffragan, and Mr Finsen, the mayor of Reykjavik. My uncle expressed his gratitude with the warmest of handshakes.

On the 2nd, at six o'clock in the morning, all our precious baggage having been safely stowed on board the *Valkyrie*, the captain led us to some very narrow cabins.

'Is the wind favourable?' asked my uncle.

'Excellent,' replied Captain Bjarne. 'A southeasterly. We'll sail down the Sound at full speed, with all sails set.'

In a few minutes the schooner, under her mizzen, brigantine, topsail and topgallant sail, cast off from her moorings and sailed at full speed through the straits. In an hour the capital of Denmark seemed to sink below the distant waves, and the *Valkyrie* was skirting the coast near Elsinore. In my nervous frame of mind, I half-expected to see the ghost of Hamlet wandering on the legendary castle terrace.

'You magnificent fool!' I said. 'No doubt *you* would approve of our expedition. Perhaps you would accompany us to the centre of the globe, to find the answer to your eternal doubts.'

But there was no ghostly shape on the ancient walls. In any case, the castle is much younger than the heroic prince of Denmark. It now serves as a sumptuous lodge for the guardian of the straits of the Sound, through which pass fifteen thousand ships of all nations, every year.

The castle of Kronborg soon disappeared in the mist, as well as the tower of Helsingborg on the Swedish coast, and the schooner passed lightly on her way, driven by the breezes of the Kattegat.

The *Valkyrie* was a splendid ship, but on a sailing vessel you can never be sure what to expect. She was carrying coal to Reykjavik, and household goods, earthenware, woollen clothing and a cargo of wheat. The crew consisted of five men, all Danes.

'How long will the passage take?' asked my uncle.

'Ten days,' the captain replied, 'if we don't encounter a northwesterly while we're passing the Faeroes.'

'But you aren't often delayed much, are you?'

'No, Mr Lidenbrock, don't you worry, we'll get there in good time.'

Towards evening the schooner rounded the Skaw at the northernmost point of Denmark, and then during the night crossed the Skagerrack, after which it skirted Norway with Cape Lindesnes to starboard and sailed into the North Sea.

Two days later we sighted the coast of Scotland near Peterhead, and the *Valkyrie* turned to head towards the Faeroe Islands, passing between Orkney and Shetland.

Soon the schooner encountered the great Atlantic swell. She had to tack against the north wind, and reached the Faeroes only with some difficulty. On the 8th, the captain made out Mykiness, the westernmost of the islands, and then set a straight course for Cape Portland, the most southerly point of Iceland.

Nothing unusual happened during the crossing. I wasn't troubled by seasickness; my uncle, on the other hand, to his great disgust and even greater shame, was ill for the whole voyage.

He was therefore unable to talk to the captain about Snæfell, how to get to it and what means of transport were available. He was obliged to put off these inquiries until our arrival, and spent the whole time stretched out in his cabin, the timbers of which creaked and shook with the pitching and tossing of the ship. I thought him not undeserving of this punishment.

On the 11th, we reached Cape Portland. The clear weather gave us a good view of Myrdalsjökull, which towers over it. The cape is merely a low hill with steep sides, standing alone by the beach.

The *Valkyrie* kept some distance from the coast, taking a westerly course amidst huge schools of whales and sharks. Soon we came in sight of an enormous rock with a hole in the middle of it through which the sea crashed furiously. The Westmann Islands seemed to rise out of the ocean like rocks sown in a field of liquid. From that point on, the schooner kept well out to sea and gave the land a wide berth as it rounded Cape Reykjanes, which forms the westernmost point of Iceland.

The rough sea prevented my uncle from coming up on deck to admire these battered and wind-beaten coastlands.

Forty-eight hours later, coming out of a storm which had forced the schooner to sail under bare masts, we caught sight to the east of us of the beacon on Skagen Point, where dangerous rocks stretch far out to sea. An Icelandic pilot came on board, and in three hours the *Valkyrie* dropped anchor close to Reykjavik, in Faxa Bay.

The Professor at last emerged from his cabin, rather pale and wretched-looking but still full of enthusiasm and with a look of satisfaction on his face.

The population of the town, thrilled by the arrival of a vessel from which everyone expected something, formed in groups on the quay.

My uncle hastened to leave his floating prison, or rather hospital. But before leaving the deck of the schooner he dragged me over, and pointing north of the bay to a distant mountain that formed a double peak, a pair of cones covered with perpetual snow, he shouted:

'Snæfell! That's Snæfell!'

Then motioning to me to say nothing about our secret, he got into the boat that was waiting for him. I followed, and soon we were standing on the very soil of Iceland.

The first man we saw was a decent-looking fellow in a general's uniform. But he wasn't a general, just a magistrate, the Governor of the island, Baron Trampe himself. The Professor realized at once who he was dealing with. He handed over his letters from Copenhagen, and there then followed a short conversation in Danish which, for a very good reason, I took no part in. But the result of this first conversation was that Baron Trampe placed himself entirely at the disposal of Professor Lidenbrock.

My uncle was just as courteously received by the mayor, Mr Finsen, whose appearance was just as military, and whose temperament and function just as peaceful, as the Governor's.

As for the bishop's suffragan, Mr Pictursson, he was at that moment engaged in an episcopal visit in the north, so we would just have to wait for the honour of being presented to him. But Mr Fridriksson, the science teacher at the Reykjavik school, was a delightful man, and his help became very important to us. This humble scholar spoke only Icelandic and Latin, and he came and offered us his assistance in the language of Horace. I felt we were well suited to understanding each other. In fact he was the only person in Iceland with whom I could converse at all.

This good-natured gentleman gave us the use of two of the three rooms in his house, and we were soon installed there with all our luggage, the quantity of which rather astonished the good people of Reykjavik.

'Well, Axel,' said my uncle, 'we're getting on, and now the worst is over.'

'The worst?' I said, astonished.

'To be sure, now we have nothing to do but go down.'

'Oh, if that's all, you're quite right. But nevertheless, when we've gone down, we'll have to climb up again, won't we?'

'Oh, I'm not worried about that. Come on, there's no time to lose. I'm going to the library. Perhaps there's some manuscript of Saknussemm's there, and I'd like to consult it.'

'Well, while you're there, I'll go into town. Won't you come too?'

'Oh, that doesn't interest me at all. It's not what's on this island, but what's beneath it, that interests me.'

I went out, and wandered wherever chance took me.

It would be hard to get lost in Reykjavik's two streets. I therefore had no need to ask the way, something that can easily lead to confusion when your only means of asking is by gesture.

The town stretches out along low, marshy ground between two hills. On one side there is an immense bed of lava sloping gently towards the sea. On the other side there is the vast spread of Faxa Bay, bordered to the north by the huge Snæfell glacier. The *Valkyrie* was at the time the only occupant of the bay. Usually English and French fisheries protection vessels moor there, but just then they were patrolling the eastern coasts of the island.

The longer of the only two streets in Reykjavik runs parallel to the beach. Here the merchants and traders live, in wooden cabins made of red planks set horizontally. The other street, running west, leads to a little lake and passes between the house of the bishop and other people who are not involved in trade.

I had soon explored these depressing streets. Here and there I got a glimpse of faded grass, looking like a worn-out bit of carpet, or of a kitchen garden of sorts, the sparse vegetables of which (potatoes, cabbages and lettuces) would have been suitable for a table in Lilliput[13]. A few sickly wallflowers were trying to enjoy the air and sunshine.

About halfway along the non-commercial street I found the public cemetery, enclosed by a mud wall, and where there seemed to be plenty of room.

Then a few steps brought me to the Governor's house, nothing much to look at compared with the town hall in Hamburg but a palace in comparison with the huts of the people of Iceland.

Situated between the little lake and the town, the church is built in the Protestant style, of calcined stones which the volcanoes themselves supply. It was obvious that in strong westerly winds the red tiles of the roof would be scattered in the air, to the great danger of the faithful worshippers.

On a neighbouring hill I spotted the national school, where, as I was later informed by our host, were taught Hebrew, English, French and Danish, four languages of which, I confess with shame, I knew not one word. In an exam I would have come last among the forty scholars being educated at this little college, and I would have been held unworthy to sleep with them in one of those little double closets where more delicate youths would have died of suffocation the very first night.

In three hours I had seen not only the town but its surroundings. The general appearance of the place was really dismal. No trees, and scarcely any vegetation. Everywhere bare rocks, the signs of volcanic activity. The Icelandic cottages are made of earth and turf, and the walls slope inward. They rather resemble roofs placed on the ground, but these roofs are meadows of comparative fertility. Thanks to the heat from inside, grass grows on them quite well. It is carefully mown in the haymaking season; otherwise the horses, cows and sheep would come and graze on these lush, green houses.

During my walk I only met a few people. On returning to the main street I found the greater part of the population busy drying, salting and loading cod, their main export. The men were robust but heavy, like blond Germans with pensive eyes, conscious of being far removed from the rest of humanity, poor exiles relegated to this land of ice, poor creatures who should have been Eskimos since nature had condemned them to live just outside the Arctic Circle. I tried in vain to detect a smile on their faces; sometimes they seemed to laugh, by a spasmodic and involuntary contraction of the muscles, but they never smiled.

Their clothing consisted of a coarse jacket of black woollen cloth known as *'vadmel'* in Scandinavian countries, a hat with a very broad brim, trousers trimmed with narrow red ribbon, and bits of leather rolled round their feet by way of shoes.

The women looked as sad and resigned as the men; their faces were pleasant but expressionless, and they wore dresses and petticoats of dark *vadmel*. If unmarried, they wore over their braided hair a little knitted brown cap; when married, they put a coloured kerchief round their heads, crowned with a peak of white linen.

After a good walk, I returned to Mr Fridriksson's house, where I found my uncle in the company of his host.

CHAPTER 10

INTERESTING CONVERSATIONS WITH ICELANDIC SCHOLARS

Dinner was ready. Professor Lidenbrock was devouring his platefuls with relish, as his forced fast on board the ship had turned his stomach into a vast unfathomable gulf. The meal was more Danish than Icelandic, and was nothing remarkable in itself; but the hospitality of our host reminded me of the heroes of old. It seemed to me that we were more at home than he was himself.

The conversation was carried on in the local language, which for my benefit my uncle interspersed with German and Mr Fridriksson with Latin. It was mostly about matters of science, as is quite fitting for scientists; but Professor Lidenbrock was very reserved, and at every sentence his eyes indicated that I should say absolutely nothing regarding our plans.

First Mr Fridriksson wanted to know what success my uncle had had at the library.

'Your library! Why, there's nothing there but a few tattered books on almost empty shelves.'

'What?' replied Mr Fridriksson. 'Why, we have eight thousand volumes, many of them valuable and rare, works in the old Scandinavian language, and we have all the new books that Copenhagen sends us every year.'

'Where do you keep your eight thousand volumes? As far as I could see . . .'

'Oh, Mr Lidenbrock, they're all over the country. We're fond of study in this icy region. There's not a farmer or a fisherman who cannot read and does not read. Our principle is that books, instead of growing mouldy behind an iron grating, should be worn out under the eyes of many readers. So these books are passed from one person to another, read over and over again and referred to again and again; and it often happens that they only find their way back to their shelves after an absence of a year or two.'

'And in the meantime,' said my uncle, rather spitefully, 'strangers . . .'

'Well, what would you have us do? Foreigners have their libraries at home, and the essential thing for working people is that they should be educated. I say again, the love of reading runs in Icelandic blood. In 1816 we founded a prosperous literary society; learned foreigners consider themselves honoured to become members of it. It publishes books which educate our fellow-countrymen and do the country great service. It would give us immense pleasure if you would agree to be a corresponding member, Mr Lidenbrock.'

My uncle, who had already joined about a hundred learned societies, accepted with a grace which clearly touched Mr Fridriksson.

'Now,' he said, 'if you will be kind enough to tell me what books you hoped to find in our library, I may perhaps assist you to consult them.'

My uncle's eyes met mine. He hesitated. This direct question went to the very heart of the matter. But, after a moment's reflection, he decided to speak.

'Mr Fridriksson, I wanted to know if amongst your ancient books you possessed any of the works of Arne Saknussemm.'

'Arne Saknussemm! You mean that learned sixteenth-century scholar, naturalist, chemist and traveller?'

'Exactly.'

'One of the glories of Icelandic literature and science?'

'That's the man.'

'An illustrious man anywhere!'

'Quite so.'

'And whose courage was equal to his genius!'

'I see you know him well.'

My uncle was absolutely delighted to hear his hero so described. He was feasting his eyes on Mr Fridriksson.

'Well,' he cried, 'where are his works?'

'His works? We don't have any of his works.'

'What – not in Iceland?'

'Neither in Iceland nor anywhere else.'

'Why is that?'

'Because Arne Saknussemm was persecuted for heresy, and in 1573 his books were burned by the common hangman.'

'Good! Excellent!' exclaimed my uncle, quite shocking the science teacher.

'Eh? What?' he said.

'Yes, yes. It's all clear now, it's all making sense. I see why Saknussemm, put into the Index of Prohibited Books[14] and forced to conceal the discoveries made by his genius, was obliged to bury in an incomprehensible cryptogram the secret . . .'

'What secret?' asked Mr Fridriksson with great interest.

'Oh, just a secret which . . .' stammered my uncle.

'Have you some private document in your possession?' asked our host.

'No. I was just imagining a possibility.'

'Oh, I see,' answered Mr Fridriksson, who was kind enough not to pursue the subject when he had noticed his friend's embarrassment. 'I hope you won't leave our island until you have seen some of its mineralogical wealth.'

'Certainly,' replied my uncle, 'but I'm rather a latecomer. Or have others not been here before me?'

'Oh yes, Mr Lidenbrock. The work of Olafsen and Povelsen, undertaken by order of the king, the researches of Troïl, the scientific mission of Gaimard and Robert on the French corvette *La Recherche*, and lately the observations of scientists who came in the *Reine Hortense*, have added a great deal to our knowledge of Iceland. But I assure you there is still plenty to do.'

'Do you think so?' said my uncle, pretending to look very modest and trying to hide the curiosity that was glinting in his eyes.

'Oh, yes. There are many mountains, glaciers and volcanoes left to study, as yet imperfectly known! For example, without going any further, that mountain in the horizon. That's Snæfell.'

'Oh!' said my uncle, as calmly as he was able, 'Is that Snæfell?'

'Yes, one of the most unusual volcanoes, whose crater has scarcely ever been visited.'

'Is it extinct?'

'Oh, yes, for more than five hundred years.'

'Well,' replied my uncle, who was frantically locking his legs together to keep himself from leaping up in the air, 'that is where I mean to begin my geological studies, there on that Seffel – Fessel – what do you call it?'

'Snæfell,' replied the worthy Mr Fridriksson.

This part of the conversation was in Latin. I had understood every word of it, and I could hardly conceal my amusement at seeing my uncle trying to control the excitement and satisfaction that were absolutely dripping off him. He tried hard to put on an innocent little expression of simplicity, but it looked like a diabolical grin.

'Yes,' he said, 'your words have made up me mind for me. We'll try to climb that Snæfell. Perhaps we may even carry out our studies in its crater!'

'I'm very sorry,' said Mr Fridriksson, 'that my commitments will not allow me to take time off, or I would have come with you myself for both pleasure and profit.'

'Oh, no, no!' replied my uncle with great animation, 'we wouldn't for the world put anyone out, Mr Fridriksson. Still, I thank you with all my heart: the company of such a talented man would have been very useful, but the duties of your profession . . .'

I'm glad to think that our host, innocent Icelandic soul that he was, was blind to my uncle's blatant trickery.

'I very much approve of your beginning with that volcano, Mr Lidenbrock. You will gather a harvest of interesting observations. But, tell me, how do you expect to get to the Snæfell peninsula?'

'By sea, across the bay. That's the most direct way.'

'No doubt, but it's impossible.'

'Why?'

'Because we don't have a single boat at Reykjavik.'

'Drat it!'

'You'll have to go by land, along the shore. It'll be a longer journey, but more interesting.'

'Very well, then. But I'll have to see about a guide.'

'I have one to offer you.'

'A sensible, intelligent man?'

'Yes, someone who lives on that peninsula. He is a collector of eider down, and very clever. He speaks Danish perfectly.'

'When can I see him?'

'Tomorrow, if you like.'

'Why not today?'

'Because he won't be here till tomorrow.'

'Tomorrow, then,' agreed my uncle with a sigh.

This momentous conversation ended a few moments later with warm thanks from the German professor to the Icelandic teacher. My uncle had at this dinner gained important information, amongst other things the story of Saknussemm, the reason for the mysterious document, that his host would not be accompanying him on his expedition, and that the very next day a guide would be at his disposal.

CHAPTER 11

THE FINDING OF A GUIDE TO THE CENTRE OF THE EARTH

In the evening, I took a short walk along the beach and came back early to my plank-bed, where I slept soundly all night.

When I awoke, I heard my uncle talking volubly in the next room. I immediately got dressed and joined him.

He was talking in Danish to a tall man, of robust build. This fine fellow clearly possessed great strength. His eyes, set in a large and ingenuous face, seemed to me very intelligent; they were of a dreamy sea-blue. Long hair, which would have been called red even in England, fell in long strands over his broad shoulders. The movements of this native were lithe and supple, but he made little use of his arms when speaking, like a man who knew nothing or cared nothing about the language of gestures. His whole appearance bespoke perfect calmness and self-possession, not laziness but tranquillity. I felt at once that he would be beholden to nobody, that he worked for his own convenience, and that nothing in this world would astonish him or disturb his philosophic calmness.

I caught these hints of this Icelander's character by the way he listened to the Professor's impassioned flow of words. He stood with arms crossed, perfectly unmoved by my uncle's incessant gesticulations. A negative was expressed by a slow movement of the head from left to right, an affirmative by a slight bend, so slight that his long hair scarcely moved. He took economy of movement almost to the level of niggardliness.

Looking at this man, I would certainly never have dreamt that he was a hunter. While he didn't look likely to frighten the game, it didn't seem likely that he would even get near it. But the mystery was solved when Mr Fridriksson informed me that this quiet man only hunted eider duck, whose under-plumage constitutes the chief wealth of the island. This is the celebrated eider down, and it requires no great rapidity of movement to get it.

Early in summer the female eider, a very pretty bird, goes to build her nest among the rocks of the fjords with which the coast is fringed. After building the nest, she lines it with down plucked from her own breast. Immediately the hunter, or rather the trader, comes and robs the nest, and the female starts her work all over again. This goes on as long as she has any down left. When she has stripped herself bare, the male eider takes his turn to pluck himself. But since the coarse, hard plumage of the male has no commercial value, the hunter doesn't bother to rob the nest; the female therefore lays her eggs in the spoils of her mate, the young are hatched, and the next year the harvest begins again.

Now, as the eider duck does not choose steep cliffs for her nest, but rather the smooth terraced rocks which slope down to the sea, the Icelandic hunter is able to exercise his calling without any inconvenient exertion. He is a farmer who is not obliged either to sow or reap his harvest, but merely to gather it in.

This grave, phlegmatic and silent individual was called Hans Bjelke, and he came recommended by Mr Fridriksson. He was to be our guide. His manners were in singular contrast with my uncle's.

Nevertheless, they soon came to understand each other. Neither considered the size of the payment: the one was ready to accept whatever was offered, the other was ready to give whatever was asked. Never was a bargain more easily concluded.

The result of the agreement was that Hans undertook on his part to take us to the village of Stapi on the south shore of the Snæfell peninsula, at the very foot of the volcano. By land, this would be about twenty-two miles, walkable, said my uncle, in two days. But when he learned that a Danish mile is 24,000 feet, he was obliged to modify his calculations and allow seven or eight days for the journey.

Four horses were to be placed at our disposal – two to carry my uncle and myself, two for the baggage. Hans, as was his custom, would go on foot. He knew the whole of that part of the coast perfectly, and promised to take us by the shortest route.

His engagement was not to end when we arrived at Stapi. He was to continue in my uncle's service for the whole period of his scientific research, for three rix-dollars a week; but it was an express article of the contract that his wages should be paid to him every Saturday evening at six o'clock. This, according to him, was an indispensable part of the arrangement.

The start was fixed for the 16th of June. My uncle wanted to pay the hunter part of his wages in advance, but he refused with one word:

'*Efter*,' he said.

'Afterwards,' said the Professor, for my edification.

The arrangement concluded, Hans silently withdrew.

'An excellent fellow,' exclaimed my uncle, 'but little does he know the wonderful role he is to play in the future.'

'So he is to accompany us as far as . . .'

'As far as the centre of the Earth, Axel.'

There were still forty-eight hours to go before we were to set off. To my great regret I had to spend the whole time preparing for the trip, as it took all our ingenuity to pack every article in the best way: scientific instruments here, firearms there, tools in this package, provisions in that. Four sets of packages in all.

The scientific instruments were:
1. An Eigel's centigrade thermometer, graduated up to 150 degrees, which seemed to me either too much or too little – too much if the heat in the Earth was to rise as high as that, for in that case we would be baked alive, but not enough to measure the temperature of hot springs or any matter in a state of fusion.
2. A manometer, to indicate extreme pressures of the atmosphere. An ordinary barometer would not have served the purpose, as the pressure would increase during our descent to a point where a mercury barometer wouldn't register.
3. A chronometer, made by Boissonnas Junior of Geneva, accurately set to the meridian of Hamburg.
4. Two compasses, one showing inclination and the other declination.
5. A night telescope.
6. Two Ruhmkorff's apparatuses[15], which, by means of an electric current, would provide a safe and handy portable light.

The firearms consisted of two Purdley More rifles and two Colt revolvers. But what did we want guns for? We had neither savages nor wild beasts to fear as far as I could see. But my uncle seemed as attached to his arsenal as much as to his instruments, and more especially to a considerable quantity of gun cotton, which is unaffected by moisture and the explosive force of which exceeds that of gunpowder.

The tools consisted of two pickaxes, two spades, a silk ladder, three iron-tipped sticks, an axe, a hammer, a dozen iron wedges and spikes and a long knotted rope. This made for a large load, as the ladder itself was 300 feet long.

And there were provisions too. This wasn't a large bundle, but it was comforting to know that we were taking a six-months' supply of dried beef and biscuits. The only liquid was spirits; we weren't taking any water with us, but we had flasks, and my uncle was depending on springs where we would be able to fill them. Whatever objections I raised about the quality, temperature or even absence of such springs were to no avail.

To complete the inventory of what we were taking with us, I mustn't forget to mention a pocket medicine chest containing blunt scissors, splints for broken limbs, unbleached linen tape, bandages and compresses, lint and a lancet for bleeding – each thing frightening in its implications. Then there was a row of little bottles containing dextrin, medical alcohol, lead acetate solution, ether, vinegar and sal ammoniac; these too afforded me no comfort. Finally, we had everything needed to power the Ruhmkorff's apparatuses.

My uncle hadn't forgotten a supply of tobacco, coarse-grained gunpowder and tinder, nor a leather belt in which he carried an adequate quantity of gold, silver and paper money. Six pairs of boots and shoes, made waterproof with a composition of India rubber and tar, were packed among the tools.

'Clothed, shod and equipped like this,' said my uncle, 'there's no telling how far we might go.'

The whole of the 14th was spent in organizing all these different articles. In the evening we dined with Baron Trampe; the mayor of Reykjavik and Dr Hyaltalin, the chief medical officer, were also present. Mr Fridriksson wasn't there: I learned afterwards that he and the Governor disagreed over some question of administration and didn't speak to each other. I therefore understood not a single word of what was said at this semi-official dinner, but I couldn't help noticing that my uncle talked the whole time.

On the 15th, our preparations were complete. Our host delighted the Professor by presenting him with a map of Iceland far more complete than Henderson's one. It was the map drawn by Olaf Nikolas Olsen, on the scale of 1 to 480,000, and published by the Icelandic Literary Society. Based on the geodesic work of Scheel Frisac and the topographical survey carried out by Bjorn Gumlaugsonn, it was a precious document for a mineralogist.

Our final evening was spent in close conversation with Mr Fridriksson, for whom I felt the warmest regard. After our chat, I, at least, had a disturbed and restless night.

At five in the morning I was wakened by the neighing and stamping of four horses right below my window. I dressed quickly and went down into the street. Hans was finishing our packing, almost, as it were, without moving a limb; and yet he did his work skilfully. My uncle was making a lot of noise to little purpose, and the guide seemed to be paying very little attention to his energetic instructions.

At six o'clock our preparations were finished. Mr Fridriksson shook hands with us. My uncle thanked him warmly in Icelandic for his extreme kindness. I made up a few fine Latin sentences to express my cordial farewell. Then we mounted our horses and with his last good-bye Mr Fridriksson treated me to a line of Virgil eminently applicable to such uncertain wanderers as we were likely to be:

'*Et quacumque viam dederit fortuna sequamur.*'[16]

CHAPTER 12

A BARREN LAND

We started out under a sky that was overcast but calm. There was no fear of heat, nor of disastrous rain. It was just the weather for tourists.

The pleasure of riding on horseback through an unknown country made me easy to please as we started off. I devoted myself wholly to the pleasure of the traveller, and enjoyed the feelings of freedom and expectation. I was beginning to feel really involved in the enterprise.

'Besides,' I said to myself, 'where's the risk? Here we are travelling through a most interesting country. We're about to climb a very remarkable mountain. At worst we're going to scramble down an extinct crater. It is quite obvious that Saknussemm did nothing more than this. As for a passage leading to the centre of the Earth, that's sheer nonsense! Quite impossible! Very well, then, let's get all the good we can out of this expedition, and let's not argue about our chance of success.'

By the time I had come to these conclusions, we had left Reykjavik.

Hans moved steadily on, keeping ahead of us at an even, smooth and rapid pace. The baggage horses followed him without giving any trouble. Then came my uncle and myself, looking not bad horsemen on our small but hardy animals.

Iceland is one of the largest islands in Europe. It has a surface area of 1,400 square miles[17], but only 60,000 inhabitants. Geographers have divided it into four quarters, and we were to cut diagonally across the south-west quarter, called the 'Sudvestr Fjordùngr'.

On leaving Reykjavik, Hans led us along the seashore. We passed poor pastures which were trying very hard, but in vain, to look green; they were yellow at best. The rugged peaks of the trachytic mountains presented faint outlines on the eastern horizon; here and there a few patches of snow, concentrating the diffuse light, glittered on the slopes of the distant mountains; some peaks, rising boldly towards the sky, passed through the grey clouds and reappeared above the moving mists, like rocky reefs emerging in the heavens.

Often these chains of barren rocks dipped towards the sea and encroached on the scarce pastureland, but there was always enough room to get by. Besides, our horses instinctively chose the easiest places without ever slackening their pace. My uncle didn't even get the satisfaction of urging his horse on by whip or voice. He had no excuse for impatience. I couldn't help smiling to see so tall a man on so small a pony, and as his long legs nearly touched the ground, he looked like a six-legged centaur.

'Good horse! Good horse!' he kept saying. 'You'll see, Axel, that there is no more intelligent an animal than the Icelandic horse. Neither snow, nor storms, nor impassable roads, nor rocks, nor glaciers – nothing stops him. He is courageous, sober and surefooted. He never takes a false step, never shies. If there is a river or fjord to cross (and we will meet with many), you'll see him plunge in at once, just as if he were amphibious, and reach the opposite bank. But we mustn't hurry him; let him have his way and we'll cover a steady twenty-five miles a day.'

'We may, but how about our guide?'

'Oh, never mind him. People like him stride on without a thought. The man moves so little, he'll never get tired; and besides, if he wants it, he can have my horse. I'll get cramps if I don't move about a bit. My arms are all right, but my legs need exercise.'

We were progressing at a rapid pace. The country was already almost a desert. Here and there, there was a lonely farmhouse, a *'boër'*, built of wood, turf and pieces of lava, and looking like a poor beggar by the wayside. These dilapidated huts seemed to be begging for charity from passers-by, and we weren't far off offering alms for the relief of the poor inmates.

In this country there were no roads and paths, and the poor vegetation, slow-growing as it was, would soon cover all trace of the footsteps of the infrequent travellers. Yet this part of the province, only a very small distance from the capital, is reckoned among the inhabited and cultivated parts of Iceland. What, then, must the other parts be like, even more deserted than this desert? In the first half mile we hadn't seen a single farmer standing at his cottage door, nor a single wild shepherd tending a flock rather less wild than he was; nothing but a few cows and sheep left to themselves. So what would these distorted regions that we were heading for be like, regions turned upside down by eruptions, born of volcanic explosions and underground convulsions?

We were to get to know them before long, but on consulting Olsen's map, I saw that we were for the moment avoiding them by following a winding route along the seashore. In fact, the main volcanic activity is confined to the central part of the island; there, the horizontal strata of superimposed rocks, called 'trapps' in the Scandinavian languages, the trachytic layers, the eruptions of basalt and tuffs and agglomerates, the streams of lava and molten porphyry, have made this a land of supernatural horrors. I had no idea what sight was awaiting us on the Snæfell peninsula where the destruction caused by fiery Nature has created frightful chaos.

Two hours after leaving Reykjavik, we arrived at the *'aoalkirkja'* ('main church') or village of Gufunes. There was nothing to see here but a few houses, scarcely enough to make a hamlet in Germany.

Hans stopped here for half an hour. He shared a frugal breakfast with us, answering my uncle's questions about the path with nothing but 'yes' or 'no'. When asked about our stopping-place for the night, he simply replied, 'Gardär.'

I consulted the map to see where Gardär was. I saw there was a small town of that name on the banks of the Hvalfjord, four miles from Reykjavik. I showed it to my uncle.

'Only four miles!' he exclaimed. 'Four miles out of twenty-eight. What a pleasant little walk this is!'

He tried to say something to the guide, but the latter, without answering, took up his place at the head of the horses again and went on his way.

Three hours later, still walking over the colourless grass of the pastureland, we had to work our way round the Kollafjord, a longer way but an easier one than straight across the inlet. We soon entered a *'pingstaær'* or 'commune' called Ejulberg, on whose steeple the clock would have been striking twelve if Icelandic churches had been rich enough to have clocks. But they're like their parishioners, who have no watches and manage perfectly well without.

There our horses were fed and watered. Then, taking the narrow path to the left between a range of hills and the sea, they carried us to our next stopping-point, the *aoalkirkja* of Brantär and, one mile farther on, to Saurboër *'annexia,'* a chapel of ease built on the southern shore of the Hvalfjord.

It was now four o'clock, and we had gone four Icelandic miles.

The fjord was at least half an Icelandic mile wide at that point. The waves rolled in and crashed on the sharp-pointed rocks. The inlet widened out between high walls of rock, precipices topped by sharp peaks 2,000 feet high, and remarkable for the brown strata which separated the beds of reddish tuff. However much I might respect the intelligence of our horses, I was little inclined to put it to the test by trying to cross an arm of the sea on horseback.

If they're as intelligent as they're said to be, I thought, they won't even try it. In any case, I intend to do the thinking for them.

But my uncle wouldn't wait. He spurred his horse on down to the water's edge. His mount lowered its head to look at the nearest waves and stopped. My uncle, who had an instinct of his own, applied his spurs again, and again the horse refused, shaking its head. Then came strong language and the whip, but the animal replied to these arguments by kicking and attempting to throw its rider. At last the clever little pony, by bending its knees, got out from under the Professor's legs and left him standing on two boulders on the shore like the Colossus of Rhodes[18].

'Confounded brute!' cried the unseated rider, suddenly demoted to being a pedestrian, and just as ashamed of it as a cavalry officer would be if downgraded to being a foot soldier.

'*Färja*,' said the guide, touching him on the shoulder.

'What! A ferry?'

'*Der*,' replied Hans, pointing to one.

'Yes,' I exclaimed. 'There is a ferry.'

'Why didn't you say so, then? Come on, let's go!'

'*Tidvatten*,' said the guide.

'What's he saying?'

'He's saying 'tide',' said my uncle, translating the Danish word.

'So we have to wait for the tide, then?'

'*Förbida*?' asked my uncle.

'*Ja*,' replied Hans.

My uncle stamped his foot, while the horses headed towards the ferry.

I perfectly understood the need to wait for a particular point in the tide before undertaking the crossing of the fjord, the point when, the sea having reached its highest level, there would be slack water. At that point, the ebb and flow of the water have no noticeable effect, and there is no risk of the ferry being carried either to the top of the fjord or out to sea.

That favourable moment didn't come till six o'clock, at which time my uncle, myself, the guide, two ferrymen and the four horses, entrusted ourselves to a somewhat fragile craft. Accustomed as I was to the steamboats on the Elbe, I found the oars of the rowers a rather slow means of propulsion. It took us more than an hour to cross the fjord, but the crossing was effected without mishap.

In another half hour we had reached the *aoalkirkja* of Gardär.

CHAPTER 13

HOSPITALITY UNDER THE ARCTIC CIRCLE

It should have been dark, but on the 65th parallel there was nothing surprising about the nocturnal polar light. In Iceland during the months of June and July, the sun never sets.

But the temperature had gone down. I was cold, and even more hungry than cold. Welcome indeed was the sight of the *boër* which was hospitably opened to receive us.

It was a peasant's house, but as far as hospitality was concerned it was the equal of a king's palace. On our arrival, the master came out to shake our hands and without further ado beckoned us to follow him inside.

Follow him was what we did, because it would have been impossible to walk with him down the long, narrow, dark passage. The building was constructed of roughly squared timbers, and along the passage were four rooms – the kitchen, the weaving workshop, the *'badstofa'* or family bedroom and the visitors' room, which was the best of all. My uncle, whose height had not been taken into consideration in the construction of the house, of course hit his head several times on the beams that projected from the ceiling.

We were shown into our bedroom, a large room with a floor of hard-packed earth and lit by a window, the panes of which consisted of sheep's bladders and therefore didn't let in much light. The sleeping accommodation consisted of dry straw thrown into two wooden frames which were painted red and decorated with Icelandic sayings. I was hardly expecting so much comfort; the only discomfort came from the strong smell of dried fish, hung meat and sour milk, which my nose didn't like at all.

When we had laid aside our travelling gear, the voice of our host was heard inviting us to come into the kitchen, the only room where a fire was lit even in the severest cold weather.

My uncle wasted no time in obeying this friendly invitation, nor was I slow to follow him.

The kitchen chimney was constructed in the ancient style: in the middle of the room there was a stone for a hearth, and over it a hole in the roof to let the smoke escape. The kitchen also served as the dining-room.

As we came in, the host, as if he had never seen us before, greeted us with the word *'sællvertu'*, which means 'be happy', and came and kissed us on the cheek.

His wife greeted us in the same manner, and then, placing their hands on their hearts, the two bowed deeply.

I hasten to say that this Icelandic lady was the mother of nineteen children, all of whom, big and little alike, were swarming around in the midst of the dense coils of smoke with which the fire on the hearth was filling the room. At every moment I saw some fair-haired and rather melancholy face emerge from the rolling clouds of smoke – they were a perfect band of unwashed angels.

My uncle and I welcomed this little tribe kindly, and in a very short time we each had three or four of these kids on our shoulders, as many on our laps, and the rest between our knees. Those who could speak kept repeating *'Sællvertu'*, in every conceivable tone; those that could not speak made up for that lack by shrill cries.

This concert was brought to a close by dinner being announced. At that moment our hunter returned; he had been seeing to the horses, which is to say he had let them loose in the fields, where the poor beasts had to content themselves with the scanty moss they could pull off the rocks and a few meagre clumps of seaweed. The next day they would be sure to come of their own accord and resume the labours of the previous day.

'Sællvertu,' said Hans.

Then calmly, automatically and dispassionately he kissed the host, the hostess and their nineteen children.

This ceremony over, we sat at table, all twenty-four of us, and therefore literally one on top of another. The luckiest ones among us only had two urchins on their knees.

But silence reigned in this little world when the soup was served, and the natural taciturnity of the Icelander took over again, even among the children. The host served us soup made of lichen, by no means unpleasant, then a huge piece of dried fish floating in butter that, having been kept for twenty years, had turned rancid and was therefore, according to Icelandic gastronomy, greatly preferable to fresh butter. Along with this, we had *'skyr'*, a sort of clotted milk, flavoured with the juice of juniper berries and served with biscuits; and to drink, we had whey mixed with water, known as *'blanda'* in this country. It is not for me to say whether this diet is healthy or not; all I can say is that I was desperately hungry, and that when it came to dessert, I swallowed every last mouthful of a thick broth made from buckwheat.

As soon as the meal was over, the children disappeared, and their elders gathered round the fire, in which was burning such miscellaneous fuel as peat, heather, cow-dung and fishbones. After warming ourselves a little, the different groups retired to their respective rooms. In accordance with Icelandic custom, our hostess hospitably offered us her assistance in getting undressed, but on our gracefully declining her offer, she didn't insist on it, and I was able at last to curl up in my bed of straw.

At five o'clock next morning, we said good-bye to our host, my uncle only with difficulty managing to persuade him to accept proper payment for his hospitality, and Hans gave the signal for us to start.

A hundred yards from Gardär, the landscape began to change in appearance. The ground became boggy, and our progress became more difficult. To our right, the chain of mountains stretched out like an immense system of natural fortifications, of which we were following the counterscarp; often we met with streams, which we had to ford with great care in order not to get our packs wet.

The deserted countryside was becoming more and more of a wasteland, yet from time to time we could make out a human figure who fled at our approach. Sometimes a sharp turn in the path would bring us suddenly within a short distance of one of these spectres, and I was filled with loathing at the sight of a huge deformed head with shiny, hairless skin and repulsive sores visible through the holes in the poor creature's wretched rags.

These unhappy beings would not come near us and offer us their misshapen hands. They fled away, but not before Hans had greeted them with the customary *'Sællvertu'*.

'Spetelsk,' Hans would say.

'A leper!' my uncle would repeat.

This word always had a repulsive effect. The horrible disease of leprosy is all too common in Iceland; it is not contagious, but hereditary, and lepers are therefore forbidden to marry.

These apparitions were not likely to add any charm to the increasingly unattractive landscape. The last tufts of grass had disappeared from beneath our feet. Not a tree was to be seen, unless we except a few dwarf birches as low as brushwood. Not an animal but a few wandering ponies that their owners would not feed. Sometimes we could see a hawk gliding through the grey cloud and then darting away south with rapid flight. I was affected by the melancholy of this wild land, and my thoughts drifted away to the more cheerful scenes I had left far to the south.

We had to cross a few narrow fjords, and finally quite a wide bay. It being high tide, we were able to cross without delay and reach the hamlet of Alftanes a mile further on.

That evening, after having forded two rivers full of trout and pike, the Alfa and the Heta, we were obliged to spend the night in a deserted building worthy of being haunted by all the elves of Scandinavia. The ice-king certainly held court there, and all night long showed us what he could do.

Nothing of note happened the next day. Just the same bogs, the same monotonous landscape, the same melancholy desert tracks. By nightfall we had covered half the distance we had to travel, and we stopped for the night at the *annexia* at Krösolbt.

On the 19th of June, we walked for about a mile – that is, an Icelandic mile – over hardened lava. This ground is called *'hraun'* in Iceland. The wrinkled surface has the appearance of distorted, twisted cables, sometimes stretched out lengthwise, sometimes twisted together. An immense torrent of lava, once liquid, now solid, flowed down from the nearest mountains, now extinct volcanoes, but the debris all around us indicated the violence of past eruptions. Here and there, there were still a few jets of steam from hot springs.

We had no time to study these phenomena; we had to continue on our way. Soon the boggy land reappeared under the feet of our horses, interspersed by little lakes. Our route now lay westward; we had made our way round the great bay of Faxa, and the twin peaks of Snæfell rose white into the cloudy sky less than five miles away.

The horses walked on well; no difficulties stopped them in their steady progress. I was getting tired, but my uncle held himself as stiff and erect as he did when we first started out. I couldn't help admiring his persistence, and that of the hunter, who was treating our expedition as nothing more than a little stroll.

On June the 20th, at six o'clock, we reached Büdir, a village on the seashore. The guide was asking for his wages, and my uncle settled up with him. It was Hans's own family, that is, his uncles and cousins, who gave us hospitality. We were kindly received, and without abusing too much the goodness of these people, I would willingly have stayed here for a while to recover from my tiring journey. But my uncle, who had no need of time to recover, wouldn't hear of it, and the next morning we had to mount our horses again.

The soil showed the effects of being close to the mountain, whose granite foundations rose from the earth like the knotted roots of some huge oak. We were going round the immense base of the volcano. The Professor hardly took his eyes off it. He waved his arms about and seemed to be challenging it, saying, 'There stands the giant that I shall conquer.' After about four hours' walking, the horses stopped of their own accord at the door of the priest's house at Stapi.

CHAPTER 14

BUT ARCTIC PEOPLE CAN BE INHOSPITABLE, TOO

Stapi is a village of about thirty huts, built of lava, at the south side of the base of the volcano. It extends along the inner edge of a small fjord, enclosed between basaltic walls of the strangest construction.

Basalt is a brownish rock of igneous origin. It assumes regular forms, the arrangement of which is often very surprising. Here nature had done her work geometrically, with set-square, compasses and plumb line. Everywhere else her art consists in simply throwing down huge masses together in disorder; you see imperfectly formed cones, irregular pyramids, a strange confusion of lines. But here, as if to exhibit an example of regularity in advance of the very earliest architects, she has created a severely simple order of architecture, never surpassed either by the splendours of Babylon or the wonders of Greece.

I had heard of the Giant's Causeway in Ireland, and Fingal's Cave on Staffa, one of the Hebrides, but I had never before seen a basaltic formation.

At Stapi I beheld this phenomenon in all its beauty.

The wall that held in the fjord, like the whole coast of the peninsula, was composed of a series of vertical columns thirty feet high. These straight shafts, of perfect proportions, supported an architrave of horizontal slabs, the overhanging portion of which formed a semi-arch over the sea. At intervals, under this natural shelter, vaulted entrances spread out in beautiful curves, into which the waves dashed with foam and spray. A few shafts of basalt, torn from their hold by the fury of storms, lay along the soil like remains of an ancient temple, in ruins that remained forever fresh, and over which centuries passed without leaving a trace of age upon them.

This was the last stage of our journey above ground. Hans had shown great intelligence, and it gave me some little comfort to think then that he was not going to leave us.

On arriving at the door of the rector's house, which was no different from the others, I saw a man shoeing a horse, hammer in hand, and with a leather apron on.

'*Sællvertu*,' said the hunter.

'*God dag*,' said the blacksmith in good Danish.

'*Kyrkoherde*,' said Hans, turning to my uncle.

'The rector,' repeated the Professor. 'It seems, Axel, that this good man is the rector.'

Our guide in the meanwhile was telling the *kyrkoherde* what we were doing there. Stopping his work for a moment, the latter shouted something that could no doubt be understood between horses and horse dealers, and immediately a tall, ugly hag of a woman appeared from the hut. She must have been six feet tall, or as near as doesn't matter. I was afraid she might treat me to the 'Icelandic kiss' but thankfully she didn't, nor did she show us into her house with very good grace.

The visitors' room seemed to me the worst in the whole hut. It was narrow, dirty and smelly. But we had to be content with it. The rector obviously did not to go in for old-fashioned hospitality. Far from it. Before the day was over, I saw that we were dealing with a blacksmith, a fisherman, a hunter, a joiner but not at all with a minister of the Gospel. To be sure, it was a weekday; perhaps he made amends on Sundays.

I don't mean to say anything against these poor priests, who after all are absolutely destitute. They receive a ridiculously small pittance from the Danish government, and from the parish they get a quarter of the tithe, which doesn't amount to sixty marks a year. Hence the need to work for their living; but after fishing, hunting and shoeing horses for any length of time, one soon gets into the ways and manners of fishermen, hunters and farriers and other uncultivated people; and that evening I found out that temperance too was not among the virtues of our host.

My uncle soon discovered what sort of a man he was dealing with. Instead of a good and learned man, he found a rude and coarse peasant. He therefore decided to start out at once on the great expedition and to leave this inhospitable rectory. He cared nothing about fatigue, and resolved to spend a few days in the mountains.

The preparations for our departure were therefore made the very day after our arrival at Stapi. Hans hired the services of three Icelanders to carry our packs instead of the horses, but as soon as we had arrived at the crater, these men were to turn back and leave us on our own. This was made absolutely clear.

My uncle now took the opportunity of explaining to Hans that it was his intention to explore the interior of the volcano to its farthest limits.

Hans merely nodded. Heading there or elsewhere, down into the bowels of the Earth or anywhere on the surface of the globe, was all the same to him. For my own part, the events of the journey had kept me amused up to this point and made me forget the evils to come, but now my fears were again beginning to get the better of me. But what could I do? The place to stand up to the Professor would have been Hamburg, not at the foot of Snæfell.

One thought, above all others, particularly alarmed me, one that would have rattled firmer nerves than mine.

Now, I thought, here we are about to climb Snæfell. Fine. We'll explore the crater. That's fine, too; others have done as much without dying for it. But that's not all. If there is a way to penetrate into the very bowels of the island, if what that foolish Saknussemm said is true, we will lose our way among the deep subterranean passages of this volcano. Now, there's no proof that Snæfell is extinct. Who can reassure us that an eruption is not brewing at this very moment? Does it follow that just because the monster has slept since 1229, it will therefore never wake again? And if it does awaken in the near future, where shall we be?

It was worthwhile considering this question, and I did consider it. I couldn't sleep for dreaming about eruptions. I had no desire to play the role of ejected scoriae and ashes.

So, at last, when I couldn't stand it any longer, I made up my mind to put the question to my uncle, as prudently and cautiously as possible, in the form of an almost impossible hypothesis.

I approached him. I communicated my fears to him, and stepped back to give him room for the explosion which I knew would follow. But I was wrong.

All he said was, 'I was thinking of that.'

What could those words mean? Was he actually going to listen to reason? Was he contemplating abandoning his plans? This was too good to be true.

After a few moments' silence, during which I dared not question him, he went on:

'I was thinking of that. Ever since we arrived at Stapi, my mind has been occupied with the important question you have just raised, because we mustn't be guilty of imprudence.'

'No, indeed!' I replied emphatically.

'For six hundred years Snæfell has been silent, but it might speak again. Now, eruptions are always preceded by certain well-known phenomena. I have therefore questioned the locals, I have studied the land, and I can assure you, Axel, that there will be no eruption.'

At this positive assertion, I just stood there, amazed and speechless.

'You doubt my word?' said my uncle. 'Well, then, follow me.'

I obeyed like an automaton. Leaving the priest's house, the Professor took a straight path, which led away from the sea through an opening in the basaltic wall. We were soon in the open countryside, if one may give that name to a vast expanse of mounds of volcanic material. This part of the country seemed to have been crushed by a rain of enormous rocks – trap, basalt, granite and all kinds of igneous rock – thrown out by the volcano.

Here and there I could see curling up into the air puffs and jets of steam, called in Icelandic *'reykir'*, issuing from thermal springs and indicating by their movement the volcanic energy below. This seemed to justify my fears, but my new-found hopes were dashed when my uncle said:

'You see all these plumes of steam, Axel? Well, they show that we have nothing to fear from the fury of a volcanic eruption.'

'Why should I believe that?' I exclaimed.

'Listen,' said the Professor. 'If there's an eruption coming, these jets redouble their activity, but they disappear altogether during the eruption, because the gases, no longer under pressure, are released through the crater instead of escaping by their normal passage through the fissures in the soil. Therefore, if these vapours remain in their usual state and show no increase in force, and if you add to this the observation that the wind and rain are not being replaced by a still, heavy atmosphere, then you may say with certainty that no eruption is coming in the near future.'

'But . . .'

'That's enough. When science has spoken, there is nothing more to be said.'

I returned to the parsonage, completely crestfallen. My uncle had bested me with the weapons of science. Still, I had one hope left, and this was that when we reached the bottom of the crater it would be impossible, for lack of a way through, to go deeper, in spite of all the Saknussemms in Iceland.

That whole night was one long nightmare. I saw myself in the heart of a volcano and thrown up like a rock from the deepest depths of the earth into interplanetary space.

The next day, June the 23rd, Hans was waiting for us with his companions, carrying provisions, tools and scientific instruments; there were also two iron-tipped sticks, two rifles and two cartridge belts for my uncle and myself. Hans, as a cautious man, had added to our luggage a leather bottle full of water, which, with what was in our flasks, would ensure us a supply of water for eight days.

It was nine in the morning. The priest and his huge harpy of a wife were waiting for us at the door. We thought they were standing there to bid us a kind farewell, but the farewell came in the unexpected form of a large bill, in which we were charged for everything, even the very air we breathed in the pastoral house, foul as it was. This worthy couple were fleecing us just like a Swiss innkeeper might have done, and reckoned their inadequate hospitality at a very high price.

My uncle paid without demur; a man who is starting out for the centre of the Earth is hardly going to quibble over a few rix-dollars.

This matter settled, Hans gave the signal to set off and we soon left Stapi behind us.

CHAPTER 15

SNÆFELL AT LAST

Snæfell is 5,000 feet high. Its double cone forms the end of a trachytic belt which stands out distinctly in the mountain system of the island. From our starting-point we couldn't make out the two peaks against the dark grey sky; I could only see an enormous cap of snow descending low on the giant's brow.

We walked in single file, led by the hunter, climbing up along narrow tracks where two people could not have walked abreast. Conversation was therefore almost impossible.

After we had passed the basalt wall of the Stapi fjord, we walked over fibrous peaty soil, created from the ancient vegetation of this peninsula. The vast quantity of this unharvested fuel would be sufficient to warm the whole population of Iceland for a century; this huge peat-bog was as much as seventy feet deep in places, to judge from the gorges in it, and consisted of layers of the carbonized remains of vegetation interspersed with thinner layers of tufaceous pumice.

As a true nephew of Professor Lidenbrock, and in spite of my worries, I couldn't help taking an interest in the mineralogical curiosities which lay about me as if in a vast museum, and I worked out in my mind a complete geological account of Iceland.

This most curious island has evidently been forced up from the bottom of the sea at a comparatively recent date. It may possibly still be rising slowly. If this is the case, its origin may well be attributed to subterranean fires, in which case Sir Humphry Davy's theory, Saknussemm's document and my uncle's opinions would all go up in smoke. This hypothesis led me to examine even more carefully the appearance of the ground, and I soon arrived at a conclusion as to the nature of the forces operating in its formation.

Iceland, which is entirely devoid of alluvial soil, is wholly composed of volcanic tufa, that is to say, an agglomeration of porous rocks and stones. Before the volcanoes erupted, it consisted of trap rocks slowly raised to the level of the sea by the action of forces in the centre of the Earth. The internal fires had not yet forced their way through.

But at a later period a wide chasm formed diagonally from south-west to north-east, through which the trachyte that was to form a mountain chain was gradually forced out. There was no violent activity in this change; the matter was thrown out in vast quantities, and the liquid material oozing out from the abysses of the earth slowly spread in extensive plains or in hillocky masses. To this period belong the feldspars, syenites and porphyries.

But with this outflow the thickness of the island's crust increased considerably, and therefore also its powers of resistance. One can easily imagine what vast quantities of gases, what masses of molten matter, accumulated beneath its solid surface, with no possible escape after the cooling of the trachytic crust. Therefore a time came when the fluid and explosive forces of the trapped gases lifted up this heavy cover and forced openings for themselves through tall chimneys. Hence the volcano that had formed in the crust, and the crater suddenly created at its summit.

Other volcanic phenomena followed. First of all, the ejected basalt of which the plain we had just left presented such marvellous specimens escaped through the outlets that had now been made. We were walking over dense and massive grey rocks, which in cooling had formed hexagonal prisms. Everywhere around us we saw truncated cones, which had formerly been so many fiery mouths.

After that, when the basalt flow was exhausted, the volcano, whose power was increased by the extinction of the lesser craters, allowed the escape of lava, ashes and scoriae, long screes of which I could see flowing down the sides of the mountain like locks of hair.

Such was the succession of phenomena which produced Iceland, all arising from the action of internal fire, and to suppose that the material within did not still exist in a state of liquid incandescence was absurd. Nothing could surpass the absurdity of imagining that it was possible to reach the centre of the Earth.

I felt a little comforted by this thought as we advanced to the assault of Snæfell.

Walking was becoming more and more difficult, and the ascent steeper and steeper. Loose fragments of rock gave way beneath our feet, and the utmost care was needed to avoid dangerous falls.

Hans carried on as calmly as if he were on level ground. Sometimes he disappeared altogether behind the huge rocks, then a shrill whistle would direct us towards him. Sometimes he would stop, pick up a few bits of stone and build them up into a recognisable shape, so making landmarks to guide us in our way back. A very wise precaution in itself, but, as things turned out, quite pointless.

Three hours of tiring walking had only got us as far as the foot of the mountain. There Hans made us stop, and a hasty breakfast was served out. My uncle swallowed his food two mouthfuls at a time in order to get on faster; but whether he liked it or not, this was time for a rest as well as for breakfast, and he had to wait till our guide decided to move on, which he did after about an hour. The three Icelanders, just as taciturn as their friend the hunter, never spoke, and ate their breakfasts in silence.

We were now beginning to climb the steep sides of Snæfell. By an optical illusion not uncommon in mountains, its snowy summit seemed very close to us, and yet how many weary hours it took us to reach it! The stones, not held together by soil or fibrous plant roots, rolled away from under our feet, and dropped down into the precipice below with the speed of an avalanche.

At some places the sides of the mountain formed an angle with the horizon of at least 36 degrees. It was impossible to climb these stony cliffs, and we had to work our way round them, not without great difficulty. At those points we helped each other by means of our sticks.

I have to admit my uncle kept as close to me as he could. He never lost sight of me, and in many difficult places his arm gave me strong support. He himself seemed to possess an instinctive sense of balance and he never stumbled. The Icelanders, although burdened with our loads, climbed with the agility of mountaineers.

To judge by the appearance of the summit of Snæfell in the distance, it seemed too steep to climb on the side we were on. Fortunately, after an hour of exhausting exercise, a kind of staircase appeared unexpectedly in the middle of the vast plain of snow in the hollow between the two peaks, and it made our ascent much easier. It was formed by one of those torrents of stones flung up by the eruptions, called *'stinâ'* by the Icelanders. If this torrent had not been arrested in its fall by the shape of the sides of the mountain, it would have carried on down to the sea and formed more islands.

Such as it was, it served us well. The steepness increased, but these stone steps allowed us to climb with ease, and even at such a speed that, having rested for a moment while my companions continued their ascent, the distance they had climbed reduced them to microscopic size.

At seven we had ascended the two thousand steps of this great staircase, and we had reached a bulge in the mountain, a kind of bed on which rested the actual cone of the crater.

Three thousand two hundred feet below us stretched the sea. We had passed the lower limit of perpetual snow, which, on account of the dampness of the climate, begins at a lower level than one might expect. It was bitingly cold. The wind was blowing violently. I was exhausted. The Professor saw that my legs were refusing to carry me any further, and in spite of his impatience he made up his mind to stop. He signalled his intention to the hunter, who shook his head, saying:

'Ofvanför.'

'It seems we have to go higher,' said my uncle.

He asked Hans why.

'Mistour,' replied the guide.

'Ja, mistour,' said one of the Icelanders in a tone of alarm.

'What does that word mean?' I asked uneasily.

'Look!' said my uncle.

I looked down to the plain. An immense column of pulverized pumice, sand and dust was rising with a whirling circular motion like a waterspout. The wind was lashing it on to the very side of Snæfell to which we were clinging. This dense veil hanging in front of the sun threw a deep shadow over the mountain. If that huge revolving pillar leant over, it would grasp us in its whirling eddies. This phenomenon, which is not infrequent when the wind blows from the glaciers, is called in Icelandic *'mistour'*.

'*Hastigt! hastigt!*' cried our guide.

Even without knowing Danish, I understood at once that we had to follow Hans as fast as we could. He began to circle round the cone of the crater, but on a slanting path so as to make our progress easier. Presently the dust storm crashed down on the mountain, which shook with the shock of it. A hail of loose stones, caught up by the irresistible blasts of wind, flew about as if in a volcanic eruption. Fortunately we were on the other side of the mountain and sheltered from harm. But for the prudence of our guide, our mangled bodies, torn and pounded into fragments, would have been carried far away like the remnants of some unknown meteor.

Nevertheless, Hans didn't think it wise to spend the night on the side of the cone. We continued on our zigzag climb. The remaining fifteen hundred feet took us five hours to cover; the diagonal path, the circuitous route, and the need to retrace our steps from time to time, must have made for a walk of at least three leagues. I could hardly keep going any longer. I was succumbing to the effects of hunger and cold. The rarefied air was scarcely enough to fill my lungs.

At last, at eleven o'clock in the sunlit night, we reached the summit of Snæfell, and before taking shelter in the crater I had time to watch the midnight sun, at its lowest point, gilding with its pale rays the island that slept at my feet.

CHAPTER 16

BOLDLY DOWN INTO THE CRATER

Supper was gobbled down, and our little company settled itself as best it could. The bed was hard, the shelter not very substantial, and our position an anxious one at five thousand feet above sea level. Yet I slept very well indeed; it was one of the best nights I had ever had, and I didn't even dream.

Next morning we awoke half frozen in the keen air, but with the light of a splendid sun. I got up from my granite bed and went out to enjoy the magnificent spectacle that lay unfolding before my eyes.

I was standing on the very summit of the southernmost of Snæfell's peaks. I could see over the whole island. By an optical effect that you get at all great heights, it seemed as if the shores had been raised up and the central part of the island had sunk down. It was as though one of Helbesmer's relief maps lay at my feet. I could see deep valleys criss-crossing each other in every direction, precipices like low walls, lakes reduced to ponds, rivers abbreviated into streams. On my right were countless glaciers and innumerable peaks, some surrounded by feathery clouds of smoke. The undulating surface of these endless mountains, crested with sheets of snow, reminded me of a stormy sea. If I looked westward, there lay the ocean spread out in all its magnificence, like a mere continuation of those fleecy summits. My eye could hardly tell where the snowy ridges ended and the foaming waves began.

I was now able to steep myself in the wonderful ecstasy which all high summits produce in the mind without any feeling of dizziness, as I was beginning to get accustomed to these sublime aspects of nature. My dazzled eyes were bathed in the bright flood of the sun's rays. I was forgetting where I was and who I was, living rather the life of elves and sylphs, those fanciful creations of Scandinavian superstition. I felt intoxicated by the sublime pleasure of lofty peaks, without thinking of the deep abysses into which I was shortly to be plunged. But I was brought back to reality by the arrival of Hans and the Professor, who joined me on the summit.

My uncle pointed out to me in the far west a light mist, a haze, a suggestion of land, on the distant horizon beyond the waves.

'That's Greenland!' he said.

'Greenland?' I exclaimed.

'Yes. We're only thirty-five leagues away; and during thaws, polar bears are carried by the ice fields from the north even as far as Iceland. But never mind that. Here we are at the top of Snæfell and here are two peaks, one to the north and one to the south. Hans will tell us the name of the one we are standing on at the moment.'

The question being asked, Hans replied:
'Scartaris.'
My uncle shot a triumphant glance at me.
'Now for the crater!' he cried.

The crater of Snæfell resembled an inverted cone, the opening of which might be half a league in diameter. It appeared to be about two thousand feet deep. Imagine what such a reservoir would look like brimful and running over with liquid fire and rumbling like rolling thunder. The bottom of the funnel was about 250 feet in circumference, so its lower edge could be reached without much difficulty down the gentle slope. I couldn't help thinking that the whole crater was like an enormous blunderbuss, and the comparison absolutely terrified me.

'What madness it is,' I thought, 'to go down into a blunderbuss, perhaps a loaded blunderbuss, to be shot up into the air without warning!'

But I didn't try to back out. Perfectly calm, Hans resumed the lead, and I followed him without a word.

To make the descent easier, Hans wound his way down the cone by a spiral path. Our route lay through rocks that were the result of past eruptions. Loosened from their beds by our feet, some of the rocks bounced down into the abyss, creating in their fall remarkable loud echoes.

In some parts of the cone there were glaciers. Here Hans moved forward with extreme caution, using his iron-tipped pole to check for crevasses. At particularly doubtful sections, we had to tie ourselves together with a long rope so that anyone who missed his footing would be held up by his companions. This was a wise move, but didn't remove all the danger.

Yet, notwithstanding the difficulties of the descent, down slopes the guide was not familiar with, it was accomplished without accident, except for the loss of a coil of rope which escaped from the hands of an Icelander and took the shortest way to the bottom of the abyss.

We arrived at midday. I looked up and saw straight above me the upper opening of the cone, framing a very small but almost perfectly round bit of sky. Just at the edge of the opening, the snowy peak of Scartaris stood out sharp and clear against the infinities of space.

At the bottom of the crater there were three chimneys through which, in its eruptions, Snæfell would have belched out fire and lava from its central furnace. Each of these chimneys was a hundred feet in diameter. They stood gaping right in front of us. I hadn't the courage to look down any of them, but Professor Lidenbrock had hastily surveyed all three. He was panting and puffing, running from one to the other, gesticulating and uttering incoherent noises. Hans and his companions were sitting on loose lava rocks, watching him; they obviously thought he was quite mad.

Suddenly my uncle gave a shout. I thought his foot must have slipped and that he'd fallen down one of the holes. But he hadn't. I could see him, arms outstretched and legs wide apart, standing in the centre of the crater in front of a granite rock that looked just like a pedestal made for a statue of Pluto. For a moment he stood like a man transfixed, but that soon gave way to delirious joy.

'Axel, Axel,' he cried. 'Come quickly, come down here!'

I ran down. Hans and the Icelanders just stayed where they were.

'Look!' cried the Professor.

And, sharing his astonishment, but not, I think, his joy, I read on the western face of the block, in Runic characters, half crumbled away with the passage of time, this thrice-accursed name:

ᛆᚱᚿᛁ ᛋᛆᚴᚿᚢᛋᛋᛁᛙ

'Arne Saknussemm!' replied my uncle. 'Do you still have doubts now?'

I said nothing, and returned in silence to my lava seat in a state of utter consternation. I was completely crushed by the evidence.

How long I remained deep in thought, I cannot say. All I know is that when I looked up again, I could see only my uncle and Hans at the bottom of the crater. The Icelanders had been dismissed, and they were now descending the outer slopes of Snæfell to return to Stapi.

Hans was sleeping peacefully at the foot of a rock, in a lava bed, where he had found a suitable place to lie down, but my uncle was pacing around the bottom of the crater like a wild animal in a cage. I had neither the desire nor the strength to get up, and following the guide's example, I dropped off into an unhappy slumber, imagining I could hear ominous noises or feel tremblings within the recesses of the mountain.

That is how we spent our first night in the crater.

The next morning, a grey, heavy, cloudy sky seemed to be hanging over the summit of the cone. This I discovered not from the darkness in the crater but from my uncle's uncontrollable anger.

I soon found out the cause of his anger, and for this reason hope dawned again in my heart.

Of the three paths that lay open before us, only one had been taken by Saknussemm. What that learned Icelander had hinted at in the cryptogram was that the shadow of Scartaris touched that particular opening during the final days of the month of June.

That sharp peak might therefore be considered as the gnomon of a vast sundial, the shadow projected from which on a certain day would indicate the way to the centre of the earth.

Now, no sun means no shadow, and therefore no indicator. And it was now June the 25th. If the sun stayed hidden by cloud for six days, we would have to postpone our visit till next year.

My limited powers of description would be insufficient to attempt a picture of the Professor's angry impatience. The day wore on, and no shadow came to lay itself along the bottom of the crater. Hans didn't move from the spot he had selected; yet he must have been wondering what were we waiting for, if the matter crossed his mind at all. My uncle said not a word to me. His gaze, always directed upwards, was lost in the grey and misty space beyond.

On the 26th, still nothing. A mixture of rain and snow fell all day long. Hans built a hut of pieces of lava. I felt a malicious pleasure in watching the thousand streams and cascades that came tumbling down the sides of the cone, and the continuous deafening noise made by the stones they struck in passing.

My uncle's rage knew no bounds. It was enough to infuriate a much more mild-tempered man than he was, because his plans were foundering just like a boat that hits some rocks when almost in the harbour.

But Heaven never sends unmingled grief, and for Professor Lidenbrock there was a satisfaction in store proportionate to his desperate anxieties.

The next day the sky was again overcast, but on the 29th of June, the last day of the month but one, with the change of the moon came a change of weather. The sun poured a flood of light down the crater. Every hillock, every rock and stone, every projecting surface, shared in this torrent of brightness and threw its shadow on the ground. Amongst them, Scartaris laid down his sharp-pointed angular shadow, which began to move slowly in the opposite direction to that of the shining globe.

My uncle followed the shadow as it moved.

At noon, now at its shortest, it licked gently at the edge of the middle chimney.

'There it is! There it is!' shouted the Professor.

'Now for the centre of the Earth!' he added in Danish.

I looked at Hans, to hear what he would say.

'*Forüt!*' was his calm reply.

'Forward!' replied my uncle.

It was thirteen minutes past one.

CHAPTER 17

VERTICAL DESCENT

Now our real journey began. Up to this point, our efforts had been equal to all the difficulties we had faced, but now new difficulties would spring up at every step.

I had still not taken a look down the bottomless pit into which I was about to plunge, but the moment of truth had arrived. I could now either take part in the enterprise or refuse to go on. But I was ashamed to turn back in the presence of the hunter. Hans was accepting the adventure with such calmness, such indifference, such a perfect disregard for any possible danger, that I blushed at the very thought of being less brave than him. If I'd been alone, I might have tried once again to argue my uncle out of it, but in the presence of the guide I held my peace. I thought of my sweet Virland girl, and I walked towards the central chimney.

I have already mentioned that it was a hundred feet in diameter and three hundred feet round. I leant over a projecting rock and looked down. My hair stood on end with terror. A dizzying feeling of emptiness gripped me. I felt my centre of gravity moving and a mounting giddiness was affecting my brain just as if I was like drunk. There is nothing more treacherous than this feeling of attraction down into deep abysses. I was just about to let myself fall when a hand took hold of me. It was Hans. Obviously I hadn't taken as many lessons in 'abyss exploration' as I should have done in the Frelsers Kirk in Copenhagen.

But, short as my examination of this well had been, I had formed some idea of its shape and structure. Its almost perpendicular walls were bristling with innumerable projections which would facilitate our descent. But even if there was no lack of steps, there was still no rail. A rope fastened to the edge of the aperture might have helped us down, but how would we unfasten it when we reached the other end?

My uncle used a very simple expedient to get round this difficulty. He uncoiled a rope which was about the thickness of a thumb and four hundred feet long. First he dropped half of it down, then he wound it round a lava block that was sticking out conveniently and threw the other half down the chimney. Each of us could then descend by holding both halves of the rope, which would not be able to unwind itself from where it was attached. When we got two hundred feet down, it would be easy to get the whole rope again by letting go of one end and pulling it down by the other. Then the exercise would be repeated, *ad infinitum*.

'Now,' said my uncle, after having completed these preparations, 'let's think about our packs. I'll divide what we have to carry into three bundles, and each of us will carry one on his back. I'm only talking about the fragile articles.'

We, of course, were not included under that heading.

'Hans will take charge of the tools and one part of the provisions; you, Axel, will take another third of the provisions, and the firearms; and I will carry the rest of the provisions and the delicate instruments.'

'But,' I said, 'what about the clothes and that pile of ladders and ropes? What are we going to do with them?'

'They'll go down by themselves.'

'How?' I asked.

'You'll see.'

My uncle was always willing to take drastic action unhesitatingly. As commanded by my uncle, Hans bundled up all the non-fragile articles, tied them firmly together and simply dropped them down the abyss that lay in front of us.

I listened to the dull thuds of the bundle as it fell. My uncle, leaning over the abyss, followed the descent of the luggage with a look of satisfaction, and only stood up when he could no longer see it.

'That's fine. Now it's our turn.'

Now, I would ask any sensible person, could anyone hear such words without a shudder?

The Professor fastened his pack of instruments to his back; Hans took the tools; I took the firearms; and our descent began in the following order: Hans, my uncle, myself. It was all done in a deep silence, broken only by the sound of loose stones falling down into the dark abyss.

I let myself drop, as it were, frantically clutching the double rope with one hand and using the other to keep myself off the wall by means of my stick. One thought almost overwhelmed me, a fear that the rock I was hanging from might give way. The rope seemed very flimsy to be bearing the weight of three people. I made as little use of it as possible, performing wonderful feats of balance on the lava projections which my feet tried to catch hold of like hands.

When one of these insecure footholds became dislodged under Hans's foot, he said in his calm voice:

'*Gif akt!*'

'Watch out!' repeated my uncle.

In half an hour we were standing on the surface of a rock that was jammed across the chimney.

Hans pulled on one of the ends of the rope, and the other rose in the air. After passing the rock up above, it came down again, bringing with it a rather dangerous shower of bits of stone and lava.

Leaning over the edge of our narrow perch, I could see that the bottom of the hole was still out of sight.

The same manoeuvre with the rope was repeated, and half an hour later we had descended another two hundred feet.

I don't suppose even the maddest geologist would under such circumstances have studied the nature of the rocks we were passing. I can tell you I didn't give them any thought. Pliocene, Miocene, Eocene, Cretaceous, Jurassic, Triassic, Permian, Carboniferous, Devonian, Silurian or Primitive, it was all one to me. But the Professor was certainly continuing with his observations or taking notes, as during one of our stops he said to me:

'The farther I go, the more confident I feel. The order of these volcanic formations strongly confirms Davy's theories. We are now among the earliest rocks, which have been subjected to chemical actions which are produced by the contact of elementary bases of metals with water. I reject the whole idea of central heat altogether. We'll see further proof very soon.'

Still the same conclusion. Of course, I wasn't inclined to argue. My silence was taken for consent, and our descent continued.

Another three hours, and I could still see no bottom to the chimney. When I looked up, I could see the opening, which was getting noticeably smaller. The walls, sloping gently inwards, were coming closer together. It was steadily getting darker.

Still we kept going down. It seemed to me that the dislodged stones were being swallowed up with a duller sound, and that they must be reaching the bottom of the abyss more quickly.

As I had been careful to keep an exact note of our manoeuvres with the rope, which I knew we had repeated fourteen times, and each descent had taken half an hour, it was easy to calculate that we had been working our way down for seven hours. With fourteen quarter-of-an-hour rests, that made ten and a half hours. We had started out at one o'clock, so it must now be eleven o'clock. And the depth to which we had descended must be fourteen times 200 feet, or 2,800 feet.

At that moment I heard Hans's voice.

'Halt!' he shouted.

I stopped dead just as my feet were about to land on my uncle's head.

'We're there,' he cried.

'Where?' I said, sliding down beside him.

'At the bottom of the perpendicular chimney,' he answered.

'Is there no way of going further?'

'Yes. There's a sort of passage which slopes down to the right. We'll take a look at it tomorrow. Let's have supper and go to sleep.'

We were not yet in total darkness. The food pack was opened, we had our refreshment, and then went to sleep as well as we could on a bed of stones and lava fragments.

When I was lying on my back, I opened my eyes and saw a bright shining point of light at the top of the gigantic 3,000-foot long tube, now a huge telescope.

It was a star which, seen from this depth, had lost all its twinkle, and which by my calculations would be the *beta* star of the Little Bear. Then I fell fast asleep.

CHAPTER 18

THE WONDERS OF
THE TERRESTRIAL DEPTHS

At eight o'clock in the morning, a ray of daylight came to wake us up. The thousand shining surfaces of lava on the walls picked it up on its way down, and scattered it like a shower of sparks.

There was enough light to make out the objects around us.

'Well, Axel, what do you say?' exclaimed my uncle, rubbing his hands. 'Did you ever spend a quieter night in our little house in Königsberg? No noise of cart wheels, no street-cries of women with baskets, no boatmen shouting!'

'Certainly it's very quiet at the bottom of this well, but there's something disturbing in the very quietness itself.'

'Come now!' my uncle exclaimed. 'If you're frightened already, what will you be like later on? We haven't yet gone one single inch into the bowels of the Earth.'

'What do you mean?'

'I mean we've only reached the level of the island again. This long, vertical tube which starts at the mouth of the crater has its lower end exactly at sea-level.'

'Are you sure of that?'

'Quite sure. Check the barometer.'

In fact, the mercury, which had risen in the instrument as we descended, had stopped at twenty-nine inches.

'You see,' said the Professor. 'What we have now is exactly one atmosphere of pressure, and it's about time for the manometer to replace the barometer.'

And in truth this latter instrument would become useless as soon as the weight of the atmosphere exceeded the pressure at sea-level.

'But,' I said, 'is there no reason to fear that this ever-increasing pressure will eventually become very painful?'

'No. We'll be descending slowly, and our lungs will become used to a denser atmosphere. Aeronauts experience a lack of air as they climb to the higher levels, but we may perhaps have too much: of the two, that's what I would prefer. Let's not waste a moment. Where's the bundle we threw down ahead of us?'

I remembered then that we had searched in vain for it the evening before. My uncle questioned Hans, who, after having looked around carefully with the eye of a huntsman, replied:

'*Der huppe!*'

'Up there.'

And so it was. The bundle had been caught by a projection a hundred feet above us. Immediately the Icelander climbed up like a cat, and in a few minutes the package was in our possession.

'Now,' said my uncle, 'let's have breakfast. And let's breakfast like people who may have a long journey ahead of them.'

The biscuit and meat extract were washed down with several mouthfuls of water mixed with a little gin.

Breakfast over, my uncle pulled out of his pocket a small notebook that he kept for scientific observations. He consulted his instruments, and recorded:

Monday, July 1.

'*Chronometer, 8.17 a.m.; barometer, $29^{7/12}$ in.; thermometer, 6°. Direction, E.S.E.*

This last observation applied to the dark gallery, and was as indicated by the compass.

'Now then, Axel,' exclaimed the Professor with enthusiasm, 'now we're really going into the interior of the Earth. This is the moment when our journey really begins.'

So saying, my uncle with one hand took hold of the Ruhmkorff's apparatus which was hanging round his neck and with the other hand made an electrical connection to the coil in the lamp, and there was a bright enough light to disperse the darkness in the passage.

Hans carried the other apparatus, which was also switched on. This ingenious application of electricity would enable us to continue for a long while by creating an artificial light even in the midst of the most highly inflammable gases.

'Now, let's go!' shouted my uncle.

Each of us shouldered his pack. With Hans pushing the bundle of ropes and clothes along in front of him and myself at the rear, we entered the gallery.

At the moment of becoming engulfed in this dark gallery, I looked up, and for the last time saw through the length of that vast tube the Iceland sky that I thought never to see again.

In the last eruption of the volcano, in 1229, the lava had forced a passage through this tunnel. It still lined the walls with a thick, glistening coat. Here the electric light was intensified a hundredfold by reflected light.

The only difficulty in making progress lay in not sliding too fast down an incline of about forty-five degrees. Fortunately, there were worn-away and blistered patches in the lava that formed steps, and all we had to do was continue downwards, letting our baggage slide before us at the end of a long rope.

But the material which formed steps under our feet had formed stalactites above our heads. The lava, which was porous in many places, had formed a surface covered with small rounded blisters. Crystals of opaque quartz, set with limpid tears of glass and hanging like chandeliers from the vaulted roof, seemed as it were to catch fire and form sudden illuminations as we passed on our way. It was as if the genii of the depths were lighting up their palace to receive their terrestrial guests.

'This is magnificent!' I exclaimed in spite of myself. 'Uncle, what a sight! Aren't the colours of the lava wonderful, blending together and changing by imperceptible shades from reddish brown to bright yellow? And aren't these crystals just like globes of light?'

'Ah, you think so, do you, Axel, my boy? Well, you'll see greater splendours than these, I hope. Now, let's move on. Let's go!'

He would have been better to have said 'Let's slide', because we did nothing but drop down the steep inclines. It was Virgil's *facilis descensus Averni*[19]. The compass, which I consulted frequently, gave our direction as southeast with inflexible consistency. This lava stream deviated neither to the right nor to the left.

Yet there was no noticeable increase in temperature. This justified Davy's theory, and more than once I looked at the thermometer with surprise. Two hours after we had set off, it only showed 10°, an increase of only 4°. This suggested to me that our descent was more horizontal than vertical. As for the exact depth we had reached, that was very easy to ascertain: the Professor accurately measured the angles of deviation and inclination on the road – but he kept the results to himself.

About eight o'clock in the evening, he indicated that we should stop. Hans sat down at once. The lamps were hung on a projection in the lava; we were in some sort of cavern where there was plenty of air. Currents of air were getting to us. What atmospheric disturbance was causing them? I couldn't answer that question at that moment. I was so hungry and tired that I was incapable of thinking. A descent of seven hours at one go is not made without a considerable expenditure of effort, and I was exhausted. So I was very glad to hear the order to stop. Hans spread out our provisions on a block of lava, and we ate hungrily. But one thing troubled me: our supply of water was already half used up. My uncle was counting on a fresh supply from subterranean sources, but up to that point we hadn't come across any. I couldn't help drawing his attention to this fact.

'Are you surprised at this lack of springs?' he said.

'More than that, I'm anxious about it. We've only got enough water for five days.'

'Don't worry, Axel, we'll find more than we want.'

'When?'

'When we've left this bed of lava behind us. How could springs break through walls like these?'

'But perhaps this passage runs to a very great depth. It seems to me that we've made no great progress vertically.'

'Why do you suppose that?'

'Because if we had gone deep into the crust of Earth, we would have encountered greater heat.'

'According to your way of thinking,' said my uncle. 'But what does the thermometer say?'

'Hardly fifteen degrees, an increase of only nine degrees since we set out.'

'Well, and what is your conclusion?'

'This is my conclusion. According to exact observations, the increase of temperature in the interior of the globe increases at the rate of one degree for every hundred feet. But certain local conditions may modify this rate. So, at Yakutsk in Siberia there is an increase of one degree every 36 feet. This difference is a result of the heat-conducting capacity of the rocks. Moreover, near an extinct volcano, through gneiss, it has been observed that there is only an increase of one degree every 125 feet. Let's assume this last case as the most comparable to our situation, and calculate on the basis of that.'

'Well, calculate away, my boy.'

'Nothing easier,' I said, jotting down figures in my notebook. 'Nine times a hundred and twenty-five feet gives a depth of eleven hundred and twenty-five feet.'

'That's right.'

'Well?'

'According to my observations, we're 10,000 feet below sea-level.'

'Is that possible?'

'Yes, or figures no longer tell the truth.'

The Professor's calculations were quite correct. We had already reached a point six thousand feet deeper than anywhere that the foot of man had trod, such as the mines of Kitz-Bahl in the Tyrol and Wuttemberg in Bohemia.

The temperature, which ought to have been 81°, was scarcely 15°. That was something to think about.

CHAPTER 19

GEOLOGICAL STUDIES IN SITU

Next day, Tuesday, the 30th of June, at 6 a.m., our descent began again.

We were still following the gallery of lava, a natural staircase and as gently sloping as those sloping floors which in some old houses are still found instead of flights of steps. And so we went on until 12.17, the precise moment when we caught up with Hans, who had stopped.

'Ah, here we are,' exclaimed my uncle, 'at the very end of the chimney.'

I looked around me. We were standing at the intersection of two paths, both dark and narrow. Which one should we take? We had a problem.

My uncle was unwilling to show any sign of hesitation in front of either me or the guide. He pointed to the eastern tunnel, and soon all three of us were in it. In any case, if we had hesitated over which path to take, there would have been no end to it: since there was nothing whatsoever to guide our choice, we were forced to trust to chance.

The slope of this gallery was scarcely perceptible, but it varied greatly in height and width. Sometimes we passed through a series of arches, one after the other, like the majestic arcades of a Gothic cathedral. Here the architects of the Middle Ages might have found specimens for every form of the sacred art which grew from the development of the pointed arch. A mile farther on, we had to bow our heads under corniced elliptical arches in the Romanesque style, with massive pillars standing out from the wall and bending under the vault that rested heavily on them. In other places, this magnificence gave way to narrow channels between low structures which looked like beavers' lodges, and we had to crawl along very narrow passages indeed.

The level of heat was perfectly bearable. In spite of myself, I began to think how hot it would be when the lava thrown out by Snæfell was boiling and working its way through this now silent path. I imagined the torrents of fire being forced round every bend in the gallery and the accumulation of intensely hot vapours in this confined channel.

I only hope, I thought to myself, that this so-called extinct volcano won't take a fancy in its old age to begin its activities again!

I refrained from communicating these fears to Professor Lidenbrock. He would never have understood them anyway. He had only one idea in his head – onward! He walked, he slid, he scrambled, he tumbled, with a persistence which one could not help but admire.

By six in the evening, after a not very tiring walk, we had gone two leagues southwards but scarcely a quarter of a mile downwards.

My uncle indicated it was time to sleep. We ate without talking, and went to sleep without much thought.

Our arrangements for the night were very simple: a travelling rug for each of us, that we rolled ourselves into, was our sole covering. We had neither cold nor intruders to be afraid of. Travellers who penetrate into the wilds of central Africa, and into the pathless forests of the New World, have to keep watch over one another at night. But we enjoyed absolute safety and total seclusion: no savages or wild beasts infested these silent depths.

Next morning, we awoke refreshed and in good spirits. We set off again. As on the day before, we followed the path of the lava. It was impossible to tell what sort of rocks we were passing. The tunnel, instead of heading downwards, became more and more horizontal; I even thought I perceived a slight rise. But about ten o'clock this upward tendency became so evident, and therefore so tiring, that I was obliged to slacken my pace.

'What is the matter, Axel?' demanded the Professor impatiently.

'I can't go on any longer,' I replied.

'What, after three hours walking over such easy ground?'

'It may be easy, but it's tiring all the same.'

'What, when we've nothing to do but keep going down?'

'Going up, with all due respect.'

'Going up?' said my uncle.

'Definitely. For the last half-hour the slope has gone the other way, and at this rate we shall soon be back on the level ground of Iceland.'

The Professor shook his head slowly and uneasily, like a man who is unwilling to be convinced. I tried to pursue the conversation. He made no reply, and gave the signal for us to start again. I could see that his silence was nothing but ill-humour.

Still, I courageously shouldered my pack again, and hurried after Hans, who was following my uncle. I was anxious not to be left behind. My greatest concern was not to lose sight of my companions. I shuddered at the thought of being lost in the depths of this vast subterranean labyrinth.

Besides, if the ascending path did become steeper, I was comforted by the thought that it was bringing us nearer the surface. I found hope in this. Every step confirmed this, and I was rejoicing at the thought of meeting my little Gräuben again.

By midday there was a change in the appearance of the walls of the gallery. I noticed it by a drop in the amount of light reflected from the sides; solid rock was appearing in place of the lava coating. The rock-mass was composed of inclined and sometimes vertical strata. We were passing through rocks of the Transition or Silurian system.

It's evident, I exclaimed to myself, that marine deposits formed these shales, limestones and sandstones in the second period of the Earth's development. We're turning away from the primary granite. It's just as if we were Hamburg people going to Lübeck by way of Hanover!

I would have been better to have kept my observations to myself. But my geological instinct was stronger than my prudence, and Uncle Lidenbrock heard my exclamation.

'What's that you're saying?' he asked.

'Look,' I said, pointing to the varied series of sandstones and limestones and the first indication of slate.

'Well?'

'We're at the period when the first plants and animals appeared.'

'Do you think so?'

'Take a closer look.'

I made the Professor shine his light over the walls of the gallery. I expected some signs of astonishment, but he said not a word and just carried on.

Had he understood me or not? Was he refusing to admit, out of self-pride as an uncle and a scholar, that he had made the wrong choice when he chose the eastern tunnel? Or was he determined to examine this passage to its very end? It was evident that we had left the lava path, and that this path could not possibly lead to the extinct furnace of Snæfell.

Yet I wondered if I was not depending too much on this change in the rock. Might I myself not be mistaken? Were we really crossing the layers of rock which overlie the granite foundation?

If I'm right, I thought, I must soon find some fossil remains of primitive life, and then he'll have to yield to the evidence. Let's look for some.

I hadn't gone a hundred yards before incontestable proofs presented themselves to me. It was bound to happen, as in the Silurian age the seas contained at least fifteen hundred vegetable and animal species. My feet, which had become accustomed to the hard lava floor, suddenly found themselves on dust composed of the debris of plants and shells. In the walls were distinct impressions of seaweeds and club-mosses. Professor Lidenbrock must realize what that meant, I thought, and yet he still pushed on with, it seemed to me, his eyes resolutely shut.

This was simply obstinacy taken to a ridiculous stage. I couldn't bear it any longer. I picked up a perfectly formed shell, which had belonged to an animal not unlike the modern woodlouse. Then, joining my uncle, I said:

'Look at this!'

'Fine,' said he quietly, 'it's the shell of a crustacean, of an extinct species called a trilobite. Nothing more.'

'But don't you conclude . . . ?'

'Just what you conclude yourself. Yes, I do, perfectly. We've left the granite and the lava. It's possible that I may be mistaken. But I can't be sure of that until I have reached the very end of this gallery.'

'You're right in that, uncle, and I would quite approve of your determination if there were not a danger threatening us more and more.'

'What danger?'

'The lack of water.'

'That's all right, Axel, we'll ration ourselves.'

CHAPTER 20

THE FIRST SIGNS OF DISTRESS

In fact, we had no option but to ration ourselves. Our water supply couldn't last more than three more days. I found that out for certain when we took our evening meal. And, to our sorrow, we had little reason to expect to find a source in these Transition Period beds.

The whole of the next day the gallery opened before us in endless arcades. We carried on almost without a word. Hans's silence seemed to be infecting us too.

The path was no longer climbing, at least not perceptibly. Sometimes, even, it seemed to have a slight downward slope. But this tendency, which was very slight, could do nothing to reassure the Professor, because there was no change in the beds, and the Transitional characteristics became more and more obvious.

The electric light was reflected in sparkling splendour from the schist, limestone and old red sandstone of the walls. You might have thought we were passing along a trench section in Devon, which gave its name to this system. Specimens of magnificent marbles clothed the walls, some of a greyish agate fantastically veined with white, others of a rich crimson or yellow dashed with splotches of red; then came dark cherry-coloured marbles relieved by the lighter tints of limestone.

The greater part of these rocks bore impressions of primitive organisms. Creation had evidently advanced since the day before: instead of rudimentary trilobites, I noticed remains of a more developed order of beings, amongst which were ganoid fishes and some of those sauroids in which palaeontologists have discovered the earliest reptile forms. The Devonian seas were populated by animals of these species, and deposited them by thousands in the rocks of the newer formation.

It was evident that we were ascending that scale of animal life in which man fills the highest place. But Professor Lidenbrock seemed not to notice.

He was waiting for one of two things to happen – either the appearance of a vertical shaft opening before his feet, down which our descent might be resumed, or some obstacle which would force us to turn back and retrace our footsteps. But evening came and neither wish was gratified.

On Friday, after a night during which I felt pangs of thirst, our little band again plunged into the winding passages of the gallery.

After ten hours' walking, I observed a strange deadening of the reflection of our lamps from the side walls. The marble, the schist, the limestone and the sandstone were giving way to a dark and lustreless lining. At one point, the tunnel becoming very narrow, I leant against the wall.

When I took my hand off the wall, it was black. I looked closer, and found we were in a coal formation.

'A coal mine!' I exclaimed.

'A mine without miners,' my uncle replied.

'Who knows?' I asked.

'I know,' the Professor stated firmly. 'I'm certain that this gallery driven through beds of coal was never cut by human hand. But whether or not it's the work of nature doesn't matter. It's dinner-time. Let's eat.'

Hans prepared some food. I scarcely ate, and I swallowed down the few drops of water rationed out to me. One flask half full was all we had left to slake the thirst of three men.

After their meal my two companions lay down on their rugs, and found in sleep a solace from their fatigue. But I couldn't sleep, and I counted every hour until morning.

On Saturday, at six o'clock, we started off again. In twenty minutes we reached a vast open space. I knew then that human beings hadn't hollowed out this mine: the vaults would have been shored up, whereas, as it was, they seemed to be held up by some miracle of equilibrium.

The cavern was about a hundred feet wide and a hundred and fifty in height. The ground had been forced apart by some subterranean disturbance. Yielding to some great power from below, it had separated, leaving this great hollow into which human beings were now penetrating for the first time.

The whole history of the Carboniferous Period was written on these gloomy walls, and a geologist might with ease trace all its diverse phases. The beds of coal were separated by strata of sandstone or compact clays, and appeared crushed under the weight of overlying strata.

During the age of the world which preceded the Secondary Period, the Earth was covered with immense plant forms, the product of the double influence of tropical heat and constant moisture. A steamy atmosphere surrounded the Earth, still veiling the direct rays of the sun.

This gives rise to the conclusion that the high temperature then existing was due to some other source than the heat of the sun. It is even possible that the daystar might not have been ready yet to play the important role it now has. There were no 'climates' as yet, and a torrid heat, equal from pole to equator, was spread over the whole surface of the globe. Where did this heat come from? From the interior of the Earth.

Regardless of Professor Lidenbrock's theories, a violent heat *did* smoulder within the body of the sphere. Its effect was felt to the outermost layers of the terrestrial crust. The plants, deprived of the beneficial effects of the sun, produced neither flowers nor scent, but their roots drew vigorous life from the burning soil of the early days of this planet.

There were few trees. Herbaceous plants alone existed. There were tall grasses, ferns and club-mosses, besides Sigillarias and Asterophyllites, rare plants now but whose species might at that time be counted in their thousands.

The coal measures owe their origin to this period of profuse vegetation. The still elastic and yielding crust of the Earth moved with the fluid forces beneath it, whence the innumerable fissures and depressions. The plants, sinking beneath the water, gradually gathered into huge masses.

Then came the chemical action of nature. In the depths of the seas, the vegetable accumulations first became peat; then, acted on by generated gases and the heat of fermentation, they underwent a process of complete mineralization.

Thus were formed those immense layers of coal, which nevertheless are not inexhaustible and which at the present rate of over-consumption will be exhausted in three centuries unless the industrial world devises some way of avoiding this.

These thoughts came into my mind whilst I was contemplating the wealth of coal stored in this section of the globe. This, I thought, will no doubt never be discovered; the working of such deep mines would involve too large an outlay, and so what would be the point as long as coal is still spread far and wide near the surface? Just as these untouched stores are as I see them now, so will they be when this world comes to an end.

But still we marched on. I alone was forgetting the length of the path we trod by losing myself in the midst of geological contemplations. The temperature remained what it had been during our passage through the lava and schists. I was, however, strongly affected by a gassy smell. I immediately recognized the presence in the gallery of a considerable quantity of that dangerous gas that miners call firedamp, explosions of which have often caused terrible catastrophes.

Fortunately, our light came from Ruhmkorff's ingenious apparatus. If we had been unfortunate enough to have been exploring this gallery with torches, a terrible explosion would have put an end to travelling and travellers at one stroke.

This trip through the coal mine lasted until night. My uncle could scarcely control his impatience at the horizontal passage. The darkness, always deep just twenty yards in front of us, prevented us from estimating the length of the gallery, and I was beginning to think it must be endless, when suddenly at six o'clock a wall very unexpectedly rose up before us. There was no way forward, neither to the right nor to the left of it, neither at the top of it nor at its base; we were at the end of a blind alley. 'That's fine. So much the better,' exclaimed my uncle. 'Now, at any rate, we know what we are about. We're not on Saknussemm's path, and all we have to do is go back. Let's have a night's rest, and in three days we shall get to the fork in the path.'

'Yes,' I said, 'if we have any strength left.'

'Why not?'

'Because tomorrow we'll have no water.'

'Nor any courage either?' asked my uncle severely.

I didn't dare reply.

CHAPTER 21

COMPASSION MELTS THE PROFESSOR'S HEART

Next day we started off early. We had to hurry. It was a three-day walk back to the crossroads.

I will say nothing of the sufferings we endured during our return. My uncle bore them with the angry impatience of a man obliged to admit his own weakness; Hans with the resignation of his passive nature; I, I must confess, with complaints and expressions of despair. I didn't have the mental strength to cope with this ill-fortune.

As I had warned, the water ran out by the end of the first day's march back. All we now had as liquid food was gin, but the infernal fluid burned my throat and I couldn't bear even the sight of it. I found the temperature and the air stifling. Fatigue paralysed my limbs. More than once I almost collapsed. Then there would be a stop, and my uncle and the Icelander would do their best to restore me. But I could see that the former was struggling with difficulty against extreme fatigue and the tortures of thirst.

Finally, on Tuesday, July 8, we arrived, half dead and on our hands and knees, at the junction of the two passages. I lay there like a lifeless mass, stretched out on the lava. It was ten in the morning.

Hans and my uncle, leaning on the wall, tried to nibble a few bits of biscuit. Long moans escaped from my swollen lips.

After some time my uncle came over to me and raised me in his arms.

'My poor boy!' he said, in genuine tones of compassion.

I was touched by these words, not being accustomed to see the excitable Professor in a gentler mood. I grasped his trembling hands in mine. He let me hold them and looked at me. His eyes were moist.

Then I saw him take the flask that was hanging at his side. To my amazement he placed it to my lips.

'Drink this,' he said.

Had I heard him correctly? Was my uncle mad? I stared at him in a daze, unable to grasp what he was saying.

'Drink it,' he said again.

And raising his flask he emptied it every drop between my lips.

Oh, infinite bliss! A mouthful of water came to moisten my burning mouth. It was just one sip but it was enough to bring back my ebbing life.

I thanked my uncle with clasped hands.

'Yes,' he said, 'a mouthful of water. But it's the last one – do you hear me? – the very last. I'd been keeping it as a precious treasure at the bottom of my flask. Twenty times, no, a hundred times, I fought off a terrible impulse to drink it. But no, Axel, I kept it for you.'

'My dear uncle,' I said, whilst hot tears trickled down my face.

'Yes, my poor boy, I knew that as soon as you arrived at these crossroads, you would collapse half dead, and I kept my last drop of water to refresh you.'

'Thank you, thank you,' I said. Although my thirst was only partially quenched, some strength had nevertheless returned. The muscles of my throat, tight until then, now relaxed again, my lips became a little less inflamed, and I was able to speak again.

'Well, now,' I said, 'there's only one thing we can do now. We have no water; we must go back.'

While I was saying this, my uncle was avoiding looking at me; he hung his head; his eyes avoided mine.

'We have to go back!' I exclaimed vehemently. 'We have to go back to Snæfell! May God give us the strength to climb up the crater again!'

'Go back,' said my uncle, as if he was talking to himself rather than me.

'Yes, go back, and there's not a minute to lose.'

A long silence followed.

'So, then, Axel,' replied the Professor in a strange voice, 'you've found no courage or energy in these few drops of water?'

'Courage?'

'I see you are just as weak-willed as you were before, and still expressing nothing but despair!'

What sort of a man was I dealing with here, and what schemes did he now have going round in his fearless mind?

'What? You won't go back?'

'Should I give this expedition up just when we have the best chance of success? Never!'

'Then must we resign ourselves to perishing?'

'No, Axel, no. You go back. Hans will go with you. Leave me here myself!'

'Leave you here?'

'Leave me, I tell you. I have undertaken this expedition. I'll carry it out to the end, and I will not go back. Go on, Axel, just go!'

My uncle was in a state of feverish excitement. His voice, which had for a moment been tender and gentle, had now become harsh and threatening. He was struggling with gloomy determination to do the impossible. I didn't want to leave him in this bottomless abyss, but on the other hand the instinct for self-preservation was prompting me to flee.

The guide watched this scene with his usual phlegmatic unconcern. Nevertheless, he understood perfectly well what was going on between his two companions. Our gestures themselves were sufficient to show that we were each bent on taking a different path. But Hans seemed to have no interest in a matter on which his life depended. He was ready either to start out at a given signal or to stay, if his master so willed it.

How I wished at this moment I could have made him understand me. My words, my complaints, my tone would have had some influence over his impassive nature. Those dangers which our guide could not understand I could have demonstrated and proved to him. Together we might have overruled the obstinate Professor. If necessary, we might perhaps have been able to force him back up the heights of Snæfell.

I approached Hans. I put my hand on his. He didn't move. My parted lips sufficiently revealed my sufferings. The Icelander slowly shook his head and, pointing calmly at my uncle, said:

'Master.'

'Master?' I shouted. 'Are you crazy? No, he isn't master over your life. We must get out of here, we must drag him with us. Do you hear me? Do you understand?'

I had seized Hans by the arm. I wanted to get him to stand up. I struggled with him. My uncle intervened.

'Be calm, Axel! You'll get nothing from that stoical servant. So listen to what I have to suggest.'

I folded my arms and faced my uncle boldly.

'The lack of water,' he said, 'is the only obstacle in our way. In this eastern gallery made up of lavas, schists and coal, we haven't come across a single drop of moisture. Perhaps we'll have better luck if we follow the western tunnel.'

I shook my head incredulously.

'Hear me out,' the Professor went on with a firm voice. 'While you were lying there motionless, I went to examine the conformation of that gallery. It goes straight down, and in a few hours it'll bring us to granite rocks. There we are bound to meet with plentiful springs of water. The nature of the rock assures me of this, and instinct agrees with logic to support my conviction. Now, this is what I suggest. When Columbus asked his ships' crews to allow him three more days to discover a new world, those crews, disheartened and sick as they were, recognized the rightness of the request, and he discovered America. I am the Columbus of this nether world, and I ask only for *one* more day. If in a single day I have not found the water we need, I swear to you we will return to the surface of the Earth.'

In spite of my irritation I was moved by these words, as well as by the violence my uncle was doing to his own desires in making so dangerous a proposal.

'Well,' I said, 'do as you will, and may God reward your superhuman energy. You have now but a few hours to tempt fate. Let's make a start!'

CHAPTER 22

A TOTAL LACK OF WATER

This time we started our descent in the new gallery. Hans led the way, as was his custom.

We hadn't gone a hundred yards when the Professor, moving his lantern along the walls, exclaimed:

'Here are some primitive rocks. Now we're on the right path. Forward!'

When in its early stages the Earth was slowly cooling, its contraction gave rise to disruptions, distortions, fissures and chasms in its crust. The passage through which we were walking was one such fissure, through which at one time granite had poured out in a molten state. Its thousand meanders formed an intricate labyrinth through the primeval mass.

As fast as we descended, the succession of strata forming the primitive foundation appeared with increasing distinctness. Geologists consider this primitive matter to be the base of the mineral crust of the Earth, and have ascertained it to be composed of three different formations, schist, gneiss and mica schist, resting on that unchangeable foundation, granite.

Never had mineralogists found themselves in such wonderful circumstances to study nature *in situ*. What the drilling machine, an ignorant and brutal contraption, was unable to bring up from the inner structures to the surface of the globe, we were able to see with our own eyes and handle with our own hands.

Through the beds of schist, coloured with delicate shades of green, ran winding threads of copper and manganese, with traces of platinum and gold. I thought to myself, what riches are buried here at an inaccessible depth, hidden for ever from the covetous eyes of the human race! These treasures have been buried at such an extreme depth by the convulsions of primeval times that they run no risk of ever being harmed by pickaxe or spade.

After the schists came gneiss, partially stratified, remarkable for the parallelism and regularity of its lamina, then mica schists, lying in large plates or flakes, revealing their structure by the sparkle of the white shining mica.

The light from our Ruhmkorff lamps, reflected from the small facets of quartz, flashed sparkling rays in every direction, and I felt as if I was moving through a diamond, within which the darting rays criss-crossed in a thousand flashing coruscations.

About six o'clock this brilliant feast of light underwent a noticeable reduction in its splendour, then almost ceased entirely. The walls took on a crystalline but sombre appearance. The mica was more intimately mixed with the feldspar and quartz to form the rock of all rocks, the hard stone that forms the foundations of the Earth and which without being crushed bears the weight of the four terrestrial rock-systems. We were walled up within prison walls of granite.

It was eight in the evening. There had been no sign yet of water. I was suffering terribly. My uncle marched on. He refused to stop. He was listening anxiously for the murmur of distant springs. But, no, there was absolute silence.

And now my legs were refusing to carry me any further. I fought the pain and torment in order not to stop my uncle, which would have driven him to despair, because the day was drawing to its close, and it would be his last.

Finally my strength gave out. I gave a cry and fell to the ground.

'Help, I'm dying.'

My uncle retraced his steps. He looked at me with his arms folded, then these muttered words passed his lips:

'It's all over!'

The last thing I saw was a terrifying gesture of rage, and my eyes closed.

When I reopened them, I saw my two companions motionless and rolled up in their coverings. Were they asleep? For my part, I couldn't get a wink of sleep. I was suffering too much, and what made my thoughts especially bitter was that there was no remedy for my condition. My uncle's last words echoed painfully in my ears: 'It's all over!' For in such a terrible state of weakness, it was madness to even think of ever reaching the upper world again.

Above us there was a league and a half of terrestrial crust. The weight of it seemed to be pressing down on my shoulders. I felt weighed down, and I exhausted myself with violent struggles to turn over on my granite bed.

A few hours passed. A deep silence reigned around us, the silence of the grave. No sound could reach us through walls, the thinnest of which were five miles thick.

But even in my stupor, I thought I could hear a noise. It was dark down the tunnel, but I thought I could see the Icelander vanishing from sight with the lamp in his hand.

Why was he leaving us? Was Hans going to abandon us? My uncle was fast asleep. I wanted to shout, but my voice died on my parched and swollen lips. The darkness became deeper, and the last sound died away in the far distance.

'Hans has abandoned us,' I shouted. 'Hans! Hans!'

But these words were only spoken within me. They went no further. Yet after the first moment of terror, I felt ashamed of suspecting a man of such extraordinary faithfulness. Instead of going up, he was going down the gallery. Any evil intention would have taken him up, not down. This thought made me calm again, and I turned to other thoughts. Only some important purpose could have induced this quiet man to give up his sleep. Was he off on a search? Had he in the silence of the night detected a sound, a murmur of something in the distance, which I had failed to register?

CHAPTER 23

WATER DISCOVERED

For a whole hour, I was trying to work out in my delirious brain the reasons which might have made this calm huntsman behave like this. The most absurd notions ran in utter confusion through my mind. I thought I was going mad!

But at last the noise of footsteps could be heard in the dark abyss. Hans was coming back. A flickering light was beginning to glimmer on the wall of our dark prison. Then it appeared at the mouth of the gallery. And then Hans appeared.

He went over to my uncle, put his hand on his shoulder, and gently woke him. My uncle got up.

'What's the matter?' he asked.

'*Vatten*,' replied the huntsman.

Under the inspiration of intense pain, no doubt everybody becomes endowed with the gift of tongues. I didn't know a word of Danish, yet instinctively I understood the word he had uttered.

'Water! Water!' I shouted, clapping my hands and waving my arms like a madman.

'Water!' repeated my uncle. '*Hvar?*' he asked, in Icelandic.

'*Nedat*,' replied Hans.

Where? Down below! I understood everything that was being said. I grasped the hunter's hands, and held them tightly while he looked at me calmly.

The preparations for our departure were not long in making, and we were soon on our way down a passage that inclined two feet in seven. In an hour we had gone a mile and a quarter, and descended two thousand feet.

Then I began to hear distinctly a new sound of something running within the thickness of the granite wall, a kind of dull, dead rumbling like distant thunder. During the first part of our march, not coming on the promised spring, I could feel my distress returning, but then my uncle acquainted me with the cause of the strange noise.

'Hans wasn't mistaken,' he said. 'What you hear is the rushing of a torrent.'

'A torrent?' I exclaimed.

'No doubt about it. There's a subterranean river flowing around us.'

We hurried on in the greatest excitement. I was no longer aware of my fatigue. This murmuring of waters close at hand was already refreshing me. It was getting increasingly loud. The torrent, after having flowed for some time above our heads, was now flowing, roaring and rushing, within the left wall.

Frequently I touched the wall, hoping to feel some indication of moisture, but I couldn't feel anything.

Another half hour passed and we'd covered another half league.

Then it became clear that the hunter hadn't managed to go any further than this point. Guided by an instinct peculiar to mountaineers and water-diviners, he had, as it were, felt this torrent through the rock, but he had certainly seen none of the precious liquid, nor had he slaked his thirst.

Soon it became clear that if we continued walking, we would increase the distance between ourselves and the stream, the noise of which was becoming fainter.

We went back. Hans stopped where the torrent seemed closest. I sat near the wall, while the waters were flowing past me violently only two feet away. But there was a thick granite wall between us and the object of our desires.

Without thinking, without wondering if there were any means of getting the water, I gave way to a feeling of despair.

Hans glanced at me with, I thought, a smile of pity.

He stood up and picked up the lamp. I followed him. He moved towards the wall, while I looked on. He put his ear against the dry stone and moved it slowly backwards and forwards, up and down, listening intently. I realized at once that he was searching to find the exact spot where the torrent could be heard the loudest. He found that spot on the left-hand side of the tunnel, three feet from the ground.

I was almost overcome with excitement. I hardly dared guess what the hunter was about to do. But I couldn't help but understand, and applaud and cheer him on, when I saw him take hold of the pickaxe to attack the rock.

'We're saved!' I cried.

'Yes,' cried my uncle, almost frantic with excitement. 'Hans is right. What an excellent fellow! Who but he would have thought of it?'

Yes, who but he? Such an expedient, simple as it was, would never have crossed our minds. True, it seemed extremely hazardous to strike this part of the Earth's structure with a hammer. What if some rocks moved and crushed us all? What if the torrent, bursting through, drowned us in a sudden flood? There was nothing foolish in these fancies. But nonetheless, no fear of falling rocks or rushing floods could stop us now, and our thirst was so intense that, to satisfy it, we would have dug down into the ocean bed itself.

Hans set about the task which my uncle and I together could not have accomplished. If impatience had given our hands the power, we would have shattered the rock into a thousand fragments. Not so Hans. Completely under control, he calmly cut his way through the rock with a steady succession of light, skilful strokes, creating an opening six inches wide. I could hear noise of flowing waters getting louder, and I fancied I could feel the delicious fluid refreshing my parched lips.

The pickaxe had soon penetrated two feet into the granite partition, and our man had been working for over an hour. I was in an agony of impatience. My uncle wanted to take stronger measures, and I had some difficulty in dissuading him. However, he had just picked up a pickaxe when a sudden hissing was heard and a strong jet of water spurted out, hitting the opposite wall.

Hans, almost thrown off his feet by the force of the shock, uttered a cry of pain, and I soon understood why, when, plunging my hands into the gushing torrent, I hastily pulled them out again: the water was scalding hot.

'The water's boiling,' I cried.

'Well, never mind, let it cool,' my uncle replied.

The tunnel was filling with steam, whilst a stream was forming, which slowly trickled away into the winding subterranean passages. Soon we had the satisfaction of swallowing our first mouthfuls.

Could anything be more delicious than the feeling that our intolerable burning thirst was easing, leaving us to enjoy comfort and pleasure? But where was this water from? It didn't matter. It was water, and though still hot, it brought back life to the dying. I drank without stopping, almost without even tasting it.

It was only after a moment of savouring the water that I exclaimed, 'Why, this spring has iron salts in it!'

'Nothing could be better for the digestion,' said my uncle. 'It's full of iron. It'll be as good for us as going to Spa or Töplitz[20].'

'Well, it's delicious!'

'Of course it is. Water should be when it's found six miles underground. It has an inky flavour, which is not at all unpleasant. What an excellent source of strength Hans has found for us here. We'll name it after him.'

'That's a good idea,' I said.

And Hans's Brook it was from that moment on.

Hans was none the prouder for this honour. After drinking moderately, he quietly went over to a corner to rest.

'Now,' I said, 'we mustn't lose this water.'

'Why trouble ourselves about that?' replied my uncle. 'I don't imagine it will ever run out.'

'Yes, but we can't be sure it won't. Let's fill the water bottle and our flasks, and then block up the opening.'

My advice was followed as far as getting in a supply of water was concerned. But blocking the hole was not so easy to accomplish. In vain we picked up pieces of granite and stuffed them in with tow; we only scalded our hands without succeeding in blocking the flow. The pressure was too great, and our efforts were fruitless.

'It's obvious,' I said, 'that the main body of this water is at a considerable height above us. The force of the jet shows that.'

'No doubt,' answered my uncle. 'If this column of water is 32,000 feet high, that is, coming from the surface of the Earth, it is equal to the weight of a thousand atmospheres. But I've got an idea.'

'Well?'

'Why bother to stop the stream coming out at all?'

'Because . . .' Well, I couldn't actually think of any reason.

'When our flasks are empty, where will we be able to fill them again? Can we know that for sure?'

No, we couldn't be sure about that.

'Well, let's let the water keep on running. It'll flow downwards, and will both guide us and refresh us.'

'That's a good plan,' I said. 'With this stream for our guide, there is no reason why we shouldn't succeed in our undertaking.'

'Ah, my boy! So you agree with me now?' exclaimed the Professor, laughing.

'I heartily agree with you.'

'Well, let's rest a while, and then we'll start off again.'

I was forgetting that it was night-time. The chronometer soon informed me of that fact. And in a very short time, refreshed and thankful, we all three fell into a sound sleep.

CHAPTER 24

WELL SAID, OLD MOLE! CANST THOU WORK I' THE GROUND SO FAST?[21]

By the next day we had forgotten all our sufferings. At first, I was surprised to find I was no longer thirsty, and I was wondering why. The answer came in the murmuring of the stream at my feet.

We had breakfast, and drank some of the excellent iron-laden water. I felt totally bucked up and quite determined to push on. Why should such a firmly convinced man as my uncle, assisted by such a hard-working guide as Hans and accompanied by such a determined nephew as myself, not succeed in his aim? This was the sort of excellent thought that was going round in my head. If anyone had suggested to me that I should return to the summit of Snæfell, I would have declined with indignation.

Fortunately, all we had to do was to go down.

'Let's make a start!' I cried, awakening by my shouts the echoes of the vaulted hollows of the Earth.

On Thursday, at 8 a.m., we started off again. The winding granite tunnel led us round unexpected bends and turns, and seemed almost to form a labyrinth, but, on the whole, its direction seemed to be south-easterly. My uncle constantly consulted his compass to keep a check on the ground we were covering.

The gallery sloped down very slightly from the horizontal, scarcely more than two inches in every six feet, and the stream ran gently burbling at our feet. I thought of it as a friendly spirit guiding us underground, and with my hand I caressed the soft water-nymph whose comforting voice accompanied our steps. With my reviving spirits, these mythological notions just seemed to spring into my mind.

As for my uncle, he was beginning to rage against our horizontal passage. He was a man for vertical paths. This route seemed to be extending indefinitely, and instead of sliding along a chord of the circle as we were now doing, he would have much preferred to drop down the Earth's radius. But there was nothing we could do about it, and so long as we were approaching the centre to some extent, we felt we mustn't complain.

From time to time, a steeper path appeared. Our naiad then began to tumble before us with a hoarser murmur, and we descended with her to a greater depth.

On the whole, that day and the next we made considerable progress horizontally, but very little vertically.

On Friday evening, the 10th of July, we were according to our calculations thirty leagues south-east of Reykjavik, and at a depth of two and a half leagues.

At our feet there now opened a terrifying abyss. My uncle, however, was not to be put off, and he clapped his hands with pleasure at the steepness of the descent.

'This will take us a long way,' he exclaimed, 'and without much difficulty, because the projections in the rock make for a good staircase.'

The ropes were fastened by Hans in such a way as to prevent any accidents, and the descent began. I can hardly call it perilous, because I was beginning to be familiar with this kind of exercise.

This well, or abyss, was a narrow cleft in the granite mass, called by geologists a 'fault' and caused by the unequal cooling of the globe of the Earth. If it had at one time been a passage for eruptive matter thrown out by Snæfell, I couldn't understand why no trace remained of it passing through. We kept going down a kind of winding staircase, which seemed almost to have been made by human hands.

Every quarter of an hour we were forced to stop for a short rest to allow our knees to recover. We would then sit down on a fragment of rock and talk as we ate and drank from the stream.

Of course, Hans's Brook was falling in a cascade down this fault, and had lost some of its volume, but there was enough and to spare to slake our thirst. Besides, when the incline became more gentle, it would naturally resume its peaceful course. At this point it reminded me of my worthy uncle, with his frequent fits of impatience and anger, while below it ran with the calmness of the Icelandic hunter.

On the 11th and 12th of July, we kept following the spiral curves of this fault, penetrating in actual distance no more than two leagues, but being carried to a depth of five leagues below sea level. But on the 13th, about noon, the fault turned towards the south-east, with a much gentler slope, one of about forty-five degrees.

Then the road became monotonously easy. It couldn't be otherwise, as there was no landscape to vary the stages of our journey.

On Wednesday, the 15th, we were seven leagues underground, and had travelled fifty leagues from Snæfell. Although we were tired, we were in perfect health, and had not yet had any reason to open the medicine chest.

Every hour, my uncle noted the readings on the compass, the chronometer, the manometer and the thermometer, exactly as he has published in his scientific report of our journey. It was therefore not difficult to know exactly where we were. When he told me that we had travelled fifty leagues horizontally, I couldn't hold back an exclamation of astonishment at the thought that we had now long since left Iceland behind us.

'What's the matter?' he exclaimed.

'I was just thinking that if your calculations are correct we are no longer under Iceland.'

'Do you think so?'

'It's easy to check,' I said, and examining the map and using a pair of compasses, I added, 'I wasn't wrong. We've passed Cape Portland, and those fifty leagues bring us out into the middle of the ocean.'

'*Under* the ocean,' my uncle said, rubbing his hands with delight.

'Can we really be?' I said. 'Is the ocean spread out above our heads?'

'Of course, Axel. What could be more natural? Aren't there coal mines at Newcastle that extend far out under the sea?'

It was all very well for the Professor to call this 'natural', but I couldn't feel entirely relaxed at the thought that the boundless ocean was rolling above my head. And yet it really mattered very little whether it was plains and mountains that covered our heads, or the Atlantic waves, so long as we were protected by an arch of solid granite. Anyway, I quickly got used to the idea, as the tunnel, at times running straight, at other times winding as capriciously in its inclines as in its turnings but constantly keeping its south-easterly direction and always going deeper, was gradually taking us to very great depths indeed.

Four days later, on Saturday the 18th of July, in the evening, we arrived at a kind of vast grotto, and here my uncle paid Hans his weekly wages, and it was agreed that the next day, Sunday, should be a day of rest.

CHAPTER 25

DE PROFUNDIS[22]

I therefore awoke next day relieved from concerns about an immediate start. And although we were in the deepest of chasms, there was something quite pleasant about it. Besides, we were beginning to get accustomed to this troglodyte life. I no longer thought about the sun, the moon and the stars, nor about trees, houses and towns, nor about any other of those superfluous things that those who live on the earth's surface consider necessities. Being fossils, we considered all those things as mere nothings.

The grotto formed an immense hall. Along its granite floor ran our faithful stream. At this distance from its spring, the water was scarcely warm, and we drank it with pleasure.

After breakfast, the Professor spent a few hours sorting his daily notes.

'First,' said he, 'I'll make a calculation to ascertain our exact position. I hope, after our return, to draw a map of our journey, which will be in reality a vertical section of the globe, containing the path of our expedition.'

'That will be very interesting, Uncle, but are your observations sufficiently accurate to enable you to do that correctly?'

'Yes. I have everywhere observed the angles and inclines. I'm sure there are no errors. Let's see where we are now. Look at the compass and tell me what direction it indicates.'

I looked, and replied carefully:

'South-east by east.'

'Well,' answered the Professor, after a rapid calculation, 'I reckon we've gone eighty-five leagues since we started.'

'And so we're under the mid-Atlantic?'

'We certainly are.'

'And perhaps at this very moment there is a storm above us, and ships above our heads are being roughly tossed about by the tempest.'

'Quite probably.'

'And there are whales lashing the roof of our prison with their tails?'

'It may be, Axel, but don't worry, they won't do us any harm here. But let's go back to our calculations. Here we are eighty-five leagues south-east of Snæfell, and I reckon that we're at a depth of sixteen leagues.'

'Sixteen leagues?' I cried.

'No doubt.'

'Why, this is the very limit assigned by science to the thickness of the crust of the Earth.'

'I don't deny it.'

'And here, according to the law of increasing temperature, there ought to be a heat of 1,502 degrees Celsius!'

'So there should, my boy.'

'And all this solid granite ought to be in a liquid state.'

'You see that it is not so, and that, as so often happens, facts arise to overthrow theories.'

'I'm forced to agree with you, but, nevertheless, it is surprising.'

'What does the thermometer say?'

'27.6 degrees.'

'Therefore the scientists are out by 1,474.4 degrees, and the theory of proportional increase in temperature is a mistake. Therefore Humphry Davy was right, and I am not wrong in agreeing with him. What do you say now?'

'Nothing.'

In truth, I had a good deal to say. In no way did I accept Davy's theory. I still held to the notion of central heat, although I couldn't feel its effects. To tell the truth, I preferred to think that this chimney of an extinct volcano, lined with lavas, which are non-conductors of heat, simply didn't allow the heat to pass through its walls.

But without stopping to think up new arguments, I simply accepted our situation as it was.

'Well, admitting all your calculations to be quite correct, you must allow me to draw one definite conclusion from them.'

'Go ahead, my boy. Feel free to speak.'

'At the latitude of Iceland, where we now are, the radius of the Earth, the distance from the centre to the surface, is about 1,583 leagues. Let's say 1,600 leagues in round figures. So, out of 1,600 leagues, we've done twelve?'

'As you say.'

'And we have gone down these twelve leagues at a cost of 85 leagues diagonally?'

'Exactly so.'

'In about twenty days?'

'Yes.'

'Now, sixteen leagues are a hundredth part of the Earth's radius. At this rate it'll take us two thousand days, or nearly five and a half years, to get to the centre.'

The Professor didn't reply.

'And what's more, if a vertical depth of sixteen leagues can be achieved only by a diagonal descent of eighty-four, it follows that we must go eight thousand miles in a south-easterly direction. So we'll emerge at some point on the Earth's circumference instead of getting to the centre!'

'Confound your figures, and your theories,' shouted my uncle in a sudden rage. 'What are they based on? How do you know that this passage doesn't run straight to our destination? And besides, there's a precedent. What one man has done, another may do.'

'I hope so, but I still have the right to . . .'

'You have the right to hold your tongue, Axel, but not to talk in that stupid way.'

I could see the terrible Professor threatening to burst out of the skin of my uncle, and I took timely warning.

'Now look at the manometer. What does it say?'

'It says we are under considerable pressure.'

'Very good. So you see that by going down gradually and getting accustomed to the density of the atmosphere, we don't suffer at all.'

'Nothing except a little pain in the ears.'

'That's nothing, and you may get rid of even that by rapid breathing whenever you feel the pain.'

'Quite so,' I said, determined not to say anything that might run counter to my uncle's prejudices. 'There's even a positive pleasure in living in this dense atmosphere. Have you observed how intense sound is down here?'

'No doubt it is. A deaf person would eventually hear perfectly.'

'But won't this density increase?'

'Yes, according to a not quite understood law. It's well known that gravity lessens as one goes lower. You know that it's at the surface of the globe that its effect is felt most, and that at the centre of the globe objects have no weight at all.'

'I'm aware of that, but tell me, won't air end up with the density of water?'

'Of course, under a pressure of seven hundred and ten atmospheres.'

'And how about even deeper still?'

'Deeper, the density will increase even more.'

'Then how will we go down?'

'Well, we must fill our pockets with stones.'

'You've got an answer for everything, haven't you, Uncle.'

I didn't dare venture any further into the realms of hypothesis, for I might eventually have stumbled on an impossibility that would have enraged the Professor.

Still, it was clear that the air, under a pressure which might reach thousands of atmospheres, would sooner or later reach the solid state, and then, even if our bodies could bear the strain, we would be brought to a halt and no amount of reasoning would be able to take us any further.

But I didn't put forward this argument. My uncle would have countered it with his inevitable Saknussemm, a precedent which counted for nothing with me, for even if the journey of the learned Icelander really was attested, there was one very simple answer: that in the sixteenth century, there were neither barometers nor manometers, and therefore Saknussemm couldn't have known how far he had gone.

But I kept this objection to myself and waited to see how things would turn out.

The rest of the day was passed in calculations and in conversations. I remained a steadfast supporter of the opinions of Professor Lidenbrock, and I envied the stolid indifference of Hans, who, without going into causes and effects, went blindly on to wherever his destiny led him.

CHAPTER 26

THE WORST PERIL OF ALL

I must confess that up to this point things had not gone badly and I had had little reason to complain. If our difficulties got no worse, we might hope to reach our goal. And to what a height of scientific glory would we then attain! I had become quite a Lidenbrock in my thinking. Seriously, I had. But was this state of affairs due to the strange place I was now living in? Perhaps.

For several days steeper inclines, some terrifyingly close to perpendicular, took us deeper and deeper into the interior of the Earth. Some days we advanced nearer to the centre by a league and a half, or nearly two leagues. These were perilous descents, in which Hans' skill and incredible coolness were invaluable. The calm Icelander gave of himself with an incomprehensible lack of concern, and thanks to him we crossed many a dangerous spot which we would never have cleared alone.

But his habit of silence was increasing day by day, and was infecting us too. External objects produce definite effects on the brain. A man shut up between four walls soon loses the power to associate words and ideas together. How many prisoners in solitary confinement become idiots, if not mad, for lack of exercise for the faculty of thought?

During the fortnight following our last conversation, nothing happened that's worth recording. But I have good reason to remember one very serious incident which took place about this time, and of which I could scarcely even now forget the smallest details.

By the 7th of August our successive descents had brought us to a depth of thirty leagues; that is, for thirty leagues above our heads there were solid beds of rock, ocean, continents and towns. We must have been two hundred leagues from Iceland.

On that day the tunnel led down a gentle slope. I was ahead of the others. My uncle was carrying one of the Ruhmkorff lamps and I the other. I was examining the beds of granite.

Suddenly turning round, I realized I was alone.

Oh well, I thought, I've been going too fast, or Hans and my uncle have stopped along the way. Well, that won't do. I must rejoin them. Fortunately there's not much of an ascent.

I retraced my steps. I walked for a quarter of an hour. I gazed into the darkness. I shouted. No reply: my voice was lost in the midst of the cavernous echoes which alone replied to my call.

I began to feel uneasy. A shudder ran through me.

'Just keep calm!' I said aloud to myself, 'I'm sure to find my companions again. There aren't two paths. I've just got too far ahead. All I have to do is retrace my steps!'

For half an hour I climbed up. I listened for someone calling, and in that dense atmosphere a voice could carry a long way. But there was a dreary silence in the whole of that long gallery. I stopped. I wanted to believe that I was just disorientated, not lost. I was sure I would find my way again.

'Come on, now,' I repeated, 'since there's only one passage, and they're in it, I'm bound to find them again. All I have to do is keep going up. Unless, indeed, missing me, and supposing me to be behind them, they too have retraced their steps. But even in that case, all I have to do is walk faster than them. I'll find them, I'm sure I will.'

I repeated these words in the fainter tones of a man only half-convinced. Besides, to form even such simple ideas into words, and think them through, took time.

A doubt then gripped me. Was I really ahead when we became separated? Yes, I definitely was. Hans was behind me, and in front of my uncle. He had even stopped for a moment to adjust the pack on his shoulders. I could remember that little incident. It was at that very moment that I must have gone on.

Besides, I thought, have I not got a guarantee that I won't lose my way, a thread in the labyrinth[23] that cannot be broken – my faithful stream? I only have to follow it back and I'm bound to meet up with them.

This conclusion revived my spirits, and I resolved to resume my march without wasting any more time.

How I then blessed my uncle's foresight in preventing the hunter from blocking up the hole in the granite. This kindly spring, after having satisfied our thirst along the way, would now be my guide through this labyrinth in the terrestrial crust.

Before starting off again, I thought a wash would do me good. I stooped to bathe my face in Hans's Brook.

To my stupefaction and utter dismay, all I could feel was rough dry granite! The stream was no longer flowing at my feet.

CHAPTER 27

LOST IN THE BOWELS OF THE EARTH

To express my despair would be impossible. No words could describe it. I was buried alive, with the prospect before me of dying of hunger and thirst.

Automatically, I swept the ground with my hands. How dry and hard the rock seemed!

But how could I have left the course of the stream? For the terrible fact was that it was no longer running beside me. Then I understood the reason for the terrible silence when I had last listened for any sound from my companions. At the moment when I left the correct path I hadn't noticed the absence of the stream. It was clear that when I had reached a fork in the path, Hans's Brook, following the whims of another incline, had gone off with my companions into unknown depths.

How was I to get back? There was no trace of their footsteps nor of my own, for feet left no marks on the granite floor. I racked my brain for a solution to this problem. One word described my position. Lost!

Lost at an immeasurable depth! Thirty leagues of rock seemed to be weighing down on my shoulders with a dreadful pressure. I felt crushed beneath it.

I tried to make myself think about things on the surface of the Earth. I could hardly manage to. Hamburg, the house in the Königstrasse, my poor Gräuben, all that busy world underneath which I was wandering about, was passing in rapid confusion through my terrified memory. I could see again with vivid reality all the incidents of our journey, Iceland, Mr Fridriksson, Snæfell. I told myself that, in such a position as I was now in, to cling to even a single glimmer of hope would be madness, and that the best thing I could do was give myself up to despair.

What human power could restore me to the light of the sun by tearing apart the huge arches of rock which joined together over my head, buttressing each other with impregnable strength? Who could place my feet on the right path, and bring me back to my company?

'Oh, Uncle!' burst from my lips in the tone of despair.

It was the only word of reproach I uttered, for I knew how much he would be suffering looking for me, wherever he might be.

When I saw myself in this way far removed from all human help, and unable to do anything to save myself, I turned to heaven for aid. Memories of my childhood, and of my mother, whom I had only known in my tender early years, came back to me, and I knelt in prayer imploring the Divine assistance I was so little worthy of.

This return to trust in God's providence made me calmer, and I was able to concentrate the full force of my intelligence on my situation.

I had three days' provisions with me and my flask was full. But I couldn't remain alone for long. Should I go up or down?

Up, of course. Always up.

That way I would be bound to arrive at the point where I had left the stream, that fatal turning in the path. With the stream at my feet, I might hope to regain the summit of Snæfell.

Why hadn't I thought of that sooner? Here clearly was a chance of reaching safety. The most pressing need was to find the course of Hans's Brook again. I got up and, leaning on my iron-pointed stick, I ascended the gallery. The slope was rather steep. I walked on with hope and without hesitation, like a man who has only one path to follow.

For half an hour I met with no obstacle. I tried to recognize my way by the form of the tunnel, by the way certain rocks projected, by the layout of the fractures. But no particular sign struck me, and I soon found that this gallery could not take me back to the turning point. It came to an abrupt end. I met an impenetrable wall, and collapsed on the rock.

Unspeakable despair then gripped me. I lay there, overwhelmed, aghast! My last hope had been shattered against this granite wall.

Lost in this labyrinth, whose winding paths criss-crossed each other in all directions, there was no longer any point in thinking of escape. Here I must die the most dreadful of deaths. And, strange to say, the thought crossed my mind that when some day my petrified remains were found thirty leagues below the surface in the bowels of the Earth, the discovery might lead to some serious scientific discussions.

I tried to speak out loud, but only hoarse sounds passed my dry lips. I was panting for breath.

In the midst of my agony, a new terror laid hold of me. When I had fallen, my lamp had been damaged. I couldn't fix it, and its light was getting dimmer and would soon disappear altogether.

I watched the luminous current growing weaker and weaker in the wire coil. A dim procession of moving shadows seemed to be slowly unfolding down the darkening walls. I hardly dared shut my eyes for one moment, for fear of losing the slightest glimmer of this precious light. At each moment it seemed about to vanish and I could feel the dense blackness come rolling in upon me.

One last trembling glimmer shot feebly up. I watched it in trembling anxiety; I drank it in as if I could preserve it, concentrating the full power of my eyes on it, as if on the very last sensation of light they were ever to experience, and the next moment I lay in the heavy gloom of deep, thick, unfathomable darkness.

A terrible cry of anguish burst from me. On Earth, even in the middle of the darkest night, light never altogether fails in its duties. It's still there, subtle and diffuse, but no matter how little there may be, the eye still catches that little. Here there was not a glimmer; the total darkness made me totally blind.

Then I lost my head. I got up with my arms stretched out in front of me, attempting painfully to feel my way. I began to run wildly, hurrying through the inextricable maze, still going down, still running through the substance of the Earth's thick crust, a struggling denizen of geological 'faults', crying, shouting, yelling, soon bruised by banging against the jagged rock, falling and getting up again bleeding, trying to drink the blood which covered my face, and expecting at any moment to shatter my skull against some wall of rock.

I will never know where my mad dash took me. After some hours had passed, no doubt exhausted, I collapsed like a lifeless lump along the wall and lost consciousness.

CHAPTER 28

THE RESCUE IN THE WHISPERING GALLERY

When I came to again, my face was wet with tears. How long that state of insensibility had lasted I cannot say. I had no means now of keeping track of time. Never was there solitude the like of this, never had any living being felt so utterly abandoned.

After my fall I had lost a good deal of blood. I felt covered in it. Ah! how happy I would have been to have died already, for death not still to be gone through. I no longer wanted to think. I chased away every idea, and, overcome by my grief, I rolled to the foot of the opposite wall.

I was already feeling another fainting fit coming on, and was hoping for complete annihilation, when a loud noise reached me. It was like the distant rumble of continuous thunder, and I could hear its deep sound rolling far away into the remote recesses of the abyss.

Where could this noise be coming from? It must be from some phenomenon happening in the great depths in the midst of which I lay helpless. Was it an explosion of gas? Was it the fall of some mighty pillar of the globe?

I continued to listen. I wanted to know if the noise would be repeated. A quarter of an hour passed. Silence reigned in this gallery. I couldn't even hear the beating of my heart.

Suddenly my ear, resting by chance against the wall, caught, or seemed to catch, certain vague, indescribable, distant, articulate sounds, like words. I shuddered.

'My mind is playing tricks on me,' I thought.

But it wasn't. Listening more carefully, I really did hear a murmuring of voices. My weakness prevented me from understanding what the voices were saying. But it was language, I was sure of it.

For a moment I was afraid the words might be my own, carried back to me by an echo. Perhaps I had been crying out without being aware of it. I closed my lips firmly, and laid my ear against the wall again.

'Yes, really, someone *is* speaking. Those *are* words!'

Even a few feet from the wall, I could hear it distinctly. I managed to catch uncertain, strange, undistinguishable words. They came as if pronounced in low, murmured whispers. The word '*forlorād*' was repeated several times in a sympathetic and sorrowful tone.

'Help!' I cried with all my might. 'Help!'

I listened, I waited in the darkness for an answer, a cry, a mere breath of sound, but nothing came. Some minutes passed. A flood of ideas exploded into my mind. I feared my weakened voice would never reach my companions.

'It's them,' I repeated. 'What other men could be thirty leagues underground?'

I began to listen again. Passing my ear over the wall from one place to another, I found the point where the voices seemed to be heard best. The word *'forlorád'* again came to me; then the rolling of thunder which had roused me from my lethargy.

'No,' I said, 'no, it's not through such a solid mass that a voice can be heard. I'm surrounded by granite walls, and the loudest explosion could never be heard here! This noise is coming along the gallery. It must be due to some remarkable action of acoustic laws!'

I listened again, and this time, yes, this time I did distinctly hear my name pronounced across the wide interval.

It was my uncle's own voice! He was talking to the guide. And *'forlorád'* is a Danish word.

Then it all became clear. To make myself heard, I had to speak along this wall, which would conduct the sound of my voice just as wire conducts electricity.

But there was no time to lose. If my companions moved but a few steps away, the acoustic phenomenon would cease. I therefore went close to the wall, and pronounced these words as clearly as possible:

'Uncle Lidenbrock!'

I waited with the greatest anxiety. Sound doesn't travel very quickly. Even increased density of air has no effect on its rate of travel; it merely increases its intensity. Seconds, which seemed ages, passed away, and at last these words reached me:

'Axel! Axel! Is that you?'
. . .
'Yes, yes,' I replied.
. . .
'My boy, where are you?'
. . .
'Lost, in the deepest darkness.'
. . .
'Where is your lamp?'
. . .
'It's gone out.'
. . .
'And the stream?'
. . .

'Disappeared.'
...

'Be brave, Axel, don't lose heart!'
...

'Wait a second! I'm exhausted! I can't answer. But keep talking to me!'
...

'Be brave,' said my uncle again. 'Don't talk. Listen to me. We've looked for you up and down the gallery. Couldn't find you. I wept for you, my poor boy. At last, supposing you were still on Hans's Brook, we fired our guns. Now at least we can hear each other even if our hands cannot touch. But don't despair, Axel! To be able to hear each other is something.'
...

During this time I had been thinking. A vague hope was returning to my heart. There was one thing I needed to know to begin with. I placed my lips close to the wall, saying:

'Uncle!'
...

'My boy!' came to me after a few seconds.
...

'We need to know how far apart we are.'
...

'That's easy.'
...

'Have you got your chronometer?'
...

'Yes.'
...

'Well, get ready to use it. Say my name, noting exactly the second when you speak. I'll repeat it as soon as it reaches me, and you will note the exact moment when you get my reply.'

'Yes. And half the time between my call and your answer will indicate exactly the time my voice will have taken to reach you.'
...

'Exactly, Uncle.'
...

'Are you ready?'
...

'Yes.'
...

'Now, pay attention. I'm going to call your name.'
...

I put my ear to the wall, and as soon as the name 'Axel' came, I immediately replied 'Axel,' then waited.

...

'Forty seconds,' said my uncle. 'Forty seconds between the two words, so the sound takes twenty seconds to travel between us. Now, at the rate of 1,020 feet per second, that's 20,400 feet, or just under four miles, more or less.'

...

'Four miles!' I murmured.

...

'It'll soon be over, Axel.'

...

'Do I need to go up or down?'

...

'Down, and I'll tell you why. We've reached a vast chamber with a large number of galleries. Yours must lead into it, because it looks like all the clefts and fractures of the globe radiate out from this huge cavern. So get up and start walking. Keep walking, drag yourself along if necessary, slide down the steep parts, and at the end gallery you'll find us waiting for you. Now, my boy, get going.'

...

These words cheered me up.

'Goodbye, Uncle.' I cried. 'I'm setting off now. There'll be no more voices heard once I've started. So goodbye!'

...

'Goodbye, Axel. See you soon!'

...

These were the last words I heard.

This wonderful underground conversation, carried on over the distance of four miles that separated us, ended with these words of hope. I thanked God from my heart, for it was He who had led me through those vast lonely places to the point where, perhaps there alone and nowhere else, the voices of my companions could reach me.

This acoustic effect is easily explained scientifically. It arose from the concave shape of the gallery and the conducting power of the rock. There are many examples of this transmission of sounds which remain unheard in the intervening space. I remember that a similar phenomenon has been observed in many places, amongst others on the internal surface of the 'Whispering Gallery' of the dome of St. Paul's in London and especially in the middle of the strange caverns in the quarries near Syracuse, the most wonderful of which is called Dionysius' Ear.

As I remembered these things, I could see clearly that, since my uncle's voice had reached me, there could be no barrier between us. Following the direction from which the sound came, I would without a doubt arrive where he was, if my strength didn't fail me.

So I got up. I dragged myself more than walked. The slope descended rapidly, and I slid down.

Soon the speed of the descent increased frighteningly and threatened to become a fall. I no longer had the strength to stop myself.

Suddenly there was no ground under me. I felt myself spinning in the air, striking and rebounding from the rocky projections of a vertical gallery, virtually a well. My head hit a sharp rock, and I lost consciousness.

CHAPTER 29

THE SEA! THE SEA!

When I came to, I was lying stretched out in semi-darkness, covered with thick coats and blankets. My uncle was watching over me, looking for the slightest signs of life. At my first sigh, he took hold of my hand; when I opened my eyes, he uttered a cry of joy.

'He's alive! He's alive!' he shouted.

'Yes, I'm still alive,' I answered weakly.

'My dear nephew,' said my uncle, hugging me to his breast, 'you're safe.'

I was deeply touched by the tenderness of his manner as he uttered these words, and still more with the care with which he watched over me. But it took trials such as this for the Professor to show his more tender emotions.

At that moment, Hans appeared. He saw my hand in my uncle's, and I may safely say that there was an expression of pleasure on his face.

'*God dag,*' he said.

'Good day, Hans, good day. And now, uncle, tell me where we are at this particular moment.'

'Tomorrow, Axel, tomorrow. You're too weak today. I've bandaged your head with compresses which mustn't be disturbed. Sleep now, and tomorrow I will tell you everything.'

'But do tell me what time it is, and what day.'

'It's Sunday the 9th of August, and it's ten o'clock at night. You must ask me no more questions until the 10th.'

Truth to tell, I was very weak, and my eyes closed of their own accord. I was needing a good night's rest. So off I went to sleep, with the knowledge that I had been four long days alone in the heart of the Earth.

Next morning when I awoke, I looked all around me. My bed, made up of all our travelling rugs, was in a charming grotto that was decorated with magnificent stalactites and whose floor consisted of fine sand. It was half-light. There was no torch and no lamp, but a certain mysterious light was coming from outside the grotto through a narrow opening. And I could also hear a vague, indistinct noise, something like the murmuring of waves breaking on a shingly shore, and at times I thought I could hear wind whistling.

I wondered whether I was awake or dreaming, whether perhaps my brain, deranged by my fall, was being affected by imaginary noises. Yet neither my eyes nor my ears could be deceived to that extent.

It's a ray of daylight, I thought, slipping in through this cleft in the rock! And that is indeed the murmuring of waves! That's the rustling noise of wind. Am I quite mistaken, or have we returned to the surface of the Earth? Has my uncle given up the expedition, or has it come to a successful conclusion?

I was asking myself these unanswerable questions when the Professor came in.

'Good morning, Axel,' he exclaimed cheerfully. 'I expect you're feeling better.'

'Yes, I certainly am,' said I, sitting up on my bed.

'You could hardly fail to be better, since you've had a peaceful sleep. Hans and I watched over you in turn, and we could see you were evidently recovering.'

'Yes, I do feel a great deal better, and I'll prove that to you in a moment if you'll let me have my breakfast.'

'You shall have something to eat, my boy. The fever has left you. Hans rubbed your wounds with some ointment or other that the Icelanders keep the secret of, and they've healed marvellously. He's a splendid fellow, that hunter of ours!'

Whilst he went on talking, my uncle prepared some food, which I devoured eagerly, notwithstanding his advice to the contrary. All the while I was badgering him with questions which he was more than willing to answer.

I then learnt that my providential fall had brought me right to the foot of an almost perpendicular shaft; and as I had landed in the midst of an accompanying torrent of stones, the smallest of which would have been enough to crush me, the conclusion was that part of the rock-face had come down with me. This terrifying conveyance had thus carried me into the arms of my uncle, where I fell bruised, bleeding and unconscious.

'It's quite incredible that you weren't killed a hundred times over. But, for the love of God, let's stay together from now on, or we might never see each other again.'

'Stay together? Is the journey not over then?' I opened a pair of astonished eyes, which immediately prompted the question:

'What's the matter, Axel?'

'I have a question to ask you. You say that I'm safe and sound?'

'No doubt you are.'

'And all my limbs unbroken?'

'Certainly.'

'And my head?'

'Your head, except for a few bruises, is all right, and it's on your shoulders, where it ought to be.'

'Well, I am afraid my brain is affected.'

'Your mind is affected?'

'Yes, I fear so. Are we back on the surface of the globe?'

'No, certainly not.'

'Then I must be mad, because I imagine I can see the light of day, and hear the wind blowing and the sea breaking on the shore.'

'Oh! Is that all?'

'Can you explain it to me.'

'I can't explain the inexplicable, but you will soon see and understand that geology has not yet learnt all that it has to learn.'

'Then let's go,' I answered quickly.

'No, Axel, the open air might be bad for you.'

'Open air?'

'Yes, the wind is rather strong. You mustn't expose yourself.'

'But I assure you I'm perfectly well.'

'A little patience, my boy. A relapse might get us into difficulty, and we've no time to lose, as the voyage may be a long one.'

'The voyage!'

'Yes, rest today, and tomorrow we will set sail.'

'Set sail?' The words made me jump up.

What did it all mean? Was there a river, a lake or a sea for us to cross? Did we have a ship at our disposal in some underground harbour?

My curiosity was greatly aroused, and my uncle tried in vain to restrain me. When he saw that my impatience would do me more harm than giving in to it would, he relented.

I quickly got dressed. As a precaution, I wrapped myself in a blanket and left the grotto.

CHAPTER 30

A NEW *MARE INTERNUM*[24]

At first I could hardly see anything. My eyes, unaccustomed to the light, quickly closed. When I was able to reopen them, I stood more stupefied than surprised.

'The sea!' I cried.

'Yes,' my uncle replied, 'the Lidenbrock Sea, and I don't imagine any other explorer will ever dispute my claim to name it after myself as its first discoverer.'

A vast sheet of water, the start of a lake or an ocean, spread far away beyond what the eye could see. The deeply indented shoreline was lined with a stretch of fine shining sand, softly lapped by the waves, and strewn with small shells which had been inhabited by the earliest creatures of creation. The waves broke on this shore with the hollow echoing murmur peculiar to vast enclosed spaces. A light foam blew over the waves on the breath of a moderate breeze, and some of the spray fell on my face. On the other edge of this slightly sloping shore, about a hundred fathoms from the waves, was a huge wall of vast cliffs rising majestically to a great height. Some of these, dividing the beach with their sharp spurs, formed capes and promontories, worn away by the ceaseless action of the surf. Farther on, the eye could discern their massive outline sharply defined against the distant, hazy horizon.

It was certainly a real ocean, with the irregularity of the shorelines on Earth, but deserted and horribly wild in appearance.

If my eyes were able to range far over this great sea, it was because a peculiar light made every detail of it clearly visible. It wasn't the light of the sun, with its dazzling shafts of brightness and the splendour of its rays, nor was it the pale and uncertain shimmer of moonbeams, the dim reflection of a nobler body of light. No, the illuminating power of this light, its trembling diffuseness, its bright, clear whiteness and its low temperature, showed that it must be of electrical origin. It was like an aurora borealis, a continuous cosmic phenomenon filling a cavern large enough to contain an ocean.

The vault that spanned the space above, the sky (if such it could be called), seemed to be made up of vast plains of cloud, shifting and variable vapours which at certain times condensed and fell in torrents of rain. I would have thought that under so great an atmospheric pressure there could be no evaporation, and yet, by a law of physics unknown to me, there were broad tracts of vapour suspended in the air. But then, one could say it was a 'fine day'. The play of the electric light produced peculiar effects on the upper strata of cloud. Deep shadows formed on their lower curves, and often, between two separated strata of cloud, there glided down a ray of indescribable brightness. But it wasn't solar light, and there was no heat. The general effect was sad, supremely melancholy. Instead of the shining firmament, spangled with innumerable stars shining singly or in clusters, I could feel above the clouds vast granite arches which seemed to crush me with their weight; and all this space, great as it was, would not have been enough for the orbit of the humblest of satellites.

Then I remembered the theory of an English captain, who likened the Earth to a vast hollow sphere, in the interior of which the air became luminous because of the vast pressure on it, while within it two heavenly bodies, Pluto[25] and Proserpina, followed their mysterious orbits. Had he been right?

We were in reality enclosed inside a vast cavern. Its width could not be estimated, since the shore continued to widen out as far as the eye could see, nor could its length, for the dim horizon limited one's view. As for its height, it must have been several leagues high. Where this vault rested on its granite base no eye could tell, but there was a cloud hanging far above, the height of which we estimated at 12,000 feet, a greater height than that of any terrestrial vapour, and no doubt due to the great density of the air.

The word cavern does not convey any idea of this immense space. Words of human language are inadequate to describe the discoveries of one who ventures into the deep abysses of the Earth.

I couldn't decide what geological theory would account for the existence of such a cavern. Had the cooling of the globe produced it? I knew of famous caverns from the descriptions of travellers, but had never heard of any of such dimensions as this. Even if the grotto of Guachara, in Colombia, visited by Humboldt, did not fully divulge the secret of its depth to him, he did investigate it to a depth of 2,500 feet and it probably didn't extend much farther than that. The immense Mammoth Cave in Kentucky is of gigantic proportions, since its vaulted roof rises five hundred feet above an unfathomable lake and travellers have explored its ramifications for ten leagues. But what were these holes compared to that one I was admiring, with its sky of luminous vapours, its bursts of electric light and a vast sea filling its bed? My imagination was powerless before such immensity.

I gazed at these wonders in silence. I couldn't find the words to express my feelings. I felt as if I was on some distant planet such as Uranus or Neptune, and in the presence of phenomena of which my terrestrial experience gave me no knowledge. For such novel sensations, new words were wanted, and my imagination failed to supply them. I gazed, I thought, I admired, with a stupefaction tinged with fear.

The unforeseen nature of this spectacle brought back the colour to my cheeks. I was receiving a new course of treatment with the help of

JOURNEY TO THE CENTRE OF THE EARTH

astonishment, and my convalescence was promoted by this novel system of therapeutics. And besides, the dense and breezy air invigorated me, supplying more oxygen to my lungs.

It will be easily conceived that after forty-seven days' imprisonment in a narrow gallery, it was the height of physical enjoyment to breathe moist air impregnated with salty particles.

I was delighted to leave my dark grotto. My uncle, already familiar with these wonders, had ceased to feel surprise.

'Do you feel strong enough to take a little walk now?' he asked.

'Yes, certainly, and nothing could be more delightful.'

'Well, take my arm, Axel, and let's follow the windings of the shore.'

I eagerly accepted, and we began to follow the coast along this new sea. On the left huge pyramids of rock, piled one upon another, created a prodigious titanic effect. Down their sides flowed countless waterfalls which wended their way in clear, gurgling streams. A few light vapours, leaping from rock to rock, indicated where there were hot springs, and streams flowed gently down to the common basin, gliding down the gentle slopes with a softer murmur.

Amongst these streams I recognized our faithful travelling companion, Hans's Brook, coming to quietly add its little volume to the mighty sea, just as if it had done nothing else since the beginning of the world.

'We won't see it again,' I said, with a sigh.

'That one or another one,' replied the professor, 'what does it matter?'

I thought him rather ungrateful.

But at that moment my attention was drawn to an unexpected sight. Five hundred yards away, along a high promontory, appeared a tall, tufted, dense forest. It was composed of trees of moderate height, umbrella-like in form, with sharp geometrical outlines. The currents of wind seemed to have had no effect on their shape, and in the midst of the windy blasts they stood unmoved and firm, just like a clump of petrified cedars.

I hurried towards them. I couldn't give any name to these singular creations. Were they among the two hundred thousand known plant species, or did they claim a place of their own in lakeland flora? No. When we arrived under their shade, my surprise turned to wonder. There before me stood products of Earth, but of gigantic proportions. My uncle immediately said what they were.

'It's just a forest of mushrooms,' he said.

And he was right. Imagine the large development attained by these plants, which prefer a warm, moist climate. I knew that the *Lycoperdon giganteum* attains, according to Bulliard, a circumference of eight or nine feet, but here there were pale mushrooms thirty to forty feet high and crowned with a cap of equal diameter. They stood there in their thousands.

No light could penetrate between their huge cones, and complete darkness reigned beneath those giants. They formed settlements of domes in close array like the round, thatched roofs of a central African city.

I wanted to walk beneath them, though a chill fell on me as soon as I came under those cellular vaults. For half an hour we wandered from side to side in the damp shade, and it was a comfortable and pleasant change to arrive once more on the seashore.

But the subterranean vegetation was not confined to these fungi. Farther on there rose groups of tall trees of colourless foliage, easy to recognize. On Earth they were lowly shrubs, but here they attained gigantic size: Lycopodia a hundred feet high; huge Sigillaria, found in our coal mines; tree ferns as tall as our fir-trees of northern latitudes; Lepidodendrons with cylindrical forked stems ending in long leaves and bristling with rough hairs.

'Wonderful, magnificent, splendid!' cried my uncle. 'Here is the entire flora of the second period of the world – the Transition Period. These, humble garden plants as they are with us now, were tall trees in the early ages. Look, Axel, and wonder at it all. Never had a botanist such a feast as this!'

'You're right, Uncle. Providence seems to have preserved in this immense conservatory the antediluvian plants which the wisdom of scientists has so sagaciously put together again.'

'It is a conservatory, Axel, but is it not also a menagerie?'

'Surely not a menagerie!'

'Yes, there's no doubt about it. Look at that dust under your feet. See the bones scattered on the ground.'

'So there are!' I exclaimed, 'the bones of extinct animals.'

I rushed to look at these remains, formed of an indestructible mineral substance, calcium phosphate, and without hesitation I identified these monstrous bones which lay scattered about like decayed tree-trunks.

'Here's the lower jaw of a mastodon,' I said. 'These are the molar teeth of the Dinotherium. This femur must have belonged to the largest of those animals, the Megatherium. It certainly is a menagerie, because these remains were not brought here by a flood. The animals they belonged to roamed on the shores of this subterranean sea, under the shade of those arborescent plants. There are entire skeletons here. And yet I can't understand how these quadrupeds appear in a granite cavern.'

'Why?'

'Because animal life existed on Earth only in the Secondary Period, when a sediment of soil had been deposited by the rivers, and taken the place of the incandescent rocks of the Primitive Period.'

'Well, Axel, there's a very simple answer to your objection, which is that this soil is alluvial.'

'What! At such a depth below the surface of the Earth?'

'Without a doubt, and there's a geological explanation for that. At a certain period the Earth consisted only of an elastic crust or bark, alternately acted on by forces from above or below, according to the laws of attraction and gravitation. Probably there were subsidences of the outer crust, when some of the sedimentary deposit was carried down through sudden openings.'

'That may be so,' I replied, 'but if there have been creatures now extinct in these underground regions, is there any reason why some of those monsters might not still be roaming through these gloomy forests or hidden behind the steep crags?'

And as this unpleasant notion gripped me, I anxiously surveyed the open spaces before me, but no living creature appeared on the barren shore.

I felt rather tired, and went to sit down at the point of a promontory, at the foot of which the waves were beating themselves into spray. From there my eye could scan every part of this bay created by an indentation in the coastline. The end of the bay formed a little harbour between the pyramidal cliffs, where the still waters slept, sheltered from the boisterous winds. A brig and two or three schooners might safely have moored within it. I almost fancied I would presently see some ship sail out under full sail, and take to the open sea in the southern breeze.

But this illusion lasted a very short time. We were the only living creatures in this subterranean world. When the wind dropped, a deeper silence than that of the deserts fell on the arid, naked rocks and weighed heavily on the surface of the ocean. I tried to see through the distant haze, and to tear apart the mysterious curtain that hung across the horizon. Anxious questions came to my lips. Where did that sea end? Where did it lead to? Would we ever know anything about its far shores?

My uncle had absolutely no doubt about it. For my part, I both wanted and feared to know.

After spending an hour contemplating this marvellous spectacle, we returned to the shore to go back to the grotto, and I fell asleep in the midst of the strangest thoughts.

CHAPTER 31

PREPARATIONS FOR A VOYAGE OF DISCOVERY

The next morning I awoke feeling perfectly well. I thought a bathe would do me good, and I went and plunged for a few minutes into the waters of this 'Mediterranean Sea', for assuredly it better deserved this name than any other sea[26].

I came back to breakfast with a good appetite. Hans was a good caterer for our little household; he had water and fire at his disposal, so he was able to vary our bill of fare now and then. For dessert he gave us a few cups of coffee, and never was coffee so delicious.

'Now, then,' said my uncle, 'high tide is due now and we mustn't miss the opportunity to study the phenomenon.'

'What? A tide?' I exclaimed. 'Can the influence of the sun and moon be felt down here?'

'Why not? Aren't all bodies subject throughout their mass to the power of universal attraction? This mass of water cannot escape the general law. And in spite of the heavy atmospheric pressure on the surface, you will see it rise like the Atlantic itself.'

At the same moment, we reached the sand on the shore, and the waves were gradually encroaching on the shore.

'The tide *is* rising,' I exclaimed.

'Yes, Axel. And judging by these ridges of foam, you may observe that the sea will rise about twelve feet.'

'That's amazing,' I said.

'No, it's entirely natural.'

'You may say so, Uncle, but to me it's quite extraordinary, and I can hardly believe my eyes. Who would ever have imagined, under this terrestrial crust, an ocean with ebbing and flowing tides, with winds and storms?'

'Well,' replied my uncle, 'is there any scientific reason against it?'

'No, I can't think of any, as soon as the theory of central heat is abandoned.'

'Then so far,' he answered, 'Sir Humphry Davy's theory is confirmed.'

'Clearly it is. And now there's no reason why there should not be seas and continents in the interior of the Earth.'

'No doubt,' said my uncle, 'but uninhabited ones.'

'All right,' I said, 'but why shouldn't these waters hold fish of unknown species?'

'Well,' he replied, 'we haven't seen any yet.'

'Well, let's make some fishing-lines, and see if the bait will draw them to it as it does in regions under the moon.'

'We'll certainly try, Axel, for we must investigate all the secrets of these newly discovered regions.'

'But where are we, Uncle? I haven't asked you that question yet, and your instruments must be able to provide the answer.'

'Horizontally, three hundred and fifty leagues from Iceland.'

'As much as that?'

'I'm confident of not being a mile out in my reckoning.'

'And does the compass still show south-east?'

'Yes, with a westerly deviation of nineteen degrees forty-five minutes, just as above ground. As for its dip, a curious fact is coming to light, which I have observed carefully: that the needle, instead of dipping towards the pole as in the northern hemisphere, on the contrary rises from it.'

'Would you then conclude,' I said, 'that the magnetic pole is somewhere between the surface of the globe and the point where we are?'

'Exactly, and it is likely enough that if we were to reach the spot beneath the polar regions, about that seventy-first degree where Sir James Ross has discovered the magnetic pole to be situated, we should see the needle point straight up. Therefore that mysterious centre of attraction is at no great depth.'

'It must be so, and there's a fact which science has scarcely suspected.'

'Science, my lad, has been constructed on many errors, but they are errors which it was good to fall into, because they led to the truth.'

'What depth have we reached now?'

'We are thirty-five leagues below the surface.'

'So,' I said, examining the map, 'the Highlands of Scotland are over our heads, and the Grampians are raising their rugged summits above us.'

'Yes,' answered the Professor, laughing. 'It's rather a heavy weight to bear, but a solid arch spans over our heads. The Great Architect has built it with the best materials, and never could man have made it arch so wide. What are the finest arches of bridges and the arcades of cathedrals compared with this far-reaching vault with a radius of three leagues, beneath which a wide and tempest-tossed ocean may flow at its ease?'

'Oh, I'm not afraid it'll fall on my head or anything like that. But now what are your plans? Are you not thinking of returning to the surface now?'

'Return? Certainly not! We'll continue our journey, since everything has gone well so far.'

'But how are we to get down below this liquid surface?'

'Oh, I'm not going to dive in head first. But if all oceans are properly speaking just lakes, being surrounded by land, this internal sea will of course be surrounded by a coast of granite, and on the opposite shores we shall find fresh passages opening.'

'How long do you suppose this sea to be?'

'Thirty or forty leagues. So we've no time to lose, and we'll set sail tomorrow.'

I looked about for a ship.

'Set sail, will we? I'd like to see my boat first.'

'It won't be a boat at all, but a good, well-made raft.'

'Why,' I said, 'a raft would be just as hard to make as a boat, and I don't see . . .'

'I know you don't see, but you might hear if you would listen. Don't you hear a hammer at work? Hans is already busy at it.'

'What, has he already felled the trees?'

'Oh, the trees were down already. Come with me and you'll see for yourself.'

After half an hour's walk, on the other side of the promontory which formed the little natural harbour, I saw Hans at work. With a few more steps, I was at his side. To my great surprise, a half-finished raft was already lying on the sand, made of a peculiar kind of wood, and a great number of planks, both straight and bent, and of frames, were covering the ground, enough almost for a little fleet.

'What sort of wood is this, Uncle?' I asked.

'It's fir, pine and birch, and other northern conifers, mineralized by the action of the sea. It's called *'surtarbrandur'*, a variety of brown coal or lignite, found mainly in Iceland.'

'But surely, then, like other fossil wood, it must be as hard as stone and won't float?'

'Sometimes that may happen. Some of these woods become true anthracites. But others, such as this, have only gone through the first stage of fossilization. Just watch,' added my uncle, throwing one of the precious planks into the sea.

The bit of wood, after disappearing, returned to the surface and swung to and fro with the movement of the waves.

'Are you convinced?' said my uncle.

'I'm absolutely convinced, although it's incredible!'

By the following evening, thanks to the hard work and skill of our guide, the raft was completed. It was ten feet by five. The planks of *surtarbrandur*, firmly tied together with ropes, formed a flat surface, and when launched this improvised vessel floated easily on the waves of the Lidenbrock Sea.

CHAPTER 32

WONDERS OF THE DEEP

On the 13th of August, we awoke early. We were now going to adopt this speedier and less tiring mode of travelling.

A mast was made of two poles spliced together, a cross-piece was made of a third pole, a blanket borrowed from our coverings made a tolerable sail. There was no lack of rope for the rigging, and everything was well made and firmly fixed together.

The provisions, the baggage, the instruments, the guns and a good quantity of fresh water from the rocks around us, all found their proper places on board, and at six o'clock the Professor gave the signal to embark. Hans had fixed up a rudder to steer his vessel. He took the tiller, I cast off. The sail was set, and we pushed off. At the moment of leaving the harbour, my uncle, who was obsessively fond of naming his new discoveries, wanted to give it a name, and proposed mine amongst others.

'But I have a better name to suggest,' I said. 'Gräuben. Let it be called Port Gräuben. That'll look good on the map.'

'Port Gräuben it is then.'

And so the cherished memory of my Virland girl became associated with our adventurous expedition.

The wind was blowing from the north-west. We sailed with it at top speed. The dense atmosphere acted with great force and drove us along quickly like a huge fan.

An hour later, my uncle had been able to estimate our speed fairly accurately. At this rate, he said, we'll cover thirty leagues in twenty-four hours, and we'll soon come in sight of the opposite shore.

I said nothing, but went and sat forward. The northern shore was already beginning to dip under the horizon. The eastern and western shores spread out wide as if to bid us farewell. Before our eyes lay far and wide a vast sea. Shadows of great clouds swept heavily over its silver-grey surface, the glistening bluish rays of electric light, here and there reflected by the dancing drops of spray, shot out little sheaves of light from the track we left behind us. Soon we entirely lost sight of land. There was no object left for the eye to judge by, and but for the frothy track of the raft I might have thought we were standing still.

About twelve, immense tracts of seaweed came in sight. I was aware of the great vegetative power that characterizes these plants, which grow at a depth of twelve thousand feet, reproduce under a pressure of four hundred atmospheres and sometimes form barriers strong enough to impede the course of a ship. But never, I think, were there such seaweeds as those we saw floating in immense waving lines on the Lidenbrock Sea.

Our raft skirted the whole length of these seaweeds, three or four thousand feet long, undulating like vast serpents farther than the eye could see. I amused myself tracing these endless waves, always thinking I would come to the end of them, but for hour after hour my patient expectation proved wrong and my surprise increased.

What natural force could have produced such plants, and what must have been the appearance of the Earth in the first ages of its formation, when, under the action of heat and moisture, the vegetable kingdom alone was developing on its surface?

Evening came, and, as on the previous day, I perceived no change in the luminous condition of the air. It was a constant phenomenon, the permanence of which we could rely on.

After supper I lay down at the foot of the mast and fell asleep in the midst of weird reveries.

Hans, motionless at the helm, let the raft run on, which, after all, needed no steering, the wind blowing directly from behind us.

Since our departure from Port Gräuben, Professor Lidenbrock had entrusted the log to my care. I was to record every observation, make entries of interesting phenomena, the direction of the wind, the rate of sailing, the progress we made – in short, every particular of our strange voyage.

I shall therefore reproduce here these daily notes, written, so to speak, as the course of events directed, in order to furnish an exact narrative of our passage.

Friday, August 14. – Wind steady, N.W. The raft making rapid progress in a direct line. Coast thirty leagues to leeward. Nothing in sight before us. Intensity of light the same. Weather fine; that is to say, the clouds are high, light and bathed in a white atmosphere resembling molten silver. Thermometer: 32°.

At noon Hans prepared a hook at the end of a line. He baited it with a small piece of meat and flung it into the sea. For two hours he caught nothing. Are these waters, then, empty of inhabitants? No, there's a pull at the line. Hans draws it in and brings out a struggling fish.

'A fish,' exclaims my uncle.

'A sturgeon,' I exclaim in turn, 'a small sturgeon.'

The Professor studies the creature attentively, and his opinion differs from mine.

The head of this fish is flat, but rounded in front, and the anterior part of its body is plated with bony, angular scales. It has no teeth, its pectoral fins are large, and it is tailless. The animal belongs to the same order as the sturgeon, but differs from that fish in many essential particulars. After a short examination my uncle states his opinion.

'This fish belongs to an extinct family, of which only fossil traces are found in the Devonian formations.'

'What?' I cried. 'Have we taken alive an inhabitant of the seas of primitive ages?'

'Yes,' says the professor, continuing his observations, 'and you will observe that these fossil fishes have no identity with any living species. To have in one's possession a living specimen is a happy event for a naturalist.'

'But to what family does it belong?'

'It is of the order of Ganoids, of the family of the Cephalaspidae, genus . . .'

'Well?'

'It's a species of Pterichthys, I'm sure. But this one shows a peculiarity confined to fishes that inhabit subterranean waters. It's blind.'

'Blind?

'Not only blind, but actually has no eyes at all.'

I took a look at it. Yes, my uncle was absolutely right. But thinking that it might be a solitary case, we baited our line again and tossed it out. This ocean is clearly well stocked with fish, for in another couple of hours we catch a large quantity of Pterichthydes as well as other fish belonging to the extinct family of Dipterides, but of which species my uncle could not say. None had organs of sight. This unexpected catch makes a useful addition to our stock of provisions.

It thus becomes clear that this sea contains nothing but species known to us in their fossil state. In the fossil records, fish as well as reptiles are the more perfectly formed the farther back their time of creation.

Perhaps we may yet meet with some of those saurians which science has reconstructed out of a bit of bone or cartilage. I pick up the telescope and scan the whole horizon. The sea is deserted everywhere. No doubt we are still too close to the shore.

I gaze up into the air. Why should some of the strange birds reconstructed by the immortal Cuvier[27] not flap their wings again in this dense and heavy atmosphere? There are sufficient fish to support them. I survey the whole space that stretches overhead; it is as deserted as the shore was.

Nevertheless, my imagination carries me away amongst the wonderful speculations of palaeontology. Though awake, I fall into a dream. I imagine I can see floating on the surface of the waters enormous Chelonia, antediluvian tortoises, resembling floating islands. Over the dimly lit strand there tread the huge mammals of the earliest ages of the world: the Leptotherium, found in the caverns of Brazil, and the Merycotherium, found in ice-clad Siberia. Farther on, the elephant-like Lophiodon, a gigantic tapir, hides behind the rocks to dispute its prey with an Anoplotherium, a strange creature which looked like a mixture of horse, rhinoceros, camel and hippopotamus, as if the Creator, in too much of a hurry in the earliest hours of the world, had combined several animals into one. A colossal mastodon twists and untwists his trunk, and with his huge tusks pounds and crushes the fragments of rock that cover the shore, whilst a Megatherium, buttressed on its enormous paws, grubs in the soil, awaking the sonorous echoes of the granite rocks with his tremendous roarings. Higher up, a Protopithecus – the first monkey to appear on the globe – is climbing up the steep slopes. Higher still, a pterodactyl darts to and fro in irregular zigzags in the heavy air. In the uppermost regions of the air immense birds, more powerful than the cassowary and larger than the ostrich, spread their vast wings and strike their heads against the granite vault that bounds the sky.

All this fossil world rises to life again in my vivid imagination. I return to the scriptural periods or ages of the world, conventionally called 'days', long before the appearance of man, when the unfinished world was as yet unfitted for his support. Then my dream goes back even farther into the ages before the creation of living beings. The mammals disappear, then the birds vanish, then the reptiles of the Secondary Period, and finally the fish, the crustaceans, molluscs and articulated creatures. Then the zoophytes of the Transition Period also return to nothing. I am the only living thing in the world: all life is concentrated in my beating heart alone. There are no longer any seasons nor any climates; the heat of the globe continually increases and neutralizes that of the sun. Plant growth becomes accelerated. I glide like a shade amongst arborescent ferns, treading with unsteady feet the coloured marls and the particoloured clays; I lean for support against the trunks of immense conifers; I lie in the shade of Sphenophylla, Asterophylla and Lycopods a hundred feet high.

Ages seem no more than days! I pass willy-nilly back through the long series of terrestrial changes. Plants disappear; granite rocks soften; intense heat converts solid bodies into thick fluids; the waters again cover the face of the Earth; they boil, they rise in whirling eddies of steam; mists wrap round the shifting forms of the Earth, which by imperceptible degrees dissolves into a gaseous mass, glowing fiery red and white, as large and as shining as the sun.

I myself am floating in the middle of this nebulous mass, fourteen hundred thousand times the volume of the Earth into which it will one day be condensed, and am being carried forward amongst the planetary bodies. My body has split into its constituent atoms, rarefied, volatilized. Sublimated into vapour, I mingle and am lost in the endless clouds of those vast globular volumes of vaporous mists, which roll in their flaming orbits through infinite space.

But is it not a dream? Where is it taking me? My feverish hand is vainly attempting to describe on paper its strange and wonderful details. I have forgotten everything that surrounds me. The Professor, the guide, the raft – all are gone from my mind. A hallucination has taken hold of me.

'What's the matter?' my uncle breaks in.

My staring eyes fix vacantly on him.

'Take care, Axel, or you'll fall overboard.'

At that moment I feel Hans' sinewy hand seizing me firmly. But for him, carried away by my dream, I would have thrown myself into the sea.

'Is he mad?' shouts the Professor.

'What's going on?' I say at last, coming to myself again.

'Do you feel ill?' asks my uncle.

'No, but I've had a strange hallucination. It's gone now. Is everything all right on the raft?'

'Yes, it's a fair wind and a fine sea. We're sailing along rapidly, and if I'm not out in my reckoning, we'll strike land soon.'

At these words I stood up and gazed round at the horizon, still bounded everywhere by clouds alone.

CHAPTER 33

A BATTLE OF MONSTERS

Saturday, August 15. – The sea unbroken all round. No land in sight. The horizon seems extremely distant.

My head is still stupefied by the vivid reality of my dream.

My uncle has had no dreams, but he's in a bad mood. He scans the horizon all round with his telescope, and folds his arms with a disgruntled look.

I notice that Professor Lidenbrock is tending to relapse into his impatient moods, and I make a note of it in my log. It took all the danger I was in and all my sufferings to coax a spark of human feeling out of him, but now that I am well again his basic nature has resumed its control over him. And yet, what reason is there to be angry? Is the voyage not prospering as favourably as possible under the circumstances? Is the raft not scudding along marvellously?

'You seem anxious, Uncle,' I said, seeing him continually with his telescope at his eye.

'Anxious! No, not at all.'

'Impatient, then?'

'One might well be, with less justification than now.'

'Yet we're going very fast.'

'So what? I'm not complaining that our speed is slow but that the sea is so wide.'

I then remember that the Professor, before starting out, had estimated the length of this underground sea at thirty leagues. Now we have covered three times that distance, but the southern coast is still not in sight.

'We aren't going down as we ought to be,' says the Professor. 'We're wasting time, and the fact is I haven't come all this way to take a little sail on a pond on a raft.'

He calls this sea a pond, and our long voyage taking a little sail!

'But,' I remark, 'since we've followed the path that Saknussemm has shown us . . .'

'That's the very question. *Have* we followed that path? Did Saknussemm reach this stretch of water? Did he cross it? Has the stream that we followed not completely led us astray?'

'At any rate we can't feel sorry to have come so far. This view is magnificent, and . . .'

'But I don't care for views. I came with a purpose, and I mean to achieve it. So don't talk to me about views and prospects.'

I take this as my answer, and I leave the Professor to bite his lips with impatience. At six in the evening Hans asks for his wages, and his three rix-dollars are counted out to him.

Sunday, August 16. – Nothing new. Weather unchanged. The wind is freshening. On awaking, my first thought is to observe the intensity of the light. I'm gripped by a fear that the electric light might grow dim or fail altogether. But there seems no reason to be afraid of that. The shadow of the raft is clearly outlined on the surface of the waves.

Truly this sea is of immeasurable width. It must be as wide as the Mediterranean, or even the Atlantic – and why not?

My uncle takes soundings several times. He ties the heaviest of our pickaxes to a long rope which he lets down two hundred fathoms. No bottom yet – and we have some difficulty in hauling up our sounding line.

But when the pickaxe is brought on board again, Hans points out deep prints on its surface as if it has been violently compressed between two hard bodies.

I look at the hunter.

'*Tänder*,' he says.

I don't understand, and turn to my uncle, who is entirely absorbed in his calculations. I prefer not to disturb him. I turn back to the Icelander. He conveys his idea to me by a snapping motion of his jaws.

'Teeth!' I cry, looking at the iron bar with more attention.

Yes, indeed, those are the marks of teeth imprinted on the metal! The jaws they line must be possessed of an amazing strength. Is there some monster beneath us belonging to the extinct races, more voracious than the shark, more fearful in its size than the whale? I can't take my eyes off this indented iron bar. Will the dream I had last night come true?

These thoughts bother me all day, and my imagination is scarcely calmer after several hours' sleep.

Monday, August 17. – I am trying to recall the peculiar instincts of the monsters of the pre-Adamite world, who, coming next in succession after the molluscs, the crustaceans and the fish, preceded the mammals on Earth. The world then belonged to the reptiles. Those monsters held mastery in the seas of the Secondary Period. They had a perfect structure, gigantic proportions, prodigious strength. The saurians of our day, the alligators and the crocodiles, are only feeble reproductions of their forefathers of primitive ages.

I shudder as I recall these monsters to my mind. No human eye has ever beheld them living. They burdened this Earth a thousand centuries before man appeared, but their fossil remains, found in the argillaceous limestone which the English call the Lias, have enabled their colossal structure to be perfectly reconstructed and anatomically ascertained.

I saw the skeleton of one of these creatures at the Hamburg museum, thirty feet in length. Am I then fated – I, an inhabitant of Earth – to be placed face to face with these representatives of long extinct families? No, surely it cannot be! Yet the deep marks on the iron pick have been made by conical teeth that certainly resemble those of a crocodile.

My eyes are fixed in terror on the sea. I dread to see one of these monsters darting forth from its undersea caverns. I suppose Professor Lidenbrock was of my opinion too, and even shares my fears, for after having examined the pickaxe, he too casts his eyes back and forth across the ocean. What a very bad idea that was of his, I thought to myself, to take depth soundings! He's disturbed some monstrous beast in its den, and now we could be attacked during our voyage . . .

I look at our guns and see that they are all right. My uncle notices, and nods his approval.

Already widely disturbed regions on the surface of the water indicate some commotion below. The danger is approaching. We must be on the look-out.

Tuesday, August 18. – Evening comes, or rather the time comes when sleep weighs down weary eyelids, for there is no night here, and the ceaseless light wearies the eyes with its persistence just as if we were sailing under an Arctic sun. Hans is at the helm. During his watch I sleep.

Two hours afterwards a terrible shock awakes me. The raft is heaved up on a watery mountain and pitched down again, at a distance of twenty fathoms.

'What's the matter?' shouts my uncle. 'Have we struck land?'

Hans points at a dark mass six hundred yards away, rising and falling alternately with heavy plunges. I look at it and exclaim:

'It's an enormous porpoise.'

'Yes,' replies my uncle, 'and there's an enormous sea lizard too.'

'And farther over a monstrous crocodile. Look at its huge jaws and its rows of teeth! It's diving down!'

'There's a whale, a whale!' cries the Professor. 'I can see its massive fins. See how it's throwing out air and water through his blowholes.'

And in fact two columns of liquid are rising to a considerable height above the sea. We stand amazed, thunderstruck, at the presence of such a herd of marine monsters. They are of supernatural dimensions; the smallest of them could crunch up our raft, crew and all, with one snap of its huge jaws. Hans wants to tack to get away from this dangerous area, but in the other direction he sees enemies no less terrible: a tortoise forty feet long and a thirty-foot serpent, lifting its fearsome head and gleaming eyes above the surface of the ocean.

Flight is out of the question now. The reptiles rise up; they wheel around

JOURNEY TO THE CENTRE OF THE EARTH

our little raft faster than an express train. They swim around us in gradually narrowing circles. I pick up my rifle. But what could a bullet do against the scaly armour these enormous beasts are clad in?

We just stand there, struck dumb with fear. They come closer: on one side the crocodile, on the other the serpent. The other sea monsters have disappeared. I prepare to fire. Hans signals to me not to. The two monsters pass within a hundred and fifty yards of the raft, and hurl themselves one upon the other, with a fury which prevents them from noticing us.

The battle is fought three hundred yards away from us. We can clearly see the two monsters engaged in deadly conflict. But it now seems to me that the other animals are taking part in the fray – the porpoise, the whale, the lizard, the tortoise. At every moment I seem to see one or other of them. I point them out to the Icelander. He shakes his head.

'*Tva*,' he says.

'What, two? Does he mean there are only two animals?'

'He's right,' says my uncle, whose telescope has never left his eye.

'Surely you must be mistaken,' I exclaim.

'No. The first of those monsters has a porpoise's snout, a lizard's head and a crocodile's teeth; hence our mistake. It is an ichthyosaurus, the most terrible of the ancient monsters of the deep.'

'And the other?'

'The other is a plesiosaurus, a serpent protected by the shell of a turtle. It's the mortal enemy of the other.'

Hans was quite right. Only two monsters are disturbing the surface of the ocean, and in front of my eyes are two reptiles of the primitive world. I can see the eye of the ichthyosaurus, glowing like a red-hot coal and as large as a man's head. Nature has endowed it with optical apparatus of extreme power and capable of resisting the pressure of the great volume of water in the depths it inhabits. It has been appropriately called the saurian whale, for it has both the speed and the rapid movements of this monster of our own time. This one is not less than a hundred feet long, and I can judge its size when it sweeps the vertical coils of its tail over the water. Its jaws are enormous, and according to naturalists it is armed with no less than one hundred and eighty-two teeth.

The plesiosaurus, a serpent with a cylindrical body and a short tail, has four flippers or paddles that act like oars. Its body is entirely covered with a thick shell, and its neck, as flexible as a swan's, rises thirty feet above the waves.

Those huge creatures attack each other with indescribable fury. Around them they create liquid mountains, which roll as far as our raft and rock it dangerously. Twenty times we come near to capsizing. We can hear incredibly loud hissing. The two beasts are locked together; I can't distinguish the one from the other. The winner's probable rage terrifies us.

One hour, two hours, pass. The struggle continues with unabated ferocity. The combatants alternately approach our raft and swim away again. We remain motionless, ready to fire. Suddenly the ichthyosaurus and the plesiosaurus disappear below the waves, leaving a whirlpool eddying in the water. Several minutes pass while the fight continues under water.

Suddenly an enormous head rises up out of the water, the head of the plesiosaurus. The monster is mortally wounded. I can no longer see its scaly armour. Only its long neck shoots up, drops again, coils and uncoils, droops, lashes the waters like a gigantic whip and writhes like a worm when you cut it in two. The water is splashed about over a long distance and blinds us. But soon the reptile's agony draws to an end; its movements become weaker, its contortions become less violent, and the long serpentine form lies like a lifeless log on the water, now calm once more.

As for the ichthyosaurus, has it returned to its undersea cavern? Or will it reappear on the surface of the sea?

CHAPTER 34

THE GREAT GEYSER

Wednesday, August 19. – Fortunately the wind is blowing violently, and has enabled us to flee from the scene of the recent terrible struggle. Hans sticks to his post at the helm. My uncle, whom the absorbing incidents of the combat had drawn away from his contemplations, begins once more to look impatiently around him.

The voyage resumes its uniform tenor, which I don't care to see broken by a repetition of such events as yesterday's.

Thursday, August 20. – Wind N.N.E., unsteady and fitful. Temperature high. Rate: three and a half leagues an hour.

About noon, we hear a distant noise. I note the fact without being able to explain it. It's a continuous roaring sound.

'There's a rock or small island in the distance,' says the Professor, 'and the sea is breaking against it.'

Hans climbs the mast, but can't see any breakers. The ocean is smooth and unbroken to its farthest limit.

Three hours pass. The roaring seems to come from a very distant waterfall.

I mention this to my uncle, who shakes his head. However, I'm sure I'm right. Are we, then, speeding forward towards some waterfall which will toss us down into the abyss? This method of progressing may please the Professor, because it's vertical, but for my part . . .

At any rate, some leagues to windward there must be some noisy phenomenon, for now the roaring is getting very loud. Is it coming from the sky or the ocean?

I look up at the atmospheric vapours and try to fathom their depths. The sky is calm and motionless. The clouds have reached the utmost limit of the lofty vault, and there they lie still bathed in the bright glare of the electric light. It isn't there that we must look for the cause of this phenomenon. Then I study the horizon, which is unbroken and completely clear of mist. There's no change in how it looks. But if this noise is being produced by a waterfall, if all this ocean is flowing headlong into an even lower basin, if that deafening roar is produced by a mass of falling water, there must be a current, and its increasing speed will allow me to estimate the danger that threatens us. I check the current: there isn't any. I throw an empty bottle into the sea: it floats to leeward of us without moving.

About four o'clock, Hans gets up, grips the mast and climbs to the top.

From there his eye sweeps across a large expanse of sea and fixes on a point. His face shows no surprise, but his eyes remain fixed on something.

'He can see something,' says my uncle.

'I believe he can.'

Hans comes down, then stretches out his arm towards the south, saying:

'*Der nere!*'

'Over there?' replies my uncle.

Then, taking hold of his telescope, he looks attentively for a minute, which seems to me an age.

'Yes, yes!' he exclaims.

'What can you see?'

'I can see a huge plume of water rising from the surface of the ocean.'

'Is it another sea animal?'

'Perhaps.'

'Then let's steer farther to the west, because we know something of the danger of meeting with monsters of that sort.'

'Let's keep going straight on,' replies my uncle.

I appeal to Hans. He maintains our course inflexibly.

But if at our present distance from the animal, a distance of at least twelve leagues, the column of water forced through its blowholes may be seen distinctly, it must be enormous. Common sense would suggest immediate flight, but we haven't come this far to be sensible.

Imprudently, therefore, we continue on our way. The nearer we get, the higher the jet of water shoots into the air. What monster can possibly fill itself with such a quantity of water, and spurt it up so continuously?

At eight in the evening we aren't more than two leagues away from it. Its dusky, enormous, hillocky body lies spread over the sea like a small island. Is it an illusion, is it something fear is creating in our minds? It seems to me to be about a couple of thousand yards in length. What can this cetacean monster be, this creature which neither Cuvier nor Blumenbach knew anything about? It lies motionless, as if asleep; the sea seems unable to move it at all, and it is the waves that are undulating on its sides. The column of water thrown up to a height of five hundred feet falls like rain with a deafening roar. And here we are scudding like lunatics before the wind, to get near to a monster that a hundred whales a day would not satisfy!

Terror grips me. I refuse to go any further. I'll cut the halliards if necessary! I stand in open mutiny against the Professor, but he says nothing in reply.

Suddenly Hans stands up, and pointing with his finger at the menacing object, says:

'*Holme.*'

'An island!' cries my uncle.
'That's not an island!' I exclaim sceptically.
'That's exactly what it is,' shouts the Professor, with a loud laugh.
'But what about that column of water?'
'*Geyser*,' says Hans.
'No doubt it's a geyser, like those in Iceland.'

At first I can't bring myself to admit that I've been so wrong as to have mistaken an island for a sea monster. But the evidence is against me, and I have to admit my mistake: it's nothing more than a natural phenomenon.

As we get nearer, the dimensions of the plume of liquid become magnificent. The little island resembles, most deceptively, an enormous whale with a head rising above the waves to a height of twenty yards. The geyser, a word that means 'fury', rises majestically at one end. From time to time, deep, heavy explosions can be heard, and then the enormous jet, even more violent than before, shakes its plumed crest and leaps up till it reaches the lowest stratum of the clouds. It stands alone. There are no steam vents or hot springs around it, and all the volcanic power of the area is concentrated in it. Sparks of electric fire mingle with the dazzling plume of liquid, every drop sparkling with all the colours of a prism.

'Let's land,' says the Professor.

But we have to take care to avoid this waterspout, which would sink our raft in a moment. Hans, steering with his usual skill, brings us to the other end of the island.

I leap up on to the rock. My uncle follows nimbly, while our hunter remains at his post, like a man too wise to be astonished by anything.

We walk on granite mixed with siliceous tufa. The ground shivers and shakes under our feet, like the sides of an overheated boiler filled with steam that is struggling to get out. We come to a small central basin that the geyser is rising out of. I plunge an overflow thermometer into the boiling water. It registers a temperature of 163°, which is far above boiling point; this water is therefore issuing from a fiery furnace, which is not at all in harmony with Professor Lidenbrock's theories. I can't help remarking on this.

'Well,' he replies, 'how does that go against my doctrine?'

'Oh, not at all,' I say, seeing that I am up against immovable obstinacy.

Still I'm forced to say that up till now we have been extremely fortunate, and that for some reason I don't know we have accomplished our journey under singularly favourable conditions of temperature. But it seems obvious to me that some day we will come to a region where the central heat reaches its highest limits and goes beyond a point that can be registered by our thermometers.

'We'll see,' says the Professor, who, having named this volcanic island after his nephew, gives the signal to embark again.

For some minutes I am still contemplating the geyser. I notice that it throws up its column of water with variable force: sometimes sending it to a great height, then not so high; this I attribute to the variable pressure of the steam accumulated in its reservoir.

At last we leave the island, sailing past the low rocks on its southern shore. Hans has taken advantage of the brief stop to repair the raft.

But before going any farther I make a few observations, to calculate the distance we have covered, and note them in my journal. We've crossed two hundred and seventy leagues of sea since leaving Port Gräuben; and we're six hundred and twenty leagues from Iceland, under England.

CHAPTER 35

AN ELECTRIC STORM

Friday, August 21. – By the next day the magnificent geyser has disappeared. The wind has risen, and has rapidly carried us away from Axel Island. The roaring becomes lost in the distance.

The weather – if I may use that term – will soon change. The atmosphere is becoming charged with vapours which carry with them the electricity generated by the evaporation of salt water. The clouds are sinking lower, and take on an olive hue. The electric light can scarcely penetrate through the dense curtain which has dropped over the theatre on which the battle of the elements is about to be waged.

I feel an odd sensation, like many creatures on Earth do at the approach of violent atmospheric changes. The piled-up cumulus clouds lower gloomily and threateningly; they wear that implacable look which I have sometimes noticed at the outbreak of a great storm. The air is heavy; the sea is calm.

In the distance, the clouds look like great bales of cotton, piled up in picturesque disorder. They gradually swell up, and gain in size what they lose in number. Such is their ponderous weight that they cannot rise from the horizon, but, under the impulse of currents of air they merge and darken, and soon present to our view a level surface of menacing appearance. From time to time a fleecy tuft of mist, still with some gleaming light left on it, drops down on the dense floor of grey and loses itself in the opaque and impenetrable mass.

The atmosphere is evidently saturated with electrical charge. My whole body is impregnated with it; my hair is standing on end just like when you stand on an insulated stool and are affected by the action of an electrical machine. It seems to me that if my companions touched me, they would get a severe shock.

At ten in the morning, the storm symptoms get worse. You would say that the wind seems to drop only to acquire even greater strength. The huge bank of heavy clouds is a vast reservoir of fearsome windy gusts and rushing storms.

I am loath to believe these atmospheric threats, and yet I can't help muttering:

'Here comes some very bad weather.'

The Professor doesn't reply. He's in a foul mood, seeing this vast stretch of ocean stretching out interminably before him. At my words, he shrugs his shoulders.

'There's a heavy storm coming,' I shout, pointing towards the horizon. 'Those clouds look as if they're about to crush the sea.'

A deep silence falls all around us. The winds that have been roaring now drop to a dead calm; nature seems to stop breathing and to sink into the stillness of death. On the mast I can already see the light play of tongues of St Elmo's fire; the outstretched sail catches not a breath of wind and hangs like a sheet of lead. The raft is sitting motionless in a sluggish, waveless sea. But if we are now no longer moving forward, why have we still got the sail up, since it could cause us to capsize at the first shock of the storm?

'Let's reef the sail and cut the mast down!' I shout. 'That would be the safest thing to do.'

'No, no! Never!' shouts my uncle. 'Never! Let the wind catch us if it will, let the storm sweep us away! Let me have at least a glimpse of a rock or shore, even if our raft should be smashed to pieces on it!'

The words are hardly out of his mouth when a sudden change takes place in the southern sky. The accumulated vapours condense into water, and the air, forced into violent action to supply the vacuum left by the condensation of the mists, turns into a hurricane. It's blowing from the farthest recesses of the vast cavern. The darkness deepens; I scarcely manage to jot down a few hurried notes.

The raft lifts and tosses. My uncle is thrown down full length on the deck; I drag myself over beside him. He has taken a firm hold on a rope and appears to be watching this awful display of elemental strife with grim satisfaction.

Hans doesn't move. His long hair blown by the storm and laid flat across his immovable countenance makes him a strange figure, as the end of each lock of loose flowing hair is tipped with little luminous radiations. This frightening mask of electrical sparks puts me in mind of pre-Adamite man, the contemporary of the ichthyosaurus and the Megatherium.

The mast is still holding. The sail is stretched tight like a bubble ready to burst. The raft is racing along at a rate I cannot calculate, but not as fast as the drops of spray which it's throwing out on both sides in its headlong speed.

'The sail! the sail!' I cry, motioning to lower it.

'No!' replies my uncle.

'*Nej!*' repeats Hans, gently shaking his head.

But now the rain is forming a rushing waterfall in front of the horizon towards which we are racing like madmen. But before it has reached us, the rain cloud splits, the sea boils, and the electricity is brought into violent action by some strong chemical reaction operating in the upper regions. Intensely vivid flashes of lightning mingle with the violent crash of constant thunder. Fiery arrows dart continuously in and out amongst the flying thunder-clouds; the vaporous mass is soon glowing with incandescent heat; hailstones rattle down fiercely, and as they strike our iron tools they too emit gleams and flashes of lurid light. The heaving waves look like fiery volcanic hills, each belching out its own interior flames, and every crest is plumed with dancing fire.

My eyes are blinded by the dazzling light, my ears are deafened with the incessant crash of thunder. I have to cling to the mast, which bends like a reed before the mighty strength of the storm.

(Here my notes become vague and incomplete. I have only been able to find a few which I seem to have jotted down almost unconsciously. But their very brevity and their obscurity reveal the intensity of the excitement I felt, and describe the actual situation even better than my memory could do.)

Sunday, August 23. – Where are we? Being driven forward at a speed beyond measurement.

Last night has been terrible; no abatement of the storm. The din and uproar never stop; our ears are bleeding; to exchange words is impossible.

The lightning flashes with intense brilliance and seems never to stop for a moment. Zigzag streams of bluish-white fire flash down to the sea and rebound, flying upward again till they strike the granite vault that arches over our heads. What if that solid roof should collapse on our heads? Other lightning flashes become forked or form themselves into balls of fire which explode like bombshells. The general level of noise doesn't seem to be increased by this. We have already passed the limit of sound intensity within which the human ear can distinguish one sound from another. If all the powder magazines in the world were to explode at once, we would hear no more than we do now.

From the under-surface of the clouds come continual emissions of lurid light; electricity is constantly being given off by their component molecules. Apparently the gaseous elements of the air are undergoing a transformation. Innumerable columns of water spring upwards into the air and fall back again as white foam.

Where are we heading? My uncle is lying stretched out at the edge of the raft.

The heat increases. I check the thermometer; it indicates . . . (the figure is illegible).

Monday, August 24. – Will there never be an end to this? Is the atmospheric condition, having now reached this density, to going to stay like this?

We are almost prostrate with fatigue. But Hans is the same as ever. The raft is still heading south-east. We've done two hundred leagues since we left Axel Island.

At noon the violence of the storm redoubles. We're forced to fasten down every item of our cargo as securely as possible. Each of us is lashed to some part of the raft. The waves rise above our heads.

For three days now, we have not been able to make each other hear a word we say. Our mouths open, our lips move, but not a word can be heard. We can't even make ourselves heard by putting our mouth close to the other person's ear.

My uncle has crawled close to me. He has uttered a few words. He seems to be saying 'We're done for' but I'm not sure.

Finally I write down the words: 'We should lower the sail.'

He signals his agreement.

He scarcely has time to nod his head again before a disc of fire appears right beside our raft. In an instant the mast and sail together fly up into the air, and I see them carried up to a prodigious height, looking just like a pterodactyl, one of those fantastic birds of the earliest ages of the world.

We lie there, our blood running cold with unspeakable terror. The fireball, half white, half azure blue, and the size of a ten-inch shell, moves around slowly while revolving on its own axis with astonishing speed due to the force of the hurricane. Here it comes, there it glides, now it is up on the ragged stump of the mast, from there it leaps lightly on to the provisions bag, descends lightly again and just touches the powder magazine. Horror of horrors! We're going to be blown up! But no, the dazzling disc of mysterious light leaps nimbly to one side; it heads towards Hans, who steadily fixes his blue eyes on it. It threatens my uncle, who drops to his knees to avoid it. And now it's my turn, as I stand pale and trembling in the blinding splendour and the melting heat. It drops at my feet, spinning silently round on the deck. I try to move my foot away, but can't.

A stifling smell of nitrous gas fills the air. It gets into our throats and lungs. We choke on it.

Why can't I move my foot? Is it riveted to the planks? Oh, I see! This electric globe falling on to our ill-fated raft has magnetized every article of iron on board. The instruments, the tools, our guns, are clattering and clinking as they collide with each other. The nails of my boots are clinging firmly to a piece of iron embedded in the timbers, and I can't pull my foot away. At last, by a violent effort, I release myself at the very instant when the spinning ball is about to grip my foot and carry me off, if . . .

Ah! what a flood of intense and dazzling light! The globe bursts, and we are deluged with tongues of fire!

Then the light disappears. I just have time to see my uncle stretched out on the raft, and Hans still at the helm and emitting sparks of fire because of the electricity that has saturated him.

But where are we going? Where?

Tuesday, August 25. – I come out of a long faint. The storm continues to rage; the flashes of lightning flicker here and there, like broods of fiery serpents filling the air. Are we still at sea? Yes, we are being borne along at incalculable speed. We've been carried under England, under the Channel, under France, perhaps under the whole of Europe.

We can hear a new noise! Clearly the sea breaking on rocks! And then . . .

CHAPTER 36

CALM PHILOSOPHICAL DISCUSSIONS

Here ends what I may call my log, fortunately saved from the shipwreck, and I take up my narrative as before.

What happened when the raft was dashed against the rocks on the coast is more than I can tell. I felt myself thrown into the waves; and if I escaped death, and if my body was not torn on the sharp edges of the rocks, it was because Hans's powerful arm came to my rescue.

The brave Icelander carried me out of reach of the waves, on to a burning sand where I found myself by my uncle's side.

Then he returned to the rocks, against which the waves were beating furiously, to save what he could. I was unable to speak. I was shattered with fatigue and emotion. It took me a whole hour to recover.

But rain was still falling in a deluge, though with that violence which generally means that a storm is nearly over. A few overhanging rocks afforded us some shelter from the storm. Hans prepared some food, which I couldn't touch; and each of us, exhausted from three sleepless nights, fell into a disturbed and painful sleep.

The next day, the weather was splendid. The sky and the sea had suddenly become calm. Every trace of the terrible storm had disappeared. The happy voice of the Professor reached my ears as I awoke; he was ominously cheerful.

'Well, my boy,' he shouted, 'have you slept well?'

Anyone would have thought we were still in our little house in the Königstrasse and that I was just coming down to breakfast, and that I was going to be married to Gräuben that day.

Alas! If the storm had only sent the raft a little farther to the east, we would have passed under Germany, under my beloved town of Hamburg, under the very street where dwelt all that I loved most in the world. Then only forty leagues would have separated us! But they would have been forty vertical leagues of solid granite, and in reality we were a thousand leagues apart!

All these painful thoughts rapidly crossed my mind before I could answer my uncle's question.

'Well, now,' he repeated, 'won't you tell me how you've slept?'

'Oh, perfectly well,' I said. 'I'm still a bit bruised, but I'll soon be better.'

'Oh,' says my uncle, 'that's nothing. You're just a bit tired, that's all.'

'But you, Uncle, seem to be in very good spirits this morning.'

'I'm delighted, my boy, absolutely delighted. We've got there.'

'To our journey's end?'

'No. But we've reached the end of that seemingly endless sea. Now we shall go on by land, and really begin to go down, down, down!'

'But, my dear Uncle, let me ask you one question.'

'Of course, Axel.'

'How about getting back?'

'Getting back? Why, you're talking about the return journey before we even arrive there.'

'No, I only want to know how we are going to do it.'

'In the simplest way possible. When we have reached the centre of the globe, either we shall find some new way to get back, or rather boringly we'll come back the way we came. I'm pretty sure the path won't have closed up behind us.'

'But then we shall have to rebuild the raft.'

'Of course.'

'Then, what about provisions? Have we got enough to last us?'

'Yes, I'm sure we have. Hans is a clever fellow, and I am sure he must have saved a large part of our cargo. But nevertheless let's go and make certain.'

We left this grotto, which lay open to every gust of wind. I cherished a trembling hope which was at the same time a fear as well. It seemed to me impossible that the terrible wreck of the raft would not have destroyed everything on board. But I was wrong. Arriving on the shore, I found Hans surrounded by an assemblage of articles all laid out in good order. My uncle shook hands with him with warm gratitude. This man, with almost superhuman devotion, had been at work all the time that we had been asleep, and had saved the most precious articles at the risk of his life.

Not that we had suffered no serious losses. For instance, our firearms were gone, but we could do without them. Our stock of powder had remained unharmed after having nearly exploded during the storm.

'Well,' cried the Professor, 'since we have no guns, we can't hunt, that's all there is to it.'

'Yes, but how about the instruments?'

'Here's the manometer, the most useful of them all, and for which I would have happily given away all the others. With it, I can calculate our depth and know when we have reached the centre; without it, we might go too far, and come out at the Antipodes!'

He was in a ferociously good mood.

'But where's the compass?' I asked.

'Here it is, on this rock, in perfect condition, and so are the thermometers and the chronometer. Our hunter really is a splendid fellow.'

There was no denying it. We had all our instruments. As for tools and appliances, there they all lay on the ground – ladders, ropes, picks, spades, etc.

Still there was the question of provisions to be settled, and I asked, 'How are we off for provisions?'

'Let's look at the provisions, then.'

The boxes containing these were in a line on the shore, in a perfect state of preservation; for the most part, the sea had spared them, and what with biscuits, salt meat, spirits and salt fish, we had enough for about four months.

'Four months!' exclaimed the Professor. 'We've time to get there and come back again, and with what's left over I'll give a grand dinner to my colleagues at the Johannaeum.'

I ought by this time to have been quite used to my uncle's ways, but he always came up with something new to astonish me.

'Now,' he said, 'we'll replenish our supply of water with the rain which the storm has left in all these granite basins, so we'll have nothing to fear as far as thirst is concerned. As for the raft, I'm going to suggest to Hans that he do his best to repair it, although I don't expect it will be of any further use to us.'

'Why not?' I said.

'Just an idea of mine, my boy. I don't think we'll be leaving by the same way as we came in.'

I stared at the Professor with a good deal of mistrust. I wondered whether he might have gone a little bit crazy. And yet there was method in his madness.

'And now let's have breakfast,' he said.

I followed him to a headland, after he had given his instructions to the hunter. There we had an excellent meal of preserved meat, biscuits and tea, one of the best meals I ever remember. Hunger, the fresh air, the calm quiet weather after the turmoil we had gone through, all contributed to give me a good appetite.

Whilst breakfasting, I took the opportunity to ask my uncle where we were now.

'That seems to me,' I said, 'rather difficult to work out.'

'Yes, it is difficult to calculate that exactly,' he said. 'Perhaps even impossible, since during these three stormy days I've been unable to keep track of the speed or direction of the raft. But nevertheless we may get a rough idea.'

'The last observation,' I remarked, 'was made on the island where the geyser was...'

'You mean Axel Island. Don't decline the honour of having given your name to the first island ever discovered in the interior of the globe.'

'Fine,' I said, 'so be it. On Axel Island. By then we had covered two hundred and seventy leagues across the sea, and we were six hundred leagues from Iceland.'

'Very well,' replied my uncle. 'Let's start from that point and count four days of storm, during which our speed can't have been less than eighty leagues every twenty-four hours.'

'That's right. And that would make another three hundred leagues.'

'Yes, and the Lidenbrock Sea would therefore be six hundred leagues from shore to shore. Surely, Axel, it may be equal in size to the Mediterranean itself.'

'Especially,' I replied, 'if it happens that we have only sailed across it and not from one end to the other. And it is a curious circumstance,' I added, 'that if my calculations are right, and we are nine hundred leagues from Reykjavik, the Mediterranean is now right above our heads.'

'That's a good long journey, my boy. But whether we're under the Mediterranean, Turkey or the Atlantic depends very much on what direction we have been travelling in. Perhaps we have deviated from our intended course.'

'No, I don't think so. Our course has been the same all along, and I reckon this shore is south-east of Port Gräuben.'

'Well,' replied my uncle, 'we may easily ascertain this by checking the compass. Let's go and see what it says.'

The Professor walked towards the rock on which Hans had laid out the instruments. He was happy and full of spirits; he was rubbing his hands together and striking poses. I followed him, curious to know if I was right in my estimate. He was behaving like a much younger man! As soon as we reached the rock, my uncle picked up the compass, laid it down flat, and looked at the needle, which, after a few oscillations, eventually assumed a fixed position. My uncle looked, and looked, and looked again. He rubbed his eyes, and then turned to me, thunderstruck.

'What's the matter?' I asked.

He motioned to me to take a look. An exclamation of astonishment burst from me. The north pole of the needle was turned to what we had supposed to be the south. It pointed to the shore instead of out to the open sea! I shook the box and checked it again; it was in perfect condition. No matter what position I placed the box in, the needle returned every time to point in this unexpected direction. Therefore there seemed no reason to doubt that during the storm there had been a sudden change of wind that we hadn't noticed and which had brought our raft back to the shore we thought we had left so far behind us.

CHAPTER 37

THE LIDENBROCK MUSEUM OF GEOLOGY

It would be impossible to describe the emotions which in turn shook the breast of Professor Lidenbrock. First amazement, then incredulity, lastly an outburst of rage. Never had I seen a man so put out and then so exasperated. The fatigues of our crossing, the dangers we had faced, had all to be repeated. We had gone backwards instead of forwards!

But my uncle rapidly recovered himself.

'Well, then! Is fate playing tricks on me? Are the elements plotting against me? Will fire, air and water make a combined attack against me? Well, they shall know what a determined man can do. I will not yield. I will not take a single step backwards, and we'll see whether man or nature is to have the upper hand!'

Standing erect on the rock, angry and threatening, Otto Lidenbrock looked like a rather grotesque parody of the fierce Ajax[28] defying the gods. But I thought it my duty to step in and attempt to restrain this crazy fanaticism.

'Just listen to me,' I said firmly. 'There has to be some limit to this ambition of yours. We can't do the impossible. We're in no state to set out on another sea voyage. Who would dream of undertaking a voyage of five hundred leagues on a heap of rotten planks, with a ragged blanket for a sail, a stick for a mast and fierce winds in our teeth? We can't steer, we'll be blown about by the storms and we would be fools and madmen to attempt to cross a second time.'

I was able to develop this series of irrefutable reasons for ten whole minutes without interruption. It wasn't, however, that the Professor was paying any respectful attention to his nephew's arguments, but because he was deaf to all my eloquence.

'To the raft!' he shouted.

This was his only reply. There was no point in me entreating, pleading, getting angry or doing anything else by way of opposing him; I would only have been opposing a will harder than the granite rock.

Hans was finishing the repairs to the raft. It was as if this strange being was able to guess my uncle's plans. With a few more pieces of *surtarbrandur*, he had repaired our ship. A sail was already hanging at the new mast, and the wind was playing in its waving folds.

The Professor said a few words to the guide, and immediately he put everything on board and arranged everything necessary for our departure. The air was clear, and the north-west wind was blowing steadily.

What could I do? Could I make a stand against the two of them? Impossible. If only Hans had taken my side! But no, it was not to be. The Icelander seemed to have renounced all will of his own and made a vow to forget and deny himself. I could get nothing out of a servant so feudally subservient, as it were, to his master. My only course was to proceed.

I was therefore going to take my usual place on the raft when my uncle put his hand on my shoulder.

'We'll not sail until tomorrow,' he said.

I made a gesture of total resignation.

'I mustn't neglect anything,' he said. 'And since fate has driven me on to this part of the coast, I won't leave until I have examined it.'

To understand this comment, it must be borne in mind that, although we had returned to the northern shore of the sea, we were not at the spot we had set out from. Port Gräuben had to be to the west of us. It therefore made perfect sense to carefully investigate the area around our new landing place.

'Now, let's go and see what we can find,' I said.

And leaving Hans to his work, we set off together. There was some considerable distance between the water and the foot of the cliffs. It took us half an hour to reach the wall of rock. We trampled under our feet countless seashells of all the forms and sizes that existed in the earliest ages of the world. I also saw immense animal shells more than fifteen feet in diameter. They had been the coverings of those gigantic glyptodons or armadillos of the Pliocene Epoch, of which the modern tortoise is but a miniature representative. In addition, the soil was scattered with stony fragments, shingle rounded by the action of water, and formed in successive rows. I was therefore led to the conclusion that at one time the sea must have covered the ground on which we were treading. On the loose and scattered rocks, now beyond the reach of the highest tides, the waves had left clear traces of their passage.

This might to a certain extent explain the existence of an ocean forty leagues beneath the surface of the globe. But, by my theory, this mass of liquid must be gradually disappearing into the bowels of the Earth, and it clearly originated in the waters of the ocean above, which had made their way here through some fissure. Yet it must be assumed that that fissure was now closed, and that this whole cavern, or rather this immense reservoir, had filled in a very short time. Perhaps this water, subjected to the fierce action of subterranean heat, had been partially converted into vapour. This would explain the existence of those clouds hanging over our heads and the development of the electricity which raised such tempests within the body of the globe.

This theory regarding the phenomena we had witnessed seemed satisfactory to me, for no matter how great and stupendous are the phenomena of nature, established physical laws can always explain them.

We were therefore walking on sedimentary soil, the deposits of the waters of former ages. The Professor was carefully examining every little fissure in the rocks. Wherever he saw a hole, he always wanted to know how deep it was. To him, this was important.

We had been following the coast of the Lidenbrock Sea for a mile when we noticed a sudden change in the appearance of the soil. It seemed to have been turned upside down, contorted and convulsed by a violent upheaval of the lower strata. In many places depressions or elevations bore witness to some tremendous power causing the dislocation of strata.

We moved with difficulty across these granite fragments mingled with flint, quartz and alluvial deposits, when a field – no, more than a field, a vast plain – of bleached bones lay spread out before us. It looked like a huge cemetery, where the remains of twenty ages mingled their dust together. Immense mounds of bony fragments rose up in the distance. They stretched out in waves as far as the horizon, and then were lost in a faint haze. Within three square miles there were accumulated the materials for a complete history of the animal life through the ages, a history scarcely sketched out in the all too recent strata of the inhabited world.

But impatient curiosity carried us forward. Crackling and rattling, our feet were trampling on the remains of prehistoric animals and interesting fossils, the possession of which is a matter of rivalry and contention between the museums of great cities. A thousand Cuviers could never have reconstructed the organic remains deposited in this magnificent and unparalleled collection.

I stood there in amazement. My uncle had raised his long arms towards the vault which was our sky. His mouth gaping wide, his eyes flashing behind his shining spectacles, his head nodding and shaking, his whole stance denoted utter astonishment. Here he stood, looking at an immense collection of scattered Leptotheria, Mericotheria, Lophiodia, Anoplotheria, Megatheria, Protopithecae, pterodactyls, mastodons and all sorts of extinct monsters gathered here together for his private satisfaction. Imagine an enthusiastic bibliophile suddenly dropped into the middle of the famous Alexandrian library that was burnt by Omar[29] and by some miracle restored from its ashes! That was my uncle, Professor Lidenbrock.

But more was to come, when, rushing through clouds of bone dust, he put his hand on a bare skull, and exclaimed with a voice trembling with excitement:

'Axel! Axel! A human skull!'

'A human skull?' I cried, no less astonished.

'Yes, my boy. Oh, Milne-Edwards, oh, de Quatrefages[30], how I wish you were standing here with me, Otto Lidenbrock!'

CHAPTER 38

THE PROFESSOR IN HIS CHAIR AGAIN

To understand this last exclamation of my uncle's, addressed to two famous French scientists, you have to know about an event of great importance from a palaeontological point of view which had occurred shortly before our departure.

On the 28th of March, 1863, some excavators working under the direction of M. Boucher de Perthes, in the stone quarries of Moulin-Quignon near Abbeville, in the department of Somme, found a human jawbone fourteen feet beneath the surface of the ground. It was the first fossil of this sort that had ever been brought to light. Not far from it were found stone hatchets and flint tools stained with a uniform patina by the passage of time.

The impact of this discovery was immense, not just in France but also in England and Germany. Several scientists at the French Institute, amongst whom were Messrs Milne-Edwards and de Quatrefages, at once saw the importance of this discovery, proved the genuineness of the bone in question and became the most ardent defendants in what the English called the 'jawbone trial'.

The geologists of the United Kingdom – Messrs Falconer, Busk, Carpenter and others – who believed the fact as certain, were soon joined by German scholars, the most eminent, the most ardent and the most enthusiastic of whom was my Uncle Lidenbrock.

The genuineness of a fossil human relic of the Quaternary Period seemed therefore to be incontestably proved and accepted.

It is true that this theory met with a most obstinate opponent in M. Elie de Beaumont. This eminent authority maintained that the soil of Moulin-Quignon was not from the diluvial period at all, but was of much more recent formation; and, agreeing in that with Cuvier, he refused to admit that the human species could be contemporary with the animals of the Quaternary Period. My Uncle Lidenbrock, along with the great majority of geologists, had held his ground, had disputed and argued, until M. Elie de Beaumont stood almost alone in his opinion.

We knew all these details of the affair, but we were not aware that since our departure the matter had developed further. Other similar jawbones, although belonging to individuals of various types and different nations, were found in the loose grey soil of certain grottoes in France, Switzerland and Belgium, as well as weapons, tools, earthenware utensils, bones of children and adults. So the existence of man in the Quaternary Period seemed to become ever more certain as each day passed.

But that was not all. Fresh discoveries of remains in the Pliocene formation had emboldened other geologists to attribute the human species to an even earlier period. It is true that these remains were not human bones, but objects bearing the traces of human handiwork, such as fossil leg-bones of animals evidently sculptured and carved by the hand of man.

Thus, in one bound, man had risen several rungs further back up the ladder of time. He was a predecessor of the mastodon; he was a contemporary of the southern elephant; he lived a hundred thousand years ago, when, according to geologists, the Pliocene was being formed.

Such then was the state of palaeontological science, and what we knew of it was sufficient to explain our behaviour in the presence of this stupendous Golgotha. Anyone can now understand my uncle's frenzied excitement when, twenty yards further on, he found himself face to face with a primitive man!

It was a perfectly recognizable human body. Had some peculiarity of the soil, like that of the St-Michel cemetery at Bordeaux, preserved it in this condition for such a long time? It might be so. But this dried corpse, with its parchment-like skin drawn tightly over the bony frame, the limbs still preserving their shape, sound teeth, abundant hair, and finger and toe nails of a frightening length, this desiccated mummy startled us by appearing just as it had lived countless ages ago. I stood mute before this apparition of remote antiquity. My uncle, usually so garrulous, was likewise struck dumb. We lifted the body. We stood it up against a rock. It seemed to stare at us out of its empty socket. We sounded his hollow frame.

After some moments' silence, the uncle gave way to the professor again. Otto Lidenbrock, reverting to character, forgot all the circumstances of our eventful journey, forgot where we were standing, forgot the vaulted cavern which held us. No doubt in his mind he was back again at the Johannaeum, lecturing to his pupils, for he adopted a professorial tone and, addressing himself to an imaginary audience, spoke as follows:

'Gentlemen, I have the honour to introduce to you a man of the Quaternary system. Eminent geologists have denied his existence, others no less eminent have affirmed it. The Doubting Thomases of palaeontology, if they were here, might now touch him with their fingers, and would be obliged to acknowledge their error. I am quite aware that science has to be on its guard with discoveries of this kind. I know what capital enterprising individuals like Barnum have made out of fossil men. I have heard the tale of Ajax's kneecap, of the supposed body of Orestes claimed to have been found by the Spartans, and of the body of Asterius, ten cubits long, that Pausanias speaks of. I have read the reports of the skeleton of Trapani, found in the fourteenth century, and which was at the time identified as that of Polyphemus; and the history of the giant unearthed in the sixteenth century near Palermo. You know as well as I do, gentlemen, the analysis made at Lucerne in 1577 of those huge bones which the celebrated Dr Felix Plater affirmed to be those of a giant nineteen feet high. I have gone through the treatises of Cassanion, and all those memoirs, pamphlets, assertions and rejoinders published respecting the skeleton of Teutobochus, the invader of Gaul, dug out of a sandpit in the Dauphiné in 1613. In the eighteenth century I would have stood up for Scheuchzer's pre-Adamite man against Peter Campet. I have held in my hands the pamphlet entitled *Giga*—'

Here my uncle encountered his unfortunate affliction – that of being unable to pronounce difficult words in public.

'The pamphlet entitled *Gigan*—'

He could get no further.

'*Giganteo*—'

It was no good. The unfortunate word would not come out. At the Johannaeum, there would have been laughter.

'*Gigantosteology*,' at last the Professor burst out, between two words which I shall not record here.

Then rushing on with renewed vigour and great animation:

'Yes, gentlemen, I know all these things, and more. I know that Cuvier and Blumenbach have recognized in these bones nothing more remarkable than the bones of the mammoth and other mammals of the Quaternary Period. But in the presence of this specimen, to doubt would be to insult science. There stands the body! You may see it, touch it. It is not a mere skeleton; it is an entire body, preserved for a purely anthropological purpose.'

I was wise enough not to contradict this startling assertion.

'If I could only wash it in a solution of sulphuric acid,' my uncle continued, 'I would be able to rid it of all the particles of earth and the shells with which it is encrusted. But I do not have that valuable solvent here with me. Yet, such as it is, the body will tell us its own wonderful story.'

Here the Professor took hold of the fossil skeleton, and handled it with the skill and dexterity of a showman.

'You see,' he said, 'that it is not six feet tall, and that we are still a long way away from the supposed race of giants. As for the family to which it belongs, it is evidently Caucasian. It is of the white race, our own. The skull of this fossil is a regular oval, or rather ovoid. It exhibits no prominent cheekbones, no projecting jaws. It presents no appearance of that prognathism which reduces the facial angle[31]. Measure that angle. It is nearly ninety degrees. But I will go further in my deductions, and I will affirm that this specimen of the human family is of the Japhetic race, which has since spread from the Indies to the Atlantic. Do not smile, gentlemen.'

Nobody was smiling, but the learned Professor was frequently disturbed by the broad smiles provoked by his learned eccentricities.

'Yes,' he pursued with animation, 'this is a fossil man, the contemporary of the mastodons whose remains fill this amphitheatre. But if you ask me how he came to be here, how those strata on which he was lying slipped down into this enormous hollow in the globe, I confess I cannot answer that question. No doubt in the Quaternary Period considerable movement was still disturbing the crust of the Earth. The long-continued cooling of the globe gave rise to chasms, fissures, clefts and faults, into which, very probably, portions of the upper earth may have fallen. I make no rash assertions, but there is the man surrounded by his own works, by hatchets, by carved flints, which are the characteristics of the Stone Age. And unless he came here, like myself, as a tourist on a visit and as a pioneer of science, I can entertain no doubt of the authenticity of his remote origin.'

The Professor stopped speaking, and his audience broke out into loud and unanimous applause. For, of course, my uncle was right, and wiser men than his nephew would have found it hard to refute his statements.

Another remarkable thing. This fossil body was not the only one in this immense catacomb. We came across other bodies at every step amongst the dust, and my uncle could have selected any of the most curious of these specimens to demolish the incredulity of sceptics.

In fact, it was an amazing sight, these generations of men and animals mingling in their common cemetery. Then one very serious question came to our minds which we scarcely dared consider. Had all those creatures slid through a great fissure in the crust of the Earth, down to the shores of the Lidenbrock Sea, when they were dead and turning to dust, or had they lived and grown and died here in this subterranean world under a false sky, just like inhabitants of the upper Earth? Until the present time the only creatures we had seen alive were sea monsters and fish. Might not some living being, some native of the abyss, still be found on these desolate shores?

CHAPTER 39

FOREST SCENERY ILLUMINATED BY ELECTRICITY

For another half hour, we walked over a carpet of bones. We pushed on, driven by our burning curiosity. What other marvels did this cavern contain? What new treasures lay here for science to unfold? I was prepared for any surprise; my imagination was ready for any eventuality, no matter how astounding.

We had long since lost sight of the seashore behind the hills of bones. The foolhardy Professor, unconcerned about losing his way, dragged me on and on. We walked in silence, bathed in luminous waves of electricity. By some phenomenon which I am unable to explain, it lit up all sides of every object to an equal extent. It was so diffuse, there being no central point from which the light emanated, that shadows no longer existed. You might have thought yourself under the rays of a vertical sun in a tropical region at midday in the height of summer. No vapour was visible. The rocks, the distant mountains, a few isolated clumps of forest trees in the distance, presented a weird and wonderful aspect under these totally new conditions of universal diffusion of light. We were like Hoffmann's shadowless man[32].

A mile further on, we reached the edge of a vast forest, but not one of those forests of fungi which bordered Port Gräuben. Here the vegetation was of the Tertiary Period in the fullest extent of its magnificence. Tall palm-trees belonging to species no longer living, other splendid palm-like trees, firs, yews, cypresses, thujas, representatives of the conifers, were linked together by a tangled network of creepers. A soft carpet of mosses and liverworts clothed the soil luxuriously. A few sparkling streams ran almost in silence under what would have been the shade of the trees, except that there was no shadow. On their banks grew tree-ferns similar to those we grow in hothouses. But a remarkable feature was the total absence of colour in all those trees, shrubs and plants, growing without the life-giving heat and light of the sun. They all merged together in a uniform brownish colour like that of fading and faded leaves. Not a green leaf anywhere, and the flowers – which were abundant enough in the Tertiary period, which first gave birth to flowers – looked like brown-paper cut-outs, with neither colour nor scent.

Uncle Lidenbrock ventured into this colossal grove. I followed him, not without some apprehension. Since nature had provided plant nourishment here, why shouldn't there be fierce animals there too? In the broad clearings left by fallen trees, decayed with age, I could see leguminous plants, Acerinae, Rubiaceae and many other edible shrubs dear to ruminant animals of every period. Then I observed, mingling together in confusion, trees of countries far separated on the surface of the globe. The oak and the palm were growing side by side, the Australian eucalyptus leaned against the Norwegian pine, the birch-tree of the north mingled its foliage with New Zealand kauris. It was enough to drive the most ingenious classifier of terrestrial botany to distraction.

Suddenly I stopped. I held my uncle back.

The diffused light made it easy to make out even the smallest of objects in the dense thickets. I thought I could see – no! I *did* see, with my own eyes, enormous forms moving among the trees. They were gigantic animals, a herd of mastodons – not fossil remains but alive and resembling the ones whose bones were found in the marshes of Ohio in 1801. I could see those huge elephants under the trees with their trunks writhing like a host of serpents. I could hear the crashing noise of their long ivory tusks boring into the old decaying trunks. Branches were cracking, and the leaves that were torn away in cartloads were going down the monsters' cavernous throats.

So, then, the dream in which I had had a vision of the prehistoric world of the Tertiary and Quaternary Periods had become a reality. And there we were alone, in the bowels of the Earth, at the mercy of its wild inhabitants!

My uncle was gazing at the scene with intense and eager interest.

'Come on!' said he, seizing my arm. 'Let's take a closer look!'

'No, I won't!' I cried. 'We don't have any guns. What could we do in the middle of a herd of these four-footed giants? Come on, Uncle, let's just get away. No human being could safely risk upsetting these monstrous beasts.'

'No human creature?' replied my uncle in a lower voice. 'You're wrong, Axel. Look, look down there! I fancy I see a living creature similar to ourselves: it's a man!'

I looked, shaking my head incredulously. But though at first I couldn't believe it, I had to yield to the evidence of my senses.

In fact, about a quarter of a mile away, leaning against the trunk of a gigantic kauri, stood a human being, the Proteus[33] of those subterranean regions, a new son of Neptune, watching this countless herd of mastodons:

Immanis pecoris custos, immanior ipse.[34]

Immanior ipse? Yes, truly more gigantic. We were no longer dealing with a fossil being like the man whose dried remains we had easily lifted up in the field of bones. This fellow was a giant, well able to control those monsters. In stature he was at least twelve feet tall. His head, as big as a buffalo's, was half hidden in the thick, tangled growth of his unkempt hair. It most resembled the mane of the primitive elephant. In his hand he held an enormous branch, a crook worthy of this antediluvian shepherd.

We stood there, petrified and speechless with amazement. But what if he saw us? We had to get away!

'Come on, Uncle, run for it!' I said, dragging my uncle away. For once he allowed himself to be persuaded.

In quarter of an hour our feet had carried us beyond the reach of this terrifying monster.

And yet, now that I can consider the matter quietly, now that I am calm again, now that months have slipped by since this strange and supernatural meeting, what am I to think? What am I to believe? I have to conclude that the whole thing was impossible, that our senses were deceived, that our eyes didn't see what we thought they saw. No human beings live in this subterranean world, no human race lives in those deep caverns of the globe, unknown to and unconnected with the inhabitants of its surface. It would be crazy to think they did.

I prefer to think that it might have been some animal whose structure resembled that of humans, some ape or baboon of the early geological ages, some Protopithecus or Mesopithecus like the one discovered by Lartet in the deposit of bones at Sansan. But this creature was far larger than any known to modern palaeontology. No matter, it had to be an ape, yes, definitely an ape, improbable as that might be. That a human being, a living person, and therefore no doubt a whole race of humans besides him, should be entombed there in the bowels of the Earth, was impossible.

Meanwhile, we had left the clear, brightly lit forest, speechless with astonishment, overwhelmed with a stupefaction which reduced us almost to the level of dumb animals. We kept on running for fear that the horrible monster might be on our trail. We really were fleeing; it was just like the feeling of being driven along in spite of oneself that one often experiences in nightmares. Instinctively we made our way back to the Lidenbrock Sea, and I cannot say into what wandering thoughts my mind might have carried me but for a circumstance which brought me back to practical matters.

Although I was certain that we were now walking on ground never before trodden by our feet, I often noticed groups of rocks which reminded me of those around Port Gräuben. Besides, this seemed to confirm the indications of the compass needle, and to show that we had unintentionally returned to the north shore of the Lidenbrock Sea. Occasionally I felt quite sure about it. Brooks and waterfalls were tumbling everywhere from projections in the rocks. I thought I recognized the bed of *surtarbrandur*, our faithful Hans's Brook and the grotto in which I had regained life and consciousness. Then a few paces farther on, the arrangement of the cliffs, the appearance of an unrecognized stream or the strange outline of a rock, threw me into doubt again.

I expressed my doubts to my uncle. Like me, he wasn't sure. He didn't recognize anything in this unvarying landscape.

'It seems clear,' I said, 'that we haven't landed at our original starting-point, but the storm has carried us a little further up, and if we follow the shore we'll find Port Gräuben.'

'If that's the case, it'll be useless to continue our exploration, and we'd better return to our raft. But, Axel, could you be mistaken?'

'It's difficult to be sure, Uncle, because all these rocks are so very much alike. But I think I recognize the promontory where Hans built our boat. We must be very near the little port, if indeed this is not it,' I added, examining a creek which I thought I recognized.

'No, Axel, we would at least find our own tracks and I can't see anything . . .'

'But I can see something,' I exclaimed, darting towards an object lying on the sand.

And I showed my uncle a rusty dagger which I had just picked up.

'Come on, now,' he said. 'Were you carrying this weapon with you?'

'Me? No, certainly not! But were you perhaps . . .'

'Not as far as I know,' said the Professor. 'I'm not aware of ever having had this object in my possession.'

'Well, this is strange!'

'No, Axel, it's very simple. Icelanders often carry weapons of this sort. This must belong to Hans, and he's lost it.'

I shook my head. Hans had never had an object like this on him either.

'Might it not have belonged to some pre-Adamite warrior,' I exclaimed, 'to some living man, contemporary with the gigantic herdsman? But no, it can't be. This is not a relic of the Stone Age. It's not even from the Bronze Age. This blade is made of steel . . .'

My uncle stopped me abruptly on this path that my new train of thought was leading me down, and said in a cold voice:

'Calm down, Axel, and see sense. This dagger dates from the sixteenth century; it's a poniard, such as gentlemen carried in their belts to give the *coup de grace*. It's of Spanish origin. It was never yours, or mine, or the hunter's, nor did it belong to any of those human beings who may or may not inhabit this inner world. Look, it was never made jagged like this by cutting men's throats. Its blade is coated with rust that is neither a day, nor a year, nor even a hundred years old.'

The Professor was as usual getting excited and allowing his imagination to run away with him.

'Axel, we're on the way to a great discovery. This blade has been lying on the shore for a hundred years, two hundred years, three hundred years, and has become chipped and notched on the rocks that surround this subterranean sea!'

'But it hasn't got here on its own. And it hasn't got bent like that on its own. Someone has been here before us!

'Yes, some man has.'

'And who was that man?'

'A man who has engraved his name somewhere with that dagger. A man who wanted to mark once again the way to the centre of the Earth. Let's have a look around.'

And our interest now well aroused, we searched all along the high wall, looking into every fissure which might open out into a gallery.

And in this way we came to a place where the shore was much narrower. Here the sea lapped the foot of the steep cliff, leaving a passage no more than a couple of yards wide. Between two projecting rocks appeared the mouth of a dark tunnel.

There, on a granite slab, were two mysterious carved letters, half eaten away by time. They were the initials of the bold and daring traveller:

'A S,' shouted my uncle. 'Arne Saknussemm! Arne Saknussemm again!'

CHAPTER 40

PREPARATIONS FOR BLASTING A PASSAGE TO THE CENTRE OF THE EARTH

Since the start of our journey, I had been astonished so often that I might well be excused for thinking myself well inured to surprises. Yet at the sight of these two letters, engraved on this spot three hundred years ago, I just stood there in dumb amazement. Not only were the initials of the learned alchemist visible on the living rock, but I was actually holding the tool with which the letters had been carved. Unless I was totally dishonest with myself, I could no longer doubt the existence of that amazing traveller and the fact of his unparalleled journey.

Whilst these thoughts were spinning round in my head, Professor Lidenbrock had launched into a somewhat rhapsodical eulogy, of which Arne Saknussemm was, of course, the hero.

'You great genius!' he cried. 'You didn't forget anything that would serve to lay open to other mortals the road through the terrestrial crust, and your fellow men may even now, three centuries later, once again trace your footsteps through these dark underground passages. You intended that other eyes besides your own should look on these wonders. Your name, carved on each stage of the journey, leads the bold follower in your footsteps to the very centre of our planet's core, and there again we shall find your name written with your own hand. I too will inscribe my name on this dark granite page. But henceforth let this cape that you discovered be known by your own illustrious name – Cape Saknussemm.'

Those, or something like them, were the glowing words I heard, and I felt myself inspired by their enthusiasm. An inner fire was kindled afresh in me. I forgot everything, both the past perils of the journey and the dangers to come during our return. What another man had done, I reckoned we too might do, and no human endeavour seemed impossible to me.

'Forward! Forward!' I cried.

I was already making for the gloomy tunnel when the Professor stopped me. Usually the impulsive one, it was he who was counselling patience and calmness.

'Let's first go back to Hans,' he said, 'and bring the raft to this spot.'

I obeyed, not without displeasure, and slipped between among the rocks on the shore.

'You know, Uncle,' I said, 'it seems to me that events have been amazingly kind to us up till now.'

'Do you think so, Axel?'

'No doubt about it. Even the storm carried us in the right direction. Bless that storm! It brought us back to this coast while fine weather would have taken us far away. Just suppose our prow (is there a prow on a raft?) had touched the southern shore of the Lidenbrock Sea, what would have become of us? We would never have seen the name of Saknussemm, and we would at this moment be stranded on a rocky, impassable coast.'

'Yes, Axel, it is quite providential that, while thinking we were heading south, we should simply have come back north and arrived at Cape Saknussemm. I must say it is astonishing, and I can think of no way to explain it.'

'What does that matter, Uncle? Our business is not to explain facts, but to use them!'

'Certainly, but . . .'

'But now we're going to head north again, and to pass below the countries of northern Europe – Sweden, Russia, Siberia, who knows where? – instead of burrowing under the deserts of Africa or perhaps the waves of the Atlantic, and that's all I need to know.'

'Yes, Axel, you're right. It's all for the best, since we have left that weary, horizontal sea, which was leading us nowhere. Now we shall go down, down, and further down! Do you know, it's now only 1,500 leagues to the centre of the globe.'

'Is that all?' I cried. 'Why, that's nothing. Let's make a start, then! Let's go!'

This crazy conversation was still going on when we met the hunter. Everything was made ready for our immediate departure. All our bags and packs were put on board. We took our places, and with our sail set, Hans steered us along the coast to Cape Saknussemm.

A raft is not designed for sailing close to the wind. The wind we had was unfavourable and in many places we had to push ourselves along with our iron-pointed sticks. Often sunken rocks just beneath the surface forced us to deviate from a straight course. Finally, after sailing for three hours, about six in the evening we reached a place suitable for landing. I jumped ashore, followed by my uncle and the Icelander. This short journey had in no way dampened my enthusiasm. On the contrary, I even suggested 'burning our boats', that is to say, our raft, to prevent the possibility of turning back, but my uncle would not agree to it. I thought him remarkably lukewarm.

'At least,' I said, 'let's not waste a minute before setting off.'

'Yes, yes, my boy,' he replied, 'but first let's examine this new gallery to see if we'll need our ladders.'

My uncle switched on his Ruhmkorff's apparatus. The raft, moored to the shore, was left to itself. The mouth of the tunnel was not twenty yards from us, and our party, with myself at the head, made for it without a moment's delay.

The opening, which was almost circular, was about five feet in diameter. The dark passage had been cut through the living rock and smoothed down by the eruptive matter which had formerly issued from it. The inside was level with the ground outside, so we were able to enter the passage without difficulty. We were following an almost horizontal path when, only six yards in, our progress was blocked by an enormous rock.

'Damn this rock!' I shouted angrily, finding myself suddenly confronted by an impassable obstacle.

We searched in vain for a way past, up and down, side to side, to the right and to the left; there was no way of progressing further. I was bitterly disappointed, and could not accept the existence of such an obstacle to our plans. I looked underneath the block: no opening. Above: just more granite. In vain Hans shone his lamp over every part of the barrier. We were being forced to give up all hope of passing it.

I sat down in despair. My uncle walked up and down the narrow passage.

'But how did Saknussemm do it?' I cried.

'Exactly,' said my uncle. 'Was he stopped by this stone barrier?'

'No, no,' I replied fervently. 'This piece of rock has been shaken down by some shock or convulsion or by one of those magnetic storms which disturb these regions, and has now blocked up the passage which lay open to him. Many years elapsed between Saknussemm's return to the surface and this huge rock blocking the path. Isn't it obvious that this gallery was once open to the lava flow, and that at that time there must have been free movement along it? Look, there are recent cracks grooving the granite ceiling. This roof itself is formed of fragments of rock that were carried along; it consists of enormous stones, as if some giant's hand laboured to build it. But at some time the downward pressure was greater than usual, and this block, like the falling keystone of a ruined arch, has slipped down to the ground and blocked the way. It's only a chance obstruction, not met with by Saknussemm, and if we can't destroy it we don't deserve to reach the centre of the Earth.'

Such was my opinion! The soul of the Professor had passed into me. The spirit of discovery wholly possessed me. I forgot the past, I scorned the future. I gave not a thought to the things on the surface of this globe into which I had dived: its cities and its sunny plains, Hamburg and the Königstrasse, even poor Gräuben, who must have given us up for lost, all were for the time being dismissed from the pages of my memory.

'Right,' exclaimed my uncle, 'let's make a way through with our pickaxes.'

'It's too hard for pickaxes.'

'Well, then, with the spades.'

'That would take us too long.'

'What, then?'

'Why, gunpowder, of course! Let's mine the obstacle and blow it up.'

'Blow it up?'

'Yes, why not? It's only a bit of rock that needs blasting.'

'Hans, to work!' shouted my uncle.

The Icelander returned to the raft and soon came back with a pickaxe which he used to make a hole for the charge. This was no easy task. It required a hole large enough to hold fifty pounds of guncotton, whose explosive force is four times that of gunpowder.

I was almost beside myself with excitement. While Hans was at work, I was helping my uncle prepare a slow match of wetted powder wrapped in linen.

'This will do the trick,' I said.

'It certainly will,' replied my uncle.

By midnight our mining preparations were complete. The charge was rammed into the hole, and the slow match uncoiled along the gallery, with its end outside the opening.

A spark would now be enough to set the whole device off.

'Tomorrow,' said the Professor.

I had to resign myself to waiting six long hours.

CHAPTER 41

THE GREAT EXPLOSION AND THE RUSH DOWN BELOW

The next day, Thursday, the 27th of August, was an important date in our subterranean journey. I never think of it without a shudder of horror that makes my heart pound. From that time on, we had no further opportunity to use our reason or judgement or skill or ingenuity. Henceforth we were to be carried along, the playthings of the fierce elements of the deep.

At six o'clock, we were up and about. The moment had come for us to clear a path for ourselves by blasting through the mass of granite that was blocking our way.

I begged the honour of lighting the fuse. This done, I was to join my companions on the raft, which had not yet been unloaded. We would then push out to sea as far as we could and avoid the dangers that would arise from the explosion, the effects of which were not likely to be confined to the rock itself.

The fuse was calculated to burn for ten minutes before setting off the explosive, so I had time enough to escape to the raft.

I got ready to carry out my task, not without some anxiety.

After a hasty meal, my uncle and the hunter embarked on the raft while I remained on shore. I was equipped with a burning lantern with which to set fire to the fuse.

'Now, on you go,' said my uncle, 'and come back to us immediately.'

'Don't worry,' I replied. 'I'll not stop to play on the way.'

I went at once to the mouth of the tunnel. I opened my lantern. I took hold of the end of the match. The Professor stood, chronometer in hand.

'Ready?' he cried.

'Ready.'

'Light it!'

I immediately plunged the end of the fuse into the lantern. It spluttered and burst into flame, and I ran back to the raft at top speed.

'Get on board quickly, and let's shove off.'

Hans, with a vigorous thrust, pushed us away from the shore. The raft shot forty yards out to sea.

It was a moment of intense excitement. The Professor was watching the hand of the chronometer.

'Five minutes to go!' he said. 'Four! . . . Three! . . .'

My pulse was beating every half second.

'Two! . . . One! . . . Down you go, you mountain of granite, you!'

What happened then? I don't think I actually heard the dull roar of the explosion. But the rocks suddenly took on a new shape: they separated like curtains. I saw a bottomless pit open up on the shore. The sea, lashed into a sudden fury, rose up in an enormous billow, on the ridge of which our unfortunate raft was lifted bodily in the air with all its crew and cargo.

All three of us were thrown down flat. In less than a second we were in deep, impenetrable darkness. Then I felt as if the raft, not just me, had nothing supporting it. I thought it was sinking, but it wasn't. I tried to speak to my uncle, but the roaring of the waves prevented him from hearing even the sound of my voice.

In spite of the darkness and noise, and my astonishment and terror, I understood what had happened.

On the other side of the blown-up rock, there was an abyss. The explosion had caused a kind of earthquake in this fissure-ridden region, a great chasm had opened up, and the sea, now changed into a torrent, was rushing us along into it.

I gave myself up for lost.

An hour passed – two hours, perhaps; I can't be sure. We clung to each other to stop ourselves being thrown off the raft. We felt a violent shock whenever we were thrown against projecting rocks. However, these shocks were not very frequent, from which I concluded that the gully was widening. It was no doubt the same road that Saknussemm had taken, but instead of walking peacefully down it as he had done, we were taking a whole sea along with us.

These ideas, you understand, presented themselves to my mind in a vague and undetermined form. I had difficulty in putting any thoughts together during this headlong race, which seemed like a vertical descent. To judge by the air which was whistling past me and making a whizzing noise in my ears, we were moving faster than the fastest express train. To light a torch under these conditions would have been impossible, and our last electrical lighting-apparatus had been shattered by the force of the explosion.

I was therefore very surprised to see a clear light shining near me. It lit up Hans's calm face. The skilful huntsman had succeeded in lighting the lantern, and although it flickered so much that it nearly went out, it threw a fitful light across the awful darkness.

I was right in my supposition. It was a wide gallery. The dim light could not show us both its walls at once. The fall of the waters which were carrying us away exceeded that of the swiftest rapids in American rivers. Its surface seemed to consist of a sheaf of arrows hurled with inconceivable force; I cannot convey my impressions by a better comparison. The raft, occasionally seized by an eddy, spun round as it flew along. When it approached the walls of the gallery, I lit them up with the light of the lantern, and I could more or less judge just how fast we were moving by noticing how the jagged projections of the rocks spun into endless ribbons and bands, so that we seemed to be held within a network of shifting lines. I reckoned we must be travelling at thirty leagues per hour.

My uncle and I looked at each other with haggard eyes, clinging to the stump of the mast, which had snapped off at the first shock of our great catastrophe. We kept our backs to the wind, so as not to be suffocated by the rapidity of a movement which no human power could restrain.

Hours passed. No change in our situation. But then I discovered something that complicated matters and made them even worse than we thought.

Attempting to put our cargo into somewhat better order, I found that the greater part of the articles we had loaded on to the raft had disappeared at the moment of the explosion, when the sea broke in on us with such violence. I wanted to know exactly what we had saved, and with the lantern in my hand I began to check. Of our instruments, none were saved except the compass and the chronometer; our stock of ropes and ladders was reduced to the bit of cord rolled round the stump of the mast. Not a spade, not a pickaxe, not a hammer remained; and – a disaster we could least cope with – we had only one day's provisions left.

I searched in every crack and cranny on the raft. There was nothing else there. Our provisions were reduced to one bit of salt meat and a few biscuits.

I stared at the remains of our supplies blankly. My mind could not take in the seriousness of our loss. And yet what was the use of worrying about it? Even if we'd had provisions enough to last for months, or even years, how were we to get out of the abyss into which we were being hurled by this irresistible torrent? Why should we fear the horrors of starvation, when death was swooping down upon us in a multitude of other forms? Would we actually survive long enough to starve to death?

However, by some inexplicable trick of the mind I forgot my present dangers to contemplate the menacing horrors still to come. In any case, was there still a chance that we might escape the fury of this rushing torrent and return to the surface of the globe? How? I had no idea. Where? It wouldn't matter. But one chance in a thousand is still a chance, whilst contemplating death from starvation left us no hope at all.

I considered telling my uncle the whole truth, showing him the dreadful straits to which we were reduced, and calculating how long we might expect to live. But I had the courage to stay silent. I wanted to leave him calm and under control.

At that moment, the light from our lantern slowly dimmed and then went out. The wick had burnt itself out. Black night reigned again; and there was no hope left of our being able to dissipate a darkness we could almost feel. We still had one torch left, but we couldn't have kept it lit. Like a child, I closed my eyes firmly, so as not to see the darkness.

After quite some time, our speed increased. I could tell by the way the currents of air were blowing into my face. The descent became steeper. I thought we were no longer slipping down, but falling down. I had the impression we were dropping vertically. My uncle's hand, and the strong arm of Hans, held me tightly.

Suddenly, after a period of time I couldn't measure, I felt a shock. The raft hadn't collided with something hard but had suddenly been checked in its fall. A waterspout, an immense column of liquid, rained down on it. I was suffocating, I was drowning . . .

But this sudden flood didn't last long. In a few seconds, I found myself in air again, which I inhaled to the fullest extent of my lungs. My uncle and Hans were still holding me firmly by my arms, and the raft was still carrying us along.

CHAPTER 42

HEADLONG SPEED UPWARD THROUGH THE HORRORS OF DARKNESS

It must have been, I reckon, about ten o'clock at night. The first of my senses which came into play after this latest assault was my hearing. All at once I could hear – and it really was something to hear: I could hear the silence in the gallery after the din which for hours had stunned me. Eventually these words of my uncle's came to me as a vague murmur:

'We're ascending.'

'What do you mean?' I cried.

'We're going up, we're going up!'

I stretched out my arm. I touched the wall, and pulled back my hand. It was bleeding. We were climbing extremely quickly.

'The torch! Light the torch!' shouted the Professor.

Not without some difficulty, Hans managed to light the torch, and the flame, rising on the wick in spite of our rapid ascent, threw out enough light to show us what kind of a place we were in.

'Just as I thought,' said the Professor. 'We're in a narrow shaft not twenty-four feet wide. The water had reached the bottom of the gulf. Now it's rising to find its level, and is carrying us with it.'

'Where to?'

'I've no idea, but we must be ready for anything. We're rising at a speed which I would estimate at twelve feet per second, which makes 720 feet per minute or a little over eight miles an hour. At that speed we could go far.'

'Yes, if nothing stops us, and if this shaft has a way out. But supposing it's blocked. If the air is condensed by the pressure of this column of water, we'll be crushed.'

'Axel,' replied the Professor with perfect calmness, 'our situation is almost desperate, but there are some possibilities of deliverance, and it is these that I'm considering. If at any moment we may perish, so equally at any moment we might be saved. So let's be prepared to grasp even the slightest opportunity.'

'But what will we do now?'

'Recover our strength by eating.'

At these words I fixed a haggard eye on my uncle. The unpleasant truth I had been so unwilling to confess now at last had to be told.

'Eat, did you say?'

'Yes, at once.'

The Professor added a few words in Danish, but Hans shook his head mournfully.

'What!' cried my uncle. 'Have we lost our provisions?'

'Yes. Here is all we have left – one bit of salt meat for the three of us.'

My uncle stared at me as if he couldn't understand what I was saying.

'Well,' I said, 'do you still think we've any chance of being saved?'

My question remained unanswered.

An hour passed. I began to feel the pangs of violent hunger. My companions were suffering too, and not one of us dared touch the wretched remains of our once plentiful store.

But now we were climbing at great speed. Sometimes the air would stop us breathing, as happens to aeronauts who ascend too rapidly. But whereas they suffer from cold in proportion to their ascent, we were beginning to feel the opposite effect. The heat was increasing in a way that was causing us great anxiety; by now the temperature was certainly up around 40°.

What could such a change mean? Up to this point, the evidence had supported the theories of Davy and Lidenbrock. Until now, the particular conditions of non-conducting rocks, of electricity and of magnetism, had tempered the general laws of nature, giving us only a moderately warm climate – for the theory of a central fire remained to my mind the only one that was true and explicable. Were we then heading to where the phenomena of central heat ruled in all their rigour and would reduce the most solid of rocks to a state of molten liquid? I feared so, and said as much to the Professor:

'If we aren't drowned, or shattered to pieces, or starved to death, there's still the possibility that we'll be burned alive and reduced to ashes.'

At this, he shrugged his shoulders and returned to his own thoughts.

Another hour passed, and, except for some slight increase in the temperature, nothing new happened.

'Right,' he said, 'we have a decision to make.'

'A decision about what?' I said.

'We must keep our strength up. If we ration our food in order to try to prolong our existence by a few hours, we will simply continue to be very weak right to the end.'

'And the end is not far off.'

'So, if there is any chance of us saving ourselves, if a moment for active exertion presents itself, where will we find the strength we need if we allow ourselves to be weakened by hunger?'

'Well, uncle, when we have eaten this bit of meat, what'll we have left?'

'Nothing, Axel, nothing at all. But will it do you any more good to devour it with your eyes than with your teeth? Your thinking is that of a man with neither sense nor spirit.'

'But aren't you in despair?' I shouted irritably.

'No, certainly not,' was the Professor's firm reply.

'What? Do you think there is still some chance of being saved?'

'Yes, I do. So long as one's heart beats, so long as body and soul stay together, I cannot agree that any creature endowed with a will need despair of life.'

Resolute words, these! The man who could speak in such a way, under such circumstances, was no ordinary man.

'Well, then, what do you mean to do?' I asked.

'Eat what is left to the very last crumb, and restore our fading strength. This meal will perhaps be our last. So be it, then! But at any rate we shall once more be men, and not exhausted, empty bags.'

'Right, let's eat it then,' I exclaimed.

My uncle picked up the piece of meat and the few biscuits which had escaped the general destruction. He divided them into three equal portions and gave one to each of us. This made about a pound of food each. The Professor ate his greedily, with a sort of feverish rage; I ate without pleasure, almost with disgust; Hans quietly, moderately, chewing his small mouthfuls without any noise, and relishing them with the calmness of a man above all anxiety about the future. Searching carefully, he had found a flask of gin; this he offered to us each in turn, and this generous beverage cheered us up slightly.

'*Förtrafflig*,' said Hans, drinking in his turn.

'Excellent,' replied my uncle.

A glimpse of hope had returned, although without good reason. But our last meal was over, and it was now five in the morning.

Human beings are so constituted that health is a purely negative state. Hunger once satisfied, it is difficult for a man to imagine the horrors of starvation; they cannot be understood without being felt.

So it was that, after our long fast, these few mouthfuls of meat and biscuit triumphed over our previous troubles.

But as soon as the meal was over, we each of us fell deep in thought. What was Hans thinking of – that man of the far West who nevertheless seemed to be guided by the fatalist doctrines of the East?

As for me, my thoughts consisted of memories, and they carried me up to the surface of the globe which I ought never to have left. The house in the Königstrasse, my poor dear Gräuben, that kind soul Martha, flitted like visions before my eyes, and in the dismal rumblings that were from time to time coming through the rock, I thought I could distinguish the roar of the traffic of the great cities above me on the Earth.

My uncle was still concentrating on his work. Torch in hand, he tried to get some idea of our position by observing the strata. This calculation could, at best, be but a vague approximation, but a scientist is always a scientist if he succeeds in remaining calm, and assuredly Professor Lidenbrock possessed calmness to a surprising degree.

I could hear him muttering geological terms. I could understand them, and in spite of myself I felt interested in this final geological study.

'Eruptive granite,' he was saying. 'We're still in the Primitive Period. But we're going up, higher and higher. Who knows where?'

Yes, who knows where? With his hand he was examining the perpendicular wall, and in a few more minutes he continued:

'This is gneiss! Here is some mica schist! Ah! Soon we'll come to the Transition Period, and then . . .'

What did the Professor mean? Could he be trying to measure the thickness of the crust of the Earth that lay between us and the world above? Had he any means of making this calculation? No, he hadn't got the manometer, and no guesswork could make up for that.

The temperature kept on rising; it felt like we were in an oven. I could only compare it to the heat of a furnace at the moment when the molten metal is running into the mould. Bit by bit we had been forced to throw off our coats and waistcoats; the lightest covering became uncomfortable, even painful.

'Are we heading up into a fiery furnace?' I cried at one point when the heat was increasing rapidly.

'No,' replied my uncle, 'that's impossible, quite impossible!'

'But,' I answered, feeling the wall, 'this wall is burning hot.'

At the same moment, touching the water, I had to draw back my hand quickly.

'The water's scalding,' I cried.

This time the Professor's only answer was an angry gesture.

Then I was gripped by an overwhelming terror from which I could not free myself. I felt a catastrophe was approaching, something so awful that the boldest imagination could not conceive of it. A vague notion took hold of my mind, and was fast hardening into certainty. I tried to repel it, but it kept coming back. I didn't dare put it into words. Yet a few involuntary observations confirmed my thoughts. By the flickering light of the torch I could distinguish contortions in the granite strata. A phenomenon was unfolding in which electricity would play the principal part. And then there was this unbearable heat, this boiling water! I took a look at the compass.

It had gone crazy!

CHAPTER 43

SHOT OUT OF A VOLCANO AT LAST!

Yes, our compass was no longer a guide to our movements. The needle was jumping from pole to pole in a kind of frenzy, it was rushing round the dial, it was spinning giddily backwards and forwards.

I knew quite well that, according to the most generally accepted theories, the mineral covering of the globe is never completely at rest. The changes brought about by the chemical decomposition of its component parts, the turbulence caused by great liquid torrents, and the magnetic currents, are continually tending to disturb it, even when the beings living on its surface imagine that all is quiet below. A phenomenon of this kind would therefore not have alarmed me greatly, or at any rate would not have given rise to dreadful apprehensions.

But other peculiar circumstances gradually revealed to me the true state of affairs. There were the explosions of increasing frequency and ever greater intensity. I could only compare them to the loud clatter of dozens of carts driven at full speed over cobblestones. There was a rumbling like interminable thunder.

Then the compass, that had been thrown out of action by the electric currents, confirmed my worst thoughts. The mineral crust of the globe was threatening to break up, the granite foundations were going to come together with a crash, the fissure through which we were being driven helplessly would be filled up, the space would be full of crushed fragments of rock, and we poor wretched mortals were going to be buried and annihilated in this terrible destruction.

'Uncle, Uncle' I cried, 'we're doomed now, utterly doomed!'

'What are you frightened about now?' was the calm reply. 'What's the matter with you?'

'The matter? Look at those shaking walls! Look at those quivering rocks. Don't you feel the burning heat? Don't you see how the water is boiling and bubbling? Are you blind to the dense vapours and steam that are growing thicker and denser with every minute? Look at the compass needle spinning. There's an earthquake coming.'

My uncle shook his head calmly.

'So,' he said, 'you think there's an earthquake coming?'

'I do.'

'Well, I think you're wrong.'

'What? Don't you recognize the signs?'

'Of an earthquake? No! I think it's something better than that.'

'What do you mean?'

'It's an eruption, Axel.'

'An eruption! Do you mean to say we're being carried up the shaft of a volcano?'

'I do believe we are,' said the indomitable Professor with an air of total self-possession, 'and it's the best thing that could possibly be happening to us under the circumstances.'

The best thing! Was my uncle completely mad? What did the man mean? And what was the point in making jokes at a time like this?

'What?' I shouted. 'Are we being carried upwards in an eruption? Fate has flung us here among burning lava, molten rocks, boiling water and all kinds of volcanic matter. We're going to be pitched out, expelled, tossed up, vomited, spat out high into the air, along with fragments of rock, showers of ashes and scoria, in the midst of a towering rush of smoke and flames. And you're saying it's the best thing that could happen to us?'

'Yes,' replied the Professor, looking at me over his spectacles, 'I can't see any other way of reaching the surface of the Earth.'

I will pass rapidly over the thousand ideas which went through my mind. My uncle was right, undoubtedly right, and never had he seemed to me more daring and more certain in his ideas than at this moment when he was calmly contemplating the possibility of being shot out of a volcano!

In the meantime, up we went. The night passed in continual ascent. The din and uproar around us became more and more intensified. I was stifled and stunned; I thought my last hour was approaching. And yet imagination is such a strong thing that even in this supreme hour I was preoccupied with strange and almost childish speculations. But I was the victim, not the master, of my own thoughts.

It was quite clear we were being rushed upwards on the crest of an eruptive wave. Beneath our raft were boiling waters, and under these the more sluggish lava was working its way up in a heated mass, together with hordes of fragments of rock which, when they arrived at the crater, would be flung out in all directions high and low. We were trapped in the shaft or chimney of some volcano. There was no doubt about that now.

But this time, instead of Snæfell, an extinct volcano, we were inside one that was fully active. I wondered, therefore, where this mountain could be, and what part of the world we were to be shot out into.

I had no doubt that it would be in some northern region. Before it had gone mad, the needle had never deviated from that direction. From Cape Saknussemm we had been carried due north for hundreds of leagues. Were we under Iceland again? Were we destined to be thrown up out of Hecla, or through another of the other seven fiery craters on that island? Within a radius of five hundred leagues to the west I could only remember on this parallel of latitude the not-well-known volcanoes on the north-east coast of America.

To the east there was only one at a latitude of 80 degrees north, the Esk in Jan Mayen Island, not far from Spitzbergen. Certainly there was no lack of craters, and there were some large enough to throw out a whole army! But I wanted to know which of them was to act as our exit from the interior world.

Towards morning, our ascent grew faster. If the heat was increasing, instead of diminishing, as we approached the surface of the globe, this was due to local causes alone, volcanic ones. The way we were moving left no doubt in my mind. An immense force, a force of hundreds of atmospheres, generated by the extreme pressure of confined vapours, was driving us irresistibly on. But to what countless dangers it exposed us!

Soon wild lights began to penetrate the vertical gallery which widened as we went up. To right and left I could see deep channels, like huge tunnels, out of which escaped dense volumes of smoke. Tongues of fire lapped the walls, which crackled and sputtered under the intense heat.

'Look, Uncle, look at that!' I shouted.

'That's all right, those are only sulphurous flames and vapours, which one must expect to see in an eruption. They're quite natural.'

'But suppose they envelop us?'

'But they won't envelop us.'

'We'll be suffocated.'

'We won't be suffocated at all. The gallery is widening, and if necessary, we shall abandon the raft, and creep into a crevice.'

'But what about the water, the rising water?'

'There is no more water, Axel, only a sort of lava paste which is carrying us up on its surface to the top of the crater.'

The liquid column had indeed disappeared, replaced by dense and still boiling eruptive matter of all kinds. The temperature was becoming unbearable. A thermometer exposed to this atmosphere would have indicated 150°. Perspiration streamed from my body. But for the rapidity of our ascent we would have been suffocated.

But the Professor gave up his idea of abandoning the raft, and it was a good thing he did. However roughly joined together, those planks afforded us firmer support than we could have found anywhere else.

About eight in the morning something new happened. The upward movement ceased. The raft lay motionless.

'What's happening?' I asked, shaken by this sudden halt as if by a shock.

'It's just a pause,' replied my uncle.

'Has the eruption stopped?' I asked.

'I hope not.'

I stood up and tried to look around me. Perhaps the raft itself, stopped in its course by a projection, was holding back the volcanic torrent. If that were the case, we would have to release it as soon as possible.

But it was not so. The blast of ashes, scoria and rubbish had stopped rising.

'Would the eruption stop?' I exclaimed.

'Ah!' said my uncle between his clenched teeth. 'That's what you're afraid of. But don't be alarmed, this pause can't last long. It's lasted five minutes now, and in a short time we'll resume our journey to the mouth of the crater.'

As he spoke, the Professor continued to consult his chronometer, and once again he was right in his forecast. The raft was soon pushed and driven forward with a rapid but irregular movement, which lasted about ten minutes and then stopped again.

'That's fine,' said my uncle. 'In another ten minutes we'll be off again. We've got an intermittent volcano here. It gives us time now and then to catch our breath.'

This was perfectly true. When the ten minutes were over, we started off again with even greater speed. We had to hold on tight to the planks of the raft so as not to be thrown off. Then once again the paroxysm was over.

I have since thought about this strange phenomenon without being able to explain it. At any rate it was clear that we were not in the main shaft of the volcano, but in a lateral gallery where there was some sort of counter-reaction.

How often this operation was repeated, I cannot say. All I know is, that at each fresh impulse we were hurled forward with much greater force, and it seemed as if we were mere projectiles. During the short pauses, we were stifled by the heat; whilst we were being thrown forward, the hot air almost stopped me breathing altogether. I thought for a moment how delightful it would be to find myself carried suddenly into the Arctic regions, with a temperature 30° below freezing point. My overheated brain conjured up visions of white plains of cool snow, where I might roll around and alleviate my feverish heat. Little by little my brain, weakened by so many constantly repeated shocks, seemed to be giving way altogether. But for the strong arm of Hans, I would more than once have had my head broken against the granite roof of our burning dungeon.

I have, therefore, no exact recollection of what took place during the hours that followed. I have a confused impression of continuous explosions, loud detonations, a general shaking of the rocks all around us, and of a spinning movement with which our raft was at one point whirled helplessly round. It rocked on the lava torrent, in the middle of a dense downpour of ashes. Snorting flames darted their fiery tongues at us. There were wild, fierce puffs of stormy wind from below, like the blasts of huge iron furnaces blowing out all at the same time. I caught a glimpse of the figure of Hans lit up by the fire. All I felt was what I imagine must be the feelings of an unfortunate criminal doomed to be blown apart at the mouth of a cannon, just before the shot is fired and flying limbs and rags of flesh and skin fill the quivering air and spatter the blood-stained ground.

CHAPTER 44

SUNNY LANDS IN THE BLUE MEDITERRANEAN

When I opened my eyes again, I felt the strong hand of our guide holding me by my belt. With the other arm, he was supporting my uncle. I was not seriously hurt, but I was shaken and battered and bruised all over. I found myself lying on the sloping side of a mountain only two yards from a gaping gulf, which would have swallowed me up had I leaned at all that way. Hans had saved me from death while I lay rolling on the edge of the crater.

'Where are we?' asked my uncle irascibly, as if he felt greatly put out by having landed on the surface of the Earth again.

The hunter shook his head in token of complete ignorance.

'Is it Iceland?' I asked.

'*Nej*,' replied Hans.

'What! Not Iceland?' cried the Professor.

'Hans must be mistaken,' I said, standing up.

This was our final surprise after all the astonishing events of our wonderful journey. I expected to see a white cone covered with the eternal snow of ages rising amidst the barren deserts of the icy north, faintly lit by the pale rays of the Arctic sun, far away in the highest latitudes known, but contrary to all our expectations, my uncle, the Icelander and myself were sitting half-way down a mountain baking under the burning rays of a southern sun, which was blistering us with its heat and blinding us with the fierce light of its nearly vertical rays.

I could not believe my own eyes, but the heated air and the sensation of burning left no room for doubt. We had come out of the crater half-naked, and the radiant orb to which we had been strangers for two months was lavishing on us from its blazing splendours more of its light and heat than we were able to receive with comfort.

When my eyes had become accustomed to the bright light to which they had been strangers for so long, I began to use them to put my imagination right. In my opinion, this had to be Spitzbergen, and I was in no mood to give up this notion.

The Professor was the first to speak, and said:

'Well, this isn't much like Iceland.'

'But is it Jan Mayen Island?' I asked.

'Nor that either,' he answered. 'This is no northern mountain. There are no granite peaks capped with snow here. Look, Axel, look!'

Above our heads, at a height of five hundred feet at the most, we saw the crater of a volcano, through which, at intervals of fifteen minutes or so, there issued with loud explosions lofty columns of fire, mingled with pumice stones, ashes and flowing lava. I could feel the heaving of the mountain, which seemed to breathe like a huge whale, and puff out fire and wind from its vast blowholes. Below, down a pretty steep slope, streams of lava ran for seven or eight hundred feet, meaning that the mountain couldn't be more than about 1,800 feet high. But the base of the mountain was hidden in a perfect bower of rich greenness, amongst which I was able to distinguish olive trees, fig trees and vines covered with luscious purple bunches.

I was forced to admit there was nothing of the Arctic here.

When my eye passed beyond these green surroundings, it fixed on a wide, blue expanse of sea or lake, which appeared to surround this enchanting island which was only a few leagues wide. To the east lay a pretty little white seaport town or village, with a few houses scattered around it, and in whose harbour a few vessels of peculiar rig were gently swayed by the softly swelling waves. Beyond it, groups of small islands rose from the smooth, blue waters, but in such numbers that they resembled ants on a huge ant-hill. To the west, distant coasts lined the dim horizon, on some of which rose blue mountains of smooth, undulating forms. On a more distant coast arose a huge cone crowned on its summit with a snowy plume of white cloud. To the north lay spread out a vast sheet of water, sparkling and dancing under the hot, bright rays, its uniformity broken here and there by the topmast of a gallant ship appearing above the horizon or a swelling sail moving slowly before the wind.

This unexpected sight was extremely charming to eyes long used to underground darkness.

'Where are we? Where are we?' I asked faintly.

Hans closed his eyes with complete indifference. My uncle looked round with dumb amazement.

'Well, whatever mountain this may be,' he said at last, 'it's very hot here. The explosions are continuing, and it would be pretty stupid to have come out on an eruption and then to get our heads smashed by bits of falling rock. Let's climb down. Then we'll have a better idea what we're about. Besides, I'm starving and parched with thirst.'

The Professor was definitely not given to idle contemplation. For my part, I could happily have forgotten my hunger and fatigue for another hour or two to enjoy the lovely scene in front of me, but I had to follow my companions.

The slope of the volcano was very steep in many places. We slid down screes of ashes, carefully avoiding the lava streams which glided sluggishly past us like fiery serpents. As we made our way, I chattered and asked all sorts of questions about our whereabouts, for I was far too excited not to talk a great deal.

'We're in Asia,' I exclaimed, 'on the coast of India, in the Malayan Islands or in Oceania. We've passed through half the globe and come out near the Antipodes.'

'But what about the compass?' said my uncle.

'Ah yes, the compass!' I said, greatly puzzled. 'According to the compass, we've gone north.'

'Has it lied?'

'Surely not. Could it lie?'

'Unless, indeed, this is the North Pole!'

'Oh, no, it's not the Pole, but . . .'

Well, here was something that baffled us completely. I didn't know what to say.

By now we were coming into that delightful greenery, and I was suffering a lot from hunger and thirst. Fortunately, after two hours of walking, a charming countryside lay open before us, covered with olive trees, pomegranate trees and delicious vines, all of which seemed to belong to anybody who liked to claim them. Besides, in our state of destitution and famine we were not likely to be choosy. Oh, the inexpressible pleasure of pressing those cool, sweet fruits to our lips, and eating grapes by mouthfuls off the rich, full bunches! Not far off, in the grass, under the delightful shade of the trees, I discovered a spring of fresh, cool water, in which we bathed our faces, hands and feet voluptuously.

While we were thus enjoying our much-needed rest, a child appeared out of a grove of olive trees.

'Look!' I exclaimed. 'Here's an inhabitant of this happy land!'

It was only a poor boy, miserably ill-clad, a sufferer from poverty, and our appearance seemed to alarm him a great deal. Naturally, only half-clothed and with ragged hair and beards, we were a suspicious-looking group, and if the people of the country knew anything about thieves, we were very likely to frighten them.

Just as the poor little wretch was going to take to his heels, Hans caught hold of him, and brought him to us, kicking and struggling.

My uncle began to encourage him as well as he could, and said to him in good German:

'What is this mountain called, my little friend?'

The child made no reply.

'All right,' said my uncle. 'I infer that we're not in Germany.'

He put the same question in English.

We got no further forward. I was very puzzled.

'Is the child dumb?' exclaimed the Professor, who, proud of his knowledge of many languages, now tried French.

Still silence.

'Now let's try Italian,' said my uncle:

'*Dove noi siamo?*'

'Yes, where are we?' I repeated impatiently.

But there was still no answer.

'Will you speak when you are told!' exclaimed my uncle, shaking the urchin by the ears. '*Come si noma questa isola?*'[35]

'Stromboli,' replied the little herdboy, slipping out of Hans's hands and running through the olive trees down to the plain.

We'd hardly been thinking of that possibility. Stromboli! What an effect this unexpected name had on my mind! We were in the middle of the Mediterranean Sea, on an island of the Aeolian archipelago, on the ancient Strongyle[36] where the god Aeolus kept the winds and storms chained up, to be let loose at his will. And those distant blue mountains in the east were the mountains of Calabria. And that threatening volcano far away in the south was fierce Etna.

'Stromboli! Stromboli!' I kept repeating.

My uncle accompanied my exclamations by clapping his hands and stamping his feet, as well as echoing my words. We seemed to be chanting in chorus!

What a journey we had accomplished! How fantastic! Having entered by one volcano, we had issued from another more than two thousand miles from Snæfell and barren, faraway Iceland! The strange fortunes of our expedition had carried us into the heart of the most beautiful part of the world. We had exchanged the bleak regions of perpetual snow and impenetrable barriers of ice for those of brightness and 'the rich hues of all glorious things'[37]. Over our heads we had left the murky sky and cold fogs of the frigid zone to revel under the azure sky of Italy!

After our delicious meal of fruit and cold, clear water, we set off again to reach the port of Stromboli. It would not have been wise to explain how we had arrived there. The superstitious Italians would have put us down as firedevils vomited out of hell. So we presented ourselves in the humble guise of shipwrecked mariners. It was not so glorious, but it was safer.

On my way I could hear my uncle murmuring: 'But the compass! That compass! It pointed due north. How are we to explain that?'

'My opinion is,' I replied disdainfully, 'that it's best not to explain it. That's the easiest way to deal with the problem.'

'Indeed, sir? The occupant of a professorial chair at the Johannaeum unable to explain the reason for some cosmic phenomenon? Why, that would be simply disgraceful!'

And as he spoke, my uncle, only half dressed, in rags, looking a perfect scarecrow, with his leather belt around him, settling his spectacles on his nose and looking learned and imposing, was himself again, the formidable German professor of mineralogy.

One hour after we had left the grove of olives, we arrived at the little port of San Vicenzo, where Hans claimed his thirteenth week's wages, which was counted out to him with cordial handshakes all round.

At that moment, if he didn't share our very natural emotions, at least his expression changed in a way very unusual with him, and while he lightly pressed our hands with his fingertips, I do believe he smiled.

CHAPTER 45

ALL'S WELL THAT ENDS WELL

Such is the conclusion of a story which I cannot expect everybody to believe, since some people will believe nothing against the testimony of their own experience. However, I'm indifferent to their incredulity, and they may believe as much or as little as they please.

The people of Stromboli received us kindly as shipwrecked mariners. They gave us food and clothing. After we had waited forty-eight hours, on the 31st of August a small craft took us to Messina, where a few days' rest completely removed the effect of our exhaustion.

On Friday the 4th of September, we embarked on the steamer *Volturno*, in the service of the French Imperial Messenger Service, and in three days we were in Marseilles, with nothing to bother us except that infernal lying compass, which we had mislaid somewhere and could not now examine. But its inexplicable behaviour occupied my mind terribly. On the evening of the 9th of September, we arrived in Hamburg.

I cannot describe to you Martha's astonishment or Gräuben's joy.

'Now you're a hero, Axel,' my blushing fiancée said to me, 'you won't leave me again!'

I looked at her tenderly, and she smiled through her tears.

How can I describe the extraordinary sensation caused by the return of Professor Lidenbrock? Thanks to Martha's gossiping, the news that the Professor had gone off to find a way to the centre of the Earth had spread over the whole civilized world. People refused to believe it, and when they saw him they would not believe him any the more. Nonetheless, the appearance of Hans and sundry pieces of intelligence gained from Iceland, tended to shake the confidence of the unbelievers.

Then my uncle became a great man, and I was now the nephew of a great man – which is a privilege not to be despised.

Hamburg gave a grand banquet in our honour. The Professor gave a public lecture at the Johannaeum, in which he described everything about our expedition, with only one omission – the unexplained and inexplicable behaviour of our compass. On the same day, he deposited in the city archives the now famous document of Saknussemm and expressed his regret that circumstances over which he had no control had prevented him from following the trail of the learned Icelander to the very centre of the Earth. He was modest notwithstanding his glory, and he was all the more famous thanks to his humility.

So much honour could not but arouse envy. There were those who envied him his fame; and as his theories, based on known facts, were in opposition to current scientific theories with regard to the question of the central fire, he maintained by pen and by speech notable discussions with scholars from every country in the world.

For my part, I cannot agree with his theory of gradual cooling. In spite of what I have seen and felt, I believe, and always shall believe, in the Earth's central heat. But I admit that certain circumstances not yet sufficiently understood may tend to modify here and there the action of natural phenomena.

While these questions were being debated with great animation, my uncle met with a real sorrow. Our faithful Hans, in spite of our entreaties, had left Hamburg. The man to whom we owed all our success, and our lives too, would not allow us to reward him as we would have wished. He was stricken with homesickness.

'*Farval*,' he said one day, and with that simple word he left us and sailed for Reykjavik, which he reached in safety.

We were very attached to our brave eider-down hunter. Though far away in the remotest north, he will never be forgotten by those whose lives he protected, and I will certainly try to see him once more before I die.

To conclude, I have to add that this 'Journey to the Centre of the Earth' caused a tremendous sensation throughout the world. It was translated into all the languages of civilization. The leading newspapers printed the most interesting passages, which were commented on, picked to pieces, discussed, attacked and defended with equal enthusiasm and determination, both by believers and sceptics. A rare privilege! My uncle enjoyed during his lifetime the glory he had deservedly won, and he may even boast the distinguished honour of an offer from Mr Barnum[38] to exhibit him on most advantageous terms in all the principal cities in the United States!

But there was one 'fly in the ointment' among all this glory and honour: one fact, one incident, of the journey remained a mystery. Now, to a man eminent for his learning, an unexplained phenomenon is an unbearable hardship. Well, my uncle was still fated to be completely happy.

One day, while arranging a collection of minerals in his cabinet, I noticed in a corner the wretched compass which we had long lost sight of. It had been in that corner for six months, little mindful of the trouble it was causing. I opened it and looked at it.

Suddenly, to my intense astonishment, I noticed something strange and uttered an exclamation of surprise.

'What's the matter?' asked my uncle.

'The compass!'

'Well?'

'Look, its poles are reversed!'

'Reversed?'

'Yes, they're pointing the wrong way.'

My uncle looked at it and checked it, and the house shook with his triumphant leap of exultation.

A light suddenly shone into his mind and mine.

'See there,' he cried, as soon as he was able to speak. 'After our arrival at Cape Saknussemm, the north pole of the needle of this blasted compass began to point south instead of north.'

'Clearly!'

'Here, then, is the explanation of our mistake. But what phenomenon could have caused this reversal of the poles?'

'The reason is obvious, Uncle.'

'Tell me, then, Axel.'

'During the electric storm on the Lidenbrock Sea, that ball of fire, which magnetized all the iron on board, reversed the poles of our magnet!'

'Aha, aha!' shouted the Professor with a loud laugh. 'So it was just a trick of electricity!'

From that day on, the Professor was the happiest of scientists – and I was the happiest of men, because my pretty Virland girl, resigning her place as his ward, took her position in the old house on the Königstrasse in the double capacity of niece and wife. What need is there to add that her uncle was the illustrious Otto Lidenbrock, corresponding member of all the scientific, geographical and mineralogical societies of the civilized world?

NOTES

1 The Tugendbund or 'League of Virtue' was a patriotic body formed in Prussia in 1808.
2 Virland is in Estonia.
3 Well-known bookbinders.
4 Verne wrongly wrote *m* in his translation of this Runic character. The rune represents a double m, not a single m, as Verne himself says further on. The translation printed here is amended to this effect.
5 In Ancient Greek mythology, Oedipus solved the difficult riddle asked by the Sphinx.
6 In the Roman calendar, the calends were the first day of the month.
7 A Leyden jar was a device for storing electricity.
8 A French league is about 4 kilometres or 2½ miles.
9 The Belts are two straits on the east coast of Denmark.
10 At this time, Iceland was not an independent country but was governed by Denmark.
11 The Sound is the stretch of sea between Zealand (Sjælland) and Sweden.
12 It is actually the south-eastern part.
13 Lilliput is a fictitious country described in the novel *Gulliver's Travels*. The people of Lilliput are tiny.
14 Formerly, a list of books banned by the Roman Catholic Church.
15 The following is Verne's note: 'A Ruhmkorff's apparatus consists of a Bunsen battery activated by potassium dichromate, which is odourless. An induction coil carries the electricity generated by the battery to a lantern of peculiar construction: in this lantern there is a spiral glass tube from which the air has been expelled, and in which remains only a residue of carbon dioxide or nitrogen. When the apparatus is operated, this gas becomes luminous, producing a steady white light. The battery and coil are placed in a leather bag which the traveller carries over his

shoulders; the lantern, outside the bag, throws out sufficient light in deep darkness; it enables one to venture without fear of explosions into the midst of highly inflammable gases, and is not extinguished even in the deepest waters. M. Ruhmkorff is a learned and most ingenious man of science; his great discovery is his induction coil, which produces a powerful stream of electricity. He obtained in 1864 the quinquennial prize of 50,000 francs reserved by the French government for the most ingenious application of electricity.'

16 'And whatever path Fortune may give us, we will follow it.'

17 These must be Icelandic 'miles'. The area of Iceland is just under 40,000 sq. miles.

18 A statue of the Greek sun-god Helios at Rhodes, according to legend built astride the entrance to the harbour.

19 'An easy path down to the Underworld.'

20 Well-known spas. (The word 'spa' comes from the town of Spa.)

21 Quotation taken by Malleson from Shakespeare's *Hamlet*.

22 'Out of the depths'; quotation taken by Malleson from the Latin version of Psalm 130.

23 In an Ancient Greek myth, Theseus used a thread to guide him out of the labyrinth where the Minotaur lived.

24 The 'Internal Sea', a Roman name for the Mediterranean Sea.

25 The planet named Pluto was not discovered until 1930. The name 'Pluto' was not attached to any body in the Solar System when Verne was writing.

26 'Mediterranean' means 'in the middle of the Earth'.

27 A famous French anatomist and palaeontologist.

28 An Ancient Greek hero who defied the Greek gods and who as punishment was shipwrecked and drowned.

29 It is said that the books in the library in Alexandria were burned on the orders of the Muslim caliph Omar in the 7th century, but the story is almost certainly not true.

30 Famous French naturalists.

31 The following is Verne's note, of interest in that it illustrates then current scientific thinking: 'The facial angle is formed by two lines,

one touching the brow and the front teeth, the other from the orifice of the ear to the lower line of the nostrils. The greater this angle, the higher intelligence denoted by the formation of the skull. Prognathism, in anthropological terminology, is that projection of the jaw-bones which sharpens or lessens this angle.'

32 The person referred to is Peter Schlemihl, the hero of Adelbert von Chamisso's tale of a man who sold his shadow to the Devil. The writer E T A Hoffmann included the character in one of his tales.

33 Proteus was the herdsman of the Greek god Poseidon (or Neptune in Roman mythology).

34 'The shepherd of gigantic herds, even more gigantic himself.'

35 'What is the name of this island?'

36 The Greek and Latin name for Stromboli.

37 Quotation taken by Malleson from Mrs Hemans' poem *The Better Land*.

38 A famous American showman and circus-owner.